THREE GREAT NOVELS
Bestselling Liverpool Sagas

Also by Maureen Lee

THE PEARL STREET SERIES

Lights out Liverpool
Put out the Fires
Through the Storm

Stepping Stones
Liverpool Annie
Dancing in the Dark
The Girl From Barefoot House
Laceys of Liverpool
The House by Princes Park
Lime Street Blues
Queen of the Mersey
The Old House on the Corner
The September Girls

Maureen Lee

Three Great Novels: Bestselling Liverpool Sagas

The Girl from Barefoot House

Laceys of Liverpool

The House by Princes Park

ORION

First published in Great Britain in 2005 by Orion,
an imprint of the Orion Publishing Group Ltd.

The Girl from Barefoot House Copyright © 2000 Maureen Lee
Laceys of Liverpool © 2001 Maureen Lee
The House by Princes Park Copyright © 2002 Maureen Lee

2 4 6 8 10 7 5 3 1

A CIP catalogue record for this book is
available from the British Library.

ISBN 0 75286 905 1

Typeset by Deltatype Ltd,
Birkenhead, Merseyside

Set in Minion

Printed in Great Britain by Clays Ltd,
St Ives plc

The Orion Publishing Group Ltd
Orion House
5 Upper Saint Martin's Lane
London, WC2H 9EA

Contents

The Girl from
Barefoot House

For
Deidre and David

Huskisson Street
1938–1940

1

'Hello, Petal. I'm home.'

'Mam!' Josie raised her arms and was lifted out of bed and hugged so hard she could scarcely breathe.

'I see you drank your milk and ate your cream crackers like a good girl.'

'Yes, Mam.' She snuggled her head against Mam's neck, into the curved space she thought of as especially hers.

'I've missed you, Petal. Now, I've got a visitor, so you sit on the stairs for a little while. Take Mam's cardy, and don't forget Teddy. I'll be out to get you in the twinkling of an eye. Then I'll make us a cup of cocoa and a jam butty, like always.'

'All right, Mam.' Josie slithered obediently to the floor, and Mam gently placed the navy blue cardigan around her shoulders.

'How old is she?' The gruff voice came from a dark corner of the candlelit room, by the door. A man stepped forward, very tall, with a bent nose and black curly hair. His face was hard, but his eyes were troubled.

'Three.'

'Bit young to be left on her own all this time, isn't she? It's not safe.'

'What do you mean, it's not safe?' Mam said tartly. She removed the long pearl pin from her brown felt hat. 'There's a fireguard, and I leave something to eat. She knows I'll always come back. Anyroad, what's it to you?'

'Nowt. Just put her outside so I get what I've come for before you pass out. You're stewed rotten, and I've been waiting all night long for this.'

'It's what I was about to do before you shoved your big oar in.' The voice changed as she turned to her child. 'Go on, luv,' she said softly, shoving her through the door and on to the landing.

Josie sat at the top of the stairs and held Teddy up so that he could see the stars peeping down at them through the skylight and the filmy cobwebs floating eerily in the light of the moon. Then she wrapped the sleeves of the cardigan around her neck, and tried to tuck her bare feet inside the ribbed hem. It was cold in her nightie on the landing. Their attic was the warmest place in the house according to Mam, because heat rose, and they got the benefit of everyone's fires, as well as their own. The attic was where the maids used to live a long time ago. It had a small iron fireplace and a triangular sink in the corner. There was a tiny window just below where the roof peaked.

The stairs in the tall house in Huskisson Street, a mere stone's throw from the Protestant cathedral, had their own special smell, a mixture of all sorts of interesting things: of food – mainly boiled cabbage or fried onions – scent, smoke, dust, a peculiar smell that Mam said was dry rot. The house had once been very grand, having been owned by a man who imported rare spices from the Orient. The rooms used to be full of fine furniture; exquisite rugs and carpets had covered the floors. Everywhere, apart from the attic, had been wired for electricity, which was very up to date, as not everyone could get light at the flick of a switch. Most people still used gas.

Mam spent ages describing how she imagined the place might have looked. 'But now it's gone to rack and ruin,' she sighed. All that remained was the opulent wallpaper in the downstairs rooms. Even the bathroom had lost its grandeur: tiles had fallen off the walls, and the taps provided water at a trickle. The chain in the lavatory was just a piece of string, and no one could remember it having had a seat.

There was a party downstairs, lots of voices, music – someone was playing a mouth organ. Josie never seemed to be awake when the house was quiet. Perhaps it never was. Perhaps there were always people having parties, shouting and screaming, fighting or laughing, crying or singing. Sometimes the bobbies came, stamping through the house as if they owned the place, up and down the stairs, banging on doors, not waiting to be asked in. When this happened, Mam would sit Josie on her knee and be reading a story when a bobby barged in and demanded she come to the station.

'How dare you!' she would say in the frosty, dead posh voice she kept specially for such occasions. 'I'm just sitting here, reading me little girl a story. Since when has reading been a crime?'

'Sorry, ma'am,' the bobby would say, touching his funny big dome of a hat, followed by something like, 'I didn't realise respectable women lived here.'

Mam would toss her great mane of brown hair and say, 'Well, they do, see.'

On Sundays, after she and Mam and some of the girls had been to Mass, everyone would be in a great good humour and they would gather in one of the downstairs rooms for a cup of tea and a jangle. There were six other girls besides Mam – fat Liz, tall Kate, buck-toothed Gladys, black Rita, Irish Rose and smelly Maude. Maude was much older than the others and going bald, but was still called a girl. She smoked a lot, and the fingers of her right hand were a funny orange colour. Mam was fondest most of Maude. Josie, in her best dress, would be in her element as she was made a desperate fuss of, passed from one knee to another and petted almost to death. The girls often bought her presents – a bar of chocolate, a hairslide or a little toy. It was Maude who'd given her Teddy for her first birthday.

'They're dead envious because I've got you,' Mam would whisper. 'They'd all like a little girl like my Petal, though they'd never admit it.' At nineteen, Mam was the next to youngest there, but the only one a mother. This made her very proud, as if she had one up on the others.

Josie was quite definitely not a burden or a cross to bear, as some of the girls suggested. Okay, she could have earned two or three times as much if she had been on her own, but she made enough to keep body and soul together, thanks very much. The Sunday before last, when the subject had come up again, Mam lost her temper when Kate said, 'Let's face it, Mabel, someone in our line of work would be far better off without a kiddie.'

'Cobblers!' Mam flashed angrily. 'You're only saying that because you're jealous. Our Josie's more important to me than anything in the world.'

'Why should I be jealous when I got rid of two of me own?' Kate countered. 'If you cared about your Josie all that much, you wouldn't be here. This is no place to raise a kid. You had a proper education, not like us lot. You're always on about that chemist's shop where you used to work. If you put your mind to it, you could get a decent job like a shot.'

Like much of the conversation that she overheard, this went completely over Josie's head, but she noticed Mam's rosy cheeks turn white. 'No, I couldn't,' she whispered. 'Not while I'm stuck on the booze.'

The door to the attic opened and the man with the crooked nose came out. He said kindly, 'C'mon, kid. I'll take you back in.' He scooped Josie up, carried her into the room and sat her on the bed. Mam was in her pink nightie, twisting her long hair into a plait, which made her look like a beautiful saint. She swayed and nearly fell.

'You may well be a good screw,' the man snapped, 'but you're a lousy ma. If you're not careful, one of these days the kid'll be taken off you.'

'You bugger off, you,' Mam said in a slurred, trembly voice. 'You'd go a long road before you'd find a bonnier child. And, anyroad, she'll be four in May.' She sat on the bed and put her arm around Josie's shoulders. 'You're happy, aren't you, luv?'

Josie looked up from tucking Teddy under the bedclothes so that just his head and arms showed. 'Oh, yes, Mam.'

'See!' Mam said challengingly.

'She looks fit,' the man conceded grudgingly. 'As to being happy, well, she don't know any better, does she? She probably don't know what happy means.'

After he'd gone, Mam filled the kettle from the sink in the corner and put it on the hob to boil, talking to herself all the while. 'I wonder if we should move, find somewhere else?' she muttered. 'Though I like it here, the girls are a scream, well mostly, and the landlord's more or less decent. But I'll have to start using a different pub. I don't want to come across that geezer tonight a second time, nosy-poke bugger that he was. I'll have a word with Maude, see what she thinks.' She suddenly flew across the room and seized Josie in her slim arms. 'I couldn't live without you, Petal. I'd kill us both before I'd let them take you away.'

'Yes, Mam,' Josie answered. She had no idea what Mam was on about, though she knew what being happy meant. She sat on the big bed, watching the candle send flickering shadows on to the sloping wooden rafters and the bare brick walls. Mam took some clothes off the line strung between rafters and put them over the fireguard. They began to steam and give off a warm, familiar smell. Then her mother mixed the cocoa, cut and margarined the bread, spread the jam, and Josie thought it would be impossible to be happier than she was now. In a minute, Mam would bring the butties to bed with her, leaving the cocoa on the floor for now, and they would eat them sitting up, leaning against each other.

'What is it we need, Petal?' Mam said, coming over with the butties on a cracked plate.

'A tray,' Josie said promptly. Every night without fail Mam brought up their desperate need of a tray.

'That's right. We could prop it on our knees, like a little table. Tell you what, we'll walk into town tomorrow, see if there's any trays going cheap in Blackler's bargain basement. We'll make a day of it, wear our bezzie clothes. We'll finish off with a cup of tea in Lyon's.'

'Yes, Mam,' Josie said blissfully. Mam turned every day into an adventure. Depending on the weather, they would go to the swings in Princes Park, or for a ride on the ferry to Birkenhead or Seacome – sometimes they even went as far as New Brighton, and if Mam was flush they'd go on the waltzer and the bobby horses. If it were raining, they would wander around St John's Market, or the big posh shops like George Henry Lee's and Bon Marché.

As Mam climbed into bed beside her, she said, 'We used to have a lovely black lacquered tray at home – you should have seen it, Petal.'

'Tell us about home,' Josie murmured.

'Again? You'd think I'd lived in Buckingham Palace, not an ordinary house off Penny Lane.'

''S interesting.'

Mam laughed. 'Interesting! That's a big word for a little girl not long off four.'

'Well, it is. What was the tray like?' Josie took a butty and snuggled into the crook of Mam's arm, careful not to disturb Teddy, who had gone fast asleep.

'I told you, black lacquered. It sort of shone, and had flowers, like orchids, painted on it. Orange and pink they were, with long, green leaves.

Me dad brought it back from Japan, I think it was. Our house in Machin Street was full of lovely things me dad brought from all over the world. The best tray was only brought out on Sundays. Weekdays, we used the horrible wooden one. Mind you, I won't turn up me nose if wooden's all they've got in Blackler's basement tomorrow.'

'What did your dad look like, Mam?'

'You know as much about him as I know meself, and what's more, you know you know.' Mam tickled her tummy, and Josie collapsed, giggling. 'He was an Irishman from County Kildare, a captain in the merchant navy, and he died in the last year of the Great War, though it was the weather, a terrible storm, that killed him, not the fighting. I was only a month old, so I never saw him, and he never saw me. Ne'er did the twain meet, as the saying goes.'

'But you saw his photo,' Josie prompted.

'So I did, Petal.' Mam grinned. 'You remember this word for word, don't you? Yes, his photo was on the mantelpiece in Machin Street.'

'And he was very handsome?'

'Very handsome indeed, my Petal. Tall, well built, with brown hair same as yours and mine and the same dark blue eyes. Not that I could tell the colours from the photo, like, but that's what me poor mam told me.'

'Poor Mam died of a broken heart,' Josie said sadly.

'More or less.' Mam shrugged. 'She was Irish, too, from the same village, and she'd known him all her life. Six years afterwards, she went to meet her maker. Our Ivy was eighteen by then, and it was her that brought me up. She was more like a mother than me real one. Until she married Vincent Adams, that is. I were twelve by then. Here's your cocoa, luv. Mind you don't spill it.' Mam's blue eyes glittered angrily. 'Three years later, she chucked me out, though she'd no right. It was a bought house, and every bit as much mine as hers. It was the only bought house in Machin Street, and the first to have electricity,' she went on grandly. 'All the rest were rented.'

'Why did she chuck you out, Mam?' Josie asked curiously. The story always got rather vague at about this time.

'She thought I'd done something wrong, but I hadn't. Someone else had done the wrong, but I was the one who got the blame. I was the one who wandered the streets, looking for a place to live, getting chucked out over and over once they realised me condition.'

'It was then you found Maude downstairs.'

'No, luv, it was Maude downstairs who found me. I'd collapsed in a back entry not far from here, and was waiting for a miracle to happen. It was Maude who brought me to her room downstairs so the miracle could happen somewhere nice and warm.'

'*Me* was the miracle,' Josie said contentedly.

'The miracle of miracles, that's my Petal, and it's "I", not "me". Now, if you've finished your cocoa, it's time we lay down and went to sleep. That party downstairs sounds as if it's going on all night. Do you want to use the po first?'

'No, ta, Mam. I used it just before you came in.'

'Well, I do.' Mam got out of bed and pulled the po from underneath. 'I hope Teddy's got his eyes closed. It's not done for a gentleman to see a lady using the chamber pot.'

'He's fast asleep, but I'll put me hand over his face, like, just to make sure.'

'Ta, Petal, but be careful not to smother him, mind.'

Mam snuffed out the candle and got into bed. 'Turn over, luv. Sit on me knee, like. It's the comfortablest way.'

They lay like that for quite a while, and Josie felt as if they'd become one person as Mam's heart beat against her own, and she could feel the warm breath on her neck. She could tell that Mam was still awake.

'Mam?' she whispered.

'Yes, luv?'

'Another miracle's going to happen one day, isn't it?'

'That's right,' Mam murmured huskily. 'Like I said, by the time you're ready for school, Mam'll be off the drink, I swear it. I'll get a proper job, and we'll get a proper little house between us. You and me will stay together nights, not like now. I'm glad it was Maude who found me in that entry, not some sanctimonious snob like our Ivy who would have had you taken away. But Maude wasn't exactly a good influence on a girl of fifteen. She got me this room and set me on a road I would never have followed otherwise, the only road she knew. Still, I'm not sorry about the way things turned out.' The voice got huskier, became a sob. Josie felt Mam's arm tighten around her waist. 'Well, not sorry much.'

Blackler's basement was an Aladdin's cave of dazzling and exceedingly tempting bargains. Mam was greatly taken with a flowered china teapot with a slightly misshapen lid and a hand-embroidered Irish linen tablecloth with nothing obviously wrong with it at all. The cheapest tray they found was brown Bakelite and rather ugly, but only elevenpence ha'penny. Mam said she'd cut a rose out of her flower book and glue it in the middle. 'Then it'll look dead pretty.' She was fond of decorating things with flowers from her book.

'You know, Petal,' she said thoughtfully as she paused in front of the cutlery, 'a new bread-knife wouldn't come amiss. Our one's so blunt it makes the bread all crumbly. They're only a tanner, 'cos the handles have got a chip out the wood.' She picked up several lethal-looking knives until she found the one with the least chipped handle. 'You can hardly count this as an extravagance.'

The shop assistant put the goods in a paper bag, and they were quickly making their way towards the exit because Mam was worried she'd spend money she hadn't got when a voice said, 'Why, if it isn't Mabel Flynn.'

Mam went very red and nearly dropped the tray. 'Mrs Kavanagh. Hello,' she said awkwardly.

'You're looking well, luv.'

'Ta,' Mam gulped.

Mrs Kavanagh seemed exceptionally nice, and Josie couldn't understand why Mam was so embarrassed. She was small and plump, with a round, kind face, pink, cushiony cheeks and brown eyes that shone with good humour. Her blue coat was extremely smart. It had a fur collar and fur buttons, and she wore a little blue veiled hat made from the same material as the coat tipped precariously over her right eye. Her hair was brown and tightly waved. Josie waited to be introduced. It was the first thing Mam did when they met someone new. 'This is Josie, me little girl,' she would say proudly. Today, though, Mam said nothing.

'How's the job going, girl?' Mrs Kavanagh asked kindly.

'The job?' Mam faltered. She was holding Josie's hand so hard it hurt. 'All right, I suppose.'

'I was surprised to hear you'd given up Bailey's Chemists – wasn't Mrs Bailey teaching you to dispense the prescriptions? – to become a live-in nanny, but according to your Ivy you love it there. Where is it over the water, luv? I forget now.'

'Er, Greasby.'

'And I suppose this is one of your little charges.' The woman beamed at Josie.

'Yes. Oh, yes. This is Josie.'

'You're very pretty, Josie.' She bent down and took Josie's hand. 'How old are you?'

'I'll be four in May.'

'I've got a little girl who'll be four next week. Her name is Lily, and she should be standing right beside me, except she's wandered off, as usual. Lily,' she called. 'Lily, where are you?'

Mam seemed to have found her voice. 'I didn't know you'd had another baby, Mrs Kavanagh.'

'Well, five's an uneven number, luv. Me and Eddie decided to make it six, but that's our lot. I'd've thought your Ivy would've told you on one of her visits. Oh, here she is, our Lily. Come on, luv, say hello to Josie here.'

A girl came bouncing up, a mite smaller than Josie. She was very like her mam, with bright pink cheeks and sparkling eyes. Her slightly darker hair fell to her waist in a mass of tiny waves. To Josie's surprise, her coat was exactly the same as her mother's – blue with fur buttons and collar. She wore a different sort of hat, a bonnet tied under her chin.

'Hello, Josie,' the girl said obediently. Her face was alive with mischief.

'Hello.' Josie twisted her body shyly. She wasn't used to children, and had never had a friend. Mam had been the only friend she'd ever wanted, but she would have quite liked to get to know Lily Kavanagh.

However, that was not to be, because Mam said in a rush, 'We'd better be

9

getting back to Greasby. I only came over to do a bit of shopping, seeing as it was such a nice day, like. Come on, Josie.'

Mrs Kavanagh looked disappointed. 'I thought we could have a little natter over a cup of tea and a scone. I've missed you in the street, Mabel. Everyone has.'

'That would have been the gear, Mrs Kavanagh, but I really must get back.'

'Oh, well, some other time, then. Tara, luv. Tara, Josie. Where's your manners, our Lily? Say tara.'

Lily's eyes gleamed impishly at Josie. 'Tara.'

'It's not fair. Oh, it's not fair a bit,' Mam raged as they walked quickly out of Blackler's into the bright spring sunshine. Her face was very red. Josie had to run to keep up, and kept bumping into people on the crowded pavements. A shopping basket nearly sent her flying. 'As if I'd've given up me good job in Bailey's to be a nanny, for God's sake. But I suppose our poor Ivy had to come up with something to explain why I wasn't there no more. After all, I was forced to think up all sorts of lies meself, else the truth might have killed the poor woman. Mind you, I never thought she'd turn against me the way she did. She's me sister, after all. I thought she'd stick by me.'

'Mam!' Josie panted. She had a stitch in her side, and felt confused. What on earth was Mam on about? Which poor woman might the truth have killed?

'I'm sorry, Petal. Am I going too fast for you? I'm the worst mam in the whole world.' She slowed down considerably, but remained just as angry. 'I'm glad we were all done up in our best gear and I had me beret on, not that horrible brown thing. Did you see the lovely coats they had on? Mollie will have made them, as well as them dead smart hats. She makes all the kids' clothes, including the boys'. Mr Kavanagh – Eddie, that is – owns the haberdashers by Woolworths in Penny Lane, so she gets the material cheap, like. She was ever such a good friend when I was little. I used to have me tea in their house until our Ivy came home from work. Their Stanley's only three years younger than me.' She stopped dead in the middle of the street. 'I would have liked a cup of tea and a natter, I really would, but I was scared she'd guess what's what.'

'What is what, Mam?'

'Never mind.' Mam sighed. 'You should be wearing coats like Lily's, not other kids' cast-offs from Paddy's market. There was money left, hundreds of pounds, and half of it were mine. Mollie Kavanagh made the frock for me first Holy Communion, something you'll be needing yourself in the not too distant future, and where are we going to get *that* from, I'd like to know?'

Josie had no idea. Nor did she know why the day, which she had anticipated being so enjoyable, should have turned so sour, all because they'd met nice Mrs Kavanagh and her daughter, Lily.

Then the day became even worse. Mam noticed they were standing outside a pub. She said, 'Hang on a minute, Petal. If I don't down something quick to calm me nerves, I'm likely to bust a blood vessel. Sit on the step, luv. I'll be out again in the twinkling of an eye.'

True to her word, Mam was only a short while in the pub, and when she came out she looked much calmer. But she had claimed that drinking was a curse, that she was determined to stop altogether so she could get a job and a little house. This was the first time Josie had known her to drink during the day.

2

Josie had been at Our Lady of Mount Carmel elementary school a year when Britain declared war on Germany, and everyone began to make a desperate fuss about things. But apart from food rationing and people having to wear gas masks over their shoulders, war made little difference to their lives as far as Josie could see. All the windows had crisscross tape to protect against bomb damage – not that anyone thought there was the remotest chance that bombs would fall. Tall Kate and fat Liz had 'pulled themselves together' and gone down south to work in a factory making parts for aeroplanes. But Josie and her mam remained in Huskisson Street, where these days there were always a few bottles of stout kept in the sideboard cupboard, and the little house hadn't been mentioned in a long while.

Josie didn't mind, not very much. They still went to Princes Park and for rides on the ferry. She liked school, and could read quite well. Night-times, when Mam was out – and she was out longer and longer these days – she looked through books with Teddy and taught him the words she knew.

After the war started, Mam's visitors were mainly young men in uniform – some gave Josie a penny, or even a threepenny bit, as they were leaving. She put the money in a cocoa tin to save up for a house.

On the last day of the summer term, the children were allowed home early. They whooped out of the gates, blissfully excited at the thought of no more school for six long weeks. Josie ran all the way home, burst into the house and was halfway up the first flight of stairs when Irish Rose emerged from her ground-floor room. She was a tiny woman – 'petite' Mam called her – with lovely ginger hair, and would have been dead pretty if she hadn't had such a dreadful squint.

'Josie,' she called urgently. 'Come in with me a minute, luv. Your mam's got someone with her. She wasn't expecting you just yet.'

'Why can't I wait on the stairs, like always?' Josie hadn't realised Mam had visitors while she was at school.

'I think your mam would prefer it if you waited with me. It might take a while. Come on, luv,' Rose coaxed in her soft, lilting voice. 'The kettle's on, and I got half a pound of broken biscuits this morning – most of 'em are cream.'

At the mention of the biscuits, Josie returned downstairs. She loved Rose's big room, with its fancy net curtains and red silk tasselled lampshade. Rose had spent several days sticking tape to the tall windows in a highly complicated pattern. The linoleum was purple with a pattern of trailing vines, and the red and blue striped wallpaper, with its sprinkling of embossed gold flowers, was a relic of the importer of rare spices – faded, torn in places, but still incredibly grand. During the summer, the marble fireplace was filled, as now, with tissue flowers that Rose had made herself. A patchwork quilt covered the single bed, and the sideboard was packed with statues, holy pictures and photos of Rose's numerous sisters and brothers and other relatives back in Ireland, who would all 'drop stone dead' for some reason if they knew what their Rose was up to on the mainland.

The kettle was already simmering on the hob, the tea was quickly made and the broken biscuits emptied on to a plate.

'You can dip your bicky in your tea if you want, luv,' Rose said kindly, before proceeding daintily to dip her own. Rose was always dressed up to the nines from early morning. Today, she wore a lovely maroon crêpe dress with sequins on the bodice. Her cheeks and lips had been painted the same colour as the dress, and her lashes were two rows of stiff flies' legs. She regarded Josie searchingly with her good eye. 'And what did you get up to at school today?'

'We did games this avvy, and Catechism this morning,' Josie said importantly. 'Did you know the Pope cannot err? What does err mean, Rose?'

Rose shrugged. 'Dunno, luv. I'm a downright eejit, me. I can't even read proper.'

'Honest? Me mam reads books all the time, big thick ones,' Josie bragged. 'She gets 'em from the library.'

'Oh, we all know how clever Lady Muck is.' Rose sniffed and looked annoyed. She went on, a touch of spite in her voice, 'But she weren't clever enough to check if her chap was wearing a johnny, were she? *I* always do. The chaps hate using 'em, and only an eejit would take them at their word. Now look where it's landed her.'

'Where's that, Rose?'

'Up shit creek without a paddle, that's where.'

Josie was about to ask if shit creek was anywhere near the Pier Head when an agonised scream came from upstairs.

'Mam!' Josie would have recognised the sound anywhere. In her panic, she dropped a custard cream in the half-drunk tea, and almost fell in her rush towards the door.

'Wait a minute, luv,' Rose leapt to her feet. 'Oh, dear God. I should've locked the effin' door,' she groaned.

At first, Josie couldn't make out what was happening when she burst into the attic room, half expecting to find Mam being murdered and ready to defend her with her life. The terrifying scene that met her was possibly worse. The bed had been covered with a black rubber sheet on which her mother lay, legs bent and wide apart. Between them was a pool of dark red blood. Mam, her teeth bared and the whites of her eyes glinting madly, was struggling to escape from Maude, who had her pinned down by the shoulders. A strange old woman was crouched at the foot of the bed. She got to her feet as Josie rushed in.

'That should do it,' the woman said, and at the same time Mam shrieked, 'Get our Josie out of here.'

'I'll get her.' Rose arrived, breathless. 'Come on, luv.'

But a terrified Josie dodged the grasping arms. She slithered past Maude and threw herself on top of her mother who screamed again. Both began to sob loudly.

The old woman, oblivious to the commotion, said in a hoarse voice, 'That'll be a quid.'

'You should'a been a butcher, Gertie,' Maude said tersely, releasing Mam, who made no attempt to escape, but fell back on to the bed, still sobbing. 'I hope that instrument o' yours was sterilised.'

Gertie ignored her. 'I'd like me rubber sheet back if you don't mind. I'll wash it meself at home. Oh, and you'd better get the girl some Aspro. She's likely to hurt for a couple of days.'

Mam did more than hurt – she caught an infection. Her temperature soared, she tossed and turned, moaned in her sleep and said things that Josie couldn't make sense of.

'Don't touch me, else I'll tell our Ivy,' she would wail hysterically. Or, 'If me sister finds out, it'll break her heart.'

It was like a nightmare, Josie thought during the night as she cuddled against the hot, damp body, made worse when the air-raid siren went several times. Its unearthly wail sent shivers up and down her spine. The drone of German planes sounded in the distance, and she held her breath, praying they wouldn't get closer. Maude said bombs had dropped on Birkenhead and Wallasey. Five people had been killed.

For eight whole days, Mam stayed in bed, only getting up to use the po, which was 'like a hot knife being stuck in me guts', she said tearfully to Maude. Josie flatly refused to leave her side for more than a few minutes. She sat on the bed, making little soothing noises and gently stroking the burning cheeks.

'I don't know what I'd do without you, Petal,' Mam said when she was lucid. Several times a day she would ask, 'Would you mind taking that little glass and nipping downstairs to ask Maude for a sup of whisky? It's the only thing that helps with the pain.'

'She's drinking more than ever,' Maude said worriedly one day, after inviting Josie into her horribly smelly room – according to Mam, Maude had yet to discover the virtues of soap and water. Yesterday's make-up smudged her anxious, good-natured face, and she wore the filthy dressing-gown with both pockets hanging off that she wore all day. Because she hadn't combed her hair, the bald patch was more noticeable than usual. 'I thought she'd vowed to give it up.'

Josie tut-tutted and shook her head, very grown up. 'She vows that nearly every day, Maude.'

'She's been doing it for years.' Maude grimaced and waved her cigarette. 'It's me own fault. I was the one that got her started. I mean, you can't sit in the ale house half the night and only sup lemonade. And your mam's far too respectable to walk the streets. At least with a pub you know exactly who you're getting. But I never thought she'd take to the drink like a duck takes to water.'

'Maude?' Josie was still puzzled by the scene she had encountered the day she came home early from school. There was a question she had been dying to ask for days.

'What, luv?' Maude said absently.

'Was that old woman trying to kill me mam?'

Maude looked grave and didn't answer for a while. Then she said, 'No, luv. She wasn't trying to kill her. She was taking something away that your mam didn't want, like lancing a boil, sort o' thing.' She patted Josie's head affectionately as she poured whisky into the glass. 'Take this up to her. By the way, luv, have you had anything to eat today?'

Josie's stomach had been rumbling for hours. Mam seemed to have forgotten about food. 'Not yet.'

'Tch, tch.' Maude shook her head. 'I'll make you a brawn and piccalili sarnie. That should fill the hole for now.'

Mam got better, but for a long while her legs felt like 'a rusty pair of scissors' and her movements were stiff and painful. Walking as far as Princes Park or the Pier Head was out of the question. She preferred to rest, get her strength back, though she went to the pub at night, always bringing back a visitor, because she had no choice, her purse being completely empty.

Josie offered the one and sevenpence halfpenny out of the cocoa tin. Mam burst into tears and said she was very kind, but it wouldn't last five minutes.

During the long holiday, on sunny days, rather than seek out the friends she'd made at school, Josie preferred to wander alone down to the Pier Head where she watched children armed with buckets and spades boarding the New Brighton ferry, huge families of them, accompanied by perspiring mams and a few dads. She envied the children's carefree faces, their obvious gaiety, and on one brilliant August day, a thought she'd never had before wriggled its way into her head. Despite the heat, for some reason she felt cold as she began to wonder about the strangeness of her own existence. Why didn't Mam have a husband?

Thinking about it now, for the first time, on this gloriously sunny afternoon, there seemed something very odd, not quite right, about the never-ending visitors and what they did while Josie was out of the room. She knew that Mam got undressed, and they lay on the bed together, making dead funny noises, and afterwards she was paid. Sometimes the visitors grumbled she'd already cost them a small fortune in ale, and Mam would reply sharply she wasn't available for the price of a few drinks, thanks all the same. And since the old woman had lanced the boil, whatever the men did hurt badly. Mam was often in tears when Josie went back, and in need of a drink to ease the pain. There was whisky in the cupboard now instead of stout, and she would take a huge swig straight from the bottle and go to bed, forgetting all about their usual cocoa and jam butties.

In fact, Josie was hungry a lot of the time because Mam mostly forgot to buy food. If it hadn't been for Maude, some days she wouldn't have eaten at all.

There were children in her class at school who smelled much worse than Maude. Their bodies, their ragged clothes, were filthy. A few had no shoes, and some of the girls didn't wear knickers. Even so, Josie would have bet that these children's mams didn't get undressed for strange men. It made her feel a little bit ashamed.

She rested her arms on the rail and watched the ferry on its way to New Brighton spewing a trail of white froth. The sun glinted blindingly on the green-grey waters of the Mersey, and her eyes began to run. There was no hankie up her sleeve, so she rubbed her cheeks with the hem of her frock, and it was only then she noticed how dirty it was. It hadn't been washed since the day school finished, and in all that time she hadn't changed her knickers and vest because there hadn't been any clean ones to put on. She only had one frock that fitted, and Mam had promised ages ago to get another from the market. And she needed shoes – the ones she had on now pinched badly.

Josie didn't know why she should suddenly think of Lily Kavanagh in her lovely blue coat, but she did. The day they'd met was as clear as crystal in her mind, and she thought how nice it would be to have a mam like Mrs Kavanagh, who would remember to feed her and make her clothes, and would never allow her to wear shoes that hurt.

Mam was lying on the bed, fully dressed and fast asleep, when she got home, and Josie thought how beautiful she looked with her rich brown hair spread over the pillow. Her cheeks were pale, and she wondered if they would ever be rosy again.

As quietly as possible, she removed her clothes, then carefully took her nightie from under the pillow and put it on. She went over to the sink, where a heap of dirty clothes underneath waited to be washed, and turned on the tap. The water was cold, and she had been strictly forbidden to touch the fireguard so she couldn't warm it on the hob, and, anyroad, the fire was out. She smeared soap on the frock, and her small frame quivered as she rubbed the material together.

'What'cha doing, luv?' Mam murmured in a slurred voice.

'Just washing me frock, Mam. It's awful dirty.'

She had thought Mam would be pleased. Instead, she sat on the edge of the bed, burst out crying, and called herself every name under the sun. 'I'm the worst mam who ever lived,' she sobbed. 'I don't deserve you, Petal. I'm neglecting you something awful. There's hardly a woman in Liverpool who wouldn't look after you better than me.'

A strange feeling, a sort of painful ache, began to roll down Josie's body, starting at the top of her head and finishing at her toes. She could hardly speak for the huge lump in her throat. She didn't care what Mam did for a living, and if Mrs Kavanagh and Lily came and begged her on their bended knees to come and live with them, nothing on earth would make her go. She loved Mam, and always would, with all her heart and soul, and never more so than at that moment. They would never be parted. One day, they would get their little house, even if it took all the years until she went to work herself.

She flung herself across the room on to her mother's knee and began to cover her face with kisses.

'Oh, your hands are wet, and they're all cold,' Mam shrieked, as she fell back, laughing, on to the bed.

Josie sat on her chest, looking down. She could see her own reflection in the dark blue eyes. 'I love you, Mam.'

'And I love you, Petal. I love you so much it hurts. Now, just give us a minute to sort out me head, then we'll do the washing together.'

The noise was so great, so penetrating, that Josie felt as if her brain were rattling in her head – the steady drone of the planes in the sky above, the sharp answering crackle from the ack-ack guns on the ground. Then came the bomb.

This raid was worse than any she'd known before. The others hadn't felt so close, so personal. The bomb sounded as if it had fallen right outside the house, and everywhere shook. The dishes rattled on the table, the rafters creaked and layers of dust drifted downwards. The candle went out, and the room was pitched into blackness.

Josie pulled the covers over her head and grabbed Teddy, shakily telling him that everything was going to be all right, though she had never felt so frightened and desperately wished that Mam were there to whisper the same comforting words to her. She wondered why the bed shook, then realised it was she herself who was shaking, and her teeth were chattering, and she was holding poor Teddy so tightly that he was almost being strangled.

Another bomb screamed its way to earth, and Josie screamed with it, then screamed again when a hand removed the blankets, and she couldn't see who it belonged to in the dark.

'Josie,' Mam said urgently. 'It's all right, luv. It's only me. Them Jerries have never struck so close to home before.' She lit the candle, and Josie, frozen, petrified, saw that she was alone. Mam picked her up and cradled her in her arms. 'There, there, luv. I came the minute that first bomb landed 'cos I was out of me mind with worry.'

'Don't leave me again, Mam,' Josie cried hysterically, clinging to her mother. 'Don't leave me by meself again.'

'Don't fret, luv. I won't.' Mam stroked her face tenderly. 'If we're going to go, we'll go together. I couldn't live without my little girl, my Petal.'

Mam stayed in for three nights in a row and finished off the whisky. There were no raids, but her nerves were on edge. 'This can't go on,' she kept saying. 'I'm stuck in a rut, taking the easy option.' She couldn't sit still, and talked frequently about 'getting a proper job. I might take a look around tomorrow'. They could move out to Speke or Kirkby, where she could work in a munitions factory. The wages were good. Though Josie would have to change schools. She said this in a tired way, as if it were an insurmountable problem.

'I don't mind, Mam.' Josie was thrilled at the idea of living in what she imagined was the countryside, preferably plumb in the middle of a bluebell wood, like a girl in one of her stories. At the same time she recognised with a very adult awareness that Mam was searching for ways *not* to go to Speke or Kirkby.

During that summer holiday, Josie had come to terms with several things. The oddness of her life, for instance, the peculiar thing, the precise nature of which she was still not sure of, that Mam did for a living. What hurt most was knowing that, although Mam sincerely meant it when she said she couldn't live without her and that she loved her more than anyone in the world, she didn't love her quite enough to get the proper job she was always on about, to move somewhere different. Perhaps it was the drink that had weakened her spirit, made her lose the courage she might once have had. What's more, Mam wasn't fit to work in a munitions factory unless she stopped drinking, something which Josie had given up all hope of happening. Kate had written to Maude. She worked on something complicated called a capstan lathe. It was all highly responsible, very difficult, and needed careful precision. But Mam's hands shook when she poured a cup of tea.

All this did nothing to make Josie love her mother less. In fact, she only loved her more.

There was a raid on the fourth night that Mam stayed in. The siren went early, just after seven o'clock. The hairs prickled on Josie's neck. She crawled on to her mother's knee, and they listened to the far-away hum of enemy planes. Fifteen minutes later the welcome sound of the all clear split the still, evening air.

'I think I'll nip out for a little while,' Mam said when it finished.

'*No!*' Josie seized her arm. She never wanted to stay in the room alone again. The aeroplanes might come back, the siren might go again, bombs might fall.

'I can't stay in for ever, luv.' Mam blushed and twisted her thumbs together on her knee, as if for the first time she felt uncomfortable with her daughter about whatever it was she did. 'I've got a living to make.'

'Then take me with you. *Please*, Mam.'

Her mother looked at her for a minute, frowning. 'I suppose I could,' she said eventually. 'It's still broad daylight. You could sit on the steps outside. Lots of kids do.'

The Prince Albert public house was on the corner of two short streets behind the Rialto ballroom. It was small, but impressive. The bottom half was shiny dark green tiles, separated from the plain brick upstairs by a wide band of masonry on which a row of diamond shapes had been carved and painted gold. The corner entrance was particularly grand. Five curved stone steps led to a pair of giant swing doors with fancy brass handles. Across one street, there was a small chandler's, the window a jumble of buckets and mops and tins of paint, a fish shop with an empty marble slab behind the glass, and a sweet and tobacconist's, still open. An elderly woman was sitting on a chair by the door, taking advantage of the evening sun.

When Josie and her mother arrived, a boy about her own age and a little girl who looked no more than two were sitting on the steps outside.

'I promise I won't be long, luv,' Mam said as she went through the swing doors – the glass in the doors and all the windows had been painted over for the blackout. A thick curtain hung over the entrance for when it grew dark, so that not even the slightest chink of light would show when people went in and out.

The boy on the steps was chirpy, with a monkey-like face and a shaven head full of sores. His left arm was withered. He introduced himself as Tommy. The little girl was his sister, and he was looking after her, otherwise he would be playing with his mates, which he would have much preferred. His sister's name was Nora. She couldn't talk yet, and was a pain in the bloody arse.

'I don't suppose you've got a ciggie on you?' he asked casually.

''Course not. I'm only six.'

She was amazed to learn that Tommy was ten. 'I'll be eleven at Chrimbo,' he boasted. 'I've been smoking for years.'

'Does your mam and dad know?'

'Well, no,' he conceded. 'Me dad'd batter me soft if he did.'

'It would be no more than you deserved,' Josie said primly. 'By the way, your sister wants her nose wiping.'

'Wipe your effin' nose, our Nora,' Tommy commanded, and Nora drew her arm across her face, spreading the offending green stuff over her cheek.

They played together amiably on the stone steps. Tommy was impressed when Josie jumped down from the fourth. 'Not bad for a girl,' he grudgingly conceded. Naturally, he could jump all five, landing lightly on his tiny feet, much smaller than hers.

Then Nora had a go, and screamed blue murder when she fell on all fours and grazed her hands and knees. Tommy opened the pub door and yelled, 'Mam, our Nora's hurt herself.'

In view of the racket going on inside the Prince Albert – the blasts of laughter, the occasional sing-song, the thud of glasses on the tables – Josie wasn't surprised when no one came. She comforted Nora as best she could when it seemed that Tommy couldn't care less. Then her own mam appeared with a glass of lemonade and a packet of crisps, which she felt obliged to share with her new friends. Nora stopped crying, but started again as soon as the crisps had gone. Josie stamped her foot and ordered her to stop. To her surprise, Nora did.

A woman arrived carrying a baby, a scantily clad little girl trailing wearily behind holding her skirt. She plonked the baby in the girl's arms, warning, 'Drop her, and you'll be in dead trouble.'

'Hello, Shirl,' said Tommy. Shirl nodded, sat on the step with the baby and promptly fell asleep.

'She mustn't half be tired,' Josie whispered.

'Yeah.' Tommy seemed oblivious to everything except exhibiting his own athletic prowess. Despite his withered arm, he swiftly shinned up a lamp-post and swung from the top. 'Look at me, Jose,' he called.

'You're nothing but a show-off,' Josie sniffed.

Tommy dropped to the ground. He seemed determined to impress her. 'Would you like to see me cock?' he offered.

'Your what?'

'Me cock, me tool, me thingummyjig. Have you never seen one before?'

'No.'

The boy undid the tweed trousers that ended just above his crab-apple knees, and proudly produced a wormlike piece of flesh. 'I'll give you a baby, if you like. I've had it off with girls before.'

Josie regarded the worm scornfully. 'Put it away. I don't want a baby, thanks all the same.' She didn't know where babies came from, only that Tommy was talking through the back of his neck.

'You're a proper ould bossy boots, Jose,' Tommy said as he fastened his trousers.

'Can I go again tomorrow?' Josie asked when they were on their way back to Huskisson Street.

Mam, flushed and bleary-eyed, was linking her arm with that of a sailor in a dead funny uniform. 'Of course, luv. Did you enjoy yourself?'

'Oh, yes, Mam. It was the gear. Tommy goes to Our Lady of Mount Carmel, same as me. I've never seen him before 'cos he's in the Juniors.'

'I'm glad. It means we've solved the problem of the air raids for now. But we can't have you hanging round once the nights grow dark. Still, we'll sort that problem out when we come to it. By the way, Petal, this is Pascal. Isn't that a lovely name? He's French, and can hardly speak a word of English.'

Pascal smiled at the sound of his name. He nuzzled Mam's cheek and said huskily, *'Je t'adore, Mabel.'*

3

Tommy had found a dog-end in the gutter. He cadged a match off a man who had paused outside the pub to light a foul-smelling pipe, and struck it between the tiles. He puffed the dog-end furiously until the end glowed red. 'That's good,' he breathed, before exhaling the smoke with the air of an expert. Nora snuffled noisily on the step beside him.

'You're showing off again,' Josie said mildly. 'Nora, wipe your nose.' She looked away when Nora wiped her nose in the usual fashion.

It was a week since she'd first come to the Prince Albert, and she had grown fond of Tommy and Nora. She felt quite touched when Nora ran to meet her and took her hand. Their father was in the army, a sergeant. Tommy said Josie was his girlfriend and had kissed her twice. Josie had told Mam, missing out the kisses. Mam laughed. 'When you're old enough for boyfriends, let's hope you can do better than *that*, Petal.'

Josie felt hurt. She was looking forward to going back to school next week and having a boyfriend in the Juniors. She watched him affectionately. He got three puffs from the dog-end, and began to look for more in the gutter. She liked him almost as much as she did Maude, and felt a motherly concern for Nora.

A small, jaunty man with a cheerful face came out of the pub. His name was Bert, and he usually exchanged a few words with the children. Tonight, he went over to the sweetshop and returned with three Mars bars. 'Here you are, kids. It's Friday, payday, so I'm flush. Don't eat it all in one bite, now.' He winked at Josie. 'Reckon you'll be carrying your mam home tonight, luv. She's in there downing gin and tonics like nobody's business.'

Josie opened one of the swing doors as far as she dared without invoking the wrath of the landlord who didn't want children on his premises for fear he'd lose his licence. She searched with worried eyes for her mother, and saw her sitting with two khaki-clad young men in one of the wooden compartments with seats each side. All three were laughing hilariously. Mam's hat was all crooked, and when she picked up her glass, liquid spilled down the front of her frock. They all laughed again. One of the men grinned, undid the buttons and dabbed her breasts with a hankie.

'They're officers, them,' a voice said in her ear. 'You can tell by the uniform. Your mam's a tart, isn't she? She goes with men for money.'

Tommy was standing behind her. Josie let the door swing shut, conscious of the Mars bar melting in her hand. She was too sick to eat it. She nodded miserably, and felt tears rush to her eyes. Then Tommy's shrivelled arm slid around her waist. 'Don't worry, kid. I won't tell anyone at school. And when we're grown up, you'll have me to look after you, so you won't end up like your mam.'

'Ta, Tommy,' she whispered gratefully.

The sky darkened early and it started to rain, only lightly. Nora cried when she finished her Mars bar, so Josie gave her hers. She ate it greedily, and cried again after she'd licked the paper clean.

They sat in a row on the top step, four children and a baby – Shirl had just arrived, and was already fast asleep with her sister on her lap. Nora whinged. Josie couldn't stop thinking about Mam and wasn't in the mood to play. Even Tommy seemed subdued by the rain. They watched the old lady lock up the sweetshop and walk away beneath an umbrella.

A woman clattered smartly up the steps in very high heels. 'Just look at them poor kids,' she said to the man with her. 'Some parents are totally irresponsible. They don't deserve to have children.'

'Fuck off,' Tommy snarled.

The man threatened to give him a good hiding, and Tommy said if he laid a finger on him, he'd call his dad who was a heavyweight boxer.

'Oh, yeah!' sneered the man. 'And I'm Clark Gable.'

'Oh, leave them, Geoff. Poor things, they don't know any better. Let's find a different pub. I don't like the look of this place.'

'What happens if the air-raid siren goes?' Josie asked as the sky became darker. She seemed to have lost track of time.

'There's a shelter just down the street,' Tommy assured her. 'Don't worry, Jose. I'll show you where.'

'But I can't go without Mam!' The whole point of coming to the Prince Albert was so that she and Mam wouldn't be parted. A lump of fear rose in her throat at the thought of waiting outside, alone, while the bombs fell.

To her relief, the pub doors opened and Mam staggered out with the two soldiers. They wore peaked caps and neat, well-fitting uniforms.

'I told you they were officers,' Tommy murmured.

Josie's relief was followed by a feeling of horror, because it quickly became obvious that *Mam had forgotten she was there!* She shrieked with laughter when the men linked arms with her and rushed her across the street so that her feet scarcely touched the ground. They had turned the corner before Josie started to follow. Her legs felt numb, and she forgot to say tara to Tommy.

Halfway along Upper Parliament Street one of the soldiers said in a loud, posh voice, 'We seem to have acquired a shadow, an extremely pretty little shadow,' and they all turned round.

'Josie! Oh, luv. I'd forgotten all about you.' Mam's eyes were glazed, she could hardly see. She broke away from the men's supporting arms. One just managed to catch her before she fell. Two women who were passing looked at her in disgust.

Mam hiccuped loudly. 'It's our Josie. It's me little girl.'

For the second time that night, Josie's eyes filled with tears. She'd never seen Mam so drunk before – legless, Maude called it. 'This chap was legless,' she said once. 'He gave me a pound note in mistake for ten bob.'

If only she were bigger, Josie thought fiercely, bigger and stronger and older. She'd chase the men away, drag Mam home and forbid her to touch another drop of drink again.

'Come on, Josie. I'll give you a piggy-back.' Suddenly, she was lifted in the air and found herself clutching the soldier's neck. To her surprise, he smelled of scent. His hair was very fair and bristly. As they walked towards Huskisson Street, he told her his name was Roger, and he had a sister, Abigail, who wasn't much older than she was. His friend was Thomas – not Tommy or Tom, but Thomas. Thomas's hair was dark, and he had a small moustache, like a hyphen in a book. They were both quite good-looking, good-humoured and, she had to concede, boyishly nice. They were completely different to the visitors Mam usually had, and she wondered if they were just seeing her safely home.

When they reached Huskisson Street Roger put Josie down, and helped his friend half drag, half carry her mother upstairs. Mam was giggling helplessly, and by the time they got to the second floor Josie sensed the men were getting angry. They were no longer boyish, and not the least bit nice, and said horrible words like 'bitch' and 'whore'.

'This had better be fucking worth it,' Thomas swore.

They reached the attic room. Mam was roughly pushed inside and the door slammed.

Josie sat at the top of the stairs and waited. Her clothes were wet from the rain, and little needles of fear pulsed through her body. The house was very quiet for a change. She went down and knocked on Maude's door, but there was no answer. Upstairs again, she wished Teddy were there as she watched the stars, pale and unblinking, appear through the skylight. Grey clouds scudded past, concealing then revealing the tiny pricks of light.

The attic door opened. Roger emerged in his shirtsleeves and took her arm. His grip was painful. 'You'll do for a shag till Thomas has done,' he muttered.

She didn't understand. He pulled her into the room, and she went willingly because she wanted to be with her mother, make sure she was safe. She no longer trusted the men she'd thought so nice.

Through the high window, the final remains of daylight offered enough illumination to see the naked figure of her mother lying face down on the bed, moaning softly. Thomas, half-dressed, was riding her like a horse, almost galloping. Josie felt a sickly throbbing in her stomach. Still unsure what was happening, she was roughly flung on the bed and Roger crawled on top of her. She felt his hand reach underneath her frock, but she ignored it, concerned only for Mam, whose face was turned towards hers, only inches away, her eyes screwed close. Was Thomas hurting her? Josie wriggled away from Roger's groping hands and touched her mother's cheek.

'Are you all right, Mam?' she asked tenderly.

Mam's eyes slowly opened, the merest crack. Then, in quick succession, they flickered briefly, closed, snapped wide open and grew very bright and alert. Josie's blood turned to ice when a sound emerged from her mother's throat that was barely human. She growled, and the growl became a howl, and the howl became a roar. She gritted her teeth, took a deep breath and raised herself on all fours like a wild animal.

Thomas was flung off the bed on to the floor. Mam turned over, raised her feet and kicked Roger in the chest. He was thrown against the wall with a sickening thud, then slid to the floor beside his friend.

'How dare you lay a hand on me daughter?' Mam spat. 'Get out! Both of you, get *out!*'

The men were momentarily stunned. After a while, they sat up and, breathing heavily, began to adjust their clothes. Thomas got to his feet. He approached the bed, grinning. 'So, you want to play games, bitch? I know a good one.' He grabbed Mam's foot, but she shoved her other foot in his stomach, and he fell back, grunting.

Roger was up. He reached for Josie, and pulled her on to her back. 'You hold the mother while I take the kid.'

'Oh, no, you don't, not while there's breath left in me body.' Mam leapt off the bed, and suddenly she was holding the bread-knife from Blackler's bargain basement, holding it in front of her, the point aimed directly at Roger. 'Let go of her, or I'll kill you. I'll kill you both, I mean it. I don't care if I swing for it, you bastards.'

Thomas hesitated. Roger released Josie.

There were footsteps on the stairs and Irish Rose burst in, accompanied by a giant black man who was bare to the waist. Muscles rippled like dancing waves on his gleaming back. 'What's going on?' Rose demanded.

Mam said shakily, 'These men are just leaving.' She waved the knife threateningly. 'Aren't you?'

The black man stepped forward. His dark eyes swept from the frightened child to the naked woman with the knife in her hands and the handsome young Army officers crouched against the wall. He nodded his giant head towards the door, and said mildly, 'Git.'

And the two men went.

They were going back to Machin Street tomorrow, Sunday, straight after Mass. They would turn up looking as fine as fivepence – Mam was buying Josie a new frock that afternoon.

Maude was all in favour. She came up in her dressing-gown after breakfast to see how they were. Irish Rose had told her about last night's events, and Mam announced they were leaving.

'You should have gone a long while ago, Mabel,' Maude said. 'You can't risk another night like last night, and the older Josie gets, the more likely it'll happen. She's as pretty as a picture, a real little Miss Pears, and getting more like her mam every day. It's either that, or turning professional, getting a proper flat, like, and a maid to look after Josie. I've said it before and I'll say it again, you could make a fortune on the game if you turned professional.'

'I've no intention of turning professional,' Mam said frostily. She looked surprisingly self-composed. Her face glowed and her mouth was set in a determined line. Last night, terrible though it had been, had brought her to her senses, made her see things clearly, she had said earlier. 'It was always only temporary with me,' she said to Maude. 'The trouble was, I got stuck on the booze, but only 'cos I hated what I was doing. In the end, it became a vicious circle. Now all that matters is our Josie. Isn't it, luv?' She smiled vividly at Josie who was busy emptying the drawers of their well-worn clothes.

'Yes, Mam.' Josie was still not quite sure what Roger had intended to do when he threw her on the bed. After all, she was only a little girl, six, not a grown-up woman.

'I'm chucking most of our stuff away,' Mam said. 'If there's anything decent, it can go to the pawnshop with the crockery, the cutlery and the bedding. I'll not redeem it, it's just that I want to get our Josie a frock and a pair of shoes in Paddy's market this avvy, and another few bob wouldn't come amiss. I'm not having our Ivy turn up her nose when she sees us.'

'There'll be one helluva kerfuffle, Mabel,' Maude said cautiously.

'I know, but I've already made up me mind what to say. She'll be given two choices – either she believes me, takes us in and gives his lordship his marching orders, or she doesn't believe me, in which case I want half of everything, including the money that was left and the value of the house.' Mam folded her arms on her chest and looked extremely fierce. Her eyes sparkled angrily. 'I was fifteen when she chucked me out, up the stick and in a state. Now I'm twenty-two, and in full possession of me senses. I know what's mine by rights. What's more, I intend on having it. If necessary, I'll threaten to have the law on her.'

'Mightn't it be a good idea to leave you-know-who with me while all this is going on?' Maude suggested timidly. She appeared to be slightly in awe of Mam, who was becoming more forceful and aggressive by the minute. Even

Josie found it hard to believe that this was the same woman who'd been legless in Upper Parliament Street the night before.

'No, it wouldn't,' Mam said crisply. 'I'll pop Josie in number thirty for a while. Mrs Kavanagh's bound to guess the truth, if not the whole truth, that's if she's not guessed already. Once our Ivy's been sorted, I'll collect Josie. We'll either have a home in Machin Street, or enough cash in me bag, or at least the promise of it, to take on the nice little house I've been on about for years. We'll live by one of them munitions factories, Kirkby or Speke. Kate said the pay's enough to make your eyes pop. Now, if you don't mind, Maude, I'd like to get on. Me and Josie have got a lot to do today.'

It was the best day Josie could ever remember, a day she never forgot, despite the fact it rained non-stop. It wasn't just the lovely blue velvet frock that Mam bought in the market for a shilling, or the patent leather shoes that pinched a bit – but it didn't matter because next week they'd buy a pair that fitted perfectly from Freeman, Hardy & Willis – or the three-quarter-length white socks with a curious knobbly pattern that were brand new, or the ice-cream cornet with a twirl of raspberry syrup on top that she ate in the rain on the way home. It was knowing that, as from tomorrow, there would be no more visitors and – this time she knew Mam truly meant it – no more drink. They might be living in Machin Street, or they might not. Josie didn't understand the complications. She knew there was going to be a row and that she was being left with Mrs Kavanagh – which she was quite looking forward to. All she cared about was that things were about to change out of all proportion for the better. She skipped along beside her mother, and felt she could easily have burst with happiness.

Mam felt it, too. Every now and then she had a little skip herself, and even when she realised she'd pawned the bedding and they had to spend another night in Huskisson Street, like with the shoes, it didn't matter.

'If necessary, Petal, we'll sit up all night and I'll burn the last of the nutty slack,' she laughed. 'Or we'll sleep on the bare mattress, and I'll ask Maude if she'll give us the loan of her eiderdown, and hope it don't pong too much. She only uses it in winter. Mind you, it could be winter today, it's so cold, yet we're only just into September.'

When they got home, Mam cleaned every surface of the attic room. She brushed the rafters, brushed the walls, brushed the floor, dusted the sideboard, the table and the chairs. She turned the mattress over and blackleaded the tiny grate. Then she lit the fire, borrowed an iron off Maude, put it on the hob to heat and carefully pressed the brown tweed costume, cream blouse and white beret she'd been wearing when she'd left Machin Street, and which were still her bezzie clothes after all this time. She buffed her brown suede shoes as best as she could with the hairbrush. 'We used to have a special brush for this in Machin Street,' she said. 'It were made of wire and called a suede brush. Oh, there's so many things there, Petal. Just wait till you see them.'

When the iron was cool, she turned Josie's new frock inside out and smoothed out the few creases.

'There, that's everything done.' She put her hands on her hips and glanced with satisfaction around the room, at the dust-free surfaces, at her costume and Josie's frock, hanging behind the door, their shoes placed neatly under the sideboard, at Teddy who was sitting on top of their gas masks, next to the brown paper bag containing Josie's books and the money from the cocoa tin which was tied in a hankie. It amounted to two and threepence. 'All that's left is for us to wash our hair, which we'll do later and dry it by the fire.'

Josie reminded her she hadn't shaken the mat, so Mam climbed on a chair and opened the window. 'Why, the sun's come out, Petal,' she announced joyfully. 'It looks dead lovely out there. I don't know about you, but I wouldn't mind a little walk. I've got dust up me nose and in me throat, and the fresh air will clear it. Where shall we go – Princes Park? It's almost autumn, the trees might have started turning gold by now.'

'Yes, but . . .' Josie hesitated.

'Yes, but what, my fragrant, my adorable little Petal?' Mam leapt off the chair, danced across the room and caught Josie in her arms. She led them in a waltz around the bed. 'But what, luv?'

'Can I say tara to Tommy and Nora?' Otherwise, she might never see them again. Our Lady of Mount Carmel was too far from Penny Lane, and even further from Speke and Kirkby.

Mam wrinkled her nose. 'That Tommy's a right scally, luv. I can't understand how you can like him. His mam's a dead horrible woman, she batters them kids something rotten. And did he tell you his dad's in jail?'

'No, Mam. But Tommy's nice. He's . . .' Josie broke off, remembering the way Tommy had put his arm around her waist the night before, promising to look after her, the various athletic feats he'd done solely to impress her. She didn't care if his mam was horrible or his dad was in jail. She shrugged. 'He's just nice.'

'All right, luv,' Mam said resignedly. 'I suppose we could carry on into town, do a bit a window-shopping. We'll get the tram home.'

Outside, the air smelled fresh and clean, and they both sniffed appreciatively. The pavements were full of puddles, and water streamed along the gutters carrying empty fag packets and sweet papers and pouring noisily through grids down to the drains.

Nora ran to meet them when they approached the Prince Albert. She took Josie's hand, and Tommy did a perfect handstand against the wall. Mam tutted, either at Nora's runny nose or Tommy's showing off, Josie wasn't sure.

Then Mam said, 'I suppose it wouldn't hurt to go inside and say tara to me mates. They'll all wonder what happened if I just disappear.'

'Mam!' Josie said warningly, and suddenly wished they hadn't come anywhere near the Prince Albert.

Mam merely laughed and squeezed her shoulder. 'Don't worry, Petal. I'll just have a lemonade. I promise on me honour.'

Predictably, Nora, who cried at the drop of a hat, burst into tears when she understood she would never see Josie again. 'Want Josie stay,' she sobbed, which, Tommy said laconically, were her very first words. He'd tell his mam later, if he remembered.

It seemed Tommy couldn't have cared less that she was going. He climbed the lamp-post and, turning his little monkey face away, refused to look at her. Josie didn't feel hurt. She hoped he would find another girlfriend very soon. She had come prepared to buy him and Nora a present – the hankie with the two and threepence in was clutched in her hand. She'd taken it when Mam wasn't looking because she didn't think she'd approve. She'd get Nora a Mars Bar, and ten Woodbines for Tommy.

The air-raid siren went, but outside, in the sunshine, with people around, the sound wasn't so terrifying as in the darkness of the night. It didn't seem real. Tommy, perched on the lamp-post, showed no sign of having heard. Josie anxiously watched the doors of the Prince Albert, praying Mam would come. A man and two women came out and sauntered in the direction of the shelter. Then Mam opened the door and shouted, 'Josie, luv. I'm going to the lavvy. I'll be out in the twinkling of an eye.'

Josie trotted across to the sweetshop. A bell rang when she opened the door. Inside it was small and dark and smelled of tobacco. The walls were tobacco-coloured. Two were lined with glass jars containing a mouth-watering array of sweets. There was no sign of cigarettes on the shelves behind the counter, and it was only then she remembered Maude saying ciggies were harder to get than gold dust.

The old woman appeared from a room at the back, putting on her coat. 'I'm off to the shelter, luv. I was just about to close up.'

'Have you got any ciggies?'

'No, and I wouldn't sell them to you if I had. You're too young.' The woman smiled at her good-naturedly.

'Can I have some sweets, then?'

The woman smiled again as she buttoned up her coat. 'Sorry, luv, but I'm not prepared to weigh them out, not while there's a raid about to start. I'm rather anxious to get to the shelter.' She cocked her head and listened. 'In fact, I think I can hear a plane now – it sounds like more than one.' She came from behind the counter and began to push Josie towards the door. 'Come with me, luv. Hold me hand. You can come back for the sweets later.'

'But I wanted . . .' Josie turned to look at the bars of chocolate at the front of the counter behind a sheet of glass '. . . three Mars bars.' One for herself, one for Nora and one for Tommy, though he would have preferred ten Woodies.

Suddenly, there was a high-pitched whine, which got louder and louder, and higher and higher, and the old woman, instead of pushing her out, was pulling her back, and she was shoved behind the counter, where she fell full length. The old woman landed on top of her, nearly knocking her out.

Then the whole world erupted with a dull rumbling sound, the floor shook, the windows shattered, a mighty wind raged through the shop and the bottles flew from the shelves. Something big and heavy thudded against the counter, wood broke, glass broke, the counter fell backwards with a creak and a groan, and propped itself against the shelves where the ciggies should have been. Josie and her protector were showered with shards of glass.

The rumbling stopped, the world stood still. There was, for a moment, silence. In that brief ensuing silence, Josie was sure she could have heard a pin drop. Then someone screamed, someone shouted, a child cried.

Nora! She prayed the child was Nora. If Nora was all right, then so was Mam. Surely. Please, God, *please, God, make Mam be all right.*

She tried to scramble to her feet, but the old woman said with bewildering calm, 'Don't move, luv. Let me edge out first. Careful you don't cut yourself, mind. There's glass everywhere.'

Mam, Mam, Mam! The word hammered through her head.

The woman was gradually crawling backwards, oh, but so slowly, too slowly. Josie felt the weight on her body ease. A minute later, ignoring the advice to take it easy, be careful where she put her hands, 'Oh, mind out, luv!', she was free to shuffle through the glass and the dozens of bars of chocolate that had slid off the counter. Her hands and arms were bleeding, she could feel glass in her hair. Her dress was torn. She didn't care.

The first thing she noticed when she stood upright was that it was so bright. When she'd entered the shop it had been dark. Now it was bright, because there was no window, no door, no front to the shop at all, and no building opposite to shut out the light.

No Prince Albert!

The shop was full of chunks of masonry. Dark green tiles glittered like emeralds in the rubble. Grey dust hung in the air. The Prince Albert lay in ruins before her. It lay in the shop and in the street outside, blown into a million pieces.

The crying child was Shirl. She cried still, across the street, standing in the rubble, holding her baby sister and crying for her mam.

Josie regarded the destruction with dull, uncomprehending eyes. A bell clanged. A fire engine was approaching, or it might have been an ambulance, she didn't know. People appeared, their faces fierce and angry, and began to pull at the debris with their bare hands.

And as it slowly began to make sense, Josie felt curiously empty, withered, like Tommy's arm, as if her heart and soul, her spirit, had flown up to heaven to be with Mam.

Machin Street
1940–1951

1

After the explosion, Josie was taken to a still, silent place where there were nuns. She refused to give her name. Either she couldn't speak, or she wouldn't speak. No one was sure, not even Josie.

The sisters were very kind. They blessed her, fed her, put her to bed, dabbed her cut hands with iodine and said hundreds of Hail Marys, rosary beads threaded through their worn fingers. They provided her with a red gingham frock much too small, and a cardigan much too big, because the clothes she had arrived in were dirty and badly torn. Josie had no idea how long she stayed in the silent place. She knew she was alive, but she felt dead.

One morning, Sister Bernadette, who looked about a hundred, came to Josie's tiny white room, with its iron bed and wooden crucifix on the wall. Maude was with her. She wore a dreadful felt hat shaped like a tin helmet, and a moth-eaten fur coat which Mam had said privately looked as if it was made from rats.

'That's her!' Maude exclaimed. 'That's Josie Flynn.' She fell upon Josie with open arms. 'Oh, luv!'

'I'm afraid she has lost the power of speech,' Sister Bernadette murmured.

At this, Maude gave a little shriek, seized Josie's shoulders and violently shook her, as if the power of speech could be restored if she was rattled hard enough. Then she burst into tears. 'She's the spitting image of her poor mam, you know, Mabel – may the good Lord rest her soul.' She bowed her head and made the sign of the cross.

According to the whispered conversation that took place between Maude and Sister Bernadette in the corridor, not everyone had died in the Prince Albert. Most customers had been pulled out of the wreckage alive. But Mam, in the lavatory, in the yard where the bomb had fallen, had taken the full blast. Josie had known the very second it happened. She had felt it in her heart.

Two children had been killed. Well, the building had virtually landed on top of them. One a boy of ten, the other his sister, only two. And, would you believe, their mam, who had suffered only a few scratches, had been seen in another pub the next night, laughing fit to bust.

Sister Bernadette said that, no, she wouldn't have believed it, ever, had she not heard it directly from Maude's lips. But she would remember the woman in her prayers, for she was obviously more in need of God's love than most.

'Huh!' Maude said disgustedly, and went on to inform the sister that the bobbies had been round to Huskisson Street looking for Josie because they'd found her identity card in her poor mam's handbag. That was when they'd learned that Mabel was dead. The whole house was stunned. 'The house is flats,' Maude went on, as if it needed an explanation. 'Quite superior flats.'

But where *was* Josie? Nobody knew. Lines of communication had become all tangled between the bobbies and the rescue services. The woman from the sweetshop was somehow involved.

'Is there someone who will take the child – a relative?' Sister Bernadette enquired gently.

'Well, Mabel had a sister living in Machin Street off Penny Lane. I don't know what number. Mind you, I'm not sure if she's fit . . . her husband's a . . .' Maude was becoming as tangled as the lines of communication. 'Knowing Ivy, not that I do, mind, but from what I've heard, she might not take her.' She began to sob again. 'She's such a lovely kid, I'd take her meself, like a shot I would. But me job wouldn't allow it. I work these dead funny hours, see.'

'The authorities will find her, this Ivy. They will sort everything out,' Sister Bernadette said with quiet confidence.

The voices grew fainter as the women walked away. Josie crept over to the door and listened, because she wanted to know everything there was to know about Mam.

'The remains . . . hardly recognisable. Well, you can imagine, can't you, Sister? The girls . . . the other residents, that is . . . making a collection . . . couldn't abide the thought of Mabel going to a pauper's grave . . . only four and sixpence in her purse . . .'

Then the voices faded altogether and Josie heard no more.

Aunt Ivy was as nice as could be, almost fawning, with the woman in a green uniform who took Josie to Machin Street by car two days later. Josie had been told the woman's name, but forgot it immediately. The sky was heavy with dark grey clouds and it was drizzling. The windscreen wipers weren't working properly, and the woman kept tut-tutting when she pressed buttons and nothing happened. She crouched over the wheel, trying to see through water-streaked glass.

They were expected at precisely half past two. The woman had been to see Aunt Ivy the day before to discuss Josie's future. 'She's looking forward to having her pretty little niece to live with her,' the woman said on the way. 'She hasn't any children of her own, so you're all the more welcome. You'll like her, dear. She's very nice.'

Josie didn't answer. Her throat felt as tight as a fist. Perhaps she would never talk again.

'We're turning into Machin Street, Josie. This is where you're going to live.'

I don't want to! She didn't want to live anywhere if it wasn't with Mam, particularly not in one of these red brick houses with square bay windows and sentry-box porches that made the street look like a fortress.

The car stopped. 'Here we are.' The woman got out. She came round and opened Josie's door, saying kindly, 'Don't look so frightened, dear. I'm sure you're going to be very happy with your auntie.'

Aunt Ivy must have been watching through the window as the door opened and she came out and waited for them on the step, clapping her hands and laughing aloud as they approached. 'You're right,' she cried. 'She's just like our Mabel.'

'I never met your sister, Mrs Adams, but one of her friends remarked on the fact to Sister Bernadette.'

'Come in, darling.' Aunt Ivy took Josie's hand. 'I'm sure you're going to be very happy in your new home.'

'That's what I just told her,' the woman smiled.

The woman stayed only a few minutes to hand over Mam's handbag, which looked remarkably undamaged. 'Josie's ration book and identity card are in there. The rest of your sister's possessions are in Huskisson Street. You can collect them any time. Ask for Miss Maude Connelly.'

'Thank you,' Aunt Ivy said, 'but I shan't bother.'

Teddy! She'd forgotten all about him. Josie thought about Teddy sitting on top of the gas masks. She remembered her new velvet frock, Mam's bezzie costume, all ready to come to this very house last Sunday after Mass. Her heart threatened to burst with sadness. If only she hadn't gone to buy sweets that night. If only she'd stayed outside the Prince Albert with Tommy and Nora, then she would be dead. More than anything in the world she wished she were dead so she could be with Mam.

The woman was going, she had a dozen things to do that afternoon. She kissed Josie's cheek and wished her every happiness, and shook Aunt Ivy's hand. 'She's such a sweet little girl. With a bit of love and kindness, I'm sure her voice will soon come back. It was almost certainly the shock that did it, the shock of the explosion, then losing her mother. I've known it happen before. If you have any problems, do get in touch. You have my card. Goodbye, Mrs Adams. Goodbye, Josie.'

'Tara,' Aunt Ivy called as she closed the door.

Josie shrank against the row of coats hanging in the hall, because in the space of the few seconds it took to shut the door and turn around Aunt Ivy had become a completely different person. No longer smiling, her eyes glittered alarmingly as she swooped upon her niece, grabbed her arm and led her none too gently into a room at the back of the house. Four chairs with backs like ladders were set around a table covered with a dark green chenille cloth. The sideboard was twice the size of the one in Huskisson Street, with shelves almost reaching the ceiling, full of darkly patterned dishes. Through the window, overlooking a small garden, she could see that a corrugated-iron air raid shelter had been built.

'Sit down,' Aunt Ivy said curtly.

'I want it understood right from the start,' Aunt Ivy went on in the same curt voice when they were seated at the table, a voice nothing like the one she'd used when the woman was there, 'that I'm only having you because it's me Christian duty. Seeing as how you're me sister's child, to do otherwise would be a sin. You'll have a roof over your head, I'll feed and clothe you, but that's as far as it goes. Have you got that, miss?'

Josie nodded. Her head was throbbing. A ball of black fear rolled around her stomach, and she was worried she might vomit all over the posh cloth. It was horrible here, she hated it. And she hated Aunt Ivy most of all.

There was nothing about Aunt Ivy to remind her of Mam. It was hard to believe they had been sisters. Neither tall nor short, thin nor fat, her aunt's eyes were the colour of dirty water. She had yellow, mottled skin and a very low hairline, rigidly straight. When she frowned, as she did now, the black hair and thick black eyebrows almost met. Her hair was neatly parted, neatly waved, and a hairclip secured the longer side. She wore a purple costume with a mauve lacy jumper underneath, high-heeled black shoes and a surprising amount of make-up – almost as much as Irish Rose, though she didn't use mascara. Her nails were very long and painted scarlet.

'Don't you nod at me, miss,' she snapped. 'I want a proper answer, using the voice that the good God gave you. You can't fool me with your silly histrionics. I said, *have you got that?*'

The fist in Josie's throat tightened further. She tried to swallow, but it wouldn't go down. Aunt Ivy pinched her wrist, the scarlet nails dug into her flesh, and her throat felt even tighter. Her eyes smarted with the pain, and she knew that she had to answer to make the pain go away. She swallowed again, almost choking on the fist, and a sound like a grunt was expelled from her mouth. 'Yes,' she croaked.

Aunt Ivy released her wrist and her face twisted in an unpleasant smile. 'I thought as much. It was all put on. Your mam was the same, always putting on an act, full of airs and graces, making eyes at people.' She placed her arms on the table and leaned forward, so that her face was only inches from Josie's own. Her breath smelled worse than Maude's. 'Now, miss, we've got matters to discuss. I've taken you in, but I'm not having the neighbours knowing me sister gave birth to a bastard, so we've got to make up a story. I want you to listen very carefully. From now on, you're only five, not six. Understand?'

Josie opened her mouth to argue, but stopped when her aunt reached for her wrist.

'You're only five, otherwise they'll guess why our Mabel left home. A year later, she was old enough to get married, and that makes you legitimate. Her husband, your dad, was killed in the Battle of Britain.'

'But Mam didn't have a husband, and I didn't have a dad,' Josie protested.

Aunt Ivy impatiently pursed her red lips. 'I know that, and you know that, but we want the neighbours knowing something different. I told you, this is a story. We're making it up. Your dad was a rear gunner in the RAF. His name was – John Smith! Mabel met him when she was working as a nanny. I'll say I didn't tell anyone because I disapproved, thought she was too young to get married. You stayed living over the water, anywhere will do – Ellesmere Port. Repeat that, miss – Ellesmere Port.'

'Ellesmere Port,' Josie said reluctantly. Mam had taught her never to tell lies.

'And what was your dad?'

'A rear gunner in the RAF. He died in the Battle of Britain.'

'And his name?' Her aunt raised her thick, black brows.

'John Smith.' It was all very difficult to take in. 'Does it mean I'm not Josie Flynn any more?'

'It most certainly does, miss. From now on, you're Josephine Smith, and you're only five.' Aunt Ivy leaned back in the chair, looking pleased. 'Good. You've got a good memory, like your mam. She could tell me things I'd said years ago, repeat them word for word. It means you should do well at school, like she did. You'll be starting Monday, it's all arranged. Sat'day, we'll go to Penny Lane and get you some clothes.'

She looked through the window at the yard and said thoughtfully, 'It's got Flynn on your ration book, so I'll have to register you with shops that don't know me, somewhere in town. I'll go in me dinner hour. It'll be a nuisance, but the shops round here know everyone's business.' She got to her feet.

'Well, miss, I'm going back to work now. I had to take two hours off because of you, and I've got a very responsible job. I'm secretary to the head of Claims at the Mersey Insurance Company. Mr Roberts can't cope if I'm not there.' She smirked. 'I'm never home before six, so someone's coming round at four to make your tea, but you can learn to do it yourself in future so that we don't have to bother people. My Vince is on afternoons – it'll be half ten at least by the time he puts in an appearance.' She looked keenly at the child crouched over the table. 'Did you know you've got an Uncle Vincent?'

'Mam talked about him sometimes.'

'I bet she did, the sly bitch.' She picked up a crocodile handbag off the sideboard. 'I'm off. You be good, and if you stay good, behave yourself and keep out me way, we'll get on just fine. You should be grateful you've got a nice, respectable home.' Her lips twisted in a sneer. 'I know what your mam was up to. If you'd stayed in Huskisson Street with that crowd of slags, you'd have ended up on the streets in time with your slag of a mam. That's right, isn't it, miss?'

Josie was pleating and unpleating the chenille cloth between her fingers, because her hands couldn't keep still. Her aunt's words, horrible words, beat against her brain, like tiny nails being tapped into her head. She felt as old as Sister Bernadette, a hundred, as memories returned, scenes flashed before her eyes and she recalled things that Mam had said.

I couldn't live without my little girl, my Petal.

Hello, Petal. I'm home.

She visualised her beautiful mother standing at the foot of the bed, arms outstretched. She used to think Mam was weak, but last Friday she'd been ready to defend her daughter with her life. Josie firmly believed she would have killed the two men if Irish Rose and the black man hadn't come. *I'll swing for you,* she'd said. Mam was strong. And *she* would be strong. No one would insult her and get away with it. *No one.* She wouldn't be sneered at or called names. And the same applied to her mother – she had no idea what a slag was, but it sounded horrible.

Aunt Ivy was still waiting for a reply. She returned to the table and tapped her foot. Josie, boosted by her newly found confidence, decided that if her wrist was pinched again, then her hand could drop off before she'd admit her aunt was right. She looked up at her, and felt hate burning in her eyes.

'Don't you *dare* call me mam a slag,' she said slowly in a voice so deep it surprised herself. 'You're the one who's horrible. You chucked her out, she told me. And I'd sooner be living in Huskisson Street any day than here.'

'Oh, Oh, I see.' Aunt Ivy was momentarily taken aback, but quickly recovered. Her face darkened. 'Oh, so now we know where we stand. You know, all I have to do when I get to work is pick up the phone and you'll be in an orphanage by tomorrow. Don't imagine I *want* you here.'

'I don't want to be here.'

There was silence. A clock ticked loudly on the wall. It was an extremely grand clock, with peculiar letters instead of numbers on its pearly face.

Aunt Ivy's face turned dark with anger. She said abruptly, 'I haven't time to argue. I'll see you later, miss.' Her heels clicked down the hall. She called, 'We'll soon see who's boss.' The front door closed.

Josie was shaking. She realised she'd won something that she hadn't wanted to win: a minor battle. But she didn't want to be at war with Aunt Ivy. Suddenly, all the hideousness, the misery, of the last few days came washing over her and she began to cry. It was the first time she'd cried since her mother died, and the sobs racked her body till it hurt. Her chest was sore, her throat was sore, hot tears scalded her eyes. She couldn't believe that she would never see Mam again, or hear her voice, touch her, live with her in the attic room. It seemed she was destined to live in Machin Street with Aunt Ivy for ever. The future, so bright a few days ago, stretched ahead of her, black, miserable and lonely. Everything had changed in the twinkling of an eye. She put her hands to her ears, to block out the future, to block out the fact that Mam was dead.

Why, then, could she hear screaming? Not so much screaming as a thin, pathetic wail, as if a small animal were caught in a trap, pleading to be rescued.

The screaming, the wail, came from herself, and she was running round the house, running upstairs, slamming doors, kicking furniture, beating the walls with her fists. And screaming. She pulled at curtains, threw pillows and cushions on the floor. In the bathroom she stopped to vomit in the sink, then rested her forehead on the cool, white porcelain rim.

After a while she lifted her eyes, and noticed the lavatory. It didn't just have a wooden seat, but a lid as well. She sat on the lid, feeling calmer. Mam would be dead ashamed if she knew the way she'd just behaved. She'd been determined to make a good impression on Aunt Ivy. 'I'm not having her turning up her nose at us,' she'd said.

Josie slid off the lavatory, cleaned the sink and went around the house straightening the curtains, putting the cushions and pillows back in place. This time she noticed the lovely things that Mam had told her about. The ornaments and little items of fancy furniture, the pictures and mats that her very own grandad had brought back from foreign countries like Japan – elaborate brass candlesticks, mosaic bowls, statues, vases. She sat briefly on the puffy green settee in the parlour and admired the carved elephant with ivory horns with a table on its back. In the big main bedroom, two lamps with shades made from little bits of coloured glass glittered on each side of the double bed, which was covered with a mountainous maroon eiderdown.

There were two bedrooms at the back, one full of cardboard boxes. The other must have been Mam's and, she assumed, would be hers. A pretty white mat with raised flowers lay beside the single bed which had a dark blue embroidered coverlet. Another brightly coloured mat hung from a pole on the wall, which seemed a most peculiar thing to do with a mat, though perhaps it was a picture: a man, a shepherd because he had a crook, was standing at the foot of a mountain, a hand shading his eyes as he stared at a rainbow.

Josie threw herself on the bed, exhausted, and stared at the ceiling. In its much smaller way, this house was as grand as the one in Huskisson Street when it had been owned by the importer of rare spices. Even so, she didn't want to live there, not with Aunt Ivy.

But where else could she go? Even if Maude was willing to have her, Josie knew that Mam, up in heaven, would strongly disapprove. And Mam would be as miserable as sin if she knew her Josie was in an orphanage. She supposed that she had no alternative but to stay with Aunt Ivy, pretend her name was Smith and that she'd once had a dad called John. Most of all, she resented having to say that she was five, because she was proud of being six.

She closed her eyes. If only she could sleep and never wake up! Sleep, however, refused to come, and she remained stubbornly awake, reliving last Saturday, hearing the bomb, the explosion, over and over. She'd *known* Mam was dead, she'd just *known*.

When someone knocked on the front door at first she considered taking no notice. But the knock came again. It was almost certainly the person to make her tea. If she didn't answer, it would be reported back to Aunt Ivy, and she'd have another black mark against her.

She trudged downstairs, wishing she'd had time to wash her face because it was probably all swollen, and her eyes felt as if they were glued together. She wished it even more when she opened the door and found a smiling Mrs Kavanagh and Lily on the doorstep, both looking extremely smart. Mrs Kavanagh wore a pink linen costume and matching hat, and Lily a grey pleated skirt and a white jersey. She had a leather satchel over her shoulder. Her long brown hair rippled, like a cloak, around her shoulders.

'Hello, Josie, luv. We've met before, remember?' Mrs Kavanagh said warmly.

'Have you been crying?' Lily demanded.

'No,' Josie said pugnaciously. 'I never cry.'

'Me, I'd cry buckets if me ma died.' Lily tossed her head and looked superior.

'Oh, do be quiet, Lily,' her mother said crossly. 'We all know you have to do the opposite of everyone else.' She turned to Josie. 'I promised Ivy I'd pop in and make your tea, but that seems a bit daft when you can have it with us. We're only just down the street. I'm surprised Ivy didn't take the afternoon off, 'stead of leaving you by yourself on your first day. Are you okay, luv? You look a bit rough.'

'I'm fine, ta.'

'Why is your frock too short?' Lily asked rudely.

'Because a bomb tore me old one,' Josie explained, thinking this would make Lily sorry for her rudeness.

Instead, Lily said smugly, '*We've* never been bombed.'

'Oh, shut up, Lily,' her mother said. 'Come on, Josie. All the kids are home, 'cept Stanley who's at work. And I've made scouse, everyone's favourite. There's treacle pud for afters.'

At the mention of scouse, Josie realised she was starving. She loved scouse – Mam made it all the time because there was a limit to the meals you could do on a hob over the fire.

The Kavanaghs' house wasn't remotely as posh as Aunt Ivy's, but she much preferred its untidy clutter. A fire burned in the parlour, where the flowered three-piece was faded and well worn. Books and toys littered the floor, and the sideboard was piled high with more toys, a pair of football boots and some ravelled knitting. A doll squinted at her from the mantelpiece, reminding her of Irish Rose. In the square bay window, a treadle sewing machine was draped with yards of bright red tulle. A wireless was on, and a woman was singing very loudly, 'Wish me luck as you wave me goodbye.'

Two very sunburnt boys with green eyes and hair the colour of butter wrestled each other on the floor. The biggest, who looked about twelve, was clearly winning, and a girl, a slightly older version of Lily, oblivious to the din, was reading a book, her legs draped over the arm of the chair. She looked up, said, 'Hello,' and returned to the book.

'H-hello,' Josie stammered. The change from the tomb-like atmosphere of her aunt's house to the noisy chaos of the Kavanaghs' was welcome, but slightly daunting. She stood in the middle of the room, not sure what to do. Should she sit down? Mrs Kavanagh and Lily had disappeared into the kitchen, and she wondered if she should follow, offer to help set the table or something.

The boys had noticed she was there. They stopped wrestling. The older one held his brother down by the throat, and asked curiously, 'Who are you?'

'I'm Josie Flynn, I mean Smith.'

The boy grinned. 'Josie Flynn-I-mean-Smith. That's a dead funny name.'

Josie drew herself to her full height and said haughtily, 'It's Josie Smith.'

'All right, you don't need to bite me head off, Josie Smith. I'm Robert, and this is our Benjamin on the floor. We call him Ben. He's only eight. Us boys are called after prime ministers, Conservative ones, natch.' His green eyes sparkled mischievously. 'The girls are only flowers. That's our Daisy over there. She's ten, and you won't get a word out of her till she's finished that book.'

'Oh, shut up, Robert,' Daisy snapped. 'I'm not likely to finish me book while there's such a racket going on.'

'So why don't you read in the bedroom?'

'Because our Marigold's trying on frocks. She's going to the pictures tonight with Gabrielle McGillivray.'

'What to see?'

Daisy sniffed. 'I dunno, do I? I haven't been invited.'

Josie was doing her best to remember the names – Marigold, Daisy and Lily, Robert, Ben, and who was the boy at work? Stanley, she remembered. She wondered if Mr and Mrs Kavanagh ever got confused when their children were all there together.

Throughout the noisy meal that followed, Mrs Kavanagh got confused all the time. 'Pass us the bread, Mar—, Dais—, *Lily*,' she would finish triumphantly when she got it right. Or, 'Our Robert's late. He should be home by now.'

The children grinned at each other. 'Robert's here, Ma. It's our Stanley who's late.'

The six Kavanaghs had been born neatly, a boy and a girl alternately, all two years apart. The girls were slightly plump like their mother, with the same dark brown eyes and the same brown hair which they wore long and parted in the middle. They looked like a set of Victorian dolls, with their pink, glowing faces, pert noses and tiny rosebud mouths.

Lily might well be the youngest, but she had more to say than the others put together. She talked in a firm, opiniated voice, to be met with, 'Oh, shut up, Lily,' from various members of the family.

At half past five, Stanley arrived home from his boring job in a bank, followed by Mr Kavanagh a few minutes later. He was very tall, very thin, very sunburnt, with pale, creamy hair like his sons. His dark suit was covered with threads, and Josie remembered Mam saying he owned a haberdasher's in Penny Lane. He had the air of a man who was seriously moidered, but smiled benignly on his large family, who were still around the table where they'd been for almost an hour, because everyone was too busy talking to leave. Only eight-year-old Ben, next to Josie, hadn't said a word.

Mrs Kavanagh went into the kitchen and fetched a plate of scouse. 'There's treacle pud for afters, Eddie.'

'Goodo,' he said, winking at Josie, and she thought it mightn't be so bad living in Machin Street, with the Kavanaghs only a few doors away.

At half past six, Mrs Kavanagh suggested she go home. 'Only because Ivy should be back by now and she'll be worried where you are. Tell her it's my fault you're late. Oh, and luv.' Josie was led into the hall, where it wasn't exactly quiet but at least they were alone. Mrs Kavanagh sat on the stairs and pulled her down beside her. 'That time we met in Blackler's basement, luv, I guessed straight away that Mabel was your mam – you're too alike to pretend otherwise. Anyroad, I never told your auntie that I'd seen you. Poor Ivy, she's not a bad woman, but she's a stickler for appearances. It means I know darn well you didn't have a dad who died in the Battle of Britain – Mabel would have been bound to mention she was married the day we met. And I remember you telling me then you were nearly four, so you can't be only five like Ivy ses. I didn't argue when she told me all that rubbish the other night. Even so, her secret's safe with me. And, Josie, whatever happens, remember you're always welcome in this house. Mabel was one of the nicest girls I've ever known, as well as the prettiest. I don't give a damn what she got up to, and she'd have wanted me to be your friend.'

'Ta.' It was a relief to know that another person knew the truth.

'Oh, and another thing, luv. You won't have met your Uncle Vince yet, but you'll find he's a real Prince Charming.'

'Will I?' Josie felt even more relieved. Mam hadn't talked much about Uncle Vince, but she'd had the feeling he'd done something bad. If Mrs Kavanagh thought so highly of him, then she must have got the wrong end of the stick. Who, she wondered was 'His Lordship', the person who had to be given his marching before Mam moved back in?

Lily offered to come with her when she realised she was leaving. 'In case you've forgotten your house, like.'

''Course I haven't forgotten,' Josie said scornfully. 'It's seventy-six.'

'Still, I'll come with you all the same.'

To her surprise, when they were outside Lily linked arms, and Josie didn't know whether to be pleased or annoyed. Since she'd got to know her, she wasn't sure if she liked Lily all that much. She was far too bossy and sure of herself.

'Ma said you're starting St Joseph's on Monday. Our Marigold left last term – she's gone to commercial college – but there's still four of us Kavanaghs left. I'll call for you, shall I?'

'If you like.'

'Pity we won't be in the same class, else I'd have told Tommy Atherton to shove off and you could have sat beside me.'

Josie wriggled her shoulders and didn't answer. Aunt Ivy had been in touch with the school and would have told them she was five, which meant she'd have to go through the whole first year again, learn to read and write and do sums when she could already do them. She was wondering how this could be avoided when Lily said, 'I think our Ben's stuck on you.'

'What?'

'Our Ben, he's got a crush on you. He didn't say a word during tea, just kept looking at you sideways, sort'a thing. Mind you, he's a soppy lad, our Ben. I wouldn't be all that flattered if I were you.'

'Don't worry, I'm not,' Josie snapped.

They had arrived at Aunt Ivy's, who opened the door to Josie's knock, her face like thunder. 'And where the hell d'you think you've been, miss? I've . . .' Her voice became a simper and she gave a sickly smile when she saw Lily. 'Oh, hello, luv. I should have known she'd be in your house. Your mam, she's all heart.'

'She's a living saint, Mrs Adams,' Lily said in sepulchral tones. Josie realised she was making fun of her aunt, and warmed to her new friend. 'And she said Josie can come to ours for tea every night. "Another mouth at the table won't make much difference," as she said to me da'.'

Josie couldn't remember Mrs Kavanagh saying any such thing, but didn't argue. Aunt Ivy began to mutter something about if she was being fed regularly she'd have to take along some rations, and Lily said, 'God bless you, Mrs Adams.' She nudged Josie playfully in the ribs, and went home.

It was hard not to think of the Kavanaghs' happy, noisy house when the door closed and she was left alone with Aunt Ivy, who remarked spitefully, 'If you hadn't been at the Kavanaghs', miss, you'd have gone to bed early. I was dead worried when I got in and you weren't here.'

'I'd like to go to bed early, please.'

Her aunt shrugged. 'Suit yourself. You'll find a nightie on the bed. I got it in Lewis's on me way home from work.'

'Ta.' She was halfway upstairs, already feeling tearful, longing to be alone so she could think about Mam which she'd hardly done at all over the last few hours, when Aunt Ivy called, 'Don't forget to draw the blackout curtains.'

'No.'

'Are you all right?'

Josie turned, taken aback by this unexpected expression of concern. 'I'm okay, ta.' Her aunt was standing at the bottom of the stairs, looking up. Her face was odd, all screwed up, as if she were about to cry.

'I suppose, well, as that woman said this morning, you've had a shock. It'll take a while to get over that business with your mam. I was dead upset when me own mam died, but I got over it eventually. You'll find the same.'

'Ta,' Josie said again. Perhaps Aunt Ivy was sorry about the way she'd behaved earlier and would be nicer in future, but this turned out not to be the case.

2

It wasn't until Saturday, at breakfast, that Josie met Uncle Vince. When she went into the dining room he was tucking into a plate of bacon and fried bread, a small, slight figure wearing a shirt without a collar and a hand-knitted Fair Isle waistcoat. Aunt Ivy, her back to Josie, was pouring tea. She glanced at her niece and didn't speak.

'Hello there, luv.' Uncle Vince turned round and chucked her under the chin. He smiled. 'You're a lovely big girl for six.'

'Five,' Aunt Ivy snapped.

'Oh, yes, five.' He winked at Josie from behind his wife's back, and she risked a little smile back.

As Mrs Kavanagh had said, he was a genuine Prince Charming, with thick, straight hair a lovely golden colour, blue eyes as pale as a misty sky at dawn, and a dead straight nose. Had his chin been firmer, he would have been perfect, but it sloped away under his mouth, making him look weak. He must have been weak, Josie thought, the way he let Aunt Ivy boss him around. Yet the funny thing was, she was mad about him.

She had still been awake last night at half ten when Uncle Vince came home from his job as a quality control inspector at the Royal Ordnance factory in Fazakerley. As he ate his tea, she could hear Aunt Ivy telling him to sit up straight, not put his elbows on the table and eat up quickly before the food got cold, but all said in a fond, dopey voice, as if Vince were a little boy, not her husband.

'My Vince' was how her aunt referred to him when she spoke to the neighbours who'd called to see 'Mabel's little girl' for themselves, and remark in amazement at how incredibly tall she was for five.

'My Vince is on afternoons this week,' Aunt Ivy would say in the same dopey voice, and with an equally dopey smile, or, 'My Vince can't stand that awful dried milk.' 'My Vince would have joined the army like a shot if it hadn't been for his dicky heart.'

When Lily called, Josie was not long home from a shopping trip to Penny Lane where Aunt Ivy had sourly bought her a grey pleated skirt, two white blouses, a navy blue cardigan, shoes, socks, underwear and a drab brown frock with long sleeves that was dead cheap but would do for church and to wear around the house until Mrs Kavanagh ran up something nicer.

'You can chuck that rag away when we get home.' Aunt Ivy nodded at the red gingham frock. 'I'd have thought Mabel would have decked up her kid a bit smarter. I made sure she was dressed nice when she was your age.'

Josie thought about the blue velvet frock from Paddy's market. A picture flashed through her mind, of Mam ironing the frock. It seemed like an eternity ago. 'There, that's everything done,' she'd said. Later, they'd waltzed around the room.

'Come on.' Her reverie was rudely interrupted by Aunt Ivy pinching her arm. 'It's time we made tracks. My Vince will be dying for a cuppa.'

They hadn't been in five minutes when Lily knocked. 'Me ma thought Josie would like to see the fairy glen in Sefton Park,' she said sweetly to Aunt Ivy.

Josie was upstairs, changing into the brown frock. 'I'm sure she would, luv,' Aunt Ivy said in a grovelling voice.

When she came down, Lily was in the parlour chattering away to Uncle Vince about football. He had a pools coupon on his knee, the wireless was on and he was waiting for the results.

'You won't win much,' Lily warned. 'Even if you get eight draws, you'll only get about fifteen hundred pounds, least so me da' says. Since the war, people have stopped doing the pools.'

'Fifteen hundred quid would do me fine, luv,' Uncle Vince replied.

Aunt Ivy ruffled his golden hair. 'I thought I told you to put your collar on, Vince,' she said fondly. 'It looks bad when people come.'

'Oh, sorry, luv. I forgot. I'll do it in a minute.'

'You better had.'

'That's a horrible dress,' Lily said the minute they were outside. 'It's the sort of thing they wear in the workhouse.' Before Josie could think of an equally rude reply, Lily put her arm through Josie's and said, 'I see you've met My Vince.'

'He's very nice,' Josie said defensively. She was convinced Vince would be even friendlier if it wasn't for his wife.

'Oh, he's dead lovely, My Vince.' Lily giggled. 'Our Marigold's madly in love with him, but me da' said Ivy would kill her stone dead if she found out. He doesn't like either of 'em.'

'Your da' doesn't like your Marigold?' Josie gasped.

'No, silly. He can't stand My Vince or your Auntie Ivy. He said *she's* besotted, though I don't know what that means, and *he's* a ponce. I don't know what that means either. Me da' thinks he only married her 'cos she had a house. It's usually the fella that supplies the house. And, according to me da', your auntie's not short of a few bob. She *bought* his services, he said. When I asked for an explanation, I was told to mind me own business. He wasn't talking to me, but to me ma.

' "Look at the clothes she's always buying him," he said before he realised I was listening. "He's got four suits." Me poor da's only got two, one for best and one for every day. Ma says he's jealous, because she doesn't wait on him hand and foot, like Ivy does My Vince, and he's not nearly so good-looking.'

They had reached Sefton Park, and Lily showed her the fairy glen, a small clearing where the surrounding trees were turning bronze, and a few leathery leaves had already fallen on to the emerald grass, dotted with buttercups and daisies. The sun shone through the trees, making yellow patterns underneath. A slight breeze shook the branches, and the patterns shivered.

Josie was instantly enraptured. They were the only ones there, and the atmosphere was magical, like something out of a book. She half expected a fairy or an elf to come dancing towards her as she wandered down the sloping bank towards a stream, where goldfish, all different sizes, swam lazily in the tinkling, silvery water. If only she could stay for ever, never see Aunt Ivy again, but hide herself in the dark, rocky place where the stream disappeared and the trees joined thickly together to make an arch.

Two ducks came paddling towards her in their ungainly way, quacking angrily. Josie backed away. Perhaps living here wasn't such a good idea.

'They won't hurt you.' Lily was standing beside her. She must have sensed that Josie was awesomely impressed by the fairy glen. Her expression was smug, as if she owned the place, had planted the trees herself and had supplied the fish and the ducks and the frog that suddenly leapt from the water on to the bank.

'Have you seen trees before?' she asked patronisingly.

''Course I have,' Josie snapped. 'Mam used to take me to Princes Park.'

'What was your mam like?'

'Beautiful.'

'I bet she wasn't as beautiful as mine.'

It seemed a futile argument. Josie didn't bother to reply. She watched the frog, which kept leaping and pausing, leaping and pausing, until it disappeared from sight.

There was silence, which she already realised was unusual when in the company of Lily Kavanagh. Then Lily said in a careful voice, 'Do you like me?'

'I'm not sure,' Josie said honestly.

'I'd like you to like me.'

'We'll just have to see.'

'You can come to the pics with us tonight,' Lily said in a coaxing voice, as if this might help Josie make up her mind.

'The pics?'

'The pictures, to see a film. Me ma's taking me and our Ben to see Deanna Durbin in *Spring Parade*. Have you never been to the pictures, Josie?'

'No. But me Auntie Ivy mightn't let me.'

'She will if I ask. She'll do anything to keep in with the Kavanaghs.' Lily puffed out her chest conceitedly. 'We're the most important family in the street. Me da's a councillor on the corpy, as well as chairman of the Conservative Party, and me ma runs the Townswomen's Guild. Our Stanley and Marigold are the Amateur Junior Waltz Champions of the North East of England.'

Lily hesitated and looked less sure of herself. 'Or it might be the North West. They don't do it so much nowadays. They used to go with a crowd in a big charabanc to places like Manchester and Blackpool, but now there isn't the petrol. You can come with us to the Grafton ballroom next time there's an exhibition. Our Stanley's got an evening suit, a proper one, and Marigold's got seven spangly frocks me ma made. You should be dead pleased that I like you and want you for a friend.'

'Oh, I am,' Josie said sarcastically. Privately, she was impressed, particularly with the waltzing bit. The sarcasm was wasted on Lily, who greeted the reply with a complacent smile.

'Anyroad,' she said, 'your auntie will be pleased if you go out tonight. Sat'days, her and My Vince go to the pics in town. She wears her fur coat, and he gets dolled up to the nines. Me da' ses he looks like one of them dummies in Burton's shop window.'

St Joseph's was already three days into the autumn term when Josie started on Monday. She noticed she was taller than all the girls in class 1 and most of the boys. When the teacher, Miss Simms, called the register, she answered clearly in a loud voice. Not normally given to pushing herself forward, she showed off outrageously, putting up her hand at every opportunity when the class was asked a question. At break time, Miss Simms asked her to remain behind.

'Would you like to read this page for me, Josie?'

The page was composed of short sentences of mostly three-letter words. The cat sat on the mat. The man had a gun. The dog lay by the log.

Josie read the entire page without a pause. Miss Simms was impressed. 'Who taught you to read, dear?'

'Me mam,' Josie said in a rush. After all, Aunt Ivy considered it all right to tell lies. 'She taught me to do sums, an' all. I can do add up and take away. *And* I've learnt some of the Catechism. I know the Pope cannot err, but I don't know what err means. Do you, miss?'

Miss Simms laughed. 'It means he can't make a mistake, and it's clever of you to ask. But I think *I* might be erring if I kept you in this class. I'd better have a word with Mr Leonard, the headmaster.'

On Tuesday morning she was moved up to class 2, which had been her objective all along. It was annoying when Mr Leonard took her into the new classroom, and Lily Kavanagh leapt to her feet and screeched, 'Can she sit beside me, sir? I'm the only friend she has in the world.'

Josie was woken at half past eleven that night by Aunt Ivy shaking her arm. 'The siren's gone. Come on, miss, stir yourself. My Vince is working. He's on nights.'

'Where are we going?' Josie stumbled out of bed, half-asleep.

'The shelter, of course. Get a move on.'

The air-raid shelter was small, with a narrow bunk each side. Aunt Ivy lit a portable fire, and the shelter immediately stank of burning oil. The light from the fire revealed a dead spider suspended from a single thread. Josie lay on a bunk, and the dead spider sprang to life, raced up the thread and disappeared behind one of the wooden struts supporting the roof. She kept her eyes firmly on the spot where it had disappeared, knowing she'd never sleep a wink while it was there. The bombs didn't bother her. She didn't care if she was killed.

A thought occurred to her. She was reluctant to speak to her aunt unless she absolutely had to, but this seemed one of those times. 'Where will I sleep if there's a raid when Uncle Vince is home?'

Aunt Ivy was adjusting a thick, flesh-coloured net over her metal curlers. She tied the net under her chin. Her head was curiously at odds with the rest of her, as she wore a glamorous black satin dressing-gown and lace nightie. She only wore the curlers when Vince was at work. Other times, she waved her hair with metal tongues which she heated on the fire. She plumped the pillow. 'I suppose you'll have to curl up with me.'

Never! Never in a million years.

Two days later, when the siren went, Josie clung to the headboard and refused to get up. 'I'm not scared, I'd sooner stay.'

'But you can't!' Aunt Ivy raged. 'It's dangerous. You might be killed.'

'I'm not going,' Josie said flatly. 'You'll have to drag me there.'

The buzz of planes could be heard, getting closer. For a few seconds, Aunt Ivy glanced wildly from her niece to the door, before giving up. 'On your own head be it, miss,' she said in clipped tones, and closed the bedroom door.

As the weeks went by the raids got worse, but the worse they got, the closer Josie felt to Mam. She could almost *feel* Mam's warm body in the bed with her as the bombs screamed to earth and exploded with deafening thuds. The house would rock.

After a while, she decided she didn't want to die after all. She would never stop missing her mother, but even though Mam was dead, incredibly, it seemed possible to be happy, at least for some of the time.

'Shove off, our Ben,' Lily said cruelly when her brother tried to sit by them in the school canteen. They were just finishing their dinner.

'Don't speak to him like that,' Josie admonished when a downcast Ben loped away, shoulders hunched. With his thin face, big, brown eyes and shaggy blond hair, he reminded her of a defenceless puppy. She felt sorry for him, and was fed up with the way he was treated by his sister. Most people quickly got fed up with Lily and her bossy ways. It seemed to Josie that *she* was the only friend Lily had in the world, not the other way round.

'He's a drip,' Lily sneered as they wandered into the playground.

'No, he's not. Cissie O'Neill said the other day he's very clever. He's expected to pass the scholarship when he's ten, and go to grammar school.'

Lily's eyes narrowed. 'Since when have you been friends with Cissie O'Neill?'

'I'm not, we were just talking. Though I wouldn't mind us being friends, she's very nice.'

'Hmm.' Lily considered this seriously and must have decided it wasn't a line of conversation she wished to continue because she said, 'Only drips pass scholarships.'

'Only thickos fail them,' Josie replied smartly. Perhaps the reason she didn't mind Lily so much was because she gave as good as she got. She wasn't prepared be told what to do, or what not to do, by someone who was shorter than she was and only a month older, not that Lily knew that.

Lily took offence at this, and marched off with her little nose in the air, but quickly returned when she could find no one else to play with. She took Josie's arm, and they smiled warmly at each other.

'Josie.'

Josie turned, and saw Ben Kavanagh galloping towards her on his long, thin legs. She was on her way home from school, by herself for a change because Lily was off with a cold and driving her mother to distraction with her non-stop demands.

Ben blushed scarlet, and mumbled something which at first she didn't catch. He licked his lips nervously and repeated the words. 'Can I carry your satchel?'

'If you like.' She gave it to him, and thought he looked a bit daft with a satchel on each arm.

'Are you coming to ours for tea?'

'Well, yes.' It was a silly question, but she reckoned he was embarrassed. She had tea with the Kavanaghs every day. 'But I've got to call home first for a pound of self-raising flour.' Last week it had been margarine, and the week before a tin of cocoa, because Aunt Ivy insisted on providing rations to make up for what Josie ate.

Ben seemed useless at conversation. His Adam's apple kept wobbling as he cleared his throat to speak, but nothing came. Josie felt desperately sorry for him, and searched her mind for something to say, but Ben's awkward silence seemed to have affected her too. 'It's a nice warm day for December,' was all she could manage.

'Yes,' Ben croaked. After an awkward pause, he went on, 'They say it will stay warm over Christmas. Not like last year. Remember last year, Josie?'

She nodded. Last year it had snowed and snowed, and the whole world had been muffled in white. The attic had felt particularly warm and cosy. Her face grew sad at the memory.

'You're very brave,' Ben said boldly.

'Brave?' Josie stared at him. He was still very pink.

He cleared his throat again. 'Ma told us about your mam and dad, both dying, like. Your face is often sad, like it was just now, but you never cry.'

'Oh!' She felt touched. He was much more perceptive than his sister. She said impulsively, 'But I do cry, Ben. I cry every night with me head under the bedclothes so no one'll hear.'

Ben's face crumpled, as if he was about to cry himself. 'That's awful,' he gulped.

Josie smiled cheerfully. 'I'll just have to get along with it, won't I? Promise you won't tell your Lily about me crying. She'd never understand.'

He looked chuffed at the idea of them sharing a secret. 'Don't worry, I won't say a word.'

There were times when Josie felt very odd, like two completely different little girls living in two completely different worlds. In one world, the outside one, lived the Josie who liked school, Lily's best friend. In the other, darker world, a silent, surly Josie lived with Aunt Ivy, and cried for her mam every night.

She never told anyone how horrid it was at home because she didn't want them feeling sorry for her, particularly Lily.

Aunt Ivy was impossible to please. If Josie put something down, it should have been put somewhere else, and she would be told so in an awful sneering voice, as if she were dead stupid. To be the object of such derision made her feel less than human.

'You're as bad as Mabel. She was never much of a one for housework. I bet that place you lived was filthy.'

Remembering how Mam had usually kept their attic spotless, Josie wanted to shout that this wasn't true, but she had given up arguing. It wasn't lack of courage, or that answering back made things worse, but her sullen silences, sullen eyes, drove her aunt wilder than words would ever do.

'Cat got your tongue?' she would scream hysterically, and shake her till her head was spinning.

For the slightest of reasons she would be sent to bed early, and sometimes for no reason at all, which she didn't mind because it was better than sitting in the parlour with Aunt Ivy and My Vince, and being picked on all the time.

Not that Uncle Vince said anything nasty. When his wife wasn't looking, he'd wink at Josie, and throw her a big smile.

And soon they were to share another secret, Josie and her Uncle Vince.

Christmas week, and the air raids were the heaviest Liverpool had known. They continued throughout the night, night after night, lasting ten hours, eleven, twelve.

The night before Christmas Eve, Josie listened to the sound of her city being blown to smithereens by Hitler's bombs. It was like hell on earth, impossible not to be frightened. Fire engines clanged, fires crackled, glass shattered, people screamed, the earth shuddered. She put her arms around the pillow and tried to pretend it was Mam.

During a lull, her aunt came in and called upstairs for her to come to the shelter, but Josie refused. She yearned for company, but not her aunt's. She wanted Maude, or Lily – any one of the Kavanaghs would have done. Most of all she wanted her mother. It didn't seem fair, she thought fretfully. Cissie O'Neill sat under the stairs with her little brother when there was a raid, and their mam read stories until they went to sleep. The Kavanaghs went to Hughes's cellar, the bakery on the corner, because their shelter wasn't big enough for eight people, and they played I Spy and the Churchwarden's Cat. Other children went to public shelters with flasks of tea and sandwiches, and sang 'Bless 'Em All' or 'We're Going to Hang Out the Washing on the Siegfried Line'.

The all clear went at a quarter past five. Her aunt and uncle came indoors, the kettle was put on, dishes rattled. After a while they came upstairs, and she could hear them talking. Eventually, the bed creaked, as they lay down to catch a few hours' sleep.

But Josie couldn't sleep. She lay, tossing and turning, wondering if any other girls and boys had lost their mams during the night. War was wicked. She couldn't understand it.

Some time later, the front door closed. Aunt Ivy had gone to work, but was finishing early, at lunchtime. My Vince must still be in bed. She almost wished it were a schoolday, that Lily would call any minute. They liked to get to school before everyone else and play ball in the empty playground.

She slid out of bed and opened the blackout curtains. A pall of black smoke hung low in the sky, which was otherwise bright and clear. The houses behind were still standing, and a woman cleaning an upstairs window gave her a little wave. Josie waved back. No matter how bad the raids, people very quickly returned to normal. She got dressed and washed her face in the bathroom. Her eyes were sticky, her knees shaky, as if they might give way any minute. She hoped they wouldn't, because she and Lily were going to Penny Lane this avvy – if Penny Lane still existed – to buy Christmas presents for each other.

Apart from the ticking of the various clocks, the house was quiet. Josie made her bed, and a feeling of terrible loneliness swept over her. She groaned, determined not to cry.

'Is that you, Josie? Are you all right, luv? That was a raid and a half, that was.'

Uncle Vince! 'I'm all right, ta,' she called.

'Why don't you come and say hello?'

Josie hesitated, then slowly crept along the landing. Uncle Vince was sitting up with the maroon eiderdown tucked around him. He wore blue and grey striped pyjamas buttoned to the neck and his bright golden hair was tousled. There was a tray of tea things on the bedside table. He smiled, and patted the space beside him. 'Come on, luv. I heard that groan. Come and tell your Uncle Vince all about it. What's up, luv?'

She sat on the bed. Uncle Vince slid an arm around her shoulders. 'We've never had a little tête-à-tête before.'

'What's that?'

'A little talk, a chinwag. Either you're in, or I'm out, or Ivy's here.' Josie assumed from this that her aunt wouldn't approve of the little talk. 'I've wanted to ask about Mabel.'

'About me mam?' Josie was startled.

'I wondered what she got up to after she left, that's all. I miss her terrible. She was like a ray of sunshine, Mabel.' He shifted in the bed and scratched his perfect nose. 'Did she ever talk about me?' he asked casually.

'Sometimes.'

His arm tensed around her shoulders. 'I hope she only said nice things.'

'I can't remember. Did someone used to live here called His Lordship? She didn't like him much.'

Uncle Vince gave a funny little gasp. 'Not since I've been here, luv.' He looked down at her with his kind, blue eyes. 'I expect you still miss Mabel, your mam.'

'Oh, yes!' Perhaps it was the arm on her shoulders, the kind eyes, the wistful, understanding expression on his face, as if he knew exactly how she felt, that made her cry – not the despairing, hopeless way she cried at night, her head under the clothes, but sad, gentle tears, more to do with the fact that she hadn't slept a wink and had been frightened out of her wits during the raid.

'There, there, luv.' Uncle Vince stroked her face and kissed her cheek, and it was so nice to think that someone actually *cared* that Josie cried for ages and ages, until she fell asleep.

'Josie, luv.' She woke up to find Vince, fully dressed, beside the bed. 'Your friend's here, Lily.' He lifted her up and sat her on his knee. 'Let's not tell anyone about our little tête-à-tête, eh? Ivy, well she's inclined to be jealous, like, and she'd only take it out on you. We'll keep it a secret, luv, just between you and me.'

The bombing of Liverpool continued for another year. It wasn't until after the following Christmas that it stopped altogether, and everyone gave a collective sigh of relief.

After that, it was easy to believe there was no such thing as war. Josie and Lily went regularly to the pictures, and Josie fell in love with Humphrey Bogart, who was, Lily said scathingly, hideously ugly. She far preferred Alan Ladd, who was a little bit like My Vince. If the film was a U certificate, they were allowed to go by themselves, otherwise Mr and Mrs Kavanagh would take them, or Stanley and his girlfriend, Beryl. The minute they got inside, Stanley and Beryl would make for the back row, where they would kiss each other extravagantly and entirely ignore the film, which Josie and Lily thought daft. Why didn't they do it outside for free?

It came as a shock when, twelve months later, Stanley received his call-up papers. He was nearly eighteen.

All the Kavanaghs, Josie and Beryl, went to the Pier Head to wave goodbye to the thin young man about to sail to North Africa, looking so vulnerable in his khaki uniform. Beryl burst into tears when the ship's horn went, and soon everyone was crying, including Josie. It was like losing a big brother. She turned, without thinking, and buried her head in Ben's shoulder.

'Don't worry, Josie. You've got me.'

She looked up in surprise, remembering Tommy, who'd once said the same thing. Ben was blushing but, then, he rarely spoke without going red. 'I'll take you to the pictures from now on.' He went even redder, and looked as if he were about to curl up and die with embarrassment.

'It would have to be a U certificate, or we wouldn't be let in,' Josie said practically. He was only ten.

Two weeks later, they went to see Will Hay in *The Ghost of St Michael's*. Josie had assumed Lily would be coming, but Ben made it plain his sister wasn't welcome. A furiously jealous Lily hardly spoke to Josie for a week.

In the cinema, they sat in the front row where the seats only cost threepence, and he gave her two warm, melting lumps of Cadbury's milk chocolate wrapped in silver paper. She felt a little thrill. This was her first date. She had one up on Lily for a change.

She peeled the silver paper off the chocolate. 'Would you like some?' she enquired, and was a bit put out when he took half.

During the interval, he told her he was going to be a scientist when he grew up, and discover something vital that would change the world, like penicillin, which she'd never heard of, or radium, which she hadn't heard of either, or electricity, which fortunately she had.

The film was dead funny, but frightening when the ghost appeared. Josie hid her head in Ben's shoulder during the scariest bits. She heard him swallow nervously, then reach for her hand, and they managed to remain hand in hand throughout the remainder of the film and all the way back to Aunt Ivy's.

'Shall we go again next Friday?' Ben gulped.

'I wouldn't mind, ta.'

'I think we should get married when we grow up.' He stood before her, suddenly not the least bit red, not at all nervous, very manful for ten.

'If you like.'

Ben nodded seriously. 'I would, very much.'

3

They pretended Uncle Vince was her dad. It wasn't often they were alone. Only in the school holidays, when he was on late shift and Ivy had gone to work, did they have the house to themselves.

'Josie,' he would call as soon as Ivy closed the front door, and she would run along the landing in her nightie. They would roll around the bed, and he would tickle her, cuddle her, kiss her, just like a dad.

'Aren't we the perfect couple,' Uncle Vince would say afterwards, looking at their flushed faces in the dressing-table mirror.

But she had learned, a long time ago, that things could never be relied on to stay the same. Within the twinkling of an eye, everything could alter – sometimes for the better, sometimes for the worse.

She was nine, and it was just after Christmas. They were looking at themselves in the mirror and, as she watched, she saw his expression change. He seemed abstracted and vague, not very pleased about something. Josie thought she'd done something wrong. She fell silent, hunched her knees and stared at her toes.

Suddenly, Uncle Vince grabbed her, roughly turned her on her side, away from him, and held her so tightly that she could hardly breathe. She felt something stiff and hard pressed against her bottom, and Vince started to make dead funny noises, like gasps. It made her feel frightened, but she daren't ask him to stop in case he got annoyed, something best avoided. Uncle Vince rarely got annoyed, but when he did he was like a child, worse than Lily. He would jump up and down, wave his fists and shout in a funny, squeaky voice, like the day Aunt Ivy scorched his best shirt, or the time he lost one of his gold cuff links. Even his wife was struck dumb when My Vince lost his temper. Josie had a feeling that telling her uncle to stop when he was making the funny noises was something that would make him very annoyed indeed.

She couldn't stop thinking about it all day and next morning pretended to be asleep when he called. After a few minutes, she gave a sigh of relief – he must have given up. Instead, the door opened and he came in.

'Who's a little sleepyhead this morning?' He smiled, but behind the smile his eyes looked strange. 'It's going to be a bit of a squash in a single bed, but never mind, eh?' Josie turned away, feeling trapped, helpless, when he climbed in. She kept her eyes shut until he finished making the funny noises.

'Don't forget, luv,' Vince whispered, 'this is our secret. It's just between you and me. Don't think of telling Ivy, 'cos she'd never believe you. She'd think you were making it up, like, and there'd be hell to pay. She might even send you to one of them orphanage places, and you'd never see your friend Lily again. And that'd be a shame, wouldn't it, luv?'

At St Joseph's, class 5 was being prepared to sit the scholarship in June. Miss Simms had left long ago to get married, and Mr Leonard had been called up, although he was forty-one. Other teachers had gone, either to join the forces or take up important war work. Their replacements were retired teachers, glad to return and do their bit.

As there was no one to know better, Josie was assumed to be nine and entered for the scholarship along with Lily. Lily had convinced herself she would pass with flying colours.

Their form teacher, Mrs Barrett, was eighty if a day. Mr Crocker, the headmaster, was even older. They had worked together before and disliked each other intensely.

Everyone had been working hard and was looking forward to the Easter holidays. Lily would be ten on Good Friday, and was having a party the next day. Mrs Kavanagh had made them a new frock each. Lily's was a genuine party frock – green taffeta with short sleeves, a heart-shaped neck and a gathered skirt. Aunt Ivy didn't believe in party frocks, they were a waste of money. 'You don't get enough wear out of them,' she said thinly, so Josie's frock was more sensible – cream Viyella, with long sleeves, a navy blue collar and matching buttons – and would do for less salubrious occasions, like church. Even so, Josie was delighted. She was having a final fitting after school. It was her own birthday in May, six weeks off. There wouldn't be a party. Josie's age was something her aunt preferred to ignore.

She sighed happily, ignored Mrs Barrett, who was enthusing about fractions, and thought instead about Ben, who'd passed the scholarship two years ago and was now at Quarry Bank Grammar School. He'd kissed her for the first time last week, but only on the cheek. They'd discussed where they would live when they were married. Would she mind leaving Liverpool? he wanted to know. Josie said she wasn't sure.

In desperation, because she felt left out, Lily had more or less forced Jimmy Atherton to be her boyfriend, and they went out in a foursome, to the Pier Head or the pictures, to the fairy glen in Sefton Park or for a cup of tea in Lyon's in Lime Street. Jimmy insisted Lily pay for herself. He was prepared to be her boyfriend, reluctantly, but not if it meant being out of pocket. Mr Kavanagh had doubled Ben's pocket money for passing the scholarship and also, he said, chuckling, 'Because he's got a woman to support.'

The Easter holiday would be the gear. There was only one fly in the ointment, an enormous one: Uncle Vince, who was part of that other, inside world, where nothing had ever been the gear.

Josie's stomach churned. She gnawed her lip and wondered how she could avoid him. If she got dressed and sneaked out of the house as soon as Aunt Ivy left, it would mean wandering around for ages until it was time to meet Lily, which she wouldn't mind. But she'd have to return home eventually, see Uncle Vince, meet his eyes, feel as if she'd let him down.

'Josie Smith! I have asked you twice what four over four equals.' Mrs Barrett's voice was sharp with annoyance. 'Your body is present, but your mind clearly somewhere else. If you could bring mind and body together for a moment, you might come up with an answer.'

'Sixteen?'

Mrs Barrett sighed. 'No, dear. I think you'll find the answer's one. I expect you're all tired, I certainly am. Thank goodness we break up tomorrow.' The class uttered a huge groan of relief, and Mrs Barrett smiled wearily. 'It might be nice to dispense with lessons on the last day, do something less taxing – a quiz, for instance. I'll see what his lordship has to say.'

'*Who*, Miss?' Josie's hand shot up.

'His lordship, dear. In other words, Mr Crocker, our esteemed headmaster.'

'Why did she call him that?' Josie whispered hoarsely to Lily, sitting beside her.

Lily looked puzzled. 'It's not rude or anything, Jose. Me ma sometimes says, "Where's his lordship?" when she wants me da', or "What's his lordship up to?" '

'Lily Kavanagh, stop talking, *please!*'

'Sorry, miss.'

'It was my fault, miss.'

'In that case, Josie, you must be an expert ventriloquist. I could have sworn the words I heard came from Lily's mouth.'

His lordship!

Either she believes me, takes us in, and gives his lordship his marching orders, or . . .

Had Uncle Vince been doing the same thing to Mam, pressing against her, making funny noises? Was that why Mam had left?

No, Aunt Ivy had chucked Mam out because she was in some sort of condition.

It was very confusing. Josie's head ached with the effort of trying to make sense of it all. She began to dread the Easter holiday even more. Vince would be home as he was on nights.

Aunt Ivy got up at six. Josie heard her pottering around the kitchen. The smell of frying bacon wafted upstairs. Her aunt came up and went straight down again. She must have put the hot-water bottle in the bed. Shortly afterwards, Vince came home.

'Oh, he*llo*, luv,' Aunt Ivy said in a warm, thrilling voice, as if she hadn't seen him in years. Vince's light voice was inaudible. Josie wondered if they were kissing, or was Aunt Ivy patting his shoulders, stroking his cheek with the back of her finger, caressing his hair, like she did all the time?

'She can't keep her hands off him,' Lily had said, who'd noticed. 'She finds him irresistible, like I find Alan Ladd.'

'Come on, luv. Your breakfast's ready. Put your slippers on, they're warming by the fire.'

The truth might have killed the poor woman.

Josie sat up. Gradually, things were falling into place. Uncle Vince must have done something bad, but Ivy was Mam's sister. Mam didn't want to hurt her by telling the truth. Ivy was 'besotted' with Vince. Lily had looked it up in the dictionary. It meant 'to be blindly infatuated'. Then she'd had to look up 'infatuated'. 'To be inspired with foolish passion', it said. If Mam had told her sister the truth about Vince, it might have killed her.

Her aunt and uncle were coming upstairs! Josie quickly got dressed. She sat on the edge of the bed and heard the springs creak as Vince lay down. Aunt Ivy went to and from the bathroom several times. Instead of bacon, the house was full of her powerful scent.

At a quarter past eight, dead on time, her aunt's heels clattered downstairs. She paused in the hall to put on her coat, the front door closed.

Josie was dying to use the lavatory. She reached the bathroom just in time, and went back to collect a cardy. She felt the hairs prickle on her neck when she turned to leave. Uncle Vince, in his pyjamas, was smiling at her from the door.

'Here's me, looking forward to the holidays so we can have our little tête-à-tetês, and you're about to run out on me. Are you deserting your Uncle Vince, Josie?'

'No, me and Lily are going to Mass, the nine o'clock one. It's Holy Week, see. She'll be here in a minute.'

'No, she won't, luv,' he said mildly. 'That's three quarters of an hour off. There's still time for a cuddle.' He came into the room. 'Come on, luv, let Uncle Vince give you a nice big kiss.'

'*No!*'

He frowned, hurt. 'No?'

Backing away, Josie furiously shook her head. 'No!'

'Why not, luv?' He shrugged, mystified.

'I don't like what you do, the other thing.'

'There's no harm in it, luv.' He came closer. Josie took another step back and found she'd reached the bed. She sat down, though she hadn't meant to. Uncle Vince sat beside her and laid his arm across her knees. She was trapped. He idly played with her hair, making curls around his finger. 'You know, luv,' he said softly, 'if you're not nice to me, I might tell Ivy one or two things, not very nice things. A word from me, and you'll go shooting out the door faster than a bullet. You'll end up on the streets like Mabel, or in one of them orphanage places I mentioned before. You'll never see your friends again.'

'But I haven't done anything.' Her voice trembled. She tried to push his arm away, but it felt like a rod of iron. He was stronger than she'd thought.

'I know, luv, but it wouldn't stop me saying I caught you nicking a quid out me wallet, or I saw you up to no good with that little boyfriend o' yours. What's his name, Robert?'

'Ben, and I don't know what you're talking about.' He was being dead horrible, worse than Aunt Ivy because he spoke so kindly and reasonably and smiled the whole time. 'Anyroad, Ben's not little,' she said heatedly. 'He's bigger than you.' She threw caution to the winds. 'You're only a little sprat, Lily ses.'

His pale eyes narrowed angrily. He shoved her back on to the bed, and began to untie the cord of his pyjamas, watching her all the while. Then his face seemed to melt. 'You're a lovely girl,' he said huskily. 'Almost a woman, almost ten, double figures. You get more like Mabel every day. Take your clothes off, there's a good girl. It's time we were a proper couple.'

'No!' She tried to push him away, but when this had no effect she remembered the way Mam had got rid of Roger and Thomas. She planted her feet forcefully in his stomach, and pushed with all her might. His blue eyes popped, he gave a funny little hiccup, folded his arms over his stomach and fell back against the wardrobe with a soft thud.

She flew downstairs. Outside the house, she panicked. Which way to go? If she didn't get a move on, Uncle Vince might come out and drag her back. No one would stop him, they'd consider he had a perfect right. She began to run towards St Joseph's. By the time she reached it she had a stitch in her side. The iron gate was padlocked, as expected, and she wondered why she'd come. A few boys had managed to climb over the high, spiked wall and were playing football in the playground. She watched them through the gate, envious. They seemed without a care in the world.

Where now? She needed somewhere quiet, to think. More slowly now, she walked towards Sefton Park, to the fairy glen.

The gently sloping banks were a carpet of yellow daffodils, and the trees looked as if they had been sprinkled with pale green confetti as buds sprouted into tiny leaves. Josie watched two squirrels chase each other up and down the branches, leaping skilfully from one tree to the next. There was a fresh, invigorating smell, springy. Could you smell the spring?

A pale sun shone weakly through a veil of light grey cloud, and it made the dew glisten like little diamonds on the grass. It was too wet to sit on, and the only bench was already occupied by a girl in a yellow frock, her face buried in a newspaper. Josie went down to the stream and watched the large goldfish moving ponderously through the water and the smaller ones dart aimlessly this way, that way, backwards and forwards.

She knelt beside the stream, and it was only then that the events of the morning caught up with her and she began to tremble. Uncle Vince had been about to rape her, she realised that now. She knew about rape because less than a month ago a friend of a friend of Marigold Kavanagh had been raped by a soldier on the way home from a dance. Lily had told her about it. She shouldn't have been listening, but Lily spent half her life listening to conversations she wasn't meant to hear. She knew all sorts of things. How babies were made, for instance – men put their John Thomas in the place where women did a wee, and nine months later a baby was born. 'It's as easy as that!' Lily had said, wide-eyed and a bit dismayed.

What had happened that morning, however, dreadful though it was, seemed less important than what was to happen now. Where was she to live? How could she possibly *tell* people what Uncle Vince had tried to do? If she could get over the embarrassment of putting it into words, they'd say she led him on. Josie had the squirmy, uncomfortable feeling that it was all her fault. She felt sick, remembering the way she'd let him touch her, press against her, make funny noises.

She shivered. The grass was cold and she hadn't got a cardy. She longed for a drink, a cup of tea. Something plopped on to her bare knees – tears. She was crying.

'Josie, is that you? I thought I recognised you from the back.'

She turned. Daisy Kavanagh was coming towards her through the wet grass, folding a newspaper. She held it up. It was called *The Daily Worker*. 'Me da' won't allow this in the house. They get *The Times*, which is dead stuffy, full of letters from retired colonels.' She lifted the skirt of her yellow frock, which went perfectly with the background of daffodils, and knelt beside the younger girl. Daisy always looked as if she were posing for the cover of a romantic novel. Her long hair was tied back with a big yellow bow. The Kavanagh girls always had matching bows, headbands, dolly bags and even hankies to go with their frocks, which their mam made from bits of leftover material. 'What's up, Jose? You don't half look sad.'

Daisy was the quietest of the girls, and spent all her spare time reading. She had just left St Joseph's, and was due to start work next week in the local library, putting books away, keeping the shelves tidy, while she trained to be a proper librarian.

'Has your Auntie Ivy been horrid? You know, I've never liked that woman.'

Josie wished that were the case. It was something she was used to. She shook her head.

'Something's wrong, Jose. I can tell by your face. Have you had a fight with our Lily?'

'No.' She quite enjoyed her fights with Lily.

'You know, a trouble shared is a trouble halved, so Ma always ses,' Daisy said wisely. 'If you tell me, I promise, on my honour, to keep it in total confidence. I won't tell a soul.'

'It's something dead awful.' Josie picked up a clump of grass and pulled it to pieces. 'You'll be disgusted.'

Daisy gave a tinkling little laugh. 'Nothing disgusts me, Jose. I've read hundreds of books, and you wouldn't believe some of the things that happen. But let's sit on that bench first before me knees freeze solid. Come on, Jose.'

'Well,' Josie began hesitantly when they were seated. Daisy seemed the ideal person to talk to, not quite an adult, not quite a child, worldly wise and not easily shocked. 'It all started last Christmas, no, four Christmases ago, when I was six . . .' It was a relief to let it all pour out. She kept making excuses for herself. 'I know it's me own fault. I shouldn't have encouraged him. But we were pretending he was me dad, see,' she finished.

'Some dad!' Daisy's face was blank. She had always seemed very grown up but now she looked a bit lost, as if Josie's story was nothing like she'd read in books. Perhaps it was too dreadful to have told someone who was only fourteen.

There was a long silence. 'Oh, I knew you'd be disgusted,' Josie wailed. 'I wish I'd never told you. Now you hate me.'

'Oh, Jose. I don't hate you. I just don't know what to say.' Daisy reached for her hand. 'Let's go home. You've had nothing to eat. You must be starving.'

'You won't tell your ma, will you?' Josie said anxiously. 'I'd hate anyone else to know.' She felt a bit worried when Daisy didn't answer.

Apart from the clink of dishes from the kitchen, the Kavanaghs' house was unusually quiet. Quarry Bank didn't break up until tomorrow so Ben was still at school. Marigold had gone to work in the solicitor's office where she was a junior secretary, and Robert to the factory where he was a trainee draughtsman – Mrs Kavanagh was praying the war would be over before he reached eighteen. Lily, still in her nightie, was in the parlour with her head buried in an exercise book. Josie thought she had started on her homework, until Daisy angrily snatched the book away.

'That's mine,' she snapped. 'How dare you? It's my novel.'

'It's very good.' Lily had no shame. 'I don't think much of the hero, though. And what's a mousetachy?'

'It's moustache, idiot. I can't see you passing the scholarship. And you should have been called Deadly Nightshade, or Garlic Mustard, instead of Lily. You're dead horrible.' She turned to Josie. 'I'll ask Ma to make us a cup of tea.'

'What are you doing out so early?' Lily enquired when her sister had gone. 'And you haven't combed your hair. It doesn't half look untidy.'

'Oh, shut up, Lily.' Josie sank into a chair. Her head was throbbing. She glanced around the untidy room. There were hardly any toys nowadays, but the typewriter Marigold had used to practise on, and now Daisy, was on the sideboard, alongside a pile of *Girl's Crystals*, which she'd borrowed and avidly read. Pieces of grey flannel were draped over the sewing machine, waiting to be turned into a pair of trousers, and there were books everywhere, dozens of them. How wonderful it would be to live here, be part of this family, she thought.

'You're very lucky,' she said.

Lily misinterpreted this completely. She tossed back her wavy hair. 'Oh, I know. I'm pretty and clever, and I'm going to pass the scholarship and be a great success. When I grow up, I shall be a famous film star or a singer or a dancer. The whole world will know who I am. Have you ever heard me sing?'

'Of course I have. It was dead awful.'

'It was not.'

'It was.'

'It was not.'

'Josie,' Mrs Kavanagh said from the door, 'would you come here a minute, luv?'

Daisy appeared behind her, looking slightly shamefaced. 'I'm sorry, Jose. I've never betrayed a confidence before, but I couldn't have kept what you told me to meself. Something's got to be done, and I'm afraid I haven't a clue.'

'What?' Lily leapt to her feet and nearly fell over her nightie. 'What's she told you? She's *my* friend – why didn't she tell me?'

'Oh, calm down, Lily,' her mother said irritably. 'This is nothing to do with you. Go upstairs and get dressed this minute, or I shall be very cross.' Lily flounced out of the room, and Mrs Kavanagh led Josie into the kitchen. 'I can keep an eye on the stairs from here, case that little madam creeps down to listen.' Her plump, good-natured face became grave. 'Now, luv, Daisy's told me everything, so you don't have to go through it again. There's just one thing I want to say – *it's not your fault*. None of it's your fault.' She gave Josie's shoulders a little shake. 'Understand?'

'Yes, Mrs Kavanagh.'

'Now, we've got to tell Ivy as soon as possible, because you can't go home the way things are.' She thoughtfully bit her lip. 'I'll meet her off the bus tonight. She's going to have to give his lordship his marching orders, I'm afraid.'

'That's exactly what me mam said!' Josie exclaimed. 'There was something Mam had wanted to tell Aunt Ivy a long time ago, but she couldn't because it would have killed her. Then something happened, and we were coming back to Machin Street, but the night before Mam was . . .' She stopped, unable to go on.

Mrs Kavanagh had gone as white as a sheet. She gave Josie another little shake. 'Try not to think about it, luv.' She turned away and took the cosy off the teapot. 'Oh, Lord,' she muttered. 'This is worse than I thought. Much worse.'

Over the next two days, Josie felt as if there was a little black cloud hanging over her. She stayed with the Kavanaghs, sleeping on the settee in the parlour, and would have enjoyed herself had it not been for the cloud. And there was another worry lurking in the corner of her mind, too awful to think about.

Lily oozed curiosity from every pore. She had been forbidden to ask questions, but Josie could tell she ached to know what was going on.

Ben took her to the pictures to see *Pinocchio*, which helped a bit. She'd never seen a picture in Technicolor before. On the way home, he said seriously, 'When we're married, everything's going to be dead fine. You'll never have a single thing to worry about again.'

On Thursday evening after tea, Mrs Kavanagh suggested gently that she go home. 'I'll take you, luv. It's been lovely having you, but you can't stay for ever.'

'But Vince'll be there, and Auntie Ivy's still at work!'

'You'll find Vince has gone, luv, and Ivy hasn't been to work in days.'

Josie hung back. 'She'll *hate* me,' she said fearfully.

'No, luv. She doesn't hate you, not the least little bit.'

Outside number seventy-six, Josie said shyly, 'Ta, very much. You've been dead kind.'

Mrs Kavanagh's eyes were watering for some reason. 'It's one of the reasons we're put on this earth for, to help each other. Least, so I've always thought. One of these days, when you're grown up, maybe you can give me a hand if I need it.' She smiled. 'The way things are going with you and our Ben, I reckon you'll be one of the family by then. Go on, luv.'

Mrs Kavanagh gave her a little shove, and Josie returned to the house she thought she had left for ever.

4

It was still light outside, but the parlour was in semi-darkness because Aunt Ivy never parted the thick, green curtains by more than a few inches in case the sun faded the carpet. Even so, Josie was able to see the numerous framed photos of Mam which were scattered around the room.

'Ooh!' she whispered. She picked up one of Mam when she was a little girl making her First Holy Communion. She wore a white frock with puffed sleeves and smocking on the bodice, white shoes and socks. Most of her hair was hidden beneath a short, triangular veil, and she was holding a white prayer book and grinning broadly. A sprinkling of snow lay on the ground outside the church, and the trees were tipped with frost.

Josie pressed the photo against her breast. 'She must have felt cold,' she said to Aunt Ivy.

'She never felt the cold, not much,' her aunt replied. 'You might have noticed. She took a lot of persuading into a vest when winter came, and I could never get her to wear a liberty bodice. I've still got that prayer book and the veil put away. You can have them if you like.'

'I'd like them very much, ta.'

Aunt Ivy was wearing the navy blue coat overall she only wore on Saturdays to clean in. Since Josie had last seen her a few days ago, she seemed to have aged twenty, thirty years. Her yellow face was wizened, she looked smaller and was hunched in the corner of the big settee, as if she'd like to disappear inside it. Josie was shocked to see the naked misery evident in the small grey eyes.

'I loved her, you know.' She nodded at the photo. 'She was six then. Same age as you the day you came. I hated you for looking so much like her. I felt she'd come back to haunt me. Every time I looked at you I felt guilty. I'd put them away, the pictures, hid them in the spare room. But I couldn't put you away, could I? You were always here, reminding me of what I'd done. Oh, God!' She put her head in her hands and began to cry.

'What did you do?' Josie felt as if they had swopped places, that she was the aunt, Ivy the child.

'I chucked her out, didn't I?' Ivy cried wildly. 'I threw me own sister on the streets, when all the time I knew it wasn't her fault. I *knew* Mabel as well as I knew meself. I'd brought her up. I knew damn well she'd never go with a fella, particularly her own sister's husband. She wasn't that sort of girl. But I put the whole thing to the back of me mind, out of sight, and whenever it came to the surface I pushed it back again, because although I loved Mabel I loved my Vince more. I refused to let meself *think* he could have done such a thing.' She raised her burning eyes. 'You know he was your father, don't you?'

Josie sat down. She held Mam's photo tight against her breast. 'I've wondered, over the last few days, but I did me best not to think about it.'

'Like me, eh?' Ivy chuckled, but it came out more like a sob. 'There's some thoughts best kept hidden, otherwise they'll drive you doolally in the end.' She gave a bitter smile. 'I met him, Vince, outside church. I was with our Mabel. She was twelve, and I was twenty-four.' She glanced at her niece, and it was the first time Josie had known a look from Aunt Ivy that wasn't filled with hatred.

'You'll never know what it's like to be plain. I don't know where me looks came from – some throwback in the family, an ugly little leprechaun. It didn't help when I caught yellow jaundice when I was a kid. Me dad, he was a fine-looking man – Mabel took after him – and Mam was dead pretty. Mind you, I assumed I'd find a husband one day, but I never thought it would be someone like Vince. He was so handsome, Josie,' she said dreamily, as if Vince were dead and Josie had never met him. Then she sighed. 'But perhaps it was Mabel he was after all along. I think that crossed me mind right from the start, but I kept it hidden in a dark cellar in me brain, like all them other things.'

She suddenly reached behind the arm of the settee and brought up a glass and an almost empty bottle of whisky. 'I think I might be just a bit sozzled. I've been drinking all day and yesterday.' She emptied the remains of the whisky into the glass, and waved the bottle. 'It's five years old, this, so you can see I don't normally indulge. Make yourself a cup of tea if you fancy one. As from tomorrow, I'll start looking after you proper. Right now, I'm not fit to walk as far as the kitchen.'

'I will in a minute, ta.' The loathing Josie had always felt for her aunt had gone. It was impossible not to feel sympathy for the poor, pathetic woman huddled on the settee. And, young though she was, she understood the need to make excuses, apologise, explain. She must have felt gutted when Mrs Kavanagh told her what her husband had been up to.

'Oh, and another thing, luv.' Her aunt drained the glass. Her voice was thick and slurred, the way Mam's used to be. 'I'd never have left you alone with *him* if I'd thought there was a chance he'd lay a finger on you. Not on his own *daughter*. He must be sick in the head. It's a crime, that is. It's called something, I can't remember what right now. That's how I got him to leave. I threatened to fetch the bobbies to him.' Her face seemed to shiver. 'Oh, I wonder where he is, if he's got a place to sleep, like?'

Josie felt her blood turn to ice. *She still loves him!* In her heart, perhaps Ivy still longed to convince herself that My Vince had done no wrong.

She made tea and took it to the lounge, where she drew the blackout curtains, discreetly hidden behind the green silk, and switched on the lamp.

Aunt Ivy was sobbing wretchedly. 'She let me put her out rather than tell the truth about Vince.'

'She thought the truth would kill you,' Josie said.

'Oh, dear God,' her aunt shrieked, and crossed herself. 'Dear God, forgive me.'

Not long afterwards Ivy fell asleep. Josie fetched the maroon eiderdown to lay over her, then went to bed herself.

Neither Josie nor Lily passed the scholarship. 'I suppose we're just not clever enough,' Josie said when the letters with the results arrived. St Joseph's had broken up two weeks ago for the summer holiday.

'I would've passed if I hadn't had such an awful headache,' Lily claimed. 'And my nib was crooked, and I'm sure Mrs Barrett hadn't taught us some of them sums.'

Josie grinned. 'And the chair was uncomfortable, the sun was shining right in your eyes and the desk kept wobbling.'

'I don't know what you're talking about. Anyroad, if our Ben can pass, then so should I.'

'Oh, Lil. Didn't you read your Ben's end-of-term report? He got top marks for everything except art.'

'If they'd had art in the scholarship, then I'm certain to have passed,' Lily grumbled. 'Mr Crocker said that picture I did of a tiger was dead brilliant.'

Mr Crocker had said all their pictures were brilliant, but sometimes it wasn't worth arguing with Lily.

Like thousands of streets all over the country, Machin Street was throwing a party. It was 8 May 1945, VE Day, and the war was finally over. Hastily made bunting fluttered in the warm breeze. Union Jacks hung from the windows, blackout curtains were taken down, the ugly crisscross tape removed. Tables groaned with food, and there was a bar of chocolate for every child.

The day was a national holiday and everyone went completely mad. Several pianos were dragged outside to accompany the singing and dancing. Neighbours who'd never spoken to each other before, or who had sworn never to speak again, shook hands and promised to be the best of friends.

There were sing-songs and dancing, and everyone got extremely emotional when they sang, 'We'll Meet Again' and 'Land of Hope and Glory'. Josie danced with Lily. She clung to Mr Kavanagh's waist when the entire street did the conga, Aunt Ivy holding on behind. They made circles and did the hokey cokey and Knees up Mother Brown. Later, when it grew quieter, Ben took her in his arms for the waltz, 'Who's Taking You Home Tonight?'

'We'll always remember this day, Josie,' Ben whispered. 'We'll talk about it when we're very old – the day the worst war the world has ever known came to an end.' His eyes glistened with emotion. 'I love you, Josie,' he gulped.

'I love you,' she replied in a small voice.

The celebrations continued late into the night. When it grew dark, the lights in every room in every house were switched on, and the whole street sang 'When the Lights Go On Again' followed by a tremendous cheer and a chorus of 'God Save The King'.

Next morning, before she went to work, Aunt Ivy offered her one and only piece of motherly advice. 'I saw you dancing with Ben Kavanagh last night, luv. You want to be careful there.'

'But he's ever so nice,' Josie protested.

'Oh, he's a lovely lad, from a lovely family. I'd be dead chuffed if you became a Kavanagh.' She closed her eyes, as if imagining herself sharing the limelight with Mrs Kavanagh at the wedding. 'But you're far too young for boyfriends, luv. Ben's obviously smitten, and if you're not careful you'll find yourself walking blindfold into marriage with a chap you don't love because you've never known anyone else. All the love will be on *his* side, and although he might think that's enough for both of you it's not true.' She pursed her lips sadly. 'It's something I know from bitter experience. I loved my Vince enough for ten women, and look at what he did.'

'I'm sorry, Auntie,' Josie sighed.

'Oh, Lord, luv, don't apologise. He tried to ruin your life, as well as mine. But at least we're still alive to tell the tale, eh, not like our poor Mabel.'

5

'Of course, we're middle-class, stupid,' Lily said furiously. 'Me da' owns his own shop, our Stanley's a sergeant in the army in Berlin, Marigold's married to a solicitor, Daisy's a qualified librarian, well, almost, our Robert manages something or other down in London, I work in an office and look at our Ben, off to Oxford or Cambridge next October.' She finished her litany with a superior sneer.

'I've got exams to take first,' Ben reminded her.

Lily tossed her waist-length hair. 'Oh, don't be silly, Ben. We all know you'll come top in everything.'

Francie O'Leary, the prime target of Lily's wrath, looked at Ben with his small, mean eyes. Lily was madly in love with him. She found him attractive in a small, mean way, like a handsome rat. Francie talked out of the corner of his mouth like Humphrey Bogart. Even though they were inside, he wore a trilby hat on the back of his head that made him look a bit of a rogue. 'What have you got to say about this, Ben?' he enquired lazily.

'Me!' Ben laughed. 'I don't believe in the class system. As John Ball said, "Ye came as helpless infants to the world, Ye feel alike the infirmities of nature, Why then these vague distinctions?"'

'Who the hell's John Ball?' Lily interceded.

'Leader of the Peasants' Revolt.'

'I thought that was Wat Tyler.' Francie had been Ben's friend at Quarry Bank. His father had been killed in the war, and he'd left at sixteen to provide for his mother and two young sisters. Josie wondered if he resented his friend going to university. It seemed very unfair that the son of a man who'd given his life for his country had been denied higher education.

Ben said, 'Wat Tyler was the brawn, John Ball the brains.'

'He can't have had much in the way of brains,' Francie said drily. 'The whole bloody revolt was a wash-out. The peasants were routed, if I remember right.'

'They were betrayed. John Ball was hung, drawn and quartered. I don't know why we're arguing, Francie. We're both on the same side. Our Lily's the only one out of line.'

'Do you mind?' Josie broke in. 'I've no idea whose side I'm on, thanks all the same. I don't know what class I am either, and, quite frankly, I don't care.' Months ago, the four of them had got into the habit of coming to town on Saturday mornings, sitting for hours in a restaurant and arguing – about politics, life, religion, the headlines in that morning's newspapers.

'You're what's called a "white-collar" worker, Jose, so you're definitely middle-class,' Lily said firmly. '*And* you live in Machin Street, which is in a middle-class area. There's already five families with cars, me da' amongst them.'

'Bollocks!' Francie snorted. 'If it were middle-class, it'd be a road, Machin Road – or Machin Avenue. Streets are only for us poor, working-class fodder.'

'What about Downing Street?' said Josie. 'And Harley Street, where the posh doctors live?'

Lily threw her a grateful smile, and Francie clutched his brow and pretended to look devastated. 'You got me there, Jose. That was a knock-out blow.'

Ben squeezed Josie's shoulders. 'Clever girl,' he whispered.

She thought it obvious, not clever. He was being a bit patronising, but she daren't say anything because he got disproportionately upset if she criticised him. She could never truly be herself with Ben.

The manageress glared at them from behind the till. They'd been there two hours and had bought only a single coffee each, and she was expecting an influx of lunchtime customers any minute.

They took the hint, drained the dregs of the coffee, now stone cold, and wandered into Bold Street. Josie pulled on a woolly hat that covered her ears, buttoned her coat against the bitter February wind and wrapped a scarf twice around her neck. Francie took Lily in his arms and they kissed passionately.

'Young love!' Ben rolled his eyes and took Josie's hand. He disapproved of such demonstrations, which he considered showy and insincere. Lily had kissed previous boyfriends with equal passion, though she swore things were dead serious between her and Francie. They hadn't yet gone all the way, but it was likely to happen any minute. Lily couldn't wait.

Ben had never tried to go all the way with Josie. He respected her too much. Although he had never discussed it, she took it for granted that they would wait until they were married, which would be after he'd got his degree and found a job. Josie felt relieved, as she wasn't particularly looking forward to it. She quite enjoyed Ben kissing her and touching her naked breasts, which he'd never properly seen because she was always fully clothed, and he merely slid his hand inside her frock or under her jumper. Pleasant though these occasions were, she had the feeling she wasn't enjoying herself remotely as much as Lily when she did the same thing with Francie, but, then, Lily was always prone to exaggeration.

'It was heaven,' Lily gushed the first time. 'I went all woozy. I completely lost control, and so did Francie. We might well have gone all the way if it hadn't been raining.'

Lily and Francie paused for another kiss. Ben said, 'Hey, folks, where are we going?'

'The Pier Head?' Francie suggested.

'It's bloody freezing.' Lily shivered. She looked up at the bleak, grey sky. 'It looks as if it might snow. Can't we go somewhere inside? Has anyone got any money?'

'I'm skint,' Francie announced. 'You gave a penny towards me coffee, remember?'

'I've only got three bob, but I need half that for next week's fares to work. Then there's tonight . . .' Josie's finances were a mess. She'd only been paid the day before, but by then she had owed Aunt Ivy her entire wages. The same thing happened nearly every week. She couldn't resist the clothes she saw as she wandered around town during the dinner hour. Last week, she'd seen a lovely black frock with embroidery on the bodice that looked like a waistcoat. Aunt Ivy had loaned her a pound towards it, and she'd had to borrow her fares for the rest of the week.

Lily was rooting through her purse. 'I've got nearly eight bob, but I need stockings and a Max Factor panstick. If there's enough over, I'll treat everyone to another coffee, as long as someone does the same for me next week.'

Ben, who had to exist on five shillings a week pocket money, took no part in this debate. Josie paid for herself at the pictures nowadays, and sometimes for Ben, though he claimed it made him feel like a kept man.

They went to Owen Owen's department store. After Lily had bought the stockings and the panstick, they decided to tour the shop for something to do. In the furniture department, Francie pushed Lily down on a fully made-up bed and kissed her again.

'Do you mind?' an elderly assistant said frostily.

'We were just trying it out, like, seeing if it felt comfortable.' Francie pulled Lily up, and patted the bed. 'What do you think, darling? Shall we buy it or not? We're getting married soon,' he explained to the assistant.

'I'd like to look around other shops first.'

All four exploded into giggles and made for the stairs.

'Would you say that was a proposal?' Lily gasped as they raced to the ground floor, the boys ahead.

'He was only joking, Lil.'

'I'll sue him for breach of promise, take him to court. You and Ben can be me witnesses.'

'I doubt if that would work.' If Lily was set on capturing Francie O'Leary, she needed to be a bit more agreeable. He wasn't the sort of chap who appreciated being called an idiot, or told he was dead stupid if they happened to disagree.

'I suppose not,' Lily sighed. 'But I'm determined to get Francie to the altar one way or another. I could get pregnant – that might do the trick.'

'The baby will look like a little rat.'

'Yes, but a very handsome little rat.'

'What are you two laughing at?' Ben enquired when they caught up.

Josie and Lily looked at each other and started to laugh again. 'Nothing,' they said together.

'Let's go to Lyon's,' said Lily. 'I've enough left for a pot of tea for four.'

Outside, Ben said, 'Where shall we go tonight?'

'Where else but the pictures.' Josie shrugged. 'It's the only place that's cheap, particularly if we sit at the front and go somewhere outside town. Oh, Ben, I wish I weren't so extravagant. Auntie Ivy takes hardly anything for me keep, and I spend a small fortune on clothes. Me new frock cost almost two pounds. But it's dead pretty. You'll love it. I'll wear it tonight, shall I?'

Ben stopped and looked down at her shining face. He glanced round to see if anyone was looking, then kissed her. 'I love *you*, Josie. I'd love you even if you wore rags.'

Josie noticed two girls about her own age eyeing her enviously from across the road. They were envious of Ben – blond, six feet two inches tall, no longer all elbows, slim instead of gawky, graceful and self-assured. He clearly didn't feel the cold. He wore flannels, a green tweed jacket and an open-necked shirt. His school scarf was draped casually around his neck. Even Lily conceded her soppy brother had become a handsome young man.

She nestled against him. 'And I love you.' She was immensely lucky. She had never had to suffer, as other girls did, the torture of praying a boy she liked would ask her out, or the awkwardness of a first date, wondering if she'd be asked again, or hoping she wouldn't because the chap had picked his nose non-stop throughout a picture you'd been dying to see for ages, as had happened with Lily during *Blood on the Moon*, with Robert Mitchum. She didn't have to worry if she would get married, because it had all been decided a long time ago. As Mrs Kavanagh had said, they were 'made for each other'.

Two years ago, when they had left school, after much discussion between Mrs Kavanagh and Aunt Ivy, Josie and Lily had been sent to the same commercial college Marigold had attended. They practised on the same typewriter. College was dead boring, but what else could girls do except work in a shop, a factory or an office? There were no vacancies in the *Liverpool Echo* for actresses or dancers or singers. No one advertised for fourteen-year-old girls to climb mountains, go to Timbuktu, drive trains or fly aeroplanes, any one of which Josie and Lily would have done like a shot.

If college had been boring, work was even worse. Lily worked for a stationery suppliers in Edge Hill. She spent her days processing orders for copy paper, bank paper, boxes of carbon, bottles of ink, pencils, all the rubbish people needed to work in other offices. Worst of all, not a single man worked there she fancied marrying, though it didn't matter since she'd met Francie two months ago.

'Sometimes I feel as if me brain's gone dead,' she moaned to Josie.

'It can't be as bad as insurance,' Josie grumbled. '*Car* insurance. Nothing but policies and premiums. The letters are as dull as ditchwater. It wouldn't be so bad in Claims. At least they have accidents to deal with.'

They yearned for adventure. One day they would get married, settle down, have children, but in the meantime it would be marvellous if only something *exciting* would happen.

Josie had already tried on the new dress several times. It fitted perfectly. She put it on again that night, twisting and turning in front of the full-length mirror in Aunt Ivy's bedroom. Sometimes it was uncanny, looking at herself. She would feel pins and needles all over because it was as if she were looking at Mam. The same eyes, dark blue and wide apart, the same over-generous mouth. The nose that had looked dead perfect on Mam, because everything about her had seemed perfect, was actually a mite too long. She wore her thick brown hair shoulder-length, and brushed it frequently, as Mam had done, to make it shine.

Only the other day, Ivy said in a puzzled voice, 'You know, when I look at you, it feels like our Mabel's never been away. She was fifteen when I last saw her. Now you're a year older, and it's almost like you've taken over and there's never been a break.'

Ivy was in the bathroom humming as she made herself up for a night on the town with her friend, Ellen. Josie walked towards the figure in the mirror and held out her arms. 'Hello, Petal. I'm home,' she whispered. She put her hands, palms facing, on the glass and pressed her mouth against the cold, reflected one. When she stepped back the glass was clouded, and it was even more spooky, watching the face of her mother reappear as the cloud began to fade. 'I love you, Mam.'

'I'm off now, luv,' Aunt Ivy shouted from the landing.

Josie jumped. She went to the bedroom door. Her aunt was wearing her fur coat and an unusual amount of diamanté jewellery. 'Which picture are you going to see?'

'I'm going to the theatre, luv, for a change. Margaret Lockwood's on at the Royal Court in *Pygmalion*.'

'I thought Ellen didn't like the theatre?'

'Ellen got herself a new fella a long while ago. I'm going with another, er, friend. That frock looks lovely. Take care, luv. Have a nice time.'

'You, too.' She wondered if Ivy's new friend was a fella, and she was too embarrassed to say.

Ben came minutes after Ivy had gone. He thought the frock was well worth the inconvenience of being broke for a whole week.

'You look gorgeous.' He slid his arms around her waist and kissed her soundly. 'Ma's loaned Lily and Francie five bob,' he said when they came up for air. 'It was only to get them out of the way while she and me da' got ready for a dinner dance, so they're coming with us. You don't mind, do you?'

'Of course not.'

They went to the Grand in Smithdown Road to see *Samson and Delilah*, which Josie and Lily thought very moving. It was annoying when the boys laughed when Samson grew his hair and pulled the temple down on top of the entire cast.

'Let's go for a drink,' Francie suggested when they came out. Tiny particles of ice were being blown about in the freezing wind, like fireflies against the yellow streetlights.

'A proper drink?' Lily squeaked. 'In a proper pub?'

'A proper drink in a proper pub,' Francie confirmed. 'We can just afford two pints of ale between us.' He grinned. 'I'll ask for four straws.'

Lily wrinkled her small nose. Josie knew she had planned on getting Francie back to the house while it was empty. 'Me and Josie aren't old enough.'

'You *look* old enough. Ben and I will get the drinks. You two sit in the corner. What do you say, Josie?'

'I don't mind.' It would bring back memories of the Prince Albert, but she couldn't avoid pubs for the rest of her life. It was only nine o'clock, too early to go home and consider the night over. She shivered, and stamped her feet on the icy pavement. 'Can we go somewhere before we all freeze to death?'

'We'll go to the first pub we come to,' Francie promised.

A welcoming fire burned brightly in the grate of the first pub. Whoever was playing the piano had their foot pressed firmly on the loud pedal as they banged out 'Bless 'em All', but perhaps the pianist was determined to be heard above the deafening singing. Inside, the air was warm and full of smoke. They looked for somewhere to sit, but every seat was taken and there were crowds standing round the bar. Lily immediately began to complain. The smoke got in her eyes, the singing hurt her ears, she was tired and wanted to sit down. And she hated war songs, she added, as if further confirmation of her discomfiture was necessary.

'Let's find somewhere else, then,' Francie said patiently.

'I bet all the pubs around here are just as rough. It's that sort of area. Every single man here is probably a crook, and the women look no better than they ought to be. This is a dead stupid idea, Francie.' She fluttered her eyelashes and put her hand on his shoulder. 'I'd sooner go home.'

The fluttering eyelashes and the hand had come too late for Francie. He lost his temper. 'Me dad used to come here.' His small eyes flashed and he gestured angrily around the room. 'These people are the salt of the earth. Who the hell d'you think you are, calling them criminals and whores?'

Lily's jaw sagged. 'But I didn't . . .' she began.

'Yes, you did,' Francie said curtly. 'You know what you are, Lily Kavanagh? A snob! A petty, mean-minded, prejudiced snob. You and I have got nothing in common, and we never will. Quite frankly, you get on me fucking nerves. Oh, and it's about time you got your hair cut. It looks daft on someone your age.'

'Eh, hold on a minute, Francie.' Ben touched his friend's arm. He and Josie had been watching the proceedings, stunned. Francie shook the arm away.

'I'm off, Ben. Enjoy your drink.'

'I haven't bought one yet. Anyroad, you've got the money.'

'So I have.' He shoved a handful of coins in Ben's pocket. 'That's the change from what your mam loaned us. Forget the drink. Take your sister home to that nice, middle-class house in Machin Street.'

'But it's *you* I want to go home with, Francie,' Lily cried. 'It's what I've wanted all along.'

'Well, you picked a bloody funny way of showing it. Tara, Ben, tara, Josie.'

Francie pushed his way out the door. 'Well, he certainly had a hump and a half,' someone said admiringly.

'What's a whore?' Lily asked, then burst into tears. 'Oh, what did I do wrong?'

Ben put his arm around his sister's heaving shoulders. 'You were dead tactless, Sis. You should think before you speak. Every time you open your mouth, you put your foot in it.'

Lily didn't listen, she rarely did. 'I'm going after him. I'll tell him I didn't mean it, that I love him.' She looked at them tearfully. 'I do, you know.'

She rushed out, and Josie and Ben looked at each other. 'What shall we do now?' he asked. 'Would you like a drink?'

'No, ta. It's not our money, it's your mam's. Anyroad, I think we should go back to yours. I doubt if Francie's in the mood for making up. Lily's quite likely to turn up any minute in a terrible state and there's no one in.'

They strolled back to Machin Street, talking quietly and feeling sorry for everyone in the world except themselves.

Lily was still in a state next morning. She cried, she screamed, she threatened to kill herself, she refused to go to Mass. Mr Kavanagh found it necessary to go to the shop and do a bit of stocktaking. Daisy remembered she'd promised to see a friend. Ben was despatched to fetch Josie in the hope she could help.

'Well, I wasn't much use last night, was I?' Lily had managed to catch up with Francie, who'd repeated the pub diatribe, along with a few more home truths.

'He likes *you* better than me,' Lily raged. Ben had made himself scarce. 'He thinks you're a far nicer person. If Ben wasn't his friend, he'd ask you out. What do you think of *that*?'

Josie thought of that, and felt a surprising – and most unwelcome – little thrill at the notion of Francie kissing her, touching her breasts. 'He was only saying it to get at you.'

'Have you been making eyes at him?'

'Of course not.' She decided to get angry. 'How dare you suggest such a thing?'

'Thank goodness you're here, Josie,' Mrs Kavanagh had said that morning when Josie arrived. 'I don't know what to do with her. She's in the bedroom. Our poor Daisy hardly got a wink of sleep. Lily wept and wailed the whole night long. See if you can talk some sense into her, there's a good girl. Oh, Lord,' she moaned. 'She's only sixteen. I hope we don't have to go through this performance every time she's jilted by a boyfriend.'

Lily was sitting up in bed when Josie went in. Her eyes were bloodshot and swollen, but she had a strange, beatific smile on her puffy face. 'I've decided to become a nun,' she announced grandly. 'I'm going to dedicate the rest of me life to God.'

'Don't be daft, you haven't even been to Mass.'

'I'll go later, the twelve o'clock. Oh, Jose, just imagine, the quiet of a convent, the peace.' Lily put her hands together, as if in prayer. 'No more boyfriends, no more having to be nice to someone so they'll ask you out. No more *men*! Just priests, *holy* men. All you have to do is kiss their rings, not ... well, that thing Francie once suggested.'

'Since when have you ever been nice to anyone?' Josie was unimpressed by this desire for a quiet life. 'You'd have to shave your head, and never wear make-up again or buy pretty clothes or wear nylons. You'd be bored out your skull within a week.'

Lily looked at her kindly and a touch disdainfully. 'You don't under*stand*, Jose. Those sorts of things wouldn't matter any more. I wouldn't even *think* about them while I was communing with God. My mind would be on a different plane. I never realised I had a vocation. I'm looking forward to shaving me head. I'd better go downstairs and tell Ma.'

'The silly girl is driving us up the wall,' Mrs Kavanagh complained a few weeks later. 'She goes around with this stupid grin on her face, as if butter wouldn't melt in her mouth, and wakes us up every morning with a hymn. If I hear "Faith of Our Fathers" once more, I think I'll scream. She can't get this idea of a convent out of her head. Have you seen her hair? She's had it cut, makes her look like Shirley Temple.'

That was Monday. On Tuesday Lily decided she liked her hair too much to have it shaved off. Instead, she was going to join the Army and spend the rest of her life serving King and Country.

'You're too young,' Josie said. 'You have to be eighteen.'

'I've already thought of that,' Lily said complacently. 'I shall pretend I'm our Daisy – she's twenty.'

'Does Daisy know?'

'No, but I'm sure she won't mind.'

'Your legs will look dead fat in khaki stockings.'

'Oh, don't be such an old misery guts, Josie Smith. Stop trying to put me off.' She preened herself. 'I'm officer material, me. I bet I'm promoted in no time.'

Josie nearly fell off the chair laughing. 'The Army won't have a cap to fit a head as big as yours, Lily Kavanagh.'

An outraged Daisy flatly refused to allow her identity to be used by her sister so she could join the Army, and Lily was forced to abandon the idea, though she claimed her heart had been broken for ever by Francie O'Leary.

It was Lily who saw the poster in Hewitt's sweetshop window. She dragged Josie round to see it the same night.

The poster was printed in bright red on yellow foolscap.

STAFF REQUIRED

KITCHEN HANDS, PORTERS, CHALET MAIDS

MAY TO OCTOBER, GOOD RATES OF PAY

ACCOMMODATION AVAILABLE IF REQUIRED

APPLY IN WRITING TO:

HAYLANDS HOLIDAY CAMP, PRIMROSE MEADOW,

COLWYN BAY

Josie's eyes sparkled. 'Adventure!' she breathed.

'And boys,' Lily said in an awed voice. 'Stacks and stacks of boys, different ones every week. I'd be over Francie O'Leary in a jiffy. Oh, Jose, it's only two months off. We'll apply to be chalet maids the minute we get home.'

Over the next few weeks, they changed their minds a dozen times. They almost didn't fill in the application forms when they came, but Josie persuaded Lily to do it, or it might have been the other way round.

Mr Kavanagh was dead set against the whole idea, 'But when did anyone ever give a fig for my opinion?' he said with a martyred air.

'I wish I'd done something like that when I was a girl,' Mrs Kavanagh said wistfully. 'I think you're showing a great deal of enterprise. You'll easily get other jobs when you come back. And it'll be nice to get rid of our Lily for a while. Anyroad, she'll only make our lives a misery if she's thwarted.'

'Oh, I will!' Lily said sweetly.

'You'll keep an eye on her, won't you, Josie, luv?'

'Yes, Mrs Kavanagh,' Josie assured her. She had no intention of doing any such thing.

'What do you think?' Josie asked Aunt Ivy several times. Ivy still saw the mysterious friend, but he or she had never been invited to the house.

Her aunt was always encouraging, so much so that Josie had the oddest feeling that she actually wanted her to go. 'As I said before, luv, it seems a good idea. I'm sure you and Lily will have a lovely time.'

'Will you be all right on your own?' Josie asked anxiously, the day the letters arrived confirming their employment.

'Of course, I will, luv.'

'I can still change me mind. It's three days before I need to give in me notice at work,' Josie assured her.

'I'll be all right,' her aunt said irritably. 'I don't know how many times I have to tell you.'

Josie turned away, hurt. Since Vince had gone, she had got on well with Ivy. It came as a shock to find her aunt so willing to see her leave. She felt very unwanted. Even Ben hasn't tried to persuade me to stay, she thought miserably.

She couldn't have been more wrong about Ben.

Josie and Ben were sitting on the same bench on which she'd told Daisy about Uncle Vince eight years ago. It was Friday, and the girls had handed in their notices that afternoon, which meant there was no going back. They would leave for Haylands a week tomorrow.

'Mr Short, me boss, said he was dead sorry to see me go. He made me promise to contact him when I get back. If there's a vacancy, he'll take me on again like a shot. I thanked him nicely, but there's no way I'd work for an insurance company again. I'd love to work for the *Echo*. It would be dead interesting, hearing the news before any one else. What do you think?'

'Since when have you been interested in my opinion?' Ben said coldly.

'I'm always interested in your opinion,' she replied. For the first time, she noticed they were sitting several inches apart, that he hadn't automatically put his arm around her shoulder when they had sat down.

'That's not true. You haven't asked what I think about you working in that camp, not once.'

'But I've discussed it with you every day,' she said indignantly.

'No, you've *told* me about it every day.' He leaned forward and folded his arms on his knees. His voice was stiff with hurt. 'You haven't asked if I *care* that you're leaving, if I *mind*.'

'But I'm not leaving for ever,' she protested. 'I'll only be gone five months. It never entered me head you'd mind. I mean, you're going away for three whole years in October. Have you asked if I mind about that?'

He gave her a curt glance. 'That's entirely different. I'm going away to learn, get a degree, so one day I'll get a well-paid job. I'm doing it for *you*, so we can have a nice house, and a nice life, and you'll never want for anything. Your only motive is to have a fine old time.'

'What's wrong with that? I bet you'll have a fine old time at university.' Josie laughed, but there was a prickly sensation in her stomach. They had never fought before, but she felt she had right on her side and wasn't prepared to give in. He was being totally unreasonable. 'And don't pretend you're doing it for me, Ben. You're doing it for yourself, you know you are.'

'No, I'm not.' His lips twisted sadly. 'I would have still gone, even if I'd never met you. But, you see, one day, I was only eight, I was wrestling on the floor with our Robert, and when I looked up there was this girl, younger than me. Oh, if only you knew how sad you looked, Josie, how frightened. I felt myself go limp. I suppose I must have fallen in love then, but I was too young to know. I just knew I wanted to be with you for the rest of me life.' He sat back in the seat, not looking at her, but at a couple with two small children by the stream.

'So, you see, I am doing it for you. I do everything for you. Whenever I sit an exam, I think to meself, I'm doing this for Josie. You're never out of me mind.' He turned and put his arm around her. He kissed her hair, her forehead, her cheeks. Then he gently kissed her lips. 'I love you, darling.'

He had never called her darling before. She saw his eyes were wet with tears, and felt ashamed of being the cause, because he was probably the best young man in the whole world. He put his other hand on her neck, and she could feel his thumb hard on her cheek. 'I love you, Ben,' she whispered.

They kissed again, and a kiss had never felt so sweet before, so loving and so tender.

'Please, don't go, Josie. If you truly loved me, you'd stay.' His voice was hoarse with passion and pleading. But Josie couldn't see the *harm*. Five months, that's all, for just five months she wanted a bit of adventure. Once it was over she'd settle down, get another job, commit herself to him entirely. She'd even try to save up for the wedding, start a bottom drawer.

But she had hesitated too long. Ben stood. His face was bleak and raw with hurt. Josie was shocked to think she could cause such hurt to another human being. With a further shock, she realised that he wasn't meant for her. No matter what Ben did, he couldn't possibly hurt *her* so deeply.

'I'm sorry, Ben.' She touched his arm, and they stared at each other. They both knew it was over.

'I'm thinking of the day I first saw you.' He almost smiled.

'And me of that day we went to the pictures. You gave me some chocolate and took half back. Ben?'

He was already walking away. He turned. 'Yes, Jose?'

'If I asked you not to go to university, what would you say?'

'I've sometimes hoped you would. Tara, Josie. I might not see you before you go, so have a nice time.'

She watched him walk away, a tall, loping, extremely nice young man with a broken heart. There was lump in her throat when she returned to the seat and watched Ben until he disappeared into the trees. She suddenly felt so lonely that it made her body ache. One minute she'd had a boyfriend, now she hadn't. And it had all happened so quickly, the way the most profoundly important things always did.

The girls were very quiet on the bus that took them from the Pier Head to Colwyn Bay. Lily kept sniffing and burying her face in a hankie. They perked up when the coach stopped outside the camp, and they saw the gaudily painted 'Haylands Holiday Camp' sign on an arch above the gates.

'You know what, Jose?'

'What, Lil?'

'Over the next few months, I'm determined to go all the way with a bloke.'

Josie smiled. 'Good luck.' She wasn't considering *looking* at a man, let alone sleeping with one. She couldn't stop thinking about Ben.

Haylands

1

'Oh, what pretty chalets.' Lily's voice throbbed with excitement. 'Can we pick our own?'

The driver of the long open trolley carrying them and their luggage looked at her drily. 'No, luv. You're in the staff quarters behind the theatre.'

'There's a theatre!' Lily nudged Josie in the ribs. 'I wonder if there'll be any famous stars.'

The pebble-dashed chalets had been built back to back, the fronts facing each other across a wide concrete path, with a strip of grass in the middle. Wooden tubs, each with an identical green shrub, had been placed neatly, about twelve feet apart. There were five long rows of chalets altogether. Like all the buildings in the camp, the chalets had been freshly painted cream.

They had already passed two bars, the Coconut and the Palm Court, a fish-and-chip shop called Charlie's Plaice, a ballroom called the Arcadia, an amusement arcade, a parade of shops, a small fairground, a children's nursery with swings and a see-saw outside, though there wasn't a child in sight. In fact, there were few campers around and they were mainly elderly. Signs pointed to tennis courts and crazy golf. A few hundred yards in front, the Irish Sea glimmered dully, like pewter, the waves as unnaturally stiff as freshly permed hair. The sky was dark and getting darker, and there was a touch of rain in the air. Despite all the gaudy entertainment on offer, the camp had a desolate, deserted air.

'I love crazy golf,' Lily remarked.

The man steered the trolley towards a large cream building with 'The Prince of Wales Theatre' over the entrance in unlit neon. A poster announced that night's play was *Strip Jack Naked*.

'I wonder who it's by?' Lily mused aloud as the trolley veered violently to the left and they clung on for dear life.

'I don't know, luv,' the driver said, 'but it ain't Shakespeare.' He veered to the right and stopped. 'This is youse lot here.'

Josie stepped off the trolley and hauled her suitcases after her. 'Oh, dear.'

'Bloody hell.' Lily went pale. 'Is this what they meant by "Accommodation Available If Required"? It looks like a concrete bunker left over from the war.'

Hidden from view, no one had bothered to paint the grey slabs of the long, single-storey building, badly joined together with lumps of cement. The windows were slits, presumably for guns, now fortunately glazed. A thin woman in a white overall came out of a door marked 'Women' and marched towards them. She regarded them sternly. 'Are you Kavanagh and Smith?'

'We're Lily Kavanagh and Josie Smith,' Josie said icily. She wasn't prepared to live in a concrete bunker *and* be treated like a second-class citizen. She vaguely hoped the woman would take offence and they'd be sent back to Liverpool on the spot. 'I didn't think we'd joined the Army.'

'Good for you, Jose,' Lily said under her breath.

To their surprise, the woman laughed. 'I'm Mrs Baxter, the women's supervisor. I *was* in the Army, so I suppose surnames have become a habit I must get out of. Come on, Misses Kavanagh and Smith, and I'll show you where you'll live for the next five months. I hope you didn't expect the Ritz, because you'll be sadly disappointed.'

'We already are.' Josie picked up her cases and followed Mrs Baxter into a badly lit corridor with numbered doors each side. She opened number five, and entered a small room in which two double bunks and four green-painted lockers had somehow been crammed. A small mirror was screwed to the wall. Josie was immediately put in mind of a prison cell.

'I told you not to expect the Ritz,' said Mrs Baxter. 'Your two companions won't be joining you till next week when the camp will be busier. There's not many people here at the moment, and you'll find they're all very old. *Very* old,' she added with a grin. 'This is the cheapest time, you see. So if you were hoping to cop off with a fella tonight, girls, you've got another disappointment in store, I'm afraid.'

'There's no sink,' Lily complained, 'and no lavatory.'

'You'll find plenty of sinks and lavatories behind the door marked "Ablutions".'

'You mean we have to get washed *in public*?'

'I'm afraid so – are you Kavanagh or Smith?'

'I'm *Miss* Kavanagh.'

'Well, *Miss* Kavanagh, I suppose it is like the Army in a way, though you won't be put on a charge. You will, however, be ordered to leave immediately if you're found with a man in your room, or you consistently fail to turn up promptly at eight o'clock for work. I don't care if you've got a hangover, as long as you turn up.'

'What's a hangover?'

'I think I'll let you find that out for yourself, Miss Kavanagh. You must be the first chalet maid I've ever met who didn't know. It's rather refreshing.' Mrs Baxter rubbed her thin hands together. 'Well, girls, the rest of today is yours to do with as you please. The staff have their tea in the dining room after the campers, around seven. Tomorrow, being Sunday, you can have a nice lie-in, otherwise breakfast's at seven, but I shall expect you in the laundry at twelve to show you round and tell you what you have to do. You'll find overalls in the lockers. Always keep the key on your person, or you might have your valuables nicked. Oh, and I'd like your ration books, please.'

'What about Mass?' Lily enquired.

'You'll find a list of church services in Reception. I think the Catholic Mass is ten o'clock.'

'Ta.' Josie made a face as soon as Mrs Baxter left the room. 'I might pray to be released. We'll never get all our clothes in them lockers, Lil. I've brought virtually everything I own.'

Lily was climbing the ladder of one of the bunks. 'Bagsy me sleep on top.' She burst out laughing. 'Oh, Jose. This isn't a bit like I imagined. What have we let ourselves in for?'

'I dunno. I'd sooner be working in car insurance any day.' To think she'd let Ben go for *this*! She banged her head throwing herself on to the bottom bunk. 'Ouch! It's worse than prison. Actually, Lil, I feel like a good cry.'

Lily's head appeared upside down. 'Never mind, Jose. We'll have a fine old time. I can feel it in me water. Let's unpack, and we'll explore.'

It was, Lily said later, the most miserable day of her life. To cheer themselves up, they bought lipsticks in the chemist's, and decided to have a go on the fairground, but found it unmanned. By now it was raining heavily, so they couldn't play tennis or crazy golf. The bars were virtually deserted. At seven they turned up in the dining room, where several tables were packed with staff who all seemed to know each other. Some had worked at the camp before, and were comparing notes on what had happened since last year. Others were locals, about to go home for the night.

'Help yourself to fish and chips, dearies,' a woman shouted. They collected the food and took it to an empty table.

'They're wearing dead funny uniforms,' Lily murmured. 'On the table next but one. And they don't half talk dead posh.'

Josie had already noticed the dozen or so attractive young people dressed in black and yellow striped blazers, the men in bright yellow trousers, the women with yellow sun-ray pleated skirts. They made everyone else look very drab, and seemed to be blessed with enviable self-assurance, talking loudly and dramatically throwing their arms about. The meal finished, the group made a great show of leaving.

'See you later, Jeremy. Have a good show.'

'So long, Barbara. Try not to kill any poor souls at bingo.'

'I loathe bloody bingo,' Barbara yawned.

'Darling Sadie, if you haven't organised an olde-time dance, you haven't lived.'

'I wish we wore uniforms like that,' Lily said inevitably. 'They've got more class than an overall.'

For something to do, they went to the theatre where, with about twenty other people, they saw *Strip Jack Naked*, in which half a dozen actors, dressed only in their underwear, rushed in and out of bedrooms that weren't their own. Lily was disgusted, but refused Josie's suggestion that they leave in the interval.

'No, as we're here, we may as well stay till the end,' she said primly. 'Did you recognise some of the cast, Jose? They're the ones we just saw in the dining room. I'd have applied to be an actress if I'd known.'

Over the next few days, the weather improved, and they slowly got used to the camp and the concrete bunker. At eight they reported for duty at the laundry, and helped sort the dirty linen. They went round the chalets, making beds, cleaning sinks, collecting rubbish, brushing floors, and were aghast to find they had to clean the communal lavatories at the end of each block. Lily worked with one hand, held her nose with the other and wished they'd never come.

By the end of the week, though, they were looking forward to July and August when, according to staff who'd been before, the atmosphere would be somewhat similar to Las Vegas, and it was humanly impossible *not* to have the time of your life. The camp would be full, the ballroom and bars crowded, and there would actually be queues for crazy golf and tennis.

The extrovert young people in the black and yellow uniforms were called Wasps. Most were in show business, and organised the dances, beauty competitions and games, or could be seen nightly on stage at the Prince of Wales. It was Josie's and Lily's job to clean their chalets – they lived in pairs in a row set aside from the main camp. Lily considered it degrading to clean up after people who were merely staff like themselves.

'Yes, but very superior staff,' Josie reminded her with a grin. Lily was insanely jealous of the Wasps.

Their room-mates turned out to be two intimidatingly tough-looking, leather-faced sisters in their thirties. Rene and Winnie ran a market stall selling second-hand clothes in Bermondsey. They were married, but their husbands had 'taken a hike' years ago, and their seven children had been left with their nan because Rene and Winnie were 'sick to death of the bleedin' sight of them, if you must know'. They'd come for a break, and another sister was looking after their stall. Over the next few months, they intended to get 'as drunk as pipers every bleedin' night, and shag every man who looks at us twice'.

It seemed strange to the girls, coming from women old enough to be their mothers. At first, they found Rene and Winnie faintly menacing, but their tough exteriors hid hearts of gold. It was rather comforting to be told, in a motherly sort of way, 'If you ever have trouble with a bloke, darlin', just tell me or Winnie here and we'll lay the bugger flat.'

A great heap of post awaited Josie when she called in Reception on her second Tuesday at Haylands. 'Is it your birthday, dear?' the woman behind the counter enquired.

'Yes, I'm seventeen.'

'Many happy returns of the day,' the woman smiled.

'Ta.' She opened the cards there and then. Her boss and two of the girls from the insurance company had remembered it was her birthday. Aunt Ivy enclosed a pretty georgette scarf with her card. There were cards from most of the Kavanaghs, but none from the person she most wanted one from – Ben. Josie turned away, knowing it was unreasonable to feel so disappointed. Since leaving Liverpool, she had missed Ben far more than she had expected. She had grown used to him just *being* there.

She was walking away when the woman cried, 'Oh, Josie – it is Josie, isn't it? Look, I've just found this little parcel on the floor. It's addressed to you. It must have been in the middle of the cards and I dropped it. Sorry, dear.'

The brown paper parcel was no more than three inches square. Inside was a velvet box containing a tiny silver locket, hardly bigger than a sixpence, with a curly, engraved 'J'. 'For my one and only girl', Ben had written in his admirably neat hand, and underneath in brackets, 'I bought this months ago. It seems a shame to let it go to waste.'

Weeks passed, and more and more people, from the very young to the very old, descended on the tight, self-contained, over-heated little oasis of pleasure that was Haylands. Only one thought was in their heads: to have the best possible time during their stay. For the young and single, this meant throwing conventional morality aside. The men hoped to copulate frequently with a member, or members, of the opposite sex. The girls looked forward to romance, passion, to meeting the man of their dreams. Many tearful goodbyes were witnessed on Saturday mornings. Whether any of the promised letters were ever written, or the fervent vows to meet again were kept, no one knew.

Lily could have gone all the way with half a dozen blokes a day, but hadn't met a single one that appealed. 'I'm too picky,' she moaned. 'They've always got something wrong with them. If it's not their looks, then they're too pushy. I want the first time to be extra-special, not some ten-minute, fumbly thing in return for a few drinks. I quite enjoy a good old necking session, but some boys don't find that enough.' Still, she lived in hope that one day the ideal bloke would turn up, and waiting didn't stop her from having a marvellous time.

Josie felt very much a wet blanket. Already, she was tired of the dances, of being asked the same old questions over and over again. 'What's your name?' 'What do you do?' 'Where do you come from?' 'Can I walk you to the chalet?' And if she let a boy take her back to the concrete bunker, she felt traitorous. They would pass rows of heaving couples lined up outside the ballroom, the chalets, in every dark corner. But after a single kiss she would flee, convinced that Ben was watching with his sad, hurt eyes. She preferred to go home alone. Lily would usually arrive about an hour later, and Rene and Winnie even later, or sometimes not at all. It was July but so far she hadn't particularly enjoyed herself. She liked playing tennis or crazy golf with Lily, but the inevitable boys would arrive, wanting to make a foursome and a date for that night. The same thing happened on the fairground or in the theatre. You weren't even safe from male attention in a shop, and she felt obliged to play along for Lily's sake. She began to wonder why they'd come. For adventure, she recalled. Lily had come for the boys, of which there'd been plenty. She herself had wanted adventure but so far there had been no sign of it.

One day Josie returned to their room after work to find a parcel the size of a small shoe box on her bed. 'I noticed it in Reception,' Winnie said. She was lounging on the bunk, drinking gin and orange. 'So I thought I'd bring it.'

'Ta. I wonder who it's from?' She didn't recognise the writing, but her name and address had been printed in large, anonymous capitals.

'Open it, darlin', and find out.'

Josie undid the string, opened the box and stared at the contents, mystified. She removed them one by one, and found a note at the bottom. 'Dear Josie, You forgot to take these with you. Love, Ivy.'

It hadn't crossed her mind to bring the photo of Mam making her First Holy Communion. Even less would she have thought to bring Mam's veil and the white prayer book, which she considered her most precious possessions. And she had deliberately left behind the watch Aunt Ivy had given her as a leaving school/starting work/fourteenth birthday present, in case it got damaged or even lost.

Winnie nodded at the photo. 'Who's that, darlin'? Let's have a decko.'

'It's me mother, me mam,' Josie said. 'She died ages ago. I can't think why me auntie sent it.'

'She's pretty, just like you.'

'Ta.' The parcel made Josie feel uneasy. It seemed such an extraordinarily strange thing for Aunt Ivy to do. Hardly a day went by when she didn't think of Mam, but seeing her picture, holding the things that Mam herself had once held, brought everything flooding back, as if Mam had died only yesterday.

Next morning, Lily received a letter from her mother which she read over breakfast. 'Our Marigold's in the club again,' she gurgled, loud enough for everyone to hear. 'And our Stanley's getting married in Berlin to someone called Freya.' Her voice rose to a shriek. 'And we're *buying* our own house. It's a semi-detached in Childwall with a big garden and a garage for me da's car. Our Daisy's staying in Machin Street with her friend, Eunice. And me brother, Ben, is going to Cambridge University. Look, Jose, Ma's sent you a note an' all.' She handed Josie an envelope. 'She's marked it "Private" – as if I'd have opened it,' she said in a hurt voice.

Mrs Kavanagh had written:

My dear Josie,

I have no idea whether Ivy has told you her news. Somehow, I suspect not, which is why I am writing this, though I hate to spoil what I hope is a happy time in the camp. I worry you might hear from someone else, and thought you should be forewarned.

Anyroad, I'll stop beating about the bush. The thing is, dear, Vincent Adams is back in Machin Street. I heard a rumour months ago that Ivy had been seen with him in town, but couldn't believe my eyes when I saw them walk by our parlour, arm in arm and as bold as brass. I can't help but wonder what she's told the neighbours.

It means you have some thinking to do about your future, Josie. Whether to go back to Machin Street in October, with all that entails, or find yourself somewhere to live, a little flat or a bedsitting-room. Or perhaps a job with accommodation would be a good idea, a hotel, for instance, or some sort of boarding school. You can stay with us in the new house while you sort yourself out – Ben will have gone by then. But he is still shattered over the break with you, and I know he misses you dreadfully. We're hoping he'll feel better about things by Christmas, so it would be best if he didn't find you here. (Are you QUITE sure it's over between you? Eddie and I still have hopes you'll be our daughter-in-law one day.)

I know this will have come as a shock, dear. My thoughts will be with you over the next few days.

Your loving friend, Mollie Kavanagh.

Aunt Ivy knew someone would tell her. She'd sent those things, her most precious things, as a sign she didn't want her back. Not that she would dream of going back, not with Vince there, but just in case, in desperation, with nowhere else to go, she returned to the only flesh and blood she had on earth.

Perhaps the penny had yet to drop, because the only feeling Josie had was pity for her aunt. Poor Ivy. Fancy loving someone so much that you excused every single thing they did, no matter how wicked. Besotted, that was the word Lily had used. Ivy was besotted with Vince. He must have been the friend she'd been meeting. Haylands had come up at an opportune time. No wonder she'd been anxious for Josie to leave.

'What did Ma have to say that's so private?' Lily sniffed.

'Nothing,' Josie said abruptly. She stuffed the letter in her overall pocket and quickly left the dining room before her friend could follow. She wanted to be by herself to think.

Outside, the camp was virtually deserted. A few hardy campers had risen early to savour the lovely July morning. The fresh, salty air was rent with the harsh cry of seagulls as they swooped on the remains of last night's fish and chips which would shortly be swept up.

She wandered over to the fairground. Without the bright lights and loud, jangly music, the rides looked rather shabby, she thought, in need of a lick of paint. She climbed on a bobby horse and found the Irish Sea within her sight – vivid, sparkling, green, the waves tipped with creamy foam.

'One day I'll sail across there, to America.' In a way, Mrs Kavanagh's letter was a ticket to freedom. She had no responsibilities, no dependants. She could go anywhere in the world.

'The world is my oyster,' she said aloud.

Climbing down from the bobby horse, she made her way to the big wheel, which was only small as big wheels went. She sat in the bottom seat, pushed her foot against the platform to make it swing and thought about the letter again. What was she going to do? Did she really want to be totally independent at seventeen?

At that moment, on such a beautiful morning, with the sun shining warmly on her back and the sea glittering in the distance, the problem didn't seem that acute. But Josie knew that with each day that passed, October growing nearer, the problem would get bigger and bigger.

She read Mrs Kavanagh's letter again. There wouldn't be enough to pay rent out of a seventeen-year-old's wages, though she'd quite like to work in a hotel. But she would feel vulnerable, living there, as well. If things went wrong, she would lose her home as well as her job. The same thing went for a boarding school, and everyone would go home in the holidays except her.

A gull had perched on the back of the seat in front, and was watching her curiously with bright, black eyes.

'No,' she said, and the gull flew away. No, she didn't want to live and work in either of those places.

'You can stay with us until you sort yourself out,' Mrs Kavanagh had written. But she mustn't be there at Christmas when Ben came home. It wouldn't be fair. 'Eddie and I still have hopes you'll be our daughter-in-law one day.'

Reading it again, Josie saw a simple way out of her problem. She would write to Ben, tell him she missed him as much as he missed her, that she was sorry she'd gone away. It was true. His shadow had haunted her ever since she'd come to the camp. Just dancing with another boy made her feel guilty, because it wasn't *him*. There was no need to wait to get married. Circumstances had changed. They could get married next year, as soon as she was eighteen, and live in Cambridge. She would find a job and support him until he was ready to work himself.

She smiled. Why hadn't she thought of it before?

*

Josie wondered why, despite having sorted everything out so satisfactorily in her head, she felt more confused than ever.

She was cleaning the chalets that housed the Wasps. So far, she had managed to avoid Lily, who was unbearable if she knew something was being kept from her. Josie wasn't in the mood for her friend's remorseless probing, followed by the predictable oohs and ahs and shrill expressions of disbelief that Vince Adams was back in Machin Street.

'And after what he did an' all!' Lily would say, having guessed a skeleton of the truth. 'What exactly *did* he do, Josie?'

Most Wasps lived in a terrible state of untidiness. A few women kept their chalets neat, their clothes hung up. Some even made their own beds. It wasn't Josie's job to tidy, so she ignored the mess, merely straightening the beds beneath the heaps of clothes on top. She brushed floors, took mats to the door to shake. She worked automatically, her mind on other things.

The next chalet she entered, Barbara's and Sadie's, was a little home from home, kept scrupulously clean. There was a teddy bear on Barbara's pillow, film posters on the walls, dried flowers and photographs on the dressing-table.

Josie bent to pick up the mat to shake it. Her eyes became level with one of the photographs. She'd never once looked at them before, though Lily took everything in, even read letters if they'd been left around.

The photo had been taken in a garden – a couple standing under trees, the man with his arm around the woman, both middle-aged, both smiling. Josie picked it up to study it more closely. The couple looked complacently happy – the woman must be Sadie's mother, she had the same dark, pretty eyes. She looked at the back. 'Mummy and Daddy's Silver Wedding' was scrawled in purple ink. There was another photo, an ordinary wedding, about twenty adults and half a dozen children grouped around the bride and groom. She recognised Sadie as a bridesmaid and noticed the middle-aged couple in the group. On the back she read, 'Jenny and Peter, 1949.'

'Aah!' Josie breathed. How lovely to have a family, a mam and dad, brothers, sisters, uncles, aunts – to *belong*.

Mrs Kavanagh's letter was stiff in her pocket, reminding her that, as from now, she was entirely alone. She had no one – unless she wrote to Ben.

There were typical mounds of clutter in the next chalet, Jeremy's and Griff's. Both beds were heaped with clothes, and the floor was full of empty beer bottles. There must have been a party the night before, as Jeremy and Griff couldn't have drunk so much between them. The sight depressed her for some reason. It seemed that with each chalet she went into she grew more and more aware of her situation and the future seemed more stark, more bleak. Unless she wrote to Ben, she reminded herself again, and wondered why she kept forgetting such an obvious way out.

'Mam,' she whispered. 'What am I going to do? Oh, why did you have to go and die on me?' She sat heavily on a bed, and began to cry.

There was a shriek. Josie screamed, leapt off the bed and a man's head appeared from beneath the pile of clothes. 'You sat on me,' he said accusingly.

'I'm sorry.' Josie, limp with fright, sat on the other bed, then quickly jumped off in case there was someone in it.

'It's all right, it's empty.'

She sat down again. 'You scared me.'

'Not half as much as you scared me. I thought the Russians had dropped the dreaded atom bomb or something.' He sat up. It was Griff Reynolds, a Jack-of-all-trades who played the piano and the double bass, acted a bit, sang a bit and told terrible jokes. He was the handsomest of the Wasps, with a face like a Greek god, lovely blue eyes surrounded by enviably long lashes and brown curly hair that was a mite too long, trailing rakishly around his perfect ears. Winnie said he was a fag, a pansy. You could tell by the way he walked and talked – the prissy little steps he took, the limp way he waved his hands, the high-pitched, effeminate voice. Winnie was then obliged to explain to the girls what being a pansy entailed. Lily had gone on about it for days.

This was the first time Josie had spoken to a Wasp, other than saying 'Hello' or 'Good morning'. They normally kept very much to themselves.

Griff rolled up his pyjamas and examined his perfectly shaped legs. 'I think you've broken one. Or at least an ankle.' He wore a white pyjama jacket with black spots, and black bottoms with white spots. 'If I have to go on stage tonight on crutches, then it'll be your fault, darling.'

'I'm sorry,' Josie said again. 'Anyroad, shouldn't you be on duty? It's half eleven.'

'I'm ill, angel,' Griff said mournfully.

Josie glanced at the bottles. 'I'm not surprised.'

He caught her glance. 'It was Jeremy's birthday, sweet. We had friends in.' He rooted through the clothes, found a pillow and propped it behind him. 'How dare you come in crying, muttering about someone having died, then have the cheek to actually sit on me?'

'You were awake? You should have said something.'

'I was only half-awake, darling. And I wasn't expecting to be used as a chair. Why were you crying? Who has died?'

Josie sensed that behind the jokey remarks, he seemed genuinely to care that she'd been crying.

'The person died a long time ago,' she explained. 'It was me mam, and I still miss her. I just think about her whenever I feel miserable, that's all.'

'And why should such an adorable young woman have reason to feel miserable when it's such a glorious day outside?' He squinted at the window where the curtains were still closed. 'I assume it *is* a glorious day?'

'It's lovely.'

'Are you homesick, poppet, is that it?'

Josie smiled. 'I haven't got a home to feel sick about.'

'You poor little homeless orphan,' he cried. 'Tell your Uncle Griff all about it.'

She got to her feet. 'I can't. I'll get in trouble if I don't finish by twelve o'clock. I'm already a bit behind.'

Griff sprang out of bed – too quickly. He clutched his head and winced. 'I'll help, sweet. Where do the bottles go?'

'In the trolley outside. Ta.'

Between them, they disposed of the bottles. Griff threw the clothes off his bed, straightened the bedding, then threw the clothes back, while Josie made the other. He shook the mat while she brushed the floor.

He giggled. 'I might come back next year as a chalet maid.'

'You'd be wasted. I've seen your shows. You're very good, particularly when you sing and play the piano at the same time.'

'What a perfectly sweet thing to say. You know, I've seen you around, but I don't know your name. I can't very well call you Little Orphan Annie, it's a bit of a mouthful.'

'It's Josie.'

'I'm Griff.'

'I already knew that.' She stared up at him. He wasn't as tall as Ben, about five feet eleven, but much broader. His shoulders and arms were heavily muscled. She remembered he was very good at tennis. For the first time since leaving Liverpool she felt a flicker of interest in the opposite sex, but if Winnie was right, Griff wasn't attracted to women. Yet there was something in his eyes . . .

'Why don't we meet up for a drink tonight after *Hit For Sex*?' he suggested.

'What?'

'The play, my love.'

Her heart beat a fraction faster. 'I'd like that, ta.'

'The curtain comes down about five past ten, then I have to change and remove my disgusting make-up, so I'll see you at about twenty past in the Palm Court?'

She nodded. 'Okay.'

For the rest of the morning, she mostly forgot about Mrs Kavanagh's letter, and thought about Griff instead.

That night, she took great pains with her appearance, brushing her hair vigorously and applying make-up with particular care. After staring at the contents of her crammed locker for several minutes, she reached for a white linen skirt with an inverted pleat at the back, a lemon silky jumper with short sleeves and a V-neck, and white sandals that showed off her tanned legs to perfection.

'You look nice,' Rene remarked. 'Lovely and fresh, like a pineapple. Are you meeting someone special tonight?'

'Not really.' She couldn't tell anyone, not even Lily, about Griff. They'd only make fun.

The girls usually caused a stir when they entered the ballroom. Lily was small and plump, with Shirley Temple hair and cheeks rosier than ever from the sun. Her brown eyes sparkled, as if she was determined the evening ahead was going to be fun. Josie was taller, slimmer, her dark blue eyes more wary than her friend's, her expression withdrawn, almost cold. She was beautiful, or so she'd been told a score of times, and supposed it was true. People who'd known them both said she was the spitting image of her mother, the most beautiful person Josie had ever known.

They were asked to dance immediately, and it continued that way for the next two hours. Josie was glad when Lily became attached to a nice young man called Harry, but unfortunately Harry had a friend, Bill, and Josie was forced to claim a headache and leave early, otherwise she would have found herself landed with Bill.

It was only ten to ten. She went for a walk around the tennis courts, entered the Palm Court at a quarter past, found an empty table and waited for Griff.

He arrived a few minutes later with his room-mate, Jeremy, who led communal sing-songs in a fine baritone voice. They stood by the door, laughing, nudging each other, as if sharing a private joke. Griff wore a blue shirt with an open neck and dark trousers. A belt encircled his narrow waist. His eyes searched the room. Josie waved, and they came towards her, Griff with his funny, wiggly walk. She noticed the campers grin and wink at each other when he passed their tables.

'*There* you are, darling,' Griff gushed. 'Josie, this is my pal, Jeremy. Jeremy, Josie. What are you drinking, precious? Lemonade! Jeremy, fetch this young lady a lemonade, and a pink gin for yours truly.' He threw himself on to the next chair, and gave her a searching look. 'Feeling better, poppet?'

'Yes, ta,' she gulped. 'How did the show go?'

'Like a dream, dear heart. The audience loved it.' He told her about his career so far, 'which wouldn't fill the back of a postage stamp. I've yet to find my niche.' He'd had a few small parts in West End revues and had played the piano on the wireless a few times. 'But the vile producer wouldn't let me sing.'

Jeremy arrived with the drinks. There was no sign of a pink gin. Instead, he put a tankard of beer in front of his friend.

As the night wore on, more and more Wasps joined their table. Josie didn't open her mouth during the fascinating conversation that went on. What on earth could she contribute of the faintest interest to people who said things like, 'Larry Olivier actually kissed me on the lips, darling. Poor Vivien, she was *livid*!'

'Tommy said – Tommy *Handley*, that is, darling, "I just *know* we'll see your name in lights one day, Stella." Such a pity he died, poor man.'

'Who's got a pantomime at Christmas?'

There was a groan and a chorus of, '*I* have!'

The strains of the last waltz drifted from the ballroom, 'When We Sound The Last All Clear'. The orchestra played the same tune every night. 'We're going to the beach, sweetheart,' Griff said. 'Like to come?'

'Oh, *yes.*' She didn't want to miss a single thing.

'Good grief,' Griff shrieked when he saw the dozens of writhing couples on the sand. 'This place is becoming more and more like Sodom and Gomorrah every day. Don't look, my pet. You're far too young.' He put a casual arm around her shoulder, and she felt a stupid little thrill.

Then Jeremy said something very strange. 'Calm down, mate. There's no need to keep up the act. We're amongst friends.'

'Phew!' Griff said in a deep, perfectly normal voice. 'One of these days, I'll forget who I really am.' He squeezed Josie's shoulders. 'That other guy is merely a performance put on to entertain the campers. You guessed, didn't you, Josie? Otherwise you'd never have come.'

'Yes,' Josie said weakly. Perhaps she had!

'We come here most nights. It's peaceful after a hectic day acting so bloody cheerful.'

'It's lovely,' she breathed, suddenly extraordinarily happy.

The midnight sky was perfect – a dark, luminous blue, cloudless, strewn with a million twinkling stars and a few dusty patches of gold. The waning moon was a tangerine segment, and the sea gleamed as if it were illuminated from underneath. She removed her shoes and the sand felt warm and powdery beneath her feet. Ahead, a bonfire burned merrily, and Josie could hear music and the crackle of flames.

The music came from a portable wireless. Half a dozen Wasps were lying around the fire and heralded their arrival with subdued murmurs. Josie didn't know where to look when four of the newcomers, three men and a girl, stripped off and ran *stark naked* into the sea. They began to kick water at each other.

Griff sank down on to the sand, and pulled her down so she was sitting in front of him, his arms around her waist. It seemed only natural to lean back, relax against him.

Little was said over the next hour as they watched the flames, watched the wood turn to brilliant red ash, watched the red ash crumble and become grey. They hummed occasionally to the music, and Josie lay contentedly in Griff's arms. Then someone yawned. Soon everyone was yawning and stretching. Jeremy said, 'One last swim for me.' He began to remove his clothes.

'I love this song,' Josie murmured. The haunting strains of 'Goodnight, Sweetheart' came from the wireless.

'Let's dance.' Griff lifted her up, and slid his arms around her waist. There was nothing to do with her arms except put them around his neck, which she willingly did. He pressed his cheek against hers as they shuffled over the sand.

She closed her eyes, and when she opened them Jeremy was entering the water without a stitch on, holding the hand of a girl as naked as himself. Sand was being kicked on the fire, parts of which still glowed dullish red. The sky looked even more beautiful, as if more stars had appeared, and the moon had got bigger and more orange.

Josie caught her breath. It was an enchanting scene, and she was part of the enchantment. Not everyone might regard the last few hours as an adventure, but it would do.

2

Next morning, Lily's eyebrows narrowed in a frown when Heidi and Barbara passed their breakfast table. 'Morning, Josie,' they called. The frown deepened when Jeremy said, 'Enjoy yourself last night?' Before she could open her mouth to demand an explanation, Griff came up. 'See you tonight, darling. Same time, same place.'

'Okay,' Josie replied weakly.

'Did you enjoy yourself *where*?' Lily looked about to burst a blood vessel. 'And you haven't got a date with *him*, surely?'

'Griff was in the chalet yesterday when I cleaned it,' Josie said haughtily. 'We had a little chat. He's very nice. I met him again last night on me way home from the dance, and he asked me for a drink. Then a big pile of us went to the sands.'

'You went to the sands with a pile of *Wasps*?' Lily's eyes gleamed jealously. 'I *crept* in last night, so as not to disturb you because you said you had a headache. I didn't even turn on the light. I thought you were in bed, but all the time you were cavorting on the sands with piles of *Wasps*.'

'We weren't cavorting. We were merely talking and listening to music. We danced a bit and some of them swam.' She didn't mention they swam in the nude, as Lily was likely to choke.

'That sounds like cavorting to me.'

'Well, it isn't,' Josie snapped. 'And quite frankly, Lily, it isn't any of your business if we were cavorting or not. Nor is it anything to do with you who I go out with. I never offer a word of criticism of your various boyfriends.'

'You said Frank from Manchester was ugly.'

'No, *you* said Frank from Manchester was ugly. I just agreed that he was as ugly as sin.'

Lily's bottom lip quivered with rage. 'Another thing, you still haven't told me what was in the letter from me ma.'

'She wouldn't have marked it "Private" if she'd wanted you to know. It's another thing that's none of your business, Lily Kavanagh.'

'You're a fine friend, Josie Smith.'

Josie wasn't sure what came over her, other than a wish to remove the wind from Lily's sails completely. She said airily, 'Me name's not Josie Smith any more, it's Josie Flynn.' With Aunt Ivy out of her life, there was no need to keep up the pretence.

Lily's face collapsed. She floundered, 'What? *What*? What on earth are you talking about?'

Josie smiled mysteriously. 'Wouldn't you like to know?'

It was the first row they'd had since they'd come to Haylands and they were both quite happy with it. They linked arms on the way to the laundry to fetch their trolleys.

'Actually,' Lily mused, 'I wouldn't mind a platonic relationship. It makes things so much easier, no wondering how far a bloke's hands are going to roam and if you should let him if they do. And I must admit that Griff is dead gorgeous.'

'Who said it was a platonic relationship?'

Lily's face collapsed for the second time that morning. 'But I thought, I thought . . .'

'Well, you thought wrong.' Josie felt smug. 'It's just an act he puts on to entertain the campers.'

'Did – did he *kiss* you?'

'Only me ear.'

'Oh, Jose. It sounds dead romantic.' Lily sighed. Later, as they pushed their trolleys towards the chalets, she said, 'You know that business of your name being Flynn, not Smith. I take it you weren't having me on, so you will tell me one day, won't you, Jose? And whatever it was me ma had to say in her letter. After all, we're *friends.*'

The tide had not long gone out, and the sand was moist beneath Josie's feet as Griff twirled her round and round in an old-fashioned waltz. They were getting further and further away from the group around the bonfire who lay uncaringly on the damp sand. There was no moon, and the only illumination came from the leaping flames and a strange, grey light that hung over the sea. The horizon was a dark, silvery blur.

Josie trod on something and yelped, and Griff led her back to where the sand was dry. They sat down and he examined her foot. 'Nothing there, darling,' he said after a while. Suddenly, he kissed her toes, he kissed her legs and her knees. He put his arms around her waist, pushed her down on to the sand and kissed her lips. Josie felt a wild, fluttery sensation in her stomach that she'd never had with Ben. She kissed him back, and willingly opened her mouth when he tried to force it with his tongue, a habit she'd previously thought disgusting. Nor did she mind when his hand crept under her jumper, under her bra, pulling it away, and he bent and kissed her breasts. In fact, it was so nice, so incredibly nice, that she wanted to scream how nice it was, and that she didn't want him to stop, not ever. There was a throbbing between her legs, and she longed for him to touch her *there.*

'Griff. Josie. We're going.' The shouts sounded far away.

Griff raised his head. 'Coming.' He looked down at Josie and lightly touched her left nipple. 'Have you done this before?'

'Well – almost.' She felt disappointed that he'd stopped. There seemed something daringly wicked about lying in the open air with her breasts bare. She stretched voluptuously.

'I thought as much.' He pulled down her jumper. 'That's enough for tonight, my darling. And don't tease.'

She thought about him the second she woke. He was on her mind all day, as she counted down the hours and the minutes before she would see him again.

That night, they wandered far away from the bonfire to the place they'd lain the night before, where they fell on the sand in each other's arms and began to kiss eagerly. Josie felt as if her body were on fire as it began to respond to Griff's touch, his hands or his lips exploring every secret part of her. Suddenly, he sat back on his haunches. She was surprised to see that he was naked – and so was she, though she couldn't remember either of them having removed their clothes. He was the handsomest man she had ever known. Her head was whirling, and she felt as if a spell had been cast upon her. Making love had been far from her mind when she'd come to the camp. She had thought it would be years away, when she was married. But now it was about to happen, on an enchanted Welsh beach under a dark sky, to the sound of the rippling tide and the faint, tinny music from the wireless.

'What are you doing?' she asked impatiently. Griff was feeling in the pockets of his trousers. She wanted him *back*.

'Looking for this.' He held up something very small. 'We don't want a little memento of Haylands arriving in nine months' time.' He straddled her, then tenderly cupped her face in his hands. 'Are you sure you're ready for this?' he said gently. 'I won't be cross if you change your mind. Well, not very.'

Josie clasped her arms around his neck. 'You'll have to put me in the mood again.'

'Willingly,' murmured Griff.

Lily was irritable next day, and it was all Josie's fault. She wasn't concentrating, she wasn't listening, she was in another world. 'You're bloody miles away,' Lily said accusingly.

'Am I?' Josie dreamily shook a mat.

'You're supposed to shake it *outside*, not in. I've just brushed that floor.'

'Sorry, Lil.' Josie shook the mat outside.

'You've already done that. I'm just brushing the muck up.'

'Sorry, Lil. What shall I do now?'

'Empty the bin, make the beds, clean the sink, same as we do every day.

What on earth's got into you, Josie?' Lily said acidly. She looked at her friend intently. 'What's happened? I've never known you so vague before.'

'Something wonderful, Lil,' Josie said in a husky voice. She had to tell someone, and there was no one else but Lily. 'Something truly incredible and . . . and, oh, *wonderful*.' She could almost hear the ticking of Lily's brain as she tried to think what the something was. Her eyes grew wide and her jaw fell as enlightenment dawned.

'You've gone all the way!' she cried. 'Did it hurt, Jose?'

'Only a bit, only at first.'

Lily's face twisted ferociously as she tried to adjust to the news. She pouted. 'I'm the oldest. I should have done it before you.'

'Oh, Lil. It's not a race.'

'Are you in love? You *look* like you're in love.'

'I'm not. It's purely sexual.' Josie sighed rapturously. 'We can't keep our hands off each other.'

'You lucky bugger!' Lily's expression changed from one of envy to concern. 'Our poor Ben, though. Does this mean you'll never get back together? Ma keeps hoping you will.'

'I'm afraid it does, Lil. I never felt with Ben the way I do with Griff.' She had forgotten the letter she'd meant to write.

Lily said wistfully, 'I love being here. It won't half seem dull when we're back in Liverpool, working in an office.'

Josie reluctantly came down to earth. She decided it was time she dropped her bombshell. 'I'm not sure if I'm going back to Liverpool, Lil.'

'Why ever not?' Lily's face was a picture of bewilderment.

'Because Vince Adams is back with Auntie Ivy. That's what the letter from your ma was about. I've got to find somewhere to live, as well as a job.' In order to get everything out of the way in one go, she explained that her mother hadn't been married and that Ivy had insisted that Josie change her surname to Smith so no one would know. 'But from now on, I'm Josie Flynn.'

The *Liverpool Echo* was on sale in the camp. Josie bought a copy every day. By the end of August, the only live-in job even vaguely suitable was as a cook in a men's hostel, which she didn't fancy, mainly because she couldn't boil an egg. Most rented accommodation was way beyond her means. Even the few affordable places meant she'd be left with scarcely anything to live on.

Lily was desperate for her friend to stay in Liverpool. 'We've got to stick together, Jose. I don't know what I'd do if you weren't around. I'd miss you far more than I would our Daisy or Marigold.'

Even Griff became involved in the search of a job for Josie. 'You could join the forces,' he suggested one night after they had finished making love. They were in his chalet because it was raining. Jeremy had been ordered not to come back for an hour. 'Become a Wren or a Wraf. Or you could marry me.'

She looked at him in surprise. 'Do you mean that?'

He appeared a tiny bit shocked. 'I'm not sure. It just sort of slipped out.'

'*I'm* sure. It wouldn't work. We hardly know each other.'

'I would have thought we knew each other better than anyone else on earth. I'm familiar with every single part of your body, and you with mine.'

Josie's stomach lurched. 'Yes, but we still don't *know* each other. We don't know what goes on inside each other's heads. I mean, we never *talk*.' She began to touch him. There was still time to make love again before Jeremy came back. 'Oh, but I'm so glad you were the first,' she cried. 'I'm so lucky it was you.' She would never see him again after October, but she would remember him all her life.

It was Lily who saw the job that might possibly do. 'Secretary/companion required by elderly gentlewoman to commence mid-October. Own large room. No cooking/cleaning/nursing. Formby area. References required. Salary: £10 per month.'

'There's a box number,' Lily announced when she read the advertisement aloud. 'It sounds perfect, Jose.'

'Would you fancy being companion to an elderly gentlewoman?' Josie said huffily.

'I'd hate it. But I don't need to find a live-in job, do I?'

'Thanks for reminding me. What's a *gentle*woman when she's at home, anyroad?'

Lily shrugged. 'Same as a gentle*man*, I suppose. In other words, dead posh. But ten pounds a month, Jose, and you wouldn't have to buy food. You wouldn't need fares.'

'Hmm, I dunno.' Josie chewed her lip. 'I couldn't very well write from Haylands, could I? It wouldn't look good to say I was a chalet maid.'

'Put our new address in Childwall, and I'll send it to Ma to post. She'll send the answer here.'

'I don't suppose it would hurt.'

A fortnight later, Mrs Kavanagh sent the reply with a short note to say the job sounded ideal, and she hoped the letter contained good news.

The letter was signed by a Marian Moorcroft and was short and to the point. 'Dear Miss Flynn, In regard to your application as secretary-companion to my mother, kindly present yourself for interview at the above address on Wednesday, 2nd September at 2 p.m. Please telephone if you are unable to keep the appointment.'

'Oh, well, that's that.' Josie threw the letter at Lily. 'I can't possibly go all the way to Liverpool for an interview.'

'Someone's not going to take you on as companion to her dear old ma on the strength of a letter,' Lily argued. 'It stands to reason she'll want to see you. You can easily get there and back in a day. Wednesday's our afternoon off, and I'm sure Mrs Baxter would you let you have the morning off as well. We've both been reliable workers. Oh, look at the address – Barefoot House, Sandy Steps, Formby. It sounds lovely. Come on, Jose,' she coaxed. 'Formby's only the other side of Liverpool. We could go out together nights and weekends. At least you'll have *friends*, which won't be the case if you move away.'

'I'll think about it,' said Josie.

It was a bright, sunny day, and Liverpool seemed incredibly *loud* when Josie got off the bus at the Pier Head, loud and very crowded. Trams clattered noisily along the metal lines. They, and the buses, seemed much bigger than she remembered, and she almost gagged when a car passed exuding clouds of black fumes. The New Brighton ferry had just docked, and people were hurrying to board down the big, floating gangway – families, mainly, the children carrying buckets and spades.

Josie paused for a second on the very spot where she'd stood once before and watched the same scene. It seemed a lifetime ago, and she found it hard to connect the small, mixed-up child with the person she was now. Yet they were the same. And she was still mixed up, but in a different way. And then she'd had Mam.

She walked to Exchange station, where the Southport train was waiting. It left almost immediately. After the wide open spaces of the camp, with its small cream buildings, the landscape she passed through seemed claustrophobic, the houses small and dark, crammed together in narrow streets. There were still bomb sites to be cleared, and the air was full of smoke. But when they reached Formby, the scenery became more countrified, the houses spaced widely apart with big gardens. Cows grazed in a field.

It wasn't quite half past one when she got off the train at Formby station. There was plenty of time to find Barefoot House – Mrs Kavanagh had been unable to find Sandy Steps on the map.

Unfortunately, the few shops were closed and wouldn't be opening again because it was half-day closing, and there wasn't a soul about. She walked along a road of large, detached houses, and approached a man working in his garden.

'Sandy Steps? Sorry, dear, I've never heard of it, or Barefoot House. Try the post office.'

'It's closed.'

Two girls on bikes couldn't help either, or a woman walking her dog, or the man about to get in his car. By then it was almost two, and the idea of having come all the way from Colwyn Bay and not being able to find the house added desperation to her search. It wasn't hot, but her hair felt damp against her neck and her armpits were wet, although she'd rubbed them with deodorant that morning. Worst of all, the canvas shoes which had always felt so comfortable, began to rub her heels.

At last! 'That's where Louisa Chalcott lives, isn't it?' exclaimed an elderly lady in conversation with another over a garden gate. 'It's at the bottom of Nelson Road, on the beach. Go back down this road, turn left, then second right. It's quite a walk,' she chuckled, 'but it won't take long on your young legs.'

As Josie limped away, she heard the other woman say, 'I thought Louisa Chalcott was dead?'

Nelson Road was lined with bungalows, and led directly to the shore, beyond which flowed the greeny-brown waters of the Mersey. At the point where the bungalows ended, the road sloped down to meet the sand, and on the right a series of steps, attached to a brick wall, led to a tall iron gate with a name on a metal plate: BAREFOOT HOUSE.

With a feeling of relief mixed with annoyance at the lack of directions, Josie hurried down the steps, through the gate, up more steps and into a small garden of withered bushes, bent reeds and long-dead trees, separated from the sand by a low wall. She almost ran towards a large, windswept, sandstone house with curved bay windows upstairs and down. The window frames had more paint off than on, and the front door, which might have once been grey, was pitted, as if gravel had been thrown against it.

She knocked, and the door was opened by a smiling woman in a flowered wrap-round pinny, a scarf tied turban-wise around her head.

'I'm so sorry I'm late,' Josie began, 'but—'

'There's no need to apologise to me, luv,' the woman said cheerfully. 'Save it for the terrible twins in the parlour. What's your name, luv? I'm supposed to announce you. Stupid bitches,' she said under her breath.

'Josephine Flynn, er, Miss Flynn.' Josie was a bit put out by the reception. She ached to go to the lavatory, and would have liked to comb her hair, see if her lipstick had smudged, have a wash. As she followed the woman across a square, spacious hall, she tried to straighten herself up as much as possible.

'Miss Josephine Flynn,' the overalled woman said regally when she opened a door without knocking. She jerked her head at Josie. 'Go on in, luv.'

Josie entered a massive, sparsely furnished room overlooking the river, where two women in pastel twinsets and pearls were seated officiously behind a table. They would have been identical, except that one wore glasses and the other didn't. Their round, narrowly set eyes regarded the newcomer with disapproval. She saw her letter on the table.

'You're late,' the woman with glasses snapped. She looked at her watch. 'It's a quarter to three. In another fifteen minutes we have to interview somebody else.'

'I'm sorry, but—' Josie began, but the other woman interrupted. 'It hardly seems worth our whiles interviewing this person, Marian. Not only was she very late, but she's far too young for Mother.'

'I agree with you there, Hilary.'

Josie plonked herself in a chair without being asked. She was seething. 'If you'd bothered to put the proper address on your letter, I wouldn't have been late,' she said spiritedly.

The women gave each other an outraged look. 'Everyone knows where Barefoot House is,' Marian said curtly. 'Our mother, Louisa Chalcott, is very well known.'

'Well, I asked loads of people who'd never heard of Barefoot House, and the only one who had thought Louisa Chalcott was dead.' Josie tossed her head. 'As to me being too young, I put me date of birth on me letter. All you had to do was work it out.' She rose to her feet, knowing that the job would never be hers, but she wasn't leaving without tearing the women off a strip. 'You're both very irresponsible and rude. I don't appreciate having me time wasted by the likes of you.'

Their faces sagged in stupefaction. Josie went to the door and opened it. 'Tara,' she said loudly, and they both jumped.

'Stay!' an imperious voice thundered.

It was Josie's turn to jump. Outside the door stood a very old, very tall, painfully thin woman with jet black hair, lightly sprinkled with grey, and black, bushy eyebrows. She had a walking stick in one hand. The other, trembling slightly, she held in front of Josie's face. She wore baggy tweed trousers, a man's shirt worn loose and carpet slippers. Her dark eyes, large and very beautiful, flashed angrily in her deeply wrinkled face. She gave a terse nod, which Josie took as an indication to return. The woman followed, leaning heavily on the stick, and sat down with difficulty, waving aside Josie's attempt to help. 'If I need a hand, I'll ask for it,' she snapped.

'Please yourself,' Josie snapped back. She wasn't in the mood to be nice to people, even if they were old and walked with a stick.

'Really!' Hilary gasped.

The older woman smiled. She took cigarettes, a holder and a silver lighter from her breast pocket, lit a cigarette and inhaled deeply. Puffs of smoke emerged from her nostrils, reminding Josie of a dragon. 'I want *her*,' she said emphatically. 'I don't want another retired schoolteacher fawning over me, or a retired nurse, or a widow with nothing to do. I want someone young for a change, someone with a bit of spirit who'll answer back. I want someone like *her*.' She nodded at a dazed Josie, then chuckled spitefully. 'I enjoyed the way she wiped the floor with you two.'

'Have you been eavesdropping, Mother?'

'I most certainly have.' The woman – presumably Louisa Chalcott – had a deep, hoarse, attractive voice, and spoke with an accent Josie couldn't identify. 'I was amused to hear some people think me dead. I am, however, very much alive, and, despite your insistence to the contrary, I am not an invalid. I am also still in possession of all my faculties, and quite able to choose a secretary for myself.'

'But, Mother, you *are* an invalid,' Marian cried. 'We were only trying to help. This ...' She waved her hand at a still-dazed Josie. 'This person is entirely unsuitable.'

'She isn't to me.' Louisa Chalcott banged her stick on the floor and yelled, 'Phoebe.'

The woman in the flowered overall must have been indulging in a spot of eavesdropping herself, because the door opened immediately. 'What, Lou?' Hilary and Marian winced.

'Show this young lady to the room that would be hers should she deign to live with us. She is quite likely to subject you to the third degree, and I'd like you to be brutally honest so she'll know what to expect. Oh, and, Phoebe, show her the lavatory on the way. She looks desperate for a pee.'

The upstairs room was the same size as the one below, and just as sparsely furnished. There was a double bed with a white cotton cover, a wardrobe and chest of drawers, both urgently in need of varnish. Two faded rugs graced the polished wooden floor, and faded cretonne curtains the big bay window. The view, overlooking a vast expanse of the Mersey, was breathtaking. Josie knelt on the window seat to watch a liner, making its stately way along the gleaming river, and several other smaller ships – tugboats and coasters. There was a single yacht, poised like a bird on the water. Fluffy clouds raced across the blue sky, much faster than the ships. Fancy waking up every morning to this!

Phoebe was standing inside the door, arms folded. 'I must say you put the twins in their place,' she said with a complacent smile. 'Me and Lou laughed like drains.'

Josie climbed off the window seat, sat on the bed and bounced a few times. It felt nice and soft. 'Who exactly is she, Louisa Chalcott? I've never heard of her meself.'

'Not many people have, luv, only intellectual types. She writes poetry, used to be quite famous in her day. Before the war this house was full of people, parties most weekends. But then poor Lou had a stroke. That's when I came to work here. She was only sixty-two, but it left her paralysed one side. She's much better than she used to be, though she never goes out and there's scarcely been a visitor since, apart from the twins. Lou doesn't want people knowing the state she's in.'

'Why does she need a companion if you're here?'

Phoebe came and sat beside her on the bed. 'I'm only the cleaner, luv. I come a few hours a day, make Lou's meals – she eats like a bird. She wasn't always so thin. She needs someone to do her typing and live here full time, case she falls, like. She has to sleep downstairs because she can't manage the stairs.' She patted Josie's hand. 'I hope you decide to take the job, luv. You're just what she needs, young and full of life. As long as you answer back, stand up for yourself, like, you and Lou will get on fine. She can't abide what she calls lickspittles or toadies. Her last companion walked out in tears. Marian and Hilary will be here till October, and they need someone to take over then.' Phoebe made a face. 'I can't wait to see the back of them, interfering pair of bitches.'

'What happened to Louisa's husband?' Josie enquired. She had, after all, been more or less authorised to ask questions.

Phoebe winked. 'Never had one!'

Josie gasped. 'But she's got two daughters!'

'Lou's never been what you'd call conventional. And she never does things by halves. She didn't just have one baby on the wrong side of the blanket, she had twins.' Phoebe shook her head. 'Lord knows what people said at the time. It must have caused a terrible scandal – she was forty an' all. Mind you, she's a Yank. Perhaps they do things different in America.'

Louisa Chalcott was waiting in the same chair, smoking a fresh cigarette. There was no sign of her daughters. Or, Josie noted with amusement, the woman who'd been expected at three o'clock. 'Well, young lady,' she said with a grin. 'I expect Phoebe has just washed all my dirty linen in front of you. Can I expect you in October or not?'

'Yes.' She didn't have much choice. 'I've got a name, you know. It's Josie Flynn.'

'And I'm Louisa Chalcott. Thrilled to meet you, Josie. You can call me Lou or Louisa. I don't mind which.'

The children had gone back to school, and with each week fewer and fewer campers came to Haylands. Once again the camp was almost deserted, the bars hardly used. The ballroom was a miserable place with so few people there, nearly all couples. Staff left, and Josie and Lily bade a tearful goodbye to their room-mates. Rene and Winnie had enjoyed themselves. The break had done them good, they were looking forward to seeing their kids. They took each other's addresses and promised to write.

The summer too had ended. September was a cold, blustery month, unsuitable for midnight sojourns on the sands. Half the Wasps had gone, back on the dole or to menial jobs in London where they could keep in touch with their agents and hope for better things. A lucky few had tiny walk-on parts in far-flung theatres throughout the country, which they hoped would lead to something better. They left, praying they *wouldn't* meet up again in Haylands, a certain sign of failure.

Griff had the chalet to himself, so they could make love whenever they pleased. But something was missing – the enchantment, the company, the moonlit beach, the music. Josie knew she had been right to dismiss the idea of them getting married.

On the final night at Haylands, she and Griff talked for a long time. They said things to each other that they'd never said before. She hadn't known he'd been a soldier in the war and that he'd hated every minute. She told him she was dreading being stuck in Formby with a horrible old woman.

They made love for the last time. It was sweet, tender, devoid of passion, like an old married couple who'd done the same thing a thousand times before.

'I'd better be going,' Josie sighed. She detached herself from his arms.

'We're catching the ten o'clock bus in the morning, and I haven't packed a thing.'

'I'll walk you back.'

'No, ta. I'd sooner go by meself.' She could feel tears behind her eyes. If he touched her again, she would only cry. She dressed quickly and went to the door. 'Tara, Griff,' she whispered. His handsome face was just visible in the faint light that filtered through the curtains from the lamp outside. He looked devastated.

'Bye, Josie, my darling. Have a nice life.'

'You, too.' She closed the door. That night, she cried herself to sleep. She was still crying next morning. Lily, who had no one to cry for and was leaving with her virginity still intact, was irritated when her friend cried most of the way home on the bus to Liverpool.

The Kavanaghs' new house in Childwall was light and roomy. It had a sunshine lounge, a breakfast room, a large, modern kitchen and four bedrooms. Josie was staying for a few days before going to Barefoot House.

The first thing Lily did was inspect her room, where she immediately found fault with the wallpaper. The flowers were too big – she'd wanted smaller ones. 'And couldn't you have found net curtains with a frillier frill, Ma?'

'Lily, luv. We did the best we could,' Mrs Kavanagh said in a hurt voice.

'Oh, I suppose it'll *do*.'

Josie knew her friend had been jealous of her relationship with Griff. Now, as if she was trying to get her own back, even things out, over the next few days she felt convinced Lily was doing her utmost to emphasise Josie's aloneness when compared to her own comfortable place within a large, loving family. As soon as Mr Kavanagh sank into his armchair, Lily would drape herself all over him and demand a cuddle. She apologised to her mother for criticising the room. 'After you'd gone to so much trouble for your little girl.'

Perhaps I'm just imagining it, Josie thought. But Lily had always wanted to be on top. It rather spoiled her stay at the Kavanaghs', which she'd been looking forward to.

One day she went into Ben's room. He had a bookcase of his own now, and a desk. She noticed that the books had been placed alphabetically on the shelves, and the desk was bare, a chair neatly placed in front. The only ornaments were the various cups he'd won at school over the years placed neatly on the window-sill. The room had a stark, monk-like air.

'This is the way he left it,' Mrs Kavanagh said from the door. 'I never needed to tidy up after our Ben.'

'I suppose you miss him.'

'More than I can say.' Mrs Kavanagh came into the room. 'I miss all me kids. Lily's the only one left. I've got two grandchildren and another on the way, but they're not the same as your own.' She smiled ruefully. 'You know, luv, Ben's still heartbroken. Is it definitely over between you two?'

Josie nodded. 'I'm afraid so. I nearly did something awful, though. When I heard Vince Adams was back, I thought about making up with Ben. I was feeling desperate, you see.' She squared her shoulders. 'I'm glad I didn't. It would have been dead unfair. It was the Kavanaghs I wanted to marry, not Ben.'

'I understand, luv.' The older woman gave her a hug. 'Anyroad, I'm a realist. Our Ben will make some girl a good husband, but not a very exciting one.' She picked up one of the cups and tenderly polished it with her sleeve. 'Children,' she sighed. She looked at Josie. 'I'm sorry about Lily, luv, the way she's behaving. I know she's me daughter and I love her to death, but always remember this – you've got more character in your little finger than our Lily's got in her whole silly body.'

Next day, Josie left for Barefoot House. She telephoned first, and Phoebe said to come at five o'clock. 'Lou's expecting the doctor around four, and she hates anyone being there.'

With each portion of the journey, her heart sank lower and lower. By the time she reached Barefoot House and entered the bleak, petrified garden, she felt totally detached from the real world of ordinary people leading ordinary lives. She had no one: no Mam, no Aunt Ivy, no Kavanaghs just along the street.

From now on, she was truly on her own.

Barefoot House
1951–1954

1

It had originally been called Burford House, Louisa said, built for someone called Clarence Burford in 1858. In those days, it had stood entirely alone on the sands. Louisa had lived there for almost thirty years.

'We landed in Liverpool from New York, and decided to spend a few days here, take a look round one of the most famous ports in the world. Chuck managed to borrow a car. He was actually driving the damn thing along the beach when we saw the house. I fell in love with it straight away, though I didn't spend much time here. I was for ever flitting off to London or New York.' The twins had called it Barefoot House, and the name had stuck. Phoebe said they were ten years old before their mother sent for them from America.

Nelson Road hadn't existed when Louisa had bought her house, and she loathed the new properties. 'Moronic,' she called them. 'Moronic little houses for moronic little people.' Fortunately, they were only visible from the back, and then from the upstairs rooms which were only used when Marian and Hilary came to stay. It was still easy to believe that Barefoot House, surrounded as it was on three sides by ten-foot-high walls, and only sand and the river visible from the front, stood entirely alone.

The doctor was just leaving the day Josie arrived. He tipped his hat. 'If you're the new companion, then you have my every sympathy, young lady. Her ladyship's in a foul mood.'

Josie went inside, deposited her suitcase at the bottom of the stairs and shouted, 'Hello, it's me.' There was no reply.

There was a rattling sound coming from somewhere at the back. Josie found Louisa Chalcott, clad in tweed slacks and a short-sleeved shirt, her black hair wild and uncombed, in the kitchen trying to support herself with her stick. At the same time she was struggling with a strange metal contraption, a sort of pan, trying to get the top off.

'Hello,' Josie said again.

Louisa, startled, dropped the metal contraption on the floor. 'Fuck!' she spat. She glared at Josie. 'Don't tell me you're a creeper. I can't stand fucking creepers. I had someone once, Miss Twizzlewit or something, who crept around like a fucking mouse.'

'I didn't mean to frighten you, but I walked in quite normally, and I shouted, too.'

Louisa ignored her. 'That stupid doctor's just told me there's something wrong with my heart. A creepy-crawly companion is the last thing I need. Since you're here, you can make some coffee. I like it black and very strong, no sugar.' She kicked the pan. 'The percolator's on the floor.'

Josie picked up the contraption. She'd never seen the likes of it before. 'What am I supposed to do with this?'

'Make coffee, stupid. You'll find it in the cupboard, and you'll find water in the tap. The coffee goes there.' She pointed to a round part with holes that seemed to fit on top. 'Fill the bottom with water and put it on the stove. I'll tell you when it should be ready.'

'Thank you.'

'I'll be in my room, and when you bring it, *don't creep*.'

'I didn't creep,' Josie said pleasantly. 'And another thing, if you ever call me stupid again, I shall leave on the spot.' She thought this might evoke an apology, but Louisa merely gave a contemptuous snort and limped heavily away.

I'll start getting the *Echo* again, look for another job, a shaken Josie vowed as she watched the pot boil and the delicious aroma of coffee filled the small, old-fashioned kitchen, with its stone floor and deep brown sink. The stove and boiler looked as if they'd come out of the ark. A grille over the small window made the room very dark. And there were draughts. It would be freezing in winter.

Her bottom lip trembled. This time last week she'd been at Haylands, but the camp, and everything that had happened there, was already beginning to feel like a lovely dream that she'd woken up from a long, long while ago.

There was a bang and a shout. 'It should be ready now.'

Louisa's room appeared to have been a study. There was a large desk and the shelves on the walls were crammed with books. A double bed was dumped uncompromisingly in the middle. She was sitting in a rocking chair, smoking, and staring out of the window at the river. She didn't look round when Josie went in.

'Getting old's a bitch,' she said gruffly. 'You'll find that out for yourself one day. When I first came here, I used to imagine myself striding along the beach at eighty. I was always very fit, you see, used to swim every morning.' She laughed bitterly. 'Now I can't even manage the stairs. The doctor comes once a month, and always finds something new wrong with me. If it's not my ears, then it's my joints or my eyes. This time it was my heart. It's beating too fast, or too slow. I can't remember which. I try not to listen. I don't want to know. If I think about it too much, I get upset, and I can't abide people who feel sorry for themselves.' She turned round and regarded Josie with her large, brilliant eyes. 'Are you a virgin?'

The question was so unexpected that Josie nearly dropped the coffee. She put it on the window seat beside her strange new employer. 'Mind your own business,' she gasped.

'That means you're not, or you would have said something like, "Of course I am," in the same outraged voice.' Louisa stretched her gaunt arms, the backs riddled with bright blue veins. 'How old are you? Seventeen? I had my first man at thirteen – he was a friend of my father's. Oh, tell me some gossip, Josie,' she cried. 'What is your young man like? What's his name? Are you still seeing him? Is he likely to come to Barefoot House courting you with flowers?' She leaned forward and said slyly, 'Or has there been more than one? Titillate me. What is going on in the world outside these four walls?'

'Have you never heard of newspapers?'

'Reading about it isn't the same. Oh, I know all about Ingrid Bergman's affair with Roberto Rosselini and her two little bastard sons. But I prefer my gossip face to face. It's juicier that way.'

'Well, you're not getting anything juicy out of me.'

Next day, Phoebe showed her the office. It had a desk and chair, a typewriter so old it could have been the first ever made, and a small shelf of books, mainly reference works. The desk drawers were full of curling, yellow paper and odd sheets of well-used carbon. The room was as small, cold and dark as the kitchen opposite, and just as draughty.

Louisa only needed two or three letters a day to be typed, which was just as well as the keys on the typewriter took all Josie's strength to press, and then there was no tail on the 'p', no top on the 'b' and the 'e' was hardly visible. She had to fill them in with a pen afterwards. Sometimes the letters were to Louisa's agents – there was Cy Marks in New York, and Leonard McGill in London – usually to do with one of her poems being used in an anthology or a magazine, or acknowledging a cheque, always very small. All her books were out of print, Phoebe said, though she still received letters from students and admirers, for which there was a standard reply.

The worst, most nerve-racking times were when she wrote to old friends. She would stand over Josie, breathing heavily and refusing to sit down, and rattle off a stream of lies. She felt fine. She was writing furiously. There'd been a house party last weekend. She'd been to the theatre. 'Have you brought last night's paper, Phoebe,' she would bawl, 'so I can check what's on? Where had I got to?' she would demand of Josie.

'I've no idea. I've only reached the bit about you writing furiously. You're dictating much too fast. I can do shorthand, you know. It would be much easier.'

'It wouldn't be so spontaneous.'

'I don't see anything spontaneous about having to repeat yourself half a dozen times. The fastest typist in the world couldn't keep up on *this* damn thing.' Josie typed 'furiously' ponderously. The 'y' seemed to have disappeared altogether.

As the weeks passed, Josie gradually got used to Louisa Chalcott's rude and demanding ways. It was hard sometimes to be rude back. She wasn't always in the mood, and would have preferred to disappear into her room for a good cry, but it would have been fatal to show any sign of weakness in front of her employer.

She quickly got into a routine. As soon as she got up, if the weather was even faintly reasonable, she would go for a walk on the shore. On her return, she would make breakfast – Louisa's a boiled egg with a single round of bread and butter, cornflakes for herself. At around ten, Phoebe arrived with the groceries, and Josie would retreat to the office and attend to that day's mail. Phoebe made dinner at noon, and all three would eat together in the parlour, the cheeriest time of the day as far as Josie was concerned as Phoebe would regale them with hilarious stories about her family – she had five children, all married, and twelve grandchildren, always getting into scrapes. Louisa would become deeply involved in the rather trivial tales, and ask numerous questions.

'It's pathetic, really,' Phoebe said privately. 'She don't half miss the outside world. She wouldn't be seen dead in a wheelchair, else you could've taken her for walks. What she needs is a companion who can drive. There's a car in the garage she used to drive herself. She'd enjoy being taken shopping.'

Josie investigated the garage behind the house, where high double gates, now firmly padlocked, opened on to Nelson Road. There was indeed a car inside, a dusty little black box on wheels. One of these days, she might suggest to Louisa that she take driving lessons.

Afternoon and evenings, Josie found herself with little to do, except make sandwiches at teatime and numerous cups of coffee. Louisa spent most of the time in her room, in bed or the rocking chair, lost in thought or scribbling away in her large, wild, execrable writing in a shiny red notebook, which she would close if anyone went near. When Josie took her in a drink, she would talk, usually about her lovers, of which there seemed to have been hundreds – poets, actors, writers, politicians and notorious playboys – or so she claimed.

Otherwise, a bored Josie sat in the parlour, reading, teaching herself to knit, staring at the view. But she was fed up with the sight of only sea, ships and sand – only a few hardy souls took to the beach in winter. She longed for company, noise, traffic, a wireless, and would have offered to do the shopping and the cooking if it hadn't meant treading on Phoebe's toes. It was actually a treat when Louisa ran out of cigarettes, and she had to walk as far as the shops, where she usually bought a newspaper to look for another job, so far without success. Marian and Hilary often telephoned, wanting to know how their mother was, but Louisa flatly refused to speak to her daughters and it was left to Josie to explain stiffly that she was fine. Louisa only came to the phone in the hall if it was an agent or her friend, Thumbelina, from New York, when she would chatter away for ages. Every month, Thumbelina would send a pile of American newspapers, which Louisa eagerly read from cover to cover.

'That's a dead funny name to give someone,' Josie said.

'I call her Thumbelina because she's so tiny,' Lousia explained with a fond smile. 'Only four feet ten. Her real name is Albertine. She's had six husbands, each one richer than the one before. I expect any day to hear she's about to marry Mr Seven, who is bound to be a multi-multi-millionaire.'

Tuesday evening and all day Saturday, Josie had off. With a feeling of exhilaration, she caught the train to Exchange station to meet Lily. Mid-week, they went to the pictures. On Saturdays they went shopping, then to the Kavanaghs' for tea and to get changed for a dance at the Locarno or the Grafton. But tea would have to stop soon because it was December, and Ben was due home any day. Mrs Kavanagh didn't want him upset.

When she got back, Louisa would ply her with questions. 'Did you meet any nice young men? What picture did you see? Did you go to George Henry Lee's? Y'know, I used to buy a lot of my clothes there once.'

And Josie would answer every question, even down to a physical description of Richard Widmark, whom she'd just seen in *Night and the City*, and display every item of her shopping for Louisa to examine, usually critically. 'I used to buy Helena Rubinstein cosmetics. The lipsticks came in big gold cases, not piddling little Bakelite tubes like that.'

'If you double me wages, I'll buy Helena Rubinstein, too.'

At Louisa's suggestion, she brought Lily to see her. At first Lily was plainly terrified of the forceful old woman, who immediately began to pry into her private life, but softened when told she had flirtatious eyes. 'I bet you have scores of young men after you,' Louisa said slyly.

'Well, quite a few,' Lily conceded, although there wasn't a single man on the horizon at the moment.

'And I bet you give them a good run for their money.'

'Oh, I do,' Lily concurred.

'Don't run too fast, though.' Louisa nodded wisely. 'You must pause and let them catch you once in a while.'

'Oh, I do,' Lily said again.

'What the hell was she on about, Jose?' Lily asked when Josie walked her to the station. 'All that talk about sex. It's peculiar coming from an old woman. Is she round the bend?'

'Possibly,' Josie said.

'Do you think I've got flirtatious eyes?'

'Possibly.'

On Christmas Day, Josie woke up with a heavy heart and a sense of gloom, knowing the day was going to be thuddingly boring – like Sundays, only worse. The weather didn't help. The sky was the colour of wet slates, threatening rain, the river brown and murky. She went early to Mass. On the way back the skies opened and she got soaked, despite her heavy mack and umbrella. Once home, she changed her clothes, hung the mack in the bathroom and lit the parlour fire. Louisa was still in bed, and the cold, dark house felt very still and quiet. All that could be heard was the sound of the rain against the windows.

What am I doing here?

Josie had an hysterical urge to scream. After Christmas, she'd seriously start looking for something else. She quickly went round the house, turning on every light – in the hall, on the landing, in the parlour – before going in to the kitchen to make tea. Phoebe had left a chicken, already stuffed and roasted, in the meat safe, and a pudding she'd made herself. All Josie had to do was prepare the potatoes and the Brussels sprouts, and make the gravy and custard.

She thought about the Kavanaghs, and how different their day would be. Marigold, her husband, Jonathan, and their three children were coming to dinner, as well as Daisy and her friend, Eunice. Robert was travelling up from London. Ben was already home. Stanley would probably telephone from Germany – Freya, his wife, was expecting their first baby. She visualised the ritual exchange of presents after breakfast, and remembered Lily's present to her was in her room, but couldn't be bothered to go upstairs and open it.

The telephone rang. It was Hilary, wanting to wish her mother a merry Christmas. 'She's still in bed. I'll wake her.'

There was no answer when Josie knocked. She went in. Louisa was lying face down under the clothes. 'Hilary's on the phone. She wants to speak to you.'

Still no answer. With a feeling of alarm, Josie shook the still figure. 'Fuck off,' Louisa snarled without moving. 'Tell Hilary I'm spending the day in bed.'

'But it's Christmas Day, you can't.'

'I know full well what day it is, and I'll do anything I want. Tell my idiot daughter to go screw herself.'

'She's still a bit sleepy,' Josie told Hilary. 'Perhaps you could call later, this afternoon.' Her gloom deepened. She wasn't in the mood to cope with Louisa in one of her fouler moods. With a sigh, she returned to the room. 'What's the matter?'

'I told you to fuck off.' Louisa hadn't moved. All that could be seen was the top of her black hair under the clothes.

'I've no intention of, of doing what you say. Would you like a cup of coffee?'

'No! Why don't you go to your friends in Childwall? Have dinner there, pull your crackers, drink your sherry, open your presents. Have a lovely time.'

'I can't,' Josie said flatly. 'I'm not welcome there today.'

At last Louisa raised her head. Her old face was full of creases from the pillow. Her eyes looked suspiciously red, as if she'd been crying. 'Why not?'

'Because me old boyfriend's there – Ben. He's home from university, and they're worried I'll upset him.' Josie knew this trite piece of information would be of interest, and she was right. She didn't offer assistance as Louisa struggled to a sitting position, knowing it would be churlishly rejected.

'Is he the one you slept with?' she asked eagerly.

'I've never said I've slept with anyone, have I?'

'No, but you have. I can see it in your eyes. You're a woman, not a girl. Oh, please, Josie,' she implored, her dark eyes glowing, 'tell me about it. These days I live through other people. I'm starved of sex, starved of romance. I'm a parasite. I feed off other people to stay alive.'

'All right,' Josie said brusquely, 'but not until you're up, dressed and in the parlour with a cup of coffee.'

Louisa thought the episode with Griff desperately romantic. 'And he actually pretended to be homosexual!'

'No, he just gave the impression. After all, he's an actor.'

'I slept with a homo once. He was okay, I managed to teach him a few things. Have you ever done it with a woman? Now, that's *really* interesting.'

'*No.* There are times, Louisa, when I suspect you only say things to shock.'

'My dear, I have never told you anything even faintly shocking.' She laughed coarsely. 'I was regarded as a nymphomaniac in my day. I could tell you things to make your blood run cold.' She glanced out of the window, and said in a voice full of envy and longing, 'I wonder where that liner's off to?'

Josie watched the large, brightly lit ship sailing past. She would have given anything to be on it herself, on her way to somewhere dead exciting, instead of pandering to a selfish, bad-tempered old woman on Christmas Day.

'I spent Christmas on a ship once.' Louisa sighed. 'We had a party that lasted three whole days. I slept with three stewards and the purser.'

'Is that all you ever thought of – sex?'

'Yes,' Louisa said flatly. 'I still do. It's the only thing that's ever mattered to me.'

'What about love?' Josie asked curiously. 'Didn't you ever fall for the men you had this never-ending sex with?'

'Occasionally, but love gets in the way. Love brings jealousy in its wake, and things quickly get nasty.' She groaned, and wrapped her arms around her sagging breasts, hugging herself. 'I still miss it, the sex. I *ache* for it. My body's grown old, but my mind hasn't. I'm still a young girl inside my head.'

Josie turned away, embarrassed. Once again, she thought about the Kavanaghs' bright, cheerful house. 'I'll go and peel the potatoes,' she said dully.

'Get some wine from the cellar,' Louisa called. 'Fetch two bottles. I think I shall get intoxicated today.'

'I was about to take a sleeping tablet this morning when you came in,' Louisa said over dinner. 'I thought of all the Christmases that had gone before, the gay times we had, the games we used to play, the flirtations, the silly presents we gave each other. I couldn't abide the thought of another Christmas in this house – so fucking *dull*. The best thing was to sleep through it. You know,' she said brightly, 'I once spent Christmas with Virginia Woolf.'

'Did you really?' Josie had never heard of Virginia Woolf. She wondered if Louisa ever had the faintest regard for anyone's feelings but her own. Had she not thought that taking a sleeping tablet would make her companion's day even more depressing than it already was?

Louisa was on her fourth glass of wine. Her cheeks were flushed. Josie collected the plates, took them to the kitchen and made custard for the pudding that was steaming on the stove. She took the bowls into the parlour, and said, 'If only I could drive, we could have gone to the Adelphi for dinner, or some posh hotel in Southport. We could even go shopping now and then.'

'I'm not prepared to be driven about like an invalid.' Louisa's cheeks flushed a deeper red.

'In that case, I'm handing in a month's notice.' She'd get an ordinary job, find a bedsit, even if she was only left with a few bob a week. 'Frankly, Louisa,' she said in a shaky voice, 'I'm bored out of me skull. You're not the only one who finds this house dull. As for Christmas, this is the worst I've ever known. It's so bloody miserable, I could *scream*.'

'Oh.' There was a long silence, broken by the shrill ring of the telephone. Marian this time, asking for her mother.

'Tell her Merry Christmas,' Louisa snapped. 'Say I'm too ill to talk.'

'That would be cruel. There's nothing wrong with you. She's just coming,' Josie said into the receiver. She watched Louisa make deliberately heavy weather of limping towards the hall.

That night, Louisa said shortly, 'I'll pay for you to take driving lessons. Whether I'll come out with you, we'll just have to see. If you're bored, take more time off. I like to hear about the dances and the films. And bring Lily round more. I like her.' For the very first time since Josie had known her, there was the suggestion of a quiver in the harsh, gruff voice. 'You're my connection to life, Josie. I don't want you to leave.'

Josie felt uneasy at the end of December when she found her wages had gone up from ten pounds a month to fifteen. 'When I gave me notice in, I wasn't trying to blackmail you,' she said hesitantly. 'You don't have to do this.'

'Don't look a gift horse in the mouth,' Louisa snarled. 'And if I'd thought you were blackmailing me, you'd have been out the door like a shot.'

2

Josie passed her driving test just after her eighteenth birthday. The same night, with a mixture of pride and nervousness, she drove all the way to Childwall in the little black Austin Seven, as it was apparently called, to tell the Kavanaghs.

They were duly impressed. Lily decided to take driving lessons herself. 'I'll save up and buy meself a car. Something more modern than that. It looks like an antique.'

'I thought I'd get a bit of practice in. Louisa said I can use it whenever I like. And she's condescended to go shopping. I'm taking her to Southport on Friday.'

It took several hours to get Louisa ready to go shopping. Her clothes were in her old bedroom, and Josie's legs ached from running up and downstairs, fetching things for her to choose from – lovely, expensive outfits, silk-lined, hand-stitched, intricately embroidered – all terribly old-fashioned, but it didn't matter when they were going shopping and she could buy more up-to-date things. There was a search upstairs for stockings, a suspender belt, underwear, jewellery. 'There's a three-strand pearl necklace and earrings in the little dressing-table drawer,' Louisa called. 'And don't forget face powder and lipstick. And scent. Oh, and shoes.'

'You look dead beautiful,' Josie said admiringly when Louisa emerged from her room – she'd insisted on dressing herself. She wore a navy blue silk suit patterned with large white orchids, white court shoes and a white toque. Despite her age and her infirmities, she looked extremely smart. She must have been outstanding in her day.

'Don't patronise me. I look ghastly. These shoes are too big, and I need a safety pin in the skirt. I tried, but I can't fasten it.' She frowned peevishly; she loathed asking for help.

Phoebe, who was also taking part in the exercise, fastened the pin. She and Josie trailed behind, making faces at each other as Louisa made her own slow, determined way out of the back door into the balmy sunshine of a late May day. They watched, longing to offer a hand, as she struggled into the passenger seat of the small black car. Phoebe picked up her shoes when they fell off.

'I don't envy you today, Josie,' she whispered.

Josie drove cautiously, never exceeding twenty miles an hour, all the way to Southport, ignoring the queue of impatient traffic that gathered behind. She managed to park in Lord Street, a wide, elegant thoroughfare with a tree-lined central reservation, full of exclusive and outrageously expensive shops. Louisa, who had been very quiet during the journey, deigned to take her hand when she alighted from the car.

She stood on the pavement, supported by her stick, and took several deep breaths, her dark, brilliant eyes raking the shop fronts, the pedestrians, the passing traffic. 'Why haven't I done this before?' she said in a dazed voice. 'So near, yet so far. I should have come years ago. Suddenly, the world feels so much bigger. We must go to dinner one night. And the movies, the theatre.' She put her arm in Josie's, crying, 'How pleased I am you came to work for me. Come, my dear, we'll do some shopping.'

Over the next few hours, Louisa went quite mad with her cheque-book. She bought a striking scarlet dressing-gown and slippers to match, two glamorous nighties, a yellow linen costume, an amber pendant on a fine, gold chain, two pairs of narrow-fitting shoes – she put on a pair straight away – a straw picture hat, kid gloves, a lizard handbag and two colourful scarves.

'There's stacks of gloves and scarves upstairs,' Josie protested, 'and at least a dozen handbags.'

'Oh, yes, but these are *new*,' Louisa said with childish glee, 'and a woman can't have too many handbags. Oh, isn't this—what is it you say in Liverpool? Isn't this the *gear?*'

'Don't overtax yourself, Louisa.'

'And don't you nag. I feel like Sleeping Beauty, just awoken from a very long sleep.' She chuckled. 'Except with me the years have taken their toll. By the way, this is for you.' She pushed the box with the amber pendant into Josie's hand.

Josie tried to push it back. 'I didn't expect a present.' But Louisa was implacable. 'I bought it with you in mind. You said how pretty it was. I wouldn't be seen dead in such an anaemic piece of jewellery.'

'Ta, Louisa. But you mustn't do this sort of thing again.'

'I shall do whatever I like with my money, dear,' Louisa said loftily.

They paused for coffee in a charming, glass-roofed arcade of tiny shops. Halfway through a cheese scone, Louisa said, 'There was a quaint little bookshop around here where I used to order books from the States. I flirted quite madly with the owner, Mr Bernstein, but he probably retired years ago. I wonder if the shop's still in business? I'd like to order that book they're making such a fuss about back home, *Catcher in the Rye.*'

The shop was three blocks away, according to the waitress, too far for Louisa to walk. They returned to the car, stowed the shopping in the boot and Josie drove the three blocks.

There was no need to order *Catcher in the Rye*. The attractive young man behind the counter of the long, narrow shop said it had been published in this country, and they had several copies in stock. Louisa was writing a cheque when an astonished voice cried, 'Miss Chalcott! Miss Louisa Chalcott?'

A small, extremely elderly man was coming towards them, arms clasped dramatically across his chest. The lack of hair on his pink head was made up for by a lustrous silver beard.

'Mr Bernstein!' Louisa said emotionally. 'Why, how lovely to see you.'

Mr Bernstein snapped his fingers. 'Ronald, fetch a chair for Miss Chalcott.' He beamed. 'This beautiful lady is a famous poet. Sit down, sit down, Miss Chalcott. Would you like a sherry?'

Josie might as well not have existed during the fulsome and mutually flattering conversation that ensued. She retreated to the counter, where Ronald whispered, 'Who's Louisa Chalcott? I've never heard of her.'

His favourite authors were Dashiell Hammett and Raymond Chandler. 'I was put off poetry at school,' he confessed. 'I never want to hear 'The Boy Stood on the Burning Deck' again.'

Josie said she felt the same about Wordsworth's 'The Daffodils', and she liked Agatha Christie and Dorothy L. Sayers. She told him she'd tried to read Louisa's poems once, but couldn't make head nor tail of them.

The conversation turned to pictures. Ronald's favourite films were thrillers, too, and Josie said that she also liked them best. 'When I was young, I had a crush on Humphrey Bogart.'

'You're not exactly old now.' Ronald had a quirky smile and lovely dark green eyes. Josie, who hadn't met a man she considered even remotely attractive since she'd said goodbye to Griff, regarded him with interest. He leaned on the counter. '*Key Largo*'s on across the road, starring your old hearthrob. Perhaps I could take you tomorrow night? I could pick you up,' he added nonchalantly. 'I've got a car.'

'So've I,' Josie said, equally nonchalantly. 'The thing is, I'm seeing me friend tomorrow, but I'm free Monday.'

'That would be even better. *Key Largo* will have finished, but they're showing the latest Hitchcock film, *Strangers on a Train*. We could meet outside at seven o'clock. If it's too early, we'll go for a coffee.'

Across the shop, Mr Bernstein was presenting Louisa with a copy of Robert Frost's *Complete Poems*. 'A little gift, dear lady. Hot off the press. It only came in this morning.'

'I always thought Robert Frost a trifle overrated, but thank you very much, Mr Bernstein. Now, don't forget, I'm expecting you on Wednesday on the dot of half past seven. We shall have a lovely little talk about literature.'

'I am already looking forward to it, Miss Chalcott.' With a flamboyant gesture, Mr Bernstein kissed her hand.

'I think that was a most satisfactory shopping expedition,' Louisa said on the way home. 'Fancy Mr Bernstein recognising me after all this time! He's become a widower since we last met. I think I might seduce him. Wives never stopped me in the past, but I think one might have stopped Mr Bernstein.'

'Oh, Louisa!'

'Take no notice of me, dear. I can dream, can't I? Now, where shall we go tomorrow in the car?'

It was summer. Josie woke up to the warm sun shining through her window, the squawk of the gulls, the tide lapping on the beach. She would leap out of bed and walk down to the water in her bare feet, glad to be alive on such a lovely day, thinking how incredibly lucky she was compared to Lily and all the other people who worked in boring, stuffy offices and factories. Being Louisa's companion no longer felt like a job. She felt slightly guilty when she took her wages.

Back in the house, she would make two cups of coffee and drink hers with Louisa, sitting cross-legged at the foot of the bed, and they would look through last night's *Echo* to see what pictures were on, or discuss a play they'd just seen, which reminded Louisa of an affair she'd once had, or several affairs.

She saw Ronald twice a week. He was a perfect boyfriend. They had plenty to talk about, and he seemed quite satisfied with a few enjoyable and passionate kisses at the end of the evening. Lily was green with envy. 'How do you do it, Jose? I only go out with a bloke once, and he never wants to see me again.' Lily had given up all hope of getting married, and was prepared for a life on the shelf.

It would have been easy to feel smug about how fortunately things had turned out, but Josie had already experienced how quickly life could change. When Lily casually announced that she and her mother were going to Germany to stay with Stanley, Freya and the new baby, Josie, who'd been expecting to go on holiday with her friend, found herself with nowhere to go and no one to go with. Once again she felt conscious of her solitariness. She would just have to spend the time at Barefoot House, carry on as normal. When Marian and Hilary came in September for their annual holiday, she would take a few days off.

It was difficult to believe that the twins, with their plain looks and severe clothes, were the daughters of passionate, extrovert Louisa. They appeared slightly aggrieved that their mother looked so well, had put on weight and was obviously much happier than when they'd visited a year ago. As if to prove she'd been right in her choice of companion, Louisa exaggerated the visits to the theatre and the cinema and the shopping trips, making it seem as if they led the life of Reilly and went out every day.

The two women did their utmost to sideline Josie. They made Louisa's meals, took in her morning coffee, fussed over her in a way Josie knew she'd hate. Phoebe said it was always the same. 'They call the doctor if she so much as sneezes, and keep telling her how ill she is, how old, reminding her she's an invalid. Oh, I won't half be glad when the pair of them have gone.'

It would have been nice to have gone away, be out of it for a whole fortnight, but all Josie could do was take time off. She went into town nearly every day and met Lily in the dinner hour.

One day Lily emerged from her office looking unusually grave. She grabbed Josie's arm. 'Ma telephoned this morning, Jose. She tried to call you, but you'd already gone. She ses to tell you that Vince Adams died yesterday of a heart attack.'

The news left Josie cold. 'I wonder if I should write to Auntie Ivy?'

'I wouldn't if I were you.'

'I'll think about it. Where shall we go for dinner? I'm starving.'

'Let's try that new place in Whitechapel. They take luncheon vouchers. Are you all right, Jose? You look a bit peculiar.'

'I'm fine.' But she wasn't fine. For some reason, when they reached the restaurant, she no longer felt hungry. Her head was full of thoughts that didn't make sense. Vincent Adams had been her *father*. It was her *father* who had died the day before. If it hadn't been for Vince, she wouldn't have been born. How could your father die and leave you feeling cold and completely unmoved? Her life had been so strange, so different to everyone else's, that she had no warm feelings for the man responsible for bringing her into the world.

She said goodbye to Lily, but didn't walk back with her to Victoria Street as she usually did. Instead, she set off in the opposite direction. All of a sudden, she felt a strong desire to see Huskisson Street, take a look at the house in which she'd lived with Mam. She hadn't seen it since the night of the bomb. Their final conversation came back as clearly as if it had taken place only yesterday.

Why, the sun's come out, Petal, Mam had cried joyfully during their last minutes in the attic room. *It looks dead lovely out there . . . I wouldn't mind a little walk.*

If only they'd gone to Princes Park as Mam had suggested!

Yes, but . . . Josie had said.

Yes, but what, my fragrant, my adorable little Petal? Mam had leapt off the chair, danced across the room, caught Josie in her arms. They had waltzed around the bed.

Josie bit her lip. 'Oh, Mam,' she breathed.

She had walked so fast that she reached Huskisson Street sooner than expected. The house had been done up. The window-frames had been painted and the front door, which was open, was bottle green.

Dare she go in? Could it possibly be that Maude, or any of the other girls, still lived there? Just now, if there was one thing she'd like to do more than any other, it was to talk to Maude, tell her about Uncle Vince.

She climbed the steps into the wide hall, which had pale cream walls and a biscuit-coloured carpet. 'Can I help you?' a woman's voice demanded sharply.

The voice came from a window in the wall, the wall of Irish Rose's room. A woman had slid back the glass and was regarding Josie balefully.

'I'm sorry to bother you, but I was wondering, who lives here now.'

'No one. It's a solicitors'. It should be obvious from the plate on the door.'

'What's upstairs?' Josie glanced at the carpeted staircase.

'Rooms. Now, if you don't mind, I'd like to get on.' The window was snapped shut.

'Thank you,' Josie said to no one at all.

If you sat on the window seat facing westwards – at least, she'd worked out it was westwards, but she could be wrong – you could see the lights of Birkenhead and Wallasey gradually being switched on.

Josie had no idea how long she'd been there, but at first it had been daylight and the shore had been crowded. Then people had begun to pick up their blankets, their sunshades, their toys and go home. Now the sands were empty and it was dark, and the lights across the Mersey twinkled brightly in the distance.

She had been reliving her childhood, every single scene, something which she had never done before. She felt immeasurably sad for all the things she had missed: going on holiday with her mother, for instance, like Lily; telling Mam about her boyfriends. What would Mam think of Ronald? Of Griff? Would she have thought it a bad idea to have married Ben? Josie remembered that she hadn't liked Tommy. She'd thought her daughter too good for him, that she deserved something better.

Apart from the creaks and groans of the old house, and the rustle of the tide, everywhere was quiet. Marian and Hilary kept very early hours. She vaguely remembered hearing them come upstairs a while ago. Louisa, so different from her daughters, usually stayed up till all hours, scribbling away in the red notebook, or they would talk – Josie hated going to bed early. On top of the usual sounds, she became aware of a faint shuffling and a tapping noise.

Rats, Josie thought, but she didn't care if the house was invaded by rats. The twins could get rid of them. She thought about making herself a cup of tea. Louisa, if she was awake, might like some coffee.

In a minute, she told herself.

The tapping and shuffling was getting closer. She was feeling a touch alarmed when the door opened and Louisa came puffing in.

'Why are you sitting in the dark?' She switched on the light. She was wearing her red dressing-gown and slippers and looked pleased with herself. 'Those stairs! That's the first time I've climbed them in ten years. What an achievement. Oh, but if I don't sit down soon, I'll collapse.' She shuffled over to the bed and eased herself down with an exaggerated sigh of relief.

Josie didn't move. 'I thought you were a rat,' she said.

'Oh, I am, I am,' Louisa panted. 'It's an insult usually reserved for men. People seem to forget there are female rats. I wonder why that is? And why are only women described as kittenish?'

'I've no idea. You can explore the contradiction in your next poem.'

Louisa clapped her hands delightedly. 'Josie! How glad I am to see you. You treat me like a normal human being. I'm sick of those silly girls fussing round. I'm openly crossing off the days before they go home on my calendar, but they refuse to take the hint. Now.' She looked at Josie sternly. 'I heard you come in. It was half past four. There's been dead silence ever since. What's wrong, dear? Is it something to do with that phone call? Phoebe said someone rang after you'd gone.'

It was no use beating about the bush with Louisa. 'It was Mrs Kavanagh, Lily's mam, to say me father died yesterday.'

'Oh, my dear! But . . .' the heavy brows puckered '. . . I could have sworn you told me your father was already dead.'

'I did. I told everyone he was dead. Mrs Kavanagh is the only one who knows the truth.' Josie swung her legs off the window seat and rested her chin in her hands. 'It's funny, but it's only today, now that he's dead, that I've thought about him as me father. He was also me Uncle Vince, you see, Auntie Ivy's husband. I told you a bit about them, too. Me father and me uncle were the same person.'

'How extraordinarily interesting,' Louisa remarked. She lit a cigarette. 'Tell me more. For instance, was your mother a willing accomplice in the deceit?'

Josie smiled. It was just the sort of reply she would have expected from Louisa who, unlike most people, would never come out with expressions of sympathy and shock. 'No, he forced himself on her. He tried to do the same with me, but I kicked him in the stomach.'

'Good for you. You should have aimed for the balls, much more painful.' She flicked ash on the floor. 'So, why are you mooning around because this despicable individual has died? I would have thought it a cause for celebration.'

'Oh, I dunno.' Josie turned to stare at the lights across the water. Louisa was reflected in the window, watching her with interest. 'It just feels unnatural not to *care* that your father's dead. I feel as if I'm missing out on something.'

'I can never understand why we are automatically expected to love our relatives,' Louisa said irritably. 'I respected my father, but I never loved him. I felt sad when he died, that's all. Mom, now, I miss her still.' Her face creased tenderly. 'She was my best friend. I was an only child, so I have no idea how I would have felt about siblings. As for my children, I expected to love them – I *wanted* to love them – but when they were born they were such an ugly little pair I asked the nurse to take them away.' She smiled ruefully as she attempted to get off the bed. 'I've rather missed being a doting mother. Come, let's go downstairs and you can make us some coffee. We can continue this conversation there.'

Eighteen months later Louisa suffered another stroke, only a mild one but she had to stay in bed for weeks. She was a fearsome patient, browbeating mercilessly the private nurse, Miss Viney, who came to see her twice a day – the only person she would allow to give her the bedpan. At other times Josie was ordered from the room, while she dragged herself to the commode, which only Miss Viney was allowed to empty.

Mr Bernstein and Lily were forbidden to visit. On Saturdays Phoebe and her husband, Alf, spent the day at Barefoot House, so Josie could have time off, to go dancing or to the pictures with Lily. The rest of the time she stayed in because Louisa couldn't be left on her own.

'I'll be all right,' Louisa growled awkwardly, the stroke having slightly impaired her speech. 'Ask that stupid nurse in.'

'I'll do no such thing. The poor woman's terrified of you. I don't want to add to her misery. Do you feel better now that you've got the telephone next to the bed?' Josie had arranged for the telephone company to move it.

'As long as you continue to answer it. I don't want to be stuck with one of my girls. But it's nice talking to Mr Bernstein or Thumbelina. Did I tell you she's just married husband number seven? He collects oil wells the way some people collect stamps.'

For something to do, Josie attacked the front garden. She dug up the dead bushes and the dried yellow grass, and broke down the crusty, clay-like soil. Alf removed the trees, sawed the dead wood into logs and stacked them in the garage.

'They should keep the fire going a treat,' he said. He was a tall, robust man with the strength of an ox. 'See you through the winter, that lot.'

Josie knew nothing about gardens. She'd assumed everything had to be grown from seed, and was thrilled to discover you could buy plants partially grown, and a ready-made lawn in the form of turfs, from a place called a nursery. Alf said there was one of these magic places not far away.

She spent her twentieth birthday pushing and pulling the rusty garden roller she'd found in the garage over the hard earth to make it smooth enough for a lawn, nearly dislocating her arms in the process. As soon as it was done, she drove to the nursery, bought dozens of hardy plants which she put in the car, and ordered turfs and a wooden bench for Louisa to sit on when the garden was finished, to be delivered next day.

That afternoon she planted the border, putting a handful of bonemeal in the hole with each plant as the woman in the nursery had suggested. The day was hot and the sun burned down on her back, so she was exhausted by the time she finished. Despite this, she was outside early next morning, impatiently waiting for the lorry to arrive, and had already begun to lay the turfs before the driver had finished unloading. At eight o'clock that night,

Barefoot House could boast a neatly laid lawn, surrounded by a border of bushes and tiny flower plants. There was a bench beneath the window of Louisa's room. Josie went inside to tell her the garden was finished. 'You can come and look now.'

'Do you think I haven't looked already? You've been bobbing up and down outside my window for weeks.' Louisa had only been allowed out of bed a few days and was in a dreadful temper. She longed to go shopping or to the pictures, but was too weak to walk more than a few yards. She flatly refused to go merely for a drive. 'It would be too fucking boring.'

Josie took her arm, noticing how thin it was again, and how bent her back had become, and how slowly she shuffled from the house, barely able to lift her feet between each step. She led her to the bench and helped her sit. 'What am I supposed to do now?' Louisa asked acidly. Her tongue was as sharp as ever.

'Look at the view, smell the fresh air, enjoy the atmosphere. It's a beautiful evening, Louisa.' Josie sniffed appreciatively. Apart from two boys some distance away, playing football, the beach was deserted. The tide was receding in a ruff of creamy-white froth, and the gleaming ribbon of wet sand left in its wake was getting wider and wider. Gulls rode the waves as lightly as bubbles.

'Would you like a coffee?'

'No, thank you. I'd like my cigarettes, though.'

'I thought it would be nice for you to sit here early in the morning,' Josie said when she returned. 'Or late at night, when it's dark, round September, like. If I put the bench by the other window, you can see the lights across the water.'

'Is that all you've got to think about?' Louisa said in a cold voice. 'Where I am to sit come September?' She lit a cigarette. 'At your age, you should be concentrating on young men, clothes, movies, having a good time. I thought of little else when I was sixty, let alone twenty. As for gardening, it was furthest from my mind, along with similar stultifyingly boring pursuits.'

'I thought you'd be pleased.'

Louisa gave her a contemptuous look. 'Oh, I am. And Marian and Hilary will be delighted. You've increased the value of the house no end. What shall you do next to get rid of your excess energy? Paint the windows, the door, decorate inside? Everywhere could do with a lick of paint, and we can both sit and watch it dry. Where's Ronald?' she asked unexpectedly, and peered around the garden, as if expecting Ronald to pop up from behind a newly planted bush.

'I gave him up.'

'Why?'

Josie squirmed. 'We didn't get on.'

'Liar! You gave him up shortly after I had my stroke. You told him you couldn't see him again because of me. He was heartbroken, according to Mr Bernstein. He had hoped one day you would get married.'

'I would never have married Ronald,' Josie said truthfully. 'Why are you getting so ratty, anyroad? I'd have thought you'd be pleased about that, too.'

'Your loyalty and devotion do you credit, Josie, but they are entirely misplaced. I am not worth it.' She stared at the river. 'You know, I can hardly see.'

'You should wear—'

'I know,' Louisa interrupted testily. 'I should wear my long-distance glasses. Or is it the short-distance ones? I can never remember. Any minute now, I'll need a hearing-aid, too. I'm finding it increasingly difficult to hear. I'm breaking down, Josie. I can scarcely walk. I hardly sleep. The only thing that works perfectly is my brain.'

'Louisa,' Josie said gently.

'Oh, take your sympathy, girl, and stuff it where the monkey stuffed its nuts,' Louisa said so nastily that Josie flushed. 'Fetch me my lizard handbag. It's on the floor beside the bed.'

The large handbag having been brought, Louisa rooted inside and took out a large brown envelope and two small white ones. She handed Josie a white one. 'I had intended giving you that on your twenty-first birthday, but circumstances have changed.'

It was a letter, addressed to her, written in Louisa's hardly discernible scrawl. Josie read it with difficulty. Her jaw dropped when she understood the message it contained. 'You're giving me a month's notice!' she said, completely taken aback.

'Got it in one,' Louisa chuckled. She handed Josie the other white envelope. 'Now read this.'

At first the typed enclosure, full of meaningless figures, was equally difficult to make sense of. 'It's a plane ticket to America,' Josie said after a while. 'To New York. Louisa, what on earth is this all about?'

Louisa was staring at the river again. Now it was almost dark, the boys had gone and the water shone a greeny-silver. The moon had appeared, not quite full, and there was a sprinkling of early stars. Except for the rustling tide, the silence was total. 'When I first came to live here, we used to go skinny-dipping in the moonlight. Do you know what that means?'

'I can guess, but, Louisa, this ticket. And why do I have to leave?' Her voice trembled.

'I've always been a very selfish person,' Louisa continued as if Josie hadn't spoken. 'I've used people all my life, men in particular, women if I felt in the mood. I dropped them the minute they'd served their purpose, satisfied my need.' She shifted irritably on the bench. 'I shall need a cushion for this. Not now, dear. Some other time will do,' she said when Josie made to get up. 'I shall only have you one more month, so sit down and hold my hand.' Josie did, and the skin on the hand felt soft and shiny, like old silk.

'I should never have taken you on,' Louisa sighed. 'The girls were right, but for all the wrong reasons. They thought you couldn't cope. I knew you could, but that's not why I insisted. I wanted you for your bright face, your fresh blood, your young soul. I hoped they might rub off on me.' She smiled ruefully. 'I'm like a fucking vampire. I should have let the girls show you the door. You would have eventually found something better to do than dance round after an egotistical old woman for three years. No, don't argue.' She wagged a gnarled finger.

'For the first time in my life, I am making a sacrifice, so consider yourself lucky because I don't want you to leave. I want you to stay so much it hurts.' Josie felt the frail hand tighten on her own. 'But leave you must,' Louisa said firmly. 'It's time you started to live, my dear. I've had you far too long. As for me, I'm dying.' She laughed a touch bitterly. 'But I'm a stubborn bitch. I shall put up a fight. I could last for years, getting blinder, deafer, more and more impossible and ill-humoured with each day. There is no way, Josie, that I will allow you to sacrifice yet more years of your young life to watch me die.'

'But I want to stay, Louisa,' Josie wailed, and was rewarded with a look of utter contempt.

'Well, you can't,' Louisa snapped. 'You have just been given your marching orders, and I want you out of this house by the end of June. The plane ticket is a leaving present. You can get a refund if you want, use it as a deposit on a flat. Otherwise, Thumbelina is off on a belated honeymoon early in July, and you can stay in her grand house in New York. You won't be alone, the staff will be there.' She chuckled. 'I promised her you're not the sort who'll take off with the silver. There is a heap of American currency somewhere upstairs. I always thought I'd go back one day, but that's not likely now.' She removed her hand. 'I would appreciate a cup of coffee, dear, though inside, I think. It's getting chilly out here.'

As she helped Louisa to her feet, Josie felt a flood of gratitude mixed with sadness and something else, possibly love, for the impossible, cantankerous, surprisingly kind old woman. 'But who'll look after you?'

'That, dear girl, is no longer any of your business,' Louisa said brusquely, and refused to discuss the matter further.

'What's this?' Josie picked up the large brown envelope, surprisingly sealed with red wax.

'Nothing much, just a few notes I've made.' Louisa looked at her enigmatically. 'You're not to open it until nineteen seventy-four.'

'Why then?' Josie asked, surprised.

'It will be obvious at the time.' She grasped the window-sill and began to make her way inside. 'Do you know, my dear, I can already smell the flowers in my new garden.'

'There aren't any yet, just leaves. They need a good watering. I'll do it in a minute.' The plants looked rather sad, she thought, as if they realised she would soon be going.

'Then I can smell the leaves.' Louisa squeezed her hand.

'I'll come and see you the minute I get back,' Josie promised as they went into the house.

'You will do no such thing,' Louisa barked. 'I don't want to see or hear from you in a long while. If you must know, it would upset me. Perhaps this time next year.' She laughed gaily. 'Yes, this time next year. Come and see how your garden grows, Josie dear.'

3

'Oh, Jose. I won't half miss you,' Lily said sadly. 'I wish I could come with you, but they'd never let me off work a whole month. Anyroad, I couldn't afford the fare.'

'I wish you could come, too, Lil. Still, I'll only be gone a month, and you've made new friends over the last few years. You had to, didn't you? You haven't seen much of me.'

'Yes, but you're me *best* friend, Jose.' They were sitting together on Lily's bed in the house in Childwall. Josie was spending two days with the Kavanaghs before flying to New York, having left Barefoot House for ever.

Louisa hadn't even turned round when she went to say goodbye. She was in her rocking chair facing the window, and said gruffly, 'Bye, dear. Have a nice time.' Josie wanted to fling her arms around her, have a good cry, but Louisa waved a dismissive arm, which Josie took as a sign she didn't want an emotional farewell. Closing the door quietly behind her, she cried on the train instead. The new companion, a retired headmistress, seemed very nice, very firm. Louisa would be safe with her, but she didn't doubt the poor woman would be reduced to a nervous wreck in no time.

Mixed with the sorrow was a feeling of relief, a sense of freedom, the awareness that Louisa had been right to let her go. Somewhere, buried deep within her mind, there'd been a dread of remaining in Barefoot House for years while she watched Louisa die.

Tomorrow, she would leave Lime Street station for London, where she would stay the night – she'd booked into a little hotel right by Euston – then make her way to Heathrow early next morning to catch the plane to New York. Thumbelina was picking her up from Idlewild airport. Josie had a passport with a horrible photo inside that made her look like a criminal, and over three hundred yellowing American dollars that had been found in an old handbag in Louisa's wardrobe upstairs. Since Louisa's second stroke, there hadn't been much opportunity for Josie to indulge her weakness for new clothes, and she'd managed to save up over fifty pounds. This she was keeping for when she came back from America. She'd have to start again then, find somewhere to live, another job.

A new beginning! It made her feel almost as excited as the holiday.

That afternoon, Marigold and her family were coming for a farewell tea, as well as Daisy and Eunice. Daisy had telephoned earlier with a message from Aunt Ivy. 'I told her about your trip to America. She'd love to see you, Jose.'

Mrs Kavanagh shook her head when asked for her advice. 'I don't think it's such a good idea, luv,' she said. 'That part of your life is well behind you. Don't rake it up.'

'I promised meself I'd never go back to Machin Street again,' Josie said, relieved. Mrs Kavanagh had promised to look after Louisa's brown envelope and Mam's Holy Communion veil and prayer book, because it seemed silly to take them all the way to America.

The front door opened, and a man's deep voice shouted, 'It's only us, Ma. I've been showing Imelda the fairy glen.'

Lily made a face. 'I wonder what she thought of *that*?'

Imelda was Ben's fiancée, who'd come for the weekend to meet her prospective in-laws for the first time. They were getting married at Christmas because Imelda had always wanted a winter wedding. She and Ben had just left Cambridge, Imelda with a first class (hons) degree in English, and Ben with the same in physics. He was due in Portsmouth in a few weeks' time to start his national service in the Navy, and would be made an officer straight away because of his degree.

The Kavanaghs had been expecting to meet a studious-looking girl with glasses, a blue-stocking. Instead, Imelda was dainty, with delicate white skin and china blue eyes. Her hair was black, shiny and very straight, and she wore it parted in the middle and tucked behind her ears, which really did resemble two little pink shells.

It went without saying that Lily couldn't stand her soon-to-be sister-in-law, who was everything Lily wanted herself to be; thin, with manageable hair and make-up that seemed willing to stay on for ever. 'And she's all over our Ben. She keeps kissing him in front of everyone. I'm sure he's dead embarrassed.'

'He doesn't seem embarrassed to me.' Last night, when Josie had first arrived, also expecting to meet someone plain, possibly with plaits and flat, lace-up shoes – how else would you expect a woman with a degree to look? – she had felt a totally unreasonable stab of jealousy when she saw an exquisite creature wearing strappy, high-heeled sandals and a stiff petticoat under her white sundress, making her look like a fairy off the top of a Christmas tree. Ben didn't seem to mind at all when she snuggled close, tucking his arm in hers as they sat together on the settee and occasionally nuzzling his ear.

'Hello, Josie.' Ben had leapt to his feet when she went in. 'It's good to see you.' He had kissed her cheek, in the friendly way you'd kiss a cousin or an aunt.

'You've changed. Oh, you've got a moustache!' She had to stop herself from reaching up and touching the pale hairs on his upper lip.

'Imelda persuaded me to grow it.'

'But he won't grow a beard,' Imelda pouted.

Ben grinned. 'One day.'

Why did I go to Haylands? Josie wondered wildly. Why did I give him up? The moustache made him look dashing and sophisticated – and older, more like twenty-five than twenty-two. He wore khaki cotton trousers and a white shirt with the sleeves rolled up, revealing tanned, surprisingly muscular arms. The mere fact that someone like Imelda found him attractive only increased his appeal in Josie's eyes.

It could have been *me* marrying him at Christmas!

She was relieved when Ben took Imelda out that night to see a play at the Royal Court, because she was worried he would guess how unsettled she felt, full of doubts and uncertainties. Had she made a terrible mistake?

During the night, as she tossed and turned in the uncomfortable camp bed in Lily's room – naturally, Imelda had been given the spare – she could have sworn she heard someone on the landing. Ben creeping into Imelda's room, or perhaps it was the other way around.

I'm being stupid, she told herself. If Imelda had been as ugly as sin, I wouldn't have felt like this – at least, I don't think so. Anyroad, if Imelda didn't exist, and Ben asked again if I would marry him, he'd be dead set against me going to New York, and we'd be right back where we started. I'd have to tell him, no.

Phew! Josie snuggled her face in the pillow and fell asleep.

New York
1954–1955

1

She fell in love with him at first sight, something she hadn't thought possible, not in real life. It was her last night in New York. In Thumbelina's magnificent house, her case was packed, and Matthew had been alerted to drive her to the airport in time to catch the ten o'clock flight to Heathrow. She had bought him and Estelle a little present each for looking after her so well. She was sorry to be leaving New York, yet looked forward to going home.

Then she met Jack Coltrane and everything changed.

Four weeks previously, just as the sun was setting, Thumbelina, tiny, dazzling, seventy-five years old but looking more like fifty, with improbable golden hair and five-inch heels, had picked Josie up from the airport in a chauffeur-driven car. Josie was introduced to the chauffeur, Matthew, a handsome, grizzled black man, then to Henry Stafford Nightingale the third, known as Chuckles, who was in the back, a mild, tubby man with a bright red face who reminded Josie of a robin. They were leaving early next morning on a round-the-world cruise, Thumbelina explained, a belated honeymoon. 'Aren't we, hon?' She gazed adoringly at her new husband, who gazed adoringly back but didn't speak.

Josie felt shaken after a bumpy flight. Her legs were like jelly, and she had never felt so hot before. She tried to concentrate while she was bombarded with questions about Louisa, about herself and about Liverpool, which Thumbelina knew well, having stayed many times many years ago at Barefoot House. It was difficult to answer when her brain was still halfway across the Atlantic, and had yet to catch up with her body.

They were driving through an area called Queens, she was told, which had a look of Liverpool about it, but then the car crossed a bridge over a shimmering green river, reaching the other side through a vast arch flanked by colonnades, and Thumbelina said, 'We're on the island of Manhattan, hon. This is Chinatown.'

All Josie's tiredness, her feeling of disorientation, vanished in a flash, and she blinked in disbelief at the brilliantly lit shops, the pagoda-topped telephone boxes, restaurants with the names written in Chinese, tiny cramped arcades hung with banners and bunting. All the shops were open, although it was late, and the pavements were packed. Some people wore genuine Chinese clothes, long, gaudy silk robes with frogging and embroidery.

'Oh!' she murmured, and Chuckles glanced at her awe-struck face, smiled and opened the window of the air-conditioned car to allow in hot, spicy smells, mixed with wafts of musky perfume, as well as gentle tinkly music that sounded slightly off key, and the buzz of a hundred voices speaking a hundred different tongues. Or so thought an open-mouthed Josie as she listened to the strange sounds and breathed in the strange smells. The world seemed to have got lighter and brighter, noisier, busier, more colourful, larger than life. She was captivated instantly. New York was undoubtedly the most fascinating, the most exciting city in the world.

Louisa had said the Upper East Side was the poshest place to live in Manhattan. The house in which Josie stayed for the next four weeks was palatial – a double-fronted brownstone off Fifth Avenue, solidly built, with a row of pillars supporting a balcony that ran the width of the front. Josie was impressed, but wouldn't have wanted to live there permanently. It was more like a museum than a place to live. Even the house in Huskisson Street in its glory days couldn't have looked so grand. 'I'm not exaggerating, Lil,' she wrote in the first letter to her friend, 'but you could live in one of the wardrobes. They're *huge*. Downstairs, the floors are marble-tiled, but the carpets upstairs are so thick my feet almost disappear. You should see my room, it's a parlour as well as a bedroom.'

Her room was about forty feet square, with an oyster silk three-piece, a four-poster bed with matching drapes, a red carpet and lots of heavy black furniture decorated with gold.

When Matthew's wife, Estelle, the matronly housekeeper, took her upstairs on the first day, insisting on carrying her case – which made Josie feel uncomfortable because she was so much older – she did a little jig when the door closed, because she had rarely felt so happy. She began to unpack her case. 'If only you could see me now, Mam,' she crowed.

Dinner was served in a room that reminded Josie of Liverpool Town Hall, where she'd once gone with Lily to hear Mr Kavanagh make a speech. After a five-course meal that was more like a banquet, Thumbelina and Chuckles, who were leaving early in the morning, bade her goodnight and goodbye. She kissed them both, and wished them a lovely holiday, and they kissed her and wished her the same. Thumbelina said she must come back one day and they'd show her a real good time. Josie felt as if she'd known them for years. She went to bed immediately and slept like a log for twelve hours.

'I looked in earlier,' Estelle said next morning when she brought in a cup of coffee, 'but you were sleeping as soundly as the sweet Baby Jesus, so I decided not to wake you. It's ten o'clock. Now, honey, do you want breakfast in that mausoleum of a dining room or in the kitchen? Me and Matthew have already eaten, but we'll share a cup of coffee with you.'

'The kitchen, please,' Josie said promptly. While she ate scrambled eggs, followed by delicious pancakes with maple syrup, Matthew explained where to find the nearest bus stop and subway station.

'You're welcome to eat with us whenever you want, honey,' Estelle said, 'but if you decide to eat out, you'll find delis and diners are the cheapest. Oh, and Macy's is the place for clothes. It's the biggest department store in the world,' she finished proudly.

Matthew gave her the key to the door and said she was to come and go as she pleased. Josie went upstairs to collect her handbag and guide book, give her hair a final brush and renew her lipstick, before setting off to explore the glorious wonders of New York.

Time flashed by. Days merged, became weeks. She went up the Statue of Liberty and the Empire State Building, sampled the gaudy, clanking delights of Coney Island, wandered along Fifth Avenue. She gaped at the prices of the clothes in the windows of the opulent shops, nipped into Blooming-dale's, sprayed herself with Chanel No 5, then nipped out again, which Estelle had done when she first came to New York. She went to Mass in St Patrick's Cathedral, to Chinatown and Little Italy, the garment district, and so many museums she forgot which was which. She stood in the sharp, black shadows and gazed up in awe at the towering skyscrapers – it was like being in the middle of a giant pincushion – gorged on hamburgers, bagels, pancakes, pizzas and exotic ice creams, discovered a penchant for peanut butter and a passion for Coca-Cola with ice, not just because the weather was so hot.

And it *was* hot, as if a furious fire raged beneath the streets of this unique, fantastic city, and the heat could be felt through the thin soles of her sandals. Her feet hurt, her legs hurt, her head hurt from the noise, the crowds, the stifling atmosphere.

But Josie loved every minute. She rode buses and the sweltering subway, and sat on the grass in Central Park where she saw *As You Like It* and *The Merchant of Venice* for nothing. She spent far too long in Macy's, where there were four floors of mouth-watering women's clothes, and bought two sunfrocks and a lovely linen jacket.

The place she liked best of all was Greenwich Village, bohemian, unconventional, with quaint, tangled little streets that made a pleasant change from the rigid block system in the rest of the city. She wondered if anyone in Greenwich Village ever slept, because no matter how late it was the shops were still open, the bars and restaurants full, the streets buzzing with an almost anarchic excitement. It was possible to enter one of the dark little coffee-bars and find a play or poetry reading in progress, or a meeting going on, usually something political, to do with banning the bomb or stopping the McCarthy witch-hunts, whatever they were. Josie would sit in a corner and listen, savouring every little thing, no matter how trivial, because it was like nothing she had ever known before.

Suddenly it was her last week, her last few days, then the final day of the most wonderful holiday anyone could possibly have had. She had bought presents for everyone at home: a pretty necklace and earring set from Chinatown for Estelle, and for Matthew a leather tobacco pouch because the one he had was wearing thin.

'What are you going to do with yourself today, honey?' Estelle asked over breakfast.

Josie had the day all worked out. 'See all my favourite places one last time – Chinatown and Fifth Avenue, St Patrick's Cathedral, then Macy's because I've got a few dollars left and it would be a shame not to spend them. Tonight, I'm going to see *A Midsummer Night's Dream* in Central Park, then have a coffee in Greenwich Village.' She sighed. 'I can't believe I'm going home tomorrow.'

'We'll miss you, honey. It's been a pleasure having you here.' Matthew vigorously nodded his assent. 'But don't forget,' Estelle went on, 'you've been invited back. We might see you again some time.'

'It would be worth coming back if only for your lovely pancakes.'

She felt sad, walking round the vivid, noisy streets of Chinatown, not sure if she would ever see them again. She could promise herself she'd come back until she was blue in the face, but fate might not allow the promise to be kept. In life, nothing could be relied on – she'd learned that a long time ago.

She stayed quite some time in the cathedral, savouring the calm, the aroma of incense just discernible in the cool air, and prayed she would find a nice place to live when she got home, a nice job, that she would be happy. She prayed for Louisa, for Lily and everyone she could think of.

It was time for lunch when she came out, so she ate in the nearest diner – hamburger, a banana split, Coca-Cola. Afterwards, she set off for Macy's, where she roamed the aisles of clothes for hours before buying a long narrow black skirt and a baggy cerise jumper. There were just enough dollars left for a dead cheap evening meal and a final coffee in Greenwich Village.

He was at the next table, a slim young man with straight, coal black hair falling in a careless quiff on his forehead. Dark eyes sparkled in his lively, mobile face, which had a slightly dusky hue. He looked Italian, Josie thought, or Spanish, something foreign. The table he was at was crowded, and the young man was clearly the centre of attention. Everyone seemed to want his opinion, vying to make him notice them, clutching his arm, shouting each other down.

His name was Jack. Or perhaps it was Jacques. He might be French. He wore black pants and a dark blue shirt with the top button undone. His check tie was pulled loose. Every now and then he would throw back his head and laugh, and there was something joyous and uninhibited about the laugh, as if it came from deep inside him.

The coffee-bar was called Best Cellar, reached down a poky stairway on Bleecker Street. She'd been there twice before. The young man – she couldn't take her eyes off him – was animatedly sounding off about something to do with politics, waving his arms about. His listeners regarded him silently, with respect.

Josie glanced at her watch. Half past eleven. It was time she was getting back, she had a plane to catch tomorrow. But she was reluctant to leave while the young man was there, which was crazy. He hadn't even glanced in her direction. Did she intend to sit there in the hope that everyone would go except him, leaving *her* to be the object of his undivided attention?

She was already feeling dead peculiar, anyroad. *A Midsummer Night's Dream* had been a magical experience. Dusk had fallen over Central Park halfway through the performance, then night came, stars appeared. The grass on which the audience sprawled, mostly couples, felt cooler, and the scent of a million flowers was almost overpowering. As the sky grew dark the stage became brighter, the actors' voices louder, more resonant, the audience more rapt. Something stirred in Josie, an acute awareness of the beauty and the clarity of her surroundings and the sheer brilliance of the lines the actors spoke. Then came something else, a longing to have someone with her. Not Lily, a man, a boyfriend, in whose arms she could lie as she watched the play draw to a close, and they would experience the beauty of the magical night together. Would she ever meet a man like that?

Then she'd come to Best Cellar, and there he was.

Suddenly, the young man leapt to his feet and removed himself from her life for ever. He raced up the stairs two at a time. The occupants of the next table seemed to droop, as if his leaving had removed a vital element from their lives, though after a while they began to talk quietly amongst themselves.

'Oh, well.' Josie gave a wistful shrug, drained her third cup of coffee, picked up her bag and made for the stairs. Halfway up, she met the young man hurtling down. 'Forgot my jacket,' he muttered. He smiled, but she could tell he wasn't actually *seeing* her.

'Some people'd lose their heads if they weren't screwed on,' Josie remarked, which, given the circumstances, was probably the most stupid thing she could have said but was all she could think of when they had to stop on the stairs to squeeze past each other.

They were standing sideways, facing, touching, and the young man was looking at her, astounded. 'Was that a Liverpool accent I just heard?'

Josie's heart thudded, unnaturally fast, unnaturally loud, as the dark eyes smiled into hers. 'Yes.'

'Oh, then please can I kiss you? I haven't kissed a girl from Liverpool in almost fifteen years. What's your name? Where are you from? I mean, what part of Liverpool?'

'Penny Lane,' she stammered. 'I'm Josie Flynn.'

'And I'm Jack Coltrane from Old Swan.' He kissed her on both cheeks. 'Pleased to meet you, Josie Flynn.'

She could hardly breathe. There was a weird sensation in her stomach, as if everything had collapsed inside. He was looking at her with a slightly puzzled expression. Suddenly he laughed. 'You're very beautiful, Josie Flynn. Can I kiss you again?'

Next day, instead of going back to Liverpool, she moved in with Jack Coltrane.

2

It was like a dream, or a film, or a book. No, it was like none of those things, but something else, impossible to describe. She had become another person, quite literally lost her senses.

He had invited her to dinner. She was about to explain that she was leaving tomorrow when she realised he meant have dinner *now*, at midnight. On the way to the restaurant the ground felt different where she walked, and the things she touched weren't real, and when she looked at people they were slightly askew. It didn't help her surreal state to be faced with spaghetti bolognese and a bottle of wine at a time when she would normally have been in bed, or at least thinking about it.

She also seemed to have lost her voice, which didn't matter because Jack didn't stop talking. Before the war, he told her between mouthfuls of spaghetti, his father had been a doctor in Old Swan. In 1939, with war threatening, the family had upped roots and moved to America, where an uncle on his mother's side already lived. They settled on the coast of Maine. At first, it was only supposed to be temporary, but his father started practising again, his mother, a trained nurse, returned to work, and by the time the war was over there was no question of going back to England. They applied for American citizenship.

'And Dad thought the new National Health Service was the work of Communists. Free health care for the masses? No way. I realised me and my family hadn't much in common. I left home at nineteen. I've hardly seen my folks since.' He grinned. 'So, that's how I ended up a Yank instead of a scouse.'

Josie listened, only half taking it in, wondering if he was as fascinated with her as she was with him. Had he only asked her for a meal because they had Liverpool in common? Would she see him again after the meal had finished?

Apparently she would. 'Let's dance,' he said, when the wine had gone and their plates were empty.

'Here?' she glanced around the crowded bistro. There wasn't a soul dancing.

He laughed. 'No, sweetheart, on a dance floor. There's a club just around the corner.'

She could easily have fainted, at the 'sweetheart' and the pressure of his thin arm around her waist when he led her out to the still busy street. He stopped on the pavement and took her in his arms and she could feel his heart beating against her own. She slid her arms around his neck, and rested her head on his shoulder, knowing this was the place where God had intended her to be. His hand moved to the small of her back, to her neck, to her face. He stroked her hair, as if he was trying to make sure she was real. Then, regardless of the passers-by, he kissed her. As she stood within the shelter of his arms, Josie had the oddest feeling that nothing real, nothing of importance, nothing that mattered, had ever happened before, that she had crossed a bridge and entered another world, a magic, brilliantly lit other world, inhabited by Jack Coltrane.

Their lips parted. Jack's dark eyes were moist. They stared deep into hers, and she felt as if he were seeing into her soul. He sighed. 'So, this is it, then?' he whispered. 'Shall we forget about dancing and go home?'

Josie nodded. But, despite his words, Josie was never truly sure if Jack had entered the other world with her.

His apartment was over a dry-cleaner's in a busy street in Little Italy. Opposite was a greengrocer's with a green and white striped awning, a tiny cinema that screened only Italian films – *Stromboli*, with Ingrid Bergman, was showing the day Josie collected her suitcase from Thumbelina's and moved in – and an ice-cream parlour with window-boxes upstairs full of bright flowers and trailing ivy.

Matthew had expressed concern when she told him she wasn't going back to Liverpool. 'Are you sure you're doing the right thing, girl?'

'Course she is. Just look at her face.' Estelle had hugged her hard. 'Be happy, honey. You'll never have that look again.'

The apartment consisted of two largish, badly furnished rooms, a bathroom and a kitchen that was only used to make coffee as Jack usually ate out or had food delivered. The gloomily patterned wallpaper looked as if it had been up for decades but, as with the awful furniture, it didn't seem to matter. It wasn't just because Jack was there, with personality enough to totally eclipse his surroundings, but the place had a warm, well-lived-in feel, full of evidence of his active life. Books and papers were piled on the floor and political posters covered the walls, as well as several paintings done by his friends. More friends had showered him with objects they had sculpted, chiselled, moulded or carved – a lovely hand-woven rug hung over the unused fireplace. The front room was a cross between a second-hand shop and a small art gallery.

'Let's christen the bed,' Jack said the very second Josie had plonked her suitcase on the floor.

'We christened it last night, oh, half a dozen times.'

He pulled her into his arms and kissed her chastely on the brow. 'Yes, but now you're permanent. It'll feel different.'

Permanent! The word gave her a thrill, yet at the same time made her feel uncomfortable. She was a good Catholic girl, who had never faintly envisaged living in sin with a man. It just wasn't *done*, at least not in Liverpool where people got married first. What on earth would she tell Lily when she wrote to say she was staying in America for good? And she must let Louisa know she was in love.

'Hey, you having second thoughts?' Jack kissed her again, this time on the lips, this time more urgently.

'Gosh, no.' She'd probably go to hell, but it was worth it. She relaxed against him. 'What are we waiting for? Let's christen the bed.'

Jack Coltrane was a playwright – there were eight scripts on a shelf to prove it. With the first six, he'd got nowhere but the next, *The Disciples*, had been taken up by an off-Broadway theatre and received excellent reviews.

'I thought I'd made it until Joe McCarthy stuck his big nose in.' Jack glowered darkly. He rarely lost his temper, but could never control his anger when he spoke about the way his play had been treated. 'I was small fry, not important enough to be called before his damn committee, but it didn't stop one of his goons having a word with the theatre, and my play was pulled. The manager was very apologetic, but a play with a socialist message wasn't appropriate in the present climate. Arthur Miller could get away with it, but not someone like me.'

Senator Joseph McCarthy was a hated figure in the eyes of every liberal-minded person in America, Josie learned. His Anti-American Activities Committee had ruined the careers of hundreds of illustrious figures from all walks of life, including many from the theatre and cinema.

Jack had since written another play. He was writing one now, sitting solidly in front of the typewriter for four hours every morning because he was a driven man with a head full of dreams, ideas, plots, that simply had to be put down on paper. But there was no point in submitting them, he said with a sigh. 'I'm only trying to say the same thing as in *The Disciples*.' He laughed bitterly. 'I'd have to send it under a different name, and I'm not prepared to hide behind a pseudonym. There isn't a theatre in America that would even *read* a play by Jack Coltrane, let alone stage it. Word gets around. I'm a bit of a pariah.'

'Only for now,' Josie said stoutly. 'Things might change.' Had it been someone else, she would have suggested they forget the politics and write a thriller or something funny, but she had quickly learned that Jack had too much integrity to write about what he didn't strongly feel. He was, he explained once, trying to get across man's inhumanity to man, the social injustice in the world, trying to fathom out why some people had so much and others had so little, yet most folk didn't seem to care.

Josie remembered reading once that couples were never equal, that one loved more than the other. There was a giver and a taker. She suspected from the start that she gave and Jack took. There was nothing selfish about it – he hadn't a selfish bone in his body – but it was the way the dice had fallen, or how the cookie had crumbled, as they said in America. Only in bed where, time after time, they brought each other to a rapturous, scarcely bearable climax did she feel totally certain that he was committed to her and her alone, that she was *extra* special.

It was an undeniable fact that Jack had the knack of making the whole world feel special. His warm smile was free to anyone, his normally sunny disposition shared with everyone he met. Josie watched his numerous friends, men and women alike, watching him, waiting for Jack to notice *them*, to smile his all-embracing smile just for *them*, to shake their hand, give them a hug, a kiss, a friendly slap on the back. They adored him.

There'd been women before her. She found hairclips and an earring under the bed, a pink jumper in the wardrobe, a half-full bottle of scent in the bathroom cabinet. Josie tortured herself with the thought that, like these other women, she was only temporary, that one day Jack would meet someone else and she would be dispensed with. Once they were in bed and he told her how much he loved her, that he'd been waiting all his life for a girl like her, the thought would vanish, then slither its poisonous way into her head next morning. She hadn't known it was possible to be so deliriously happy one minute and so abjectly miserable the next.

She got a job in Luigi's, the dry-cleaner's downstairs, where she worked from two till ten, the same hours as Jack worked in a local bar. To her horror, she discovered she was classed as an illegal immigrant, but Luigi didn't give a damn that she didn't have a green card allowing her to work legally in the States. Anyroad, she'd have been useless in an office, where she could have earned more, because they never went to bed before dawn.

For Jack Coltrane, the good times started late. New York was a sleepless city, with plenty of all-night clubs and all-night bars. All-night parties were the norm. He always knew where a party was being held, and there was never a more welcome guest. Within seconds he would be surrounded by people, wanting to touch him, wanting to know his opinion on this or that, hanging on to his every word, and Josie would be left with mixed feelings. This slight, not very tall, delightful, handsome man, this man in a million, loved *her*. She would feel a glow of possession, particularly when Jack put his arm around her shoulders and drew her into the crowd.

What she wanted more than anything was for them to get married, for him to be truly hers in the eyes of God and the law. She was careful never to drop the slightest hint. Marriage might be the furthest thing from Jack's mind.

When, one Sunday in October, Miranda Marshall arrived at Jack's apartment Josie pretended not to care. Every Sunday from midday on, people began to drop by, armed with a bottle of wine. They came to talk, to argue, to sort out the world. Around teatime, Jack would send for a Chinese or an order of pizzas.

Miranda, though, was different. She hadn't come to talk, she'd come for Jack.

She was a sleekly attractive woman with a feline, sharply angled face. Glossy maroon lipstick made her lips look wet, and gold shadow adorned her almond-shaped eyes. Her dark brown hair was tied in a ponytail, not at the back of her head but over to one side, giving a jaunty and slightly eccentric impression.

Miranda was an actress, and had appeared in Jack's off-Broadway play. They had been great friends for years, and she was just back from Hollywood after an unsuccessful attempt to get into movies.

'I'm going back, I'm not giving up, but I just felt like a few days in New York to see my friends. I thought I'd lay claim to your couch for a few days, Jack.' The almond eyes rested fleetingly on Josie. 'I didn't know you had company. I'll find somewhere else.'

'You'll do no such thing,' Jack said. He looked at Josie. 'You don't mind, do you, sweetheart?'

'No,' Josie lied.

She minded terribly. She minded so much she wanted to cry, particularly when Miranda went to the bathroom and came back waving the scent from the cabinet. 'So *this* is where I left it,' she crowed.

They must have been lovers! Miranda had been hoping to take up with Jack where they'd left off. Laying claim to the couch had been a lie. It was Jack she wanted. Josie burned with inner fury.

That afternoon a whole crowd of them went to a political rally in Central Park to protest against the Chinese occupation of Tibet. Miranda came with them. She accompanied them to Pogo's, a blues club in SoHo, then to a party in Canal Street, where she seemed to know everyone. Josie watched closely, sensing that no one liked Miranda much. They made faces behind her back, which pleased Josie so much she felt ashamed.

By the time all three returned to the apartment, her head was spinning and she felt sick, imagining Jack creeping out of bed in the middle of the night to make love to Miranda on the couch. Wouldn't most women protest if their lover invited his old lover to stay? They'd never had a row before, but she'd have it out with him that night.

When they went to bed Jack immediately reached for her, but she gripped his hands. 'I want to ask you something.'

He nuzzled her neck. 'Ask away.'

Josie took a deep breath. 'Have you had an affair with Miranda?'

'Yes,' he said lightly. 'It didn't mean anything but, yes, I have.'

'Would you mind if one of my old lovers turned up and I let them sleep on the couch?'

'Sweetheart, you're *jealous.*' He laughed and tickled her waist. Josie squealed and put her hand over her mouth in case Miranda heard. Their guest was in the bathroom getting washed.

'I didn't say I was jealous.' Josie pushed his hands away and did her best to sound reasonable. 'I asked a direct question. How would you feel if the situation were reversed?'

'I'm not sure.' There was a long silence, during which he rested his face against hers. 'How many lovers have you had?' he said eventually.

'Only one. I had a fiancé, too, Ben. We were going to get married when he finished university, but I gave him up.'

'What was the lover's name?'

'Griff. He was an actor. Still is, I expect.'

Jack lay on his back, staring at the ceiling. 'I don't know why, I thought you were a virgin, that I was the first.'

'I hope you're not going to say you're disappointed.' She adopted a slightly amused tone. 'I was probably the twenty-first for you, or the hundred and first, for all I know.'

He turned and grabbed her by the shoulders. 'I know it's unreasonable, but I can't stand the thought of another man touching you,' he said gruffly. 'I want to ask stupid questions, like how was it with this Griff – was he better than me?'

'He wasn't. It was just a holiday romance. Was Miranda better than me?' she asked, more flippantly than she felt.

'Don't joke.' He shook her and said urgently, 'There's never been anyone better than you, and there never will. I love you with all my heart and soul. I've told you that a million times.'

'But I've told you the same,' she cried as she clung to him. 'It didn't stop you getting cross about Griff. I think I've a right to worry about Miranda. I can't stand the thought of you having slept with her. I can't stand the thought of you having slept with *any* woman. I don't want you to so much as *touch* another woman again, only me.'

'As if I would,' he said softly, kissing her. 'You're for me, and I'm for you, and that's the way it's going to be till the end of time.'

They made love, and it was as if they'd never made love before and were discovering each other's bodies for the first time. When it was over, and she nestled in his arms, he said, 'I'll tell Miranda to go in the morning.'

'There's no need,' Josie said contentedly. From now on she would never feel insecure again.

Of course, she did. Even when she discovered the couch was empty, and Miranda had done a midnight flit, the doubts had already begun their stealthy return. It seemed she would never feel fully happy with Jack Coltrane unless they spent the rest of their lives in bed!

Autumn had arrived in New York. The trees in Central Park shed their leaves to make a crisp, golden carpet. The air became fresher, cooler, with a hint of champagne. The endless hooting of the traffic sounded slightly muted. People had begun to wear coats, scarves, boots.

When Josie bought a fur coat for five dollars from a thrift shop, she thought longingly of the smart winter clothes she'd left in Lily Kavanagh's wardrobe. She bought a pair of dead cheap boots, one a slightly darker grey than the other, but at least they hadn't been on some other woman's feet. Luigi paid peanuts in the dry-cleaner's, and she was always short of money.

On 25 November Jack abandoned his precious play, and took her to see the Thanksgiving Day parade. The entire length of Broadway appeared to be covered in balloons, thousands of them, millions, of every conceivable colour. Josie watched, entranced, as float after float drove by, each more glorious, more eye-catching and inventive than the one before. This was the day Santa Claus arrived in New York, and he finished off the parade in a white fur coach, clanging his bell, already wishing everyone a Merry Christmas.

'That was wonderful,' she breathed when everything was over and the crowds began to disperse. Jack was standing behind her, his arms around her waist, his chin resting on her shoulder. He kissed her neck.

'How about a coffee?'

'I'd love one.'

'Then a coffee it is.'

They linked arms. Jack began to walk quickly, his step slightly ahead of hers so she had to hurry to keep up. He did everything quickly, combed his hair, washed, dressed, undressed, typed, ate – as if worried the world might end before he'd finished. She had something to tell him. Perhaps over coffee? But should she tell him yet that she was pregnant?

She hadn't taken much notice when she'd missed her August period. Although she'd always been as regular as clockwork, one missed period wasn't worth getting worked up about. But two! When nothing happened in September she began to worry, but convinced herself she couldn't possibly be pregnant because she felt so well. There'd been no morning sickness. She didn't go off her food, or get a hankering for peculiar things like treacle butties, as Marigold Kavanagh had. Then she'd missed October, and yesterday another period had been due ...

There was no doubt about it – she was four months pregnant. Her waist was starting to thicken. She was expecting Jack's baby, and didn't know whether to be glad or not.

It must have happened the night they met on the steps of Best Cellar, because since then he'd always taken precautions – he was so careful that she took it for granted he didn't want a child. Their lifestyle would have to change drastically. She had tried, but she couldn't see Jack content to stay home at night, happy to relinquish the parties, the clubs, the politics. The apartment wasn't big enough for a baby, and she'd have to leave work. Jack's wages weren't much. He made as much again in tips, but not enough to pay the rent and support a wife and child.

She imagined telling him, imagined his face lighting up. 'I've always wanted a child, a son.' Men always seemed to want a son. That was the best scenario. But he might be horrified, might even suggest an abortion. He was a Catholic, but didn't go to church. Perhaps that's why she hadn't told him. She was leaving it until it was too late even to discuss getting rid of her child, *their* child, because it was something she would have flatly refused to do, even for Jack.

Josie sighed. 'The bar will be busy today,' Jack said. 'The parade's over, but not the celebrations. Hey, this place looks interesting.' He steered her inside a diner with a real skeleton in the window. It was called Bones. 'What was that big sigh for, sweetheart? I felt it shudder right through me.'

'Nothing.'

Josie's waist was becoming thicker, her stomach bulged slightly. Hardly anything fitted. She tried to avoid Jack seeing her naked, reaching for something to put on before getting out of bed, because she still hadn't told him. Though he was bound to notice soon ...

'Sweetheart ...' he said one morning. It was a week after the Thanksgiving Day parade, and he was seated at the table, typing like a madman. She emerged from the bedroom, having only just got up. 'Sweetheart, I think you should cut down on the spaghetti. You're getting quite a tummy on you.'

Josie didn't answer. She looked down at the baggy cerise jumper she'd bought in Macy's on what she'd thought would be her last day in New York. It wasn't baggy enough to hide the ever-growing bump. 'If I didn't know better, I'd say you were in the club, girl,' Jack went on in the pretend Liverpool accent he occasionally used as a joke.

'I *am* in the club, Jack,' Josie said softly. 'That's the reason for the tummy.' She sat on the other side of the table and watched his thin, expressive face.

He looked stunned, then he frowned and opened his mouth to speak, but nothing came out at first except a groan. Then he said, 'Of course, that first night!' He tried to smile. 'You must be very fertile, sweetheart,' he said lightly. 'If we're not careful, we could end up with twenty kids.'

'Do you mind?' It was a silly question, because he obviously minded very much.

'To be honest, I'm not sure.' He laughed, not his usual, wholehearted laugh. 'I'm twenty-six. I suppose it's about time I settled down.'

'But you weren't planning on settling down just yet?' He didn't want the baby. She felt her veins turn to ice, and cursed herself when two solitary tears trickled down her cheeks.

'Sweetheart! Come here.' He patted his knee, and she crept into his arms. 'This is my fault. I should have been more careful. How far gone are you?'

'A bit over four months.' She began to cry properly.

'Aw, shit, Josie,' he said angrily. 'Why didn't you tell me before?'

Because I was worried you'd react in exactly the way you're reacting now, she wanted to say. Instead, she whispered, 'I don't know.'

Suddenly he grinned. Nothing could keep Jack down for long, not even an unwanted baby. 'Will you marry me, Miss Josephine Flynn?' He tipped up her chin with his finger. 'Please say yes.'

Josie nodded. 'Yes.' But she felt sure he would never have asked if she hadn't been pregnant. She would never be sure of anything with Jack Coltrane.

So that the priest wouldn't be shocked by a bride on the verge of motherhood, the wedding was arranged to take place as soon as possible.

The bride's outfit came from a thrift shop – a pink, silkily soft velvet skirt with a long, matching jacket to hide her swollen stomach.

On the morning of the wedding a letter came from Lily, enclosing a cutting from the *Echo*. Louisa Chalcott, the American poet, who had lived in obscurity in Liverpool for more than thirty years, had died peacefully in her sleep a few days before.

'Miss Chalcott's cerebral writing was well before its time. The day may well come when she will be recognised as one of this century's major poets . . .'

There was more, about Louisa's unconventional lifestyle, her legendary lovers, that she had never married but had borne twin daughters to a man she refused to name.

'That's because she didn't know who it was,' Josie said, showing the cutting to Jack. She felt incredibly sad, but at the same time relieved that Louisa had departed from this world painlessly, and in her sleep.

'Try not to let it worry you, sweetheart. She's gone to a better place, as my mother would say.'

'Louisa would do her nut if she thought I'd let it spoil me wedding day. As regards her being in a better place, I doubt it. She's probably in hell, trying to seduce Old Nick as we speak.'

The ceremony was held at midday in a little Italian church off Hester Street, only a short walk from where they lived. Jack had borrowed a respectable suit, black and white pinstriped. He looked like a member of the Mafia. The church was crowded with his friends, whom Josie had never come to regard as hers. She had always felt very much in his shadow, and sensed they resented her, as they would have resented any woman their hero had chosen to fall in love with.

Now they would resent her even more. Not only was she marrying him, but she was taking him to England, to London, though it was Jack's idea, not hers.

He had come bursting into the apartment days ago, his dark eyes alight with excitement. 'Hey, I've had a brainwave. Let's go live in England. That's what two of the blacklisted directors did – Joseph Losey and Carl Foreman. No one there gives a shit about your politics. I can start again, submit my plays – and boast of a Broadway production under my belt.'

'Off-Broadway,' Josie reminded him, at the same time trying to get her brain to adjust to the idea of them living somewhere else. Jack, she felt, was *part* of New York. He belonged here, every bit as much as the Empire State Building and the Statue of Liberty. Would he be happy in a place that was so utterly different? She reminded herself that he'd been born in Liverpool. England was his country as much as hers.

'Don't be a wet blanket. Off-Broadway, on-Broadway, it still sounds impressive.' He began to pace the floor, his excitement growing. Josie sometimes wondered if electricity rather than blood flowed through his veins. 'Oh, God, Josie. Why didn't I think of it before?' he whooped. 'It makes even more sense now with the baby – no medical fees, for one. I don't want some makeshift midwife delivering the little chap in here, and we couldn't afford a hospital.' He came over and kissed her tenderly. 'We'll live in London, where the contacts are – the agents, the actors, most of the theatres. I'll get a job, and you'll be a lady of leisure in our little apartment in Mayfair overlooking Park Lane.'

'A lady of leisure – with a baby!' she spluttered.

'You know what I mean. What do you say, sweetheart? It makes perfect sense, don't you think?'

She would have gone anywhere in the world with Jack Coltrane even if it made no sense at all. 'Of course it does.' She smiled. 'As soon as we're married, we'll go to England.'

The sun was shining brightly enough to crack the pavements, but inside the church it was dark. Light struggled unsuccessfully to penetrate the gloomy stained-glass windows, probably thick with dust and too high to clean.

The young priest looked very serious as he went through the motions of joining Josephine Flynn and Jack Frederick Coltrane together in holy matrimony.

'For richer, for poorer ...'

'In sickness and in health ...'

'Do you take this woman ...?'

'I do,' Jack said gravely.

'Do you take this man ...?'

'I do.' Josie's voice was little more than a whisper.

'I now pronounce you man and wife. You may kiss the bride.'

'Hi, there, Mrs Coltrane.' Jack kissed her warmly on the lips. He looked happy enough, she thought, as if the day had been inevitable since they met. He didn't *have* to marry her. But he had, whether out of a sense of honour or because he loved her as much as she loved him. The baby chose that moment to give its first, extremely violent kick. She rested her hands on her stomach. She was married. She was Mrs Jack Coltrane, and with that she would have to be content.

From Cypress Terrace . . .
1955–1957

1

As usual, the hall was awash with leaflets and old letters. A few weeks ago, not for the first time, she'd collected everything together, thrown the leaflets away and put the letters in a neat pile on the window-sill in case old tenants returned to see if there'd been any mail, which happened occasionally. Since then the letters had managed to get back on to the floor, and there were more leaflets, dozens of them. No one else living there seemed to give a damn about the state of the hall. There was a notice on the battered pay phone. OUT OF ORDER.

Josie plodded wearily up to the second floor. The office had been exceptionally busy today. Peter Schofield had wanted an urgent quotation to catch the post, and she'd had no alternative but to stay till half past six because two girls in the typing pool were off.

'Don't worry, darling. You'll find an extra few quid in your wage packet on Friday,' Peter said. He was very generous. 'Now you go home to that nice hubby of yours. I'll post this.'

'Ta.' Josie managed to squeeze her face into a tired smile. Peter didn't know about Laura.

The couple in the first-floor back room were having a fight, screaming at each other at the tops of their voices. Thank God we don't live over them, she thought. The man in the room below them made hardly a sound, unlike the young man on the ground floor who had friends round every night and played music till the early hours. The woman in the basement seemed quite respectable, but there was something wrong with her. More than once Josie had heard the sound of desperate weeping coming from the flat. She might have investigated had she not felt much like weeping herself. Jack said the woman's name was Elsie Forrest. She was a retired nanny, and often admired Laura. There were other tenants she didn't know – they kept changing all the time.

It was time Mr Browning got someone in to give this place a good scrub. She scowled at the dirt encrusted in the corners of each linoleum-covered stair. And a few repairs wouldn't have gone amiss. Several bannisters were missing, the light in the hall didn't work and there was a cracked window in the communal bathroom, where hot water was just a far-off dream. But all Mr Browning was interested in was collecting the rent. Still, he hadn't turned them away when she was obviously pregnant, like so many other landlords and landladies had done. But, then, Mr Browning didn't live on the premises, and probably didn't give a damn if a crying baby disturbed the other residents.

Josie reached the second floor. Before opening the poorly fitting door with gaps top and bottom, she threw back her shoulders and fixed a bright smile on her face. She turned the knob, and went in. 'Hi,' she sang out. 'How've things been?'

Jack was pounding away at the typewriter, and Laura was fast asleep in her cot at the foot of the bed. Josie bent over her beautiful six-month-old daughter, half resentful, half thankful she was asleep. She longed to give her a cuddle, yet ached to sit down and relax with a cup of tea.

'Everything's fine, sweetheart.' Jack abandoned his typing to give her a hug. 'You're late. I was getting worried.'

'I had this quotation to do. I tried to phone, but it's out of order again.'

'You can't hear this far up, anyway, particularly if I'm typing. The kettle's boiled. Fancy a cuppa?'

'I'm *dying* for a cuppa.' She sank thankfully on to the lumpy settee, her head swimming. 'How's the play going?'

Jack made a face. 'Okay, but two came back this morning, one from the Liverpool Playhouse.' He grinned. 'Bastards! No loyalty to a fellow scouse.'

She knew the grin was fake, like her smile. Every play he had submitted had been returned – even *The Disciples*, in which he'd had such faith – usually with unfavourable comments. 'Not tense enough.' 'The characters have no depth.' 'Where is the plot?' one director had rudely demanded.

'Perhaps you're before your time,' Josie had suggested once. 'Like Van Gogh, for example.'

'Well,' Jack drawled, 'let's hope I don't have to wait as long as he did, like long after I'm dead.'

He was unhappy in London. He missed his friends and the buzz and excitement of New York. Instead of looking out over a row of busy shops and a cinema, their large, dingy bedsitting-room in a Fulham cul-de-sac was opposite an abandoned factory with smashed windows and graffiti on the walls. Unlike New York, where Jack's radiance made everything around him seem pale in comparison, this ugly room with its bits and pieces of well-used furniture and faded, fraying lino diminished him. He seemed smaller, slighter, less important, just an ordinary man struggling, unsuccessfully, to make something of himself. Moving to London had been a disastrous mistake.

He brought a mug of tea. 'I thought I'd send a play to the BBC,' he said. 'Bob knows someone who knows someone there. He said they're always looking for new writers.'

'It wouldn't hurt,' Josie said encouragingly. She didn't say it would hurt their finances. With ten plays constantly in circulation, the cost of postage both ways, and envelopes and paper, bit deeply into her wages. But the whole point of this very unsatisfactory way of life was so Jack could concentrate on nothing but writing.

During her pregnancy, and for two months after Laura was born, he had worked for a pittance in a pub in Fulham. There had been scarcely enough to pay the rent and buy basic food. Josie didn't know how she would have managed if Mrs Kavanagh hadn't sent a huge parcel of baby clothes from Marigold, with a tactful note to say, 'It seems a shame to let these go to waste. Some haven't even been worn.'

'I could kick myself for not staying at college, getting a degree,' Jack complained frequently. He was completely unskilled. All he knew was bar work.

Josie was the one with a trade, but she hadn't worked as a shorthand-typist since leaving the insurance company four years ago. When Jack was out, she sharpened her skills by retyping his plays, with the excuse that the manuscripts had got shabby during their constant journeys in the post. As she typed, she had the worrying thought that the plays weren't very good. They seemed too wordy, rather dull, a bit preachy. Even *The Disciples*, of which he was so proud, had copies of the reviews clipped to the cover, and they weren't all *that* marvellous. Only two, from badly printed magazines she'd never heard of, had flattering things to say. When a play was returned with the comment, 'Where is the plot?' she couldn't help but agree.

She brought her shorthand back to speed by taking down the news from the wireless. As soon as she felt up to it, she suggested Jack give up the pub. *She* would work so *he* could write.

'I can earn more than you. It seems the sensible thing to do.' It was the hardest decision she had ever made in her life, to desert her lovely baby.

Jack's reaction still upset her when she thought about it four months later. He had gazed at her wretchedly. His body seemed to shrink before her eyes. 'Oh, Christ!' The sound, a mixture of a groan and a cry, seemed to come from the very depths of his being. 'I'm no good at this.'

Josie felt as if she were shrinking herself, melting away to nothing in the face of his despair. 'At what?' she asked shakily.

He gestured round the room. 'At looking after a wife and kid. It's not *me*. It's not what I had planned, at least not until I was *someone*. Back home I was a playwright who worked in a bar to make a few dollars. Now, I'm a fucking *barman*! Sometimes I feel too damn dispirited to write.'

'I'm sorry,' Josie said tightly. The doubts she'd had on her wedding day had been confirmed. He hadn't wanted to marry her. He didn't want to be a father. He may well love her, and he adored Laura, but both were burdens to this rather splendid, rather immature, intensely good-humoured man. She remembered the first time she'd seen him in the coffee-bar in New York, without a care in the world. That man no longer existed, though he still put up a front, but now, with his guard down, he looked destroyed.

'It's not your fault, sweetheart.' He dropped his head in his hands and didn't speak for several seconds. Then he looked at her dully. 'Look, why don't I find something else? One of those smart West End places might well snap up a Yankee barman, and if I smile nicely at the customers, I'll make a load in tips.'

'You're not a barman, Jack. You're a playwright.' Her voice was sharp. 'You expected to take London by storm, but maybe the storm's a long time coming. Oh, does that sound stupid?'

He smiled. 'A bit.'

'Anyroad,' she said seriously, 'our best plan is for you to concentrate on writing, and *I'll* work. It shouldn't be for long. Laura won't give you any bother. You'll just need to take her for a little walk around lunchtime, that's all.'

She would have to stop breast-feeding. That would be the hardest part. She had so much milk, gallons of it, and breast milk was so much healthier for a child. The best times of the day were when she watched her daughter suck furiously on her white, overlarge breasts, sometimes grabbing the flesh with her tiny hands, squeezing it. It was the oddest sensation, almost sensual and at the same time totally natural. Mother and child, joined together, one nourishing the other.

Everything about leaving Laura was hard. On her first day as a secretary with Ashbury Buxton, a civil engineering company in Chelsea, she cried the whole way on the bus. She couldn't stop thinking about her little daughter.

She'd told all sorts of lies to get the job, apart from the glaring omission that she had a child. She'd been working as a secretary in New York, she told Peter Schofield, and tried to look confident, at the same time praying he wouldn't suggest sending for a reference to the mythical company she'd invented. He'd been impressed, didn't mention a reference and employed her on the spot. There was a good atmosphere in the office, though the work was hard, and there was never time to stop for a chat with the other women.

Four months later, Josie still hadn't got used to leaving her child. When she got home Laura was usually asleep. She'd always been a perfect baby, and rarely woke during the night.

I'm missing so much, she thought as she watched Jack move the typewriter to the floor, then take the casserole she'd made the night before from the oven and put it on the table. She'd been at work while Laura had spent a whole hour trying to pull her fingers off one by one, and when she'd sat up unaided for the first time and held out her arms to be picked up. At weekends, when she nursed her, she noticed Laura's eyes turn to Jack. Who is this stranger? Josie imagined her thinking. Who the hell is this funny woman whose knee I'm sitting on? In another few months Laura would start talking, and her first word wasn't likely to be 'Mummy'.

The graffiti-covered factory served as a background to their meal. If there had ever been cypress trees in Cypress Terrace, there was no sign of them now. 'I was wondering,' Jack said, 'if we could run to a television? Not buy one,' he added hastily. 'I mean get one on hire. It only costs about a dollar a week. It's just that, if I'm to approach the BBC, I'd like to see a few plays first. Bob said they have on at least two a week. You might enjoy having a set, sweetheart.' Bob was someone he'd met in the corner pub, his only social outlet and so utterly pathetic when compared to the frantic clubbing and partying in New York.

She would never have time to watch TV. There was always ironing to do, Laura's nappies to wash and soak before they went to the launderette, things to mend, next day's meal to prepare – the inevitable casserole or stew – tidying, cleaning. She was lucky if she managed to snatch an hour with a book before it was time for bed, where Jack always wanted to make love, and she had to pretend it was wonderful when all she wanted to do was sleep.

He was looking at her pleadingly, and she couldn't stand it. She hated being the breadwinner and her husband asking for money.

'Of course we can afford it,' she said cheerfully.

'I'll arrange it tomorrow.'

She took her empty plate over to the sink, and noticed a canvas holdall on the floor. 'Jack, did you take the washing to the launderette?'

'Christ, I forgot.' He jumped to his feet. 'I'll take it now – they're open till ten.'

'You might as well have a drink while you're waiting.'

He planted a kiss on her cheek. 'I suppose I might. Bye, sweetheart. See you later.'

'Bye.' Josie let out a long, slow breath when the door closed. She put the dishes in to soak and sat at the foot of the bed beside the cot. Laura was on her back, her hands raised in a position of surrender. Josie lifted the quilt. Her knees were spread, feet together, making a perfect diamond.

'I love you,' she whispered. Laura uttered a tiny cry, opened her brown eyes – Jack's eyes – stared unseeingly at her mother, then closed them. She was Jack's child, with his eyes, his fine nose, fine eyebrows, the same coal black hair.

The nurses had exclaimed in surprise at the amount of hair she'd had when she was born. 'This baby already needs a haircut,' the midwife said. The birth had been as easy as the pregnancy – no complications, no stitches, hardly any pain.

'You're a dream baby,' Josie told her, 'which is just as well. If you were like some babies I've heard of, your dad would hardly get any writing done. Mind you, I wouldn't mind if you had a little cry in the middle of the night, so I could pick you up and give you a bit of a cuddle, like. But then, frankly, luv, I feel more than a bit worn out, so ignore that.'

Two months later, Josie came home to find Laura standing up in her cot, clutching the bars and grinning fiendishly. 'She did that herself,' Jack said proudly. 'You should have seen the look of determination on her face. She was going to stand up or die in the attempt. She's enormously pleased with herself.'

'I wish I'd been here,' Josie said wistfully.

'So do I.' His expression changed to one of mild irritation. 'Lately, her favourite game is throwing her toys out the cot, and expecting them back straight away so she can throw them out again. I must have got up at least twenty times.'

'She can't stay in her cot for ever. She'll be crawling soon.' Josie knelt beside the cot. 'Won't you, darling?'

Laura did a little jig. 'Bah!' she cried.

'Would you like a rusk?'

'Bah!'

'I've already fed her,' Jack broke in. 'Don't give her any more. She'll get fat.'

Josie stroked her daughter's plump arm. 'She's already fat. Shall I change her nappy?'

'She had a fresh diaper about half an hour ago.' He put the kettle on. 'Hey, despite the trials and tribulations of the day, I finished that play for the BBC. It took some discipline, trying to fit the whole thing into an hour and a half.'

'Good.' Josie picked Laura up out of the cot and carried her to the settee, half expecting Jack to tell her not to. The baby immediately made a grab for her necklace of multicoloured beads. 'What's it about, the play?' He was unwilling to discuss plots until he'd finished.

She only half listened as he explained that it was about a pit disaster somewhere, followed by a famous strike, aware only that it sounded dead dull, as Jack's plays usually did. It was strange because he was basically a happy soul, yet everything he wrote was as miserable as sin.

How much longer would this go on? she wondered as Laura tried to strangle her with the beads. They'd been in London fourteen months, yet Jack was no nearer success than the day they'd arrived.

Suddenly, the beads broke. They fell on the cushions of the settee and rolled on to the floor.

'Damn!' Jack exclaimed.

'It doesn't matter, they're only cheap ones.'

'I don't give a shit about the necklace,' he said irritably. 'I'm worried Laura's got one in her mouth. You should have stopped her chewing it.'

'I didn't notice she was,' Josie said in a small voice.

Laura, conscious that something was happening she didn't understand, raised her arms and looked nervously at Jack. He came over and plucked her off Josie's knee. 'It's all right, honey. Open your mouth for Daddy. Let's see what you've got in there. Good girl, four perfect little teeth, another two on the way and not a bead in sight.'

It was all Josie could do not to burst into tears.

It was Friday. Josie came out of the office, and saw Jack waiting on the other side of the road. He smiled, waved and came striding across, lightly dodging the traffic. For the first time in ages she felt a tiny thrill. There was something about the confident, bouncing walk that reminded her of the Jack of old.

'Where's Laura?' she demanded as soon as he arrived.

'I left her with Elsie Forrest,' he said easily. 'I've got some great news.'

'Elsie Forrest, the woman in the basement?' Josie hurried towards the bus stop. 'She's not quite right in the head, Jack. Haven't you heard the way she cries?'

Jack laid a restraining hand on her arm. 'Josie, I told you ages ago, she used to be a nanny. She's looked after dozens of children. Laura's completely safe. Elsie only cries because she's lonely, that's all.'

'But, Jack ...' Entirely against her will, she found herself being steered into a pub. 'I'm worried about Laura.'

'I've told you, she'll be fine. What do you want to drink?'

'I don't want a drink.'

'Well, you're having one, so sit down. We've got something to celebrate.' He brought her a sherry and a beer for himself.

'What have we got to celebrate?'

His dark eyes danced. 'This morning, I was leaving the apartment to take Laura for her walk when the phone rang. It was a woman from the BBC, wanting to talk about my play. The long and the short of it was, she asked if I was free for lunch. It was too good an opportunity to miss, so I said yes. I was going to call your office, ask you to come home, but thought about Elsie Forrest. She was only too pleased to oblige. I've been home since,' he said quickly when Josie opened her mouth to speak. 'Laura didn't want to know me. She's fine with Elsie. Anyway, back to this afternoon. Matty took me to a very smart restaurant in Mayfair.'

'Mattie?'

'Mathilda Garr, Mattie, the woman from the BBC.' He waved a dismissive hand. 'She's old. Although she didn't think much of the play, she reckons I've got a way with dialogue. She wants me to write a pilot for a series she has planned. My play arrived quite fortuitously while she was casting around for a writer.'

'What sort of series?' She was doing her best to relax. Surely Laura wasn't likely to come to harm with an ex-nanny?

'A crime thing. An American cop, a detective, joins the Metropolitan Police. There's all sorts of resentment until he becomes accepted.' He put his hand over hers. 'Oh, sweetheart, I've a feeling this is it. By this time next year we'll have that flat in Mayfair that I promised.'

'But, Jack, it doesn't sound your sort of thing,' Josie said cautiously.

His lip curled. He leaned back in the chair and shook his head. There was a hard look on his face she'd never seen before. It made her feel very sad. 'I don't think anyone's interested in my sort of thing, sweetheart. If Mattie likes my script, there'll be a four-figure advance for seven episodes. I say, fuck plays, I'd sooner have the cash.'

Josie felt even sadder. If they had never met, he would be in New York, still full of ideals, writing plays that *meant* something. What would his old friends say if they knew the noble Jack Coltrane had sunk to writing for money?

Still, it would be more than welcome, the money. She felt guilty that she'd been so preoccupied with Laura that she wasn't as excited as she should have been at his news which, now she thought about it, was dead marvellous. He looked a bit let down, she thought. He'd have expected her to be as thrilled as he was.

She put her hand over his and squeezed it warmly. 'Congratulations, luv. Let's buy some wine on the way home. We'll drink to your success tonight.'

Josie was relieved to find her daughter sitting contentedly on Elsie Forrest's floor, surrounded by her toys and scribbling furiously in a pad. She completely ignored their arrival.

Elsie, a small, neat woman with lovely silver hair, wore a navy blue pinafore dress and a white starched blouse and apron, almost a uniform. The basement flat was clean, probably cleaner than the Coltranes', and Elsie was smiling radiantly. 'That's Mummy she's drawing.' She looked fondly at Laura. 'I never thought I'd care for a baby again. I'm so happy.'

Jack gave Josie a challenging look. There! I told you it would be all right, it seemed to say.

'Why don't you leave her a little longer and have a nice dinner to celebrate?' Elsie suggested. 'She'll fall asleep soon. She's been too busy all afternoon to take a nap.'

They went to a small Italian restaurant in Soho with red gingham cloths and candles on the tables. The owner, Marco, was the brother of someone Jack had known in New York, and it was almost like old times when he introduced himself. Marco slapped him on the shoulder and shook his hand for a good five minutes.

'Course I hearda Jack Coltrane. Frankie tolda me you come to London. You Mrs Coltrane? Sit down, sit down, here, nice, private corner.' He produced a menu and waved his arms expansively. 'Meal's on the house for Frankie's besta friend.'

Josie couldn't remember having met anyone called Frankie, but in New York everyone regarded themselves as Jack's best friend. The wine arrived, and with it some of the old magic. She knew it would never return completely, not after the hard look she'd seen on Jack's face. Circumstances had changed him, as they had probably changed her. She had never been a happy, carefree person, not like Jack, she had too many painful memories. She was too introverted, she took everything too seriously, but over the last eighteen months she'd felt as if she was carrying the weight of the whole world on her shoulders.

. . . to Bingham Mews, Chelsea
1957–1960

1

They had moved less than a mile, to another cul-de-sac of tall terraced houses, but it was like moving to the other side of the world. The yellow brick residences were brand new, and the estate agent described them as 'town' houses, not terraced. There were twelve altogether, six each side, built on the site of an unused church off the Kings Road, Chelsea. They were mostly occupied by young couples like the Coltranes.

It was an area that reminded Josie a little bit of New York. She loved the boutiques with their outrageous clothes, and the coffee-bars and pubs where she frequently glimpsed faces she'd seen in films or on television.

The ground floor was a garage in which they kept the blue Austin Healey convertible. There was a small room at the back that Jack used as a study. The living-cum-dining room was on the first floor, with a window that took up the entire wall. Behind, overlooking a paved courtyard, was a kitchen, with matching units, a refrigerator, a Hoover twin-tub washing machine and an alcove with padded seats and a table, where they ate if they didn't have guests. Three bedrooms and a bathroom were on the floor above.

Everyone in Bingham Mews was friendly. In summer, they held cocktail parties in the open, drifting in and out of each other's houses in search of snacks and drinks – Jack was an expert at mixing cocktails. There was sometimes a drinks party on Sunday afternoons, and they invited each other in small groups to dinner, gravely discussing the Suez crisis, the enforced desegregation of schools in America, the revolution in Cuba led by a man called Fidel Castro.

Josie didn't care that she was the only woman in the mews who did her own cleaning, but found it nerve-racking having to make meals for half a dozen dead posh people – her previous culinary experience extended no further than casseroles and shepherd's pie from the cheapest mince. But she had no intention of letting down the working classes. She bought a 'Good

Housekeeping' recipe book and learned how to make chicken marengo, turkey blanquette, venison and all sorts of gateaux and meringues, as well as discovering thirty different ways to use an orange.

Elsie Forrest, now their regular babysitter, usually came to help. Elsie was frequently 'borrowed' by other residents with children. She had moved to a much nicer flat in Fulham, and considered Jack entirely responsible for her change in fortune. 'If he hadn't trusted me with your darling Laura, I'd still be wasting away in Cypress Terrace.'

Josie had made a friend in Charlotte Ward-Pierce, a gaunt woman with large, sick eyes, who had two small children and lived next door but one. She came for coffee on Monday mornings, and Josie went to her on Fridays. Charlotte's father was Lord Lieutenant of somewhere, and her husband, Neville, managed an Arabian bank. The two young women were grateful for each other's company at the various social functions held in Bingham Mews.

Josie waited until all the carpets and curtains had been fitted, and every item of furniture bought, before inviting Lily Kavanagh to stay. It was December 1957, three and a half years since she'd last seen Lily, and although they corresponded regularly it felt more like a hundred.

Lily had wanted to come before, and couldn't understand why Josie didn't visit Liverpool. Josie had felt obliged to tell her the truth. 'Because I don't want you to see the dead awful place where we live.' She had tried to make it sound bohemian. 'Quite frankly, Lil, I'm too exhausted to travel. I'm supporting an artist, remember? I'm working full time.'

She had had to work another six months before Jack's pilot script had been deemed suitable for production by the BBC and a series had been commissioned. With a sense of overwhelming relief, Josie handed in her notice. Laura quickly got used to being looked after by her mother, though she retained an especially close relationship with Jack.

Her little girl was a joy to be with. Laura had an impish sense of humour, and kept her mother entertained during the long hours Jack was downstairs in his study, at meetings, at script conferences or lunching with Mattie Garr.

After living in one room for almost two years, the new house felt incredibly spacious. For the first few weeks Josie used to go for walks, in and out of rooms, up and down stairs, hardly able to believe it was *theirs*.

They weren't rich, not yet, but no expense had been spared when it came to furnishing their new home – a beige leather three-piece, a walnut table with six matching chairs, two of them carvers, a maple bedroom suite. Nearly everything came from Peter Jones in Sloane Square, one of the poshest shops in London.

What would Mam say if she could see me now? Josie wondered as she ordered furniture costing hundreds of pounds. She found the change from being dead poor to seriously well off somewhat daunting. People came to measure for curtains and carpets, and she had swatches of material and samples of carpet to choose from.

Laura's room was painted pink, and had a glossy white junior bed, wardrobe and chest of drawers. Josie stuck transfers on the walls, and bought a fairy castle nightlight to keep her little girl company in the dark.

It was lovely, splashing money around like there was no tomorrow, but it was accompanied by the scary knowledge that the more successful Jack became, the further apart they grew.

Jack Coltrane was now a name to be reckoned with at the BBC. A second series of *DiMarco of the Met* had been commissioned and would start in the new year. They'd bought his play, *The Disciples*, though Mattie Garr had insisted on numerous alterations, and it was due to be shown at Easter. Now there was talk of a completely new series, and Jack was spending a lot of time in discussions with Mattie before he wrote the pilot.

There was nothing Josie could put a finger on. They made love almost as often as they used to, with almost the old fervour. It was just a feeling in her bones that something was wrong. She would catch a far-away expression on his face, as if he were thinking, What the hell am I *doing* here? She'd had the same disturbing thought herself that first Christmas at Louisa's. Despite everything, Josie suspected he would sooner be living in the apartment opposite an Italian cinema and an ice-cream parlour, working in a bar and writing plays with a message that no one wanted to hear. Having a wife and child had led to a lifestyle the old Jack would have despised.

On the day she was due to meet Lily at Euston station, Josie got dressed up to the nines in a green suede coat and matching high-heeled shoes she'd bought in the Kings Road. Underneath, she wore an orange polo-necked jumper and a slightly flared tweed skirt with orange flecks nestling in the green. She dressed Laura in her white hooded fur coat and tied her black hair in bunches with white ribbons.

'Me take Blue Bunny,' Laura said as they were leaving. It was a statement, not a question.

'Mind you don't lose him.' Laura and Blue Bunny were inseparable. Josie had felt the same about Teddy.

'Look for your Auntie Lily, luv,' Josie said later when the Liverpool train drew in. 'She's small and plump with short curly hair. Oh, look! She's grown it long again. She's got a bun.'

Lily was walking towards them in a black fitted coat and long boots, smiling and waving. Outside the barrier, Josie waved frantically back, and Laura waved Blue Bunny's paw. It was so lovely to see a familiar face that the long gap shrank rapidly, and it was as if she'd only seen Lily's pert, pretty face yesterday. The two girls embraced warmly. Not to be outdone, Laura curled a fur-clad arm around her new aunt's neck.

'You suit a bun, Lil,' Josie said. 'It looks nice.'

Lily took a long, deep breath, and smiled rapturously. 'Oh, it's good to see you, Jose. You look dead smart. And you . . .' She chucked Laura under the chin. 'You're beautiful, you are. Can I hold her?'

'Bootiful,' Laura agreed as she was passed from one set of arms to another. 'Kiss Blue Bunny,' she commanded, and Lily duly complied.

Josie took her friend's arm. 'You haven't changed a bit, Lil.'

'You've aged, Jose. You look older than twenty-three.'

It was quite like old times. 'I've had a baby,' Josie remarked tartly. 'And things haven't exactly been easy over the last few years.'

They arrived at Bingham Mews, and Lily had never seen such funny-shaped houses before. 'Fancy living over the garage! Were the builders short of space? I bet these were dead cheap.'

Josie assured her they were three times the cost of a house in Liverpool, which Lily found hard to believe.

'If you don't believe me, there's a famous model living opposite. Her name's Maya, and she's in all the posh magazines. There's an actor next door, and there's stockbrokers and bankers.' She tossed her head. 'And there's us!'

They went up to the lounge. 'Where's that famous husband of yours?' Lily enquired. 'I'm dying to meet him.'

'At lunch, which can go on for hours. He probably won't be home till six.' The lunch was usually accompanied by several bottles of wine, and Jack was likely to come home ever so slightly drunk.

She went to make tea, leaving Laura with a badly smitten Lily. Like father, like daughter, Josie thought ruefully. Laura, with her all-embracing smiles and beguiling ways, could charm the birds off the trees.

'I don't look all *that* much older.' She regarded her reflection in the little mirror behind the kitchen door. There were no wrinkles – not that you'd expect them at twenty-three – but she didn't look *young*. It was something to do with the expression in her blue eyes, as if she'd seen too much, known too much that she would have preferred not to. Perhaps it had been there since the day the bomb had fallen on the Prince Albert, and she'd never noticed before.

Trust Lily to point it out!

'Tell me all the news,' she demanded, returning to the living room with a tray of tea-things. Laura was dozing off on Lily's knee.

'I've told you everything there is to know in me letters. Oh, except this. I only heard it yesterday.' Lily's eyes gleamed and her voice rose to a squeak, a sure sign she was about to impart something of remarkable significance. 'Your Auntie Ivy's got married again. He's a policeman, Alfred Lawrence, and really huge, about six feet six.'

Josie grimaced. 'I hope he turns out a better bet than Vincent Adams.' She didn't want to talk about Aunt Ivy. 'What's the girl like your Robert's engaged to? Is there any sign of your Daisy getting married? Is Imelda still as horrible? How's your Ben? It must be awful, being married to someone no one likes.' Josie snuggled into a leather armchair. 'This is nice. I haven't had a gossip in years.'

'Imelda's pregnant again, and she's completely round the bend,' Lily said flatly. 'You should hear the way she nags Ben something rotten when they come to visit. Did I tell you they're living in Manchester? Ben's got a job there in a laboratory. Poor lad, he can't do a thing right. Ma daren't say a word in case Imelda won't come again, and it's Ben who'd suffer most. At least Sunday dinner at ours gives him a break – he goes for a drink with me da'. Anyroad, we're all dead fond of Peter. He's a super little boy, only a few months younger than this little one.' She removed a lock of hair from Laura's eyes. 'Imelda doesn't hesitate to have a go at him as well.'

Poor Peter. And poor Ben, so nice, so polite, so innocent, always anxious to do the right thing. It wasn't fair that he should end up with someone like Imelda.

'As for our Robert,' Lily was saying, 'Julia seems okay but, then, so did Imelda. Ma said she'll give her judgement in another five years. And our Daisy shows no sign of getting married.' Her voice fell, as if she might be overheard. 'Frankly, Josie, I'm beginning to wonder if she's a lesbian. She and that Eunice seem awfully close. They're always off on holiday together, and neither has ever had a fella.'

'She's only twenty-seven.' Josie laughed. 'Your Daisy's a career woman. She's bent on being chief librarian of Liverpool. There's plenty of time for her to get married.'

Lily sniffed. 'It was you that asked. Actually, Jose, would you mind taking Laura? I'm desperate to go to the lavatory.'

Josie carried Laura up to her pink and white bedroom, then went down to the ground floor, through the little door at the bottom of the stairs which led to the garage. She rolled up the garage door for when Jack came home so he could drive straight in. When she returned, Lily was coming out of the bathroom, full of admiration for a change. 'I've never seen a blue suite before, it looks dead pretty.'

'I'm glad we've got something you like.'

'Everywhere's nice.' Lily flushed. 'The house is lovely.' She sighed as they returned to the lounge. 'I'm jealous, that's all. When I saw you waiting by the barrier with Laura, I wanted to kill you stone dead, I envied you so much. Our Ben wanted to marry you, and that chap you met at Haylands, Griff. Now you're married to someone who had his picture in the *Radio Times*. He's *gorgeous*, Josie. I took it to show the girls at work.' Lily hunched her shoulders. 'I want a husband and children so much I can't think of anything else most of the time.'

'Haven't you met anyone you fancy, luv?'

'Oh, loads,' Lily said promptly. 'The trouble is, they don't fancy me. Remember Francie O'Leary? I would have married him like a shot.' Her eyes grew frightened. 'I'll be twenty-four next April, Jose. I'm worried I'll be left on the shelf.' She sort of smiled. 'I'm still a virgin, you know.'

Josie poured more tea. She said slowly, 'If only you knew how much I envied *you* over the years. I would have given anything for a mam and dad, a family.' She smiled. 'I even envied your coat the first time we met in Blackler's basement before the war. It was exactly the same as your ma's, blue with a fur collar, though I wasn't exactly crazy about your hat.'

'I suppose the grass is always greener . . .'

'On the other side of the fence.'

A car drove into the mews, and she recognised the harsh roar of the Austin Healey. The garage door was pulled down, and a few minutes later Jack came in to the room.

'You're fatter than I expected,' Lily told him plainly when they were introduced. 'You looked much thinner in your photo in the *Radio Times*.'

Josie glanced at her husband. Lily was right. She hadn't noticed, but his once-lean cheeks were fuller, and he was becoming jowly. He looked well fed, a touch prosperous. When he removed the jacket of his expensive suit, the black trousers were tight around his waist. She had a moment of fear. He looked a stranger.

He seemed slightly taken aback. 'I like a woman who speaks her mind,' he said, politely shaking Lily's hand, though Josie sensed he was annoyed. But no one liked to be told they're growing fat, particularly by someone they'd only just met. Lily was incorrigible.

She herself felt annoyed with Lily, then with Jack, who announced he had work to do and went down to his study. She was even more annoyed when Lily said, 'He's not quite as gorgeous as I thought. Is he a bit pissed, Jose? His hands were shaking.' It would have been easy to have had one of their famous rows, but Josie resisted the temptation. They were older, and it might not pass off as easily as their frequent childish ones.

Lily stayed for five days. With Laura in tow, Josie took her to see the sights, most of which she hadn't had time to see herself – the Tower of London, the Houses of Parliament, Madame Tussaud's. They lunched in Lyon's Corner House, went for walks through Hyde Park, along Oxford Street, Regent Street, Piccadilly, all decorated for Christmas.

They took the opportunity to buy each other presents, and Josie searched for something expensive and unique for Mrs Kavanagh, who had been the nearest thing she'd had to a mam over the years. She decided on an antique cameo brooch in a gold setting which cost twenty-five pounds. 'It's second hand but, then, you can't buy a new antique, can you?' Lily promised to give it to her mother on Christmas morning.

What should she buy Jack? Last Christmas and the one before they'd been poor. They'd bought each other things like chocolates and scarves. She'd knitted him gloves, but the fingers were all the wrong size. This year she could afford to buy something dead expensive.

'What about one of those?' They were in Selfridge's menswear department. Lily pointed to a rack of pure silk dressing-gowns in dark colours – maroon, navy blue, bottle green.

'Hmm! I'll keep them in mind.' The Jack Coltrane she'd met in Greenwich Village three years ago hadn't owned pyjamas, let alone a dressing-gown, and he would have laughed at the idea of silk. It shocked her that Lily considered such a *poncy* garment suitable for the Jack of today.

Later, as they walked through the art department, looking for the lift, she noticed a large framed picture of New York. Close up, she saw it was a photograph, taken at night. The sky was dark, the soaring buildings black, the river oily. But every light in every window was switched on, and the effect was dazzling. As Josie stared, the yellow lights seemed to be winking back at her, as if she were *there*.

She bought it immediately, and arranged for it to be delivered. Jack would love it. He could hang it in his study.

Jack managed to remain invisible during most of Lily's stay. In the privacy of their bedroom, he confided he couldn't stand her. 'In spite of what I said, I *don't* like people who speak their minds, not if it's hurtful.'

Josie was sitting up in bed. 'In Liverpool, it's called not being polished. It was one of me Auntie Ivy's favourite sayings. "You know me, I'm not polished." Were you hurt?'

He made a face as he climbed in beside her. 'I suspected I was putting on weight, but not so that you'd notice. Since your unpolished friend pointed it out I've tried a few exercises. I must be out of condition. I can hardly touch my toes.'

'It's all those lunches, Jack, and all the wine. Lily noticed you were drunk.'

'Bitch!' Jack said savagely, and Josie wondered why she kept comparing one Jack with the other, as if they were two entirely different people. The other Jack would have merely laughed. This one swore.

She would have liked to have continued the conversation. Having spent the first six years of her life with an alcoholic, Jack's drinking worried her. She thought it wrong that he should drive. But he switched off the bedside lamp, wished her an abrupt goodnight and pulled the bedclothes around his shoulders. He lay with his back to her. Josie stayed sitting up. For some reason, she wanted to cry.

The Liverpool train was packed. Lily raced ahead, peering through windows for a seat. Josie followed with a reluctant Laura, who dragged her feet because she didn't want Aunt Lily to leave and seemed to think if she made her miss the train Aunt Lily might stay for ever.

Lily must have spied a seat. She hoisted her suitcase on board, and by the time Josie arrived a slender young man with a sweet face could be seen through the window, helping to put the case on the overhead rack. He smiled, and put a book in the place where she was to sit. Lily appeared in the corridor and leaned out of the window.

'He looks nice,' Josie remarked. 'He's keeping you a seat.'

'He's a bag of bones,' Lily said dismissively, 'and you should see his Adam's apple. It don't half wobble. I hope he doesn't talk to me. I want to read my book.'

Laura had begun to cry. 'Want Auntie Lily stay,' she sobbed.

Josie picked her up to be kissed by a suddenly tearful Lily. 'You will come at Easter, like you promised, Jose? Everyone will be thrilled to see you, particularly Ma.'

'I promise absolutely.'

The guard's whistle sounded. A few seconds later the train began to move, and Laura's sobs increased. 'Have a lovely Christmas,' Josie shouted.

'The same to you, Jose.' Lily blew kisses with both hands until the train disappeared.

The young man Lily sat next to on the train was called Neil Baxter. When Josie went to Liverpool at Easter, she was matron of honour at their wedding.

'I don't love him,' Lily said flatly the day before the wedding, 'but he loves me, and I like him *ever* so much, Jose. He's got a good job with the post office, and we have loads to talk about and never argue. Oh, and we're both mad about Elvis Presley. We want a family, two kids at least, a boy and girl. We'll call them Troy and Samantha, but we're leaving children until we've moved up a notch in the housing market. The place we're buying in Orrell Park is nice, but there's no garden. And it's a bit run-down. We're going to do it up and sell it at a profit in a year or so's time. I'll keep on working, natch, so there'll be two wages coming in.'

'You've got everything worked out for years.' Josie thought it sounded very hard-headed, not at all romantic. Yet for a woman who claimed not to be in love, Lily looked radiant the following morning when she walked down the aisle of the church of Christ the King in the brocade Victorian-style wedding dress her mother had made. Her shoulder-length veil was secured, somewhat appropriately, by a wreath of lilies of the valley, and the delicate flowers mingled with the white roses and trailing ferns in her bouquet.

Neil Baxter's eyes glowed tenderly as he watched his bride come towards him on the arm of her da'. Mr Kavanagh looked quite emotional, though the night before he'd claimed to be as pleased as punch to be finally shot of his loud, argumentative daughter.

Josie was the sole attendant, as Lily wanted to avoid the expense of bridesmaids. She wore a plain yellow costume and a black straw picture hat with a circle of yellow flowers on the crown, both from Harrods, black shoes and gloves, and carried a posy of yellow roses. Her only jewellery was the amber pendant that Louisa Chalcott had bought in Southport, nestling within the deep V of her collar.

All the Kavanaghs had turned up for the wedding of their baby sister. Stanley and Freya had flown from Berlin with their two children. Stanley was going bald, Josie noticed when they were outside and the photographs were being taken – Lily had got someone from the office to do them on the cheap. She'd last seen Stanley the year the war ended, and supposed it was silly to expect him to look the same thirteen years later. And Marigold cut a rather matronly figure in the severe navy costume she hoped would make her look slim. She was only thirty-one but, then, she'd had four children since they'd first met when Josie had gone to Machin Street to live with Aunt Ivy.

Robert still lived in London doing something in the City, and it was impossible to imagine him aged twelve, wrestling on the parlour floor with his little brother. His fiancée, Julia, was dressed smartly in a grey costume and a little pillbox hat with a pink veil. She'd been impressed to learn that Jack was responsible for *DiMarco of the Met.* 'We must meet up in London some time, go to dinner,' she gushed earlier. Jack had greeted the suggestion with a charming smile that Josie knew was false. He was here under sufferance and hating every minute.

Only Daisy Kavanagh hadn't changed at all. In a glorious cream and purple frock and a dramatic picture hat, she looked no different from the girl in the fairy glen who'd asked what the matter was. Perhaps being single isn't such a bad thing, Josie thought. No husband to worry about, no kids, no money problems. Daisy's face was smoothly serene, contented. Her friend, Eunice, seemed equally content.

Her eyes searched for Laura and Jack. Of Jack there was no sign, but Laura was playing with Heidi, Stanley's and Freya's youngest, who couldn't speak a word of English, yet somehow they seemed to understand each other. Her three-quarter-length white socks were filthy, and Josie was wondering if she could get back to the house for a clean pair before they went to the reception when a voice said in her ear, 'She's beautiful.'

She turned. Ben was looking down at her. He nodded towards Laura. 'Quite beautiful.' His lips twisted in a wry smile. 'And so are you.' He took her hands. 'You look stunning, Josie.'

'You're not so bad yourself.' She gave a small, lying laugh. He looked *terrible*. His brow was creased like an old man's, his eyes were tragic. He was stooped, yet he used to hold himself so very straight, so erect. 'How's things, Ben?' she asked, which was a silly question, because she knew things were dead awful. There was something inherently wrong with Imelda.

He shrugged. 'Oh, you know, okay, I suppose. I like my job. Manchester's a nice place to live. Imelda, well, Imelda's . . .' His voice trailed away. 'Have you seen Peter?' His face suddenly brightened. 'He's about the same age as your little girl. He's around somewhere . . .' He stopped again, and she felt his hands tighten on hers. 'Oh, Josie,' he said in an anguished voice. 'If only you hadn't decided to go to that damn holiday camp.'

She wanted to say, if only you hadn't tried to stop me. But that would only be rubbing it in, and he was miserable enough already. He had seemed to regard it as a test of his manhood to make her stay. And if she had stayed, or if he had let her go, how would things have turned out?

He continued to hold her hands, more loosely now, like two old friends together. 'Where's this famous husband of yours?'

'Around somewhere.' She'd had a terrible job persuading Jack to come. They'd fought for days. 'What's the point of having a husband,' she angrily demanded, 'if he won't come with you to important things like your best friend's wedding?'

'You know I can't stand Lily,' Jack said reasonably. 'I feel sorry for the poor guy she's managed to drag to the altar.'

In the end, he had agreed to come just for the day. He was returning to London straight after the reception. Josie was staying with the Kavanaghs until Wednesday.

'There you are!' A very pregnant Imelda came out of the church, dragging a small boy by the hand. Her pretty face was screwed in a scowl, and the child's bottom lip was trembling, as if he was about to cry. 'He's your child as well as mine,' she said acidly to Ben, completely ignoring Josie. 'I just caught him at the candles. He could have burnt himself.' She virtually flung the little boy in the direction of his father. 'It's your turn for a while.'

Ben released Josie's hands and she felt his body droop beside her. He lifted up his son. 'Have you been a naughty boy, Peter?'

'He was being curious, not naughty,' Josie said. 'Come and introduce him to Laura.' Seeing Ben, she was almost sorry herself she'd come to the wedding.

Jack must have been watching for them. When the taxi stopped, he came out while Josie was paying the driver.

'Daddy!' Laura launched herself upon him. She squealed in delight when he swung her small, squirming body above his head.

'Did you miss me?'

'Oh, *yes*, Daddy,' Laura confirmed.

Jack propped her in the crook of his arm and put his other arm around Josie. He kissed her, and it was more than just a welcoming kiss. There was something hungry about it. 'And I've missed you, both of you. It's been very quiet and lonely here by myself.'

In the lounge, all three sank together on to the settee, which squeaked in protest. 'Did you enjoy yourselves after I'd gone?' Jack asked.

'We had a lovely time. I took Laura to New Brighton and Southport. There was a party last night for Stanley and Freya – they left the same time as us.'

'I won a game, Daddy. I got a prize, a box of chocolates.'

'Only because you cheated. It was musical chairs,' Josie explained. 'She couldn't quite get the hang of it.'

'Did you eat them, the chocolates?'

'No, Daddy. Blue Bunny ate every single one.'

Josie went to put the kettle on. It had been nice, meeting everyone again, but sad, seeing how much older they were. Mrs Kavanagh's hair had turned completely grey over the last three years, and she was wearing glasses, quite thick ones. She thought about Ben and his tragic eyes. She hadn't realised how much she missed Liverpool till she'd gone back. It was where she fitted in, felt at ease, which she would never do in Bingham Mews if she stayed for the rest of her life.

She returned to the lounge. 'I think the wedding went off very well, don't you? Lily looked radiant, and you'd think Neil had won a million pounds.'

'Poor guy!' Jack made a face. 'Did they go somewhere exotic for the honeymoon?'

'No.' She giggled. 'They had a weekend in the Lake District, and were home by Monday. They're spending the next two weeks doing up their new house.'

Jack shuddered. 'Not exactly romantic.'

'It doesn't *sound* romantic, but it is in a way. They both seem so *happy*, Jack, like it didn't matter where they were, as long as they were with each other.'

He laughed shortly. 'You almost sound envious.'

Perhaps she was. There'd been something about the faces of the newly married couple that had filled her with a sense of longing. She and Jack had looked like that when they'd first met.

When they were getting ready for bed, he said gruffly, 'Don't put your nightdress on. I want to touch you all over.'

Josie had never been able to understand why things had gone wrong, or how they'd gone wrong, but after they'd made love everything seemed right again. He stroked her body, tenderly at first, then more and more feverishly, kissing her nipples, caressing her breasts until she wanted to scream.

'I love you,' he whispered, over and over again. 'I love you.' Then he knelt over her, thrust himself inside her, and Josie's body responded, arching rhythmically against his as they climbed, higher and higher, until everything burst in a scarcely bearable climax.

We should spend time apart more often, was her last thought before she fell asleep.

She felt convinced their marriage had been rejuvenated. Jack was unusually attentive. Not that he'd neglected her, but he'd never bought her flowers before or unexpected gifts of jewellery. He came home one night with a pair of amber earrings in a velvet box. 'To go with that pendant you always wear.'

'Oh, I've always wanted some.' She threw her arms around his neck, delighted.

'I would have got them before if I'd known.'

On Monday he left early for a script conference, and an hour later she found the compact down the side of the settee. It was gold, with a pattern of red enamelled flowers. She opened it – the powder was dark, for a brunette. Josie felt herself grow cold. She shivered, snapped the compact shut, threw it back on the settee and rubbed her hands against her skirt, as if the thing were contaminated.

Charlotte Ward-Pierce was due any minute for coffee. Josie picked up the phone to tell her not to come, just as there was a knock on the door. She was too late.

'Auntie Charlie's come,' Laura sang out from the kitchen where she was drawing a picture of the wedding.

As Josie ran downstairs she told herself she was being silly, too suspicious. The compact might belong to anyone in the mews. Every single woman who lived there had sat on the settee at some time over the last few months. But surely they would have remembered where they'd last had it? Women used their compacts every day. She paused behind the door, her hand on the latch. Bile rose in her throat when she remembered feeling down the side of the settee for Lily's wedding invitation the day before they'd gone to Liverpool.

She remembered smiling, thinking to herself, she might not let us in without it. The invitation had been addressed to 'Mr & Mrs J. Coltrane, and Laura'.

Charlotte's mournful face twisted in a mournful smile when Josie opened the door. Her usually limp hair was arranged in tiny ringlets pinned on top of her head with a diamanté clip. It looked incongruous with her cotton slacks and shirt.

'We're going to a ball tonight,' she explained. 'I hope it won't have dropped by then. I left it too late to book an appointment with the hairdresser, and he was full this afternoon. Neville was cross with me as usual.' Neville Ward-Pierce was a brusque, impatient man, who never hesitated to disparage his wife in public.

'Where are the children?' Tristram and Petronella were on holiday from their preparatory school in South Kensington.

'Elsie's got them. She's taken them for a walk.'

Josie stood to one side, aware she was blocking Charlotte's way. 'Come in.'

She made coffee, gave Laura a glass of milk, filled a plate with chocolate digestive biscuits and admired Laura's picture of the wedding – Lily wouldn't exactly be pleased to know she had one eye bigger than the other.

Charlotte was on the settee, having put the compact on the coffee-table.

'I don't suppose that's yours?' Josie said casually, knowing it couldn't possibly be, otherwise she would have found it when she searched the settee last week.

'No, I've never seen it before.' Charlotte opened the compact. 'It's not my colour, much too dark.'

'Nor mine.'

There was silence. Josie couldn't take her eyes off the compact. She kept telling herself there must be a simple explanation for it, and wished she could think what it was.

Charlotte said, 'You look – what is that phrase you sometimes use? – as if you've lost a pound and found a sixpence. Is there something wrong, Josie?'

She would never be friends with Charlotte the way she was with Lily, yet Charlotte was easier to confide in and had already told intimate things about her own unhappy life. Josie nodded at the compact. 'I found it down the side of the settee, but I know it wasn't there before I went away.'

'It could be Elsie's.' Charlotte's long, gaunt face went red. The cup and saucer rattled in her hand, and she hurriedly put them on the table.

'What is it, Charlotte?' Josie said urgently. 'It's not Elsie's, she doesn't use make-up. Have you remembered whose it is?'

'No, no.' The woman lowered her head and clutched her knees, as if she were trying to roll her long body into a ball. 'I didn't intend to mention this, Josie,' she said in a small voice, 'but on Sunday morning the children got me up about half six wanting their Easter eggs. There was a noise outside. When I looked, Jack was taking the car out the garage. There was a woman in the front seat.'

Josie went over to the window and looked outside, as if half expecting to see the same scene. Her heart was drumming in her throat. 'What was she like?'

'Old,' Charlotte whispered. 'At least forty, very dark, with glossy black hair. She wore tons of make-up.' She picked the compact up, looked at the contents and put it down again.

Mattie Garr! Josie had met Mattie twice, and the description fitted perfectly. 'Perhaps they talked all night,' she said half-heartedly.

'Perhaps.' Charlotte nodded eagerly, as if she hoped this was the case. Her face fell slightly. 'I heard the same noise on Monday morning. I didn't bother to look, so couldn't swear if it was Jack. But I remember hearing a woman laugh.'

'She turned up late Saturday night,' Jack said easily. 'I'd just got back from Liverpool. We were discussing script changes for the new series. The hours just seemed to fly by. Before we realised where we were, it was morning. I took her home. That's all there was to it.'

'For two nights in a row?' Josie tried not to sound too incredulous.

His face didn't change. 'Well, yes, as a matter of fact. It's easily done when there are important things to talk about.'

She had inspected the bed in the guest room, hoping to find Mattie had slept there, but the sheets were virginally smooth. Then she'd changed the sheets in their room in case they'd made love there. *If* they'd made love.

'Why did Mattie turn up when me and Laura were away? She's never been before.'

'She came *because* you were away,' he said patiently. 'It gave us a chance to talk without being disturbed.'

'Oh, so me and Laura are in the way?' Josie could hardly contain her anger. 'If it was all so innocent, why didn't you mention it? You said the house was quiet, that you felt lonely.'

'Because it didn't seem worth mentioning. And the house *was* quiet most of the time, and I *did* feel lonely.'

For three nights, she slept in the spare room. On the fourth she was woken by Jack's hand gently caressing her beneath the sheets.

'I would never be unfaithful to you, sweetheart,' he said softly. 'I should have told you Mattie had been. Incidentally, she's one of the most unappealing women I've ever met.' His hand curved over her hip and circled her breast. He kissed her neck. 'Why would I want to sleep with someone else when I've got you? Come back to bed, Josie, please.'

Josie went, because she couldn't sleep in the spare room for ever, otherwise their marriage would quickly be beyond repair. She wanted to believe him more than anything on earth. The magic might have gone, but she was still as madly in love with Jack Coltrane as she had ever been.

2

'I used to write that sort of thing,' Jack said boastfully. 'I went into television instead.' He was standing only a few feet away, and Josie could barely hear him above the clamour of other voices and the too-loud music from Maya's gramophone. 'Do not forsake me, oh my darling', Tex Ritter pleaded.

There must have been at least sixty guests. As well as the residents of Bingham Mews, Maya had invited people from the world of fashion to her New Year's Eve party – magazine editors, photographers, models, male and female.

'You can hardly compare *DiMarco of the Met* with *Look Back in Anger*,' a bearded man Josie had never seen before replied scathingly. 'John Osborne's play was a real breakthrough. There'd never been anything like it before. It started a whole new trend.'

'I wasn't comparing them, was I?' Jack sounded truculent, a sign he'd drunk too much. Josie thought tiredly that these days Jack spent more time drunk than sober. He never got completely plastered, though tonight seemed to be an exception – he must have downed at least five large whiskies. The man had apparently irked him. He gestured angrily with his glass, and the liquid spilled on the sleeve of his maroon corduroy jacket. Jack was envious of John Osborne and Arnold Wesker and the other new young playwrights whose work had blown a blast of fresh air through the staid world of British theatre. They were the sort of plays he wrote himself, he groaned.

'I always said you were before your time.' Josie had tried to comfort him, though she could see little similarity between kitchen-sink drama and Jack's high-minded, rather tedious work.

'Did you see my play, *The Disciples*, on TV?' He glared belligerently at the man.

'Never heard of it.' The man walked away. Jack, staggering slightly, went over to the bar and poured himself another whisky. Maya, in a bright red curly wig, a gold lamé top and tight matching slacks, linked her arm in his and led him to a group in the corner, where Neville Ward-Pierce's penetrating voice drowned all those around him. He was bemoaning the fact that America seemed likely to elect the left-wing Senator Jack Kennedy as its next President.

'I think your husband and mine could well come to blows,' Josie said to Charlotte. They had taken refuge on the uncomfortable white plastic and chrome settee under the window. 'Jack thinks the sun shines out of Senator Kennedy's arse.'

'I quite like him myself.'

'So do I.' Josie's eyes followed the slightly Oriental figure of Maya. 'I'd love to try on wigs, see what I looked like with different colour hair.'

'I quite fancy her outfit, not gold lamé. Crêpe would look nice, black. But Maya's a model. I'd probably look awful.'

'You'd suit that sort of thing,' Josie said truthfully. It would hide her sharp knees and protruding elbows. 'Do I look like a tart in this?' She was wearing a purple Mary Quant mini-dress and showing an awful lot of leg.

'No, you look lovely,' Charlotte said admiringly. 'Neville said if I ever bought a mini-dress he'd divorce me. Do you think we should circulate? After all, it's a party.'

'Nah. You can if you like. I'd sooner stay put.' Where she could keep an eye on her husband.

Maya's lounge, exactly the same shape as every other lounge in Bingham Mews, was sparsely furnished in white and red with a black carpet, already littered with crumbs. Josie looked at the clock. Only an hour before the start of a new decade.

Charlotte left, and her place on the settee was immediately taken by the bearded man who'd been talking to Jack. 'Hi, I'm Max Bloch, photographer. Who are you and what do you do?'

'I'm Josie Coltrane, wife and mother of one.'

'Boy or girl?'

'Girl, Laura. She'll be six in April.'

'Do you work?'

'Is housework counted? If so, I work.'

He looked at her appraisingly. 'Have you ever thought of taking up modelling? You have very good bone structure. I bet you're very photogenic.'

Josie hooted. 'I'm also size fourteen, far too big to be a model. Look at Maya – she's taller than me and her hips are about six inches smaller.'

They both turned and regarded the statuesque Maya as she swayed elegantly around the room. 'She looks like a beanpole in a wig,' Max said disparagingly. 'I wasn't suggesting you become a fashion model – there's different sorts, you know. I'll give you my card. That's what I do, prepare portfolios for models and actors. If you decide to go ahead, get in touch.'

'Oh, so you're just touting for business.' Josie smiled. 'I bet you've told every woman here she'd make a good model.'

He looked hurt. 'I've done no such thing. I'm very proud of what I do. I regard it as an art form. When I'm taking photographs I feel at one with my subjects. I hope it stays that way, otherwise I shall feel as if I've sold my soul to the devil.' He gestured. 'Like that chap over there.'

'Which chap?'

'The guy pinning back the ear of the girl in the white dress. I can't remember his name.'

Josie glanced across the room to where Jack was talking animatedly to a beautiful blonde in a white mini-dress with legs up to her ears, almost certainly a model.

'Writes some muck for television, but claims to be a great playwright,' Max Bloch continued disgustedly. 'He's sold out. No commitment, I guess. People like him make me want to puke.'

'Perhaps he has a family to support.' Josie felt the blood rush to her head. 'It takes a lot of courage to sell out if you're genuinely committed to what you do. If you're living in one room with a baby, your wife's working to support you and you're putting all your heart and soul into your writing but getting nowhere, then I wouldn't blame anyone for selling out. Anyroad, *DiMarco of the Met* isn't exactly muck. It's quite highly thought of, not just in this country but all over the world.' Numerous other countries had bought the rights.

Max Bloch looked uncomfortable. 'You know the guy?'

Josie smiled icily. 'He's my husband. His name's Jack Coltrane, by the way.'

He left to fetch her a drink, and she wasn't surprised when he didn't come back. She turned to look out of the window, still shaken. It was snowing heavily. The light was on in their house, where Elsie was looking after Laura, who'd pleaded to stay up till twelve o'clock. They'd be watching television. She'd go over in a minute to make sure they were all right. No, she'd leave it until after midnight, till 1960, then she'd wish them a happy new year and make sure Laura went to bed.

She'd surprised herself the way she'd spoken to Max Bloch. Why have I never looked at it in that way before? She wondered if Jack ever regretted that they had met. He had given up his apartment, his friends, then the plays that meant so much, for her, and Laura. She had taken for granted the rich, comfortable life that had cost him so much to provide.

She made up her mind that tomorrow they would have a long talk. She would persuade him to start writing plays again, even if only part time. It might be possible for them to go back to New York, where there was much greater scope for television writers. They had dozens of channels over there.

The party was getting a bit wild, the laughter too piercing, the voices too loud. Nearly everyone had drunk too much. Charlotte returned and reported a man was throwing up outside. She'd been to the bathroom and had found a couple engaged in what she called 'hanky-panky' in the bath, and she'd had to go home to use the lavatory. 'And there are some very peculiar noises coming from the bedrooms. I hope it isn't going to turn into one of *those* sorts of parties.'

'We'll go home if it does.' At a recent party in Bingham Mews the host suggested the men throw their car keys in a bowl.

'What for?' Neville Ward-Pierce demanded suspiciously, concerned for his silver-grey Daimler.

'We pass the bowl around,' the host explained with a wink. 'Whichever keys the bloke picks out gets the wife of the owner.'

'No way, old chap,' Neville said, stiffly indignant. 'Come, Charlotte,' he snapped. 'We're leaving.'

'I wouldn't dream of indulging in such gross behaviour,' a woman gasped in outrage.

Jack Coltrane merely laughed. 'Are you ready, sweetheart? I don't think this is quite us.'

Five couples had stayed, and it had given Josie and Charlotte something to talk about for weeks.

The girl in the white dress looked bored. She kept glancing around, as if hoping someone would rescue her from this drunken man in the maroon jacket. Josie felt sad as she watched the girl wriggle uncomfortably against the wall. She didn't realise it was the great Jack Coltrane she was talking to, one of the most popular men in New York. There, some people would have given their right arm to be in her position.

Maya swayed over to the gramophone and turned it off, then turned the television on. 'It'll be midnight in a minute,' she announced. A silent Big Ben appeared on screen, and within a few seconds the great clock began to chime.

Neville Ward-Pierce came and took Charlotte's hand. Other couples hastily began to seek each other out ready for the first chime of the New Year, a sound that always seemed so significant and full of hope.

Josie and Jack had always greeted the New Year in each other's arms. Perhaps he hadn't realised the time. Josie felt a knot in her stomach as she tried to push her way through the packed room towards her husband.

'Jack,' she called, but he was too engrossed in the blonde to hear, though the room was strangely silent except for the chimes of Big Ben, which struck midnight before she reached him. There was a deafening cheer, and roars of, 'Happy New Year.' 'The sixties, here we come!' a man yelled.

'Happy New Year,' Josie whispered when the same man grabbed and kissed her. At least someone wanted to, if not her husband. *He* was kissing the blonde, and there was something desperate and pathetic about it, something demeaning, as if he were trying to find his lost youth or his lost dreams in the reluctant embrace of a stranger. The girl's eyes were open. Help! they pleaded.

Josie ran downstairs and into the snow that was falling in heavy, wet clumps, just as the party began to sing 'Auld Lang Syne'. She stopped, the key in the door, and looked at the bright upstairs window of Maya's house. Had Jack noticed she'd gone? A sensation of aloneness which she'd had before, but had thought she'd never have again, enveloped her like a cloak. She shivered. Her feet in the thin strappy sandals were wet, and she'd forgotten her stole.

Elsie and Laura had fallen asleep in front of the television, which showed the crowds in Trafalgar Square rowdily welcoming 1960. She managed to carry Laura up to bed, glad she'd changed her earlier into her nightclothes.

'Good night, my darling girl.' She placed a visibly ageing Blue Bunny on the pillow and stroked her daughter's smooth forehead. The long, dark lashes quivered in response, and Laura uttered a long, breathy sigh of contentment, before turning over. Josie tucked the eiderdown around her shoulders and switched on the fairy light.

'What's going to happen to us – to you and me?' She sank into the white wicker chair in which she sat when she read Laura a story.

It couldn't go on, not like this, not with Jack drinking so much and them growing further and further apart. She remembered that, earlier, she'd vowed to talk to him, urge him to spend more time writing plays, suggest they return to New York, say that she hadn't realised the sacrifices he'd made. After tonight it was even more important that she say these things.

She got to her feet with a sigh. 'Good night, luv,' she whispered, closing the door.

In the lounge, Elsie Forrest was just waking up. She jumped when Josie entered the room. 'I didn't hear you come in.'

'Happy New Year.' Josie kissed the rosy, withered cheek of their babysitter.

'The same to you, dear.' She glanced at the television. The revellers in Trafalgar Square had been abandoned for a club in Scotland, where a man in a kilt was singing, 'On the Bonnie Bonnie Banks of Loch Lomond'. 'I've missed everything, haven't I? Oh, well, never mind. Did you have a nice time at the party?' she asked cheerily. 'Where's Jack?'

'Still there. I'll go back meself in a minute. You go to bed, Elsie.' Elsie was staying the night in the spare room.

'I wouldn't say no. I'll make myself a cup of milk to take up. Would you like something?'

'A cup of tea would be lovely. Ta, luv.'

As soon as Elsie left, Josie dialled Lily's number, but there was no reply. She and Neil were probably at the Kavanaghs', and she preferred not to ring there. It would look as if she had no one to talk to on New Year's Eve. Lily was thrilled to bits because she was three months pregnant. Even morning sickness gave her an odd sort of pleasure. 'Twenty-seven is the perfect age to have a baby. We're going to try for Samantha three months after Troy's born.' Everything was so certain with Lily nowadays.

Elsie came in with the tea. 'Here you are, dear. I'm off to bed. I might be gone in the morning by the time you're up, so Happy New Year again.'

''Night, Elsie.'

Josie wandered over to the window. The sounds from the party were subdued. The white curtains had been drawn and smudged bodies moved slowly behind the thin, gauzy material. They must be dancing. Maya's front door opened and a couple came out. The woman put her coat over her head and they ran through the snow to number eleven. Strange, she thought. The Maddisons are usually the last to leave a party.

After a while she supposed she'd better go back, if only to get Jack home before he passed out. She fetched a coat and left it hanging loosely over her shoulders when she went back into the snow. She rang Maya's bell, hoping someone would hear above the strains of 'Some Enchanted Evening' and let her in. The door was opened almost immediately by Neville Ward-Pierce, who was ushering out a clearly embarrassed Charlotte.

'You don't want to go in *there*, Josie,' she said quickly. 'They've already started pairing off, and there's a floor show. I daren't tell you what they're up to.'

'I've never seen anything so depraved since I was in Cairo during the war,' Neville boomed. 'It's utterly repulsive.'

'But Jack's still there,' Josie said hesitantly.

'Jack's in the kitchen, vomiting his heart up.' Neville pursed his lips disapprovingly. 'He'll come home as soon as he realises what's going on.' He slammed the door and took his wife's arm. 'That's the last party *we* go to in Bingham Mews.'

For some reason Josie waited until they'd gone indoors before she rang the bell again, but although she pressed the buzzer for ages and ages no one came.

It was gone six o'clock when Jack came home. Josie, still wide awake, heard him stumble upstairs. He lurched into the room, removed his jacket and trousers and fell on top of the covers, half-dressed. She got up and put on her dressing-gown because she couldn't stand the thought of lying beside him.

She went down and made tea. The central heating had just switched itself on and the house was still cold. She took the tea into the lounge, but found she couldn't sit down. Perhaps it was lack of sleep that made her head feel so fuzzy and thick, as if there were a tight band around her forehead preventing her from thinking, for which she was grateful because she didn't want to think about last night. She drank the tea as she walked to and fro across the room, and found comfort in the scalding liquid coursing down her dry throat. There were dirty dishes in the kitchen, which she washed and dried, hardly aware of what she was doing, just knowing that she had to do something to keep herself busy, not think. Then she polished the walnut table and the six chairs, two of them carvers, rubbing the satiny wood until it shone as it had never shone before.

Elsie came down when Josie was clearing out the cupboard under the sink. 'The paper was dirty,' Josie explained. 'I thought I'd put a new piece in.'

'Yes, dear.' Elsie nodded. Josie could tell by her eyes that the older woman had guessed something was wrong.

'There's tea made.'

'Shall I pour you a cup?'

'Please.'

They sat on the padded benches and chatted about perfunctory things. What would the sixties bring? Elsie wondered. 'At least we're not at war,' she said thankfully, 'not like in nineteen-forty. In nineteen-fifty, we were still on rations, and there weren't enough houses for people to live in. Can you remember the squatters? I reckon we're all better off these days, and things can only improve.'

'Let's hope so.'

She refused Josie's offer to phone for a taxi. 'I'd sooner walk, dear. It's not very far.' It had stopped snowing, and none had stuck to the ground.

Josie finished cleaning the cupboard. She made more tea and took up a cup to Laura, who was disappointed to learn there was no snow. 'I was going to play snowballs with Tristram and Petronella.'

'Happy New Year, luv.' Josie kissed her forehead. 'It's a new decade. Today is the first of January, nineteen-sixty.'

'I'm getting old,' Laura said glumly.

Her mother laughed. 'Is such an old lady in the mood to accompany me to the pictures this afternoon to see *Snow White and the Seven Dwarfs*?'

'Will they sing "Whistle While You Work"?' Laura forgot her age and bounced excitedly on the bed.

'It'll be exactly the same as when you saw it before. Mummy saw the same picture when she was a little girl. I went with Auntie Lily and *her* mummy.'

'Mrs Kavanagh?'

'That's right, luv. You can wear your new blue velvet dress.' It was almost identical to the one Mam had bought in Paddy's market.

'Will Daddy come? He liked *Snow White* the first time.'

'We'll just have to see. Your dad's got a bit of a cold coming on. He might prefer to spend the day in bed.'

There was no sign of Jack when they got back from the pictures. Laura raced up to the bedroom to tell him about the film. She came down again, her face crestfallen. 'Daddy's not there.'

'Wait here, luv. Perhaps he's in his study.'

Jack was still in his dressing-gown, elbows on the desk, staring at the typewriter which had no paper in. He raised his head when Josie went in. His eyes were swollen and puffy, half-closed, he was badly in need of a shave and his chin was bluish. He looked utterly wretched. She felt a pang of longing for the man he used to be.

'Didn't you hear us come in?' she asked sharply from the door. 'Your daughter would like to see you, even if I wouldn't.'

'I didn't do anything last night, you know.' His voice was as wretched as his appearance. 'I fell asleep on the settee. I kept waking up and dozing off again. There were things going on, I thought I must be dreaming.'

'If Neville Ward-Pierce was right, you must have had some dead peculiar dreams. I think pornographic is the word.'

'I knew you wouldn't believe me.' He rested his head on his fists.

Josie closed the door in case Laura could hear. 'I've only got your word for what went on after midnight, Jack,' she said tightly, 'just like that episode with Mattie Garr three years ago. But I've got the evidence of me own eyes for what went on before. You were as drunk as blazes, and too attached to that blonde to wish me a happy new year. You still haven't.' Her voice broke. 'It really hurt, Jack.'

He raised his head again and said mockingly, 'Happy New Year, sweetheart.'

'Is there any need to say it like that?'

'What other way is there to say it in this house?'

'And is that your fault or mine?'

Jack stretched his legs under the desk and put his hands behind his head. He grinned. 'Mine, I suppose.'

She itched to slap the grin off his face, though she knew it was merely bravado. Her eyes swept the room, looking for something to attack instead of him, and they lighted on his plays, neatly stacked on the top shelf of the bookcase. She went over and swept them to the floor, then turned on him. Her face felt ugly with anger.

'You know, you need your head examined. There's thousands of writers who'd give their eye teeth to be in your shoes, but you? Oh, you've written a few lousy plays, and you're so bloody childish that you've decided to ruin your life, as well as mine and Laura's, just because no one wants them. Grow up, Jack, count your blessings. You're a very lucky man.'

He grinned more widely. 'So, you think my plays are lousy?'

'If you must know, yes.' Josie folded her arms and glared at him. 'They're hectoring and lecturing, not the least bit entertaining.'

'Oh, well, now that the esteemed critic Josephine Coltrane has given my work the thumbs down, I might as well burn it.'

'It wouldn't be a bad idea, except we don't have a fire.'

They stared at each other challengingly across the small room. Then Jack swivelled the chair around until he was looking at the door. 'Have you never wanted to *do* something? Something magnificent that would set people talking, change things.'

'No.'

'Have you never wanted *anything*, Josie?'

'Yes.' She wished there was another chair so she could sit down. 'I wanted a family, a mum and dad, sisters and brothers. I wanted to *belong*. I always felt terribly alone, rootless. But I met you, we got married, we had Laura and the feeling went. Last night it came back again.'

His lips curved in a wistful smile. 'I'd always hoped I'd change things with my plays. They gave me a sense of purpose, a reason for being alive. They were part of me, almost like Laura.'

'Have plays ever changed things? Did Shakespeare?'

He smiled again. 'You're very down to earth all of a sudden. Are you intent on destroying all my dreams today?'

Josie gestured impatiently. 'I think it's time you stopped dreaming, came down to earth and counted your blessings.'

'You've already said that.'

'Well, I've said it again.' She took a deep breath. 'Things can't go on like this, Jack. You're hardly ever sober, we hardly ever talk. If you don't stop behaving like some silly . . .' She paused, searching for words. 'Like some silly prima donna, then I shall leave you.'

The chair swivelled round, and his eyes were like black holes in his puffy face. 'And take Laura?'

'I'm not likely to leave her with a drunk, am I?' His eyes both frightened and repelled her. She recalled having planned to say quite different things today. It wasn't too late to say them, suggest they go back to New York. She took a hesitant, placatory step towards him, but her foot caught on one of the cardboard folders she'd swept off the shelf, and she was shocked by the scorn and disgust she felt as she stared down at the scattered plays. Stupid things, she thought. Fancy mucking up everyone's lives on account of *them*. It's time he grew up and lived in the real world.

Laura burst into the room. 'Why are you so long? Laurel and Hardy are on television.' She threw herself on Jack's knee. 'Happy New Year, Daddy.'

Jack refused anything to eat. He also refused to meet his wife's eyes. 'Black coffee's all I want,' he said shortly to the wall.

'There's loads of Christmas cake left, Daddy. And a big tin of biscuits with only half gone. Would you like a ginger cream, your favourite?'

'No, thank you, darling.' He reached out for his daughter and held her tightly in his arms. 'I love my little girl. Always remember that, won't you?'

Laura looked slightly startled. 'I knew that already, Daddy,' she solemnly replied. 'I love you, too.'

It was pitch dark. Laura had gone to bed and it had started to snow again when Jack announced he was going out. They had spent the hours since the row ignoring each other. Josie was already regretting some of the things she'd said. She shouldn't have criticised his precious plays.

'Where to?' She felt a pang of concern.

'For a drive, to clear my head.' He put his hands to his forehead. 'I can't think straight.'

'Don't have anything more to drink, Jack,' she pleaded. 'It's not safe to drive if you've been drinking. You might have an accident.'

'Would you care?' He looked at her sardonically.

She stamped her foot. 'Of course I'd care. I worry about you all the time when you're driving.'

'Oh, well, that's something, I suppose.'

'You'll need a coat.' She went upstairs to fetch it, but when she came down Jack had gone, and she heard the inside door to the garage slam. Then there was the grating roll as he pulled up the main door. A few minutes later the car backed out, and Jack drove away. The sound of the engine seemed to go on for ever in the stillness of the night.

'What have I done?' Josie whispered to the empty room.

Jack stayed away for almost two days, and during most of the time it snowed. On the first night Josie slept soundly as she hadn't slept a wink the night before. She wasn't surprised when he wasn't in bed when she woke up, or particularly bothered when the spare room proved empty when she looked. He was probably indulging in a long, drawn-out sulk. She regretted telling Laura that he'd be back any minute when she demanded to know where Daddy was, because the child visibly itched with worry as the hours passed and he didn't return.

On the first afternoon the Ward-Pierce children called, and Laura helped to build a snowman. It had black stones for eyes, and Charlotte made something resembling a pipe out of cardboard.

'Have you heard from Daddy?' she demanded the minute she came back.

'Not yet, luv,' Josie said brightly.

Her face fell. 'Mummy, everything in our garage is covered with snow.' She frowned. 'It looks funny, like a Christmas grotto, but there's no Santa Claus.'

'I left the door up so Daddy can drive straight in.' In fact, she hadn't been outside the house all day and had forgotten it was open. It didn't seem worth closing it now.

When darkness fell, and Jack had been gone twenty-four hours, Josie began to worry herself. Laura was fast asleep in the double bed with Blue Bunny clutched in her arms. If Jack had had an accident, surely the police or the hospital would have been in touch. He had his driving licence in his wallet. Maybe he'd holed up with a friend, not that he had many friends these days, or maybe Mattie Garr had offered him shelter from his ogress of a wife. She actually hoped this was the case, and the Austin Healey wasn't buried in a ditch in the depths of the countryside covered in snow, with a dead Jack draped over the steering-wheel. If she rang the police, they'd want to know where he'd gone, and she had no idea. He could have gone north, south, east or west. He might be hundreds of miles away or hundreds of yards.

Why didn't he pick up a phone and let her know he was all right? *If* he was all right. And if he was, she would never forgive him for putting her and Laura through the mill like this. He'd passed the point of no return, she thought angrily. As soon as he came back, she would leave. But where would she go?

Liverpool, obviously. She felt hungry for the place where she was born. Jack would never see his daughter go short, even if he didn't give a damn about his wife. He would let them have an allowance, then she would rent a nice little house and look for a part-time job. Jack could come and visit whenever he pleased. Life would seem dead peculiar without him, but she welcomed the peace it would bring. She was fed up with the non-stop worry, the guilty feeling that she had ruined his life. It was all her fault that he had become a successful, highly paid writer when the poor man preferred to write lousy plays for nothing at all!

Josie woke up next morning and met the brown eyes of her daughter on the pillow next to hers. 'Daddy's still not home. I've just been to look.' The eyes, normally so shining and full of fun, were wet with tears. 'He's coming back, isn't he, Mummy?'

She inwardly cursed Jack Coltrane with all the invective at her command for causing such misery to a five-year-old child. Reaching out, she took the small figure in her arms and wanted to cry herself when she felt Laura's heart beat anxiously against her own.

'Daddy telephoned,' she lied. 'He called last night, long after you were asleep. The car broke down miles from nowhere in a place called Essex. He had to walk for ages through the snow to find a garage, but they didn't have the parts to fix it. He's staying in a hotel until they arrive. He doesn't know when he'll be back, but there's no more need to worry.'

Laura regarded her gravely. 'Are you sure, Mummy?'

'I wouldn't have imagined all that, luv, would I?'

'You're not just saying it to make me feel better?'

'Ask Daddy yourself when he gets home.'

Throughout the day, Laura inundated her with questions. Where exactly had Daddy phoned from? Had they got a map so Josie could show her the precise spot?

'The road atlas is in the car, luv. It was somewhere round Chelmsford, I think.' She had a feeling Chelmsford was in Essex.

'Is it a nice hotel where he's staying?'

'It's more a pub than a hotel. He said it's nice and warm.'

'And they'll make him something to eat?'

'Of course.' She wondered if Laura was trying to catch her out, expose her lie, and wished she could tell herself a lie and stop worrying.

The day wore on. She made dinner, and forced herself to eat for Laura's sake. For tea they had soup and finished off the Christmas cake. By then it was dark again, and the snow fell relentlessly against the blackness of the sky, obliterating the outline of the houses opposite. The windows were bright blurs in the midst of nowhere. Josie couldn't have felt more isolated in her expensive home if she were living at the North Pole, hundreds of miles from the nearest neighbours.

She made up her mind that, as soon as Laura went to bed, she'd ring Mattie Garr. She'd ring every single person who had anything to do with Jack and ask if they knew where he was. If they didn't know, she'd call the police.

Laura was ready for bed in her nightie and dressing-gown. She lay on the settee with her head on Josie's knee, sucking her thumb, which she hadn't done for years, and idly watching television. The nightie was fleecy white cotton with a pattern of tiny rosebuds. It had long sleeves and a lacy frill at the neck. Josie had bought another at the same time, and they'd cost a mint. That would have kept me and Mam for a few months in Huskisson Street, she recalled thinking in Peter Jones.

She picked up the swathe of black silky hair that was spread like a fan over the blue dressing-gown. It lay like a rope in her hand. Laura gave a little bothered sigh, as if she were half-asleep with her mind on her missing daddy. It was nice to be in a position to buy anything she wanted for her daughter. Mam would have loved doing the same for her. She'd been thinking about Mam a lot over the last two days. Perhaps it was because the house seethed with the same sensation of dread she'd felt when she'd looked across the street and seen the ruins of the Prince Albert. She had known then that something terrible had happened. She had known life would never be the same again.

And life would never be the same if Jack was dead. She would miss him for ever. In the two days since he'd gone, her emotions kept changing by the minute – she loved him, she hated him, she would leave, no, she would stay. Just because *she* had never wanted to write, she reasoned, or paint, or act, or do anything creative, what right had she to judge someone who did? It was impossible for her to comprehend how Jack felt about his plays. When he came back, and he *had* to come back, she would make everything right again. Somehow.

'I love you, darling,' she whispered.

Laura wriggled on her knee. 'I know, Mummy.'

From outside, there came the sound they'd been waiting so long for, the harsh whine of the Austin Healey turning into Bingham Mews, the wheels muffled by the snow.

'Daddy!' Laura raised her head and stared, starry-eyed, at her mother. 'Daddy!'

'Not so fast, luv,' Josie cried when Laura leapt to her feet and raced out of the room. 'Wait till he stops,' she called, when she heard Laura's light footsteps running down the stairs. But the little door to the garage opened, and the car's engine roared, as if in relief at the end of a long journey and the sight of home. There was an unfamiliar bump then the engine was switched off, followed by a silence that went on too long, far, far too long.

Josie tiptoed downstairs, her hands clasped mutely against her breast. 'Please, God, you can't do this to me,' she whispered. 'Say something, Laura. *Please*, God, make Laura say something.'

The first thing she saw was Jack. He was getting out of the car, and his face was a mask of horror. 'I skidded on the snow,' he said in a voice she'd never heard before.

'Back up, back up,' Josie screamed when she saw the body of their daughter jammed between the front of the crookedly parked car and the breeze-block wall. Her head had fallen forward, lying sideways on the bonnet. Blue Bunny was still clutched in her hand, and she was smiling because Daddy had come home.

It was all over. Everything was over – the inquest, the funeral, their marriage. She couldn't live with Jack again. He had murdered their daughter, though the coroner had called it a tragic error which Jack would have to live with for the rest of his life. Only Josie knew that Laura had never run to meet her father like that before. It was only because Jack had disappeared for two whole days that she'd been so anxious to see him, to touch him, to be kissed and cuddled by her dad.

She didn't tell him this, because she loved him too much to cause more suffering. He had suffered enough. Perhaps he blamed her for not closing the garage door, for allowing the snow to drift in and make him skid. He didn't say anything, and neither did she. They hardly spoke to each other in the days that followed the death of their beloved only child.

Josie felt as if her body was a bloody open wound that would never heal. She was sore all over, and her head threatened to explode with unbearable grief. Sometimes it was impossible to believe that it had happened, *impossible*. She would go into Laura's room and expect to find her asleep in the white glossy bed or arranging her dolls in a row so that she could give them a lesson. But the room would be empty, the truth would assault her like a physical blow and she would double up, clutching her stomach, as the awareness sank in that she would never see her daughter again.

Their grief was suffered separately and alone. Josie slept in the spare room. During the day Jack remained in his study, the typewriter silent. He had shrunk inside his clothes, and they hung loosely on his rapidly thinning frame. She never glimpsed him without a drink in his hand, yet he appeared to be stone cold sober. She never asked, and he never said, where he'd been during the time he was away.

The house in Bingham Mews was put on the market to be sold fully furnished. They couldn't live there any more, it held too many bad memories. Jack was returning to New York, Josie to Liverpool. She would go first, and he would wait until the house found a buyer. People had already been to look round, and several had expressed interest.

'According to the estate agent, we'll make a profit.' Jack's thin lips quivered in what might have been a smile. 'It's worth thousands more than we paid. I'll finish off the mortgage and send you what's over.'

'I don't want a penny,' Josie said quickly. It would feel like blood money. That night she tore up the cheque-book for their joint account and threw it away. She had enough money in her bag for the fare to Liverpool. Once there, she'd start again on her own.

'As you wish,' Jack said dully.

Elsie Forrest was distraught. She had loved Laura deeply. 'I felt like her grandma,' she sobbed. 'As if she were partly mine.'

'She loved you, too.' There would be other children for Elsie to love, but not for her, Josie thought bitterly. Laura was her one and only child. She would never have another.

She was grateful Elsie was willing to clear the house of their possessions. 'What about the dishes, the cutlery, all your lovely ornaments and pictures?' Elsie wanted to know.

'I don't give a damn what happens to them,' Josie said listlessly. Her suitcase was already packed with a few clothes, a few photographs.

Charlotte had been a tower of strength. It was Charlotte who telephoned Mrs Kavanagh to relay the tragic news, because Josie couldn't possibly have done it.

'I can't begin to imagine how you must feel, my dear, dear Josie,' Mrs Kavanagh had written. 'Your friend said you're coming back to Liverpool. You know you're welcome to stay with us as long as you wish.'

It was her last day in Bingham Mews. The house had been sold. The final contract would be signed shortly. She said goodbye to Charlotte and promised to write, though she knew she never would. She made the same promise to Elsie, avoiding the woman's kind, worried eyes.

Jack was in his study when she went to bed. Tomorrow they would say goodbye for ever, and she wasn't sure if she could stand it. If only they'd stayed in New York. The 'if onlys' could go right back to the start of time. If only she hadn't worked for Louisa, she wouldn't have gone to America in the first place. If only she hadn't wanted to say goodbye to Tommy, then Mam wouldn't have been in the Prince Albert when the bomb struck.

'Comfort me,' Jack was saying in a muffled voice which was almost a sob. 'Comfort me, sweetheart. Say you forgive me. I already hate myself enough without knowing that you hate me, too.' He began to weep. 'I want to die, Josie. I want to *die*.'

At first Josie thought she was dreaming, that it was part of yet another nightmare, but when she opened her eyes Jack was kneeling beside the bed.

Without hesitation she put her arms around his neck and drew him to her. 'I don't hate you, Jack,' she whispered. 'I know you would never have done anything to hurt our darling Laura.'

'I adored her,' he wept.

'I know, luv.' She patted his back, as if he were a child. 'We both did.'

'I love you, sweetheart.' She had never heard such anguish in a voice before. 'Can't we try and get through this together? Come back with me to New York. *Please*, Josie.'

'No.' She shook her head implacably. It was easy to dispense forgiveness, but she would never cease to blame him for Laura's death. If he hadn't been so childish, so foolish, as to disappear, Laura would be fast asleep in her room now. 'I don't think it would work,' was all she said. Then she herself began to cry, and it was Jack's turn to comfort her, to take her in his arms, stroke her cheek and kiss her eyes and say that she was his lovely girl, his sweetheart, and he was sorry, so sorry, for the way he had behaved, because he loved her more than words could possibly say.

'Remember the night we met?' he said huskily.

'I'll never forget it, Jack.'

He kissed her, and she felt his lips quiver against her own. Incredibly, her body began to respond. Little hot darts of desire coursed through her veins, and she pressed herself against him, while all thoughts of everything fled from her brain, and all she wanted was for Jack to take her, swallow her up, so she would no longer exist.

There was something raw and uninhibited about the way they made love, something desperate and tragic, as if they were the only two people left in a world that was about to explode in one last almighty bang.

Afterwards, they clung to each other silently for a long while. Then Jack took her face in both hands and pressed a final kiss against her trembling lips. 'Goodbye, sweetheart. I won't be around when you leave in the morning.'

'Goodbye, Jack.'

Josie lay against the pillows and watched him leave. The door closed, and she slid under the bedclothes, sobbing uncontrollably. It was a long time before she fell into a restless, jerky sleep. At one point she woke up when she banged her arm against the wall, and a thought drifted through her head – Jack hadn't used anything when they'd made love. But she wasn't likely to conceive, not like that first time in his apartment. Her body felt barren, as juiceless and dead as the plants she'd pulled from Louisa's garden.

She looked at her watch. A quarter past six. This time tonight she would be in Liverpool. For good.

Princes Avenue
1960–1961

1

Josie had been back in Liverpool a week, living with the Kavanaghs, and had no idea what to do with herself. She felt as if her body had seized up, like pipes in winter. She couldn't read, she couldn't watch television and conversation was impossible. Lily came to see her, as did Daisy and Marigold. She could hear them speak, but the meaning went over her head.

She regretted her impulsive decision to tear up her cheque-book, because she had no money. When she telephoned the bank in London to ask for another, the joint account had been closed. Although Jack was the last person she wanted to talk to, she telephoned Bingham Mews, and was perversely disappointed when there was no reply. She called several more times over the next few days, and eventually Elsie Forrest answered.

'Jack's gone, dear.' Elsie's voice was husky with sadness. 'He signed the final contract the other day. I'm just giving the place a final going over. The new people move in tomorrow.'

He'd gone! Her heart turned over, and she knew she had made a terrible mistake. 'Did he leave an address?'

'No, dear. He didn't know where he would be living. He said it might not be New York. He mentioned California.'

'I see. Well, thank you, Elsie.' She rang off before Elsie could ask how she was, how was she feeling, how was she coping.

Everyone thought she was coping extraordinarily well. 'Gosh, I'd be devastated, me,' Lily had said. Or something like that. Only a tiny part of Josie's brain was working, the part that coped with getting dressed, getting washed, getting from one room to another, and now money.

It was ironic because last week she'd had hundreds of pounds at her disposal and now there was only a few pounds left. She was almost grateful to have something important to concentrate on. It meant she'd have to find a job and support herself, which had been her intention all along, she recalled.

'Are you sure it's not too soon, luv?' Mrs Kavanagh said cautiously when Josie brought up the subject of work.

'It will always be too soon, but I need to occupy me mind.'

The older woman looked dubious. 'You're not letting yourself grieve properly, Josie. I haven't heard you cry once. You need to let go, get everything out of your system. Once that's done, you'll find time will heal.'

'I daren't let go,' Josie said simply. 'I'd go mad if I did. I try to pretend it didn't happen. Not that Laura isn't dead, but that she never existed, that I never had her, that I never met Jack. It's seems the easiest way.'

'That won't work, luv. You'll have to grieve some time.'

'It's worked so far.'

She found a job with relative ease, with a builder, Spencer & Sons, in Toxteth, no distance from Huskisson Street where she'd lived with Mam. They wanted someone straight away.

'The missus usually looks after the paperwork.' Sid Spencer had interviewed her in the office, a wooden shed in the corner of the yard where the materials were kept. He was fiftyish, with a tough, kind, weatherbeaten face and an expansive grey moustache. She liked him immediately. 'But now all three of me lads are in with me, and work's growing all the time. Chrissie gets herself in a right ould tizzy. She can only type with two fingers, and me books are in a terrible mess. I don't know what's been paid, or what hasn't, or if a bill was sent out in the first place.' He indicated the desk, piled high with pieces of paper. 'Nothing's been filed for months.'

'I'll sort things out for you.' She welcomed something she could concentrate all her attention on. The typewriter was a Remington, relatively modern, and there was a two-bar electric fire and an electric kettle. The shed was warm and cosy, and she could make tea whenever she felt like it. It was far better than a carpeted office, an officious boss breathing down her neck, other women who'd want to talk.

Sid coughed, embarrassed. 'I wasn't expecting someone as posh as you after the job, luv. You look like the secretary to a millionaire. I'm afraid the lavvy's outside. There's only the one, and it's in a disgusting state. I'll get one of the lads to clean it up and put a bolt on the inside.'

'I just want a job, any job,' Josie said quietly. 'And the pay's good.' She probably looked overdressed in the only coat she'd brought with her – camel with a fur collar, which she'd got in the Kings Road, and brown suede boots. Her handbag had cost more than she would be earning in a week.

'Well, if something comes up in a nice, plush office, I'll understand if you leave, luv.'

'I won't leave.'

She put her mind and all her energy into the new job: made new files, giving one to each of the jobs in hand; typed orders, quotations, invoices, the occasional letter, and dealt with calls from customers, mainly wanting to know why someone hadn't turned up as faithfully promised to instal a new bathroom or lay a new floor, or when on earth they would finish the extension started weeks ago – there'd been so sign of a bloody workman in days.

Sorting through the papers, trying to tie quotations to invoices to payments received, Josie discovered that Sid was owed over five hundred pounds. 'And you paid the builders merchants twice for those sheets of plywood you ordered last November.'

Sid was thrilled. 'That's enough to pay your wages for over a year. You're worth your weight in gold, Josie, luv.' He looked at her respectfully. Josie sometimes felt like the employer, not the employee. His three curly-haired sons, Colin, Terry and Little Sid, called her 'miss'.

Chrissie Spencer came to inspect the paragon of a secretary her husband had hired. It was during Josie's second week, just before dinner time. She was a glamorous woman with dyed blonde hair and a good-natured face, wearing a beaver lamb coat over a smart tweed costume. 'I got done up in me bezzie clothes, so's not to feel at a disadvantage, like,' she grinned. 'Sid ses you turn up looking like a fashion model every day. All he does is go on and on about you. Every time he ses "Josie", I want to scream. D'you fancy a cup of tea, luv? It's bitter outside.'

'I've already had five this morning, but I wouldn't mind another.'

'And where's Mr Coltrane?' Chrissie asked.

'In America. We're separated.'

'Really!' She looked over her shoulder, eyebrows raised. 'You were married to a Yank?'

Josie nodded, dreading that the next question would be about children because she didn't know how to answer. Instead, Chrissie asked, 'D'you take sugar, luv?'

'No, ta.'

She brought the tea. 'Here you are, luv, a nice hot cuppa. Where is it you're living? Sid said you're staying with friends.'

'Childwall, but I'm looking for a place of me own.' She yearned to be alone, ached for it. The Kavanaghs couldn't possibly have been nicer or more sympathetic, but she felt in the way. They turned off the television if something funny was on, and Marigold hadn't brought her children round once since Josie had come to stay. Lily's pregnancy was never mentioned. Everyone was treading on eggshells, all because of her. Josie felt as if she'd cast a blight on their normally happy, easygoing life.

And she wanted to be alone for her own sake, so she wouldn't have to put up a front. She could look as miserable as she felt, get up in the middle of the night, *do* things, make tea when she couldn't sleep, which was most nights, rather than creep around, worried she'd wake someone up.

'You should ask Sid, luv,' Chrissie said helpfully. 'He's just done up this great big house in Princes Avenue for some property company, turned it into flats, like. You never know, one of 'em might do you.'

'I'll ask Sid next time I see him.'

Sid had a key to the house in Princes Avenue. 'Have a look round, luv, it's only five minutes' walk. It's empty, I've still got bits and bobs to do. I'd take you meself, but if I don't get on with Mrs Ancram's kitchen, she'll do her bloody nut.'

Josie went at dinner time. Princes Avenue was wide and stately, with a line of trees running down the centre. Like Huskisson Street, the houses had been owned by the Liverpool wealthy – importers and exporters, owners of shipping companies and factories. Josie could tell by the different curtains on each floor that most had now been turned into flats.

The house she was looking for was dark red brick, semi-detached, huge, with a wild, overgrown garden that showed signs of once having been carefully cultivated. The massive front door was freshly painted black, with three stained-glass panels in the upper half. There was a row of bells, seven altogether, she counted, with a little blank space beside each for a name. She found the lock stiff and awkward when she tried to turn the key. Once inside, she slipped the latch in case she couldn't get out. Although the February day was dull, the hall and the wide, elegant staircase were speckled with vivid spots of colour from the stained glass. The woodwork was cream, the walls a pale coffee colour. Sid had said the owners intended to carpet the communal areas. 'It won't be let to riff-raff,' he'd said. 'You're just the sort they want. I'll put in a word if you're interested.'

There were doors left and right. Josie opened the one on the right. The flat consisted of two immense rooms, a small kitchen and bathroom. The one opposite was identical. Sid had left the original fireplaces and painted the elaborately moulded ceilings white. On the first and second floors the rooms were just as large, the fireplaces and windows smaller. The walls were the same pale coffee colour as the hall, the woodwork cream.

Her footsteps echoed eerily through the empty, unfurnished rooms, and the higher she went the narrower the stairs became. Steep steps, no wider than a ladder, led to the third floor and a doll's-house door which she had to stoop to get through, to discover an attic that had been given an entirely new floor and dormer window at the back.

'This is for me.' Josie surveyed the long room that ran the length of the house. The peaked ceiling sloped down to walls no more than four feet high. 'I bet this is the cheapest,' she said aloud. There were kitchen units, a cooker and a sink at the front end, and a small square portion had been sectioned off with hardboard at the back. She opened the door and found a shower room, with a lavatory and small sink.

'It wouldn't need a carpet, just a few cheap rugs. I could get a bed and a settee on hire purchase.' She closed her eyes and tried to imagine the room furnished, but felt herself go dizzy. Perhaps it was the empty house, the silence, the echoes, or that she was alone, properly alone, for the first time since she'd come back to Liverpool, but her brain suddenly went into free fall, as if she were in a lift in a New York skyscraper and the mechanism no longer worked. Downwards, downwards, she zoomed, until she could no longer stand. She fell down on all fours. There was an explosion in her brain, and Josie went completely insane.

Laura was dead, Jack had gone!

Josie screamed. Why should she care where she lived when ahead there was only a living death because she had lost her husband and her child? She screamed and beat the floor with her fists. 'Laura, come back!' she groaned, and raised her arms skywards, as if God had the power to restore her daughter to her arms. She beat the floor again when Laura didn't come, because she was dead, and Josie had been at the funeral and seen with her own eyes the tiny coffin being lowered into the ground, leaving her with no reason to go on living. She cursed God, using words, foul words, that had never crossed her lips before, for being so cruel as to have first taken Mam, and now Laura.

Suddenly there were arms around her, and a soft, vaguely familiar voice was murmuring, 'Let it all go, luv. That's right, let it all go. Cry all you like. I'm here now.' Josie pressed herself against the unknown breast and sobbed until her heart felt as if it were breaking, and the voice kept murmuring, 'There, there, luv. Cry all day if you want. It'll do you good. There, there.'

Her chest and ribs were sore, and still Josie cried, while the soft voice continued to make soothing little noises. A hand lightly stroked her hair. Eventually, when she could cry no more, because she felt completely dry, empty, Josie stopped. She was exhausted and, for the first time in weeks, longed for sleep. If a bed had been available, she was sure she could have slept peacefully for hours.

'Better now?' enquired the voice.

Josie realised she was still clinging to the owner of the voice, and that she had no idea who it was. She moved away from the strange arms, and found herself staring into the soft gentle eyes and serene face of Daisy Kavanagh, looking like a Christmas card in white fur earmuffs and a fluffy scarlet coat. She stroked Josie's swollen, tear-stained face. 'Better now, Josie, luv?'

'I don't know,' Josie croaked. 'How did you get in?'

'You left the door unlatched. I called in the yard to invite you to lunch, it's me half-day off, see. A very nice young man told me where you'd be, so I decided to keep you company, like.' She smiled sweetly. 'Mind you, I thought you were being murdered when I first came in.'

'I'm sorry if I gave you a fright.' She felt embarrassed that her outburst had been witnessed, even if it had been by Daisy Kavanagh, so kind and understanding. 'You always seem to be around when I'm in a state.'

'It's only been the twice, luv.' They were sitting cross-legged on the floor now, facing each other in the big empty room. Daisy took both Josie's hands in hers. 'It'll have done you good to get if off your chest, well, some of it. I don't doubt you'll cry again.' She glanced around the room. 'It's nice here. Are you going to take it?'

With an effort Josie switched her mind from the tragedy of the past to the practicality of the present, which had perhaps been Daisy's intention. She sighed. 'If I can afford the rent. I'll need all sorts of furniture.'

'We've got bits of stuff in Machin Street you can have. Eunice is always saying the place is over-furnished.'

'Ta.'

Daisy released her hands and scrambled to her feet. 'Lunch is still on offer, Jose. My treat. We'll go somewhere with a licence so you can have a drink. I reckon a double whisky would do you the world of good.'

Sid Spencer contacted the company that owned the house in Princes Avenue to ask about the rent for the top-floor flat. It was just within Josie's means. 'They're being dead official. You can move in the first of March, but you have to sign a year's lease.'

'That's all right,' Josie said easily.

'It means you can go home for your dinner.' He regarded her with a fatherly eye. 'I don't like the idea of you sitting in this place all day without a break.'

'It's too cold for a walk, and too far to get to Childwall.'

'I know. Princes Avenue is just right.' He looked pleased.

Mrs Kavanagh understood completely that Josie would prefer to be on her own. She came with Lily to see the flat the day the stair carpets were being laid. Josie had signed the lease the day before.

Lily was five months pregnant and beginning to show. She was wearing a voluminous maternity frock, as if she wanted the whole world to know she was expecting. 'It's very pleasant,' she conceded, walking the length of the room, jutting out her stomach as far as it would go, 'but you can't compare it to a house. There's no privacy.'

'Honestly, Lily!' Her mother rolled her eyes impatiently. 'I sometimes wonder if you're dead from the neck up.'

'I don't need privacy, do I?' Josie said with a wry smile. 'I'll be living on me own.'

'It'd be a job lugging a baby up them narrow stairs.'

'*Lily!*' Mrs Kavanagh snapped.

'I meant when I bring Troy to see Josie, that's all.' Lily patted her stomach and looked hurt. 'Can I christen the lavatory, Jose? I'm aching to go.'

'Of course.'

The door to the lavatory closed. Josie looked out of the small window at the front. It was strange, but the other side of Princes Avenue was called Princes Road. She wondered if the postman ever got confused.

'Lily doesn't mean anything, luv, but she was back of the queue when the good Lord handed out tact.'

'I don't take any notice.' The hairs were tingling on Josie's neck. It was the mention of lugging a baby up the stairs that had done it, made something click in her weary brain. She'd been too wrapped up in misery to notice that she hadn't had a period since December, and she knew, more surely than she had ever known anything before, that she was pregnant. It had happened on the last night with Jack, just as Laura had been conceived on the first. Her body shuddered with revulsion. She didn't want this child.

2

'Daisy,' Josie cried hysterically. 'Oh, Daise, hold me hand, there's another contraction coming.'

'There, luv.' Daisy gripped her hand. 'It'll soon pass. It'll soon be all over and done with.'

'I didn't have pains like this when I was having Laura.' Josie gasped as the contraction mounted and swelled, reaching a pitch that was barely tolerable, before gradually fading. She tried to relax, impossible when she was dreading the next pain, knowing it would be worse.

'You didn't have backache with Laura either,' Daisy said in her light, sweet voice. She looked coolly beautiful in a sage green costume and tiny matching hat. 'Or veins in your legs, or swollen feet. Having Laura was as easy as pie, or so you keep saying, but all babies are different, Josie, before they're born and after.'

'Your Lily's terrified of having another baby.' It helped to fill the gaps between the pains with conversation. 'She was going to show everyone how easy it was. Instead, she yelled her head off when the time came.'

'I know, Jose. I was there, unfortunately. It was dead embarrassing. Not only that, she was outraged when Samantha appeared and it should have been Troy. We all thought she was going to tell the midwife there'd been a mistake. Neil was delighted, but he's delighted with everything Lily does.'

'I hope I have a boy, Daise.'

'I know, luv.' Daisy stroked her brow.

It was ten past two in the morning, and they were in Liverpool Maternity Hospital, in a side ward. The main light was off, and a small lamp with a green shade gave off a ghostly glow, making the room, with its cream and green walls and green window-blind, seem dismal and depressing.

The contractions had started six hours ago, eight days before the baby was due. Josie was lying on the settee, reading, when it gave the first sign it was on its way, a very strong sign, but this was only the beginning – the contractions could go on for hours. She made tea and tried to drink it calmly, pretending to admire how the late evening sunshine added a light golden lustre to the attic room, lingering on the pale coffee walls, turning the vase of plastic sunflowers on the table into yellow flames.

The table, like everything except the bed, was second hand, other people's cast-offs. Nothing matched – the chintz-covered settee clashed with the curtains, which clashed with the faded patchwork quilt – but the room looked pretty, almost striking, with the addition of loads of plastic flowers and statues bought for coppers which she'd painted bright red. She'd had more satisfaction from making the room look nice than she'd had from furnishing Bingham Mews when money had been no object, though she often thought wistfully about the television that had been left behind, as well as the twin-tub washing machine and the steam iron. She could have really done with those things now.

The cot beside the bed she would have sooner done without. The white-painted bars made her think of a prison – for herself, not the baby it would shortly hold.

Another contraction started. She gasped and looked at her watch – twenty minutes since the first one. Adding a hairbrush and some make-up to the suitcase that had been packed for days, she caught a bus to the hospital. She was still pretending to be calm. The pregnancy hadn't been easy, and she was glad the time had come. Working for Sid, which she'd done almost to the end, had helped to occupy her mind.

When she reached the hospital she phoned Daisie Kavanagh. Eunice answered and said Daisy was round at Childwall and she would phone her there.

'Don't tell Mrs Kavanagh, will you? Daisy's the one I want. She knows why.'

'I understand, luv. She'll be along in a flash.'

Eunice wished her good luck. Josie hoped she hadn't sounded rude but, much to the chagrin of Lily who regarded it as a betrayal of friendship, she'd grown close to Daisy over the last few months. She was the only person who knew how unwelcome the baby was. Everyone else regarded it as a miracle, a replacement sent by God for her darling Laura, when Josie regarded it as a trespasser, an intruder in her life. It wouldn't be so bad if it was a boy, but a girl ...

Daisy didn't judge her harsh, muddled emotions, didn't criticise, just seemed to understand.

A nurse popped her head around the door. 'How's she doing?'

'I don't think it will be long now,' Daisy said.

The door closed, busy footsteps sounded in the corridor, babies cried, there was a muffled scream. Someone else was going through the ordeal of giving birth.

'Don't ever have a baby, Daisy,' Josie groaned.

'I nearly did, once.' The soft lips twitched in amusement at the sight of Josie's shocked, astonished face.

'When?' Josie briefly forgot her own discomfiture. 'How? What do you mean by nearly?'

'I had a miscarriage,' Daisy said placidly. 'The father's name was Ralph. He was an assistant librarian where I worked. I knew he had a wife, but I was too much in love to care. I was only twenty, and I suppose you could say he seduced me. I believed him when he swore he loved me. I thought we'd get married one day. I didn't care if it wouldn't be a church wedding because Catholics aren't allowed to marry divorcees.'

'What happened?' It was hard to imagine tranquil Daisy Kavanagh being passionately in love, having sex with a married man.

Daisy smiled a touch sardonically. 'Oh, he dropped me like a hot brick when he discovered I was pregnant. It turned out I was just a girl in a whole line of girls.' Her grip on Josie's hand tightened slightly. 'His poor wife was going out of her mind. She came round to Machin Street to have it out with me. Fortunately, it was the time Ma and Da were moving to Childwall so they were round at the new house. *Un*fortunately, perhaps it was the shock of being jilted, the shock of the wife turning up, but I suddenly had these dreadful pains, just like you're having now, Jose, and my dear little baby was flushed down the lavatory.'

'You mean, while the wife was there?' Josie gasped. There was another muffled scream from outside, followed by a sharp, triumphant shout, then a baby's angry wail.

'Yes, but she was a brick. She held me in her arms, comforted me, and we called the father every name under the sun.'

'I can't imagine you calling anyone names.'

'Still waters run deep, Jose.' Daisy gave an enigmatic smile. 'Me and Eunice spent many a happy hour planning Ralph's murder, but we were too scared of being caught so we gave up on the idea.'

'Eunice! You mean . . .'

'Yes, I mean Eunice. When the family moved, I stayed in Machin Street and Eunice left Ralph and came to live with me.' She chuckled. 'I know some people, our Lily for one, think there's something odd about it – well, I suppose there is, but it's not what they think. Anyroad, Jose, you are now privy to one of the best kept secrets in the world, and I trust you'll keep it to yourself. I only told you so you'd know how much I'd like to be in your shoes at the moment.'

'Oh, Daisy!' Josie was about to say something else, but another contraction started that seemed to go on for ever, and Daisy called the nurse.

The midwife was black, brusque and efficient. 'It's a girl,' she announced, holding up an ugly, red, baby-shaped object for Josie to see. 'What are you going to call her?'

'I don't know.' Josie ached all over and wanted to be sick. She had intended to call it Liam if it was a boy, but couldn't bring herself to consider girls' names. 'What's your name?'

The midwife frowned unbelievingly. 'Dinah.'

'Then Dinah it is.'

'Me mother's called Shelomith. I bet you wouldn't have latched on to that quite so quick.'

'Oh, I don't know.' Josie closed her eyes. 'I really don't care.'

She had loads of visitors, so different from when she'd had Laura and there'd only been Jack. Mr and Mrs Kavanagh, Marigold and a moidered and extremely cross Lily, who complained that Neil wasn't doing his share with the new baby. She had to get up and feed Samantha twice a night.

'Are you still breast-feeding?' Josie asked.

'Of course I am. Mother's milk is best for baby.' Lily spoke as if she was quoting from a book.

'Then what on earth do you expect Neil to do – grow breasts?'

'He could at least wake up and *talk* to me.'

Chrissie and Sid Spencer arrived with flowers, and presents from Colin, Terry and Little Sid. Daisy came every night. Charlotte Ward-Pierce had kept the Kavanaghs' telephone number, and had called months ago to see how Josie was when she didn't write. Mrs Kavanagh must have rung to tell her about Dinah, because there were cards from her and Neville, and Elsie Forrest.

'I'm so happy for you, Josie,' Elsie wrote. 'It's a miracle, another little daughter, and so soon. How I wish that I could see her. Does Jack know? Has he been in touch?'

Jack knew where the Kavanaghs lived. He could easily have got in touch. But he hadn't. He would never know he had a new daughter, and she wondered how he would feel if he did. She thought about him more than usual the day Elsie's card arrived. The time in New York, the years in Cypress Terrace and Bingham Mews seemed to belong to a different world altogether from the one she lived in now, but she still longed to see him.

The evening visitors poured into the ward, the new fathers stiffly formal in their best suits, a few awkwardly bearing flowers. Josie's attention was drawn to one man who stood out from the rest. He wore a trenchcoat with the belt tightly buckled, and a black trilby perched precariously on the back of his head. He was chewing gum, and his hands were stuffed mutinously in his pockets, as if he wouldn't be seen dead carrying flowers or a bag of fruit. She thought he looked vaguely familiar. Their eyes met when he passed the foot of her bed and they stared at each other. Then the man grinned broadly, and said out of the corner of his mouth, 'Well, if it isn't Josie Flynn!'

'Francie O'Leary!'

He came and sat on the edge of the bed, which was strictly forbidden. Visitors were supposed to use the chairs. 'What are you doing here, luv?'

'What do you think? It's a maternity hospital, Francie.' He was still the handsome rat she remembered from the Saturdays when they'd sorted out the world over a cup of coffee, and she was really pleased to see him. He carried with him the aura of that carefree time when she'd got on well with Aunt Ivy and was going to marry Ben.

He seemed equally pleased to see her. 'Someone told me you lived in America, or was it London?'

'Both, but now I'm back in Liverpool for good.'

'You've had a baby?'

Josie smiled. 'They wouldn't have let me in if I hadn't.'

To her surprise, he picked up her hand and kissed it. 'Congratulations, Jose. Where's the proud father? He's a writer, isn't he?'

'Yes. He's back in America. It ...' She shrugged. 'It didn't work out. What about you? Are congratulations due?'

His small eyes widened in amusement. 'Jaysus, no, luv. I'm not married. It's our Pauline who's had the baby. She's over there with me Mam and the doting husband.' He winked. 'I'll get an ear-bashing for not fetching in a bunch of grapes.'

'Are you still working in the same place?' she asked conversationally, reluctant to let him go. He'd worked as a clerk for a shipping company on the Dock Road.

He took out his wallet, removed a business card and held it in front of her eyes. 'Francis M. O'Leary, Printer', she read, followed by his address and telephone number. 'Wedding Invitations, Tickets, Letterheads, Business Cards, etc.'

'What does the "M" stand for?' she asked.

'Money, girl,' Francie said with a wicked grin. 'I thought, seeing as we live in a capitalist society, I may as well be a fully paid up member. It means *I* get the benefit of me hard graft, not some cruddy employer. I put the printing machine in the bedroom after our Pauline and Sandra left home. Not doing bad for meself either.'

Daisy had arrived, along with Mrs Kavanagh, who fortunately didn't remember this was the man who had nearly sent her youngest daughter to a convent. Before he left, Francie said nonchalantly that if Josie would like to give him her address, he'd drop in sometimes, and she said she was already looking forward to it.

Mrs Kavanagh wanted to know how Dinah was getting on now that she was five days old.

'Fine.' Josie didn't haunt the nursery like the other mothers, looking through the glass to reassure themselves that *their* baby wasn't crying. Nor did she welcome having the child thrust at her several times a day to breast-feed. She felt no connection, no relationship, to the tiny, pale, fair-haired infant, almost two pounds lighter than Laura, who bore no resemblance to either her mother or her father. In another five days she would be sent home with a baby she still didn't want.

Spencer & Sons were doing their best to hang on to the typist whom Sid claimed kept the firm afloat. Josie said he was being ridiculous – there were dozens of typists around, as good as her or better – though she appreciated a pile of invoices or estimates arriving via Chrissie or one of the lads which she would type on the machine that now stood on her table, something that would never have happened with the insurance company she'd worked for, or Ashbury Buxton in Chelsea. Not many women with a newly born baby were in a position to earn a wage, but she flatly refused to accept the amount she'd had before. 'It's too much. You'll have to pay someone to be in the office and answer the phone.'

Chrissie claimed she missed the office, but not the typewriter. 'I didn't mind answering the phone. It gave me something to do while Sid and the lads were at work.'

Everyone agreed on two pounds less a week, and everyone was happy.

Dinah was a fractious baby. She cried if she was wet, if she was dry, if she was hungry, if she was full. She cried for no reason at all as far as her anxious mother could see. Josie nursed her, cursed her and poured gripe water down her throat, because Daisy had consulted a book in the library which suggested she might have three-month colic. If so, it would stop in another five or six weeks.

'I don't think I can stand another week,' Josie groaned, 'let alone five or six. Laura hardly cried at all.'

'That was Laura, this is Dinah,' Daisy said patiently. 'She's such a sweet little thing, so pretty.' She toyed with the white fingers which quickly curled around her own. Dinah gave a little shuddering breath and fell asleep in her arms.

'You seem to have a knack with her.'

Daisy looked Josie full in the face. 'She knows I love her, that's all.' She turned her gentle gaze to the baby. 'I don't half wish she were mine.'

Josie turned away, ashamed. She didn't love her daughter, and doubted if she ever would. Perhaps that's why Dinah cried so much. It wasn't gripe water she needed, but her mother's love.

She'd been half expecting someone to complain about the noise. 'I know it can't be helped, dear,' the smart, middle-aged woman who lived in one of the flats below said when she came upstairs to point out that neither she nor her husband had had a wink of sleep the night before. 'All babies cry, though yours seems to be a champion. We were wondering if you intended to stay, renew your lease. If so, we thought we'd look for somewhere else because I dread to think what it'll be like when she starts teething, and that can go on for months.'

'I *am* moving,' Josie said tiredly. She hadn't had a wink of sleep either, and the woman had woken up Dinah, who'd started to cry, just as she was attempting to get on with some typing. 'I'm looking for a house. Until then, I'm afraid you're going to have to put up with me and me baby. Tara.'

She closed the door, without mentioning she'd had a letter from the agent who managed the property informing her that the lease strictly forbade children under sixteen and, while he wouldn't evict a mother and baby, he'd had several complaints, and would be obliged if she would find somewhere else as soon as possible.

Josie would have moved the next day had she been able to find a house, where the neighbours could complain until they were blue in the face about a crying baby but there was nothing they could do, and she would have a proper kitchen and hang the nappies out to dry. As things were, she was spending a small fortune in the launderette. And Lily had been right about the stairs. Coming up wasn't so bad, but going down was treacherous. She had to take Dinah all the way to the bottom floor, put her in the pram which she kept in the hall – no doubt someone had complained about *that*, too – then go all the way back for the washing or her shopping bag. Coming home, she did the same thing in reverse. It was worse than Cypress Terrace in a way. Although this room was incomparably nicer, in London Jack had been writing, and there'd been a *point* to all the inconvenience they'd had to put up with.

Francie O'Leary had taken to dropping in at least once a week. He arrived that night with a bottle of wine and cheered her up somewhat. She switched off the light in favour of the white shaded lamp, which made the room look smaller and more cosy. It was raining outside, and a blustery wind kept throwing the rain against the windows. The glass creaked and squeaked in protest. Dinah was fast asleep in the shadows at the other end, and Josie prayed she'd stay that way.

Francie still found it incredible that there was a man alive who had been willing to marry Lily Kavanagh. 'Does she hang him on a crucifix at night to sleep?'

'No.' Josie giggled.

'I visualise him with an arrow through his chest, like a martyr.'

'Don't be silly.' She sipped the wine. Francie always made her feel young again. He reminded her there was a world outside that could be fun. 'Neil's a perfectly nice, normal young man. He loves Lily to death.'

He grinned. 'That's appropriate. The poor guy signed his death warrant when he married her. She'll nag him into the grave in no time. Eh, what about Ben? I understand he got hitched to a cracking-looking girl. I can't remember her name.'

'Imelda. They've got two children, a boy and a girl.' She hadn't seen Ben since Lily's wedding, since which time things had got worse. Lily said that Imelda was completely unstable, regularly threatening suicide. She was on tablets for her nerves.

'I liked Ben, he was a nice guy. I wouldn't mind getting in touch with him. Have you got his address?'

'No, but I can get it for you. I think he'd appreciate that, Francie.' She wrinkled her nose. 'He's not very happy.'

'Marriage!' Francie snorted. 'I wouldn't get married if they paid me, not even if it were Marilyn Monroe on offer. *Especially* if it were Marilyn

Monroe. She's already on her third husband. Marriage is an unnatural state. How can people be expected to get on with each other for a whole lifetime? It'd be okay if you could change partners every few years.'

'So you're going to remain a bachelor gay?' Dinah made a noise, a little hiccup, and Josie turned to watch the cot, praying the bedclothes wouldn't move, indicating that the baby had woken up, hungry for a meal, and poor Francie would have to be surrendered to the rain, which was coming down in buckets, while she breast-fed. She was enjoying their conversation.

'I'd sooner be a bachelor-dead-miserable than be married,' Francie said with an elaborate shudder. 'Talking of Marilyn Monroe, *Some Like It Hot* is on at the Forum. Let's go one night. I've been told it's the gear.'

'Go to the pictures?' Josie looked at him, astounded.

'People do it all the time,' he said airily. 'It's quite a common practice. Some people even do it two or three times a week. In fact, I've known *you* go to the pictures before now, Josie, so don't look so surprised. I distinctly remember you were there when I saw *Samson and Delilah*.'

'You spoiled it,' she pouted. 'It's just that I can't imagine doing anything *normal*, like going to the pictures, for years.' She couldn't imagine reading a book, painting her nails or going shopping for anything that wasn't to do with babies.

'Get someone to babysit, and we'll go next week.'

She'd drunk too much wine, but it was a pleasant, hazy feeling, relaxing. Francie had managed to make her feel vaguely happy. Before getting into bed, she fed Dinah, rubbed her back and raised a satisfactory burp, then changed her nappy. 'Now, look here,' she said sternly. 'Mummy feels exceptionally tired tonight, and she's a little bit drunk, too, so I'd appreciate a good night's sleep, if you don't mind.'

Dinah was an unresponsive child. She didn't gurgle or wave her arms, as Laura used to, but regarded her mother coolly when she was put in the cot. Josie climbed into bed and immediately fell asleep.

It was still dark when she woke up and, apart from the rain which had become a deluge, the room was silent. But she knew what was about to happen. After a few minutes there was a little cry, like a kitten's mewl, followed by another, slightly more urgent. It was as if her brain was connected to her child's, and it recognised when she had awoken and was about to cry.

Josie groaned. She'd been having a lovely sleep, the bed felt exceptionally comfortable and she would have given anything on earth to stay under the warm covers, particularly on such a stormy night.

The cries rose in volume, and she could barely drag her lethargic body out of bed. She swayed dizzily, staggered to the cot, picked up Dinah and carried her back to bed. Halfway through the feed she fell asleep, and woke up to find an irritable Dinah sucking at an empty breast. She transferred her to the other breast, and managed to stay awake until the baby had had her fill. The rain thundered on the roof, and she could have sworn she could hear the slates move.

Josie sighed. She always found these dead-of-night feeds lonely and depressing, sorely missing Jack's warm presence in bed beside her, reminding her that she shouldn't have let him go, not for ever. But she'd been in such a state, sick with grief over Laura. Why, she thought fretfully, hadn't Jack understood she wasn't herself when she said she didn't want to see him again? But he had been sick with grief and guilt himself. The best plan would have been to part for a while, see how she felt, how he felt, in a few months. She considered putting an advert in a newspaper, asking him to contact her, but there were probably hundreds of papers in California, and he might not even be there. Like the time he had disappeared for two days, he could be anywhere. Anyroad, if he wanted to see her again, *he* was in a position to contact *her*.

'I'll burp you and change your nappy in a minute,' she muttered tiredly, leaving Dinah in the bed and covering her with the eiderdown while she went to get a drink of water. It must be the wine – her mouth felt like the bottom of a birdcage.

She drank two glasses thirstily, but on the way back from the sink she felt dizzy again and had to sit on the settee.

It was the slamming of a door that woke her, voices on the stairs. The rain had stopped. Cold December sunshine glimmered through the curtains, and Josie, waking up on the settee, remembered *she'd left Dinah in the bed.*

She might have choked on her vomit, smothered under the eiderdown. Terror gripped Josie like an icy fist. 'No!' she screamed. '*No!*' Somehow she got to the other end of the room. The bottom half of the baby's face was covered with the eiderdown. Josie snatched it away. Dinah lay completely still, eyes closed, very pale.

'*Dinah!*' The tiny body felt cold when she picked it up. She pressed her daughter against her breast, her cheek against the pale one. Dinah stirred and uttered a little sigh, the most welcome sound Josie had ever heard. 'Dinah, oh, darling, I thought you were dead.' She sat on the bed and rocked to and fro, her child clutched in her arms. 'I love you, darling. Mummy loves you more than words can say.' She was trembling, and rocking like a mad woman. 'I love you, I love you,' she said in a hoarse, shaky voice, over and over again.

She moved her arm so that they faced each other, and her eyes met the light blue, almost lavender-coloured eyes of her daughter. There was something about her mouth she'd never noticed before, something determinedly serious, almost wilful, about the small pink lips. 'You're going to be a little madam when you grow up,' Josie said, and could have sworn that Dinah smiled.

'It was bound to happen some time, Jose,' Daisy said that night. 'Having Dinah happened too soon, while you were still grieving for Laura. If the circumstances had been different, it would have been best to wait a year or so before you had another child.'

'I'll never stop grieving for Laura,' Josie said quickly. 'Dinah's just blunted the edges a bit, that's all.'

'I know, luv. But it's not as intense as it used to be, I'll bet. I didn't want to go on living when Ralph jilted me and I lost me baby in the space of a few weeks. It took a while before I realised the world hadn't ended, that life was still there to be lived and I could still enjoy meself, as it were. The world would be a miserable place, Josie, if everyone gave up the ghost when someone dear to them died.'

'I feel terrible.' Josie glanced at the cot, where Dinah was peacefully sleeping. 'I hope she doesn't grow up with the feeling I don't properly love her.'

'You've always loved her, Josie. It just took a while for it to sink in, that's all.'

The sun continued to shine the next day. It was shining at one'clock when Josie's doorbell rang. She hoped it was Lily with Samantha, and they could take the babies for a walk in Princes Park.

A strange, elderly woman was standing on the step. She wore a fur coat and too much jewellery, and her stiffly permed hair was the colour of iron. She's pressed the wrong bell, Josie thought. It's someone else she wants.

'Hello, Josie,' the woman said, however, and there was something terribly sad, terribly lost about the dark eyes in the yellow face when Josie's face showed no sign of recognition.

'I'm afraid—' Josie began, but the woman interrupted with, 'It's Ivy, luv.'

Her last contact with Aunt Ivy had been in the holiday camp, when she'd sent a note more or less telling her to get lost. What was she supposed to say? How was she supposed to act? 'Hello,' she said stiffly. After a long pause, when Aunt Ivy showed no sign of going away, she muttered, 'You'd better come in.'

It was horrible, really horrible, watching the blunt yellow fingers pick up Dinah from the cot and Aunt Ivy stroke the pale cheeks of her great-niece. 'I think that's what she is. And I'm her great-aunt.' Josie prayed Dinah would cry, so she'd have an excuse to snatch her away, but Dinah sat uncomplainingly on Aunt Ivy's knee, letting the horrible woman maul her.

'She's the image of me mam.' Ivy looked up, beaming. 'There's a wedding photo on the mantelpiece in the parlour. Do you remember, luv? I'll bring it round next time I come,' she said when Josie shook her head.

She intended coming again! Not if I can help it, Josie vowed. She wouldn't let her in. No way did she want Aunt Ivy back in her life, the woman who had betrayed her own sister, then her sister's child.

Aunt Ivy sighed. She gently put Dinah in her cot, and glanced at Josie. 'I'm not exactly welcome, am I, luv?'

Josie didn't answer. Aunt Ivy sighed again, and there was that same sad, lost look in her eyes. 'I don't blame you. I let you down more than once.

Trouble with me, I've never been much of a judge of character. I turn the good people away, and welcome the bad ones with open arms.'

Still Josie didn't answer. What else could she do but agree?

'Do you mind if I take me coat off, luv? It's hot in here.'

'Of course not.' She mustered every charitable bone in her body and said, 'Would you like a cup of tea?' Anyroad, she longed for one herself.

'I'd love one.' Aunt Ivy removed her coat and came and sat on the settee. She glanced around the room. 'It's nice, this place, but a bit cramped for a baby.'

'I signed the lease before I realised I was pregnant, didn't I?' Josie said shortly. 'I'm looking for a house.'

'Daisy Kavanagh said you'd been given notice to quit.'

'Yes.'

Aunt Ivy raised her yellow hands for the tea. Josie took hers to the table and sat on a wooden chair. Her aunt looked at her almost slyly. Josie remembered the look well from her first years in Machin Street, and her stomach curled again. 'I can help with the house,' Ivy said. Her voice was surprisingly timid.

'You know where there's one to let?' Her spirits rose. 'I can only afford a dead cheap place.'

'No, but there's plenty around that you can buy.'

'Oh, yeah.' She made no effort to keep the sarcasm out of her voice.

'I said I can help.' Aunt Ivy put her tea on the floor and reached for her handbag. 'I've just been to the bank. I told the manager weeks ago that I wanted to take everything out. You've got to give notice with long-term investments – they don't just hand the cash over at the drop of a hat.' She reached into the bag, drew out a cheque and handed it to Josie. 'This is for you and Dinah.'

Josie ignored the cheque. It was pathetic. Ivy was trying to buy her way back into her affections, not that she'd ever truly been there. But Aunt Ivy had always been pathetic. 'I don't want your money, thanks all the same.'

'But it's *your* money,' Ivy said eagerly. 'When Mam died, there was over six hundred pounds in the bank. Half belonged to Mabel, as well as half the house. The way things went, well . . .' a spasm of pain crossed her face '. . . she never got it, did she?'

'No, she didn't.'

It were a bought house, and half of it were mine. And there was money, too, hundreds of pounds . . .

'You know I got married again, don't you, luv?'

'Lily told me, years ago.'

'I knew from the start Alf only married me to get a roof over the head of him and his kids. I didn't mind. I only married him for the company, so I reckon that makes us equal. We don't get on too bad.' She smiled ruefully. 'He was a copper, see, and about to retire, which meant he'd lose his nice police house. Trouble is, Alf's rather keen on the horses, so his pension goes up in smoke, which leaves me the only one working. I'm still in the same place, you know,' she said proudly.

'I thought his grown-up children lived with you?'

'Oh, they do, but they're in and out of jobs by the minute, and more often out than in. I often come home and find one or other of the nice things me dad brought from abroad have disappeared to the pawn shop. I don't mind, not much.' She looked anxiously at Josie, and gave the cheque a little shake. 'Alf knows nothing about this, luv. It'd be gone with the wind if he found out. I've made a will, leaving the house to him and the kids. In the meantime, you and Dinah can have the money. That seems only fair, doesn't it, luv?'

'I suppose it does.' After all, it was *Mam's* money. 'Thank you very much, Aunt Ivy,' Josie said politely, 'though I'm afraid six hundred pounds wouldn't buy a house.'

'For goodness' sake, girl,' Aunt Ivy cried. 'I told you, it's been invested since before the war, moved from one account to another to earn higher interest.' She puffed out her chest conceitedly. 'I even had some shares once in this big electrical company that went bust, but not before I sold the shares at a profit. This cheque's for over five thousand pounds.'

The house was at the end of a row of five, dead in the centre of Woolton, once a little village on its own but now very much part of Liverpool. The tiny houses were invisible from the busy main street less than a hundred yards away. They were reached down a narrow gravel path called Baker's Row, which ran between a shoe shop and a greengrocer's, and had been built almost two centuries before the shops and the main street existed.

Josie's house was the only one not modernised. The others had had their kitchens extended, bathrooms added. They had pretty latticed or bow windows, shutters, wrought-iron gates, glazed front doors. Josie's front door hadn't seen a lick of paint in years, and the wooden gate only had one hinge. The gardens, front and back, were a wilderness of overgrown grass and weeds. Her kitchen still had a deep, brown earthenware sink. The only attempt at modernisation was that the washhouse and outside lavatory had been knocked into one and made into a bathroom which was accessed from the kitchen.

When she tried to scrape the wallpaper off the walls, she discovered five thick layers, each pattern more hideous than the one before. Sid Spencer said soaking the paper with warm water would help, and loaned her Little Sid to give a hand.

The house was the cheapest she could find in a place she liked. It had cost fifteen hunded of the five thousand pounds from Aunt Ivy. It would have been easy to buy a place much grander, but Josie wanted to conserve as much as possible. Sadly, she was too far from Spencer & Sons to do their typing, and she needed money to live on. She felt a bit guilty when she bought a television and washing machine, and resolved that as soon as Dinah went to school she would look for a part-time job.

Josie felt very odd, slightly depressed, the day she moved in with the things she had acquired for the attic room. There were times when she was scared she didn't know who she was. The woman she should have been had died with Laura and when Jack had gone away. That woman would never return – only her shell remained.

She would never love another man the way she had loved Jack. She had his child, his little girl, so different from Laura. She loved Dinah, but suspected that Laura would always have first place in her heart.

At twenty-seven, she had many years ahead of her, at least she prayed so for Dinah's sake. But what did those years hold, now that the adventures were all over and the romance had gone?

Baker's Row
1965–1974

1

'Eh, Jose. I wish you'd get a phone.' Lily came puffing into the house with Gillian on her reins. Lily's plans had gone madly awry a second time. It had taken three years for her to pluck up the courage to have another baby, to be blessed with pretty, roly-poly Gillian instead of Troy. She blamed Neil.

'I can't afford one, can I?'

'I thought you were going to get a job when Dinah went to school?' Lily said crossly.

'Give us a chance, Lil.' Josie went to put the kettle on. 'She's only been gone a week. Anyroad, I'm waiting to hear from the accountants round the corner. They want a part-time shorthand-typist, though I'm useless at figures. Anyroad,' she shouted, 'why is it suddenly so important that I have a phone?'

'It's always been important.' Lily looked at her irritably. 'I don't know how anybody can *live* without a phone. Look at this morning. I had to take our Samantha to school, and she screamed blue murder. She hates it, not like your Dinah. I reckon it's because she's more sensitive. Then I had to race over to me ma's for the letter, bring it here and I'll have to drive you back to ours to make the phone call. You're a terrible nuisance, Jose. You've really mucked up me schedule. Tuesday's the day I clean the fridge and vacuum upstairs.'

'What letter? What phone call? What are you on about?'

Lily took an envelope from her bag. 'Some firm in California has written to me ma and da' wanting to know where you are. Your whereabouts, they call it. Hang on a mo, I'll read it out.'

'"Dear Mr & Mrs Kavanagh,"' Lily read out a touch pompously, '"I am anxious to trace the whereabouts of Mrs Josephine Coltrane (née Flynn), and have been given to understand you may be able to help. Should this be the case, I would appreciate any information you are able to provide with all possible speed. It may even be that Mrs Coltrane herself is in a position to respond. In the case of a telephoned response, please reverse the charges. I look forward to hearing from you. Yours sincerely, Dick Schneider."'

'It's from Crosby, Buckmaster & Littlebrown – Jaysus, what a mouthful. I wonder if the Crosby's any relation to Bing? Their address is 17 South Park Boulevard, Los Angeles, California, USA. They're lawyers. Fancy a lawyer calling himself Dick. If it were me, I'd call meself Richard in me letters, wouldn't you, Jose?'

Josie's blood had got colder and colder as she listened to the letter. She burst into tears. 'Jack's dead!'

'Don't be morbid, Josie,' Lily said impatiently. 'Anyroad, it beats me why on earth you should give a fig if the bugger's dead or alive. You haven't seen him in years, and who'd have given them our address if he's dead?' The kettle boiled and she went to make the tea. 'Come back to ours and you can phone from there. Though make sure you reverse the charges.'

'But what on earth can it be about, Lil?' Josie cried frantically. Perhaps he was dying, and wanted to see her one last time. Or he just wondered how she was, might even want to come and visit. But if that was the case, there was nothing to stop him from writing to the Kavanaghs himself.

They drank the tea hurriedly, Lily just as eager to know why a firm of Californian lawyers wished to contact her friend as Josie herself was.

Josie sat on the stairs of the Baxters' smart new house in Woolton Park, less than a mile from her own. Lily found the code for the international operator in the book and told her what to dial. 'Don't forget to reverse the charges.'

'You've already said that half a dozen times.' Josie raised her eyebrows. 'I wouldn't mind some privacy,' she said, when Lily looked set to stay.

'I know when I'm not wanted.' She picked up Gillian and flounced into the kitchen. The letter from America on her knee, Josie dialled the operator . . .

Ten minutes later Lily crept into the hall and found Josie in exactly the same position at the bottom of the stairs. 'I didn't realise you'd finished. Why didn't you say? I've made tea. You look a bit sick, Jose. What's happened?'

'He wants a divorce,' Josie whispered dully. 'They said Jack wants a divorce. He's going to marry someone else. Honestly, Lil, I love him so much, I don't think I can bear it.'

They went into the kitchen. Lily did her best to be sympathetic, but she had disliked Jack as much as he had her, and couldn't understand how you could still love someone you hadn't seen for nearly six years.

'I just do,' Josie sobbed. 'I don't know how or why, I just do.'

'It means you can get married again yourself,' Lily said comfortingly.

'Oh, really? Who to? Not only have I no intention of getting married again, but there isn't exactly a horde of would-be husbands beating their way to me door.'

'There's . . .' Lily's face contorted painfully and she virtually spat out the next words. '. . . Francie O'Leary.' It was a sore point that Josie and the first man Lily had ever loved had become such close friends.

'Don't be ridiculous, Lil.' Josie managed to raise a smile. 'I don't think of Francie that way. Anyroad, he's a confirmed bachelor.'

'I wish he'd told me that when we first went out, before he broke me heart, like.'

Josie went back to her own little house, where she could be alone, think, though it was torture to imagine Jack in another woman's arms, marrying another woman, smiling at her, touching her, saying the things he'd said to *her*.

'You're stupid,' she told herself angrily. 'Dead stupid.' She made tea – one of these days, she'd turn into a packet of tea – and carried it out to the deckchair in the garden. It was a lovely warm September day, and she hoped it would stay nice for Dinah's fifth birthday party on Saturday. Best to think about the party instead of Jack.

The narrow garden looked dead pretty. She'd cleared the wild grass and the weeds, grown a new lawn from seed and a neat privet hedge from cuttings off the woman next door. The rose bushes in each corner were from the same source, and this year they'd come on a treat, with big, bulging pink and yellow blooms. Dinah collected the petals and kept them in a bowl in her room. The front garden had been turned into a rockery and the heathers were spreading nicely.

Josie sipped the tea, trying not to think of Jack. Inside the house it was just as pretty. There was still the earthenware sink and the claw-toothed bath. She'd had no improvements made, but the walls were covered with delicately flower patterned paper and all the woodwork was white. She'd gone mad with indoor plants, and Aunt Ivy had let her have one of the lovely, colourful, glass-shaded lamps from Machin Street.

'They're called Tiffany lamps,' she said. 'Me dad brought them from America. One's already gone – to the pawn shop, I presume. I thought I'd give you the other before that goes, too. They have them in George Henry Lee's and they cost the earth.'

Life was so unpredictable and topsy-turvy. Aunt Ivy was a regular visitor nowadays. She adored Dinah, and Dinah, such a strange little girl, regarded Ivy as one of her favourite people.

Josie finished the tea, sighed and went indoors to wash the dishes. She stacked everything on the wooden draining-board, very unhygienic accord-ing to Lily, who had stainless steel and couldn't understand why everyone oohed and aahed in admiration over Josie's house, so titchy and run-down, when hers was much nicer – modern, miles bigger and full of G-plan furniture. She even had an Ercol three-piece, bought when Neil was promoted to under-manager, or it might have been over-manager, at the Post Office.

'And you have so many visitors,' she pouted. 'Hardly anyone comes to ours, except me ma and da'.'

It was probably because Josie didn't expect visitors to remove their shoes before being allowed on the carpets, or frown if they wanted to smoke, or watch them like a hawk in case a drop of tea spilled on the furniture.

On Monday nights, Daisy, Eunice and Francie came and played poker for halfpennies. Josie hoped she wasn't showing her daughter a bad example by letting her join in for a while before she went to bed. Dinah had caught on quickly and usually won. At some time during the week, usually Wednesdays, Josie went with Lily to the pictures or the theatre. The same with Francie. Aunt Ivy was only too willing to babysit. Chrissie and Sid Spencer often popped in on Sunday afternoons to see how she was – two of their lads were now married, and they had three grandchildren. Mrs Kavanagh came frequently, her husband less often now that he was plagued with arthritis and had had to sell the shop.

Josie went upstairs to make the beds, still doing her best not to think about Jack. She had a lovely house, and loads of friends, which was rather surprising as she'd never thought of herself as a sociable person. She'd been careful with the money from Aunt Ivy, and there was still plenty left if she didn't find a job immediately. As she plumped up Dinah's pillow, Josie wondered why, despite this undeniably pleasant, even enjoyable existence, she felt only half alive.

It rained on Saturday morning, but the sky had cleared and the sun was shining by two o'clock when it was time for Dinah's party.

'I hope no one fetches me dolls. I hate dolls,' Dinah had said earlier as they'd wrapped tiny gifts in sheets of newspaper for pass the parcel.

'I know, luv.' Josie's present had been, by special request, a xylophone. Dinah could already pick out 'Silent Night'.

'Auntie Ivy's got me a trumpet. Francie said he had a lovely surprise. He's bringing it tonight.' Dinah frowned. 'Samantha and Gillian have got me a doll. Samantha told me, though she wasn't supposed to. It opens its mouth and says "Mama".'

'You mustn't let anyone guess you don't want it, luv,' Josie warned. 'Pretend to be dead pleased.'

'Oh, I will, Mummy,' Dinah assured her seriously. 'It's called being polite.'

Dinah was a very serious little girl. Her conversation, her reasoning, was almost adult. Josie had never discussed where soil came from, how flowers grew, what clouds were made of, why the Queen was the Queen with Laura. Yet she was conscious that there wasn't the same intimacy between her and Dinah as there'd been with her other child. Dinah was too self-contained. She liked her privacy.

Josie often got up in the morning and found her sitting up in bed looking at a picture book, or lying on the floor, her pretty, pale, rather tight little face hidden behind a curtain of creamy hair, doing a jig-saw or some other puzzle and talking to herself. It never crossed her mind to jump into bed with her mam. A few weeks ago Josie had walked into the bathroom when Dinah had been on the lavatory, and her little tight face had got tighter with obvious annoyance. 'You should knock first, Mummy.' Since then she'd fastened the bolt.

Perhaps Josie over-compensated for those first few months when she had resented Dinah so much for taking Laura's place. It was hard to believe, now, that she could have been so stupid, so insensitive as to resent a tiny baby. She must have been unbalanced, sick in the head. Ever since, she had tried to make up by cosseting Dinah too much, fussing over her endlessly, finding it hard to leave the child to her own devices. Sometimes she wondered if she got on Dinah's nerves!

She glanced at the clock. 'It's time you changed into your new frock, luv. People'll be arriving soon.'

'Why didn't Mrs Kavanagh make my frock like always?'

'She's had to give up sewing, hasn't she? Poor Mrs Kavanagh can't see that well any more.' It was sad. What with arthritis and glaucoma, the couple she'd regarded as a substitute mam and dad for most of her life had suddenly become very old and frail.

Lily and the girls were the first to arrive, dropped off by Neil on his way to a football match, followed by two little girls from Dinah's class at school. Then Aunt Ivy appeared bearing the trumpet, and Mrs Kavanagh a sewing set. Everyone went into the garden, where deckchairs were provided for the older women and Lily sat on the grass. Josie took the presents into the minuscule dining room where the table was set for tea – the big, rather ugly doll squeaked 'Mama' whenever it was moved. She wasn't looking forward to organising games for five little girls to fill in the time before the birthday tea.

It was difficult, trying to ensure that Gillian, three years younger than the others, wasn't left out, particularly with her mother watching keenly. And stopping Samantha from cheating, something that the same keen-eyed mother didn't notice. Josie prayed the children weren't as bored as she was. She was slightly relieved when Aunt Ivy shouted that there was a knock on the door, seeing it as an opportunity to collapse, exhausted, on the grass.

'I'll go.' Lily returned minutes later with a tall, sad-faced man. Two excessively thin children followed timidly behind, a boy of about twelve, a girl a few years younger. 'Look who's here,' Lily said in a funny voice. 'It's our Ben, with Peter and Colette. They've been home, and me da' sent them here.'

'Ben, is that our Ben?' Mrs Kavanagh tried, unsuccessfully, to struggle out of the deckchair, and for some reason Josie recalled the sprightly woman in the blue coat she'd met in Blackler's bargain basement where she and Mam had gone to look for a tray. 'Ben, son, I haven't seen you in ages.'

Before his mother could get up, Ben did the most surprising thing. Every muscle in his face seemed to collapse, and he strode across the grass, knelt in front of his mother's chair and buried his face in her breast. Mrs Kavanagh gently stroked the fair hair of her youngest son. Lily looked set to burst into tears. Ben's children watched, their faces showing not the slightest flicker of emotion. The five little girls stood awkwardly on the grass, knowing something strange was happening. Josie, shaken by the pathos of the situation, had no idea what to do. Should she take the little ones inside?

It was Aunt Ivy who saved the day. She stood and clapped her hands. 'How about a little walk to the sweetshop?' she cried. 'You two an' all, Peter and Colette. Colette, you take Gillian's hand, she's only a little 'un. Peter, you can keep an eye on the others. Come on. We won't be long,' she sang gaily.

They left. Ben stayed with his head buried in his mother's breast. Josie couldn't tell if he was crying. It seemed ages before he looked up. His dead eyes searched for Josie, and he said in a cracked voice, 'I'm sorry if I've spoiled the party.'

'You haven't—' Josie began, but Lily interrupted.

'That bloody Imelda – what's she done now?'

'Shush, luv,' Mrs Kavanagh chided.

'I will not shush. She's ruining our Ben's life. Did you see the faces of them kids? They look set for a nervous breakdown.'

'Lily, girl, please shush.'

'No, Ma. Why don't you leave her?' Lily demanded angrily of her brother. 'Why put up with it all this while?'

Ben sat on the deckchair Aunt Ivy had vacated. 'I can't leave Imelda, she's sick.'

'No she's not, she's evil,' Lily said flatly.

'Lily!'

'Be quiet, Ma. Anyone with an ounce of spunk would have left years ago. I wouldn't have stood it for a minute, me.'

Josie went to put the kettle on, but could still hear the argument raging on her lawn. She hoped the neighbours weren't listening.

'I can't walk out and leave the children, Lil,' Ben was saying. 'I can't just take them away either. Imelda's their mother. Believe it or not, they love her. Peter's old enough to guess there's something wrong. He used to be frightened, but now he gets protective when she has one of her rages.'

'Rages! Huh!' Lily said contemptuously. 'How did you manage to escape today? Did she write you a pass or something? What time have you got to be back?'

'She took another overdose last night,' Ben said wearily. 'She's in hospital again. I know I should be with her, but I had the children to think of. She'll sleep all day, and I'll fetch her home tomorrow.'

'Oh, no, son!' Mrs Kavanagh's voice quivered like an old woman's.

Lily was unimpressed. 'She never takes enough to finish herself off, does she? Next time she decides to *kill* herself, I hope she lets me know first, and I'll encourage her to take a fatal dose. Good riddance to bad rubbish, I say.'

'Have a heart, Lil. The doctors say it's a cry for help.'

'I'm all heart, Ben,' Lily said virtuously, 'but where Imelda's concerned, it's made of iron.'

There were footsteps down the side of the house and Francie O'Leary appeared. Josie dragged him into the kitchen. 'Don't interrupt. It's a family row.'

'Is that Ben?' Francie said, aghast. 'Jaysus, he looks about eighty. He's only thirty-four, same as me. I wrote to him, years ago, but never got an answer. What's happened to the party? Where are the kids?'

'Gone to the shops with Auntie Ivy.' She closed the door to shut out the row. Lily had started to shriek. 'As you can see, there's been an upset. What are you doing here, anyroad? I wouldn't have thought a children's party was your scene.'

Francie gloomily stuffed his hands in his pockets. 'Anything's my scene these days, Jose. The house seems like a morgue since me mam died. I feel so lonely, I'm thinking of getting married.' He grinned. 'Who should I ask?'

She grinned back, knowing he was only joking and glad he was there to lighten the mood of the day which had suddenly turned so tragic. 'I don't know, Francie. As long as it's not me, because I'd turn you down.'

'I wouldn't dream of asking you and spoiling a perfect friendship!' he said in a shocked voice.

'Mind you, you'd be a good catch, especially since your printing business has taken off.' He now employed six people. She looked at him appraisingly. He was still attractive in a lean, pinched way, and his black outfit – leather jacket, polo-necked sweater, flared trousers, boots – gave him an appealingly sinister air. Since the Beatles had taken Liverpool and the whole world by storm a few years ago, and long hair had become fashionable, Francie had acquired a dashing ponytail.

'You're the first girl I ever fancied.' He leered at her and winked. 'I mean, *really* fancied. I used to be dead envious of Ben.' He went over to the window. Ben was staring at the grass, his arms folded, his long face inscrutable. Mrs Kavanagh was crying, Lily shouting and waving her arms. 'The way things change, eh!' Francie said softly. 'I feel dead sorry for him now.'

The party turned out a success after all. Aunt Ivy came back, having bought the children each a present. 'We found a toy shop,' she smiled. 'I thought it might cheer them two up.' She nodded at Peter and Colette. Peter was earnestly studying a travel chess set, and Colette was nursing a fluffy dog, more suitable for a child half her age. They looked almost happy. 'Before you say anything about the money, Alf would only have cadged it off me for the horses. It's better spent this way.'

Josie had never appreciated Aunt Ivy so much before. She felt sufficiently moved to bestow a kiss on the yellow cheek. 'Ta. I don't know what I'd have done without you today.'

The drama in the garden seemed to be over, though Lily was in a mood for the rest of the afternoon. Josie brought a chair from upstairs and the stool from the bathroom to accommodate the extra guests, and the children sat down to tea. Ben brought his mother inside for a welcome cup of tea, and was astonished to find his old friend Francie skulking in the kitchen.

'It's good to see you, mate.' They shook hands and punched each others' shoulders, and Josie was touched to see the lines of strain on Ben's face melt away. He looked almost like the Ben she used to know.

At six o'clock the mothers of Dinah's two schoolfriends came to collect them, and Aunt Ivy supposed she'd better get back to Alf. Neil arrived, and Lily offered her mother a lift home.

'Ben can take me,' Mrs Kavanagh said. 'You're coming back to ours, aren't you, son?'

'I thought me and Ben could go for a drink later,' Francie said quickly.

'Would you mind having the children, Ma?'

'Of course not, son. I hardly ever see them nowadays.' Mrs Kavanagh seemed drained after the trauma of the day. She patted Ben's arm. 'You have a nice time, now.'

'I'll take you home, then come back. I wonder where I left the car?' Ben looked slightly harassed.

'Don't worry, I can squeeze everyone in. It's only a minute to our house. I'll drop Lily and the girls off, then take your mam and the kids home.' Neil Baxter's earnest, good-natured face glowed with a willingness to help. 'Are you ready, love?'

Lily's eyes flickered from Josie to Francie to Ben, as if she resented leaving them behind. Gillian pulled at her skirt. 'Want beddy-byes, Mummy,' she whined. Lily turned on her heel and left the room without a word.

Dinah thanked her guests nicely for the presents, and Josie went to the door to say goodbye as her house suddenly emptied. 'Why don't you come back later?' she said to Lily. 'It would be like old times, the four of us together. Neil wouldn't mind.'

'I'm a married woman,' Lily said stiffly, 'Not a free agent like you.'

'Thanks for reminding me, Lil.'

'I didn't mean it like that.' Lily's cheeks went pink. 'It's just there's the children to bath and put to bed, Neil's tea to make, the pools to check, the telly to watch, and I always make a cup of cocoa before we go to bed at about eleven.' Her voice was surprisingly harsh. 'Next Saturday will be exactly the same, and the Saturday after that, and so on. I don't know why I was so keen on getting married, Josie. It's more dead bloody boring than working in an office. I sometimes wish I were a lesbian like our Daisy. She has loads more fun than I do.'

Josie hid a smile. She glanced at Neil, waiting patiently for his wife, Gillian in his arms. 'You've got a husband in a million there, Lil. You don't realise how lucky you are.'

'I don't call it lucky to have landed a chap as dull as the proverbial ditchwater,' Lily snapped. 'I should never have married him. I don't love him, and I never will.' She marched away, turned round and marched back again. 'Don't take any notice of me, Josie. It's seeing Francie that's made me feel like this. He looks so gorgeous, so *exciting* in that outfit. Neil wouldn't grow a ponytail if you paid him, and he wouldn't be seen dead in a leather jacket. Yet he's worth ten Francie O'Learys.' She grinned. 'I must remind meself of that when we go to bed.'

Ben and Francie decided to start off the night with a Chinese meal. They left a few hours later to catch a taxi into town, on the assumption they would both be too drunk to drive home. Dinah went to bed with Francie's present, a rubber date stamp and pad that had fascinated her so much when Josie had taken her to the small print works a few weeks previously. The house seemed unnaturally quiet, welcome after the chaos of the day. Aunt Ivy had washed the dishes, everywhere was tidy. It was time to read properly the contents of the fat envelope which had arrived by air mail that morning from Crosby, Buckmaster & Littlebrown in California.

Dick Schneider's letter was couched in friendly tones. His client was pleased to learn she was in agreement to an amicable divorce. Would she kindly read the enclosed papers carefully and sign those places marked with a cross? If she would prefer to take advice from her own lawyer first, then all expenses would be paid. Whatever the case, he would appreciate her treating the matter with some urgency.

Jack was obviously in a hurry to marry his new wife, Josie thought bitterly. Lily had tried to persuade her to ask for alimony, but Josie didn't want a penny.

'Tell them about Dinah,' Lily had urged. 'After all, she's Jack's child every bit as much as yours. He should take some responsibility.' Then, more grudgingly, she added, 'He has a right to know, Jose, particularly after what happened with Laura. And Dinah has rights, too. She's started school, and any minute now she'll want to know why she hasn't got a dad like the other kids. Are you prepared to tell her he doesn't know she exists? It was different before. You didn't know where he was, but now you do, at least this lawyer does. You could send a photograph.'

Dinah had thought Francie was her dad, he was around so much. She didn't seem to mind when told he wasn't, and the subject hadn't come up again. Though Lily was talking sense for once. Dinah would want to know one day, and it would be unfair on her, and Jack, to deny them knowledge of each other.

Josie took a deep breath, signed the forms in the places marked with a cross, then wrote a brief letter informing Jack he had a daughter, Dinah, whose fifth birthday it was that very day. She enclosed a snapshot of their little girl in a bathing costume on Birkdale sands. Dinah, posing stiffly, spade in one hand, bucket in the other, had treated the camera to one of her rare, sweet smiles. Her pale hair was being blown into her eyes. She looked fragile, yet there was a toughness about her stance, an air of confidence, that plump, fun-loving Laura had never had. She put the letter and the photograph in an envelope marked 'Jack Coltrane, Strictly Confidential' and enclosed it with the papers in the large, self-addressed envelope Dick Schneider had sent. She sealed it, and stamped the flap with her fist.

'There!' she said aloud. There might be more forms to sign, she didn't know, but in a few weeks or months she would be a single woman again, 'on the market', as Lily had put it.

Except she didn't want to be. She sat on the tiny settee and tried not to go through all the 'if onlys'. If only she hadn't done this, said that, gone there. The trouble was, most people needed two chances at life so they could do things right the second time around.

Still, it was too late for a second chance with Jack. She got resolutely to her feet and went upstairs to check on Dinah, who was fast asleep, having stamped the date several times on her new doll's forehead. Downstairs, she watched a play on television, and wondered if Ben and Francie would come back to hers or return for their cars in the morning.

At half eleven, when there'd been no sign of either, she went to bed, and had just read the first page of an Ed McBain thriller when there was a knock on the door. She groaned, slipped into a dressing-gown and went downstairs to answer it.

Ben was outside, grinning at her stupidly, looking young, very boyish and extremely drunk. 'I've come for my children.'

'They're at your mother's. Oh, you'd better come in,' she said, too late, as Ben had virtually fallen inside the door.

'Francie said they were here. Or was it my car?'

'Your car's around somewhere.' She helped him to his feet. 'I'll make some black coffee, sober you up.' She went into the kitchen. If only she'd had a phone, she would have called a taxi. After he'd had the coffee, she'd get dressed and call one from the box on the main street.

She was running water in the kettle when Ben came lurching in. To her astonishment, he grabbed her by the waist and said hoarsely, 'I don't want coffee, I want you. That's why I came back – not for the kids or the car, but for you.'

For one mad, wild moment she felt a surge of desire. It was so long, too long, since she'd made love, and the pressure of his hands on the curve of her hips reminded her of what she had been missing. But common sense returned, and she moved out of his reach. 'Don't be silly, Ben,' she said shortly.

He dragged her back against him, his hands grasped her breasts, he groaned. 'I love you, Josie.' He buried his head in her neck. 'Not silly, love you, love you, love you.'

'You're drunk, Ben. You'll feel dead embarrassed tomorrow.' She tried again to move away, but his hands tightened on her breasts. She was trapped. She jerked her elbow sharply back into his stomach, but it had no effect.

'I've never loved anyone but you,' he was saying, almost sobbing against her neck. 'You were my girl, my special girl. We were going to get married. What happened, Jose? Why didn't we?' He turned her round so they were facing each other, and she stared, shocked, at the ravaged face, the haunted eyes. 'What happened, Josie?'

Life, she wanted to say. Life happened. Wrong decisions, right decisions. You said no when you meant yes, or the other way around. Someone else might have married Imelda, another woman might have married Jack Coltrane. Laura might not have been born, Laura might not be dead.

Ben was kissing her, kissing her roughly, hungrily, trying to force her mouth open with his tongue. She resisted and felt his teeth grind against her own. This wasn't the Ben she used to know. She didn't like this Ben at all. His hands were tugging at the belt on her dressing-gown, undoing it, caressing her body, hurting it, through the thin material of her nightie, telling her all the time how much he loved her, missed her, wanted her, that she was on his mind every minute of every day. She was the only woman for him, always had been, always would, and she was so beautiful, so precious.

Now he was touching between her legs, and she felt him shudder powerfully against her. She contemplated screaming. The walls of the house were paper thin. Someone would hear, someone would come, rescue her. The police would be called. But she didn't want to do that, not to this tragic, unhappy man. Not to Ben. Nor did she want to frighten Dinah.

Josie stopped struggling and let herself go limp. She gently clasped his face in her hands and said in a soft voice, 'Are you going to rape me, Ben?'

He froze. He stayed completely still for a long time. Then he removed his hands, stepped back. 'Jesus Christ, Josie. I'm so sorry.' He didn't meet her eyes.

She picked up the kettle. 'Go and sit down, and I'll make us both a cup of coffee.'

The kettle rattled on the ancient gas stove so she didn't hear the front door open and close, and when Josie went into the parlour with two cups of coffee, Ben had gone.

He came early next morning to apologise, extremely shamefaced, highly embarrassed. She'd had a feeling he would. Dinah had gone to Mass with Aunt Ivy. Josie, her head still spinning after the previous day, intended to go later.

'I walked home last night, sobered myself up,' he said on the doorstep.

'This time I really have come to collect my car – if I can remember where I left it.'

'Come in.' She half smiled, and he gave a sigh of relief.

'I thought I'd blotted my copybook for ever. I don't know what came over me last night, Josie. I've never behaved like that before. Mind you, I've never been so drunk either.'

'Let's put it down to a single aberration.' They went into the parlour and he glanced appreciatively around the tiny room.

'I like it here. It's so calm and comfortable, like a fairy-tale house.' His lips twisted slightly. 'A fairy-tale house for a fairy queen. Remember the fairy queen in *The Wizard of Oz*, Jose? We saw it together. You said you'd love a frock like hers.'

'She was a good witch, not a fairy.'

'Was she?' He looked oddly troubled. 'I thought I could remember everything we did with complete clarity.'

'I've seen the film twice since, first with Laura, then Dinah.'

He gave a rueful smile. 'It keeps me going, reliving the times we spent together. Some mornings I wake up and try to imagine it's *you* in bed beside me, that we got married after all. I drive home from work, and think what it would be like if *you* opened the door.'

'Ben,' she said warningly, 'I wouldn't have let you in if I'd known the conversation would turn this way.'

'Sorry, Jose.' He glanced at her curiously. 'But we've both made a complete cock-up of things. You're separated, my marriage isn't exactly what you'd call happy. Aren't you ever sorry *we* didn't get married?'

She shook her head firmly. 'No, Ben.' She had thought about it sometimes, but never with regret.

'I just wondered.'

Aunt Ivy and Dinah could be heard coming in the back way. Ben got up to leave. 'Can I come and see you occasionally? Just to talk?'

'I'd sooner you didn't, Ben.' He might take it as a sign of encouragement.

'Oh, well.' He shook hands formally. 'See you around some time, Jose.'

2

Josie had told Dinah about Laura years ago, when she was still too young to understand, to grasp the concept of death and the passage of time, and the things that had happened before she was born. Josie had thought this the best way, rather than spring the fact of a dead sister later, right out of the blue.

Dinah was eight when she began to plague her mother with questions, about Laura, about Jack. She demanded pictures, descriptions. Why didn't Jack come to see her? Was Laura clever, was she nice, was she pretty?

'Not as clever as you, luv, but every bit as nice, and just as pretty, though in a different way. She was dark, like your dad. You take after my side of the family.'

'I'm like Auntie Ivy's mummy. Was she me grandma?'

'No, luv, she was mine. Your grandma ... gosh!' It was impossible to imagine Mam being a grandma. 'Your grandma was dead beautiful. Her name was Mabel. She was only twenty-two when she was killed.'

'Did you love Laura better than me?'

Josie gasped. 'Of course not, luv. I loved her exactly the same way as I love you.' She reached down to stroke the creamy hair, but Dinah shrugged the hand away.

A fire blazed in the black metal fireplace with its fancy tiled surround. The Tiffany lamp was on, casting jewel-coloured shadows on the walls and ceiling of the small room. Dinah lay face down on the mat, drawing. Josie held a Sunday paper on her knee. It was a gloomy December day, but cosy inside. She might put the decorations up later. It was only a week off Christmas.

'What are you drawing, luv?'

'Laura. I remember what she looks like from the photo you showed me. The one she had done at school.'

'Ah, yes.' It had been a state school, but the children had worn uniforms. Laura's tie was crooked, her hair a mess, but she was grinning from ear to ear. She'd been such a happy little girl. The only time Josie could recall her otherwise were those final two days when Jack had disappeared.

Dinah looked over her shoulder. 'Will me dad send a Christmas card from America?'

'I doubt it, Dinah. He never has before.' There'd been no reply to the letter she'd sent three years ago, telling Jack he had a daughter and enclosing her photograph.

'I think that's rude,' she said primly.

'So do I.'

'I don't think me dad is very nice.'

'Oh, he's all right. But I've told you before – he's got another wife now, perhaps more children. I reckon you and me are very far from his mind.'

'He's still rude. If he comes, I won't speak to him.'

'Join the club, luv. I mightn't speak to him meself.' She knew she was talking rubbish. Hardly a day passed when she didn't think of Jack Coltrane. She was still as much in love with him as she had ever been.

Dinah got to her feet. 'Can I ring Samantha? Auntie Lily took her to town yesterday to buy her a dress for Christmas. I bet it's not as nice as mine.'

'Tell Auntie Lily I'll be round tomorrow after work. Say about one o'clock.'

'Okay, Mum.'

Josie had got the job with the accountants, only a minute's walk away but tedious beyond words, typing never-ending columns of figures. She would never get used to figures, but the wages were good and had paid for the installation of a telephone, and the subsequent bills which she tried to keep small. Lily looked after Dinah in the school holidays. It would be nice, she thought wistfully, to have a job you could get your teeth into, something stimulating. But all she could do was type!

She went over to the window. The view was dead miserable – the back of someone's hedge and the path, which ended outside her house so no one ever walked past. Still, it looked pretty in the summer when it was almost like living in the heart of the countryside, instead of busy Woolton. Perhaps it was the weather, or talking about Jack and Laura, but today Josie felt unusually discontented. She wished the house were somewhere else, somewhere busy, where there were cars and people to be seen, noise. She wished everything about her life was different.

With a sigh, she returned to the settee. Dinah's drawing of Laura lay on the floor, and her heart turned over when she picked it up. Dinah had drawn her sister with a great deal of skill, particularly the dark, tousled hair, the pretty mouth, but why had she felt compelled to spoil it with a stark, black, jagged cross, completely obliterating Laura's smiling eyes?

'Oo-er,' Lily said next day when Josie told her about the drawing. 'That's dead peculiar, that is. Did she say why she did it?'

'I thought it best not to mention it.'

'I would have given our Samantha a clock around the ear if she'd done that to a picture of Gillian.'

Josie made a face. 'I doubt if that would have been the best approach, Lil. It would have only made things worse.'

'What things?'

'I dunno, do I? I'm not a psychiatrist. Her feelings for Laura, I suppose. Perhaps I should have talked to her about it,' she said thoughtfully. 'Maybe she left it there deliberately, knowing I'd see it, like. I just put it back where I found it, and didn't say a word.'

'I shouldn't take any notice,' Lily said lightly. 'Kids do ever such peculiar things when they're little. I remember cutting all the buttons off our Stanley's best suit. I've no idea why.'

'I put a bad spell on me Auntie Ivy loads of times, but none of them ever worked.'

'Oh, I don't know. She married Vincent Adams, didn't she?'

'That was before I was born. It was nothing to do with me.'

'Try not to think about the drawing. Maybe she crossed it out because she didn't think it good enough. You're reading too much into it. By the way, Josie, would you mind putting your coffee on a coaster, please? That's what they're there for.'

Christmas passed pleasantly enough. On Boxing Day afternoon, Josie threw a drinks party. Lily had never heard of such a thing before, but came willingly enough with Neil and the girls. Aunt Ivy came early to help prepare the food, and Francie O'Leary brought a new girlfriend, Kathleen, a divorcee with long, dramatic, black hair and an hourglass figure. The Spencers were there. All the Kavanaghs were home for Christmas, and the old people managed to make a joke of the fact that one could hardly see and the other barely walk. Stanley and Freya, Marigold and Jonathan, Robert and Julia – all arrived with their children, so that Josie's tiny house bulged at the seams. Ben was the only Kavanagh absent.

It was the day Daisy and Eunice announced they were getting married.

'To each other?' Lily spluttered.

'No, idiot.' Daisy's laugh tinkled through the house. 'Eunice has been quietly courting for ages. He's a teacher, same as her. I met Manos in Greece last summer, and we've been writing to each other ever since. He proposed over the phone last night.'

There was a chorus of cheers and congratulations. 'I never thought you'd do it, girl,' Stanley whooped.

Mrs Kavanagh was close to tears. 'I'm so happy for you, Daisy, luv. Get married soon, won't you?'

'As soon as humanly possible, Ma.'

The Kavanagh children looked fearfully at each other. Their mother wanted an early wedding while she had the sight left to see.

All the Kavanaghs were back again in Liverpool on St Valentine's Day, when Daisy married Manos Dimantidou. She looked like a Greek goddess, in a simple white dress with a silver cord tied around her slim waist. Manos was a tall, suntanned man, sporting an awesome amount of black, curly hair with a sprinkling of silver in the long sideburns.

'Ah, well, that's the last of the children off our hands,' Mr Kavanagh said at the reception. 'Six down and none to go.'

His wife laughed. 'Now I can die happy. Though the grandchildren's weddings will soon be starting. Our Marigold's Colin will be twenty next year. He's already courting.'

And Laura would have been fifteen, Josie thought with a pang, old enough to be thinking about boys. She looked for Dinah, and saw her playing with Samantha in the corner of the hotel ballroom. She'd never mentioned the drawing of Laura and, since Christmas, Dinah seemed to have lost interest in both Jack and her sister.

'Hi. We only seem to meet at parties and weddings.' Ben appeared beside her.

'Hi, yourself. You're looking well.' He wasn't nearly as tense as the last time she'd seen him at Dinah's party. 'Is Imelda here?'

'She wouldn't come. Too tired, she claimed. I promised to be home by four, which is a shame. Peter and Colette are having a great time.' He regarded her soberly, and there was a message in his eyes she would have preferred not to see. 'You look beautiful, as usual. I like your frock. You always suited blue. It goes with your eyes.'

'It's only C & A.' It was a suit, not a frock, cornflower blue wool with satin lapels and cuffs on the fitted jacket and a slightly flared skirt.

'I expect you know what I'm thinking.'

That they'd come to the wedding together as man and wife? 'I'd sooner not know, Ben,' she said stiffly. 'We all make choices of our own free will. It's no good looking back and wishing we'd chosen different.'

She walked away, but was sorry for the rest of her life that she'd been rude. Ben remained at the reception until half past six, by which time the newly married couple had left for their honeymoon. The family decided not to tell them yet that when Ben arrived home, Imelda was dead, having taken what turned out to be a final fatal overdose.

'She was expecting Ben back in time to save her,' Lily sneered. 'I'm glad he was late. Good riddance to bad rubbish, I say.'

'You can be awful hard when you like, Lil,' Josie remarked.

'Oh, I'm as hard as nails, me. I believe in putting meself, me kids and me family first, and that means our Ben. I always said he was a soppy lad. He should have given Imelda her cards years ago. There's no way I'd let someone ruin me life the way she did his.'

Imelda had only been buried a month when Mollie Kavanagh fell the full length of the stairs in the house in Childwall. She never regained consciousness and died two minutes before midnight the same night, with her husband and four of her children at her bedside, having been given the Last Sacraments just in time. Stanley and Robert arrived too late to be with the mother they had loved so dearly.

Josie waited anxiously by the phone. Lily had rung earlier to explain what had happened. She longed to be there, to say goodbye to the kind, loving and immensely generous woman who had been such a significant presence in her life, but would have felt in the way.

The telephone went at half past twelve. 'She's gone, Jose,' Lily said in a ragged voice. 'She went half an hour ago. Me poor da's in a terrible state. Our Marigold's taking him home. Oh, Josie! Why don't nice things ever happen? Why is everything always so bloody sad?'

The funeral was held on the first of April. It rained solidly, all day, without a break. Francie O'Leary was one of more than a hundred mourners; Mrs Kavanagh had made many friends over the years. Josie was grateful for his presence beside her during the Requiem Mass and, later, in the house in Childwall in which she'd known so many happy times.

'Can I come and see you tonight?' Francie asked when it was time for him to leave for his printing business, now occupying a small factory in Speke.

'Why the formality? You don't usually ask.' He turned up at all sorts of unlikely hours, and she was always glad to see him. Francie managed to make everything seem more cheerful than it actually was. Tonight he would be more than welcome.

He gave an enigmatic smile. 'Tonight's different.'

It was just gone eight when he arrived, having changed from a formal suit into jeans, a loose Indian shirt and a long, padded, velvet jacket. He'd recently had a perm, and his narrow face was framed in loose, bouncy waves.

'Where's Dinah?' he asked.

'In bed. She went early with a book. She can read ever so well, Francie. At school, they reckon she's bound to pass the eleven plus and go to grammar school.'

'Good.' He settled in a chair and looked at her intently. 'I'm not going to beat around the bush. Will you marry me?'

She smiled. 'No.'

'It's not a joke, Josie. I mean it. I seriously think we should get married. We get on perfectly together, we never row.'

'That's because we're not married.' She still thought he was joking. 'What happened to Kathleen?'

'I ditched her.'

'Poor girl. She was mad about you.'

'Stuff Kathleen. It's us I want to talk about.' He cleared his throat. 'I'm not in love with you, Jose.'

'I'm not in love with you, Francie.'

'Though I fancy you something rotten, always have.'

'I quite fancy you,' she conceded. 'Though you don't suit a perm. You look like a Cavalier.'

'That's a pity.' He gave an amiable, laid-back grin. 'I would have been on the side of the Roundheads. We're both getting on, you know, Jose. I'm thirty-seven, you're thirty-five. Why spend the rest of our lives apart when we can be together? It's a terrible waste. I really am serious, Josie. Honest.'

'Would you like a cup of tea?'

'Don't change the subject. I'll have tea when you've said you'll marry me.'

'Then you'll never drink another cup of tea again, Francie O'Leary,' she cried. 'I wouldn't dream of marrying you. I like you too much.' She looked at him curiously. 'If you really are serious, why ask now, after all this time?'

'Because I want to snap you up before Ben Kavanagh does,' Francie said surprisingly. 'He's crazy about you, Jose. After a decent interval he's bound to propose.'

'Then I shall tell him no, same as you.'

'Are you sure?'

Josie nodded furiously. 'Positive.'

'In that case, I'll have a cup of tea. Strong, two sugars, to steady me nerves.'

'You don't have nerves, Francie.' She went into the kitchen.

'Are you still in love with that husband of yours?' he shouted.

'Ex-husband.' She returned to the parlour. 'Yes, though I know it's hopeless. It's strange, because we weren't exactly happy a lot of the time.'

Even in New York, which she looked back on as having been perfect, she'd nevertheless been full of doubts and uncertainties.

He looked at her curiously. 'What's it like, being in love? It's never happened to me.'

'It's . . . it's indescribable, Francie.' She clasped her hands against her breast, smiling, remembering the night she'd met Jack. 'Everything seems different, the whole world. It's agony and ecstasy at the same time.'

'It doesn't sound too healthy to me,' Francie said drily.

She thought about Ivy and Uncle Vince. 'It isn't always.'

The kettle boiled and she went to make the tea. Francie appeared in the kitchen doorway. 'I meant what I said earlier, that we should get married. I don't expect an answer now, but think about it, Jose. Another thing . . .' He winked at her suggestively. 'I reckon we'd be good together in bed.'

Josie thought about it, and decided it wasn't a bad idea. Whenever Francie got a new girlfriend she didn't feel jealous, but she was always worried she would lose him as a friend. He'd become part of her life, like Lily and Aunt Ivy, like Mrs Kavanagh had been. Francie touched a side of her that no one else did. He made the world seem funny and young. They had a good laugh together. Was that enough to make a marriage? Well, she'd never know if she didn't try. And they might grow to love each other one day, you never knew.

'But would you mind if we left it until next year?' she said to him the night she accepted his proposal. 'It's been such an awful year so far. We've known each for half our lives, so another few months won't make much difference. And, if you don't mind, I'd sooner we kept it between ourselves for now.'

'In case you get cold feet?'

Josie chewed her lip. 'I'm not sure, Francie, to be honest. I mean, this isn't exactly a romantic situation we're in, is it? It's almost a business arrangement. *You* might get cold feet. Say you fall madly in love with some girl next week, for instance?'

'I don't think I'm capable of falling in love,' Francie said glumly. He folded his arms over his lavishly embroidered waistcoat, and looked at her challengingly. 'Okay, so we get married next year. In the meantime, what about the bed bit?'

'What *about* the bed bit?'

'Do I have to wait for that until next year, too?'

'Oh, I dunno, Francie. Let me think about it.'

They made love the first time in Francie's new house in Halewood, because it would have been impossible in Baker's Row with Dinah in the next room. He was a fervent, inventive lover, who still managed to make her laugh, even at the height of passion, and Josie felt enjoyably exhausted when it was over. They leaned against the pillows and finished off the wine they'd brought with them to bed. Francie looked even more sinister naked, with the faintly blue bones of his ribs showing through a surprisingly hairy body.

'Now we've broken the ice, we must do this more often,' he said. 'Twice a night would suit me fine.'

'You'll be lucky.' Josie stared around the bare room. 'You could do with some pictures up, Francie. And those curtains are dead dull.' The curtains were a sickly beige, to go with the carpet and the walls.

'It needs a woman's touch.' Francie grinned. He pulled her hand under the bedclothes. 'Like me.'

'Nineteen-seventy,' Lily said gloomily. 'It'll be nineteen-seventy in a few hours. Where have the years gone, Jose?'

'I dunno.' All day, Josie's mind had kept going back to the eve of the last decade. She glanced at her watch. It was just gone six. Ten years ago she was putting on the purple mini-dress ready for Maya's party, waiting for Elsie Forrest to arrive. Laura was running around the house in Bingham Mews, excited that she was being allowed to stay up till midnight. Jack had already started to drink.

'It's been the most miserable Christmas I can ever remember.' Lily's eyes were moist.

'I know, Lil.' Stanley had stayed in Germany, Robert in London. Daisy and Manos had gone to Greece to spend Christmas with his family. There'd been no sign of Ben. It was as if Mrs Kavanagh had been the thread that had held her children together.

Now it was New Year's Eve. Francie had got tickets for a dinner dance, but Josie had felt obliged to spend the evening with Lily, who had been deeply depressed since her mother died. Dinah was in the lounge, watching television with Samantha and Gillian. Neil had gone to the pub, but had promised to be back before Big Ben chimed in the New Year. Francie, being Francie, hadn't minded being forsaken for the woman he most loathed. There were plenty of parties he could go to.

'I mean,' Lily was saying, 'what's it all for? We're born, we get married, we have children, we get old, then we die! It hardly seems worth it, Jose.'

'Not if you put it like that. We're supposed to enjoy ourselves along the way, be happy.'

'Are you happy, Jose?'

Josie shrugged. 'Well, yes. I think I am. A bit.'

'*I'm* not, not the least bit, and it's not just because of Ma. It's, it's . . .' Lily searched for words. 'It's *Neil.*' The name came out like a gasp. 'Oh, I know he's a bloke in a million, you said that once, but . . .' She seemed lost for words again. 'Remember that day in Haylands? It was the day after you'd been with that Griff for the first time. Your face, Jose. I often think about your face that day. It was sort of lit up – radiant, I think you'd call it. And your eyes were so bright, almost as if you'd been crying, except they were such happy eyes, shining.' Lily looked shyly at Josie. 'My face has never looked like that, Jose. Making love with Neil is a bit of an ordeal nowadays, and it's never exactly turned me on. Oh,' she cried, 'I missed so much, marrying him. I should have waited. Look at our Daisy, madly in love at forty.'

'Lily, you would have been unbearable if you'd had to wait to get married until you were forty. You'd have had all of us nervous wrecks by now.'

'I know.' Lily sighed. 'I'm too impatient. I grabbed the first man that asked. Neil's good and decent, but I should have turned him down. He would have been hurt, but not as much as he'll be hurt now.'

Josie looked askance at her friend. 'What do you mean?'

'I'm going to chuck him out, Jose,' Lily said in a shaky voice. 'Ask him to leave. I'll suggest we sell the house, get rid of the mortgage and I'll buy something smaller for me and the girls. I don't want the poor bloke on the streets. Then I'll get a job like you. Anything's better than being stuck in a dead boring marriage for the rest of me days. I always said our Ben was daft, sticking by Imelda. Well, the same rule applies to me. I'm wasting me life with Neil.' Lily glared at her friend, her small face knotted in determination. 'And do you know what else I'm going to do, Jose?'

'What's that, Lil?'

'I'm going to chase Francie O'Leary like he's never been chased before. I'll get him to the altar if it's the last thing I do. I could never understand you still being in love with Jack, until I realised I've been in love with Francie since I was sixteen. I'm going to marry him, Josie, or die in the attempt.'

There was a significance about 1974, but Josie couldn't remember what it was. It wasn't to do with turning forty, which she didn't regard as significant, but something else. A long while ago, 1974 had been mentioned as a year when something would happen. She had racked her brains every day since the year began, but nothing would come.

She got ready for work on a crisp, February morning, making up her nearly forty-year-old face in the dressing-table mirror. Now she worked for the accountants from nine till four, with half an hour for lunch, almost full time. She kept promising herself she would leave, but it was convenient and well paid.

I'm wasting me life, she told herself. Though perhaps I expect too much. There was always a nagging feeling that she was missing out on something.

'Dinah,' she yelled. 'It's half past eight. You should be on your way to school by now, not still in bed.'

There was an answering thump. Josie went downstairs and made herself a bowl of cornflakes. It was no good putting food out for Dinah, she rarely had time in the mornings to eat. A few minutes later her daughter appeared, looking surprisingly neat in her gymslip, blouse and tie, considering the short time she'd had to get dressed.

'Don't want breakfast, Mum.' She disappeared into the bathroom. Water briefly ran, the lavatory flushed. Dinah reappeared. 'Where's me satchel?'

'Don't ask me, luv. It's wherever you left it last night.'

'Where did I do me homework?'

'I can't recall you doing any.'

'I read a book, didn't I?' Dinah looked at her defiantly.

'I didn't realise they set *True Confessions* as homework these days.'

'I read a chapter of *Vanity Fair*, if you must know.'

She must have read it awfully quickly. Josie held back the comment, and found the satchel on the floor beside the settee.

Dinah swung the bag on to her shoulder. 'Ta, Mum. I might be late home from school.'

'Where are you going, luv?' Josie asked anxiously. Dinah was late home most nights. Sometimes it was seven o'clock by the time she put in an appearance.

'Round Charlie Flaherty's house.'

'A boy! Will there be other girls there, Dinah?'

'Oh, Mum. Get with it. Charlie's a girl – Charlotte. We're only going to listen to her record player. Where's me coat?'

'Behind the door, where it always is.'

'Well, it's not there now!'

The navy blue duffel coat was on the floor on the other side of the settee. Dinah picked it up, muttered a curt, 'Tara,' and left the house, only half into the coat.

Josie stood at the window and watched the tall, slim figure of her daughter go running down the path, still struggling with the coat. She sighed. It was a sad fact, but she didn't get on with Dinah. They never really had, but things had gone from bad to worse since she'd started at the local comprehensive school three years ago. She'd failed the eleven-plus, Josie suspected deliberately, out of sheer bloody-mindedness, because everybody, her mother included, had expected her to pass, or it might have been because she didn't fancy the long journey each day to the nearest grammar school. Whatever the reason, Dinah had failed, and now they seemed at daggers drawn most of the time.

She went into the dining room and finished off the cornflakes, then drained the pot of tea. She couldn't help but wonder what Laura might have been like at fourteen. Josie felt sure she wouldn't have spoken to her mother the way Dinah did, so impatiently, so rudely. They would have done things together – gone shopping, to the pictures, had little confidential chats. Perhaps Dinah would have been different if she'd had a father. Well, she *did* have a father, but he'd decided to ignore her existence, which only made it worse. It can't have done the girl much good.

'Oh, well, it's no use sitting here thinking about what might have been. I'll be late for work,' she said to the empty room.

She would have missed it if it hadn't been for Mr Kavanagh, still living with

Marigold and bedridden most of the time. He telephoned one Sunday morning in July. 'Do you get the *Sunday Times*, dear?'

'No, the *News of the World*.'

'Well, I should get *The Times* today if I were you. There's an article about that writer you used to work for, Louisa Chalcott. It's very interesting. It's her centenary, you see. She was born a hundred years ago this month.'

1974! Louisa had given her a brown envelope sealed with wax which wasn't to be opened until 1974. Josie thanked Mr Kavanagh, and began to search for the envelope. She couldn't remember where she'd put it. She ransacked the house, waking up an irritable Dinah who liked to lie in on Sundays, and found it at the bottom of the wardrobe drawer, underneath the spare blankets. She knelt on the floor and took the envelope out.

'Oh, gosh!' She recalled the night Louisa had given it to her. She'd just finished the garden, and they were sitting on the bench outside. The sea, the sky, the sand, had looked so beautiful, peaceful.

The envelope looked remarkably new. Josie broke the wax, and withdrew three shiny red exercise books. She flicked through them. Every page was crammed with Louisa's scarcely decipherable scribble. It wasn't poetry. She managed to read a page, thought it might be a highly risqué novel, then realised it was the story of Louisa's life, her autobiography.

'Oh, gosh!' she said again. *Lady Chatterley's Lover* was probably mild by comparison. She noticed a slip of paper had fallen from one of the books. 'This book,' she read, 'is both dedicated and gifted to my dear friend, Miss Josephine Flynn, to do with whatsoever she may please.'

'Well, I'm not likely to throw it away, am I, Louisa?' Josie said aloud. 'All I can do is read it, if I can make sense of your lousy writing, that is.'

'Who are you talking to?' Dinah, in the skimpiest of nighties, was at the bedroom door.

'Meself. I'm just going to get the Sunday paper.'

'What are those?' Dinah asked as Josie returned the books and the slip of paper to the envelope.

'Just something written by an old lady I used to work for. She was a poet. Her name was Louisa Chalcott.'

'Can I have a look?'

'Well,' Josie said doubtfully, 'it's not suitable for young eyes, luv. It's pretty hot stuff, as they say.'

Dinah pouted. 'You don't mind me reading *True Confessions*.'

'I do, actually. And this is *True Confessions* with knobs on. Oh, go on.' She shoved the envelope at her daughter. 'You probably won't be able to make head or tail of her writing. Be careful with it. I'd like to try and read it meself some time.'

The article in the *Sunday Times* repeated much that had been in Louisa's obituary twenty years before. She was before her time, her scandalous lifestyle had caused a furore in turn-of-the-century New York, and even later, in the twenties, when she had given birth to twins but had refused to name the father. The writer went on to say that the twins, Marian Moorcroft and Hilary Mann, now living in Croydon, England, had refused to discuss their mother. Lousia Chalcott's raw, earthy poetry had seen a renaissance of late. The unsuspected power of her work was only now beginning to be recognised, and would shortly be republished in full. There was, however, one choice piece of work the public would never see. According to her agent, Leonard McGill, Miss Chalcott had written her autobiography, but unfortunately it appeared to have been lost.

'"She assured me, several times, in the years prior to her death, that she was writing her life story," Mr McGill told me. "But although I and her daughters made a thorough search, the manuscript has never come to light."'

'Dinah,' Josie said urgently. 'Where's that scrap of paper that fell out the books?'

'Here.' Dinah was reading a red exercise book, mouth open, eyes shocked. 'Shit, Mum. This woman was an *ogre!* A nyphomaniac ogre! She must have been hell to work for.'

'She was, and she wasn't.' Josie searched for somewhere safe to put the paper. 'I might need that if it comes to a battle with the twins. And don't swear, luv. It's not very nice.'

3

Next day, she rang Directory Enquiries during her dinner break to get Leonard McGill's telephone number. She could actually remember his address in Holborn.

'He's at lunch,' she was told. 'Would you like to leave a message?'

'Yes, please. It's about Louisa Chalcott. He'll probably remember me.' They'd spoken over the phone often enough. 'I used to be Josie Flynn. Tell him I've got Louisa's manuscript.'

'Have you really?' remarked the disembodied voice. 'He *will* be pleased. He'll return your call the minute he gets in. Can I have your number?'

Josie reeled off the number. 'I'm going back to work, I'm afraid. I won't be home till four o'clock.'

'Oh, dear. I shall have a very agitated gentleman on my hands for the next three hours,' laughed the voice.

The phone was ringing when Josie unlocked the door two minutes after four. The years seemed to fall away when she heard the familiar, cultured tones of Leonard McGill. He courteously asked how she was before mentioning the manuscript, which she could tell he was dying to do. 'So, madam left it with you, did she? The twins will be thrilled. I'm over the moon. I long to read it, find out what that awful woman got up to.'

'Actually, she left it *to* me, not *with* me. I didn't realise I had it until yesterday. It was in an envelope which Louisa asked me not to open until nineteen seventy-four.'

There was silence, followed by a strange noise, like water gurgling down a drain, and she realised Leonard McGill was laughing. 'The twins will be as sick as dogs, and I'm even further over the moon. What a turn-up for the books, eh? Dreadful pair, those two. I'm not sure who was worse – the mother, or her frightful daughters.'

'Oh, the daughters,' Josie said promptly. 'At least Louisa was honest.'

'I'll let the press know. Offers of publication are bound to come pouring in. Now,' he said, and she could imagine him mentally rubbing his hands together with glee, 'I hesitate to abandon something so precious to the tender mercies of the Royal Mail, and I can scarcely ask you to bring it all the way to London. I think it best if I came personally to collect it as soon as possible. If I cancel my appointments, I could come tomorrow. Would that suit you?'

'No,' Josie said firmly. The manuscript was *hers*, and she wasn't prepared to let it out of her possession, not yet. 'I tell you what – the firm where I work has just got one of them new photocopying machines. I'll do a copy tomorrow and post it straight away.'

He was clearly disappointed, but Josie didn't care. She rang off. She was holding something very important, with which Louisa had said she could do 'whatsoever she may please'. Knowing Louisa, she'd had publication in mind, and had obviously wanted Josie to have the benefit of the royalties it would earn, which wouldn't be much, if her previous royalties were anything to go by, but better than nothing. But a principle was involved and, with the twins hovering on the horizon, it seemed important to hold on to the original until an agreement, or a contract, or whatever it was called, was signed.

She sank into a chair, feeling elated. At last something exciting had happened, and it was all due to Louisa.

In the nine years she had worked for Terence Dunnet, a small, reserved man with skin like parchment, half-moon spectacles and very little hair, they had never had a proper conversation. She felt slightly nervous when she asked if he would mind if she used his new copying machine. 'It's quite a few pages, hundreds, but I'll pay for the ink and paper. And I wouldn't do it during working hours, naturally.' She had told Dinah she might be late home, but Dinah said it didn't matter, she'd be even later.

'Well . . .' He looked from her to the gleaming new machine that stood in the corner of the main office. 'I don't suppose it would hurt. I get a discount the more paper that's used.'

'Ta, very much,' she said gratefully.

It was a slow job, and took much longer than expected. She was still hard at work at six o'clock when Terence Dunnet came out of his own office, ready to lock up and go home.

'I'll have to finish tomorrow.' She wiped her brow. It was a hot day, and continual use of the photocopier had turned the room into an oven. 'I'm only two-thirds of the way there.' There was still another exercise book to copy.

'What is this?' He looked with interest as a double page of barely legible scribble emerged from the machine and plopped on to the pile already there.

'It's a book, written by a friend of mine. I'm doing a copy for her agent,' Josie felt bound to explain.

'Has she had anything published before?'

'Yes, but only poetry.'

'*Only* poetry!' He smiled his dry-as-dust smile. 'My wife is something of an amateur poet, Mrs Coltrane. She would be annoyed to hear it referred to that way. What is your friend's name? If she's been published, Muriel may have heard of her.'

'Louisa Chalcott.' Josie herself did her best not to be annoyed. 'And I said "only" poetry, because this is something different, that's all. I wasn't being offensive.'

Terence Dunnet's glasses nearly dropped off his nose. 'This surely cannot be the manuscript that was mentioned in the *Sunday Times*? Louisa Chalcott is one of Muriel's favourite writers, and she gave me the article to read.'

Josie nodded, and explained she'd been Louisa's secretary, and had only known she held the missing manuscript on Sunday.

'How remarkable.' He looked dazed. 'How absolutely remarkable. And it's actually in *my* office! Muriel will be knocked for six when I tell her.' He put his briefcase on the floor, removed his jacket and rolled up his snow-white sleeves. 'It is obviously important that this reaches Miss Chalcott's agent with all possible speed. The last post goes from Whitechapel at eight o'clock. You look exhausted, Mrs Coltrane. Make us both a cup of tea while I finish this off. You know where the large envelopes are kept. Why not get one ready? *I* will make sure the post is caught. And forget about paying for the paper and the ink – a copy of the book when it's published would suffice.' He smiled again. 'Signed by you, of course.'

The twins consulted a solicitor, but according to Leonard McGill had been advised they hadn't a leg to stand on. 'I sent them a copy of Louisa's note,' he told Josie on the phone, 'and they tried to claim it was a forgery. I said if that was the case, the entire book must be a forgery because the writing is identical. By the way, I've had another offer – two and a half thousand pounds. The publishing trade are vying with each other for Louisa's last work. Sex and art.' He chuckled. 'A highly volatile combination.'

Josie gulped. She'd had no idea you got paid for books before they were published – half on signing the contract, the rest when it was published.

This was the third offer, five hundred pounds more than the last. 'Will you accept?'

'Will *you* accept, Josie?' Leonard said smoothly. 'It's entirely up to you. As your agent, I would recommend against it. It's early days yet.'

'It makes me feel uncomfortable,' she confessed. 'After all, it's not as if I wrote it.'

'Would you feel uncomfortable had Louisa left you a valuable antique that was up for auction?'

'Probably not.'

'Well, this is no different, my dear.'

By the end of August, the bidding had reached twelve thousand five hundred pounds, and Leonard McGill phoned.

'It's a new company, Hamilton & Ferrers. I know nothing about Ferrers, but Roger Hamilton is a well-known entrepreneur. He's been in oil, plastics, mining, owns a racehorse or two. The company have already published half a dozen works that haven't exactly set the world alight. He hopes to create a stir with *My Carnal Life*. I have tentatively accepted on your behalf.'

'Do you think the title's okay? It's the way Louisa described it more than once.'

'It's perfect, Josie. Oh, Roger Hamilton would like to meet you. I thought if I brought him to Liverpool one day soon, we could sign the contract over dinner and you can hand over the original manuscript at the same time.'

'Can I come?' Dinah demanded.

'You'd feel out of place, luv, with a crowd of old people.'

'You're only forty, Mum. And who's to say this Roger chap mightn't be young? Anyroad, I'd quite enjoy it. And you need someone on your side.'

'It's not a battle,' Josie argued. 'There won't be sides. If there were, Leonard McGill should be on mine. He's me agent.'

'He's also a man. It'll be two men against one woman if I don't come with you.'

'As I said, it's not a battle ... Oh, all right. I'd like to have you with me. I'll ask Leonard to book a table for four.'

She felt touched that Dinah seemed protective all of a sudden, and bought them a new outfit each for the occasion. They actually ventured into George Henry Lee's, where the prices were normally way beyond her reach. It meant being temporarily overdrawn at the bank.

'Gosh, this brings back memories.' She searched through a rack of elegant suits, possibly a bit warm for early September.

'Memories of what?'

'Of shopping in the Kings Road when money was no object. You should have seen the things I used to buy, Dinah! You know me camel coat with the fur collar? I bought that in the Kings Road. It's older than you are, and still in good condition.'

'I suppose Laura had lovely clothes, too,' Dinah said.

It was a long time since she'd mentioned Laura, and Josie was upset by the bitterness in her voice. She touched the slim, white arm. 'You didn't exactly go short, luv. I always made sure you were as well dressed as Lily's Samantha.'

For once, Dinah didn't shrug her away. 'Are you going to buy one of these?'

'No, I'd prefer something not so heavy.'

She settled on a violet shot silk suit with a straight skirt and boxy jacket, with a black lace blouse to go underneath. Dinah refused to be talked out of a brief green linen frock that barely covered her behind.

'You'll have to wear tights,' her mother advised as she gritted her teeth and wrote the cheque, 'else your thighs will get stuck to the seats if they're leather.'

The dinner was arranged for five days later. That afternoon they went together to the hairdresser's. Dinah was still on holiday from school, and Terence Dunnet willingly gave Josie the time off. He had been dining out on the story of a famous lost manuscript being photocopied in his office, and she had kept him abreast of the various bids. He had offered to read the contract before it was signed. 'As an accountant, I often read through agreements, contracts, that sort of thing. I can check if you're getting a good deal.'

'I'm signing it at dinner, but I trust Leonard McGill – that's the agent – completely. He's entitled to ten per cent, I know that much.'

'Well, if you need help or advice, I'm at your service.'

'Ta.' She was pleased that they had become friends. They'd started to call each other Terence and Josie. His wife, Muriel, had been to see her, wanting to know all about Louisa Chalcott.

'Do I look all right?' she anxiously asked Dinah that night when she was ready to go.

'Gorgeous, Mum. That suit makes your eyes look a lovely dark blue. I wish mine were darker. What colour did me dad have?'

'Brown – still does, I expect. You've got lovely colour eyes, Dinah, there's a touch of lilac in them.' She looked sophisticated, and at the same time very young and fresh, in the green dress. Her fair, rather fine hair, tucked behind a green band, was shoulder length and turned up at the ends. She wore lipstick for the first time, a light coral, and her normally pale cheeks were slightly flushed. She was obviously excited at the thought of the evening ahead.

Relations with Dinah had improved enormously over the last few weeks. It was as if, since the discovery of Louisa's book, she was seeing her mother in a new light, with an interesting past, not just someone who nagged her to get up or wanted to know what time she'd be home. Had she been a different sort of girl, Josie would have told her about Louisa – and all sorts of other things – before, but Dinah had never seemed interested in talking to her mother.

Leonard McGill had booked a table at The George in Lime Street, expensive and discreet. Josie had never set foot in the place before. Dinah insisted they be five minutes late. 'You don't want to look too anxious.'

'I want to look polite, that's all.'

'Let them be waiting for us, not us for them.'

The restaurant was barely half-full. Two men were sitting at a corner table, set slightly apart from the others. Waiters hovered attentively, and there was the subdued clink of dishes, the mouth-watering smell of food. One of the men stood, waved and came towards them.

'Josie! We meet at last. Leonard McGill, how do you do?' He shook hands effusively. 'And this must be Dinah!' He turned back to Josie. 'Why, you were scarcely any older than this when we first spoke on the phone all those years ago. How lovely to see you both. Let me introduce you to Roger.'

Roger Hamilton was equally effusive. Both men were remarkably similar in appearance – early fifties, silver-haired, wearing dark suits and dark ties. Roger Hamilton's clothes were clearly more expensive than those of a mere literary agent, and his face redder, his chin jowly. Josie wondered if the large green stone in his tie clip was a real emerald. She was immediately struck with the feeling that she'd seen him before, and also that she didn't like him much. Behind the smiling eyes she sensed a hardness. This man could be very cruel and ruthless, she suspected, but perhaps that went for all entrepreneurs.

Throughout the meal she felt she was being slightly patronised by both men. 'I suppose this will be your first and only venture into the world of literature,' Roger Hamilton remarked over the main course, delectable roast beef and melt-in-the-mouth vegetables.

'It's not her first.' Dinah spoke up. 'My father used to be a famous television writer, and she used to do his typing. What was it he wrote, Mum?'

'*Di Marco of the Met*, and a few other things.'

'He's in Hollywood now. He writes scripts for films. Mum divorced him because she didn't like living in London. Before that, they lived in New York.'

Under the table, Josie kicked her daughter's ankle, but was glad she'd spoken, even if she'd made half of it up. She was regarded with new respect. They had probably thought they were dealing with an ignorant peasant. She said to the publisher, 'I've a feeling I've seen you before, but can't remember where.'

'On television? I'm often interviewed about this and that. I'm on the book programme shortly, promoting *My Carnal Life*.'

'No.' She shook her head. He hadn't had silver hair. It was more the cut-glass accent she remembered, the rather jerky gestures. 'It'll come to mind eventually.'

The meal ended, more wine was ordered, glasses filled, including one for Dinah who'd drunk lemonade so far. 'To toast the signing,' said Leonard

McGill. He produced a sheaf of papers from his briefcase. 'The contract, Josie. Do you have the manuscript with you?'

'Of course.' Terence Dunnet had loaned her a leather document case to carry it in. 'It's here.'

'Fair exchange is no robbery.' He laughed. 'Read through this, my dear. Initial each page at the bottom, and sign on the dotted line at the end.'

'I'm sure there's no need to read it.' Josie began to flick through the pages, conscious of Roger Hamilton watching, almost licking his lips, as he waited for her to sign.

'I have been long awaiting this moment, but I'm afraid nature calls. Please, excuse me.' The agent left the table.

Josie reached inside her handbag for a pen. The man opposite was playing with a knife, turning it over and over in his hand. She stared at the knife, then at his face. 'I've definitely seen you before. Have you ever been to Liverpool?'

'During the war, yes. My regiment stayed overnight before sailing for Cairo.' He smiled charmingly at her. 'But you would have been just a babe in arms then, possibly not even born.'

'You've got a sister called Abigail.'

He dropped the knife. 'How can you possibly know that? She died years ago.' His face went ghostly white, his jaw wobbled. He picked up a glass, drained it, smoothed back the silver hair with a hand that shook.

Josie's eyes never left his face. He'd remembered, too! 'You called me mam a whore,' she said softly. 'You nearly raped me. I wasn't a babe in arms, but I was only six.'

There was silence, and it seemed to go on for ever. A waiter appeared, and went away when everything seemed to be in order. Across the room someone laughed. A cork popped.

'Look, that was a long time ago.' His voice was hoarse, uneven. Saliva oozed from the corners of his mouth. 'We were living on the edge. We did things we wouldn't normally dream of doing. We weren't ourselves.'

'Nothing can excuse what you tried to do.'

He swallowed, recovered slightly, became belligerent. 'If I recall rightly, your mother *was* a whore.'

'*I* wasn't,' said Josie. 'I was six.' She stood, collected her things together, put them in her bag and picked up the document case. 'Goodbye, Mr Hamilton. I think Louisa would have preferred her book to be published by someone else.'

'Look!' He was angry now, so angry that it scared her. 'If this gets out, you won't look whiter than white. Your mother was a prostitute. It's not something to boast about.'

'It's not something to be ashamed of either. But it won't get out, Mr Hamilton. I'm going to put it to the back of me mind again, where it's always been until tonight when I met you.'

'Mum, Mum. You left without me.' Dinah caught her up at the door and grabbed her arm.

'I'd forgotten you were there! Oh, luv!' She could have wept. 'You shouldn't have heard all that stuff.' Dinah wasn't fourteen until the end of the month.

'Are you all right?'

'No, luv, I'm not. Me legs seem to have disappeared, and me head feels like someone else's. I need a drink – a cup of tea, dead strong.'

They emerged into Lime Street. Dinah linked her arm in Josie's for the very first time. Josie said shakily, 'Let's go to the Adelphi lounge, hang the expense.'

'What was all that about, Mum?'

'I reckon you've already got the gist of it, Dinah.'

'Grandma was a prostitute?' The girl's face was bright with curiosity, and Josie was relieved there was no sign of disgust.

'Yes. Look, once I've got a pot of tea in front of me, I'll tell you the whole thing.'

'Did the dinner go well?' Terence enquired next morning.

'It went abysmally.' Josie made a face. She'd hardly slept, reliving the awful meal, worrying about Louisa's book. 'The publisher chap was dead rude, so I walked out. I'll call Leonard McGill when I get home. He'll have to get someone else.'

'What a dreadful pity. Call him from here if you wish,' he said generously. 'The sooner the better. Muriel can't wait for that book to be in print.'

'Ta, very much. Oh, I've got the contract. I was so mad I stuffed it in me bag without thinking.'

'Ah, do let me see.'

She handed him the contract, then dialled the London number. The friendly receptionist answered as usual. 'What did you do to him, Josie? He's like a bear with a sore head this morning. Hold on a minute, I'll put you through.'

The extension rang. 'Josie! What on earth happened last night? Poor Roger, he claimed you took umbrage over something trivial. I said that wasn't like you.' His voice was strained, as if he was finding it hard to be his courteous self.

'Poor Roger's talking rubbish, but I'd sooner not talk about it if you don't mind. I'd like you to find another publisher.'

'That's easily done, though the advance won't be as large.'

'I don't mind.' Josie was conscious of something very odd happening. Terence Dunnet was doing a war dance in front of her eyes, mouthing, 'No, no, no,' and waving his arms, jumping up and down. To her complete astonishment, he suddenly snatched the phone out of her hand in mid-sentence and slammed it down.

'Sorry to be rude,' he gasped, 'but you don't just need another publisher, Josie, you need another agent. Did you agree to sell the book outright to this Hamilton chap?'

'I didn't agree to anything in particular.' She looked at him, alarmed. 'Is something wrong?'

'There most certainly is,' he said grimly. 'No author in their right mind sells a book outright. If you had signed this, you would have given up all rights to the work. You wouldn't have received a penny in royalties.' He waved the contract. 'It would seem that Hamilton and McGill took advantage of your ignorance, did a deal, signed a private contract of their own. Either that, or a very large backhander was involved.'

She was back to square one, no further than that. At least in the beginning she'd had an agent to negotiate on her behalf. How did you acquire an agent? Terence offered to find out.

'Do you *need* an agent?' Dinah queried that night. 'Why can't you send it to a publisher yourself?'

'Terence said that might be tricky. Leonard McGill had offers from most major publishers, so he'd consider himself entitled to ten per cent. He rang earlier, and wasn't half mad when I told him nicely to get stuffed.' She wasn't prepared to let him have a penny, and still bristled with indignation at how close she'd come to being conned.

'Another agent might find it tricky, too.'

'I know.' Josie sighed. She was beginning to wish Louisa hadn't left her the damned book.

'Mum?'

'Yes, luv?'

'I'm sorry.'

'For goodness' sake, luv.' Josie laughed. 'None of this is your fault.'

'I know, Mum.' Dinah came and sat beside her on the settee. 'It's that stuff you told me last night. I've been thinking about it all day. I've been horrible, haven't I? I was a hateful little girl, and now I'm a hateful big girl.'

'Dinah, luv! You've never been horrible. I must concede you've been a bit awkward from time to time, but horrible and hateful? Never!'

'Yes, I have, Mum.' Dinah seemed to hesitate, before laying her head on her mother's shoulder. 'You didn't have a mum or dad, and today I realised how lucky I was, having you.'

'And I'm lucky, having you.' Josie's heart turned over. Was it possible that after fourteen strained years they might become friends?

'When I was little,' Dinah said in a small voice, 'I used to have this dead funny feeling that you didn't want me, that I was in the way. When I got older I was convinced you kept comparing me to Laura, wishing I was nicer, more like her. I *was* awkward. I did it deliberately, I don't know why.'

'I was *glad* you weren't like Laura,' Josie cried. Guilt almost choked her. Fancy, a tiny baby sensing it was unwanted. 'I preferred to have a little girl different to Laura. It was wonderful, you know,' she said softly, 'to find meself pregnant only a few weeks after Laura died. Like a miracle. I would have been dead lonely without you, what with your dad gone an' all.' It came to her how empty the last years would have been, spent alone. 'Mind you, it was me own fault your dad went, I told you that last night. He didn't want to go, I made him. If we'd known about you, nothing would have made him leave.' Last night, she'd told her daughter just about everything except the murky part Uncle Vince had played in her own and Mam's life. She wasn't quite old enough to know *that* yet!

'And you nearly married Ben Kavanagh!' Dinah wrinkled her white nose. 'He's a bit of a drip, Mum. I'm surprised he didn't propose again when his wife died.'

'Oh, he did, but I turned him down. He's not a drip, Dinah, just a very sensitive man.'

'Huh! I always thought you'd marry Francie O'Leary. I've always liked him.'

'So has your Auntie Lily.' Josie grinned. 'And now she's got him, hasn't she?'

Directly after that New Year's Eve four years ago, when Lily had claimed it was her intention to chase Francie O'Leary to the ends of the earth, Josie had told him she didn't want to marry him. She didn't add that Lily's need was much greater than hers.

Francie's face was tragic. 'Why ever not, Jose?'

She looked at him in surprise. 'I didn't think you'd care. I mean, we don't love each other.'

'I *don't* care,' Francie wailed. 'That's what's so bloody tragic. I *want* to care, about something, someone. I've got a gene missing, Jose. The gene that makes a person fall in love.'

'Don't be so ridiculous, Francie. You just haven't met the right person yet, that's all.'

'What about the bed bit? I *do* care about that.'

'The bed bit's over and finished with. We're not getting married, and I'm not the sort of woman who sleeps around.'

'Oh, Jose! But we'll still be friends, won't we?'

'The best of friends,' Josie assured him.

A distraught and tearful Neil Baxter left the house by Woolton Park and got a flat in Anfield as close as possible to Liverpool Football Club. Lily was a bit put out when, after an indecently short interval, he started going out with his landlady's daughter, almost twenty years his junior. They got married two years later, as soon as the divorce came through.

In the meantime, Lily ruthlessly set about wooing Francie O'Leary with all the wiles at her disposal. She and Josie developed a code. When Francie came to Baker's Row, Josie would dial Lily's number and let it ring three times. Shortly afterwards, Lily would arrive, as nice as pie, usually with the children who had been trained to call him 'Uncle Francie' and sit on his knee whenever possible. Invitations were printed for Samantha's and

Gillian's parties, which required Lily calling on Francie at his place of work, and also for the headed notepaper she suddenly found essential. She threw grown-up parties, and played nothing but Louis Armstrong records, Jellyroll Morton, King Oliver – Francie's all-time favourite music.

One night, Francie arrived at Baker's Row, and collapsed in a chair. 'Lily's proposed,' he said in a strangled voice.

'Are you going to accept?' Josie held her breath. She'd known a proposal was on the cards.

'It's either that, or move to another country. Or another planet.' He smiled slightly and stretched his legs. She thought he looked a bit smug. 'Actually, Jose, it wouldn't be such a bad thing to have someone like Lily Kavanagh on your side. She's come up with all sorts of ideas for the business, quite good ones. But I won't be nagged,' he said warningly, as if Josie had the power to prevent it. 'I will not be nagged or pissed around or told off in public – in private either, come to that. By the way, Jose, you've never told her about us, have you?'

'Lord, no, Francie.' Lily would have killed her.

And so it came to pass that Lily became Mrs Francis O'Leary, twenty-two years, almost to the day, since she'd been so publicly jilted by him in a noisy pub in Smithdown Road.

'I've been thinking, Mum,' Dinah said three days after the fateful dinner. 'You could publish Louisa's book yourself.'

'Oh, yeah! On Terence Dunnet's photocopying machine?'

'No, get Francie to do it. He does books, at least he does booklets. Marilyn brought one to school one day. It was a history of Liverpool Docks.'

'He won't do it for free, luv.'

'Get a loan from the bank,' Dinah said promptly. 'Francie got a loan when he expanded, I remember him saying once.'

'I'll talk it over with Terence.'

'It's not such a bad idea.' Terence smiled. 'Your daughter has a good business head on her shoulders. This is not a first novel by an unknown author, it's a book that comes with its own advance publicity. It doesn't need to be promoted. A circular sent to every bookshop in the land, a few advertisements in the press, should do it. It's a venture I would very much like to invest in, Josie. Get a quotation from your friend, and I'll draw up a business plan. We mustn't forget postage and packing, and I'm sure there will be other things to take into account.' He rubbed his dry hands together. 'This is getting rather exciting. Wait till I tell Muriel!'

'How many copies would you want, Jose?'

'I haven't a clue, Francie. Thousands, I expect.'

'That's a great help. I'll do two quotes – one for five thousand, another for ten. Once the machine's set up, it's a simple matter to run off more.

Have you thought about the cover? The more colours you have, the more expensive it'll be. And would you like it glossy?' He punched the air. 'Actually, Jose, I've never done such a big job before. It's dead exciting.'

Daisy said there was a directory in the reference section of the library listing bookshops in the British Isles. 'It's not supposed to be borrowed, but I'll make an exception, seeing as it's you. Let me have it back as soon as possible, though.'

Terence Dunnet's clients were neglected as Josie spent several days typing the envelopes for the circulars announcing the publication of *My Carnal Life* in November. There was a cut-off section at the bottom for orders.

'Don't forget to send advance copies to the critics,' Mr Kavanagh advised from his sickbed.

'Can I have ten copies for Christmas presents?' enquired Muriel Dunnet.

Lily, heavily pregnant with what she prayed was a son, borrowed a typewriter from Francie's works and typed the manuscript out. She kept ringing Josie every time she reached a particularly juicy bit. 'Louisa went on a cruise once, and she slept with three stewards and the purser.'

'I remember her telling me that.'

'Will you dedicate the book to me after all my hard work?'

'I'll do no such thing. It's already dedicated to me.'

'It's a miserable cover, Mum,' Dinah remarked.

'No, it's not. It's dead tasteful.' The cover was plain grey, with Louisa's name in black and *My Carnal Life* embossed in gold. 'That gold cost an arm and a leg.'

'Another thousand!' Francie gasped. 'That'll be twenty altogether. You're going to have a bestseller on your hands. By the way, Jose, your company needs a name.'

'What company?'

'Your publishing company. Even if it's only a one-off, it needs a name. Coltrane Press would do.'

Josie cogitated overnight. 'Make it Barefoot House Press,' she told Francie next day.

'That's a bit of a mouthful. What's wrong with just Barefoot House?'

'Nothing,' she agreed.

'I'll sue,' Leonard McGill threatened when news of the imminent publication reached him.

'So sue. I'll tell everybody how you tried to rook me.'

'I am Louisa's agent.'

'You *were* Louisa's agent. You're not now.' Josie slammed down the phone.

This is better than sex, she thought one morning, feeling a surge of pleasure when even more envelopes than usual were pushed through the letter box. Well, no, not better. Not even as good. But close. One of the orders was from a shop in Knightsbridge where Louisa had ordered books when she'd stayed in London before the war. There was a letter enclosed. 'One of our assistants, Miss Whalley, can actually remember Miss Chalcott coming in. All our staff wish you well with your venture, and look forward to having the book on our shelves.'

Oh, Lord! There was an order from W.H. Smith for 6000 copies. Josie whooped. She quickly got ready for work and rushed to tell Terence.

It was a dreary November morning. The air was wet with drizzle, and banks of ominous black clouds slowly rolled across an already grey sky. But the six people gathered in the glass-partitioned office in the corner of a print works in Speke were oblivious to the weather. Lily and Francie O'Leary, Muriel and Terence Dunnet, and Josie and Dinah Coltrane had something to celebrate. The first pages of *My Carnal Life* had just begun to roll off the press. Francie produced a bottle of champagne. Lily had brought glasses.

'To Louisa.' Francie raised his glass.

'To Louisa.'

That night Lily gave birth to a boy weighing eight pounds six ounces. Francie called Josie from the hospital. 'She wanted to call him Louis, in memory of Louisa, like, but I talked her out of it. I mean, Louis O'Leary is a helluva moniker to wish on a kid. We're calling him Simon instead.'

Some critics thought *My Carnal Life* disgusting, but confessed they couldn't stop turning to the next page. Others said Louisa's life was reflected in her dark, passionate poetry. Or that she had been a feminist before the word had been invented. That she had been a greedy, arrogant, over-sexed woman, who'd known what she'd wanted and hadn't cared who she'd hurt in the process of getting it. But they all agreed she wrote like a dream.

By Christmas, Louisa's book had already been reissued three times. Josie had given several interviews to the press about her part in Louisa's life and the publication of the book. She'd gone all the way to Broadcasting House in London to be interviewed on the wireless.

'Radio, Mum,' corrected Dinah. 'Don't say "wireless", they'll think you've come out of the ark.'

By March, the orders had virtually dried up, the foreign rights had been sold, the interviews were over, the excitement had died down. Terence Dunnet's loan had been repaid with interest and all the bills had been settled, leaving Josie with a reasonable sum in the bank, more than enough to have her house modernised and extended or buy somewhere else, as well as get a car. It was nice to be well off, but life seemed emptier than ever after the last tumultuous months. She still worked for Terence, and the job was much more pleasant since they'd become friends, but it wasn't enough to occupy her mind. She badly missed finding heaps of post on her doormat, the endless phone calls, typing letters late into the night on her *own* behalf. The portable typewriter she'd bought hadn't been used in weeks.

She badly wanted back the turbulence, the excitement. But how?

The manuscripts had started to arrive when Louisa's book had hardly been out a week, poetry mainly. Sometimes only a single poem was sent, or two or three. 'In case you should ever decide to publish an anthology,' the authors wrote. They were addressed to 'The Editor', as if Barefoot House were a huge company with loads of staff.

Josie always sent them back with a polite letter, explaining that Louisa's book had been a one-off and there would be no more. A few novels came which, out of interest, she began to read, but gave up when she realised they were awful. There was a murder mystery from a man in Somerset that was so good she read it right through to the end, returning the manuscript with a flattering letter saying she was sure he would find another publisher for his excellent book.

She came home from work one day and found a large, fat envelope on the mat, obviously delivered by hand. It was from a William Friars of Bootle, she discovered when she read the badly typed covering letter. The more than three hundred pages, entitled *The Blackout Murders*, were just as poorly typed. She made a cup of tea and began to read. She was still reading when Dinah came home from school to find there was no meal made, and she was despatched for fish and chips. Josie read while she ate, and was still reading at midnight. She took the book to bed and read there.

'Phew!' she gasped when she had finished. Her eyes were hurting, her head was aching, but she had never read anything so gripping before. It was a thriller, set during the last war, in which a killer stalks the blacked-out streets and back alleys of Bootle, secreting his hapless victims in the rubble left by the blitz. The hero, Edgar Hood, a sensitive, disturbed young man with a club foot, rejected by the Army and longing to do his bit, has set up his own private detective agency by the time the novel ends.

Josie visualised more books involving the same character – Edgar Hood could be another Hercule Poirot or Lord Peter Wimsey. She went downstairs and made tea, too excited to notice it was almost two o'clock, then found the carbon copy of the letter she'd sent to the man in Somerset who'd written the thriller, not quite as good as *The Blackout Murders*, but still highly readable. She wrote there and then and suggested he kindly send his novel back.

Tomorrow she would hand in her notice, and ask Terence to draw up another business plan. It would be harder this time as the authors would be unknown, but Barefoot House was about to become a proper publishing company of crime fiction. She knew nothing about poetry, and only liked it if it rhymed, but she'd been reading thrillers all her adult life.

Huskisson Street
1974–1984

1

'That was dreadful.' Dinah yawned and threw the manuscript to the floor.

'Be careful, luv. I can see it's beautifully typed.'

'That's the only thing good about it. I could tell who "dun" it by page five. I'll get Bobby to send it back tomorrow.' Dinah read through every piece of work received by Barefoot House, the small but highly respected publishing company located in Liverpool. Sometimes a few pages were enough to judge if it wasn't suitable. The more promising ones she passed over to her mother.

'I'd better get ready. Me and Jeff are going to the Playhouse.' She got to her feet. Dinah hadn't stopped growing until two years ago when she was seventeen, and she was now three inches taller than Josie, slender and graceful in her jeans and T-shirt. 'Actually, Mum . . .' She sat down again. 'There was something I wanted to talk to you about.'

'I'm all ears, luv.' Josie felt sleepy, curled up in a chair in front of the realistic flames of an electric fire.

'I'm thinking of moving to London.'

She was suddenly wide awake. 'London! But why, Dinah? I thought you and Jeff were serious?' She found it difficult to keep track of Dinah's young men, but Jeff had lasted longer than most. He was twenty-four, a quantity surveyor, almost handsome. She quite fancied him for a son-in-law.

Dinah wrinkled her nose. 'Jeff's serious. I don't want to settle down, Mum, not like Samantha, with a husband and baby at nineteen. There's a whole world out there I've yet to see.'

'I know, luv.' She sighed. She'd felt the same when she was young. 'But what about a job? Unemployment's soaring.'

'I can type, Mum, and I have experience in publishing. In fact . . .' She looked ever so slightly uncomfortable. 'You know that agent, the new one – Evelyn King? Well, she's offered me a job, doing more or less what I do now

229

– reading manuscripts, corresponding with authors, that sort of thing. She even said I can stay in her flat till I find somewhere of me own.'

'When was this?'

'A few months ago.'

Josie smiled. 'So you've been plotting and planning behind me back, have you?' Despite the smile, she was hurt.

'Not exactly, Mum. I didn't take much notice till Jeff asked me to marry him, and I realised it was the last thing I wanted.' Dinah leaned forward in the chair, her blue eyes bright with hope and excitement. 'I haven't *lived*, Mum. At least London's a start. I thought I might go after Christmas. One day I'd like to go to New York, like you.'

'Well, I'll not stand in your way, Dinah.' Josie smiled again. 'Not that you'd let me if I tried. It's your life, and you must do with it exactly as you please.'

'I knew you'd understand.'

Dinah went upstairs, and returned fifteen minutes later in different jeans and T-shirt. She was also wearing a short, fake-fur coat, which seemed a dead funny outfit to wear for the theatre but, then, Josie had worn a few dead funny outfits in her day.

'Tara, Mum.'

'Tara, luv. Have a nice time.'

Josie listened to the footsteps racing swiftly down the stairs. The front door opened, and again Dinah yelled, 'Tara.' The door slammed.

'Tara, luv,' Josie whispered. A lump came to her throat. She felt incredibly sad, as if Dinah had gone for good.

She didn't want her daughter to go to London. Over the last few years, with Lily preoccupied with Francie, Dinah had become her best and closest friend. It was selfish, but Josie wanted her to get married, live in Liverpool and have children so she could visit her, the way Lily visited Samantha and her grandson.

Tea! She urgently needed a cup of tea. The new fitted kitchen was in Maude's room. Ever since she'd bought the house in Huskisson Street, four doors away from where she'd lived with Mam, with exactly the same layout, she couldn't help but think of the girls. Irish Rose's room was Reception where Esther, her secretary, worked, as did the office junior, Bobby, who staggered to the post office twice a day with returned manuscripts.

Fat Liz's room had been split into two – one half Josie's office, the other Dinah's and Richard White's, who was in charge of publicity and circulation. What had been a very large cupboard now housed Eric, who'd been made redundant by the English Electric Company and worked part time, organising the wages, paying the bills and keeping the books in tiptop condition for Terence Dunnet, who did the firm's accounts and read through contracts to make sure they were correct. The more complicated legal work Josie passed on to a solicitor. Lynne and Sophie, the proofreaders, both graduates and married with small children, worked from home.

The kettle boiled. How many times in her life had she stood and watched a kettle boil? Millions. She made tea, furiously stirring the pot, but instead of taking the mug back to the lounge she went up two flights of stairs to the attic, to Mabel's and Josie's room! The house had been renovated throughout before she'd moved in, but there seemed little point having the little black grate and the corner sink removed.

This was where the rubbish was kept – the odds and ends of furniture she didn't want to throw away, the books she'd read but might read again, Dinah's school books which she preferred to keep, despite the fact she hadn't exactly been a star pupil. With her record, she'd been dead lucky to have a job waiting for her in Barefoot House when she left. There was a box of Dinah's toys, the trumpet Aunt Ivy had given her on her fifth birthday on top, its shine long gone.

It had been a shock, Aunt Ivy dying so suddenly without any apparent reason. It turned out her heart had just decided to stop beating one night as she lay beside Alf who, with his children, had stripped the house in Machin Street of everything nice. Josie had been surprised to find herself in tears at the funeral. Perhaps it was because she was gradually losing all links with the past – Mr Kavanagh had died not long before, and Sid and Chrissie Spencer had retired to Morecambe. According to Daisy, who still lived in Machin Street with Manos, Aunt Ivy's house had been sold to pay Alf's debts with the bookies. No one knew where the family had gone.

'Well, Mam,' she said loudly, 'Your daughter's about to be left on her own again. What are you going to do about it, eh?'

Mam didn't answer, and Josie's own heart might well have stopped beating if she had. She switched off the light and closed the door. At the top of the stairs she paused on the plush green carpet and watched the cold December stars blinking down at her through the skylight, the same stars she'd shown Teddy forty years ago.

'This is making me feel even sadder!'

She went down to the bottom floor, pausing in Maude's room on the way for another mug of tea. In Dinah's office she found a manuscript with a yellow sticker, indicating it had been read but Dinah was in two minds as to whether it was any good. She tucked it under her arm to read. A red sticker meant very good, a green one that the work showed promise, and a rare gold one that the novel was a knockout. Black was the death knell for any hopeful author, and their work was returned with a letter of rejection. Dinah was an excellent judge for someone so young. She'd do well with Evelyn King's literary agency. She knew as much about publishing as Josie, admittedly only on a small scale.

In her own office, Josie sat at her desk and began to read. After a few minutes she gave up, unable to concentrate for thinking about Dinah. Perhaps if she made her daughter a partner, signed half of the company

over to her, she might stay. But that would be unfair. She would almost
certainly see it as a desperate move on her part but, knowing Dinah, she still
wouldn't stay, and it would create tension. Best let her go, with smiles and
best wishes for a better, more exciting life in London.

Josie glanced at the shelf of Barefoot House publications: seventy-three
books so far. There'd been only five the first year, ten in the second. Now
they were putting out twenty-five novels a year, all with the same bright red
glossy covers, the author's name in black, the titles embossed in gold.

The Blackout Murders, their first publication, had put Barefoot House on
the map. The paperback had sold more than a hundred thousand copies
within three months, but William Friars, the author, lately of Bootle, now
living in a smart residence in Calderstones, had turned out to be a pain. A
retired schoolteacher, he contested every alteration the copy editor made,
complained about the covers always being the same, demanded ever-
increasing advances which were only just met by the admittedly huge sales.

His latest offering, *Death By Stealth*, was on her desk. It was the first he'd
set post-war, and she didn't think it very good. The others, written with a
terrible war raging in the background, had had a darkness, a compelling
atmosphere of fear. His new book seemed pale by comparison. She had
tactfully told him that he would be better off sticking to the war years, but
he had lost his temper and demanded an advance that made her wince.

'I have been approached by another publisher,' he said pettishly, 'a firm
much bigger than yours, who are prepared to meet my demands.'

Josie wasn't too keen on being blackmailed. 'I'll think about it,' she
promised, with a feeling that she would shortly be telling William Friars to
get stuffed.

Still, he had contributed to the so far modest success of Barefoot House.
Without William Friars, she wouldn't have been able to buy this house,
centrally situated in the shadow of the Protestant cathedral, a perfect place
to live and run a company under the same roof.

She returned to the spacious first-floor lounge, tall Kate's room. If only
Mam could see it, with its pink and cream striped wallpaper and a four-
seater settee covered with matching material. The armchairs were pink
velvet. Lily had said she should buy Regency furniture, but Josie preferred
pine, even if it was out of period. There was a pine bureau, coffee-table,
chests, two bookcases, both full. The carpet was a lovely warm brown. She
threw herself full length on the settee. Gosh, she'd never thought she'd end
up in such a grand house. Mind you, she thought drily, she'd started off in
one exactly the same.

Christmas was very quiet. Esther, fifty, unmarried, and living alone, came to
dinner, along with a miserable Jeff, who still lived in hopes of persuading
Dinah to stay in Liverpool.

On New Year's Eve, Lily and Francie held a family party. Lily, at the
remarkable age of forty-two, had produced a second son, Alec, now three,

the image of his sinisterly handsome father. Simon was five and blond, like all the Kavanagh boys. Gillian was home from university in Norwich, where she was studying politics. She had brought a boyfriend, a spotty youth called Whizz who got more and more drunk as the night progressed. Samantha came with her husband, Michael, and their three-month-old son.

'Gosh, Lil. You're starting a dynasty of your own,' Josie remarked in the kitchen as she helped make more sandwiches when they ran out, Whizz having devoured far more than his share. Except for Lily and Daisy, it was ages since she'd seen another Kavanagh. Ben and his children had apparently disappeared off the face of the earth.

'I know.' Lily was starry-eyed. 'When I think of the way I used to envy you, Jose. You were so beautiful, you still are, and you never went short of boyfriends. Yet look at the way things have turned out! Oh, I know you've got a dead successful company, but it's nothing compared to me.'

For a moment Josie felt tempted to tell her friend that she wouldn't have had the opportunity to establish such a large dynasty if she hadn't given up Francie O'Leary on her behalf. She was also tempted to tell her she was getting much too fat, that it was about time she did some exercises so she didn't look six months pregnant all the time. Francie wasn't the sort of husband who'd take kindly to a wife who let herself go. She succumbed to neither temptation, contenting herself with a tart, 'You say the nicest things, Lil.'

'Why didn't your Dinah and Jeff come? They were invited.'

'Jeff preferred to have Dinah to himself. She's off to London in a few days.' Dinah hadn't realised – no one had except Josie – that she was leaving twenty years to the day that Josie had lost her other daughter.

It would soon be 1980, another decade gone. The years seemed to be leaping by. Josie excused herself and went upstairs. She wished Dinah had come to the party, so she'd have had someone there of her own, instead of being surrounded by Lily's children, husband, grandson, son-in-law and a possible prospective and extremely spotty second son-in-law.

She sat on the bed in Francie's and Lily's room and looked at herself in the mirror. For some reason, she recalled doing the same thing in Aunt Ivy's bedroom when she was sixteen and about to go to the pictures with Ben. It was the first time she'd realised she was beautiful, because she looked so much like Mam. She hadn't changed much since then. Apart from looking thirty years older, she thought wryly. She wore her brown hair in much the same style, loose and bouncy on her shoulders. There were a few strands of grey, hardly noticeable. She still took the same size clothes, but it was undoubtedly a middle-aged woman who stared back at her from the mirror across the room, despite the fact she was too far away to see the wrinkles under her eyes.

'You know, I still fancy you something rotten,' said a voice, and Francie O'Leary came in. He wore tight jeans, a navy V-necked sweater, no shirt. A thick gold chain nestled in the dark hairs on his chest and there was a gold hoop in his left ear. His hair was combed in a fringe on his forehead to disguise his slightly receding hairline, making him look a touch evil, Josie thought, a bit like Old Nick, but dead dishy all the same.

'You're not supposed to say things like that, Francie,' she said reprovingly.

'Can't help it, Jose.' He sat down beside her. 'I still miss the bed bit.'

'Francie!'

He winked. 'Don't you?'

'I wouldn't say if I did.' But she did, she did! If the door could have been locked without anyone noticing, if she had been capable of temporarily throwing her conscience to the wind, she would have welcomed half an hour of the bed bit with Francie.

'Lily's not exactly appealing these days,' he said glumly. 'I keep falling off her belly.'

'Francie! What a horrible thing to say.'

'I'm a horrible person. I've never pretended to be anything else. Lily knew that when she proposed.' He sighed. 'I love the lads. In fact, I'm mad about the lads. But life's a bit tedious nowadays, Jose. All we talk about is carpets and wallpaper and kids' shoes. Did you know that little boys wear their shoes out at a rate of knots? Lily's on about it all the time. I say, "Chuck 'em away, kiddo. Buy more. Money's no object," but she goes on about it all the same. Apparently – and this will fascinate you, Jose – since cobblers became shoe repairers, they charge the earth.' He put his hand on the bed over hers, and said wistfully, 'You used to make me feel young.'

She snatched her hand away. 'You made *me* feel young, Francie, only because we had nothing that really mattered to talk about. You and Lily have shared responsibilities. Shoes matter.'

'I'm not old enough for responsibility, Jose. I'm only forty-eight.'

'What are you two up to?' a sharp voice demanded.

Francie groaned and got to his feet when his wife came in. 'Nothing, Lil,' he said in a pained voice. 'I was checking to see if Simon and Alec were asleep, and found Josie sitting on the bed all by herself. We were talking, that's all.'

'Well, you can talk downstairs.'

Josie was shocked to see the naked suspicion in Lily's eyes. Did she actually think there might be something going on? If so, it would serve her right, pay her back for the awful thing she'd said earlier, which Josie had found deeply wounding. It was a long time since she and Lily had had a row, but New Year's Eve wasn't exactly a good time to start one. She said coldly, 'I think I'll go home. Dinah might be there, and I'd like to see in the New Year with me family.'

She waved frantically at Dinah's Mini as it turned the corner of Huskisson Street on its way to London. Dinah gave one last wave and the car disappeared. Josie returned to the house, ready to sink into a decline, to be met by a grim-faced Esther emerging from Reception.

'I've just had William Friars on the phone. He refused to wait and speak to you. He's transferring to another publisher, Havers Hill. He said would you kindly send them *Death by Stealth*. He only has a carbon copy.'

'Does that mean they haven't read it?'

'I assume not. Actually . . .' Esther grinned '. . . he didn't say "kindly", he said "tell her" to send the original.'

'I shall do no such thing,' Josie said indignantly. 'Send it back to Friars, Esther. Tell him to send his lousy book to his new publisher himself.' She chuckled. 'They'll do their nut when they read it. It's not a patch on the others. Oh, it'll sell well – he's acquired a loyal following, who will be sadly disappointed. I bet it gets a mauling from the critics.'

Esther returned to Reception when the phone began to ring. 'It's for you, Josie.' She looked impressed. 'New York.'

'I'll take it in my office.' Her heart missed a beat. New York! She picked up the receiver. 'Josie Coltrane.'

'Hi, Josie,' said a friendly American voice. 'Val Morrissey, Brewster & Cronin, publishers. Read one of your books last week on the plane back from good old Blighty, *Miss Middleton's Papers*, a really creepy tale of good and evil in Victorian England. I wondered if we could do a deal?'

She had actually thought it might be Jack. 'What sort of deal, Mr Morrissey?'

'Call me Val. Brewster & Cronin are a bit like Barefoot House – small output, nothing but crime fiction. I wondered, if we took some of yours, would you take some of ours? I've checked – none of your books are published in the States. The same goes for us the other way round. We don't seem to be able to break into the UK market.'

'We've tried to sell in the States, but no luck,' Josie confessed. 'Except for *My Carnal Life*.'

'Those big companies, they've got no imagination,' Val Morrissey said disgustedly. 'It's us little ones who are the innovators.'

Josie agreed wholeheartedly. 'I love American thrillers. Ed McBain is my favourite.'

'Mine's the little lady who wrote *Miss Middleton's Papers*, Julia Hedington. Great book, Josie! We'd like to take it. Can't offer much initially, I'm afraid – five hundred dollars. We'll only be dipping our toe in the water with a couple of thousand copies to begin with, see how the market takes it. If that's agreeable, I'll have a contract in the post by tomorrow.'

'I'll have to ring Julia first.'

Julia Hedington screamed with joy when told an offer had been made for the American rights of her first novel. She was a widow, with five school-aged children, who had been writing the book for years, scribbling away in a notebook whenever she had a rare, spare minute.

'It's only five hundred dollars, Julia,' Josie said, alarmed when the screaming became hysterical. 'And Barefoot House takes ten per cent of that.'

'I don't care if it's only five dollars. I don't care if you take a hundred per cent. My book's going to be published in *America*. Oh, Josie, I can hardly believe my luck.'

She called Val Morrissey back. 'The author's delirious. So, if you'd let me have that contract?'

'It'll be on its way tomorrow.' They rang off, promising to send each other a selection of books.

Josie went into the next office, where Richard White was typing away on the latest model electric typewriter which had cost a bomb. Dinah's desk was piled high with manuscripts that had arrived that morning – Barefoot House received about fifty a week and, on average, accepted one every two weeks.

'I've just done a deal with an American publishing company,' she said.

'Goodo.' Richard didn't look up. A calm, bespectacled young man, hard-working and conscientious, she'd rather hoped he and Dinah would hit it off.

'We need more staff.'

'I know. We definitely need someone in place of Dinah.'

'I should have advertised.' She'd kept putting it off. 'Do you know anyone?'

Richard shook his head and continued typing. How on earth could he concentrate on two things at the same time? She concluded he must have two brains.

She sighed. 'I hate interviewing staff.'

'I would, too.'

'I might pick the wrong person.'

'It happens sometimes.'

'Then I'd have to sack them, and I'd hate that more.'

'So would I.'

'I'll put an advert in the *Echo* tonight.'

'That mightn't be a bad idea.'

She made a face at his back. Bloody workaholic.

She missed Dinah, but didn't have time to mope. The contract came from Brewster & Cronin, and she sent it to Terence Dunnet to appraise. She hired a replacement for Dinah. Cathy Connors had moved to Liverpool eighteen months ago when her husband's firm had relocated to Cheshire and she had been forced to resign her job as editor with a publisher in London.

'I'm working for a bank at the moment, producing their house magazine, but quite frankly I find it mind-bogglingly boring. Give me fiction any day. I never thought I'd find a position up North with a genuine publisher.'

'Well, you've found one now,' Josie said contentedly. Cathy would take some of the load off her own shoulders, giving her more time to travel round the country, meeting her writers, taking them to lunch, trying to make them feel as if they were part of a family, not just anonymous assets of a large, impersonal company.

April arrived, and Josie realised that Lily was avoiding her. She was cold and unforthcoming when Josie phoned, and hadn't been to see her once since the New Year's Eve party. Lily was too thick-skinned to have taken offence because she'd left early. It must be something else. She recalled the suspicion in her eyes when she'd come into the bedroom and found her talking to Francie. It wasn't that, surely!

Francie's workforce had grown larger, mainly due to regular orders from Barefoot House. She needed to speak to him, warn him that two of their books would be reissued shortly so that he would be prepared. It could have been done by phone, but she decided to go in person for a change.

It was impossible to carry on a conversation in a glass office with no roof while the presses thundered away. Francie took her outside, into the soft mist of a spring morning, and they sat on a wall and talked.

'It's not exactly an ideal place to consult with me best customer, but I'm afraid it'll just have to do.' He looked a bit down in the mouth, unusual for Francie, who rarely let anything bother him.

She told him about the reissues, and he promised to drop everything as soon as he heard from her. He knew how important it was that orders were met with minimum delay.

'What's the matter?' she asked, when he got to his feet and began to walk up and down, hands in pockets, kicking at stones.

'Your friend's the matter, Lily Kavanagh.'

'I thought she was known as Mrs Francis O'Leary these days?'

'Yeah, and it's Mr O'Leary's bad luck that she is. Honestly, Jose . . .' he sat down again '. . . I wouldn't dream of saying this to another soul, but we've always been completely open with each other. She's a pain in the bloody arse. If you must know, she thinks you and me are having an affair. I wish to God we were. It would be worth the endless nagging.' He leered at her weakly.

'Just because she found us talking in the bedroom?'

'She said there was an "air of intimacy" about us. I said why the hell not? I've known the bloody woman for over thirty years, she's me friend. Lily said she'd prefer it if I weren't, and I told her to get lost. I'm not giving up me friends because she's got a dirty mind.'

'You said some very intimate things that night, Francie.'

'I wish I'd done them, not just said them.'

Lily was her own worst enemy. Josie didn't know what to say.

'I wouldn't mind if I'd done anything wrong,' Francie continued irritably. 'You know, Josie, I swore to meself I'd never get married because I wanted to avoid this type of thing. I'm a laid-back sort of guy, I like to get on with people. I never cause trouble. If people like me ruled the world, there'd never be another war. If it weren't for the lads, I'd do a runner. I can't take much more.'

It was *that* bad! She'd speak to Lily, if she'd let her. Try to talk some sense into her bad-tempered friend.

She kept putting it off. Lily would be taking Simon to school, collecting Alec from playgroup, making dinner, making tea, just sitting down to the television, on the point of going to bed.

In the end it was Lily who rang her, early one morning when Josie was about to go down to her office. 'I've got a lump, Jose,' she whispered fearfully.

'Oh, no, Lil! Where?' Josie cried.

'In me breast.' She began to cry. 'Will you make sure Francie looks after the boys properly when I'm gone? I don't want to ask our Samantha. She's only young, and she's expecting again. Not that I'll see it,' she wept. 'I'll go in that hospice near Ormskirk. I'll not let me family watch me suffer. I'm going to be dead brave, Jose. And don't send flowers to the funeral. I'd sooner the money went to cancer research.'

'Is it much of a lump, luv?'

'Well, actually, I can't find it,' Lily sniffed, 'though I've felt all over. But I had a mammogram last week, and they've written and said to come back this avvy for another. They've found something on the X-ray. Oh, Jose. I don't want to die.'

'You bloody idiot!' Josie gasped with relief. 'That might mean nothing at all, just that the X-ray hasn't come out properly or there's some quite innocent shadows. Even if there is a lump, the chances are it's benign. It's a bit early to be planning your funeral, Lil.' The same thing had happened to Esther only last year. Mind you, Esther had been worried sick when she'd got the letter asking her to go back. She said, more kindly, 'I'm not surprised you're upset, but try not to worry. Would you like me to come with you to the clinic?' She had arranged to drive to Rhyl to take a new author to lunch, but it would have to be changed. Lily came first.

'*Please*, Jose. I don't like worrying Francie.'

Another X-ray and a thorough physical examination revealed Lily's breasts to be completely lumpless. They went to town to celebrate, and got slightly tipsy over a pub lunch. Then they linked arms and went shopping.

'This is just like old times,' Lily said. 'But Liverpool's so different from how it used to be. There's no Owen Owen's any more, where Francie threw me on a bed and sort of proposed. It's Tesco's instead.'

'There's no Blackler's either, or Reece's, where we used to go dancing.'

'The Rialto burnt down,' Lily reminded her.

'Most of the cinemas have closed. And we're two middle-aged women with grown-up children and greying hair.' Josie laughed. 'Everything changes, Lil. Us and Liverpool included. Come on, let's have coffee in St

John's Market. That's not half changed, too, since I used to go there with me mam.'

'I'm sorry I haven't been in touch for a while,' Lily said when they were on their second coffee. 'I've been rather busy, what with the boys. I thought . . . Oh, it doesn't matter. I haven't exactly been meself lately.' She crumbled the remains of her scone. 'I think Francie's a bit fed up with me.'

'That's not like Francie,' Josie said carefully. 'He's not the type who easily gets fed up.'

'How would you know?' Lily was immediately suspicious.

'For goodness' sake, Lil. We've both known him since we were sixteen. He doesn't like people making waves. Remember when he walked out of that pub in Smithdown Road?'

Lily pursed her lips. 'There was no reason for that.'

'Yes, there was. You were moaning your head off over just about everything in sight. He couldn't stand it so he left.'

'I'd die if he left again.'

'Then don't make waves,' Josie said simply.

'Who said I was?'

'You, in effect, when you claimed he was fed up. He wouldn't get fed up without a reason.'

'As I said, I haven't been meself.' Lily scowled. 'He drives me mad when he walks away and all I want to do is talk.'

'You mean nag?'

Lily suddenly grinned. 'Probably. Anyroad, I'm going to be as nice as pie to everyone now that I'm not going to die. I was ever so scared, Jose, when that letter came. I'm glad I've got you.' She squeezed Josie's hand. 'Thanks for coming with me.'

'Think nothing of it. Now, let's go try on those frocks we saw in that boutique in Bold Street. You'd really suit the red one. And I'll treat you to a shampoo and set. I could do with a trim meself. Oh, and another thing, this new woman who works for me, Cathy, goes to a gym in the lunch hour. I thought I'd do the same in the evenings. I'm getting a paunch.' She patted her stomach which was as flat as a pancake. 'Why don't you come with me, Lil?'

'I must admit me figure's not what it used to be.'

'Then it's a date. We'll go together, twice a week.'

Dinah was homesick in London, but now she had a flat of her own and was determined to stick it out, become an international executive and travel the world.

'Well, your room's always here for you, luv,' Josie assured her whenever she rang.

'I know, Mum. It's that thought that keeps me going, knowing I've got a real home in Liverpool if things go wrong. Is Barefoot House busy?'

'Incredibly busy.'

Brewster & Cronin had bought the US rights to five books, and she had bought British rights to six of theirs. It meant Barefoot House would soon be producing a book a week. Josie was sometimes in her office until midnight, writing letters, reading manuscripts, making phone calls to New York where the time was five hours behind.

One of her books reached number five in the bestsellers chart, and stayed there for almost two months, an achievement only surpassed by William Friars, whose transfer to Havers Hill she'd read about in *Publishing News*, though there was no mention of when his new novel would be coming out.

My Carnal Life was reprinted for the eighth time. Val Morrissey reported that *Miss Middleton's Papers* was being seriously considered by a Hollywood company, Close-up Productions, for a film. Josie rang Julia Hedington when she knew her children would be home, in case she fainted at the news.

One hot, clammy morning in July, Cathy Connors came into Josie's office holding a manuscript. Josie recognised the look on her face straight away. She'd read something that wasn't merely a run-of-the-mill enjoyable thriller, suitable for publication but unlikely to set pulses racing throughout the land. She'd read a 'breaking new ground' book, as Josie called them, different, exciting, innovative.

'This is marvellous,' she said in a rush. 'I read it last night – all night, in fact. My husband thought I'd fallen asleep downstairs when he woke up at four o'clock and I wasn't in bed. The thing is, Josie, the author's only twenty-one. He lives in Northern Ireland.'

Josie looked at the cover. *My Favourite Murderer*, by Lesley O'Rourke. 'It's a woman,' she said. 'The man's name is spelled differently.'

'Of course! I'm so tired, I can hardly think.'

'I know the feeling. Go home, why don't you? Have some sleep. I don't expect my employees to work all night. I'll read this later. I'd start now, but I'd never get a minute's peace.'

Cathy said she'd slip off at midday. 'You'll enjoy that, Josie.' They smiled at each other. 'I almost envy you, having it to read for the first time.'

'There can't possibly be a better recommendation than that!'

Everyone felt lethargic with the heat, despite the open windows and electric fans. The front door was propped open. Even Richard's typing wasn't at its usual fast pace. The telephone hardly rang; perhaps all over the country people felt the same. Cathy went home, Richard and Bobby went to lunch. Eric was still to arrive. There was only Esther in Reception when Josie went upstairs to take a shower and change her soggy clothes. It was one of the advantages of living over the office.

She emerged from the shower, feeling only slightly fresher and longing for a little nap. The heat was debilitating. Half an hour wouldn't hurt, on the bed in Dinah's room, which was at the back of the house, much quieter. She put on the alarm in case she slept all afternoon.

The high-pitched beep sounded thirty minutes later. Oh, Lord! She felt worse, not just tired but groggy. Her head seemed to be stuck to the pillow, she could hardly lift it. And she'd had a terrible dream, a nightmare, in which Francie had slain Lily with an axe, and Laura had been watching, laughing. Then the dream changed. Mam appeared, crying bitterly, and Josie began to cry with her. 'Stop that!' Aunt Ivy screamed, pinching her wrist. The dream changed again. She was with Jack in the snow-covered garage in Bingham Mews. 'I love you,' Jack whispered. 'I don't want you to go.' But Josie had flown away, soaring up into the night sky until the world below disappeared, and she was alone in the stark, black wilderness, knowing she was destined to stay for ever, that she would never see another human being again.

She rolled off the bed, put on a towelling robe, went downstairs and made tea. Her cheeks were wet with tears. She dried them with her sleeves, blinking because the room looked so weird. The units, the taps, the kettle – all seemed to have two outlines, the real one and another, slightly fainter, behind. She couldn't wait to go down to the office – talk to Esther, ring Lily, do some work – so everything would seem back to normal.

'Is anyone there?'

The voice, a man's, came from downstairs. Josie went on to the landing and peered over the white bannisters. A blurred figure, framed by a halo of dazzling sunlight, was standing in the doorway, clutching a travelling bag. Not many people came to the office without an appointment. It was probably a salesman, offering stationery at a discount, or office machinery. Esther would see to him. At any other time Josie would have done it herself, but she was wearing a bathrobe. It would give a most unbusinesslike impression, even if only to a salesman.

Esther must have gone to sleep. The man's eyes, probably blinded by the sun, hadn't yet adjusted to the change in light, and he hadn't notice the door marked 'Reception'.

'There'll be someone with you in a minute,' Josie called.

The man stepped inside and shaded his eyes with his hand. He looked up, saw Josie, smiled. 'Hi, sweetheart,' he said.

It was Jack Coltrane.

2

Over the years, Josie had sometimes imagined how she would greet her ex-husband should they meet. Coolly, she had decided, even though the longing to see Jack again was never far away. But she had her pride. He'd made no attempt to contact her. 'Why, hello, Jack,' she would say with a warm, slightly distant smile.

Never had she thought she would burst into tears, race downstairs, throw herself in his arms and hungrily kiss him, as if it were only yesterday they had parted.

'Jack, Jack, Jack.' She kept saying his name over and over between kisses. 'I've just been dreaming about you. Oh!' she wept, 'I felt so sad. I flew away, and you wanted me to stay.'

It really was only like yesterday when he held her face in both hands, kissed the tears, then her trembling lips. He touched her hair, pressed his cheek against her burning forehead. She felt his body shudder. 'I'm sorry,' she said, drawing away, embarrassed. 'I'm feeling a bit . . . weird! You must think I'm mad, throwing myself at you like this. It's been twenty years . . .'

'Hey.' He pulled her back in to his arms. 'I like you weird. I expected to be shown the door. This is a welcome surprise.'

Esther opened the door of Reception, blinked and quickly closed it. Richard and Bobby's voices could be heard outside, returning from lunch.

'Let's go upstairs.' Lord knew what they'd think if they found their employer in her bathrobe with a strange man. She pulled Jack towards the stairs.

Had he come another day, had she not just had the awful dream, felt so distinctly weird, no doubt she would have greeted Jack with the warm but distant smile. Instead, when they reached the landing, out of sight from down below, they kissed again.

'Let me look at you,' Jack said huskily, and undid the knot on her robe. It fell in folds around her feet. His eyes travelled slowly over her body, and she felt every single nerve quiver, turn to liquid, and was filled with desire. 'You're as lovely as ever. I've missed you, sweetheart. You'll never know how much.'

'I do, Jack. I've missed you.' She looked at him properly for the first time. He looked tired, she thought. His face was thin and drawn, and there were tiny crinkles beneath the warm brown eyes, perhaps slightly duller than they used to be. Deep, craggy lines ran from nose to jaw. But his hair was as black and thick as it had always been, and lay in the same careless quiff on his forehead. His skin was brown, from the Californian sun, she assumed. The off-white linen suit he wore over a plain white T-shirt was crumpled, but worn with such casual panache it looked smart. Some men were lucky, she thought enviously. Age served them well. Jack was fifty-one, but as charismatic and attractive as he'd always been, possibly more so.

He reached out and began to caress her breasts, brought her closer, stroked her waist, her buttocks, slid his hand between her legs. Oh, this is mad, she thought wildly. This is quite mad. It's been twenty years . . .

'Come.' She drew him up another flight of stairs, to the bedroom, where she lay on the bed, inviting him. He kissed every part of her body, made her come with his tongue, with his hand.

'Jack!' she said urgently. She badly wanted him inside her.

He laughed joyfully and began to remove his clothes. 'I can't believe this is happening,' he said incredulously, and the familiarity of his smile, his closeness, the way his hair flopped down in front of his eyes, made Josie gasp. He bent over her, and she stroked the brown skin of his arms, his chest, noting somewhere at the back of her mind that he'd lost a lot of weight, too much.

When he entered her, it was as if a miracle had occurred. This was something she had thought would never happen again. But it had, and it was almost too much to bear. She giddily wondered if it was just another dream, like the one she'd had before, and any minute she would wake up and he wouldn't be there.

But then it was over. She was lying in Jack's arms, and it wasn't a dream. It was real.

'What I'd like now,' he said comfortably, 'is one of your famous cups of tea. I'm still in throes of jet lag.' He gently kissed her lips. 'You're a very demanding woman, Mrs Coltrane.'

'I'll get dressed.'

He watched her find clean pants and bra, and slip into a thin white cotton frock and sandals, then began to put on his own clothes. Two floors down a phone rang, and she realised she had forgotten all about Barefoot House, which could manage perfectly well without her.

'The kitchen's on the floor below.' In Maude's room! She went down, put the kettle on and was waiting for it to boil when she heard his footsteps on the stairs and smiled at him through the open door.

He smiled back, but she wondered why he was walking so stiffly. Why did he have to concentrate so hard, hold so tightly to the bannister, as if he was worried he'd fall? At first she thought it was the jet lag, but a chill ran through her bones when she realised he was drunk. He'd been drunk when he'd arrived, and he was drunk now. Not mildly, not even moderately, but completely, totally inebriated. And he was so used to it, it was so much a part of him that he'd learnt to cope, to converse, to pretend, when he'd probably been drunk for days, for months or it might even be for years.

'What made you come?' she asked over the tea. His hand, holding the cup, was shaking slightly. They were in the lounge, sitting together on the pink and cream settee.

'Two things. Remember Bud Wagner? He was always round at the apartment.'

She shook her head. 'No.' She remembered hardly anyone from those days.

'Well, he remembers you. He runs a literary agency in New York. We've kept in touch, and he sent an article from the trade press about a company – I don't recall the name – buying the US rights to books published in Britain by a firm called Barefoot House. That rang a bell. You'd told me that's where you lived with Louisa Chalcott. When I read that the firm belonged to Josephine Coltrane, I knew it could only be you.'

'What was the other thing?'

His lips twisted ruefully. 'Dinah.'

She remembered, too late, one of the reasons for the cool reception she had planned, the warm, distant smile. He had ignored the letter telling him about Dinah. 'You took your time, Jack.' She tried not to spoil things by sounding cold. 'I wrote to you about Dinah on her fifth birthday. She's twenty in September.'

'I only got it last week, sweetheart. I showed Jessie Mae the article, told her who you were and she gave me the letter. It's Mae with an "e", by the way, she's particular about that.'

She'd actually forgotten he had a wife! If only he'd arrived yesterday, or tomorrow, when she was fully dressed, with a clear head, when she hadn't felt so damn *weird*.

'Coral used to open mail that came from the lawyers about the divorce,' Jack was saying. 'We were living together by then.'

'Who's Coral?'

'My wife. She died two years after we were married. Leukaemia.'

'I'm sorry.' It was horrible to hear him say, 'my wife', when it wasn't *her* he was referring to. 'Then who's Jessie Mae?'

'She's my daughter, stepdaughter. She's nineteen, same as Dinah. I have a stepson too, Tyler. He's twenty-one.'

'Really!' Josie muttered. How fortunate for Tyler and Jessie Mae to have had the benefit of a father all these years, she thought cynically, when his real daughter had been deprived.

She seemed to have lost the thread of the conversation. 'You mean Coral, your wife, opened my letter, but didn't show it to you?'

'Yes,' he said simply.

'But it was marked "Strictly Confidential".' She could actually remember writing the words on the envelope.

'All the more reason for her to open it. She would have guessed it was from you, and was worried it might say something that would stop us getting married. She gave it to Jessie Mae, said to let me have it when she thought the time was right.' He put the cup and saucer on the floor, which seemed to require much frowning concentration, then took Josie's hands in his. 'Coral was dying, sweetheart, she wanted a father for her kids. We met on the set of this movie we were making. She was the continuity girl, divorced. Her ex was a bastard, she was terrified he'd get his hands on Jessie Mae and Tyler when she died. We weren't in love, but I was prepared to take on the kids.' His mouth twisted wryly. 'You can guess why.'

She guessed straight away. 'Because of Laura?'

He nodded. 'I wanted to give something back for what I'd taken away.'

It had been a supremely kind, very noble thing to do, but Josie felt herself withdrawing slightly from him. She felt resentment for the woman who had kept her letter, and even more for Jack for understanding why. She'd been the victim of an underhand trick, conned out of the husband she loved. Then she remembered that five years had passed before he had met Coral, five years during which he hadn't thought to get in touch, see how she was. She was about to ask why, tell him she'd tried to contact him in Bingham Mews and he'd already left. But what was the point of raking over the past?

She'd told him she never wanted to see him again, and he'd taken her at her word.

'Where is Dinah?' he asked.

'She works in London. I'll ring soon, tell her you're here.'

He gave a nervous grin. 'How is she likely to take it? It's a bit of a bombshell.'

'I don't know,' Josie said truthfully. 'I've never been able to guess how Dinah will react. She's a law unto herself.' She picked up the cups. 'I'll get more tea.'

In the kitchen, she leaned on the sink and took several deep breaths. It was hotter than ever, and the afternoon air felt sticky and humid. Her head was whirling. She almost wished that Jack hadn't come, that she was downstairs in her office dealing with the mundane affairs of Barefoot House.

'I'm getting too old for this sort of trauma,' she muttered.

But then she took in the tea, and there was Jack Coltrane sitting on her settee, and she felt a wave of love that took her breath away. He looked up. 'Have you been happy, sweetheart?'

She paused before answering. 'I haven't been *un*happy, not for most of the time,' she said seriously. 'How about you?'

He shrugged tiredly. 'It's been difficult. Tyler's always been a sweet, laid-back kid, but Jessie Mae was badly damaged by the divorce and Coral's death. She had problems at school.' He shrugged again. 'Poor Jessie Mae, she's had problems more or less every damn where.'

It hardly seemed fair that Jessie Mae's problems should be *his*. 'You said you were working on a film?'

'I'm a script editor. It's reasonably well paid. We've got a neat little house in Venice with a pool. You must come and stay some time, Josie.'

She almost dropped the tea. 'That would be nice.' She put both cups on the coffee-table and went over to the window, where she clutched the curtains to steady herself. What on earth had possessed her to assume he had come back for good? How long did he plan to stay, she wondered, a few days, a week, a month?

'Where's the bathroom, sweetheart?' He stood, holding himself determinedly erect. 'I need to freshen up.'

'On the floor above, at the back.'

He glanced around the room. 'I had a bag when I came.'

'I'll go and look.' She found the leather holdall at the top of the stairs. Bottles clinked when she picked it up. Aftershave, perhaps? Mouthwash?

Josie returned to the sanctuary of the curtains, and watched a sharp black shadow creep across the street. Soon the house would be in the shade. She wished, more than she had wished anything in her life before that she had never met Jack Coltrane. I ruined his life, she thought bleakly, and he ruined mine. I thought we were meant for each other, but we weren't. And now I'm lost, because I still love him. I'll love him till the day I die.

He returned to the room, having combed his hair and changed the T-shirt for a black one, looking reinvigorated.

'What happened to your plays?' she asked.

'The last time I saw them, they were on the floor of the study in Bingham Mews where you'd thrown them.' His eyes twinkled at her. 'Then you kicked them.' He held out his arms. 'Sweetheart, come here.'

She ran across the room and buried her face in his shoulder. 'Have you written any more?'

'No.' He gave an exaggerated sigh. 'Been too busy, too uninspired, had too many burdens, needed to earn a crust.'

'It's not too late to start again.' She gave him a little shake.

'I might, one day.'

Later, she went down to her office so she could phone Dinah in private. 'Are you sitting down? More importantly, are you alone?'

'I'm sitting down, entirely alone. Evelyn went home early. The heat and the menopause were getting her down, and it didn't help when I handed in me notice this morning. That job came up, the one I told you about with the much bigger agency. I was going to ring you later. Anyroad, what's up?'

Josie told her that her father was there, and about the complications with the letter she had sent all those years ago, finishing with, 'He's dying to see you.'

There was a long pause, then Dinah said, 'I feel as if I should come rushing home, but I don't want to.'

'Then don't.'

Another pause. 'This Coral sounds a selfish bitch, if you ask me,' she cried passionately. 'I don't care if she *is* dead. And Jessie Mae, stupid name, seems just as bad. It's not *fair*, Mum.' Dinah was close to tears. 'He would have come to see me if it weren't for them.' The voice became plaintive. 'He would have, wouldn't he, Mum?'

'Like a shot, luv.'

'I might come, I dunno. How long will he be there?'

'I haven't got round to asking yet.'

That night they went to dinner, and she showed him the house where she had been born and had lived with Mam. 'In the attic. I never told you before, but she was – what do you say in the States? – a hooker.'

He placed an arm around her shoulders and squeezed hard. 'You've come a long way, sweetheart.'

'Only four doors,' she said drily.

They strolled into town, and ate in a little dark pub in North John Street. 'You know,' Jack said when they had finished, 'I never dreamed it would be so *easy*, us being together, talking naturally, like old times. I thought I'd be straining to think of things to say, then saying the wrong thing, and there'd be all sorts of awkward silences. I always got on with you better than anyone. We were best friends as well as lovers.'

He was looking back through rose-coloured glasses. They hadn't got on all that well in Bingham Mews, where he'd been frustrated by success he hadn't wanted. She realised, sadly, that something in him had died. This was the old, easygoing Jack, the charming, twinkling Jack she'd married in New York, but now resigned to the fact he would never be a successful playwright. The need to survive – earn a crust, as he'd put it – had killed any ambition he used to have. It was the way of the world, no doubt full of middle-aged men and women who'd long ago given up their dreams of becoming famous at something or other.

'I think another bottle of vino is called for.' He went over to the bar. It was the fourth bottle he'd ordered. Josie had had two glasses and was toying with her third. His brain seemed surprisingly unaffected by the amount he'd drunk. He was lucid, witty, clear-headed. There was merely that slight stiffness in the way he walked. She decided to say nothing. Criticising his drinking, mild in comparison to now, had caused tension when they'd lived in Bingham Mews.

It was almost dark when they came out of the pub, and they wandered, arm in arm, down to the Pier Head, then caught the bus back to Huskisson Street.

She showed him round the offices downstairs. 'We have only six staff, and one of them's part time, though I'll have to take on some new people soon. Production's increased, everybody's working their socks off at the moment.'

'You've done incredibly well.' He eyed the rows of Barefoot House books in their bright red covers. 'Strange,' he said in an odd voice. 'It was me who wanted to be someone, not you. You once said all you wanted was a family. Now look at us! I'm a third-rate script editor on third-rate movies, and you're a successful businesswoman.'

'Perhaps this . . .' Josie waved a hand at the books, '. . . is instead of a family. Anyroad, I've got Dinah. *She's* me family, even if she's the only one.'

'That's nice to know,' a voice said brightly, and Josie turned, startled. Dinah came sauntering into the room. 'I decided to shut up shop and come home.' She stared at them defiantly. She must have got changed since she arrived, as Josie recognised the yellow cotton frock as one she'd left behind when she went to London. Her long legs were bare, and she wore Indian sandals, the sort that fitted between the toes, which Josie had never been able to wear because they were so uncomfortable. The long fair hair was slightly damp, brushed away from her slightly flushed face. She looked exquisitely fresh and lovely.

'Hello, luv! What a nice surprise.' Josie kissed her daughter's cheek. She stayed, holding her hand, concerned that the defiant look was because she and Jack gave the impression of being a couple, and Dinah felt excluded. 'This is your dad.'

Jack didn't move. Oh, but the look on him! Josie could have wept as myriad emotions chased across his handsome, mobile face: astonishment, followed by admiration for the beautiful young woman who was his daughter; anger for some reason Josie couldn't define, perhaps because he'd never been told of her existence until now; sadness, possibly for the same reason; then the soft, gentle, fond look that people gave, usually women, when they set eyes on a small baby. 'Hi, Dinah,' was all he said.

'Hello,' Dinah replied. 'The kettle's on, Mum. It'll have boiled by now. Shall I make tea?'

'Please, luv.'

'Like mother, like daughter, the same passion for tea,' Jack commented as Dinah ran lightly upstairs. Then he turned away, his back to her. It was a while before he spoke, and when he did his voice was thick. 'Christ, Josie! When I think of what I've missed. What we've *both* missed. We could have been together all this time, raised Dinah between us. We could have had more children, the family you've always wanted.'

'Don't think like that, Jack,' she said softly. 'It's too late.' Or was it? It was too late for children, but not for them to be together. She had plenty of money. She could turn the attic into a study, he could write full time. Twenty years ago she had made the mistake of sending him away. Now she would ask him to come back. 'Jack,' she said hesitantly.

'Yes, sweetheart?' He faced her, and her heart ached when she saw the tears in his eyes.

'Why don't we get married again?'

He smiled his dear, sweet smile. 'We can't, sweetheart. There's all sorts of reasons why we can't.'

'I can't think of a single one.'

'There's Jessie Mae,' he said. 'I can't leave Jessie Mae. She'd go to pieces without me.'

'Bring her to Liverpool. She can live with you, with us, here.'

He slid his arms around her waist and shook his head. 'That wouldn't work, sweetheart. She's Hollywood born and bred, and she would never accept another woman in my life. She'd be impossible to live with.'

They stood in each other's arms, their chins resting on one another's shoulders. It felt so comfortable, Josie thought, so natural. This is where God intended me to be! She remembered thinking the same thing the night they'd met.

'You've given this girl twenty years of your life, Jack,' she said reasonably. 'Isn't it time you had a life yourself?'

'I promised her mother on her deathbed that I'd always care for Jessie Mae. I can't go back on that.'

Not even for me? she almost said, but it would have sounded childish, and she knew that Jack Coltrane would never go back on his word to a dying woman. 'I suppose I'll have to wait until Jessie Mae finds a husband. Will you marry me then?'

She leaned back so that they were face to face, and was cut to the quick when he suddenly pushed her away with a curt, 'No!'

'Why not?' she asked, startled.

'Christ, Josie!' His face was dark with anger. 'Are you always so persistent? Hasn't it entered your head that I might not want to get married again?'

'But you said earlier . . .'

'I was lamenting the years we'd lost, that's all. I've had it with relationships, up to here.' He held a hand to his chin. 'When Jessie Mae gets married I want to live alone, in peace.'

It was too much. It had been such a peculiar day, what with the strange dreams earlier, the heat, Jack coming, being so strangely drunk, having to tell Dinah her father was there, then Dinah herself coming all the way from London and behaving so coolly, upstairs now, making tea. There'd been a brief vision of happiness, imagining living with Jack again, and now the brutal rejection, which wasn't a bit like the Jack she used to know.

Josie burst into tears, wild, racking tears that tore at her body and made her chest want to burst.

'Sweetheart!' Jack threw himself in the chair behind the desk and dragged her on to his knee. 'Oh, my darling girl. I love you so much. I didn't remember how much until earlier when you came running downstairs. You're *part* of me. I love you with all my heart and soul. There is nothing on earth I want more than for us to be married, to spend the rest of our lives in each other's arms. But it's not to be, my love.'

'Why not?' she sobbed. 'I love you just the same. I always have, Jack. I want what you want. I understand if we can't have it right this minute, but surely we can have it in the future?'

His arms tightened around her so that she could hardly breathe. 'I'm no longer the guy you first met,' he said savagely. 'I haven't been in a long time. I'm a physical and emotional wreck. I get depressed. I have terrible black moods. I'm on pills for my nerves.'

'I don't care, I love you. Anyroad, you wouldn't need pills if you were with me. I'd make you better.'

'Josie, I ruined your life once, I don't want to ruin it a second time.' He gestured around the office. 'You've got a great business, a lovely daughter, a nice life. The last thing you want is me fucking everything up for a second time.'

Josie began to cry again. 'This afternoon was wonderful. Oh, Jack, half of our lives are already over. Why can't we spend what's left with each other?' With all his faults, she would sooner have Jack Coltrane than any other man on earth.

He stayed for six days, Dinah left after two, by which time they were getting on reasonably well. They talked mainly about films, which seemed to be a cover for things the more wary Dinah would prefer to avoid for now. She left for London on Wednesday morning, having kissed her mother and shaken Jack's hand. 'I hope we'll meet again one day,' she said politely.

'Well,' Jack said with a grin after she'd gone, 'I suppose a kiss and a "Dad" was too much to expect after only two days.'

'A kiss might be on the cards, but I'm afraid "Dad" is most unlikely. She talked to me about it yesterday. "Jack" is the most you can look forward to.'

'That's better than nothing, which is all I've had so far. Oh, I'm not complaining,' he said hastily, when Josie opened her mouth to say he was expecting too much too soon. 'I feel privileged that such a stunning, autocratic and supremely confident young woman was so nice to me.'

'She's not quite as confident as she appears.' Josie didn't want him getting the wrong impression of their daughter. 'She was a very withdrawn little girl. It was my fault. I didn't want her, Jack. She came too soon after Laura. I think she sensed she wasn't welcome, even though she was only a tiny baby.'

'Ah, Laura!' Jack said the name reverently. They had hardly mentioned their other daughter. 'She would have been twenty-five. I wonder what she would have looked like?'

'I often wonder the same thing,' Josie said softly. 'I reckon she would have been a female version of you and driven the boys wild.'

'Why did we call her Laura?' He looked puzzled. 'I've tried to remember, but I can't. It drives me crazy sometimes.'

'We saw that film together in a little cinema in New York – *Laura*, with Gene Tierney and Dana Andrews. When I was expecting, we decided on Laura for a girl, Patrick if it was a boy.'

'We had a girl, but then we lost her.' Jack's face was tight with pain. 'Since that day I've never driven a car. I'm not surprised you never wanted to see me again.'

'I wanted to see you again within a week. But you'd already gone, to California, according to Elsie Forrest. If it had been New York, I would have tried to find you.'

'Don't say things like that!' he groaned. 'I went through hell over the next few years, and it doesn't help to find I could have been with you – and Dinah.'

'By the way, should Dinah ever bring the subject up, she's named after Dinah Shore, your favourite singer.'

He looked taken aback. 'Did I say I liked Dinah Shore?'

'No, but I couldn't tell her she was called after the midwife because I couldn't be bothered to think of a name meself, could I?'

'Where are we going today?' he asked when they were outside, after she had checked that Barefoot House was working smoothly without her. Cathy reminded her of the manuscript, *My Favourite Murderer*, that she'd been given to read.

'I'll read it this weekend,' Josie promised. 'My friend, well, actually, it's my ex-husband, goes back to California on Saturday morning. I'll be looking for something to do.'

'We're going to New Brighton on the ferry,' she told Jack. The day before, they'd gone to Southport, and she'd showed him the arcade where she'd had tea with Louisa, and where Mr Bernstein's little bookshop used to be, now a burger bar. They'd been to Old Swan to look for the house where he used to live, but it was no longer there. 'Tonight I thought we could go and see Lily.'

He made a hideous face. 'Are you two still friends? How's that poor guy she married? Assuming he's not already dead.'

'Neil was dispensed with ages ago. She's got a different husband, Francie, and two lovely little boys, as well as two grown-up daughters.'

The weather had remained hot and humid all week, and New Brighton was packed with day-trippers. There wasn't even the suggestion of a breeze drifting across the crowded beach from the Mersey. They bought fish and chips and ate them out the paper, then an ice-cream cornet with a chocolate flake. Josie wanted to go to the fairground, but Jack complained he felt queasy. 'I need a drink to settle my stomach.'

'I would have thought a drink would make it worse.'

He smiled. 'You don't know my stomach.'

She agreed that she had little acquaintance with his stomach. In the big, busy pub she found two seats, and her eyes searched for Jack in the hordes waiting at the bar. He was ages getting served. She'd asked for coffee, and wondered why two large glasses of spirits were placed in front of him when at last he caught the bartender's eye. To her dismay, she saw him quickly swallow one in a single gulp while waiting for the coffee. Her heart sank. He was drinking massively more than he'd done in Bingham Mews. She had investigated his bag and discovered two bottles of Jack Daniels. This morning there'd been only one. There was also a bottle of mouthwash, which he must have used to disguise the fact that every time he went to the bathroom he had a drink. Or two.

'Here we are.' He put a glass and the coffee on the table. 'You've got a cookie with yours, on the house.'

'Ta.' She grabbed his hand. 'I love you.'

'I love you, sweetheart.' He kissed the hand that was tightly holding his. 'I wish you could stay.'

'So do I, but it's not possible, I told you . . .'

'I know.' She grimaced. 'Jessie Mae.' One day, though, she would get him back. She was set on it. In the meantime, she could have cheerfully strangled bloody Jessie Mae, particularly when, after only a few minutes, Jack returned to the bar and gave a repeat performance with the two drinks.

'He looks ill,' Lily declared when the two men went to the pub. Francie and Jack had taken to each other instantly, and it had been Francie's idea to go out. 'And he isn't half thin, Jose.'

'The first time you met, you told him he was fat!'

'He looked healthier fat.'

'Francie's no more than skin and bone,' Josie said tartly.

'Yes, but he's healthily thin. Jack's like death warmed up.'

Josie rolled her eyes. 'Talking about skin, why is it you always manage to get under mine?'

'Mind you . . .' Lily winked '. . . he has a *ravaged* sort of look. It's dead sexy.'

'I would prefer it if you didn't describe my ex-husband as sexy, Mrs O'Leary. It's just not done.'

'Is the ex likely to become an ex-ex soon? How do you describe a husband you marry a second time?' Lily regarded Josie with a beady eye. 'He's obviously mad about you. He can't take his eyes off you, in fact. And you're just as bad, I can tell.'

'I dunno, Lil.' Josie sighed. 'I took a leaf out of your book and proposed but, unlike Francie, he turned me down, at least for the time being.' She explained about Coral, Jessie Mae and Tyler. 'Gosh,' she sighed, 'I won't half miss him. I was jogging along quite comfortably before, enjoying me business. He's disturbed me equilibrium, Lil.'

She was determined not to make a show of herself when he left on Saturday morning. They embraced silently behind the big front door, the offices either side eerily empty.

'I'll miss my plane,' Jack said after a while.

'I don't care. I don't know how I'm going to live without you,' she said bleakly.

'You managed very well for twenty years.'

'Not really.' She sniffed, fighting to hold back the tears.

'I'll give you a call as soon as I'm home. I'll call every month. No, every week. Oh, Christ!' He looked at her despairingly. 'I'll call every single day.'

'Once a week will do fine, and I'll call you.'

They kissed passionately. 'We'll see each other at Christmas, won't we?' he said huskily. 'Try and persuade Dinah to come. I'll pack Jessie Mae off to stay with Tyler, so there'll just be us three. Our first family Christmas together.' He reached for her wrists and removed her arms from around his neck. 'Goodbye, sweetheart.'

With that, the door closed and he was gone!

Dinah telephoned a few minutes later. 'Have I timed it right? Has he gone? He called last night, just to say goodbye. He said he had to leave prompt at ten o'clock, which is why I'm ringing at ten past. I thought you'd be dead miserable.'

'I'm as miserable as sin, Dinah,' Josie said shakily. She swallowed hard. 'What did you think of your dad?'

'He's lovely, Mum. I really liked him. I can understand why you fell for him so hard. Oh, but I wish he'd been around when I was little. It would have been great to have had a dad like him.'

'Did he mention staying with him at Christmas?'

'Yes.'

'Will you go?' Josie enquired cautiously.

'Just try and stop me, Mum.'

3

On Monday, Josie threw herself back into work in the hope that it would take her mind off Jack. It worked, to a degree. She read manuscripts while she ate, in the bath, in bed, on trains. There were inevitably times when she was left to her own thoughts, and she would pray that Jessie Mae would soon get married or take up a career, and Jack would be free to spend the rest of his life with her. Until then she would just have to make do with his frequent phone calls – and seeing him at Christmas. Dinah was already looking forward to it, and Josie could hardly wait.

My Favourite Murderer was a vivid and telling account of the conflict in Northern Ireland. There was no indication whether the young narrator, a girl, was Catholic or Protestant. She referred to 'our side' or 'the other side'. The murderer was her terrorist father, whom she loved, but she couldn't understand why she should hate other people because of their religion. Should she protect her father, or betray him, when she knew he was guilty of a heinous crime?

'You're right,' Josie said to Cathy Connors. 'It's brilliant. Write to Lesley O'Rourke and offer her a five thousand advance. I think we've got a bestseller on our hands.'

Lesley O'Rourke turned out to be a pseudynom, and the writer refused to reveal her real name or where she lived. They corresponded through a box number. 'If my address is known, then so will my religion,' she wrote to Cathy. 'I'd sooner not appear to be on anyone's side.'

'She's probably protecting her father, too,' Cathy said, showing Josie the letter. 'I bet the book is autobiographical. Shall I slot in publication of the hardback for January? Richard's already preparing next year's catalogue.'

'Yes. I'd like to get it out as soon as possible. It's got something meaningful to say, not that it'll make any difference to Northern Ireland. I don't think anything will.'

William Friars's *Death By Stealth* appeared in hardback in September, and was slated by the critics. Josie tried her best not to be pleased.

Later that month Val Morrissey rang from New York. Close-Up Productions had offered one hundred thousand dollars for the film rights to *Miss Middleton's Papers*. 'So our little enterprise has paid off in spades, eh!'

he said triumphantly. 'Now, William Friars's *The Blackout-Murders.* I'm not convinced a thriller set in the Liverpool blitz would sell in the States, but I'm intrigued by this guy's uptight private eye. I'd like to give it a go with a couple of thousand copies – see how the cookie crumbles. The usual advance applies.'

'I'll contact both authors. By the way, I bought two plane tickets for Los Angeles this morning. My daughter and I are spending Christmas with my ex-husband. Pity New York's on the other side of the country. We could have met up.'

He guffawed delightedly. 'It so happens *I'm* spending Christmas in Los Angeles – Long Beach. Where will you be based?'

'Venice. Is that far?'

'Twenty, thirty miles. Chickenfeed. I'll only be staying a couple of days, but we could meet for a drink.' He expressed envy for what was obviously an amicable divorce. 'My ex-wife and I are still conducting the Third World War.'

Josie rang off and called a dazed Julia Hedington, who seemed less concerned with the money than the fact that well-known actors would be speaking *her* lines. 'Do you know who will be in it?'

'It won't have been cast yet.' She promised to let her know as soon as she heard.

'I hope it's Meryl Streep and Al Pacino. They'd be perfect.'

Josie asked Esther to send Julia a bouquet of roses, and dictated a letter to William Friars. Barefoot House still owned the rights to his earlier work. He replied by return of post, a stiff, condescending letter conveying his willingness to be published in America but expressing dismay at the small advance.

'You'd think he was doing us a favour,' Josie said disgustedly.

The downstairs dining room, so far unused, was converted into an office. Three new desks were ordered, and all the paraphernalia required by a modern business in the eighties. A second secretary arrived to assist the overworked Esther. Another editor was hired, Lynne Goode, happy to transfer from her job with a large London publisher to work for Barefoot House, as well as a young woman straight from university whose first job it was to study rights, because requests for foreign rights, book club rights, audio rights, large print rights, even TV rights, were flooding in.

Sometimes, when everyone downstairs had gone and she was alone, and the deathly silence was broken only by the creaks and groans of the old house, Josie would feel quite literally terrified by what she had created. It was getting too much, too big, too successful. She wouldn't be able to cope. She would shiver, imagining the whole edifice one day tumbling down about her ears.

But next morning the postman would deliver a mountain of post and manuscripts, the staff would arrive, the phone would ring for the first time, and would probably ring a hundred times again before the day was out, and the calls could be from anywhere in the world.

This is mine, she would think with another shiver, this time of pride. All mine. It would never be as good as sex. But it came close.

Christmas at last! The plane tickets were already tucked inside the handbag she was taking, her passport had been renewed and one acquired for Dinah, and her suitcase had been packed for days. Jack said the weather in Los Angeles was magic – brilliantly sunny and warm.

'We'll buy summer clothes there,' she said to Dinah. They phoned each other constantly. 'I'll treat you. American clothes are gorgeous, and dead cheap.'

'Just imagine, sunbathing in December!' Dinah sighed rapturously. 'It's snowing in London at the moment.'

'There's a blizzard blowing in Liverpool.'

'We can swim in Jack's pool!'

'You can, luv. I've never learned. I'll just sit in the sun and watch.'

'Oh, Mum. I can't wait!'

'Me neither.' She was longing to see Jack again and lie in his arms. For weeks now she'd been useless in the office, her stomach on fire with anticipation, her mind miles away in sunny Los Angeles.

Two days before they were due to leave, Josie felt an ominous tickling in her throat. Then her joints began to ache, and she had a throbbing headache. On the day they should have flown to Los Angeles, she was in bed with a virulent attack of flu.

'I'll catch a flight to London tonight,' Jack said instantly when she called and told him in a cracked voice she wouldn't be coming.

'You'll do no such thing. The weather's awful here, and you'll only catch my germs. Dinah's coming to look after me.'

'Are you sure? Are you absolutely positive? I'll be there like a shot if you like.'

'No, we'll come to you as soon as I'm better.'

'If you say so.' He sounded disappointed, and she was always to regret not taking up his offer to come and visit.

'Did Jack say I called on Christmas Day as we had arranged?' Val Morrissey enquired early in January.

'Yes. I'm so sorry I wasn't there. I didn't think to let you know. Jack said he explained what had happened.'

'Are you better now?'

'Still a bit weak, that's all.' Josie smiled at the receiver. 'Jack said you came in for a drink, anyroad.'

'I did indeed. Great guy, your ex. Great constitution, too. He drank me under the table, but it had no effect on him.' There was a pause, and Josie assumed he was about to discuss their mutual business interests, but he continued, 'That girl, Jessie Mae. She's his stepdaughter, right?'

'Right.'

'I hope you don't mind my asking, but how old is she?'

Jessie Mae had recently had a birthday. 'Twenty.'

Val whistled. 'Wow! She looks fourteen, but acts older. Do you think it would be okay if I made a move?'

'What sort of move?' Josie asked mystified. 'Oh, I see. You mean you fancy her?'

'That's a cute way of putting it,' he laughed. 'Yes, I do. It's not often you meet a real old-fashioned girl like that.'

'I'm afraid Jessie Mae and I have never met, but I'm sure Jack would have no objection if you made your move.'

'You'd love her,' Val Morrissey said enthusiastically. 'In that case, I'll send some flowers, and I'm sure I can think up an excuse for going to L.A. in the near future.'

She didn't mention the conversation to Jack, who reported that the guy from New York, whose name he had forgotten, was inundating Jessie Mae with flowers and phone calls. 'She's quite chuffed. What she needs is a father figure, and this guy's still on the right side of forty. I'm sure Coral would have approved.'

Josie didn't say that *she* approved wholeheartedly. If Val Morrissey married Jessie Mae, Jack would have no excuse when she badgered him to marry her. And badger him she would, even if it meant going to Los Angeles and *dragging* him to the altar.

The reviews for *My Favourite Murderer* were glowing. One critic wrote, 'The saying is that "small is beautiful". Barefoot House, the diminutive publishing company based in Liverpool, seems to prove this point with every book they produce, but never more so than with Lesley O'Rourke's compelling tale of violence in Northern Ireland.'

Three companies made offers for the film rights, and vied with each other, increasing their offers until the final bid had reached half a million pounds.

Lily arrived just as Josie was reading the letter. She had phoned that morning to ask if they could lunch together. 'Please, say yes, it's rather important. I need someone to talk to.'

Josie showed her the letter. 'Just look at this! It makes me go all funny. Half a million *pounds*.'

'Very impressive,' Lily said dully. She sank in the chair in front of her friend's desk.

'What's up? You don't exactly *sound* impressed.'

'I'm pregnant.'

Josie gasped. 'You can't possibly be. You're forty-six. You've made a mistake, Lil. It's probably the menopause. You can have the same symptoms.'

Lily gestured impatiently. 'It's been confirmed. I'm bloody pregnant. Five months gone, if you must know. I mean, I'm a grandmother twice over, Jose. I'm not exactly thrilled at the idea of providing a new aunt or uncle for me grandkids. And I've just got the boys off me hands – Simon's at school, and Alec's at playgroup. I'll feel daft, buying nappies and stuff at my age.'

'What does Francie have to say?'

'Oh, *him*! Well, you know Francie. Nothing seems to shake him. The thing is, it's all his bloody fault.'

'What did he do?'

'What the hell d'you think he did to make me pregnant?'

'Maybe he thought you were still on the Pill,' Josie said reasonably. '*I* did.'

Lily scowled. 'I came off the Pill months ago, didn't I? There didn't seem much point. Me and Francie aren't exactly Romeo and Juliet these days. I don't know what got into him the night this happened.' She pointed to her bulging stomach, which bulged no more than it had done six months ago – the visits to the gym hadn't lasted long. 'He must have been drunk.'

'Did Francie know you weren't taking the Pill?'

'I didn't tell him, no, but you'd think he'd have noticed the box wasn't on the kitchen window-sill any more.'

The telephone rang. Josie went and told Esther to get someone else to deal with it. She returned to her office. 'Come on, Lil, let's go to lunch and get a bit pissed. It'll do you good.'

'I'm not supposed to drink,' Lily said sulkily. She got to her feet, a bulky, shapeless figure with dull, listless eyes. Josie felt sad, remembering the bright-eyed young woman she'd accompanied to Haylands Holiday Camp.

Lily aimed a kick at the chair. 'Oh, I suppose I'll just have to have it, won't I? But I'm not looking forward to it, I'll tell you that for free.'

Neither was Josie nor, she suspected, was Francie or any other people likely to have anything to do with Lily over the next few months. She'd made a huge meal out of her four other pregnancies, and was likely to turn this one into a banquet.

Lily had always been house-proud, but now it became an obsession. Not a speck of dust was allowed to rest for a second in the house in Halewood. Windows and mirrors were polished daily, the bathroom cleaned, carpets vacuumed, towels changed, clothes washed.

'I thought you had a squeegee mop,' Josie said when she called one day in the lunch hour and found Lily on her hands and knees scrubbing the kitchen floor.

'It doesn't get in the corners,' Lily puffed.

'And what are the dishes doing in the sink when you've got a dishwasher?'

'I don't trust the thing to get them properly clean.'

'I suppose you'll be doing the washing by hand next,' Josie said laconically.

'What do you mean by that?' Lily struggled to her feet and wiped her brow. She opened the kitchen door and dumped the bucket outside.

'Come off it, Lil. You're not fooling me. You're deliberately wearing yourself out to make everyone suffer, particularly poor Francie. There's no need for any of this.' She nodded at the sink and the wet floor. 'If you're so concerned about being clean, pay someone else to do it.'

'Do you seriously think I'd let another woman clean my house?' Lily glared at her, enraged.

'I don't see why not. Another woman cleans mine – two, actually. They come on Saturday morning and clean the offices at the same time.'

'That's different.'

'No, it's not, Lil.' Josie led her friend into the spotless living room and sat her down. 'Stop making such a martyr of yourself. It's driving all of us doolally.'

Lily got to her feet. 'I'll make some tea.'

Josie pushed her down again. 'I'll make it. Do you want me to collect Alec from playgroup?'

'No, ta. Our Samantha's getting him. Those flowers in the window are crooked.' She made to get up. Josie shoved her back.

'I'll do it. Now, you stay there while I make the tea. When I come back, if I find you've moved an inch I'll biff you.'

While she waited for the kettle to boil, she put the dirty dishes in the dishwasher. In a perverse way Lily was enjoying being overworked and miserable. Francie claimed to be at his wits' end. 'The only thing I can do to please her is allow meself to be endlessly nagged. She snaps at the lads, even when they try to help. One of these days, so help me, I'll kill the bloody woman, baby an' all.'

Lily rowed with both her sisters. 'Our Daisy had the cheek to tell me I was *lucky* to be having a baby at my age. Just because *she* couldn't have one, it doesn't mean *I* have to be glad. I said to her, I said, "You don't know what it's like to bear a child, Daise. You're talking through the back of your neck." Now she's taken umbrage. Not that *I* care,' she finished haughtily.

And Marigold had the nerve to admonish Lily for chastising her own boys. '"I beg your pardon," I said to her, "I *beg* your pardon. Just who do you think you are? These are *my* children, and I'll talk to them however I please. If you don't like it, you can lump it somewhere else." So she did!' Lily gave a fiendish grin. 'I don't give a damn. Some sisters *they* are.'

Even Samantha found reasons for giving her mother a wide berth, and Gillian, at university, no doubt forewarned, found something else to do during the Easter holidays rather than return to Liverpool. Francie was suddenly inundated with orders, all urgent, and had to work late. Only the two little boys were left but, then, they had no choice, and Josie. She came every lunchtime and most evenings to sit with her friend because she had the miraculous knack of coping with Lily's tantrums, of never taking offence, of giving as good as she got and somehow managing to love Lily, despite her numerous faults.

Lily's blood pressure rose alarmingly at eight months, her ankles swelled, her head ached. The doctor, who came every day, ordered her to rest. Only Lily could make resting an ordeal for everyone around. She was bored. 'I can never get to grips with a novel, you know that,' she said when Josie brought her a pile of books to read. She didn't like magazines, they were too bitty, she announced when Josie brought them instead. Daytime television was nothing but rubbish. She couldn't sew, she couldn't knit or embroider. 'I'd write a letter, but who is there to write to?'

'There's your Stanley and Robert,' Josie said helpfully.

For some reason they wouldn't do. 'I'd write to our Ben if I knew where he lived. I wonder where he went, Jose?'

'I don't know, Lil.' Ben hadn't been heard from in years.

'Give us his address and I'll write to Jack.'

'My Jack?' Josie's jaw dropped. 'Jack Coltrane?'

'How many Jacks do we know?'

'All right, Lil. I'm sure Jack will be pleased.' Jack would probably faint with shock.

Jack phoned a week later. 'I've had this very odd letter from your pregnant pal, Lily. Is she okay?'

'As okay as she'll ever be. What did she have to say?'

'In a nutshell, that you're a walking saint, and we should get married again immediately. She goes on in a muddled way about life being short and it shouldn't be wasted. It's rather touching in a way.'

Josie said nothing, and Jack went on, 'I suppose she's right, about life being short and stuff, though I don't go along with the walking saint bit. Saints don't throw a guy's plays on the floor and kick them.'

'I'm sorry,' she said abjectly.

'Too late, I'm afraid.' She imagined him grinning, and was surprised when his voice suddenly became harsh. 'Josie, you're a beautiful, vital woman. You should have married again years ago.'

She cradled the receiver in both hands. 'You weren't here to marry, Jack.'

'Forget about me, damn you!' he yelled. 'I made a lousy husband the first time, and I'd make a worse one now. You must meet a whole heap of eligible men when you're running that business – marry one of them, for Chrissake.' There was a pause, then a noise that might have been a sob. 'Sweetheart, my sweetheart,' he groaned, 'I love you too much to marry you. You deserve something better than an old, washed-up has-been like me. I've had it, Josie. I'm finished, over the hill. Forget me, my dearest love, and find someone else.'

'Jack!' she cried, but the line had gone dead, and when she tried to ring back she got the engaged tone, and continued to do so the next day and the day after. A week later the receiver was still off the hook. In desperation she rang Val Morrissey in New York to ask if there was anything wrong. He might know. He'd been seeing a lot of Jessie Mae.

'Didn't Jack tell you?' he gurgled happily. 'Jessie Mae and I flew to Las Vegas last weekend and got married. I've written to you, expressing my everlasting gratitude. We wouldn't have met if it hadn't been for you. You won't have got the letter yet.'

She was conscious of her heart beating rapidly in her chest. 'Did Jack go?'

'No, but Jessie Mae came to me with his warmest love.'

'So he should be at home?'

'I don't see why not. He didn't say he was going away.'

If it hadn't been for Lily, she would have flown to Los Angeles there and then. As soon as the baby's born, she vowed, we'll go, me and Dinah. They'd hoped to go at Easter, but Dinah had changed jobs again to become an assistant editor with a leading publisher, and was unable to take time off. Josie had no intention of giving up so lightly on Jack Coltrane, not this time.

'Did Jack get my letter?' Lily enquired. It was the last night Josie would spend with her pregnant friend in the house in Halewood. The baby wasn't due until the fourteenth of May, two weeks off, but Lily was going into hospital the next day so that her blood pressure could be regularly monitored. It was still too high.

'Yes, luv. He was very pleased.'

'I hope he takes my advice. I'd like to see you happy, Jose.'

'I'm already quite happy.'

'Happier, then.'

Josie didn't say that the letter had probably arrived at the worst possible time for Jack – and for herself. Jessie Mae had just married and Lily rambling on about life being short, time being wasted, had unsettled him. He'd said things that, without the letter, it might never have entered his head to say. She changed the subject. 'I've brought you a prezzie – two prezzies, actually.'

'Goodie! I love prezzies. What are they?'

'Open them and see.' Josie handed her a George Henry Lee's bag. 'One's so you'll look dead gorgeous when you've had the baby. The other's so you'll smell like a dream.'

'Oh, Jose. It's lovely.' Lily held up a filmy pink nightie, thickly trimmed with ivory lace. 'And Opium! I *love* Opium. It's me favourite.' She sprayed behind her ears, and heady, exotic musk perfumed the air.

'That's why I bought it.'

They were sitting together on the settee and Lily grabbed her hand. 'You've been the best friend in the world, Jose,' she said in the clear, sweet voice she rarely used. 'No one could have had a better friend than you. You've always been there for me, ever since we were six.'

'And you for me, Lil.'

'No.' Lily shook her head. 'No, I haven't. I've always been too selfish to think of anyone but meself. But everything's going to change after I've had the baby. These last few weeks, I've had nothing to do but think.' She sighed massively. 'Poor Francie, I couldn't wait to get me hands on him, but I've led him a terrible life. Yet he's a husband in a million. Neil was, too.' Her face softened. 'And me kids! They're lovely kids, Josie. I'm never going to snap at them again. Our Marigold was right to tell me off, and I was horrible to our Daisy. I'll write to them from hospital and say how sorry I am. I'm going to turn over a new leaf, Jose.'

Josie had heard all this before and didn't believe a word of it. 'You're all right as you are, Lil,' she lied.

'Light the candle and I'll try and relax. Do you mind nipping upstairs first, make sure the lads have settled down? They're both a bit upset about me going to hospital. Oh, and switch on the landing light. It's getting dark.'

The boys were fast asleep in their bunk beds. The walls were full of *Star Wars* posters, and Simon was clutching a plastic Darth Vader to his chest. The younger Alec slept with a teddy in his arms, his feet protruding from under the duvet. She covered them, suddenly feeling tearful at the sight of the perfect childish feet, the still pearly toes. It was many years since she'd done the same thing for her little girls.

When she went downstairs, Lily had already lit the candle and drawn the curtains. 'I don't find it all that relaxing,' she said. 'The doctor suggested it, said it might calm me mind, but I keep wondering where the draughts come from that make it flicker. It reminds me of when we had candles during the war, in that cellar we used as a shelter.'

'Aunt Ivy had an oil lamp. Phew, it didn't half stink. I only used the shelter once. There was a spider.' Josie shuddered. 'It was *huge*.'

Lily set off on a long, winding journey of memories. 'Remember the fairy glen, Jose? . . . Remember when you had a crush on Humphrey Bogart? . . . Remember that boyfriend I had, Jimmy something? Or was it Tommy? . . . Oh, and the pictures we used to see! I'm sure they were funnier in those days, and the men were much more handsome – except for Humphrey Bogart!' Remember this, remember that, when this happened, when that.

'Remember Haylands. Oh, we had a glorious time, didn't we, Jose?'

'Wonderful.' Josie felt hypnotised by the flickering candle. She couldn't take her eyes off it. The scenes, the memories, seemed unnaturally real. She could smell the flowers in the fairy glen, the salty sea air at Haylands, the cigarette fumes in the picture-houses they'd gone to, the choking tang of yellow fog that used to hang heavily over the Liverpool streets, sometimes for days.

Lily's voice was getting sleepy. 'Remember the time I came to Bingham Mews? I met Neil going home on the train. Laura was such a sweet little girl,

Jose. You must be very proud of her, having such a responsible . . . job . . . in . . . London.' Lily's head fell on her chest. She was asleep.

'Laura's dead, Lil. Dinah's in London,' Josie murmured under her breath. She longed for a cup of tea, but felt too indolent to move, still fascinated by the dancing flame which cast agitated shadows over the room. She tried to think of reasons to make herself get up, but if tea wouldn't do it, nothing would.

I'll ring Jack! She blew out the candle, and was on her feet in an instant, swaying dizzily because she'd risen too quickly. It was half past ten, but only half past two in Los Angeles. In the hall, she dialled the number with stiff fingers, and felt a surge of relief when she heard the dialling tone, which meant the receiver had been replaced. A woman answered after three rings. 'Hi! Shit, I can't read the number. Sorry about that. Hi, again.'

'I'd like to speak to Jack, please. Jack Coltrane.' She was too relieved to wonder why a woman was answering the phone.

'Sorry, honey. He doesn't live here any more. I'm Lonnie Geldhart from the realtors. This property is up for sale.'

'Where has he gone?' Josie cried frantically. 'Do you have his new address?'

'No, honey. I've never even met the guy.'

'But when the house is sold, you'll be sending him the proceeds. Oh, please, I have to know.'

'Gee, honey. I'd love to help,' the woman said sympathetically, 'but the money's being split between his kids – Tyler and Jessie Mae, I think their names are. I can give you their addresses if you like.'

'It's all right, I know where Jessie Mae is. Thank you for your help.'

'Any time, hon. I hope you manage to find the guy.'

Josie replaced the receiver. 'You've done it again – disappeared,' she whispered. 'Val Morrissey said he didn't know where you were.' She stamped her foot, forgetting the sleeping children upstairs and their pregnant mother on the other side of the wall. 'You *bastard*, Jack Coltrane!'

Francie entered the house through the back door. Josie was in the kitchen, on her third cup of tea. 'Been working late,' he said brazenly.

'You've been drinking.' Josie curled a caustic lip. 'Don't deny it, Francie. I can smell it on your breath.'

'Only a couple of beers after work, Jose. How's her ladyship?'

'Asleep, not that you'd care.'

'I *do* care, quite deeply, as a matter of fact, but caring does me no good, Jose.' He grinned. 'The other day she called me a rapist.'

'You probably are, amongst other things.'

'Apparently, I raped me own wife, though she was perfectly willing at the time. I thought the bloody woman was on the Pill, else I wouldn't have touched her. I'll feel like a pervert every time I look at the new baby, even when it's twenty-one.'

'You'll be pleased to know she's turning over a new leaf when she's had the baby.'

They smiled at each other. 'In a pig's ear, she will,' Francie said.

Josie rinsed her cup. 'I'm dead on me feet. I'm going home.'

'Ta, Jose.'

'What for?'

'For everything.' He kissed her forehead and gave her a brief hug. 'You're a cracking girl, you know. I'm dead lucky Lily's got a friend like you. You've kept me sane over the last few months.'

'I'm hardly a girl, Francie. I'll be forty-seven next week.'

He winked suggestively. 'You'll always be a girl to me.'

'Oh, shurrup, you.' She gave him a shove. 'Tara, Francie. I'll go and see Lily in the hospital tomorrow.'

She was climbing into her car when she heard the scream, and she paused, unsure where it had come from. Then Francie opened the front door. 'It's Lily,' he shouted. 'The baby's coming. I'm taking her to the hospital straight away.'

The scream had woken the little boys. They came creeping downstairs, looking scared, just as Francie's car screeched away. 'What's the matter with Mummy?' Simon asked worriedly. A wide-eyed Alec sucked his thumb.

'She's had to go to hospital a bit early. By this time tomorrow you'll have a lovely little sister or brother. Won't that be the gear?'

'When will Mummy be home?'

'In a few days. Come on.' Josie held out her hands and they each took one. 'Shall I make you some warm milk?' It would be better if they didn't return to bed immediately, with Lily's scream still ringing in their ears. 'Would you like a biccy?'

'Yes, please, Auntie Josie,' they said together.

They sat together on the settee, their small bodies tucked against hers. She had got on well with all Lily's children.

'Will the new baby make Mummy scream again?'

'No, Simon.'

'It'll be a nuisance. Mummy said it will be a nuisance.'

'She didn't mean it.' She stroked Simon's pale hair, and wished Lily were there so she could give her a piece of her mind. What a thing to say! She thought how beautiful the love was that young children had for their mothers, who could do or say the vilest things yet the love persisted – unconditional, loyal, totally committed. 'The children love her,' Ben had said once of Imelda. And she had loved Mam, oh, so much, so much.

'Back to bed,' she sang out when the milk had gone. 'It's school and playgroup in the morning.'

Simon was obviously a worrier. 'Who'll take us if Daddy's not here?'

'Daddy will almost certainly be back by then. If not, I'll take you meself.'

Alec lisped, 'We making cakes tomorrow, with currants.'

'Shall I take one to the hospital for Mummy?' Josie offered.

'*Please*,' Alec said eagerly. 'And one for the new baby, too.'

After they had been tucked up in bed, Josie wandered round the house, trying not to think of Jack, failing utterly, thinking about him, cursing him, loathing him, loving him. I'll find you, she vowed. You're not getting away from me again.

She was about to make tea, but felt the urge for something stronger, so searched for bottles. There was beer in the fridge, but she hated beer. She found a bottle of gin in the sideboard, and wondered how much the legal limit was for when she drove home. A double – she'd risk a double, mixed with orange squash.

The hours crept by. She drank more gin, lay on the settee and tried to sleep, couldn't, got up, had another gin, thought about Lily, thought about Jack, thought she heard a burglar, but it was next door's cat scratching at the door, no doubt attracted by the light. She gave it milk and let it out again – Lily would have a fit if she knew, she hated cats.

Four o'clock! A child started to cry. She went upstairs. Alec, in the bottom bunk, was sobbing hopelessly.

'What's the matter, luv?' She held the small, shaking body in her arms. 'Have you had a bad dream?'

'Feel sad, Auntie Josie.' He could hardly speak. 'Feel dead miserable. Want my mummy.'

Simon turned over. 'Shurrup,' he muttered.

Alec quickly fell asleep, and Josie sat at the top of the stairs in case he woke again. Gosh, it was creepy, so quiet and so still. Alec's wretched crying had disturbed her. She longed to be in her own house in her own bed. Hurry up, Lil, and have your baby, she urged.

The phone went just after half four. She raced downstairs and picked it up before it woke the boys. 'Francie!'

'Hello, Jose.' His voice was curiously calm.

'How's Lily?'

'Dead, Jose. Lily's dead. She went into a fit or something, then she haemorrhaged, then she died. The baby's dead, too. It was a little girl. We were going to call her Josephine, after you.' He laughed. 'I can't believe I'm saying this. Lily's *dead*.'

4

They had put Lily in the pink nightgown trimmed with ivory lace that Josie had bought. Her lips were painted a delicate pink, her hair brushed away from the forehead made smooth by death and arranged in waves on the white satin pillow of the best coffin money could buy, which would have pleased her no end. Her hands were crossed over her breast. She looked peaceful, serene, as she had never done in life. It was hard to imagine a cross word had ever emerged from the pink mouth, Josie thought in the funeral parlour as she gazed down at the still, silent figure of her friend. She still couldn't believe Lily was dead. She half expected her to sit up and bark, 'Who d'you think you're staring at? Is that all you've got to do, Josie Flynn?'

The crematorium chapel was half-full – Lily's children, her husband, her brothers and sisters, a few nieces and nephews, their husbands and wives. Josie was the only person not a relative. Lily had had few friends. Dinah hadn't come. The new job was making her paranoid about taking time off.

At first, Josie didn't recognise the tall, tanned, athletic man in the front pew, blond, fiftyish, in an expensive grey suit. Then she realised it was Ben. Ben Kavanagh!

So all the Kavanaghs had turned up for the funeral of their baby sister. Were they looking at each other, wondering whose turn it would be next? Their ma and da had gone, now Lily, the youngest. For which Kavanagh would the next funeral be held?

Daisy and Marigold felt guilty. They shouldn't have taken offence and neglected their sister while she was pregnant. They should have made allowances. After all, Lily hadn't been herself.

'She realised it was her fault.' Josie told them. 'She was going to write from hospital and apologise.'

'Well, she might have,' Marigold said with a dry smile.

'It would have been a first,' muttered Daisy.

It was strange. No one seemed all that upset, as if they, like Josie, couldn't believe Lily was dead. She had been so noisy, had made her presence so forcefully felt, that it didn't seem possible she had been silenced for ever.

Francie grieved for his lost wife, but felt no guilt for having found her a pain to live with, a fact that couldn't be challenged just because she was dead. He arranged for the most lavish of funerals, because it was what Lily would have demanded had she known she was going to die. 'I keep hearing this nagging voice in me head telling me what to do,' he confided to Josie. '"I want roses on me coffin, red ones, shaped like a cross. Make sure you wear a clean shirt and a black tie for me funeral. And don't drink too much afterwards, Francie O'Leary. Don't forget, I've got me eye on you."'

She would always be grateful to Francie for making life seem not quite as tragic as it really was.

Everyone went back to Marigold's house in Calderstones for a drink and something to eat. Marigold's children were grown up, long married, and numerous grandchildren cluttered the rooms.

Josie grabbed a sandwich and a glass of wine, and hid in a corner. Perhaps because Lily wasn't there, for the first time she felt out of place within the hubbub of this large family.

'I wanted a word with you.' Daisy approached, elegant in floating black chiffon. 'It's rather sad, I'm afraid. In a few weeks, Manos and I are leaving Liverpool to live in Greece.'

'Oh, Daisy!' Josie cried. 'You've always been a permanent fixture in me life, almost as much as Lily.'

'I know, and you in mine.' Daisy smiled tremulously. 'It was our Lily going that did it. Stanley and Robert live so far away, and I had no idea where Ben was. Marigold's wrapped up in her family. There seemed no reason left to stay, and Manos has this huge extended family in Crete. I miss being part of a family.'

Josie kissed her on both cheeks. 'I hope you and Manos will be very happy in Crete. Twice in me life you've come to me rescue when I've been at rock bottom. I'll never forget that, Daise.'

'Promise you'll come and stay some time, Josie. You'll always be welcome. You're one of Manos's favourite people.'

'I promise.' Josie nodded vigorously, knowing she almost certainly wouldn't. It was just that partings were much easier if you promised to see each other again.

'I've been trying to escape from our Stanley for ages.' Ben arrived in her corner. 'You look great but, then, you always do. Have you sold your soul to the devil in return for permanent youth?'

Josie opened her mouth to laugh, but quickly closed it. Lily wouldn't approve of people laughing at her funeral. 'You can talk! You look wonderful, like a Nordic god.'

'I've taken up tennis. I'm rather good at it. I'm champion of the local club.' He grimaced. '*Senior* champion, in the section for the over forty-fives.'

'Where exactly is the local club?' she asked curiously. 'It's something all of us have wanted to know for a long time.'

'Isle of Wight. Come on, let's find somewhere quieter to talk.' He took her arm and led her into the garden. It was full of children, but there was a bench right at the bottom, half hidden by an apple tree iced with pink blossom. 'After Imelda died,' Ben said when they were seated, 'I felt I wanted a change of scene, for myself and the children. We drifted round the country for a while and I worked as a supply teacher. I kept meaning to write to say where I was, but never got round to it.' He shrugged. 'I was pretty mixed up for a while. Then I got a job with an aeronautic design company on the Isle of Wight. We settled down, and it seemed too late to let people know, so I never bothered.'

'Who told you about Lily?'

'Read it in the *Echo*,' he said surprisingly. 'About this time last year, I felt dead homesick. Colette was already married and living in Dorset – I'm a grandfather of twins, by the way – and Peter discovered the social conscience I used to have myself. He's in Cuba, working on a farm. I decided to look for a job in Liverpool, come home. I've been getting the paper ever since.'

'It'll be nice to have you back.' She meant it sincerely. A Kavanagh coming, a Kavanagh going, and one gone for ever!

'I can't wait to be back,' he said, 'though I was expecting a right earful from our Lily when I showed my face. Instead, I feel gutted. I thought the Grim Reaper would have to drag Lily to her grave kicking and screaming when she was a hundred.'

Josie was glad of the buzz of activity in Barefoot House when she returned next day. William Friars had called when she was away. Havers Hill had decided not to publish *Death By Stealth* in paperback because of its initial mauling by the critics and the subsequent small sales.

'He said he would graciously allow us to publish it.' Cathy grinned. 'I said I'd talk to you.'

'Write and tell him to get stuffed,' Josie said curtly. 'I didn't want the book in the first place. Tell him if he'd like to write another set in the war, we might take it.'

'With pleasure. Have you had any further thoughts about that suggestion Richard made?'

'I haven't had time to think for weeks.' Barefoot House seemed to have reached a plateau. There was only a limited amount of good crime fiction available. She didn't want standards to drop by accepting work she might once have rejected, and Richard had come up with the idea that they extend their range to another genre of novel – science fiction, romance, war or historical, books for children. 'I don't know, Cathy. I don't think I want to become a millionaire. I'm content with things as they are.'

Cathy left, looking disappointed. Josie chewed her lip and worried that she was letting down her staff by being too unadventurous. She should be looking for ways to go forward, not be content with standing still. Mind you, it would be *her* taking the risk, not Cathy, Richard or the others, and she wasn't in the mood just now.

She scanned the post. There was a letter from Brewster & Cronin in New York, marked 'Personal'. Val Morrissey had hired a private detective to trace Jack's whereabouts, but had had no luck so far. 'I'm worried about Jack myself,' he wrote. 'After all, the guy's my father-in-law of sorts. I really liked him the few times we met. I'll not give up until every avenue has been exhausted.'

There was no mention of Jessie Mae being worried about her stepfather. Josie opened the top drawer of her desk and took out the photo Val had sent in January. She was glad to have a face to put to his familiar voice. He was smaller than she had imagined, going slightly bald, very ordinary and rather nice. He was smiling happily at the camera but, then, this had been his wedding day. Yet the bride wasn't smiling. Jessie Mae's plump, pretty face was expressionless. She didn't glare at the camera, she didn't smile, merely stared. She didn't look happy, she didn't look sad, or excited, or even faintly pleased that she had just married a relatively wealthy man who was crazy about her. Josie didn't think she had ever seen such dead eyes before. 'Jessie Mae's had problems,' Jack had said.

Well, at least his real daughter was upset. Dinah was hurt and angry that the father she had only just met had vanished from her life again. 'I can't have meant much to him, can I?' she said bitterly whenever she called to ask if Jack had been found.

At six o'clock, Ben came to take Josie to dinner. He was staying the week with Marigold. 'You didn't say yesterday you had your own business. Our Marigold told me this morning. Who'd have thought it, eh? I've actually read two of your books.'

'Don't sound so surprised,' she said indignantly. 'Did you think I was too thick to start a business?'

'I never considered you even vaguely thick, Jose. You didn't seem the type, that's all.'

'I suppose it was born of necessity.' She glanced around the office, at the rows and rows of bright red books. 'I was in a rut, and the thing just grew and grew.'

Ben had come in his car – the latest model BMW, she noticed. The job on the Isle of Wight must pay well. They drove into the countryside and ate in a little seventeenth-century pub near Ormskirk, with beams and an inglenook fireplace. Over chicken and chips, she told him about Richard's suggestion. 'But I'm not as entrepreneurial as I look. Barefoot House became a success despite me. It happened so gradually I hardly noticed. If I'd known I'd end up handling things like film rights and TV rights, I'd have probably backed off.'

'I doubt it,' he said comfortably. 'Anyroad, most businesses start from nothing. Didn't Marks & Spencer grow from a stall selling candles? Or was that Harrods? Great oak trees from little acorns grow, so it's said. Would you like to finish off this wine, Jose? I've already had two glasses, and I'm driving.'

He emptied the bottle into her glass. It had been an enjoyable, relaxing evening. They had talked, without a hint of strain, about when they had been children living in Machin Street, the things they'd done together, the times they'd had, about Lily and the tantrums she used to throw. He seemed to have got over the passion he'd once had for her, and she was glad. He had spoken about Imelda, how painful the marriage had been, how he and the children had suffered from her moods.

'It would have been so easy to blame her, hate her, but the poor woman couldn't help it. She was sick. If she'd had a physical illness, everyone would have been sympathetic, but people have no patience with the mentally ill.'

She was reminded of how kind he'd always been, how understanding. 'Imelda was lucky to have had someone like you.'

'It wasn't easy,' he muttered. 'There were times when I felt at the end of my tether. I'm the sort who likes a quiet life.'

Mrs Kavanagh had remarked once, 'Our Ben will make some girl a good husband, but not a very exciting one.'

'He's a soppy lad, our Ben,' Lily had said.

He took out his wallet and picked up the bill. Josie watched his face as, frowning slightly, he counted out the money. It was a sensitive face and, despite all he'd suffered, the green eyes were guileless and innocent, like a child's. He was a good man, through and through.

'If you can spare the time before you go back, perhaps I could treat *you* to dinner,' she said impulsively.

His face lit up. 'I've always got time to spare for you, Jose. Not tomorrow, I'm seeing Francie. The night after?'

'It's a date.'

Josie woke suddenly with the eerie feeling that she'd just been sharply prodded in the ribs. The room was pitch dark, and the electric alarm clock showed thirteen minutes past three. She reached out a shaking hand to switch on the bedside lamp, terrified that another hand would grab it. She would never get used to sleeping alone in the big old house.

'Who's there?' she enquired timidly.

No answer. Josie gritted her teeth and sat up. The bedroom was empty. She rubbed her left side, where there was the definite sensation of having been poked. Lily had had the irritating habit of poking people if she thought they weren't listening, or had said something she didn't like, a habit Josie had suffered from more than most. It had driven Francie to the verge of murder, as his ribs were unnaturally exposed.

It dawned on Josie that Lily was dead. *Lily was dead?* She would never see her friend again. 'Lil,' she wailed. 'I want you back.' She began to cry for the first time since Francie had called from the hospital to say Lily and the baby had died. The tears flowed for the girl who had been her best friend since they were six, whose death she'd been unable to grasp. Until now, when she'd been poked awake by an unseen finger.

'You bitch, Lily Kavanagh,' she whispered through the tears. 'You did that on purpose.' She'd like to bet that, all over the country, various Kavanaghs and a somnolent Francie O'Leary had been awoken by a red-faced, bad-tempered Lily, waving her arms and stamping her feet because no one had acknowledged the fact that she was dead. No one had cried. No one had mourned, only her daughters and her two little boys.

'You've left a great big hole in me life, Lil, and I'll always miss you.' Josie snuggled back under the bedclothes. 'But if you do that again, I'll bloody kill you.'

Two months later, on the first of July, Ben Kavanagh returned to Liverpool, having procured a job with a chemical company over the water in Birkenhead. He bought the top half of a large Victorian house in Princes Park which had been converted into two flats.

The evening after his furniture had arrived from the Isle of Wight, Josie helped arrange it in the big, elegant rooms.

'You've got excellent taste,' she said as she straightened the cushions of the comfortable three-piece, upholstered in coarse, oatmeal wool. The carpet was new, mustard tweed.

'I got most of the stuff from Habitat. I like the modern look – plain colours, no curly-wurly bits on the furniture, white walls.' He was stacking books in alphabetical order on a natural wood bookcase.

'Shall I hang the curtains?'

'Please. I put the fittings up last night. The rings are already in.'

The navy blue curtains took only a few minutes to slide on the pole. She found a screwdriver and secured the pole at each end, then took the screwdriver and another set of curtains, brick red, upstairs to hang in the bedroom. Here the carpet was grey. The bed had a slatted base, a polished plank for a headboard and was covered with a grey duvet. A wardrobe and six-drawer chest were equally unadorned.

She hung the curtains, secured the pole and sat on the bed to admire her handiwork. A bit Spartan, but what you'd expect of a man. Well, some men. Jack's apartment in New York had looked as if he were about to hold a jumble sale.

Ben came in. 'I'll hang my clothes up tonight. They're still in boxes.'

'What else shall I do? What about ornaments?'

'Don't believe in them. I prefer the cool, uncluttered look.' He sat beside her on the bed.

'That chest looks very bare. It needs something.'

'It'll have a bowl for my small change, and that's all.'

'What about a little vase on the window-sill? I've got things in my attic you can have.'

He grinned. 'They can stay in your attic, thanks all the same. Ornaments need dusting. I can live without them very well.'

'You've always been so sensible and organised,' she said admiringly.

'It doesn't seem to have got me anywhere.' He laughed shortly. 'So far, my life has been extraordinarily chaotic. My wife killed herself, and I've spent years living in places I didn't want to live.'

'Well, you can settle down now.' She patted his knee. 'You're home.'

He put his hand over hers before she could remove it. 'I'm looking forward to it, Jose. But I'd look forward to it even more if I were settling down with you.'

'Ben!' She tried to remove her hand but he wouldn't let go. Instead, he took her other hand, placed her arms around his neck, and drew her towards him.

'I won't kiss you,' he whispered. 'I want you to listen, that's all. I still love you. I know you don't love me, and I won't come out with all that guff about me having enough love for both of us.' He drew in a deep breath, and let it out slowly.

'You just said I was sensible, and it makes perfect sense for us to be together. I don't want a commitment, I'm not going to propose. Instead, I'd like us to conduct a little experiment, which is what I do all the time in my job. When you feel ready, if you ever do, I'd like us to be lovers, not just friends. Let's see how we get on, you and me, together, as a couple.' He released her so suddenly, she almost lost her balance. 'I'm not being very sensible now, am I?' he groaned. 'That was totally impetuous, and I've probably alienated you for ever.'

Josie didn't speak. She went over to the window which overlooked the back of the house. A very old man was mowing the grass in the garden next door, and a woman about the same age, presumably his wife, was fetching in washing. She wondered what it would be like to have been married to the same person for forty or fifty years. Had she married Ben, they would have clocked up their silver wedding anniversary by now. Their children might be married, they might have grandchildren. She would never have experienced the ecstatic highs and the tragic lows there'd been with Jack Coltrane.

There was still no trace of Jack. It could be another twenty years before he resurfaced. But Ben was here, loving her still, loving her for a whole lifetime. He had always made her feel safe and secure, even when she was a child. But he hadn't understood her need for adventure, even if it was only a few months at Haylands, because he wasn't adventurous himself. But Josie was forty-seven, and Barefoot House provided all the excitement she needed. Jack Coltrane had never made her feel remotely safe or secure, but Ben would.

'Ben.' She turned. He was still sitting on the bed, watching her, and the love in his eyes made her heart melt. 'Oh, Ben!' She sat beside him, laid her head on his shoulder. 'I don't deserve you. You make me feel a desperately horrible woman.'

'You're the woman I want.' He kissed her lips, softly, gently, and she laughed. 'You were always a good kisser. You haven't changed.'

Nothing much had changed. He undid her blouse, caressed her breasts, kissed them, and Josie found it pleasant, slightly arousing, but that was all. She felt more aroused by his own mounting passion, which was catching, and the tenderness of his touch, the lovely things he said between kisses. He made her feel a uniquely special person, the most beautiful woman who had ever lived. She felt cherished and very fortunate that a man like Ben regarded her body, possessing it, as equivalent to finding the Holy Grail.

They reached orgasm together. 'Darling,' Ben panted. 'Oh, darling, that was wonderful.' He folded her in his arms, and she was conscious of his pounding heart, his body shuddering against hers. 'Was it all right for you?' he said anxiously.

'More than all right, silly.' It had been sweet and enjoyable. She would quite like to do it again.

5

Josie was founder and managing director of Barefoot House, but didn't want to appear an autocrat so she called a staff meeting. Everyone crowded into her office, and she asked for their views on the company branching out to include another genre of novel.

'What do you think? It's ages and ages since Richard suggested it, but I've had a lot of things on my mind lately, personal things.'

'Why don't we do westerns?' This came from Bobby, the post-boy, who Josie was surprised to see there as he hadn't been invited. But he was a cheeky character, blissfully unaware of his place in the office hierarchy. 'They're me fave.'

To her surprise, there was a rumble of agreement. 'Westerns are like thrillers, always popular,' someone murmured.

Josie thought westerns old hat, but didn't say so. It was quickly turning into one of those times when she felt inferior to her staff, who were mostly far more experienced and knowledgable about publishing than she was herself. She folded her arms on the desk and tried to look cool and in charge of the situation.

'Josie, do you know Dorothy Venables?' asked Lynne Goode, who had come to Barefoot House almost a year ago.

'I've heard of her, naturally.' Dorothy Venables wrote women's sagas that sold by the cartload. Her name was always near the top of the year's bestselling writers.

'I was going to talk to you about this anyway. She had a three-book contract with my old company,' Lynne explained. 'I was her editor. It was the only thing I regretted about leaving, parting with Dottie. We still keep in touch. She's uneasy about signing a new contract since they've been taken over by this big, soulless American company. It's the reason I left myself. I think I could persuade her to come to us.'

There was an even louder rumble from the assembled staff, this time of excitement. 'I can't believe you have *that* much influence, Lynne,' Cathy Connors said jealously.

'No one can influence Dottie. She's more than capable of thinking for herself.' Lynne smiled. 'I've told her about Barefoot House. She's a right-on feminist, though you'd never tell by her books. She likes the idea of being published by a woman.'

'Would she want a massive advance?' Josie enquired.

'Probably, but you'd get every penny back, and more.'

Josie swallowed nervously. Women's sagas! Dorothy Venables! Was she getting in too deeply? Would she be able to cope? She was aware of a dozen pairs of eyes, watching her intently, and felt a sudden thrill of excitement. *Dorothy Venables!* 'Sound her out,' she said to Lynne. 'If she's willing, I'm willing, as long as she doesn't want an advance that will bankrupt us.' She grinned. 'Or even if she does.'

Dorothy Venables telephoned an hour later. She spoke quickly and aggressively in a hoarse, gruff voice, with a strong North Country accent. 'I've read about you, and I like the sound of you,' she growled. 'Come from a working-class background meself. We drank our tea from jam jars in my part of Yorkshire.'

Josie was unable to match such depths of poverty. She promised to draw up a contract. The advance agreed on was less than expected. Lynne said later it was only half what she had received for her previous novel.

'She realised a figure like that might cause problems. She's very kind underneath all that bluster. I'm sure you two will become great friends.'

'Dorothy Venables!' she crowed that night.

'Never heard of her,' Ben said.

'She's published all over the world in umpteen different languages. It's like signing up the Queen. I'm going down to London next week to take her to lunch. Lynne, one of me editors, is coming with me. They're old friends. I sent Bobby out to buy some of her books. I want to read the lot before we meet. Gosh, Ben. Sometimes I can't believe this is happening.' She still felt nervous and strung out. She was lying on the pink and cream settee, her legs draped over his knee, and she smiled up at him. 'I'm glad you're here to talk to.'

He laid his hand flat on her stomach. 'Pleased to be of service, ma'am.'

Since Dinah had gone, she had missed having someone there with whom to discuss the events of the day. Ben was particularly soothing to be with. They had been together three months, and he was a perfect companion, utterly reliable. She would have trusted him with her life. If Ben said he would telephone at six, or arrive at seven, he would keep his promise to the dot. He looked up timetables for her, met her off trains, made sure her car was serviced and filled with petrol, kept an eye on when insurance premiums were due, found things she had lost. He even brought her tea in bed each morning, and generally looked after her in a way no one had ever done before. She felt dearly loved and very precious.

They were virtually living together in Huskisson Street, though he hadn't properly moved in. He returned to his flat in Princes Park to change his clothes, do his washing, keep the place dusted and tidied. He wanted to move in permanently, but Josie had put him off. 'Not just yet, let's leave it a while,' she had said gently.

'Hmm. That's nice.' She sighed dreamily when he began to rub his hand in a circle on her abdomen. Closing her eyes, she immediately began to worry that she was using him. At the back of her mind there was a feeling that the relationship wouldn't last, which was why she hadn't wanted him to move in, give up his home. He knew she didn't love him, not in the way he loved her, but it still felt wrong.

Dorothy Venables turned up in a leather jacket and well-worn jeans. She was in her fifties, thin and lanky with dark, burning eyes and a badly scarred chin. She looked as tough as old boots. A cigarette dangled from her narrow, unpainted lips. Having been forewarned by Lynne, Josie had booked a table in a restaurant that didn't have a dress code.

Books were one of the few subjects not mentioned throughout the meal. Dottie – Josie had been told to call her Dottie – smoked between courses, slagged off the government, the aristocracy, royalty, the stock exchange, banks, building societies and any other bastions of the establishment that came to mind, using the sort of language that never appeared in her novels. Unmarried, her most scathing criticism was directed at men, most of whom she unreservedly loathed. Josie found it incredible that such tender love stories could have been nurtured in so cynical a mind. Even so, she liked down-to-earth Dottie Venables very much. Lynne was right. Josie just knew they would become great friends.

Josie and Lynne had come by train, and would make their own way home. Lynne went to see her mother in Brent, and Josie to the West End to do some shopping, then to Holborn to meet Dinah after work.

Her daughter emerged from the high-rise office building carrying a briefcase, looking anxious and flustered. 'I don't like leaving so early,' she said.

'Early!' Josie looked at her watch. 'It's twenty-five to six.' She thought Dinah looked rather pale and much too thin.

'Yes, but everyone works all the hours God sends, Mum. I felt dead conspicuous, being the first to leave. I hope no one noticed, else it'll be a black mark against me.'

'People should work to live, Dinah, not live to work.' Josie took her arm and ushered her inside the first reasonable-looking restaurant they came to. 'I'm sure not everyone works as hard as you say,' she said when they were seated, 'otherwise they'd have no home life.'

'Well, no, not everyone,' Dinah conceded, 'but I'm the youngest assistant editor there, and the only one who didn't go to university. I have to put in more effort than the others if I'm to get anywhere.'

'And where exactly is it that you want to get, luv?'

'I've told you before – to the top,' Dinah said promptly. 'Some of the senior editors fly all over the world, meeting writers. I'd like to work in the States one day, become an executive, edit a top magazine. I want to get *on*, Mum.'

'Well, while you're getting on, I wish you'd eat properly. You look as if you haven't had a decent meal in ages.'

'I'm too busy to eat,' Dinah muttered.

'I suppose you'll be too busy to come home for your birthday.' Dinah would be twenty-one in a fortnight's time. It was a long while since she'd been to Liverpool. 'We can have a party,' Josie said coaxingly.

'I can't see me managing it, Mum.'

Josie would have liked to discuss the matter more, but Dinah rushed the meal. She pointed to the briefcase and said she had stacks of work to do at home.

The journey back seemed to take for ever, and Josie worried about Dinah the whole way. There'd been a hardness about her daughter that she hadn't liked, yet beneath the hardness had been an air of vulnerability that touched her mother to the core. And she was admirable in her way. She could have had a cushy, secure job at Barefoot House, but preferred to make her own way in the publishing world. Josie sighed. Perhaps she was old-fashioned, but she felt a young woman of twenty should be out and about having a good time, not working herself to death in an office, skipping meals.

Ben had been primed as to when the train would arrive, and was waiting at Lime Street station. 'I've had some great news,' he said joyfully. 'I had a letter today from Cuba. Our Peter's coming home for Christmas. I haven't seen him in over two years.'

Twelve people sat down to dinner that Christmas in Huskisson Street: Josie and Ben; a very tense Dinah; Peter Kavanagh, now a lovely bronzed young man, the image of Imelda; Francie O'Leary and his two little boys; Esther, Josie's secretary, still alone; and Colette, Ben's daughter, with her husband, Jeremy, and their twin daughters, Amy and Zoe. They were staying in Ben's flat.

'Bloody hell!' Josie swore, as she struggled with pans of vegetables and a giant turkey in the steaming kitchen. 'I can't believe I wanted a big family. I would have had this lark every sodding year.'

'Need a hand?' Francie poked his head around the door.

'No, that's the problem. You're not the first to offer help, but I don't know what to give people to *do*! Colette's set the table, Ben's organising the drinks.'

'Can I peel a potato or something?' He sidled into the room.

'I did them last night, idiot. Can you see the white dish I was going to put the sprouts in?'

'Is this it?'

'I think so. I need one like it for the carrots.'

'What's wrong with your Dinah? I think this might be the carrot dish.'

'Ta, Francie. She's working too hard, that's what.' She suddenly noticed Francie's bizarre outfit. 'Why have you come to Christmas dinner at my house wearing a nightshirt?'

'It's the latest fashion, Jose.' He did a little twirl. The long white shirt almost reached the knees of his black velvet trousers. 'Hey, I knew you and Ben were seeing each other, but I didn't realise you were such a close item. I'm dead envious. If I'd known he was going to make a move, I'd have proposed to you at Lily's funeral.'

'Oh, Francie. You only say things like that to shock. If you're not careful, I'll find someone else to print me books.'

'I let you go once, I'm determined not to let it happen again.'

She snorted. 'It's a bit late. Anyroad, Mr O'Leary, it was the other way around. It was *me* that let *you* go.'

'Whatever.' He waved his hand. 'Seriously, Jose, Ben's a decent guy, but I hope you're not going to marry him or anything daft like that. He'll bore you rigid after a while. Here, let me help you with that.' Together, they lifted the sizzling turkey out of the oven. 'Me, now, I'm a different proposition altogether, but you already know that. And we were great together when we did the bed bit.'

'Shush!'

There were footsteps outside and Ben appeared. 'I thought you might need some help. Will dinner be long? It's chaos back there. The twins are starving, Simon and Alec are squabbling over something out of a cracker, Esther's worried dinner might be so late she'll miss the Queen's broadcast, and our Peter and Dinah are having a flaming row about Fidel Castro.'

'I think I might treat meself to a holiday,' Dinah said somewhat surprisingly over breakfast on Boxing Day. Ben had left early for Princes Park to see Colette, and Peter, who was staying in Josie's spare room, had risen at some unearthly hour to go for a walk. 'I've enough money saved. I've never been abroad. We never managed to get to Los Angeles, did we?'

'No, luv.' Josie sighed. 'But what about work? You can't just take time off without telling anyone.'

'Oh, I'll give my boss a ring,' Dinah said carelessly, which was even more surprising.

'Would you like me to come with you?' Josie offered. 'Cathy Connors and her husband have gone to the Seychelles for Christmas. She said the weather's perfect this time of year.'

Dinah blushed. 'Actually, Mum, I'm going to Cuba.'

'Cuba!' Josie's face burst into a delighted smile. 'With Peter Kavanagh?'

'Yes, but there's nothing in it. He said it's a wonderful place, and I said I didn't believe him. It's a dictatorship, however benign. He invited me to come and look for meself. I'm only going for a fortnight.'

Josie couldn't have been more pleased. 'I hope you have a lovely time.'

'I doubt it,' Dinah said darkly. 'Peter's a dead irritating guy. He has these really peculiar opinions. All we do is argue.'

A fortnight passed, and Dinah didn't come back from Cuba. She wrote to say she had telephoned the company she worked for to say that she'd left, and had no idea when she would be home. She'd got a job in a hospital and was learning to speak Spanish. Peter had turned out okay after all, and they were sharing a flat. The Americans were shits, the way they treated the Cubans. Would Josie mind driving down to London and collecting her belongings from the flat? She'd given the landlord a month's notice. The dishes were hers, the pots and pans were the landlord's. In the oven there was a lovely casserole dish which she didn't want left behind.

'Why the hell should she give a damn about a casserole dish when she's in Cuba?' Josie wanted to know. 'Your son has a lot to answer for, Ben Kavanagh.'

'You don't mind, do you?' Ben said anxiously.

'Of course not. He's a lovely lad. Though I wish he lived a bit nearer.' Josie smiled wistfully.

'So do I. I wonder if our children ever miss us as much as we miss them?'

'I doubt it.'

As soon as it became known that Dorothy Venables had transferred to Barefoot House, the company was deluged with women's sagas. Josie engaged two more editors, an assistant for Richard in Publicity, and another secretary, by which time space had become a problem. There were too many desks in too few rooms. She could have afforded to move into a spacious office block in town, but preferred the more intimate accommodation of Huskisson Street. She solved the problem by giving up her lovely lounge and elegant dining room for offices, and moving up a floor. The attic was ruthlessly emptied, decorated and turned into a bedroom, and Josie slept with Ben in a room identical to the one she'd lived in with Mam, just four doors and more than forty years away.

The following year, Josie and Ben went to the Odeon in Leicester Square to attend the premiere of *Miss Middleton's Papers*. Great Britain was at war in the Falklands, but war was far from the minds of the expensively dressed guests that night as they strolled across the red carpet into the cinema.

Ben looked dead handsome in the evening suit hired for the occasion. 'Distinguished,' Josie declared. 'I feel quite proud to have you as me escort.' Her own frock was a blue crêpe sheath with long sleeves – she felt convinced the tops of her arms were getting fat. She hoped it looked worth the extravagant amount of money it had cost.

She found the evening very pretentious, the way people fell upon each other and called each other 'darling'. She rather traitorously wished Francie O'Leary were there instead of Ben, because he'd have poked fun at everyone and made her laugh. Ben was very much in awe of the well-known faces, very reverential when people spoke to them. There were times when she wouldn't have minded swopping Ben for Francie. Just for a week or two!

In another month she would be fifty. Fifty! She looked at Ben, aghast. 'I can't believe it! I've been alive half a century. It doesn't feel nearly that long.'

He suggested she throw a big party, invite her staff and all their friends, but Josie demurred. 'I'm not sure I want the staff to know I'm fifty.'

'Have a little dinner party, then. Get caterers in. We'll ask Francie and his latest woman, our Marigold and her husband, that peculiar friend of yours, Dorothy. How many's that?'

Josie counted on her fingers. 'Seven with us, but Daisy and Manos are due home shortly for a few weeks, and I'd like to ask Terence Dunnet, me accountant, and his wife, Muriel. I hardly see them these days.'

'That's eleven. Twelve would make a perfect number. We need another man to partner Dorothy.'

'She'd prefer a woman.'

Ben's eyebrows raised in surprise. 'I didn't know she was that way inclined.'

'She's not. She prefers women's company, that's all. Men are only allowed to do their duty in her bed.'

'Ugh!' He pulled a face. 'Some things are beyond the call of duty. Anyroad, Jose, dinner for twelve. I'll pay, it'll be half my present.'

'What's the other half?' she asked greedily.

Ben went over and switched off the television, which she found slightly irritating as she'd been waiting with the sound turned down for *EastEnders*. 'I thought you'd like a ring,' he said. 'A wedding ring.'

If it had been Francie, she would have said, 'Turn the bloody television back on, and we'll talk about wedding rings when *EastEnders* has finished.' But you could never say things like that to Ben. Even when they were little, she'd had to be careful because his feelings were so easily hurt. Oh, God! She still felt annoyed that he'd proposed just as one of her favourite programmes was about to begin. She remembered he was still waiting to know if she'd like a wedding ring.

'I'd sooner continue as we are,' she said lamely.

'In other words, you don't want to marry me?' His voice was icy.

'I never said that.'

'We're not married and you want to continue as we are. *Ergo*, you don't want to marry me.'

'What does *ergo* mean? We didn't do Latin at St Joseph's junior and infants school.'

'It means therefore, and don't be so sarcastic.'

'Then don't argue with me in Latin,' she said furiously. She had been looking forward to a relaxing evening watching television, and wasn't in the mood for a fight. 'Things are fine as they are. Why change them? Why rock the boat?'

'As far as I'm concerned, things will never be fine until you're my wife.' He folded his arms stubbornly.

'Too bad, Ben.' There was something about his face, the way his lips were drawn in an angry line, almost prim, that brought back memories of the only other row they'd had. 'You know what this reminds me of? That time I wanted to go to Haylands and you decided to put your foot down for some reason I never understood. Just because I wasn't prepared to do your bidding on one, small, unimportant thing, you were equally prepared to ruin everything. Any minute now you'll threaten to leave if I don't marry you, and ruin everything again.' He was easygoing to a fault, but seemed to find it necessary once in a while to put up a hoop for her to jump through. She hadn't jumped the last time, and she had no intention of jumping now.

'Darling!' Suddenly, he was on his knees in front of her, holding her hands. 'I want you to be *mine*. I'm terrified you'll meet someone else during one of the times you go flitting off all over the country. I want you to have my ring on your finger when you take strange men to lunch. I want you to be Mrs Kavanagh, not Coltrane.' His voice broke, and he sounded just like the young man who'd pleaded with her on a bench in the fairy glen. 'I love you, Josie. I love you so very much.'

'Oh, Ben.' She put her cheek against his. He was so sweet, so nice, comfortable to live with, a truly decent man, entitled to some happiness. If they married, the comfortable life would continue. She imagined the years stretching ahead, serene and contented, as they no doubt would have passed had she married him in the first place. 'All right,' she said in a small voice. 'We'll get married.' She had jumped through the hoop after all.

His face broke into a delighted smile. 'When?' he demanded. 'I know, let's do it on your birthday.'

'Not quite so soon,' she said quickly. She was about to say, 'Let's leave it till next year,' but remembered it was what she'd once said to Francie because she'd felt so uncertain. 'In a few months,' she said to Ben. 'I'd like time to get used to the idea.'

'We'll announce it at the dinner,' Ben said jubilantly. 'I'll buy you an engagement ring instead.'

It was three days before her birthday. Ben was down in London at a conference and was coming back tomorrow. The caterers would be arriving at six o'clock on the day and would take over the kitchen. Dinner would be served at half seven. Josie had wasted a lot of time deciding which floral centrepiece she preferred. Dorothy Venables was coming up from London and would stay for two days. The obvious person to make up twelve guests was Lynne Goode, another friend, though she'd been asked not to breathe a word to Cathy Connors who might feel hurt at being left out.

Daisy and Manos were already in Liverpool, and looking forward to the evening. Francie still hadn't decided which of his women to bring. 'If *you* can't be me partner, Jose, then I'm bloody stuck.' Josie hadn't told him about the engagement, knowing he'd laugh like a drain. In bed that night, she sighed wistfully and wished he were bringing Lily. She'd have hurt everyone's feelings, but she'd sooner Lily were coming than anyone.

She was fast asleep when the telephone rang, and immediately felt fearful. It wasn't quite three o'clock, and a call at such an unearthly hour could only be bad news. She gingerly picked up the receiver. 'Hello.'

'Josie, it's Val Morrissey. Sorry, I've just realised it's some ungodly hour in the morning over there. I'm a bit drunk, if the truth be known. I should have left it till tomorrow.'

'Val!' Josie was wide awake, knowing there could be only one reason why he should call at such a time. She swung her legs on to the floor, and sat tensely on the edge of the bed.

'I've found him, Josie. I've found Jack Coltrane. Me and a few guys were watching this video after office hours. I'll leave you to guess what sort. His name was on the credits. I rang the film company. He's still works for them, and they gave me the name of his hotel. The manager confirmed he's a permanent guest.'

'Where is this hotel?' She could hardly speak.

'Miami. I'm not sure what to do, Josie. I don't want to go down there, scare him off.'

'Don't do anything, Val. *I'll* go. I'll go tomorrow – today. As soon as there's a flight.'

'Not by yourself, Josie. Not Miami. Look, when you arrive, check in the Hotel Inter-Continental. It's in downtown Miami, not far from Jack's place. I'll reserve two rooms. Try and let me know your schedule, and we'll meet up there. Okay?'

'Okay,' she agreed. 'See you, Val. And thanks.'

She dialled Directory Enquiries for the number of Manchester airport, then called and made a reservation. She would have to change planes at Orlando, Florida, she was told. Her hand shook as she wrote down the times. A taxi – she needed to book a taxi for six o'clock in order to check in on time. There was the number of a reliable firm in the telephone book downstairs. She went down in her nightie, made the booking, put the kettle on, waited for it to boil, remembered her birthday dinner, remembered Ben!

The kettle boiled. Josie took the tea into the living room, opened the bureau and quickly scribbled letters of apology to all her dinner guests. It had had to be cancelled due to 'unforeseen circumstances', she wrote, and worried that the words sounded too stiff and formal. She put the letters in Esther's tray in Reception with a note asking her to have them sent by first-class post the minute she came in.

Now Ben! What on earth should she tell him? Even if she didn't find Jack, she knew it was over between her and Ben. She had forgotten him too quickly when the call had come from Val. What did you say to someone whose heart you were about to break a second time?

'My dearest Ben,' she wrote, then paused and chewed the pen. Time was getting on. She needed to get dressed, pack a few things. Her eyes lighted on the little blue box in a pigeonhole of the bureau. The engagement ring Ben had bought that she'd intended to wear for the first time at the dinner! She'd never had one before. She opened the box, and the diamond solitaire winked back at her. Oh, Ben! She wanted to weep for the little boy, wrestling on the floor with his brother, scarlet with embarrassment as he carried her satchel home from school. The young man she'd sat with in restaurants all over Liverpool while they'd argued about politics with Lily and Francie. She'd missed him so much when she'd gone to Haylands, but had quickly been distracted by Griff.

Josie could think of nothing to put in the letter that didn't sound cruel. 'I'm so sorry,' she wrote, 'but I've gone to Miami to meet Jack Coltrane.' She had to get across to him that it was over, just in case he was there when she came back, hurt, disillusioned, but still living in hope that they had a future together. 'I've always loved you, Ben, but never enough,' she added. How to finish? After gnawing her lip for several seconds, she signed the letter simply, 'Josie.'

The Last Post
1984–1989

1

It was hot in Miami. The streets reminded her of New York, choked with impatiently honking traffic, pavements teeming with people. She caught a taxi from the airport to the hotel, and sat numbly in the back, feeling as if she wasn't really there. Her body felt as heavy as lead, her head like a balloon. She ached for a long, cold drink, then a lie-down, somewhere cool and quiet. She stared through the window, scarcely taking in the colourful sights, and wondered why she'd come. To see a man who had shown no interest in seeing her, a man who had gone out of his way to avoid her, who had advised her to marry someone else? She must be mad.

This is the last time, she vowed. I'll never do it again. If Jack tells me to get lost, I'll put him out of me mind for ever, get on with me life. I'm fifty today, or it might be tomorrow. It could have been yesterday. She had flown through several time zones and had no idea what day it was.

The foyer of the Hotel Inter-Continental contained a huge sculpture by Henry Moore. Josie checked in at reception, and was told she was in room 33 on the third floor. 'A Mr Morrissey in thirty-two has asked to be advised when you arrive. Is it okay to tell him you're here?'

'Yes, of course.'

Val Morrissey was waiting when she got out of the lift. He tipped the bell-hop and took her bag. 'You look shattered. It's nice to meet you after all this time, but I wish the circumstances were different.'

'So do I.'

They kissed affectionately. Their relationship had been conducted entirely by phone, but she looked upon him as a friend. He seemed less brash and sure of himself in the flesh. He showed her to her room. 'It's lovely,' she remarked. It was large, airy, very modern. The bed looked inviting. Josie looked at her watch – a quarter to nine. 'You'll think me stupid, but I don't know if it's night or morning. It never seemed to get dark on the plane.'

'It's morning. Jack will be at the studios by now. I went round to his hotel yesterday. The manager said he's been there two years, and he really likes the guy. The only trouble he has is getting rid of the bottles.'

'Nothing much has changed, then?'

Val shrugged. 'Doesn't seem like it.'

'This film company he works for . . .' She struggled for words. 'You know, I can't see Jack getting involved in porn.'

'It's only soft porn, Josie,' Val said quickly. 'The sort you can rent in any video store. There's nothing illegal about it. Me and the guys in the office wouldn't know where to get the hard stuff. I drove out to the studios yesterday, managed to get talking to a guy in reception. Jack does the scripts, helps with the sound system. He's popular there, too. Rumour is he used to be a well-known playwright till he hit the sauce.'

'He had a play produced off-Broadway,' Josie said proudly. 'It got wonderful reviews. And he wrote one of the best crime series ever seen on British television.' She sat on the bed, and Val regarded her worriedly.

'You look all in. Why don't you rest? I'll do some sightseeing, buy Jessie Mae and Melanie gifts from Miami.'

'How are Jessie Mae and Melanie?' she asked politely.

'I told you Jess was pregnant again, didn't I? We're hoping for a boy this time. She's fine. Having Melanie did her the world of good. She smiles a lot these days.' He made a rueful face. 'She didn't smile all that much when we first got married.'

'I'm glad she's so much happier.'

'We're both happy, Josie, and it's all due to you.'

She hoped he would be returning the favour. He had found Jack, but whether there would be a happy ending was yet to be seen.

He came into the hotel lobby, only slightly unsteady on his feet. The cream linen suit looked like the same one he'd worn in Liverpool, and the T-shirt underneath was white, unironed but clean. He badly needed a shave. There were streaks of grey in the black hair that hung over his eyes. He looked ill, very ill, with dull eyes and a face ravaged by deep, craggy lines.

Josie and Val Morrissey had been waiting for almost an hour in the lobby, sitting side by side on a shabby settee. She got to her feet, and felt the same thrilling sensation course through her veins as the night thirty years before when she'd first seen him in a New York coffee-bar. She went to meet him, stopping a few paces away. 'Hello, Jack.'

'Sweetheart.' He said it without surprise, as if they'd only seen each other yesterday. Then he smiled the smile that would never cease to charm her. 'I knew you'd find me, Jose. I guessed one day you'd track me down.'

'Did you want to be found, darling?'

'I think so.' His head drooped. 'I'm awfully tired, Jose.'

'Then come home with me.'

She bought a house in Mosely Drive, a four-bedroomed bungalow overlooking Sefton Park, not far from the fairy glen. It had belonged to a retired colonel who had called it 'The Last Post'. Josie thought it a silly name and took the sign down. The house had a number, it didn't need a name, though over the years circulars continued to arrive addressed to 'The Occupier, The Last Post'. The decoration inside was ultra-conventional – cream paint everywhere, anaemic flowered wallpaper. She had the walls stripped and painted dusky jewelled colours – deep rose pink, turquoise, amethyst, garnet red, topaz – with curtains to match made from lustrous silks. Much of the furniture was bought from a warehouse in London that imported from all over the world – a wicker bedroom suite, a cane three-piece, an Indian carved table and matching chairs, embroidered rugs and wall hangings. Japanese lanterns hung in every room, and there was always a joss stick burning somewhere, so that the house smelled of musk, orange blossom, sandalwood.

The lounge was at the back, with French windows opening on to the large, somewhat bizarre garden, filled by the retired colonel with statues and tubs, trellises and arches, a fountain and a fish pond, and steps up and down to various levels. It was a cross between a jungle and a maze, with strange plants with curious blooms and prickly leaves that emitted sweet, heady scents.

As the house was painted and furnished, Lily's voice was constantly in her ear. 'Why on earth d'you want to buy *that*, Jose? I couldn't live in the same house with such a peculiar colour/picture/chair.'

It *was* unusual, she had to admit, like one of those Arabian palaces in the Sinbad and Aladdin films she'd seen with Ben when she was little. Jack's study was a restful green, with the latest word processor installed on the desk and a comfortable settee to rest on while he waited for the Muse to strike.

'It's lovely, sweetheart,' he said when everything was done and she showed him round for the first time. 'Exotic, that's the word.'

Until then they'd been living in Huskisson Street, and she had been making him better. When she'd found him in Miami he'd been close to a physical breakdown. Now he was her lover, her child, her patient. She made him rest and fed him, but she couldn't stop him from drinking, and didn't try.

There were times when he tried to stop himself. She could tell when they occurred. He would be scratchy and bad-tempered. He would forget things that had happened the day before, things she'd said. After a while he would break out in a sweat and his face would glisten, as if he had a fever. His hands would shake. 'I think I'll have a drink,' he would say, and go over to the pine sideboard where she openly kept the whisky and brandy – the drinks she knew he liked best – pour himself a large glass and immediately be all right again.

He needed drink to keep going as much as he needed oxygen to breathe.

He never had hangovers. He had a drink instead. As he seemed able to function normally after drinking an amount that would have made Josie senseless for a week, she reckoned it was sensible to leave him alone. He knew about Alcoholics Anonymous. If he wanted to go, he would. At the same time, she knew it was killing him. She went to the library, and read with mounting horror the various ways alcohol could kill. It could stop the liver working, damage the heart, cause all sorts of cancers. She thought angrily that he wasn't being fair on her. She had him back, and she wanted to keep him, but she realised there was nothing she could do.

They had been in the new house a week when Dinah and Peter came home from Cuba. Dinah had come especially to see her dad.

'In case you disappear again.' She hugged Jack tearfully. Josie had never known her normally withdrawn daughter be so demonstrative. Perhaps being in love had done it, broken down an emotional barrier. She and Peter were obviously crazy about each other, though they weren't married. Josie would have liked her daughter to become a Kavanagh. There was a chance they might stay in England. Peter had an interview with a trade union in London in a few days' time.

'I'll never go away again,' Jack said. Was it just her imagination, but did he look sad when he said that? She was concerned that he regarded the house as a prison. He'd been very low in Miami, allowing himself to be bundled on a plane, virtually kidnapped. After the glamour of Miami and Los Angeles and the hubbub of New York, how on earth could she expect him to settle in a bungalow, no matter how exotically it was decorated, in a quiet suburb of Liverpool?

It must have been her imagination, the sad look. Not long afterwards Jack declared he hadn't felt so fit in a long time. His eyes had begun to sparkle with the old, irresistible warmth. All of a sudden life in Mosely Drive became almost as good as it had been in New York thirty years ago.

Josie was working mornings only at Barefoot House. After much consideration, she had made Richard assistant managing director. Cathy Connors was more experienced, but she and Lynne Goode didn't get on, and giving her the job would have created waves. Anyroad, Richard had been there from the start, when they'd only been producing a few books a year. He knew as much about the company as Josie.

One dull October day when she and Jack planned to go shopping in town, then to the cinema, followed by dinner, she came home at one o'clock, and the music was audible when she turned into Mosely Drive, even though the car windows were closed. I wouldn't like to live next door to *them*, she thought, and was horrified to discover her own house was the culprit. It was Irish music, the sort she loved – but possibly the neighbours didn't.

In her lounge, two young men were playing the fiddle with an awesome brilliance, and a girl was shaking a tambourine and singing 'The Isle of Innisfree' in a clear, sweet voice.

'Hi, sweetheart.' Jack gave her a hug, and yelled, 'This is Mona, Liam and Dave. I met them at the pub. They're singing at another pub tonight in Dingle. I thought we'd go.' The young people nodded at Josie, but didn't stop playing. She noticed a man, much older, sitting in an armchair, tapping his feet to the music. 'Oh, and this is Greg. He played at the Cavern when it first opened, New Orleans jazz. The group still play occasional gigs.' Greg smiled and nodded.

'Out of interest, will Greg be using our house to rehearse in, as well as Mona, Liam and Dave?' Josie enquired.

'They're not rehearsing, sweetheart. This is by special request, it's my favourite.'

'I see.' She went into the kitchen and put the kettle on, not sure whether to be annoyed or not. The music stopped, and suddenly it was, 'What did you think, Jack?' 'Would you like us to play something else, Jack?'

His head appeared around the door. 'What's your favourite Irish song, sweetheart?'

'"Molly Malone",' she said automatically, and minutes later the fiddles began to play, and Mona began to sing, '"In Dublin's fair city, where the girls are so pretty . . ."'

And Josie began to cry, because it was so much like New York and never, in her wildest dreams, had she imagined she would have those days back again. But it seemed she had.

By Christmas, Jack was at the centre of a network of friends. The house seemed to have become a meeting place for people of all ages, and the phone never stopped ringing. Nine times out of ten it was for him, inviting him to a party, a gig, for a drink, for a meal, to a concert or a play – and the wife, of course. They had tickets for this, tickets for that, and would Jack and the missus like to come? They had friends over from the States, or Australia, or some other country, and would very much like them to meet Jack. Oh, and Josie, too. Their brother or sister was up from London, and had been told about Jack Coltrane. Could Jack pop over for a drink and a chat? And don't hesitate to bring Josie if she'd like to come.

Josie always went. Life had become almost surreal, she was never without a sense of déjà vu, or the feeling it was all a dream and one day she'd wake up and Jack would be gone, and she would be living somewhere other than their little palace on Mosely Drive. She felt very much in Jack's shadow, but didn't care. With the same glow of pride she'd had thirty years before, she watched people fussing over him, wanting his opinion on everything under the sun. She noticed the way women tried to grab his attention, flirt, but it didn't bother her. He was *hers*. Everyone assumed they were married, and she supposed they still were in the eyes of God. Jack seemed to have forgotten they were divorced, and always referred to her as his wife, so she called him her husband because in her heart she'd always felt he was.

She and Jack shared history. They'd had two children and one had died, and only she knew he was a hopeless drunk.

Dottie Venables came to stay, having driven from London in her battered Mini. She wore her leather jacket and jeans, and had brought a few bare necessities in a plastic bag. She was immediately bowled over by Jack and he by her. They told each other dirty jokes, tore the government to pieces, went to the pub together when Josie was at her desk in Barefoot House, and matched each other, drink for drink.

Francie arrived on one of the nights she was there. He brought his new girlfriend, Anthea, who would never see fifty again. Francie was already best mates with Jack. They had the same taste in music, and went to football matches together. Josie had never known such an hilarious evening. They swopped outrageous stories. Dottie told them about the time she'd slept with an orang-utan.

'Not a real one?' Josie gasped, worried the conversation was taking an unhealthy turn.

'Of course not. I met him at a party. I didn't realise he looked like an orang-utan till I woke up next morning. I told him to get lost, go swing from a tree, and he wanted to know if my chin had been gnawed by rats.'

'I remember a party once,' Jack said. 'I fell asleep on the couch, and when I woke up it had turned into an orgy. I thought it was a dream and went to sleep again.' He laughed. 'My one and only orgy, and I slept the whole way through.'

He was describing the party they'd gone to at Maya's on New Year's Eve, Josie realised.

'I've always fancied an orgy,' Francie said longingly. 'But they don't seem to have them in Liverpool.'

'You're very lucky,' Dottie said. She nestled in a chair, a glass of whisky in one hand, a cigarette in the other. Francie and Anthea had gone, Jack was in his study, writing an article. It was a new venture. He'd already sold two on the theme of an American's impression of Britain in the eighties. 'You've got a bloke I'd sell me soul for. A great improvement on the other one, the stuffed shirt.'

'Ben?'

'Yeah, Ben. Not your type, not like Jack. Mind you, he's everyone's type.' The leathery face creased in a suggestive smile. 'I could eat the bugger.'

Josie frowned. 'Do you mean he's like a chameleon? He's all things to all men sort of thing?'

'I don't mean any such thing.' Dottie paused. 'Oh, I don't know. Perhaps he *is* all things to all men. It's not that Jack changes, but men see him as the person they want as their best friend, and women the romantic lover they've always desired. I've never envied a woman before because she was married, but I envy you being married to Jack Coltrane.'

'He drinks far too much, Dottie. You must have noticed.' Dottie was one of the few people she felt she could open up to. 'I worry about it all the time. I should stop him, but I don't know how.'

'Leave him be,' Dottie said brusquely. 'It's his body, not yours. You might find Jack the reformed alcoholic an entirely different kettle of fish to Jack the drunk. The drink keeps him going, it's fuel for his engine. Without it, the engine will pack up and die.'

'He's going to die, anyroad, at the rate he drinks.'

'Let him die his own way.' Dottie waved her cigarette. 'These are shortening me life, but I've no intention of stopping. I enjoy them too much, I need them. I'd sooner go to an early grave than give up me fags.'

There'd been no sign of Ben since she'd come back from Miami, not surprising under the circumstances. When Jack had first wondered why Peter's father didn't come to visit when he lived less than a mile away, Josie told him they had lived together for three years. 'You advised me to marry someone else, remember?' she said virtuously. 'Well, me and Ben didn't quite go that far.'

On Saturday Ben had been invited to Mosely Drive for tea, because now the two families had a grandson between them and they couldn't go on not meeting for the rest of their lives. Josie wasn't looking forward to it.

Peter had got the job in London with the trade union, just as Dinah discovered she was pregnant. It was May again when Josie and Jack went to London to be with their daughter when she had Oliver, nine pounds six ounces, and the most beautiful baby boy Josie had ever seen.

'Pleased to meet you, luv,' she whispered to the fat, lobster-coloured ball that was her first grandchild. 'You'll have lots more, won't you?' she said to Dinah, who was sitting proudly up in bed, despite having had three stitches. Peter looked exhausted, as if it had been he who'd given birth.

'I'm not sure whether to have another two or three. What do you think, Pete?'

'I couldn't stand another one,' Peter groaned.

'Come on, Pete.' Jack slapped him on the back. 'I'll treat you to a cup of tea.'

The men left, and Dinah said, 'Mum?'

'Yes, luv?' Josie was examining the tiny fingers, the pink toes. 'He's perfect,' she breathed.

'Mum, you've no idea how much it's meant to me, you and Dad being around when I was having Oliver. For the first time in me life I feel part of a proper family.' Dinah's eyes were unnaturally bright.

'I know exactly how much it's meant, luv,' Josie said softly. 'I feel the same. I've got you, your dad, a grandson, Peter.' She sighed blissfully. 'It's a long time since I felt so happy.' Jack had probably made an excuse to go to the Gents to swig half the contents of the little flask he carried in his hip pocket. But, then, you couldn't have everything.

It was an awkward meal. Ben turned out to be the first person in the world to hate Jack Coltrane on sight. He hardly spoke, and then only to mutter a reply to something said to him. Josie found herself paying an awful lot of attention to Oliver, now a month old and already smiling broadly. 'Isn't he gorgeous?' she said several times.

'Yes,' Ben would grudgingly agree.

Jack didn't seem to notice anything amiss. He drank glass after glass of wine and regaled them with bits of gossip from his time spent in the film industry.

For some reason Ben's normally good-natured face got darker and darker. As soon as the meal finished he pushed back his chair and declared he had to go. 'Perhaps you and Dinah could bring Oliver to see me while you're home?' he said stiffly to his son. He clearly had no intention of returning to Mosely Drive.

Josie went with him to his car. 'Thank you for coming.'

'Thanks for asking.' He unlocked the door, opened it, then angrily turned on her. 'I don't take kindly to being dumped for such a . . . a *blaggard*,' he snapped, almost choking on the words. 'And I've never known anyone down so much wine with a meal. Is he an alcoholic?'

'Mind your own business,' Josie said coldly.

'Then I take it that he is.'

'Take it any way you like.' She went back into the house and slammed the door.

That night they had dinner in a new vegetarian restaurant in town, where one of Jack's friends had an exhibition of paintings – one of the garish offerings already hung in their hall. Before long their table was packed, and Jack was at the centre of an admiring audience.

'Is it always like this?' Dinah enquired.

'Always, luv. Here, give us Oliver, so you can eat your pudding in peace.'

'It makes me feel quite proud he's my father. It's like having Robert Redford for a dad, or Paul Newman. I'm sure everyone's dead envious.'

'It's a nice feeling, isn't it?' No one asked Josie what she did. They didn't know she owned one of the most successful small publishers in the country. She was Jack Coltrane's wife, which was enough as far as they were concerned.

'Christ, Josie, that guy's a dork,' Jack said disgustedly when they were in bed. 'Why didn't you and he get hitched?'

Because he's a dork, Josie wanted to say, but held her tongue. It was unfair to make fun of a nice, decent man like Ben. 'It just never seemed the right time.'

'He's still in love with you. His eyes followed you everywhere. And he hates me.' He spoke matter-of-factly, with a certain amount of satisfaction. 'Come here!' He folded her in his arms. 'Whose woman are you?'

'Yours, Jack,' she whispered.

'What was the dork like in bed?'

'Not very good,' she said truthfully. 'He never turned me on, not like you.' She stroked his face. 'There's never been anyone like you. Kiss me, Jack, quickly. I can't wait.'

On Monday Ben came to Barefoot House to apologise. 'I'm sorry about the way I behaved,' he said stiffly. 'It got to me, I suppose, seeing you and him together.' His lips pursed. 'I won't pretend to like him, because I don't. He's not worthy of you.'

'And you are?'

He went red. 'I didn't mean it like that. If you were going to leave me, I wish it had been for someone ... different.'

'We're together because we love each other, Ben,' Josie said gently, and immediately wished she hadn't because he looked as if he was about to burst into tears.

'I realise that.' He nodded. 'I've just got to learn to live with it, that's all.'

Another May, Josie's fifty-fourth birthday, and the day Dinah had a second son, Christopher, two ounces heavier than Oliver. 'Though I only had two stitches this time,' she said happily when Josie went to see her in hospital. During the birth she'd stayed in their small house in Crouch End looking after Oliver, who would be three next week.

'Another two babies, and you mightn't need stitches at all. The more grandchildren the better, as far as I'm concerned.' She already haunted Mothercare, buying toys and clothes for Oliver. The dark-eyed, dark-haired baby in her arms reminded her very much of Laura, though she didn't say so. She tearfully kissed the sleepy face.

Dinah wrinkled her nose. 'Two's my lot, I'm afraid. Peter thinks it's wrong to over-populate the world. There's hardly enough food for the people there are now, though I intend to try and change his mind. I'd like to have another two babies – a daughter would be nice, for a change, like.'

'I'll get your dad to work on him.' Peter took far more notice of Jack than he did of his own father. They shared the same radical views. Ben, once the champion of the Peasants' Revolt, had become very pro-establishment over the years, whereas Jack remained a die-hard Socialist.

Dinah looked worried. 'Is Dad okay? I wish he was here.'

'He wanted to come, I told you, but he was feeling tired. He'll be sixty next year, Dinah. He's slowing down.'

'He drinks too much, doesn't he, Mum? You can't help but notice, though I've never seen him pissed.' Dinah pleated and unpleated the sheet between her fingers. Her eyes were scared. 'I wish you'd make him stop.'

'Nothing on earth can stop your dad drinking, Dinah. I've reached the age when I realise it's no use trying to change people. They are what they are, and there's nothing you can do about it.'

When Josie got back to Mosely Drive it was almost dark, and Jack appeared to be out. Their little Arabian palace was unnaturally quiet, unusually cold. The bell mobile in the living room was tinkling eerily – she must do something about the draught from the French windows. There was a musty smell, as if the place had been empty for weeks. For some reason she shivered. This was a house that was rarely still, and silence sat uneasily on the warmly coloured rooms with their foreign furniture and exotic ornaments.

She switched on lights, and went into the kitchen to put the kettle on. In the lounge, she turned on the gas fire with real flames. 'That's better,' she muttered. 'More like home.'

Where was Jack? She searched for a note to tell her where he'd gone. When she'd called from London to say what time she would be home, he'd promised to have a pot of tea waiting. He'd been in the study when she'd phoned.

With a feeling of alarm she went into the hall and opened the study door – and a great black hole seemed to open in front of her. Jack was lying on the settee, and she knew straight away that he was dead. His face was sickly pale, his lips curved in the slightest of smiles. He had rested his head on a green satin pillow, one hand cupping his chin, the other hanging limply. His body, from head to toe, seemed to be covered in a grey veil, like the finest of cobwebs. A half-empty bottle of whisky was on the desk.

'Jack!' She screamed, and the veil disappeared. Jack opened his eyes, and said blearily, 'Hi, sweetheart. I must have dropped off. Hey, guess what, I've started a play.'

'You bugger!' She sank, shaking, into a chair, her hand pressed to her crazily beating heart. 'I thought you were dead!'

'I'm very much alive, Josie. Well, almost. I've got pins and needles in my legs.' He tried to stand, laughed and fell back. 'They'll go in a minute.'

Perhaps it was because she had thought him dead, or that she had been away for ten whole days, but Josie was suddenly struck by how old he looked, and so very frail. She hadn't realised that his hair had turned quite so grey, or that he had a slight stoop, or that the flesh on his neck was hanging loosely. Had his wrists always been so thin, with the bones protruding sharply, like little white doorknobs? His eyes, though, his eyes were just the same – warm, brown, smiling at her from the face more heavily lined than she remembered.

He made another attempt to get up, and Josie said, 'Stay there, darling. The kettle's just boiled. I'll make some tea.'

She put milk in cups, two sugars for Jack, none for her, and spread a plate with chocolate biscuits. She'd make a proper meal in a minute, something quick from the freezer. In the lounge the bell mobile tinkled, and she thought again about the draught, but all the while there was a buzzing in her head, a feeling of dread in her bones, because she knew, somehow she just knew, that Jack was dying. She had seen it in his face, as if death were lurking somewhere near, waiting to pounce. There'd been a feeling in the air when she came in, a haunted quietness, like the calm before the storm. If she hadn't arrived when she did, she felt convinced that death would have taken from her the man she loved.

He was passing blood. She found it on his clothes, but he flatly refused to see a doctor. 'I don't want to know what's wrong,' he said, so airily that she wanted to thump him.

'You might only need a few tablets.'

He smiled sweetly. 'I don't think so, sweetheart.'

She stamped her foot. 'Since when have you been such an expert on medical matters?'

'I'm an expert when it comes to treatment for myself. No doctors, no tablets. And kindly don't mention the words "hospital" or "operations" in my presence. I'm having no truck with either.'

Josie rang Dottie and told her about Jack's intransigence.

'I don't blame him,' Dottie said gruffly. 'It's his body. I said that to you once before. It's up to him how it's treated.'

'That's stupid,' Josie wept. She told her about the blood on his clothes. 'What can it mean?'

'Do you want me to be brutally honest?'

Josie hesitated. 'Yes, please.'

'It might be something quite innocent, but Jack's drunk so much for so long that his insides have probably rotted. It could be cancer.'

'Oh, God, *no!*'

'It's probably why he won't see a doctor. He doesn't want all that radiotherapy rubbish. In fact,' Dottie said thoughtfully, 'we talked about it once. We both agreed we'd sooner die than have treatment that can drag on for years. Relatives suffer as much as the patient. I said I'd like to meet me maker with a fag in my hand, and Jack said he wanted to go holding a glass of Jack Daniels.'

He was visibly getting weaker and weaker, day by day. He ate scarcely anything. They didn't go out much. Francie came round on Saturday afternoons with half a dozen cans of beer, and they watched football on television.

It had happened, like every major event in her life, in the twinkling of an eye. Josie had gone to London to see a new life being born, and returned to find another life being slowly snuffed out.

'*Make* him go to the doctor, Mum,' Dinah raged on the phone.

'I can't, luv. He refuses to budge.'

'Then get the doctor to come to *him*.'

'I did, and your dad refused to see him. He went into his study and played New Orleans jazz at top blast.'

'Is he depressed?' Dinah asked curiously.

'No, he's perfectly happy. There's people dropping in to see him all day long. He's busy writing his play, and drinking like a fish, which is probably why he doesn't have any pain. It's almost as if . . .' Josie paused.

'As if what, Mum?'

'As if he *doesn't care*.' She suppressed a sob.

'But, Mum,' Dinah cried despairingly, 'he's always been so full of life. Why on earth should he not care?'

'I don't know, Dinah. I wish I did.'

They had begun to talk openly about death. 'No Requiem Mass, no priests, no prayers, no hymns,' he said lightly. 'If there must be music, I want Louis Armstrong, Jelly Roll Morton and Ella Fitzgerald singing "Every Time We Say Goodbye".'

'Fuck off,' Josie said.

He looked at her, pretending to be shocked. 'I've never heard you use that word before.'

'I never have. How dare you sit there, dictating the music for your funeral? Have you got no thought for me?' She burst into tears. 'I haven't the remotest idea how I'll live without you.'

'You'll get over me in time, Jose,' he said, so complacently that she nearly threw her book at him. 'Everyone gets over everything in time.'

'Have you got over Laura? *I* haven't. A day never goes by when I don't think about her.'

His thin face paled. 'That day is indelibly etched in my mind. It will be a relief to escape. I don't believe in an afterlife but, you never know, sweetheart, if there's a heaven, I might meet our little girl.'

'Oh, *God*, Jack. I don't think I can take any more of this.'

By now, he was housebound. Every part of him was gradually breaking down. His legs wouldn't carry him far, his hands could barely grasp a cup. He felt the cold acutely, even though it was a fine, warm summer. His study was a hothouse, where he worked feverishly on his play, still able to type. 'It's the best thing I've ever done,' he gloated. You would never guess from his voice, from his laugh or the warm brown smiling eyes that he was a dying man.

'Can I read it?' Josie asked.

'No, you cannot. I'll not forget the way you treated my other plays. You kicked them, if I remember rightly.'

'I won't kick this one,' she promised.

'You're not touching this play until it's in a sealed envelope.' He grinned. 'Then you can post it. Now go away. I'm in a hurry to finish.'

His meaning was obvious. Josie went into the kitchen and threw a cup at the wall.

She had forgotten she was supposed to be running a busy publishing company, but Barefoot House seemed to be coping quite well without her. Dottie Venables produced a charming saga every year, and each one sold in its hundreds of thousands; William Friars's Bootle thrillers continued to be hits, particularly in the States, where he had a large cult following. The anonymous young Irish writer who called herself Lesley O'Rourke never wrote another book, but *My Favourite Murderer* continued to sell well in the shops. There were other new writers that she'd never met. One of these days I must catch up on them, she thought, and remembered what would have to happen before she did.

The play was done. It was called *The Last Post*. 'You called it after the house?' Josie was startled. 'What's it about?'

'Mind your own business.'

'Am I allowed to know where you're sending it?'

'I can't keep that a secret, it's on the envelope. It's going to Max Stafford-Clark at the Royal Court. I met him once. Tomorrow I shall run off a copy and send it to another theatre, and another the day after, and the day after that. This play is going to every theatre in the country.'

Josie hurried to the post office with the large brown envelope under her arm. She would have given everything she possessed in return for Jack's play being accepted before he died.

She rang Francie. 'Can you do me a letterhead, just one sheet?'

'It must be for a very important letter, Jose.'

'It is.' She explained what it was for. 'I'll send you the particulars – I got them from the London phone directory. I'll type the letter meself.'

'I'll get it done today, Jose.'

'There's no need to rush.' There had to be a decent interval between the play's arrival and acceptance by the theatre. She prayed Jack would last that long.

Dinah rang. 'Mum, I'm pregnant,' she said in a small voice.

'Good heavens, Dinah.' Josie sat down quickly. 'I'm thrilled to bits, but Christopher's only four months old. You're going to have two babies on your hands. I thought you didn't want to over-populate the world?'

'One of the reasons the world is over-populated is that some women think they can't become pregnant if they're breast-feeding and not having periods.'

'You mean they can?'

'I'm living proof. Not that I mind, but Peter's a bit fed up. Anyroad, that's only half me news. The other half is we're getting married.'

Josie's hand tightened on the receiver. If only they'd thought of it before, when Jack ... 'That's marvellous, luv. I wish your dad was well enough to be there.'

'I wouldn't dream of getting married in London. We've booked the registry office in Brougham Terrace for half past two on the fourteenth of September, two weeks on Friday. Can you put us up? If Dad can give me away, it'll be the best wedding *ever!*'

2

Only close friends and relatives had been invited to the actual ceremony – Ben, obviously, Colette, Jeremy, and the twins, Marigold and Jonathan, Dottie Venables, Richard White from Barefoot House who'd once worked with Dinah, Francie O'Leary and his sons, Lily's two girls and Oliver, in new shorts and his first proper shirt. Josie would carry Christopher.

Every single person they knew was coming to the reception, which would be held in Mosely Drive – Josie's staff, Jack's friends and their neighbours either side so they wouldn't complain about the noise. Josie didn't bother to count the numbers. She ordered enough food and drink for a hundred and fifty, hoping there'd be enough and that the weather would be fine so people could go in the garden. If everyone had to stay inside, they wouldn't be able to breathe.

The Irish group were coming, as were Greg and his jazz band. Francie was bringing his sixties records, and Josie made sure there was a spare stylus for the turntable on the music centre.

She had never known a week like it before in her life. The air tingled with bitter-sweet excitement. Her husband was dying, her daughter was getting married and she never seemed to be without a lump in her throat. The phone scarcely stopped ringing; people kept dropping in with wedding presents. She had Jack try on his suits and discovered they were all too big, so a tailor was persuaded to come round and measure for alterations. He took away the mid-grey flannel she liked best, and promised to have it ready by Friday morning. He was so nice and helpful that she invited him to the wedding.

There was a posy to order for Dinah, buttonholes for the guests, flowers for the house, bedrooms to get ready. She still hadn't bought herself an outfit. A problem cropped up at Barefoot House and she told them she didn't want to know. The firm could go bankrupt for all she cared. This coming Friday represented a full stop in her life, and she didn't give a damn what happened afterwards.

Dinah arrived with Oliver and Christopher on Tuesday, Dottie on Wednesday to 'give a hand'. Peter wasn't coming till Thursday evening.

'Did you give him that letter to post?' Josie said to Dinah anxiously. 'It's got to have a London postmark.'

'He's posting it Thursday morning.'

Josie gazed out of the window, where Jack was sitting on a bench with Oliver. Her heart turned over. There was hardly anything left of him. His face was calm, as if he were at peace with himself. With each day that passed she sensed he was growing further and further away, from her, from everyone, that he was holding himself together until Friday.

She took Dinah and the children to the fairy glen. 'I used to bring you in a great big pram when you were Christopher's age,' she told her daughter. The baby was fast asleep in his carrycot on wheels, which would have been dead useful when she'd lived in Princes Avenue. Oliver chased the ducks, and Josie showed Dinah the bench where she'd had the argument with Ben, and where Daisy Kavanagh had been sitting the morning she'd rescued her from a great dilemma.

'What sort of dilemma?' Dinah wanted to know.

'I can't remember now,' her mother lied. It had been all to do with Uncle Vince, and Josie found it hard to believe she was still the same person who'd lived in Machin Street with the man who had been both her uncle and her father. Or the little girl from Huskisson Street whose mam was on the game. She hardly ever thought about Mam these days, yet there'd been a time when she'd thought of her every day.

'Mum, what's wrong? You look as if you're going to cry.'

'I dunno, luv. It's the passing of time, growing old. It's all so terribly *sad*. Oh,' she cried angrily, 'I wish people didn't have to die!'

'But then there'd be no space for babies to be born.' Dinah sounded very practical. 'One of these days Peter and I will die, by which time our children will have had children. Even this one in here.' She patted her stomach. 'It's the way of the world, Mum.'

'There's still no reason why it has to be so bloody *sad*.'

She went shopping alone and bought a dress of ivory sculptured velvet, very fine. The material clung to her hips, swirling around her ankles in soft folds. Her own wedding outfit had been pink velvet, she remembered, and she'd got it in a thrift shop. When Dinah's wedding was over, she would put this dress away and never wear it again, nor the delicate, high-heeled, strappy shoes and the hat that was like a large flower, the petals framing her face. She was buying everything especially for Jack.

'You'll look more like the bride than the real one,' Dottie commented when Josie got home and showed her everything.

'Dinah won't mind.' Dinah had decided on a plain blue suit that would 'do again'. 'What will you be wearing, Dottie?' She was praying that one of the country's bestselling novelists didn't intend to turn up to the wedding in her customary leather jacket and jeans.

Dottie must have guessed her thoughts. She hooted raucously. 'I won't let you down, Jose. There's a smart check suit hanging in the wardrobe.' She winked. 'I got it in Harrods. By the way, has Lynne told you not to expect a book from me next year?'

'No, but I've deliberately cut meself off from Barefoot House all week.' That could have been the problem they'd wanted to discuss the other day. Josie didn't care if Dottie never wrote another book again.

'Don't you want to know why?' Dottie pretended to look hurt.

'Of course, Dottie. Why can't I expect a book from you next year?'

'Because I'm trekking round the world, that's why.' The small eyes twinkled wickedly.

'Trekking!' Josie giggled. 'In a pith helmet and khaki shorts?'

'Forget about the helmet, but I've already got the shorts. And, no, I'm not really trekking, but I'm going to visit the most out-of-the-way places where there's no chance of being murdered or kidnapped, so Barefoot House doesn't have to worry about paying a ransom.' Dottie sighed rapturously. 'I intend to cross America by Greyhound bus, travel through Canada by train, learn to play the didgeridoo in Australia. I'm fifty-five, Josie, same as you, and I've never seen an iceberg in the flesh, walked through a jungle, crossed a desert on a camel, sailed down the Nile. Before I get too old I want to do every single one of those things, and a few more I haven't mentioned.'

Josie said it sounded marvellous, and she was looking forward to lots of postcards, though she was unable to imagine a time beyond Friday.

She woke at half six on the day Dinah was to marry Peter Kavanagh. The glimmer of light showing between the curtains looked ominously dull. When she got out of bed to look out of the window, her worst suspicious were confirmed. It was raining, not heavily but a steady drizzle, and dark clouds rolled across the leaden sky.

'What's it like?' Jack was struggling to sit up.

'Horrible!'

'It's only early. There's plenty of time for it to improve.'

Josie got back into bed and curled up against him. 'How do you feel?'

'Great.'

'Are you sure you're up to going to the register office?'

He looked at her, amused. 'I just said I felt great. I mean it, Jose. This is a day I never in my wildest dreams thought would happen. My daughter is getting married and I'm giving her away.' He kissed the top of her head. 'Thank you for the last five years, sweetheart.'

'Thank *you*, Jack. They've been wonderful.'

They stayed leaning against the pillows for quite a while, neither speaking. Questions chased each other through Josie's head. How many more times will I do this? How many more times will I hear him call me 'sweetheart'? They were questions to which she didn't want an answer.

The post came. There was a letter for Jack with a London postmark. Josie had typed the envelope herself a few days before. He was in the bathroom, no doubt having the first drink of the day. For some reason he had always shut himself away for the early morning drinks. She knocked on the door and sang out, 'Letter for you. I'll put it on your desk.'

By nine o'clock the sun was struggling to come out. By ten it was a shimmering golden ball, and the clouds had miraculously disappeared. The garden was like a fairy tale, engulfed in a mist of steam as everything began to dry in the heat. Dinah's posy and the buttonholes were delivered, along with a great heap of russet chrysanthemums. Josie mustered every vase she possessed and arranged them around the house. The caterers were bringing the buffet while the wedding was in progress – the woman next door would let them in. Jack still hadn't opened his letter.

She went with Dinah for a shampoo and set, and Dottie looked after the children – nothing on earth could persuade Dottie inside a hairdresser's. Peter had stayed the night with his father. It had been Josie's idea. 'It's unlucky for the groom to see the bride before the wedding,' she stated. Dinah thought the idea daft. They'd been living together for years and had two children and another on the way. 'Don't tempt fate, luv,' Josie warned.

'Oh, *Mum*,' Dinah said impatiently, but nevertheless agreed.

They returned from the hairdresser's to find the tailor had delivered Jack's suit. Jack was in the shower, and emerged shortly afterwards, wearing the trousers and a new white shirt, a leather belt around his much too narrow waist. He looked ten years younger, and fitter than he'd done in weeks. There was colour in his cheeks, and he held himself sternly erect. 'Which tie, do you think?' He held up three.

'Let Dinah choose, it's her wedding.'

Dinah frowned at the ties. 'The light grey one, Dad.' She went to give Christopher his midday feed.

'She called me "Dad".' Jack's smile was sweet and grateful. 'Your hair looks nice.'

'I thought I'd have it tucked behind me ears for a change. It'll look better with the hat.'

'When am I going to see this incredible hat?'

'Later, when I'm completely ready. Who was that letter from?' she asked casually.

'I haven't opened it yet. Probably an acknowledgement from one of the theatres for my play.'

Josie looked at her watch and screamed. A quarter past one! 'I'd better get changed.'

She took particular care with her make-up, outlining her eyes with black kohl, which she hadn't done in years, smoothing pale gold shadow on her lids, giving the lashes several coats of mascara. She lightly powdered her face, stroked her cheeks with blusher, painted her lips a shade similar to the chrysanthemums that filled the house. There were new tights, very pale, bought specially to go with the ivory dress. No need for a slip as the dress was lined. The cold material was icy when she put it on, making her shiver. The strappy shoes felt uncomfortable straight away, but she didn't care because they went perfectly with the dress. She searched through her jewellery box for Louisa's amber pendant, and the earrings Jack had given her to match. Finally, the hat, which cast shadows over her face, making her look enigmatic and aloof, like Greta Garbo.

She was ready, and her full-length reflection stared back at her from the wardrobe mirror. I *am* beautiful, she thought, but I will never be as beautiful again as I am today.

Jack was in his study. There was no sign of the letter that she was so anxious for him to open. 'How do I look?' She gave a little twirl.

He caught his breath, and the expression of tender, naked love on his face made her heart turn over. His lips trembled slightly when he smiled. 'Was that a Liverpool accent I just heard?'

She remembered the way his dark eyes had smiled into hers when he'd asked the same question on the steps of Best Cellar. 'Yes,' she replied now, as she had done then.

'Please, can I kiss you? I haven't kissed a girl from Liverpool in years.' He took her in his arms, ever so gently.

'I can't remember what I said then.' She rested her cheek against his. 'It's thirty-five years since the night we met.'

'I asked your name and where you came from. You said you were Josie Flynn from Penny Lane. I decided there and then to change your name.'

She didn't think that was true. 'Have I ever told you I'd been watching you for ages?' Watching the handsome, animated young man across the tables of the basement coffee-bar in New York.

'Hmm. We only met because I'd forgotten my coat.'

And if he hadn't! Oh, what would have happened then? Things couldn't possibly have turned out more tragically if they'd both married someone else. Yet there was nowhere else on earth she'd sooner be at this moment than in the arms of Jack Coltrane.

He seemed to have found a mysterious inner strength. His voice in the registry office was steady when he gave his daughter to Peter Kavanagh. He firmly held Josie's arm for the photographs, kissed Dinah, shook hands with Peter and Ben, shared a joke with Dottie and Francie.

They went back to Mosely Drive. Guests had already started to arrive. Champagne was opened, toasts were drunk, food began to rapidly disappear. Mona, Liam and Dave played Irish songs and encouraged everyone to join in the choruses. Greg and his group of grey-haired musicians belted out 'Sidewalk Blues', 'Beale Street Blues', 'Snake Rag' ... Francie put on his Beatles records, Dottie did an imitation of Mrs Thatcher, the tailor, whose name was Maurice Cohen, sang a haunting Yiddish ballad, and quite a few people cried.

The day wore on. Josie had removed her hat and shoes, Dinah had combed her hair loose and changed from the blue suit into something lilac and filmy. She looked heartbreakingly lovely.

Dusk began to fall, music continued to play, the children went to bed, and everyone lit the hundreds of candles which had been placed inside the house and in the garden, and it was like walking through stars.

But none of the stars shone as brightly as Jack. Josie couldn't take her eyes off the man she had married. He seemed almost to float among the guests, a glass in his hand, everyone anxious to have a word with him, just catch his eye. Perhaps she had drunk too much, perhaps time was going backwards, but the more she watched, the younger he seemed to be, as if a miracle was happening.

'He's okay.' Ben appeared at her side, slightly tipsy. He nodded towards Jack. 'He's okay.'

'I know, Ben.' She linked his arm in hers. 'Can we be friends?'

'Always, Jose. Always.'

Midnight. People started to leave. They shook Jack's hand, pressed his shoulder, even hugged him, as if the men knew this was the last time they would see this very special person they regarded as their best friend and the women the lover they had always dreamed of.

Francie put on a Frank Sinatra record, and the vibrant, tender voice began to sing 'Smoke Gets In Your Eyes'. The few people left were in the living room, where the French windows opened on to a carpet of candles, fluttering low now. Gradually, the flames began to go out, one by one by one.

Dinah and Peter were dancing, wrapped tightly in each other's arms. Oh, she was so pleased their daughter was happy. Then Jack held out his hand, and Josie drifted into his arms. She could hardly think. There was too much emotion in the room, and she couldn't bear it.

'I don't want to leave you, sweetheart,' Jack whispered.

'My darling, I don't want you to go.' Over his shoulder she could see the last remaining candle flicker out, and the garden was plunged into darkness. 'They asked me how I knew, our true love was true,' Frank Sinatra sang.

Jack was beginning to flag. It must have come over him very suddenly. She could feel his body heavy against hers. She was virtually holding him up. 'Go to bed,' she urged softly. 'I'll join you in a minute.'

'That mightn't be a bad idea.' He jerked himself upright, one final effort to get through his daughter's wedding day. The music finished, Jack said goodnight.

'Goodnight, mate.' Francie pumped his hand. He was nodding for some reason, nodding over and over.

Dottie kissed him. 'Sleep well, Jack.'

Ben shook his hand, Peter gave his father-in-law a hug, Dinah flung her arms around his neck. 'Night, Dad.'

Jack touched her chin. He said something Josie couldn't hear, then left the room.

Dinah's eyes were bright with tears. 'He called me Laura,' she said.

'Do you mind?' Josie asked anxiously.

'No.' Dinah shook her head. 'That's what the drinking's always been about, isn't it? He killed Laura and he's never got over it.'

'Probably, luv.' For some reason she thought about the other children there might have been if only she and Jack had stayed together. She said her own goodnights, and apologised if it looked rude but she'd like to be with Jack.

He was already in bed when she went in. She noticed he'd managed to put the grey flannel suit neatly on a chair. 'Nice try, sweetheart,' he said.

'What?'

'Nice try, with the play, that is.' He chuckled. 'The Royal Court wrote last Monday and turned the play down. A few days later they write on a completely different letterhead, saying they'd be pleased to put it on.'

'I'm sorry.' Josie removed her clothes and slipped, naked, into bed. She pressed herself against him. One of these days she'd read his play for herself. 'Are you mad at me?'

'I'm mad about you, sweetheart, always have been.' He yawned. 'I think I'll sleep now. Have you enjoyed the day?'

'It's been wonderful, Jack.'

He was already asleep. Josie woke up during the night, and he was making love to her with all the energy of a young man. His brown eyes were smiling warmly into hers, his hair flopped on his forehead. She could feeling herself coming, coming . . . Oh, this was the best she had ever known, exquisite. Her body was on fire, and Jack was pouring himself into her, loving her . . .

It must have been a dream because when she woke Jack was barely conscious, and he never got out of bed again.

Over the next few days he slipped in and out of reality. Now and then he could carry on a perfectly lucid conversation, then his eyes would close and nothing could rouse him.

'Ben would make a good husband,' he said one day. He even managed a rusty laugh. 'He'll cut your meat up for you when you get old. Francie would make you laugh. Did you know you're the first girl who turned him on?'

'He told you?'

But he had drifted away. Next time he woke up, hours later, he asked for Laura. 'She's not here, darling. Shall I fetch Dinah?'

He had gone again. Josie called the doctor when he began to have hallucinations and a sedative was injected. 'It's a pity we didn't meet before,' the doctor, an elderly man, said drily. 'I would have told him how much my late wife and I used to enjoy that television series of his. What was it called?'

'DiMarco of the Met.'

'That's right. We could never get our little son to bed the night it was on.' He promised to come again that night.

'He should have injected a triple whisky,' Dottie said. Like Dinah and

Peter, Dottie had stayed in Mosely Drive. Francie and Ben came every day. People kept telephoning. 'He's stone cold sober for the first time in years.'

'What can I do?' Josie cried frantically.

'Nothing. Just pray the end will be quick.' Dottie wasn't inclined to beat about the bush.

Jack Coltrane died when his daughter was with him, and his son-in-law was holding his hand. It was ten past two in the morning. Josie was snatching a few hours' sleep on the settee in the study when Dinah woke her. 'He's gone, Mum. It was very peaceful. One minute he was breathing, then suddenly it stopped.'

They embraced each other, then Josie went into the bedroom. She pressed Peter's shoulder. He kissed her and left the room, and she was left with Jack. She knelt beside the bed, laid her head on his chest and wept.

Somehow she got through the days before the funeral. Jack had wanted to be cremated, and the service was in the same chapel as Lily's had been held. There was no Mass, no hymns, no prayers, no priests, just people taking turns to say a few words about their friend. The rather rusty strains of Louis Armstrong, Jelly Roll Morton and King Oliver drifted from the loudspeaker, but Josie hadn't mentioned he'd wanted Ella Fitzgerald because listening to 'Every Time We Say Goodbye' just wasn't on. She would have broken down, along with everybody else.

She didn't look when the curtains closed on the coffin and it slid into the flames. Jack had dismissed the idea of flowers, so there were no wreaths to admire when they emerged into the pale sunshine of a mid-September day. Everyone stood around awkwardly, talking in subdued voices. Dinah said, 'Do you mind if Peter and I go, Mum? I'm worried about leaving the children with the woman next door. Francie or Ben will give you a lift home.' She squeezed Josie's hand. 'I'll have tea made.'

'I've invited a few people back.' Only a few. It would be such a contrast to last week's wedding.

She shook dozens of hands, thanked people for coming, her voice cold with grief. Would she ever feel normal again?

Nearly everyone had gone, just a few old friends left. Marigold and Jonathan kissed her and said goodbye, then Terence and Muriel Dunnet, both now very old, Cathy Connors and Lynne Goode from Barefoot House, Richard White, all terribly sad.

Josie was left with Dottie and the two men who had featured so largely in her life – Ben Kavanagh and Francie O'Leary. They walked over to their cars, unlocked the doors, looked at her expectantly, waiting for her to choose.

Dottie said, 'See you back at the house, Jose.' She took it for granted that Josie wouldn't want a lift in the decrepit Mini with rusting doors and an engine that sounded a bit like its owner's gruff voice.

There's nothing left for me! Josie thought despairingly, as she glanced from Ben to Francie, from Francie to Ben. Then, from nowhere, came a vision of leafy jungles, hot arid deserts, trains and buses to far-away places, strangers speaking languages she didn't understand.

She caught her breath. Dottie was about to slam the door of the Mini. 'Dottie,' she called.

'Yes, Jose?'

'Can I come with you?'

Laceys of Liverpool

For Paul,
May the force always be with you.

Prologue
Christmas 1940

The woman lay listening to the rain as it beat against the hospital windows. She and Alice hadn't picked a good night to have their babies. As had become the custom in Bootle over the last few months, there'd been an air raid, a bad one, and they'd all been moved down to the cellar. Alice's lad had been born only minutes after the All Clear, at a quarter past eleven. Her own son had arrived almost three hours later, so they'd have different birthdays. Later, there'd been an emergency. Some woman had been found in the rubble of her house about to drop her baby. Since then, things had quietened down.

In a bed opposite, her sister-in-law was fast asleep, dead to the world, like the other six women in the ward. 'Why can't *I* sleep like that?' the woman murmured fretfully. 'I can never sleep.' Her mind was always too full of plans for the future, schemes: how to get this, how to do that. How to make twenty-five bob last the whole week, including paying the rent and buying the food. Oh, how she'd love new curtains for the parlour! But new curtains, new anything, were an impossible dream.

Unless she stole something, pawned it, bought curtains with the money. She'd stolen before, her heart in her mouth, sweat trickling down the insides of her arms. The first time it was only a string of beads that looked like pearls. The price ticket said a guinea. The pawnbroker had offered a florin, which she'd accepted gratefully and bought four nice cups and saucers in Paddy's Market.

One day she'd walked all the way into town and nicked a cut-glass vase from George Henry Lee's, which she kept on the mantelpiece, though she was the only one who knew it was cut glass. Billy thought it was just a cheap old thing. The silver candlestick she'd robbed from Henderson's had paid for a nice mat in front of the parlour fireplace. Some things she kept, some she pawned. She'd become quite skilled at shoplifting. The trick was to stay calm, not rush, smile, make your way slowly to the door. Stepping outside was the worst part. If spotted, it was the time you'd be nabbed. But she'd got away with it so far.

The woman didn't care how she looked as long as it was respectable, or what she ate, but she liked pretty things for the house: curtains, crockery, cutlery, furniture. Furniture most of all. She'd give anything for a new three-piece: velveteen, dark green or plum-coloured. She licked her lips and thought about brocade cushions with fringes, one at each end of the settee, on each of the chairs.

Most of all, she'd like a nice big house to put the lovely things in. She was sick to death of living in a two-up, two-down in O'Connell Street. But if curtains were an impossible dream, then a big house was – well, out of the question. Being married to a no-hoper like Billy Lacey, she was just as likely to fly to the moon.

She shoved herself to a sitting position. The red light on the ceiling cast a sinister glow over the ward, over the prone bodies beneath the faded cotton counterpanes. 'It looks like a morgue,' she thought. Paper chains criss-crossed the room and she remembered it was Christmas Eve. 'Everyone's dead except me and that fat bitch in the corner snoring her head off.'

The clock over the door showed a quarter past four. A cup of tea should arrive soon. Alice, who already had three kids, all girls, and knew about such things, said the tea trolley came early, around five o'clock, which seemed an unearthly time to wake anyone up. In the meantime she'd go for a walk. If she lay in bed till kingdom come, she'd never go asleep.

The rain was lashing down, making the windows rattle in their frames. It drummed on the roof and she hoped Billy would keep an eye on the loose slates over the lavatory. She'd been at him to fix them for ages, but would probably end up fixing them herself. She fixed most things around the house. Her lips twisted bitterly when she thought about Billy. His brother, John, had stayed in the ozzie with Alice until an hour before their lad was born. He'd only left because the girls were being looked after by a neighbour who was scared of the raids. But Billy had left *her* on the steps outside the ozzie when she was about to have their first-born child. Off to the pub, as usual. He didn't know yet if she'd had a boy or a girl.

There was a nurse in the glass cubicle at the end of the ward where a sprig of mistletoe hung over the door. She was at a desk, head bent, writing. The new mothers were expected to remain confined to their beds for seven whole days, not even allowed to go to the lavatory, but the woman slid from under the bedclothes and crept past, opening one half of the swing doors just enough to allow her through. The nurse didn't look up.

The dimly lit corridor was empty, silent. Her bare feet made no sound on the cold floor. She crept round corners, through more doors, dodged into the lavatories when she heard footsteps coming towards her. The footsteps passed, faded, and she looked both ways before coming out, hoping it wasn't someone on their way to her ward who'd notice the empty bed, though it was unlikely. The hospital was understaffed. Some nurses had joined the Forces, or gone into better-paid jobs. There were a lot of part-timers and older nurses who'd retired and come back to do their bit.

She arrived at the place that had been her destination all along: the nursery. Five rows of babies, tightly wrapped in sheets, like little mummies in their wooden cots. Most were asleep, a few grizzled, some had their eyes wide open. Like her, they couldn't sleep.

Her own baby had been whisked away because of the emergency and she'd barely seen him. Now she did, she saw he was a pale little thing. He looked sickly, she thought. There was yellow stuff in his eyes. As she stared at her sleeping child, she felt nothing. She was twenty-seven, older than Alice, and had been married longer. But she hadn't wanted a baby. The sponge soaked in vinegar she'd inserted every night, which Billy knew nothing about, hadn't worked for once.

The child couldn't possibly have come at a worse time. Just when she'd worn Billy down, ranted at him mercilessly for month after month, until he'd conceded that letting his missus get a job wasn't a sore reflection on his masculine pride. Not with a war on and women all over the country working in ways they'd never done before. Why, there were women in the Army, on the trams, delivering the post, in factories doing men's jobs.

It was a job in a factory on which the woman had set her eye, making munitions. You could earn as much as four quid a week, three times as much as Billy. And as she said to him, 'Any minute now, you'll be called up. What am I supposed to do then? Sit at home, twiddling me thumbs, living on the pittance I'll get from the Army?'

His face had paled. He was a coward, not like his brother John, who'd volunteered when war broke out, but had been turned down because he was in a reserved occupation. John was a centre lathe turner, Billy a labourer. There was nothing essential about *his* menial job. John, anxious to make a contribution towards the war, had become a fire-watcher. Billy carried on as usual and haunted the pubs waiting for his call-up papers from the Army to land on the mat.

She'd only been in the munitions factory a fortnight, packing shells. It was hard work, but she liked it. If she felt tired, she thought about the pay packet she'd get on Friday, about the things she'd buy, and soon perked up. Then she discovered she was up the stick, pregnant and, stupid idiot that she was, she told the woman who worked beside her and next minute everyone knew, including the foreman, and she'd got the push.

'This is not the sort of job suitable for a woman in the family way,' the foreman said.

The woman glared through the glass at her baby. She hadn't thought what to call him. She wasn't interested. Billy wanted Maurice for some reason if they had a boy, but she had no idea if Maurice was a saint's name. Catholics were expected to call their kids after saints. Alice's girls had funny Irish names and she didn't know if they were saints either. The new kid would be called Cormac. 'No "k" at the end,' John had said, smiling. He humoured his silly, dreamy wife something rotten.

Where was Cormac? There were cards pinned to the foot of each cot with drawing pins. 'LACEY (1)' it said on the cot directly in front of her. Her own baby was 'LACEY (2)'. Alice had yet to see her little son. It had been a difficult birth and she'd been in agony the whole way through. John had been close to tears when he'd had to go home. Afterwards, with seven stitches and blind with pain, Alice had been given something to make her sleep.

Her own confinement had been painless – she wouldn't have dreamt of making a fuss had it been otherwise. She hadn't needed a single stitch. Her belly still felt slightly swollen and she hurt a bit between the legs, but that was all.

Even though she didn't give a damn about babies, the woman had to admit Cormac was a bonny lad. He had dark curly hair like his dad, and he wasn't all red and shrivelled like the other babies. His big brown eyes were wide open and she could have sworn he was looking straight at her. She pressed her palms against the glass and something dead peculiar happened in her belly, a slow, curling shiver of anger. It wasn't fair: Alice had the best Lacey, now she had the best son.

From deep within the bowels of the hospital, she heard the rattle of dishes. Tea was being made, the trolley was being set. Any minute now, someone would come.

The woman opened the door of the nursery and went in.

1
Christmas 1945

Alice Lacey sang to herself as she swept a cloud of Florrie Piper's hair into the corner of the salon. 'Away in a manger, no crib for a bed . . .' She brushed the hair on to a shovel and took it into the yard to empty in the dustbin.

'They say you can sell hair like that for a small fortune in the West End of London,' Mrs Piper yelled from under the dryer when Alice came back.

'Who to?'

'Wig makers. They're always on the lookout for a good head of hair.'

'Really,' Alice said doubtfully. The hair she'd just thrown away was more suitable for a bird's nest: dry as dust, over-permed, full of split ends and dyed the colour of soot.

'You can comb Mrs Piper out now, Alice,' Myrtle said in a slurred voice.

'About time too,' Florrie Piper said, tight-lipped. 'These curlers are giving me gyp.'

'I don't know how you stand it to be honest.' Alice switched off the dryer, and Mrs Piper heaved her large body out of the chair and went to sit in front of a pink-tinted mirror.

'We can't all have naturally wavy hair, Alice Lacey, not like you.' Florrie Piper chose to take offence. She sniffed audibly. 'You shouldn't work in a hairdresser's if you can't take what's done to the customers.'

Alice removed the net and yelped when her fingers touched a red-hot metal curler. It must be torture, sitting for half an hour with bits of burning metal pressed against your scalp. 'I'll take them out in a minute,' she muttered. 'Would you like a mince pie?'

'Well, I wouldn't say no,' Mrs Piper said graciously. She'd already had three. Food wasn't usually provided in Myrtle's Hairdressing Salon, but it was Christmas Eve. Some rather tired decorations festooned the walls and a bent tinsel star hung in the steam-covered window. There'd been sherry earlier, but the proprietor had finished off the lot by dinner time. Myrtle was as tipsy as a lord and had made a terrible mess of Mrs Fowler with the curling tongs. The waves were dead uneven. Fortunately, Mrs Fowler's sight wasn't all it should be and she refused to wear glasses. Hopefully, she wouldn't notice.

Mrs Piper had recovered her good humour. 'What are you doing for Christmas, luv?' she enquired when Alice began to remove the curlers. Her ears were a startling crimson.

'Nothing much.' Alice wrinkled her nose. 'John's mam's coming to Christmas dinner, along with his brother Billy and his wife. They've got a little boy, Maurice, exactly the same age as our Cormac. Me dad usually comes, but he's off to Ireland tonight to spend Christmas with his sister. She's not been well.'

'Your Cormac will be starting school soon, I expect.'

'In January. He was five only yesterday.'

'And how are your girls? You know, I can never remember their names.'

'Fionnuala, Orla and Maeve,' Alice said for the thousandth time in her life. 'They're at a party this avvy in St James's church hall. Something to do with Sunday School. I made them a cake to take. I managed to get some dates.'

Mrs Piper eyed the remainder of the mince pies. 'Would you like another?' Alice enquired.

'I wouldn't say no,' Mrs Piper repeated. 'It would be a shame if they went to waste. You're closing early today, aren't you? I must be one of your last customers.'

'We've got a couple of trims, that's all. Here's one of 'em now.' The bell on the door gave its rather muted ring – it probably needed oiling – and Bernadette Moynihan came in. She was a vivacious young woman with an unusually voluptuous figure for someone so small. Alice smiled warmly at her best friend. 'Help yourself to a mince pie, Bernie.'

'I thought we were having sherry an' all,' Bernadette cried. 'I've been looking forward to it all day.'

'I'm afraid it's gone.' Alice glanced at Myrtle who seemed to have given up altogether on hairdressing and was staring drunkenly at her reflection in the pink mirror.

Bernadette grinned. 'She looks like a ghoul,' she whispered.

Myrtle was a tad too old for so much lipstick, eyeshadow, mascara and rouge. Now, everything was smudged and she looked like a sad, elderly clown. Her grey roots were showing and the rest of her hair had been peroxided to a yellow frizz. She made a poor advertisement for a hairdressing salon.

'Don't comb it out too much, luv,' Mrs Piper said when the curlers were removed. 'I like it left tight. It lasts longer.'

Alice loosened the curls slightly with her fingers and Mrs Piper said, 'How much is that, luv?'

'Half a crown.'

'And worth every penny!' She left, tipping Alice threepence, with her head resembling the inside of an Eccles cake.

The door closed and Alice looked from Bernadette to Myrtle who was slowly falling asleep, then back again. 'I'm not supposed to give trims, not official, like.' She usually went to Bernadette's to trim her hair, or Bernadette came to hers.

'Well, if you don't cut me hair, it doesn't look like anyone else will.' Bernadette seized a gown and tied it around her neck. 'I just want an inch off. Anyroad, Al, you've got the knack. You couldn't do it better if you were properly trained. I only came 'cos it's Christmas and I was expecting mince pies and a glass of sherry. To be sadly disappointed,' she added in a loud voice in Myrtle's direction, 'in regard to the sherry.'

Alice giggled. 'Sit down, luv. An inch you said?'

'One inch. A fraction shorter, a fraction longer, and I'll complain to the management.'

'You'll be lucky.' Alice attacked Bernadette's smooth fair hair, draped over one eye like Veronica Lake, with the scissors. 'Are you looking forward to tonight?'

Bernadette grinned. 'Ever so much. I've always liked Roy McBride. He works in Accounts. I was thrilled to pieces when he asked me out – and to a dinner dance on Christmas Eve!'

'I hope you have a lovely time.' Alice placed her hands on her friend's shoulders and they stared at each other in the mirror. 'Don't be too disappointed if he turns out like some of the others, will you, luv?'

'Like *most* of the others, you mean. All *I* want is company, all *they* want is . . . well, I can't think of a polite word for it. Men seem to think a young widow is game for anything.' Her usually cheerful face grew sober. 'Oh, Al, I don't half wish Bob hadn't been killed. I feel guilty going out with other men. I get so lonely, but not lonely enough to jump into bed with every man I meet. If only we'd had kids. At least they'd make me feel wanted.'

'I know, luv,' Alice said gently.

'We kept putting them off, kids, until we got a house. We didn't want to start a family while we were still in rooms. Then the war started, Bob was killed, and it's been horrible ever since. And I'm still living in the same rooms.'

Alice squeezed her shoulders. 'Don't forget, you're welcome round ours tomorrer if you feel like a jangle. Don't be put off 'cos it's Christmas Day.'

'I'm going to me mam's, Al, but thanks all the same.' Bernadette reached up and touched Alice's hand. 'I'm sorry, luv, for being such a moan. You've got enough problems of your own these days, what with John the way he is. It's just that you're the only person I've got to talk to.'

'Don't you dare apologise, Bernadette Moynihan. You're the only person I've told about John. Today was your turn for a moan. Next time it'll be mine.'

The final customer of the day arrived; Mrs O'Leary, with her ten-year-old daughter, Daisy, who was in Maeve's class at school and whose long, auburn ringlets were in need of a good trim. By now, Myrtle was fast asleep and snoring.

'Would you like me to do it?' an embarrassed Alice offered. 'I won't be long with Bernie.'

'Well, I haven't got much choice, have I?' Mrs O'Leary laughed. 'At least you'll probably cut it level both sides. Myrtle's usually well out. I sometimes wonder why we come. I suppose it's because it's so convenient, right at the end of the street, but I think I'll give that place in Marsh Lane a try. Each time we come Myrtle's worse than the time before. And it's not just the drink. She's every bit as useless if she's sober. If it weren't for you, Alice, this place would have closed down years ago.'

'Hear, hear,' cried Bernadette. 'It's Al who keeps it going.'

Alice blushed, but she had a feeling of dread. If Myrtle's closed, what would she do? She'd started four years ago, just giving a hand: sweeping up, wiping down, putting women under the dryers, taking them out again, washing hair, fetching towels, putting on gowns. Lately, with Myrtle going seriously downhill in more ways than one, she'd been taking on more and more responsibility. It was impossible to work in a hairdresser's for so long without learning how it was done. Alice was quite capable of giving a shampoo and set, a Marcel or Eugene wave, a perm – the new method was so much simpler than having to plug in every curler separately, a procedure that took all of four hours – and she seemed to have a knack with scissors. It was just a question of holding them right.

She only lived in the next street. It was easy to pop home when business was slack to make the girls their tea, keep an eye on them during the holidays. She usually brought Cormac with her. An angel of a child, he'd been quite happy to lie in his pram in the kitchen, play on the pavement outside when he got older, or sit in the corner, drawing, on the days it rained. But it wasn't just the convenience, or the extra money, useful though it was. Nowadays the hairdresser's provided an escape from the tragedy her life had become since last May. For most people the end of the worst war the world had ever known was a joyful occasion, a reason to celebrate. For the Laceys it had been a nightmare.

Myrtle's was an entirely different world: a bright, cosy, highly dramatic little world behind thick lace curtains and steamed-up windows, quite separate from the one outside. There was always something to laugh about, always a choice piece of gossip doing the rounds. The women had sorted out the war between them – it would probably have ended sooner had Winston Churchill been privy to the sound advice of Myrtle Rimmer's customers.

Most women were willing, even anxious, to open up their hearts to their hairdresser. There were some very respectable men in Bootle who'd have a fit if they knew the things Alice had been told about them. She never repeated anything, not even to Bernie.

Bernadette waited until Alice had cut Daisy O'Leary's ringlets so they were level both sides and Mrs O'Leary pronounced herself satisfied. She wished them Merry Christmas and departed.

Alice locked the door, turned the 'Open' sign to 'Closed' and between them the two women half carried, half dragged the proprietor to her flat upstairs and laid her on the bed.

'Jaysus,' Bernadette gasped. 'It don't half pong in here. She's not fit to live on her own, Al, let alone run a hairdresser's.'

The bed was unmade, the curtains still drawn. Alice covered her employer with several dirty blankets and regarded her worriedly. 'I'll pop round tomorrer after dinner, like. See if she's all right. She said something about going to a friend's for tea.'

'Has she got any relatives?' Bernadette asked.

'There's a daughter somewhere. Southampton, I think. Myrtle's husband died ages ago.' She heard someone try the salon door, but ignored it. There was a notice announcing they closed at four.

They returned downstairs. After Bernadette had gone, Alice brushed the floor again, gave it a cursory going over with a wet mop, wiped surfaces, polished mirrors, straightened chairs, arranged the three dryers at the same angle and tied the dirty towels in a bundle ready to go to the laundry when the salon reopened after Christmas. She glanced around to see if there was anything she'd missed. Well, the lace curtain could do with mending, not to mention a good wash, the walls were badly in need of a lick of paint, and the oilcloth should be replaced before a customer caught her heel in one of the numerous frayed holes and went flying. Otherwise, everywhere looked OK. She could go home.

Instead, Alice switched off the light and sat under a dryer. Go home for what? she asked herself. The girls weren't due till five. Her dad had taken Cormac to the grotto in Stanley Road. John was finishing work at three. He'd be home by now. Alice shuddered. She didn't want to be alone with her husband.

John Lacey regarded what was left of his face in the chrome mirror over the mantelpiece. It had been a handsome face once. He wasn't a conceited man, but he'd always known that he and his brother Billy weren't at the back of the queue when the Lord handed out good looks. Both were tall, going on six feet. John's dark-brown hair was curly, Billy's straight. They had the same rich-brown eyes, the same straight nose, the same wide brow. His mam, never one to consider anyone's feelings, used to say John was the handsomer of the two. He had a firmer mouth, there was something determined about his chin. Billy's chin was weak.

Mam didn't say that now, not since her elder son had turned into a monster. John stroked the melted skin on his right cheek, touched the corner of the unnaturally angled slit of an eye. If only he hadn't gone to the aid of the seaman trapped in the hold when the boiler had exploded on that merchant ship. The hold had become a furnace, the man was screaming, his overalls on fire. He emerged from the flames, a blazing phantom, hair burning, screaming for help.

The irony was he hadn't managed to save the chap. He had died within minutes, writhing in agony on the deck, everyone too terrified to touch him. Everyone except that dickhead, John Lacey, who'd dragged him out, burnt his own hands, burnt his face. The hands had mended, but not the face.

A further irony was that the war was virtually over and the accident had had nothing to do with the conflict. The firefighters were on duty at Gladstone Dock, as they had been every night over the past five years, when the boiler had gone up. They'd come through the war unscathed, all his family, his brother's family, his mam, his father-in-law. Amber Street itself hadn't been touched, not even a broken window, while numerous other streets in Bootle had been reduced to rubble. Then, in the very last week, John had lost half his face.

He stared at the grotesque reflection in the mirror. 'Fool!' he spat through crooked lips.

Where were his children – his three girls, his little son? More important, where was his wife? He remembered the girls had gone to a party. His father-in-law had Cormac. But there was no explanation for why Alice wasn't home.

'She don't fancy you no more,' he told his reflection. 'She's with another fella. He's giving her one right now, sticking it up her in the place that used to be yours.'

John groaned and turned away from the mirror. He'd never used to think like that, so coarsely, lewdly. Making love to Alice used to be the sweetest thing on earth, but now he couldn't bring himself to touch her, imagining her shrinking inside, hating it.

The back door opened and his wife came in. Until last May, until a few days before the war ended, until his accident, he would have lifted her up, kissed her rosy face, stared into her misty blue eyes, told her how much he'd missed her, how much he loved her. They might have taken the opportunity, the kids being out, of going upstairs for a blissful half-hour in bed. Instead, John scowled and said gruffly, 'I tried Myrtle's door on the way home, but it were locked. That was more than half an hour ago. Where have you been, eh? With your fancy man?'

She looked at him reproachfully. 'I haven't got a fancy man, John.'

Oh, she was so lovely! She was thirty-one, though she didn't look it: tall, gawky like a schoolgirl, a bit too thin. He used to tell her she had too many elbows, she was always knocking things over. Her face was long and oval, the skin flawless, the eyes very large and very blue. They were innocent eyes, guileless. Deep within his soul, he knew she would never be unfaithful, but the new John, the John Lacey who now inhabited his body, found it just as hard to believe that such an attractive woman, a woman born to be loved, hadn't found someone else since her husband had become so repulsive.

'So, what have you been doing with yourself for the last half-hour?' he sneered.

'Tidying up. I remember hearing someone try the door when me and Bernadette were upstairs with Myrtle. She drank all the sherry and ended up incapable.' She sighed. 'I'll make some tea.'

He grabbed her shoulder when she turned to leave. 'I don't believe you.'

'There's nothing I can do about that.' She was about to shrug his hand away. Instead, she bent her head and laid her face against it and he could feel the rich-brown hair fluttering on his fingers. The gesture touched his heart. 'I don't need a fancy man, luv,' she said softly. 'I've got you. Why don't we go upstairs for five minutes? I can get dressed in a jiffy if the latch goes.' Alice missed making love more than she could say. She didn't care about his face. For his sake, she would prefer it hadn't happened. But it *had* happened and she loved him just as much, if not more. Sadly, it was impossible to convince John of this. Anyroad, his face wasn't nearly as bad as he made out. The right side was a bit puckered, that was all. The burn had slightly affected his eye, the corner of his mouth, but he looked nothing like the monster he claimed. She reached up and stroked the puckered skin. 'I love you.'

If only he could believe her! He wanted to, so much. But he knew, he was certain, she was forcing herself to touch him. She was a good, kind woman and felt sorry for him. She was probably feeling sick inside. The tender, loving look on her face was all put on. He seized her wrist and pushed her hand away. 'I don't want your sympathy,' he said gruffly.

He truly hadn't meant to be quite so rough. He noticed her wince and rub her wrist when she went into the kitchen. Water ran, the gas was lit and John Lacey realised he had just hurt the person he loved most in the world. He looked at himself in the mirror. Sometimes he wondered if it would be better for all concerned if he did himself in.

Alice had borne three daughters within two and a half years of her marriage to John Lacey. Fionnuala was only two months old when she had fallen pregnant with Orla and Maeve had arrived when Orla was still on the breast.

Her husband realised something had to be done. Alice was barely twenty-one. At the rate they were going, they'd have a couple of dozen kids by the time she reached forty. Although strictly forbidden by the Catholic church, for the next five years, with Alice's approval, he took precautions. Then the war started and they decided to try for a son. Nine months later, Cormac was born. Four children was enough for anyone and John started to take precautions again. It was easier now, with French letters available over the counter at the chemist.

They were an exceptionally happy family. The girls were the image of their mam with the same brown hair and blue eyes. Cormac was a lovely lad, a bit pale, a bit small, rather quiet compared with his sisters. He had his mam's blue eyes, if a shade or two lighter. Apart from that, no one was quite sure whom he took after, with his straight blond hair and neatly proportioned features.

John didn't mind when his wife went to work in the hairdresser's in Opal Street. He earned enough to feed his family, keep them comfortable, but the girls were mad on clothes and it didn't seem fair that the eldest was the only one who had new things. Anyroad, Orla was a little madam and would have screamed blue murder at the idea of always having to wear her sister's hand-me-downs. Alice worked to dress her girls and she was happy at Myrtle's. And if Alice was happy, so was John.

At least that used to be the case. Now, it was the first war-free Christmas in six years. It should have been the best the Laceys had ever known, but it turned out to be the worst.

Orla had made a show of herself at the Sunday School party, Fionnuala claimed. She'd sung 'Strawberry Fair' and 'Greensleeves'. 'Though no one asked her. I felt dead embarrassed, if you must know.'

'Miss Geraghty asked who'd like to do a turn,' Orla said haughtily. 'I put me hand up, that's all.'

'Perhaps our Fionnuala didn't hear what Miss Geraghty had said,' suggested Maeve, the peacemaker.

On Christmas Day, after dinner, when everyone was in the parlour, Orla offered to sing again.

'That'd be nice, luv,' Alice said quickly, hoping a few songs might lighten the atmosphere. It had been a miserable meal and though she didn't like to admit it, not even to herself, it was all John's fault. He glowered at everyone from the head of the table, snapped at the children, was rude to his wife. Even Billy, his brother, normally the life and soul of the party, had been subdued. By the time the pudding stage was reached the conversation had dried up completely.

As soon as the food was eaten, Billy escaped to the pub. John wasn't a drinker, but he used to like the occasional pint, particularly at Christmas. This year, he'd churlishly refused. He rarely left the house, except for work, when he wore a trilby with the brim tipped to show as little as possible of his face. At Mass he sat at the back.

Cora was watching everything with a supercilious smile, as if she was enjoying seeing the Lacey family fall to pieces. Alice had never got on with her sister-in-law. Cora was so cold and reserved. She had made it obvious from the start that she didn't want to become friends. She had, possibly, softened a little since Maurice was born, but Maurice himself seemed the sole beneficiary of this slight improvement. Yet she was strict with the boy, too much so. Alice had seen the cane hanging on the wall in her sister-in-law's smart house off Merton Road, but had also witnessed the soft look in

Cora's strange brown eyes, almost khaki, when they lighted on her handsome son.

Maurice was a Lacey to his bones. His gran doted on him. Meg Lacey carried a photo in her handbag of John and Billy when they were little, and either one could have been Maurice they were so alike.

Meg had Maurice on her knee, stroking his chubby legs – she made it obvious she had no time for Cormac. 'Who's my favourite little boy in the whole world,' she cooed.

Cora didn't look too pleased. Her small, tight face was screwed in a scowl. Alice wondered what she would look like with her hair combed loose, instead of scraped back in a knot with such severity that it stretched the skin on her forehead. Except for the odd brown of her eyes, there wasn't a spot of colour in her face. Cora scorned make-up and nice clothes. Today, she wore the plain brown frock with a belt that had been her best since Alice could remember.

Orla sang 'Greensleeves' in a fine, strong voice. If there'd been the money, Alice would have sent her to singing lessons – Mrs O'Leary's Daisy went to tap-dancing classes – but then Fionnuala would have demanded lessons in something or other and it wouldn't have been fair to leave out Maeve, although her placid youngest daughter wouldn't have complained.

'Any requests?' Orla enquired pertly when she'd finished her repertoire.

'Yes, shurrup,' Fionnuala snapped. It was said so viciously that Alice was dismayed. The girls had always got on well with each other. Perhaps, because the house was so full of love, they hadn't found it necessary to compete. Lately, though, Fion, who Alice had to concede could be dead irritating at times, had become resentful of Orla, making unnecessarily spiteful remarks, like the one just now. It didn't help when Orla, eleven, started her periods and the older Fion showed no sign. Alice wondered if it was the change in atmosphere that had done it. The house may well have been full of love once, but it certainly wasn't now.

Oh, God! This was a *horrible* Christmas. Normally, she never let Cora bother her, nor the fact that John's mother made such a fuss of Maurice and entirely ignored her other grandson. Alice was fond of Maurice, but it would have been easy to get upset. Instead, she and John usually laughed about it. Other Christmases, John organised word games. He sometimes sang, usually carols, in a rather fine baritone voice. He made sure everyone had a glass of sherry and told them amusing things that had happened at work. In the past, John had even been known to make Cora laugh. Now, Alice wasn't sure what she wanted to do most, burst into tears, or scream, as two of her daughters squabbled, Maeve looked bored, Cora scowled, her mother-in-law cooed and John's face was like thunder. Only Cormac was his usual sunny self, playing quietly on the floor with a truck he'd got for Christmas. If only her dad were there! He'd see the funny side of things and they could wink at each other and make faces.

Suddenly, John grabbed Fion and Orla by the scruffs of their necks and flung them out of the room. 'If you're going to fight, then fight somewhere else,' he snarled.

Alice got up and left without a word. The girls were in the hall, holding hands, she noted approvingly, and looking shaken.

'I *hate* Dad,' Orla said spiritedly.

'Me, too,' echoed Fionnuala.

'We weren't exactly fighting.'

'It was more an argument.'

'Your dad gets easily narked these days.' She put her arms round both her girls, they were almost as tall as she was. 'You need to humour him.'

Orla sniffed. 'Can I go round Betty Mahon's house, Mam? She got Monopoly for Christmas.'

'If you want, luv.'

'Can I come?' Fionnuala said eagerly.

Orla hesitated. Why couldn't Fion find friends of her own? Not only was she getting dead fat, but she was a terrible hanger-on. She remembered her sister had also been unfairly treated by their dad. 'OK,' she said.

Alice sighed with relief when the girls left; two less people to worry about. She opened the parlour door. 'Maeve, would you like to help me make some tea, luv?'

'I *hate* Christmas,' Maeve declared in the kitchen. 'It used to be nice, but now it's awful. Will Dad ever be in a good mood again?'

'Of course, luv. He's still getting over the accident.'

'But Mam, it wasn't *our* fault he had the accident. Why is he taking it out on us?'

Alice had no idea. Maeve had inherited her mother's easygoing nature. It wasn't like her to complain. John was gradually alienating every member of his family. Only Cormac seemed sweetly oblivious to the change in his dad.

She made tea and Spam sandwiches, spread a plate with biscuits, took them into the parlour, told Maeve that, yes, it would be all right if she stayed in the back and read her new Enid Blyton book, then excused herself from the company, saying she had to go round to Myrtle's and make sure she was all right.

The acrid grey fog that had enveloped Bootle earlier in the day was beginning to fall again. On the nearby River Mersey, ships' foghorns hooted eerily. The pavements glistened with damp, reflecting the street lights in glittering yellow blurs. It was lovely to see the lights on again after five years of blackout.

Hardly anyone in Amber Street had closed their parlour curtains. Alice passed house after house where parties were going on. She had been born only a few streets away, in Garnet Street, in another cramped terrace house that opened on to the pavement, and had known most of these people all her life. They felt like family. The Fowlers were having a riotous time, doing the 'Hokey Cokey'. Their two lads had returned unharmed after years spent in the Navy. Emmie Norris had all her family there, including the twelve grandchildren. The Martins were playing cards, a whole crowd of them in paper hats, laughing their heads off.

Everywhere Alice looked people were having the time of their lives. The strains of 'Bless 'Em All' came from the Murphys', 'We'll Meet Again' from the Smiths'.

Apart from Orla, no one had sung at the Laceys'. They had pulled crackers, but hadn't bothered with the paper hats, not even the children. It just didn't seem right for some reason. For the first time Alice felt like a stranger in the street that was as familiar to her as the back of her hand, as if she no longer belonged, as if her life was no longer on the same keel as those of her friends and neighbours.

She sighed as she went through the entry into Opal Street. Myrtle's was in darkness, upstairs and down. She remembered being at school with the girl who had lived there when it had been an ordinary house. It was more than twenty years since Myrtle had moved in and it had become a hairdresser's. The wall between the parlour and the living room had been knocked down and turned into one room. Mam had taken her there to have her hair cut. Myrtle had seemed old then, going on sixty. She claimed to have worked for some posh place in London doing rich people's hair.

'Debutantes,' she boasted, 'titled personages.' No one had believed her.

Alice unlocked the door. 'Myrtle,' she shouted. There was no reply. She went up to the bedroom, where the bed was empty, still unmade. Myrtle must have gone to tea with her friend, which was a relief.

Downstairs again, she sat under the same dryer as she'd done the night before, the middle one. She was even more miserable now than she'd been then. What was to become of her, of John, of their children? How was she to convince John that she loved him? Would she continue to love him if he remained the angry, glowering, suspicious person, nothing like the man he used to be? Could you love someone who made your children unhappy? Did he love her? What had happened was awful, but as Maeve had wisely said, he had no right to take it out on his family.

'White Christmas' was being sung not far away. 'Just like the ones we used to know ...' Not any more, we don't, Alice thought bleakly. This Christmas has been nothing like the ones we used to know. The first after Mam died had been bad enough. Dad was gutted, but he'd done his best to brighten things up for his daughter. He'd bought her a new frock, taken her to the pantomime on Boxing Day. She was eight, an only child.

Alice knew she wasn't a clever person. She hadn't a single talent she could think of. She was often tongue-tied, stuck for something to say, slow-witted. She had achieved just five things in her life: she had married John Lacey, whom all the girls at Johnson's Dye Factory had been mad about, and she'd had four beautiful children.

But if she was to get through the years to come and stay sane, she needed to do something else. Time passed so quickly. Pretty soon the girls would start getting married. There'd only be Cormac left and what if John was still the same? Things at home were unbearable now and they'd be even more unbearable with the girls gone.

Yes, she had to *do* something. But what? At the moment, even her job was on the line and it wouldn't be easy getting another, not with servicemen coming home, wanting back their jobs in the factories, and women all over the place being given the sack – women used to earning a wage and unwilling to return to being housewives. Bernadette said there'd been forty-two applications when the Gas Board where she worked had advertised for a wages clerk. Most were from women who'd been in the Forces, but it was a man who'd got the job. Not that Alice was fit to be a clerk of any sort, she couldn't even add up.

'We'll not go round our John's next Christmas if things there don't improve,' Billy Lacey said as he walked home through the fog with his family. 'I'm glad you said we were having someone round to tea, luv, even if it were a lie. I couldn't have stood another minute in that house.'

'It wasn't a lie,' Cora said coolly. 'Mr Flynn's coming to tea.'

'Mr Flynn, the landlord!'

'The very same.'

Billy grimaced at the idea of another meal accompanied by stilted conversation. They were passing O'Connell Street where they used to live and which Billy much preferred to where they lived now. 'I think I'll drop in on Foxy Jones. I haven't seen him since he came out the Army. I'll be home in time for tea, luv.'

'Like hell you will,' Cora muttered as her husband, hands in pockets, whistling tunelessly, made off down the street. She wouldn't see him again until the pubs closed. Not that she cared. The less she saw of Billy the better.

'Dad!' Maurice called plaintively, but his dad ignored him.

Cora gave her son a little shake, annoyed he wanted his dad when he had her. 'I've got a bone to pick with you.'

Maurice took the words literally. 'A bone, Mam?'

'How many times have I told you not to sit on your Grannie Lacey's knee? I can't stand to see her maul you.'

The little boy felt confused. Gran had sat him on her knee. He'd had no choice in the matter. 'I'm sorry, Mam.' He apologised to his mother a hundred times a day. He was always getting things wrong, though was often mystified as to what they were.

'You will be sorry when you get home.'

His stomach curled. He knew what the words meant and could tell by the way Mam walked, very quickly, shoulders back, lips pursed, that she was going to hit him with the cane. For the rest of the way home he did his best not to cry, but the minute the front door closed he started to bawl. 'Don't hit me, Mam. Please don't hit me.'

His mother ignored his cries. 'In here,' she said imperiously, opening the door to the living room. 'Come on!' She tapped her foot impatiently.

Maurice walked slowly into the room, dragging his feet. What had he done wrong? He never knew what he'd done wrong. He was shaking with fear as his mam told him to bend over a chair and the cane swished three times against his bottom. It hurt badly. The little boy sobbed helplessly, knowing his bottom would sting for ages. He could understand being beaten if he broke windows, did something really bad, but although he tried very hard to be on his best behaviour, somehow he always managed to make Mam angry.

'You can get to bed now.'

It was too early. He hadn't had any tea. Still crying, the child made his way upstairs. In the living room his mother listened to the faltering steps. There was something very touching about the way he climbed, drawing his feet together on each stair. Her heart turned over as she imagined the sturdy little figure clutching the banister. She heard him reach the top, go into his room, then flew after him. He was sitting on the bed, knuckles pressed into his eyes.

'Maurice!' She fell on her knees, clutched him against her breast. 'Don't cry. Oh, don't cry, luv. Your mammy loves you. She loves you more than anyone in the whole wide world.'

He felt hot, his small body shuddered in her arms, his heart thumped loudly against her own. Two small arms curled around her neck. Cora held him closely as wave after wave of raw, savage emotion coursed through her veins. There was nothing, absolutely nothing on earth comparable to the love she felt for the child sobbing in her arms, clinging to her, and it was made even sweeter by the knowledge that he loved her back, unquestioningly, wholeheartedly, because she was his mother.

'Do you love your mam, son?'

'Oh, yes.'

'Shall we go down and have some tea?'

Maurice hiccuped. 'Please, Mam.'

'Would you like some Christmas cake?'

He nodded. 'Yes.'

'Let Mam carry you.' She picked him up, laughed and said, 'Lord, you're a weight. Pretty soon you'll be carrying me.'

She carried him downstairs like a baby. Maurice, more confused than ever, wondered what it was he'd done right.

It was three years since Cora and her family had moved from O'Connell Street to Garibaldi Road. The new house was a great improvement on the old: semi-detached, with three good bedrooms, a proper hall, small gardens front and back. There was a bathroom and separate lavatory upstairs. Even Billy, who hadn't wanted to move, appreciated having a lavvy inside.

'But we'll never be able to afford the rent on a place like that,' Billy protested. He was home on leave from the Army where he appeared to be having a whale of a time.

'It's twelve and six a week, half a crown more than we pay now.' Cora was no longer prepared to be dictated to by her husband. If Billy wanted, he could stay in O'Connell Street on his own.

'Only twelve and a tanner for a house in Garibaldi Road!'

'According to the landlord, yes.'

Billy looked dubious. 'I don't want us to move, then have that Flynn geezer shove up the rent.'

'He won't,' Cora assured him. 'I work for him, don't I? I told you. He calls himself Flynn Properties. I keep the books.'

She'd been badgering Horace Flynn for a better house for years. They couldn't afford it, but she'd take in washing, she'd do anything to get out of O'Connell Street. Then, he'd owned just over thirty properties. Now there were forty. Every few months he bought another house.

'We're good tenants, aren't we?' she'd reasoned years ago. 'We're never late with the rent.'

'No and I don't know how you manage it, not with your husband in the Army. I've had to give notice to quit to half a dozen of me tenants since their hubbies were called up. What is it you get; a shilling a day, and twenty-five bob a week allowance?'

'I'm good at managing with money.'

Mr Flynn glanced around the neat parlour of O'Connell Street. He was small and tubby, shaped like a ball, with exceptionally short arms and legs. A fringe of greying hair went from ear to ear at the back of his otherwise bald head, which was covered with brown blotches, like over-large freckles. From what she could gather, he wasn't married.

'I must say you keep the place nice.' He shook his head. 'But no, Mrs Lacey. I'm not prepared to move tenants up a notch until I feel assured they're in a position to pay the increased rent.' He smiled a touch sarcastically. 'Perhaps one day, when the war's over and your husband's in a well-paid job.'

If she had to wait for Billy to get a well-paid job, she'd be in O'Connell Street until the day she died. Cora gnawed her bottom lip. She was still shoplifting. It was easier with a baby in a pram, then a toddler in a pushchair. Like before, some things she kept, some she pawned. Once, when it was winter, she'd taken a fur coat from C & A Modes, not an expensive one, it being C & A, though she'd got five quid for it from the pawn shop. But she couldn't very well tell Mr Flynn *that*.

Maurice was two, and she'd already bought the cane, hung it on the wall and had used it a few times, when once again she had a go at Horace Flynn about a house. There was a lovely one going in Garibaldi Road and she knew it was one of his because she'd seen him collect the rent. The previous tenants were two old maids in their fifties who'd gone to live in America. She asked him into the parlour to remind him how nicely it was kept.

'I've got a job,' she lied, 'serving in a shop.'

'Which shop?'

Cora thought quickly. 'Mercer's the newsagent's in Marsh Lane.'

'I'd like to see some proof; a wage slip, a letter from the manager, if you don't mind, so I'll know you can afford the rent.'

'I'll ask the manager for a letter. I don't get wage slips.' She didn't want to admit she'd lied. Next week, she'd just pay the rent and keep her gob shut. If he mentioned Mercer's she'd say she'd left.

There was silence. Mr Flynn was staring fixedly at the wall at the cane. 'What's that for?'

'Me little boy. I'm a firm believer in discipline.'

He licked his lips. 'So am I.'

Cora saw a gleam of perspiration on the round bald head, a craving in the round wet eyes. She also saw something else: a way of getting the house in Garibaldi Road. It was the way she was to use to get the lovely furniture that went in it, the reason why it was many years before she shoplifted again.

She smoothed back her hair, curled her lip disapprovingly, said sternly, 'Have you been naughty, Mr Flynn?'

He nodded eagerly. Saliva oozed from his mouth. 'Very naughty, Mrs Lacey.'

'Then we shall have to do something about it.' She unhooked the cane from the wall.

2

For more than a month, Alice virtually ran Myrtle's on her own. The girls took turns to give a hand on Saturdays and after school. Orla complained loudly that it was dead boring and the smells made her sick, particularly the ammonia, but sixpence a week was too good to miss. Fionnuala loved it. She would have done it for nothing, because it made her feel important. Maeve didn't care what she did as long as she was left to do it in peace.

Only occasionally did Myrtle put in an appearance. She looked terrible, usually wearing tatty carpet slippers, her face grey and mottled. Once she came down in her dressing gown, a filthy plaid thing without a belt. Alice turned her round and sent her back upstairs.

'She's lost her mind,' one of the customers at the time pronounced. 'I reckon it's 'cos the war's over. It was the war that kept her going. Remember when we had to bring our own towels?'

Alice smiled. 'And we made shampoo by grating soap and boiling it in water. I was reduced to using Lux soap flakes on the customers once.'

'I remember you setting me hair with sugar and water when you'd run out of setting lotion. Myrtle used to open dead early or dead late, even on Sundays, to accommodate the women working in factories, otherwise there'd never have been time for them to get their hair done. She never charged extra.' The woman sighed. 'We all pulled together then. I wouldn't want the war back, not for anything, but there was a nice friendly spirit around. People put themselves out, like Myrtle.' She jerked her head towards the stairs. 'Is anyone seeing to her, like?'

'I usually make her a bite to eat for breakfast and dinner, and her friend, Mrs Glaister, comes round every day to make her tea and put her to bed. She's written to Myrtle's daughter in Southampton to say she needs looking after permanent.'

'You'll soon be out of a job, then?'

'Looks like it.'

Olive Cousins, Myrtle's daughter, took her time coming from Southampton. It was over four weeks later, at the beginning of February, that she turned up; a sharp-faced woman in her fifties, wearing too much pink face powder and a beaver lamb coat that smelt of mothballs. Even then, she didn't go straight upstairs. Alice was in the middle of a perm and was forced to listen while she explained in a dead posh voice, that occasionally lapsed into broad Scouse, that Christmas had been so hectic she was fair worn out and had needed time to recuperate. Her son had been home from university, her daughter had not long married a doctor and his parents had come to stay – she emphasised 'university' and 'doctor', in the obvious hope Alice would be impressed. Alice was, but decided not to show it. She disliked Olive Cousins on the spot.

'Where is mother?' Olive enquired, glancing around the salon as if expecting mother to pop up from beneath a chair.

'Upstairs, in bed,' Alice replied briefly.

'Well, I don't like the look of *her*,' the recipient of the perm announced as Olive Cousins's high heels clattered up the lino-covered stairs.

She stayed for three days, eating and sleeping in a bed and breakfast place on Marsh Lane, not that anyone blamed her for that, considering the state of upstairs. On the second day she came into the salon and announced that next morning she was taking mother back with her to Southampton.

'That's nice of you,' Alice remarked, revising her opinion of the woman, but not for long. Myrtle would be going into an old people's home in a strange part of the country where none of her friends and neighbours could visit. It was, however, more convenient for her daughter.

'She couldn't possibly live with us, there isn't the room, and I can't be doing with travelling halfway across the country every time something goes wrong.'

'You'll let us have the address, won't you? Of the home, that is, so we can write to her.'

'Of course. It'll be nice for her to get letters, but I doubt if she'll be up to reading them,' Olive said brightly, as if they were discussing the weather not her mother's health. 'Now, about the salon. I'd been expecting to sell it as a going concern, but' – her lip curled – 'no one would give tuppence for a dump like this, so I've written to the company that owns the premises. The salon will close today.'

'Today!' Alice's mouth dropped open. She probably looked dead stupid. The thing was, the appointment book was full for weeks ahead, and quite a few women had booked months in advance for weddings and the like. There was a sinking feeling in her belly. She'd have to put a notice on the door.

'Today,' Olive Cousins repeated firmly. 'I don't doubt you'd have liked more notice, but you must have seen this coming for a long time.'

'I suppose I have.'

'Of course, you could always take the place over, assuming you could afford the lease.'

'What's a lease?' Alice felt even more stupid.

'Like rent, only more long term,' Olive explained brusquely, obviously realising that if someone didn't know what a lease was it was unlikely they could afford it. 'Mother appears to have signed a new seven-year lease only last year and it still has six years to run. There was a letter upstairs from the property company asking for this year's payment and complaining about the state of the place. Me mam, I mean mother, hasn't kept it properly maintained.' She sniffed derisively. 'Instead, she's let it go to rack and ruin.'

'She hasn't exactly been well,' Alice said. 'How much is the lease?'

'A hundred and seventy-five pounds for seven years. That's cheap at the price. My hubbie's in business, so I should know. Mam, mother, paid at the rate of twenty-five pounds a year.'

Twenty-five pounds! Alice had never even *seen* twenty-five pounds. She glanced around the shabby room and imagined the walls repainted – mauve would look nice – new curtains on the windows, new oilcloth on the floor. The chairs needed upholstering, but could be patched up for now, and the dryers looked as if they'd come out of the ark, but a good polishing would bring them up a treat. She wasn't sure what came over her when she said to Olive Cousins, 'Have you posted the letter yet to the property company?'

'It's in me, *my* bag, to post as soon as I go outside.'

'Would you mind leaving it till morning? If I'm not round by nine o'clock, post it then.'

The wireless was on in the living room of number eight Garnet Street. Geraldo and his orchestra were playing a selection of Cole Porter songs.

'Night and day,' Danny Mitchell hummed as he ironed his favourite shirt: blue and white striped with pearl buttons. He grinned as he thought about the evening ahead. In an hour's time he would call for Phyllis Henderson, a widow in her forties. They would go to the pub, have a few drinks, Phyllis would play hard to get, but end up inviting him back to her house for a mug of cocoa and thence into her bed.

Danny had a well-deserved reputation as a ladies' man. During the ten years he'd been married to his beloved Renee and the ten years after Renee's death, when he'd had a daughter to bring up, Danny had never given another woman a second glance, but then Alice had got married and he began to sow his wild oats, if rather late.

He was fifty-one, an electrician on the docks, and as lean and fit as a man half his age, with a full head of wavy hair the same colour as his daughter's. There was nothing particularly handsome about his face, but he had a quirky smile that people found attractive and a look in his blue eyes that made women go weak at the knees. There were numerous widows and spinsters in Bootle whose main aim in life was to tie the knot with Danny Mitchell.

'Night and Day' ended. 'You were never lovelier,' Danny sang under his breath. He was thinking of Phyllis in her black satin nightie when the back door opened and his daughter came in. All thoughts of Phyllis and the evening ahead fled from his mind and he looked anxiously at the face of his only child. He was relieved to see her eyes were brighter than they'd been in a long while. Perhaps things had started to improve between her and John.

'I've brought a couple of mince pies, Dad. There was mincemeat in a jar left over from Christmas.' She put a paper bag on the table. 'They're still warm.'

'Ta, luv. I'll have them in a minute. There's tea in the pot if you fancy a cup. Pour one for me, if you don't mind. I've only got the cuffs of this to do.' He turned the cuffs back, ready for the studs, and hung the shirt behind the door. Then he folded the badly singed blanket he used to iron on, put it away and took the iron into the yard where he left it on the step to cool, by which time Alice had poured the tea. They sat opposite each other across the table, Alice in the place where her mother used to sit.

'How's Cormac getting on at school?' Danny asked the same question every day since his grandson had started, mainly because he liked hearing the answer.

'As I said before, Dad, he's taken to reading like a duck takes to water. The teacher's ever so pleased. He was sitting up in bed looking at a book when I left.'

'Good.' He smacked his lips with satisfaction. His grandson had always lived in the shadow of his cousin, Maurice, and it was nice to know Cormac was better at something for a change. From what he could gather Maurice was only average at school.

'Our Orla wants to see you to ask about the Great War. It's something they're doing at school.'

'Tell her to come round Saturday. I'll get some cakes in.' He would never have admitted it to a soul but Orla, with her enthusiasms and quick temper, was his favourite of the girls. He was already looking forward to Saturday.

'You'll do no such thing,' Alice remonstrated. 'If you want cakes I'll make 'em for you. I'll send some round with Orla.'

At the mention of cakes, Danny remembered the mince pies. He removed one from the bag, ate it with obvious enjoyment and quickly demolished the other.

Alice regarded him suspiciously. 'Have you had anything to eat since you came home from work?'

''Course, luv,' he assured her. He could only be bothered with making himself a Piccalilli sarnie.

'I wish you'd come round to ours for your meals.'

'You've enough to do, luv, without having another mouth to feed. And I'm always there for me dinner on Sundays, aren't I?'

She reached across the table for his hand. The eyes that had seemed so bright when she came in had dulled. 'I'd sooner you were there all the time.' There was a catch in her voice. John was apt to mind his tongue in the presence of his father-in-law and it was nice to have someone on her side, someone who would never turn against her, no matter what happened.

'It wouldn't be right, Alice,' Danny said gruffly. He knew why she wanted him, as a buffer between her and her husband, but the situation in Amber Street had to be worked out between the main participants. Lately, though, he felt increasingly tempted to give John Lacey a piece of his mind. It wasn't right, him taking things out on the folks who loved him most, particularly when the folks concerned were his dearly beloved daughter and his grandchildren.

Within the space of months, Danny had seen Alice turn from a happy, tranquil young woman into a sad, listless creature who rarely smiled. Lord knew how she'd feel when the hairdressing job went, which was likely to happen any minute. At least it provided some respite from the atmosphere at home. If only he could *do* something to put things right.

Alice released his hand. 'Anyroad, Dad. I'm here on the cadge.'

'Just say the word, luv. What's mine's yours, you know that.' He would have given his life for her and her children.

'I need some money.'

Danny didn't show his surprise, though he knew John earned reasonable wages and had never kept her short. He dug into his pocket. 'How much?'

'I need more than you'll be carrying in your pocket, Dad.'

'Me wallet's upstairs.' He got up. 'I'll fetch it.'

To his horror, she put her head in her hands and burst into tears. 'I must be daft,' she sobbed. 'I must need me head examining. I told the woman to leave the letter till tomorrer, but I couldn't get twenty-five pounds together in a month of Sundays, let alone a few hours.'

He felt himself go pale. 'Twenty-five pounds, luv? It'd take me all me time to scrape together five, and then I'd have to wait till tomorrer when I get paid. What the hell d'you need all that much for?'

'For Myrtle's. The salon's closing, it already has, but I can take over the lease if I want. It costs twenty-five pounds. Oh, Dad!' She turned and put her arms round his waist, pressing her face against his rough working shirt. 'I'd give *anything* if Myrtle's could be mine. I'm good at hairdressing, everyone ses. I'd've hated to leave, anyroad, but now, with the way things are at home ...'

'I know, luv,' Danny said gently. His mind rapidly assessed his few possessions. What could he pawn? Nothing worth anything much, he realised. There was only the furniture, the bedding, oddments of crockery and cutlery, a few ornaments, his books. He felt guilty for having so many shirts, for not having put away a few bob a week for a rainy day. But he was a man who liked a good time, a man free with his money. His hand was always first in his pocket when it came to a round of drinks. He enjoyed buying presents for his grandchildren. He liked feminine company, perhaps a bit too much, and the various lady friends he'd had over the years hadn't come cheap. There was a ten-shilling note in his wallet upstairs. At that minute he was worth about twelve and a tanner.

'It's so horrible at night, Dad.' Alice's hands tightened round him. 'The girls go out, not that I blame them. I encourage them to. I put Cormac to bed as early as possible. He doesn't mind if I leave the light on, so there's just me and John downstairs. He won't even have the wireless on nowadays. It's as if he can't stand anything cheerful. I stay in the back kitchen as much as possible, but there's a limit to how long you can wash dishes and do a bit of baking for tomorrer, so I try to get on with some sewing. It's hopeless trying to read. I can't concentrate, knowing John's glaring at me. Oh, Dad!' she cried. 'He accuses me of having affairs. He's got this thing in his head that I'm having it off with other men. As if I would! He's the only man I've ever wanted. Now Myrtle's has gone,' she groaned. 'At least it was something to look forward to. I loved it there. It was like a fairy-tale world, all bright and shiny.'

'There, there, luv.' Dan stroked her hair. He'd definitely be having a word with John Lacey. He'd never known his daughter in such a state, as if she were at the end of her tether. He furiously tried to think of a way of getting twenty-five pounds and wondered if there was a bank he could rob and get away with it. He thought of a possible solution and his nose wrinkled with distaste. 'What about asking that Cora woman?' he said. He couldn't abide Cora Lacey.

'Cora!' Alice stopped crying and looked at him. 'It didn't cross me mind. We're not exactly friends.'

'She's never been exactly friends with anyone,' Danny said curtly. 'But she never seems short of a few bob, though Christ knows where it comes from. Billy earns a pittance clearing bomb sites. There's no way he could afford to pay for a house in Garibaldi Road.'

'She works for the landlord, Horace Flynn,' Alice explained. 'She does his books, whatever that involves. I suppose he let her have the house as a favour.' Horace Flynn was one of the most notorious landlords in Bootle, who chucked people on to the streets without so much as the blink of a fat eyelid.

'I reckon it involves more than doing his books.'

'Oh, Dad!' She sounded shocked. 'You've got a dirty mind. I've never known anyone so strait-laced as Cora.' She put a finger thoughtfully to her chin. 'I might go round and ask her. It won't do any harm. All she can do is say no.'

'And she might say yes. Would you like me to come with you?' He entirely forgot about Phyllis Henderson.

'No, ta, Dad. It would be best if I went on me own.'

'You'd better get a move on. It's almost half past seven. Does John know where you are?'

'I said I was coming round to yours with the mince pies.' She laughed bitterly. 'He probably thinks they're for one of me secret lovers. I'll be cross-examined when I get back, particularly if I'm late.'

'Does he know about the twenty-five pounds?'

She shook her head. 'No, he might have stopped me coming if he had.

John doesn't like me working no more. He wants me safely at home where I can't get up to mischief.'

Danny Mitchell swallowed an expletive. He hadn't realised things were quite so bad. 'He won't be all that pleased if Cora comes up with the cash and you start the hairdressing on your own,' he said cautiously, worried that Alice was getting into a situation that would only make things worse.

'I don't care, Dad.' Her face tightened in a way he'd never seen before. 'I'm entitled to something out of life and I'm not getting it now. I wish with all my heart John had never had the accident. I love him, I always will, but I've given up trying to make him believe it. He's impossible to live with, so I'll just have to make a life for meself outside the house.'

Danny hadn't thought his normally timid daughter capable of such determination. He nodded approvingly. 'Right thing too, luv.'

Come in,' Cora said in surprise when she opened the door and found her sister-in-law on the step.

Alice rarely came to Garibaldi Road, mainly because she was rarely asked and Cora wasn't the sort of person you dropped in on uninvited for a jangle.

'What can I do for you?' Cora asked when they were seated in the nicely furnished living room, as if she realised it wasn't a social visit and Alice had only come for a purpose for which an explanation was due.

'Where's Billy?' She didn't want John's brother blundering in.

'At the pub, where else?' Cora sneered.

Alice nodded. 'Right. I want to borrow some money,' she said bluntly. She wasn't prepared to beat about the bush, engage in chit-chat to pass the time, then tactfully come up with a request for a loan.

'Really!' Cora laughed. It must be for something of very great importance. Under normal circumstances, Alice wouldn't have asked her for the time of day, let alone money. 'What for?'

In a cool voice Alice explained about Myrtle's. 'I'll pay you back the twenty-five pounds as soon as possible with a fee on top, for borrowing it, like.'

'You mean interest?'

'Do I?' Alice said, confused.

'Interest is what you pay for borrowing money.'

'Then I'll pay interest.'

'At what rate?' Cora asked, in order to confuse her sister-in-law more.

But Alice understood what Cora was up to. 'At whatever rate you say,' she replied, cool again.

The older woman smiled unpleasantly. 'Why should I loan you a penny?'

'Because you'll make a penny in return.'

Cora smiled again. Then her voice became hard. 'It would have to be a business arrangement.'

'That's all right by me,' Alice said nonchalantly. Inwardly, she was desperately trying to keep her wits about her. She didn't trust Cora Lacey as far as she could throw her and wished she had taken up Dad's offer to come with her. What on earth was a business arrangement?

'I'll lend you the twenty-five quid, but I'll draw up an agreement and we'll both sign to say we'll share the profits till the loan's paid back.'

'*Share* the profits!' Alice exlaimed. She wanted Myrtle's more than anything on earth, but sharing the profits seemed a bit rich. 'You mean half each? That hardly seems fair. It's me who'll be doing all the work.'

'OK, you have two-thirds, I'll take a third.' Cora had known Alice, dim as a Toc H lamp though she was, would be unlikely to agree to half. A third was what she'd wanted all along. It was the easiest way she'd ever come across of making money. 'I'll just go in the parlour and write it down. I won't be long.'

Alice waited on the edge of her chair. She'd done it! Tomorrow morning Myrtle's would be hers, but she wished it hadn't been necessary to involve Cora Lacey. It left a nasty taste in the mouth. A third of the profits! She held out her hands to warm them in front of the small coke fire. It was cold in here. She shivered. The fire gave off scarcely any heat. Cora surrounded herself with nice things, but had no regard for creature comforts. No wonder Billy took himself to the pub night after night.

She knew nothing about her sister-in-law other than that her maiden name was Barraclough, her mother had died when she was born and she'd been brought up in Orrell Park by two spinster aunts, both long dead. Nothing was ever said about a father.

It was a constant wonder what she and Billy had seen in each other. Billy was hardly ever in, Cora rarely went out. In company they ignored each other. Billy seemed nervous in the presence of his cold-eyed wife, Cora contemptuous of her childish, good-natured husband.

Her legs were numb with cold. Alice got up and walked around the room to bring them back to life. She picked up a glass vase off the mantelpiece. It shone like diamonds as she turned it back and forth in the dim light. She flicked it with her fingernail and it gave off a sharp, tinkling sound, like a bell. Cut glass! How on earth could Cora afford such a thing? Where had she got the twenty-five pounds from, come to that? Off Horace Flynn?

'I reckon she does more than keep his books,' Dad had said, or something like it. Alice shivered again at the thought of fat, greasy Horace Flynn coming within a yard of her, let alone doing his books – or far more intimate things if Dad was right.

There was a child's book on the table; a colourful cardboard alphabet book with an animal beside each letter. A for Antelope. She turned to the back page: Z for Zebra. A piece of paper fell out on which had been written several simple sums: $1 + 1$, $2 + 2$, $2 + 1$. The answers had been filled in by a clumsy, childish hand. Cora must have written the sums, Maurice had filled in the answers. She must be teaching him at home.

For some reason Alice glanced at the wall where the cane usually hung. It wasn't there. She noticed it propped against the green tiled fireplace. Her stomach turned. Was Cora whipping her little boy to make him learn?

Alice suddenly longed to get away from this lovely, cold room with its expensive ornaments and return to her own comfy, warm house, where there wasn't a single ornament costing more than sixpence, but which was far preferable to here. Hang Myrtle's. Cora could keep her money and her business arrangement.

She made for the door – and remembered John who would be sitting in the chair under the window waiting for her, glowering, wanting to know where she'd been, how many men she'd allowed to touch her. The accusations were getting wilder and wilder, more and more offensive. She couldn't bring herself to tell Dad some of the things John had said. How many men had she serviced? Did they stand in line? How much had she made? Terrible accusations from the man she had thought would love her for ever. Alice suppressed a sob, just as Cora came into the room with a piece of paper torn from a writing pad.

'Sorry I was so long, but it had to be worded carefully. Just sign here where I've drawn a line of dots. I've brought the ink with me and a pen.'

'I'd like to read it first.'

'Of course,' Cora said smoothly. 'You should never put your signature to anything you've not read first.'

'I, Alice Lacey,' Alice read aloud, 'acknowledge receipt of the sum of twenty-five pounds from Cora Lacey, entitling the said Cora Lacey to a third share in perpetuity of the business presently known as Myrtle's Hairdressing Salon.' She frowned. 'What does "in perpetuity" mean?'

'Till the money's paid back.'

'That's all right, then.' It wasn't often she put her signature to anything. She sat down and carefully wrote 'Alice M. Lacey' on the dotted line.

'What's the M. for?' Cora enquired.

'Mavoureen. It was me mam's name. Me dad called her Renee.'

Cora nodded. 'Well, here's your money.' She held out a small piece of paper.

Alice regarded it vacantly. 'What's that?'

'It's a cheque for twenty-five pounds.'

'But I need the money, not a cheque!' She'd only vaguely heard of cheques and had never seen one before.

'A cheque's the same as money,' Cora said with a superior smile. 'Just give it to Myrtle's daughter. She'll know what to do with it.'

Alice wanted to protest, but it would only show her ignorance. She took the cheque, thanked Cora and said she had to be getting home.

Outside the house she paused. She felt uneasy. How could a piece of paper be worth the same as twenty-five pound notes? Oh, if only she could ask John! He seemed to know everything worth knowing. Alice sighed. But the days were long gone when they could discuss things – should they have a day out in New Brighton on Sunday if the weather was fine, for instance?

Or perhaps Southport, easier to get to on the electric trains that ran from Marsh Lane Station? Was it possible to squeeze another bed into the girls' room now that they were getting older? Orla constantly complained about sleeping three to a bed.

The cheque thing was bothering her. She would have gone back to Dad's, but he'd be out by now, probably with Phyllis Henderson, his latest woman. But Bernadette would know. Unlike Alice, she was clever. Although they'd started St James's Junior and Infants together, Bernadette had passed the scholarship at eleven and gone to Seafield Convent. She lived no distance away in rooms in Irlam Road. Hopefully, Bernadette would set her mind at rest. It would make her late home, but she was already late and by now John was probably doing his nut.

'Oh, well! I may as well be hung for a sheep as for a lamb.'

'Of course a cheque's all right, silly.' Bernadette laughed. She was already in her dressing gown ready for bed although it was only half past eight. Since Christmas she'd been feeling low. Roy McBride had turned out like all the other men she'd known, except for Bob, and had tried to get his hand up her skirt in the taxi on the way home from the dance on Christmas Eve. She had decided to give up on men altogether and rely on books for company.

'We get loads of cheques in the Gas Board. What's it for, anyroad?'

For the third time that night, Alice explained about Myrtle's, then described her meeting with Cora. 'She made me sign an agreement of some sort – and she wants a third of the profits, but never mind. As from tomorrow Myrtle's will be mine, that's all that matters.'

'Oh, Alice!' Bernadette looked dismayed. 'I wish you'd asked me first. I would have loaned you the money and you wouldn't have had to sign anything. I wouldn't have demanded a share of the profits, either. Just the money back when you could afford it, that's all.'

Alice regarded her friend, equally dismayed. 'It never entered me head you were so flush, Bernie.'

Bernadette shrugged. 'It's why Bob and I never had kids, isn't it? I stayed at work so we could save up for furniture for our house. Since he was killed I couldn't bring meself to touch a penny. It didn't seem right, buying clothes and stuff, so the money's been lying in the Post Office for years. There must be going on for forty pounds by now. You could have had the lot and used some to do up Myrtle's place a bit. It certainly needs it.'

'Oh, Bernie! I wish I'd known.'

'Tell Cora to stuff her cheque and I'll arrange to draw the money out tomorrow.'

'I can't, can I? I told you I signed an agreement.'

Bernadette looked at her doubtfully. 'What did it say?'

'I can't remember.'

'You're too trusting by a mile, do you know that, Alice Lacey? Anyroad, how about a cup of tea? Better still, a glass of sherry to toast your new business venture.'

'You make it sound very grand.' Alice smiled.

'It *is* very grand. I feel dead proud that you're my friend. Hold on, I'll just get some glasses from the kitchen.'

While she was gone, Alice glanced around the big, rather gloomy room that was at least warm. A big fire burnt in the massive fireplace. The book Bernadette had been reading was lying face down on the floor alongside an empty cup that had obviously contained cocoa. She wouldn't have wanted to be in Bernie's shoes, not for a moment, but just then she felt a certain amount of envy for her friend for being able to do as she pleased – go to bed when she liked, stay out as long as she cared to without someone breathing down her neck wanting to check up on her every single moment. She squirmed guiltily when she considered how much nicer life would be without John.

Oh, Lord! Alice felt sick. According to the sideboard clock it was ten to nine. But, she reasoned, if John was worried it was his own fault. She couldn't confide in him any more, tell him about Myrtle's. Even when she got back she could tell him where she'd been, but not *why*. He would be quite likely to tear up the cheque, say he didn't want her working. Best to leave telling him till Myrtle's was actually *hers*.

'Hey! I've just thought of something.' Bernadette returned with the glasses. 'How did Cora know who to make the cheque out to?'

'I've no idea.' Alice took the cheque out of her bag and read it properly for the first time. 'It ses "Pay Flynn Properties".' She read it again, frowning. '*Flynn Properties*?'

Bernadette shrieked, 'The bitch! Myrtle's belongs to Horace Flynn. *He's* the owner of the property company that awful daughter was on about. Oh, Al! Right now, I bet Cora Lacey's laughing up her sleeve.'

Myrtle came into the salon wearing a slightly bald astrakhan coat with a brown fur collar, a dusty black hat shaped like a turban and fleece-lined ankle boots. The lace on one of the boots was undone. Alice made her sit under a dryer while she tied it. 'In case you trip over, like.' She stroked the creased, bewildered face. 'Take care, Myrtle, luv. Look after yourself, won't you? We're not half going to miss you.'

'Here, here,' echoed Florrie Piper who had just arrived for her weekly shampoo and set.

A taxi drew up outside and Olive Cousins came downstairs dragging a large, shabby suitcase. 'Gerra move on, Mam,' she snapped. She went pink. 'I mean, do hurry, Mother.' She turned to Alice. 'Good luck with the salon,' she said shortly. 'I hope you do better with the place than Mother did. I must say you could have knocked me down with a feather when you turned up this morning with that cheque.'

Mrs Glaister, Myrtle's friend, appeared. 'You forgot your handbag, luv,' she said gently. 'I've put a clean hankie inside and a quarter of mint imperials, your favourite.'

'Ta.' Myrtle smiled tremulously at everyone. 'Can I have a cup of tea?'

'No, you can't, Mother. The taxi's waiting. Say goodbye to your friends.' Olive roughly dragged the old woman to her feet. She glanced sneeringly around the room. 'It won't exactly break my heart not to see *this* place again.'

The door closed and Myrtle Rimmer left Opal Street for ever. Mrs Glaister burst into tears. 'It won't exactly break my heart not to see *her* again either. Expecting to find Myrtle had saved thousands of pounds, she was, when all she'd saved was hundreds. Mind you, she's taken every penny.'

'It wouldn't be a bad idea to make that cup of tea, Alice,' Florrie Piper said. 'Forget about me and me hair for the minute, though I wouldn't mind a cuppa meself.'

Alice hurried into the dingy back kitchen to put the kettle on, remembering that Olive Cousins had emptied the till last night, but hadn't thought to pay her. She'd worked four days for nothing. But never mind, from now on she would be paying herself. The sadness she felt for Myrtle was mixed with jubilation. She didn't care what underhand things Cora might have got up to with the cheque, nor did it matter that Horace Flynn owned the building. *She*, Alice Lacey, was now the proprietor of a hairdressing salon. Apart from her wedding day and the times she'd had the children, this was the proudest day of her life.

'That's a nasty bruise you've got on your cheek, luv,' Florrie Piper remarked when Alice came back.

Alice touched the bruise as if she had forgotten it was there. 'I walked into a door,' she explained.

'You should be more careful.' Had it been anyone else, Florrie would have taken for granted that the bruise had been administered by her feller, but everyone knew that John Lacey would never lay a finger on his wife.

He hadn't meant to hit her. He never meant to hurt her, either by word or deed. But she was out such a long time and by the time she got back he was genuinely worried and as mad as hell.

One by one the girls came in. He didn't see much of them nowadays. They seemed to spend a lot of time in other people's houses. As soon as they realised their mother wasn't there they went straight to bed. He could hear them chattering away upstairs, laughing and giggling, and he felt excluded, knowing they were avoiding him, knowing *he* was the reason why they were out so much and never brought friends home as they used to. It was the same reason why Alice put Cormac to bed so early – so the lad wouldn't witness the way his dad spoke to his mam.

John went to the bottom of the stairs and listened to his daughters fight over who would sleep in the middle, knowing Maeve would be the loser, always wanting to please. What was needed was an extra bed. It could be squeezed in somehow. A chap at work had told him you could get bunk beds and John wondered if he could make a set, or a pair, or whatever they were called. He liked working with wood, so much more natural than metal. There'd be fights over who'd sleep on top, which was reached by means of a small ladder, but he'd organise a rota. He'd talk it over with Alice.

No, he wouldn't! With a sound that was almost a sob, John Lacey sat on the bottom of the stairs and buried his monstrous face in his hands. He had forgotten, but he and Alice didn't talk any more, and it was his fault, not hers. John felt as if he'd lost control of his brain. His brain made him say things, do things, that the real John found despicable and wouldn't let him do the things he knew were right.

The clock on the sideboard chimed eight, which meant Alice had been away an hour. But she'd said she was only going round Garnet Street to see her dad! John's lip curled and hot anger welled up in his chest. He'd like to bet she was up against a wall in a back entry with some feller. In fact, he'd go round Garnet Street and check, prove beyond doubt that he'd been right in his suspicions.

'I'm just going out a minute,' he shouted upstairs.

Only Maeve deigned to answer. 'All right, Dad,' she called.

John grabbed his coat and hurried out into the gaslit streets. It took just a few minutes to reach Garnet Street and even less to establish that there was no one in Danny Mitchell's house. To make sure, he went round the back and let himself in, but the house was as dark as it was empty.

Afterwards John was never quite sure what happened to his head. There was a glorious feeling of triumph, a quickening of his heart and a shiver ran through his bones at the realisation that he'd been right all along. Now he had a genuine reason to hate her.

He returned home, sat in the chair under the window, tapping his fingers on the wooden arm, waiting for Alice, his slut of a wife, to come home.

It was half past nine when she arrived and by then he was beginning to worry that she'd left him, though common sense told him she would never leave the children – certainly not with him.

He had rarely seen her look so lovely. Any man would be suspicious if his wife came in all starry-eyed and pink-cheeked, as if she'd just won a few hundred quid on the pools. It was the way she used to look when they made love. Something must have happened to make her eyes shine like that. Whatever it was, it was nothing to do with her husband.

'I'm sorry, luv,' she said in a rush, 'but after I'd been to me dad's I decided to drop in on Bernadette because she's been feeling dead low since Christmas. We had a drop of sherry each and I seemed to lose track of the time.'

'You've been gone two and a half hours,' John said icily.

'I know, luv. As I said, I'm sorry.'

'You've been with a feller, I can tell by your face.' Why, oh why, did he so much want this to be true? It was as if he wanted to wallow in his misery, make it worse.

She sighed. 'Oh, don't be silly, John. Go round and ask Bernadette if you don't believe me.'

'Do you think I'm daft enough not to know you've fixed a story up between you?'

'Think what you like,' she said tiredly and went into the kitchen where she put the kettle on. 'Did the girls have drinks when they came in? I can still hear them talking upstairs. Perhaps they'd like a cup of cocoa.'

Had he been the sensible man that he used to be this would be the time to mention the bunk beds. Instead, the man he had become followed his wife into the kitchen and grabbed her arm. 'I want to know where you've been. I want to know why you've got that look on your face. How much did you make? How much have you got in your purse?' He released her arm. She had hung her handbag on the knob of the kitchen door. It was one of those shoulder things that had become popular during the war. He undid the zip and turned it upside down. A gold enamelled compact smashed on to the tiled floor, followed by her purse, a little comb, two neatly ironed hankies, the stub of a pencil, a couple of tram tickets and a scrap of paper.

'John! Me dad bought me that compact for me twenty-first. Oh, look, the mirror's broke.' She was close to tears, kneeling down, picking up the broken bits of glass. 'That's seven years bad luck.'

'I'll get it fixed.' Jaysus! He looked like a monster – and he acted like one. Kneeling beside her, he began to put the things back in the bag. Their shoulders touched and he longed to take her in his arms, dry her tears. Dammit, he *would*. It was now or never. Things couldn't possibly go on like this. He would just have to take the risk of seeing the disgust on her face. He said humbly, 'I don't know what gets into me some ... what's this?'

'It's a cheque,' Alice said in an odd voice. She snatched it away before he could see who it was from and all John's suspicions returned with a vengeance he could scarcely contain.

'So, you get paid by cheque, eh? It must be some posh geezer you do it with? Let's see.'

'No!' She stubbornly put the cheque behind her back. 'It's nothing to do with you.'

'Oh, so me wife can sleep around all over the place and it's nothing to do with me!' He laughed coarsely. 'Let me see that fuckin' cheque.'

Alice shuddered. He'd never sworn in the house before, not so much as a 'bloody'. She suddenly felt sick and knew it was no use keeping the cheque from him. He was stronger than she was and could easily take it off her. 'It's from Cora Lacey,' she said. 'She's loaned me twenty-five pounds for Myrtle's salon. As from tomorrer it'll be mine.'

A year ago John would have been delighted. A year ago he would have borrowed the money for her. A mate of his had borrowed from a bank to set up his own small engineering company. But now, a year later, John felt only blinding rage, accompanied by tremendous fear. He didn't want her independent, having her own business, no longer reliant on him for money. Lately he'd even resented the few bob she earned at Myrtle's. He wanted her at home. If he could, he'd have stopped her going to the shops. He raised his hand and struck her across the face, so hard that she stumbled and almost fell. She screamed, then stopped the scream abruptly, her hand over her mouth, worried the children would hear. The cheque dropped to the floor and he grabbed it.

'Are you all right, Mam?' Orla called.

'I'm fine, luv. Just knocked meself on the kitchen cupboard, that's all.' She looked at her husband. 'If you tear that up,' she said in a grating voice, 'I'll only ask Cora for another. You're not me keeper. And as from tonight, I'll not think of you as me husband either. Go on, hit me again,' she said tauntingly when he raised his fist a second time. 'Hit me all night long, but you won't stop me from having Myrtle's.'

It was the first time she had answered back and, staring at her flushed, angry face, John Lacey realised that he'd lost her. With a groan that seemed to come from the furthest depths of his being, for the second time that night he buried his face in his hands. 'I don't know what's got into me, Alice,' he whispered.

Had Alice's cheek not been hurting so badly she might have felt sorry for him, but for ten months she'd been treading on eggshells, trying to get through to him, putting up with his rages, his moods and, worst of all, his insults, all because she loved him. Perhaps she still loved him, she didn't know, but he had gone too far. Hitting her had been the last straw. He had frightened her girls away so they were hardly ever in. Only Cormac had been spared his bitter anger. She took the cheque and left the room.

Seconds later she was back. She felt extremely powerful, as if it was her, not him, who was in control. 'I'd sooner sleep on me own from now on,' she said curtly. 'I'll kip in the parlour. You can have the bed to yourself.'

3

On Sunday, after early Mass, Alice and the children changed into their oldest clothes. Armed with several paintbrushes, a large tin of mauve distemper, a smaller tin of white, silver polish, rags, and various cleaning fluids and powders, and leaving behind a silent, brooding John, they made their way to Myrtle's.

Even Orla, not usually willing to lend a hand, found it very exciting. 'The girls at school will be dead envious when I tell them we own a hairdresser's,' she said boastfully.

'We don't exactly own it, luv. I only lease the place,' Alice told her.

'Oh, Mam, it's just the same.'

Bernadette Moynihan arrived just as Alice was unlocking the door. She wore old slacks and her long fair hair was tucked inside a georgette scarf. She grinned. 'Just in time.'

Alice grinned back. 'Thanks for helping, Bernie.'

'I wouldn't have missed it for worlds. What shall I do first?'

'Can I start painting the walls, Mam?' Fionnuala pleaded.

'Not yet, luv. Let's get the place cleaned first including the kitchen. There's years of dirt out there and I daren't look at the lavvy in the yard. I used to feel ashamed when customers asked if they could use it. Meself, I went home and used ours whenever I felt the urge.'

Bernadette offered to clean the lavatory. 'You can't very well ask one of the girls and you need to stay here and keep an eye on things.'

'Ta, Bernie. You're a mate. There's bleach somewhere.' Alice handed out various tasks. 'Fion and Orla, you wash the walls, Maeve, clean the sinks, there's a luv. Cormac . . .' She tried to think of something suitable for a five-year-old to do. Cormac looked at her expectantly, his small face puckered earnestly, his blue eyes very large. He was such an adorable little boy. Unable to resist, she picked him up and gave him a hug. 'You can wipe the leather chairs for your mammy.' The chairs weren't leather but leatherette and she was going to make enquiries about having them re-covered.

Everyone sang happily as they worked, all the old war songs: 'Run Rabbit Run', 'We'll Meet Again', 'We're Going to Hang Out the Washing on the Siegfried Line' . . .

At half past eleven they stopped for lemonade and meat paste butties. By one o'clock Maeve, who tired easily, had begun to wilt and Orla complained she was fed up to the teeth with cleaning. Cormac was kneeling on a chair playing with the big old-fashioned till that Alice had always thought entirely unnecessary in a hairdresser's. Fion was scrubbing away in the kitchen, longing to get her hands on a paintbrush. Having finished the lavatory, Bernadette was now brushing the yard. Alice had polished the dryers until they sparkled, though there was little she could do about the paint chipped off the hoods.

'When are we having our dinner?' Orla wanted to know.

'Four o'clock. I told you before it would be late today. Go home if you want. You too, Maeve. Your grandad will be here in a minute to distemper the ceiling.'

'Oh, Mam!' Fion cried from the other room. 'I wanted to do the ceiling.'

'You can do the walls, luv. A ceiling needs an expert hand. I did our kitchen ceiling once and I ended up covered in distemper and looking like a ghost.'

Maeve went home to read a book, but Orla decided to stay when she realised Grandad was coming. They stopped and finished off the sandwiches, and Alice made tea in the amazingly clean kitchen. 'You've done a wonderful job with this stove,' she told Fion. 'It looks like new.'

'Can I do the walls now?'

'Not yet, luv,' Alice said patiently. 'But I tell you what you can do, go upstairs and look for some old sheets to spread around while the ceiling's being done. We don't want paint spilling everywhere.'

'What are you going to do about upstairs, Ally?' Bernadette enquired.

'What d'you mean?' Alice looked at her vacantly.

'Well, it's a flat, isn't it, soft girl. You can let it, make a few extra bob a week. Once it's cleaned up it'd be nice and cosy up there. It might ...' She paused.

'It might what?'

Bernadette glanced sidelong at Fion and waited until the girl had left the room before continuing. 'It might do for the person who give you *that*!' She nodded at the bruise on her friend's cheek that was gradually turning from purple to yellow.

'Bernie!' Alice gasped, shocked to the core.

'I loved my Bob to bits, but he'd have been out the door like a shot if he'd so much as laid a finger on me.' Bernadette folded her arms and regarded her sternly. 'Say he hits you again or lashes out at one of the kids?'

'He'd never hit the kids!'

'This time last year would it have crossed your mind he'd hit you?'

'Well, no,' Alice said soberly.

'It's not right, Alice. No woman should be expected to put up with violence from her husband.'

Alice was trying to think of what to say in reply when the bell on the door gave its rusty ring and her dad came in. He climbed into a pair of greasy overalls and proceeded to paint the drab ceiling a lovely sparkling white.

Bernadette had turned bright pink and seemed to have lost the power of speech, Alice noticed with amusement – she'd had a crush on Danny Mitchell since she was eight.

At last Fion got her hands on a paintbrush and started on the walls. Alice began to rip up the tatty linoleum, aided by Cormac and Orla – a man was coming at eight o'clock in the morning to fit the lino she'd bought on tick yesterday in Stanley Road: black, with a faint cream marble effect, the sort she wouldn't have wanted in her house, but that was perfect for a hairdressers.

She'd got a length of white lace curtaining and two lampshades at the same time, which she'd put up when the distemper was dry. She felt a tingle of excitement. Everywhere was going to look dead smart when it was finished.

Bernadette and Danny came back to Amber Street for their dinner. For once, John's glowering face wasn't allowed to dampen the atmosphere during the meal. Everyone was too full of the hairdresser's and what they had achieved.

'What are you going to call it, Mam?' Maeve enquired.

'Why Myrtle's, luv. I wasn't thinking of changing the name.'

'I think you should,' said Bernadette.

Danny nodded. 'So do I.'

'Why don't you call it Alice's,' suggested Orla.

Alice thought that sounded a bit clumsy and wondered how anyone could be as stupid as she was; fancy not thinking about a new name and not realising the upstairs flat was included in the lease! 'You're as thick as two short planks, Alice Lacey,' she told herself.

'You could call it Lacey's,' said Fion.

'That has a nice ring to it.' Bernadette nodded her approval.

Danny said it sounded classy, Maeve thought it perfect, Cormac remarked it would go with the lacy curtains, Alice looked pleased, John merely scowled and Orla pulled a face, cross that Fionnuala's suggestion had been taken up, not hers.

And Fion glowed. She had actually christened a hairdresser's and felt very proud of herself.

After the table had been cleared and the dishes washed, Bernadette announced she was going home. Danny offered to walk with her as far as Irlam Road.

'There's no need.' Bernadette went all pink again. She never knew what to say to Danny Mitchell.

'Actually, there's something I wanted to ask you,' Danny said when they were outside. 'Where did that bruise come from on our Alice's face? She claimed to have walked into a door, but I'm not sure if I believe her.'

'John did it.' Bernadette had no intention of protecting John Lacey from his father-in-law's wrath. She was slightly disappointed that Danny was only walking her home because he'd wanted to ask about Alice. 'It was on Thursday night, when Alice came back with the cheque.'

Danny swore under his breath. 'I'll be after having a word with him as soon as I get the opportunity.' Later that night, maybe. Alice had said something about going back to the hairdresser's to put up the curtains so there was a good chance John would be alone.

Thinking she was being helpful, Bernadette told him about the flat over Myrtle's. 'I said it would do for John, but Alice wouldn't hear of it.'

'Quite right, too.' He sounded even more shocked by the idea than his daughter had. 'You can't chuck a man out of his own home, no matter what he's done,' he said, outraged.

'Huh! No matter if he'd put your Alice in hospital or done the same to one of the kids?' She forgot her awe of him and lost her temper. Men! The world would be a far better place without them. There'd only been one good one and he'd been killed in the war.

'It's not the way things are done,' Danny said testily. He was beginning to wish he hadn't offered to take her home. He'd always thought her a rather quiet little thing. He wasn't used to women arguing with him. They usually agreed with his every word.

'Well, it's about time it was. Are you suggesting women are born to be punchbags?'

He was flummoxed. What could he say to that? 'I'm suggesting nothing of the kind.'

'Yes, you are. You're saying a woman can be knocked to bits and nothing should be done about it.'

'She can always leave.' He regretted the words as soon as they'd left his mouth, because the quiet little thing burst into sarcastic laughter.

'In that case, if John hits your Alice again, I'll suggest she ups with the four kids and parks herself on you.'

Both seething, they walked the rest of the way to Irlam Road in silence.

Alice finished hanging the white lace curtains and imagined the reaction of the customers tomorrow when they saw the changes that had been made to Myrtle's – she corrected herself – *Lacey's*. She must get a signwriter to change the name over the window and pushed to the back of her mind the knowledge that there'd been a time when John would willingly have done it.

There were other things she must do – buy new towels, for instance, mauve if you could get them. And she needed a clock, a little cheap one – how on earth had Myrtle managed without a clock for all those years? And she'd have price lists printed on little cards, like wedding invitations.

She rubbed her hands together excitedly. She'd have to engage an assistant, someone to do the same things she'd been taken on for herself. A woman with school-aged kids would be ideal because Fionnuala was only too willing to come and help when she finished school, as well as on Saturdays.

All the pictures of the beautiful, dead smart coiffures that Myrtle couldn't have managed in a month of Sundays had been removed from the wall so it could be painted. Alice began to put them back with the drawing pins she'd saved, along with the adverts for various shampoos, setting lotions and hairdressings – she liked the one for Rowland's Macassar Oil the best. Her arms were aching. But it wasn't just the hard work she'd put in today, but that she'd been sleeping on the settee in the parlour since Thursday and it was extremely uncomfortable, much too short and much too hard.

Things couldn't continue at home the way they were, but once again Alice refused to think about them. Instead, she sat under the dryer and regarded Myrtle's – *Lacey's* – with satisfaction. Tomorrow it would look even nicer with the lino laid.

Across the street, well away from the street lamp, a dark figure stood watching the woman at her various tasks. He saw her sit in the centre of the three dryers, saw the way her face glowed when she glanced around the salon, which he had to concede had improved out of all proportion for the better.

John Lacey felt sick with love for the woman who was his wife, along with stirrings of anger and jealousy, never far away these days. The bloody salon had taken *his* place in Alice's heart, but then he only had himself to blame for that.

For the first time in his life he felt the urge to get drunk, to get totally inebriated, forget everything. He'd only been that drunk once before – at a mate's wedding when he was eighteen. It hadn't been a very pleasant experience, but right now the idea of forgetting everything was infinitely appealing.

Where to go to achieve this agreeable state of mind? Not a pub where he was known, or a quiet, respectable place where they'd stare at his face. One of those rowdy ale houses on the Dock Road would be ideal. They were usually packed to the gills with foreign seamen and prostitutes. No one would take a blind bit of notice of him.

John took a final look at Alice, turned up the collar of his coat, pulled his hat down over his scarred face and hurried in the direction of the Docky.

Hours later Danny Mitchell, on his way to have a stern word with his son-in-law, was still seething over the conversation he'd had with Bernadette. If she were older, she'd probably have been one of them damned, stupid suffragettes, chaining herself to railings so women could have the vote.

A little worm of reason penetrated his stubborn brain. It wasn't exactly fair that women *shouldn't* have the vote. After all, whatever those fools of politicians got up to affected them just as much as it did men. And they'd been worth their weight in gold during the war. And if a man knocked a woman about, was she supposed just to stand there and let him?

Danny squirmed uncomfortably. It niggled him that the little girl who'd been his daughter's best friend for as long as he could remember had caused him to have such disturbing thoughts. He felt like a traitor to his sex and tried to concentrate on his meeting later with Phyllis Henderson. Phyllis would butter him up no end, restore his equilibrium, as it were.

To his surprise, when he entered his daughter's house the light was on, but it appeared to be empty. 'Is anyone home?' he called.

'Only me, Grandad,' Cormac shouted from upstairs.

'Surely you haven't been left all on your own!' Danny exclaimed on his way up to the boxroom where his grandson slept.

'Dad said Mam or the girls'd be back soon.' Cormac was sitting up in bed, his slightly too big wincyette pyjamas buttoned neatly to the neck. He put down the book he was reading when his grandad came in.

'Your mam'll be dead cross if she finds you all by yourself. I'll stay till someone comes.' Danny sat on the edge of the narrow bed. 'What's that you're reading, son?'

'I'm not 'xactly *reading* it, Grandad,' Cormac explained gravely. 'I'm trying to do the sums.'

Danny gaped. The lad, only five years old, was actually studying an *arithmetic* book. His heart swelled with pride. Wait till he told Phyllis and his mates in the pub! 'Need any help, son?' he enquired, though beyond the twelve times table he needed help himself.

'What's that word?' Cormac turned the page and pointed to the heading.

'Multiplication. It means . . .'

'I know what it means, Grandad. It means "times". I didn't know how it was said. The next page is "long" something. I don't know how that's said either.'

'Long division, son.' He was beginning to think his grandson was a genius. 'Can you do all these things – the long division and the times?'

'Only with little figures,' Cormac confessed sadly.

'Can the whole class do them?' Danny asked.

Cormac shook his fair head. 'Acshully, Grandad, school's a bit fed-upping. I wish it weren't so dead easy.'

He should be moved up to a higher class, Danny thought indignantly. He'd have a word with Alice when she came in.

Not far away in Irlam Road, Bernadette Moynihan also felt indignant. To think that all these years she'd been sweet on such a rampant misogynist! Even when she'd been married to her darling Bob she had continued to find Danny Mitchell slightly disturbing.

It had started when his wife died and Danny had appeared so devastated. She was eight, same as Alice, and had resolved to marry him, take care of him, when she grew up. He was only twenty-nine and, as Bernadette grew older – became twelve, sixteen, twenty – in her eyes Danny remained the same. One of these days she'd catch up with him, he'd notice her and ask for her hand in marriage. She had spent many happy hours imagining what it would be like being Danny Mitchell's wife. This was one of the few dreams she hadn't confided to Alice, who might not care to have her best friend as a stepmother.

Then Bernadette had met Bob Moynihan and all thoughts of Danny Mitchell had fled from her mind – except when she met him in the flesh, when her knees were still inclined to grow weak and her cheeks to turn pink. She used to pray Bob wouldn't notice and he never had.

But now! Now she had completely gone off him. 'You can't chuck a man out of his own home no matter what he's done,' he'd actually said. Oh, really! She'd have flattened John Lacey with a frying pan if she'd been in Alice's shoes, then dragged him outside and had the locks changed so he couldn't get back in.

She hated men, every single one of them, and she hated Danny Mitchell the most.

At the next table a black man had pulled a girl on to his knee and was touching her breasts beneath her green jumper.

The girl laughed and pulled away. Her face was orange with powder and her mouth a vivid scarlet. She had a green bead as big as a marble dangling from each ear. 'Eh, mate. I don't usually let fellas do that for free.'

The man leered, showing large, very white teeth. 'How much you charge?'

'Five bob and I'm all yours for half an hour.'

'Where we go?'

'Outside, I'll show you where, but give us the five bob first.'

The couple left and John Lacey felt something stir in the pit of his stomach. After ten chaste months and half a dozen pints of ale, he was badly in need of a woman. In the past the idea of using a prostitute would have disgusted him, but right now perhaps it was the drink that made him consider the idea not all that repugnant.

Jaysus! Did he really intend to sink so low? Well, why not? To have set foot inside this den of iniquity wasn't the act of a man who cared how low he sank. There'd already been a fight – two men had produced knives and gone for each other. They'd been thrown out, leaving behind quite a lot of blood. The fight had been over a woman, a gaunt young woman with hollow cheeks and vacant eyes who had followed them outside.

The place was called the Arcadia and when he'd first set foot inside the large, square room with its worm-eaten pillars, the low ceiling blackened by age and smoke, it had made him think of a scene from hell. The wooden floor was scattered with sawdust, the tables long, full of stains and cigarette burns, with benches either side. It was packed, as he had expected. Noise assaulted his ears, hurt them. Men and women shouted at each other in order to be heard above the din – the women's shrill voices seemed the louder. Directly in front of him a man with a black patch over his eye swept his arm across a table and dozens of empty glasses smashed to the floor. There was the pungent odour of dirt, unwashed bodies, cheap scent. The smoke that hung in the air smelt musky and sweet – it wasn't just tobacco.

His first instinct had been to turn on his heel and leave, but he remembered he'd wanted a place where no one would know him. What did it matter where he got plastered? Two hours later he knew his first instinct had been right. He was only half drunk, he had forgotten nothing and the ale had made him feel even more depressed. The tragedy that was now his life seemed worse, more insoluble, even less bearable, than ever. In such alien surroundings he found it hard to believe he was a married man with a lovely wife and four equally lovely children.

Another thing, sex had been furthest from his mind when he came in, but now he could think of little else. He had tried to, but couldn't, take his eyes off the grotesquely painted women in their tight frocks and short skirts. He imagined doing things with them that he had never done with Alice. He thought about what the black man was doing with the girl in the green jumper and felt himself swell.

A woman slid on to the bench opposite. 'Like a spot of company, luv?' she asked in a coarse, gruff voice. She was twice his age, with hair dyed an unnatural red, almost purple, and a gaudily painted face. John's eyes were drawn to the breasts that swelled over the top of her black blouse, the nipples prominent through the thin, gauzy material. She was wearing nothing underneath.

He shook his head, though his heart was pounding and he longed to reach out and touch the bulging breasts. 'No, thank you.'

'Just come for a gander, have you?' she sneered and went away, muttering, 'Filthy bugger.'

All it needed was courage. Men and women kept disappearing and reappearing half an hour, an hour, later. All he had to do was approach a woman – he didn't even have to say anything, just show the money and nod towards the door. But he was terrified that even these women, the lowest of the low, would turn him down because of his face. Even worse, they might take his money with the same expression of distaste on their faces that he'd seen on Alice's, though she flatly denied it.

Someone older might be less choosy. He regretted sending away the woman who'd asked if he wanted company – clearly, his face didn't bother *her*. He wondered where she'd gone so he could say he'd changed his mind. His eyes searched the packed room for her red head, but she was nowhere to be seen.

Then he saw the girl. She was two tables away, sitting demurely with her hands clasped on her lap, head bent, as if she was closely studying something on the table. Her hair was long and straight, and so fair it was almost white. Even from this distance John could see the long, pale lashes surrounding a pair of large grey eyes. The girl raised her head, as if aware she was being watched, and through the crowds their faces met – the faces of the man with the melted skin and the girl who would have been pretty if it hadn't been for the ugly hare lip.

Her name was Clare he learnt after they had made love. She'd written it down because he couldn't understand the strange, guttural sounds that came from her mouth. She had a cleft palate, no roof to her mouth. She gestured a lot, her face fierce with concentration, pointing to herself, to him. When he asked her age, she wrote 'twenty' in the air with her finger.

John liked her. He liked the fact that she never smiled, because he himself hadn't felt much like smiling in a long time. He sensed that she found life as burdensome as he did. He admired her for not painting her face or wearing revealing clothes – she had on a plain black frock and flat black shoes, no jewellery. She was very clean and her room, on the top floor of a narrow three-storey house just round the corner from the Arcadia, was neat and tidy.

He hadn't done the disgusting things he'd imagined with the other women. He made love to her as he would have done to his wife – gently, with some passion, quite satisfyingly. Other than wrapping her legs around his waist, she didn't respond, but nor did she give the impression she found the act objectionable.

When they had finished he felt as if a great load had been lifted from his shoulders. For the first time since he'd been fire-watching and that damned ship had gone up in flames, he was able to relax. He lay beside her on the bed, watching the cold moon shining through the small window. Stars twinkled in the dark sky.

'Do you want to go back to the Arcadia?' he asked after she had answered his questions as best she could and they had lain there for a while. He was stopping her from earning her living.

She shook her head and pointed to the door, indicating that he could go if he liked.

'D'you mind if I stay? I feel dead tired.'

Closing her eyes, she gave a tiny sigh, which he understood to mean she was tired too.

John reached out and touched her twisted lips with his finger. 'You're very pretty.'

There was surprise in the intelligent grey eyes when she turned towards him. She seemed to hesitate, then lifted her hand and stroked his melted cheek. He decided he could quickly get used to her painful pronunciation when she said in her awkward way, 'You're very handsome.'

Alice had been cross the night before when she came home and discovered that, unusually for him, John had gone out, which she didn't mind, but he shouldn't have left Cormac on his own.

Her dad thought he'd almost certainly gone for a drink. 'Do him good, if you ask me.'

'Yes, but he might have *said*.'

Danny left, rather late, to meet his lady friend. The girls came home. Alice made cocoa and several rounds of toast, and they sat round the fire, giggling helplessly, telling each other silly jokes. They made so much noise that Cormac came down to see what was going on and told the unfunniest joke of all: 'Why did the chicken cross the road?'

'To get to the other side!' everyone screamed.

'Oh,' gasped Maeve, bent double with laughter. 'It's a pity Dad isn't out more often. It's much better fun without him.' She went very red and everyone fell silent as they contemplated the truth of this remark.

'Well,' Alice said eventually, 'I think it's time we went to bed. I'm fair whacked and I need to be up early tomorrer to let the man into Myrtle's with the lino.' There didn't seem much point waiting up for John. Since last Thursday they'd hardly exchanged a word.

'Lacey's,' Fionnuala reminded her.

'Oh, yes, Lacey's.'

Alice fell asleep immediately on the uncomfortable settee and was woken by the sound of clinking bottles. The milkman had arrived. She went into the living room in her nightie and felt cross again when she discovered John hadn't lit the fire as he normally did before going to work – he'd used to wake her up with a cup of tea, but those days were long gone.

She lit the fire herself, made tea, woke Cormac, then the girls. 'I'll have to be going in a minute,' she told the three sleepy faces. I'll trust you to make sure your brother eats his cornflakes and that he's properly dressed for school. He's inclined to forget his vest if you don't watch him.'

'OK, Mam,' they chorused, and she thought what lovely children they were and how nice and cheerful last night had been without their father's brooding presence. Perhaps he'd go for a drink more often, she thought hopefully.

The linoleum had been dead cheap and the man cut it into shape in no time. 'It's not going to last all that long,' he warned, 'not in a hairdresser's with so much traffic.'

'It's only temporary,' Alice assured him, 'just to make the place look respectable until I can buy some of that inlaid stuff.'

He wished her luck, promised to recommend Lacey's to his missus and Alice tipped him sixpence.

'You've worked a miracle, Alice,' the first customer gasped when she arrived for her nine o'clock appointment. 'Mauve, white and black go together perfect.' Throughout the day, customers continued to express their astonishment at the transformation that had taken place in Myrtle's – now called Lacey's, Alice informed them. She didn't feel the least embarrassed when a few asked to use the lavatory. At least it was clean and as soon as she could she'd paint the walls.

Late in the afternoon Mrs O'Leary popped her head round the door to ask if their Daisy could possibly be squeezed in for a trim. She regarded the salon with amazement. 'It looks lovely and bright, like a grotto. After Christmas Eve, I swore I'd never set foot in here again, but now I'm glad Gloria's in Marsh Lane were too busy to take us. Our Daisy's got a concert tomorrer night and she needs a trim dead urgent.'

Daisy tossed her auburn curls. 'I'm an elf,' she announced.

'I'm afraid you'll have to wait a bit.' Alice was halfway through a perm, and there was a customer under a dryer who would shortly need combing out. She was doing the work of two women and felt worn out.

'You look puffed,' Mrs O'Leary remarked as she sat down. 'What you need is an assistant.'

'I know. I keep meaning to put a notice in the winder, but I've been too busy all day to write it out.'

'I'd apply meself, but our Kevin's only five – he started school with your Cormac – and I'm not prepared to let him and Daisy wander the streets until you close, and on Saturdays an' all. Me neighbour's got Kevin at the moment, but I couldn't ask her every day.' She pulled a face. 'I could do with the money. The cost of Daisy's dancing class went up in January and her costumes cost a mint. Me husband claims we can't afford it and keeps threatening to make her stop. The thing is, the dancing teacher ses she's got talent.' She chucked Daisy under the chin. 'You want to go on the stage when you grow up, don't you, luv?'

'Oh, *yes*, Mam,' Daisy concurred.

'Mmm,' Alice said thoughtfully. Mrs O'Leary was always nicely dressed, and she had a warm smile and a pleasant manner. She used to get on Myrtle's nerves, boasting incessantly about Daisy and her dancing, but Alice could do much worse for an assistant. She said, 'Actually, the job would only be during school hours. Our Fion's helping out the rest of the time. In fact, she should be here any minute. Ah, here she is now.'

Fionnuala burst into the salon, eager to start work properly as a hairdresser. She pouted when her mother told her to sweep the floor. 'Oh, *Mam!*'

'Just get on with it, luv. You're not ready to give a perm just yet.' She turned to Mrs O'Leary. 'What do you say, about the job, that is?'

'I'd *luv* it,' the woman said breathlessly. 'When can I start?'

'Tomorrer wouldn't be too soon.'

'Tomorrer it is. Me name's Patsy, by the way. You can't very well call me Mrs O'Leary and me call you Alice.'

I might as well be invisible, John Lacey thought sardonically when he arrived home from work and realised no one had noticed he'd been out all night. As far as his family were concerned he didn't exist.

He'd spent the night with Clare, feeling guilty, but at the same time hoping Alice would worry herself sick – he'd worried himself enough over her. He had concocted a story – he'd met a mate, drunk too much, gone back to his house and fallen asleep. But the story wasn't necessary. All Alice did was rattle on and on about hairdressing and the marvellous day she'd had, and you'd think Fionnuala had given Queen Elizabeth herself a shampoo and set from the way she spoke, when all she'd done was wash some woman's hair.

'I'm going out,' he said in a surly voice after he'd finished his tea.

'Have a nice time, luv,' Alice said brightly.

John saw Orla wink joyfully at her sisters as he left the room and longed to turn round, tell his family how much he loved them, make everything better. But it was too late. They hated him. He'd passed the point of no return.

Cormac had followed him into the hall and John wondered if the divil now possessed his soul. How could he have thought his little lad could hate anyone, let alone his father?

'Got ten out of ten for me sums today, Dad. I've brought the book home to show you.'

Tears stung his eyes as he sat on the stairs and lifted Cormac on to his knee. 'Let's have a dekko, son.'

'They're add up and take away.'

'So I see. Gosh, that's dead neat writing.'

'The teacher said it's the best in the class.'

He stroked Cormac's soft cheek. 'I bet she did, son.'

Alice poked her head round the door. 'I was wondering if you'd gone or not. I didn't hear the door slam.'

John put Cormac down and reached for his coat. 'I'm going now. By the way,' he said gruffly, 'you have the bed from now on. I'll use the settee.'

The Docky was always busy. The offices of the shipping merchants, the importers and exporters, were closed and there was less traffic than during the day. But at seven o'clock the pavements were still full of seamen and sailors of myriad nationalities. Behind the high walls of the docks activity could be heard – the shouts and thuds as ships that could have come from anywhere in the world were being loaded or offloaded in the bright glare of floodlights.

Particles of ice were being blown crazily about, this way and that, by the bitter wind that blew in from the Mersey. John could hear the water slushing noisily against the walls of the docks. He drew up his scarf around his neck.

He arrived at the Arcadia, where two small children, a boy and a girl, were cuddled against each other on the steps outside, shivering in their thin clothes. He gave them a penny each.

'Thanks, mister,' the boy said with remarkable cheerfulness.

Clare was sitting at the same table as the night before, her back to him. John's heart lifted and he began to push his way through the crowded room. He'd been looking forward to this moment all day, a day when he'd felt at ease with himself for the first time in months. He slid on to the bench beside her. 'Hello, there.'

She frowned. At first he thought she was annoyed with him for coming until he recognised the frown was one of disbelief. Her cheeks went pink and he realised she was pleased and flattered that he was back.

She nodded furiously. 'Hello.' She hesitated, as she had done the night before, then reached for his hand. 'Glad,' she whispered. 'Glad you're here.' And then she smiled and the smile made her look almost beautiful.

John smiled back and thought what a miracle it was that he had met a woman who was as damaged as himself and that they could make each other smile.

Cora Lacey came into the salon at the end of Alice's first week. The hairdresser's was just about to close. Fionnuala was cleaning the sinks and Cormac was kneeling on a chair in front of the big till ringing up numbers.

'Had a busy week?' Cora enquired.

'I've been run off me feet if you must know.' Alice collapsed under a dryer. 'Thank the Lord it's Sat'day. I've just sent our Orla and Maeve round for fish and chips. I haven't the strength to make the tea.'

'Good,' Cora said with satisfaction. It meant the takings must be considerable. 'Shove over, son.' She gave Cormac a little nudge with her hip and he reluctantly climbed off the chair. 'Is this all there is?' She glanced suspiciously at her sister-in-law. 'Not a single note?'

'The notes are at home,' Alice explained. 'I empty the till each night, don't I? And I hardly ever take notes, anyroad, except for perms and I didn't do one today.'

'Then I'll come back to the house with you to collect me share.'

Fionnuala had stopped work to listen. She glared at her aunt whom she had never liked. 'What's she on about, Mam?'

'It's none of your business, luv.'

'Why is she taking money out the till? It's *our* salon.'

'Your Auntie Cora put money into the business,' Alice explained patiently. Her eldest daughter usually managed to test her patience sorely. 'She's entitled to some of the profit.'

'But there won't be profit for weeks and weeks, Mam,' Fion exclaimed. 'You said so only the other day, what with the price of paint and everything.'

'Yes, but ...' Alice paused. Fion was right. The cost of improvements shouldn't just be borne by her, but shared with Cora, too. And the wages – she wondered if she was entitled to claim a wage for herself? Oh, Lord! She must be the stupidest woman in the world for not having grasped the blatantly obvious.

She swallowed hard – Cora always made her feel dead nervous – and said in a firm voice, 'I'm afraid you can't just come in and help yourself. I need to work things out first, what comes in and what goes out, like.'

'And what exactly goes out apart from the price of a few tins of paint?' Cora wanted to know. She had been expecting to go home with a few quid in her pocket and was annoyed at being thwarted.

Alice was about to reel off the things she'd bought and those she intended buying, when Fionnuala said aggressively, 'She said she'd write them down, didn't she? It's *our* hairdresser's. We don't have to answer to you for everything we buy.'

'Shush, luv.' Alice squeezed her daughter's arm.

The door opened and Orla and Maeve came in, each carrying a parcel of fish and chips wrapped in greasy newspaper.

'Shall we take them home and put them in the oven, Mam?' Maeve enquired.

'Please, luv. We'll be there in a minute.'

Orla's bright, curious eyes went from her mother to her aunt, then to her sister's red, angry face. 'What's going on?'

'There's nothing going on, luv. Just get them fish and chips home before they turn cold.'

'We'll wait for you.' Orla and Maeve came into the salon and stood alongside their mother. Cormac bent his head against his mam's hip and Alice idly began to stroke the soft fair hair.

Faced with the girls' hostile eyes, it dawned on Cora that she wasn't going to find their gormless mother the easy touch she'd expected. She also felt disturbed at being presented with such a united front, conscious she had no one on her side. She wished she'd brought Maurice so she could stroke his hair the way Alice was stroking Cormac's and she wouldn't look so very much alone.

'I'll be in Monday for a statement,' she muttered.

'It might not be ready by then.' Fionnuala smirked. She was thoroughly enjoying protecting Mam from the horrible Cora. It was *her* who had reminded Mam the hairdresser's wouldn't show a profit for ages, *she* who had given it its name. She felt annoyed and very unappreciated when Mam tugged her sleeve and told her again to 'shush'.

'I'll have the statement ready for Monday,' Alice promised.

She had been born, Clare informed him, when her mother was forty-seven. By then her three brothers were in their twenties; all married, all living in different parts of the country. They rarely came home. Her parents' marriage had broken down years before. John was astonished to learn her father had been, possibly still was, a solicitor's clerk.

'My mother said she only had me because he raped her. She hated me right from the start.' She conveyed this in a mixture of gestures, facial expressions, sounds and the pad on which she wrote. Her full name was

Clare Frances Carlson. 'They were ashamed of people knowing I was their daughter.'

She'd been sent to a special boarding school, returning home at fourteen when her education was complete. Within months she had run away – she came from Widnes – but couldn't think of a job someone like her could do apart from cleaning. Even then, 'People don't like this.' She pointed to her mouth, then wrote, 'They think I'm an imbecile.'

'You're anything but.' John took her hands in his. She was a very clever young woman – he wouldn't have known how to spell imbecile. There were books on the sideboard, pencil drawings on the walls that he was surprised to learn she'd done herself. They were mostly of the Dock Road, which could be seen from the window – the traffic, the teeming pavements, the funnels of ships protruding from behind the dock walls. A few were sketches of the crowded interior of the Arcadia that she'd done from memory.

Her short life story was told without a shred of self-pity. She hadn't drifted into prostitution, no one had coerced her. She just heard it went on and it seemed a good way for someone like her to make a living. She didn't like it, but she didn't hate it either.

'Surely there were other things that you could have done,' John said, conscious of a note of reproof in his voice.

'What would you have done if you'd been born with your face like that?' she scribbled, underlining the 'born'.

For some reason he seized the pencil. 'Hidden from the world,' he wrote.

'That's what I'm doing in my way,' she wrote back.

'You deserve better,' he wrote in turn. He'd never been greedy for money. A few extra bob a week wouldn't have come amiss for the odd luxury, but as a skilled tradesman he earned slightly more than the average man. There'd always been enough to keep his family comfortably warm and fed, and the bit Alice got from hairdressing was merely the icing on the cake. But he longed to take Clare away from this run-down house full of tarts, find her somewhere respectable to live, support her, so that she could come off the game and belong to him alone.

But without money none of these things was possible. It gnawed at his gut, knowing that before he came, or after he'd gone, she was in the Arcadia touting for customers, yet he had no right to ask her to stop. He couldn't have afforded to see her more than once or twice a week, had she not refused to let him pay after the first night.

'I said you're different. We're friends,' she wrote, turning away the five shillings he offered. She was a curious mixture of hardness and innocence.

He thought 'friends' described their relationship perfectly. They were friends drawn together by adversity and loneliness. At the back of his mind there was always the awareness that a year ago he wouldn't have dreamt of going near the Arcadia or sleeping with a prostitute. He had told Clare he was married, but still worried that he was using her. Having broken through her hard shell, he was taking advantage of the soft, generous woman inside.

He worried that he might hurt her, let her down, that she would become too dependent on him. If things ever improved between him and Alice, for instance . . . But – he sighed – things never would, particularly now that she was so deeply involved with that damned hairdresser's.

The nightly visits to the pub were doing John the world of good. Alice only wished he'd gone before. He was nicer to the girls, and after tea he'd put Cormac on his knee and discuss the things he'd done that day at school. He'd even deigned to speak to his wife in a civil manner, suggesting he build bunk beds for the middle bedroom.

'The girls are getting too big for three in a bed,' he said and actually smiled.

Alice opened her mouth to say that Maeve had been sleeping with her since she'd occupied the double bed, but quickly closed it. 'Them bunk beds sound the gear, luv,' she said warmly. 'The girls will be dead pleased.'

'I'll get the wood this weekend.'

'John!' She laid her hand on his arm and was dismayed when he quickly moved away as if disgusted by her touch. She regarded him sadly, thinking how much she'd once loved him, then felt even more dismayed at the realisation she didn't love him now. He had spurned her too often. He had driven her away.

'What?'

Alice sighed. 'Oh, nothing.'

4

Christmas 1951

'Who'd like another mince pie?' Alice cried.

'Me!'

'Apart from you, Fionnuala Lacey. I thought it was your intention to lose a few pounds. Any minute now and you'll need a bigger overall.' The overalls were lilac nylon – 'lilac' sounded so much nicer than 'mauve', Alice thought, more tasteful.

'Oh, *Mam!*'

Alice virtually danced across the room to pass the plate beneath the noses of the three women under the dryers. They each took one.

'You look happy, luv,' Mrs Curran remarked. 'Did you make these yourself?'

'I was up till midnight baking,' Alice said cheerfully. 'It's home-made mincemeat too. I managed to get a pound of sultanas in Costigan's. I think it's disgusting. The war's been over six whole years and the country's still on rations. Do you fancy a drop of sherry with the pie?'

'Ta all the same, luv, but no. Drink plays havoc with me gallstones. I wouldn't mind a cup of tea, though.'

'Fion, make Mrs Curran a cup of tea, please.'

'On the Empire, she was,' Patsy O'Leary was saying as she combed out Mrs Glaister's wet hair ready for Alice to set. 'All the dancing schools in Liverpool took part, but our Daisy was the star of the show. Wasn't she, Alice?'

'Oh, yes,' Alice dutifully lied.

Fionnuala looked at her mother and winked. Alice must have been asked the same question a hundred times since the concert last week. Daisy had been good, but a few other girls and one or two boys had been better.

'Poor Myrtle, she wouldn't recognise this place if she saw it now,' Mrs Glaister said sadly.

'Do you ever hear from her, luv?'

'No. I always send a Christmas card, but I haven't had one back for years.

I still miss her, even after all this time. She was a good friend, Myrtle.' Mrs Glaister's old eyes grew watery. 'I reckon she must have passed on.' She crossed herself.

'It happens to us all,' Patsy O'Leary commented.

'Fion,' Alice called, 'put a gown on Mrs Evans. I'll be ready for her soon.'

'Come on, Mrs Evans, luv,' Fionnuala said in a sickly, sugary voice, and proceeded to help the woman, who was barely fifty and as fit as a fiddle, to her feet, and shove her arms inside the sleeves of the lilac gown as if she hadn't the strength to lift the arms herself.

'I can manage on me own, thanks,' Mrs Evans snapped.

It was Alice's turn to wink at Patsy. Fionnuala persisted in treating anyone over forty as if they had one foot in the grave. She would help women down to the lavatory in the yard, wait for them outside and help them back again. Even when asked by one woman, admittedly elderly, but resentful at being fussed over, if she was waiting to wipe her arse, it hadn't prevented Fionnuala from assuming that most of her mother's customers were helpless invalids. Still, Alice thought, her heart was in the right place.

Alice went over to a chair facing the mirror and laid her hands on Mrs Evans's shoulders. 'What is it you want, luv? Explain to me again.'

'Frosting. Just the tips of me hair bleached. I would have thought you'd have heard of frosting, Mrs Lacey,' the woman said sniffily, 'you being a hairdresser, like.'

'Of course I've heard of frosting. I get *Vogue* every month to keep up with the latest styles and products, don't I? I just wasn't sure if you knew what it was.' Bleached ends wouldn't suit someone as dark as Edna Evans. But then, the customer was always right and if she wanted to end up looking dead stupid it was up to her.

'I wouldn't have asked for it if I didn't know what it was.'

'Just making sure, luv,' Alice said serenely. Some customers could be really difficult.

'You're obviously very busy,' Edna Evans said grudgingly.

'I've had to turn customers away. We've been booked solid for weeks, but then Christmas Eve is always busy. Patsy's only helping today as a special favour.'

The door opened, the bell chimed sweetly and Bernadette Moynihan came in. 'Oh, it's like a little oasis in here,' she sang. 'It's dead gloomy outside. The lights in the window look the gear, Al. Lovely and bright.'

'They actually spell "Lacey's". It took me ages to do. Patsy,' she called, 'would you comb out Mrs Curran, then put a gown on Bernie and wet her hair.'

'I'm here for a Peter Pan cut, Al. It doesn't need wetting.'

'I read the other day that hair cuts better if it's wet. I thought I'd experiment on you.'

'Oh, ta! Friendship can have its limits, Alice Lacey. If you spoil me hair, I'll never speak to you again.'

The dryers gradually emptied. Edna Evans went away looking as if she'd been sprinkled with icing sugar, tipping Alice sixpence, so *she* must be pleased. Mrs Glaister seemed reluctant to leave the warm, brightly lit salon with its silver decorations and coloured lights. Feeling sorry for the old woman, knowing that after five years she still missed Myrtle, Alice suggested she stay and have another glass of sherry. The salon would be closing in half an hour.

'And there's still a few mince pies left, luv. Help yourself. Fion, start cleaning the sinks, there's a good girl. Patsy, you can go if you want. Thanks for coming.'

Patsy O'Leary wished everyone Merry Christmas and went home. Mrs Glaister realised her time was up when Alice turned the 'Open' sign to 'Closed'. Fionnuala went to tidy the kitchen and Bernadette examined the Peter Pan cut in the mirror. It was a big step, going from very long to very short in the space of a few minutes. Her neck felt cold, she complained. Alice gave her a towel to keep it warm.

There were footsteps on the stairs and a stocky young woman with a vivid, smiling face entered the salon. She wore a warm tweed coat and a knitted mohair tam-o'-shanter. 'I'm off now, Mrs Lacey.'

'Miss Caddick!' Alice kissed the woman on the cheek. 'Have a lovely Christmas and I hope the wedding goes really well. Good luck for the future.'

'Same to you, Mrs Lacey. I couldn't have wished for a nicer landlady. I've just given upstairs a good clean, ready for the new tenant.'

'Ta, luv. I wish you were getting married in Bootle. I'd have come to the church for a look.'

'If I was getting married in Bootle, you'd have been invited, Mrs Lacey, but Durham's a long way to ask someone to come.' She shouted, ''Bye, Fionnuala,' bestowed a glittering smile on Bernadette and left.

'So, you've got to find a new tenant for upstairs,' Bernie said.

'I've already got one. The teacher taking over Miss Caddick's class at St James's is taking over the flat as well. Nell Greene, her name is, with an "e" on the end. I take it she's a "miss". She comes from London.'

'What's she like?'

'Dunno, I haven't seen her. It was all arranged by letter.'

Bernadette worriedly regarded her hair. 'Does this look too boyish? And I don't like the look of me ears.'

'Peter Pan was a boy, so it's bound to. As for your ears, I'll give them a trim if you like.'

'You say the nicest things. Albert'll have a fit tonight when he sees it. We're going to Reece's to a dance.'

'Albert Eley hasn't got the strength to have a fit. And I'm surprised he can dance, if you must know.'

Bernadette pretended to look angry, then her face collapsed in a loud sigh. 'He'll probably not even notice me hair or me new dress. He's a good dancer, though. He had lessons in some place in Spellow Lane.'

'Tap-dancing? Like Daisy O'Leary?'

''Course not, idiot.' She giggled. 'Ballroom dancing. He went with his mam.'

'I don't know what you see in him,' Alice said bluntly. Albert Eley was a bachelor of forty who lived in Byron Street with his mother. He was the most uninteresting man she had ever known.

Bernie shrugged. 'He's company. At least he's never tried anything on.'

'Only because he wouldn't know how. Seriously, Bernie. You're only thirty-seven, you're still dead pretty. There must be loads of men out there who'd be an improvement on Albert Eley.'

'Until I met Albert, I never came across a single one who didn't want to jump into bed with me within the first five minutes. He's easy to be with, very polite, free with his money. The only thing that gets me down is him going on and on about his bloody mother. It's mam this and mam that until I could scream.' Bernie giggled. 'Anyroad, *you're* only thirty-seven and still dead pretty. There's a few men around who'd be an improvement on John Lacey.'

'Shush!' Alice put her finger to her lips and nodded towards the kitchen where her daughter could be heard washing dishes. 'Me and John get on fine nowadays.'

'Not all that fine,' Bernie said in a hoarse whisper. 'He still sleeps in the parlour. The kids must have guessed there's something up by now.'

'They think it's his back, he ricked it and he has to sleep on his own.'

'A likely story!'

'It *is* a story, Bernie, and as long as the kids believe it, that's all that matters. Anyroad, it doesn't bother me, not much. I've got used to it by now.' She gave her friend a little shove. 'Stop trying to make me miserable. I love having me own salon. I'm dead happy, even if things aren't exactly perfect at home. Now shove off and make yourself beautiful for Albert. Oh, and by the way, when you come to Christmas dinner tomorrer, try not to rile me dad. All you two ever do is argue.'

Bernadette opened the door. 'Tell him not to rile me,' she said pertly before closing it.

'Phew!' Alice locked the door and collapsed in a chair. 'It's been a day and a half, today has. Have you nearly finished, Fion?' she called. 'It's time us two went home.'

'I've only got to dry the dishes, Mam.'

'Just leave them on the draining board to dry themselves.'

Someone tried the door. 'We're closed,' Alice shouted, but the person banged on the glass. 'Oh, Lord,' she groaned. 'It's only your Auntie Cora.'

'Tell her to sod off, Mam.'

'Don't be silly, luv.'

'I've just come to wish you Merry Christmas and discuss the lease,' Cora said when Alice reluctantly let her in. Her light skin was becoming sallow and her colourless hair was scraped back in its usual sparse bun. She wore an unflattering camel coat.

'Merry Christmas, Cora,' Alice said coldly. 'What about the lease?' The seven-year lease expired at the end of the month and was due to be renewed. No doubt Cora had come on Horace Flynn's behalf to announce the cost of a new one.

'It's going up,' Cora said.

'I expected it would.' It seemed only fair.

'A new seven-year lease will be fourteen hundred pounds.' The small eyes gleamed with pleasure. She clearly enjoyed being the purveyor of such grim news.

'Fourteen hundred!' Alice gasped. 'I can't afford that much, Cora! The rates went up earlier this year and the last electricity bill made me eyes pop.'

'You'll just have to cut down on expenses,' Cora said. 'Get rid of that assistant, for one.'

'Not our Fion!'

'No, the other one. That Patsy woman. You haven't needed her since Fionnuala's been full-time.'

'I couldn't possibly. She needs the money. Her husband's dead mean and she's desperate for their Daisy to go on the stage.'

'There's no room for sentiment in business, Alice.'

'There is in mine,' Alice cried. 'There's no way I'd get rid of Patsy. Anyroad, we're often in need of three pairs of hands.'

Cora shrugged her narrow shoulders. 'Take it or leave it – the lease, that is.'

'We'll leave it, thanks all the same,' said a voice. Fionnuala came in from the kitchen. Cora shrank back. She wouldn't have come if she'd known the girl was there. While she could wrap her gutless wonder of a mother around her little finger, she was nervous of Fionnuala who somehow always seemed to get the better of her. It was Fionnuala who, years ago, had demanded a copy of the agreement that her stupid mam had signed and pointed out Cora was only entitled to a third share of 'the business presently known as Myrtle's Hairdressing Salon', so wasn't due a penny from the upstairs flat: it was Fionnuala who made sure Cora bore her share of every single expense incurred by Lacey's, down to things like lavatory paper and hairpins and even the tea the customers drank. Fionnuala had laughed like a drain when Cora tried to suggest that tips were part of the takings.

However, even Fionnuala couldn't claim that 'in perpetuity' didn't mean just that. In perpetuity. For all time. For ever.

'But I asked you at the time, and you said "till the money's paid back",' a shocked Alice had said, years ago, when she thought she had repaid the twenty-five pounds with interest.

'I did no such thing.' Cora had contrived to look indignant. 'I assumed anyone in their right mind would know what "in perpetuity" meant. I didn't just give you a loan. I invested in the business. A third of it's mine. It ses so on the agreement.'

'You're not half an idiot, Mam,' Fionnuala had groaned and Cora couldn't help but silently agree.

Now, Fionnuala looked contemptuously away from her aunt towards her mother. 'Mam, someone said the other day that Gloria's in Marsh Lane is closing down. That agreement you signed was for Myrtle's. If we moved somewhere else it would be null and void.'

Null and void! Alice wondered where her daughter had got such a grand phrase from. 'That's right,' she said to Cora.

Cora's lip curled. Fionnuala wasn't quite as clever as she thought. 'That's funny,' she said. 'Mr Flynn holds the freehold of Gloria's and he's never mentioned anything about it closing down.'

Fionnuala was only momentarily taken aback. Her eyes flickered slightly. 'Then maybe I heard wrong, but we could still move somewhere else.'

'What, and lose all your custom?' Cora sneered. 'Don't forget, if you upped and left, this place could still be let to another hairdresser. It doesn't have to close down.'

'Oh, no!' Alice flung her arms around a dryer. 'I wouldn't want anyone else to have Lacey's.'

'Well, there you are, then.' Cora smacked her lips. 'As I said, you'll just have to cut down on expenses. It's much too warm in here, fr'instance, and you don't need so many lights on, not now you're closed. Get rid of that Patsy woman and stop being so free with the cups of tea.' She eyed the single mince pie left on a plate and the remains of the sherry. 'I bet women don't get given stuff like that when they get their hair done in Mayfair.'

Fionnuala almost exploded with rage. 'How dare you tell us how to run our business?'

'Shush, luv. Goodnight, Cora,' Alice said with false brightness. 'I'll tell you after Christmas whether I'll take up the new lease or not. It needs some deciding, like.'

'Honestly, Mam,' Fion groaned after her aunt had gone. 'You were dead stupid signing that bloody agreement.'

'Horace Flynn could still put up the lease whether I'd signed the agreement or not.'

'Yes, but we could *afford* it if we didn't have to give Cora such a big chunk of what we earn.'

'Hmm,' Alice said thoughtfully. Her dad still maintained Cora did more for the landlord than keep his books. Alice wouldn't have touched him with a bargepole, but there were more ways than one to get round a man like Horace Flynn.

Next day all the Laceys, along with Bernadette Moynihan and Danny Mitchell, sat down to Christmas dinner in the parlour of the house in Amber Street. It was a happy, festive occasion, occasionally hilarious.

Bernadette and Danny pretended to be nice to each other – they'd even bought each other presents – a loud check scarf and a frilly pinafore.

From the head of the table, John Lacey beamed proudly at his family. The girls, once so similar, had acquired their own, singular features as they approached adulthood. Orla was dead pretty, the spitting image of her mother. A real heartbreaker, she already had a steady boyfriend of whom John disapproved. She'd got herself a job with the *Crosby Star*. At first, all she'd done was run messages and the like while she learnt shorthand and typing at night school. Now she was taking letters and had her own desk and typewriter. She was going to be a reporter one day, she said boastfully. 'With a big London paper.'

Maeve seemed to have stopped growing at the age of twelve. Small, dainty, quietly self-assured, she worked at Bootle General Hospital in Derby Road, just skivvying to be blunt, but with the intention of training to be a proper nurse when she was old enough.

He sometimes worried about his eldest daughter, Fionnuala, who, at only eighteen, had become matronly stout and didn't appear to have a friend in the world. She was an awkward, graceless girl, tactless – always saying the wrong thing – and over-effusive when there was no need. Perhaps it wasn't good for her to work with her mother, mixing with women two, three, four times her age and not a lad in sight.

And Cormac! John beamed most proudly of all upon his son, eleven the day before yesterday and certain to pass the scholarship next year and go to St Mary's grammar school. He used to worry that his lad, so quiet and studious, his head always buried in a book, would be bullied at school, particularly when he'd been moved up a class and put with children a year his senior. But Cormac, with his sweet smile and gentle face, never made a show of his cleverness, never bragged. And he was good at games, not so much footie, but his slight, fragile frame could move like the wind. If the school played rugby he'd be a star.

'John, Bernie would like some more wine.' Alice smiled. 'You were in a little world of your own just then.'

'Sorry, Bernie.' John refilled her glass. 'Alice was right. I was miles away.'

Alice! His wife had ripened over the years. No longer gawky, her movements were confident, self-assured. And she was growing more and more confident by the day. He felt proud of Alice too. He hadn't thought she'd had it in her to run her own business. But, he thought drily, perhaps he'd driven her to it. She'd been given the choice of Myrtle's or staying at home and, like any sane, sensible person, she'd chosen Myrtle's. He watched her, flushed and lovely, blue eyes sparkling animatedly as she discussed hairstyles with Bernadette. She had her own hair in something called a French pleat, which he didn't like – it made her look sophisticated, a bit hard, he thought.

'Not so much, luv.' Alice put her hand on Fionnuala's arm as she was about to take a third helping of Christmas pudding.

Did he still love her? John wondered. Probably. Probably just as much as he'd ever done. But now he felt they belonged to two different worlds – the world of the damaged and the world of the perfectly formed. He smiled to himself. And ne'er the twain shall meet!

The meal finished, the table was cleared and they played cards – Cormac could wipe the floor with everyone at poker.

At four o'clock John announced he was going out. 'To the yard. I'd like to get a bit of painting done so it'll be dry by tomorrer. I've got this urgent order, see.'

'But it's Christmas Day, luv,' Alice wailed. 'And surely you're not working Boxing Day as well?'

'I can't let these people down, Alice. It's the first time I've actually had an order from a big shop.'

'And it's dark, John. You should have done it this morning if it's all that important. It's blowing a gale out there.'

'I didn't want to miss seeing the kids open their presents. I'll probably go for a drink later, so I'll be late home.'

She fussed around, tying his scarf round his neck, buttoning his coat, and he tried not to show his impatience. Across the room his father-in-law was eyeing him suspiciously. He was so used to clandestine assignations himself that he automatically assumed John was off on a similar mission.

Alice came with him to the door, bemoaning the fact that he had to go all the way to Seaforth. 'I'm surprised you couldn't have found a more suitable place much nearer home in Bootle.'

'I tried,' John said and closed the door.

When Alice returned to the parlour, Bernie and Danny were in the middle of an argument. Why had he bought her a pinny? Bernie wanted to know. Had he done it deliberately to emphasise a woman's place was in the kitchen?

Danny winked. 'I might have.'

'Well, it won't work. I'll never wear it.'

'I'll not wear that jazzy scarf. I don't know what made you think I had such dead awful taste.'

'You,' Bernadette said furiously, 'are the most maddening man in the whole world.'

'And you're the most abominatable woman.'

Bernadette wrinkled her nose haughtily. 'It's abominable, actually.'

Danny chuckled. 'Whatever it is, you're it, particularly with that hairstyle. It makes you look like a convict.'

The girls and Cormac were listening with interest to the inevitable squabble between Grandad and Mam's best friend. They found them highly entertaining. 'Why don't you two like each other?' Maeve wanted to know.

'It's a long story, luv.' Danny shook his head resignedly.

'They're only *pretending* not to like each other,' Cormac wisely said. 'They like each other really.'

'Don't be so ridiculous, luv.' Bernadette blushed beetroot red. Danny found something tremendously interesting on the back of his left thumb, and Alice stared at her father and her friend, flabbergasted.

'It's time for tea, Mam,' Fionnuala reminded her.

'Oh, yes.' Alice came down to earth. 'Mind everyone while I set the table.' They had guests coming – Orla's boyfriend, Micky Lavin, and two girls from the hospital, friends of Maeve.

While she prepared the sarnies, Alice tried to discern how she would feel if Cormac, clever little chap, were right. She'd always known Bernie was keen on her dad – not that she'd ever mentioned it – but it hadn't crossed her mind the feeling was reciprocated. Danny was twenty-one years older than her friend, but still a vital, attractive man, a bit like Clark Gable, though not quite so tall and less broad – much preferable to the lacklustre Albert Eley. She'd not minded Danny's never-ending stream of women in the past, because she'd always known they weren't serious. But Bernie, only the same age as herself! Would she take her own place in her father's heart?

Oh, what did it matter? Alice laughed out loud. They were two of the people she loved most in the world and it would be the gear to see them happy together. She began to plan what she would wear for the wedding.

It must have been a ten-force gale. John had to battle his way through the streets on his way to Seaforth.

These days, Alice wasn't the only Lacey with her own business. Five years ago John had built bunk beds for his girls, which had become the subject of much interest. In an area of mainly small houses and generally large families, space was always at a premium. The Murphys down the street were the first to ask if John could spare the time to make them a set of bunk beds, or two sets if he had even more time.

John had obliged and the Murphys had insisted on paying, not only for the wood, but for his labour. Before long, orders for beds stretched ahead for months. Then he made a bed for himself in the parlour, because sleeping on the old settee was crucifying for a chap as tall as he was. It was a very simple design and he managed to upholster it himself – a settee, with a seat that pulled forward and a back that slid down to make a double bed.

With many a parlour used to accommodate growing children, ageing grandads and grannies, spinster aunts and lonely uncles, even married sons and daughters, John Lacey's folding beds quickly became as popular as the bunk beds.

Instead of months, he was deluged with orders that would have taken years to complete. It seemed only sensible to give up regular employment and concentrate on making furniture.

He had rented a yard, an old dairy, and there was more than one reason why he'd chosen Seaforth, so far away from Bootle. It wasn't only because he wanted to avoid the neighbours and his family dropping in for a chat, preventing him from getting on with his work.

The wind was less fierce within the shelter of the narrow streets of Seaforth. The yard was on the corner of Benton Street and Crozier Terrace, the latter a cul-de-sac. Next door was the shop that used to be the actual dairy where milk and eggs had been sold. It had been empty for years.

John undid the padlock on the double gates. There was no sign yet announcing the name of the company inside, but the heading on the order books and invoices he'd had printed was B.E.D.S. It had been Fionnuala's suggestion and he thought the capital letters and full stops gave the name a certain authority – much better than just 'Beds'.

There was another padlock on the two-storey building inside the yard that had once housed the dairyman's horse. John used the top floor as an office and kept the finished furniture downstairs. He climbed the ladder, turned on the light and removed a paper carrier bag from beneath the table he used as a desk. Then he locked the stable, locked the yard gates and hurried away. He had no intention of doing a mite of work on Christmas Day.

The bag in his hand, John walked quickly along Crozier Terrace, his eyes fixed on the end house where light gleamed through the flowered curtains. The houses were even smaller than those in Amber Street, with only two bedrooms and no hall – the front door opened straight from the parlour.

The key already in his hand, John inserted it in the lock and went inside. The aroma of roasting chicken greeted him and music, which he had heard from outside – something classical and very grand.

Clare immediately rose from the chair in front of a roaring fire. The other chair was empty, waiting for him. She held a tiny baby in her arms. Another child, about two, with white-blond hair like his mother, was playing with bricks on the floor. He leapt to his feet.

'Dad!' He flung his arms round John's legs.

John's eyes met smiling grey ones across the room. 'Merry Christmas, Mrs Lacey.' He held up the bag. 'Prezzies.'

Meg Lacey had been round for her Christmas dinner. Billy had gone missing the minute the meal was over and Cora did her utmost to encourage his mother to follow suit – Mrs Lacey still insisted on mauling Maurice, something which made Cora's stomach curl.

'I think I'll pop round and see me friend, Ena. Her husband only died last July, so it's her first Christmas on her own. You don't mind, do you, luv?' Meg seemed as anxious to escape as Cora was to see her go. 'I'd call round our John's, but that Danny Mitchell will be there. I can't stand that man, forever making eyes at me.'

You'll be lucky, Cora thought cynically. Danny Mitchell liked his women glamorous – he wouldn't be seen dead with a plump, grey-haired sixty-year-old like Meg Lacey. For women interested in such things, she supposed Danny Mitchell was dead attractive.

Only one man interested Cora and it wasn't Danny Mitchell. It wasn't her husband either. Not long after Maurice was born she'd begun putting Billy off: pretending to be asleep, claiming a headache, not going to bed until he was snoring fit to bust. She'd always had trouble sleeping, was usually awake at the crack of dawn, and up by the time Billy stirred himself and got ideas. She could only assume he paid for it if he needed it, or had a girlfriend. Either way, she didn't care as long as he left her alone.

His brother, John, though, was a different kettle of fish. She'd always considered him the best of the Lacey brothers and would have much preferred him to Billy, but since the accident, she'd felt even more drawn to the man with the destroyed face. She visualised touching the puckered red skin, being kissed by the twisted mouth, when she'd always thought kissing disgusting and the thing that was done in bed beyond the pale. But now, when she imagined doing it with John Lacey, there was a fluttery feeling in her belly that she'd never had before.

She didn't see much of him these days, only the times he came to visit Billy. He would nod at her curtly and not say a word. Cora was no longer welcome in Amber Street, hadn't been for years, not even at Christmas.

It's not fair, she thought. Alice was desperate for that twenty-five pounds. If it weren't for me, she'd never have got that bloody hairdresser's. Why should *I* take the blame just because she was too thick to understand a perfectly straightforward business agreement?

Cora was never usually in need of company. She enjoyed being alone, plotting and planning, thinking of things she'd like for the house. But it was Christmas Day, Billy was out, Meg had gone, Maurice was in his bedroom, where he'd been sent to avoid his grandma's mauling hands, and the house seemed much too quiet. It didn't seem right that it should be so itchily silent, not on Christmas Day. Horace Flynn was coming to tea, and she remembered what would inevitably happen afterwards once Maurice was in bed and gave an involuntary shudder, though she didn't usually let it bother her.

In Amber Street they'd probably be playing cards by now, or them parlour games she'd always considered stupid. But she wouldn't have minded being there right now, part of the noise and bustle.

There *was* something she could do to become part of it. She could go round Amber Street with the paper Alice had signed and tear it up, throw it on the fire, redeem herself in everyone's eyes, even Fionnuala's, whose loathing for her aunt was palpable.

Cora felt an odd, unexpected pang at the thought of Alice's warm smile welcoming her back into the fold. She fetched the agreement from the elegant bureau in the parlour. The words 'in perpetuity' seemed to stand out from the rest. She *had* told Alice a lie, misled her. But Alice was too trusting by a mile. Anyone with half a brain would have double-checked before putting their signature to a legal document.

Why should I tear it up? she asked herself. Why should I give up a regular income just because the house is a bit quiet? It'll be all right tomorrer. Sod the Laceys, I don't give a damn whether they like me or not. A little voice insisted she did, but Cora ignored it.

She went to the bottom of the stairs and called Maurice. 'Would you like to go for a walk?' she asked when he appeared, such a handsome, strong lad, at the top of the stairs.

'OK,' he said dully. Slowly he plodded down towards his mother.

'How are you getting on with the Meccano set you got for Christmas?'

'I'm still wondering what to make, like.' Maurice couldn't understand the instructions. He had no idea what bolt went where. What he would have liked was to take the kit round to his cousin, Cormac, and ask him. Cormac would no doubt knock up a crane or a lorry in no time. But it was more than Maurice's life was worth to ask if he could go to Amber Street on Christmas Day.

'When we get back, we'll do sums together till teatime,' Cora said.

'Yes, Mam.' Maurice sighed. He dreaded to think what would happen if he didn't pass the scholarship with Cormac. He reached the hall, glanced through the door of the living room, saw the cane hanging on the wall and decided if he didn't pass he'd run away. 'Can we go down the Docky?' he asked hopefully.

Cora was about to refuse – she would have preferred Merton Road with its big, posh houses. But it was Christmas Day and Maurice looked a bit downcast. 'All right,' she said charitably. 'We'll go down the Docky.'

At half past seven Danny Mitchell went to meet his latest woman, Verna Logan, in the King's Arms, with a rather bewildered glance at Bernadette on his way out. Orla disappeared into the parlour with Micky Lavin and stern instructions from her mother to 'leave the door open, if you don't mind'.

Maeve and her friends went up to the bedroom to discuss their future nursing careers and Cormac's head was buried in the encyclopaedia he'd got for Christmas. Every now and then he would lift his head and announce some astounding fact. Toboggan was another name for a sledge; that the proper name for salt was sodium chloride; and Guy Fawkes really had existed.

'Everyone knows that,' Fionnuala said tartly in response to the last.

'*I* didn't,' said her mother.

Bernie shook her head. 'Nor me.'

Fionnuala wondered why everything that came out of her mouth sounded wrong, either the words or the way she said them. She could have said, 'Everyone knows that' and laughed, and it would have sounded quite different. Instead, it appeared as if she was belittling Cormac, something she hadn't intended. She couldn't communicate like normal people, she thought tragically. It was the reason no one liked her, why people preferred Maeve or Orla – particularly Orla, who was everyone's favourite, including Dad and Grandad, with the gift of saying the cheekiest, most outrageous things and everyone adored her. On the occasions Orla came into the salon the customers' eyes would brighten and they'd be dead flattered if she so much as remembered their names. Yet Fionnuala, who was as nice as pie, had the horrible feeling she got on their nerves.

'This is nice,' Alice remarked pouring out a fifth, or it might have been sixth, glass of sherry. 'D'you want filling up, Bernie?'

'No, ta. I'll never find me way home at the rate I'm going.'

'I'll make some tea and sarnies in a minute.'

Bernie didn't answer. Instead, she stared into the fire. 'They're only *pretending* not to like each other,' Cormac had said earlier. 'They like each other really.'

Was it possible, was it truly possible, that she was still attracted to Danny Mitchell after he'd revealed himself as such an out-and-out misogynist? Was it possible that Cormac was right and Danny was attracted to *her*?

Well, he had another think coming if he thought she'd have anything to do with a man who'd give a woman a pinny for Christmas because he considered her place was in the kitchen. Oh, Lord! She'd had too much to drink, because all of a sudden she was imagining herself *in* Danny's kitchen, wearing the bloody pinny, making his bloody tea. Jaysus! *She was wearing nothing BUT the pinny*, and Danny was stroking her bottom and telling her she was beautiful. Bernadette moaned with delight.

'Are you all right, luv?' a concerned Alice enquired. 'I hope you're not going to be sick.'

'I'm fine,' Bernie replied in a choked voice.

In the parlour, Micky Lavin was trying to force his hand up Orla's jumper.

'No,' Orla said firmly. He could touch her breasts outside the jumper, but not in.

'Oh, come on,' Micky said coaxingly. He was nineteen, dead gorgeous, with jet-black curly hair, wickedly dirty eyes and a sexy mouth. Had the door not been open, Orla might easily have succumbed.

Micky transferred his hand to her knee and it began to creep up her skirt.

'Stop it.' She slapped the hand away. 'Why can't you just kiss me like a normal man?'

'Normal!' Micky laughed. He had lovely teeth, large and very white. 'You don't know the meaning of normal.'

'I'm not sure I want to if it means all this silly fumbling about.'

'Silly!' He laughed again.

'If you're just going to echo every word I say, then you can go home,' Orla snapped, knowing he wouldn't.

'All right, then. I'll just kiss you.'

At the touch of his lips, Orla's head began to swim and she couldn't bring herself to stop him when his hand returned to her breasts, *inside* her jumper, because it was so incredibly nice.

'Let's get married,' Micky said hoarsely when they came up for air. 'I know you're only seventeen, but your dad'll let you, won't he?'

'That's something you'll never know, Micky Lavin, because I've no intention of asking me dad any such thing. I don't want to get married, not yet. Ask me again in another ten years.' It wasn't the first time he'd proposed. He was never put off by her repeated refusal, but would ask again a few weeks later. Perhaps he was trying to wear her down, which could be easily done if he kissed her and stroked her breasts for much longer. Orla pushed him away and jumped to her feet. 'I think I can hear me mam making tea.'

She had the horrible feeling she was in love with Micky Lavin with his wicked eyes and sexy mouth. If so, she was determined to resist it. Only the other day at work the editor, Bertie Craig, had said she had an aptitude for writing racy little news items and thinking up suitable headlines. He had complimented her on her shortand and suggested that, in the very near future, she might be sent to cover council meetings.

Orla badly wanted to be a reporter like Rosalind Russell in *His Girl Friday*. She longed to leave the narrow confines of Amber Street, of Bootle, and move to London. She would live in a smart little flat somewhere dead posh and report on big criminal trials – even murders – or be sent to interview royalty and famous film stars.

Micky Lavin, who was an apprentice something or other in a foundry in Hawthorn Road, didn't feature anywhere in the plans Orla had for this exciting and fascinating future.

On Boxing Day, Alice put on the cornflower-blue frock she'd bought especially for Christmas. It had a satin bow at the neck and a long, straight skirt. She buckled the stiff wide belt as tight as it would go. Yesterday's gale had lessened, but it was still cold. Even so, Alice decided to wear a navy-blue boxy jacket rather than her winter coat and high-heeled shoes instead of boots. She carefully made up her face and coiled her hair into a French pleat.

'Where are you going all dolled up to the nines?' Fionnuala enquired when her mother came downstairs.

'Never you mind.'

'Can I come with you?'

'Sorry, luv, but this is something I've got to do on me own. What are you doing here, anyroad? You should have gone to the pantomime with Grandad and our Cormac.'

'The seats were already booked, weren't they?' Grandad had asked weeks ago if she'd like to go to the pantomime, but Fionnuala thought it a drippy thing for a girl of eighteen to do on Boxing Day. She had imagined something far more interesting would turn up. Except it hadn't and now she was about to be left all on her own – Maeve had gone with her friends to see Joan Fontaine in *From This Day Forward*, Dad was working and Orla was out somewhere with Micky Lavin. This last fact caused Fionnuala considerable heartache. She had always envied Orla – her slim figure and her confident manner – but nothing like as much as she envied her having Micky Lavin for a boyfriend. Fionnuala desperately wanted a boyfriend, any boyfriend, but to have someone as handsome and desirable as Micky Lavin panting after her seemed little short of heaven.

The rotund figure of Horace Flynn came to the door wearing a crumpled shirt without a collar and baggy trousers supported by a pair of frayed braces. He didn't look well, his face a sickly grey and slightly moist. He regarded the visitor with shrewd, hostile eyes.

'Hello, there,' Alice said in her sweetest voice and with her sweetest smile. 'I wanted to see you about something. I'm Alice Lacey, from the hairdresser's in Opal Street,' she went on when the landlord looked at her vacantly, which wasn't surprising, as they'd never spoken before and she only knew him by sight. He stood to one side and nodded down the hallway, which she took as a signal to come in, though she had the feeling that if it hadn't been so cold he would have left her to have her say at the door.

The large house in Stanley Road was more comfortably furnished than she would have expected from a man living on his own. He led her into a room at the back overlooking a white-painted yard. A fire burnt brightly in the black-leaded grate, in front of which two plush upholstered armchairs were set at an angle either side. The black wooden dresser was full of hand-painted plates, various items of brassware, an assortment of china vases and pretty figurines. A wireless was on, not very loud, and Nelson Eddy was singing 'September Song'.

'D'you mind if I sit down?' As she was nodded towards a chair, Alice began to wonder if he'd lost his voice. He sat his corpulent frame in the chair opposite.

'Seeing as it's Christmas, I thought I'd bring you a few bits and bobs to eat, like, knowing you lived on your own.' She put two paper bags on the table. 'There's a few mince pies and a piece of Christmas cake there, as well as a steak and kidney pudding, which'll need a bit of warming up. I made them all meself.' Her voice faltered in the face of the man's still hostile expression. This was going to be harder than she'd thought. It was said that the way to a man's heart was through his stomach and, as Horace Flynn's stomach was such a notable part of him, she had hoped to soften him up with food.

He spoke at last. 'What d'you want?' he grunted. People only came to see Horace Flynn if they wanted something. Although Alice didn't realise it, he was quite appreciative of the food. He'd been offered many things over the years in lieu of rent – women's bodies, expensive ornaments: most of the stuff on the dresser had come by way of hard-up tenants – but no one had ever thought to suggest a good meal.

And this woman wasn't the plaintive, wheedling sort of creature he usually came across. She was extremely attractive, well-dressed, with her own successful business. He was well aware how much the property in Opal Street had improved since she'd taken over the lease.

'It's hot in here. D'you mind if I take me coat off?'

He shook his head, furtively taking in her slim waist and the way her skirt rode up when she crossed her trim ankles.

'It's about the lease for the hairdresser's,' she said. 'To be blunt, I can't afford it. I expected it to go up, naturally, but not from a hundred and twenty-five pounds to fourteen hundred. The salon can't stand it. I mean, it's no good squeezing things till the pips squeak, if there's no pips left to squeeze.' Alice winced. That last bit sounded dead stupid.

Horace blinked. He was a greedy man, he was cruel and heartless, but he wasn't a fool. It wasn't good business to demand more than the market could stand. And, unlike a house which could go overnight, if a shop was vacated it could stand empty for months, if not years. He had told Cora to increase the lease to seven hundred pounds. Who did the little tart think she was, going against his wishes, demanding double! He recognised a family feud, remembering this woman was Cora's sister-in-law. Was Cora trying to put her out of business?

Apparently not, otherwise she'd be cutting off her nose to spite her face, because the woman said, 'I might, only might, be able to afford it,' she continued in her sweet, lilting voice, 'if me sister-in-law didn't take such a large share of the profits.' She rolled her eyes and laughed girlishly. 'Silly me! I was dead ignorant in those days. I signed this agreement I didn't understand and now I'm beholden to Cora.'

Horace had the uncomfortable and alarming feeling that he'd been done. He needed Cora, but he wouldn't have trusted her as far as he could throw her. She'd never mentioned she had a share in Lacey's hairdressing salon and he wondered if *he* would have seen the extra money she was asking off this rather nice woman who worked hard running her own business and had thought to bring him food. With her smiling face and sparkling eyes, she had brought a breath of fresh air into an otherwise dull and lonely Boxing Day.

On the wireless, Dooley Wilson began to sing 'As Time Goes By'. 'I love this song,' Alice cried. 'Did you see the picture, *Casablanca*? I went to see it with me husband. It was the last . . .' She paused. It was the last picture she and John had seen together before he'd had the accident. She remembered they'd walked home, hand in hand. 'You must remember this,' John had sung. It was rarely she thought about John now. She'd grown used to their loveless relationship. The fact that they were friends seemed enough, but the song had brought back tender memories and her eyes filled with tears.

'Oh, gosh, you must think me an idiot.' She jumped to her feet and struggled into her coat. 'I'm sorry, Mr Flynn, to have forced meself on you, right in the middle of Christmas too. It was thoughtless and rude. I'll go home and leave you in peace. Forget about the lease. I'll pay it somehow, even if it means sacking one of me staff. Thanks for your time.'

She was already in the hall when he called, 'Mrs Lacey!' She went back. He was still sitting in the chair, his back to her. 'A hundred pounds a year will do.'

'What?'

'A hundred pounds a year for seven years. I'll bring the papers round meself in the new year.'

She gasped with delight. 'Thank you very much, Mr Flynn. It's much appreciated. When you come, I'll make you a nice cup of tea.'

Outside, Alice undid the belt that was killing her and let out a long, slow breath. She'd done it! He'd reduced the cost of the lease. She felt quite shameless, recalling the way she'd rolled her eyes, fluttered her lashes, even showed a bit of leg. She fished in her bag for a hankie and rubbed her wet cheeks. The tears, though, had been real.

5

The door of the salon opened and a man's voice with a cut-glass accent said cheerfully, 'Hello, there!'

Men rarely set foot inside Lacey's. Occasionally one might come to make an appointment for his wife, usually scarpering pretty sharpish at the sight of so many strange-looking women, like characters out of a Buck Rogers science fiction picture.

'Good morning.' Alice went over to the appointment book.

'Are you Mrs Lacey?'

'I am.' She thought it wasn't fair that a man should have such lovely hair. It appeared to have been spun from pure gold and was in bountiful curls all over his head. He had warm brown eyes, a perfectly straight nose and pink lips that could only be described as pretty. He wore corduroy trousers and a thick hand-knitted jumper. A colourful striped scarf was thrown carelessly round his neck. He looked about twenty-five. Fionnuala was staring at him, mouth hanging open, as if any minute she'd start to drool. 'What can I do for you?' Alice asked.

'I'm Neil Greene. By tonight I hope to be living in your upstairs flat.'

'Neil!' Alice exclaimed, flustered. 'I thought your name was Nell. I was expecting a woman.'

'I'm so sorry, it's my frightful writing. I'm afraid you've got a man. I hope you don't mind. My car's outside, loaded to the gills with all my stuff. Is it all right to start bringing it in?' He beamed at the assembled customers who were regarding him, wide-eyed. 'How do you do, ladies?'

Embarrassed, the three women under the dryers patted the thick net-covered curlers as if trying to make them disappear. Mrs Slattery, in front of the sink with her head covered in blue paste, was trying to slide down the chair out of sight.

'Of course you can bring it in.' Alice nodded, still dazed.

Fionnuala darted forward. 'Would you like a hand?'

'How terribly kind.' He smiled angelically as he unwound the scarf to reveal a slender white neck. 'But only if you can be spared.'

'I can, can't I, Mam?' Fionnuala pleaded.

'Yes, luv, but not for long.'

'Well, isn't he a regular Prince Charming!' one woman remarked when the door closed.

'He looks like a right pansy to me,' said another, Mrs Nutting, whom Alice had never much liked.

'I wish my hair were that colour.' Mrs Slattery sighed. 'And doesn't he talk nice? Dead posh.'

'More like he's got a plum in his gob,' sneered Mrs Nutting.

'I thought he'd be a woman,' Alice gasped.

'I reckon he almost is.'

'What's he here for, Alice?'

'He'll be teaching at St James's, the infants.'

Fionnuala returned, carrying a box of gramophone records, Neil Greene behind with two large suitcases. 'Don't worry, I haven't brought the kitchen sink,' he sang.

'Can we have a gramophone, Mam?'

'Perhaps, one day.'

'Isn't it time this tint was washed off, Alice?' Mrs Slattery said.

'Oh, yes. Sorry, luv. I'm a bit taken aback, if you must know. It looked just like Nell on the letter.'

'I wonder if he's related to that film star, Richard Greene? He's dead handsome too, though he's dark, not fair. Have you ever seen him, Alice?'

'No. Me and John didn't get to the pictures much when the kids were little. Nowadays we both seem to be working all the hours God sends.' She had to pretend things were normal, that they would have gone to the pictures had they had the time.

'I suppose one day soon you'll decide Amber Street's not good enough and you'll be off somewhere more select. You could easily afford it with all the money that must be rolling in.'

'I wouldn't dream of it, Mrs Nutting,' Alice said stiffly. 'Amber Street is quite select enough, thank you. It's where I live and it's where I'll die. We're having the wash-house turned into a bathroom, so we won't have to go outside to the lavvy no more. That's enough for me.'

'Oh, well, it's nice to know the money for me shampoo and set is contributing towards an indoor lavvy for the Laceys. I'll sleep better tonight, knowing that.'

Alice was amazed that the horrible woman managed to sleep at all and that her nasty mind didn't keep her wide awake all night long. She kept the thought to herself, sometimes difficult with customers who were particularly unpleasant.

'He's so *handsome*,' Fionnuala said dreamily over tea. 'A bit like the Angel Gabriel. There's not a single film star who comes near him. And you'll never guess what he did when I finished helping him move in. He only *kissed me hand*!'

'Honest!' Maeve looked impressed, but Orla, at whom the words were directed, seemed miles away.

'He's got a gramophone,' Fionnuala continued, willing her sister to listen, 'loads of records and hundreds of books.'

It was Cormac's turn to look impressed. 'What about?'

'Oh, all sorts of things. Too many to remember. He said I can borrow them, though, whenever I like.'

'Would he let me borrow some too?'

'I'll ask him if you like.' Fion gave a superior smile. 'We're already friends. Aren't we, Mam?'

'Well, yes, luv. I suppose you are.' The new upstairs tenant seemed determined to be friends with everyone.

'He asked if he could call me "Fion" and I said yes, and when I called him Mr Greene he said to call him Neil, even though he's a teacher.'

Orla came to life. 'I should think so too,' she said indignantly. 'He's not *your* teacher, so you're equal. Why should he expect to be called mister by someone your age? You're not a child.'

'I call Mr Flynn Mr Flynn,' Fionnuala said lamely.

'Yes, but Mr Flynn's *old*. How old is this Neil?'

'Twenty-seven, he told me.'

'*There* then,' Orla said, as if this proved her point. 'And I don't like the name Neil.'

Fionnuala went red. 'Well, I don't like Micky.'

'I don't care.'

'Neither do I.'

'Girls!' Alice said tiredly. 'Please can we have our tea in peace?'

'Then tell our Orla to leave me alone,' Fionnuala said sulkily.

'Orla, stop being so sarcastic with your sister.'

'Was I being sarcastic?' Orla looked around the table with pretend innocence, but no one answered.

Once the meal was over and the table cleared, Cormac started on his homework. He seemed able to concentrate no matter how loud the noise around him. Fion washed the dishes and Maeve dried them. Alice started to make pastry for a mincemeat and onion pie for tomorrow.

Micky Lavin called for Orla. They were going for a walk, which Alice considered a mad thing to do in the depths of an icy winter, but then she and John had done the same sort of silly things when they were courting. Young people in love wanted only to be with each other. The weather, no matter how awful, didn't matter.

Alice rolled out the pastry and hoped things weren't serious between Orla and Micky. He was a nice lad, considering his background: the middle child of a family of nine, whose dad was hardly ever in work and whose mam could only be described as a slattern – never seen without a pinny, even at the shops. The eldest lad was currently in jail for thieving. Coming from such a family, Micky had done well for himself, somehow managing to become an apprentice welder.

Even so, Alice wanted someone better for her daughter – for all her daughters, come to that. She wondered if it was possible something might develop between Fion and Neil Greene, but thought it most unlikely. Once his presence became known, every young single woman in Bootle would be setting her cap at him, as well as some of the married ones.

She put the pastry in the meat safe to keep cool. Fion appeared in a tweed coat and a headscarf, and announced she was going to confession.

'You only went on Friday. What awful sins have you committed that you need to confess again so soon?'

'None, Mam. I just feel like going to church.'

'Don't stay out too long, luv. It's awful cold outside.' It seemed pathetic that all a girl of Fion's age had to do was go to church.

Maeve, who was on early shift at the hospital and had to be up at the crack of dawn, went to bed early with a book. Alice offered to bring her up a cup of cocoa shortly. Cormac finished his homework and also went to bed, in his case armed with an encyclopaedia.

At last Alice was left alone. She turned on the wireless – there was a play on soon. There'd be no sign of John till all hours. She was usually in bed by the time he came home. That horrible Mrs Nutting had been talking through her hat, going on about all the money rolling in. After allowing for the overheads, Alice took little more than she'd have done in a factory and John made a surprisingly small amount considering all the hours he put in. Still, he was generous with what he did get, witness the planned new bathroom.

Sometimes Alice felt guilty, sitting in a nice warm house with her feet up, listening to the wireless or reading, knowing John was hard at work in the yard. If only he'd got a place somewhere closer she'd have popped round evenings with a flask of tea and a nice warm pie. As it was, she hardly saw him. Her face grew sad. Their marriage had become a travesty, a joke. They treated each other with friendly politeness.

The play started and she turned up the sound. She'd sooner not think about John and the way things were now.

'I love you, Orla,' Micky whispered. 'When I'm at work, all I think about is you. I can't get you out me mind. It's driving me up the wall.'

And I love you, Orla wanted to say. I feel exactly the same. I can't wait for you to kiss me. I think about you all the time.

However, Orla said none of these things. She didn't want him to know she found him so disturbing. Instead, she said, 'I don't like it in this entry, Micky. It's dark and dirty, and smells of wee-wee.'

'Where else can we go?' Micky said helplessly.

'Why can't we just walk?'

'I'm tired of walking. I'm desperate to kiss you. Would your mam let us use the parlour, do you think?'

'What for?' Orla asked tartly.

'You know what for.'

'I feel uncomfortable in our parlour, knowing me mam's just on the other side of the wall.'

'We could do harmless things like kiss.'

'I hope you're not suggesting we could do less harmless things elsewhere?'

Unexpectedly, Micky began to walk away. 'I wouldn't dream of it,' he said coldly.

She watched the boyish, not very tall figure recede along the entry. The lights from the rear of the houses either side shone on his black hair, his broad shoulders. Even from the back he looked dead handsome. She knew he was hurt because she refused to take him seriously. Something twisted in her heart and she found herself shaking, as strange sensations she had never felt before swept through her body.

'Micky!' she called when he was about to turn the corner. 'Oh, Micky!'

'Orla!'

They ran to meet each other. Micky swept her up in his arms, kissed her, swung her around, kissed her again, undid her coat, grabbed her waist. His hands pushed under her jumper and she could feel them hard on her ribs through the thin material of her petticoat.

'Micky,' she breathed rapturously when his thumbs touched her nipples. Somehow, straps were moved, her bra undone and Orla groaned in delight when her breasts were exposed to Micky's seeking hands.

Oh, my God, she was wetting herself! And Micky was pulling up her skirt, stroking the bare flesh at the top of her legs, feeling inside her pants.

Orla could never quite remember exactly what happened next, only that it was mind-shatteringly thrilling and quite wonderful. Afterwards they walked back to Amber Street, Micky's arm round her shoulders, hers round his waist. She was still shaking and felt extremely odd, as if she'd entered a different world from the one she used to live in. She'd left the house a girl and returned a woman.

At the door, Micky said huskily, 'We're made for each other, Orla. We've got to get married now.'

'Did you have a nice walk, luv?' Alice enquired when her daughter came in.

'OK,' Orla said in a bored voice. 'I think I'll make meself a cup of cocoa and take it to bed. I've got a busy day tomorrer.' She was being sent on her very first assignment – some person off the wireless, whom admittedly she'd never heard of, was coming to Waterloo to open a shop.

'Mind you don't disturb Maeve. She's got an even busier one.'

'I won't, Mam.' As Orla waited for the kettle to boil she made up her mind that, after tonight, she would never see Micky Lavin again. It was too dangerous.

It was Cora's birthday, not that anyone knew or cared except herself. Billy had forgotten, as usual. Alice used to send a pretty card – 'From John and Alice, the girls and Cormac' it always said. Cora missed the cards, but they'd stopped five years before, along with the invitations to Christmas dinner and other events, like birthday parties.

Since Christmas, Cora had been in a terrible state. For one thing, the least important as it happened, she was fed up with the house – there was a limit to how nice it could be made to look and she felt she'd reached it. What she would like more than anything was to start afresh in a different house, this time bigger – a detached one in a wider road with trees. She wouldn't mind moving as far afield as Waterloo or Crosby. Months ago, Horace Flynn had acquired a lovely bungalow right on the shore in Blundellsands. The elderly widower he'd bought it from was a penny short of a shilling and had let it go dead cheap. Horace was having the place done up before he let it.

Cora had intended demanding it for herself in return for services rendered and would have done if it hadn't been for her sister-in-law. Because of her, going behind her back, telling tales, she'd lost favour with the fat, greasy slob of a landlord. Cora's blood boiled when she thought about it. Her hands twitched, as if she'd like to get them round her sister-in-law's neck and squeeze. She'd only seen Horace once since Boxing Day and then he'd torn her off a strip.

'How dare you countermand my orders?' he'd demanded. She'd never seen him look so cross. 'Did you intend keeping the extra money for yourself?'

'Of course not,' Cora insisted, though she had been wondering if she could get away with it. It would have depended on whether Alice paid by cheque or with cash.

'Have you done anything like this before?' His little round eyes flashed angrily.

'I only did it the once,' she said humbly. 'Only because it was personal.'

'Ah, yes, that reminds me. Why didn't you tell me the hairdresser's partially belongs to you?'

'I didn't think it mattered, if you must know.'

'Of course it matters,' he snapped impatiently. 'It was clearly your intention to cause your sister-in-law some harm. You made the mistake of letting your emotions cloud your judgement.' He left, saying he intended going very carefully through the books to make sure he hadn't been done. It was a pity, but he didn't trust her any more.

Since then, he hadn't given her any more work, nor dropped in for a spot of titillation and to give her the five quid that always followed. Even worse, one day she'd seen him coming out of Lacey's hairdresser's, so had kept watch and seen him twice again.

It was a good job she had the money from the hairdresser's, because all of a sudden she found herself paying the full rent for Garibaldi Road, which she could never have afforded on the pitiful amount Billy earned.

It was vital she get back in with Horace Flynn. He wasn't particularly old, only in his fifties, but he was a sick man – you could tell by his unhealthy colour. There was something wrong with his heart. It didn't beat proper. She wouldn't be a bit surprised if he dropped dead any minute. In fact, she often hoped he would, because he hadn't a close relative in the world, just some far-off cousins in Ireland. They'd actually talked about it once.

'I don't like the idea of some person or persons I've never met benefiting from all my hard work when I pass on,' he'd said.

'Surely you know someone closer you could leave it to,' Cora had said innocently, knowing there was only her.

'Hmm.' He'd eyed her speculatively. 'In that case I would have to make a will.'

Since then, whenever she went to his house and he wasn't looking, she'd searched for a will, but if he'd made one it must have been left with his solicitor, because she never found it.

'I'm sorry, luv, but she's gone to the pictures,' Alice said to the distraught young man outside.

'Again!' Micky Lavin said wildly. He ran his fingers through his black hair, as if about to tear it out. 'She went to the pictures last night. I stood outside the Palace in Marsh Lane until the picture finished, but I didn't see her come out.'

'She didn't go to the Palace last night, she went to the Rio in Fazackerly with some girl from work. I'm not sure where she's gone tonight,' she added, in case Micky stood outside again.

'Can I come in and wait?' His bottom lip quivered like a child's.

'I was just about to go to bed, luv,' Alice lied. 'It's not really convenient.'

'I'll sit on the step, then, till she comes.'

'I'm not sure if she'll come in the back way or the front.'

'I'll do me best to keep an eye on both.'

Alice felt dreadful as she closed the door on his desperate, unhappy face. She went to the bottom of the stairs and called, 'Orla?'

'Yes, Mam?'

'That's the last lie I'm telling Micky Lavin on your behalf. He's a nice lad and he's obviously mad about you. If you don't want to see him again, then tell him so to his face. D'you hear me, our Orla?'

'Yes, Mam.' In the bedroom, Orla buried her face in the pillow so no one would hear her cry. It had been awful listening to Micky's anguished voice. She tried not to imagine him walking down Amber Street, as miserable as sin – as miserable as she felt herself, if the truth be known. It was all she could do not to rush out of the house and call him back. But look what had happened when she'd called him back the other night! Jaysus! It had been out of this world, totally wonderful. She ached for it to happen again.

But, she reminded herself, she wasn't the sort of girl who made love in back entries. She was going to *be* someone one day, someone dead important. Why, only yesterday Bertie Craig had suggested she practise her shortand, make it faster, so that she could become a verbatim reporter.

'When you're interviewing a politician, say, it helps if you can take down every word. If he later denies he said a certain thing, you can flourish your notebook and prove he did.'

A politician! One of these days Orla Lacey might actually interview a politician, beside which marrying Micky Lavin came a very poor second.

Oh, but if only she could get him out of her mind!

'I didn't realise until yesterday that you were the mother of the genius,' said Neil Greene.

'Eh?' It was Saturday and the salon had just closed. Alice was transferring the takings to her handbag to tot up later.

Neil had obviously been shopping in town. He was carrying several Lewis's and Owen Owen's carrier bags. 'Cormac Lacey, he's your son, right?' He raised his perfect eyebrows.

Alice swelled with pride. She nodded. 'He is so.'

'Going to pass the scholarship with flying colours, so I understand. They're always talking about him in the common room. I knew you had a son at St James's, but I thought it was the other Lacey, Maurice. He has the look of Fion.'

'Maurice is me nephew. We don't know who Cormac takes after.'

Fionnuala emerged from the back where she was washing cups, eager to bathe in some of her brother's reflected glory. Alice felt slightly irritated by the look on her face, like a sad little puppy waiting to be noticed by its lord and master. Fion was useless on Saturdays, on edge waiting for Neil to pop in and out.

'Ah, Fion!' Neil's smile was wonderful to behold. The customers claimed it made them go weak at the knees. 'I've bought you a present.' He rooted through one of the bags and took out a little red box.

Fionnuala almost collapsed with gratitude before she even knew what the present was. 'Oh, ta,' she gasped. She opened the box and took out a large silver brooch in the shape of an 'F'. 'It's lovely,' she breathed. 'Oh, and it's got a little diamond in.' She clasped the brooch against her chest. 'I'll treasure it all me life,' she said shakily.

'I'm afraid the diamond isn't real. It's called a zircon.' Neil beamed as he handed Alice a green box. 'And one for you. It's an "A".'

'Thank you very much.' Alice deliberately didn't look at her daughter's face, knowing that she would be shattered that Neil hadn't bought a present just for her.

'That's by way of an apology,' Neil said.

'Apology for what?'

'For not putting "Mister" on my letters, for inadvertently letting you think I was a woman. With the flat, situated as it is over a hairdresser's, you might have preferred having a female of the species upstairs. You showed admirable restraint when I turned out to be the wrong sex.' He grinned. 'Another person might have given me a good bollocking and told me to take my bags elsewhere. I just hope I don't disturb the customers too much when I come in and out.'

Alice assured him he was no bother and he went upstairs. 'That was nice of him, wasn't it?' she said warmly to Fion. 'And he must think a lot of you, buying you a brooch as well as me. I mean, if it's by way of apology like he ses, there was no need to include you, was there?'

Fionnuala's face brightened – she was very easily pleased, Alice thought sadly.

'Not really, Mam.' Fion couldn't wait to show the brooch to Orla who didn't have a boyfriend at the moment, having gone completely mad and ditched that gorgeous Micky Lavin.

She'd had to tell him to his face eventually. She'd taken him into the parlour because she didn't trust herself in a place where he could take her in his arms and touch her the way he'd done before. They'd only end up doing that crazy, wonderful thing again and she'd be lost.

Oh, his expression when she told him! She would never forget it – shocked, disbelieving, close to tears. His eyes were black with despair.

'But I love you,' he'd said, as if this were the end of the matter.

'Well, I don't love you,' Orla said spiritedly.

'You do! Of course you do. You know you do. I can tell. What we did together was magic. Wasn't it, Orla?' He shook her arm. 'Wasn't it?'

She looked straight into his eyes. 'No,' she said. 'It was all right, that's all. I quite enjoyed it.'

'You're lying. You thought it was magic, same as me.'

Orla shrugged and longed for him to go, get out of the house, out of her life, for ever. She folded her arms and wished him goodnight.

'And that's it, then?'

'That's it.'

'So it's tara?'

'Tara, Micky.'

'You've broken me heart,' he said in a cracked voice.

'It'll soon mend,' she said carelessly.

The front door slammed. Arms still folded, Orla began to rock backwards and forwards on the settee. Tears dropped on to her knees, her skirt, made wet patches on her shoes and the floor around them.

It was Cormac who found her, rocking like a maniac and flooding the parlour with her tears. 'Why have you told Micky to go away when you want him to stay?' he wanted to know, which only made Orla cry even more. Her alarmed mother came in, did her best to soothe her, then sent her to bed with cocoa and a couple of Aspro.

That was weeks and weeks ago, and Orla still couldn't forget Micky's face, though now she hated it. She hated every single thing about Micky Lavin.

His face was in front of her now, staring at her from the sheet of paper in the typewriter. She resisted the urge to pull the paper out, rip it to shreds, because the face would only appear again when she put more paper in.

Another woman worked with her in the small office, Edie Jones, Bertie Craig's secretary. Edie and Orla didn't get on. The older woman seemed to resent the younger one being such a favourite of her boss.

'What's the matter with you?' Edie asked as Orla sat scowling at the typewriter.

'There's nothing the matter with me,' Orla snapped.

'Then why do you look as if you've lost a pound and found a sixpence?'

'Perhaps I have, that's why.'

Edie shrugged. 'I was only asking.'

Orla wondered what her reaction would be if she shouted, 'I think I'm pregnant, *that's* what's the matter. I bloody well think I'm bloody pregnant. And I don't want to be. I don't want to be bloody pregnant more than anything in the world. I *hate* Micky Lavin. Men are supposed to take precautions, wear things. But Micky didn't and now I'm bloody well pregnant.'

'Are you sure you're all right, Orla?' Edie sounded worried. 'Now you look as if you're about to burst into tears.'

'Wouldn't you if you'd lost a pound and only found a sixpence in its place?'

'I'm only trying to help, dear.'

Perhaps it was the 'dear' that made Orla start to weep. 'I'm sorry for being rude,' she sobbed. 'There *is* something wrong, but I can't possibly tell you what it is.'

'Why don't you go home? I'll tell Bertie you weren't feeling well. He'll understand.'

'I think I will. Ta, Edie.'

She wandered along Liverpool Road towards Bootle. She'd missed two periods, which had never happened before. She was definitely up the stick, had a bun in the oven, as some people crudely put it. Approaching Seaforth, she passed a doctor's surgery and contemplated going inside and asking the doctor to examine her. But she looked so young and wasn't wearing a wedding ring. What would the doctor say?

Orla had never cared particularly what people thought, but having a baby without a husband was just about the most shocking thing a girl could do. There was a girl in Opal Street who'd done it. That was ten years ago and the girl was now a woman, but it was still talked about as if it were only yesterday. The baby had been sent to an orphanage.

'*Mine won't.*' Orla clutched her stomach. It was no use asking a doctor, because she knew in her bones that there was a tiny baby curled up in there waiting to be born. She also knew that she had to keep it, that to have it taken away would be wrong. And if she didn't want her baby growing up with the stigma of having an unmarried mother, the equivalent of having a sign saying 'bastard' hung round its neck, then she would have to marry Micky Lavin. Furthermore, she was only seventeen and needed her parents' permission, so she would have to tell Mam and Dad.

A young woman approached, pushing a large, shabby pram. The baby inside was shrieking, as if it was being severely tortured. 'Oh, for Christ's sake, shut your gob,' the woman said in a despairing voice as she passed by.

Orla turned and watched her walk away, bent and weary. 'That will be me in a year's time,' she thought with horror. 'I'd sooner be like them.'

She glanced across the road at two girls, slightly older than she was, strolling along arm in arm, talking animatedly. They were smartly dressed in tweed costumes and little felt hats. One carried a big grey lizard handbag that Orla badly coveted. The girls were everything that she had one day planned to be herself.

Horace Flynn had taken to dropping in at the hairdresser's at least once a week. 'Just to see how things are going, Mrs Lacey,' he would say.

'Things are going fine, Mr Flynn. Thanks for asking.'

'He's got a crush on you,' announced Fionnuala. 'What on earth did you do on Boxing Day when you went round to ask about the lease?'

'I just fluttered me eyelashes a bit, that's all,' Alice replied uneasily.

'If you'd fluttered them some more, we might have got the lease for nothing.'

'Oh, Fion, don't!' Alice squirmed. 'Anyroad, it's your fault he comes so often. There's no need to make quite such a desperate fuss of him, taking him into the kitchen, plying him with cups of tea.'

'I feel sorry for him. He's got sickly skin. He probably comes because we're the only people in the world who are nice to him. Everyone else hates his guts.'

'With good reason, luv. He's a horrible man.'

'Horrible or not, I prefer having him on our side rather than Auntie Cora's.'

'There's no need to talk about sides, Fion. There isn't a war on.'

'Oh, yes, there is,' Fionnuala said darkly. 'We're on one side, Cora's on the other. One of these days we're going to win.'

These days, John Lacey considered the world darn near perfect. He rarely thought about his face. It had happened, there was no going back. He felt no guilt about having two families. It had been a question of survival and Clare had given him the ability to live with himself.

At six o'clock he locked the yard and went down Crozier Terrace to the end house where he let himself in. Robby came running towards him from the kitchen, demanding to be picked up. John hoisted the little boy on to his shoulder.

'Been for walk in park, Dad,' he gurgled. 'Lisa cried all day. She's growing tooths. Did I cry when I was growing tooths?'

'All the time,' John assured him. 'Hello, luv.'

Clare emerged from the kitchen looking slightly harassed. She wore a gingham pinny over a plain brown frock. Her long fair hair was pinned back with a slide. She rolled her eyes towards the stairs and made a guttural sound, which John immediately understood. His daughter, Lisa, was upstairs, asleep for once.

'Been getting you down, luv?'

She made a face and nodded furiously, then suddenly smiled, folding both him and their son in her slim arms. 'But happy,' she said. 'Very happy. Tea ready.'

He had learnt to read the expressions on her face, translate the strangled sounds that came from her mouth into proper English. 'Good.' He smacked his lips. 'I'm starving, and I think I can smell liver and onions.'

She nodded again and he followed her into the tiny kitchen where the table was set for three. As they ate, John wondered if he had ever felt so blissfully contented during the first years with Alice and remembered that he had. The memory disturbed him. He was doing a terrible thing, betraying his wife and their four children with a woman who had once been a prostitute.

Clare lightly touched the back of his hand with her finger. 'You all right?'

'Yes.'

She seemed able to read his mind as easily as he understood her awkward speech and facial expressions. On the pad she always kept beside her she wrote, 'Conscience?' There were some words she didn't even attempt.

'I'm afraid so.'

'Go home early,' she wrote. 'See your family.' She shook her head. 'I don't mind.'

'You're a saint.'

Her eyes sparkled. 'I'm anything but.'

'I'll see how I feel.' He knew he wouldn't go home early to the house where nowadays he felt like a stranger. Alice had adapted very easily to his absence, he thought cynically. She never reproached him for being being away so often. His girls showed no sign of missing him. Only Cormac seemed to mind his dad not being there, a fact that caused John some heartache.

Still, there was nothing to be done. It was a question of survival, he reminded himself for the umpteenth time. He glanced around the table, at Clare, at his white-blond other son. A small cry came from upstairs, and he and Clare smiled at each other. She went upstairs to fetch Lisa. In six months' time there would be another baby.

This was his family now. These were the people who accepted him for what he was, what he had become. One of these days he would abandon the other family altogether – once the girls were married and Cormac was old enough to understand. Alice would be all right. She had the hairdresser's to keep her busy.

It was midnight when John rose from the bed he shared with Clare, got dressed and returned to Amber Street. To his surprise, Alice came into the hall to meet him. He'd never known her stay up so late before.

'Something's happened,' she said.

He noticed her eyes were red with weeping. 'Are the kids all right?' he asked, alarmed.

'Sort of. Can we talk?'

'Of course.'

She led the way into the living room. There was a teapot with a striped cosy on the table, two cups and saucers, sugar in a bowl, milk. He felt slightly guilty. She must have been waiting a long time for him to come.

'What's up?' His heart was beating rapidly in his chest.

'It's our Orla, she's in the club.' She poured tea and handed him a cup.

'Pregnant?' The cup jerked in his hand and tea slopped into the saucer.

'Pregnant,' Alice confirmed.

'The little bitch! I'll bloody kill her . . .' He rose to go upstairs and drag his daughter out of bed, shake her till her teeth rattled.

'John! Leave her. You'll only wake Fion and Maeve, and they don't know yet. Orla only told me tonight.'

He hadn't realised people actually did see red when they were angry. 'Is it that Micky chap?'

'Yes, and it was only the once. She hasn't seen him in weeks.'

'It only needs the once,' John spat. 'You should have kept a closer eye on her.'

'Oh, so it's my fault!' Alice laughed incredulously. 'You're hardly ever here, but it's *my* fault if our daughter falls for a baby. What was I supposed to do, follow her and Micky wherever they went?'

He knew she was right, but wasn't prepared to admit it. 'Did she know the facts of life?' he growled.

'Yes, she did, as it happens. I told all three of them at the same time. I trust you'll do the same with Cormac,' she added pointedly. 'Assuming you can find the time. Look,' she said reasonably, 'why can't we discuss this like civilised people? Things have to be done, said.'

'Such as?'

'We have to go round the Lavins, all three of us; you, me and Orla, talk it over with Micky's family. He hasn't been told, but Orla's convinced he'll marry her. The thing is, he's only nineteen and an apprentice welder. He earns peanuts. What are they going to live on?'

'He should have thought about that before he poked my daughter.'

Alice winced at the coarse expression. '*Our* daughter,' she said firmly. 'And it's the present we have to deal with, not the past. Orla thinks he'll give up the apprenticeship and get a proper job – he's a decent lad, John, no matter what you think. That means he'll just end up a labourer like your Billy. They need supporting for the next couple of years until he's finished his training. I wondered, could we put them up in our parlour?' Putting aside the rather unfortunate circumstances, Alice quite fancied having a baby in the house.

He was completely taken aback. 'What!'

'Our parlour, John.'

'What about me?'

'You can sleep upstairs. I'll sleep with the girls. There'll be an empty bed.'

'I'll do no such thing,' he gasped, outraged. 'Why should we have to put ourselves out because Orla's behaved like a little whore?'

'John!' Her eyes widened in shock. 'That's a terrible thing to say.'

'It's a terrible thing she's done.' He couldn't adjust to the fact that the prettiest of his girls, his favourite, had actually let a man touch her in that way. It was disgusting. 'Where did it happen?' he asked, almost choking on the words.

'I don't know, do I? I didn't ask. But whatever she's done, John, she's still *ours*. We've got to stand by her. Now, about the parlour . . .'

'She's not having the parlour,' he said brutally. 'If this house had twice as many rooms, I wouldn't have her, or that Micky, under me roof. She's made her bed, let her lie on it.'

'I see.' Alice's voice was cold. 'You know, John, when that fire burnt your face, it burnt something else an' all. It sounds a bit daft to say it burnt your heart, but that's what it seems like. There's not a drop of charity left in your body. You're as hard as bloody nails. It's not fair. You've no right to behave like this with your family.'

His wife and daughters all seemed part of the accident. When his face had been destroyed, something had happened to the love he felt for the people in this house, even Cormac. It had been damaged, perverted in some way, riddled with suspicion. He had changed from Dr Jekyll into Mr Hyde.

He wanted shot of them. They were no longer his concern, more like an intrusion into his present happiness. He felt like fleeing Amber Street there and then. He longed for Crozier Terrace, for Clare and his other family with whom he felt completely at ease.

He stood abruptly. 'I'm going to bed.'

'Will you come with us to the Lavins tomorrer night?'

'No! I'll sign the necessary forms so she can get married and off me back, but Orla can rot in hell for all I care.' He couldn't believe he'd just said that. He stopped at the door, turned to say he hadn't meant it. He was confused. He always felt confused in Amber Street. But Alice had picked up the cups and was taking them into the kitchen, and he couldn't be bothered calling her back.

The following evening Orla went on her own to Micky's house in Chaucer Street to tell him he would shortly become a father. Alice followed an hour later, apprehensive and nervous, worried the Lavins would react as badly as John had and there'd be a scene. She was surprised to find Micky had already told his mam and dad and they were delighted at the news.

She was taken into the shabby parlour, which had obviously been given a quick dusting because there were still smears of dirt left on the sideboard. A broken orange box burnt in the grate. To her further surprise the room contained one of them new-fangled television things, which she later learnt had fallen off the back of a lorry – one of the Lavin lads just happened to be there at the time.

'They'll be wed with our blessing,' Mrs Lavin said grandly. 'Won't they, Ted? We can have the do afterwards in the Chaucer Arms – our Kathleen works there as a barmaid.'

'I doubt if Orla will want much of a do. Will you, luv?'

'No, Mam.' Orla was sitting as far away from Micky as she could in the small space provided by the parlour. She looked pale and subdued, as if they were planning her funeral rather than her wedding. Micky was watching her anxiously. He was crazy about her, Alice realised, and a lump came to her throat. Were two lives about to be destroyed by this marriage? Three, if you counted the unborn child. Last night she had suggested Orla forget about Micky and go away to have the baby.

'And what would happen to it?' Orla asked thinly.

'It would have to be adopted.'

Orla shook her head. 'No, Mam. That would be dead irresponsible. I'd feel terrible for the rest of me life.'

'So would I, if the truth be known. I couldn't stand the thought of me first grandchild being brought up by strangers.'

One of the younger Lavins was being despatched to buy a bottle of sherry so a toast could be drunk to the about-to-be-married couple. Mrs Lavin wondered aloud if it was too late to go round St James's church that night and post the bans: 'So they can get spliced at the earliest, like.'

Alice found herself warming to the good-natured, red-faced woman, with her kind, generous manner and her equally kind husband. She felt deeply touched when the subject of where the young couple would live was raised and Mr Lavin said instantly, 'They can sleep in the parlour. We don't want our Micky giving up his apprenticeship and we wouldn't ask a penny off him, would we, luv? Not when he's got a wife and a kiddy on the way.'

Mrs Lavin's plump, worn face creased into a broad smile. 'The good Lord always seems to provide sufficient food for the table. At least, so I've found.'

It was so different from John's attitude the night before. 'John and I will help out, of course,' Alice said, feeling obliged to include her husband in the offer.

'They'll get by,' Mrs Lavin said placidly.

Orla uttered a strangled cry and fled from the room.

They got married, Orla Lacey and Micky Lavin, on the first Monday in March. The Nuptial Mass was at ten o'clock. Although the bans had been called for the last three weeks, few onlookers turned up at the church at such an early hour. There were no wedding cars to attract attention, no bouquets or buttonholes, no bridesmaids.

In place of the bride's father, who had unfortunately been struck down a few days before with a severe bout of flu – or so Alice told the extravagantly sympathetic Lavins – Danny Mitchell gave his granddaughter away. Lacey's hairdresser's was closed for the day. Maeve was on afternoon shift at the hospital, so had no need to ask for time off. Cormac, who found the whole situation completely baffling, stayed away from school. He'd thought people only got married because they made each other happy, but all Orla did was snap people's heads off every time they spoke, particularly Micky's.

Bernadette Moynihan took the morning off to be with her friend on such a stressful day.

'I'd imagined having a great big bash when the kids got married,' Alice confessed tearfully as she got ready. 'Y'know, picking the bride's and bridesmaids' dresses, ordering flowers and the cake, arranging a nice reception with a sit-down meal. But this is going to be awful and John not being there only makes it worse.'

'What's Orla doing about her job?' Bernie asked.

'She's given in her notice. She had no choice, did she? Any minute now she'll start to show.'

Orla looked like death in the simple blue suit her mother had bought. She held a white prayer book in her white-gloved hands. Throughout the ceremony, Micky couldn't take his troubled eyes away from her stony face.

'She's going to make his life hell.' Alice's heart sank. This was a nightmare of a wedding.

6

'The letter came this morning to say he'd passed, which means he'll be off to St Mary's grammar school in September. You should see the list of things we've got to buy!' Alice laughed and made a face. 'He was a bit put out to find he's got to wear a cap, but he's going to keep it in his blazer pocket till he gets to school.' Blazer! She never dreamt she'd have a son who'd wear a blazer.

'I suppose it's nice to have some good news for a change,' said Mrs White who came once a month for a shampoo and set. 'Your Cormac passing the scholarship makes up a bit for Orla.'

'What exactly do you mean by that?' Alice enquired in an icy voice.

'Well . . .' Mrs White must have been put off by Alice's tone. 'Nothing, really.'

'We're all very happy for Orla, if you must know. Micky Lavin is a fine lad who'll make a good husband. And we're dead pleased about the baby.'

'Yes, but . . .'

'But what?'

'She's so young to be a mother,' Mrs White said lamely.

'She's seventeen. I was only a year older when I had our Fionnuala.'

'You're fastening the curlers too tight, Mrs Lacey. Would you mind undoing the last two and rolling them up a bit looser.'

Alice sniffed. 'Sorry.'

'I understand you're about to expand.' Mrs White must have decided this was safer ground. Alice Lacey was a brilliant hairdresser, the best in Bootle, and it wouldn't do to annoy her. She was relieved to be rewarded with a smile.

'Yes, I'm taking on a trained assistant, if you can call that expanding: Doreen Morrison, only part-time. She used to work in this exclusive salon in town till she retired.'

'She's old, then?'

'Only fifty. She retired because of a heart complaint, but feels she can manage four afternoons a week and Sat'days. She only lives down Cowper Street, so she won't have that big journey into town.'

The salon was getting busier. Women were coming from further and further afield, and Alice was often booked solid for weeks ahead. As well as taking on an assistant, she had felt obliged to have a telephone installed.

She placed a net over Mrs White's curlers, tucking two large cotton wool pads inside to cover her ears, sat her under the dryer, then went into the kitchen to make herself a cup of tea, leaving Fion in charge. Though not for long – there was a trim arriving any minute, followed by a tint, and Mrs Nutting would shortly need combing out.

It was a lovely, hot August day. The schools had broken up a fortnight ago – Cormac had gone to Seaforth sands with his mates and stern instruction only to paddle, not swim. Alice took her tea into the backyard to drink, glad to escape from the salon for a few minutes and not just because it was so warm in there.

The trouble with Bootle, which she loved with all her heart, was that everybody knew everybody else's business. She was sick to the teeth with women making remarks about Orla, who'd only been married five months, but was already as big as a house. The baby was due at the end of next month and she wondered, grimly, what people would have to say *then*.

It was annoying that Mrs White had taken some of the sheen off Cormac's achievement – she must go round and tell Orla as soon as the salon closed. It might cheer her up a bit.

Only might! Alice sighed. Orla was behaving as if the world had ended, giving poor Micky a terrible time. His mam, whose patience seemed inexhaustible, was full of sympathy.

'I was out of sorts when I was having a couple of mine. She'll be all right by the time the baby comes.'

Somehow Alice doubted it. Being confined to the Lavins' cramped, noisy parlour with a baby to look after was likely to make Orla even worse. What was it that film star, Jimmy Durante always said? 'You ain't seen nothing yet!'

If only she could afford to rent them a little house! Hopefully, once Doreen Morrison started, the profits would go up and she'd ask Horace Flynn if he had a place going.

There were all sorts of 'if onlys'. If only John earned a bit more from the business. Instead, he gave her less housekeeping than when he'd been working as a turner. He was always vague when he handed over the money, muttering about needing new tools, more stock, increasing overheads. If it hadn't been for the hairdresser's, Alice wouldn't have been able to manage. She would, though, insist John contribute towards the cost of Cormac's uniform and all the other stuff required – she remembered there was a tennis racquet on the list.

'When will I see Dad so I can tell him?' Cormac had asked that morning when the letter came.

Alice pursed her lips, angry that John was never there when something nice happened – or something bad, like that business with Orla, with whom he had cut off contact altogether. 'I dunno, luv. Not till Sat'day, probably.'

It mightn't even be then. They seemed to be seeing less and less of him, even at weekends. 'I'll wait up late and give him the news,' she promised.

'Can I come down if I'm still awake?'

'Of course, luv.'

There was yet another 'if only'. If only she hadn't been so stupid as to sign away a third of the business to Cora! It was galling to think that the money her sister-in-law took every week would have been enough to pay the rent on three, or even four, small houses.

'Mam!' Fion yelled. 'Geraldine O'Brien's here for her trim.'

'Coming, luv.'

Maurice Lacey had had nothing to eat or drink all day, having been confined to his room ever since the letter had come to say he'd failed the scholarship. Now he reckoned it was nearly teatime, and he was starving hungry and aching for a drink.

'You're bloody thick, you are,' Mam had screeched. 'Get up to your room, I'll punish you later. I daren't do it now, else I might kill you I'm so bloody mad. I thought you'd be dead clever like your dad.'

This was a very strange remark, as Mam usually claimed his dad was as thick as two short planks. He wondered if Cormac had passed and would like to bet he had. He'd also like to bet that Auntie Alice wouldn't have made a huge big scene if Cormac had failed. He felt envious of Cormac, having Auntie Alice for a mam. She didn't hug him and squeeze him and kiss him, the way his own mam did, but nor did she hit him either – there was no sign of a cane in Amber Street.

For the first time in his eleven years, Maurice was struck with the thought that life wasn't fair. There'd been nearly forty children in his class, but only a few had been expected to pass the scholarship. Were all those others who'd failed shut in a dark bedroom with the threat of the cane hanging over their heads? They were more likely playing football in the street or in the park, or had gone to the shore, like Cormac. Why was he always treated differently from everyone else?

'It's not fair!' A ball of misery rose in his parched throat, where it stuck and he couldn't swallow. He badly wanted to cry because he felt so unhappy.

The front door slammed, indicating his mam had gone out. Maurice tried his own door, but it was locked from the outside. He glanced out of the window, where the sun was shining brightly enough to split the flags, and felt a longing for fresh air, the company of his mates from school. He was rarely allowed out on his own.

In a garden behind he could hear the sound of children playing and through the trees he spied a swing. They actually had a swing of their own!

His heart in his mouth, he slid open the window, climbed out on to the kitchen roof, then shinned down the drainpipe to the ground.

He was free! There'd be hell to pay when Mam got back and found him gone, but right now Maurice didn't care. He'd always done his best to be good. He was never naughty, never got into trouble, never answered back. He'd tried with all his might to pass the scholarship. It wasn't his fault that the questions were too hard. Anyroad, his brain had gone numb. He couldn't think.

Without any idea where he was going, Maurice began to run. If he went to North Park he'd be sure to find someone to play with. Instead, some ten minutes later, he found himself outside Auntie Alice's hairdresser's. He wanted to see her pretty, kind face light up in surprise when he went in. She was fond of him, he could tell. He'd only been in the hairdresser's a few times, but he liked it very much. It was a cheerful place and everybody there seemed happy.

He opened the door and a bell chimed. His cousin, Fion, was brushing the floor and another lady was washing another lady's hair. There was no sign of his aunt.

'Hello, luv,' Fion exclaimed. 'Is your mam with you?'

Maurice shook his head. He liked Fion, who was inclined to make a fuss of him, but it was her mam he wanted.

'You look hot. Would you like a glass of cherryade?' Fion enquired. 'We've got some in the kitchen.'

'Yes, *please!*'

'I'll get it you in a minute, as soon as I've finished this floor. Me mam's in the yard, having a quick breather. It's been like a Turkish bath in here today. Fortunately, we'll be closing soon. Why don't you go and say hello.'

Maurice trotted down the salon, through the kitchen and into the yard, where Auntie Alice was sitting on a chair. Her face was a bit sad, he thought, but brightened considerably when she saw him.

'Hello, Maurice, luv.' She beamed. 'Are you out on your own? That makes a change.'

He had no idea what came over him, because all of a sudden he'd thrown himself at his aunt and she'd dragged him on to her knee, and he was sobbing his heart out, and she was stroking his face and saying, 'There, there, luv. Tell your Auntie Alice what's wrong.'

'I've failed the scholarship,' he bawled. 'Me mam shut me in me room and tonight she's going to kill me.'

'Oh, she is, is she!' his aunt said in an ominous voice.

'I didn't mean to fail. I tried dead hard, honest.'

'I'm sure you did, luv. The best anyone can do is try.'

'I'm dead stupid.' He sobbed.

'If everyone who failed the scholarship was stupid, then the world would grind to a halt,' his aunt said wisely. 'None of our girls passed, nor did I, nor your Uncle John. Neither did your mam, come to that. Anyroad, you're good at other things – footy, for instance. You're a much better player than our Cormac.'

'I suppose so,' Maurice conceded with a hiccup.

'And you're dead handsome.' She ran her fingers through his dark curls. 'I bet you'll break lots of hearts when you grow up, by which time you'll find yourself good at all sorts of things. Me, now, I used to think I was as daft as a brush, until I discovered I was good at doing women's hair.' She hugged him very tight. 'Now, don't you ever call yourself stupid again, do you hear?'

The bell went on the door and his aunt said, 'That's probably me final customer. All she wants is a trim. You can keep me company in the salon for a while, then I'll take you home.'

He pressed himself against her. 'I don't want to go home!'

'I'm afraid you'll have to, luv, otherwise your mam will call out the bobbies and I'll be charged with kidnapping.'

'I'm hungry, Auntie.'

'In that case I'll give you your tea, *then* I'll take you home.'

It's not right, Cora,' Alice said. 'To deprive an eleven-year-old of food and drink all day just because he didn't pass a silly exam ... well, it's just not right.'

'It's none of your business,' Cora argued hotly. 'How I treat me son is nobody's affair but me own.'

'It *is* my affair when I become involved,' Alice replied just as hotly. 'The poor little lad was forced to come to mine for summat to eat. He drank a whole bottle of cherryade and I don't know how many glasses of water. His throat must have been as dry as a bone.'

Cora cast around for something to say in excuse, but could think of nothing. She'd thought about Maurice with mixed feelings while she'd been out at the shops. She was slightly uneasy that he hadn't been fed all day, but at the same time her blood was boiling because he'd let her down and failed the scholarship. If Cormac had passed, which seemed likely, it meant Alice Lacey had got one up on her again. She'd give Maurice a good thrashing when she got home, teach him a lesson. A little thrill ran through her when she thought about afterwards, after she had forgiven him. He would fling his arms around her neck, tell her how much he loved her and she would hold him close, so very, very close. Then they'd have a lovely tea.

She went into the greengrocer's and bought a pound of new potatoes and a pound of peas, then to Costigan's for four slices of boiled ham, but remembered she had a husband and increased the order to six. Finally she bought a large cream cake in Blackledge's, Maurice's favourite, with raspberry jam as well as cream.

She was at home, putting the things away, unaware that Maurice wasn't in his room, when there was a knock on the door and Alice Lacey was outside, looking very cross indeed and holding a sulky Maurice by the hand. Cora had always thought her sister-in-law wouldn't say boo to a goose and hadn't realised she had such a temper.

She stood in the parlour, angrily waving her arms. 'It's not right,' she kept saying. 'In fact, it's cruel.'

It was a good half-hour before a strangely inarticulate Cora got rid of her. She slammed the door and stood with her back against it, breathing deeply. With each breath her own anger mounted – anger that it was no use directing against Alice. Anyroad, it was Maurice who was the cause of her shame.

She advanced on the living room, where he'd been sent out of earshot of the shouting women, and found him standing by the window. Children were playing in the house behind and their cries carried sharply on the calm evening air, emphasising the stillness and quietness of their own house.

'Don't you dare go round that bloody hairdresser's again,' Cora said in a grating voice. 'And if I shut you in your room, you bloody stay there. Do you hear me, lad?'

'Yes,' Maurice said distantly.

'Yes, what?'

'Yes, Mam.'

'You made a right show of me today, going to see Alice, telling her you were hungry. What the hell must she think of me?'

Maurice shrugged. 'Don't know, Mam.'

She had never known him appear so indifferent to her words and it only made her more angry still. Her head throbbed and she felt dizzy with rage. Hadn't he realised what he'd *done*? Didn't he understand she had to feel better than everyone else? She *had* to. As a child, dirty and unkempt, always hungry, the continual butt of her two elderly aunts' brutality, she had vowed to herself that one day she would *be* someone. She'd hardly ever gone to school, though hadn't minded, because the other kids made fun of her ragged clothes and lack of shoes, the nits in her hair and the fact that she smelt and was useless at every single lesson.

'It won't always be like this,' she used to tell herself as she lay down to sleep in the bedroom that was bare of everything except a mattress and a few flea-ridden blankets. 'When I grow up I'll live in a palace.'

She'd seen off her aunts in the end, but the following years had been hard. She had slept on the streets for a while, because no one wanted to give a job to a girl who couldn't add up, couldn't read, who didn't even know how to behave proper.

Eventually she'd got a live-in job cleaning for a woman who owned half a dozen lodging houses.

'Did no one ever teach you how to use a knife and fork?' the woman asked on her first night – Cora was eating the food with her fingers.

She'd learnt how to use cutlery, when to say 'please' and 'thank you', to wipe her bum when she went to the lavatory, to change her clothes before they began to smell. She'd learnt also to read and write, do sums. The woman she worked for had helped. She said Cora had a quick brain. It was a shame she hadn't learnt all these things before. She would have done well at school.

When she was twenty she'd met Billy Lacey, very personable and far better-looking than the men who'd shown interest in her so far. By the time he proposed, Cora had already realised he was a loser. She far preferred his brother, John, who was the dead opposite, but apart from being polite, otherwise he showed no interest in his brother's fiancée. Still, if she married Billy she'd get her own house. For a while it didn't matter that it was in O'Connell Street.

It hadn't been long before wishy-washy Alice Mitchell appeared on the scene, hanging like a leech on to the arm of John Lacey. Apart from her aunts, Cora didn't think she'd ever hated anyone before as much as she hated Alice on the day she married John and changed her name from Mitchell to Lacey.

The urge to *be* someone, to have beautiful things, was just as strong, but stronger still was the need to be one up on Alice Lacey. Cora thought she had achieved this with her handsome, stolen son, with the house in Garibaldi Road, with the third share she had wangled in the hairdresser's, but somehow Alice always seemed to go one better.

Cora stared balefully at the son who'd let her down so badly. She reached for the cane and flexed it between her hands. Nodding towards a chair, she said curtly, 'Bend over.'

To her everlasting surprise, Maurice ignored her.

'Bend over,' Cora insisted, aware a note of hysteria had crept into her voice.

'No.' He stuffed his hands in the pockets of his grey shorts and looked at her stubbornly.

'In that case . . .' She raised the cane and whipped it against his shoulders. It must have hurt through the thin cotton of his shirt, but it was like rainwater off a duck's back as far as Maurice was concerned. Cora raised the cane again and was taken aback when he caught the end in his hand. For several awful seconds they tussled over possession, but he was a big, strong lad for eleven, stronger than she was, and he easily won.

For a horrible moment, Cora half expected the cane to be turned on her. She cowered against the wall, arms raised protectively, but Maurice merely bent it till it broke in two. He threw the pieces on the table and stared at them for a long time, as if wondering why he'd never done it before.

'Huh!' he muttered and walked out of the room. She assumed he was on his way upstairs to sulk in his bedroom. Instead, seconds later, the front door slammed. Cora flew down the hall and opened it.

'Where are you going?' she called shakily.

'To the park to play with me mates.'

She'd lost him! Her body froze with horror. He was the only person in the world she had ever loved, the only person who had loved her in return.

She wanted him back, would do anything to get him back, but had a horrible, sickly feeling that it was too late.

And, as usual, it was all the fault of Alice Lacey.

She felt as if she'd been pregnant for ever. She could hardly walk she was so big. Maybe she was expecting quins like that woman in Canada. The bed creaked like mad every time she turned over and she turned over all night long, waking Micky, who was red-eyed with tiredness in the mornings.

But Orla didn't care. She didn't care if his eyes fell out or his head dropped off. All she cared about was herself and her predicament.

She hated Micky, whose fault it was that she was in this mess, and she hated her dad for not letting them have the parlour in Amber Street, a much nicer place to be. She hated her sisters: Fionnuala looked so superior, as if trying to say, '*I'd* never get in a mess like you,' which was probably true, as there wasn't a boy in Bootle who'd go near her, and you'd think Maeve had delivered hundreds of babies the way she kept offering advice, yet there wasn't a maternity ward in Bootle hospital.

Most of all, she hated the Lavins for . . . oh, for all sorts of reasons. There was always a row going on for one thing, or two or three rows, come to that, with people screaming at each other at the tops of their voices from rooms all over the house. She hated the way they came into the parlour to watch the bloody telly when she was trying to rest and instead she had Gilbert Harding or Barbara Kelly or Lady-stinking-Barnet bawling down her ear. She hated the fact that Mrs Lavin sent one of the kids every morning to pinch a bottle of milk off someone's step for the expectant mother, then sat, watching the same expectant mother while she drank every bloody drop, oozing bloody sympathy and acquainting her with the gory details of her own nine births.

It was horrible, sitting down to a nice meal of roast beef, or lamb chops, or chicken, to have Mr Lavin wink and say, 'You'll never guess where this came from!'

Orla had guessed months ago – well, who wouldn't! The food was stolen, it had 'fallen off the back of a lorry'. She imagined Mr Lavin running after a speeding lorry, picking up the joints of meat that were being scattered in its wake. All Mrs Lavin ever bought was vegetables. The other day there'd been a trifle, a huge thing in a fluted cardboard case.

'You'll never guess where that came from!' Mr Lavin winked.

How the hell had he managed to nick a *trifle*?

Orla groaned. If she were still working for the *Crosby Star*, she might be interviewing a politician right now, or have been sent to cover a murder.

The lovely chiming clock on the mantelpiece, which had no doubt come the same way as virtually everything else in the house, struck five o'clock. Mam would be back in Amber Street soon, and she'd go round and see her. It was the only place where she got any peace and Mam was the only person in the world whom she didn't hate. Oh, and their Cormac.

Alice was just unlocking the salon door on a drizzly morning in September when Micky Lavin skidded to a halt outside on a rusty bicycle. 'It's Orla,' he gasped. 'She's gone to the hospital. The pains started about an hour ago.'

'Oh, dear!' It meant the baby was going to be a fortnight early, or two and a half months early if people were expected to believe Orla had remained virtuous until her wedding night. People never would! She prayed the baby would be small so she could claim it was premature.

It was a terrible way to think when her daughter was about to give birth. Alice nudged the thought to one side and said anxiously to Micky, 'Is she all right?'

Micky rolled his eyes. 'Is Orla ever all right? She was screaming blue murder when I came to get you.'

'I'll look after the salon, Mam,' Fion offered. 'Patsy'll be along shortly and Doreen's in this avvy. We'll manage between us, don't worry.'

'Ta, luv.' There were times when Fion could be extremely capable. 'I'll try and ring from the nursing home, tell you what's happening, like.' To Micky she said, 'You get along back, luv. I'll catch a tram. I'll be there in no time.'

Orla was in a side ward still screaming blue murder, when her mother arrived, out of breath, excited and at the same time dreading the next few hours.

'It hurts,' Orla yelled. 'Oh, Mam, the pains hurt really, really bad.'

Alice's heart sank when she saw Mrs Lavin sitting in a chair next to the bed. She was holding Orla's hand and singing a lullaby for some reason. 'Rock-a-bye baby, on the tree top . . .'

No wonder Orla was screaming.

'Why don't you go home, Mam, and see to the brekkies,' Micky suggested, as if sensing the presence of his mother wasn't helping.

'. . . when the tree falls, the baby will stop,' Mrs Lavin crooned. 'Or is it drop? Hello, Mrs Lacey. She's having a wicked time, just like I did when I had quite a few of mine. Our Micky, though, he just popped out, like a pea from a pod.'

'*Mam!*' Orla screeched.

'I'll take over now, shall I, Mrs Lavin? You've got little 'uns to see to, not like me.'

'Well . . .' Mrs Lavin seemed reluctant to give up Orla's hand or her seat beside the bed.

'I think they only allow two visitors, Mam,' Micky said.

'Oh, I'll be off then.' Mrs Lavin left after making Micky promise to come and tell her the minute the baby arrived. 'I'll bring some flowers and a bunch of grapes,' she said generously.

'Only if she finds a lorry for them to drop off,' Orla said through clenched teeth when the door closed. 'I'm more likely to get a side of beef or a chicken already trussed.'

'Try not to talk, luv.' Micky tenderly stroked the brow of his young wife. 'Save your breath for the pains. They're called contractions,' he said to Alice as if she didn't already know. 'They get closer and closer as the time comes for the baby to be born. I read it in a book,' he said proudly, 'that I got out the library.'

Orla had got a bloke in a million, Alice thought. It would take time, he was only twenty, but if she stuck it out she'd do well with Micky Lavin.

'Shurrup, Micky,' Orla snapped. 'Oh, there's another pain coming! Oh, Mam!'

Alice became quite impatient with her daughter as the morning progressed and she continued to scream and yell. There were two other women having babies at the same time and between them they didn't make half the fuss that Orla did. Alice suspected the screams were directed at Micky in an attempt to make him feel guilty.

The labour lasted five and a half hours and Orla was whisked to the delivery ward the minute the midwife judged her ready to give birth.

Alice and Micky sat in the corridor outside and waited for the screams to start again. To their surprise, in no time at all, the door opened and the midwife appeared. 'It's a girl,' she said jubilantly. 'She's absolutely beautiful and a whole seven pounds, two ounces. I've never known such a swift and painless birth. Congratulations – Dad! Would you like to come and see your daughter?'

Micky looked wistfully at Alice. 'Now it's all over, I wonder if she'll be happy? Will she stop blaming me, do you think? I love her, Mrs Lacey. I love her more than anything on earth.'

'I know you do, luv.' Alice kissed him, but felt unable to offer a single hopeful promise for the future. Her wilful, strong-minded daughter apparently considered this rather decent young man had ruined her life for ever.

'I'll go and see her now.' Micky was scarcely gone a minute, when he came out again. 'She wants you,' he said. His eyes were bright with tears.

'Why don't you nip home and tell your mam?' Alice said.

'I'll do that.' He looked relieved to have something to do.

The midwife had been right! The new baby was beautiful, a perfectly formed little girl, not the least bit red or crumpled like some babies and already with a fine head of dark, curly hair. Her eyes were wide open and her tiny body wriggled impatiently against the tightly wrapped blanket.

'She's going to be a lively one,' her grandmother whispered. 'I suppose it's all right if I pick her up.'

As she nursed her first grandchild, Alice wished with all her heart that John were there, not the John of now, but the one she had married. This was a unique moment, the sort a woman should share with her husband. She sighed. *Her* husband seemed no longer interested in his family.

'Have you decided on a name yet?' she asked Orla. Names for the baby had been the only thing that had sparked her interest over the last months.

'Lulu,' Orla said listlessly.

Alice had never heard Lulu mentioned before and thought it awful, like a music hall turn or a silent film star. However, it seemed wise to keep her trap shut.

'Hello, Miss Lulu Lavin,' she whispered. The baby stirred in her arms and uttered a tiny cry. 'I think she might want a feed. Are you up to it, luv?'

'I'm not sure. I feel as if I've just been dragged through the mill and back again,' Orla said weakly.

'The midwife said she'd never known such a swift and painless birth.'

'How would she know?' Orla demanded in a voice that was suddenly weak no more.

Alice shrugged. 'Through experience, I guess. What was it you said to Micky to make him leave so quick?'

'I told him I didn't want to see him, that I wanted you. Frankly, I don't care if I ever see him or the Lavins again.'

'Then why did you marry the poor lad?'

Orla pouted. 'I didn't have much choice, did I?'

'You didn't have many choices,' Alice conceded, 'but you didn't *have* to marry him. Nor, I might remind you, did *he* have to marry *you*. Another chap might have run a mile, or claimed the baby wasn't his. But Micky did the honourable thing and you've made his life a misery ever since.' Oh, it was hard, speaking so sternly to her pretty, distressed daughter, who was probably expecting buckets of sympathy, not a lecture, off her mam. 'I take it the . . . er, the time you conceived, he didn't rape you, that you were just as much a willing partner as him?'

Orla blushed and didn't answer.

Alice was all set to continue with the lecture, but two nurses arrived to move the new mother to a ward and take the baby to the nursery, so she excused herself and went to look for a telephone. She rang Fion to let her know she was now an aunt.

'Nip home as soon as you've got a minute,' she said, 'and let our Maeve know. She'll be back from the General by now. She can tell Cormac when he gets home from school. Tonight, we'll all come together to visit Orla and the baby.'

Maeve wrinkled her pert little nose. 'It seems dead peculiar, having a sister who's a mother.'

'I know.' Fion nodded her head vigorously. 'Dead peculiar.'

'Have you ever done, you know, the thing Micky did with Orla to make her have the baby?'

'Lord, *no*!' Fion gasped. 'Have you?'

'What? And end up living in the Lavins' parlour with people sitting on the bed watching telly while you're trying to sleep? No, thanks, I wouldn't dream of it. You'd have to be mad.'

'Perhaps our Orla *is* mad!'

'Perhaps. Though I wouldn't mind *kissing* Micky Lavin,' Maeve said thoughtfully. 'He's a dish.'

'What's a dish?' enquired Fion, who wouldn't have minded kissing Micky Lavin either.

'Someone who's dead gorgeous. Montgomery Clift's dishy, and Frank Sinatra.'

'Neil Greene's dishier than both of them,' Fion said. She fancied kissing Neil even more than she did Micky Lavin.

In mid-afternoon Mr and Mrs Lavin arrived at the hospital, laden with fruit and flowers, and accompanied by four of the children. Visiting time was almost over. Before a nurse could complain there were too many visitors around the bed Alice left, promising to return that night.

Outside, the morning's drizzle had become a steady downpour and she wished she'd brought an umbrella. She stood in the rain and wondered whether to go home or to the salon. She didn't feel like doing either. Her nerves were on edge after the conversation with Orla. It worried her that the girl would refuse to see sense and eventually Micky would snap. There was only so much a person could stand. So far, Micky had been dead patient. But he wasn't a saint.

If only she could talk to someone – her dad or Bernie, but they'd be at work for hours yet.

She could talk to John. He might not agree, but it was every bit as much *his* problem as it was hers. Anyroad, despite the way he'd acted with Orla, he had a right to know he'd become a grandfather. And she wouldn't wait till tonight. She'd do it now while she was in the mood, go round to the yard and see him. You never knew, his attitude might change if he could be persuaded to see Lulu, who was without doubt one of the loveliest babies ever born. It was a pity the poor child had been blessed with such a dead silly name.

Alice had only a vague idea where the yard was situated: somewhere in Seaforth not far from the playing fields. Benton Street rang a bell. For some reason John had always discouraged them from going there. She caught the tram to the terminus in Rimrose Road, walked under the railway bridge and emerged in Seaforth.

The first three people she asked had never heard of Benton Street, nor a firm called B.E.D.S. The fourth, a woman, had an idea the street was near the playing fields.

'That's right,' Alice said eagerly.

The directions were complicated. Turn right, then left, then right again at a big pub the woman couldn't remember the name of. Go half a mile down Sandy Road, turn left at a greengrocer's and Benton Street was the second turning on the right, or it might be the third.

Alice got wetter and wetter as she negotiated the complicated maze of streets. She thought about giving up, but decided she couldn't, not after having made it this far.

She was soaked to the skin by the time she turned into Benton Street and hoped John had a towel so she could dry herself. A wooden sign with B.E.D.S. painted on it was attached to a pair of tall iron gates, just round the corner in a place called Crozier Terrace, a cul-de-sac with no more than ten tiny houses either side.

Her heart sank when she tried the gates and found them locked. Surely John didn't lock himself in! Behind the gates a two-storey building had a light on upstairs. It was probably the office. Alice rattled the gates in the hope of attracting her husband's attention, but to no avail.

Disappointed, she turned away. After coming so far! She wondered where he could be. Maybe he'd gone to the timber yard for wood. Alice frowned. If that was the case, what was that smart green van doing parked inside the gates? Did it belong to John? It looked new, but he'd never mentioned having a van. She noticed a wire strung across the street attached to the top half of the building, the office. He hadn't mentioned having a telephone either.

'You'll find him at home, luv.'

'I beg your pardon?'

A woman had emerged from one of the tiny houses in Crozier Terrace. She was sensibly shielded from the rain in a plastic mac and hood. 'Mr Lacey, he's gone home to see his missus. I saw him pass me winder less than ten minutes ago.'

'You can't possibly have!' John had never been known to come home during the day. Anyroad, he'd have to go the other way, down Benton Street, not past this woman's window. There was no way out of Crozier Terrace.

'Please yourself, luv.' The woman shrugged. 'But I don't doubt the evidence of me own eyes. You'll find Mr Lacey in the end house, number twenty.'

She must be mad. Alice watched the woman walk away, then gave the gates another shake. Still no one came. She was about to walk away herself but, feeling curious, went down Crozier Terrace to number twenty. She took a step back and looked it up and down. It was a perfectly ordinary house, identical to the others, with pretty, flowered cretonne curtains. There was a vase of dried leaves in the window. The front door and the sills were painted maroon.

The woman had been talking nonsense. She couldn't possibly be right. On the other hand, how could she possibly be wrong? She'd referred to 'Mr Lacey'. She lived within spitting distance of the yard, so she must know John well. And another thing, Alice's heart began to pound painfully in her chest, it was John who insisted on maroon every time he painted the outside of their house in Amber Street. She would have preferred bottle green herself.

'His missus,' the woman had said. 'He's gone to see his missus.'

'But that's *me*,' Alice said aloud. She wondered if she should go home, *run* home, forget the house, what the woman had said, just wait for John tonight and tell him about Orla. She would never mention having been to the yard. Perhaps it would be best not to know whatever secrets might lie behind this door.

But she *had* to know. She would never rest until she did. There was still a chance that the woman had got things wrong, that it was another man who looked like John who'd passed her house. Except she'd called him Mr Lacey.

Maybe there were two Mr Laceys and they were similar!

Alice took a deep breath and knocked on the door.

After a few seconds it was opened by a young woman, heavily pregnant, with lovely soft fair hair. Through the door Alice glimpsed a simply but comfortably furnished parlour with a plain brown fitted carpet – she'd always fancied fitted carpets in her own house. There was something wrong with the young woman's face – she had a hare lip. Without it, she would have been extraordinarily pretty. A tiny girl, little more than a baby, clung to her leg and Alice felt herself go cold. The little girl could have been Orla at the same age. The young woman smiled, but didn't speak.

'John Lacey,' Alice said in a cracked voice. 'I've come to see John Lacey.'

'He's upstairs.' A little boy appeared. He had his mother's fair hair.

'Would you mind giving him a call, luv.' Alice still retained a shred of hope it was another man entirely upstairs.

'Dad!' the boy obediently yelled.

'Who is it, son?' John's voice called.

'A lady.'

There were footsteps and John came to the door. Alice, sick to her soul, was presented with the perfect picture of domesticity: the little girl, so like Orla, the boy with the fair hair, her husband, John, his arm laid casually round the shoulders of the pregnant woman.

When he saw Alice his face hardened and she glimpsed hostility in the brown eyes. He bundled his family out of sight, came outside, closed the door.

But by this time, Alice had already reached the end of Crozier Terrace and was running, racing, flying home. She didn't stop until she reached Amber Street.

Alice lay curled up in the armchair, knees pressed against her chest. There was something terrifying about her blank, staring eyes in a face that had lost all trace of colour. She looked like a ghost. Every now and then her body convulsed, as if she was about to have a fit, and the sobs that emerged fom her pale lips were strangely subdued.

A frightened Cormac had begun to cry, something he had hardly ever done when he was little. Maeve was visibly shaking.

Only Fionnuala, who could always be relied on to act sensibly in a crisis, managed to remain calm. 'What's wrong, Mam?' She shook her mother again and again. 'Mam, what's wrong?' But Alice seemed incapable of understanding, let alone providing answers.

'Perhaps our Orla's baby has died?' Maeve suggested.

'Or Orla herself?' Cormac's lip trembled.

'No,' Fion said. 'She would have told us. No, it's something different from that. She's had a terrible shock.'

Cormac managed to crawl on to his mam's knee, which he still did occasionally, despite the fact he was eleven and at grammar school. 'Mam!' He tenderly stroked her face. 'Oh, Mam!'

'Maeve,' Fion commanded, 'make a pot of tea. That might bring her round.'

Maeve hurried into the kitchen to put on the kettle. 'Should we fetch someone?' she asked when she came back.

'Who?' Fion asked simply. 'Anyroad, there's no need to fetch someone, she's got us. You know what I think we should do?'

'What?'

'Throw cold water on her. She's having a fit of some sort. I saw it once in the pictures. It's either water, or slapping her face and I don't know about you, but I couldn't bring meself to slap our mam. I prefer the water idea. She's already soaking from the rain, so it won't exactly hurt her.'

'Shall I fetch a bucketful?'

'A cup will do. *You're* the one who wants to be a nurse, Maeve Lacey. You should know about these things. Cormac, mind out the road, there's a good lad, we're going to throw a cup of water on our mam.' Fion dragged her brother off Alice's knee when he appeared not to hear.

'You do it.' Maeve handed Fion the water.

'You're going to make a hopeless nurse.' Fion took a deep breath and threw the water in her mother's face.

Alice screamed and violently shook her head for several seconds. 'Oh, my God!' she screamed again when she saw three of her children standing anxiously over her. 'What have I been saying?'

'Nothing, Mam. All you did was sort of cry.' Although relieved to see her mother all right again, Fion felt suspicious that things were being kept from her. Why should Mam be worried about what she might have said? 'Has Aunt Cora been at you over something?' she asked.

'No, luv.' Alice held out her arms and the children fell upon her. They might find out one day what their father had been up to, but they'd never hear it from her. She hugged them fiercely. 'I love you. I love you so much it hurts. Now, if someone doesn't make me a cup of tea soon, I think I'll bust.'

'The kettle's already on, Mam,' Fion and Maeve said together and disappeared into the kitchen. Cormac, with his mother all to himself, snuggled his face in her shoulder.

Alice felt dead ashamed. She had only a vague memory of being in the chair, having lost all grip on reality. There'd just been that awful feeling you had when you woke up from a horrific dream, unsure whether it was true or false. For the first time in her life the dream had turned out to be true.

Perhaps her brain and her body had been fighting against the truth, praying for the dream to turn out to be just that, a dream.

John! Till the end of her days she would never forget the look on his face, as if she were a trespasser on his happiness. It would have been far preferable if he'd just walked out of Amber Street, left them. But to set up another home, with another woman, other children!

Fion and Maeve came in with tea on a tray and a plate of digestive biscuits. 'Is Orla all right?' Fion demanded.

'She's fine and the baby's lovely.' Alice realised she'd have to explain the hysteria. Now seemed the time to tell them their dad wouldn't be coming home. 'I went round the yard to tell your father about Orla and we had a big bust-up. He's not coming back.'

'But what about us?' Cormac wailed. Fion and Maeve didn't appear particularly upset.

'We never got round to discussing you, luv. I know' – she had an idea – 'you can telephone him from the salon, arrange to meet somewhere.' She hoped John would be nice to the son he'd once loved so much, that he wouldn't regard him as a trespasser as he had done his wife. She remembered the other little boy and wondered what his name was. 'Son,' John had called him. 'Who is it, son?'

'A lady,' the child had replied.

It would be easy to cry again, but not now, not with the children there. She'd already frightened them enough. Cormac was still on her knee. She hugged him hard. He adored his dad and would miss him more than any other member of the family. Well, *this* family, she thought drily. From now on, John's other family would have him all to themselves.

'She looked so pretty, so nice,' Clare wrote quickly in her neat, precise hand. She started to weep again. 'I feel terrible. So should you,' she added, underlining the 'you'.

'I do,' John said in a heartfelt voice. He did indeed feel terrible, but he also felt very hard. He couldn't get Alice's shocked white face out of his mind, but there was no way he would let her spoil things between him and Clare.

Clare was writing again. 'We should have lived further away. It was always dangerous here.'

'We'll move as soon as possible.' He didn't want Danny Mitchell or one of the girls coming round to make a scene. They could yell at him all they liked, but he wasn't prepared to let Clare or his children be subjected to abuse, though he had a feeling Alice would keep things to herself. She'd be too ashamed and embarrassed to tell anyone, not even her dad or Bernadette.

He wondered aloud why she'd come to the yard in the first place and Clare wrote, 'Perhaps your daughter has had her baby?'

John smiled and stroked her swollen belly. If that was the case, it was possible he would become a grandfather and a father again within a single week.

'You should go to see the baby.' Clare supported the stumbling words with a movement of her hands, as if shooing him out of the house.

'I can't, not now.' He shook his head. 'Alice might be there. Anyroad, I'm not particularly interested.'

'Should be.' She nodded fiercely. 'Should be. Not right.'

'I'm the person to judge what's right or not.'

'I think we should wait a few days before we tell Orla about your dad,' Alice said when the children were ready to visit their sister. 'It's said every cloud has a silver lining, and your dad going means Orla and Micky can move into the parlour. That'll be nice, won't it, eh?'

Maeve and Cormac thought it a great idea, but Fionnuala wasn't so sure. 'Will the baby cry much?' she wanted to know.

'We'll just have to see, luv. Now, are you sure you don't mind me not coming with you? I don't feel as if me legs will carry me far tonight. Just tell Orla I'm a bit off colour, but I'll be at the front of the queue of visitors in the morning.'

'Are you sure you'll be all right on your own?' Fion asked.

Alice couldn't wait for them to go, to be on her own, to think. 'I'll be fine,' she said heartily. 'I'll be even better after a rest. Now, are you sure you've got your tram fare? Maeve, be careful how you hold them flowers, else you'll have the heads off. Cormac, put some stouter shoes on. It's still raining outside.'

She ushered them into the hall – her legs felt as heavy as lead – waved to them from the step, returned to the house, slammed the door, then let go.

'You bloody hypocrite, John Lacey!' she screamed. 'You made me life a misery, accusing me of having affairs, when all the time . . .' She aimed a kick at the skirting board and hurt her foot. 'You even called our Orla names.' What was it? A little whore. In that case, what was the women he lived with?

Unless she didn't know he was married! Perhaps he was a bigamist. If he was and if it hadn't meant she'd never be able to hold up her head in Bootle again she would have reported him to the police.

No wonder he handed over such a pitiful amount of housekeeping every week – he was buying fitted carpets for his other house, buying vans, having a telephone installed in the office. She would have loved a fitted carpet in the parlour. And it would have been nice for the whole family to have gone places at weekends in the van. When Cormac passed the scholarship, she could have rung him from the salon, not stayed up till midnight to let him know. In fact, if she'd known about the telephone she would never have discovered his double life – she would have merely rung to tell him about Orla.

Alice went into the parlour and kicked the bed that he'd slept on, then collapsed upon it, sobbing. Oh, God! It *smelt* of him. The whole house smelt of him: not just the bed, but the chairs, the very air. She had to get out of here and there was only one place she could go and think in peace, a place where there was nothing to remind her of John.

She sat in her favourite place under the middle dryer. The nights were fast drawing in, it was almost dark. But it had been dull and miserable all day.

'It's been the worst day of me life,' Alice whispered.

Her anger had been replaced by, of all things, guilt. Guilt that he'd felt the need for another woman because his own wife hadn't been sufficiently understanding. She'd tried but, somehow, in some way, she'd let him down. Perhaps she'd been selfish, taking over the hairdresser's when he would have preferred her at home. Mind you, it had seemed dead unreasonable at the time and still felt unreasonable when she thought about it now.

The young woman at the door had had something wrong with her face, a hare lip. Perhaps he felt more comfortable with someone imperfect, like himself. But it was still no excuse for having betrayed his wife and children, for taking the coward's way out.

Alice jumped when there was the sound of a key being turned in the salon door. It turned several times before it was opened and Neil Greene said, 'It wasn't locked. Alice must have forgotten.'

He had someone with him, a woman, who was laughing helplessly. Alice wondered bleakly if she herself would ever laugh again. She prayed the light wouldn't be turned on – she'd look an idiot, sitting in the dark on her own.

'I can't see a thing,' the woman giggled.

'Just a minute,' Neil said, 'the switch is over here.'

The room was flooded with light. Neil took a startled step backwards and his companion uttered a little cry when they saw the red-faced, red-eyed, swollen-faced Alice, who remembered she hadn't combed her hair since morning and it had got soaking wet, as well as her clothes, which she hadn't changed. She must look like a tramp who'd broken in, in the hope of finding a night's shelter.

'Alice!' Neil's face was full of concern. 'Are you all right?'

'I'm fine. Our Orla had the baby and I didn't manage to get in earlier. I thought I'd come and tidy up a few bits and bobs.'

'In the dark?' Neil's companion looked considerably put out. She was smartly dressed in a grey flannel costume, yellow blouse and hat. Her hair was perfectly set in a series of stiff, artificial waves. Alice would never have allowed a customer to leave Lacey's with such unnatural-looking hair.

'I must have dozed off.' Alice stood up, too quickly. She swayed, nearly fell and had to sit down again.

Neil said, 'Jean, I think it would be best if you went home. I'll drop in at the bank at lunchtime tomorrow.'

Jean made a little moue with her mouth. 'But, darling . . .'

'Tomorrow, Jean.' Neil put his hands on her shoulders and propelled her towards the door. 'Goodnight.' The door closed and he turned to Alice. 'What on earth is wrong? You look like shit.'

'Don't swear,' Alice said automatically, then remembered he wasn't one of her children. 'I'm sorry.'

'You're quite right. Teachers shouldn't swear.' He regarded her sternly. 'Alice, will you please tell me what's the matter?'

'Put the light out.'

He switched off the light. 'Is Orla's baby all right? Is Orla herself?'

'Orla's fine, the baby's beautiful.'

'Girl or boy?'

'A girl. She's calling her Lulu.'

'That's a pretty name. Lulu Lavin, sounds like a flower.' He came and sat beside her. 'Are you going to tell me now that it's dark?' His voice sounded very close, only inches from her ear.

'I can't, Neil,' she said brokenly. 'You're being very kind, but I can't tell anyone, not even me dad or me best friend. It's something truly awful.'

'A trouble shared is a trouble halved, so people say.'

'I've said it meself more than once, but I'm not sure now if it's true.'

'If it's really so awful, Alice, you should tell someone. It doesn't have to be me. You shouldn't keep it all to yourself.'

Alice said wryly, 'You sound as if you know about such things, but I can't imagine anything awful's ever happened to you.'

He was always cheerful and extraordinarily good-humoured, as if he found the world a wonderful place to be. She understood he was an excellent teacher – everyone at St James's liked him, though it was considered a mystery what he was doing there when he could have been teaching at a public school, or in a different job altogether. He'd been to university and had a Classics degree, whatever that was. He came from somewhere in Surrey and wasn't short of a few bob – one of her customers who knew about such things said his suits and shoes were handmade. His car was an MG sports.

His mam and dad were referred to as 'moms' and 'pops', and he had an elder brother called Adrian and a sister, Miranda, whose twenty-first birthday it had been in August. Instead of a party, Miranda had had a dance at which some well-known orchestra had played: Ted Heath or Ambrose or Geraldo, Alice wasn't sure. It wasn't that Neil showed off, but he sometimes talked about his private life.

It could have been embarrassing, having someone so dead posh living in the upstairs flat, but Neil hadn't an ounce of side. Alice had always felt completely at ease with her tenant. And he was always gentle with Fionnuala, whose crush on him was plain for all to see.

'What are you doing tomorrow?' he asked.

'Why, coming into the salon, like normal,' she said, surprised at the question.

'Act as if nothing dreadful has happened, laugh, smile, be your usual sunny self?'

'Well, yes, of course.'

'We all do that, Alice,' he said with a dry laugh. 'We all put on a show, no matter how we feel inside. What makes you think I'm any different?'

'I'm sorry, luv.' Alice impulsively laid her hand on his. 'I was being insensitive. It's just that you act as if you don't have a care in the world.'

'It wasn't always so. Seven years ago I wanted to kill myself.' He put his other hand on top of hers. 'If I tell you about it, will you tell me in turn why you are looking so utterly wretched? I got the fright of my life when I turned on the light. I thought the hairdresser's must be haunted.'

'I'm sorry,' Alice said abjectly. 'And I made you get rid of poor Jean.'

'Poor Jean will already have got over it.' He pulled her to her feet. 'If we're going to exchange confidences, let's go upstairs where it's comfortable and we can do it over a cup of coffee or, better still, a glass of brandy. A drink will probably do you good.'

'Give us a minute first to comb me hair.'

There were still a few pieces of furniture in the flat that had belonged to Myrtle – a sideboard, a glass-fronted china cabinet, the bedroom suite, though Alice had bought a new mattress. The two armchairs, the small table with matching chairs and the kitchen dresser were good quality second-hand.

She'd been upstairs a couple of times since Neil moved in. He had added things of his own – some exotically patterned mats that had come all the way from Persia, lots of bright pictures, a pair of table lamps that cast a rosy glow over the rather gloomy room. The china cabinet was full of books and there was a statue of an elephant on top, which Neil said was made of jade. There were more jade statues on the mantelpiece.

'It's lovely and cosy up here,' she said when he switched on the lamps.

'That was my intention. Would you like coffee or brandy? I suggest the latter.'

'That would be nice, though not too much, else it'll go to me head.'

He grinned. 'That mightn't be such a bad thing. Now, sit down, I'll get the drinks, then I'll tell you the story of my life.'

Instead of an armchair, Neil sat on the floor with his back against it, his long legs stretched out across the mat. He turned on the electric fire, not the element, just the red bulb behind the imitation coals. The room looked cosier still.

'You know I was in the Army, don't you?' he began.

Alice nodded. 'You joined in nineteen forty-two when you were eighteen.' She also knew he didn't have to join. He'd been accepted by Cambridge University and could have stayed to finish the course, by which time the war would have been over.

'What you don't know, Alice, is that I got married when I was twenty.'

'Married!' she gasped, startled. He appeared to be one of the most *un*married men she'd ever known.

Neil wagged his finger. 'Don't interrupt. I'd like to get this over with as quickly as possible. I married my childhood sweetheart, Barbara. Babs everyone called her. She was, still is, no doubt, quite gloriously pretty. Our parents had known each other for years before we were born. Even now,' he said thoughtfully, 'I'm not sure if we ever loved each other, or it was a case of doing what was expected of us. It *seemed* like love, it *felt* like it and we were happy to go along with our parents' expectations – superbly happy, I might add.'

He stared into the fire, as if he'd forgotten Alice was there. 'We married the year before the war ended. I was stationed in Kent at the time. I got special leave – we even snatched a weekend's honeymoon at Claridge's. That's a hotel in London,' he added in case Alice had never heard of it, which she hadn't. 'Babs worked for a government department, something to do with rationing. She had a little mews cottage in Knightsbridge. From then on, it's where I spent my leave, though she claimed to feel lonely when I wasn't there.' His lips twisted. 'Now that she was a married woman, she didn't lead the wild social life she'd done before. So I used to tell my fellow officers when they were going to London, "Drop in on my Babs. She'll make you feel at home for a few hours." And they did. Would you like more brandy, Alice?'

'Not yet. Perhaps later.'

'I think I'll replenish my glass.'

He got to his feet, a tall, extremely good-looking and suddenly rather tragic young man, Alice thought, even though she didn't yet know the end of the story.

'Nine months after the wedding,' he continued when he had returned to his place on the floor, 'we were posted to France. The Brits had taken it back by then. Soon we were in Germany, on our way to Berlin. We were in Berlin on the wonderful day the war was declared over. That night we had a party in the mess. Everyone drank too much, me included. Things got wild. Then a chap I hardly knew, I'd never spoken to before, mentioned this "little tart", as he called her, who he'd slept with in London. He intended calling on her the minute he got back. Her name was Barbara Greene and she'd been recommended to him as a "good lay" – that's an American term, so I understand. The chap said he felt sorry for her poor sod of a husband. Then another chap butted in who also knew Barbara Greene – she'd taught him a few tricks he didn't know, he said.' Neil laughed bitterly. 'Before long, it seemed as if the entire bloody regiment was claiming to have slept with Babs.'

'Oh, luv!' Alice breathed. 'That's terrible. What did you do?'

'I got blind drunk. I was probably the only Englishman on earth who wanted to kill himself on such a momentous night.'

'What did you do – *after* that night?'

Neil shrugged. 'Saw out the rest of my service, got demobbed, went to see my lovely wife and told her it was over. She wasn't particularly upset. We went our separate ways. A few years ago she asked for a divorce, but I refused. We're both Catholics, you see. I don't think a divorced teacher would be acceptable to a Catholic school board.'

'So, you're still married?'

'Yes. As I have no intention of ever marrying again, what does it matter?' He shrugged once more. 'Would you like another drink now? I definitely would.'

'I wouldn't mind a little bit. You're not going to get blind drunk tonight, are you?' Alice asked anxiously.

'No.' He stretched his arms, put them behind his neck and grinned. Suddenly he looked his old self again. Alice felt relieved. 'I'm over getting plastered. I'm over Babs, if the truth be known. But I shall never get over the sense of betrayal. How could she *do* such a thing? I still ask myself that from time to time.'

'What made you become a teacher?'

'I'm not sure.' He considered the question. 'After I finished Cambridge, I felt the urge to escape from the world I'd always known, do something entirely different. I took up teaching, much to my folks' horror. They thought it a terribly middle-class thing to do. They regard themselves as very much upper-class, you see.' He looked at Alice, his eyes sparkling with merriment. 'I've never told you this, but my father is Sir Archibald Nelson Middleton-Greene.'

Alice burst out laughing. 'That's a mouthful. Am I supposed to have heard of him?'

'No. I'm pleased you're amused rather than impressed.'

'Oh, I'm impressed all right.'

'Are you feeling better?'

'Loads better.'

'Me too. I've never told anyone all that before.' He refilled her glass for the third time. 'Now it's your turn to bare your soul.'

'It doesn't feel so bad now. I mean, it's still awful, it just doesn't feel as bad inside.' She told him the story right from the beginning, about how happy she and John had been with their four lovely children, then when John had burnt his face and everything had changed. She told him the awful things he'd called her. 'Then suddenly he changed again.' He'd started staying out a lot. They hardly saw him.

'Today I went round to the yard to tell him about Orla. He'd always discouraged us from going before. You'll never believe what I found.' She described knocking on the door and it being opened by the very pregnant young woman with fair hair and a toddler attached to her knee. 'She smiled at me ever so nicely.' Then the little boy came and shouted upstairs for his daddy. 'By then, I knew it must be John, but it still knocked me for six when he appeared. And his eyes! They were dead horrible. I felt about *this* big.'

Alice held up her thumb and forefinger about quarter of an inch apart. 'But do you know what gets me more than anything?'

'What, Alice?'

'It sounds daft, but she had a fitted carpet. John knew I'd always wanted a fitted carpet for the parlour. It made me realise how much he put this other family before his real one. It's as if we don't matter any more.' She sniffed. 'Oh, Lord, Neil. I think I'm going to cry again and I haven't got a hankie.'

'I'll get you one.' Neil leapt to his feet and returned with a clean, but unironed, white handkerchief. To her total astonishment he knelt beside her and began to dry her eyes, which she thought a trifle unnecessary. There didn't seem any real need to kiss them either, so that she felt her lashes flutter against his lips. It was years since John had touched her and it made her feel uncomfortable, even though it was undeniably very pleasant.

'You don't have to do this, you know,' she mumbled.

'I'm doing it because I want to, not because I have to.' Neil slid his arms around her waist. 'I've been lusting after you, Mrs Lacey, since the day I first set foot in the salon.'

'But I'm thirty-eight,' Alice gasped.

'I don't care if you're eighty-eight, you're utterly adorable.' He pulled her towards him and hugged her very tight.

'Neil.' She tried to struggle out of his arms. 'You've had too much to drink.'

'No, it's you who hasn't had enough. Stay still, Alice. I promise I won't touch you anywhere that's out of bounds.'

Alice sat stock still, knowing she should leave, but curiously reluctant to move an inch, while Neil traced her eyebrows with his finger, then her ears, her cheeks, her nose. The world had gone very quiet and, apart from the ticking of a clock somewhere, there wasn't a sound to be heard. Neil's firm finger traced her jaw and she could smell soap on his hand. John had always been a tender lover, but he'd never done anything like this. The finger moved to her lips and Alice felt as if her bones had melted inside her body. Then Neil bent forward and kissed her gently, ever so gently, on her forehead and she couldn't resist another minute. She flung her arms round his neck, feeling like a wanton woman, but not caring a bit.

7
1956

Maeve Lacey got engaged on her twenty-first birthday. Her fiancé, Martin Adams, was a colourless, fussy young man who was a radiographer at Bootle hospital. They had been courting two years, but weren't planning to get married until Maeve was a State Registered Nurse and they had saved up a deposit for a house.

Alice was pleased that it all sounded so very sensible when compared with Orla's shotgun wedding. She remarked as much to her friend, Bernadette, who was helping prepare the food for what would be the party to end all parties that night.

'Me and Bob were sensible, and look where it got us?' Bernadette said darkly. 'Absolutely bloody nowhere.'

'Yes, but you're all right now.' Alice giggled. 'Mam!'

'Oh, shurrup.' Bernadette nudged her friend's ribs. 'Stop being so cheeky, else you might get your bottom smacked.'

Three years ago, when Alice had held a similar party on the occasion of her father's, Danny's, sixtieth birthday, Bernie had taken her courage in both hands and proposed.

'Neither of us is getting any younger,' she said to the astonished birthday boy. 'I can't stand you, Danny Mitchell. If the truth be known, you drive me wild, but at the same time I think we'd be good together. I fancy you something rotten and I know you fancy me, so don't look so outraged.'

Danny had spluttered something incomprehensible in reply.

'If you're agreeable,' Bernadette went on, 'I think we should get wed as soon as possible while we've both got a bit of life left in us. And before you accept, I should tell you I'd very much like a baby. I'm thirty-nine, so if we go at it hammer and tongs, there's still time for you to put me in the club.'

Danny had spluttered something incomprehensible again.

'Think about it,' Bernadette said kindly, patting his arm. 'Take your time, but try and let me know before the party's over, so we can announce it, like, while everyone's here.'

Four weeks later Bernadette became Mrs Danny Mitchell and stepmother to her best friend. Within a year Alice was presented with a brother, Ian, and a sister, Ruth, the year after.

Danny was rarely seen in the pub these days, only on Sundays after Mass. He was content to stay indoors with his pretty wife and two young children, and watch the new telly at night, much to the chagrin of the numerous women who'd had their eye on him.

'You've made me dad very happy,' Alice said as she rolled sausage meat into a length of puff pastry. 'And he thinks the sun shines out Ian's and Ruth's little bottoms. I never thought I'd see the day when he'd take two kids in a pushchair for a walk in North Park.'

'Well, he didn't have much alternative, did he?' Bernadette sniffed. 'I'd promised to give you a hand.' She removed a baking tray from the oven. 'How many jam tarts do you want? There's a dozen here and another dozen just on finishing.'

'Well, there's thirty coming,' Alice said thoughtfully, 'but not everyone will want a tart. I reckon that's enough.'

'What shall I do now?'

'Pipe some cream on those little jellies, then sprinkle them with hundreds and thousands. Oh, by the way, could you bring some teaspoons when you come tonight? I haven't enough to go round. And some glasses too, if you've got any.'

'Of course we've got glasses. What do you think we drink the sherry out of at Christmas – mugs?'

The two women worked in contented silence for a while, each preoccupied with her own thoughts, while the smell from the kitchen became more and more mouthwatering. Two cats sat on the backyard wall, enjoying the crisp November sunshine and hoping they might be thrown the odd sausage roll.

'Who's looking after the salon today?' Bernadette enquired. 'Sat'days are your busiest day.'

'Our Fion. She's going to manage the new branch in Marsh Lane when it opens after Christmas, did I tell you?'

'Yes.' Bernadette rolled her eyes. 'New branch! Get you, Alice Lacey.'

'To think I used to look up to you when you had that good job with the Gas Board.' Alice wrinkled her nose and looked superior. 'Now you're just a housewife and I'm about to have me own chain of hairdressers.'

'I'd hardly call two a chain.'

'It's a *little* chain.' She laughed happily. 'It seemed a shame not to take on Gloria's when I discovered it was closing down – we were overstaffed once Fion got her certificate and I couldn't possibly have got rid of Doreen to make way for her. Doreen's going to Marsh Lane with Fion and I'm taking on another qualified assistant for meself. Patsy'll stay with me, naturally.'

'Their Daisy never got on the stage, did she?'

'No, she's married now, with two kids. Her husband's a chimney sweep if you'd believe it.'

'Well, I suppose chimney sweeps need wives the same as other men.'

'I think', Neil said, 'that I could become quite a fan of Elvis Presley.'

'He's OK,' Alice conceded. 'Our Fion's mad about him. She's got all his records. I prefer Frankie Laine meself.'

'This is a great party.' Neil put his hands on her hips and squeezed.

'Don't!' Alice said in a scandalised voice. 'Someone might come in.' They were in the kitchen in Amber Street and the party was going full swing. Elvis Presley was singing something about his blue suede shoes. 'Get out the way, Neil, while I make a pot of tea.'

'Don't you think people will have guessed by now how things are? It's been five years.'

'There's no reason for people to have guessed anything,' Alice said primly, 'and I've no intention of providing them with proof. I've got me reputation to consider and you've got your job. You'd be out on your ear if you were found having an affair with a married woman.' Like her, Neil was usually very discreet about their relationship and she wondered if he'd had too much to drink. 'Anyroad, me daughter's twenty-one today and I've got things to do,' she said brusquely. '*And* she's got engaged. Oh, hello, Cormac, luv. What can I do for you?'

'Are there any more jam tarts, Mam?'

'Sorry, luv. I thought two dozen'd be enough. There's plenty of jellies, though, some iced fairy cakes and loads of chocolate biccies. You'll find them on the sideboard in the parlour.'

'Ta, Mam.' Cormac vanished.

'He's not going to grow very tall,' Alice said. 'Not like his dad.'

'He's only sixteen, time to grow taller,' Neil said comfortably.

Maeve came in, her face flushed with happiness. 'Are there any clean glasses, Mam?'

'There will be if you fetch some dirty ones for me to wash.'

'I'll get some. Oh, by the way, Neil. Thanks for the scent. It's lovely.'

'I didn't know whether to buy a present for your birthday, or the engagement. Perhaps I should have bought one for each.'

'The scent's perfect. I haven't begun a bottom drawer yet.'

'She seems so certain of everything,' Alice said when her daughter had gone. 'It hasn't crossed her mind that things might change, not always for the better. Mind you, I was just as certain at her age.'

'So was I.' Neil sighed. 'But it's only natural that we expect our lives to pass smoothly along without a hiccup. If we were waiting for everything to fall around our ears, as it did with you and me, we'd all go bonkers.'

Alice opened her mouth to speak, but a girl she had never seen before came in and asked for the lavatory, Maeve brought the dirty glasses, someone asked if there were any more jam tarts and a lad rushed into the yard to be sick. Alice had the worrying feeling it had been Maurice Lacey, who wasn't old enough to be drinking.

Before he disappeared Neil blew her a kiss, which she affected to ignore in case anyone was watching. She poured a glass of sherry and decided to circulate, make sure the guests were enjoying themselves.

In the living room, Fion was conversing with Horace Flynn, whom she had insisted on inviting. Apparently it was all part of the war she had declared on Cora. Alice would have preferred her daughter in the parlour where everyone was dancing. She despaired of Fion ever finding a friend, let alone a man friend – other than their revolting landlord.

Cormac was doing card tricks for an admiring audience, Micky Lavin and Bernadette among them.

She found her dad sitting on the stairs with Orla. 'The ancient and the pregnant are having a bit of peace and quiet,' Danny quipped.

Orla was in the club again with her fourth child. The girl was sorely in need of advice on birth control, but had bitten her mother's head off when she had broached the subject. Still, the family now had a nice little house in Pearl Street since Micky had finished his apprenticeship and was earning a proper wage.

'How are you feeling, luv?' Alice asked sympathetically. It must be galling for someone only twenty-two and heavily pregnant to be surrounded by people mostly the same age who were all single, childless and obviously having a good time.

'How do you think I feel?' Orla snapped. She sometimes wondered if all she had to do was be in the same room as Micky to conceive. She'd heard it was unlikely to happen if you did it standing up. Well, *they'd* done it standing up and Lulu had arrived nine months later. The rhythm system had produced Maisie, the withdrawal system Gary. After Gary, Micky had worn a French letter, but here she was, once again looking like a bloody elephant. Micky must have bought the only French letter ever made that leaked. Every time a baby was born, they forced themselves to hold fire for at least six months, otherwise there'd be children popping out twice a year. When the six months was up, they'd leap upon each other the way people dying of thirst would leap upon a glass of water, draining the glass and wanting more. It wasn't a bit fair and she was fed up with Mr Lavin joking it was about time Micky tied a knot in it.

In future they'd just have to abstain, like priests. The trouble was, she loved Micky to death, though she wouldn't have dreamt of telling him. It was torture to lie in the same bed and not touch each other. And the children were too beautiful for words. Even so, it still wasn't fair.

Nothing seemed fair to Fionnuala either. Everyone was having a great time, but she'd been stuck with Horace Flynn the whole night because there wasn't another person in the house willing to speak to him. Of course, it was her own fault for asking him, but he'd seemed grateful and flattered – Fion suspected she was the only one in Bootle who treated him like a human being. She was definitely the only woman who allowed him to pinch her bum, something he did every time he came to the hairdresser's, which was often. Fion would grit her teeth and pretend to smile. 'Ooh, Mr Smith, don't be naughty!' she would say and move out of the way.

Mam didn't realise the sacrifices she was making to keep Horace Flynn on their side – he never went round to Garibaldi Road these days. The lease would be renewed again in a year's time and Fion hoped they might get it for nothing if she continued to let him pinch her bum. She just prayed he'd never stroke it.

It was galling to think that it was *her* records being played in the front room. 'Love me tender, love me do,' Elvis Presley crooned. Yet not one of those lads had thought to ask her to dance. Didn't they realise she was a fully qualified hairdresser who would be managing her own salon after Christmas?

Oh, if only she didn't feel so *old*! Old and fat, wretched and lonely. Her youth was passing her by, had already passed. She was twenty-three, but had never been kissed by a boy, yet one of her sisters was pregnant for the fourth time and the other had just got engaged. It was even more galling to think they were both younger than she was.

It was a relief when Mr Flynn decided to go home because it was getting too hot. He courteously shook her hand and rolled out of the house on his fat little legs. Seconds later, Neil Greene came and sat beside her, and Fion suddenly didn't know what to do with her hands. He was so handsome, yet not the least bit conceited and very kind. Talking to Neil always made her feel warm inside. She often wondered if he was in love with her, but too embarrassed to say. She fluttered her eyelashes at him encouragingly, but all he talked about was mundane things like the weather and what a great party it was, and he'd like to bet she was really looking forward to being in charge of the new Lacey's in Marsh Lane.

Alice, who happened to be passing, thought with a pang how pathetic Fion looked. The poor girl would feel betrayed if she ever discovered what was going on between her and Neil.

She'd never dreamt she was the sort of woman who'd have an affair, but Neil had caught her at a particularly vulnerable time and it had turned out to be quite wonderful. She had forgotten what it felt like to be loved, to feel feminine and wanted. And it was dead exciting, pretending to work late at the salon and going up to see Neil instead. Or remembering during the evening that there was something she'd forgotten to do. 'I'll just nip round to Lacey's,' she would say, giving a mythical reason, and Neil would be waiting for her, sometimes already in bed, because Alice wasn't prepared to stay long. He wasn't a masterful lover like John. Neil was always concerned that she was enjoying herself as much as he was.

So, what harm was she doing, apart from committing a sin? She wasn't sure if it was a mortal or a venial sin and there was no way she was going to ask a priest. Anyroad, it was only temporary, though it had already gone on longer than she'd expected. Somewhere in the world, she felt convinced, there was the perfect girl for Neil, someone bright and attractive who would give him children, the sort of girl he'd gone out with before but had been too scared to get serious with in case she turned out to be like Babs. *She* was nothing like Babs, *he* was completely different from John and she suspected that was where the attraction between them lay. But one of these days Neil would meet the perfect girl and have no use for Alice any more.

Alice wasn't sure how she would feel when that day came. Devastated, she suspected. She would miss him for as long as she lived. Perhaps that's why she was always so brusque with him, always in a hurry to get back home, because she didn't want him to feel guilty when the time came for him to let her go.

John Lacey had forgotten that today his daughter, Maeve, was twenty-one. He didn't know she had got engaged, or that Orla was expecting her fourth child, that Fion was now a qualified hairdresser and that Cormac had achieved six top-grade O levels before going into the sixth form at St Mary's in September. He wouldn't have known his mother, Meg, had died, had he not read it in the paper. He had decided not to attend the funeral.

It was years since Cormac had rung the yard, asking to see his dad. John had refused, though it had hurt. Cormac had been the favourite of his children, but he felt the need to shed his first family, leave them behind, concentrate on the new.

'Would you like more tea?' Clare said stiffly.

'I wouldn't mind.' He pushed the empty cup across the table. The atmosphere was thick with bitterness and suspicion.

'Is this how you treated Alice?' Clare curled her pretty pink mouth. 'Did you accuse her of going with other men, call her a prostitute, ask how much she'd earned?'

John ignored the question. 'I'd still like to know why the hell you were so late getting home,' he growled.

'I've already told you half a dozen times. It was such a lovely evening. Instead of catching the train from Exchange Station, I walked along the Docky as far as Seaforth and caught the train to Crosby from there. I watched the sunset. Is that a crime?'

'Did you call in the Arcadia, look up some of your old customers?' he sneered.

'No, I did not. I merely enjoyed a pleasant shopping trip to town. I bought a few early Christmas presents. I had a nice time. It's a pity you had to spoil it.' Her voice was as clear and tinkling as a bell.

It was happening all over again, the same thing that had happened with Alice. It was too late now, but he desperately wished he hadn't persuaded Clare to have surgery. He had read about it in a magazine. 'What do you think?' he asked, showing her the article. At first she had been reluctant. 'I have you, I have the children, I'm quite happy as I am,' she had written on her pad. How many pads had she completed in her short life? he had wondered.

'Yes, but you hardly ever go out,' he said. 'Have it done for the children's sake, if not for mine. They've never heard you speak, not properly. It doesn't affect them now, but it will when they grow older. Let at least one of us be perfect.' He remembered smiling.

Clare had reached out and touched his scarred face. 'What about you?'

'Nothing can be done about me, I'm afraid. The surgeon actually insisted it didn't look too bad.'

She shook her head. 'Surgeon right.' Then she wrote, 'Hardly noticeable, becoming weathered, like a tree or a house.'

The treatment had taken two years, it was more difficult for an adult. She was in and out of different hospitals as bit by bit her mouth and face were repaired with dental surgery, plastic surgery, reconstructive surgery to her palate. At first her voice had been hesitant, whispery, gradually becoming louder, clearer, more confident. She was left with a slight, attractive lisp.

Throughout the two years, during the times she was away, John had been totally supportive. He had arranged for a woman to look after Lisa and David who had yet to start school when the treatment started. He left the yard early to collect Robbie from school, make the tea. They'd been living in Crosby for years, in a large, semi-detached house not far from the shore – he could afford it; B.E.D.S. was doing extremely well.

She hadn't complained, not once, when she returned from various hospitals with her face swollen or badly bruised or in obvious pain or unable to make the slightest sound, though sometimes she looked frightened.

The time came when there was no more bruising, no more pain, no more operations. She began to say the words she'd always known, but could never say before. He'd always understood she was clever, but hadn't realised how clever until she began to talk – about politics, literature, religion, of things he didn't know about himself. She seemed to have opinions on anything and everything, as if she'd been storing them in her head, unable to express them before.

John suddenly realised she was an attractive, clever woman, with steady grey eyes, a small straight nose and a perfect, absolutely perfect, mouth. Even her hair looked different – fuller, shinier, more flattering around her face.

He must have been mad! If *he* thought her so attractive, so would other men. How stupid to have allowed, actually encouraged, her to become an object of admiration! Would he be able to trust her now that people didn't avert their eyes or regard her with an unhealthy fascination? How long would it be before she realised how lovely she was?

His brain was being split in two again, as it had been after that damned fire. He knew in his heart that Clare would never be unfaithful, just as he had known the same about Alice, but there was a different message in his head. He'd already started coming home from the yard at unexpected times to check on her. If she was out shopping, he'd wait until she came back, examining her face to make sure it didn't contain an expression that shouldn't be there. Once she'd been upstairs when he let himself in and he'd later searched the bedrooms, looking under beds and in wardrobes in case there was a man hidden there.

Clare wasn't as patient with him as Alice had been. She quickly lost her temper if he became suspicious. He wondered if her true personality was beginning to emerge, if the real Clare had been hidden until now.

'What did you buy in town?' he asked, doing his best to make his voice pleasant.

'Jumpers for Robbie and David, a woollen frock with smocking on the shoulders for Lisa. I thought I'd keep them for Christmas. I also bought a few small things for their stockings. Oh, and some more decorations. We hadn't enough last year.'

'Didn't you buy anything for yourself?'

Her eyes sparkled. She must have forgiven him for the things he'd said before. She leapt to her feet – even her movements seemed to have altered, she was more lively, more alert – and delved among the carrier bags on the floor. 'I bought myself a frock, almost a party frock. I've never had one before. I thought we could go somewhere on New Year's Eve, a dinner dance, maybe. The woman next door's always offering to babysit. I got it from Lewis's. What do you think?'

She held the frock up against her. It was black velvet, with a ruched bodice, a gently flared skirt and a scooped neck. The sleeves were long and tight, ending in a point. It was an entirely modest frock, but John felt a tightness in his chest when he visualised her wearing it. She would look a knock-out, turn every man's head.

'Oh, and I bought some high heels,' she said excitedly. 'Not very high, I'm not used to wearing them. They're black suede. See!' She slipped out of her old flat court shoes into the new ones and held out a foot for him to admire.

John could stand it no longer. 'Get them off!' he snarled. 'You're not going outside wearing them damn things, nor that frock. And we're not going to no dinner dance either. We'll stay at home on New Year's Eve like we always do.'

She looked at him with curiosity rather than anger. 'What's the matter with you? Did I have my face done for your eyes only? Am I supposed to stay indoors for the rest of my life just to please you?'

'You were quite happy to stay in before.'

'I was.' She nodded gravely. 'I was happy about everything before, but one of the reasons you persuaded me to have the operations done was so I could go out more. Today was the first time I've gone shopping on my own and been able to ask for things without feeling a freak. Why are you so intent on spoiling everything? Would you prefer I had the treatement reversed, be made the way I was before?'

There was much truth in the last remark. It had all been his idea and now he resented the result. As ever, pride prevented him from explaining how he felt. 'I'm going to bed,' he muttered.

He had reached the door when Clare said softly, 'John.'

'What?' He turned.

She was looking at him pityingly. 'I'm grateful for everything you've done for me,' she said in the same soft voice, 'although I realise it was done solely for selfish reasons. There was a time when you wouldn't have given me a second glance, when you wouldn't have set foot inside the Arcadia. But you did and we met, and the years since have been the happiest of my life.'

She gestured towards a chair, and he returned to the room and sat down. There was a feeling in his bones that what she was about to say was of tremendous importance. His legs were unsteady.

'I've grown to love you,' she continued, 'though I suspect you've never loved me. Please don't interrupt, John,' she said imperiously when he opened his mouth to argue. 'Let me have my say. If you truly loved me you wouldn't act the way you do. You would want me to be happy, not resent me. John.' She leant on the table and stared at him intently. 'I would like us to grow old together, but I am not prepared to be bullied and made a prisoner in my own house.'

'But . . .' he began, but Clare seemed determined not to let him get a word in edgeways.

'If you continue being so suspicious, cross-questioning my every move, then I shall take the children and leave, because you are making our lives unbearable. And that's not the only reason,' she went on. 'I shall leave before you go somewhere like the Arcadia, find a woman you don't feel inferior to and end up betraying me in the same way that you betrayed Alice.'

Where was he? Cora fretted. It was two o'clock in the morning and she'd never known Maurice stay out so late before. Billy's snores rumbled through the house. The snoring had been the reason she'd given for sleeping in the spare room over the last few years. Billy hadn't seemed to mind. Sometimes she wondered why he bothered coming home. It could only be for the warm bed and hot dinners – it certainly wasn't for his wife.

And now Maurice was going the same way. He'd become a labourer, just like Billy, though she hoped, unlike Billy, he'd learn a trade: bricklaying, plastering, something. Now he was earning money of his own and she hardly saw him. Even at weekends he went to the football with his mates and didn't reappear till all hours. Sundays he did the same disappearing act after a late Mass. She suspected he haunted pubs – well, he'd been shown a good example by Billy. Only sixteen, he could have passed for twenty.

There were times when she could have cried at the way things had turned out, but she'd never been given to crying and wasn't sure if she knew how.

Feeling restless, Cora edgily circled the room, picking up the occasional ornament that had given her so much pleasure to buy, but gave no pleasure now. What point was there in the place looking nice when she was the only one who saw it? Whom was she impressing with the house in Garibaldi Road, so much superior to the one in O'Connell Street? No one except herself.

There should be people to show it off to – friends, relatives, but Cora had never had a friend and she'd seen off her only relatives, the Laceys, years ago. Maeve Lacey was twenty-one today and getting engaged at the same time. Perhaps that was where Maurice was, at the party. He continued to be friendly with Alice and her kids, despite his mam's coldly expressed disapproval.

She'd heard about the party on the grapevine. Cora shopped in Marsh Lane and found it a simple matter to keep up to date with the Laceys' affairs. She knew Alice was taking over Gloria's and that Cormac had done so well in his exams that he was likely to go to university.

The key turned in the front door and Maurice came stumbling into the hall. 'Where have you been?' Cora demanded. He looked drunk, she thought.

'A party, Mam. Had a smashing time.'

'Was it Maeve Lacey's?'

'Yeh. I'm going to save up for a gramophone, buy some records. Fion had records and they were really the gear. Elvis Presley.'

'*I'll* buy you a gramophone,' she said. It would be painful, drawing the money out of the bank, but she was often driven to buying him things in the hope of winning him back, though nothing so far as expensive as a gramophone.

She was pleased when his face brightened in gratitude, but would have appreciated a kiss. 'Ta, Mam,' he said. 'I'm off to bed. I'll sleep in tomorrer, go to midday Mass.'

'I'll bring you up a cup of tea around half-eleven,' Cora promised. She watched him go up the stairs two at a time. He was every bit as good-looking as his dad, but was turning out to be a bitter disappointment. But how was she to have known that?

It was time she went to bed herself, except she hardly slept. Her mind never felt rested, never at ease. It used to be full of plots and plans for the future, but now it was more concentrated on the resentments of the present and the past.

It would have been nice to have gone to the Laceys' party. Much better than being at home by herself, with no one to talk to and the house like a tomb. Orla was likely to drop her baby soon and there'd be another big do for the christening. Cora wouldn't have minded going, buying a new frock, even getting her hair set.

Well, she knew what had to be done if she was to get back in with the Laceys. She'd have to tear up that agreement, rip it in two in front of Alice's eyes and give her the bits. After all, the investment, if you could call it that, had been returned a thousand times. It might even result in a resumption of relations with Horace Flynn – these days he only came round to Garibaldi Road to collect the rent.

She'd do it Monday, call in the haidresser's when she went to Marsh Lane shops. She might even buy a present for Orla's baby so they'd feel obliged to ask her to the christening.

Her mind wasn't at its normal feverish pitch when she went to bed and she fell asleep with unusual speed. During the night she was woken by the familiar creak of the third-to-top stair. Either Billy or Maurice was going to the lavvy. But the lavvy was on this floor and there was no need to go downstairs. The creaking sound must have come from the landing, though she could have sworn it was the stairs.

'I think,' Alice announced, 'I'll nip round the salon and practise a bit with them new mesh rollers.'

'Why don't you practise at home?' enquired Fion.

'Because the rollers are at the salon. They only arrived yesterday.' Alice wished she'd thought of another excuse. On reflection, this one seemed rather weak.

'Can I come with you?' Fion said eagerly. 'I quite fancy a bouffant hairdo. They're all the rage in London.'

Alice tried to think of a reason for saying no, but couldn't. It was Sunday afternoon and, as usual, Fion was the only one in the house besides herself. Apart from two cigarette burns on the parlour carpet, the house was pristine after Maeve's party the night before.

She was about to say, 'All right, luv,' because it would have been cruel to say anything else, when Maurice Lacey came in the back way, apparently to see Fion for some odd reason, and she was able to escape.

Alice always felt as if she was entering a different world from the one she knew when she went into Neil's flat. Wedding lines had given her and John permission from the Lord to make love, but lying in Myrtle Rimmer's old bed with Neil made Alice feel another person altogether, as if she'd removed her cloak of conventionality and left it outside Neil's door.

There was something faintly indecent, yet at the same time totally delicious, about letting Neil's tongue flutter against her nipples, his hands caress her body, every single part of it. Sometimes the sensations were so intense, so amazing, that she cried out, which Neil said later when she expressed embarrassment was perfectly all right and women did it all the time.

On the Sunday after Maeve's party Alice unlocked the salon door and went inside.

'Is that you?' Neil called.

'No, it's me.' Alice laughed and ran upstairs.

She couldn't find it anywhere. In the end, Cora removed every single piece of paper from the bureau and went through them one by one, but there was no sign of the agreement Alice Lacey had signed ten years before.

Could she have put it somewhere else? No, Cora decided. The bureau in the parlour was where she kept all the paperwork – the electricity and gas bills, receipts for this and that, Maurice's vaccination card, birth certificates. Everything.

It *had* to be here somewhere. She went through the papers again, emptying envelopes in case it had been mistakenly put inside. She was frantic by the time she'd finished and it still hadn't come to light. Perhaps it had been thrown away. Every now and then she sorted out the papers, threw away the old bills, but she surely wouldn't have been so daft as to throw away that agreement, even accidentally.

Mind you, finding the paper wasn't important. All she had to do was *tell* Alice she'd torn it up, that she wouldn't be asking for her share no more – and she'd be accepted back into the Lacey clan. Today was the day she called for her cut, but today she'd tell them they could keep it, though in a nicer way than that.

Cora fetched her shopping bag from the kitchen, put on her camel coat and zip-up boots, tied a headscarf round her pale, greying hair and set off for Marsh Lane.

She did her shopping first. Outside a shop that sold baby clothes she paused and examined the window display. A matinée coat would be nice for Orla's baby, white or lemon so it would do for a boy or a girl, booties to match. She'd get them tomorrow and ask for them to be wrapped in tissue paper before they were put in the bag.

There was a funny sensation in her belly when she turned into Opal Street. She'd made a mint out of that agreement, but it had caused a lot of bad blood and she wasn't sure if it had been worth it. Alice Lacey might be out of pocket, but *she* was the one who'd suffered most.

The bell tinkled when she opened the door. The salon was getting smarter with the years. There were tiles on the floor that looked like polished wood and three gleaming black dryers with leather chairs underneath. The colour scheme had been changed from mauve to orange, though Alice referred to it as 'apricot'. Just inside the door an elegant white desk housed a telephone and the appointment book. The old sinks had been replaced with shallow cream basins on which fat, stubby taps sparkled beneath the neon strip lights.

Although it was Monday morning, the place was already busy. The dryers were all occupied and two of the sinks. That Patsy woman, whom Cora had never been able to take to, was collecting dirty cups.

Alice looked up at the sound of the bell. Her eyes went cold when she saw

Cora. 'The envelope's in the left-hand desk drawer as usual,' she said shortly.

'I'd like to talk to you,' Cora said eagerly.

'I'm busy right now, as you can see.'

'*I'll* talk to her.' Fion abandoned the tint she was applying and made for the kitchen.

Cora followed. It wasn't quite what she'd planned, but she couldn't very well say what she'd come to say in front of a crowded salon. And Fion would do just as well as Alice to be told the agreement no longer stood, perhaps better. She quite looked forward to seeing the girl's face collapse when she heard the news.

A kettle simmered in the kitchen. Cora coughed importantly, 'I've come . . .' she began, but Fion interrupted.

'I know quite well why you've come. Aunt Cora, to collect the money you've been doing me mam out of for years.' Fion glared at her aunt. 'You're not getting another penny off Lacey's and I'll tell you why.' She smiled unpleasantly. 'No, I won't tell you, I'll *show* you.' She produced a yellowing sheet of paper from the pocket of her overall and waved it in front of Cora's eyes. 'Recognise it? It's the agreement me mam was daft enough to sign. Now just watch, Aunt Cora.' The girl was clearly enjoying herself. She thrust the paper in the flames spurting from beneath the kettle and it immediately caught alight.

Cora watched numbly as the burning paper was thrown into the sink where it quickly became a few charred scraps. Fion turned on the tap and the scraps disappeared down the drain.

'There!' she said with a loud, satisfied sigh.

'Where did you get it from?' Cora whispered.

'I'll leave you to work that out for yourself.'

'Maurice! Maurice gave it you.' She remembered the footsteps on the stairs on Saturday night. Fion must have asked him to get it at the party, to *steal* it, actually to steal it from his own mam. Cora felt sick to her stomach. 'Can I use the lavvy?'

'You know where it is.'

'Fion,' Alice called. 'What are you doing? Mrs Finnegan's only had half her tint.'

'Coming, Mam.' Fion smiled slyly at Cora. 'Mam's going to be dead pleased, I'll bet.'

'Yes.' Cora scarcely heard. Everything had been turned upside down. Maurice had betrayed her. Her son's loyalty lay, not with her, but with Alice and her family. No one wanted her: not her husband, not her son. No one.

He was beautiful, but then all her babies had been beautiful. Orla looked proudly down at Paul, her new son.

'He's a fine little chap,' Micky said, equally proud. 'Can I hold him for a bit?'

Orla carefully put the baby in his arms. 'I suppose your mam's spoiling the other three something rotten.'

'Well . . .' Micky grinned. 'Not quite as much as me dad. They're being stuffed with sweets that came from you know where.'

'I know exactly where. The lorry some Lavin or other always seems to be at the back of.'

'Your mam's having them all day tomorrow. She said the salon's overstaffed at the moment, so she can take time off. We're very lucky with our families, Orl.'

'I know,' Orla said soberly. 'We're dead lucky with the kids, too. Some woman had a baby just before me and it died within an hour.'

'Are we dead lucky with each other, though?' Micky glanced at her from beneath his long black lashes.

Orla hadn't thought it possible to blush in front of a man by whom you'd borne four children, but blush she did. 'I reckon so, Micky,' she said in a subdued voice. 'I reckon we're lucky all round in every possible way.'

Their lips met over the new baby and Orla felt the inevitable swirl of desire. She realised that, even if she wore an iron chastity belt, Micky would only have to sneeze and she'd get pregnant.

After he'd gone, the midwife came in. It was the same one who'd delivered Lulu five years ago. 'You're becoming quite a familiar figure in these parts,' she said with a grin. 'I see from your notes this is your fourth.'

'If you work here long enough you'll be present at me twenty-fourth,' Orla said gloomily – it was actually possible to feel happy and gloomy at the same time.

'Have you considered birth control?' the midwife said helpfully. 'I know it says on your chart that you're a Catholic, but I hope you don't mind my saying this, the Pope's not likely to lend a hand if you have a child a year for the rest of your life.'

'We've tried birth control, but nothing works.'

'Have you heard of the Dutch cap?'

'No.'

'And there's something new, a birth control pill. It only came out last year, so I don't know much about it.'

'We'll try *anything*,' Orla said eagerly. 'Just tell me where to go.'

8

It was surprising, but the Lacey's in Marsh Lane was attracting only a very small clientele. Business had been good at first, but had gradually petered off until the salon was doing only half the business of the one in Opal Street.

Whenever she had a spare minute, Alice went round to see if she could recognise what the problem was. She'd had the salon painted in the same warm apricot shade as the other, the same wood effect tiles laid on the floor. There were new lace curtains on the windows and strip lights fitted to the freshly painted ceiling. It looked very different, but the new decoration was a definite improvement on the old. No one could possibly have taken offence.

Yet, as the weeks passed, fewer and fewer women came. Why? Alice wondered.

She got her answer in April when the Marsh Lane Lacey's had been open for four months and Doreen Morrison handed in her notice. Doreen was in her fifties, unmarried, with platinum-blonde hair, always perfectly made up. She was never without a man friend and, years ago, had gone out with Danny Mitchell more than once. She still worked part-time, afternoons and all day Saturday.

'It's not your heart, is it, luv?' Alice said anxiously. Doreen was a top-class hairdresser and she'd be more than sad to lose her.

'My heart's fine, Alice, it's . . .' Doreen paused.

'It's what, luv?'

The woman looked embarrassed. 'I don't like to tell you.'

'If something's wrong, Doreen, I've a right to know.'

'Well . . .' She still looked reluctant. 'Well, to tell the truth, Alice, it's your Fion. She's impossible to work with. Chrissie's also talking about handing in her notice.' Chrissie O'Connell was the junior, a helpful, friendly girl.

'What does our Fion do that makes her so impossible to work with?' Alice enquired coolly, torn between wanting to side with her child, yet knowing Doreen wouldn't leave without good reason.

'See, I knew you'd be upset. I can tell by the tone of your voice.' Doreen sounded upset herself. 'I wish I hadn't told you.'

'I'm glad you did.' Alice nodded encouragingly. 'Go on.'

'It's just that she's so rude, Alice: to me, to Chrissie, to the customers, except if they're old and then she gushes over them so much the poor dears can't stand it. It was all right when she was working alongside you. You probably didn't notice, but you kept her in line, kept laughing and apologising for her. I tried that a couple of times, but she put me firmly in me place. Told me *she* was the one in charge.' Doreen warmed to her theme, clearly having been smarting over the situation for a long time. 'There's one customer couldn't stand the dryer too hot, kept switching it down every now'n again. Fion was very short with her, told her off in no uncertain terms, and the woman's never come back again, yet she'd been coming to Gloria's for ages. If a customer asks for a one-inch trim, Fion will take off two or three because she thinks it would look better. Or she'll argue over the colour of a tint, or insist someone doesn't suit a fringe when they've had a fringe for years. I often feel – you must, too – that I know better than the customer, but you've got to be dead tactful if you suggest they try something else.'

'I see.' Alice sighed. On her visits to the salon she had noticed Fionnuala was a little brusque, but perhaps she was so used to her daughter's ways that she hadn't realised how much it would grate on other people. She had hoped making her manageress would give the girl the confidence she so obviously lacked, but clearly Fion couldn't be left to run the business into the ground. 'I'll have a word with Fion tonight,' she told Doreen. 'In the meantime, will you think twice about giving in your notice?'

'Of course I will, Alice. I never wanted to leave, it was just that Fion . . .' The woman paused and didn't continue.

'I don't suppose you feel fit enough to work full-time?' Alice said hopefully. 'I'll need someone straight away to manage the place and Katy's only twenty-one and not long qualified.' Katy Kelly was Alice's assistant.

Doreen's beautifully made-up face flushed with pleasure. 'Well, actually, Alice, I wouldn't mind. I was rather hoping you'd ask when the new branch opened. It's only across the road from where I live and it never gets hectic like it did in town. The customers are nicer too, not so demanding. They don't mind waiting a few minutes if there's the occasional rush on. There's just one thing, though, you won't be leaving Fion with me, will you? That would be dead unfair on the girl, us swopping places, like. Despite what I said, I'm quite fond of her. Her heart's in the right place and she means well. She just doesn't know how to cope with people.'

'I'll let you have Katy. Fion can work with me so I can keep an eye on her.'

'But it's not fair!' Fion raged. 'Oh, Mam, it's not fair a bit. Doreen Morrison has never liked me. She's just making it up.'

Alice's heart went out to her gauche, bungling daughter, who was on the verge of tears. 'Fion, luv, Doreen wouldn't have gone to the extent of handing in her notice if she was just making it up. That would be cutting off her nose to spite her face. And is Chrissie making it up? Because she's thinking of leaving too. And what about the customers? Every week there's fewer and fewer. They're not staying away just to get at you, luv. You're not old enough for the responsibility yet, that's all. You make them feel uncomfortable for some reason.'

'I'm twenty-four.' Fion sniffed.

'It's all my fault.' Alice decided to put the blame on herself. 'Managing a hairdresser's was too much to ask of someone quite so young.'

But this only made things worse, because Fion said tragically, 'Our Orla's got four children and Maeve's a nurse. Running a crappy hairdresser's isn't much when compared to them and I can't even do that properly.'

'Do you really think it crappy?'

Fion laid her head on her mother's shoulder and began to cry. 'No, I loved it. It made me feel grown up and important. Oh, Mam!' she cried, 'what's wrong with me? No one likes me. Everything I say comes out wrong, unnatural, like. I can even hear it meself, this dead false voice.'

'You don't sound false to me, luv.' Alice stroked her daughter's brown hair. 'And don't forget how brilliant you were with Cora. You really knew how to put her in her place. Me, I was willing to lie down and let her tread all over me.'

'You were dead annoyed when I got Maurice to steal that agreement.'

'Well, I must admit I was upset at first, but it wasn't nearly as bad as what Cora did to me in the first place. I realised that after a while. It's nice to have all the money to ourselves.' She'd been so shocked when she heard what Fion had done that she'd actually considered letting Cora continue to have her share, but everyone – her dad and Bernadette, the children – said she was stark, raving mad even to think of such a thing. 'Anyroad, luv, as from tomorrow you'll be back in the old Lacey's with me. It'll be just like old times, won't it?'

Fion nodded forlornly. 'I suppose so.'

Alice told Neil what had happened when he commented on Fion's return to the salon. It was Thursday night and they were in bed together, having just made very satisfactory love.

'Poor kid,' Neil said sadly as he smoothed his hand over the curve of her hip. 'It must be awful to be so self-conscious.'

'The thing is, Orla, Maeve and Cormac have always been so sure of themselves, which can't have helped Fion much. It doesn't help that she eats like a horse, either. She's the same height as Orla, but her waist's at least six inches bigger.'

'When I heard about Babs, I drank like a fish for months,' Neil said thoughtfully. 'I suppose some people do the same thing with food. Fion only eats so much because she's unhappy.'

'Then what on earth can I do to make her happy?' Alice wailed.

'I've no idea.' Suddenly, Neil pinched her waist and she gave a little scream. 'The other day I was offered tickets for a dance at Bootle Town Hall. I turned them down,' he said with an exaggerated sigh, 'because the only person I wanted to take refuses to be seen in public with me. Why don't I take Fion? It might cheer her up a bit.'

Alice looked doubtful. 'Oh, I don't know, Neil. She might get ideas.'

'What sort of ideas?'

'That you're keen on her. She's definitely keen on you, I've told you so before.'

'I could say she was just doing me a favour, getting me out of a hole, because the girl I planned to take had let me down and I didn't want the tickets to go to waste. Actually, I wouldn't mind going,' he said in injured tones. 'I have no social life because of you.'

'Don't tell lies, Neil. You're always off to this and that.'

'Anyroad, about this dance – did you notice I just said "anyroad", which means I've become a genuine Liverpudlian – shall I ask Fion or not?'

'It might cheer her up, as you say – I can take her into town and buy her a new frock – but don't build up her hopes, Neil. She's miserable enough as it is. I don't want her heart broken as well.'

Fion had virtually stopped eating altogether. She had a slice of dry toast for breakfast, nothing for dinner and more dry toast for tea, because she was determined to squeeze into a size 40 frock for the dance at Bootle Town Hall instead of the usual 42. Alice had agreed to leave it till the very last minute before buying the dress and was actually closing the salon early on the day of the dance, at two instead of four.

'I want something black and slinky,' Fion said excitedly. 'Or really, really bright red, with straps as thin as shoelaces.'

'We'll just have to see,' Alice said, looking at her sharply. 'Why are you getting so excited? It's only a dance.'

'Yes, but I'm going with Neil,' Fion replied dreamily.

'Only as a replacement for the girl he really wanted to take.' Alice hoped she didn't sound too cruel, but it seemed her worst suspicions had been confirmed – Fionnuala was behaving as if Neil had proposed marriage.

Fion said, 'I think that was only a ruse, Mam. I think Neil's always wanted to ask me out, but didn't have the nerve.'

'Neil's never struck me as being short of nerve. Anyroad, he's much too old for you.'

'Oh, Mam, don't be daft. He's only ten years older. Grandad's twenty-one years older than Bernadette and you didn't turn a hair when they got married.'

Alice wondered if she should ask Neil to withdraw the invitation, but Fion would be bitterly disappointed. But she'd be just as disappointed when she realised Neil had no intention of asking her out again. She supposed that as, either way, Fion was bound to feel let down, she might as well enjoy the dance and feel let down afterwards rather than before.

She pleaded with Neil to be gentle with her daughter and he looked at her, hurt. 'As if I'd be anything else.'

Fion felt as if she was, quite literally, walking on air. The dance was all she talked about – the clothes she would wear, what sort of shoes and that if she kept on starving herself she might manage to squeeze into a size 38. She persuaded Orla's Micky to teach her how to foxtrot and they practised in the parlour of the little house in Pearl Street. She endlessly discussed with her mother exactly how she should do her hair: in one of the new bouffant styles, or the smooth look favoured by Lauren Bacall, or piled on top of her head in little curls. Or dare she risk one of them shaggy Italian cuts like Claudia Cardinale?

'For goodness sake, Fion,' her mother said impatiently, 'it's only a dance, not a reception at Buckingham Palace.'

Mam just didn't seem to comprehend the awesome significance of Neil asking her out. Fion had long been convinced that he was attracted to her. He was always so incredibly nice, so warmly understanding. Whenever they spoke, he gave her his undivided attention and asked all sorts of questions. Of course, Neil was nice to everyone, but she could tell she held a special place in his heart. He probably hadn't asked her before because he thought Mam might disapprove or Fion might turn him down. She didn't delve too deeply into exactly why he'd asked now, but he'd asked and that was all that mattered.

It was easy to imagine a bright, starry future – marrying Neil in about a year's time – she'd be down to size 36 by then and would wear one of those wedding dresses with a three-tiered skirt and have a bouquet of white roses with trailing ribbons. Orla could be a matron of honour and Maeve a bridesmaid – gosh, she'd, actually be getting married *before* Maeve! They would live somewhere dead posh like Crosby or Blundellsands, because teachers didn't normally live in places like Amber Street, except if they were unmarried, like Neil – like Neil was *now*.

The dance was three weeks away, two weeks, then only seven days. Fion continued to starve herself. Mam made her drink a glass of milk night and morning, and said it wouldn't do her any harm to lose a few pounds, dance or no dance. Mam positively refused to get into the spirit of things.

Only twenty-four hours to go. Fion lay on the bed in her room, her face covered in a mud pack and her feet on the headboard, which made the blood rush to the head and was good for the hair or the skin or the brain. Something.

Mam shouted up the stairs, 'I'm just nipping round to the salon for a few minutes. One of the dryers is playing up. I think it needs adjusting.'

'OK, Mam,' Cormac shouted from his bedroom in the new, deep voice he'd recently acquired. He was studying for yet more exams, but never seemed to mind.

'Tara, Mam,' Fion said tightly for fear she'd crack the mud pack, which felt like concrete and still had another five minutes to go.

The five minutes seemed to take for ever. Fion went downstairs and splashed the mud off in the kitchen. She went into the living room and examined her face in the mirror over the mantelpiece, and tried to decide if her skin looked softer, clearer, healthier, firmer, all the things it had promised on the packet. She wasn't quite sure. Mam had said the mud pack was a waste of time and money because Fion already had beautiful skin.

She had nice hair, too, thick and brown. But it was a very *ordinary* brown. Perhaps if Mam used one of them Tonrinzes when she set it tomorrow morning, auburn, say, it would bring out the highlights. She wondered if Mam had auburn in stock. She'd ask the minute she came home. No, she wouldn't. She'd go round now and check and, if necessary, call in the chemist's first thing tomorrow and buy one.

There was no need for a coat, not even a cardy, on such a lovely May evening. The sun was sliding behind the roofs of the houses, a great, flaming ball, briefly turning the grey slates into sheets of gleaming gold. Fion hummed to herself as she hurried along the street and through the entry into Opal Street. She opened the door of the salon, expecting to find her mother fiddling with a dryer – she hadn't noticed one was giving trouble. She was surprised to find no sign of Mam, either in the salon or the kitchen. The back door was locked, so she wasn't in the lavvy.

Perhaps she'd decided to call on Bernadette and Grandad, or she might have gone round to Orla's. Fion checked the box of Tonrinzes, found an auburn and was about to leave, when she realised she hadn't brought a key to lock the door – and why had it been unlocked in the first place? Mam must have forgotten to lock it when she left. Never mind, Neil would do it when he came home. She assumed he was out as there wasn't the faintest sound from the flat, no gramophone, no wireless.

She was about to leave a second time when she heard a woman laugh. The woman laughed again and Fion recognised Mam's warm, rusty chuckle.

From upstairs? Fion frowned. There was nothing wrong with Mam being upstairs, but why had it been so quiet until she laughed? And there was something odd about the laugh, something *intimate.*

Fion went to the bottom of the stairs. For some reason she felt reluctant to call out, announce her presence. She crept up a few steps until her eyes were level with the landing floor and glanced through the banisters. Neil's parlour, once a bedroom, was at the front. The boxroom was now the kitchen and the bedroom overlooked the backyard.

The doors to the parlour and kitchen were wide open, the one to the bedroom firmly closed and it was from behind this door that Fion heard her mother laugh again. Then Neil said something in a tone of voice she'd never heard him use before, soft and tender, throbbing with passion.

Mam was in bed with Neil Greene!

She could never remember leaving the salon, going home, but she must have done, because she was lying on the bed again – not crying, because she would never cry again, just staring at the ceiling, cold and shivering, numb with shock. Neil was in love with Mam, not her. He'd probably invited her to the dance because he felt sorry for her. It might even have been Mam's idea, to sort of make up for being demoted, for no longer being manageress of Lacey's in Marsh Lane.

'My life is a failure,' Fion said aloud.

'Did you just say something, sis?' Cormac shouted.

'No,' she shouted back.

'A complete failure.' She was whispering now, though there was no need to whisper, because everyone knew. Doreen Morrison and Chrissie O'Connell had refused to work with her, the customers hated her, her family felt sorry for her. 'I'm useless. There's something wrong with me.'

Fion felt overwhelmed by a black cloud of hopelessness and despair. When Mam came home, she shouted that she had a headache and had gone to bed early, and no, she didn't want an aspirin, thanks.

'I think you should start eating properly again as from tomorrer,' her mother called. 'I reckon you're overdoing it.'

'Yes, Mam.'

Maeve came home from her night out with Martin and Fion pretended to be asleep. She remembered she'd planned on having Maeve as a bridesmaid and wanted to curl up in embarrassment at even thinking such a thing. What a fool she'd been! And what was going to happen tomorrow? There was no way in the world she would go to that dance with Neil, and what reason could she give for refusing? If only she hadn't gone on about it so much to everyone she knew.

There was only one thing for it, Fion decided after a while, she'd just have to leave home.

When Fion woke up it was daylight, bright and sunny, though when she looked at her watch it was only six. The house was silent. She lay watching the sun filter through the curtains and asked herself if she still wanted to leave home.

She decided she did and that she would leave now, without telling anyone, before they got up, though she'd write a note. If she told Mam first, she'd only try to talk her out of it. Anyroad, she liked the idea of giving everyone a shock. Once she'd gone, they might appreciate her a bit more. She would come back in a year's time having made her fortune. Fion visualised herself with 36-inch hips and wearing a dead smart costume – black and white check with a velvet collar. She would be nice to everyone, not a bit toffee-nosed.

Unfortunately, the family didn't possess a suitcase. She managed to squeeze her underwear and a nightdress into the leatherette shopping bag that hung behind the kitchen door, and two frocks, a cardigan and some stockings into an Owen Owen's carrier bag with a string handle. She'd just have to wear her coat, which was a pity, because the day looked as if it was going to be a scorcher. It took some time deciding which shoes to wear, because sandals would look silly with the coat and heavy shoes equally silly in hot weather. In the end she decided on the shoes and managed to squeeze a sandal into each of the bags.

What to say in the note? One of Cormac's exercise books lay on the table. Only a few pages had been used. She tore a page out of the middle, picked up Cormac's fountain pen and sat staring at the blank paper. She wanted to write, 'I'm going because I'm dead miserable and no one loves me,' so they'd all feel guilty and sorry for the way she'd been treated. But it might be better to leave them full of admiration for her bravery and spirit of adventure. 'I'm off to see the world,' she could put. 'Don't know when I'll be back.'

Upstairs, the springs creaked on the double bed and Fion wasn't sure what got into her, because all she wrote on the paper was, 'I know about you and Neil. Tara for ever, Fion.' She folded it up and tucked it behind a statue on the mantelpiece, because if Mam found it straight away she'd only come chasing after her. Flinging her handbag over her shoulder, she picked up the bags and left by the back way, which was quieter.

A few minutes later Fion had reached Marsh Lane, already having doubts and wishing she'd left the note in a more conspicuous place. She kept looking back, praying Mam would appear and persuade her to come home. If only she had a friend in whom she could confide, who would give her some encouragement, say she was doing the right thing. Or even talk her out of it, which would be even better. But there was no one.

Except Horace Flynn! He was the only person who didn't make her feel stupid, who was always pleased to see her. It was very much out of her way, but she'd call on him and say tara.

Horace Flynn didn't welcome the knock on his door at such an unholy hour. It was barely seven. If he hadn't thought it might be the postman with a registered letter containing someone's unpaid rent – it happened occasionally – he would have ignored the knock and stayed in bed.

Wrapping his roly-poly body in a plaid dressing gown, he went downstairs and found Fionnuala Lacey outside. Had it been anyone else in the world, he would have given them the sharp edge of his tongue, slammed the door in their face, but he'd always had a soft spot for Fionnuala, though even she wasn't exactly welcome at such an early hour.

'I'm running away from home,' the girl said breathlessly. 'I've come to say tara.'

The landlord was a lonely man, entirely friendless until he'd struck up a sort of relationship with this unsophisticated and rather naïve young woman. He felt hugely flattered that she'd come out of her way to say goodbye and stood aside to let her in. 'I'm very sorry to hear it,' he said, which was true. 'Would you like a cup of tea?'

'I'd love one. There wasn't time at home. I had to leave before anyone got up, see.'

'Is there any particular reason why you're running away from home?'

Fion followed him down the hall into the nicely furnished living room. She couldn't very well tell him about Mam and Neil. 'I'm twenty-four,' she said. 'I thought it was about time. I'm going to have lots of adventures.'

'I hope you do,' said Horace Flynn, who'd left Ireland forty years before in search of adventure and ended up a landlord whom no one liked. He noticed Fion's two inadequate bags. 'Would you like a suitcase?'

'If you've got one to spare. Call it borrowing. I'll bring it back one day.'

'Keep it. I doubt if I'll ever need it.' Horace put the kettle on and went upstairs. He returned with a leather case with straps, which someone had once given him in lieu of rent.

Fion looked pleased. 'That's big enough to take me coat. I'll change me shoes, if you don't mind, put me sandals on.'

'Go ahead.' The kettle boiled. Horace made the tea and returned with two dainty cups and saucers on a tray. 'Do you take sugar?'

'I did till a few weeks ago. I don't now.'

'I thought there was a big dance tonight? You were buying a frock this afternoon, getting your hair done. You seemed to be looking forward to it, if I remember right.'

'I was, but I'm not now.' Fion shrugged nonchalantly. She was kneeling on the floor, folding her clothes inside the case, trying not to let him see her underwear in case it inspired him to pinch her bottom.

Horace sighed. 'I'll miss you.'

'I'll miss you too.'

It was worth being dragged so early out of bed for that. 'Have you got enough money?' Horace was astonished to hear the words come from his lips.

'Yes, thanks. I've got twelve pounds. It's me birthday money. I mean, it's what I've been saving up to buy presents.'

'That won't go far – where are you going, London?'

'I hadn't thought about it. I suppose London seems the obvious place.' People didn't run away to Birmingham or Manchester or Leeds.

'Just a minute.' Horace went into the parlour and opened the strong box which he kept hidden inside an antique commode. He removed twenty pounds, returned to the other room and handed the money to Fion.

She blushed scarlet. 'I can't take all that! It wouldn't be right.'

'It wouldn't be wrong either. If you like, look upon it as a loan. Once you're on your feet, you can pay me back. You don't want to come running home with your tail between your legs because you're out of money, do you?'

'No.'

Horace had the feeling that she didn't want to run away, that she wouldn't have minded being talked out of it. He felt tempted to dissuade her, because he would have preferred her to stay, but was prevented by a feeling of unselfishness that surprised him. He glanced at her fresh, innocent, unhappy face. It would do her good. She'd make proper friends, learn to be independent, find herself.

'Good luck,' he said.

Fion gulped down the remainder of her tea and got to her feet. 'I'd better get going.'

'You'll find plenty of cheap bed and breakfast hotels around Euston Station. They usually have the prices in the window. It would be best to stay there until you find somewhere permanent to live. Don't speak to any strange men,' he added warningly, suddenly concerned that the station would be teeming with men waiting for young girls like her to prey on, offering somewhere 'safe' to live.

'I won't. Thank you, Mr Flynn.'

He picked up the suitcase and took it to the door. 'Good luck again.'

'I'll send you a card as soon as I'm settled.'

'I'd appreciate that. I shall worry about you.'

'I know about you and Neil. Tara for ever, Fion.'

Alice's heart thumped painfully when she read the note that had been left on the mantelpiece. It was the first thing she'd noticed when she came downstairs.

How did Fion know? It could only be that she'd come to the salon last night and heard Neil and her upstairs. She remembered thinking she'd heard a noise.

'I'm sure the salon door just closed,' she'd said.

'As long as it didn't open,' Neil had replied lazily. 'Come here! It's been a good five minutes since I've kissed you.'

She'd let him kiss her, forgotten about the noise. Until now. Poor, poor Fion! She'd be heartbroken. Alice, overwhelmed with guilt, was desperately trying to think of the best way of dealing with the situation when it dawned on her that Fion had written 'Tara for ever'.

She went to the bottom of the stairs. 'Fion!' she called, hardly able to breathe as she waited for an answer.

It was Maeve who shouted back. 'She's not here. She woke me up at the crack of dawn creeping about. That wardrobe door creaks like mad, Mam. It needs oiling.'

'Oh, my God!'

'What's up, Mam?' Cormac had woken.

'It's our Fion. I think she's run away.'

But she wouldn't run away for long, Alice told herself, not Fion. Fion was too clinging. She needed her family far more than the others. She wouldn't know how to manage on her own. Alice would like to bet she'd be back before the day was out – it might even be within a few hours, because she hadn't the nerve to go too far. Why, she might even be wandering around North Park at this very moment, already thinking about coming home.

When she did, she would have to be told what had happened between Neil and her mother as tactfully and as gently as humanly possible and then hope they would be able to keep the secret between the three of them.

Alice tried not to worry too much as the hours passed and still Fion didn't come home.

The hotel was called St Jude's, merely a large terraced house amid a long row of identical properties. It was spotless, but cleanliness was its only good point, unless you counted the strong smell of disinfectant that pervaded every nook and corner. Fion had never seen such a miserable room as the one in which she had just unpacked her case, transferring the clothes on to wire hangers in the wardrobe. A bottle-green candlewick quilt with bare patches covered the double bed and the heavy curtains were the same gloomy colour. The walls were possibly gloomier, a pale, muddy brown. There wasn't a single picture or ornament, just a dressing table and tallboy, that didn't match each other or the wardrobe. The floor covering was cheap and shiny, and boasted a faded rug beside the bed. She hadn't exactly been expecting luxury for 12/6d a night, but this was soulless, infinitely depressing and suprisingly cold, considering it was such a lovely warm day outside.

'I'll go home tomorrer,' she said to herself. 'I've made me point, staying away a whole night.' She would give Mr Flynn his twenty pounds and his suitcase back.

When she arrived at Euston, she had contemplated catching the same train back, but something had prevented her, she wasn't sure what. Shame, perhaps, at the idea of running away and returning home the same day. Orla would laugh her head off, Maeve would disapprove, even Cormac would be cross with her for upsetting Mam. And poor Mam was probably doing her nut. She shouldn't have mentioned Neil in that note. After all, your mother having an affair wasn't a justifiable reason for leaving home. Neil was only being kind, asking her to the dance. And Mam had offered to do her hair and buy her a new dress. She was even closing the salon two hours early so they'd have time to shop.

Fion looked at her watch: seven o'clock. She'd taken ages wandering around, trying to pluck up courage to enter a hotel, and had chosen this one because it was called after a saint, though she'd never heard of Jude and he mightn't even be a Catholic saint. Then she'd taken just as long sitting on the bed and trying to pluck up more courage to go out. It was twelve hours, almost to the dot, since she'd walked out of Amber Street. She shivered, feeling very odd and out of place in this miserable, anonymous room.

It was too early to go to bed because she wouldn't fall asleep for hours. She glanced from the bed to the door and decided she couldn't possibly stay in, not on such a beautiful evening. She'd have a wash first, but remembered she'd forgotten to bring soap and a towel, a hairbrush, lipstick, her toothbrush.

Fortunately there was a linen towel as stiff as cardboard folded over the sink and a tiny slab of yellow soap. Fion splashed her face, and rubbed her finger on the soap and cleaned her teeth. It tasted dreadful. After changing into one of her frocks, she ran her fingers through her hair, collected her bag and left to explore London.

There was a notice behind the front door announcing, THIS DOOR WILL BE LOCKED AT 10.30 p.m. Fion was about to leave, when the door marked RECEPTION opened and the woman who'd taken her money poked out her head.

'Have you read the notice?' she demanded.

'Yes, thank you.' She was a horrible woman, all sharp corners, even on her face.

'Well, just make sure you remember. I don't open the door to no one after half past ten.'

'I'll remember,' Fion said politely, wondering what on earth she was doing in this strange city, being spoken to by a strange woman as if she were a piece of dirt, when she could have been at home. She must be mad.

Outside, a huge, glittering sun hung low in the sky. This was the very same sun that was setting on Amber Street the day before when she'd been on her way to the salon. Things had changed so much since then.

Fion made her way back to Euston Station, then wandered along Euston Road, which was busy with traffic, though there were few pedestrians. She came to a road full of shops, all closed, naturally, though there were more people around. It was called Tottenham Court Road, she noticed as she crossed towards it, and it was very long.

At the end she reached a busy junction where a man was selling newspapers, shouting in what could have been a foreign language for all the sense it made. There was a cinema with a large queue outside, several cafés and a stall offering souvenirs of London: mugs and tea towels and replicas of London buses. People were pouring up steps from the bowels of the earth. Fion rounded a corner and found herself in Oxford Street.

She'd heard of Oxford Street. She must be in the very epicentre of London. Regent Street was probably not far away and Piccadilly Circus. Returning to the kiosk, she bought a map of London, despite it being a waste of money. After all, she was going home tomorrow. She noticed the film on at the cinema was *War and Peace* with Henry Fonda and Audrey Hepburn, which she'd planned on going to see with Mam when it came to Liverpool.

There was a self-service café at the top of Oxford Street. Fion went in for something to eat and to study the map – she must have lost pounds today, all she'd had was Horace Flynn's tea.

After she'd devoured two ham sandwiches and drunk a pot of tea, she found Piccadilly Circus on the map and began to wander towards it, pausing frequently to stare at the beautiful clothes in the very expensive shops. Regent Street was particularly grand and even more expensive.

The sun was setting lower now, casting sharp black shadows across the street, and the pavements were crowded with pedestrians, some wearing evening dress, obviously off to nightclubs or cocktail parties or theatres, or wherever people went in London on Saturday nights. As she passed a place called the Café Royal, a big, black car drew up and two women alighted, both wearing long satin frocks and smelling richly of perfume. One woman had a white fur cloak draped round her shoulders, which Fion thought was showing off a bit, as it was far too warm a night for furs.

She found she had arrived at Piccadilly Circus, which was drenched in golden sunshine and throbbing with life. The steps around the statue of Eros were crowded and neon lights flashed palely in the evening sunshine. Fion glimpsed a Boots chemists, still surprisingly open. She went in and bought the toiletries she'd forgotten to bring, which made a big hole in her money. Then she dodged through the traffic towards Eros, climbed a few steps, and sat down between an elderly couple with a small dog and a young man with a haversack at his feet. The dog, on a lead, came waddling towards her. She stroked it and the couple smiled. 'He won't bite,' the woman said. 'Lovely evening, isn't it?'

'Lovely,' Fion agreed and found herself smiling broadly for no reason, conscious of a strange mechanism behind her eyes making them sparkle brilliantly. She gasped and excitement coursed through her body like an electric shock, accompanied by a feeling of enormous triumph. Maeve might well be a nurse and Orla have four children, but neither had ever made it to London on their own. No one she knew had sat on the steps of Eros on Saturday night, breathing in the heady atmosphere, the *foreignness* of it all.

The young man beside her thrust a bar of chocolate in her direction. Fion took a square and muttered her thanks. It was dark and tasted bitter. It turned out the young man, like the chocolate, came from Belgium. He spoke only a few words of English and Fion didn't know a word of French, so communication was limited, though very pleasant. He left after a while, saying something about a youth hostel. Fion remembered she had to be back at the hotel by half-ten. Somewhat reluctantly, she started back. She'd probably walked further than she'd thought and had better give herself at least an hour. According to the map, the steps leading down to the bowels of the earth that she'd passed several times were stations on the London Underground. The system looked very complicated and this wasn't the time to try it out for the first time.

She would disentangle the workings of the Underground tomorrow and hoped it would be a nice day to explore the further wonders of London.

Fion entirely forgot that tomorrow she had made up her mind to go home.

While Fion was on her way back to the hotel, in Liverpool in the flat above Lacey's hairdressing salon Alice and Neil Greene were having an argument, something that didn't happen often. They usually got on exceptionally well. Had things gone as planned, Neil and Fion would have been at the dance by now.

They were in the parlour, fully dressed, sitting separately on each side of the empty fireplace. Alice had flatly refused to go to bed. She'd come for one reason only, to tell Neil their relationship must end.

'Just because Fion found out?' His jaw sagged.

'No, of course, not,' Alice snapped. 'Well, yes, in a way, I suppose it is. If Fion found out, then so can other people. I'm surprised we've gone a whole five years without anyone finding out before.' The trouble was, time had flashed by. It was half a decade since she'd confronted her husband in Crozier Terrace and discovered he was leading two lives, yet it felt like only yesterday. 'She must have heard us, Fion, last night when we were upstairs. Remember I said I thought I heard the door close?'

'Hmm.' Neil stared at the ceiling, then said casually, 'Why don't we get married?'

'Oh, don't be stupid, Neil,' Alice said more brutally than she intended. 'In case you haven't noticed, you've already got a wife and I've got a husband.'

'Babs regularly asks me to divorce her. You could divorce your husband; you've got enough grounds.'

'Oh, yes, and have me dirty linen washed all over Bootle. I'd look a right fool, wouldn't I? Me husband sets up house with another woman, has another family. What would people think?'

Neil said gently, 'Is that all that matters to you, Alice? Your reputation, what people think? Surely happiness, yours and mine, comes first?'

'I wouldn't be happy, knowing people were laughing at me behind me back,' Alice replied. 'And what about me kids? I've never told them what their dad got up to. They think he just left home, full stop. I'd sooner they never knew. They've already been hurt enough, particularly Cormac.'

'In other words there's no hope for us.' His face looked very drawn all of a sudden. 'I suppose it's no use asking you to come away with me so we can live together somewhere else?'

'No use at all, Neil. I belong here, with me family.'

'Have you ever loved me? You've said it enough times.'

'I *do* love you, Neil.' But not enough to get divorced. Even if the divorce went through without a public scandal, she wasn't the type of woman who got rid of her husband. She'd married John for better or for worse. They were joined together in the eyes of God for ever and a day. 'Oh, luv,' she said, more gently now, 'I shouldn't have let it go on for so long. I've been wasting your time, preventing you from meeting someone else. Even if there was nothing to stop us, I would never marry you, Neil. You're too young, I'm too old and I could never bring meself to meet your family, not with me speaking the way I do. I'd like you to marry someone young enough to give you children. Mind you, if word got round you were getting divorced, you'd lose your job. You work in a Catholic school, remember.'

Neil almost laughed. 'I suppose that means I'm stuck with Babs for the rest of my life.'

'Unless you get another, different kind of job, I suppose it does.'

'So, this is the end?'

'No, luv, it's just the beginning. It's been very nice, but we've been wasting each other's time all this while.'

'I certainly haven't been wasting *my* time and I would have described it as more than just nice,' he said drily.

'Oh, Neil, so would I!' Alice ran across the room and threw herself on to his knee. 'It's been truly wonderful, I'll never forget you, but all good things have to come to an end.'

He kissed her softly. 'Not necessarily, my darling.'

'This good thing has, Neil.'

'Do you have to sound so sensible?'

'It's about time one of us did. I'm almost glad our Fionnuala found out. It's made me see things clearly at last.'

He began to kiss her more passionately and she couldn't find the strength to push him away – perhaps the truth was she didn't want to find it. She wished she weren't so sensible, so religious, so cautious, that she could find the courage to live with him openly and not give a damn about being respectable and what anyone thought. Or that she were harder, like John, able to leave the people she loved behind without a second thought.

But she was none of these things. She was Alice Lacey, who had four children, who lived in Amber Street, Bootle and owned her own hairdressers'. Somehow Alice knew she would never escape these simple facts, because deep down in her heart she didn't want to. She was her own jailer, bound by conventions she would never break. Even her love for Neil, which was far greater than she had ever admitted either to him or to herself, wasn't enough to change her.

He was carrying her into the bedroom and she didn't protest.

'We didn't know last night we would never make love again,' he whispered, 'and I'd like the last time to be special. Promise you'll never forget me, Alice.'

'I promise,' she cried.

It was an hour later when Alice crept out of the flat, leaving behind a shattered lover and some part of herself.

She prayed he'd soon see sense, realise he was wasting his time with a woman who wasn't willing to be seen with him in public, a woman who could never marry him, bear his children.

Oh, but she would never forget him, Alice thought as she hurried home, fighting back the tears.

She increased her pace. Neil wasn't the only person who made her want to cry. There'd been no sign of Fion all day. Perhaps she was home by now . . .

But when Alice got back to Amber Street, Fion wasn't there. A worried Orla was, as well as Maeve and Martin, who'd been to the pictures and come back early just in case Fion had shown up.

The only person seemingly unconcerned was Cormac. 'She'll be all right,' he'd said earlier. 'Our Fion will manage better on her own than any one of us.'

'What makes you say that, son?' Alice asked curiously.

'Because she's unhappy, not like us. She's searching for something we've already found. Of course, she might come back today or tomorrow, but if she manages to stick it out for longer, then I doubt if we'll see her in a long time.'

Which didn't exactly cheer Alice up on top of everything else.

9

The girl who served Fion's breakfast next morning was a distinct improvement on the woman she'd met the previous night. 'How would you like your bacon, darlin'?' she enquired, smiling sweetly, when she removed the cornflake bowl. She was about eighteen, not exactly pretty, but with big, velvety brown eyes. Her brown hair was badly cut, as if she'd hacked it off herself.

'Well, I don't like it crisp.'

'Neither do I. I'll do it medium, shall I? I won't be a jiffy.'

The dining room was every bit as miserable as the bedroom, possibly worse, with a depressing painting of a frantic-looking stag in the middle of a forest hanging above the blocked-up grate. There were only five other people there: a middle-aged couple, two Chinese girls and an elderly man who wished her good morning when she entered.

Fion sat in the window and ordered cornflakes, bacon and egg, and a pot of tea. Having this admittedly small control over her life gave her a heady feeling of adult responsibility.

The girl arrived with a slice of pink bacon, a neatly fried egg and half a tomato on a plate, as well as a rack with four triangular slices of toast. There was a saucer containing pats of butter and a small bowl of marmalade already on the table.

'Thank you, that looks lovely.'

'Let's hope it tastes as nice as it looks.'

'It did,' Fion said when the girl came to collect her plate. By now, only the elderly man remained, having finished eating and smoking a cigarette. 'Taste as nice as it looked, that is. Do you make the meals as well as wait on tables?' It seemed a lot for one person to do, especially one so young.

'Only on Sundays, when there's not usually many guests. Are you on holiday?'

Fion wasn't sure why she was there. 'I'm going sightseeing today,' she said, which didn't really answer the question. 'I thought I'd start off at Marble Arch and walk through Hyde Park.'

'Well, you've picked a smashing day for it. I hope you see all you want to see. Oh, by the way, Mrs Flowers wants to know if you're staying another night. She said you only paid for the one.'

Mrs Flowers seemed a most unsuitable name for the sharp-cornered woman. 'That's right, I wasn't sure. I'll definitely be staying another night. I'll knock on Reception and pay on me way out, if that's all right.'

'That'll be just fine.'

It genuinely was a smashing day, Fion thought outside, just as the girl had said. For some reason she could smell blossom, though there was no sign of any trees. At Euston Station she bought a guidebook – more waste of money if she didn't intend to stay – then located the entrance to the tube.

She felt quite proud, after buying a ticket, of being able to negotiate her way to Marble Arch, emerging in sunshine that seemed to have got brighter during the short journey underground.

Large crowds were gathered just inside the park and she noticed several men perched on boxes loudly sounding off about all sorts of things – according to the guidebook, this was Speakers' Corner. One man appeared to be arguing that the world was flat. Fion listened for a few minutes and decided he was daft. She was about to explore the vast greenness of Hyde Park, when at the edge of the crowd she noticed a woman speaker surrounded by about a dozen men, all heckling so ferociously that the poor woman could scarcely be heard above the chorus of insults being thrown in her direction.

'And why shouldn't women be paid at the same rate as men?' the woman wanted to know in a dead posh voice. 'Equal pay for equal work. It's already happening in the public sector, the NHS, the Gas and Electricity Boards, the Civil Service, so why not in the private sector too? It makes sense if you think about it.'

'Rubbish!' yelled a man. '*I've* just thought about it and it makes no sense to me.'

'Women are the weaker sex. They can only manage half the output of a man,' another man yelled.

'Now it's *you* who's talking rubbish,' the woman countered. She didn't seem the least bothered by her voluble and antagonistic audience. She was very tall, with intense black eyes and greying hair. 'During the war, women did the work of men. They worked on lathes and milling machines, they riveted, they welded ...'

'They screwed,' one man interjected to gales of male laughter.

'They drove lorries and tractors,' the woman continued as if she hadn't heard, 'dug fields, planted corn, joined the Army, the Navy and the Air Force, worked in field hospitals, delivered post ...'

'Took off their knickers,' the same man shouted and was greeted with more hearty laughter.

'Why don't you take *yours* off, luv? Give us an eyeful.'

'She's nothing but a bloody lesbian. I bet she only shows herself to other women.'

Fionnuala, at the back of the crowd, was aware of the same hot feeling inside her head that she'd had when Cora Lacey tried to bully Mam. 'You're worse than animals, youse lot,' she screamed. 'If it weren't for women, not one of you would be here. Men like you ought to be strangled at birth. You're not fit to live, not one of you. Haven't you heard of free speech? It's what we fought for during the war, but you're not willing to listen to a word you don't agree with.'

The men had turned from the speaker and were regarding Fion with glazed eyes. 'Now, you look here . . .' One took a threatening step towards her, but Fion took an even more threatening step towards *him*.

'Don't like it, do you?' she sneered. 'Don't like it when someone insults *you*. You're lily-livered cowards, that's why.'

'If you were a bloke, I'd give you a punch on the nose.'

'Oh, yeah! Just because me opinion's different from yours?'

The men began to drift away, having lost interest, or perhaps they preferred their own rude heckling to being verbally assailed by a woman, particularly one so young with a Liverpool accent.

'Well, you were a great help, I must say,' the speaker remarked when the men had gone and she was surrounded by just Fion and fresh air. 'It's best to have an audience, even if they're an unpleasant lot, than to have no audience at all. I might have got through to at least one of them.'

'I'm sorry.' Until then, Fion had been feeling very proud of herself, expecting the woman to welcome support from a member of the same sex.

'That's all right.' The woman grinned cheerfully. 'I know you meant well but, in future, try to structure your thoughts, make pertinent points, don't just come out with mouthfuls of invective. It doesn't get us anywhere. By "us", I mean women.'

'I'm sorry,' Fion repeated.

'That's all right. I'll just have to start again. Here, take a leaflet, so next time you let off steam you'll have the facts at your disposal.'

Fion wandered away. When she looked back, the woman was once again surrounded by a small group of men, several of whom were already shaking their fists.

She tried not to let the incident spoil her day, though every now and then she would find herself thinking up more insulting things she wished she'd said and tried to structure the insults into pertinent points. She read the leaflet, which had been issued by the Equal Pay Campaign.

The park was gradually becoming fuller. People had come to sunbathe, to fish, talk, watch their children play, to sit and lean against a tree and read the Sunday paper, or just stroll across the emerald-green grass on what was undoubtedly a glorious morning.

After studying the map, Fion realised she was now in Kensington Gardens and there should be a café around somewhere. She was longing for a cup of tea, after which she'd go to the Natural History Museum, then catch the tube to the Tower of London. Tonight she'd have a meal in Lyons Corner House, which she'd noticed by Marble Arch, then go to see *War and Peace* in the cinema at the top of Tottenham Court Road.

Late in the afternoon she remembered it was Sunday and, for the first time in her life, she hadn't been to Mass. She caught the tube to Westminster Cathedral and went to Benediction instead. It didn't make up for Mass, but would do just for today.

The room in St Jude's was beginning to look a bit like home. On the dressing table there were a hairbrush, a lipstick and a *Woman's Own* with a picture of Princess Margaret on the front: toothbrush, paste and a pink flannel on the sink, and that day's pants hanging underneath to dry. On the bedside table the guidebook and map were waiting for her to study when she got into bed, so she could decide where to go tomorrow.

It was strange, but she had felt much lonelier in Liverpool, living within the bosom of her closely knit family, than she did in this anonymous city where she didn't know a soul. It was as if she was no longer her mother's daughter, no longer sister to Orla and Maeve. She badly missed Cormac because he was the only person who'd never done or said anything that made her feel bad about herself.

Before opening the guidebook Fion counted her money. She hadn't touched Mr Flynn's twenty pounds, but the twelve pounds she'd saved for presents had almost gone. Twelve pounds! In only two days! At this rate there'd be no money left by the end of the week. And what was she supposed to do then?

There were two obvious answers: return to Liverpool, or obtain more money, and the only way to do that was to get a job. Fion found it a tiny bit disturbing that she much preferred the second answer to the first.

'I'm sorry, Missus,' the police sergeant said portentously, 'but your daughter's an adult. She can leave home if she wants. You can't expect us to go chasing after a woman of twenty-four. Under eighteen, yes. Over eighteen, folks can do as they please and it's no one's business but their own.'

'But she's only a very *young* twenty-four. She's never even been to the pictures by herself.'

'She's still twenty-four. And she didn't just disappear into thin air, did she? You say she left a note. Have you got it with you?'

'No.' Alice had only shown the note to Neil.

'Did it say where she was going?'

Alice sighed. 'No.'

'Well, it would seem she doesn't want you to know.' The policeman suddenly softened. 'Try not to worry, Missus. She'll soon realise which side her bread is buttered and come back.'

'Let's hope so,' Alice muttered as she left the station.

Fion had been gone almost a week. Alice would have worried more had not Cormac been so convinced she was all right. As it was, she felt guilt-stricken that she'd allowed Neil to ask the poor girl out, build up her hopes, then have them dashed so cruelly. Fion was such an impressionable girl. How must she have felt when she heard her mother and Neil together? She must have come round to the salon for some reason and it could only be to do with the dance the following night. She'd been so excited, *too* excited.

Her other daughters shared their mother's guilt, particularly Orla. 'I should have been nicer to her,' she wailed. 'I was horrible most of the time, yet I felt dead sorry for her.'

'Perhaps she left because she didn't want people feeling sorry for her,' Cormac suggested.

'*I* dropped her like a hot brick when I met Martin,' Maeve moaned. 'We always went to the pictures together on Sunday nights, but we haven't gone for months.'

'It was wrong of me to have made her manageress of the new salon, then just snatch the job away. I should have thought before I acted. She was far too young.' Then there was the business with Neil, which she couldn't reveal. Alice wondered what Fion was doing right now, on Friday night, six days after she had so abruptly left. Whatever it was, wherever *she* was, the poor girl was bound to be alone and as miserable as sin.

Fion was in a pub, the Golden Lamb on Pentonville Road, with Elsa, Elsa's dad, Colin, and Elsa's grandma, Ruby. The pub was bursting at the seams, there was sawdust on the floor, a spittoon in the corner and most of the customers were already sociably drunk. Hidden from view, a pianist was thumping out 'Somewhere Over the Rainbow', his or her foot stuck firmly on the loud pedal.

Elsa was the girl who served the breakfasts in St Jude's – and cleaned the rooms and made the beds, Fion discovered after she'd been there a few days.

'I need to find somewhere to live,' she had confessed to Elsa a few days ago when the money from Horace Flynn was reduced to half. 'Do you know of anywhere?'

They had already started to chat while the breakfast tables were being cleared. She had told Elsa that she'd left home, not run away, which sounded a bit silly at her age.

The hotel was almost full, mainly with commercial travellers – one had given Fion a folding clothes brush and a window leather.

'I'll ask around, darlin',' Elsa promised. 'Do you want lodgings or a place where you look after yourself?'

'Which is cheapest?'

'Lodgings. You get breakfast and an evening meal for an all-in price.'

'Lodgings, then. I prefer the other, but I'll wait till I'm settled in a job.'

'What sort of job?'

'I'm not sure.' Fion made a face. 'Any sort of job as long as it's not hairdressing.'

'Elsa, dear!' Mrs Flowers called from the kitchen. She was always very nice to Elsa. At first, Fion had been surprised, until she realised Elsa was an exceptionally hard worker and very reliable.

'See you tomorrow,' the girl said.

Fion drained the teapot, put the two remaining triangles of toast in her bag to eat later and set off for another day of sightseeing. She wouldn't spend a single penny she didn't have to, so the remaining money would last as long as possible. It meant no more pictures, which was a pity, as she'd be stuck for something to do at night. Yesterday, she'd seen *Seven Brides for Seven Brothers* and fallen in love with Howard Keel, the day before ... *And God Created Woman* with Brigitte Bardot.

The weather was still fine and the busy London streets were flooded with sunshine. Fion mingled with tourists and shoppers, with office and shop workers, and felt extraordinarily happy. At one o'clock she went to Piccadilly Circus, bought coffee in a cardboard cup and sat on the steps of Eros, eating the toast and feeling on top of the world.

In the Golden Lamb Ruby Littlemore enquired, 'How's the digs, darlin'?' Ruby was mildly drunk on Guinness. She had jet-black, tightly permed hair, purple-painted lips and too much mascara. She was young to be Elsa's grandma, fifty-seven, but then Colin, Elsa's dad, was only thirty-eight and looked young enough to be her brother.

'Not so bad,' said Fion. 'The room's a bit small and nowhere's very clean, and I got tripe and onions for me tea, which I can't stand. Mrs Napier looked a bit put out when I asked her not to give it me again, as if she doesn't know how to cook anything else.'

'She'll think of something,' Ruby said. 'Blimey, you don't need more than one set of brains to come up with sausage and mash. Are you hungry, darlin'?' she asked in a concerned voice. 'Come back to ours later and I'll knock you up a plate of something.'

'Thanks, but I bought a meat and potato pie on the way.' It had been absolutely delicious.

'Come round tomorrer for your dinner, anyway. Sat'days, I usually make a stew with all the leftovers. Elsa doesn't work Sat'days. I don't know if she told you.'

'Yes, she's taking me to Camden Market to buy some dead cheap clothes. I didn't bring enough with me. We're going dancing at the Hammersmith Palais tomorrer night. I'm cutting her hair before. And I'd like to come to dinner, ta.' A midday meal wasn't included in the thirty-five shillings a week Mrs Napier charged.

'Elsa ses you're starting work Monday.' Colin Littlemore, sitting on Fion's other side, couldn't possibly be described as handsome. He was desperately thin, with brown, haunted eyes, hollow cheeks and a soft, curvy mouth. Nevertheless, Fion thought him enormously attractive, far more so than

Neil Greene, who hadn't an ounce of character in his face. She thought it odd that she hadn't noticed that before. During the war, Colin had been taken prisoner by the Japanese and put to work building a railway. He had managed to stay alive, but returned home an invalid, unable to work, his health in ruins. There was something wrong with his lungs, he couldn't breathe properly and could only eat the tiniest of meals. He was sitting with an untouched glass of orange juice in front of him. His wife, Elsa's mother, had been killed during the war when the factory in which she worked was bombed.

Fion said, 'I saw a notice outside a factory just along the road. It said "Packers Wanted". It's called Pentonville Medical Supplies. I just walked in and they took me on straight away. I start Monday,' she finished proudly. She had a job and somewhere to live in London, and it was as if Liverpool and her family had never existed.

Colin wrinkled his thin nose. 'That company pays terrible rates.'

'Four and six an hour, but I don't care as long as it keeps me going.'

'You *should* care. The labourer's worthy of his hire. I knew a bloke who worked there once. He said they refused to recognise a union.'

Fion wasn't interested in unions. No one had ever talked about unions or politics at home, mainly about hairdressing. She was reminded of the leaflet she'd been given in Hyde Park, which was still in her bag. She took it out and showed it to Colin.

'Quite right, too,' he said after he'd read it. 'Equal pay for equal work; it makes sense.'

'That's what the woman said who gave it me. I suppose it does when you think about it; make sense, that is. Anyroad, I got really mad with the men who were trying to shout her down. I shouted them down instead.'

Colin smiled his gentle, boyish smile. 'Good for you, darlin'. If more people lost their tempers when they thought something was unfair, then the world would be a much better place.' He raised an eyebrow. 'What if Pentonville Medical Supplies are paying men more for doing the same job as women?'

'Oh, gosh! I hadn't thought of that. I suppose I'll get mad, like I did in Hyde Park.'

'Let's hope so.' He suddenly got to his feet. 'I'll have to go.' His voice was suddenly hoarse. 'This smoke don't do me lungs no favours.' The smoke was rising towards the ceiling in white, wavy layers.

'I wouldn't mind an early night. I've had a busy week and I'm dead tired. I'll come with you – that's if you don't mind.'

'It'll be a pleasure, darlin'.'

'I'll just say goodnight to Elsa.'

The pianist was playing 'We'll Meet Again', when Fion and Colin Littlemore left the Golden Lamb and began to stroll down Pentonville Road. He was hardly as tall as her and as slight as a shadow. The tiny terraced house where he lived with his mother and his daughter was two streets along. Fion's digs were down a street almost opposite.

It seemed entirely natural for Fion to link her arm in his thin one. She thought how nice and uncomplaining he was, compared with her own father who'd made the whole family suffer for the injury he'd received during the war, finally doing a bunk and completely disappearing out of their lives.

They walked in companionable silence until arriving at the street where Colin lived. 'Would you like me to come in and make you a cup of tea?' Fion asked.

'I'd appreciate that, darlin'.' Colin patted her hand. He didn't think he'd ever met anyone so vulnerably innocent as Fionnuala Lacey. He remembered reading once that newly born chicks attached themselves to the first human being they clapped eyes on because they didn't have a mother. Fion had left home and attached herself in the same way to Elsa, then to Elsa's family, because she felt friendless and unbearably lonely. At the same time, he reckoned that if circumstances called for it, she could be quite tough.

'I'll send me mam a card tomorrer,' Fion said as they turned the corner. 'She's probably dead worried.'

'She's more likely climbing the walls.'

'I won't give her me address, though. I'll just say I'm all right.'

'That'll put her mind at rest. Actually, darlin',' he panted, 'I think I'll have to sit on the step a minute, get me breath back, before I go in the house.'

Fion sat on the step beside him. 'Is there anything I can do? Rub your back, or something?'

'No, but you can go in and put the kettle on. Here's the key.'

'Ta.'

He heard her run down the hall, anxious to help, then the rush of water in the kitchen, and thought she would make a good, caring mother – and a wonderful wife. With someone like Fion Lacey at his side, a man could conquer the world.

Colin smiled, then gave a little sigh. If only he were younger and in better health . . .

The young woman emerged from the art college into the grey drizzle of the late October day. She carried a large folder, the sides tied together with tape, underneath her arm. In her black and white striped slacks and baggy red jumper, and with her fair hair loose about her face, she looked like a teenager, but the man concealed in the doorway further down Hope Street knew that she was thirty and had three children, all old enough to be at school.

It was for this reason, to collect the children on time, that she was walking so swiftly and purposefully. He knew, because he had watched before, that she would walk all the way to Exchange Station rather than catch a bus somewhere more convenient like Skelhorne Street. A bus could get caught up in traffic and she might be late. She was a conscientious mother to her children.

More students came out of the college. One, a young man in his twenties, saw the young woman hurrying away. His face broke into a smile as he ran to catch her up. The woman smiled back, but didn't pause in her stride. The watching man shrank into the doorway when they passed on the other side.

What were they talking about? Would the chap accompany her all the way to the station? They might even catch the train together. The man in the doorway took a deep, shuddering breath. He smelt danger.

Clare and the young man parted on the corner of Lime Street and he went to catch the train to Rock Ferry. She wondered if John was still watching. Had he followed her this far? Or was he racing back to the factory in the van preparing for tonight's interrogation, starting with, 'Did you talk to anyone today?'

'Of course,' she would say. 'I couldn't very well spend the entire day at art school without speaking to a soul.'

'What about on the way home?'

As he'd seen her with Peter White, she'd have to concede that she had indeed spoken to someone on the way home. It was no good trying to laugh the questions away, because he would just persist and persist until he got an answer, even if it was an answer he didn't want.

'Yes, I spoke to someone on the way home. His name is Peter White, he lives in Rock Ferry and he's twenty-one. His mam and dad are Quakers. Anything else? Would you like his chest measurements? What he has for breakfast? How often he has his hair cut?'

But she wouldn't say all those things, because she'd done it before and John had called her 'insolent' and hit her. She would answer the question simply and leave it at that.

Passing St George's Hall, two men whistled at her approach. She felt, rather than saw, them both turn and watch her walk away, and was aware of letting her hips swing more widely. It was more than a year since she'd had the operation and her perfectly mended face still gave her a thrill of delight when she caught sight of her reflection in a shop window or an unexpected mirror.

She would always be grateful to John, but he seemed to want more than gratitude and she didn't know what it was – to cocoon her from life, to hide her away out of sight of other human beings. It had been like a red rag to a bull when she said she wanted to go to art school because she'd longed to learn to draw – properly, not the scrawly, amateur things she'd done before.

John had done his utmost to stop her: threatened, bullied, refused to give her the money for the fees. Hit her!

'It's either art school or I'll get a job,' Clare said coldly. 'I'm not staying in the house by myself for the rest of my life.' She was bored out of her mind, full of unusual energy, the urge to explore, get to know people. But it was as if she'd escaped from the prison of her deformity and found herself in another, private, prison with John the warder.

'Meet anyone today?' John asked casually that night when she came downstairs after reading the children their story.

'I meet all sorts of people all day long.'

'I meant anyone special, that is.'

'I don't know what you mean by "special".' She knew she was being awkward, but 'special' seemed a strange word to use. Perhaps it was the only one he could think of to describe the short walk she'd taken with Peter White.

She could tell he was struggling to think of another way to pose the question and felt sick to her soul at the idea of having to relate in detail the entirely innocuous things she'd said to Peter. She wondered what his reaction would be if he knew Peter had asked her out! Imagine telling him *that*!

'I'm going to bed.' She got up abruptly. 'I feel very tired.' It was only half past eight and she resented having to go so early, but it was the only way to escape further interrogation. She would have liked to practise her drawing.

'I'll be up in a minute. I'm fair worn out too.'

Don't hurry, she wanted to say. Please don't hurry. These days, she couldn't stand him touching her. His eager, exploring fingers made her stomach turn. There was something so *possessive* about the way he made love. He made her feel like a thing, not a person.

This can't go on, Clare thought as she pulled the bedclothes around her shoulders. I can't put up with this much longer. I *won't* put up with it. She'd cast out on her own before and would do it again, though this time she wouldn't be on her own but would have three children. She thought of disappearing to another country, Canada or Australia, but the children had Lacey on their birth certificates and she didn't have wedding lines to prove she was their mother. John's authority would be required before they would be given passports and he mustn't know they were leaving. She had the uneasy feeling he might kill her if he found out.

She would finish the art course first so it would be easier to get a job. And she would need money. Fortunately, John was generous with the housekeeping. She'd start putting a few pounds aside each week. It would take a while, but she already felt better, knowing there was a future in which John Lacey no longer figured. She would be free.

'Our Fion? Oh, she's living in London,' Alice announced gaily. 'She went weeks ago. She's having the time of her life.'

'Is she working in a hairdresser's?' the customer enquired.

Patsy O'Leary answered: 'Yes, in this dead posh place in Knightsbridge, not far from Harrods, as it happens.' Patsy was innocently relaying the lie Alice had told her to explain Fion's sudden disappearence.

Alice went into the kitchen and the customer winked at Patsy. 'I suppose she'll be back in six or seven months and the population of the world will have increased by one.'

'Oh, no,' Patsy said, annoyed. 'Not Fionnuala. She's not a bit like that.'

The woman looked suitably chastened and changed the subject to one close to Patsy's heart. 'How's your Daisy's Marilyn?'

'Oh, she's fine. You'll never believe this, but she's only nine months old and already walking . . .'

As Patsy had predicted, the customer didn't believe a single word.

Orla only had to mention once to her father-in-law that she would very much like a typewriter for him to arrive at the house in Pearl Street within a week, bearing an old, battered Royal. He winked. 'You'll never guess where this came from!'

'Oh, yes I do.' Orla had known where it would come from when she'd asked him to get it. The backs of lorries proved a useful source of supply whenever they needed something they couldn't afford. Lulu's new bike had come the same way and several other of the children's toys.

'It works OK,' Bert said. 'I've tried it. Managed to type me own name, though it took a good ten minutes. Where would you like it, luv?'

'In the parlour. Thanks, Bert.'

'Any time, luv. All you have to do is ask.'

Orla was about to joke she wouldn't have minded a mink coat, but held her tongue in case one appeared.

'Now, you look here,' she said sternly to the children that night. 'This is not a toy to be played with. This is *mine*. Do you understand that?' She spelt the word out carefully. 'M – I – N – E. It belongs to your mum.'

'Can you get toy ones?' Lulu wanted to know.

'I'm not sure. I'll ask Grandad.'

'What's it for, luv?' Micky asked when he came home. Maisie and Gary were attached to his legs, and he was holding baby Paul in his arms. Lulu, her arms resting on the table, was taking far too much thoughtful interest in the typewriter.

'To make pastry with.' Orla rolled her eyes. 'What the hell d'you think it's for, Micky Lavin? It's to type on, you great oaf. People used to send little items of local news to the *Crosby Star* and I thought I'd do the same, as well as to the *Bootle Times*. I could even try and write articles. I wouldn't make much from it, but every little helps.'

'We're not short of money, are we?' Micky looked alarmed. Every week he handed over every penny of his wages and Orla gave him five bob back for himself. Otherwise, the housekeeping was a mystery to him.

'We're all right. Not exactly flush, so a bit extra's useful. It means we might be able to afford a holiday. In a caravan, say, somewhere like Southport.'

Micky's dark eyes brightened. 'That would be the gear.'

'Wouldn't it!' Their glances met and Orla's insides did a somersault, though there was nothing remotely romantic about a caravan holiday in Southport. By now, Orla had expected to be living in Mayfair, interviewing famous people for a top newspaper or magazine. Instead, she was stuck in a little house in Bootle with a husband and four children. She didn't know if she was happy or not.

The children, Micky and Orla collapsed together on to the settee and hugged each other lavishly. Orla wasn't sure if this was happiness, but it would do for now.

Alice was in the throes of buying the lease on a hairdresser's in Strand Road that was closing down.

'Why do you do it, Mam?' Orla asked curiously. She had come round to see her mother one Sunday afternoon. Micky had taken the children to North Park and she felt bored on her own.

'Do what, luv?'

'Keep buying new hairdressers?'

'For goodness sake, Orla. I took over Myrtle's fourteen years ago. There's only been Marsh Lane since then.'

'You might soon have one in Strand Road. That'll be three.'

Alice shrugged. 'I'm not sure why. It's not the money. I suppose I find it exciting. Anyroad, our Fion's gone, and by this time next year Maeve will be married and Cormac at university. I need something to keep me busy, fill up me life, as it were.'

'Oh, Mam!' Orla cried. 'That sounds really sad.'

'Sometimes I feel really sad.' Alice glanced around the room which still had the same furniture that Orla remembered from her childhood. 'I sometimes wonder how things would have gone if your dad were still at home. If only he hadn't had that accident.'

'I'm fed up hearing about the stupid accident,' Orla said hotly. 'Anyroad, it wasn't that that mucked everything up. It was the way he behaved afterwards. There was a girl at school whose dad lost both legs in the war, but he didn't take it out on his family. People are funny . . .' Orla paused.

'Funny in what way, Orla?'

'Things happen and it brings out the worst in people, or it brings out the best. If Dad hadn't burnt his face, we would never have known he was capable of behaving the way he did, or that you were capable of running three hairdressers.'

Alice sighed wistfully. 'We were so happy until that ship went up in flames. From then on, the world just fell apart.'

Orla hurled herself across the room and knelt beside her mother. She slid her arms around her waist and laid her head upon her knee. 'No, it didn't, Mam. You kept the world together for us. We were still happy, despite Dad – and even more happy after he'd gone.'

'You never know people, do you? I thought I knew everything there was to know about your dad.'

'Sometimes people turn out nicer than you'd expect,' Orla said encouragingly. She felt worried; it was most unlike her mother to be so despondent. 'Look at Horace Flynn. He brought you flowers the other day.'

'I know, he still comes round the salon. He misses Fion. They were friends, though I can't think why.'

Because they were two misfits together, Orla thought, but didn't say. 'Our Fion was always very kind,' she lied. Fion could be a bitch when she was in the mood.

'I wish she'd write,' Alice said fretfully. 'Oh, I know she sends cards from London, but they never say anything much. I want to know if she's happy, where she's living so I can write back. I want to know how she *is!*'

Two more years were to pass before Alice received news of her daughter. It arrived in a letter from Neil Greene and was dated November 1960.

Dear Alice,

I know we agreed not to write to each other, but something has happened I thought you'd like to know. Firstly – this is not the 'something' – my divorce from Babs came through the other day. You may not think this relevant but it is, because to celebrate my brother, Adrian, who incidentally became a fully fledged MP following last year's election, invited me to tea at the House of Commons.

I arrived at the House at about five thirty and wondered why there was such a commotion going on. It seemed as if hundreds of women, though it was probably only a few dozen, were gathered outside carrying placards, all shouting and screaming abuse at everyone in sight apart from themselves.

'A Woman's Right to Choose', the placards said, or 'Whose Body Is It Anyway?'. I remembered Adrian saying a Private Member's Bill to legalise abortion was being discussed that day. Although fully in sympathy with the Bill – unlike Adrian, who opposed it – my heart sank a little at the thought of fighting my way through a crowd of such vociferous females. It sank even further when one of the women grabbed me and I thought I was about to be attacked, or at least debagged and subjected to something shameful and possibly degrading.

But no! 'Hello, Neil,' the woman said. It took some time before I recognised it was Fionnuala. She looks wonderful, Alice. Very slim, taller somehow, long wild hair, rosy cheeks and lovely bright, bright eyes.

It was impossible to say much in such circumstances and I shall always regret not suggesting we meet some other time, but then I have always been a bit slow-witted. I managed to ask what she was doing. 'I'm a union organiser,' she said, which I found quite staggering as I can't recall her being interested in politics. I was about to ask where she was living when we were both swept away by the crowds and lost sight of each other.

Fion may have made contact with you by now and you know all this but, in case not, I thought I'd write and let you know she looks fine and you have nothing to worry about.

As for me, I miss Bootle terribly. It was where I felt at home. One day I shall return, I swear it. I miss teaching, too, but it was unfair of me to continue to deny Babs a divorce, and divorce and teaching in a Catholic school were incompatible. I'm working in the City, doing something frightfully dull and frightfully unimportant in Insurance – having a father with a title and a brother in Parliament can work wonders when you're seeking a job. I'm seeing a woman called Heather, divorced like me. We sort of like each other.

An old colleague from St James's continues to send me the *Bootle Times* each week, so I keep myself abreast of what goes on. Congratulations on the new salon – I saw the advert announcing the opening and tried to imagine exactly where in Strand Road it is. How does it feel to have three?

I also saw the news about Maurice Lacey. He seemed a nice boy, though not exactly bright. It came as a shock to read he'd been sent to prison. What was it? Breaking and entering – a newsagent's, if I remember rightly.

I closely study the Birth, Marriages and Deaths columns. I have been holding my breath, but there has been no mention of Orla under the first, though I noticed the announcement of Maeve's wedding under the second and saw the picture the following week. Was Martin as nervous as he looked? I see Horace Flynn has died. Such a strange man! I trust his properties haven't fallen into the hands of someone who will cause problems for you with leases.

My colleague told me Cormac was accepted at Cambridge. You must feel inordinately proud.

Well, I think that's all, so goodbye, my dearest Alice. You are rarely far from my thoughts.

Your glum and rather lonely friend,
Neil.

She found Neil's letter upsetting and wished they had never become lovers, just remained good friends. Then they could have remained friends when Neil moved away. Alice missed having someone to confide in, even if it were only by letter. These days, Bernadette was completely wrapped up in Danny and the children. Although she and Alice were the same age, Bernadette had had babies when Alice already had grandchildren and seemed to be growing younger as Alice grew older.

Even worse, although she was relieved to hear that Fion was safe and well, it shocked her to the core to learn she had actually been outside the House of Commons waving a placard in support of abortion. Alice was possibly more opposed to abortion than to divorce and the idea of one of her daughters promoting legalised murder filled her with revulsion. Still, no matter what Fion had been up to, she longed for her to come home.

December came, Cormac arrived from Cambridge and she put the contents of the letter out of her mind to concentrate on her son.

Cormac was twenty. He had never grown tall like his father, but had filled out a little. His shoulders were neither broad nor narrow, but they looked strong and the tops of his arms were surprisingly muscled – he'd played tennis all summer, both at Cambridge and, during the holidays, on the courts in North Park, and the long hours spent outdoors had turned his pale skin a lovely golden brown. His hair, a mite too long in Alice's opinion, hung over his forehead in a casual quiff, streaked with white by the sun. He kept pushing it out of his eyes with a brown hand. He looked sophisticated, but at the same time his face still retained the guileless, trusting expression he'd had when he was a little boy. Even then, no one had tried to take advantage of Cormac. He was genuinely liked by everyone and everyone seemed to want him to like them in return.

Alice had been worried university would change her son, that he would grow ashamed of Amber Street and his family. But university had done nothing of the kind. Cormac was proud of his roots. He'd spent weekends in other chaps' houses and they were big, cold morgues of places, where he said he'd hate to live all the time. Most of the chaps had spent their childhoods in boarding schools, which sounded dead horrible and which he would have hated even more. He still talked with a Liverpool accent, possibly not quite so pronounced as before.

Of course, other graduates made fun of the way he spoke, but he didn't give a damn. 'I tell them I'm working class and proud of it, and make fun of the way *they* speak – they call their folks Mater and Pater.' He said he was pleased to be home among normal people.

Working class or not, Cormac must have been popular in view of the number of Christmas cards that arrived for him from all over the country, even more than last year. On Boxing Day he'd been invited to a drinks party in a chap's house in Chester. He might go, or he might not, he wasn't sure.

The young woman came into the salon a few days before Christmas. Alice and her assistants were at their busiest and the windows were blurred with steam. Alice looked up briefly, then turned away. Patsy was seeing to her. Then Alice looked again and wondered where she had seen the young woman before. It was the hair, more than anything, that looked familiar: very fair, very smooth, silky. Perhaps the woman had been to the salon before, though she didn't often forget a customer and this one was quite outstandingly pretty.

'Alice,' Patsy called. 'Someone would like a word with you.'

'Half a mo.' Alice was combing out Florrie Piper, still a regular customer and still insistent that her hair be dyed the colour of soot, even though she was gone seventy.

'Leave me be, luv,' said Florrie. 'I don't mind waiting a few minutes and admiring the decorations. And it's lovely and warm in here.'

'Ta, Florrie.' Alice went over to the newcomer who wore a smart double-breasted navy coat with a half-belt at the back and navy boots. 'How can I help you, luv?'

'Mrs Lacey? I'd like to speak to you in private.' The request was made so brusquely, without a 'please', that Alice blinked.

'Well, there's only the kitchen.'

'That'll do.'

Alice was aware of Patsy's curious eyes following as they walked through the salon. She felt just as curious herself. 'What's this all about?' she enquired when they were in the privacy of the kitchen.

'I'm leaving John.'

'I beg your pardon?'

'I'm leaving John, your husband. I'm going today. I shall pick the children up from school in an hour's time, then catch a train somewhere far away. I shan't tell you where because I don't want John to know.'

Alice's head reeled. She swayed, reached for a chair and sat down before her legs gave way. She felt confused and very old. 'What's all this got to do with me?' She could hear the tremor in her voice.

'I thought someone should know because he's bound to be very upset and I shall worry about him.'

'I don't understand. Who *are* you?' The woman looked much older close up, at least thirty. Alice remembered where she'd seen her before. '*You're* the girl from Crozier Terrace! You've got a nerve, coming here. There's some women who'd tear your eyes out.' She stared at the face, which had gone very pink. 'I thought you had . . .'

The girl tossed her head. 'I had a hare lip, but it's been fixed and ever since John has made my life unbearable. I wasn't prepared to put up with it any longer. It's taken ages to get the money together, find a place for us to live, get a job. But now I've done it and I'm leaving today. I knew, somehow, you wouldn't tear my eyes out from things John's said. I got the impression your marriage was over long before he met me.'

'Perhaps it was.' Alice was beginning to get her wits back. 'Just let me get this straight,' she said carefully. 'You're walking out, but it makes you feel guilty, so you've decided to plonk the responsibility for what you're doing in *my* lap?'

The woman's face went pinker. 'I suppose I have.'

'That's very nice of you, I must say. What makes you think I give a damn what happens to John?'

'Is there another chair?'

'No.'

'The thing is' – she leaned against the sink – 'in a way, I still love him. I feel terrible for what I'm about to do. I imagine him coming home tonight, finding us gone.' She twisted uneasily. 'He'll be devastated.'

'And you think me turning up with buckets of sympathy will make him feel less devastated?' Alice laughed in disbelief. 'I never want anything to do with him again.'

'I thought you might possibly care.'

'Well, I don't. And if you love him all that much, then why are you walking out?'

'Because I think one day I might hate him.' She stared at the older woman almost angrily. 'Surely you understand? I love him because I know how kind and gentle he can be. He's wonderful with the children.' She pointed to her lovely face. 'John was responsible for this. It's changed my life, but the trouble is it changed him too. He became a different person. He couldn't bear me out of his sight. Did he ever hit you?'

'Just the once.' It all sounded very familiar. Alice frowned. 'Has he hit you?'

'Rather more than just the once.'

Patsy stuck her head round the door, her ears almost visibly flapping. 'Your next customer's here, Alice, and Florrie's still waiting to be finished off.'

'I'll have to go.' Alice got to her feet. Her legs still felt as if they were filled with jelly.

'I hope I haven't upset you.'

'Of course you've upset me. Who wouldn't be upset under the circumstances? All *right*, Patsy, I'll be out in a minute.' Patsy disappeared with obvious reluctance. 'I tell you what, I'll ask me dad to go round and see John, make sure he's all right. I'm not prepared to go near him.' It meant she'd have to tell Dad what had happened, that John had got himself another family, that he hadn't just walked out. Neil was the only person who knew the real truth. 'Are you still living in Crozier Terrace?'

'No, we moved ages ago. We're in Crosby now, 8 Rainford Road. Thank you. I appreciate you being so nice about this.'

'I don't feel a bit nice,' Alice said drily. 'Out of interest, what's your name?'

'Clare Coulson.' She paused at the kitchen door. 'Goodbye, Alice.'

'Good luck, Clare.'

Danny Mitchell didn't think he'd ever been asked to carry out a task that filled him with such revulsion. If he arrived at Rainford Road and found John Lacey with a rope and about to hang himself, his first instinct would have been to help him tie the knot. But it was a long time since Alice had asked for his help, possibly too long. Danny was uncomfortably aware that he had neglected his daughter, so wrapped up had he been in his young wife and their children. Alice hadn't exactly lost her dad and her best friend when Danny married Bernadette, but as good as. Neither was available for her in the way they'd been before.

His heart was full of loathing for his son-in-law. Alice had explained to him and Bernadette the real reason why the marriage had broken down.

'Oh, luv! You should have told us all this a long while ago,' Bernadette cried. She looked anguishedly at Danny and he could see his own guilt reflected in her eyes.

'I felt ashamed,' Alice said simply. 'I didn't want anyone to know.'

'It's nothing to be ashamed of.' Danny's voice was gruff. 'John's the one who should be ashamed. He brings misery on everyone he touches.'

'Anyroad, Dad. This girl, this Clare Coulson, she's worried about him.'

'She's got a nerve!' Danny and Bernadette said together.

'Actually, I quite liked her. She's got spunk, which is more than I ever had. I just sat back and let things happen.'

'You say he actually hit her?'

'Yes, Dad.'

'I'll sort him out,' Danny said grimly.

'No one wants you to sort him out, luv,' Bernadette put in. 'You're just going to make sure he's all right, that's all, like Alice promised.'

'I'd like to sort him out with me fists.'

'John's years younger than you, Danny Mitchell. I don't want you coming back here with a black eye and a broken nose. Forget your fists and use your mouth instead.'

'Yes, luv,' Danny said meekly.

Danny had barely taken his finger off the bell when the door opened and he didn't think he'd ever seen a look of such naked misery on a face when John saw who it was. He'd clearly been expecting someone else.

'Can I come in a minute?'

John seemed to collect himself. He shrugged and stood to one side. 'If you must. I can only spare you a minute. I've got things to do.'

The business must be doing all right, Danny thought as he walked down the spacious carpeted hall into a large, charming room, which had clearly benefited from a woman's touch. There were vases of rushes, bowls of dried flowers, a cosy blue moquette three-piece, rugs and numerous pictures on the walls. Danny tried to take everything in without making it too obvious, knowing Bernadette would subject him to the third degree when he got home. Perhaps it was because he knew the circumstances, but the room had a sad, deserted air, as if all the life had gone out of it. The fire was a mountain of grey ash with only the occasional glowing coal. It felt very cold.

'What can I do for you, Danny?' John stood, legs apart, in front of the fireplace. He didn't ask the visitor to sit down. Danny sensed he was coiled as tightly as a spring. It wouldn't take much to make this man explode. He longed to be at home in his own comfortable little house with his comfortable little wife.

'I'll come straight to the point,' Danny said bluntly. 'I'm only here for one reason, to make sure you're all right. Once you've assured me that you are, then I'll be off.'

John frowned slightly. 'Is there any reason why I shouldn't be all right?'

'I understand someone walked out on you today, someone called Clare. She came round and asked Alice to see to you, as it were.' Danny glowered. 'I don't appreciate our Alice being dragged into your affairs after all this time. I thought we'd done with you once and for all.'

The man's face had gone a dark, ugly red. 'Clare came to see you?'

'She came to see Alice.'

'She left a note. She didn't mention Alice. When the doorbell went I thought she'd ...'

'Come back for another beating? I doubt it, John. I doubt if you'll see that girl again.'

'She actually told ...' He turned away, put his hands on the mantelpiece, stared into the fire. Danny wondered if he was ashamed, embarrassed, or just angry. 'Did she say where she was going? She took the children. I'm worried ...'

'No, she didn't. If she had, I wouldn't tell you. I don't have much time for men who hit their women.'

'I didn't mean to hit her.'

Danny gestured impatiently. He wasn't interested in anything John Lacey might have to say. All he wanted to know was how the man was bearing up before he made his departure.

Perhaps John had read his thoughts, because he turned round and said coldly, 'I can't think why Clare went to see Alice. I was a bit surprised, that's all, when I came home tonight and found she and the kids had gone. We haven't exactly been getting on in a long time. It'll feel strange for a while without the children, but even that has its compensations. They were dead noisy and I've always liked a quiet life.'

He was lying, it was obvious, but Danny didn't care. He'd asked and the man claimed to be all right. His task was done. 'I'll be off, then.'

'I'll see you out.'

'Don't bother. I'll make me own way. Tara, John.'

The front door closed. John Lacey fell to his knees on the rug in front of the fire. His mouth opened in a silent scream and he beat the floor with his fists. He wanted to roll up in a ball of pain.

Clare had gone, the children. He knew in his heart he would never see them again. He had driven them away, just as he drove everyone away. He prayed to God to make him die.

Minutes later, or it might have been hours, when God seemed unprepared to answer his prayer and John hadn't the courage to take matters into his own hands, he got to his feet and went round the house gathering together a few possessions, which he threw in the back of the van parked outside.

The landlord could have his house back, as well as everything in it. From now on he'd live in the office at the yard. From now on nothing mattered any more.

10

Cora bought the *Liverpool Echo* especially. She opened it as soon as she got home and searched for Twenty-Firsts.

'LACEY, Cormac John. Many Happy Returns, son, on your twenty-first. With all my love, Mum,' she read.

There were three more entries for Cormac: from Maeve and Martin, from Orla and Micky and the children, and the last from Grandad, Bernadette, Ian and Ruth: 'Congratulations to a fine young man on reaching his majority.'

There would be no entries tomorrow for Maurice Lacey. Anyone who knew him would have laughed, because Maurice was in Walton jail.

Oh, the shame of it! Since the court case Cora had hardly left the house. She did the shopping Strand Road way where she wasn't known, rather than in Marsh Lane.

She still didn't know what had got into Maurice. He'd lost his job – he was 'unpunctual', according to his boss. Cora had considered it fortunate that he'd been called up to do his National Service almost straight away. It would do him good, teach him the discipline that Cora had failed to do. But the minute he came out he'd started hanging around with a girl, Pamela Conway, who had a reputation for being no better than she ought to be. It was Pamela's brothers who'd led Maurice astray, of that Cora was convinced. They were much older than him, with convictions for breaking and entering behind them. One had threatened a shopkeeper with a knife and wasn't long out of jail himself.

They'd *used* Maurice. He was a soft lad, easily led. He'd broken a window to get into the shop and it hadn't entered his daft head that someone might hear and call the bobbies. They were waiting for him when he came out, laden with boxes of cigarettes and baccy, almost certainly for the Conways to sell in the pubs at half price. He refused to clat on them. Cora suspected he was frightened.

For once, Billy had been in when the bobbies arrived and requested they come to the station, where he'd leapt at Maurice and had almost throttled him by the time he was pulled off. He wanted nothing more to do with him, he said. But when had Billy had anything much to do with his wife and son?

She recalled her own criminal past, though she'd been too clever to get caught. Perhaps thieving was inherited, like the same coloured eyes and hair. But if that was the case, Cormac . . .

Sometimes she forgot what the truth was.

By now, Cormac would be home from university for Christmas and there was bound to be a birthday do somewhere tonight – Alice threw parties at the drop of a hat.

Restless, Cora wandered round the house, touching things. It wasn't fair. Nothing was fair. Nothing had gone the way she'd expected. Horace Flynn had popped his clogs last year, but hadn't left her a thing. The chap who came to collect the rent said a nephew back in Ireland, a priest, had inherited the lot and wanted everything left the same. All the chap did was collect the leases and the rents, and send cheques to some church in County Antrim. When Cora asked why Horace's big house in Stanley Road remained empty, he knew nothing about it.

She wondered if Cormac's do would be held at home or whether Alice had booked somewhere bigger, seeing as how it was a twenty-first. Wherever it was, she wouldn't mind going and waiting outside so she could take a peek, see who was there – if she could do it without being noticed, that is.

They'd probably know in the Strand Road salon – she looked inside whenever she passed. It was always busy, but she'd never once seen Alice there. It looked a posh place, much bigger than the Laceys' in Opal Street and Marsh Lane. But she couldn't just barge in asking questions, she'd have to have something done to her hair. She'd get a trim, though she usually cut it herself, and give a false name. It wouldn't do to say she was a Lacey.

The thought cheered her up somewhat. It gave her a reason for getting out of the house. She'd go now.

Cora went into the hall and lifted her camel coat off a hook. It was twelve years old, but good quality and she wouldn't have dreamt of buying another until it wore out. She pushed her small feet into a pair of stout suede boots that were even older than the coat, then tied a scarf round her head. For some women, appearance was everything, but Cora didn't give a damn. She fastened the buttons in front of the full-length mirror. She was fifty-one and looked neither younger nor older. Not a soul in the world would have given her a second glance.

The woman in Lacey's who was doing her hair was called Enid. Cora would suit it shorter, she said. It would give it more texture and she'd look like June Allyson. 'She's a film star,' she went on in response to Cora's puzzled look. 'She was in *Little Women* and *Executive Suite.*'

'I don't get to the pictures much.'

'Don't you, luv? Me, I go at least three times a week.'

Cora said she'd prefer to stick to just an inch off, thanks all the same. She was about to add sourly that she had more important things to do with her time than go to the pictures three times a week, but remembered she wanted to pump the woman for information. This proved easy when she mentioned she was an old friend of Alice whom she hadn't seen in years. 'How's her kids getting on? Four she had, didn't she? Three girls and a boy – he was almost exactly the same age as me own lad.'

'In that case your lad must be round twenty-one, like Cormac. It's his birthday today. He's a smashing lad – I sent him a silver key meself. We're all going to his party tonight.'

'And where would that be?'

'You know Hilton's Restaurant on Stanley Road? Well, it's in the room above. There's at least fifty of us going. Alice has invited all the staff and Cormac has asked some friends from school and university. Did you know he's at Cambridge, luv? He's taking Chemistry, if you'll believe.' The woman couldn't have sounded prouder had Cormac been her own son. 'After he's got his degree, he's going to stay and get more letters after his name. When he leaves he'll be called doctor.'

Cora waited until eight o'clock before stationing herself across the road from Hilton's, a large restaurant well known as a venue for wedding receptions and parties. It was situated on the corner of busy Stanley Road and Greening Street. The double-fronted downstairs was in darkness. She could hear the noise of the party upstairs, the music and the chatter, the laughing and the singing, from all this way away, despite the passing trams and other traffic.

Why was she doing this, cowering in a doorway on a freezing cold night in December, listening to other people enjoying themselves? Because this night had been stolen from her, she told herself. This night should be *hers*. It should be *her* throwing the party for Cormac.

She waited a good hour, huddled inside her coat, stamping her feet, her gaze fixed hypnotically on the lighted upstairs windows opposite. There was no way she'd see a thing from here and she wanted to know what was going on. Spots of ice blew against her face as she crossed over and went down Greening Street to the side door of the restaurant where people had been going in. Hopping from one foot to the other, she stood hesitantly outside before pushing the door open, though she didn't go in. Narrow stairs led upwards and the noise here was deafening, a whooping and stamping of feet, as if people were doing some strange sort of dance. Cora had never been to a dance.

Dare she go in? Sneak upstairs, just peer through the door, so she didn't feel totally excluded from Cormac's twenty-first?

Well, even if she was discovered, she was unlikely to be chucked out on her ear. Alice would never be rude. Fion would have been, except she wasn't there. The woman in the salon said she was still living in London.

Cora crept upstairs, making not a sound in her crêpe-soled boots. To her left at the top there was a Ladies and a Gents, a kitchen and a door marked 'Office'. The whoops and stamping came from behind the door to her right.

Someone – it was Bernadette Mitchell – was coming out of the kitchen carrying a birthday cake with the candles already lit, too concerned with watching her feet in case she tripped over to notice Cora, who shot into the Ladies, heart thumping.

The music and the stamping suddenly stopped. There was utter silence for a minute, then 'Happy birthday to you, Happy birthday to you, Happy birthday, dear Cormac . . .'

They loved him. Everyone loved Cormac.

Cormac, Maurice. Maurice, Cormac. The names chased each other around Cora's brain. She'd thought she was doing a good thing all them years ago, but she'd done a bad one. If only she'd left things as they were, it would be Alice with a lad in Walton jail, not her. If only she could go back twenty-one years and put everything right.

The Ladies was a large room that doubled as a cloakroom. Two sides of the walls were full of coats, and there were two lavatories. Cora went inside one and closed the door. She pulled down the seat to sit on. They were singing 'For he's a jolly good fellow' now. Alice was probably hanging on to his arm, looking gormless. She didn't deserve Cormac for a son.

Oh, it wasn't *fair*!

There was a sudden rush of women into the Ladies. They kept trying Cora's door. 'Who's in there?' someone said. 'They've been ages.'

A few minutes later there was a knock. 'Are you all right?' It was that bloody Patsy woman who worked for Alice.

'Yes,' Cora replied gruffly.

The Ladies emptied. The music started again, quieter now, romantic music. She imagined the lights turned low and everyone dancing, and wondered if Cormac had a girlfriend with him.

Not long afterwards the women returned to collect their coats. The party must be over. From their conversation, they'd had a dead good time. After about fifteen minutes of bustle there was silence. Alice hadn't been in for her coat, Cora would have recognised her voice. Unlatching the door, she came out to find only a handful of coats left on the hooks and wondered if she could make it from the lavatory to the stairs without being seen, otherwise she might end up being locked in the building all night.

There was no one in the kitchen. Cora had reached the top of the stairs and was about to creep down as quietly as she'd come, when she noticed the door to the big room was open and there was still music, very faint, so faint that it was almost drowned out by the noise of the traffic outside.

She paused. At the far end, Orla and Maeve were dancing with their husbands: that no-mark Micky Lavin and the one who had a good job at the hospital, Martin. Danny and Bernadette were standing by a radiogram, sifting through records. Cora edged closer until Alice came into view. She wore a lovely bottle-green dress with a fluted hem and was sprawled on a chair, legs stretched out in front, clearly worn out. But Cora didn't think she'd ever seen such a look of perfect contentment on a face before. Alice quite literally glowed. Her face seemed to be exuding darts of electricity and Cora felt her own face prickle, as if from tiny electric shocks. Her sister-in-law was experiencing the happiness that was *her* due, the happiness that had been denied her all these years.

She edged closer, her eyes searching for Cormac. He appeared, inch by inch, bending over Alice. He wore black trousers and a white shirt that looked too big for him, she thought. It was all bunched up round the waist where it was tucked inside a narrow belt. He might have started off the evening with a tie, but wasn't wearing one now. The collar of the shirt was open, emphasising his slender neck. Cora's heart missed a beat. He looked dead handsome. He and Alice were laughing together about something. The whole scene looked like a painting of Happy Families. Then Cormac suddenly reached out and stroked Alice's hair.

Something snapped in the watching woman. Her head felt as if it was full of smoke: thick, black smoke, that swirled around and got hotter and hotter.

By now, Maurice would have kipped down in his cell. 'Lights Out' would have been called. Everywhere smelt of pee, he claimed. The food was awful. After a few months, Cora had stopped going to see him. She didn't know what to say and the other visitors were scum. She felt ashamed, mixing with them. She wasn't sure if she wanted Maurice back home. She wasn't sure if she loved him any more.

This was her son, her lad, the fruit of her womb, this fair-haired, clever, extremely dashing young man.

'Drat!' Alice had kicked something over. A glass of wine. The liquid spilled like blood on to the polished floor.

'I'll get a cloth from the kitchen.' Cormac began to hurry towards the door, towards Cora, the son towards his mother. God must have arranged for that glass to be knocked over.

Cora backed up so that she was in the kitchen when Cormac came in. He jumped, startled. 'Aunt Cora! I didn't know you were here. Why don't you go in the big room with me mam?'

She fixed her eyes squarely on his neat, good-looking face. 'You're mine,' she said in a deep, passionate voice that she didn't know she possessed.

'I beg your pardon?' Cormac said courteously.

'I said, you're *mine*,' she continued in the same unnatural voice. 'The night you were born, I swapped you round for Maurice. I went for a walk in the hospital. Everyone was asleep, 'cept me. When I came to the nursery, Maurice was in the cot marked Lacey 1, and you were in Lacey 2. I changed you round.'

Cormac was actually smiling. 'Don't talk rubbish, Aunt Cora. I don't like to be rude, but I've never heard such ridiculous nonsense.'

'It's not nonsense, luv. It's true,' Cora insisted hoarsely.

He laughed. 'Things like that aren't allowed to happen in hospitals.'

'They happened that night. There was a raid. It was like hell on earth, women and babies all over the place: in the cellar one minute, in the wards the next.' Cora clutched his arm, but he shrugged her away.

'This is going beyond a joke.' His voice had become icy cold. 'I'm sorry about Maurice being in prison, Aunt Cora, but it doesn't mean you have to spoil *my* twenty-first for me.'

He thought she was saying things out of spite! 'Oh, luv,' she cried. She reached for him, but he moved away with an expression of distaste. 'I don't want to spoil anything, I just thought it was time you knew the truth. I told you, it was bedlam in the hospital, nurses rushing around like lunatics. There was this emergency. Alice wasn't shown her baby till next morning, when they gave her you 'stead of Maurice. It's not your twenty-first till tomorrer. It's Maurice who's twenty-one today.'

It seemed as if the reference to the birthdays, trivial in comparison with the other things she'd said, had sown a seed of doubt in Cormac's mind. He went as white as a sheet. 'Just supposing,' he said carefully, 'just supposing there's a grain of truth in what you've said, what on earth would possess you to do such a wicked thing?'

Cora smiled slyly. 'Because I thought Maurice looked the better bet, but it turned out I was wrong.'

'Jaysus!'

She felt slightly uneasy at the sight of his gentle face contorted with horror and disgust. Perhaps she should have approached it differently, or at least thought things through before she opened her big mouth. Perhaps it would have been best if she'd told Alice first. Alice knew the way things had been that night and would have been easier to convince.

'Cormac!' Alice shouted. 'Where's that cloth?'

'Won't be a minute, Mam.' His face had cleared, become devoid of expression. 'I don't believe you. You're just making trouble, something you're very good at, going by past experience.'

'Just take a look at yourself in the mirror, son,' Cora said softly. She'd upset him badly, which was only to be expected. She felt a surge of sympathy that made her body ache, but no way was she going to deny that what she'd said was true. She'd already suffered enough for that one silly mistake. 'It's never crossed anyone's mind to notice, but you're the spitting image of me, your mam – the same shaped face, the same little hands.' Alice had long, thin hands, John's were broad. She held out her own hands, spreading the small fingers, regarding them impassively. 'See, son.'

For the first time in Cormac's life his legendary calm deserted him. 'Don't you dare call me "son". I'm not your son. I'd sooner die than be your son. I want nothing to do with you.' He could hardly speak. The words came out thickly, as if his tongue had got too big for his mouth.

Cora chewed her bottom lip. She didn't like seeing her boy in such a state, but what had she expected? For him to throw himself into her arms?

All this must have come as a terrible shock. 'Why don't we get Alice out here?' she suggested.

'Does Mam *know*?'

'No, but it's about time she did.' She thought Cormac was about to hit her. He reared over her, pushed his face in hers. 'Don't you *dare* breathe a word about this to me mam, d'you hear? It would kill her. I don't want anyone else to know. Do you hear me, Aunt Cora. *I don't want anyone else to know.*'

'But,' Cora began, disappointed, because she wanted the whole world to know that *this* was her son: Maurice, the jail bird, belonged to someone else.

Then Cormac put his small white hands round Cora's scraggy neck and began to squeeze. 'If you tell another soul, Aunt Cora, so help me, I'll kill you. I swear it. No matter where I am, I'll come back and kill you stone dead.'

She was gagging. 'Leave go, son. I won't tell a soul.'

He removed his hands. 'You'd better not,' he said threateningly. 'And don't, don't ever call me son again.'

With a sense of perverse pride, Cora realised that soft, gentle Cormac, who everyone thought wouldn't have hurt a fly, who had never been heard to raise his voice in anger, meant every word. She herself had killed, a long time ago, two people. A chip off the old block, she thought. He's his mammy's son, that's for sure. She sighed happily. Cormac knew the truth and that was all that mattered. One of these days he'd come round and learn to love his mam.

Cormac went into the Gents and stared at himself in the mirror. Within the space of a few minutes the bottom had dropped out of his world. He hadn't realised how swiftly life could change, that you could be completely happy one minute, in the depths of despair the next.

He had never liked Aunt Cora. She gave him the jitters. There was something unhinged about her. As he grew older, he'd become convinced that she was mad and, if she truly was his mother, then he, Cormac, could easily become mad himself. He hadn't, for instance, considered himself remotely capable of murder, yet minutes ago he'd grabbed a woman by the throat with the intention of strangling her. He wondered if he would have done it if there hadn't been other people around.

By some obscene coincidence her name could actually be made from the letters of his: Cormac, Cora, as if, inadvertently, there'd been a connection between them all along.

The idea that everything that had happened so far in his life was due entirely to the quirk of a crazy woman wandering around a hospital in the dead of night made his stomach curl with horror. It was enough to make anyone lose his mind.

On the other hand he supposed he was lucky. It could have been *him*, not

Maurice, brought up in the house in Garibaldi Road with a cane hanging on the wall.

Poor Maurice! Cormac shuddered.

He no longer felt sure who he was, whom he belonged to, which family was his. He told himself that Aunt Cora was talking rubbish, as he'd first thought, except that the person staring back at him from the mirror had the cold eyes and the nothing face of his detested aunt. The eyes were a different colour, that was all.

Oh, God! Why hadn't he noticed before? Why hadn't anyone? Until now, he'd always considered himself at least averagely good-looking, but the face in the mirror looked like that of a corpse.

'We don't know who on earth he takes after,' Mam said when people remarked Cormac was nothing like the rest of the family. No one had noticed the remarkable resemblance between the woman who now claimed to be his mother and himself. He would never, never be able to get his head round the fact that Alice wasn't his mam.

There was a knock on the door. 'Cormac, are you all right, son? I hope you haven't made yourself sick with all that beer. Oh, by the way, I've got a cloth meself.'

'I'm all right.' He couldn't bring himself to say 'Mam', he just couldn't. 'I'll be out in a minute,' he called.

11
1965

Cormac lay flat on his back within a circle of brittle corn. He stared at the sky through the corn tunnel that grew narrower and narrower until the top seemed no bigger than his eye. The flattened plants beneath him stuck sharply into his body through his thin Indian top and flared cotton pants, though they didn't hurt. His arms were spread as wide as they would go and his hands were hidden within the yellow stalks. The tips of his fingers touched those of Wally on one side and Frank the Yank, snoring his head off, on the other.

He imagined himself a bird passing overhead and seeing himself and his friends spread out like a row of little paper men.

'Why is the sun red?' Wally murmured.

'I don't know,' Cormac answered. 'Why is everywhere so hot?'

'Because the sun is so red, man. It's on fire.'

'I need a drink.' Cormac sat up and experimentally touched his bare toes. The fact that he was physically capable of such an act meant he was badly in need of a joint as well as a drink so that his senses would become sufficiently blurred.

He got to his feet and staggered towards a luridly painted coach that was parked in the corner of a field in Suffolk, Sussex or Surrey, he couldn't remember which. He knew they were on their way to play at a pop festival in Norwich, which would start the day after tomorrow. The farmer whose field they were on was so far unaware he had trespassers. If he noticed before they left that night, they would be turfed off sharpish with the aid of a couple of savage dogs, a shotgun, or possibly both.

Inside, the coach buzzed with flies. When bought, it had already been converted into a mobile home with six bunks, three each side, as close as shelves, a tiny sink and a table at the rear with fitted, plastic-covered benches. Behind a screen a chemical lavatory remained unused because no one was prepared to empty it and there was a tiny fridge that no longer worked. The windows had been painted over to provide privacy, apart from the one in the roof, which wouldn't open. The sun scorched through the glass like a blowtorch, turning the cramped space into an oven.

Cormac could hardly breathe in the suffocating heat. He opened the fridge and remembered it was broken when he came face to face with half a mouldy tomato. Nothing came out when he turned on the tap over the sink – the water tank must be empty. He searched everywhere, in the cupboard under the sink, under bunks, under the clothes that littered the bunks, but could find nothing except a few empty beer bottles that yielded not a drop when he attempted to drain them. In the process he knocked over a guitar, which fell to the floor with a hollow boom and he noticed one of the strings was broken.

Then he recalled that the girls had gone into the village to buy supplies: Tanya and Pol, but his memory was hazy as to the time they'd gone. It could have been five minutes ago or five hours.

Jaysus, the smell in here was foul. Someone had been sick the night before and everywhere reeked of vomit. Perhaps that was what attracted the flies. There was another smell, quite strong, and Cormac realised it was paint. The fiery sun was burning the paint off the outside of the coach.

He'd die if he didn't have a drink soon. Perhaps a joint would lessen his thirst. He remembered a joint was one of the reasons he was there and reached under the pillow on his bunk for the battered Golden Virginia tin in which he kept his stuff.

'Hello, friends,' he said affectionately to the contents of the tin: a packet of red Rizla papers and a book of matches nestling within a bed of tobacco and, most important, a lump of hash that felt warm. He spread the tobacco on a paper and shredded a portion of the hash with his fingernail so that it was evenly spread, then put back the remainder carefully. He lit the spliff, took a long, deep puff, then went out and sat in the shade of the coach, his back against it. It didn't feel even vaguely cool, but at least he was out of the sun.

'Hi, man.' Wally appeared. 'Is there anything to drink in there?'

Cormac shook his head. 'Not a drop, man.'

'Where's Tanya and Pol?'

'Gone somewhere. Where's Frank?'

'Asleep.'

'Shouldn't someone wake him? He'll get sunburn.' Did you get sunburn or catch it?

'I suppose someone should.' Wally must have decided it wasn't going to be him. He sat beside Cormac and gestured towards the joint. Cormac handed it to him. They shared everything, including the girls. Cormac and Wally had shared each other, only the once, but had decided it wasn't for them.

Frank the Yank provided most of the money. His pa had sent him abroad to escape the Vietnam draft and wherever they went, Frank only had to find a Lloyds bank and produce his passport, and massive amounts of cash would be handed over. It was Frank who'd bought the coach and they'd painted it together. The others signed on the dole if they stayed somewhere long enough, but that didn't happen often.

A pleasant fog had formed inside Cormac's head. He was no longer thirsty. This hazy sensation of wanting nothing, needing nothing, was something Cormac wished to retain for the rest of his life. His ambition was to get from one day to the next in the deepest possible daze without actually becoming unconscious – unconsciousness appealed, but was impractical.

The girls returned, loaded with shopping. Cormac feebly raised a hand in greeting. Pol smiled, but Tanya eyed them balefully.

'You're stoned,' she said accusingly. 'I bet you haven't cleaned up inside.' Tanya was tall, breathtakingly beautiful and extremely bad-tempered for most of the time. She wore a full-length flowered skirt and a skimpy T-shirt. Her mother was a famous model.

'Cleaned up inside?' Cormac and Wally said more or less together. They looked at each other. It was the first they'd heard of it.

'It stinks in there. It wasn't Pol or me who was sick. You promised you'd clean it.'

'Did we?'

'I'll do it.' Pol was short and slight, and merely pretty. She had crisp brown curly hair and a heart-shaped face. In her limp, shapeless cotton frock, she looked no more than sixteen, though she was twenty-one, three years younger than Cormac. 'As my horrible mother used to say, "If you want something done properly, then do it yourself".'

'Alice used to say something like that.' Cormac grinned.

'Where's Frank?' Tanya demanded.

'Asleep,' Wally said.

'In there?' She pointed to the coach.

'No, over yonder,' Wally said poetically and gave a vague wave in the direction of the field.

'Tsk, tsk. He'll get sunburnt.' Tanya marched away, her back rigid, like a schoolmistress. Cormac supposed that someone had to keep them in order. He was glad Tanya was around. And Pol. Particularly Pol.

'I'll put these away.' Pol staggered as she picked up one of the bags laden with shopping.

Cormac's innate courtesy came to the fore and he stumbled to his feet. 'I'll give you a hand with those.'

'Ta, Cormac. Phew, what a smell!' Pol gasped when they were inside the coach. She tripped over the guitar and it slid along the floor until it stopped under the table with a thump. 'We need to find a launderette and wash the sleeping bags. There's bound to be one in Ipswich, and they're usually open till late. I'll chuck everything outside for now.' With that, she began to grab the sleeping bags and the scattered clothes, and to throw them out of the door. The worst of the smell went with them.

Where on earth did she get the energy from? Cormac wondered. He himself would have found it a simple matter to wallow in filth for the rest of his life rather than wash a sheet. 'Is that where we are, Ipswich?' He'd only vaguely heard of the place before.

'About five miles away. Are you thirsty?' She was putting the food away under the sink.

'I think I might well be.'

'Would you like some lemonade?'

'That would be most acceptable.'

'Sit down, then, and I'll pour you some.'

'Thank you, Pol,' Cormac said gravely.

'When we stop in Ipswich to do the washing, it wouldn't hurt if you washed your hair, Cormac. It's getting quite matted. You could do it in a Gents toilet.'

'I like it matted.' Cormac touched the hair that went halfway down his back. It felt greasy and unusually thick.

Pol shrugged, easygoing. 'Please yourself.'

'I'll wash me hair for *you*.' He liked Pol very much, perhaps a bit too much. He was beginning to resent having to share her with Wally and Frank. Perhaps they should find another girl and split into three separate couples. 'I think I love you, Pol,' he said seriously.

'Oh, Cormac! You're too stoned to think most of the time.' She looked at him curiously. 'Why do you do it? I mean, I like a spliff myself, but you seem to be on a permanent high.'

'It's a long story, Pol. Something happened.' Cormac spoke slowly, carefully enunciating the words, hoping they made sense. 'One day, no, one minute, everything was perfect, next minute it was shit.'

'What was it that happened?'

'I discovered I wasn't the person I'd always thought meself to be.'

Pol looked impressed. 'That sounds deeply disturbing, Cormac.'

'Intensely deeply.' Cormac was about to reach for her, pull her on to a bunk, when Wally fell into the coach, followed by Frank, who was being led by an irritable Tanya. Frank's face and arms were as bright red as his hair and slightly puffy.

'I'm all right, man,' he protested. 'Stop making a fuss.'

'You won't feel all right tomorrow. You'll be as sick as a dog. Is there calamine lotion in the first aid box, Pol?' It was Tanya's idea to have a first aid box, and Cormac had to concede it came in useful from time to time.

'I don't think so, no.'

'Then I suggest we leave now, straight away,' Tanya said briskly. 'We'll call in Ipswich, do the washing, fill the water tank, buy some calamine lotion. Are any of you three fit to drive?'

Cormac occasionally drove, even though he'd never had a lesson. 'I'm ferfectly pit,' he announced.

'Oh, yeh!' Tanya glared at Wally who had collapsed on the floor. Frank had started to shiver violently for some reason. 'It looks as if I'll have to drive myself. One of these days we'll be stopped by the police and I haven't got a proper licence.'

The surface of the large field had baked as hard as clay. It was impossible to imagine the soil having been soft enough for the huge tyres of tractors to have made such perfect moulds – they made comfortable seats, Cormac discovered, just wide and deep enough for his bottom to fit.

Pol sat between his legs, leaning against him. His hands lay limply on her lap. They sprawled at the very edge of the field, where they could hardly see the group playing beneath an awning that fluttered not an inch on such a windless day. The music stopped and there was a smattering of applause from the crowds that dotted the field like confetti. The audience included many children, most of them naked. A few of the women were bare to the waist. The numerous dogs seemed to have been trained to defecate and piss as frequently as possible.

Today, Pol wore a different frock, just as shapeless. He nuzzled her hair, which smelt of soap. His own hair, beautifully clean, was wondrous to behold: clouds of pale-blond locks held together at the back with an elastic band.

'Where do you come from, Pol?' he asked. She'd probably told him before, but he'd forgotten.

'Lancashire, same as you. Blackpool.'

'I went to Blackpool once. There was something called the Golden Mile.' He'd gone on the big wheel with Fion and Orla. Maeve had been too scared. Grandad had been there. It was before he'd married Bernadette.

'You should see the Blackpool Lights in a few weeks' time, they're terrific.'

'Shall we go together?'

'No chance, Cormac. I might meet my mother.'

'Would that be so awful?'

'Awfully awful. She's a bitch.'

'So's mine.' Cormac shuddered.

'I thought you said your mother was lovely.' She turned her face towards him and he kissed her nose. 'You're always on about Alice.'

'Alice isn't my mother, she just thinks she is.'

'Oh, Cormac, you don't half talk rubbish. Were you adopted or something?'

'No, I was given away at birth.'

'Who by, a bad fairy?'

'Well, yes, as it happens. Very bad.'

'You're something of a mystery, do you know that, Cormac?'

'I'm a mystery to meself,' Cormac said darkly.

'Are we playing here tomorrow?'

'I doubt it, not if Frank's still laid low with sunburn. And I think one of the guitars is broken.' The Nobodys were usually the first on the bill, hired to keep folks amused while they looked for somewhere to sit, or searched for their seats if the concert was indoors. Frank and Wally played guitar not very well. The only decent musician was Tanya who was brilliant with the fiddle. Pol had a sweet, high voice and Cormac could rattle a tambourine as well as anyone. He was the group's manager-cum-roadie. At least, he was when he remembered. The Nobodys were unusual in that they recognised their limitations and weren't interested in either fame or money. It was just something to do, giving occasional point to their otherwise meaningless lives.

'I think I'll go back to the van, bathe poor Frank's head, or something,' Pol said.

'I'll come with you,' Cormac said with alacrity. He didn't want her alone with Frank, who might not be one hundred per cent incapacitated by the sunburn.

'There's no need, Cormac.'

'This group are shit and I need a rest.'

'What from? You've been sitting in that rut virtually all day.'

'I need a rest from sitting in this rut.'

Vehicles were parked nose to tail along the narrow country lane: buses, caravanettes, lorries, large vans, small vans, ambulances with the word 'Ambulance' painted out, the occasional car. According to the radio, it was the same for miles around. The police had decided to let the festival go ahead rather than turn hundreds of vehicles away. It would cause less hassle. On the radio, several local residents had huffed and puffed, and said it was disgraceful. Why weren't these people at work? How dare they descend on a peaceful, law-abiding community and create havoc? Pubs, restaurants, one or two garages, had signs outside, 'No Festival Goers'. The Nobodys were out of water again and it was impossible to get more.

'My skin won't let me move, man,' Frank complained bitterly when Pol and Cormac climbed into the coach. He was poised stiffly on a bench, elbows on the table, wearing only a pair of shorts with a pattern of butterflies. The skin on his upper half was less livid, but still looked painful. His red hair looked crisp, as if it had been fried. 'My chest hurts when I breathe.'

'Shall I douse you in calamine?'

'Please, Pol.'

Cormac reached under the pillow for his stuff and began to roll a joint. The first puff brought on a sensation of enormous lethargy. He lay down and within seconds was asleep.

It was dusk when he awoke, slightly cooler. He could hear music thumping away in the distance. The spliff had burnt a perfect round hole in the nylon sleeping bag, but there was still half left. He was searching for the matches when he noticed Frank and Pol squeezed together on the bunk opposite, both asleep. Pol was naked, her small, perfect body glistening with perspiration, and Frank's shorts were around his knees. His red skin was splattered with pink calamine.

Cormac groaned. He'd come back with Pol to keep an eye on her, yet she and Frank had made love directly in front of his closed eyes. They badly needed another girl, someone for Frank. Wally could have Tanya, Cormac would have Pol.

Another girl! He made his unsteady way outside and began to walk in the direction of the music to look for another girl. Dusk was falling. There were lights on in some of the vehicles and he could hear the clink of dishes. The smell of food made him feel nauseous, though he'd had nothing to eat all day and possibly yesterday, for all he knew. A police car came zooming down the lane, blue light flashing. Cormac pushed a small child and an exceptionally hairy dog to safety. The child cried and the dog growled ungratefully.

Cormac had no idea why he should cry as he walked towards the music. He wasn't even conscious of crying until one of the great, bulbous tears pouring down his face landed on his bare foot and he thought it was raining. He looked up into the clear, dusky blue sky and realised he was crying and the rain was a tear. He was thinking about Pol and Alice and Grandad and his sisters, about Amber Street, about Bootle, Lacey's hairdressers, the schools he'd gone to, the friends he'd made. He thought about university and the fact that he hadn't gone back to finish his degree, about Alice's face when he told her. He thought about Cora Lacey.

'Here, look where you're going, luv.'

He'd collided with a woman coming from the opposite direction, leading two children by the hand.

'I'm sorry.' Cormac wept. 'So sorry.'

'It's not the end of the world, luv,' the woman said kindly.

Still crying, Cormac walked on, when a voice said incredulously, 'Is that you, Cormac?'

He turned. The woman with the children had stopped and was looking at him, her face as incredulous as her voice. She was tall, well built, but shapely and her long, wild hair was tied in a knot on top of her head. She wore a black T-shirt with a white CND sign on the front and narrow black pants. She was, unfortunately, too old for Frank, about thirty, and there was no room for the children in the coach.

'I'm Cormac, yes,' he conceded in a whisper.

'It's Fion, luv. Fionnuala, your sister.'

'Fion!' Cormac had never, in all his life, been so pleased to see anyone. He stopped crying, grabbed his sister and showered her face with kisses. She hugged him tightly in return and rubbed his back, as if he were a baby. One of the children, the boy, tried to pull her away.

'It's all right, Colin. This is Cormac, your uncle. Oh, Cormac, you look bloody awful. Are you sick or something? C'mon, luv, we're only along here.'

The children ran ahead, stopping outside a smart white caravanette. Fion, holding Cormac firmly by the arm as if worried he'd run away, opened the door and pushed him through. Inside, the vehicle was cheerful and scrupulously tidy. Red gingham frills framed the tiny windows and there was a matching cloth on the table, as well as a small bowl of roses. The miniature stainless steel sink sparkled and a red carpet graced the floor. There wasn't a dish or an item of dirty washing in sight.

The grip of his sister's hand on Cormac's arm made him feel as if he had suddenly been plugged back into the normal world and the scene of domestic neatness reminded him of a time when he had known nothing else, when it had been a simple matter to get washed, wear clean clothes, brush his teeth, sit down to proper meals.

'Blimey, Cormac, you don't half pong,' Fion said bluntly. 'Have a wash, there's a good lad, while I make some tea. I'll find you a clean T-shirt in a minute. This is Colin and Bonnie, by the way. He's nearly five, she's nearly four. Say hello to your Uncle Cormac, kids, then get into your pyjamas. It's nearly time for bed.'

Bonnie pushed herself boldly forward. 'Hello, Uncle Cormac.' The boy hung back and sucked his finger.

'Hello, kids,' Cormac said, doing his best to sound like a proper grown-up uncle. 'Where's their dad?' he said to Fion.

'Dead. He died two years ago. His name was Colin too.'

'Oh, hell! I'm sorry.'

'So am I,' Fion said matter-of-factly. 'I loved him more than words can say, but he'd been in a Japanese prisoner of war camp and was dying when I met him. When we got married we never thought he'd last six whole years, but he did and they were the best years of me life.' She gestured towards him with soap and a towel. 'Take your shirt off, luv, and chuck it away before you stink the place out. Are you hungry?'

'I wouldn't mind some bread and butter.'

'I think we can manage that.'

Cormac had never had a favourite sister, but had always felt more drawn to Fionnuala than he had to loud, aggressive Orla and quietly confident Maeve. There had been something very vulnerable about tactless, hopeless Fion, forever putting her foot in it, saying the wrong thing. To find his wretched self plucked off a country lane in Norfolk by the sister he hadn't seen in years and put down in this neat, cool place, where there was fresh water, healthily smelling soap, roses on the table and a kettle boiling for tea, was little short of a miracle.

'What are you doing here?' Fion asked while he was getting washed. The children watched with interest as they changed into their pyjamas.

'I belong to a group, the Nobodys. We're on tomorrow's programme, but Frank's too ill to play.'

'Never heard of you.'

'Nobody ever has, hence the name.'

'Mummy, he hasn't cleaned behind his ears.'

Fion grinned. 'Bonnie says to clean behind your ears, Cormac.'

'Sorry, Bonnie.'

'And under your arms.'

'Yes, Bonnie.' Cormac was beginning to feel vaguely happy.

In quick succession Fion opened a tin of beans, shoved toast under a grill, poured water on the pot. Within minutes the children were sitting down to beans on toast, and Cormac was drinking a mug of scalding tea and wearing a T-shirt with Amnesty 61 on the back. There seemed to be plenty of provisions. A loaf appeared, a plastic butter dish, a tin of cocoa, a bottle of milk, a packet of biscuits – custard creams. Cormac couldn't remember having seen such a rich assortment of food in years.

'Is the van yours?' he asked.

'No, it's hired. We're on holiday, on our way to Scotland. Some of my friends were coming here, so I thought I'd make a detour and let the children see what a rock concert's all about. Bonnie thought it great, but Colin hated it, didn't you, luv?' Colin had yet to open his mouth and merely nodded. Fion ruffled his hair and for some reason the gesture made Cormac want to cry again.

'Me and Colin,' Fion continued, 'big Colin, that is, though he wasn't all that big as it happens, went touring every year. It's the cheapest way of seeing the country. We didn't come last year, so it's our first holiday since he died.'

'Did you ever get near Liverpool on one of your tours, sis?' Cormac said mildly. 'Alice gets dead upset whenever your name's mentioned. She misses you. We all do.'

Fion glanced at the children who had eaten the beans on toast, drunk their cocoa and were now munching biscuits, listening avidly to the conversation between their mother and their newly discovered uncle. 'Come on, you two, bed.' She clapped her hands. 'I'll leave the light on and you can take the biscuits with you as a treat, seeing as how we're on holiday, like. Mind a minute, Cormac, there's a good lad.'

She folded down the leaves of the table, which was surrounded on three sides by thickly cushioned benches covered with red moquette, with storage spaces underneath. Several items of bedding were removed and laid on two of the benches. The children obediently lay down and Colin immediately began to suck his thumb. Then Fion produced two folding stools out of thin air and took them outside, round to the back of the van, out of the way of any traffic that might go speeding past. It was almost dark by now and the air was slightly cooler.

'They don't usually go so willingly to bed, but they're dead tired. Colin's quiet because the holiday reminds him of when his dad was alive. He still misses big Colin something rotten. It doesn't bother Bonnie, she can hardly remember him. Would you like some orange juice, Cormac? It's lovely and cold.'

'I'd love some.'

'Won't be a mo.'

Cormac glanced in the direction of the field where the concert was being held. By now, it was almost dark and searchlights criss-crossed the sky. Through the intervening hedges he glimpsed a blur of coloured lights and the thumping music could be clearly heard. It was a familiar number played by a familiar group whose name he couldn't remember.

Fion was back with two glasses and a carton of juice. 'Here you are, luv.'

'Ta.'

She sat on the stool, their arms touching. 'You asked why I've never been home, Cormac. The thing is, I don't rightly know. I've sent cards from time to time so Mam would know I was all right, like. I didn't give me address in case someone came and tried to persuade me to go back. A year later, when I married Colin, it seemed too late, too embarrassing, to let anyone know and the longer it went on the more embarrassing it got.'

'Alice wouldn't have felt embarrassed.'

'I know,' she said abjectly. 'I *should* write, break the ice, as it were, because I'll be coming home to Liverpool soon. Ruby, Colin's mother, died last month and Elsa – she's his daughter from his first marriage – married a soldier and went to live in Germany.' She sighed. 'So there's nothing to keep me in London any more. Me neighbours are lovely, but it's not the same as having your own flesh and blood around. I'd like the children to have a grandma, aunts and uncles, cousins. Colin's due to start school at Christmas and it'd be best for him to start in Liverpool, rather than have him change in a few months' time.'

'There's plenty of room for the three of you in Amber Street, sis.'

'Oh, I've already got a house,' Fion said suprisingly. 'Remember Horace Flynn? He left me his house in Stanley Road. He was the only one who knew I was leaving. I wrote and told him where I lived when I sent back this twenty quid he loaned me and he promised never to tell Mam. We wrote to each other often – he sent a present when me and Colin got married. The house has been rented out for years. It seemed like fate when I got a letter from the tenants giving a month's notice the same week Ruby died. Anyroad . . .' She refilled his glass with juice. 'How is everyone? Has our Maeve had any children yet? Has Orla had more? How are Grandad and Bernadette?' Her voice dropped, became husky. 'And how is our mam, Cormac? I've missed her, you know, every bit as much as she's missed me.'

Cormac didn't doubt it. He knew how easy it was to love someone to distraction, yet treat them with terrible cruelty. At this very moment he was breaking Alice's heart, but his own heart was cold and he didn't care. 'Maeve and Martin haven't had children so far,' he said. 'They're too wrapped up in their house in Waterloo. Orla still only has the four – they're growing up, Lulu's already a teenager. Grandad's retired. He's seventy-two, but as fit as a fiddle, and Bernadette and the kids are just fine.'

'And Mam?'

'How do you think, sis?' Cormac shooed away the dog whose life he'd saved and that had repaid him with a growl. 'You walked out seven years ago and haven't been seen since and her only son has more or less resigned from the human race.'

'Hmm.' Fion gripped her knees. 'I never visualised you becoming a hippy, Cormac. I've always imagined you working in a laboratory, mixing noxious liquids, or whatever it is you do in laboratories, having left university loaded with honours and distinctions. You did, didn't you?' she said anxiously when Cormac pulled a face.

'I didn't finish my degree, Fion. I didn't go back for the last two terms. Alice did her nut. I just missed having to do National Service, I'm pleased to say, otherwise I would have had to register as a conscientious objector.'

'Why do you keep calling her Alice, Cormac? She's our mam.'

He'd love to tell someone, share the knowledge that had been gnawing away at his soul for three and a half years.

'Why, Cormac?' Fion persisted.

'If I tell you, will you promise never to repeat it to a living soul?'

'Cross my heart.'

Cormac took a deep breath. His head felt lighter as he began to relate the story of his twenty-first birthday party, finding Aunt Cora in the kitchen, the terrible things she'd said. 'I can't describe how I felt afterwards. My feet no longer felt as if they were on firm ground. I felt unreal, like a ghost. Living in Amber Street was a great big lie. I couldn't talk to Alice any more. I didn't know what to say, and what I did say sounded stiff and unnatural.' He shook himself, as if trying to rid himself of the memory of that dreadful period. 'I knew it was a waste of time going back to university; my brain seemed to have frozen solid and refused to work. The only place that I could stand was the Cavern, where I was able to drown in the music, it was so loud and I didn't have to think. It was there I met an old mate from St Mary's who was trying to get a pop group together to rival the Beatles. I joined as general dogsbody and chief tambourine player. I've been on the road with different groups ever since. I'm afraid none has come even remotely close to rivalling the Beatles.'

'No other group ever will.' Fion rocked back and forth on the stool. She didn't look as shocked as Cormac had expected. She said, slowly and thoughtfully, 'If I were you, Cormac, I wouldn't believe Cora. I reckon she's jealous, that's all, what with you doing so well and their Maurice being in prison – I met Neil Greene once in London and he told me. She was always trying to stir things up. Look at what she did to Mam with that agreement thing.'

'But, Fion,' Cormac wailed. 'I look so much like her. No one's ever noticed before. When you think about it, it's obvious she's my mother.'

Fion regarded him in the light falling through the window of the caravanette. 'I don't see a resemblance meself. You're probably just imagining it.'

Cormac shivered. 'I can't stand the thought of her being me mother. I have nightmares about it.' He often dreamed of how it might have happened, of Cora slithering through the sleeping hospital, arriving at the nursery, changing him over with Maurice. 'Maurice looked a better bet,' she'd said.

'If I were you,' Fion said again, 'I wouldn't take any notice of Cora. I'd try and pretend she never told you all that stuff.' She linked her arm in his. 'I'll never think of you as anything other than me brother, Cormac, and I know Orla and Maeve feel the same. Grandad thought the sun shone out of your arse. And Mam – you're not being very fair on Mam, luv.'

'Could you forget if it were you it had happened to?'

'No, but I'd want someone to talk to me the way I'm talking to you. It's almost quarter of a century since you were born and whatever happened that night isn't important any more. It's what's happened since that matters.' She gave him a little shake. 'You're Mam's son, our brother, Colin's and Bonnie's uncle.'

'But say if I'm not, Fion?'

'You *are*,' Fion said confidently. 'I remember the day Mam brought you home from hospital. You felt like me brother then, every bit as much as you do now. We all laid claim to you, Cormac. You're *ours.*'

Cormac was beginning to feel as if there was a way out of the morass in which he had been wallowing for so long. If he could just hold on to the fact that what Cora said didn't matter after all this time, that it was how things were *now* that was important. 'What about Uncle Billy,' he said, 'and Maurice?'

'I doubt if Uncle Billy gave a damn who Cora brought home from the hospital. As for Maurice . . .' She paused.

'I owe him a debt worth more than a kingdom,' Cormac said softly.

'*You* don't owe him a thing. If it's all true, not that for a moment I think it is, then I suppose it's hard luck on Maurice.' She wrinkled her nose. 'Well, worse than hard luck, having Cora for a mam.'

'Particularly instead of Alice. He would have grown up a different person altogether in Amber Street. He wouldn't have gone to prison for a start.'

'You can't say that for certain.'

'Yes, I can,' Cormac assured her.

'What's he doing now?'

'Living in the flat over the hairdresser's, where Neil used to live. Cora chucked him out.'

'She's mad,' Fion said flatly. 'She's not likely to say anything about this to Mam, is she? That would really put the cat among the pigeons.'

'I doubt it. I told her if she did I'd kill her. I meant it, Fion. It makes me wonder if one day I might go mad too.'

'Don't be silly. You're the sanest person I've ever known.'

'Once maybe, not now.'

'I'm going to tell *you* a secret, then I'll make us some tea and sandwiches.'

Fion regarded him slyly. 'You'll never guess, but Mam was having an affair with Neil Greene. It was the reason I left home. I heard them in bed together and it made me feel such a fool.'

Cormac smiled. 'I already knew that, sis. You couldn't help but notice the way her eyes went all starry when she announced she was "popping round" to Opal Street for some reason. They were even starrier when she came back.'

'Jaysus, Cormac Lacey! Nothing escaped your gimlet eyes.'

Fion went to make the sandwiches. Cormac leant against the back of the van, suddenly conscious of the music in the distance. He'd forgotten where he was. The lane was busy. Children were being brought home from the concert and latecomers were on their way towards it. Two girls, conventionally dressed, rode by on bicycles – he'd like to bet the young people of the area weren't as opposed to the festival as their elders.

The sky above was as clear as sapphire with a twinkling of stars and a perfectly round moon, but at the edges, just above the horizon, black clouds were banked, looking as impenetrable as mountains. This effect of nature, both impressive and oppressive, made Cormac feel very small, insignificant, in the great scheme of things. Looked at one way, the bombshell that had been dropped on the night of his twenty-first seemed trivial, not worth bothering about.

He wouldn't have minded a spliff, but his stuff was under his pillow in the coach and he didn't feel like going back, not yet. Anyroad, Fion might not approve of spliffs. He was grateful to his sister for bringing him down to earth, showing him there was a future.

As soon as he could, without letting down his friends, he would extricate himself and Pol from the life they were leading – from the life they were *wasting* – and . . .

Cormac paused in his reverie. Two young men were walking past, bare to the waist, supporting a girl between them. In their free hands the men wielded bottles of the local cider, a lethal concoction. The girl stumbled. The men roughly hoisted her upright. One squeezed her bottom through the thin cotton frock that looked ominously familiar.

Pol! She rarely drank. Half a bottle of that lethal brew and she'd be senseless. It was possible she was being taken back to the coach for her own safety, but somehow Cormac doubted it. He leapt to his feet. He had to rescue Pol.

It meant that when Fion emerged from the van with tea and sandwiches, her brother had gone.

It might have continued for ever and a day: the spliffs, the drink, missing gigs, driving nowhere, doing nothing, had it not been that Pol discovered she was pregnant.

'I can get the bread together for an abortion,' Frank said when they sat round the table for a conference. Everyone had been on tenterhooks waiting for Pol to start her period, but she'd missed two and was definitely pregnant. They wore a motley assortment of coats and jackets because it was November, and no one had any idea how to keep the coach warm, apart from using an oil heater, which brought on Wally's asthma. Being on the road had its disadvantages in winter. 'Abortion's legal in this country, isn't it?'

No one knew.

'I don't want an abortion whether it's legal or not,' Pol said defiantly. 'I want my baby.' She laid her hands on her stomach, as if she could already feel its shape inside.

'Don't be foolish,' Tanya snapped. 'This is no life for a baby.' A baby would clutter up their already cluttered lives. Tanya was very conventional. Cormac sometimes wondered if she was only there to annoy her family and had the firm intention of returning home when she felt she'd annoyed them long enough.

'I'll go away,' Pol said. 'I'll find a place to live, a bedsit, probably in London. The state will support me. I mean, us.'

'Who's the father?' Wally asked.

'I don't know, do I? It's either you, you, or you.' Pol nodded one by one at the three men.

'I'm afraid I can't offer monetary support, Pol.'

'No one's asked you to, Wally.'

'I'll buy the pram and the diapers and stuff, honey.'

'Thank you, Frank.'

'Come back to Liverpool and live with me, Pol,' Cormac said, wincing as he massaged the wrist that had been broken months ago when he'd rescued Pol from the two louts who turned out not to be taking her back to the coach, but to their own ex-Post Office van. The plaster had only been removed last week.

Everyone looked at him in surprise, including Pol. 'Hey, man. Isn't that a bit heavy?' Wally murmured.

'Live with you, Cormac?' Pol's grey eyes smiled into his. 'Why, I'd like that very much.'

'Oh, well, that's settled,' Tanya said, as if they'd just decided which pub to go to. 'Would anyone like a cup of tea?'

12

Billy Lacey strolled along the Dock Road, a woman on his arm whose name he couldn't remember. It was August and still very hot, despite the lateness of the hour – at that moment Cormac Lacey was sitting in a remote Norfolk lane with his sister, Fionnuala.

The Docky wasn't nearly so busy as it had been when Billy was a lad and he'd come with his brother, John, to look at the ships. There was hardly any traffic, hardly any ships to look at. Even the smells had gone: the musky aroma of spices, coffee, perfumed teas and the strange, dusty smell that turned out to be carpets. He considered it a poor show that such a vital, throbbing part of Liverpool was being allowed to waste away and die. Only the moon, swinging freely – Billy was drunk – in the navy-blue sky and the soaring brick walls of the docks, the giant gates, remained the same.

Despite the jowly cheeks and the monstrous beer gut that had long ago cancelled out his waist, leaving his trousers somewhat perilously supported by a narrow leather belt, at fifty-four, Billy was still a fine figure of a man, with his thick, dark hair and broad shoulders. A cheap suit adorned his burly body, the jacket hanging open because it wouldn't meet round his swollen belly. Yet he carried himself well. Not a few female eyes were cast in his direction as he swaggered along, linking the arm of his anonymous companion. She was taking him home for a nightcap. Billy wasn't sure which he was most looking forward to, the drink or what was to follow.

'Have you got a missus?' enquired the woman who was leading him towards the longed-for nightcap and her bed.

'She's left me,' Billy lied. For years now, possibly since the day after the wedding, he'd wished Cora would leave. He would have left himself, except he couldn't be bothered looking for somewhere else to live. Anyroad, he'd have to cook his own food, make his own bed, do his own washing. It was comfortable in Garibaldi Road, if nothing else. He and Cora hardly talked, but he wouldn't mind if she never opened her mouth again for the rest of her life. It was sad about Maurice: first jail, then leaving home, but Billy had never really felt that Maurice was his son. He belonged to Cora, who spoiled the poor lad rotten when she wasn't thrashing him with that bloody cane.

He'd probably ended up dead confused. Billy knew he should have put a stop to it, but he'd never been much of a match for his wife.

He had no idea why he'd married her, Cora. He must have been pissed when they met, pissed when he proposed and pissed the day they got married – he could never actually remember saying 'I do', though his mam claimed he'd behaved impeccably at the wedding. Still, it had been done and it was a long time ago now. Billy had quite enjoyed his life, Cora or no Cora. He still did. Another woman mightn't have let him do as he pleased, be so glad to see the back of him. Mind you, it would have been nice to have had a few more bob in his pocket. As it was, Cora took scarcely a penny off him, but he still had to rely on finding some poor woman like the one on his arm, desperate for company, poor cow, to keep his belly primed nightly with ale. He had no idea where Cora got the cash from to keep things going and had never bothered to enquire.

'Are we nearly there, luv?' he asked.

'Yes, Billy. It's just round the next corner.'

The pubs had not long ago called time, otherwise there was no way Billy would have been out in the open, breathing in the fresh, warm air. They were approaching the Arcadia, a pub with such a wicked reputation that even Billy had never dared enter its doors, despite intimate knowledge of most of the ale houses in Bootle. A man and woman came out, arguing furiously. At least the woman was furious, the man appeared to be drunk, but not the boozy, mild sort of drunk that Billy knew. This geezer was paralytic. You could have cut off parts of his body and he wouldn't have known. The woman gave him a shove. 'You're bloody useless, you are,' she sneered. 'I'm giving you a wide berth in future.'

The man collapsed on to his knees, wobbled, then crumpled into the gutter. His eyes, staring upwards, were glazed, unseeing. His face looked as if it had been made of stone.

'Here, mate, let's give you a hand,' Billy said sympathetically. He leant down, put his hands under the man's armpits and hoisted him to his feet. 'Jaysus, you're as light as a feather.'

The man's head hung down, like a scarecrow's, as if he too needed a pole to keep it straight. It wasn't until they were face to face that Billy realised that the man he was supporting was his brother, John, whom he hadn't seen in years.

'Don't tell anyone I'm here,' John said to Cora next morning.

'Not if you don't want me to, luv.'

Cora was in her element. This was the man she had desired all her adult life and now she had him under her roof, at her mercy, you might say.

She had never seen anyone so thin. No wonder Billy had been able to walk all the way from the Docky with his brother over his shoulder like a sack of coal. Last night they had conversed, she and Billy, for the first time in ages.

'Look who I found!' Billy said when she opened the door, him being unable to use his key, like. 'It's our John. I found him collapsed in the Docky.'

Billy looked upset. If things had been different he might have loved his wife and son, but his brother had been the only person he'd ever felt real affection for. 'I'm taking him upstairs, to Maurice's room,' he said gruffly. He stared defiantly at his wife, as if expecting her to object, but Cora flew ahead to put clean, aired linen on the bed and open the window of the stuffy, unused room.

'He hasn't a pick on him,' Billy said with unexpected tenderness when he laid John down. 'Is there a spare pair of pyjamas?'

'I'll get some.' When Cora came back, Billy was stripping John of his clothes. He looked as if he might object when Cora started to help, but must have decided two pairs of hands were better than one. John moaned once or twice as his clothes were removed and he was lifted into a pair of far too big pyjamas. Cora tucked the bedclothes around his waist.

'What shall we do now, Billy?'

'Leave him be. Let him sleep it off. He's as drunk as David's sow. He'll have a head on him in the morning.'

'He needs building up, Billy. He needs to stay in bed a week and be fed proper. He looks as if he's been neglecting himself something awful.'

'Do you mind if he stays?'

Cora shook her head vigorously. 'I always liked your John. Alice hadn't enough patience with him after the accident. I'm not surprised he left. Where's he been living?'

'I've no idea.'

'I wonder if he's still got that business of his?'

'I don't know, luv. I wrote to him twice at that place in Seaforth, didn't I? But he didn't answer. Mind you, that was years ago.'

They went to bed in their separate rooms. During the night Cora, even less able to sleep than usual, got up and went to look at their guest. The curtains had been left open to allow fresh air through the window and the room was brightly bathed in moonlight. She knelt beside the bed and gently stroked the damaged cheek, which by now was scarcely noticeable. The skin was no longer red and one side of the thin, sombre face was merely slightly more wrinkled than the other. Once he had more meat on him, it would be even less obvious.

Cora breathed a kiss on the thin lips of the man she had always wanted, then went through his pockets, the jacket first. He had three pounds, ten shillings in a wallet, along with a photograph of a fair-haired girl and a separate one of three young children, none of whom she recognised. There were some grubby business cards, including several for B.E.D.S. In another pocket she found a packet of ciggies, a lighter, a dirty hankie, a bunch of keys. His trouser pockets held nothing but change. She rubbed the material between her thumb and forefinger: good quality, but it smelt sour and was badly in need of dry-cleaning.

John was still asleep when his brother went to work next morning. Cora kept popping her head round the door, but it wasn't until midday that she found him staring vacantly at the ceiling. His head, his arms, lying loosely on the covers, were in exactly the same position as the night before, as if he hadn't the strength or will to move them. His eyes turned fractionally when Cora went in, but showed no surprise. He didn't appear particularly bothered where he found himself.

'I was wondering where I was,' he whispered. 'How did I get here?'

'Your Billy found you on the Docky and carried you all the way back. Would you like a cup of tea, luv?'

'I think I might, thank you, Cora.'

She put extra milk in the tea so it wasn't too hot, and had to support his head with one hand and hold the cup for him with the other. It gave her a feeling of intense satisfaction to have John Lacey so dependent on her.

When he'd finished he said, 'Don't tell anyone I'm here.'

'Not if you don't want me to, luv,' Cora assured him.

That afternoon she made him bread and milk, and fed it to him with a spoon. By the time Billy came home he was sitting up, propped against a heap of pillows, smoking a cigarette.

'I didn't know you smoked, mate,' Billy remarked.

John shrugged. 'I started years ago.'

'How are you feeling?'

'Exhausted,' John said thinly.

'What were you doing in the Arcadia, mate? It's a dump.' Billy regarded his older brother with concern. He'd missed John badly since he'd left Alice and had been hurt when his letters hadn't been answered. He found it upsetting to see this once strong, vital man lying like a shadow in the bed. Billy had been raised with the dictum 'Why can't you be more like your brother' constantly in his ear. Mam had made no bones about the fact she liked John best, that she was proud of him, whereas Billy was the family black sheep, the failure. Now it seemed their positions had been reversed and it made Billy feel uncomfortable.

'I can't remember going to the Arcadia,' John confessed. 'In fact, I can't remember anything much about yesterday.'

'Been on a bender, eh!'

'One bender too many, I'm afraid.'

Billy chuckled, though there was nothing to laugh about. He put his hand over his brother's thin one, slightly embarrassed. 'What's up, mate? How did you get yourself in such a state? You look like shit.'

'I feel like shit.' John took a long puff on the ciggie. 'Things happened, Billy. Things I'd sooner not talk about.'

'Whatever you say. Where are you living these days? What's happened to that company of yours?'

'I still do a bit of business – I've been living in the office for quite some time.'

'I'd've come and seen you if I'd known.'

John gave a curt nod of appreciation, but Billy had the odd feeling he wouldn't have been welcome and the even odder feeling that he wasn't particularly welcome now, that John would much prefer to be alone.

'You're looking well, though, Billy,' John said with an obvious effort. 'There's enough fat on you for both of us.'

Billy patted his monstrous stomach. 'It's the ale.'

'You always had a weakness for the ale.' John's mouth curved drily. 'I didn't have any weaknesses, did I? I was the perfect husband, the perfect father, a good provider for me family. Then this happened' – he pointed to his face – 'and I turned out to be weaker than most men. Another bloke would have taken it in his stride and got on with things. I let it ruin me life instead. Nothing's been the same since.'

'It was a brave thing you did that day, John.' Billy had had little experience with conversations of this sort. There was a break in his voice when he said, 'There's hardly another man in the world who would have tried to save that sailor. You should have got a medal.'

'They offered me a medal, but I turned it down, just like, in a way, I turned Alice down, as well as me children. I was determined to suffer and I wanted everyone to suffer with me.'

'Perhaps there's time to put things right yet. Alice is still on her own.'

John didn't answer. Cora came in with a bowl of home-made soup and announced Billy's tea was ready downstairs.

Cora was disappointed when John insisted on feeding himself. She sat on the bed, watching. 'There's jelly and custard for pudding,' she said when he'd finished.

'Maybe later. Thank you, Cora. You and Billy are being very kind. Where's Maurice, by the way? Isn't this his bed I'm in?'

He mustn't have known Maurice had been in jail. Cora wasn't about to tell him now. 'He wanted his independence. He's got his own place. It's in Opal Street, over Lacey's, as it happens.'

Later, Billy came back upstairs and Cora went down. For the first time in years, Billy didn't go to the pub. John softened slightly and the brothers reminisced, reminding each other of things that had happened when they were children. Billy had the most to say, his voice was the loudest. His laughter boomed through the normally silent house, awakening it.

Cora sat with the television on, but the sound turned down, listening, planning tomorrow's menu and the other things she'd do. She'd get John's suit cleaned – his shirt and underclothes were already washed and ironed, his tie sponged. She'd ask if he'd like some books from the library. Unlike his brother, John Lacey had always been a reading man.

John couldn't possibly have been looked after more tenderly and efficiently.

'You should have been a nurse, Cora,' he said when, after seven days of cosseting and being fed bland though nourishing meals, he felt up to coming downstairs for his tea.

It was possibly the first time in Cora's life that she had blushed. 'You just needed a bit of building up, like,' she mumbled. 'You'd let yourself go.'

'I've been letting meself go for years.'

'There's no need for it any more,' Cora assured him eagerly. 'You can stay with us for always. There's plenty of room.' It would be one in the eye for Alice when she discovered her husband was living in Garibaldi Road. Cora had promised not to breathe a word, but it was bound to get out some time.

'We'll just have to see,' John said, lighting a ciggie.

A few days later John announced he felt like a walk. Cora accompanied him round the block, proudly linking his arm. By now, August had turned into September and the air felt cooler. The flowers in the gardens smelt as sweetly as wine. She sniffed appreciatively. Normally, she never noticed such things.

'I enjoyed that,' he said when they got back to the house. 'I might go again tomorrow, further afield.'

'I'll come with you.'

'That would be nice.' His face was filling out, his suit already fitted better. He looked dead handsome, she thought. He had yet to smile, but John Lacey was a dignified, serious man, not much given to laughing and smiling. She wished there were a way of getting shot of Billy, so there'd be just the two of them left in the house.

She bought John a shirt because he only had the one and Billy's swam on him. It had a striped body and a white collar. 'The man in Burton's said it's the latest fashion.'

'Cora! You've made me feel dead embarrassed.' She could tell, though, that he was pleased. It was probably a long time since a woman had made a fuss of him, got him a prezzie.

'This is very smart. I'll wear it tonight.'

'Let me iron the creases out first.'

Billy said John looked like a stockbroker or a solicitor in the shirt and addressed him as 'Sir', while they ate their tea. When the meal was over John announced he was going out. There was someone he wanted to see.

Cora's blood turned to ice. She knew for certain he was going to see Alice and her heart seethed with jealousy. Something told her he intended asking Alice if she would have him back.

'Will you be long?' she asked when he was ready to leave, hair combed, freshly shaved, wearing the shirt *she'd* bought.

'I've no idea, Cora.'

Alice was sitting with her feet on a stool. She'd had a busy day, but then all her days were busy. It was something of an anticlimax to enter the unnaturally quiet house. The emptiness always reminded her of her two missing children. Where was Fion? she wondered fretfully. Why didn't she come home, if only to visit? And she worried constantly about Cormac. At least she saw him from time to time, but something had happened to him that she didn't understand. He appeared withdrawn, almost sullen, yet he was a lad who'd always looked upon the world with such obvious delight.

She hadn't been home long when, much to her relief, the back door opened and Bernadette yelled, 'It's me.'

'Put the kettle on while you're out there,' Alice yelled back. 'How's me dad and the kids?' she asked when her friend plonked herself in an armchair with a deep sigh.

'Everyone's fine. How's yourself?'

'A bit bored, if the truth be known. I quite fancy some excitement.'

'How about the pics? Danny's given me the night off. We could go into town. Henry Fonda's on at the Odeon. I could *eat* Henry Fonda.'

'Oh, we all know the things you'd like to do to Henry Fonda, but when I said excitement I meant something a bit more personal, not watching Henry Fonda having all the excitement.'

'Well, I'm afraid, Ally, that it's the pics or nothing.'

'I suppose the pics are better than nothing,' Alice grumbled. The kettle whistled in the kitchen. 'You can make that tea while I get changed. I won't be a mo.'

Alice had changed into a green linen costume with a fitted jacket and pleated skirt and was brushing her hair when the knock sounded on the door.

'I'll get it,' Bernadette shouted.

There was a long silence. Alice was about to ask 'Who is it?' when Bernadette came into the bedroom. Her face was white.

'It's John,' she said.

'John who?'

'John Lacey, daft girl. Your husband. I'll be getting along home.'

'Don't go, Bernie!' Alice cried, but Bernadette mutely shook her head and ran downstairs. Alice stared at her own white face in the mirror for several seconds before going downstairs herself, holding tightly to the rail to support her trembling legs.

John was standing in the living room. He looked fit enough, she thought, though showed every one of his fifty-six years. He'd also lost a bit too much weight. She would have had to look at him twice if she'd met him in the street before recognising him as the man who was still her husband.

He inclined his head. 'Hello, luv.'

'Hello, John.' She would have preferred it if he hadn't called her 'luv'. It didn't seem right after they hadn't seen each other for so long a time. 'Sit down,' she said politely. 'How are you?'

'Ta, luv.' He sat in his old place under the window. 'I've felt better, but I've felt worse, too. I've been living the last few weeks at our Billy's.'

'I didn't know.' Her voice was very cool – and perfectly steady, she noted with relief. She didn't want him to know how badly she was shaking inside. She prayed she looked as calm as he appeared to be.

'You've hardly changed a bit,' he said.

Alice squirmed uncomfortably when she saw the obvious admiration in his eyes. She didn't reply.

'How are the kids?' he asked.

'Fine. Fion's in London. I'm not quite sure where Cormac is right now. He travels a lot, like. Maeve's married and Orla has four kids, two boys and two girls.' She remembered it was the day Lulu was born that she'd discovered he'd got himself another woman and a brand-new family.

'I suppose our Cormac's in a dead good job. I take it he went to university?'

The 'our' Cormac was another mistake. 'He decided not to in the end,' Alice said coldly. If his father had been around he might have been able to talk his son into completing the last two terms. 'He went into the music business instead. He's in a group that plays all over the country.'

He didn't ask what the group was called, what Fion was doing in London, where did Orla and Maeve live. Alice sensed he'd come for a purpose and it wasn't to know how his family were.

'Would you like some tea? Bernadette made some just before you came.'

'Please, luv.'

She went into the kitchen, poured the tea and wished he'd stop calling her 'luv'. It was getting on her nerves.

'You've got the place looking nice, luv,' he said when she came back. 'All this furniture's new, isn't it? I remember you going on about how much you wanted a fitted carpet.' His eyes swept approvingly around the room. 'Hairdressing must pay well.'

'I've got three salons now.' She resented being reminded of the days when she'd been dependent on him. 'I'm able to buy me own carpets.'

John gnawed his bottom lip. He glanced at her covertly. The coolness of her tone must have got through to him. 'I suppose you're wondering why I'm here?'

'It had crossed me mind.'

'Well, luv, I won't beat about the bush. I'll be totally honest with you. Do you mind if I smoke?'

Wordlessly, Alice fetched an ashtray, though the request surprised her. In the past he'd always claimed smoking was a complete waste of money: 'You may as well set light to a ten-bob note every week or so.' She noticed he'd lost some of his composure. His hands were unsteady as he lit the cigarette.

'The truth is, luv,' he said in a rush, 'I've been going further and further downhill over the last few years until a few weeks ago when I hit rock bottom. I don't want to stay at our Billy's for ever.' He paused. 'I was wondering if you'd mind if I came back home?'

Alice folded her arms over her chest, pressing them against herself so hard that it hurt. At least he'd been honest, as he'd promised. He didn't want to come back because he loved her or he'd missed her, or he wanted to be near his children. He wanted to return because he'd reached rock bottom and had nowhere else to go.

'It's bloody miserable on your own, luv,' he said forlornly.

'I already know that, John. I've been on me own for thirteen years.'

'Well, it'll be nice to have a man around the house for a change,' he said with an attempt at jocularity.

She looked at him directly. 'Not if the man is you. Am I so pathetic that you think *any* man will do for me? Including one who walked out on me for a younger woman and wouldn't be here if that woman hadn't walked out on *him*!'

'It was nothing like you think with Clare. I wouldn't have had anything to do with her if it hadn't been for me accident.'

'Your accident!' Alice laughed bitterly. 'Oh, we all know about your bloody accident. I'm surprised you didn't put a notice in the papers and announce it to the world. You'd think you were the only person who'd ever been hurt. In turn, you hurt everyone who loved you. I'll not forget when you moved in permanently with Clare. Cormac kept ringing the yard. He wanted his dad, but you'd have nothing to do with him. You were dead cruel, John. Cruel and selfish. People don't go that way because they've had an accident. It must have been there always. You just hadn't shown it before.'

'I'm sorry, Alice.' His body had gone limp. He lit another cigarette from the stub of the first and seemed to have trouble making contact.

'So you should be,' Alice said brutally, then immediately regretted it. 'Look,' she said more kindly. 'There's nothing to stop you coming round now and then for a cup of tea. I could arrange for Maeve and Orla to be here.'

'I doubt if they'd want to see me.'

On reflection, Alice doubted it too. 'You could still come round. I could make you a meal.'

'Do you really want me to?'

She couldn't meet his eyes because she could think of few things she wanted less. Until that night she hadn't realised he meant so little to her, that she actually disliked him. 'Of course,' she said.

It was John's turn to laugh. 'I think I get the picture. Perhaps I should have said I wanted to come back because I love you.'

'It wouldn't have made any difference. And it wouldn't have been true.'

'Oh, yes, it would, Alice. I *do* love you. I've never loved anyone else the way I love you.' His face collapsed. He was almost crying and it was horrible seeing a man like John Lacey so close to tears. He dropped the cigarette. The glowing end fell on his shirt, and she leapt to her feet and knocked it away before it burnt a hole, then picked up the ciggie off the carpet. She was still holding it when John grabbed her legs and laid his head against her stomach. 'I do love you, Alice.' He sobbed. 'I can't go on living the way I am.'

She pushed him away, wanting to cry herself. 'But I don't love you, John.' She only wished she did. Then she would have been happy to take him back.

He collapsed into the chair. 'What am I to do?' he asked pitifully. 'Where am I to go?'

'Home.'

'I haven't got a home.'

'Back to your Billy's, then.'

'I can't stay there for ever. You know how much I've always loathed Cora.'

Alice had reached the point where *she* had begun to feel cruel and selfish. 'I'll find you a home, a little house somewhere,' she said desperately. 'I'll give you the money for the furniture if you're short.'

It was a genuine offer, made because she felt genuinely sorry for him, but it immediately brought her husband to his senses. His face turned to stone. 'Do you really think I'd take money off a woman?'

'I'm offering to help, John, that's all.'

'I don't want your help, or your sympathy.'

'What else do you expect when you start crying?'

He got to his feet. 'I have the distinct feeling I've made a fool of meself. I think I'll go now.'

'John.' She put her hand on his arm, but he shrugged her away. Alice had a sense of déjà vu. In the past, he'd done the same thing when she'd been trying to reach him and had been rewarded with the same churlish rejection.

'Goodnight, Alice.'

Alice shut her eyes until the front door closed. She didn't open them until she heard someone coming in the back way.

Seconds later her dad barged in, livid with anger. 'Is he still here?' he demanded.

'No, Dad. He's gone.'

'What did he want?'

'To come back.'

'The nerve of the bugger. I hope you told him to go . . . to go . . .' Danny paused, trying to think of a way of putting it without using an unacceptable expletive. 'To go and jump in the lake.'

'I just said no, Dad.'

'He's upset you, hasn't he? I can tell by your face.'

'Oh, Dad,' Alice cried. 'He seemed so *tragic*. I feel sorry for him. What's going to happen to him now?'

'That's no longer any of your concern, girl. You're too soft, you are. If John Lacey's tragic, then it's his own fault. He's already put you through enough. Come on, luv.' He put an arm round her shoulders. 'Come back to ours and have a cup of tea, then you can go to the pictures with Bernadette. Even better, go somewhere and have a nice meal and a jangle.'

Alice willingly allowed herself to be led away. Anything would be better than being left with her own thoughts. She just wished she didn't have the horrible feeling that she'd let John down.

If only you could relive certain scenes in your life and do them differently! He should have been more controlled with Alice, more practical. He shouldn't have broken down, made himself look pathetic. Perhaps he should have asked more questions about the children, then approached the subject of him coming home more casually, skirting round it, like, as if the idea had just come to him. As it was, he'd made a terrible show of himself. His flesh crawled, thinking about it.

She'd looked so lovely, too: fresh and young, elegant in that green costume. She'd changed, though, since they used to live together. She'd never have said the things then that she'd said tonight – 'Do you think *any* man will do me?' – as if he was just a piece of shit.

In Marsh Lane, John paused outside an off-licence and realised how much he needed a drink. A sup of liquor hadn't passed his lips since the night Billy had carried him home from the Docky. He'd sworn never to get in such a state again, but now he felt like getting smashed rotten. He went into the shop and bought a bottle of whisky, the cheapest there. Outside, he stopped in the first doorway, unscrewed the top, put the bottle to his lips and swallowed deeply. The alcohol seemed warmly familiar as it poured down his throat and he immediately felt better, more in charge of himself.

He walked towards Garibaldi Road, only slightly unsteady on his feet, anger mounting. Who did Alice think she was? Had she forgotten that they were still man and wife, that he had rights? It could be she had no lawful right to turn him away. It could be that the house in Amber Street was still legally his. It was *his* name that used to be on the rent book. He might go and see a solicitor tomorrow.

Cora opened the door as he was struggling with the key. 'I'll give you a key if you like, luv.' She nodded at the one in his hand. 'That must be for somewhere else.'

'Sorry.' He frowned at the key. It was for the padlock on the gates of the yard.

'You weren't gone long,' Cora said, slyly pleased. There'd obviously been no great reconciliation.

'Where's Billy?' John lurched into the hall.

'He went out not long after you. Why don't you come and watch telly till he comes home?'

'I'd sooner go to bed early, if you don't mind. I feel very tired.'

'Anything you like, luv.'

Cora could smell the drink on him. As he went unsteadily upstairs, she saw the whisky bottle protruding from the pocket of his jacket. Alice must have turned him down.

What John didn't realise was that the woman who was perfect for him was directly under his nose – herself. They thought the same black thoughts, they looked darkly upon life, they didn't suffer fools gladly, they took great risks.

For the next two hours she sat in front of the empty grate, hands clasped on her lap, unmoving. Billy came in and wanted to know if John was home, and she told him he was in bed, but didn't mention the whisky.

'I think I'll turn in meself,' Billy announced, yawning.

Within minutes she could hear him snoring. And still Cora sat, shoulders tense, arms stiff, hands held together tightly, like a knot in a rope. Dare she show John, that very night, how exactly right they would be for each other? Billy wouldn't hear. The house could fall down around Billy's ears, but you'd still have to shake his arm to wake him.

Dare she?

She'd known he was for her the very second she'd set eyes on him. She felt certain something had passed between them. But he wasn't the sort of man who'd steal his brother's girl. He'd pretended to ignore her, but she could tell he wanted her as much as she wanted him. Alice, wishy-washy, gormless Alice Mitchell, was merely a substitute for the woman he really loved.

Cora went upstairs and changed into her best nightie. It was blue, that brushed-nylon stuff, and she'd got it in a sale in T. J. Hughes's. She undid her bun and combed her greying hair loose around her shoulders. There was scent somewhere, Californian Poppy, that Alice had given her for Christmas in the days when she'd been made welcome in Amber Street. She found the tiny bottle in a drawer under her stockings and dabbed some behind her ears.

Then she crept along the landing to the room where John Lacey slept.

He lay sprawled on the bed in his vest and underpants, his suit and the shirt she had bought him thrown carelessly on the floor. On the bedside table the whisky bottle was three-quarters empty and the clean ashtray she'd provided earlier overflowed with butts. The smell of smoke, of whisky fumes, only increased Cora's desire. She leant over the bed and started to touch him.

'Darling!' John reached for her and began to stroke her body through the scratchy nightdress. Cora pulled it over her head, leaving herself entirely exposed to him, giving herself, touching him as he touched her. Her body arched and shuddered with pleasure beneath his exploring hands. Then he thrust himself inside her and she had to hold back a shriek as a feeling, impossible to describe, began to grow and grow in her gut, like a firework, sizzling away, getting brighter and brighter, louder and louder, as it prepared to explode in a shower of stars and sparks.

Then the explosion came and her body, from head to toe, was encased in a silent scream of ecstacy. Cora had been waiting all her life for this day, for this hour, for this single minute.

She fell back on the bed, blissfully exhausted. John grunted, collapsed beside her and immediately fell asleep, but she didn't care. She snuggled against him and put her arm round his waist.

'That was nice, luv. It was never that way with your Billy,' she whispered. 'Later on, we'll do it again. We'll do it again and again for the rest of our lives. We're soulmates, you and me. I bet I could tell you things and you wouldn't be the least bit shocked.' She looked at his face, wondering if he could hear. 'I've never breathed a word about this to a soul, but I killed two people once. They were me aunties, Kate and Maud. You see, luv, me mam wasn't married when she had me and she died right after I was born. I never knew who me dad was. Kate and Maud, they took me in, but they didn't like me. Oh, no, they didn't like me a bit. I was a "badge of shame", they said. They treated me worse than an animal, fed me scraps, hit me and kicked me whenever they felt like it. I got hardly any learning. I never even learnt how to be happy, like. So, you know what I did?'

She paused, half expecting him to say, 'What, luv?' but there was no answer. 'I murdered them. I set fire to the house we lived in. I waited in the backyard till I heard them scream, then I waited till the screaming stopped, then I ran away. Sometimes, in the dead of night, I can still hear them screams. I can even smell the fire. It's the reason I can never sleep.' Cora sighed. 'Are you comfy, luv?' She adjusted the pillow beneath his head, pulled the sheet over them both. 'You have a nice rest, now, and when you wake up I'll make you feel dead happy again.'

Cora had never known what it was to relax, for her body to feel rested, her soul to be at peace, her brain to feel as light as air, and free for once of the thoughts and memories that plagued her. Before long, although it was the last thing she intended, she, too, was fast asleep.

The palest of grey light was creeping through the window when John Lacey woke. The birds in the garden had just begun to sing. For a few seconds he felt disorientated.

He recognised the lampshade hanging above him and remembered he was at Billy's. It took several more seconds before he realised there was someone in bed with him: a woman. For one mad moment he thought it might be Alice. He'd been to see her the night before. But the hair just visible in the still dusky shadows of the morning was the wrong colour. Anyroad, Alice had turned him down and he'd bought a bottle of whisky. He'd obviously gone somewhere, met a woman and couldn't remember a thing about it – it had happened before. He must have been plastered out of his mind to have brought her back to his brother's house.

Jaysus! He was longing for a fag. As soon as he'd smoked it, he'd get rid of his companion of the night as quietly as possible. Gingerly he eased himself out of bed. The ciggies were on the bedside table. He lit one, breathed in deeply, then noticed the blue nightdress thrown over the foot of the bed.

His reflexes must be working dead slow this morning, because it took John quite a while to realise the significance of this. There was only one person the nightdress could belong to.

Cora! He stumbled backwards, horrified. Cora Lacey was lying in his bed, naked. They must have . . .

Christ! He wanted to be sick. Something stirred in his sluggish brain, a memory, of hands touching him, of him touching back. He could remember them making love – and that it had actually felt good. He gagged. He had to get out of here.

Frantically he picked up his clothes, the ciggies, the remainder of the whisky and carried them on to the landing, where he clumsily got dressed, thrusting his foot into the wrong trouser leg, buttoning up his shirt all crooked. As he did so other memories returned, of a voice in his ear talking about murder, about burning people alive in their beds, listening to their screams.

Outside, a fine grey mist hung in the air and he could feel the moisture on his face as he walked towards Seaforth, towards the place that had been his home since Clare had left with their children.

Every now and then he stopped and took a mouthful of whisky. If he drank enough for long enough it might drown out the memory of last night.

By the time he reached the yard the whisky had gone and he could hardly walk. He flung the empty bottle into the gutter, where it smashed into a thousand brilliant shards. It took some time to fit the key into the padlock on the gates, more time to unlock the door of the two-storey building that was a store room, an office and the place where he lived – there was little use for an office these days. B.E.D.S. was all washed up. He'd been neglecting the firm for years. He owed money for the materials going rotten in the yard.

Somehow he managed to climb the stairs, where he collapsed on the filthy bed and immediately lit a ciggie.

The place stank, but he couldn't be bothered getting up and opening a window. He couldn't remember when it had last been cleaned. For years, now, he had let himself wallow in his misery, in the dirt of his surroundings. He had let B.E.D.S. collapse around his ears.

It never ceased to amaze him that a man as sensible as he'd always considered himself had made such a total and completely unnecessary mess of his life, culminating in last night's misadventure with Cora. He squirmed at the memory and wondered if he'd just imagined the things she'd said. Was his brother's wife a murderer?

In a minute he'd look for something to drink. He'd drink himself completely senseless, so he wouldn't be able to think. There were times, like the night Billy had found him on the Docky, when his mind was nothing but a blank.

The fag had burnt so low he could feel the heat on his lips. He spat it out and reached for another. The effort of stretching made his head swirl crazily and John didn't mind a bit when he found himself sinking into welcome unconsciousness.

The stub of the cigarette had landed on the bed, rolled under the pillow. John Lacey was too far gone to notice when the pillow began to smoulder.

13

The police were still trying to trace the relatives of John Lacey, the man whose charred body had been found after the fire in the timber yard had been extinguished, when Fionnuala Littlemore returned to Liverpool with her children.

It was Sunday afternoon, and Fion came in the back way just as Alice was preparing a salad for Maeve and Martin who were expected later for tea.

'Hello, Mam,' Fion said, as casually as if she'd been gone five minutes, not several years.

'Fion!' Alice dropped a slice of ham on the floor. 'Oh, Fion, luv. It's good to see you.' She flung her arms round her eldest daughter, stroked her face. 'How are you, luv? Where have you been? And who are these?' Only then did Alice become aware of the children.

'This is Colin and this is Bonnie, and we've been living in London. Say hello to your grandma, kids.'

'They're yours?' Alice dropped more ham.

'Very much mine, Mam. And before you ask, their dad, me husband that is, died two years ago.'

'Oh, luv!' Alice burst into tears for the son-in-law she'd never met and hadn't even known existed. 'Oh, they're lovely children,' she said tearfully. 'Let's take a look at you.' She knelt down and examined Colin's face. 'You must take after your dad, because you're nothing like our family. And you' – she turned to Bonnie – 'are the image of your mam.'

Both judgements seemed to please the children inordinately. Alice forgot the salad and took them into the living room.

Fion immediately made herself at home. 'I'll put the kettle on, Mam. I'm dying for a cuppa.'

'I wouldn't say no to a cuppa either.' Alice drew her new grandchildren on to her knee. They went willingly. 'You're prettier than Ruby,' Bonnie said.

'Who's Ruby?'

'Ruby was their other grandma,' Fion said as she came in. 'She was much older than you. She died a few months ago. That's why we're back home.'

She'd come home for good! Alice did her best not to feel glad that the unknown Ruby had died, otherwise Fion, who'd clearly not acquired an ounce of tact in her absence, would still be in London. Her daughter had acquired one thing, though – confidence. Alice watched as Fion unzipped a small travelling bag and began to root swiftly and efficiently through the contents. She seemed very sure of herself. She was slimmer and had grown her hair, which was gathered in an untidy knot on top of her head. Long wavy tendrils had escaped and trailed over her neck and ears. Her outfit was a bit peculiar: black slacks and a thin black jumper under a brightly coloured patchwork waistcoat. Neil Greene, who'd met her in London, said she worked for a union.

'Oh, it's good to see you, Fion,' Alice cried. 'You look wonderful.' Her mind went back to the day Fion, her first child, had been born. She'd arrived two weeks late, after a long, tiresome labour, very early in the morning. At almost nine pounds, she was the biggest of Alice's babies – and the biggest in the maternity home, she remembered. John had been so proud. She recalled him taking his daughter in his arms, looking down at her, his eyes filled with love. It had never crossed her mind that one day that love would disappear.

'It's good to see you, Mam,' Fion said practically. 'And you don't look so bad yourself.'

'Where's your luggage, luv? You won't last long out of that small bag.'

'I've got more than luggage, Mam. I've got furniture. It's coming in a van tomorrow.'

Alice felt alarmed. 'But there isn't the room here for furniture, Fion.'

'I know that.' Fion snorted. 'I'm not an idiot. The furniture's going to me house on Stanley Road.'

'You've got a house!'

'It's Horace Flynn's old house that he left me in his will.'

'Bloody hell!' exclaimed Alice, who usually managed not to swear if children were present. 'Who'd have thought it, eh? Wonders will never cease.'

'Is our Orla still living in Pearl Street?'

'Yes, luv,' Alice said weakly, still trying to come to terms with the incredible fact that Horace Flynn's house in Stanley Road now belonged to Fion. 'Maeve's in Waterloo. Her and Martin are coming to tea.'

'I'll go round and see Orla in a minute. I'll leave the kids with you, if you don't mind.'

'As if I'd mind being left with these two little darlings,' Alice cried, hugging the children to her. 'Ask Orla and everyone back to tea. I'll take Colin and Bonnie round me dad's and see if Bernadette can lend us some food. Oh, I can't remember when I last felt so happy.' Fion's return more than made up for John's recent visit, the memory of which still haunted her.

To make things even better Fion had news of Cormac. 'I think he might soon be back as well.'

'Did he say what was wrong?' Alice asked anxiously. 'I think something must have happened at university to make him not want to go back. He was doing so well, too.'

'He didn't say anything, Mam. Perhaps he'd been studying so much his brain got tired. I've heard it can happen.'

Alice sighed blissfully. 'I can't wait to have him home. It'll be just like old times, all four of you here. And these two little 'uns will make it absolutely perfect.'

'Oh, so you saw fit to show your face again, Fion Lacey.' Orla's face was cold when she opened the door to find her sister on the step. 'You know, Mam was dead upset when you walked out.'

'She was dead upset when Micky Lavin put you up the stick,' Fion said, grinning. 'So I reckon we're even when it comes to upsetting Mam. And it's Fion Littlemore, if you don't mind. I'm a mother now of two small children.'

Orla's cold expression vanished and she grinned back. 'It's great to have you home, sis. You look marvellous. Our Maeve's become a real pain since she got married. All she talks about is her bloody house.'

'It's good to *be* home, Orla. Now, are you going to let me in, or must I stand on this doorstep for ever?'

An impromptu party took place at the Laceys' that night. Danny Mitchell went to the off-licence and returned laden with wine, beer and crisps. Bernadette quickly made two dozen sausage rolls. Orla, never an expert in the kitchen, coaxed Lulu into making a tray of fairy cakes. Maeve was telephoned and asked to bring whatever was available.

'I bought a tin of iced biscuits for Christmas the other day. I'll fetch them and anything else I can find,' Maeve promised. 'Tell our Fion I can't wait to see her.'

'Jaysus! She's become so *efficient!*' Orla groaned. 'Who in their right mind buys biscuits for Christmas in September?'

'Our Maeve does, obviously. It's no worse than someone with four children not being able to rustle up a fairy cake.'

'You've not changed, Fion. You were always one to call a spade a spade.'

'I could never understand why anyone would want to call a spade anything else. Are my Elvis records still around, Mam?'

'They're in the parlour, luv. You'll find Cormac's there too. He was fond of Gerry and the Pacemakers and Herman's Hermits – and the Beatles, of course.'

It's quite like old times, Alice thought as she prepared a mountain of sandwiches and listened to her daughters bicker. But there was no spite behind it now. Fion wasn't jealous of Orla any more. She felt her equal.

Eight o'clock. Most of the adults were slightly tipsy. Colin and Bonnie were upstairs, tired after the long journey from London, fast asleep in their mother's old room. The other children were in the parlour playing something that seemed to require a great deal of noise.

The weather had changed. The long Indian summer had ended late that afternoon when the sun abruptly disappeared and the sky became a solid mass of black, leaden clouds. Thunder rumbled in the distance, lightning flashed. Every now and then there would be a splattering of rain against the windows. A downpour was expected any minute.

In Amber Street the lights were on and the weather did nothing to dampen spirits. The three men were contemplating going to the pub for a pint.

'But we've got beer here,' Alice pointed out.

'It tastes different in a pub,' Danny claimed.

'What happens if it rains?' Orla wanted to know. 'I'm not pressing your best suit if it gets soaked, Micky Lavin.'

Maeve looked reproachfully at Martin. 'Fancy deserting me for a pint of beer!' the look said. Martin affected to ignore it.

'Well, will we or won't we?' Danny demanded.

Micky slapped him on the shoulder. 'I say we will.'

'Me, too.' Martin was still avoiding Maeve's accusing stare.

Lulu appeared in the doorway, her blue eyes round and slightly scared. 'There's a police car stopped outside,' she said. 'The man's just got out.'

There was a knock on the door.

Alice still felt shattered next day. 'It's all my fault,' she said hoarsely. 'If only I'd taken him back!'

'Don't be daft, Mam. If I'd come home and found him here I'd have been out the house again like a shot.'

'Don't say things like that, Fion.'

'Well, don't you go saying stupid things like it's all your fault. It's nobody's fault but his own. The police said the fire was started by a cigarette. He could have done the same thing here and it wouldn't have been just him who'd gone up in smoke, but you as well.'

Alice sighed. 'You sound awfully hard, luv.'

'I'm just being sensible, Mam,' Fion said more gently. 'Why don't you go in to work, try and forget him.'

'As if I could forget your dad! He was everything to me once.' Alice looked imploringly at her daughter. 'You'll come to the funeral, won't you, luv? I wish we could get in touch with Cormac, tell him.'

'I'll come for your sake, Mam, not his. Orla and Maeve are coming for the same reason, and Grandad and Bernadette. As for Cormac, he's lucky to be out of it. I only wish I'd left coming back another week and I'd've been out of it too.'

Billy Lacey was the only person to cry at his brother's funeral. His sobs sounded harsh and bitter across the deathly wastes of Ford Cemetery. It was a strange morning, neither warm nor cold, not quite sunny, not quite dull.

Billy's wife made no attempt to comfort him. The other mourners would have been surprised if she had. Cora's face was as strange as the morning. She gave no sign to show that she cared her brother-in-law had gone.

It was left to Maurice who, at twenty-five, could have been the double of the young John Lacey, to step forward and put his arm around the broad, heaving shoulders.

'Never mind, Dad,' Maurice mumbled awkwardly, and father and son embraced, as they had never done before.

Alice wouldn't let herself cry, because the tears would have been for herself, not John. They would have been hypocritical tears. She was sorry John had died such a horrible death, but her prime emotion was guilt that she might have stopped it.

John's daughters were there purely for their mother's sake. Alice was a stickler for appearances. It mattered to Mam what people, particularly the neighbours, thought. However, so far, none of the neighbours had guessed that the John Lacey, whose death in a fire in Seaforth was reported in the local paper, was the John Lacey who had once lived in Amber Street.

Good riddance to bad rubbish, Danny Mitchell thought as the coffin was lowered into the grave. Our Alice should be glad to see the back of him.

Bernadette Mitchell thought more or less the same.

Only one piece of paper remained that had belonged to John Lacey. All the rest had been destroyed in the fire, every scrap; the unpaid bills, the files, the audited accounts going back for years, every single letter John had ever received and the carbon copies of those he had sent, the photos of Clare and their children.

The paper that remained had been lodged in a bank. It was a deed, confirming that John had owned the freehold of the piece of land fronting the corner of Benton Street and Crozier Terrace. Alice, as the lawfully wedded wife of the deceased, was now the legal owner, so the bank informed her in a letter.

'I don't want it,' she said with a shudder when she showed the letter to her dad.

'Then get the place cleaned up. It's bound to be in a mess. And sell it,' Danny advised.

What would she do with the money? There was money piling up in the bank from the three salons, but none of her children was prepared to take a penny. Maeve and Martin had refused help with their mortgage, and Micky Lavin had been indignant when she'd offered to buy him and Orla a house. Cormac had lived happily on his grant at university and she had a feeling Fion wouldn't let her pay for Horace Flynn's old place to be done up – it was dead shabby and the plumbing made some very peculiar noises.

Why was she bothering to make all this money when there was nothing to spend it on? She was fed up with her customers wondering aloud why she was still in Amber Street, why she hadn't bought herself a nicer house in a nicer place.

'Because I'm perfectly happy where I am,' she would reply. She felt very dull and unimaginative.

Fion was looking for someone to care for the children so she could go to work. Alice could sell the salons and become a full-time grandma.

'No, I need more than that,' she told herself. 'I may well be dull and unimaginative, but I need to *be* someone, not just a mother or a grandmother, not just a wife. I need to be special in me own way.'

Since John's death, Billy Lacey had taken to calling on his sister-in-law on his way home from work. Alice was the closest link to the brother he had lost, found, and finally lost again.

He couldn't understand why John had left the house in Garibaldi Road, he said repeatedly. 'He was in bed when I came home the night before, but gone next morning, without a word of explanation. I thought he was happy there. He *seemed* happy. Cora liked having him. He could have stayed for ever as far as we were concerned.'

Alice didn't mention it was the night before that she'd turned John away. She already blamed herself enough and she didn't want the burden of Billy's blame as well.

'Have you ever been to that timber yard place?' Billy asked.

'Just the once.'

'I should have gone meself. It's not far. I shouldn't have let him sink into such a state, me own brother, like.'

'Don't reproach yourself, Billy. John knew where you lived. It was him who walked out, on all of us, including you. It was up to him to keep in touch, not for you to search him out.' Alice wished she could take her own sensible advice. She showed Billy the letter from the bank.

'Do you mind if I take a look at the place?' His face brightened. 'I'll tidy it up if you like.'

He would have been hurt if she'd turned him down. She accepted his offer with a show of gratitude, though she didn't give a damn what happened to the yard. Billy perked up considerably and decided to go round to Seaforth there and then.

'I'll call for our Maurice on the way. The two of us can do the job together.'

At least one good thing had come out of John's death: Billy and his wayward son were now reunited.

The iron-barred gate was secured with a padlock and chain. The men peered through the bars at the dismal remains of John's once thriving business. The building he had lived in had almost completely burnt away. There were no walls and only the skeleton of the roof remained, the beams silhouetted starkly against the livid evening sky – more rain looked inevitable later.

The yard itself was covered with ash and soot, mixed with other debris, including curls of black tar paper, like apple peelings, from the roof. Pools of black water reflected the angry yellow sky. The few lengths of timber stacked around the walls had been badly singed. There was a rusty van with a flat tyre.

'We'll have to get a key from somewhere to match the padlock,' Billy said.

'It'll be a job and a half, clearing this place up,' said Maurice.

'You don't mind though, do you, son? After all, it's not as if you've got anything else to do.'

'I don't mind and no, I haven't got anything else to do.' Maurice's voice was bitter. A prison record didn't help when you were looking for a job. Maurice hadn't worked since he'd come out of Walton jail, though he'd never stopped trying.

'I didn't mean it like that, son.'

'I know, Dad. I was a fool to break into that newsagent's. I only did it to impress some girl – I can't even remember her name. I know I shouldn't make excuses. I was an adult. I should've known better, but her brothers talked me into it.' Maurice laughed drily. 'They made it sound so easy.'

They began to walk back towards Bootle. 'You know,' Maurice said after a while, 'we could do something with that yard.'

'Such as?'

'I'm not sure. Remember that place I used to work, the builders' merchants? Something like that.'

'We'd need money to get started, son.' Billy jangled the coins in his pocket. They were all he had until he got paid on Friday.

'You can borrow money from the bank to start a business. Not that they'd lend it me,' Maurice said hastily. 'Not with my record. But they might lend it you. After all, we've already got the premises.'

'Who said we've got the premises. Alice wants the place sold.'

'She won't sell if we tell her our plans,' Maurice said with utter conviction. 'Not Auntie Alice. Anyroad, once we get going we'll pay rent. We might even buy the site off her one day.'

'What plans?' Billy asked, bewildered.

'The plans you and me have to start our own business. Dad.' For the second time in a week Maurice placed his arm round his father's shoulders. 'I wonder if that van goes?'

Cormac came into the salon wearing an Afghan coat that looked as if it had been gnawed by a hungry animal, red cotton trousers and open-toed sandals, despite it being November and very cold. His long fair hair was tied back with a ribbon. He looked a sight.

Alice was torn between the joy of seeing him again and worry that her customers would recognise who he was. She rushed her once-perfect son into the kitchen. 'Fion said to expect you one day soon.' She longed to kiss and hug him, but Cormac seemed to have gone off that sort of thing. 'Are you hungry, luv? Shall we go home and I'll make you something to eat?'

'I've just eaten at Fion's, thanks.'

'You went to see Fion first?' Alice felt hurt.

'I wanted to put my stuff there.' For some reason he refused to meet her eyes. 'I'll be living at Fion's, on the top floor. I hope you don't mind.'

'Of course not.' Alice minded very much, but didn't show it. 'Your room's always there if you change your mind.'

'The thing is' – he shuffled his near-naked feet – 'I've brought a girl. We'll be living together.'

Alice swallowed and reminded herself that young people did this sort of thing nowadays. 'I hope she's nice. What's her name?'

'Pol. She's very nice. She's also pregnant.'

To Alice's surprise she burst out laughing and at the same time thanked God he hadn't expected to live in Amber Street with his pregnant girlfriend. 'What else are you going to tell me, that she's got two heads?'

Cormac smiled for the first time. 'No, just one head, Mam. Fion said to come round tonight so you can meet her.'

It might have been a mistake, but he'd called her Mam, something else he avoided these days, along with the hugs and kisses.

Horace Flynn would have turned in his grave if he could have seen the state of his house, which hadn't seen a lick of paint in years. The few pieces of expensive furniture still remaining were covered in cigarette burns and the scars of too hot cups. Cats – Fion already had two strays – had scratched curves in the legs of the mahogany table, the six chairs that went with it and the lovely sideboard that used to house Horace's pretty ornaments.

Fion's own furniture was cheap stuff, similarly marked with years of wear and tear. Alice suspected it had been bought second-hand.

She had insisted on paying for the curtains to be cleaned – they were too thick and heavily lined to wash – because they made the rooms smell musty. 'Regard it as a prezzie,' she said to Fion. 'People usually buy each other house-warming presents.'

The long velvet parlour curtains had emerged from the cleaners in tatters. 'They were rotten,' the woman assistant announced when Alice went to collect them. 'I'm afraid we can't pay compensation.'

Alice had bought replacements, but Fion didn't notice that the curtains that went up in the parlour were different from the ones that came down. Fion seemed oblivious to her surroundings. The shabby furniture didn't bother her. Neither did the clanky, grumbling plumbing, the ancient bathroom, the tatty carpet on the stairs, the grimy ceilings, the wallpaper peeling in the corners . . .

And it wasn't just stray animals Fion had started to collect, but human beings too. Alice had no idea where she found them. The three Littlemores lived on the vast ground floor. On the floor above, in the front bedroom, a Mrs Freda Murphy spent her days knitting unwearable garments for the children.

'Where did she come from, luv?' Alice asked curiously when Freda first turned up. Fion had scarcely been living in the place a week.

'Her son was all set to throw her out. The thing is, Mam,' Fion said indignantly, 'the rent book used to be in her name, but he persuaded her to change it.'

How had Fion *known*? Alice didn't bother to pursue the matter.

Not long afterwards the Archibalds arrived, Peter and Geoffrey, twin brothers in their thirties, who occupied the bedroom at the back. 'They've been in a mental home, poor things,' said Fion.

'Are you sure they're safe, y'know, with the children, like?' Alice asked nervously.

'There's nothing wrong with them, Mam. They went in the mental home by mistake. Anyroad, it's only temporary. The corporation have promised to find them a proper house.'

Now Cormac was moving into the top floor with a pregnant girl called Pol and there were still two bedrooms empty. Alice dreaded who might turn up next.

Yet the strange thing was that she loved being at Fion's. The fire in the living room was always lit, the shabby chairs were comfortable, tea was permanently in the pot for anyone to help themselves. The telephone rang non-stop, because Fion, who never used to have a single friend, now seemed to have dozens. Alice discovered she was a member of numerous organisations and charities, and was always in the throes of arranging fund-raising events: jumble sales, coffee mornings, parties, lectures. She had persuaded her mother to help at a Christmas bazaar early in December. A few weeks ago she had taken the children down to London for a CND march.

'What's CND?' Alice asked.

'The Campain for Nuclear Disarmament. Honestly, Mam, you're dead ignorant. All you know about is hairdressing.'

Alice humbly agreed.

She felt very nervous the night that she went to meet Cormac's pregnant girlfriend. She prayed that they would like each other and that Pol would make a suitable wife – she assumed they would get married one day – for Cormac, who was a remarkable lad and would make a wonderful husband.

Freda Murphy opened the door to Alice's knock, the long needles of her untidy knitting tucked under her arms. Two strange children were playing in the hall with Colin and Bonnie.

In the living room a woman with a black eye was talking in a high-pitched, angry voice to Fion.

'Hello, Mam,' Fion said calmly. 'This is Jenny. She's staying with us a while until the police do something about her louse of a husband. Our Cormac's upstairs with Pol. Tell them to come down in a minute; I've made some scouse.'

'You gave birth to an angel when you had that girl,' Freda remarked when Alice reappeared.

'Did I really?' She went up two flights of stairs. The top floor was merely one large room with a sloping ceiling and windows at both ends.

'Come in,' Cormac shouted in answer to her knock.

Alice took a deep breath, opened the door, and found Cormac and a young girl sitting crossed-legged on the floor, facing each other and holding hands.

'We're doing breathing exercises,' Cormac said. 'We've bought a book on what to do when you're having a baby. This is Pol, by the way. Pol, say hello to ... to my mother.'

'Hello, Mrs Lacey,' Pol said in a breathless, childish voice. She scrambled to her feet, a rosy-cheeked girl, with guileless eyes and curly brown hair. She wore an ankle-length cotton skirt and a coarse woven top. Her feet, like Cormac's, were bare. She looked no more than sixteen.

'Call me Alice.' They shook hands. Pol's hand was very small and limp. 'How are you feeling, luv? When's the baby due?'

'I feel fine. I haven't been sick or anything. I'm not sure when it's due.' She looked vague.

'Well, the doctor should be able to tell,' Alice said comfortably. 'He'll send you to the clinic where they'll keep an eye on you.'

Pol gave a tinkling little laugh. 'Oh, there's no need for doctors and clinics, Alice. As long as I look after myself, eat properly and do the breathing exercises I shall be OK.'

'I see.' Alice was horrified. She glanced at her son, still sitting cross-legged on the floor, eyes closed, apparently in a trance. He must approve of Pol's plans for her pregnancy. Still, she had always made a point of not interfering in her children's affairs and wasn't going to start now. 'Oh, well, but you need to book into hospital, so they'll be expecting you.'

'There's no need for that either.' Pol regarded her pityingly. 'Cormac's going to deliver the baby here.'

'He'll sew you up, will he? If you need stitches, like.'

'She won't need stitches,' Cormac said without opening his eyes. 'She'll be too relaxed to tear.'

Jaysus! Alice announced the scouse would be ready soon and escaped downstairs. The pair were crazy, out of this world.

Fion was alone, stirring pans in the old-fashioned kitchen. A cat watched with interest from its unhygienic position on the draining board. She looked up when her mother came in. 'What did you think of her?'

'She seems very nice, but awfully young.'

'She's twenty-one, older than she looks.'

'Has she told you her plans for having the baby? They're not very sensible, Fion. I'm worried.'

'She'll change her mind nearer the time.'

'Lord, I hope so. Our Cormac's a clever lad, but I'm not sure if he's up to delivering a baby.'

The Christmas bazaar was to raise funds for an orphanage in Ethiopia. Fion put Alice in charge of the bottle stall. The main prize was a bottle of whisky. Every bottle had a raffle ticket attached, the numbers ending in a nought. People bought tickets for sixpence each and if they picked one that matched the number on a bottle it was theirs.

Naturally, everyone wanted to win the whisky. The trouble was the winning ticket wasn't in the box. Fion had taken it to put in later when most of the bottles had gone.

'You can't do that!' her scandalised mother gasped.

'Of course I can, Mam. If the whisky's won right at the start, no one will want a go any more. Don't forget, it's all in a good cause.'

Alice had been hoping to enjoy herself. Instead, she felt like a criminal as she tended her colourfully decorated stall. Carols issued from a loudspeaker and their innocent message made her feel even more sinful. She was very busy, always surrounded by a crowd, and the prizes – the bottles of chop sauce, vinegar, shampoo, lemonade, mayonnaise – rapidly diminished as the afternoon progressed. The more they diminished the more the eager participants saw their chance of winning the whisky, which had started to look very lonely, not quite by itself but almost.

Where the hell was Fion? She couldn't leave the stall and look for her. Alice began to panic. Any minute, now, someone would guess the ticket for the whisky wasn't there and she'd be driven from the hall by a justifiably angry crowd. She felt conscious of her burning face, her racing heart.

'Are you all right,' said a voice. 'It's Mrs Lacey, isn't it? Fion's mum.'

She'd noticed the slightly balding man who seemed to be in charge of things. He was about her own age, casually dressed in a black polo-necked jumper and baggy corduroy pants, his craggy face deeply tanned, as if he'd spent many years abroad. He had a slow, gentle, very patient smile.

'No, I'm not all right,' Alice said in a cracked voice. 'I need our Fion urgently.'

'I'll find her for you.'

Fion arrived seconds later. Alice stared at her accusingly over the heads of the crowd surrounding the stall.

'Can I have a go, Mam?'

'I think you better had.'

Only Alice noticed the ticket already in Fion's hand when she dipped it into the box. 'If she brings it out again and claims the whisky I'll bloody kill her,' she vowed. Luckily for Fion, she withdrew a losing ticket. Not long afterwards the whisky was won by a little boy and immediately appropriated by his delighted father. Alice breathed a sigh of relief.

'Would you like a cup of tea?' The man in the black jumper was back.

'I'd give my right arm for a cup of tea, ta.'

'There's no need for such extremes.' He smiled. 'You can have one for nothing.'

Now the whisky had gone, so had all interest in winning the motley collection of bottles that remained. Alice sank on to one of the chairs against the wall behind.

The helpful man returned with two cups of tea and sat beside her. 'My name's Charlie Glover. Do I call you, "Fion's Mum" or "Mrs Lacey"?'

'I'd prefer Alice and I don't know what I would have done without you earlier. You were a great help.'

'Pleased to be of service, Ma'am.' He smiled his lovely smile. His eyes were dark-grey with little shreds of silver.

Alice wondered why she was noticing a strange man's eyes, his smile. She was fifty-one, for heaven's sake. She'd lost all interest in men years ago. 'Have you been living abroad?' she asked conversationally.

'Yes, Ethiopia. I used to run the orphanage we're raising funds for.'

'Used to?'

'I thought it was time I had a rest and a change,' he explained. 'I'm staying with my brother and his wife in Ormskirk.' His voice was deep and pleasing, and Alice detected the faint trace of a Lancashire accent. He spoke slowly, with the air of a man unused to being interrupted. 'In another three months I'm off to the Transvaal, this time to take over a hospital on the borders of Swaziland.'

'You're a doctor?'

'Yes. I work for a charity called Overseas Rescue.'

'Gosh! It all sounds very exciting.'

'It's more worthwhile than exciting.' He half smiled. 'My wife used to love it when we moved somewhere new, but she sadly died ten years ago.'

Alice put her hand on his arm. 'I'm so sorry.'

'That's kind of you. Fion told me her father died recently. You're being very brave about it.'

She felt uncomfortable. 'Me and John hadn't lived together in a long while. I was upset he died, but not devastated. Mind you' – her lips twisted wistfully – 'I would have been devastated once.'

'You obviously have good memories to look back on.' He got to his feet. 'Duty calls. I'm due to draw the raffle any minute.' To her surprise he sat down again. 'Look, are you doing anything tonight?'

'Nothing particular. I'll probably watch television,' Alice replied, taking the question literally and wondering why he seemed so pleased by her answer, why his grey eyes lit up.

'Then why don't I take you out to dinner instead?' he said eagerly. 'Somewhere in Southport would be nice.'

'Dinner!' she exclaimed, immediately flustered. 'Oh, no. No, I couldn't possibly. Thanks for asking, but no ... excuse me. I've just seen my other daughter. Orla!' she called and almost ran over to the door that Orla had just entered by. 'What are you doing here?' she asked breathlessly.

Orla waved the notebook in her hand. 'Covering the bazaar for the paper. Have you been trying to run a four-minute mile, Mam? You're all puffed out and as red as a beetroot.'

'I've been working hard on a stall, that's all.'

'Where's our Fion? I need to know how much she raised, then I've got to interview a chap called Charlie Glover. He wants to appeal for funds for some hospital abroad.' She made a face. 'I once envisaged meself interviewing film stars and politicians, not reporting on a grotty bazaar. You know how much I'll get for this?' She waved the notebook again. 'Tuppence a line!'

'Oh, stop moaning, luv.'

Orla was jealous of Fion, with her active social life, loads of friends and part-time job at Liverpool University where she worked in the Students Union. Beside that of her sister, Orla considered her life hideously dull and uneventful, and the Lavins' house in Pearl Street poky in the extreme compared with the one in Stanley Road. 'Ta, Mam. You're all sympathy,' she said tartly.

'Tell Fion when you see her I've gone back to Stanley Road, and that I've taken Colin and Bonnie. They look dead bored. And by the way, that's Charlie Glover over there, about to draw the raffle.'

Alice was gently frying sausages when Fion arrived home, looking flushed and exhausted. 'We raised over two hundred pounds,' she said triumphantly. 'Where's the kids?'

'Watching telly. They said they were starving, so I've fed them. All I could find in the fridge was sausages, so I've done the same for us. You've got no spuds, either, only frozen chips.'

'I need to do some shopping,' Fion said vaguely. 'By the way, what did you do to poor Charlie?'

Alice nearly dropped a fork in the sausages. 'Nothing that I know of. We just chatted a bit, that's all. Why, what did he say I'd done?'

'Nothing, but he talked about you non-stop while we were packing up. He obviously fancies you dead rotten, but when I invited him back to tea and said you'd be here he claimed you wouldn't be too pleased.' She stared accusingly at her mother. 'Why on earth should he say that, Mam?'

'He asked me out and I refused.' Alice went red.

'Idiot!'

'I am not an idiot, Fion. I didn't want to get involved, that's all. I wouldn't have known what to say. I'm quite happy staying in and watching television.'

'Well, you shouldn't be.' Fion lit the gas under the chip pan, already full of fat that hadn't been changed in weeks. 'You're not exactly old and Charlie's quite decent-looking for somone in his fifties. You should have grabbed the chance to enjoy yourself for a change. Our Orla agreed.' Her eyes narrowed calculatingly. 'If you'd played your cards right, you could have gone with him to the Transvaal in a few months' time.'

'What as, one of the cleaners in his bloody hospital?'

'No, as his wife. You're not half daft, Mam. He fell for you like a ton of bricks.'

Alice's heart gave a little lurch. 'Are you after getting rid of me, Fion?'

Fion laid her chin on Alice's shoulder. 'No, Mam. I just want you to be happy, do something interesting and exciting for a change. I don't like you living on your own in Amber Street. You're going nowhere fast. Why don't you tell Charlie you've changed your mind? Give him another chance; he'd leap at it.'

'He might be a Protestant.'

'For God's sake, Mam,' Fion said, exasperated. 'As if that matters at your age.'

'I'll think about it,' Alice promised, though she had no intention of doing any such thing.

That night the television was on but Alice wasn't watching. Instead, she was going over the events of the afternoon. She didn't want to leave Amber Street, let alone travel to the other side of the world. She didn't even want her humdrum life interrupted by having dinner with a man she hardly knew.

She wasn't particularly happy, but nor was she particularly sad. She just existed, went from day to day, living a life in which little happened that was exciting or remarkable. Babies were born; people died; there was an occasional juicy bit of gossip in the salon; she sometimes went to the pictures with Bernadette; her children and *their* children came to tea on Sundays. Every now and then she threw a party. She'd got used to being the proprietor of three hairdressing salons and they had long ceased to be a source of pride.

It wasn't much of a life, but it was the life she wanted.

No one thought to close the curtains when Alice Lacey held a party on Christmas Eve. From the parlour a sharp ray of yellow light fanned across the dimly lit street. There were other parties in Amber Street that night, other lights, making the unlit areas darker and more starkly defined, shadowy. It was a beautiful night, calm and tranquil, not particularly cold for the time of year. There was no moon, but the black sky was littered with stars.

The solitary figure of a woman lurked in the shadows outside the Laceys', peering through the window, dodging from one side of the glass to the other. The woman wore the same camel coat, the same clumsy fur-lined boots that she'd worn four years before when she'd spied on Cormac's twenty-first. She spied on him now, watched him lounging against the wall, looking a bit fed up, she thought.

She was disappointed in her son, who'd given up university for some reason and had actually been seen in the labour exchange, shamelessly queuing for his dole money. She didn't approve of his long hair and the way he dressed, like he'd just picked stuff out of a ragbag. The girl, Pol, was there, obviously in the club. No one knew if she and Cormac were married. By all accounts Alice kept her mouth firmly buttoned when she was asked.

In fact, Maurice looked far more presentable, in a blue check shirt and nicely pressed grey pants. He and the Pol girl seemed to be getting on like a house on fire. They'd been laughing together on the settee for almost an hour.

Cora's lips bared in a snarl when Fionnuala came into the room with a plate of sandwiches. She'd very much like to know what favours Fion Lacey had done for Horace Flynn so that he'd seen fit to leave her his lovely big house, yet hadn't thought to let *her* have a penny.

Billy was there! Billy had come into the parlour supping a can of beer. Her own husband had been invited to Alice's party and hadn't said a word – not that they normally exchanged many words. There'd just been those weeks while John was living with them. Since then the usual silence had prevailed.

John!

She hadn't cried much in her life, but she still cried when she thought about John and the future that had been denied them – the future *together*. It would always remain a mystery why he'd left Garibaldi Road so suddenly. That morning she'd woken up, felt for him, but he wasn't there! After Billy had gone to work she'd rushed around to the yard. But it was already on fire, blazing away, throwing sparks into the sky. Someone must have called the fire engine, because it arrived almost straight away. She had stayed for hours, watching the building fall to pieces, watching the flames gradually subside, watching the firemen carry out something on a stretcher.

There didn't look to be much left of John under the tarpaulin. She longed to snatch it off and kiss the burnt remains of the only man she had ever loved. Cora clenched her fists and her nails bit into the soft flesh of her palms.

A burst of laughter came from inside the house whose occupants interested her so greatly. Billy, of all people, had made a puppet out of his hand and was making it talk. She couldn't hear what it was saying, but everyone was falling about.

Fion suddenly leapt to her feet and closed the curtains, and Cora was left desolate, with nothing to see.

In the parlour Fion shuddered and said to nobody in particular, 'It's funny, but I felt as if there was someone watching us from outside.'

14

It was April Fool's Day and the baby had taken it into its head to fool them by arriving early, though Pol had always been vague about the date. Cormac opened the window, put a tape of soothing music in the tape recorder and lit a fresh joss stick.

'Take deep breaths, Pol. Really deep now,' he instructed when the labour appeared to be reaching a climax. He sat on the edge of the bed and took several deep breaths himself to demonstrate how. 'Sing your song. "Here we go round the mulberry bush, the mulberry bush, the mulberry bush. Here we . . ."' he warbled very much out of tune.

Pol screamed.

'I didn't think it was all that bad,' Cormac joked.

Pol screamed again. There was a veil of perspiration on her brow and her body was rigid with fear.

'Push,' he commanded, determined to stay calm. 'No, don't push. Oh, where's that bloody instruction book?'

'On the table,' Pol yelled. 'Cormac, I think I need to go to hospital.'

'But we were going to do this by ourselves!'

'No, Cormac. *I* was going to do it by myself. *You* were going to help and you're not helping a bit. Ooh!' she groaned. 'I never knew you could be in such pain. Fetch your Fion. She might know what to do.'

'She's gone to a coffee morning.' Cormac felt a stir of panic. 'I'll ring for the ambulance.'

'Do it quickly, Cormac. Please!'

Two hours later Pol was delivered of a perfect baby girl weighing six pounds, two ounces. Mother and baby seemed unharmed after what had turned out to be an unexpected ordeal.

'Who does she look like?' Pol asked Cormac when he was allowed in to see her and the new baby. 'Wally, Frank the Yank, or you?'

Cormac had thought he wouldn't care, but when he stared at the little, round, scrunched-up face discovered, somewhat surprisingly, that he did. 'Me. She looks like me,' he claimed, despite the fact that the baby had red hair exactly the same shade as Frank the Yank's.

Pol touched her on her tiny ball of a chin. 'Say hello to mummy and daddy, Skylark.'

Cormac groaned. 'Oh, no, Pol. Not Skylark.' He thought they'd dispensed with Skylark. It had been Buttercup for a girl the last time they'd discussed names.

'It's a lovely name, Skylark.'

'Except this is Liverpool. It isn't full of flower people like San Francisco. Everyone will poke fun at her at school. I suggest we call her something else as well, say ...' He said the first name that came into his head: 'Sharon! Skylark can be her second name.'

'All right, Cormac,' Pol said, easygoing to a fault.

'That girl of Cormac's, she had her baby this morning,' Billy told his son when he called in Lacey's Tyres at teatime, 'TYRES FITTED ON THE PREMISES' it said on the newly painted board outside.

Maurice drew in a quick intake of breath. 'What did she have?'

'A girl. A pretty little thing, according to Alice. Going to call her Sharon.'

'That's nice.'

'Business good today?' The plan was for Billy to continue going out to work until the firm was doing well enough to keep them both busy.

'Not exactly.' Maurice pulled a face. 'Two cars, that's all, and only three tyres between them.'

'Things'll improve, son,' Billy said stoutly. 'Once word gets around how cheap we are.'

'It takes time for word to get around, Dad. We need to advertise now.'

'Can't afford it, Maurice, lad. We've used up all the bank loan to buy stock and do up the yard. They're expecting us to start paying the loan back in the not too distant future.'

'I know, Dad.' Maurice glanced fearfully around the yard that had once housed B.E.D.S. The cheap retreads from Hungary were stacked in neat heaps around the wall – it hadn't exactly been cheap to buy so many. Then there was the smart hut that had been erected in place of the burnt-out building because it was essential to have an office of some sort; the telephone; the sign; the second-hand van, bought when John's old van proved beyond repair; the chicken-wire roof they'd had put up when they discovered two boys fishing over the wall for tyres with a giant hook.

He wasn't making enough to live on, let alone pay back the loan. Dad didn't realise you could go to prison for defaulting on a loan – it was *him* who'd go, not Maurice, because it was taken out in his name. He'd been getting on well with his dad since Uncle John's funeral. There hadn't been the opportunity when he was growing up to discover how kind Billy was – and he'd worked like a Trojan getting the yard ready. Over the last few months Billy's support for his son had been rock solid.

Maurice felt nausea rise, like a ball, in his throat. Everything was his fault. He'd thought all you had to do to start a business was find the premises, stock them with whatever you wanted to sell and that was it. You were made; the customers would come flocking in. Perhaps they would have if there'd been adverts in the press, or the site weren't so much out of the way. As it was, hardly anyone knew they were there. Every day Maurice felt more desperate and the feeling of nausea was never far away.

'Which hospital is Pol in?' he asked when Billy emerged from the hut with two mugs of tea.

'Liverpool Maternity. Why? Are you thinking of going to see her?'

'I might,' Maurice muttered. It was another thing that added to his misery, thinking about Pol. Maurice wasn't sure, but he had a feeling he was in love with her. They'd first met at Alice's party on Christmas Eve and he'd been unable to stop thinking about her since. He'd started going round to the house in Stanley Road on the pretence of seeing Fion, but in reality to see Pol. Something about her childish fragility struck a chord in his heart. He wanted to look after her, cherish her, keep her warm at night. He had stupid visions of them growing old together, stupid because she belonged to his cousin, Cormac. There was a saying, 'All's fair in love and war', but Maurice was fond of Cormac and couldn't bring himself to steal his girl from behind his back, always assuming Pol was willing to be stolen in the first place.

Mind you, Cormac was no longer the person he used to be. He looked a proper ponce in those daft clothes and had made no attempt to get a job. Although he hadn't been successful, at least Maurice had tried to find work. These days he didn't feel as inferior to his cousin as he used to.

'I think I'll close early tonight, Dad.' Lacey's Tyres was open twelve hours a day, from seven in the morning till seven at night.

'No,' Billy said stubbornly. 'I'd sooner we stuck to the hours it ses on the board. You sod off, son. I'll lock up.'

Alice and her daughters were just leaving the hospital when Maurice arrived bearing a meagre bunch of flowers that was all he could afford. Cormac had gone in search of tea, he was told, and baby Sharon was in the nursery.

'You can keep Pol company till the new dad comes back,' Alice suggested.

'Hello, Pol. Congratulations.' Her eyes lit up as he approached the bed, but Pol's eyes lit up for everyone. She wore a faded cotton nightie that hadn't been ironed. He wished he could have bought her something rich and silky, trimmed with lace, but not only did he not have the money, it wasn't done for men to buy nighties for other men's girls.

'Thank you, Maurice. Are those for me?' She gasped, as if he'd presented her with a magnificent bouquet of roses. 'They're lovely. What are they?'

'Dunno.'

'They're very pretty, whatever they are. I'll ask the nurse to put them in water after you've gone. How's business?'

Pol was one of the few people in whom Maurice had confided the true state of Lacey's Tyres. If anyone else asked he would reply modestly, 'Not bad.'

'Bloody awful,' he said gloomily. 'I'm worried sick, if you must know.'

'Oh, you poor thing,' she said, her blue, doll-like eyes so full of sympathy that Maurice easily could have cried. He longed to bury his head in her small breasts and sob his heart out. 'Things will buck up soon, Maurice. They're bound to.'

'I hope so.' He explained about not earning enough to pay back the loan. 'It's me dad who worries me. He's the one who'll get into trouble, not me.'

'Perhaps you should expand, Maurice, sell more than tyres.' She waved her arm vaguely. 'Other bits for motor cars, fr'instance: brakes and stuff.' She patted his hand, when it should have been *him* patting *her* hand, her being the one in hospital, like.

'Gosh, Pol, I hadn't thought of that.' It was a good idea, but he hadn't the cash to buy so much as a tyre gauge. Still, she meant well. 'You're very clever, Pol,' he said admiringly.

'Me!' She laughed. 'What a lovely thing to say. Everyone usually thinks I'm very stupid.'

'You're anything but stupid,' Maurice said, meaning it sincerely.

Cormac was about to enter the ward when, through the glass panel in the swing door, he saw his cousin, Maurice, sitting beside Pol's bed. He always felt uncomfortable with Maurice, as if he had stolen from him something of incalculable value. One of these days, when Alice was dead, he might tell Maurice the truth about their parentage, something that was out of the question while Alice remained alive. He, Cormac, had lived twenty-one enjoyable years of Maurice's life, while Maurice had endured twenty-one years on *his* behalf with Cora.

Once again Cormac went to push open the door and once again he paused. Maurice was leaning on the bed, arms crossed, laughing at something Pol had said. Unaware he was being watched, his face was naked, showing everything, hiding nothing, and Cormac realised with a shock that his cousin was head over heels in love with Pol.

Was he jealous? No, Cormac decided calmly, standing aside to let a nurse into the ward. What was the point of being jealous over something that couldn't be helped?

Did he mind? Cormac wasn't sure. He was in love with Pol himself. He had assumed that one day they would get married, have more children and spend the rest of their lives together, that they would be happy. It wasn't until now that it came to him that something was lacking, because he had never looked at Pol the way Maurice looked at her now, so *absolutely*. Cormac felt almost envious. Would he ever look at a woman like that?

And Pol? Sometimes he wondered if Pol would have gone just as willingly with Wally or Frank the Yank, had they asked. Pol loved everybody. She was like a kitten, happy any place where she was warm, comfortable and petted. She could just as easily be in love with Maurice as with Cormac.

He owed his cousin so much. Justice would be partially done if Maurice were allowed to steal Cormac's girl, just as Cormac had, inadvertently, stolen Maurice's mother.

A man came out of the ward and nearly hit him with the door. 'Sorry, mate,' he muttered and rolled his eyes in disgust when he noticed Cormac's rainbow knitted jumper, full of snags, his green flared trousers, dirty feet, his sandals. For the first time since he left Amber Street Cormac felt slightly ashamed of his clothes. He smiled ruefully. Alice used to keep him so neat!

It was time for another cup of tea. He'd return to the ward five minutes before the bell went to indicate visiting time was over. And from now on he'd give his girlfriend and his cousin every encouragement. He'd invite Maurice round to Fion's, then make excuses to go out, leaving him and Pol together.

After all, it was only fair.

It didn't *feel* very fair, not right now, not to Cormac. In fact, he felt quite depressed. Sniffing audibly, he wished Maurice hadn't come to the hospital, that he'd never discovered he was in love with Pol.

Lord, he'd give anything for a spliff to blunt the rawness of his misery. He had been looking forward to life with Pol and his daughter. Well, there was a one-in-three chance she was his daughter and probably no chance at all if you took into account the red hair.

The debt to Maurice had to be paid some time.

'Christ, Mam, you're not half bad-tempered lately,' Lulu said acidly. 'Every time anyone opens their mouth you bite their head off.'

'Don't you dare swear in this house!' Orla screeched.

'I hate you, Mam.' Maisie's lip curled.

'So, hate me. I don't care.'

'I hate you too.' Paul's lip wobbled. He was the most sensitive of the Lavin children.

'Join the club,' Orla snarled.

'I'm leaving home,' announced Gary. 'I'm going to live with Nana Lacey.'

'Well, don't let me stop you. Shall I pack a suitcase?'

Orla and her four children glared at each other across the breakfast table. Then Orla's face collapsed and she held out her arms. 'Oh, come here. I love you! I adore you! You are the most beautiful children in the world and I am the most horrible mother. I don't deserve you. I truly don't deserve you. I'm sorry. I'm sorry, sorry, sorry.' She kissed their heads one by one. 'So sorry,' she whispered.

'Are you in the club, Mam?' Lulu asked. 'Nana Lavin said you might be.'

'No, luv.' Orla sobbed. 'I'm not in anything as far as I know.'

'Is it an early mennypause?' enquired Gary. 'Granny Lavin thought it might be that as well.'

'It can't be both, luv. It can only be one or the other and it's neither. It's just that your mother's been in a state with herself lately.'

'What sort of state?'

'An upside down, inside out, up in the air, down in the dumps, topsy-turvy sort of state.'

'Wow!' said Gary, impressed.

'I promise not to be bad-tempered again, least not till tonight, then you'll just have to excuse me and tell yourselves I don't mean it.'

The children went to school. Orla washed the dishes, dried them, made the beds, dusted, threw herself on to the settee in the parlour, burst into tears, cursed her husband . . .

'I *hate* you Micky Lavin,' she said aloud.

No, she didn't. She loved him. But she wished he'd try to understand just how *unhappy* she was, how unutterably and stultifyingly bored she was with life. The trouble was, putting it bluntly, Micky was too thick to understand. Micky felt exactly the opposite and was so lacking in imagination that he couldn't understand anyone feeling different. He was as happy as a sandboy. He enjoyed his lousy job without a future, he was perfectly content living in this grotty little house. Going to see Liverpool or Everton play football at weekends was the ultimate joy, particularly if they won. Micky didn't want a car, holidays abroad, flash clothes, posh furniture. He didn't mind seeing the occasional film as long as lots of people in it got killed, but as for the theatre, it belonged in an alien world, as did books that contained words of more than one syllable, anything intellectual on television, politics and newspapers that weren't littered with pictures of naked girls.

It meant they had nothing to talk about. Even sex had lost its thrall and become a tiny bit tedious with someone who was essentially a moron.

Micky had refused to let Mam buy them a house somewhere nicer with a garden for the children to play.

'Why not?' Orla screeched. She seemed to screech an awful lot these days.

'I've got my pride,' Micky said huffily.

'You weren't too proud to fill this house with stuff that had fallen off the back of a hundred bloody lorries.'

'That's different.'

'In what way is it different?'

He shuffled his feet. 'I dunno, it just is.'

She'd grown past him. He wanted to spend his life standing still, but she wanted to go forward. She would have got a proper job, but it would mean giving up the newspaper and the extra money wouldn't have been enough to make a difference. Besides, although she would have denied it till she was blue in the face, she got a thrill out of attending various pathetic functions and announcing, 'I'm from the press,' and occasionally seeing her name under the headline of a news item she'd sent in. She kept hoping the *Crosby Star* would take her back in the office so she'd be a real reporter, but there hadn't been a vacancy in ages.

This afternoon, she was interviewing some stupid ex-Everton footballer – anyone willing to take up kicking a ball up and down a field as a career *had* to be stupid. She'd only been asked because Dominic Reilly came from Pearl Street. His parents still lived in the house opposite. His mam, Sheila, had had twelve children. Orla shuddered delicately: *twelve!* Dominic, who at thirty-two was the same age as herself, had come back from Spain for the wedding of one of his numerous brothers and was returning that night. She had no idea what he'd been doing in Spain, but it was the first on the list of questions she'd prepared. At least it broke up the tedium of the day.

She went out and bought the *Guardian*, and read everything except the sport. Would that great intellectual Micky Lavin be interested in the fact that the war in Vietnam was escalating? No, he bloody wouldn't. Nor would he care that Mrs Gandhi had become Prime Minister of India, or that Great Britain had just elected a Labour government led by the vaguely dishy Harold Wilson. Orla had sent him out to vote, but he'd met a mate and gone for a game of billiards instead.

Seething, Orla rolled the paper into a ball and flung it across the room. It was time she got ready for the interview.

It was also time she had some new clothes, she thought irritably when she examined the miserly contents of her wardrobe. Except there wasn't the money.

'You'd look lovely dressed in rags,' Micky insisted when she complained.

In that case she was bound to look lovely, because there was nothing but rags hanging on the rail. Orla sulkily removed a black skirt and a white blouse that mightn't look so bad if they were ironed. She didn't just need new clothes, but a new house, a new husband, a new life.

She left her long brown hair loose, made her face up carefully and, promptly at three o'clock, knocked on the Reillys' front door. Sheila Reilly opened it. She was a pleasantly pretty woman, lumpily overweight, though anyone would be overweight if they'd had twelve children. Sheila was as old as her mother, but had children younger than Orla's. Two toddlers hung silently to her skirt who, unless Sheila had had more babies when no one was looking, were grandchildren – she had hordes.

'Hello, Orla, luv. I suppose you've come to see our Dominic.'

'If he's available, Sheila. I'm from the press.'

'I know, luv. He's expecting you, though where you'll find the quiet to talk I don't know. I've half a dozen of the grandkids here to see their Uncle Dominic.'

'We can go over to our house if you like.'

'I'm sure he'd appreciate that, if only for a bit of peace.'

Dominic came into the hall. He was casually dressed in pale blue linen slacks, a white, short-sleeved shirt and white canvas shoes. 'Hi, there. I've seen you around, but I don't think we've ever spoken before. I vaguely remember you from school.'

'We didn't move in till you'd left home. I vaguely remember you from school too.'

They shook hands. Orla hadn't realised he was quite so good-looking, quite so tall, quite so tanned. He reminded her a bit of Robert Redford, with his dark-blond wavy hair and broad build, his dazzlingly warm smile.

'Orla said you can use her house for the interview, luv.'

'That's a relief, otherwise I won't be able to hear meself think.'

They crossed the street to the Lavins'. Orla felt super conscious of Dominic's arm brushing against hers when she showed him into the parlour. She asked if he'd like a cup of tea. 'Or sherry?' There was sherry over from Christmas.

'Tea would be grand, ta.'

When she returned he was sitting on the settee, arms stretched along the back, legs crossed. A gold watch glinted on his brown wrist, muscles bulged in his arms, his waist was very slim.

Orla swallowed and looked away. She settled in a hard chair, pad on her knee, pencil poised, coughed importantly and asked her first question: 'What were you doing in Spain?'

For some reason Dominic choked on the tea. She hoped it wasn't too hot. 'Playing football,' he replied.

'They play football in Spain? I didn't realise. What part of Spain?'

'Barcelona.' His face had gone very red.

'They have stadiums there, just like in Liverpool?'

'Just like in Liverpool.' He nodded and she wondered why his brown eyes were glinting with amusement.

'And what made you go to Spain in the first place? Couldn't you get a job playing football in this country?'

He regarded her silently for several seconds. 'That's right,' he said eventually. 'I was on me uppers, if the truth be known. The offer from Barcelona was a lifeline.'

'You poor thing,' Orla said sympathetically, making a note in her pad. She glanced at him surreptitiously. He looked very odd, as if he was about to bust a gut. Perhaps he was dying to use the lavatory.

'Is this for publication?' Dominic asked.

'Of course.' Orla tossed her head importantly.

'In that case I think we'd better start the interview again, otherwise you're going to make a right fool of yourself.'

'Am I, now!' she said huffily. 'In exactly what way?'

'For one, you clearly know nothing about football. Barcelona is one of the leading clubs in the world, with a stadium every bit as good as those in this country, if not better. For another, I was offered a hundred quid a week to play there, twice as much as I was getting with Everton. I live in a flat overlooking the Mediterranean, I drive a sports car, I have a beautiful girlfriend – though she's not as beautiful as you. All in all, I live the life of Reilly – appropriately, considering me name.' He burst out laughing and didn't stop till tears ran down his cheeks. 'Oh, Gawd!' he gasped, wiping them away with the flat of his hands. 'I haven't enjoyed meself so much in a long time. It makes a change to have a reporter feel sorry for me; they're usually so sycophantic it makes me want to puke.'

Orla felt dizzy with shame and embarrassment. If only she had condescended to tell Micky about the interview he would have filled her in on Dominic's background. 'Jaysus!' she muttered, unable to meet his eyes. 'I wish the floor would open up and swallow me.'

'I don't, because then I wouldn't be able to look at you any more.'

She found herself blushing on top of everything else and remembered he'd said something about his girlfriend not being as beautiful as she was. There was silence in the world for a while as Orla stared at her shoes and Dominic Reilly stared at *her*, and her stomach trembled in the way it had done in the early days with Micky. Then Dominic gave her a challenging look and patted the cushion beside him and Orla knew that if she responded to the challenge everything would change, even if it appeared nothing whatsoever had altered when the children came home from school and Micky from work.

The notebook and pencil fell to the floor as Orla got up and moved into Dominic's welcoming arms. After a while they went upstairs to the bed where she'd lain with Micky for almost fifteen years.

She was sorry afterwards – deeply, wholeheartedly, wretchedly sorry. Perhaps she wouldn't have felt like that if it hadn't been so wonderful. For half an hour, an hour, she'd glimpsed another world, a world of blue seas and golden sands, of beautiful clothes, good times, parties, a world in which every day was different from the day before, where exciting, unexpected things happened, as opposed to the drab, colourless world she occupied now, in which every day was the same as the next, counting Sundays when she went to church and to tea with Mam or one of her sisters, or they came to tea at hers.

Then Dominic rose from the bed, kissed her gently and went home, and the wonderful world came crashing down around her ears.

After a few minutes she went and soaked in the old-fashioned bath that had fallen off the back of a lorry, using the last of the bath salts Micky had bought her for Christmas. At the time she'd thought how little imagination he showed: he gave her bath salts, talc, cheap perfume, every year, usually Boots' own brand. She noticed a scratch on her wrist from Dominic's watch. He'd had to take it off. She'd put disinfectant on it when she got out.

The events of the afternoon hadn't made her love Micky more, she wasn't suddenly counting her blessings, appreciating what she already had. On the contrary, she would much sooner not have glimpsed that other magical world. It made the one in which she lived seem drabber, even more colourless than it had been when she woke up. There were so many things she would never know, never do, sights she would never see if she lived to be a hundred.

She was gentle with the children when they came home. Nothing that happened would ever make her love them less. Lulu was the reason she'd been stuck with Micky, but that wasn't Lulu's fault but her own.

'What's the matter?' Micky asked that night when they were watching telly – least he was watching. Orla was miles away.

'Nothing.'

'You're very quiet. It's not like you.'

'Isn't it?' She looked at him and noticed his hair was receding slightly at the temples, that he had a small paunch. He also had a hole in his sock that needed mending. 'Shall we go to bed early tonight?'

'I wouldn't say no.' He grinned and, for a moment, she saw the teenager who'd charmed her all those years ago. Perhaps if she could lose herself in him, recapture the magic of those days...

They went upstairs. There was a time when they would have leapt naked into bed, but now Orla put on her nightdress, Micky his pyjamas. He went to put out the light, stopped and said in a voice she'd never heard before, 'Who does this fuckin' watch belong to, Orla? And what's it doing beside our bed?'

Orla turned up in Amber Street late one Sunday night just as Alice was thinking about going to bed. Unusually for Orla, who was inclined to arrive in a flaming temper over something, she appeared pale and listless.

Alice sat her down and made her a cup of cocoa. 'What's wrong, luv?' she asked sympathetically.

Orla didn't look at her mother but stared at her shoes. 'Mam, don't get mad at me, but I've done something awful.' There was a pause. 'I've slept with someone and Micky found out.'

'Jaysus, Orla!' Alice's sympathy vanished, to be replaced with anger and alarm. 'You stupid girl,' she snapped. 'Who was it?'

'It doesn't matter who it was, Mam.'

'Then why are you here? What d'you expect me to do about it?'

'Nothing, Mam,' Orla said in a subdued voice. 'I just wanted to tell someone, that's all. Micky's making me life hell.'

'I'm not surprised. Most men would if they found their wife had been sleeping around.' Alice frowned. 'He's not hit you, has he?'

'No, Mam. He just won't talk to me, that's all.'

'You can hardly blame him, luv.' Alice thought what a perfect world it could be if only human beings, including herself, could bring themselves to behave sensibly. 'When did this happen?'

'Last Monday. Micky hasn't spoken to me since. Not that I mind, to be frank, but there's a terrible atmosphere at home. The children have noticed and it's making them dead miserable.'

Alice remembered Sheila Reilly had been in Lacey's the Saturday before last having her hair done for her son, Niall's, wedding. She'd mentioned Orla was seeing Dominic, her eldest, before he went back to Spain. Alice immediately put two and two together. Micky Lavin was a nice, hard-working lad, but as dull as ditchwater and without an ounce of Dominic Reilly's glamour. She didn't approve of what her daughter had done, but could understand Orla being bowled over by a man so entirely different from her husband.

'I should never have married Micky, Mam,' Orla cried tragically. 'I wish things had been different then, the way they are now. No one's nagging our Cormac and Pol to get married.'

'No one nagged *you* to get married,' Alice reminded her.

'No, but it wasn't on in those days to have a baby out of wedlock. I felt obliged to marry Micky for Lulu's sake. If I had me time over again, I wouldn't go anywhere near an altar.' She buried her face in her hands and began to cry. 'I'm ever so unhappy, Mam. I have been for years. All those dreams I used to have are dead and I feel all dried up inside. I ache for something nice to happen, something interesting or unusual or enjoyable. I long to go out and have a good time or go on holiday abroad, somewhere like Spain. I wish we had a car so I could learn to drive, and I'd just drive and drive and drive till I came to the end of the rainbow. I wish – oh, Mam,' she sobbed. 'I wish all sorts of things.'

'I know, luv.' Alice patted her daughter's knee. She was like a beautiful wild animal trapped inside a cage, the exact opposite of her mother who gave the slightest opportunity of excitement a wide berth. 'I'll buy you a car if you like. As long as Micky doesn't mind.' She knew she was being too generous, too indulgent. After all, Orla shouldn't be rewarded for her bad behaviour. But a car would make things better for the whole family.

'Oh, *would* you, Mam?' There was something terribly pathetic about Orla's excited reaction, as if Alice had opened the door of the cage a few enticing inches. 'It would help with me job as a reporter. I could go further afield, not just stick to Bootle. And I could take the kids out weekends, to Southport and Chester and places. I'd take them on the train, except I can never afford the fares. As for Micky, I don't give a fig if he minds or not.'

'Sweetheart, I don't want to make things worse between you two.' She remembered Micky had adamantly refused to let her buy them a house and wasn't likely to take kindly to a car – he had more character than people gave him credit for.

'Oh, you won't, Mam. A car will make me happy and if I'm happy then so is Micky.'

Alice thought this an exaggeration. No doubt Orla had been happy making love with Dominic Reilly, but it hadn't exactly sent her husband into paroxysms of delight. Her main concern, though, was her daughter, who'd arrived wan and pale, and now looked happy and excited, as if she'd just been handed a million pounds.

15
1970

The air on Easter Saturday was as heady as wine: pure and sparkling, with that exceptional clarity only evident in spring. When the Nuptial Mass was over and the bride and groom posed for photographs in St James's churchyard the sharp, fresh aroma of recently cut grass combined with the earthy smell of upturned soil, adding to the flavour of the day.

Lulu Lavin made an exceptionally pretty bride. There were appreciative murmurs from the waiting crowd when she stepped out of the grey limousine in her simple white voile frock with short sleeves and a drawstring neck. Calf-length, the hem hung in points, each decorated with a tiny rosebud. More rosebuds were threaded through her dark hair arranged earlier that morning in Grecian style by her Nana Lacey. Her shoes were white satin, flat, like a ballerina's. She looked for all the world like a nymph, as did the bridesmaids, in the palest of green: her sister, Maisie, her cousin, Bonnie, and Ruth Mitchell, great-grandpa's daughter, who was Lulu's great-aunt, though three years her junior.

From across the churchyard Orla Lavin, fiercely proud, watched her daughter while the photographs were being taken. Lulu was about to escape the narrow, suffocating streets of Bootle. In two weeks' time, after their honeymoon in Jersey – a present from Alice – Lulu and Gareth would live in his tiny one-bedroomed flat in an unfashionable part of London and Gareth would continue with his ambition to make a living as an artist, though he hadn't so far sold a single painting. The people who had seen his strange, incomprehensible pictures anticipated he never would. The couple had met on a demonstration in London that Lulu had gone to with her Aunt Fion.

Everyone, except Orla, considered it a most inauspicious start to married life: the husband not earning a bean and reliant on his eighteen-year-old wife to put food on the table.

But Orla had given her daughter every encouragement. 'Go for it, girl,' she whispered, more than once. 'Even if things fail, you've given it a try.

You've had your fling. You won't spend your life thinking that you've wasted every minute, that there's a million things out there to do and you haven't done a single one.'

'Things won't fail, Mum,' Lulu had assured her, clear-eyed and full of confidence. 'I love Gareth and he loves me. I can't wait for us to be together.'

And now it was done. Lulu was Mrs Gareth Jackson and would shortly be starting on a great adventure.

'Can I have the parents of the bride and groom?' the photographer shouted.

Micky nodded curtly at Orla and they posed for several photographs with the newly married couple; with the bridesmaids; with each other; and with Gareth's widowed mother, Susan, a feisty, bizarrely dressed woman, something of an artist herself, according to Fion, with whom she'd immediately become friends.

Orla was making awkward conversation with Susan, hoping she hadn't noticed the tension between the bride's parents, when she saw the middle-aged, strikingly good-looking man lurking just round the corner of the church. He grinned when their eyes met, then stepped back, out of sight. What one earth was he doing here? she wondered fearfully. How did he know about the wedding? How the hell was she going to get rid of him, not just from the church, but from out of her life?

'I want a photie with Great-grandpa,' Lulu announced.

'Go on, luv.' Bernadette pushed Danny forward. 'It's you she wants, not me,' she insisted when Danny tried to pull her with him.

Bernadette watched the erect, silver-haired figure of her husband stand stiffly between the bride and groom. It was obvious he was making a determined effort to hold himself together and her heart filled with aching sadness. In the not too distant future she was going to lose him. He hadn't told her what was wrong. She hadn't asked. But for the last two months he'd eaten like a bird and hadn't touched the ale he'd always been so fond of. In bed at night he held her tightly in his arms, as if worried he might never hold her that way again.

Alice came up. She nodded at the wedding group. 'How is he?'

'Not so good, Ally. He was sick again this morning. I thought he'd never stop vomiting.'

'It still might not be too late for him to see a doctor.' It had become a bone of contention between the women, whether Danny should, or should not, seek medical attention.

Bernadette shook her head firmly. 'Danny's the most intelligent man I've ever known. He knows where the doctor lives, but when it comes down to it, he'd sooner die in his own way, luv, quickly and as painlessly as possible, not have long-drawn-out treatment and operations. He'd hate me and the children to see him an invalid.'

'Whatever you say, Bernie.' Alice tried not to sound cold. She had no more wish to lose Danny than did Bernadette and she longed to interfere. She felt an outsider in the relationship between her father and her best friend.

'Your Cormac's girlfriend looks very studious,' Bernie remarked, changing the subject. 'What's her name?'

'Vicky. She's not a girlfriend, just a colleague from work. She's the one he's starting the business with.' Alice's gaze drifted from her son towards Pol and Maurice Lacey. Pol was expecting her third baby. Alice still found it shocking the way Pol had transferred her affections from Cormac to Maurice not long after baby Sharon was born, though Cormac had taken it incredibly well and there was a surprising lack of animosity between the cousins. Of course, the switch had caused no end of gossip at the time. It was hard for people of her age to get used to the way some young people behaved these days. Morals seemed to have gone out the window during the Sixties. In Alice's opinion it had started with rock'n'roll, and men growing their hair long and wearing earrings.

'As soon as they've finished the photographs I'll show you the three Lacey salons,' Cormac said to Vicky. 'We're lucky, starting off with an outlet, even though it's only small.'

'Have you discussed it with your mother yet?' Vicky enquired. She was a serious young woman wearing an ill-fitting brown costume, flat shoes and round, horn-rimmed glasses. Her dark, crisp hair was boyishly cut.

'Alice was all for it. We're an entrepreneurial family, Vic. My father had his own business. So does my cousin, Maurice. Mind you, his is just ticking over.' At that moment a beaming Maurice didn't appear concerned that he just managed to scrape a living from Lacey's Tyres.

'Why do you call your mother Alice?'

'It's just a habit I've got into,' Cormac explained.

'I've not long turned me house into a refuge for battered women,' Fion was informing Susan Jackson, the bridegroom's mother. 'Why don't you come and take a look after the reception? You can stay the night if you like. It's a big house and there's plenty of room.'

'Don't the neighbours mind, about the refuge, that is?' Susan asked.

'Oh, yes. They're forever complaining, to me and to the corpy. I just don't take any notice.'

'Good for you. I'd love to stay the night, save rushing home on a late train. And next time you're in London you must stay with me.'

So many children, thought Maeve Adams as she watched them bent like birds searching for confetti, swinging on the railings, getting their new clothes dirty. The older children tried to look grown-up in the new gear bought specially for the wedding. By this time next year Orla could be a grandmother, yet her . . . She was thirty-five, getting on. But there were still so many things needed for the house – a bigger freezer for one – and she and Martin had always promised themselves they'd have a garage built on the side. And Martin didn't like driving a car that was more than a few years old, worried it might be unreliable. And the kitchen was getting a bit old-fashioned – she'd like plain white units for a change – and while the workmen were there, they might as well have the floor retiled; terracotta would look nice.

But none of these things would be possible if she stopped work to have babies.

Martin came over and took her hand. 'Penny for them, darling.'

'I was watching the children,' Maeve said wistfully. All of a sudden the kitchen and a new freezer didn't seem to matter.

'We don't need children when we've got each other.'

'Don't we?'

'No, we jolly well don't,' Martin said. Perhaps he didn't mean to sound so irritable. 'I hope you're not getting broody on me, Maeve. Our lifestyle would have to change drastically if we only had my salary to live on. We'd have to go without all sorts of things.'

Maeve sighed and supposed that, to keep Martin happy, she'd have to go without children.

Orla managed to escape the guests and make her way round to the side of the church where Vernon Matthews was leaning against the wall, smoking. He threw the cigarette away when she approached and tried to take her in his arms.

She pushed him away and said angrily, 'Don't you dare touch me!'

'Worried your hubby might see?' His smile was almost a sneer.

'Naturally, but I wouldn't want you touching me if we were stranded alone together on a desert island.'

'You didn't always feel like that.'

'Well, I feel like that now.' She had been mad to sleep with him. It had happened two years after the incident with Dominic Reilly. In all that time Micky hadn't touched her – he still hadn't, though Orla had got used to it by now. But this was before she'd got used to it, when she used to drive the second-hand Mini Mam had bought deep into the countryside, singing to herself, feeling liberated. Mixed with this was a sense of gut-wrenching frustration, a longing for something even faintly interesting to happen.

After a while she got into the habit of stopping at out-of-the-way pubs for a drink of lemonade or orange juice. It made her feel sophisticated, a woman of the world. She would get out her reporter's notebook and pretend to make notes, so people would think she was a businesswoman on her way to an important meeting.

The second time she stopped a man approached and asked to buy her a drink. Orla told him politely to get lost. A few weeks later, when she was approached again, she accepted the drink. The man turned out to be a commercial traveller who'd been on the stage in his youth. He was interesting to talk to and asked if he could see her again. Orla refused, though she had quite enjoyed the illicit excitement of the occasion. She hadn't felt like herself, but a different person altogether.

The next man who bought her a drink asked if she'd like to come upstairs with him to his room.

'You mean, you're staying here?'

'No, but I very quickly could be.'

'I'd sooner not.' Orla was beginning to feel like a character in a novel. She called herself unusual, romantic names whenever she met a man, which was happening regularly: Estella, Isabella, Madeleine, Dawn.

Micky wanted to know where she took herself every day in the car. 'Nowhere in particular,' Orla said vaguely. 'Just around. Sometimes I interview people for the paper.'

'I suppose anywhere's better than home,' Micky said nastily.

'You said it first,' Orla snapped.

They were nasty to each other most of the time. They slept in the same bed, their backs to each other. They got dressed and undressed in the bathroom.

She told Vernon Matthews her name was Greta. They met just before Christmas in a little thatched pub in Rainford that did bed and breakfasts. There were silver decorations and a lighted tree in the lounge. He was about fifty, with dark hair and dark eyes, and a Clark Gable moustache. He told her he was a representative for an engineering company and always used the pub as a base when he was in the north-west.

He also told her she was one of the most beautiful women he'd ever met. His dark eyes glistened with admiration when he said this and Orla's stomach twisted pleasantly. She felt very strange, almost drunk, though she'd only had orange juice. Afterwards, she felt convinced he'd slipped something in her drink.

Orla couldn't remember agreeing to go upstairs, but she must have, because the next thing she knew she and Vernon were lying naked on a bed together, making love. Her first thought was how to escape, but she knew it was no use trying to push away the heavy body on top of hers. She thought about screaming, but if someone came they might call the police and it could get in the papers – it was the sort of situation she was always on the lookout for herself in her role as a reporter.

Eventually, Vernon reached a noisy, gasping climax and collapsed on top of her. Orla slipped wordlessly from beneath, got partially dressed and went into the bathroom where she washed herself from tip to toe. When she came out, Vernon Matthews had emptied her bag on the bed and was going through the contents.

'How dare you!' she expostulated.

He merely laughed and picked up her driving licence. 'Orla Lavin, 11 Pearl Street, Bootle,' he read aloud. 'So you're not Greta, after all. And according to this, you're married. Does your hubbie know you spend your afternoons playing the whore?'

'I don't think that's any of your business.' She snatched the licence out of his hand.

'I could make it my business pretty damn quick.'

Orla began to push the things back in her bag. She said threateningly, 'If you say anything to me husband he'll kill you. He might kill me first, but then he'll kill you, I promise you that.'

Vernon laughed again. 'Oh, I'm shaking in my shoes, I really am.'

He lay on the bed and watched her leave, and Orla drove back to Bootle like a maniac. It was weeks before she could bring herself to use the car again, and then it was to do some genuine reporting for the *Crosby Star*.

She thought the whole horrible experience was over and done with until three months later, when she got the first phone call.

'Hello, it's me, Vernon. Love in the afternoon, remember?'

Orla was alone in the house and the hairs prickled on her neck. 'What do you want?'

'To see you. I keep thinking of those happy hours we spent together. I can't wait for a repeat.'

'Then I'm afraid you'll have to wait for ever,' Orla said shortly. She put the phone down.

It rang again almost immediately. She left the receiver off the hook until the children came home from school.

The phone calls continued for ten days, usually in the mornings. Perhaps he had too much sense to ring when Micky was home. They stopped for three months and Orla thought she was rid of him, until they started again. He must call when he was in the Liverpool area and he only called to torment her, have some fun. Orla would be reminded of their afternoon together, which Vernon would describe in sickening detail if she held on and tried to plead with him to stop.

Sometimes he wrote letters: horrible, explicit letters that she burnt immediately, without opening, once she realised who they were from. It was awkward when Micky was home and he picked up the post before she could get to it.

'Aren't you going to read it?' he would ask when she stuck the letter on the sideboard, unopened, waiting to be burnt.

'I'll read it later. It doesn't look important.'

One day, not long ago, she'd driven to Crosby to deliver some reports, wondering why a grey Marina stuck to her tail the whole way. When she came out, Vernon had been waiting, smiling, holding out his arms.

'You're crazy,' Orla had shrieked hysterically. 'Haven't you got a job to go to? Why won't you leave me alone? I never want to see you again.' She'd got in the Mini and driven away before he could reply, terrified, knowing she was trapped in a situation entirely of her own making and unable to think of a way out.

Now he'd had the brass cheek to turn up at her daughter's wedding, to spoil everything, at least for her. He must have seen the announcement in the *Bootle Times*.

'I'd like you to go,' she said shakily.

'And I'd like to stay.' She could tell he enjoyed getting under her skin, hearing her voice shake. 'I was wondering if I could inveigle my way into the reception.'

'I'd stop wondering if I were you. I'm not the only person who knows exactly who's been invited.'

His mouth twisted. 'That's a pity.'

'You're the one who needs the pity. You're crazy. Anybody sane would have better things to do with their time. Perhaps it wouldn't be a bad idea if I found out where you lived and told your wife what you were up to.'

'I haven't got a wife.' His eyes flickered and she knew he was lying. She felt she had got one up on him for a change, but it was useless knowing he was married. There was no way she could discover where he lived.

'Orla!' Bernadette came round the corner of the church. 'They're going to take a photie of everyone together.' She smiled at Vernon. 'Hello.'

'Hello, there,' he said charmingly. ''Bye, Orla. See you again one day soon.'

Cormac and Vicky managed a quick tour of the three Lacey's salons before sitting down to a ham salad in Hilton's Restaurant, where the reception was being held and where Cormac had celebrated his twenty-first.

'The salon in Opal Street is a bit off the beaten track, but the other two on main roads will make wonderful showcases for our products,' Vicky enthused.

Cormac grinned. 'Our products! That sounds very grand and business-like, Vic.'

Vicky went pink, something she was apt to do very easily, particularly if Cormac was around. 'I suppose it does, for a business about to be started in my parents' garage. Still, I think grand and businesslike is what we should aim for, Cormac.'

'I think so too. And "Lacey's of Liverpool" sounds very grand indeed. You don't mind your name being left out, do you?' Cormac said anxiously.

'Not under the circumstances – and I've never liked the name Weatherspoon. If our products are associated with an already long-established hairdresser's it will help get them off the ground.'

'You talk like a business manual, Vic.'

Vicky tried to discern if there was the faintest hint of flirtatiousness in Cormac's tone, but decided there wasn't. She was nearly thirty and Cormac was the first man she had fallen in love with. Not that he knew. Not that he would *ever* know, because she would never tell him. She might have done had she been as remotely pretty as any one of his three sisters. Even his mother looked gorgeous in a lacy lilac dress and little matching hat. Vicky sighed. If Cormac so much as suspected she was in love with him he'd probably run a mile.

They'd met three years before when Cormac had started work in the research department of Brooker & Sons, a large company in St Helens where Victoria Weatherspoon had worked since she finished university with a degree in chemistry. Brooker's, a household name, were primarily the manufacturers of domestic cleansing agents: washing-up liquid, washing powder, scourer, bleach, soap. They were also famous for their baby products and produced a small range of cosmetics, including shampoos and conditioners.

For most of the three years Cormac and Vicky had done no more than pass the time of day. They had never been involved in the same research project. While Vicky concentrated on ways of making the washing-up liquid more bubbly or the scourer more ruthless, Cormac was involved in different experiments which could lead to the world being rid of every speck of dirt and every known germ.

Two and a half months ago – Vicky remembered the day precisely, it was January the fourteenth – she and Cormac happened to be working late together. He was sitting on a stool at a table at the far end of the laboratory, writing, presumably a report on his current project. Vicky was using the shaker, a piece of machinery that gripped containers and tossed them about crazily for two minutes so that the contents were thoroughly mixed.

'What's that you're doing, Vic?' Cormac enquired.

'Mixing shampoo for my mother. Sorry, is the noise getting on your nerves?'

'No. I was wondering what the smell was, that's all.' Cormac sniffed appreciatively. 'It's very nice. What is it?'

'Geranium oil.'

'Do we make geranium oil shampoo?' He put down his pen and came towards her.

Vicky felt her heart quicken. 'No. This is Brooker's basic mixture before the perfume's added. I didn't steal it, Cormac. It's been paid for, I can assure you.'

'Gracious, Vic. I wouldn't give a damn if you pinched a ten-ton container. I'm just interested in what you're doing, that's all.' He looked with surprise at the row of plastic bottles on the worktop. 'There must be enough there to last your mother the rest of her life. Sorry, Vic,' he said apologetically, putting his hand on her arm. 'I'm being dead nosy. It's just that I'm bored witless writing up a report. I was looking for a diversion, that's all. Even so, I wouldn't mind knowing what your mother's going to do with so much shampoo.'

'She sells it, Cormac. She belongs to the Women's Institute and they have a sale of work every month to raise money for charity. Aromatherapy oils have a heavenly smell. The shampoos go like hot cakes. I usually make a couple of dozen a month, using different fragrances. This time I'm using geranium, lavender, lemongrass and rosemary.' Vicky wondered if her dull, monosyllabic tone was as evident to him as it was to herself. She sounded as if she was reading the lesson at a funeral.

'Aromatherapy oils?'

'The Egyptians first used them, possibly as long ago as 3000 BC. They can be used for massage and, oh, for all sorts of things, as well as making cosmetics.'

'Hmm! Interesting.' Cormac rocked back on his heels. 'Fancy a drink when you've finished, Vic?'

Over the next few weeks they went for several more drinks after work. Vicky could hardly believe it when he told her about his life on the road belonging to a group called the Nobodys.

'I must have smoked every known substance. We didn't know where we were most of the time.'

'I would never have guessed.' His neat good looks didn't fit in with the life he'd just described.

'What about you, Vic? What have you been up to since you left university?'

'Working in Brooker's,' she confessed, slightly ashamed.

'Ah, an upright, conscientious member of society, unlike myself.'

'I wish I'd been a bit more adventurous, if only in my job. Brooker's is so ... so ...'

'Mindnumbingly dull?' Cormac suggested, making a face, and she laughed. The more they saw each other, the more relaxed she became.

'I suppose so. I once had visions of doing something as spectacular as splitting the atom.'

'Or discovering penicillin. I know, Vic, me too.'

A few days later Cormac said, 'Is there anything unique about Brooker's shampoos, Vic?'

'No. Most shampoos contain the same basic substances: aqua, sodium laureth sulfate, cocamide, hydroxypropyltrimonium, glycerine.'

'Wow!' Cormac looked impressed. 'Could we mix all those various chemicals ourselves?'

'I beg your pardon?'

'Could we buy the cocamide and the glycerine and the other unpronouncable chemicals and make our own shampoo?'

'Of course, Cormac.' She looked at him wonderingly. 'You mean you and me? But why should we want to?'

He answered her question with another. 'Do you want to stay at Brooker's for the rest of your life, Vic?'

'Well, no.' She had always hoped to get married and have children, and Cormac was the person she'd like to achieve this ambition with. Fortunately, they were both Catholics, so religion wouldn't be an obstacle. The only obstacle was the fact he hadn't shown the slightest interest in her as a lifelong companion. 'No, I definitely don't want to stay at Brooker's.'

'Neither do I,' he said with a heartfelt groan. 'I'll never get the sort of job I wanted when I was at Cambridge because I didn't finish the course. I was lucky Brooker's took me on, but I want more than a career trying to make bleach thicker and whites whiter. I thought we could go into business together making aromatherapy shampoo and conditioner. I was virtually brought up in a hairdresser's, so I suppose it's only natural I feel drawn to the idea. I'm not suggesting we give up work. That can wait till things catch on, which might be months or years.' He wrinkled his nose. 'It could even be never.'

Had it been anyone else but him, Vicky would have pronounced him mad and walked away. But it *was* Cormac, whom she loved and who had actually suggested they do something together. She would have preferred it to be something other than starting their own business, but it was better than nothing at all.

As the weeks went by, however, she began to catch some of his enthusiasm. They would start off with a thousand bottles each of shampoo and conditioner of several different fragrances. His mother was thrilled to bits at the idea and had promised to use them in her salons – providing they were satisfactory – and display them for sale. Vicky still lived at home in Warrington with her parents and her own mother was equally thrilled. She had offered the garage to use as a workshop.

'Daddy won't mind. He can leave the car outside,' Mrs Weatherspoon said dismissively – her mother had always worn the trousers in the Weatherspoon household.

They only needed a small amount of equipment, which was fortunate as they only had a small amount of money between them, a few hundred pounds of savings. Initially there would be a lot of tedious work to do by hand. It should be a simple matter to obtain the formula for Brooker's shampoo and conditioner, and they would change a few of the basic elements so theirs would be different.

Sample bottles were ordered, a brand name decided upon: Lacey's of Liverpool.

'It has a ring to it,' Cormac mused. 'A few years ago Liverpool was the most famous city in the galaxy. Lacey's and Liverpool go perfectly together. It's not exactly gimmicky, but it's unusual.'

'We still haven't decided what colour bottles,' Cormac reminded her at the wedding as a waitress removed their plates. The best man, a friend of Gareth's, was nervously studying the speech he had written beforehand.

'I like the opaque white ones best. White with gold lettering.'

'I'm not sure if I don't prefer the black.'

'Black's showy, white's tasteful,' Vicky said stubbornly. It wasn't often she got her own way in the enterprise.

'We could have black bottles for the man's shampoo, the sage.'

'That's a great idea.'

He smiled broadly and put his hand over hers. 'We make great business partners, don't we, Vic?'

'Oh, yes, Cormac. Great.'

If you ask me, Sarge,' the driver of the police car said out of the corner of his mouth, 'women whose blokes have given them a good hiding have almost certainly asked for it.'

'Shush, Morgan.'

'She can't hear, Sarge, not with that howling baby and the screaming kids.'

'D'you think they asked for it too, the children?'

'Possibly. I've boxed me own kids' ears before now. Sometimes kids – and wives – need to be shown who's boss.'

Sergeant Jerry McKeown glanced over his shoulder at the woman on the back seat who was trying to quieten the baby and soothe two small children at the same time. Her face was covered in blood. 'Have you ever blacked your wife's eye and split her lip?' he asked sarcastically.

'Well, no, Sarge. 'Course not.'

'That's what's happened to Connie Mulligan in the back. So, get a move on, Morgan. She needs a doctor quick and afterwards a place to sleep, out of danger, like.'

'The woman who runs this women's refuge is probably a right ould cow,' Morgan said derisively. 'One of them feminists, I bet, and a lesbian too. All they do is run men down and that's only because they're too ugly to catch one for their selves.'

'You're full of worldly wisdom, Morgan. That's the place, over there. I think it might be a good idea to stop and deliver our passengers safely, not just speed past and chuck 'em on to the pavement.'

'Whatever you say, Sarge.'

The car stopped. Jerry McKeown jumped out and tenderly helped the injured woman and her terrified children out of the back. 'You'll be safe here,' he assured them. The woman recoiled from his touch and didn't speak.

He vaulted up the stone steps and knocked on the front door. It was opened almost immediately by a tall women in black jeans and T-shirt. Her bountiful hair was knotted on top of her head, cascading around her face and neck in feathery tendrils. She had large, beautiful eyes, a strong nose and mouth, and he had never seen anyone look so kind, so concerned, as the woman enfolded Connie Mulligan in her lovely long arms and drew her into the house. 'Come on, luv. I've been expecting you. The police phoned to say you were on your way. There's tea made and a nice, warm room ready for you. The doctor will be here soon – it's a woman.'

She glanced at Jerry McKeown and made to close the door. 'Thank you, officer,' she said briefly.

'Can I come in, make sure she's settled?' It hadn't been his intention to go inside, but he'd quite like to get to know this woman more.

'I'm sorry, but men aren't allowed on the premises. It's a rule. I had to put me own brother out not long ago and he was forced to find a bedsit near where he works.' Another woman had appeared and was taking the injured woman and her children to the back of the house. The tall woman made to close the door again, but Jerry put his foot in the way.

'Can I have your name, please? For the records, like.'

'I thought you already had me name on your records, but never mind. It's Mrs Littlemore. Mrs Fionnuala Littlemore.'

'Ta.' Jerry McKeown returned to the car.

'You might like to know, Morgan, that the woman who runs the place isn't old, isn't a cow and definitely isn't ugly. I wasn't there long enough to establish whether or not she's a feminist.' As for Fionnuala Lacey being a lesbian, he very much hoped not.

He went back to the house early next morning wearing plain clothes. A boy of about ten, with a grave, grown-up expression, opened the door.

'I thought Mrs Lacey said men weren't allowed on the property,' Jerry remarked with a smile.

'I'm her son, so she makes an exception.' The boy didn't smile back.

'What's your name?'

'Colin.'

'Well, Colin, does your mum make an exception for your dad as well as you?'

'Me dad's dead.'

'I'm sorry about that, Colin.' Jerry had never been so pleased about anything in his whole life.

'Who is it, luv?' Fionnuala Littlemore came into the hall wearing the same clothes as the night before. 'What do you want?' she asked abruptly when she saw the policeman on the step. 'Connie's in no position to make a statement yet. Anyroad, she'll only talk to a woman police officer, so you're wasting your time if you come again.'

She was looking at him, but not *at* him. She wasn't seeing him properly. If they met in the street tomorrow, she wouldn't recognise him from Adam. But Jerry had come prepared to make her notice him.

'I've brought some toys for Connie's kids. I got them last night in Tesco's. They close late Fridays.' He held out a plastic bag. 'I hope they like them.'

'I'm sure they will. Thank you very much, officer.'

'The name's Jerry.'

'Thank you, Jerry. Connie will be pleased. Well, tara. It was nice of you to come.'

'Also ...' He stuck his foot in the door before she could close it. The bloody woman still hadn't *seen* him. 'I'd like to make a contribution towards the refuge. You're doing a great job. I admire you. I hope you'll find this ten quid a help.'

'Oh, we will. Thank you, er, Jerry.' She took the note and tucked it in the pocket of her jeans.

'Also,' Jerry continued desperately. 'I wondered, do you ever have fund-raising events, jumble sales, like? If so, I'd be willing to give a hand.'

'Well, there's nothing planned at the moment.'

'In that case, when the bloody hell can I see you again, other than on this bloody doorstep?'

'Oh!' She blinked and took a step backwards.

She'd seen him at last!

Fion saw a very tall, broad-shouldered, rugged man in his thirties, smartly dressed in a navy-blue suit. The skin on his face was weather-beaten and his nose was slightly crooked, as if it had been broken. His lips were scarred – he either boxed or played rugby. Very short brown hair stuck up in little spikes around his crown. He was anything but handsome, but he wasn't ugly either. In fact, taking in the quirky smile and the warm brown eyes, she thought him very attractive and liked his air of dependability. She could trust this man.

'Are you married?' she asked.

It was his turn to blink. 'Divorced, no children.'

'I never go out with married men.'

'Does that mean you will, go out with me, I mean?' He couldn't believe his luck.

'Mondays are supposed to be me day off.'

'Then I'll pick you up Monday at half-seven. OK?' He removed his foot and Fionnuala Littlemore closed the door.

'I'm meeting Sammy tonight and going straight from work to the pictures, Mum,' Maisie said as she was leaving. 'Don't do me any tea.'

'And when are we going to meet this Sammy?' Orla enquired.

'I dunno, Mum. It's not as if it's serious. I'm not going to be like our Lulu and get married at eighteen. I want to have a good time first. By the way, what's wrong with Dad? He was coughing and sneezing all night long.'

'He's got a cold, luv. One of those terrible summer ones. It doesn't help working in a foundry and he wouldn't dream of taking a day off. Anyroad, have a nice time tonight.'

Gary left not long afterwards. She was glad he'd managed to avoid manual work, not that there was much future in a shoe shop, but at least it was clean. Paul, her baby, left it right till the very last minute before leaving for school where he was in his final term.

Orla breathed a sigh of relief and made a fresh pot of tea. She took it into the yard to drink because it was such a lovely July morning and wished for the millionth time they had a proper garden. It was good to be alone at last and think about the phone call she'd had last night from Cormac.

'Hey, sis. Me and Vic have just decided you'd be perfect.'

'What for?'

'For selling Lacey's of Liverpool hair products. You've got a car, you've got the personality and you wouldn't have to give up your job with the paper.'

'I might be interested, Cormac. What sort of salary are we talking about?'

There was something about the tone of his voice that made her anticipate what the answer would be.

'We weren't thinking in terms of salary, Orl, just commission,' he said sweetly. 'Twenty per cent, same as Mam gets, plus your expenses, i.e. the cost of petrol.'

'Make it twenty-five per cent,' Orla said promptly. 'I'll be putting meself out a bit more than Mam. But I'm only doing it because you're me brother and I expect to be given a high-powered job one day when you're successful.'

'You'll be head of international sales, sis,' Cormac said with a chuckle. 'It's a promise.'

She would be the only sales rep because, although he and Vic were working flat out, they couldn't produce enough bottles to cater for a larger market. 'It's a bit of a chicken-and-egg situation,' Cormac said. 'We can't take orders until we turn out more and we can't turn out more till we've got the capacity to do it, though we'll have to bite the bullet soon and get some proper equipment. Me and Vic are working ourselves to a standstill turning out stuff by hand.'

A few Liverpool shops had ordered, and since reordered, quite large supplies. Mam usually sold out within days of fresh stock being delivered. An advert in *The Lady* had produced dozens of orders in the post.

Orla would be supplied with leaflets and samples. She would start with Lancashire and Cheshire, and go further afield when they'd been covered. Chemists and small supermarkets would be her main target. Big supermarkets ordered centrally and would be approached when the company felt able to cope with a large amount. 'I don't suppose expenses would cover the cost of a nice business suit?' she asked wistfully. 'I don't possess anything remotely smart, Cormac.'

'Sorry, Orl. Anyroad, you always look nice, whatever you wear.'

'Oh, yeah! That was a typical man talking.'

She would start on Monday and was already looking forward to it. Tonight she'd tell Micky, not that he'd be interested. It might prove difficult when she went far enough away to have to stay overnight, but she'd cross that bridge when she came to it. She finished the tea and went to check the pathetic contents of her wardrobe in case anything needed washing. On her way downstairs with a denim skirt and two white blouses she heard the backyard door open and footsteps in the yard. Micky must have come home, which didn't surprise her, as his cold was really bad.

To her horror, when she entered the living room by one door, Vernon Matthews was coming in by the other. He must have waited for Micky and the children to leave. He looked overdressed for the warmness of the day, in a dark suit, collar and tie, black, highly polished shoes.

'Thought I'd give you a surprise.' He smirked.

'Get out of this house immediately!' She could hardly control her rage, which was mixed with panic and a feeling of fear. There was no one in the houses on either side.

She might as well not have spoken. 'I thought we could have a little chat.' He sat in Micky's chair under the window and, although he must have known he was less than welcome, he had the air of a man who felt entirely at home in the strange surroundings. Orla, disorientated and confused, could almost believe he belonged there.

'I don't want to talk to you – *ever!*' But she had already learnt it was a waste of time trying to reason with him. He didn't listen, or he didn't want to know, or perhaps it was just another way of tormenting her, taking not a blind bit of notice of what she said.

'Oh, come on, Orla. We had a lovely talk that first time, didn't we? Followed by an experience I shall never forget. I'd very much like to do it again, in fact. Now seems an appropriate time, when there's no one around.'

Orla leant limply against the sideboard, wondering what to do. If she ran down the hall and out of the front door, she could scream for help. Or she could dial 999 and ask for the police. Except what would she tell people: the police, whoever came to help if she screamed?

He was watching her through lowered lids, still smirking, as if he recognised her predicament. 'Have you met this man before?' was the first question she'd be asked and it would all come out, the details of the afternoon they'd spent together in the pub in Rainford. Even if she tried to deny it, how could she explain how he knew where she lived? She had no idea what would happen then, whether he would be arrested, charged. Birds' wings of panic fluttered in her chest.

'Oh, come on, Orla. What harm would it do?'

He was actually getting up, coming towards her, smiling. Orla seized a large statue of Our Lady off the sideboard, ready to strike if he so much as touched her.

'Let's go upstairs. Just for a little minute, eh?'

'I'll swing for you first.' She raised the statue but he easily caught her wrist in his hand. The statue dropped to the floor but didn't break. The birds' wings were beating madly now, painfully. He slid his other arm around her waist and tried to pull her against him, groaning. 'I've been waiting too long for this.'

Orla tried to raise her knee and thrust it in his stomach, but her legs, her body, were trapped by his weight against the sideboard. She spat in his face instead.

'*What's going on here?*'

Micky! Feverishly red, face glistening with perspiration, eyes black with anger and tinged with incomprehension. He must have felt too ill for work after all.

'Just trying to renew my acquaintanceship with your wife,' Vernon said lightly.

'Out!' Micky seized his collar, flung him through the kitchen, into the yard, into the entry that ran along the back, as if Vernon had only the strength and weight of a small child. Orla had never dreamt her husband was so strong, though she realised it was a strength born of uncontrollable rage.

Micky slammed the yard door and slid the bolt. He returned inside and Orla shrank back in the face of his anger. 'How long's he been coming round?'

'He's never been before, Micky, honest,' she stammered, more terrified of him than she'd been of Vernon. Micky looked as if he could easily kill her. 'He came when I was upstairs, just walked in.'

'Then what was that about renewing his acquaintanceship with me wife?' Micky snarled.

'I met him once, more than a year ago. He's been pestering me ever since.'

'Why didn't you tell me?'

'Because . . . because . . . oh, I don't know, Micky.' She had no idea about anything any more.

'You slept with him, didn't you?' His eyes had narrowed to slits.

She hadn't the strength to deny it. She nodded.

All Micky's rage subsided in a slow hiss of breath. He sank into the chair Vernon had recently vacated and buried his face in his hands. 'I used to love you once, Orla,' he whispered.

'I *still* love you, Micky.' She had never felt such total love as she did now, staring at him, hunched in the chair in his shabby working clothes. He had started to shiver. In a minute she'd make tea, get him aspirin, put him to bed. She wouldn't take the job Cormac had offered. And she'd give up reporting, find an ordinary job in an office not far away. The car could be sold. She'd never feel fed up or bored again. Somehow, in some way, she would talk Micky round into them starting again. She had been sorry about Dominic Reilly, but at the same time was too annoyed with Micky to care that they hardly ever spoke, never made love. This time she would work on him, *make* him love her again. She felt a surge of excitement at the idea of them recovering the feelings they'd had for each other when they were teenagers, when they'd first moved to Pearl Street.

'I'll just pack a bag,' Micky said, easing himself out of the chair.

'Why?' she asked, bewildered.

'I'm leaving, that's why. Surely you don't expect me to stay after what happened today?'

'But I love you, Micky!'

He looked almost amused. 'You have a funny way of showing it, Orla.'

'I've been a terrible wife, Micky. But I learnt me lesson today.' She took hold of his hands. 'Let's start again. Remember what it used to be like? Remember the first time in the entry behind our house in Amber Street?'

He removed his hands from hers, none too gently. 'I remember. You made me life hell and you've been making me life hell ever since. You always thought yourself too good for me, didn't you?' He looked at her thoughtfully, head on one side. 'Perhaps you were, still are. All I know is, luv, that I've had enough of you. I was going to hang on till the children were a bit older, till Paul reached eighteen. Under the circumstances I'll be off today. We'll sort out the divorce later.'

Orla felt herself go cold. 'You mean there's someone else?'

'There's been someone else for two years.' He smiled gently. 'If you hadn't been so wrapped in yourself you might have noticed.'

'Who is she?'

'Just an ordinary woman without your airs and graces who makes me feel good about meself for a change.'

Orla's voice rose. 'Who is she, Micky?'

'I hope you're not going to lose your temper, luv.' Micky's voice was mild. 'It doesn't sit well, considering what's just happened. If you must know, it's Caitlin Reilly from Garnet Street who used to live across the road. Her husband was killed in an accident on the docks when they'd hardly been married a year. She's got a lad the same age as our Paul.'

'She was in our Maeve's class at school. She used to come round to our house sometimes. Her married name is Mahon.' Caitlin was a pretty, round woman, the image of Sheila, her mother. 'You've got a nerve, Micky Lavin,' Orla said hotly, 'going on about what happened today when you've been having an affair for two whole years.'

'We've both done wrong, Orla, though don't forget you were the first. I was bloody mad earlier, I admit it, but what man wouldn't be if he came home and found a strange bloke trying to rape his wife?'

Wordlessly, Orla went into the kitchen and put the kettle on. Over the years, despite the contempt she felt for Micky, the impatience, deep inside she still loved him. The fact that he no longer loved her shook her to the core. There had always been an unshaken conviction in her heart that, no matter what she did, no matter how much she riled or offended him, Micky would remain steadfastly loyal through thick and thin. She considered pleading with him to stay, coaxing him to bed so that she could show him how much she cared.

But common sense prevailed. If Micky stayed, in a few weeks' time, when she'd got over her fright that morning, she would feel discontented again and start nagging him to do things she knew he never would.

The kettle had boiled. Orla made the tea, found the aspirin and took both into the living room, where Micky was leaning against the mantelpiece, staring into the empty grate.

'I'd like you to stay,' she said. When he opened his mouth to argue, she said quickly, 'I'll leave instead. Ask Caitlin and her son to come and live here. It'll set a lot of old tongues wagging, but who cares?'

Micky's jaw dropped. 'It'd break the kids' hearts if you left, luv.'

'They'd be just as upset to lose you. Anyroad, I won't be far away. I'll find somewhere nearby to live – Mam'll put me up for now.'

'But what will you do with yourself all on your own?'

'Our Cormac's offered me a job. I was going to tell you about it tonight. I'll do me best to make something of it.'

She would put her heart and soul into the job with Lacey's of Liverpool, drive all over the country, stay away for as long as she liked, knowing her children would be safe with Caitlin Reilly.

Orla's spirits soared. She was free to do the sort of things she'd planned on doing twenty years ago before she'd met Micky Lavin.

16

'Where are you off to today, luv?' Alice enquired.

'Bury, Rochdale, Bolton,' Orla said briskly. She wore a smart black costume and was thrusting the new leaflets Cormac had brought the night before into a briefcase, checking she had enough samples. 'I'll probably be home dead late, Mam, so don't wait up.'

'I wouldn't dream of waiting up, luv, considering the hours you keep. I don't know how you keep going to be frank.'

'Enthusiasm keeps me going, Mam: commitment, ambition. The things you felt when you started Lacey's.'

'I didn't feel any of them things, Orla. I just wanted to get out the house away from your dad.' Alice smiled. 'I'm glad you're happy, though. I thought you'd be dead miserable, breaking up with Micky, though you never stopped complaining about the poor lad since the day you married him – and before, if I remember right.'

Orla closed the briefcase with a snap. 'I miss the kids,' she said soberly. 'I miss them coming in for their tea, making cocoa at bedtime. I even miss – only a bit – doing their washing. Still, Lulu's gone and I think our Maisie's more serious about this Sammy than she'll admit. Gary was talking about joining the Navy. Soon, there'll only be Paul left.'

'And he'll have Caitlin's lad, Calum, for company.' Alice always made a point of not sounding as shocked as she felt by all this switching around, as if marriage, relationships, were just a game of musical chairs. Pol had left Cormac for Maurice Lacey, Orla had walked out on Micky and, before you could blink, Caitlin Reilly had moved in and there was talk of divorce. She knew of other respectable women whose children were divorced or living in sin. That policeman, Jerry McKeown, that Fion had taken up with, had been married before, leaving Maeve the only one of Alice's children who led a conventional married life. At least, so far!

'Are you off now, luv?'

'Yes, Mam.' Orla kissed her. 'I'll see you when I see you. D'you realise what time it is? You'll be late for work.'

'I'm taking the morning off.' Alice flushed. 'I'm having another driving lesson.'

'Good for you, Mam,' Orla sang as she slammed the door.

An increasing number of cars were appearing in Amber Street, so Alice didn't feel too ostentatious buying one herself. It was only a little car, a Citroen Ami, though she was beginning to wonder if she'd ever get the hang of the damn thing.

She was on edge, waiting for the instructor to arrive in his own car, when the telephone rang.

'Mrs Alice Lacey?' a male voice enquired.

'Speaking.'

'I'm calling regarding a Mrs Cora Lacey. She's your sister-in-law, so I understand.'

'That's right. Is something wrong?'

'You could say that, Madam. We would be obliged if you would come to Bootle Police Station straight away.'

'Why?' Alice asked irritably and immediately regretted it. Cora might have had a bad accident.

'Because the lady concerned has been apprehended and gave your name as her closest relative.'

'Apprehended! Why?'

'That will be explained at the station, Madam.'

Cora was in a cell, hunched in her camel coat as if it were a blanket, her small, sallow face expressionless. She'd been caught shoplifting, according to the desk sergeant, trying to nick two woollen vests from a shop in Strand Road. It was a first offence, so charges wouldn't be pressed, but Cora had better keep her hands to herself in future, he said warningly, else she'd find herself behind bars.

'Cora!' Alice said reproachfully when the women were alone. 'What on earth possessed you?'

'Needed vests for the winter, didn't I?' Cora shrugged her shoulders churlishly. 'Me old ones were in shreds. It must be twenty years since I last bought some.'

'I would have bought you vests, Cora.'

Cora snorted. 'Oh, you would, would you?'

'Rather than see you steal them, yes. Look, can we go home? I feel uncomfortable here.' Alice glanced at the barred window, the hard bench on which prisoners were supposed to sleep. 'I've come in a car, not mine, the driving school's. The instructor turned up for me lesson just as I was leaving. I'll just have to forget about this week's lesson.' Lord knows what the instructor would think, being asked to take her to the police station – such a nice young man too.

Cora didn't speak on the way home. Alice got out of the car when she stopped in Garibaldi Road – Cora had given her name to the police, and she felt obliged to see her safely home and find out why she had been driven to steal.

Inside the house, Cora seemed to sag. 'I'm going to the lavvy,' she numbled.

Alice realised she was far more affected by the events of the morning than she pretended. She went into the scrubbed kitchen to make tea and was shocked to find the cupboards bare: no tea, no sugar and not a drop of milk on the premises. Was Cora so skint she couldn't afford even basic food? Later, she'd buy the woman some groceries. It was years since she'd given a thought to Cora – someone had mentioned seeing her outside the church at Lulu's wedding, but that was all.

Cora came in, looking more composed. 'You can go now,' she said belligerently. 'There was no need to have come in the first place.'

Alice had no intention of going. 'Why are you so short of money that you need to go thieving? I always thought you had private means – and Billy's working.'

'The "private means", as you call them, dried up a while ago. And Billy's never given me more than a few bob a week in years.'

'Why not ask for more?'

The yellow face twisted in a scowl. 'He's hardly ever here to ask. These days, Billy spends most of his time in Browning Street with Maurice and his family. 'Stead of the ale, most of his wages go on propping up that useless business of Maurice's.'

'Then what on earth are you living on?' Alice asked, alarmed. Now that she had removed her ancient coat, Cora, always thin, looked no more than skin and bone.

'Nothing, if you must know.'

'But a person can't live on nothing, Cora,' Alice cried.

Cora turned on her angrily. 'Look, I'd appreciate it if you got out me house and minded your own business. How I manage is nowt to do with you.'

'Then why did you give the police my name?'

'Yours was the only name I could think of. I didn't want Billy or Maurice knowing, did I?' Cora swayed and would have fallen had not Alice leapt forward and caught her.

'Have you had anything to eat this morning? Come on, let's go into the other room and sit you down.'

Alice settled her sister-in-law in an armchair and fetched a glass of water. 'What you need is a cup of hot, sweet tea, but all you've got is the water. How long has this being going on, luv?'

The near-collapse seemed to have broken Cora's spirit. 'Since earlier this year, when I turned sixty,' she said in a hoarse, frightened voice. 'Apart from the few bob I get off Billy, which pays the rent, I haven't had a penny piece. The 'leccy bill's not paid, nor the gas. I can't remember when I last ate.' She looked at Alice, her strange eyes terrified. 'When they stopped me outside that shop I nearly died, imagining me name in the papers, everyone knowing.'

'There, there,' Alice soothed, but there was something not quite right about what Cora had just said. 'I thought women were entitled to a pension at sixty?'

'Oh, Alice.' Cora had begun to shake with fear. 'I've done something terrible, worse than a bit of shoplifting. The thing is, I'm scared to claim me pension. I've got the book, they sent it months ago, but I daren't take it to the post office.'

'Why on earth not, Cora?'

Cora was wringing her hands agitatedly; spittle drooled from the corner of her mouth. 'When we first moved here,' she said in the same hoarse voice, 'I found a Jacob's biscuit tin full of papers in the fireplace cupboard. Two spinsters used to live here, sisters, about fifty. They went to America during the war. I've no idea what happened afterwards, whether they came back or not. The tin was full of private things, birth certificates, like, insurance policies, some shares. I kept them, they weren't taking up much room, in case they wrote one day and asked for them back.

'Years later,' Cora went on, 'I got a letter from the government to say one of the sisters, the oldest, was due for her old age pension. They sent a form for her to sign.' She paused.

'Oh, Cora, you didn't sign it!' Alice gasped.

'I needed money. I was desperate for money. By then, there was nothing but Billy's wages coming in. I signed the woman's name and filled in something to say I was her niece and she'd given me authority to collect the money from the post office. Two years later a form came for the other sister, so I signed that too. And I cashed the insurance policies and sold the shares.'

'You could go to prison for a long time for that, Cora,' Alice said primly. 'It's called fraud.' She was shocked to the bone. Shoplifting was one thing, but this was far more serious.

Cora grabbed her arm. 'Do you think the police will check up on me, now they've got me name and address, like?'

'I doubt it. I take it you've stopped taking the pensions?'

'Months ago, when I heard about me own pension. I got frightened. I thought it would look suspicious, collecting three pensions from the post office, all at the same address.' The small hand tightened, claw-like, on Alice's arm. 'I'm worried I'll be asked for death certificates, seeing as the pensions aren't being taken any more. I'm worried someone from the government will wonder why I'm not taking me own.' Cora released Alice's arm and collapsed back in the chair. Her eyes had almost disappeared into their sockets. She looked like death. 'What am I going to do?'

'I have absolutely no idea, Cora,' Alice said coldly. She got to her feet. 'I'll be off now and buy some groceries. I'll not see you starve. And I'll give you a few bob to be getting on with.' She emptied the contents of her purse on to the coffee table. 'There's nearly three pounds there. When I come back, let's have the electricity and gas bills and I'll see they're paid. But that's as far as I'm prepared to go. If you must know, I'm thoroughly disgusted by what you just told me. I haven't a clue what advice to give. It might help if you moved to a smaller house that's cheaper to run. And I suppose you could collect your pension from a different post office.'

Alice paused at the door. 'When you feel better, I suggest you look for a job. We need a cleaner at the salons. It's either early in the morning or late at night, whichever suits best. You can let me know if you're interested when I come back with the food.'

The door closed. Cora swivelled her head and watched Alice go down the path. She turned to shut the gate.

Cow!

She had never hated anyone as much as she hated her sister-in-law at that moment. *I'm thoroughly disgusted by what you just told me.* Oh, was she, now! What did she know about being on your beam ends, not knowing where your next meal was coming from? Alice Lacey had always had it soft.

Still, there'd been no need for her to have been so understanding, Cora thought grudgingly. Oh, she'd gone on a bit, but another person might have ranted and raved, and washed their hands of Cora altogether when they heard the criminal things she'd done. There was money on the table and food on its way. She'd even offered her a job. It meant that Alice cared, even if it was done with a sickly air of being holier than thou that made Cora want to puke.

We need a cleaner at the salons.

Well, Cora had cleaned before and she'd clean again. In fact, she'd spent her whole life cleaning. She glanced round the shining, spotless room. The furniture was probably out of fashion, but it had been lovingly cared for, tenderly polished. The net curtains were the whitest in the road. Cleaning was what Cora was good at. She'd take the job because she had to live. Anyroad, soft-girl Alice would almost certainly pay more than most employers.

Cora enjoyed cleaning the three hairdressers. So there would be less chance of being seen by the neighbours she started early, at six o'clock. Each salon took just over half an hour, and she felt enormous satisfaction when she'd finished and the plastic surfaces shone, the mirrors sparkled, the sinks gleamed.

She didn't mind working on her own. She was used to it. Most of the time she preferred her own company and early in the morning, with few people around and hardly any traffic, it was easy to pretend she was the only person in the world, a situation Cora would very much have preferred. Sometimes she even sang as she worked.

Billy didn't know she was working. Billy knew nothing about her. He never had. Cora had been cleaning the salons for a fortnight when he came home one night at about half past seven. They hadn't spoken to each other in a long while and she was surprised when he came into the living room and asked if she'd make him a cup of tea.

She was about to tell him to make it himself, but remembered he didn't ask for much, probably knowing he wouldn't get it.

'Is something wrong?' she asked. He looked on edge, jingling the coins in his pocket as if he needed something to do with his hands. His face was hot and red, and she noticed his mouth kept twitching. 'Is Maurice all right?'

He didn't answer. Cora made the tea sweet and strong, the way Alice had wanted to make it for her the day she'd been arrested for shoplifting.

'What's the matter, Billy?' she asked, putting the tea beside him on the coffee table.

'I've done something dead wicked, Cora.' Tears trickled down his fleshy cheeks. At sixty-three, he was still a good-looking man, with thick, iron-grey hair and a clear complexion. His paunch had almost disappeared since he'd come off the ale. 'I've set fire to the yard.'

Cora gasped. 'You've *what*?'

He was looking at her with round, scared eyes, like a little boy, the way Maurice had done many years ago. 'I've set fire to the yard. I suppose I must have got the idea from our John, though in his case it wasn't intentional.'

'But *why*?'

'Because it was the only way out. He was losing money hand over fist, our Maurice. He's no businessman, Cora. He was making scarcely enough to feed his family, while the overdraft got bigger and bigger, and I was the one paying it back.' He swallowed nervously. 'The writing's been on the wall a long time. Six months ago I pumped up the insurance on the premises, so now Maurice can claim he's lost his livelihood. As I said, it seemed the only way out.'

'You mean you've been planning this for six months?' Cora was impressed.

'I reckon I must have.'

'Had the fire properly taken by the time you left?'

Billy nodded. 'The smoke was black. I could see it rising over the rooftops. The fire engines came, I heard them.'

'What happens if they blame our Maurice?' Cora frowned.

'There's something happening at Sharon's school, a concert. I deliberately waited till a night when he'd have – what d'you call it, luv?'

'An alibi.'

'That's right, an alibi.'

'And what about you, Billy? Have you got an alibi?'

Billy looked at her pleadingly. 'Only if you swear I've been home with you for the last few hours.'

'Of course I will,' Cora said instantly. It was the first time Billy had done something she admired. He was smarter than she'd given him credit for. She regarded the slumped figure in the chair and gave the shoulder a little squeeze. 'Come on, Billy, cheer up. Everything's going to be all right, I can feel it. In fact, it's going to be better than before, with Maurice out of trouble and you without an overdraft to pay.' She stood. 'Shall I make you something nice for your tea, luv? Fish and chips? Or there's bacon and eggs if you prefer it. Afterwards, we can watch telly. There's some good programmes on tonight.'

'Fish and chips would go down a treat, luv.' Billy sat up and squared his shoulders. He smiled. 'I never thought you'd take it so well. You're a good sort, Cora.'

At the end of September Danny Mitchell died quietly in his sleep. Bernadette woke and found him by her side, his body as cold as ice, smiling peacefully. She allowed herself a little cry before telling Ian and Ruth. If only she'd been awake to kiss him goodbye, so that he would have felt her arms around him as he slipped from this world to the next, and she could have kept him warm for a little while longer.

Then she woke up the children and rang Alice.

At the funeral there was a stiffness between the wife of the deceased and his daughter. Alice was convinced she'd been sidelined during her father's last few months on earth, prevented from seeing him as much as she would have liked.

Bernadette had thought Alice too interfering. Danny didn't want to be nagged to see a doctor, brought tonics, asked in a maudlin voice how he felt. They had played a game between them, she, Danny and their children. The game was that he was temporarily out of sorts but would get better very soon. It meant that even when he was on his deathbed they could laugh when otherwise they might have wept. The game had continued until the night Danny died. But Alice was a spoilsport and refused to play along with them.

'He's asleep,' Bernadette would claim whenever his daughter came to see him. 'I'd sooner he wasn't disturbed.'

She didn't like doing it. Alice was her best friend, but Danny was her husband. He came first.

'We're a rapidly expanding company,' Orla informed the middle-aged, impeccably dressed manager of the small, exclusive Brighton department store. At first he'd been slightly irritated at being interrupted, but she'd soon brought him round. 'We've recently moved to a new factory in Lancashire with the very latest equipment.' This wasn't strictly true. The new factory was a dilapidated building on a run-down trading estate near St Helens and the equipment was second-hand. However, it was the case that the company was rapidly expanding. In a few weeks' time, at Christmas, two new lines were being introduced: skin freshener and cleansing lotion. Perfume was on the cards for next summer.

'I like the look of it,' the manager said. 'And I like the name too: Lacey's of Liverpool. It has a nice ring to it.'

'That's what everybody says.' Orla smiled her most dazzling smile. 'I use it meself.' She ran her fingers through her shining brown hair. 'I'm a walking advertisement for our products.'

'And an excellent advertisement, I must say.'

'Would you like me to leave some samples?' She smiled again.

'I'd sooner place an order.' The manager's answering smile was more speculative than dazzling. 'Are you free for dinner tonight?'

Orla giggled. 'Depends on how much you're going to order.'

'How about a hundred bottles of each?'

'Then I'm free for dinner.'

Cormac and Vicky would be pleased: another two hundred bottles on top of the order for two hundred and fifty she'd taken that morning, making over a thousand she'd sold during her two days on the south coast.

Orla was a first-class sales representative for Lacey's of Liverpool. Within the space of six months she had sold the company's products in virtually every city and major town in the country, charming the male managers and buyers, and flattering the women. 'You've found your niche,' Cormac had declared appreciatively. He and Vicky had taken the plunge and were working out their notices with Brooker's.

Life sometimes got a little lonely on the road, staying in shabby hotels with nothing much to do at night-time. There was always the pictures, but Orla felt even more lonely in a cinema by herself when the rest of the audience were in couples. She missed her children. Occasionally she even missed Micky, particularly his warm presence in bed beside her. But next morning she always woke up refreshed, looking forward to the day ahead and the feeling of achievement when she took a big order.

When Lacey's of Liverpool became properly established, Orla would become Head of Sales and have her own office, a secretary. She visualised having charts on the wall showing the movements of reps all over the country. And when the company became more successful still, there would be no more need for reps. Orders would automatically come flooding in on reputation alone, or so everyone hoped, and it would then be Orla's job to seek markets abroad, in Europe and the States, all over the world.

She hugged herself when she thought about travelling to America to introduce Lacey's of Liverpool's products to discerning customers there. She wasn't doing exactly what she'd planned all those years ago when she was a teenager, interviewing famous people, but this was even better. One of these days a reporter might want to interview *her*.

The manager of the Brighton department store sat unnecessarily close throughout dinner. He kept putting his hand on her thigh, or grasping her arm, and she could feel his knuckles press into her breast. Orla didn't particularly mind. In its way, it was rather thrilling. She'd let him kiss her when the evening ended, but that was all. After Vernon Matthews, kissing was as far as Orla was prepared to go.

'Would you like something to eat, Maeve?' Fion enquired.

'No, thank you.'

'Well, it's time I made the kids' tea. I'm starving meself, as it happens.'

'I'll come and help.'

The sisters went into the big shabby kitchen of Fion's house in Stanley Road. A woman was already there, furiously mashing potatoes. Sausages sizzled on the stove. A small boy was squirting washing-up liquid on the floor.

'Don't do that, Tommy, luv,' Fion said mildly. 'It'll make people slip over.'

The woman turned and slapped the child's ear, hard. 'I'm sorry, Fion. I didn't realise what the little bugger was up to.' Maeve gasped and the little boy started to howl.

Fion said, not quite so mildly, 'Olga, don't you dare let me see you hit Tommy again. You're only here because someone did the same to you. This is a refuge, for children as well as their mothers.'

'I don't know how you stand it,' Maeve said when a sullen Olga and a sobbing Tommy had gone.

'I feel as if I'm doing a bit of good.' Fion was wiping off the fat Olga had splashed all over the stove. She took a big packet of fish fingers out of the fridge.

'Doesn't your nice policeman mind?'

'Jerry? Oh, he minds a lot. He wants us to get married. I said I'd marry him as soon as I found someone to take over the refuge.'

'I couldn't stand it meself. I'd feel as if me house wasn't me own. And Martin . . .' Maeve paused.

'And Martin what?'

'Martin couldn't stand it either.'

'Speaking of Martin, won't he be home from work by now and wanting something to eat?'

'Possibly.'

'Is something wrong, Maeve?' Fion regarded her small, neat sister searchingly. Maeve hadn't been to work that day. She'd arrived at one o'clock and they'd sat talking about nothing in particular ever since. Fion had expected her to go home ages ago to make Martin's tea, but Maeve had stuck to the chair and continued with the conversation that was rapidly running out of steam, mainly because she seemed unable to concentrate on one subject for more than a few minutes. She looked on edge, kept glancing at her watch, couldn't keep still.

'Everything's fine,' Maeve said in the sort of voice that indicated everything was nothing of the sort.

The telephone rang and Maeve said, 'If that's Martin, don't tell him I'm here.'

'Why ever not, sis?'

'Just don't, that's all.'

Fion went to answer the phone and came back a few minutes later. 'It wasn't Martin, it was Mam. Martin's just phoned to ask if you were there. She said he sounded worried. I didn't say you were with me.'

Maeve didn't answer. The phone rang again. When Fion returned she said, '*That* was Martin. He sounds even more worried. What's up, sis?'

'I'm pregnant!' Maeve burst into tears. 'I had a test this morning and it was confirmed.'

'That's marvellous, luv.' Fion flung her arms round her sister. 'I'm so happy for you.'

'So am I.' Maeve wept. 'But Martin won't be happy, he'll be livid. Oh, Fion! He'll be so cross. Can I come and live with you?'

'Of course, but surely it won't come to that? Martin will be thrilled to pieces. After all, how long is it you've been married? Going on thirteen years.'

Maeve shook her head wildly. 'I told you, Martin will be livid. He doesn't want children. He wants holidays and garages and new fridges, new cars.'

'Then it's about time he grew up and lived in the real world,' Fion said crisply. 'How did it happen? Did you forget to take your pill or something?'

'No. I *stopped* taking the pill.' Maeve sniffed and managed a tiny smile. 'I haven't taken it since Lulu's wedding. I decided I wanted a baby more than I wanted Martin.'

'Then why are you so worried about him finding out?'

'Because I still love him.' Maeve started to cry again. 'Least, I think I do.'

The phone went. It was Mam. Martin had rung a second time and was about to contact the police. 'I told him she's only a couple of hours late, but he said she hasn't been in work today. He's climbing the walls, Fion, and I'm getting a bit worried meself. This isn't a bit like our Maeve. I mean, where on earth can she be?'

'Actually, Mam, she's with me,' Fion confessed and explained the circumstances.

Mam listened in silence, then said, 'I'm pleased about the baby, but I never realised it was mainly Martin's idea they didn't have children. It'll do him good to climb the walls for a while longer. He might have come to his senses by the time he discovers where she is.'

Fion replaced the receiver soberly. How peculiar fate was, so topsy-turvy! She recalled Maeve's engagement party when she'd been stuck with Horace Flynn and everyone else seemed to be having a whale of a time. She'd felt so grateful that Neil Greene had condescended to talk to her. Yet, years later, when she'd met Neil in London he'd looked as miserable as sin and she'd wondered what she'd seen in him. Now Maeve was in a state because she was pregnant when by rights she should be on top of the world. And Orla!

Gosh, she used to be so envious of Orla, who had married Micky Lavin and was everything Fion herself wanted to be. Now Orla was wandering the country like a lost soul selling crappy make-up, trying to pretend it was fantastically adventurous, when it was in fact a desperately pathetic life for a thirty-six-year-old woman to lead. Poor Orla. Poor Maeve. And poor Neil.

I never thought I'd feel sorry for a single one of them, Fion mused, let alone all three. She felt very lucky, totally fulfilled. There was hardly another thing she wanted that she could think of. Colin had been a wonderful husband and Jerry would make another.

She resolved that tonight she would suggest she and Jerry got married straight away, because it seemed silly to waste time living apart. Anyroad, there *was* something she wanted – more children. But she wasn't prepared to move into his modern flat in Litherland. It would be too cramped. Besides, she loved this house that had been bequeathed to her by Horace Flynn. She'd been the only person who'd liked him, except when he pinched her bum. Another house would have to be found for the refuge. It would be her next project and she'd put everything she had into it. Fion mentally ticked off all the things she'd have to do: badger the council for an empty property, bring the local MP on board, start fund-raising, contact the press and get them on her side.

She returned to the kitchen. Maeve had made a cup of tea and started to fry the fish fingers.

'These look nice,' she said. 'Me and Martin have never had fish fingers.'

'They're lovely with beans and tinned tomatoes. Jerry's mad on them.'

'We always have posh, three-course dinners. They take ages to cook.'

'Well, that'll stop once you've got a baby to look after.' Fion grinned.

Maeve pulled a face. 'Martin will do his nut.'

'Stuff Martin. Any man who prefers three-course meals to babies wants his bumps feeling.'

'Hmm. If I have one of these fish fingers, will it make you short?'

'Have as many as you like. There's another packet in the fridge.'

The evening wore on. There were more phone calls from a frantic Martin. The police had refused to take action. Mam phoned to say she was beginning to feel sorry for him and could Fion persuade Maeve to go home, put the poor chap out of his misery?

Fion agreed that mightn't be a bad idea. 'I think our Maeve might welcome it by now. She's a bundle of nerves. It's best to get the confrontation over and done with.'

At eight o'clock Jerry McKeown arrived – the rule 'no men on the premises' had been relaxed on his behalf. He offered to fetch Martin in a police car with the blue light flashing.

'Can I go with you?' Bonnie demanded eagerly.

'Perhaps it would be best if Maeve went,' said Fion. 'How about it, sis?'

Maeve considered this silently for a while. 'Will Jerry wait outside the house until after I've told him? Just in case I have to come back here to live if he chucks me out.'

'If there's any such suggestion as chucking out, it'll be Martin out on his ear, not you,' Jerry said darkly.

Maeve Adams had never created a fuss during her entire neat and tidy life, had never given her mam and dad, or her husband, a moment's worry. She would have been embarrassed to think she had. Maeve strongly disapproved of the way her sister, Orla, behaved – though she wouldn't have dreamt of saying so – throwing herself all over the place and complaining loudly over just about everything in sight. She had thought it dead selfish of Fion to run away to London and give her family so much heartache. Even Cormac, whom everyone considered an eminently sensible person, had had a brainstorm and refused to finish university, then gone wild for several years.

Now, not only had Maeve missed a day's work at the hospital without phoning in an excuse, but she had disappeared for several hours, causing her husband a great deal of grief. In Maeve's eyes this behaviour was on a par with that of her sisters and brother.

She didn't want to lose Martin, who would be angry when he discovered she'd stopped taking the pill without discussing it with him first. But she'd only not discussed it because she knew he wouldn't agree. Martin's priorities didn't allow for children. They were still saving to have a garage built and only the other day he had complained that the car was getting old.

'*I'm* getting old,' Maeve said to herself as the police car – without its blue light flashing – made its way to Crosby through the evening traffic. Jerry thoughtfully remained silent. 'In a few years' time I'll be too old to have babies. And I'm not prepared to go without children just so Martin can have the latest car and a garage to put it in.'

He could be as angry as he liked. Maeve folded her small hands protectively over her stomach. She would have the baby with him or without him, it was up to him to decide.

Jerry stopped outside the Adamses' immaculate modern semi, though it looked entirely different from the house Maeve had left that morning. All the lights were on, including the coach lamp outside. The front door was wide open, the car was idling in the path, headlamps on, white smoke pumping from the exhaust. Martin was about to get in the car, leaving the house open and brightly lit for any passing burglars to help themselves. Normally as neat as his wife, his hair was on end, he was tieless and had forgotten to put a coat on, despite it being a bitingly cold November night.

He turned when the police car drew up and his face seemed to collapse with horror, which turned to relief when Maeve climbed out of the passenger seat.

'Darling! Oh, my darling Maeve. I thought you were dead. I thought you'd had an accident. Are you all right? Tell me you're all right.' He stroked her arms and neck, as if expecting to find broken bones. 'Where have you been?' He suddenly frowned when he noticed the driver of the car. 'Is that Jerry? Why is he bringing you home? Maeve, what's going on?'

Maeve decided not to beat about the bush. 'I'm having a baby, Martin. If you want, I'll go straight back to our Fion's with Jerry once I've collected some clothes – that's where I've been all day.'

'You've been at Fion's! Oh, Maeve,' he said reproachfully. 'I've been out of my mind with worry.' His jaw dropped. 'Did you just say you're having a baby? How on earth did that happen?'

'The same way it happens with everyone,' Maeve said cheerfully. 'I stopped taking the pill months ago and if you don't like it, Martin, then you'll just have to lump it. As I said, I'll live with Fion.'

'Can't we discuss this indoors?'

'There's nothing to discuss.' Maeve smiled sweetly. 'I'm having a baby and that's all there is to it. Once you accept that fact and promise not to complain about the age of the car, our lack of a garage, how much you fancy a colour telly and an even more expensive holiday next year than we had last, then I'll stay. Otherwise, I'll collect me clothes and be on me way.'

Martin's relief had turned to cold annoyance. 'I never dreamt you could be so deceitful, Maeve. Having a baby should be a mutual decision, not one the wife takes for herself. I'm very disappointed with you.'

'Not half as disappointed as I am with you, Martin Adams. Mind out me way while I go and collect a few things. I'll come back for the rest tomorrow while you're at work.'

'No!' Martin grabbed her shoulder. Jerry McKeown got out of the police car and leant against it, folding his arms. He watched the couple intently. Martin gasped and let go of his wife when he realised Jerry was concerned he might hurt her. He said quietly, 'The last thing on earth I want is for you to leave, Maeve. Come inside. We can talk there.'

'I'll come, but there's nothing to talk about. I'm having a baby and the sooner you get used to the fact the better.' Maeve marched up the path.

Jerry McKeown watched them go inside. They had forgotten all about him. He got out, switched off the engine of Martin's car, locked the doors and put the keys through the letter box. He then drove back to Stanley Road and, for the umpteenth time, asked Fion to marry him and was delighted, though slightly taken aback, when she accepted straight away.

Orla was the first person Lulu and Gareth had had to dinner in their tiny London flat. Orla watched her daughter fondly as she set the little round table in the window. It reminded her of when she was little and she'd played house with Fion and Maeve. The young couple hadn't enough dishes and the ones they had were cracked. None of the cutlery matched. The chairs were odd. The room smelt of oil paints and there was a half-finished painting on an easel in the corner – Gareth couldn't afford a studio. So far, the painting consisted of several dead fish pegged, like washing, on a line.

'What will you call it?' she asked him.

'I haven't thought of a name yet.'

They sat down to a tasty chicken and mushroom casserole followed by trifle. Orla had brought a bottle of wine.

'I'd've done something more ambitious, Mum, but the cooker's useless.'

'This is lovely, Lulu,' Orla said sincerely. A candle stuck in an old wine bottle flickered in the draught. The window of the fourth-floor room overlooked a landscape of Camden roofs glistening icily in the moonlight. It was December and painfully cold. 'I never realised roofs were so many different colours,' she remarked.

'I shall paint that scene before we leave,' Gareth remarked. '*If* we leave.'

Orla looked from her daughter to her son-in-law. 'Are you thinking of moving?'

Lulu wrinkled her nose. 'We *might*, but not till after Christmas. Last week we met this chap who owns an art gallery in New York, only a titchy place, badly run-down. He thinks the Americans would go for Gareth's paintings and has promised to show half a dozen on a regular basis – you wouldn't believe the price he suggested asking, Mum.'

'I don't want to compromise my integrity,' Gareth growled.

'Painters only paint paintings in order to sell them, surely,' Orla said. 'The money you earn merely proves their worth. There's no point otherwise, unless it's just a hobby and you don't mind giving them away.'

'See,' Lulu said triumphantly. 'I knew Mum would be all for it. Gareth's worried that if he earns money he'll have sold out.'

'I'm probably more scared no one will buy my work,' Gareth confessed glumly.

Orla tried to convince him he was talking rubbish. At Lulu's age – at any age – she would have gone to New York like a shot. She didn't want her daughter to miss out on what sounded a wonderful opportunity.

After dinner, quite a few friends dropped in, bringing more wine: artists mainly, male and female, not all of them young. The lights were turned off, leaving the flickering candle and the brilliant silver moon to illuminate the shabby room, and they talked about a myriad things – art mainly, politics, the latest films, the latest shows . . .

God, how I would have loved this, Orla thought longingly. I've missed so much. I've missed everything.

It was midnight when she returned to the small hotel in Victoria. To her surprise, there were half a dozen men in the lounge and the tiny bar was still open. She bought a double whisky and the men suggested she join them. Orla thought of her small, cold room with its small, cold bed and agreed. Five of the men were reps like herself, much older. Their clothes were cheap, their laughter false, their voices much too loud. They exuded an air of faint desperation as if this wasn't the life they had envisaged twenty or thirty years before. By now, they had expected an office with their name and title on the door, their own staff, respect.

The sixth man was very different. Better dressed than the others, quietly spoken, he exuded confidence rather than desperation. Orla gathered he was an engineer working for a French tool company, calling on firms by invitation to quote for new, highly expensive machinery. He said very little in a quiet voice with only the suggestion of an accent. The other men called him Louis. Orla was particularly intrigued because, unlike his friends, he completely ignored her. He was a small, slender man, dark-haired, thin-lipped, with a tight, unsmiling face. She hadn't felt so immediately attracted to someone since she'd first met Micky. She kept looking at him in the hope of catching his eye, but he never once glanced in her direction.

An hour and two more whiskies later, she announced she was off to bed. The other men bade her a noisy goodnight, but Louis merely stared at his highly polished shoes and didn't speak.

17

'This room is like a fridge,' Vicky Weatherspoon muttered. 'If I were a pint of milk, I'd keep for weeks.' She glared at the ice on the metal-framed windows, wondering if it was inside or out, and rubbed her numb hands together, but they had lost all feeling.

It was useless trying to write. She threw the pen on to the desk and tucked her hands inside the sleeves of her jumper. They felt only slightly warmer.

A plumber was coming to install second-hand central heating at the end of December. He was a very cheap, highly sought-after plumber, which meant they'd had to wait months until he was free. It hadn't been so bad in October when they'd first moved in and had spent most of their time decorating the shabby, run-down building inside and out, while Mary Gregory and Robin Hughes, both eighteen and with A levels in Chemistry, were in the workshop turning out thousands of bottles of Lacey's of Liverpool shampoo and conditioner. A business had never been started on so short a shoestring, Cormac had said, laughing.

Lucky Cormac! Vicky made a face. Cormac was at that moment in a nice warm restaurant in Liverpool, lunching with a girl called Andrea Pryce, a model, who would become the face of Lacey's of Liverpool in an advertising campaign in the press, starting January. It would swallow up all the profit the company had made so far, but hopefully be worth it in the end. Andrea was startlingly pretty and ten years younger than Vicky, who wasn't only envious of Cormac being warm. Say if he fell in love with Andrea! Say if she tried to seduce him!

Vicky tried to imagine how a woman went about seducing a man, but her imagination wouldn't stretch that far. She thought miserably that Cormac was no more attracted to her now than a year ago when they'd gone into partnership. They couldn't possibly have got on better. They were friends, they went to dinner together, had even gone to a hotel in Yorkshire on a weekend business course; they sometimes shared quite intimate thoughts. The only thing missing was romance. Cormac had shown not the slightest sign of wanting to kiss her – she didn't count the triumphant kisses he planted on her cheek when they received a big order, or the hugs he gave her for the same reason. It was a sad fact that Cormac didn't regard her as a woman, but as a mate, a business partner. He would have been just as fond of her had she been a man.

Yet with each day they spent together, Vicky only loved him more. She'd tried to make herself attractive by growing her short, crisp hair longer, but was forced to cut it off when it became a halo of wire wool. Her mother warned her she looked like a clown when she tried using make-up. 'Stick to lipstick, Victoria, and then make it pale. You've got too big a mouth for such a bright red.'

Vicky blushed at the memory and wondered if Cormac had noticed her turning up for a whole week looking as if she was about to join a circus. Did he ever notice anything about her?

The new clothes had also proved a disaster. She was short and dumpy. She didn't suit flowing frocks and pleated skirts. And, 'Your legs are too sporty for high heels,' claimed her mother. By sporty, Vicky assumed she meant her overdeveloped calves. She would never know why she had acquired such heavily muscled legs when she'd been useless at games at school.

Then she'd spent a fortune on contact lenses so she could dispense with her glasses but, try as she might, she couldn't get used to the damn things.

Still, on New Year's Day Cormac's sister, Fionnuala, was getting married and Vicky had been invited to the wedding. Naturally, she and Cormac would go together. If they spent enough time in each other's company, she thought hopefully, he might get so used to her that he'd want them to get married because he couldn't visualise another woman in his life.

Cora and Billy Lacey had also received an invitation to Fion's wedding. Cora breathed a sigh of relief that she'd been accepted back into the Lacey fold. She'd buy herself a new coat and wear that diamanté brooch in the lapel that she'd nicked from Owen Owen's a long time ago. It wouldn't hurt Billy to have a new suit – he'd lost so much weight that his best one hung round him like a tent. Perhaps they could go to town on Saturday, have a meal afterwards.

There was an odd sensation in Cora's breast when she thought about going shopping with Billy. Another person would have recognised it as happiness, but Cora wasn't used to being happy and couldn't have explained what the sensation was.

After forty years of ignoring each other, she and Billy had suddenly started to get along. Billy had more or less given up the ale and most nights they spent watching telly. One night they'd even gone to the pictures to see *The Sound of Music* and enjoyed it no end – that girl, Julie something, had a lovely voice.

Money was no longer a problem since the yard had burnt down and Billy was able to keep all his wages. As expected, Alice paid far over the odds for cleaning the salons and Cora had started collecting her pension from the post office in Marsh Lane. Maurice and Billy between them had settled all Lacey's Tyres' outstanding debts with the money off the insurance and Maurice seemed much happier working as a driver for Bootle Corporation. He'd come to tea last Sunday, bringing Pol and the kids, and Cora realised she was quite fond of the lad even if he was a loser, unlike her real son who was very much on the up and up. The kids got on her nerves a bit with their noise, but she felt like a proper grandma and had actually bought them some odds and ends of clothes.

In a few weeks' time they'd be even better off. Alice Lacey was looking to buy a house and would be leaving Amber Street for ever once she'd found one. It was Billy who'd suggested him and Cora take over Amber Street from Alice who'd had the place done up dead smart. The rent was thirty bob a week cheaper than Garibaldi Road.

Cora was surprised to find she didn't mind, not much, living in the house of the woman she'd always hated. Nowadays, there wasn't all that much room for hatred in her heart.

Fionnuala Littlemore married Sergeant Jerry McKeown on the first day of January 1971. It was snowing and Fion wore a cream fitted coat over a matching dress – Jerry had offered to buy her a fur coat as a wedding present, but Fion didn't approve of animals being slaughtered for their skins.

Over ninety guests had been invited to the reception at Hilton's Restaurant. It wasn't until six o'clock that the newly married couple left for their honeymoon in London.

Alice waved them off tearfully, though she wondered why young people bothered with honeymoons any more. In her day a honeymoon was the time you got to know each other properly. There used to be all sorts of jokes about the first night. She remembered feeling dead nervous herself, but John had been a gentle, tender lover right from the start. Nowadays, the first night happened long before the honeymoon and people knew each other far better than God had intended by the time they condescended to get wed.

She returned upstairs to where the air was fuggy with cigarette smoke and several couples were dancing to a recording of 'A Whiter Shade of Pale', which was being played loud enough to be heard several streets away.

Orla came up. 'You look dead miserable, Mam. Have a drink. What would you like, sherry?'

'Just a little one, luv.'

Orla looked as if she'd already had too much to drink herself and there were four more hours to go before the reception ended. She also looked much too thin, Alice thought worriedly. Her eyes were unnaturally bright. She seemed to laugh a lot at things that weren't remotely funny. It was an unnatural life she led, particularly for a woman: on the road, staying in strange hotels in strange places. Still, it would all change in a few months' time, when she would be based in her own office in St Helens: Head of Sales.

Alice wondered if the time would ever come when she would stop worrying about her children. At least Fion was happy, the one she'd least expected to be, and Maeve was like the cat that ate the cream since she'd fallen pregnant, though Martin didn't exactly look too pleased.

Her son appeared on top of the world, the business doing so amazingly well, but Cormac had turned thirty a week ago and it was time he got married, started a family. Of course, he already had a daughter, Sharon, Pol's eldest girl, but Alice wasn't the only one who suspected Cormac had had nothing to do with the lovely red-haired child who resembled neither her mother nor her supposed father. She'd always hoped things would get serious between Cormac and Vicky, but he'd brought that model, Andrea Pryce, to the wedding. She was a nice girl, if a trifle empty-headed.

She looked for Vicky, saw her sitting alone on a chair, looking rather downcast, and went to sit beside her. 'Would you like a piece of wedding cake to take home for your mam and dad, luv?'

'That's very kind of you, thanks.'

'I'd have sent an invitation for two if I'd known you were coming on your own. You could have brought someone with you.'

'There's no one I could have brought. I thought . . .' She paused and said no more.

'Thought what, luv?'

'Nothing.' There were tears in the girl's eyes.

Alice realised that she'd thought she'd be coming with Cormac. The poor thing was almost certainly in love with him – he chose to dance past at that moment with Andrea in his arms, clearly more impressed with beauty than brains, stupid lad. 'Would you mind helping me make everyone a cup of tea, luv?'

Vicky jumped to her feet with alacrity, obviously glad to be rescued from her lonely chair.

In the kitchen, Cora was finishing washing a mountain of dishes. 'I've just put that urn thing on to make a cup of tea,' she said when she saw Alice.

'Thanks, Cora. I was about to do the same thing meself. I think I'll use them cardboard cups, save more washing.' Alice and Vicky began to spread the cups into rows.

'I've sent Billy out to buy some sugar 'case we run short.'

Cora looked very smart in a tweed costume with a white jumper underneath. Her hair had been set that morning in the Stanley Road Lacey's. That shoplifting incident, dreadful though it was at the time, had done her the world of good, brought her to her senses. She was much more friendly nowadays, almost human.

'I was wondering,' Cora said, 'if you'll be leaving the carpets behind when you move. We've carpets of our own, naturally,' she added hurriedly, 'all fitted, but it seems daft to take them up and cut them down.'

'I'm leaving all the fixtures and fittings, curtains included.' Alice sighed. She was dreading leaving Amber Street, but circumstances and her children were forcing her out. The circumstances were that the salons were making a mint, not just from hairdressing, but she was the only stockist in Bootle of Lacey's of Liverpool products and they sold like hot cakes. She had never been so flush, yet nearly every one of her neighbours had to struggle to keep their heads above water, which made her feel dead uncomfortable.

As for the children, they'd been nagging her to buy a place of her own for years: Southport, or near the sands, Ainsdale or Formby way. When they were little she'd taken for granted she knew better than her kids, but since they'd grown up they seemed to think they knew better than *her*. Perhaps it was only natural. After all, she'd constantly tried to rearrange her dad's life, much to the chagrin of Bernadette.

It reminded her for the umpteenth time that she hadn't seen much of her friend since Danny died. There remained a stiffness between them. Bernadette was at the wedding, naturally, a pale, rather sad figure, surprisingly old, Alice thought when she'd come into the church with the children. This was the first big occasion that she'd attended as a widow.

'Excuse me, Vicky. I won't be a minute.' Impulsively, Alice went back into the reception. Bernadette was standing with a group, yet somehow looking very much alone, watching Ian and Ruth dance together. Alice was struck by how closely seventeen-year-old Ian resembled his father. Tall and lithe, he had the same appealingly wicked smile. She touched Bernadette's hand. 'He's going to be a heartbreaker one of these days, just like me dad.'

'I think he already is. I'm not sure if it's a good thing or a bad one that he looks so much like Danny.' Bernadette gave a rueful smile. 'It means I'm reminded of him a hundred times a day.'

'I reckon it's good.'

'I suppose so.'

They looked at each other. Alice wrinkled her nose. 'I'm sorry, Bernie.'

'For what?'

'For barging in when me dad was ill, trying to take control, insisting he see a doctor.'

'You only had his best interests at heart, luv. Trouble was it wasn't what Danny wanted. Perhaps I should have been a bit more tactful meself.'

Alice linked her friend's arm. 'Why don't we go to the pictures next week? We can have a meal beforehand. *Butch Cassidy and the Sundance Kid* is on at the Forum. I've been dying to see it for ages.'

'So've I.' There was an expression of relief on Bernadette's face. 'I'd love that. Ally. I'll pop in the salon and we'll arrange a time.'

'Come to tea tomorrer and we can do it then. Bring Ian and Ruth, except they'd probably find it dead boring. None of me grandchildren want to come to tea any more, not even Bonnie and she's only nine. I'll be glad when our Maeve has her baby and I'll have a little 'un again.'

Sheffield in January! Anywhere in January when it was snowing hard and freezing cold made you yearn to be somewhere else, like the South of France.

Or Spain.

Orla thought about Dominic Reilly, living in Barcelona. He'd married the girlfriend he'd said wasn't as beautiful as she was – it had been on the front page of all the papers. As soon as she could afford it she'd go on holiday to Spain. Perhaps Mam would come with her. She didn't fancy going on her own. In fact, she was fed up to the bloody teeth with being on her own and couldn't wait for April when Cormac had announced the company would go through a sort of minor relaunch and she would be working permanently in St Helens. A lot depended on how well the press campaign went with that model. If it went well, there would be no more need for her to roam the country, thank the Lord.

She trudged through the slush towards the hotel. At least it had a more-or-less decent lounge and she could sit in comfort until it was time to go to bed in an icy room with icy sheets.

The hotel also had a bar. By the end of the evening other reps would arrive, some of whom she'd be bound to know and she'd have people to talk to, make her laugh.

What a lousy day! The weather was vile, the street lamps a depressing sickly yellow, the traffic horrendous, and her car was parked miles away. Even worse, half the places she'd called in, mainly chemists, had refused to see her, even the ones where she'd made a prior appointment: people were off with colds and flu, and they were too busy.

She was beginning to hate this job. This wasn't adventure. It was no longer the least bit exciting. Maybe she was a bit run down because she seemed to have lost all her initial enthusiasm.

The hotel at last! The usual seedy establishment that looked as if it hadn't seen a lick of paint in years. Lots of plastic flowers and oatmeal paintwork. Orla hung her heavy trenchcoat on a rack in the hall. Underneath, she wore a smart black suit which no one had seen all day because this was the first chance she'd had to remove the mac. She went into the empty lounge with her briefcase. There was no fire, but an elderly radiator emitted moderate heat. The bar was in the corner and there was no one behind the tiny counter. Orla rang the bell, a woman appeared and she ordered a whisky.

'Sit down and I'll bring it over.'

'Ta.' Orla chose the armchair closest to the radiator and tucked her legs against it. The woman brought the whisky. As soon as she'd gone, Orla drank it in a single gulp. She felt in the briefcase for the half-bottle she'd bought on impulse on her walk back, the first time she'd ever done such a thing, but tonight, for some reason, she felt exceptionally depressed, what with the weather and a completely wasted day.

Refilling the glass, she drank the contents, slower now, before filling up the glass again. She wasn't trying to avoid the bar prices, just the embarrassment of reordering so quickly.

It had become a habit, starting off the evening with a couple of whiskies. They helped her forget about the present and think about the future, which looked particularly rosy when she'd had a few drinks, though she'd never had three before in such a short space of time. She drained the glass, closed her eyes and felt a pleasant warmth swill round her stomach, which reminded her how empty it was because she'd forgotten to have dinner. She'd eaten nothing since she'd left another hotel that morning – where had it been? Rotherham.

'Good evening.'

Her eyes shot open to find the sombre figure of Louis Bernet staring down at her. He wore a grey suit and a very white shirt that contrasted agreeably with his brown skin and smooth black hair. This was the second time they'd met since the night in London when she'd had dinner with Lulu and Gareth. On the last occasion they'd chatted amicably, only about trivial things. He wasn't as unfriendly as he had first seemed, more reserved, a bit shy.

'Hello.' She tried to smile.

He nodded at her empty glass. 'Would you like a drink?'

'Yes, ta.' Another drink wouldn't hurt. Not tonight, when she felt so unusually miserable.

'Whisky?'

'Please.' He'd remembered what she drank, her 'tipple', as Grandad used to say. He went over to the bar and for some reason Orla's eyes filled with tears. It must be thinking about Grandad, which made her think of Bernadette, Mam, her sisters, her children. And Micky.

Bootle seemed worlds away from this cold, crummy hotel. In Pearl Street there'd be a roaring fire in the grate, the telly would be on, the kids would be home from work desperate for their tea – and Caitlin Reilly, or whatever her name was now, would be bustling in and out of Orla's kitchen getting food ready.

Jaysus! 'What am I doing here?' Orla asked herself. 'Why did I leave?' At that moment. Pearl Street with her husband and children seemed the most desirable place on earth. 'I must be mad. I'm searching for rainbows, but you can only *see* a rainbow. You can't touch it.'

Louis Bernet returned with the drinks. He sat in the armchair next to hers. 'We seem to be the first here.'

Orla nodded and pulled herself together. She reminded herself that she was with a devastatingly attractive man. The first minute she'd set eyes on him, she'd sensed a magnetism about him. Now they were alone together and it was her opportunity to . . . to do what?

To make eyes at him over the whisky, flutter her lashes, lick her lips and pretend she was a scarlet woman? Except she wasn't a scarlet woman. She was Orla Lavin from Bootle, married, with four children whom she badly missed.

'What company do you work for?' Louis asked. He had the faintest of French accents. 'I didn't ask the time we met before.'

'Lacey's of Liverpool. It's my brother's firm. We make cosmetics. As from April, I'll have me own office back home. Would you like some samples? You can give them to your wife.'

'I haven't got a wife. Do you have a husband?'

'Sort of.' Orla paused. 'We're separated.'

'He must be mad, this husband, allowing himself to be separated from a woman like you.' His narrow lips twisted in a smile.

Orla forgot the house in Pearl Street and its occupants. She traced the rim of her glass with her finger as she'd once seen an actress do in a film, someone like Ava Gardner or Elizabeth Taylor. 'I'm not very nice,' she said seductively. 'That's why me and me husband parted.'

'I don't believe that.'

'It's true.'

'You seem exceptionally nice to me.' He moved his legs so that their knees were touching.

Orla's flesh felt as if it was on fire. A pulse throbbed in her throat. She was trying to think of an answer, when Louis said, 'Have you eaten yet?'

'I forgot to eat.'

'Would you join me for dinner here?'

'They serve meals?'

He shrugged and spread his hands, a very foreign gesture. 'Not very good meals, but edible. There aren't any restaurants nearby and it's too awful a night to go searching for one.'

'In that case I'll be pleased to join you for dinner.'

Louis was right. The meal was just about edible: badly cooked lamb, very dry roast potatoes, frozen peas. He ordered a bottle of wine to make the food go down more smoothly.

On top of the whisky, it also made Orla more than a little light-headed. She began to see the romance of the situation: two virtual strangers, stranded in a third-rate hotel, snow whipping against the windows. All that was needed was some haunting music.

During the meal he told her about himself. He'd been born in a little village north of Paris. His parents had a smallholding. The village was very dull, nothing ever happened. He'd been taken on by a local engineering firm to train as a draughtsman. At twenty-one, he'd gone to work in Paris. He kissed his fingers and threw the kiss into the air. 'Ah, Paris!' He pronounced it Paree. 'Paris is *très* beautiful. Very, very beautiful. And so full of life. It has everything a man – or woman – can possibly want.'

'I'd love to go there,' Orla breathed.

His brown eyes smiled into hers. 'I'll show it to you if you like.'

'I *would* like.'

'In the spring?'

She felt dizzy. 'Yes, in the spring.' She'd never met anyone like him before. He seemed so grown-up and sophisticated compared with the other men she'd known, particularly Micky, who was a child by comparison.

No one else had come into the dining room by the time they finished the meal. They returned to the lounge where an elderly couple had bagged their armchairs by the radiator. Otherwise the room was empty. The other reps must have wisely stayed in town and found bars with a bit more life in them. The clock showed half past nine – the last few hours had raced by.

Louis took her elbow. 'Would you like another drink?'

'A whisky and soda,' she replied, though she'd already drunk far too much. 'Just a little one.' She swayed and almost fell into an armchair.

'One more drink and I think we should go to bed.' He regarded her challengingly, eyebrows raised.

'If you say so,' she said demurely. Every nerve in her body felt alive. She couldn't possibly sleep on her own after tonight. A memory returned, of the night in a Bootle entry when she'd first made love with Micky. She had the same feeling now, of wanting to be touched all over, but this time by Louis Bernet.

Orla quickly drank the whisky. Louis held out his hand and helped her to her feet. She wondered if he felt the same pounding excitement as she did. She could hardly stand and it wasn't all to do with the amount of alcohol she'd drunk.

Her room was on the third floor. They took the lift, where they kissed for the first time and Orla felt a rush of raw desire when she felt him pressed against her.

In the corridor she stumbled and Louis grabbed her arm. He supported her as far as her room where, to her surprise, he paused. There was a look of what might have been irritation on his face. 'I didn't realise you'd drunk enough to get in this state and I find drunken women rather unappealing. Tonight you'd go to bed with any man who asked.'

'That's not true!' Orla cried. She didn't want to be alone. She couldn't stand it, not tonight. 'I don't usually make a habit of this sort of thing. I'm only doing it because it's you.' There was a sob in her voice. She unlocked the door, put her hands round his neck and drew him into the chilly room. Snow was whirling crazily against the windows and the traffic outside was muted. 'I'm more tired than drunk, but not too tired to . . .' She paused, blushing. '. . . To make love with you.'

Perhaps it was the blush that convinced him she was, at least partially, telling the truth. He sighed and said huskily, 'You're also extremely beautiful – and very hard to resist.'

'Please don't try.' She removed the jacket of her black suit. The blouse underneath was blue and very frilly.

He came over and took her in his arms, buried his head in her shoulder. She could feel his lips through the thin material of the blouse. Then he began to undo the buttons, so slowly and deliberately that she wanted to scream at him to hurry. He slid the blouse off her shoulders, his hands warm on her skin as he pushed her down on to the bed and her head swam. He took off his jacket and kissed between her breasts, then pulled down the straps of her underskirt and bra so that she was exposed to him. She felt both vulnerable and wanton as she took his head in her hands and directed his lips on to her right nipple. He sucked greedily, kneading the flesh around with his fingers. Then he transferred to the other breast and Orla moaned.

Suddenly he released her and lay back on the pillow, all passion apparently spent.

'What's the matter?' Orla asked, bewildered.

'Nothing. Let me hold you, come here.' He slid an arm round her shoulders and put the other across her waist.

Orla began to touch him, but he caught her hand and held it tightly. 'Let us lie still a minute, *chérie*,' he said softly.

'But why?' What had she done wrong? It can't have been anything all that bad, because he was being so gentle with her. But it was very mysterious all the same.

'Because there are times when it is good to stop and think, just stay quiet for a while.'

She began to catch his mood, her own passion having vanished with his, and relaxed against him. He was still almost fully dressed and he felt warm and comfortable.

'Do you ever get lonely, Orla?' His voice was little more than a whisper.

'Lately I feel lonely all the time,' she said with a sigh.

'Me, also. All the time. But unlike you, I have no family to return to.'

'You poor thing!'

'I am very much a poor thing. I have spent the last ten years travelling across Europe, searching for something I have yet to find.'

'Love?'

He nodded. 'Love, possibly. Happiness, maybe. Who knows what? It might be God. And what are you searching for, *chérie*?'

'I'm not searching for anything. I'm just doing me job.'

'No, you're searching, like me. I could see it in your eyes.' He laughed quietly. 'I've seen the same expression in my own, that's how I know. You weren't satisfied with what you had. It's why you left your husband and children. After a while, the searching can become very tedious.'

'I suppose it can.' She wondered what he was getting at. Was he leading up to something? He had turned out to be a very strange man. She liked him more now than she did before, even if she couldn't understand him.

The hotel was exceptionally silent and it would have been easy to believe they were the only two people in it. Apart from the traffic, there wasn't another sound to be heard.

'You are a lovely woman, Orla.' He caressed her face and touched her hair with his lips. 'I like you very much. I think I could very easily fall in love with you if given half a chance. You pretend to be so sophisticated, but you're not. You're vulnerable, like a child. I shouldn't have asked you to come to bed with me. I was taking advantage of your need, not for sex, but for something else: romance perhaps, which is a very different thing. I feel ashamed, but I only did it because, like you, I didn't want to spend the night alone.'

'Why are you saying all this, Louis?' Orla whispered. 'Why didn't you take advantage? What stopped you? Was it something I did?'

'No, I just wanted to say these things before I told you. I want you to realise how hopeless your search is, so you'll understand you're not missing anything when you go back home to your family.'

'Told me what? And I can't go home till Saturday, and then it's only for the weekend.'

'I think you should go now. You see, *chérie*, you have a lump in your left breast, a large one. Now is the time for you to return to the people you love – and the people who love you.'

All she wanted was for him to leave. She appreciated being told so kindly, if rather strangely, about the lump – another man might have noticed, made love and said nothing. But now she knew and all she wanted was to be with her mam.

Louis understood how she felt. He helped her pack and took her in his car to where hers was parked. It was still snowing.

'I meant it about Paris,' he said when he had put her things in the boot and came round to the driver's side to say goodbye. Orla rolled down the window. 'I hope and pray it might still happen. Here's my card in case you feel like getting in touch when you're better.'

'Thank you. Thank you for everything, Louis.'

As she was driving out of the car park, Orla threw the card out of the window, then closed it.

The journey to Liverpool was a nightmare. Snow kept sticking to the windscreen. The wipers were useless. Lorries thundered past, spraying her with slush. She couldn't see. The car kept skidding on the icy surface, but she managed to steady it. She wasn't sure if she cared if the car crashed or not. Would her children, her family, find it easier to cope with her death in an accident rather than a long, slow death from cancer? She reminded herself that the lump might be benign and, even if it wasn't, you could have treatment. Patsy O'Leary, who worked for mam, had had breast cancer and recovered. She'd had a breast removed. But Patsy was nearly sixty. Orla was only thirty-seven and to lose a breast would be the end of everything.

'This is a funny time to come home, luv,' Mam said when Orla came in just as she was making the first cup of tea of the day. 'It's only just gone seven and I'm not long up. Don't tell me you've driven all night in this weather? No wonder you look exhausted.'

Mam looked so welcoming and comfortable in her candlewick dressing gown, her greying hair all mussed. Orla burst into tears. 'Will you come to the doctor's with me later, Mam. I'm too frightened to go on me own.'

A week later and tests showed that the lump was malignant. And there was a smaller lump in the right breast that was malignant too. Orla was advised to have a double mastectomy.

'Oh, Mam!' she screamed in the hospital when the doctor conveyed the terrible news.

'I wish it was me, luv,' Alice whispered. 'Oh, dear God, I wish it was me.'

'You can wear a padded bra,' Fion said practically later that night when the family gathered together in Amber Street for a conference. 'No one will know.'

'*I'll* know,' Orla yelled. 'I'll be deformed for the rest of me life.'

'Orla, you'll still be as beautiful as ever,' Cormac assured her. 'After the operation you can carry on with the job exactly as planned, with your own office in St Helens.'

'I'll be as ugly as sin. And you can stuff the job, Cormac. I don't want it.'

'I'll pray for you, Sis,' Maeve said softly. 'I'll pray every minute of every day, I promise.'

'It's too late for prayers.' Orla wept. 'It's happened. Anyroad, I don't believe in prayers. They don't work. I used to pray for all sorts of things, but I never got them.'

Instead, she'd got a husband in a million and four lovely children, Alice thought sadly. Enough to make most women happy, but Orla had always wanted the impossible.

'I imagined one day I'd get married again, but no man will ever want me now.'

Cormac shuddered and turned away. How would he feel about Andrea if both her breasts had been removed?

Alice glanced at her other daughters. Fion made a face and Maeve shrugged. No one quite knew what to say.

'Jerry, I want a baby. I want to conceive tonight,' Fion told her new husband when they got into bed.

'I'll do me best, darling. I'm already trying hard, but I'll try twice as hard if you like. Anyroad, why the urgency all of a sudden?'

'I'm not sure.' It was something to do with Orla, something stupid, as if a new life growing inside her would act as protection against what was happening to her sister. Or perhaps it was a wish to grab at things that mattered before it was too late. 'Just a minute.'

'Where are you off to?' Jerry enquired patiently when Fion got out of bed.

'I'm going to kneel the way we used to do when we were little and say a proper prayer for our Orla.' At the end of the prayer, Fion slipped in a little one for herself. 'Please God, please make me conceive tonight.'

'How's Orla?' Martin enquired stiffly when Maeve came home. He was sitting in the lounge with a typed letter on his knee.

'In a state, as you can imagine. I'd be in a state meself if I was in the same position. She's having an operation next week.'

'I'm sorry to hear that. Oh, by the way . . .' He waved the letter, 'This is from that double-glazing firm who contacted us last year. Remember we said we might be interested in the spring? I rang and told them it's off because my wife has given up work. Another thing, I think the clutch might be going on the car. We really need a new one – car, that is – but I suppose we'll just have to do with a new clutch instead.' He sniffed disdainfully.

'Did you tell the double-glazing firm exactly why I'd given up work?' Maeve enquired. 'That I'm having a baby in three months' time?'

'It was none of their business.'

'Nor is the fact I've given up work. I suspect you didn't tell them that at all. It's just another little dig at me for getting pregnant without your permission. You'd sooner have double glazing and a new car than a baby.' Maeve's usually serene face darkened with anger. Normally she was patient with him, but tonight, thinking about Orla, she wasn't in the mood. Her voice rose. 'You've got your priorities all wrong, Martin.' If he didn't buck up his ideas, there'd soon be another divorce in the Lacey family.

Orla opened her eyes. A familiar face was bending over the hospital bed. A kiss brushed against her lips. 'Micky!'

'Hello, sweetheart. How are you feeling?'

'Still a bit dopey. You look well.' She'd forgotten how handsome he was, even if his dark hair was slightly thinner and his face had filled out somewhat.

'You probably won't believe me, but so do you. A bit pale, that's all.' He stroked her cheek. 'Do you mind me coming to see you?'

'Of course not. For a moment I thought you were here because I'd had a baby. Doesn't Caitlin what's-her-name mind you coming?'

'Caitlin left a while ago, Orla. She couldn't compete.'

'Against who?'

'You, luv. She said I still loved you and always would. I couldn't help but agree.'

'What about the divorce? I've kept expecting to get a solicitor's letter.'

He looked sheepish. 'I never got round to seeing a solicitor.'

'Micky.' She took a long, shuddering breath. 'Has me mam told you?'

'Yes and I want you to come home with me. I'll do everything for you, wait on you hand and foot. I've already arranged it with work. I've got leave of absence until . . .' He bit his lip.

'Until I die?'

'Sorry, luv. I didn't mean to put it like that.' He began to weep. His tears stung her face and she left them there to mingle with her own. 'Don't die, Orla,' he pleaded. 'The kids are going crazy back home. Lulu keeps ringing up from New York. She's ready to get on a plane at the drop of a hat.'

'It's going to happen, Micky. The lumps have been removed, but the cancer's everywhere. I'm too far gone to operate. They're going to try something called radiotherapy, but they don't hold out much hope.' She was amazed that she could speak so sanely and sensibly when she knew that she was going to die in the not too distant future.

'Will you come back to Pearl Street with me and the kids, luv?' His good-natured face was screwed up anxiously, as if nothing before had mattered to him as much as her reply.

'Have you discussed it with Mam?'

'She says it's up to you. You must do as you think best.'

'I'm in an awful mess on top, Micky,' she whispered. 'Lord knows what I'll look like when the dressings come off.'

He began to cry again. 'Oh, Orla. I know it's terrible for you, but it doesn't bother me. You're still the best-looking woman I've ever known.'

'And you're the best-looking man.' To her amazement, she managed a dazzling smile. 'I'll come back to Pearl Street and be with you and our children, Micky.'

It was still surprising, the things that could fall off the back of a lorry: an electric blanket, for instance; a lovely, spongy Dunlopillo cushion to lean against in the armchair; delectable items of food; pretty little bits of jewellery; perfume; filmy scarves; a lovely nylon bed jacket – things that Mrs Lavin, her mother-in-law, brought round frequently, to 'cheer you up, like'.

She hadn't realised how much she had come to love her in-laws, who bore her no ill will for having walked out on their son, only returning because she was dying. Neither did Micky, nor her children.

In the past, Orla had been too wrapped up in herself, in her own needs and desires, to notice how nice people were. But now there was no future to think about and she was able to see things in a less self-centred way. She had never before been in receipt of so many hugs and kisses from her children, no doubt because they knew they would have been impatiently shrugged away in the past. Now Orla wanted to be hugged and kissed as much as possible because there was so little time left – six months, maybe a year.

Lulu came home from New York for a week to see her mother. Gareth's paintings were selling like hot cakes, she announced, and they were buying an apartment in Greenwich Village. She also announced that she was expecting a baby late in October. 'You'll be at the christening, won't you, Mum?' She squeezed her mother's wrist, as if daring her to say no.

'In New York, luv?'

'It costs the earth to have a baby in America. I'll have it here, in Liverpool.'

'Then I'll be at the christening, luv. I promise.'

The house was besieged by visitors: family, friends, neighbours. Orla had passed the point of thinking she would get better, that there was hope. It made things easier for the visitors, not having to pretend. She imagined being the star of a terribly moving drama that would make a fantastic film – Vanessa Redgrave would be marvellous in her part.

Once she had got over the trauma of the operation, she felt well enough to go out, though she tired easily. She bought a stiff padded bra and filled it with cotton wool, so no one would guess she had no breasts when she went with Micky to the pictures and to the theatre when a couple of tickets managed to flutter off a lorry. After two visits to the hospital for radiotherapy, she decided not to go again. It made her feel washed out and she knew it was a waste of time.

The actual act of dying Orla tried not to think about. Only in the dead of night, lying in the double bed with Micky asleep beside her and the glimmer of the street lamps peeping through the gap in the curtains, would she let herself visualise closing her eyes for the very last time on the people she loved most dearly. She would never see them again. She would be gone from their lives for ever. They would miss her, grieve for her, but after a while they would have no alternative but to get on with their own lives and it would be as if she had never existed.

Sometimes she would start to cry, waking up Micky, who would take her in his arms and she would sob that she didn't want to die, to leave him and the children. But what could Micky say except, 'Shush, luv. There, there, sweetheart, don't cry.' He never said, 'Everything's going to be all right,' because they both knew it wasn't.

Micky was a saint for taking her back. When she thought about her moods and tantrums in the past, the bad-tempered scenes that were all her fault, she felt ashamed and embarrassed.

'I was horrible to you, wasn't I?' she said one night when the children had gone to bed and they were sitting on the settee in the parlour having just watched an old Humphrey Bogart film on television.

'You certainly were,' he agreed.

'I'm sorry,' she said penitently. 'I decided the other night that you're a saint for putting up with me for so long.'

He smiled ruefully. 'I'd sooner have married you, luv, than any other woman on earth. I just wish I'd been able to make you happy.'

'No one could have made me happy. I wanted too much.' She linked his arm. 'But you're making me happy now, Micky. I feel wonderful, being home. I remember thinking, it was the night in Sheffield, just before I came back, about how much I was missing Pearl Street and me family. I longed so much to be here I felt an ache in me heart.' The encounter with Louis

Bernet she kept to herself. She'd told everyone she'd noticed the lump when she was having a bath. 'Though I'm worried about the children. It's not good for them, watching their mother die in front of their eyes. Our Maisie hardly ever goes out these days – I remember I used to nag her for never being in – and Gary's put off joining the Navy until ... well, you know. Poor Paul's forever on the verge of tears. He's more sensitive than the others. As for Lulu, I daren't think what her phone bill will be like. She calls every other day.'

'We can't shield them from reality, Orla, luv.'

'I suppose not.' She chuckled. 'I'll be a grandma, won't I? If I live long enough. It's strange, because our Fion, who's a year older than me, has just announced she's in the club and Maeve's only got another six weeks to go. I wish ...'

'Wish what, luv?'

'Oh, nothing.'

Later, in bed, Orla said, 'I've been thinking, Micky.'

'I thought as much, you've been dead quiet.'

'I'd like a baby too.'

Micky gasped. 'Don't talk daft, luv. You can't guarantee ... That's a stupid idea, Orla.'

'You were going to say I can't guarantee I'll be alive in nine months' time, but I will be, Micky, I swear it. I'll *keep* meself alive to see Maeve's and Fion's babies born, as well as me granddaughter and me own baby.'

'That would be dead irresponsible,' Micky said, outraged. 'Who'd look after it, for one thing?'

'Everybody,' Orla said promptly. 'Mam would and me sisters would, and your mam and dad would. And you would, Micky, as well as our children. It would be the dearest loved baby in the world.'

Orla coaxed and cajoled for the next half-hour, but Micky remained implacable. But still Orla persisted, giving all the positive reasons she could think of for having a baby. 'It would make me so happy, Micky. I wouldn't feel as if I was dying if I had a baby growing inside me. It would be like knowing me soul would be passed on to me child.'

'That's nonsense, Orla.'

After another half-hour of persuasion, Micky said reluctantly, 'Let's see what the doctor has to say.'

'No. The doctor will advise against it. I know he will.'

'There!' Micky said triumphantly, as if this proved his point.

'The doctor can't do anything else. If he said "go ahead" and things went wrong, he'd be open to blame.'

'So, you concede things can go wrong.'

'Things won't go wrong, but the doctor can't be sure of that. He'll advise against it to protect his back.'

'You might not conceive.'

'If I don't, I don't. But I'd like to try.' She began to touch him. 'Please,

Micky,' she whispered. 'Anyroad, I'm not the delicate invalid you seem to think, not yet, and I feel like making love.'

'All right,' he said in a choked voice, 'we'll make love tomorrer – after I've bought some French letters. As for a baby, I'd prefer you thought about it for a bit longer than a few hours. We'll talk about it again next week. Oh, don't stop, luv. Don't stop. I've been dying for you to do that ever since you came home.'

18

Bernadette Mitchell looked up in surprise one morning when her best friend came storming through the backyard into kitchen.

'You'll never guess what our Orla's gone and done,' Alice raged. 'She's only got herself pregnant. I've never known anything so irresponsible in all me life. If circumstances were different, I'd have torn her off a strip a mile wide. As it was, I felt obliged to keep me mouth shut.'

'You'd think Micky would have been more careful,' Bernadette gasped, equally shocked.

'Orla wouldn't have let herself get in the club if she hadn't have wanted to – she learnt birth control the hard way, didn't she? She could always wrap poor Micky twice around her little finger. I'd like to bet it's all her idea.'

'It's a funny idea to have, Ally.'

'Well, you know Orla. She always has to be different. *She* can't just die like ordinary people.' Alice clapped her hand to her mouth. 'Jaysus, Bernie, that was a terrible thing to say. It's just that I'm so upset. And you know what she said, our Orla? "It will be like being born and dying at the same time, Mam." Oh!' Alice burst into tears. 'It's so sad, I could cry for the rest of me life.'

'What does the doctor at the hospital have to say?'

'She hasn't told him yet. I reckon he'll have a blue fit.'

'They might make her get rid of it.'

'Over my dead body, they will. It's a daft thing Orla's done, but it's done, and that's all there is to it. There's no going back. Is that kettle on for tea, Bernie? If I don't have a cuppa soon, I'll faint. Kids!' Alice sniffed and dried her eyes. 'They worry you sick when they're little and you think it'll stop when they grow up, except it gets worse. There's something dead funny going on between our Maeve and Martin, and Cormac's been moping around like a lovesick rabbit ever since that Andrea girl went back to London. Then there's Orla . . . I sometimes wish I'd never had children, I really do.'

'No, you don't, Ally. We women would be lost without our kids. Here's your tea. Let's take it into the other room. Shouldn't you be at the salon?'

'No, I should be at me new house in Birkdale measuring for curtains. I'm signing the final contract on Friday.' Alice sighed. 'Oh, Bernie. I hate signing things. Remember that bloody agreement Cora had me sign? Ever since, when I've signed anything I've been worried what I'm letting meself in for.'

'I wish it were me signing for a lovely bungalow overlooking Birkdale golf course,' Bernadette said wistfully.

'I wish it were you too. I'm dreading it, me. Anyroad, only toffs play golf. I'd sooner look out over Anfield football ground or Goodison Park.' Orla's news had put her in a bad mood and she was exaggerating. The bungalow was beautiful, with large, luscious gardens front and back, a lounge big enough to hold a dance in, two bedrooms and a dream kitchen. Alice had gasped in admiration when she saw the cream fitted units, matching tiled walls, the plum-coloured floor. There was a pine table almost as big as her present kitchen. The fridge, cooker and automatic washing machine were being left by the vendors, an elderly couple off to live in Spain.

Mind you, she still felt as if she had been badgered into moving by the children. It didn't help, either, when she casually mentioned to Billy Lacey she was only *thinking* of moving and he'd leapt on the idea of taking over her old house. In a weak moment she'd agreed it would be a good idea, though she felt certain Cora wouldn't. Unfortunately, Cora had, and both her and Billy had been in and out of the place like yo-yos ever since wanting to know what she was leaving behind. She wouldn't need a van to move. The few things Cora and Billy hadn't collared would fit in the boot of the car.

'Have you ever been in love, Vic?'

'Yes, Cormac. Very deeply in love.'

'Was it reciprocated?'

Vicky shook her head. 'No.'

'The chap must be a fool.'

'He's a complete idiot.'

'You're a prize, Vic. You'd make some man a wonderful wife.'

'You're drunk, Cormac. In your present state you'd make some woman a lousy husband.'

Cormac stared gloomily into his beer. He wasn't drunk, just mildly inebriated, but Vicky was still fed up with him. They'd come for a drink after work because he claimed he couldn't bear to be alone and all he'd done, for the umpteenth time, was ask questions about Andrea. Why hadn't she phoned? Why was she never in when he phoned her?

How was Vicky supposed to know? She was glad the affair had ground to a halt when Andrea had gone back to London – she took it for granted it had been a *proper* affair from the sickening way they mauled each other when they thought no one was looking. Now there was talk of using Andrea again when they promoted their perfume, Tender, in the spring. After all, Andrea was the face of Lacey's of Liverpool. It would be daft to have a different face, or so Cormac claimed, sensibly as it happened.

Vicky was dreading it because she knew the affair would start all over again. She had no idea whether Andrea was as smitten with Cormac as he was with her, but she was the sort of girl who probably liked having a man dancing constantly in attendance. No doubt she'd been thrilled to bits to find a good-looking single male available when she'd come to Liverpool for the press campaign.

'Do you think I should go down to London and look for her?' Cormac asked.

'Whatever you like, Cormac. I can't possibly pass an opinion.'

'Why not?'

'Because it's none of my business, is it? You must do what you think is best.'

'You're a lot of help, I must say. I haven't a clue what's best.'

Vicky scowled and quickly changed it to a smile – she looked plain at the best of times. She'd look hideous if she scowled. 'If I were in your position, I'd go to London.'

'There!' Cormac looked delighted. 'I knew you'd come up with an answer. I'll go tomorrow after we've seen that rep about the boxes.' They were contemplating selling their products in sets, covered with cellophane in pretty cardboard boxes.

'Glad to be of help,' Vicky said and immediately regretted sounding so sour.

He turned up next morning in his only suit to go to see Andrea: light-grey flannel with a blue shirt and navy tie. At midday, after they'd placed an order for boxes and the rep had gone, they went together out to his car.

'Will you be able to manage on your own?' he asked cheerfully and Vicky wondered if he'd give up the idea of Andrea and London if she said she couldn't.

She preferred not to find out. Anyway, she'd been left by herself loads of times before. 'I won't be on my own, will I?' Since Christmas, Lacey's of Liverpool had taken on four more staff. There was a secretary, to type the letters and answer the phone, in an elegant reception office by the door; a young man for the newly formed packaging department; two women for the large room now referred to as the workshop. 'I thought I might go and see your Orla tonight, take her some samples of Tender.'

He kissed her chastely on the forehead. 'Give her my love if you do.'

'I will, Cormac. Have a nice time.'

She watched him leave with tears in her eyes. In a few hours' time he might well be holding Andrea in his arms. Tonight, they would go to bed together. It hurt so much, just thinking about it, that she got a pain in her chest and wondered if her heart was breaking into a million little pieces.

While Cormac was driving down to London, his sister, Orla, was being examined by an astounded doctor who had just been informed that she was pregnant. Across the room a nurse glared at her, shocked and angry.

'An accident, I assume,' the doctor said coldly. 'You should have been more careful in your condition. I'll arrange for a termination straight away.'

'It wasn't an accident,' Orla said cheerfully. 'It was deliberate. And I don't want a termination, I want the baby, if that's all right with you.'

The doctor gasped, the nurse snorted. 'Since you ask, it's not all right,' the doctor snapped. 'It's one of the most stupid things I've ever heard. To be blunt, Mrs Lavin, you're dying. You might not live long enough to bring the baby to full term. Having a child in your condition is quite mad.'

'I *am* mad,' Orla agreed. 'And I will live long enough for me baby to be born. I *will*. I swear it.' She grinned. 'Though I might not breastfeed.'

The nurse rudely butted in, 'And who'll look after it?'

'The whole of Bootle.'

'What brought this on, pray?' the doctor enquired while the nurse tut-tutted. 'The wish to have a child under such dire circumstances.'

'Well, both me sisters are expecting, as well as me eldest daughter. I didn't want to be left out. Besides . . .' Orla paused.

'Besides what?' the doctor prompted.

'Normally, I wouldn't have dreamt of having another baby. But things aren't normal, are they? I'll be bringing a child into the world that wouldn't have been born otherwise. It seems to be a fruitful thing to do with me last few months on earth.'

The doctor's face broke into an unexpected smile. 'That's rather tortured reasoning, Mrs Lavin. Even so, I admire your spirit. I'll have your notes transferred to the maternity hospital straight away where my friend, Dr Abrahams, will look after you from now on. I'll ask him to keep me informed of your progress. You can be assured he will do all he can to see you have a healthy baby.' He went over to the desk and behind his back Orla stuck out her tongue at the nurse.

Alice opened the door to the house in Pearl Street in answer to Vicky's knock. 'Hello, luv. Come in. Orla will be pleased to see you.'

Vicky gasped when she was ushered into the parlour. 'I didn't realise you were having a party.' Every chair was occupied and there were people sitting on the floor. The light was switched off and dozens of candles and night lights burnt steadily on the mantelpiece. The flames flickered wildly from a sudden draught. There was music, very subdued, from a record player in the corner: Frank Sinatra singing 'Pennies from Heaven'. Voices came from the living room, the rattle of dishes from the kitchen.

'It's not a party,' Alice said. 'It's often like this. You must come more, luv. The world and his wife are welcome as far as Orla is concerned.'

'Vicky!' Orla shouted from across the room. Her cheeks were flushed, her eyes brighter than the candles. She looked more alive than anyone else in the room, in a white satin kimono, vividly patterned, and high-heeled red shoes. Her face was heavily made up and she wore too much jewellery. 'Give us a kiss. Everyone who comes has to give me a kiss. What would you like to drink? Micky, someone, get Vicky a drink.'

'I'd like a glass of white wine, please,' Vicky said to the young man who was Cormac's cousin. His name was Maurice, she remembered. She went over and kissed Orla on the cheek. 'I've brought you some samples of our new perfume. It's called Tender.'

'Tender is the night,' Orla crooned. 'Let's try some.' She unscrewed the tiny bottle and dabbed behind her ears. The heady scent of spring flowers mingled with the smell of melting wax. 'Oh, it's the gear. You and Cormac will be millionaires one day.'

'You've given me an idea for our next one. It's going to be more musky than this, for evenings. We could call this one Tender Mornings and the other Tender Nights. It would probably be best if we brought them out together.'

As was her way, Vicky melted into the background and found Maurice by the door with her wine. Fion was smiling up at her from the settee. She patted the arm. 'Sit down, Vic.'

'Thank you,' Vicky whispered. 'Who are all these people?'

'Laceys, mostly. Don't forget, there's fourteen of us altogether, seventeen with Bernadette and her kids, and twenty-five if you include Uncle Billy's lot. Some people are neighbours, some are friends from school.' Fion laughed. 'When I was young I could never understand why our Orla was so popular. She was horrible to everyone as far as I could see, yet they all liked her. I used to be as nice as pie, but no one liked me a bit.'

'I'm sure that's not true.'

'It is. It might still be true for all I know. The thing is, I don't care any more.'

'You'd never think Orla was . . .' Vicky blushed. She'd been about to say something very tactless.

'Dying?' Fion supplied. 'Oh, it's all right. You can say it quite openly. We all do. Orla doesn't mind. You've heard of people who make a drama out of a crisis, well that's what Orla's doing with knobs on. The sicker she gets, the more dramatic the crisis will get. She's even got her stage make-up on, see! In a few months' time we'll all be gathered round her bed waving candles and singing hymns, and she'll be smiling at us angelically from the pillow. She's enjoying herself no end.' Fion's voice changed, became softer. 'I don't half admire her. I didn't realise how much I loved her till the last few weeks. She's got more character in her little finger than most people have in their whole body. Did you know she's expecting a baby?'

'Yes, Cormac said. It's incredible news. And you are too – congratulations.'

'Ta. Can you feel it?'

'The baby?'

'No, the atmosphere. The whole house is throbbing with emotion. It's almost tangible. Every now and then I have to catch me breath.'

'Yes, I think I can, feel it, that is.' But she wasn't part of it. Vicky felt more like an observer than a participant in the tragic, enchanted events taking place in the tiny house in Pearl Street. She wished with all her heart she were a Lacey and these people would belong to her and she to them.

Cormac stared up at the third-floor window of the house in Camden. It was an elegant house, slightly shabby, situated on a busy road full of traffic on its way to and from the centre of London. The curtains on the window that so attracted his attention were tightly drawn against the brilliant sunshine of a lovely May morning. Perhaps Andrea was still asleep after her night out with her brute of a boyfriend. Perhaps they were *both* still asleep.

He'd looked like a brute to Cormac. His name was Alex and he had a remarkably heavy build for a banker, as well as a coarse face, a rasping voice and a plummy accent. He'd hated him on the spot.

Worst of all, Andrea hadn't been the least bit pleased to see him. She'd actually been reluctant to let him in, turning her face away when he tried to kiss her – he'd arrived in London late afternoon the day before and had driven straight to her flat. Alex had yet to make an appearance.

'I didn't answer your letters because I didn't want to,' she said coldly. She wore tight black trousers and a long silky blouse. Her perfect feet were bare, the toenails painted crimson. 'Anyway, I've been away for most of the time since Christmas, in the States doing a fashion shoot. We went all over the place. I didn't find your letters till I got back last week. Did you need to send so many?'

'I thought we were in love,' Cormac stammered. 'I thought . . .' He stared at her lovely cold face. 'Weren't we?'

'You may have been, darling. I certainly wasn't.'

'But you said . . .'

'People say all sorts of things in the heat of passion. They don't have to mean them.'

'*I* did.'

Her expression softened slightly. 'I'm afraid *I* didn't, Cormac. I thought we were just having a nice little affair to pass the time. I won't deny that I enjoyed it. But it meant nothing.' Her smooth brow puckered in a frown. 'I could have sworn you felt the same, darling. You didn't give the impression of being madly in love.'

A key had turned in the door, and a figure in a pinstriped suit carrying a bowler hat, a brolly, and a briefcase lumbered in: Alex.

'Who's this?' he said suspiciously – and rudely, Cormac thought.

'Remember that little job I did a few months ago for a company called Lacey's of Liverpool?' Andrea trilled. 'Well, this is Cormac Lacey. Cormac, meet my boyfriend, Alex Everett.'

'How do you do,' Cormac said courteously as he shook hands with a reluctant Alex who didn't speak. 'Let me know, won't you, Andrea, if you'd like to do the job again? As I said, we're launching the perfume in June.'

'I'm sure I would, Cormac.'

'Why doesn't he get in touch with the agency?' Alex growled.

'Don't be such a sourpuss, darling. It's only natural he should approach me personally. I was best friends with Cormac and his partner, Vicky. Wasn't I, Cormac?'

'The very best,' Cormac agreed.

He'd left the flat, thought about driving back to Liverpool straight away, but felt too tired, so booked into a hotel nearby. He lay in bed for ages, staring impassively at the ceiling, feeling curiously empty, trying to discern what was wrong with him. Dawn was breaking by the time he fell asleep. Even so, he woke little more than an hour later, too early for breakfast. He left immediately to come and stare at Andrea's window.

Something in him was missing, a chemical in his brain maybe, because Andrea was right. He hadn't been in love with her. He'd realised almost straight away, as soon as he'd left the flat, expecting to be heartbroken, but finding he didn't care. He'd *thought* he was in love. He'd badly wanted to be. It was what men and women did: fall in love, get married, have children. The same thing had happened with Pol with whom he'd expected to spend the rest of his life, yet hadn't minded too much handing over to his cousin, Maurice.

Andrea was a shallow human being, he told himself, and if he hadn't been so anxiously looking for a soulmate he wouldn't have allowed himself to be so easily taken in.

Why was he gazing at the window of this shallow human being who could well appear any minute accompanied by her brutish banker boyfriend in his bowler hat?

Cormac had no idea. It was as if he expected the window, glinting so brightly in the sunshine, to send him back an answer, tell him what was missing.

The thing had gone, the link that was missing, the night of his twenty-first when Aunt Cora had informed him Alice wasn't his mam. He hadn't been able to love anyone since then. There was a coldness in his heart. He wasn't sure who he was any more, where he came from, precisely where he stood in the world.

If only Vicky were there and he could tell her how he felt. He could talk to Vicky about anything on earth in a way he'd never talked to anyone else. He'd never discussed what Aunt Cora had told him because he'd never felt the need. But he felt the need now. Vicky would tell him what was was wrong with him. She had answers, solutions, for every problem on earth. He urgently wanted Vicky and it would take hours to get back to St Helens when they could speak. In which case he'd telephone. There was a call box in the lobby of the hotel where he'd stayed.

Cormac ran like the wind back to the hotel. In the lobby he emptied his pockets of change and arranged the coins in little piles on the box: pennies, sixpences, shillings. He was about to dial the factory when he remembered it wasn't yet eight o'clock and Vicky would still be at home.

'Hello.' Her voice was quietly efficient when she answered.

'Vicky, it's Cormac.' The words tumbled over each other. 'I need to talk. I'm in a terrible state, Vic. There's something wrong.'

'Cormac! Have you had an accident or something? Is Andrea all right? Are you still in London?'

'No to the first question, yes to the others. Oh, damn! This thing needs more coins already. Hold on a mo.'

'Give me the number and I'll ring back,' Vicky said crisply. 'A long-distance call will eat money as fast as you speak.'

Cormac shoved a pile of pennies in the box, reeled off the number, put down the receiver and snatched it up again a few seconds later when it rang.

'You know you asked once why I called Alice Alice?' he said immediately, sinking down on to a black plastic chair. The long leaves of a pot plant brushed against his cheek.

'I remember, Cormac. And you're calling now, a whole year later, all the way from London, to tell me why?'

'Because she isn't me mother. Aunt Cora is. I was born the same night as Maurice and she swapped us over in the hospital.' His voice rose to a wail. 'Oh, Vic! I don't know who I am. Least I do, but I'm not the person I want to be, the person I always thought I was. I'm someone else entirely.'

There was silence from the other end of the line for quite a while as Vicky took in this startling fact. 'Don't be silly, Cormac,' she said eventually. 'You're Cormac Lacey and you always have been. You belong to Alice. They put you in her arms in the hospital and she took you home and brought you up. As far as Alice is concerned, you're her son.'

'And as far as Auntie Cora is concerned I'm *her* son.'

There was another pause, then Vicky said in a strangely puzzled voice, 'But you can't be.'

'Yes, I can, Vic. Somehow, I believed Cora when she said she switched me and Maurice around. It's the sort of thing she would do.' Cormac shuddered. 'She's evil.' And she was his mother!

Then Vicky said in what Cormac called her 'schoolmistressy' voice, 'I'm surprised at you, Cormac. You're supposed to be so clever. How could you not know such a basic fact?'

'What are you talking about? What basic fact?'

'That a brown-eyed couple can't have blue-eyed children. It's something to do with genes. I thought it was something everyone knew. Your Uncle Billy has brown eyes and so does your Aunt Cora – I remember noticing what a strange brown they were at your Fion's wedding.'

'Not everyone's got a mind like an encyclopaedia, Vic,' Cormac snapped. 'People can't be expected to know everything.' He gulped. 'Does that mean . . .?'

'It means that if it's true your aunt swapped you round with Maurice, you weren't actually her baby to swap in the first place.'

'Then whose baby am I?' Cormac shrieked. A man had come into the lobby with a suitcase and was staring at him strangely.

'Maybe the nurses got confused and put the two Lacey babies in the wrong cots in the first place,' Vicky said sensibly. 'Cora merely put you back in the right one.'

'I'd love to believe that, Vic. Except – Mam told us this loads of times – it was hell on earth in the hospital the night I was born. There was an air raid and everyone was moved down into the cellar and back again. A woman was brought in who'd been found in the wreckage of her house about to give birth. I could belong to any bloody one.'

The man with the suitcase clearly thought he was sharing the lobby with a lunatic. He hurried into the dining room.

'Oh, Cormac, don't think about it now. Come home. But drive carefully. We'll talk about it tonight over dinner.'

'All right, Vic.' His voice trembled. 'I can't wait to see you.'

'Nor me you, Cormac.'

He replaced the receiver. Vicky had created more questions than answers, but he felt better after talking to her. In fact, he felt better all round. He sniffed. The smell of fried bacon came from the dining room and he suddenly felt very hungry. Mistakes had been made when he was born, but what did it matter after such a long time? And perhaps, you never knew, Cora had put him in the right cot after all. If so, he had much to thank her for. After he'd eaten he'd give Mam a ring; he still had plenty of change. They'd hardly spoken since she'd gone to live in Birkdale in her posh new house. Then he'd go home to Vicky.

It made Alice feel dead peculiar to get out of bed, pull back the curtains, and be met with nothing but the sight of her own back garden and miles and miles of sky. Apart from the birds, there wasn't a sound to be heard. She'd been used to coming face to face with a row of tightly packed houses across the street, hearing the clink of milk bottles, cars, voices as people went to work.

Every morning she found herself leaving earlier and earlier for the hairdresser's, coming home later and later. Pretty soon she'd be sleeping there! What would it be like in the winter? She dreaded to think.

She missed having friends in the same street or the next one, the library and the post office being just round the corner, as well as every sort of shop a person could possibly need. Instead, she had to drive everywhere, even to Mass.

Bernadette claimed she wasn't giving the bungalow a chance. She came to visit and ran her fingers along the cream worktop, looked out of the window at the pretty garden where Ruth and Ian were playing, and said, 'It's beautiful here, Ally. You'll soon get used to it.'

'I suppose so, Bernie. I'm trying hard.' She sniffed. Bernadette was the only person who knew she hadn't settled in. 'What have Cora and Billy done to me old house?'

'I don't know, luv, and I'm not likely to, am I? I can't see them asking me inside.' She regarded Alice sternly. 'The trouble with you, Alice Lacey, is you've made a ton of money but don't know how to enjoy it.'

Alice sighed. 'I'd give it away, except no one will take it. Only Orla let me buy her a car.'

'Talking of Orla, how is she? I haven't seen her for a day or so.'

'Driving everybody mad, including Micky, though he loves it. I wouldn't have thought it possible for a woman in Orla's state to get on so many people's nerves.'

Maeve Adams felt the first twinge of what might have been a contraction soon after breakfast. Martin had just gone to work. She glanced at her watch, calmly made a cup of tea and waited for the next twinge. It came half an hour later and was stronger than the first. The baby was on its way!

Glancing at her watch again, she washed the dishes and was just making the beds when a wave of pain passed through her tummy that couldn't possibly be described as a twinge.

She cautiously made her way downstairs, took the suitcase, already packed, out of the understairs cupboard and, in quick succession, rang for a taxi, the hospital in Southport to say she was coming, Martin at work to tell him he was about to become a father – should he be interested, that was – then her mother at the hairdresser's. Finally she rang her sisters to let them know that the first of the four Lacey babies due to arrive that year was already on its way.

'Good luck, sis,' Orla sang. 'As for me, I do believe me bump's starting to show a bit.'

In the taxi, she took deep breaths all the way. The driver assured her he'd once delivered a baby on the back seat, so there was no need to worry if it came early. Maeve worried all the same. The contractions were getting closer and more painful with each mile.

'You look very calm.' The nurse smiled when she walked into the hospital, the taxi driver coming behind with her case.

'Well, I don't like to make a fuss.'

The labour was swift and very painful, but still Maeve didn't make a fuss. She just gritted her teeth, took more deep breaths and got on with it. Her little boy was born within the hour. He weighed eight pounds, three ounces.

'He's beautiful,' said the midwife.

'All babies are beautiful,' Maeve said serenely. 'Can I hold him? I've been waiting nearly thirty-six years for this.'

'Only for a minute, dear. We've got to get you sewn up. You need at least three stitches.'

Maeve was propped against the pillow, her baby wrapped in a sheet and placed in her arms. He felt big and warm. He was real. He was a real, live baby, with real hands and feet and perfect little fingers, a snub nose, a tiny rosebud mouth, hardly any hair and sleepy blue eyes. And he could move. He could wave his hands and wriggle his body. He could make a noise, the sweetest sound she had ever heard, a squeaky croak. And he was hers! Maeve Adams was a mother at last. Her calm deserted her and she burst into tears, just as Martin walked into the delivery room, slightly dishevelled, his tie crooked and his usually neat hair on end.

He stood at the foot of the bed, looked at her, then at the baby. 'So, you've done it,' he said in a voice devoid of expression.

'Yes, I've done it, Martin. This is our son. I thought we might call him Christopher.' Maeve wiped her eyes with the corner of the baby's sheet. 'Isn't he beautiful?'

Martin edged closer. 'He's got no hair.'

'Lots of babies are born without hair. It'll soon grow. Would you like to hold him?'

'I'm not sure. I might drop him.' He came closer still. 'He doesn't look like either of us.'

'There's plenty of time,' Maeve said placidly. 'I thought he looked a little bit like Grandad.'

'He's got my mother's mouth.' Martin suddenly sat on the edge of the bed and gathered his wife and his new son in his arms. 'Oh, Maeve, I'm so *scared*,' he said hoarsely. 'I'm scared you'll love him more than me, that he'll take my place in your heart. I'm scared to love him myself in case he dies, babies do sometimes. What if he's unhappy at school, gets bullied? What if he goes off the rails when he gets older, the way your cousin, Maurice, did? Or he runs away like Fion? How must your mother feel about Orla? We're going to worry about him for the rest of our lives and I don't think I can cope.' He began to cry. 'We were so happy before, darling. Why did you have to spoil everything by having a baby?'

'*I* wasn't happy, Martin, and I suspect you weren't either. No, don't argue.' She put her hand over his mouth when he opened it to speak. 'We cared about such trivial things. Our baby's *real*. Oh, yes, he'll be a worry, but the world would come to an end if everyone stopped having babies because they were scared of the future. If your parents and mine had felt like that, neither of us would have been born. As to loving him more than you, I'll love him differently, that's all. You'll find the same.'

The door opened, the midwife came in and clapped her hands. 'Would you mind waiting outside, Mr Adams. I'm about to sew your wife back together. I'll take baby into the nursery and you can admire him through the window. There are more visitors outside who can't wait to see this lovely little chap.'

Alice was in the corridor with Bernadette and Fion. A few minutes later Orla and Micky arrived, Orla proudly displaying her bump. Then Martin's parents, and later on his sister and his niece. Cormac came with Vicky. By then, Maeve had been wheeled into a ward, exhausted but extremely pleased with herself.

Martin felt dazed as he was hugged and kissed, his hand was shaken, his shoulder punched, and he was congratulated so many times he felt as if he must have done something uniquely remarkable to deserve such approbation.

The men decided there was just time enough to wet the baby's head before the pubs closed. On the way out, they passed the nursery, where Martin paused and looked at his son lying wide awake in his cot. By God, he was a magnificent baby, far superior to every other one there. He longed to pick him up and cuddle him. He caught his breath. In another week's time, Maeve would bring him home and he could pick up his son whenever he pleased.

'What it is to be a Lacey!' Vicky remarked to Cormac on the way back to St Helens in his car. 'There's always something going on. If there isn't a new baby, or several new babies, in the pipeline, then someone's getting married or a party's thrown for no reason at all as far as I can see. All my family's ever celebrated is my parents' silver wedding. We merely went to dinner on my twenty-first because there weren't enough people to make a party.'

'We have funerals too,' Cormac said soberly. 'I think there's one on the cards in the not too distant future.'

'I hope not. Your Orla looks as if she could live for ever. What's coming next? Whose baby is due first, Fion's or Orla's?'

'Neither. Lulu's due in October. At least that's when she's coming back to England. The other two are expected to make an appearance about a month later. By the way,' he said, changing gear, 'you forgot about the wedding.'

'I didn't know there was a wedding. Who's getting married?'

'I can't tell you yet because the woman hasn't agreed.'

'You mean, there might not be a wedding?'

'Not if the woman doesn't agree.'

'You're talking in circles, Cormac,' Vicky said patiently. 'Is she having trouble making up her mind?'

'No, it's more a matter of her not having been asked.'

She laughed. 'Then why doesn't the man ask her?'

'D'you think he should?'

'Of course he should, if he wants to marry her.'

'In that case, Vicky Weatherspoon, will you marry me?'

'I beg your pardon!'

'You heard, Vic.' He grabbed her knee, removing his hand immediately when they had to turn a corner. 'I want you to be my wife and I desperately hope you want me for a husband, because I can't live without you.' He looked at her sideways. 'What do you say?'

'Yes, I'll marry you, Cormac.' She was amazed her voice sounded so sensible when she really wanted to scream with delight. It was the question she'd been aching for since the day, years ago, that they'd first met. In her wildest dreams she never thought he'd ask. Now he had and she would savour the words for the rest of her life. She would have preferred the surroundings to be more romantic: a candlelit restaurant, champagne and for Cormac to have gone down on one knee. Maybe in real life that didn't often happen.

'When?' he demanded. He was grinning. He looked incredibly happy and all because Vicky Weatherspoon had said 'yes'.

'Before all the babies are due so everyone's sure to be there. Say September.'

'September it is. We'll buy an engagement ring on Saturday. What sort would you like?'

A round one, she wanted to say. Any sort of stone. In fact, a piece of string would do. 'A diamond solitaire,' she said dazedly.

'What will your folks have to say?'

'Oh, they'll be thrilled. *I'm* thrilled.' She turned to him to explain exactly how thrilled she was that they were getting married, to tell him how much she loved him, always had, always would, but something prevented her. She merely pressed her shoulder against his and said nothing. Theirs would be an unequal partnership. He looked happy, but there'd been something casual about his proposal, as if he had taken for granted what her answer would be. They were comfortable together and, on his side, there wasn't the passion he'd clearly felt for Andrea. He hadn't told her that he loved her. There was still time for that, but Vicky knew he would never love her as much as she loved him – it might embarrass him to know how much. She would have to hold back a little, stay calm, be cool, match his emotion with her own.

Despite this, Vicky's heart throbbed with a dazed, exultant happiness. Before the year was out she would be Mrs Cormac Lacey and, whatever the circumstances were, she couldn't wait.

19

The three sisters had never been so close. Every afternoon Fion and Maeve, with baby Christopher, would arrive in Pearl Street to sit with Orla and gossip, play cards for pennies, swap jokes – Orla had learnt some that were very near the knuckle during her time on the road. Fion laughed heartily and Maeve winced.

Micky had given the backyard a fresh coat of paint and a set of white plastic garden furniture had fallen off the inevitable lorry accompanied by a red and white striped umbrella. Baskets of flowers hung on the walls. There was a tub of hydrangeas in each corner. On sunny days the women sat outside – it was like a pavement café in Paris, Orla said once. Micky grinned foolishly before escaping to the pub for a drink, as he was inclined to do when the house was taken over by three women and a baby.

'I bet it's not a bit like Paris,' Orla said after he'd gone. 'But it pleases Micky no end to hear me say it. I'm learning to be nice, though it's a bit late in the day.'

Alice usually managed to join them for an hour and when Cormac discovered his family met every day, he came over from St Helens whenever he could, so that the five Laceys could be together – after all, time was precious. In a matter of months there would be only four of them left. They talked about the years when they'd only had each other, before husbands and children had appeared on the scene. They talked about John. Alice found it upsetting that they could remember so little of the time when everything had been perfect in the house in Amber Street, before their father had had the accident and everything had changed.

'In my mind, there was always a horrible atmosphere,' Fion claimed.

'Same here.' Maeve nodded.

'I remember hating him so much,' said Orla.

'I loved him.' Cormac made a rueful face. 'Trouble was, I always had the feeling he didn't love me back.'

'He had other things on his mind.'

'What do you mean, Mam?' asked Cormac. 'What other things?'

Alice hesitated before deciding they were old enough to know the truth, old enough for it not to hurt them any more. She told them about the day

Lulu was born when she'd gone round to B.E.D.S. and found John with a new young family.

'You mean he dumped us for another lot?' Orla gasped, outraged.

'No, it wasn't you, his children, that he dumped, it was me, his wife. He found a girl as damaged as himself. But she got better and he began to treat her the same way as he'd done me, and she left him.'

'Poor dad,' Cormac said, always the softest. She was glad he was engaged to Vicky who she felt sure would never hurt him as his father had done.

It was strange that Fion, thirty-eight, but a strapping, healthy woman, was the one who suffered most during the early months of pregnancy. She was often sick, her legs swelled, she had dizzy spells, went off her food. Whereas Orla, the invalid, bloomed. Her hair was thick and glossy, her eyes star bright. Her skin had the texture of the thinnest, finest china and she had never smiled so much. The baby was growing well in her womb.

'She's a blessed baby,' Orla cooed. 'She's charmed.'

'She?' said Micky.

'Oh, it's a girl. She's another me. She's coming to take my place after I've gone.'

'No one can ever take your place, sweetheart.' Micky knelt in front of the chair and laid his face against her stomach. He felt the sharp bones of her hips under his hands and could have sworn he could hear his baby's heart beating. He wondered how he would manage to get through the next few months without completely breaking down. It was a tremendous effort always to appear composed, to look after the endless guests, engage in conversation, when he was being torn apart inside.

Orla was the only woman he'd ever wanted. He'd loved her since they were fourteen and they'd been in the same class together at school. But this love, burning, wholehearted and totally committed, hadn't been enough to make her happy. She had slept with other men. She had walked out on him. If it weren't for the cancer, she would be in an office in St Helens dreaming of even better things. She'd only returned to him and their children because she was dying.

It made him feel guilty for being so glad that she was back. For Micky, a dying Orla was better than no Orla at all and there would be nothing left for him after she had gone.

She ran her fingers through his hair. 'Cheer up, luv. Life is for enjoying, not enduring.'

'Don't say things like that.'

'Why not? It's true.' She lifted up his head, rather painfully, by the ears, and slid into his arms. 'If I'd had a bit more sense, I would have enjoyed meself more when I had the opportunity. And I'd like to think you've got a lot of years left to enjoy. I'll be keeping me eye on you, Micky Lavin, from up in heaven.'

He kissed her. 'They'll never take you in heaven, Orla. You'll be keeping an eye on me from a place much warmer than that.'

Lacey's of Liverpool perfumes were proving a great success. Tender Nights and Tender Mornings came on to the market in June. The lovely face of Andrea Pryce featured prominently in a press and television advertising campaign carried out from London. Andrea and Cormac never met again.

All the big Liverpool stores had extensive displays of the local products: Lewis's, Owen Owen's, George Henry Lee's. Cormac and Vicky were looking for a bigger factory so they could expand their range to include lipstick and face powder.

'In a few years' time we'll do an entire range of make-up,' Cormac boasted.

'How can you have aromatherapy mascara and eyebrow pencil?' Orla wanted to know.

'Don't ask awkward questions, sis. We're working on it.'

'Do you wish you were part of it, luv?' Micky asked when Cormac had gone.

'I'm having a baby, Micky, which is far more important.'

Cora Lacey helped herself to a couple of perfumes while she was cleaning the Strand Road salon, the morning one and the night one, though personally she couldn't tell the difference. They would do as a birthday present for Pol, save buying something.

Alice noticed, but tactfully kept her mouth shut. Cora was an excellent cleaner and as long as she didn't make off with one of the dryers she didn't care.

At the end of August, six months into her pregnancy, Fion started to feel better. The feeling of constant nausea went away, along with the dizziness and the swollen legs. She ate like a horse and developed a passion for apples, which were at least healthy.

Fion, though, would have preferred to remain sick, or indeed feel much worse, if it could have prevented her sister's sudden deterioration.

Orla was rapidly losing weight, getting thinner and thinner, almost daily it seemed to concerned onlookers. She was having pain more severe than she had known humanly possible. Every nerve in her body shrieked in raw agony. It was the cancer, not the baby.

The baby was all right. The baby was fine. Dr Abrahams, who had adopted her as his special project, confirmed that her child was coming along well when Orla went to see him at the hospital.

'Would you like some painkillers?' he asked for the fourth week running.

'No, doctor.' Orla shook her head violently. 'I'll not forget what Thalidomide did to unborn babies. There's no way I'm taking so much as an aspirin in case it harms me little girl. I'd sooner have pains than tablets, any day.'

'You're a very brave woman, Mrs Lavin.'

'No, I'm not, doctor. I'm a realist. Anyroad, I've learnt that, if I notch meself up a gear, the pain goes away and I can't feel it any more.'

The doctor looked at the starry eyes in the thin face. 'You're a very remarkable woman then, Mrs Lavin. Will you allow me to say that?'

'I've always wanted to be remarkable at something, doctor. I'm glad to have managed it at last.'

Micky's sole reason for existing was to take care of Orla. The children felt the same. They came straight home from work every night to sit with their mam and hold her hand, to fetch and carry, to bring her anything on earth she wanted.

To please them, to make them feel needed, to make up for the hurt that she had caused them, she asked for a daily newspaper and made a show of reading it, requested cups of tea and glasses of lemonade she didn't feel like drinking. Maisie massaged her feet which she found extremely irritating. She pretended an interest in football, which she loathed, but Micky and the boys were passionate about it. It meant they could watch the – far too many – matches on the telly without feeling they should be watching something on another channel that Orla would in fact have found ten times more interesting.

September, and the weather was sunny, gently warm. The trees in North Park began to shed their russet leaves and the flowers in the Lavins' backyard bent their heads and died. The big petal balls on the hydrangeas turned brown. Pretty soon they would become brittle. Next spring they would have to be pruned to make way for new blossoms.

Orla sat on a white plastic chair, knowing she would never see this happen. But her baby would. She laid her hands on her stomach. The baby had been very still this morning. She felt a moment of fear, closed her eyes, concentrated hard and directed all the goodness left in her emaciated body on to the baby, now fully formed in her womb. Her little daughter gave her an almighty kick. Orla gasped with pain and relief.

The other pain she'd learnt to live with. It didn't matter any more. She'd stepped outside it.

Alice woke up every morning in the silent bedroom of her silent house with a deep sense of foreboding. The next few months would be nightmarish. What would Christmas be like with one of her children gone for ever? She also felt unreasonably depressed that Cormac, her baby, was getting married, which she might not have done if it hadn't been for Orla. There was a saying: 'A daughter is a daughter for the rest of her life. A son is a son until he takes a wife.' She was losing two children. She wouldn't be needed any more. It only emphasised the fact that she was on her own. The future seemed very bleak.

Then she would get up, pull herself together and prepare for the day ahead. She never let anyone, not even Bernadette, know how low she felt.

Lulu Jackson came back from America a few days before the wedding. Gareth was to fly over nearer the time the baby – Alice's first great-grandchild – was expected the following month. Alice picked her up from Manchester airport, took her to Pearl Street to see her mother, then to the bungalow where she was to stay. There was plenty of room and she was glad of the company.

'I like your frock, luv,' she remarked. Lulu wore a spectacular yellow garment lavishly trimmed with lace with its own little lace bolero.

'It's Indian and it's not really a maternity dress. I can wear it afterwards. I brought one for Mum in cream. I thought she might like to wear it to the wedding. Oh, and I've got you a scarf, Gran. There's this lovely Indian shop right by where we live in Greenwich Village.'

As soon as they'd eaten, Lulu asked if she'd mind if she returned straight to Pearl Street. 'I'd like to spend the evening with Mum. She looks well, doesn't she? Far better than I expected. A bit thin, that's all.'

'Your mam always manages to put on a show, Lulu. And I wouldn't build up your hopes too much that she'll be at the wedding. It's not exactly close, way over the other side of Warrington. Apart from the hospital, she hasn't been outside the house in months.'

Lulu's pretty blue eyes filled with tears. 'She was always bursting with life, me mum. She was the only person who encouraged me to marry Gareth. Everyone else thought marrying an artist was daft. And she thought going to New York was a great idea.'

'She saw you doing the things she'd wanted to do herself,' Alice said sadly. 'Anyroad, luv, come on. I was intending to spend the evening at Pearl Street meself. You'll find the house bursting at the seams.'

It was raining steadily on the Saturday of the wedding. The sky was a miserable grey, heavy with clouds, and there wasn't the faintest sign of blue.

Lulu emerged from her room in an even more magnificent frock than the one she'd arrived in: tangerine silk with an embroidered bodice and long, loose sleeves. Her hat was merely a circle of velvet trimmed with net.

'You make me feel very drab,' Alice remarked as she glanced in the hall mirror at her plain blue suit and conventional flowered hat.

'You look lovely, Gran. But then I can never remember a time when you didn't.'

The young woman and the much older one kissed lovingly. Alice smiled. 'That's a nice thing to say, but I can't help noticing me hair's as grey as the sky outside.'

'You *still* look lovely. I hope I look as beautiful when I've got grey hair.'

'Flattery will get you everywhere, Lulu. I'll be changing me will in your favour as soon as I get back. We'd better be off. The coach is due in Marsh Lane at half past ten and I've promised to show meself in the hairdresser's before we leave.'

A coach had been hired for the bridegroom's guests. The men were pleased. They wouldn't need their cars so could drink as much as they liked.

Alice parked outside the Lavins', where the door was wide open, despite the rain. She waved at Fion and Jerry who were just about to go inside – Fion looked big enough to be carrying half a dozen babies.

'Tell your mam I've nipped round Opal Street. I'll be back in a minute,' she said to Lulu. 'Pass us that umbrella out the glove compartment, there's a luv.'

'My, don't you look a sight for sore eyes,' Patsy O'Leary gushed when Alice entered the salon. Patsy was silver-haired now. Her daughter, Daisy, with the long, gleaming ringlets, had never gone near the stage when she grew up. Nowadays Patsy boasted endlessly about her grandchildren, all of whom were exceptionally talented in their various ways, or so she claimed. She had never ceased to get on Alice's nerves, but she had grown fond of the woman who had worked for her for more than a quarter of a century.

She nodded at her other staff and promised to bring them a piece of wedding cake on Monday. They were mostly new. How many staff had she had over the years? How many customers? How many heads of hair had been permed, shampooed and set, trimmed, dyed a different colour?

'Oh, someone rang about the upstairs flat,' Patsy said. 'A man. I don't know where he heard about it. I told him it wasn't available yet. It had to be decorated.'

'I must get someone in to do it,' Alice murmured. 'I've been meaning to for ages.' Since the last tenant left in July.

'Well, you've had other things on your mind, haven't you?'

'Actually, in here could do with a coat of paint at the same time.' She glanced at the walls, where the paint was peeling off in places. 'I hadn't noticed before. I'm usually too busy working.' It worried her that she was letting the place fall to pieces around her ears, the way Myrtle Rimmer had done, and another, younger woman would end up taking it over, bringing it back to scratch. She suddenly laughed.

'What's so funny?' asked one of the customers.

'Nothing. I was just having a flight of fancy, rather a morbid one.'

'This is no time to be morbid,' Patsy admonished. 'Your only son's getting married today.'

'So he is. I'd better be going.'

Orla was wearing the cream dress Lulu had brought from America. The thin material lay over the bulge in her stomach and Alice felt concern for the tiny child curled up inside the tissue flesh, the fragile bones.

For once, Orla looked very down. Apart from Micky, Alice was the only other person there. Everyone else must be waiting in the coach. 'I wish I was coming, Mam.'

'So do I, Orla, luv.'

'We're going to have a fine ould time,' Micky said heartily, though Alice sensed a strain of desperation in his voice. 'On our own for a change, nice and quiet. There's a match on the telly this avvy.'

'Did you see the children, Mam? *Our* children. Didn't our Lulu look a treat in that frock? It's funny to think I'll be a grandma soon. And Maisie's wearing a mini-dress – I hope Vicky's family aren't too disgusted. It hardly covers her behind.' Orla's mouth twisted and Alice realised she was trying to laugh. 'It's just the sort of frock I'd have worn meself at her age. And the lads, they had new suits – I bet you can guess where they came from. They looked dead handsome. Oh, I'm so proud of me kids, Mam.'

'And I'm proud of mine, particularly this one.' She stroked her daughter's face. 'You know Cormac and Vicky are coming to say goodbye before they leave for their honeymoon, don't you? Vicky's keeping her wedding dress on so you can see her in all her glory – are you listening, luv?'

Orla's eyes seemed to be floating backwards into her head. Alice touched her arm, frightened, and the eyes flickered and fixed on her mother's face. 'Yes, Vicky's coming. Have a nice time, Mam. I'll see you later.'

'She's been doing that all morning,' Micky said worriedly as he showed Alice out. 'Drifting away, as it were, not hearing.'

Alice hesitated by the door. 'Perhaps it would be best if I stayed.'

'Cormac will only cancel the wedding if you don't turn up. Go and have a nice time, like Orla said.'

She managed to stay dry-eyed throughout the entire ceremony, mainly because Mrs Weatherspoon, who looked so fierce and capable when she marched into church, made a desperate show of herself, sobbing helplessly, getting louder and louder, until the noise resembled a banshee's wail. The guests on the bridegroom's side began to smile, the children giggled and the noise woke up six-month-old Christopher, who started to howl. Cormac could hardly keep a straight face and the bride's shoulders heaved.

Alice was glad that what she had expected to be a touching occasion had turned into something resembling a pantomime or farce. She wasn't exactly in the mood for tears, particularly her own.

The light mood continued throughout the afternoon at the reception, held in a modern, rather featureless hotel. Even a shamefaced Mrs Weatherspoon was able to see the funny side of things. 'I don't know what came over me,' she said to Alice. 'I really hadn't expected to cry.'

'I expected to cry buckets, but I think it's the first wedding I've been to when I haven't shed a tear.'

The best man, Maurice Lacey, made a far better speech than anyone thought him capable of.

Cora watched him, feeling unexpectedly proud. Maurice would never be a success like Cormac, but he'd become a solid citizen, with a lovely family, a nice house in Browning Street and a reasonably well-paid job with prospects of promotion. Pol had obviously decided a long while ago that he was a better bet than Cormac, and Pol was prettier than that Vicky by a mile. Vicky had a face like the back of a bus. It was said that all brides managed to look beautiful on their wedding day, but Vicky proved an exception to the rule. Cora wouldn't have fancied having her for a daughter-in-law.

Alice was pleased to see Orla's children enjoying themselves. It would do them good to have a break, forget the tragedy they had been witnessing for so many months.

At five o'clock, Cormac came over. 'Vicky and I are leaving in a minute, Mam. We're going to Orla's first. Vicky will get changed upstairs, then we'll be off to the airport and Majorca.'

'I'll come with you, if you don't mind,' Alice said with alacrity – she was pleased that Cormac had begun to address her as 'Mam' again lately. She could never understand why he'd stopped.

'Why don't you stay and enjoy the reception? It's going on till all hours and everyone's having a whale of a time.'

'I think Micky might like some company back in Pearl Street. Orla didn't seem quite herself this morning. I'll just say goodbye to Mr and Mrs Weatherspoon.'

On the way to Bootle, Vicky sat in the back of the car, where her massive brocade crinoline dress with long puffed sleeves could be more easily accommodated. Personally, Alice thought she would have suited something much plainer so she didn't look too much like the cake but, naturally, no one had asked for her opinion.

It was still raining steadily when the car drew up in Pearl Street – it hadn't stopped all day. Alice jumped out and knocked on the door of number eleven and was surprised when no one answered. She was about to go round the back when Sheila Reilly came out of her house across the street.

'Alice. I've been keeping a lookout for you. I'm sorry, luv, but your Orla went into a coma early this avvy. Micky rang for an ambulance and she was taken to the maternity hospital. He said to tell you the minute you came back.'

'Ta, Sheila. I'll go straight away.' Alice was already on her way to her own car, which she had left parked outside the house that morning.

'Would you like a cup of tea first?' Sheila called. 'Steady your nerves, like.'

'No, thank you.'

Cormac was standing on the pavement. 'What's up, Mam?'

In a trembling voice she explained the situation. 'You go off on your honeymoon, luv. Vicky will just have to get changed in the Ladies at the airport.'

'I'll do no such thing,' Vicky said. She had rolled down the car window and was listening. 'Cormac, drive Alice to the hospital. It doesn't matter about us.'

'Get in, Mam,' Cormac said in a voice that brooked no argument and Alice did as she was told.

Micky was walking up and down the hospital corridor like a wild man. He looked as if he had, quite literally, been trying to tear out his hair. His eyes were mad with grief and Alice wondered if he'd lost his reason.

Mr and Mrs Lavin were there, Mrs Lavin sobbing uncontrollably. Alice immediately assumed the worst. Her body seemed to seize up, she could hardly speak.

'What's happened?' she croaked.

'Orla's having a Caesarean at this very minute,' Micky said raggedly. 'They don't hold out much hope for the baby. As for Orla, they think this is the end.'

'Aah!' The cry came from her very soul. Orla had invested every shred of herself into this baby. If it died, it would all have been in vain.

Cormac had been searching for somewhere to park. He came rushing up with Vicky, still in her bridal gown. Mr Lavin explained the situation and went to fetch everyone cups of tea.

They had to wait over an hour for news, though it felt more like twenty. No one spoke. It was almost seven o'clock before a nurse appeared. Alice searched her face, trying to discern from her expression if the news was good or bad. She didn't look particularly grave.

'The baby has arrived safely,' she announced and there was a concerted sigh of relief. 'It's a girl and she appears to be in surprisingly good shape, though she's only tiny, barely three pounds. She's gone straight into an incubator. Her dad can see her later on, but no one else, I'm afraid. As far as the mother is concerned, I'm sorry to say there's no change.'

Micky made no sound. He hid his face in his hands for several seconds. When he removed them his face was pale, but he was himself again. His eyes were normal. 'Orla will be pleased about the baby,' he said. For the first time he seemed to notice Cormac and Vicky. 'Isn't it time you two were on your way?'

'We'd sooner stay.' Vicky's dress rustled as she went over and embraced him and Alice thought she'd make a fine Lacey. She was pleased and proud the girl was now a member of the family.

'And I'd sooner you went,' Micky growled. 'If Orla was asked for her opinion, she'd say the same.'

'I think so too,' Alice put in. 'There's enough of us here.'

'Would you like me to ring the reception, tell the children?' Cormac asked.

'No, leave the kids be.' Micky shook his head. 'Let them enjoy themselves as long as possible. They'll know soon enough. Tara, Cormac. Tara, Vicky. Good luck.'

The newly married couple left, albeit reluctantly. Cormac said he'd telephone as soon as they reached Majorca.

Mr Lavin left to fetch more tea. A young woman walked past in a dressing gown, heavily pregnant. 'I'm just going for a walk,' she said, 'to try and bring it on. It stopped coming the minute we got here.'

Another nurse arrived and said Micky could see his new daughter. He came back after only a few minutes. 'She's so tiny,' he said gruffly, holding out his hands about twelve inches apart. 'Pretty, like a doll, with lots of fair hair.'

Mrs Lavin began to cry again. Voices and footsteps could be heard approaching and Orla's children came hurrying round the corner, their faces anxious, their eyes bright with fear.

'How's Mum?'

'Can we see her?'

'Has she had the baby?'

'Are you all right, Dad? You should have told us.'

They crowded round their father. Micky hugged them one by one and tried to answer their questions. It seemed to Alice that he'd aged since morning, when she could have sworn he didn't have a stoop. His features were blurred. He looked middle-aged. For some reason she remembered the desperate young man who'd called at the house in Amber Street all those years ago asking for Orla who was hiding upstairs and Alice was obliged to tell him lies, send him packing, though she'd tried to do it kindly.

She left the group, feeling in the way. No one had taken a blind bit of notice of her, which she found quite understandable. No doubt Fion and Maeve would arrive shortly – they'd probably taken the children home first. She found a padded bench in a quiet corridor by the closed X-ray department where she sat, feeling extremely alone, wondering how John would have felt if he were there, knowing his favourite daughter was dying. Well, once she'd been his favourite. Perhaps another daughter had taken her place, just as another woman had taken hers.

'Alice! We've been looking for you everywhere.'

It was Billy Lacey accompanied by Cora. He sat beside her and put his arm round her shoulders. 'Are you all right, luv? You look dead lonely all by yourself.'

'I'm fine.' Alice sniffed. 'Just felt like a bit of peace and quiet.'

'I don't blame you. That Mrs Lavin doesn't half go on.'

Cora sat opposite. She saw Alice grit her teeth, as if determined not to cry, unlike that other woman, Micky's mam, who was making a terrible scene, not helping things a bit. It struck her that Alice had never made a scene, not even when John had left. She'd just gritted her teeth, like she'd done now, and got on with things. When you thought about it, John Lacey hadn't been much of a catch, not compared with Billy who'd stuck by his wife through thick and thin. It had taken a long time for the penny to drop, but Cora realised she'd married the right brother after all. As for Cormac,

Alice was welcome to him and his ugly missus. She'd prefer Maurice and Pol any day.

Thinking about it, Cora couldn't remember anything that Alice had done to spite her. In fact, she'd only tried to help. It was Alice who'd collected her from the police station that time, then given her a job even after she'd heard about the pensions Cora had been fraudulently collecting all them years.

There was a funny sensation in her stomach as she leaned over and patted Alice on the knee. 'Everything's going to be all right, luv,' she said consolingly, even though she knew, and Alice and Billy knew, that it wasn't.

Then Billy stood up and slapped his thigh. 'Come on, ould girl. We'd better start making tracks. It's still raining cats and dogs outside and I don't know if there's any buses running at this time of night.'

Cora stood up and linked his arm, and they went home together to Bootle.

During the long night that followed the relatives were allowed to see the patient once, a few at a time. Alice went in with Fion and Maeve.

Orla was lying peacefully still, long, dark lashes resting on her white cheeks, lips curved in a slight smile. Fion gasped. 'I've never seen her look so beautiful!'

'She looks about sixteen,' Maeve whispered.

Alice said nothing. She bent and kissed the cold, smiling lips, and wondered if she would ever kiss them again.

In a hotel room in Majorca, which smelt of strangely scented blossoms and chloride from the pool below, and where the blue, luminous water of the Mediterranean could be seen from the balcony, Cormac put down the phone. 'No change.' He sighed. 'There are times when I wish I smoked. I have a feeling a cigarette would be a great help at the moment.'

'It would also be very bad for you,' Vicky said primly.

'I've heard there are people around who say the same thing about sex.'

'Oh!' Vicky looked nonplussed. She was sitting up in bed with nothing on, a sheet chastely covering her breasts – she'd only been a married woman for a matter of hours and nudity took some getting used to. 'Oh, they can't possibly be right about sex.'

Cormac grinned. 'If those people are so very wrong – about sex, that is – then I assume it would be OK if we did it again.'

She blushed. 'It would be OK as far as I'm concerned.'

'As we are the only two people whose opinion matters, I suggest we do it immediately, though it will be necessary for you to remove that sheet.'

Vicky removed the sheet.

The hospital was very quiet. Occasionally a baby cried, there were footsteps in other corridors far away. Outside the room where Orla lay, her husband, her children, her sisters and her mother hardly spoke, and when they did it was in subdued murmurs. Mr and Mrs Lavin had gone home long ago.

Fion felt ashamed of how much she longed to be at home, under her own roof, with Jerry's warm body in bed beside her and the kids safely asleep not far away. They weren't the sort of couple who lived in each other's pockets, but she badly missed her husband right now. She squeezed the hand of Maeve, sitting beside her.

Maeve must have been having the same thoughts. 'You really appreciate your own family in situations like this,' she whispered. 'I shall never feel irritated again if Martin changes Christopher's nappy wrongly or complains about the car.' He still did occasionally.

'We're ever so lucky, sis.' Fion sighed. 'We've got everything.'

'I know, but it's a pity it takes a tragedy to make us realise it.'

Sunday afternoon, and Micky and Alice were persuaded to go home and rest. Jerry drove them. It was still raining heavily and the clouds were even greyer than they'd been the day before. Jerry stopped at the end of Pearl Street, where Micky got out, and Alice said quickly, 'I think I'll go and see Bernadette before she leaves for the hospital. She sent a message to say she was going this avvy.'

'Are you sure? I'll take you home if you prefer. It's no trouble.'

'It's kind of you, Jerry, luv. But I prefer Bootle to Birkdale at the moment. Anyroad, me own car's around here somewhere.' She couldn't possibly go back to her smart bungalow at a time like this, even though she would have liked to get rid of her hat, collect a mac and change her suit for something more comfortable. She got out of the car, kissed Micky and almost ran, not to Bernadette's, but to the dark, silent salon in Opal Street, where she let herself in and sat under the middle dryer – something she hadn't done in years.

She hadn't realised she was quite so tired. Almost immediately, she fell awkwardly asleep, a sleep full of horrible dreams, which she couldn't remember when she woke up, but she knew her mind had been preoccupied with things unpleasant.

Jaysus! Would the rain never stop! She could see nothing, not even her watch, because by now it was completely dark, but the downpour sounded even heavier, as if the rain was bouncing off the pavements.

It would have been better to have gone to Bernadette's, where she could have slept in a proper bed, had something decent to eat, not be stuck here with nothing but her own miserable thoughts to keep her company.

Mind you, what other thoughts could you expect to have at a time like this? Alice found herself dredging up every single memory she could of Orla. Orla being born, walking for the first time, saying her first word, her first day at school – she'd come home and informed her mother she was the prettiest in the class, as well as the cleverest.

'Arrogant little madam.' Danny chuckled when he was told – she'd been her grandad's favourite, as well as John's. Alice had never had a favourite. She loved all her children the same and would have felt just as devastated had any one of them been in hospital in a coma.

'Oh, I feel so *sad*!' The sadness rolled up into a ball at the back of her throat. In a minute she'd make a cup of tea – except there'd be no milk. At weekends Patsy usually took home what was over in case it went sour.

Perhaps it wouldn't be a bad idea to turn the light on, go round to Bernie's who might be home again by now. She was only making it worse, sitting by herself in the pitch dark, longing for a drink. She was about to heave herself out of the chair when the key turned in the lock and someone came in. She held her breath. It was a man, she could just make out his bulky form against the window.

He reached for the light, turned it on and uttered a startled cry when he saw her. 'Alice! I am feeling a definite sense of déjà vu.'

'Who are you?' For some reason, she didn't feel the least bit frightened.

'Have I changed so much?' the man said dejectedly.

She stared at him. He wore a well-cut tweed suit and looked about fifty. Once he had been handsome, still was in a way, but his face was deeply lined, his expression careworn. Iron-grey hair, slightly receding and wet from the rain, was combed back from his forehead in little waves. He was smiling and it was a nice smile that involved his entire face, including his very blue eyes, which were dancing merrily in her direction. Despite everything that was happening in her life, despite the fact that she didn't recognise the man from Adam and he had just walked uninvited into her salon, that somehow he had a key, Alice smiled back.

'I remember doing precisely the same thing,' the man said. 'Coming in, finding you in the dark – oh, it must be twenty years ago. You gave me a fright then. Mind you, this time I deserve it.'

'Neil!' She stared at him in disbelief. Suddenly he looked achingly familiar and she couldn't understand why she hadn't known him straight away.

'Whew! Recognition at last. How are you, my dear Alice? If you knew how many times I have longed for this moment you would be deeply flattered.' He came and sat beside her.

'How did you get in?' she stammered. 'Well, I know how you got in. I mean, how did you get the key? No one's supposed to have it.'

He dangled the key in front of her eyes. It was attached to a St Christopher medal keyring that she remembered well. 'This is my original key. I forgot to give it back and have kept it all these years. I was hoping it would fit, that you hadn't had the lock changed, because I wanted to see the flat. I intended sneaking in and out so no one would know I'd been, but you seem to make a habit of sitting under a dryer in the dark.'

'What if there'd been someone living upstairs?'

'I knew there wasn't,' he said surprisingly. 'I heard from a friend in Bootle that the flat was vacant, but when I phoned I was told it was badly in need of decoration. I wanted to see exactly how bad it was in case I could manage it myself.'

'Patsy said someone had phoned.' Alice frowned. 'Have you taken up painting and decorating?'

'Only of the upstairs flat.' His smile faded. 'Things haven't gone exactly well for me over the last few years, Alice. In fact, nothing's gone well since I left Liverpool all those years ago. I suddenly decided I'd like a little bolt-hole to hide in when I felt particularly low. And what better place than the one where I spent the happiest years of my life.'

They'd been happy years for her too. Looking back, the time they'd spent together seemed unreal. The flat had also been her bolt-hole, a place where she'd felt able to leave all her troubles outside and relax in Neil's arms. It felt like a million years ago.

'Would you mind having me as your upstairs tenant a second time?' he was saying. 'It would only be for occasional weekends.'

'I don't think I would mind that at all, Neil,' she said, and wondered if she was still dreaming and, if so, how much of the past had been a dream and how much had actually happened. At what point in her life would she wake up?

He smiled at her delightedly. 'Well, now that's settled, enough about me. What about you, Alice. How are Cormac and the girls and your multitude of grandchildren? How many do you have now?'

'Seven,' she said automatically. 'No, eight.' She'd forgotten about the tiny girl who'd been born the night before. Her eyes filled with tears when she thought about Orla, whom, incredibly, she'd almost forgotten since Neil had arrived. Just as she had done the other time he found her in the dark, Alice started to cry. She told him about Orla, the baby in the incubator, the wedding yesterday. Time fell away, the years merged to nothing, as he held her hand, patted her cheek and agreed that it was all quite unbearably sad, but that one day, a long time off, it would be bearable again, incredible though that might seem right now.

'God works in mysterious ways that I don't pretend to understand,' he said.

'Me neither.' She sighed. 'What time is it?'

'Just gone nine.'

She must have been asleep for hours. Her neck ached from having been in an uncomfortable position and she had pins and needles in her legs. 'I'd better be getting back to the hospital.'

'Can I come with you?'

'Oh, yes, please'. She didn't care if it sounded too eager, she just wanted him there. She didn't care about anything much at the moment. It didn't matter that she was fifty-seven and he was ten years younger. It didn't matter if they got back together again though she had a feeling it was what he wanted. Nor did it matter if they didn't. It would be nice to have him in the upstairs flat again, but if it all fell through, that didn't matter either.

Nothing mattered except the moment, now, when she was about to return to the hospital to see her child who would shortly die.

She got tiredly to her feet and went over to the window. The street lights were reflected, wobbling slightly, in the wet pavements. 'It's stopped raining,' she remarked. 'The stars are out.' She noticed that Neil's bones creaked as he came to stand beside her. Together, they watched the stars.

Then one star, more vivid than the others, left its mates and shot across the sky. Alice turned off the light so she could observe more clearly the bright, twinkling point passing over the earth, soaring silently towards who knew where. She pointed. 'See that one! It must be a shooting star.'

'I can't see anything.' Neil shook his head.

Alice knew then that Orla was dead and, for the Laceys, nothing would ever be the same again. The star had been her daughter's final flamboyant gesture to the world.

She held her breath. One day, very soon, she would go abroad, to a place that Orla would have enjoyed. She would go by herself, but she wouldn't feel lonely, because Orla would be with her in her heart. She'd like that.

'I hope Micky was with her when she passed away,' she murmured softly. 'Or at least I hope he saw the star.'

The House by Princes Park

For Patrick

Olivia

1
1918–1919

Olivia had only been to London once before, on her way to France, and she'd liked the busy, bustling atmosphere. But now, she hated it. She hated everyone looking happy because the war was over. Surely there must be people around who'd had relatives killed? And women who felt as empty and desolate as she did.

There might even be women, single women, single *pregnant* women, who could advise her, tell her what to do, how to cope, where to go.

Because Olivia didn't know. She didn't know anything except that she couldn't look for work in her condition. She'd always planned on going straight from France to Cardiff when the fighting ended. Matron had promised to take her back at the hospital where she'd been a nurse. But she'd got off the train in London and there seemed no point in going further. Matron wouldn't want her now. She was ashamed of feeling so helpless when, since leaving home, she'd thought of herself as strong.

Never before had she had to think about money or somewhere to live or where the next meal would come from. The small amount of money she'd earned was more than enough to buy occasional clothes and over the years she'd managed to save a few pounds. Now, the savings had almost gone on accommodation in a small hotel in Islington. She was eking it out, eating only breakfast which, as a nurse, she knew wasn't enough for a pregnant woman.

Despite this, she felt well and had never had a moment's sickness. It was one of the reasons she hadn't suspected she was pregnant when she missed her August period. She'd thought it was because she was upset over Tom. It could happen to women; their periods ceased when they were faced with tragedy. For the same reason, she wasn't bothered when there was still no period in September, but by October she had started to feel thick around the waist, and the terrifying realisation dawned that she was expecting a child. At that point, her brain seemed to freeze. She became incapable of thought.

With November came the Armistice. Olivia was glad, of course, but instead of rejoicing, she felt only despair.

She still despaired, weeks later. New clothes were needed because she could hardly fasten the ones she had. Soon, she wouldn't be able to go out, and the proprietor of the hotel, a woman, was looking at her oddly because she was in her fifth month and seemed to be growing bigger by the day.

It was strange, but she rarely thought about Tom. If it hadn't been for the baby squirming lazily in her womb, she wondered if she would have thought of him at all. The ring he'd given her that had belonged to his grandfather was in her suitcase. It wasn't that the memory of him hurt, but it was impossible to believe the night had actually happened. It seemed more like a dream. She couldn't remember what he looked like or the words he'd said or the things they'd done.

Mrs Thomas O'Hagan! She recalled whispering the words to herself the day he'd left.

'What was that?'

Olivia was eating breakfast in the dingy dining room of the hotel. She looked up to find the proprietor glaring down at her. 'Sorry, I must have been talking to myself.'

'I've been meaning to have a word with you, Miss Jones,' the woman said officiously. 'I'll be needing your room from Saturday on. I've got regulars coming, salesmen.'

'I see. Thank you for telling me. I'll find somewhere else.'

'Not in a respectable place you won't,' the woman sniffed as she went away.

It had been bound to happen; either she'd run out of money or be asked to leave. Olivia's thoughts were like a knot in her head as she walked towards the city centre. She preferred the noise of the traffic to the quiet streets, even if the West End clatter was horrendous. There were homes for women in her condition. They were terrible places, so she'd heard, but better than wandering the streets, penniless. But how did you find where they were? Who did you ask?

If only she didn't feel so cold! Specks of ice were being blown crazily about by the bitter wind. She turned up the collar of her thin coat, pulled her felt hat further down on her head, but felt no warmer.

On Oxford Street, one of Selfridge's windows had a display of warm, tweed coats, very smart. Olivia stopped and eyed them longingly. Even if she'd been working, they would have been way beyond her means, but she hadn't enough to buy a coat for a quarter of the price from a cheaper shop.

She could, however, afford a cup of tea. She made her way towards Lyons' Corner House, noting all the shops were decorated for Christmas – only a few weeks away – and trying not to think where she would be when it came.

A large black car driven by a man in uniform drew alongside the pavement in front of her. Two young women got out the back, wrapped in furs, silk stockings gleaming. Their matching handbags, gloves and shoes were black suede. They swept across the pavement into a jeweller's shop in a cloud of fragrant scent.

Olivia had always been perfectly content to be a nurse, earning a pittance. She'd never envied other women their clothes or their position in life. But now, standing shivering outside the jeweller's, watching the two expensively-dressed women seat themselves in front of a counter, the assistant bow obsequiously, a feeling of hot, raw jealousy seared through her body. At the same moment, the baby inside her decided to deliver its first lusty kick.

'Are you all right, darlin'?'

A man had stopped and was looking at her with concern as she bent double clutching her stomach with both arms.

'I'm all right, thanks.' She forced herself upright.

He nodded at her bulging stomach. 'You'd be best at home in a nice warm bed.'

'You're right.' She appreciated his kindness. Perhaps he wouldn't be so kind if he knew that beneath her summer gloves she wasn't wearing a wedding ring.

She recovered enough to make her way to Lyons. As she drank the tea, Olivia realised with a sinking heart that there was only one way out of her predicament. She would have to ask her parents for help.

She couldn't just turn up, not in her condition. Mr and Mrs Daffydd Jones could never hold up their heads in public again if it got out that their unmarried daughter was having a baby. Her father was a town councillor, her mother given to good works which she carried out with a stern, disapproving expression on her cold features. Olivia, an only child, was already in disgrace. There'd been a row when she gave up her job in the local library to take up nursing in Cardiff, and an even bigger one when she announced her decision to nurse in France. She daren't go near the place where she was born, let alone the house in which she'd lived.

A letter would have to be sent, throwing herself on their mercy, and it would have to be sent today, so there would be time for a reply before Saturday when she left the hotel.

The tea finished, she searched the side streets for a shop that sold inexpensive stationery, then went to the Post Office and wrote to her mother and father, explaining her plight. She didn't plead or try to invoke their sympathy. She knew her parents well. They would either help, or they wouldn't, no matter how the letter was framed.

The reply came on Friday morning. She recognised her father's writing on the envelope. Although he wrote neatly, he had managed to make the 'Miss' look as if it might be 'Mrs' – or the other way round. The proprietor didn't look impressed when she handed the letter over. It crossed Olivia's mind that she could have bought a brass wedding ring and signed the register as Mrs O'Hagan, claiming to be a widow if anyone asked, but she'd been so confused it hadn't crossed her mind. Still, all it would have avoided was the indignity of, in effect, being thrown out. She would have had to leave in another few days when she came to the end of her savings.

The envelope contained a rail ticket and a curt note.

'Catch the 6.30 train from Paddington Station to Bristol on Saturday night. I will meet you. Father.'

Bristol wasn't far from where she'd lived in Wales. Relief was mixed with a sense of sadness as she re-read her father's note. No 'Dear Olivia.' He hadn't signed 'Love, Father'.

At least now she was leaving she could treat herself to a decent meal with what was left of the money.

Her father was waiting under the clock at Temple Meads station, legs apart, hands clasped behind his back, glowering. He was rocking back and forth on his heels, a big, broad-shouldered man, in an ankle-length tweed overcoat and a wide-brimmed hat that made him look rather louche, though he would have been horrified had he realised. His coat hung open, revealing a pinstriped waistcoat and a gold watch and chain.

There was something forbidding about the way he waited, as if his thoughts were very dark. Olivia had always been frightened of him, although he'd never laid a hand on her, either in anger or affection.

He nodded grimly at her approach and had the grace to take her suitcase. He made no attempt to kiss the daughter he hadn't seen for two and a half years. Even if she hadn't been returning home under a cloud, Olivia wouldn't have found this surprising.

She followed him outside and he stowed the case in the boot of the little Ford Eight car that was the only thing she'd known him show fondness for. He would pat it lovingly when it had completed a journey and murmur, 'Clever little thing!'

'Where's Mother?' Olivia asked as they drove out of the station.

'Home,' he said brusquely.

There was a long silence. The gaslit streets of Bristol were mainly deserted at such a late hour. They passed a few pubs that had recently emptied and where customers still hung noisily around outside.

'Where are we going?' Olivia asked when the silence began to grate. She wondered if she was being taken to a home for fallen women. It would be horrid, but she'd put herself in a position where she had no choice.

'A Mrs Cookson, who lives near the docks, will look after you until . . . until your time comes.' His voice was grudging. 'It's most unlikely anyone we know will visit the area, but I would be obliged if you would stay indoors during daylight hours in case you're recognised. Mrs Cookson has been given money to buy you the appropriate garments. You'll be comfortable there. When everything is over, you will leave. I'll make arrangements for the child to be taken care of, if that is your wish. If you decide to keep it, don't expect your mother and me to help. We never want to see you again.'

Although she'd had no wish to see them, either, the bluntness of his words upset her. They made her feel dirty. She opened her mouth to tell him about Tom, but before she could say a word, her father said tonelessly, 'You're disgusting.'

She didn't speak to him again, nor he to her. Shortly afterwards, he turned into a little street of terraced houses, and stopped outside the end one. He got out, leaving the engine running, and knocked on the door.

It was opened by a gaunt woman in her fifties with hennaed hair and a vivid crimson mouth. She had on a scarlet satin dress and a black stole. Long jet earrings dangled on to her shoulders and she wore a three-strand necklace to match. Her long fingers were full of rings – if the stones were real, she must be worth a fortune, Olivia thought.

Her father grunted an introduction, almost threw his daughter's suitcase into the hall, and left. The Ford was already in motion by the time Mrs Cookson closed the door. She folded her arms and looked Olivia up and down.

'Well, who's been a naughty girl?' she said archly.

Olivia couldn't remember the last time she'd smiled. She'd been expecting to be treated like a wanton woman over the next few months and, although Mrs Cookson wasn't quite her cup of tea, it was a pleasant surprise to be greeted with a joke.

'Come along, dearie,' the woman seized her arm, winking lewdly. 'Come and tell us all about it. Would you like a cuppa? Or something stronger? I've got some nice cherry wine. I'm about to have a bottle of milk stout, myself. Oh, and by the way, call me Madge.'

Madge Cookson was the unofficial midwife in the area of Bristol known as Little Italy because of the street names. Her own house was in Capri Street, and there were other similar streets of tiny houses: Naples, Turin and Venice, as well as a small cul-de-sac called Milan Way, all off Florence Road. She had a weakness for milk stout and a rather brittle manner that hid a soft, generous heart. Olivia was to grow quite fond of her over the next few months.

'How did my father know about you?' she enquired after she'd been living in Madge's house for a week.

'He must have asked around. You're not the first well-bred young lady I've had under similar circumstances to your own.'

As a young woman, Madge had been a singer on the music halls and there was a poster in her bedroom listing Magda Starr fourth on the bill at the London Hippodrome.

'That was the highest I ever got,' she told Olivia sadly. 'I always wanted to be top, but it wasn't to be. I got married soon afterwards and had our Des.'

Her husband had died years ago, but Desmond had followed in his mother's footsteps and was a ventriloquist on the halls, although he had never reached such an exalted position as fourth on the bill. Desmond Starr's name was usually in small print at the bottom.

'Was your name really Starr?' Olivia asked. She would never cease to be intrigued by Madge's fascinating and varied life.

'No, my maiden name was Bailey, but Magda Starr looked better on posters than Madge Bailey.'

'How did you become a midwife?'

'I'm not a proper midwife, am I, dearie? I worked in a hospital for a while after my husband died and saw how it was done. I helped deliver a couple of babies and word got round, that's all.'

The house was comfortable, as her father had promised. Madge's exotic taste in clothes was reflected in the furnishings. Instead of a conventional runner, a garish shawl covered the sideboard on which stood a vase of enormous paper flowers. A bead curtain separated the kitchen from the living room, and there were numerous satin cushions embroidered with silver and gold thread scattered around. The covers had come from India, said Madge, as had the big tapestry over the mantelpiece in the parlour and the black and gold tea service with fluted rims that was brought out for best.

A fire crackled in the living room from early morning till late at night. On Sundays, a fire was also lit in the parlour for Madge's visitors; women about her own age, who came in the afternoon to play whist and drink milk stout.

Olivia stayed in the other room on these occasions reading one of Madge's collection of well-thumbed romantic novels. Sometimes she went upstairs for a nap in her room at the back with its lovely springy double bed.

She was as happy as anyone could be in her position. It would have been nice to have gone for a walk in the bright winter sunshine, or even the winter fog, wearing the new, warm coat, bought by Madge with money provided by her father but Madge, usually very easygoing, was strict about her staying indoors while it remained light outside.

'I promised your father you wouldn't go out until it was dark. It's what he's paying me for. I can't force you to stay in, but I'd feel obliged to let him know if you didn't.'

'I'm not likely to meet anyone I know round here,' Olivia said sulkily.

'The world is made up of coincidences,' Madge said. 'You could walk out and come face to face with the sister of your mother's best friend.'

'My mother doesn't have friends.'

'Well, her next-door neighbour, then.'

'Has my father given you his address?'

''Course. I'm to send him a telegram when the baby's born, aren't I? "Package Delivered" I've to put, case anyone reads it. Unless you decide to keep the baby, that is, in which case he doesn't want to know.'

'I wouldn't dream of keeping it.' Olivia shuddered. Once it arrived, she intended putting the whole episode behind her and finishing her training, to become a State Registered Nurse.

Madge looked at her thoughtfully. 'You might feel different when it's born.'

'If I do,' Olivia said harshly. 'I want you to tear it out of my arms and let my father have it.'

'Your father can do the tearing, dearie. Not me.'

The baby seemed even less real than Tom. It might well be in her womb, but it had nothing to do with her. She didn't care what happened to it as long as it didn't come to any harm.

Christmas came and went, and soon it was 1919, the first New Year in half a decade with Europe at peace with itself, celebrated with a joy and enthusiasm that was infectious. Madge and Olivia watched fireworks on the River Avon and sang 'Auld Lang Syne' at midnight in Victoria Park.

January became February, and February turned into March. The baby was due at the beginning of April.

Desmond Starr, Madge's ventriloquist son, came home for Easter, a cheerful, outgoing young man, just like his mother. He was booked to appear all summer at a theatre in Felixstowe and invited Madge and her guest. He could get free tickets.

'Well, I'll try,' Olivia lied. By summer, she would have started afresh. She was fond of Madge, but never wanted to see her or her son again.

She knew she had become very hard, very selfish. In days gone by, she'd been regarded as a soft old thing, too sympathetic for her own good. But now, there seemed to be a barrier in her brain, stopping all thoughts from entering that weren't concerned solely with herself.

The baby signalled it was on its way one lovely sunny Sunday afternoon in April, dead on time. Olivia was reading one of Madge's torrid romances when she had the first contraction, a strong one. It wasn't long before she had another, stronger and more painful. She'd spent time on a maternity ward during her training and recognised it was going to be a quick birth.

Madge was playing whist with her friends in the parlour. Olivia calmly made a cup of tea and waited for the friends to leave. She boiled two large pans of water and laid a rubber sheet on the bed. The worn sheets Madge had boiled to use as rags she put ready on a chair.

She gritted her teeth when another contraction came, worse than the others, but was reluctant to disturb Madge while her friends were there. Not that Madge could do anything, but she wouldn't have minded the company. The contractions were coming every ten minutes by the time the visitors were shown out.

'By, God! You're a cool customer,' Madge gasped when Olivia called her upstairs where she was lying on the bed, already in her nightdress.

'I've got a couple of hours to go yet.'

'You're too cool, d'you know that?' She sat on the bed and took Olivia's hand. 'My other young ladies have cried themselves silly during the entire confinement, but there hasn't been a peep out of you.'

'I haven't felt much like crying,' Olivia confessed, wincing when another contraction gripped her stomach like a wrench.

'It's time you did. Didn't you cry when your young man was killed? What was his name? Tom! You hardly ever talk about him.'

Olivia permitted herself a wry smile. 'I slept in a dormitory with the other nurses. There was no place where I could cry in private. And I don't talk about Tom because he doesn't seem real. I can't even remember what he looked like.'

Madge sniggered. 'Well, the baby's real enough. You can have a good old yell, you know,' she said when Olivia winced again. 'Let yourself go. Next door's deaf as a post and the street won't mind.'

'I'd sooner not. And I don't feel all that bad. Most of the births that I remember were much worse than this.'

The time passed slowly. Children could be heard playing in the street outside. Someone knocked on the door but Madge ignored it. A woman in a house behind was singing, her voice carrying clearly in the still, evening air. 'Keep the home fires burning . . .'

It was the song the men used to sing in France, Olivia remembered. It could be heard late at night, from miles away across the fields, when the fighting had finished for the day. Some nights, the nurses and the patients joined in. They'd been singing it the night when she and Tom had made love . . .

. . . the sky had been spectacular, she recalled; deep, sapphire blue, as lustrous as the jewel, and powdered with a myriad glittering stars. The waning moon was a delicate lemon curve.

Although not yet completely dark, it was dark enough to disguise the fact that the French landscape was a battlefield on which more than a million men had died. In daylight, the flat ground was a sea of dried mud, a jigsaw of trenches, empty now that the fighting had moved on.

Spurts of white smoke could be seen on the horizon, where the battle now was, where shells were landing, killing yet more men. The smoke occasionally turned to flames, indicating a building had been hit. On such a night, the flames even added something to the splendour of the view, flickering as they did like giant candles at the furthest edge of the world. A few broken trees were silhouetted like crazy dancing figures against the lucid blueness of the sky.

People had come outside the hospital to marvel at the magnificent sight amidst so much mayhem; staff, a few of the walking wounded. There was the faint murmur of voices, the occasional glimmer of a cigarette.

'Olivia! I've been looking everywhere for you.'

'Tom!' Olivia turned and instinctively lifted her arms to embrace the man limping towards her. She dropped them as he came nearer and hoped he hadn't noticed. He was her patient. He mustn't know how she felt, though she sensed he had already guessed. After all, she had a strong suspicion he felt the same, something of a miracle when he was so attractive and she so plain.

'Great night,' he said, panting slightly. The walk had been an effort.

'Beautiful,' she breathed. She nodded towards the smoke and the flames in the distance. 'That spoils it rather. And there's something sinister about not being able to hear the explosions.'

'Or the screams,' Tom said drily. He took her hand, his fingers curling warmly inside her own. She made no attempt to pull away. 'So, this is it! Our last night together.' He gave the glimmer of a smile. 'Or should I say, our last night in the near vicinity of each other. I'm sorry my leg is better. I feel tempted to take off my clothes, wander into the darkness, and pray I catch pneumonia again.'

'Not if I have anything to do with it!' She pretended to be outraged. He was joking. He was American, and the Americans joked all the time. They seemed exceptionally good-humoured. 'I'm a nurse. I want my patients to get better, not worse.'

'Don't be so practical.'

'Nurses are always practical, they have to be.' She didn't feel practical, not now, with her hand held so tightly in his.

He gave another tiny smile. 'Couldn't you be impractical just for tonight?'

'Not if it means you catching pneumonia, no. Anyway, it's exceptionally warm. You're not likely to catch anything except a few insect bites. Mind you, they can be nasty.'

'In that case,' he said lightly, 'Maybe we could forget about war, explosions in the distance, illnesses, hospitals, doctors and nurses, and just talk about each other?'

She should really say no, that's impractical too. Instead, she murmured, 'There's nothing much to say.' She already knew quite a lot about him. He came from Boston. His parents – he called them 'folks' – were Irish. He was twenty-three, worked in a bookshop owned by his father, and had volunteered to fight when America joined the war in 1917. His full name was Thomas Gerald O'Hagan and he had two sisters and five brothers of which he was the youngest. She also knew she wasn't the only nurse attracted to the tall, thin Irish–American with the laughing face, black curly hair, and peat-brown eyes. She was, however, the only one in love. He occupied her mind every waking minute of every day.

He had come into the hospital three weeks ago with a badly gashed leg and a dose of double pneumonia. Tomorrow, he was being sent to convalesce in a hospital in Calais. As soon as he was fit, he would return to an American Army unit to fight again. As a reminder of his imminent departure, there was a clanking sound as the ambulance train was shunted into place on the railway sidings behind them, ready for morning.

By comparison, he knew little about her, just that her name was Olivia Jones and she was the same age as himself. She had been born and bred in Wales and had never left its borders until she'd come to France two years ago as a nurse. He also knew, because he could see, that she wasn't even faintly pretty, almost insipid with her pale face and pale blue eyes.

'What will you do when the war is over?' Tom asked casually.

'Finish my training. I hadn't taken my final exams when I left Cardiff.'

'Would it be possible to finish training in the States?'

She caught her breath. 'Why should I do that?'

'Because it's where I'll be.' His voice was very low, intense. 'It's where my job is. And it's where I'd like *you* to be. Will you marry me, Olivia?'

'But we hardly know each other,' she gasped, though it was silly to sound so surprised when it was a question she'd hoped and prayed he'd ask.

He gestured impatiently. 'My darling girl, there's a war on, a hideous war, the worst the world has ever known. There isn't time for people to get to know each other as they would in normal times. I fell in love the first time I set eyes on you.' Pressing her hand to his lips, he said huskily, 'You are the loveliest woman I've ever known.'

He must be in love if he thought that! It was time she answered, said something positive, told him how she felt. He was kissing her now, her neck, her cheeks. He took her face in both hands and kissed her lips.

She was a timid person, withdrawn, and this was the first time she had been properly kissed. She pressed herself against him and felt her body come alive. 'I love you,' she whispered.

He held her so tightly she could hardly breathe. 'The minute this damn war is over we'll get married,' he said hoarsely. 'I'll write you every day and let you know where I'm posted so you can write me. Have you a photograph I can have?'

'I've one taken with the other nurses a few months ago,' she said breathlessly. 'I'll let you have it before you go.'

'I'll let you have something of mine.' He held out his hand. A circle of gold glinted dully on the third finger – she had noticed the ring before, and had thought he was married until she realised it was on his right hand. 'It's my grandpop's wedding ring,' he explained as he removed it, dark eyes shining. 'He gave us all something before he died. I got his ring. It'll be too big, but might fit your middle finger. Or you can wear it around your neck on a chain.'

The ring was too big for any of her fingers. She put it in the breast pocket of her long white apron. As soon as she could, she'd buy a chain.

'I feel as if we're already married.' Her voice was thick in her throat. It was almost too much to bear. She wanted Tom to kiss her again, do the things that, until now, she'd thought wrong. She slid her arms around his neck and began to pull him along the side of the hospital building. He put his hands on her waist and they moved as if they were doing some strange sort of dance. In the distance, the troops began to sing, a desolate, haunting sound.

Tom said, 'Where are we going, honey?'

'Round here.'

They reached the corner of the building. About a hundred feet away, a tangle of railway lines shone silver in the light of the moon. Beyond the lines stood a small, single-storey building without a door.

'This used to be a station,' she said. 'That building was the waiting room.'

'And is that where we're going?' There was incredulity in his voice.

By now, she felt utterly shameless. Every vestige of the respectability and conformity that she'd been fed over her entire life had fled. In just an instant, the world had turned 180 degrees. 'If you want,' she said.

'If I want! Gee, I can't think of anything I want more. But you, Olivia, is it what you want?'

Her answer was a laugh. She grabbed his hand, and they began to step over the silver lines. The stars continued to shine in their hundreds and thousands, the troops continued to sing, but Olivia and Tom were aware of none of these things as they entered the small, unused building into an intoxicating world of their own.

The war would be over in a few months' time, so everybody said: the experts, the newspapers, the pundits, the tired, hopeful men on the ground. But people had been saying the same thing for the last four years, ever since the fighting had begun.

It was something they wanted to believe, Olivia Jones included. But now she had her own pressing reason for wanting the fighting to end, to be over before Tom returned to battle.

Next morning, she saw him off, slipping him the promised photograph when no one was looking – she would get into serious trouble if Matron discovered the magical thing that had happened the night before. A few nurses in their shoulder-length voile caps, dark-blue gowns, and full-length aprons, came out of the hospital to wave goodbye to the men they had tenderly nursed back to health. Tears were shed on both sides as the train puffed away in the brilliant sunshine towards Calais.

Olivia hadn't thought it possible to feel both unbearably sad and blissfully happy at the same time; sad that Tom had gone, happy thinking about their future together. She fingered the ring in her pocket as she watched the train disappear round a bend. She'd examined it the night before. Inside was engraved, the words worn away until they were barely legible: RUBY TO EAMON 1857.

'If – no, *when* me and Tom have children, we'll call them Ruby and Eamon,' she decided, rubbing her hands together in anticipation.

The vacated beds weren't empty long. Later that morning, a horse-drawn ambulance arrived full of casualties who'd already been cursorily seen to in a dressing station on the front line. The rest of the day was spent re-bandaging wounds, comforting those for whom there seemed no hope because their injuries were too severe. Some were taken to the operating theatre to have limbs removed, returning, dopey from the anaesthetic, waking later, shattered and terrified.

As she walked from bed to bed, smiling at the stricken men, fetching water, making them as comfortable as possible, Olivia cursed the politicians who were responsible for the slaughter, who'd allowed it to continue for so long. A generation of young men had been sacrificed for no real reason, and a generation of women had lost husbands, fathers, sons.

The injured men would never have guessed the little nurse with the sweet smile – Olivia wasn't quite as plain as she thought – was so preoccupied with thoughts of the previous night, a night when she'd taken a lover, become a woman, and had promised to become a wife.

'Mrs Thomas O'Hagan!'

She practised saying the words underneath her breath.

'What was that, darlin'?' a little Cockney with a broken arm enquired.

'Sorry, I was talking to myself.'

He grinned. 'Well, that way you won't get no arguments.'

She grinned back, tucked the sheet tightly around his waist, and told him to rest.

It was after tea by the time the men had been seen to and those able to eat had been given a meal – the inevitable bully beef accompanied by mashed potatoes. While they ate, a dozen weary nurses collected in a windowless recess outside the ward which they regarded as their staffroom, for a hot drink, the first since morning.

The conversation turned, as it often did, to rumours that the fighting would soon end. After all, someone said, the Battle of Amiens had just been won, mainly by Australian and Canadian troops, and there'd been only 7000 casualties on their side.

'Only seven thousand!' someone else remarked sarcastically.

'There's been ten times that number before now.'

Olivia hardly listened. She held her hand against her breast and, through the pocket of her apron, could feel Tom's ring pressing against her palm. For the hundredth time that day, she went over the events of the previous night.

'What's the matter, Olivia?' said a voice. 'You look as if you might cry.'

'Nothing.' *She couldn't see him any more.* His face, so clear all day, had suddenly become a blur. The hairs on her neck prickled and she felt convinced something was dreadfully wrong.

It wasn't until the following day, after a sleepless night, that she learnt that Thomas O'Hagan was dead. The ambulance train had been passing over a bridge that had been heavily mined by saboteurs operating behind Allied lines. Not everyone had died when the bridge exploded and the train and those on board had plunged into the river below.

But Tom had and, for Olivia, it was the end of everything.

She sighed and wriggled uncomfortably on the bed. She was perspiring freely and the clothes felt damp. The contractions were only minutes apart, painful, but bearable.

Suddenly, she felt her stomach heave and she no longer had control of her body. There were a series of violent spasms, followed by a cloud of pain, so savage that she nearly fainted. Then the heaving stopped and she felt empty.

'It's a girl,' Madge cried triumphantly.

'A girl!'

'A lovely girl, very dark. I'm cutting the cord. Do you want to look at her, Olivia?'

'I'm not sure,' Olivia whispered. She half closed her eyes and saw a creamy-skinned baby being picked up by its feet. Madge gave the plump bottom a sharp slap, and the baby responded with an angry howl. 'She looks fat.'

'No, she's just right. She's a fine, healthy baby. I'll clean you up, then take her downstairs, make a bottle of tepid water and give her a cuddle. She deserves it after all that effort. Is there a name you want to call her?'

'I never gave a thought to names.' She half saw Madge wrap the baby in a sheet and put her in a basket, then she lay back and allowed herself to be washed and patted gently dry. The bedclothes and her nightdress were changed, her hair quickly combed.

'I'll make us both a cup of tea in a minute,' Madge muttered. 'I need one as much as you.' She picked up the basket and made her way carefully downstairs, leaving an exhausted Olivia warmly tucked in bed with only a feeling of soreness as a reminder of her ordeal.

She lay, watching the sharp line between light and shade creep across the wardrobe with its dusty suitcases on top as the sun gradually disappeared from sight. The singing had stopped. The children had gone indoors. The world seemed to have paused for breath and Olivia paused with it.

She had just had a baby!

Tom's baby. His daughter.

And now she felt oddly incomplete. She had to see Tom's daughter so as always to remember what she looked like. Otherwise, she would wonder until her dying day.

It hurt, getting out of bed, going downstairs, not making a sound in her bare feet. The basket was on the floor in front of the living-room fire. Olivia saw a tiny foot appear and kick away the sheet. Another foot appeared, followed by a little flower-like hand. The baby was making faint chirruping noises, like a bird. Madge was humming to herself in the kitchen as she prepared the bottle.

Olivia crept into the room and knelt beside the basket. The baby was naked and, oh, she was so pretty! Dark curly hair, dark creamy skin, rosebud mouth, a perfect nose, not squashed like some babies. Her limbs were smooth and round, unwrinkled. The baby regarded her calmly with big blue eyes, though she'd been told that babies couldn't focus for weeks.

'You're beautiful,' Olivia whispered. She put her finger inside the diminutive hand and it was gripped with surprising strength. As the flesh of the mother touched that of the child, Olivia shivered, and the parts of her that she had thought had died with Tom, became magically alive. She knew then she would never bring herself to give up her daughter. Never!

She slipped the nightdress off her shoulder, reached down and picked up her baby, cradling her in her arms. 'Are you thirsty, darling? Would you like a drink?' She put the child to her breast and she began to suck noisily. Olivia smiled and began to sway from side to side.

'Olivia! Oh, no, dearie. No!' A shocked Madge had come into the room with the bottle. She sank into a chair. 'That's torn it,' she groaned.

'Oh, Madge!' Olivia cried, eyes shining. 'I remember now what Tom looked like, just like his daughter. And Madge. I'm going to call her Ruby. It was Tom's grandmother's name. Ruby O'Hagan.' She stroked the soft cheek with her thumb. 'Don't you think that's lovely?'

'Lovely,' Madge agreed, sighing.

She was slightly unhinged. The emotions that had been suppressed for months bubbled to the surface. She couldn't stop smiling as she nursed her baby hour after hour, cooing, stroking and kissing, marvelling at her fingers, her toes. Entranced, she watched the blue eyes gradually close as Ruby fell asleep.

Eventually, Madge told her sharply to put the child down. 'You're wearing her out. She needs rest. And so do you. You're much too excited.'

'I'm happy, that's all, happier than I've been in ages.' Olivia reluctantly laid the sleeping Ruby in the basket. 'I want to keep her, Madge,' she said quietly.

'I thought as much.' Madge's lips tightened.

'I think that's best, don't you?'

'I've no idea what's best, Olivia.' Madge looked sober, not a bit her cheerful self. 'Whether you keep her or not, either way misery lies. Keep her and you'll have to find somewhere to live, not easy with a baby, even less without a husband. Little Ruby will grow up without a dad. You'll need money, but with a baby you'll find it hard to get a job. You can't go back to nursing. You'll feel trapped. You might come to resent Ruby for ruining your life. You might start thinking, "If only I hadn't kept her, everything would be fine".'

Olivia shuddered. 'Tell me about the other way?'

'With the other way,' Madge continued, 'You can go back to nursing, pass your exams, maybe get promoted. You'll have friends, money, nice clothes, enough to eat. You'll be respected. You might get married, have more children you won't be ashamed to call your own.'

'You make that way sound so much better,' Olivia cried.

'I hadn't finished, dearie. Despite all the good things, you'll never forget your little girl. Every time you see a child of Ruby's age, you'll wonder how she is, what she looks like now she's four, ten, twenty. You'll wonder where she is, how she is, is she being properly looked after? Is she happy? Is she sad? Does she ever think about her mother, her *real* mother? You might try to find her, even if it's only to have a little look to set your mind at rest.'

'Oh, Madge! How do you know all this?'

'I've made the same speech a dozen times before, dearie, that's how. I've another young lady coming at the end of May and I'll probably be making it again.'

'What do you think I should do?' The idea of being free, able to do anything she wanted without the burden of a baby was tempting. But the thought of giving up Ruby was intolerable.

'Don't ask me, Olivia. I don't even know what *I'd* do in the same position. It's a decision for you and no one else to make.'

In the early hours, Ruby, in her basket on the floor beside her mother's bed, woke up and began to howl and still howled after she'd been fed and her nappy changed. Olivia was rubbing her back when Madge appeared in an emerald green dressing gown.

'If you were in rooms, there'd be people hammering on the walls shouting for you to keep the baby quiet.'

'What's wrong with her?' Olivia asked fretfully.

'Nothing's wrong. She's behaving like a perfectly normal baby.'

'But why is she crying, Madge?'

'Maybe you haven't brought up all her wind.'

'She's burped twice.'

'She might want to burp three times.'

Ruby fell asleep and woke up at six for another feed. Olivia fed her. There was something almost sensual about the sound the baby made as she sucked on her breast. A thrill of emotion swept through her, almost as intense as when she'd made love with Tom.

'We're starting on a big adventure soon, you and me,' she whispered. She could look for a job as a housekeeper, say she was a widow.

Madge appeared again, much later, this time wearing a hat and coat. 'I'm going out a minute, dearie. I won't be long.'

Olivia dozed, the baby in her arms. Madge came back and made a cup of tea. She'd hoped she would offer to look after Ruby while she had a proper sleep, but Madge made no such offer. Perhaps she was making a point instead – this was how it would be when she and Ruby were on their own with no one to help.

Midday. She'd bathed her baby, marvelling again at how perfect she was, how beautiful. Ruby made cooing sounds and waved her arms. Olivia dried her, dressed her in the new white clothes Madge had bought, hugging her tightly. 'I love you,' she said. 'I love you so much.'

There was a knock on the front door, followed by Madge's footsteps in the hall, then whispering that went on for a long time. Then the whispering stopped and someone came upstairs, not Madge, because the tread was too heavy. Her heart did a somersault when her father came into the room. Madge must have sent him the promised telegram.

Olivia wasn't sure if, for the briefest of seconds, she glimpsed a softness in his stony eyes when he looked down on his daughter nursing her tiny, dark-haired baby.

Father and daughter stared at each other across the room, neither speaking. Olivia kept her eyes on his, willing the softness to return. If only she could talk to him, he might offer to support them, come and see them, bring her mother.

Instead, her father strode across the room and tore the baby from her breast. Ruby whimpered and Olivia heard someone give a thin, high-pitched scream that seemed to go on and on and on as if a single note was being played on a violin.

Then Madge seized her shoulders and shook her hard and the screaming stopped. '*RUBY!*' Olivia screamed as her father and her baby vanished from the room.

'Shush, dearie. It's for the best. It's what you asked of me, isn't it?'

But that was then, and this was now. She loved Ruby with all her heart, she wanted to keep her. Even so, Olivia made no attempt to leap out of bed and try to get her baby back. Afterwards, during the dark weeks that followed, she wondered, horrified, if in some secret, horribly selfish, part of her mind, she didn't want Ruby after all, that she was relieved she'd been taken away.

Now, though, she felt only desolation and despair.

It was the second occasion the little Ford Eight had made the long journey from the south to the north of Wales. This time, there was a baby in a basket on the back seat who made not a sound for most of the way. The driver had almost reached his destination when it began to cry. Instead of stopping to give it the bottle Mrs Cookson had prepared, Daffydd Jones pressed his foot harder on the accelerator. Nearly there.

He recognised the white convent when it came into sight, perched on a hill three miles from Abergele. He had been before. The Mother Superior knew him, but not his name. Daffyd Jones wasn't a Catholic, he had no truck with Papist nonsense, but the convent was also an orphanage and had agreed to take the child if it was a girl. Arrangements had been made elsewhere in the event his daughter's bastard turned out to be a boy.

The small car groaned its way up the hill and seemed to breathe a sigh of relief when it stopped outside the convent's thick oak door. He got out, pulled the bell, and returned to collect his tiny passenger whose cries by now had become screams of rage.

An ancient nun, as curved as a question mark, was waiting for him, nodding, like a puppet, when he came back and handed her the basket.

She nodded at him to come inside. He refused, saying gruffly, 'I've to give you this.' He handed her the scrap of paper Mrs Cookson had given him. 'After all, what harm will it do?' she'd said.

Tipping his hat, he bade the nun goodbye. She nodded again and closed the door.

Daffydd Jones watched the door close and wondered why there were tears in his eyes.

Inside the convent, the nun peered at the paper. Her eyes were old, but she could still see, particularly when it was nice, clear print like this.

'Ruby O'Hagan,' she read. Well, at least the child had a name, even if the poor, wee mite had nothing else.

Emily

2
1933–1935

The Convent of the Sisters of the Sacred Cross near Abergele was renowned for its orphan girls, all superbly trained by the age of fourteen to enter the world of live-in domestic service. They could sew the neatest of seams, embroider, cook, clean, launder, even garden. They were respectful, healthy, extremely moral, highly religious, and had perfect manners.

The girls made ideal housemaids, nursemaids, cooks, seamstresses. Well adjusted and apparently content with their lot, they had been brought up, if not with love, then with kindness. Physical punishment was strictly forbidden in the convent.

Their education was confined to subjects that would be of use to girls whose role in life would be to serve others until they eventually married a man from the same class as themselves, usually another servant. Apart from domestic skills, they were taught to read and write and do simple arithmetic. They learnt a smattering of history and geography. It was considered a waste for the girls to study science, literature, art, current affairs, or politics. No one was likely to ask a servant girl what she thought of the situation in Russia or which Shakespeare play was her favourite, though she could, if asked, recite the catechism, reel off the names of the last ten Popes, sing several hymns in Latin, and accurately describe the fourteen Stations of the Cross which she had made every Good Friday for as far back as she could remember.

There were applicants anxious for a convent girl from as far away as London, though the girls mainly went to wealthy Catholic homes across the Welsh/English border: Cheshire, Shropshire, Lancashire. Occasionally, a girl stayed and took the veil.

Until they left, the girls spent most of their time within the confines of the convent. They were taught there. They went to Mass in the tiny chapel in the well-tended grounds, the service taken by a priest from a seminary twenty miles away. If the girls were ill, unless it was something contagious or requiring surgery, the young patients were cared for by the nuns themselves.

On Sunday afternoons, they went for a walk in the quiet, secluded lanes, proceeding in a crocodile, two by two, seeing only the occasional car or cyclist.

Twice a year, on a nice day in spring or autumn, when there were few holidaymakers about, the older girls were taken to the sands at Abergele, marching through the small town, fascinated by the shops, amazed and slightly scared by the traffic, particularly if a single decker bus drove by, chugging smoke from its rear. They had never seen so many people and tried not to stare at the women with uncovered heads and bare legs, lips painted red for some reason. So far, men had hardly featured in their lives. The priests who took Mass were old. For a long time they had assumed the world to be peopled mainly by women. Yet here were young men, strange creatures, with deep, loud voices. Some even had hair on their faces which the girls took to be an affliction and said a quick prayer. And there were boys, with short trousers and scabby knees, who grinned and shouted at them rudely, even whistled. The girls, in their antiquated brown dresses and long white pinafores, walked demurely past, hands clasped, eyes fixed on the girl in front, as they had been taught.

The convent might have been considered a gloomy place, with its stone walls and stone floors and high, cavernous ceilings. Cool in summer, freezing in winter, the furniture was sparse and as plain as the food. There were no adornments apart from holy pictures, statues, and numerous crucifixes that hung on the white-painted walls. Nor was a clock evident, but someone, somewhere, must have known when to ring the bells, indicating it was time for classes, time for meals, time to pray.

However, the presence of so many children, obviously happy, despite their tragic backgrounds, dispelled any gloom the occasional visitor might have felt when they entered the big, oak door.

'Cannon fodder,' said Emily Dangerfield to her sister, Cecilia, Mother Superior of the convent, one breezy day in March. Trees could be glimpsed through the high window of the always chilly office, the long branches curtseying this way and that against the bright blue sky. 'You're producing cannon fodder.'

'Are you suggesting that one day my girls will be shot out of guns?' Reverend Mother smiled from behind her highly polished desk. She'd had the same argument with Emily before.

'You know what I mean,' Emily said crossly. 'The girls are being raised for one purpose only: to serve others, do their washing, cooking, cleaning, wait on them hand and foot. You're like a factory, except your products happen to be human.'

'What do you suggest I do with them?' Reverend Mother smiled again. She rarely lost her temper, but was secretly annoyed. What did Emily know about running an orphanage? 'Encourage them to become actresses, doctors, playwrights, politicians? How many do you think will succeed after they've been let loose into the world on their own? Our girls have no family. We ensure they have the security of a home where they will be made welcome and be of use to others.'

'Of use!' Emily laughed shortly. 'You make them sound like chairs. I saw a picture a few years ago, *Metropolis*, all about a mechanized society. It reminded me very much of here.'

'Don't talk nonsense, Emily.' Reverend Mother tried hard not to snap. 'I see age hasn't taught you to consider other people's feelings.'

'And age never will.' Emily got up and began to wander round the room. She was a tall woman who had once been beautiful, fifty-seven, smartly dressed in a houndstooth check costume and a little veiled hat on her dyed black hair. A fox fur was thrown casually over the chair she had just vacated. She was proud of her still slim, svelte figure. Her sister was two years older and similarly built, though her shape was little evident beneath the multitudinous layers of her black habit. Her face, unlike Emily's, was remarkably unlined.

'Out of interest, sister dear, why are you here?' Reverend Mother enquired. 'Have you driven all the way from Liverpool just to lecture me? We nuns are only allowed one visit a year for which notice has to be given beforehand. I couldn't bring myself to turn you away, but you've made me break my own rules.'

'It isn't just a visit, sis. I came because I want a girl.'

'I beg your pardon?'

'A girl. I want one of your girls.'

'Excuse me, but aren't you being a trifle hypocritical?'

'No. I shall educate her, broaden her mind, teach her all the things you've managed to avoid.'

'If you want to conduct an experiment, Emily, I suggest you buy a Bunsen burner.'

Emily returned to her chair. She removed a silver cigarette case and lighter from her bag, then replaced them when she saw her sister frown. 'Sorry, I forgot you disapprove. Mind you, you smoked like a chimney when you were young.'

'There are all sorts of things I did when I was young that I haven't done in many years.'

'And smoking was one of the mildest.' Emily winked.

Reverend Mother refused to be riled. 'Those things are long behind me.' She didn't go on about the sinner that repenteth, because it would have only made Emily laugh.

'Seriously, though,' her sister said. 'About a girl. Since Edwin died and the children left home, I've felt terribly lonely in Brambles by myself. It's so big, so isolated. Since I became a widow, my so-called friends have deserted me. I haven't been invited out socially in ages.'

'Why not sell Brambles and move?'

'I can't.' Emily made a face. 'It's not mine to sell. Edwin left it to the boys, but they can only have it if I leave – or die. I think he had visions of me getting married again to some awful cad who'd inherit the place and deprive his children of their inheritance.'

'I always thought Edwin very wise.'

Emily ignored this. 'I'm nervous on my own. I have servants, naturally, but they're part-time. I hear noises during the night and can't sleep.'

Reverend Mother raised her brows sardonically. 'And you think a fourteen-year-old child will protect you?'

'She'll be company, and I'll feel better, knowing there's another human being under the same roof.'

'I'm not sure if I'd trust one of our girls with you, Emily. You'll corrupt her. She'll be smoking and drinking within a week.'

'What shallow principles you must have taught them, Cecilia, that they can be dispensed with so swiftly.'

The sisters laughed.

'Why not employ a companion?' Reverend Mother suggested.

'Gawd, no.' Emily shuddered. 'Not some poor, pathetic woman without a home of her own. She'd agree with every single word I said, scared I'd sack her.'

'And you think one of our girls will disagree? Doesn't that rather contradict the cannon fodder theory?'

'I'll teach her to disagree as well as smoke and drink.'

Reverend Mother opened a drawer and took out the book in which she kept a list of applicants for her girls. She always vetted them carefully, insisting they come for interview beforehand. She pretended to study the book while considering her sister's request. It would be the worst sort of nepotism if she let Emily go to the top of the list. Yet Emily was the only flesh and blood she had and Cecilia loved her. Their only brother had been killed in the final days of the Boer War and their parents were long dead. Could she indulge her love for Emily by letting her have a girl whose head she would stuff with nonsense?

Looked at another way, it would be an opportunity for one of the more intelligent children to escape what was, let's face it, a life of drudgery, and make something of herself.

'Well?' Emily folded her arms and subjected her sister to a fierce stare. 'I know you, Cecilia. Stop pretending to read and give me an answer. Can I have a girl or not?'

Reverend Mother suddenly had a brainwave, seeing an opportunity to help her sister and herself at the same time. 'We do have someone,' she said carefully. 'She's fourteen next month. But I must warn you, she's impudent, naughty, loud, opinionated, and completely unbiddable. We do, rarely, have girls who are difficult, if not impossible, to place. She's a hard worker, but has too much lip – remember Nanny used to tell you that?'

Emily made a face. 'Has she anything nice about her?'

'She's generous, kind-hearted, amusing, curious about everything, and completely fearless.'

'Hmm! What do you know about her background?'

'Very little.' The nun shook her head. 'Fourteen years ago I was visited by a man, middle-aged, Welsh, well-dressed, rather pompous. He refused to give his name and told me one of his wife's parlour maids was expecting a child and would I take it when it arrived in a few weeks' time if it were a girl. I agreed, of course.'

'Did you believe him?' Emily asked curiously.

'Not for a minute. He looked the sort who would have shown the door to any parlour maid he discovered was pregnant. I thought it might be his own child from an illicit liaison, but he didn't look that sort, either. I decided it was almost certainly a relative's, his daughter's, maybe.'

'Has this unbiddable child got a name?'

'Of course she's got a name. What do you think we've been calling her by all these years?'

'I meant, did she *come* with a name? Or has she got one of your made-up ones?'

'She came with a name. Ruby O'Hagan. Shall I send for her?

'Why not!'

Ten minutes later, there was a knock on the office door. Reverend Mother called, 'Come' and a nun entered accompanied by a girl much taller than Emily had expected for a not-quite-fourteen-year-old. Had she not known the children were more than adequately fed, she would have suspected the child hadn't eaten in weeks. She looked pale and starved, with great dark eyes set in a peaky face, a sharp nose, and wide thin lips with an exaggerated bow. The brown uniform dress was too short, the sleeves and the hem, and her wrists and ankles were almost pathetically slight, the bones protruding as white and glossy as pearls. She had a great mane of black wavy hair tied back with brown ribbon, and she gave a bewildering impression of both fragility and strength.

The nun departed, bowing wordlessly, and the girl came and stood in front of Reverend Mother's desk, hands clasped behind her back. 'Have I been naughty again, Reverend Mother?' she asked in a loud, deep voice with an Irish accent – not surprising as most of the nuns were Irish. She didn't look concerned that the answer might be in the affirmative.

'Well, you should know that more than I, Ruby.'

'I don't *think* I have,' Ruby said earnestly. 'But sometimes I do things that don't seem the least naughty, but I'm told they are.'

Reverend Mother raised her fine eyebrows. 'Such as?'

'Such as on the way here. Sister Aloysius told me off for skipping. She said it wasn't ladylike, but she didn't answer when I asked why.'

'Young ladies are expected to conduct themselves with a certain amount of decorum, Ruby, that's why.'

It was on the tip of Emily's tongue to query this statement, but she thought better of it. 'Decorum' was such a boring word, so inhibiting. If the child wanted to skip, why shouldn't she?

Her sister spoke. 'If you have been naughty, Ruby, unwittingly or otherwise, I haven't been told. You're here because I would like you to meet Mrs Dangerfield.'

The girl transferred her big bold eyes on to the visitor. 'Hello,' she said easily.

'Hello, Ruby.' Emily smiled.

'Am I to work for you?'

'Would you like to work for me?'

'No,' Ruby said baldly, glancing briefly at Reverend Mother, who rolled her eyes heavenwards, as if asking God for patience.

'Why not?' asked Emily, taken aback.

'Because I don't want to go into service.'

'How will you support yourself, dear?'

Ruby tossed her head and her thin nose quivered. 'I'd sooner find a job on my own, like in a clothes shop, or one of those tea shop places I've seen in town. And I'll find somewhere to live on my own too. I don't like being bossed around.'

Reverend Mother's expression was grim. 'You'll be "bossed around" as you put it, in a clothes shop or a cafe, Ruby. Have you not thought of that?'

'Yes, but I won't *belong* to them, will I?' The dark eyes blazed. 'Not like in service. I don't want to belong to anyone except myself.'

Hear, hear, Emily echoed silently. Aloud she said, 'I don't want a servant. I want a live-in friend.'

It was Ruby's turn to look taken aback. She put her narrow head on one side and thought a moment. 'I'd make a good friend,' she said eventually. 'I've got friends already, lots.'

'Would you like *us* to be friends, Ruby?'

There was a choking sound from behind the desk. Reverend Mother rose and said coldly, 'Please leave, Ruby. I would like to talk to Mrs Dangerfield alone.'

The girl looked mutinous. 'But I want to be her friend!'

'I said, leave.'

'There was no need to bite her head off,' Emily said lightly when Ruby had gone.

'What on earth do you think you're doing?' Her sister's voice shivered with anger, anger mainly directed at herself for having allowed the situation to proceed this far. Emily was an entirely unsuitable person to have a child and she should have told her so straight away. 'Ruby's not a toy, or a piece of furniture to decorate your home. She's a child, a human being. How long is she likely to remain your friend? Until you decide to go on another round-the-world cruise? What happens if you get married again?'

'If I go away I'll take Ruby with me. And the idea of remarrying horrifies me. I'll treat her as a daughter, honest. Let's face it, sis,' Emily said reasonably, 'You've got an awkward customer there. Put into service she won't last a week. We'll be doing each other a favour if you let me have her.'

'That's putting it very crudely, Emily.'

'And very wisely, Cecilia. By the way,' Emily twinkled. 'Are you allowed to lose your temper? God *will* be annoyed. I think this calls for an extensive bout of flagellation tonight.'

The other residents of the convent, nuns and girls alike, would have been alarmed had they witnessed the calm, controlled face of Reverend Mother turn such a deep red. 'You're impossible. Please go. As regards Ruby, I'll think about it.'

Ruby prayed extraordinarily hard over the next few weeks that Mrs Dangerfield would come back. It wasn't that she wanted a grown-up friend, but the idea of going into service, being at the beck and call of a houseful of strangers, made her sick. She'd run away before she'd do it. Sister Finbar had once said she was no good at being good, and then got cross when Ruby had agreed. Ruby had no intention of being good unless she felt like it.

Reverend Mother also prayed. She asked God for guidance in her dilemma. Would she be denying a child the chance of a better life by refusing her sister's request? Or would the child be damaged if she acceded to it? And did it make a difference that the child concerned was Ruby O'Hagan who would present an equally troublesome dilemma next month when she reached fourteen and it was time for her to leave the walls of the convent?

She couldn't visualise the girl settling in the kindest, most accommodating of households. She would question the simplest order if she couldn't see a reason for it. The sisters were always complaining. Why couldn't she make her bed her own way? Ruby wanted to know. Why did all beds have to be made the same? Why did everyone's shoes have to be laced identically? Why did her hair have to be tied back when she would have liked it loose? What difference did it make to God how she did her hair? Why couldn't she wear her long winter socks if it was cold in September? It made no sense waiting until October just because it was a rule. Reverend Mother had changed the rule because she couldn't see the sense in it either.

Maybe the world needed people who wanted to change the rules. Ruby O'Hagan would undoubtedly be better off with Emily than in a place where unnecessary orders had to be obeyed. She wrote to her sister and suggested she visit again in the middle of April, after Ruby's birthday. 'It will give you plenty of time to get her room ready,' she put at the end.

Emily Dangerfield didn't pray. She didn't believe in it. It would be a bore having to drive Ruby to Mass at St Kentigern's, the pretty little Catholic church in Melling, where she hadn't been since Edwin died, a fact her sister was unaware of. Cecilia assumed her faith was as strong as it had always been and Emily saw no need to disabuse her. They met so rarely and she preferred to reproach Cecilia about the regressive policies of the convent about which she didn't, in fact, give a damn, rather than have Cecilia reproach her for her loss of faith.

What had praying ever done for her? She'd prayed for happiness, but look what she'd ended up with – a dry-as-dust husband who showed no interest in physical contact of the most basic sort once he'd sired two sons, forcing Emily to go elsewhere. And the sons! Adrian was in Australia, sheep-farming of all things, and she was unlikely ever to see him again. Rupert lived in London, but may as well have been in Australia with his brother for all she saw of him and his wife. She'd met her grandchildren, Sara and James, just twice.

If Ruby came, she would treat her as a daughter. Bestow all the love that no one else apparently wanted on a fragile, orphan child. And perhaps it wouldn't hurt to start going to Mass again, either.

Four weeks later, on a cool, sunny, spring day, Ruby emerged from the convent carrying a brown paper parcel tied with string and accompanied by a tearful nun. There was no sign of Reverend Mother, Emily hadn't been invited inside. The girl's eyes were dazzling. She joyfully threw back her narrow shoulders, ready to face the world.

Emily opened the passenger door of her grey Jaguar car and patted the leather seat. Ruby put her hand on the door and looked curiously inside. Then she slid on to the seat with a quiet smile and the ease of someone who had been getting into expensive cars all her life. She threw the parcel on to the back seat and waved to the nun. 'I haven't been in a car before,' she said.

'I'd never have guessed,' Emily said drily. She started up the engine and they drove away. 'Aren't you sad?' she enquired.

'A little bit,' Ruby conceded, taking the brown ribbon off her hair and tossing it loose. 'But it's silly to feel sad over something that can't be helped.'

'Very sensible, but not a concept that can be taken literally throughout one's entire life.'

'What's a concept? And what does "literally" mean?'

'I'll give you a dictionary when we get home and you can look it up for yourself.'

'What's a dictionary?'

'You'll see when you get one.'

At first, Ruby found going fast exciting, but a bit scary. She tensed whenever another car came towards them, convinced they'd crash, but the cars easily passed and she quickly forgot her fear. She said little, but her eyes sparkled with interest, even if the countryside they drove through was the same as that she'd been used to all her life: vast green fields, undulating hills, untidy hedges full of birds. They came to the occasional village that looked dull compared to Abergele.

'We're in England now, dear, Cheshire,' Emily said – she'd been told to call Mrs Dangerfield 'Emily'. 'We've just crossed the border.'

'You mean we're in another country!' Ruby was impressed.

'Yes. In a few years, people won't have to drive such a long way round to Liverpool. There's a tunnel under the River Mersey, but it isn't ready for cars yet.'

'Reverend Mother said I was going to live in Liverpool. It's where Sister Frances comes from. She said it's bigger than Abergele.'

'Much, much bigger, but it isn't exactly Liverpool where you'll live. My house is on the outskirts, a place called Kirkby. Tomorrow, we'll go to town and buy you some clothes. I'm sure you'll be pleased to get out of that ugly brown frock.'

'Clothes from a shop?'

'Of course, Ruby. Where else?' Emily thought the girl's naivety utterly delightful.

'I've always wanted to go in a shop.' Ruby gave a blissful sigh.

'I must warn you, dear, that Liverpool is terribly noisy. There's loads of traffic and crowds of shoppers. You mustn't be frightened. Cities are very busy places.'

'I'm never frightened,' Ruby said stoutly, having forgotten her recent fear that the car might crash. 'Are we nearly there?'

'We've still got some way to go.'

Ruby snorted and began to twiddle her thumbs, bored. England looked exactly the same as Wales. She visibly perked up when the scenery became more industrialised and squealed with delight when they reached Runcorn and the car drove on to the transporter bridge and they were carried across the shimmering Mersey on a metal sling, a process that Emily always found daunting.

They drove through a forest of tall chimneys spewing black smoke into the blue sky. 'They look ugly,' Ruby opined.

Emily nodded agreement. 'This is Widnes.'

'Ugly, but interesting. Everything's interesting. Are we nearly at Kirkby?' she said impatiently.

'Not far.'

The countryside became flatter, houses more frequent. Ruby bobbed up and down at Emily's side, exclaiming at every single thing, asking so many questions that Emily's head began to spin.

'What's that little boy doing?'

'He's riding a scooter.'

'I've never seen a scooter before. What's that building there?'

'A church, dear.'

'It's *big*. The church in the convent was only little. Can I go there to Mass on Sunday?'

'No, Ruby, it's too far away, and it's not a Catholic church.'

'What was it then?'

'I didn't notice,' Emily said desperately. 'A Protestant church of some sort.'

Ruby screamed. 'Look! What's wrong with that man's face?'

'Nothing. He's got a beard.'

'He looks like an animal. Are we nearly there, Emily?'

'In a minute.'

Emily gave a sigh of relief when she turned the car into the drive of Brambles, the house that wasn't hers any more, but belonged to her sons. If it hadn't been for that she would have sold up the minute Edwin died and moved somewhere more exciting: London, Brighton, or even abroad, Paris, or Berlin which was said to be fascinating, although this Hitler business was worrying. Edwin had left her well provided for, but she was scared to give up the security of her home and rent a place – the sort she aspired to would eat up a goodly portion of her income.

'Is this it?'

'Yes, Ruby, this is it.' Emily opened the car door and got out. Ruby collected her parcel and followed.

'It's not as big as the convent,' she said, a touch disparagingly Emily thought.

'Maybe not,' she said defensively, 'But it's bigger than most houses. It has twelve rooms, six upstairs and six down, that's not counting the kitchen and two bathrooms. Let's go inside so you can see.'

It was a relief to enter the empty house accompanied by another human being – the staff had all gone home by now. Emily felt grateful for Ruby's loud cries as she ran in and out of the rooms, admiring the furniture, the ornaments, ending up back in the hall, where she examined herself critically, from top to toe, in the full-length mirror, twisting and turning, peering over her shoulder at her back.

'We didn't have mirrors in the convent.' She glanced pertly at Emily. 'We used to look at ourselves in the windows when it went dark. The nuns got cross if they saw us. Vanity is a sin, they said. *I* said, surely God wouldn't mind a person wanting to look nice.'

'And what did they say then?' Emily asked, interested.

'They said it was one thing to look nice, but quite another to dwell on it. I still think that's rubbish, but they got annoyed if I argued too much.' She pointed. 'What's that?'

'A telephone, dear. I'll show you how to use it one day.'

'Can I see where I'll sleep?'

Upstairs, Emily threw open the door of the pretty white and yellow room she'd had prepared next to her own bedroom. 'This is yours.'

Ruby flung herself joyfully on to the bed, oohed and aahed over the yellow flowered curtains that matched the dressing table skirt, and had another hard look at herself in the wardrobe mirror.

'Will you mind sleeping by yourself?' Emily asked. 'You're used to a dormitory, aren't you?'

'I *hate* dormitories,' Ruby said with feeling. 'We were made to go to bed awful early and had to be quiet even if we couldn't sleep. It wasn't so bad in summer, 'cause you could read under the covers, but when it was dark and they took the paraffin lamp away, you couldn't see a thing.' She smiled cajolingly at Emily. 'Will you let me have a lamp to read in bed? After all, I'm your *friend.*'

Emily laughed. 'You can read to your heart's content, Ruby. And you don't need a lamp, you switch the light on here, just inside the door.'

'Jaysus, Mary and Joseph!' Ruby gasped when the already bright room was flooded with more light. 'What's that when it's at home?'

'It's electricity, and please don't ask me to explain it to you, dear. You can look it up in the encyclopaedia. That's a book, and you'll find it with the dictionary in the room that used to be my husband's study,' she added quickly when Ruby opened her mouth to ask what an encyclopedia was. 'Shall we go down and see what Mrs Arkwright has left for tea?'

On her way to bed that night, Emily paused outside Ruby's door, her hand on the knob, about to go in and make sure the child was all right after the day's upheaval. But say if she *wasn't* all right. She might be upset, even crying. She'd never known how to comfort people, not even her own boys when they were little. A nursemaid had carried out the task on her behalf until her sons went to boarding school at the age of seven. If they required sympathy of any sort during the holidays, they'd never said. Even when Edwin was dying, she hadn't known what to say. Emily removed her hand from the knob and hurried into her own room.

Unusually, that same night Reverend Mother couldn't sleep for the worry that bobbed about in her mind, like a yacht in a stormy sea. A memory surfaced, of when Emily was eight and she was ten. It was Christmas and they each found a doll beside their bed when they woke up, huge dolls, bigger than a real baby and dressed as an adult, in bunchy, silk, lace-trimmed frocks, frilly bonnets, underclothes, and even tiny necklaces. Emily's doll was blonde, its clothes pink, Cecilia's had dark hair and wore blue.

Emily had glanced from one doll to the other and announced in a weepy, whining voice that she wanted the blue one. Cecilia had held out, wanting her own, but gave in eventually, preferring a quiet life to a blue doll on Christmas Day. Anyway, the pink doll was quite nice. They swapped dolls, Emily calmed down, and the girls played happily with their presents throughout the day.

Nanny was putting them to bed, when Emily burst into tears and said she preferred the pink doll after all. This time Cecilia refused, having grown quite fond of the doll which she had christened Victoria after the Queen.

Emily screamed, Nanny pleaded, 'After all, it's the one she was given, Cecy, dear.'

'All right, she can have them both. I don't want the blue one back.'

Emily had played with the pink doll all Boxing Day, then abandoned it for something else. The dolls had been put in a cupboard and Cecilia couldn't remember having seen them again.

The same thing had happened on numerous other occasions, but none stuck in her mind quite so clearly as the case of the two dolls. Emily wanted things to the exclusion of everything else, but once she got them, used them, played with them for a while, she lost all interest.

Reverend Mother had no idea what time it was when she eventually fell into a restless sleep. She woke with a start when Sister Angela knocked on the door at five o'clock, interrupting a vivid dream. The dolls, she'd been dreaming about the dolls, the blue one and the pink one. Emily had thrown them away in the little woods not far from where they lived and Cecilia had gone to rescue them. She'd found them face down at the foot of a tree amid a pile of rotting leaves and when she turned them over both dolls had the thin, pale face of Ruby O'Hagan.

The nun got out of bed, knelt on the hard stone floor, and began to pray.

3

Ruby always woke up long before Emily. She would sit up straight away, stretch her arms, and look to see if the sun was shining through the yellow curtains. Whether it was or not, she would leap out of bed, get washed – she actually had her own little sink in the corner – and put on one of the frocks Emily had bought for her in Liverpool or Southport.

Of these places, Ruby preferred Liverpool. She liked the big, crowded shops, the bustle and noise. She loved the tramcars – there seemed to be hundreds and hundreds of them trundling along the metal lines making a terrible din and throwing off showers of sparks. She envied the occupants of these wonderful vehicles and longed to ride in one – Emily went everywhere by car. Liverpool buildings were magnificent: the Corn Exchange, the Customs House, the Town Hall, and her favourite, St George's Hall which, according to Emily, was famous throughout the world for its elegant design.

Emily preferred Southport, which Ruby thought all right, quite pretty, but very limited, and a bit too posh. She couldn't take to posh people, which Emily said was due to the way she'd been brought up.

'What do you mean?' Ruby demanded.

'The convent made sure you didn't have ideas above your station,' Emily explained. 'The girls weren't encouraged to have ambitions beyond becoming head cook or marrying the butler. You can't take to posh people, as you call them, because they make you feel inferior.'

'No, they don't,' Ruby argued. 'I just don't like the way they look down their noses at people who aren't as posh as themselves. I had no intention of being a cook, or marrying a butler come to that.'

Emily had merely shrugged, which Ruby took to mean her argument was inescapable. She considered herself as good as anyone in the world.

One morning, when Ruby had been living in Kirkby for just over three months, she woke to find the August sunshine dancing through the window of her room, turning it into a grotto of golden light. She scrambled out of bed, drew back the curtains, and surveyed the back garden, which consisted of a vast square lawn surrounded by neat flower borders, an orchard, a tennis court, and a vegetable patch tucked away at the bottom. Everywhere was surrounded by birch trees with silver leaves which she'd been told would turn gold in the autumn. There wasn't another house in sight, the nearest was over a mile away.

What would she do today?

A few weeks ago, Emily had suggested she might like to go to school in September. At some schools, girls could stay until they were sixteen or even eighteen. Ruby had made a face and said she'd learnt enough, thanks all the same. Emily said she could do whatever she liked, it was up to her.

Emily didn't mind if she did, or didn't do, all sorts of things. She could stay up as late as she liked, read all night if she wanted, not eat her vegetables, have two helpings of pudding if there was enough, go out to play, or come back, whenever she pleased. Ruby found this a tiny bit unsettling and she quite missed the rules she'd been so fond of breaking at the convent. It was as if Emily didn't *care*, a suspicion that grew as the weeks passed and Emily seemed to lose all interest in taking her out, whether to go shopping or just for a ride. She'd made new friends, the Rowland-Graves, who'd just come back from India to live a few miles away in Knowsley. The Rowland-Graves threw loads of parties: bridge parties, cocktail parties, theatre parties, and parties that could go on all night. Emily was forever getting her hair done and buying new clothes, going out almost daily, draped in furs, even when it was hot. Despite this, she was always very glad Ruby was there to talk to when she came home.

Ruby decided to go to Humble's Farm for the milk and eggs, to save Mr Humble delivering them. She put on what Emily called a housefrock: red cotton patterned with big white flowers and white piping on the collar and sleeves. Emily said her taste was garish and she hoped she'd grow out of it one day. She liked flowery patterns too much. 'Plain clothes are so much more tasteful, Ruby.' Even so, she was allowed to have whatever caught her eye. She pulled on white ankle socks, pushed her feet into sandals, and collected a jug and basin from the kitchen.

It was going to be another scorching day, already hot as Ruby ran along the edge of the fields planted with an assortment of crops. Mr Humble's farm wasn't big, more a smallholding. He had a few cows, a few sheep, a few pigs, quite a lot of hens, a plough horse called Waterloo, a downtrodden wife, five grown-up children who had left home – 'And who could blame them?' said Emily – and a farmhand called Jacob whom Ruby found quite interesting, mainly because he was the only other young person she knew.

Jacob Veering was eighteen, not enormously tall, but broad and solid, with hair a lovely buttery shade and eyes the colour of bluebells. He was very dirty, very handsome, and also, said Emily, a bastard. 'Just like you, I expect,' she added.

Ruby had looked up 'bastard' in the dictionary. It meant 'illegitimate', so she looked *that* up, and it meant 'out of wedlock'. Wedlock meant, 'in a wedded state'. By this time, Ruby had rather lost track and given up.

Jacob's mother lived in a little cottage opposite Kirkby church. Her name was Ruth, and she was a 'fey creature', according to Emily, supporting herself by making coloured candles that were sold in big shops like George Henry Lee's and Henderson's. She wasn't interested in Jacob, and he'd lived on Humble's Farm over Waterloo's stable since he was twelve.

'Is Jacob a Catholic?' Ruby enquired. 'So I can talk to him?'

'For goodness' sake, Ruby, dear. You can talk to Jacob if he's a heathen, which I suspect he is.'

Mrs Humble was collecting eggs when Ruby arrived, out of breath having run all the way. Everywhere in the area of the farmyard was thick with dirt and smelled strongly of manure, particularly when it was hot. Ruby dreaded to think what it would be like in winter when it might smell less, but the caked dirt would turn to mud.

'The usual?' Mrs Humble asked in her sad, beaten voice. She was as bent as an old woman, yet only forty-nine. She wore a frayed shawl, holding the ends together with a gnarled, red hand.

'Yes, please. Six eggs and a jug of milk.'

'Jacob's doing the milking right now.'

'I'll just say good morning.'

Ruby approached the cowshed on tiptoe, though wasn't sure why. Unusually for her, she felt nervous around Jacob. He was polite, but a bit reserved, and she always got the feeling she was in the way. She reached the door and said shyly, 'Hello.'

Jacob wore grubby corduroy trousers tied up with a rope and a frayed collarless shirt with half the sleeves cut off. His arms and face were very brown and his unlaced boots were planted in the straw, as if he'd grown there like a tree. He didn't look up from the task of pulling expertly at the teats of a black and white cow, each teat squirting a thin stream of creamy milk into a metal bucket.

'Hello,' he said, in a voice that wasn't exactly friendly, but wasn't unfriendly, either.

'It's a nice morning.'

'Known few better,' he grunted.

Ruby searched her mind for something to say. Jacob never started a conversation, only speaking when he was spoken to. 'Do you ever listen to the wireless?' she enquired.

'Haven't got one,' Jacob replied.

'We've got one in the house. And a gramophone, too.'

'Have you, now.'

'They play music. Do you like music?'

'Music's all right,' Jacob conceded.

'You can come and listen, if you like. Come on Saturday, after six o'clock. Emily's going to the theatre – that's a place that puts on plays,' she added, in case Jacob didn't know.

Jacob showed no sign of having known or not. 'I'll think about it,' he said.

Mrs Humble came in with a ladle, scooped milk from the bucket and poured it into Ruby's jug. 'The eggs are ready,' she said dully.

'Ta.' Ruby looked anxiously at Jacob. 'See you Saturday?'

'You might.' He still didn't look up.

Ruby sighed and made her way slowly back to Brambles, where Mrs Arkwright, the cook, was just hoisting her stout, perspiring body off her bike.

'Got the eggs and milk,' Ruby announced.

'Have you, now,' Mrs Arkwright replied, tight-lipped, before wheeling the bike round to the back. Ruby followed. The two didn't get on. Months ago, on Ruby's first visit to the kitchen, she had helpfully pointed out the ham currently boiling on the stove would taste better with the addition of a bay leaf – something she had learnt in the convent – and Mrs Arkwright immediately saw her as a threat, intent on taking over her job if she wasn't careful. From thereon, Ruby was discouraged from entering the kitchen.

The cleaner, Mrs Roberts, was just as discouraging. She was old and weary and made it obvious that Ruby's constant chatter got on her nerves.

At least Ernest, the gardener, was friendly, even if he couldn't hear a word she said, being totally deaf. He'd thrown a rope over one of the apple trees to make a swing.

Ruby was badly in need of a friend. She found the countryside very dull. There was plenty to do, but she would have liked someone to do it with – she got no satisfaction from playing in the orchard by herself. Tennis was frustrating when there was no one to hit the ball back. She wondered if it was too late to agree to school, though she'd like to bet it was full of posh girls whom she wouldn't like and she'd regret it straight away. If only Emily would *make* her go. There was a world of difference between being made to do something you didn't want, and taking the decision yourself. If it turned out horrid you had someone else to blame.

She went through the kitchen, deposited the eggs and milk on the table and made a face at Mrs Arkwright's disapproving back.

For the next half hour, she studied the dictionary in Emily's late husband's study. Edwin Dangerfield had been a solicitor specialising in conveyancing which meant transferring things, usually property – Ruby had looked it up. The dictionary was her favourite book and every day she learnt six useful words. Last week, she'd reached 'B'. She was wondering if there was any point in remembering 'bacterium', when she heard Mrs Arkwright make her heavy way upstairs with her employer's morning coffee. She put the book away and, as soon as the cook came down, she flew up the stairs to see Emily.

'Oh, Gawd!' Emily groaned when Ruby put her smiling face around the door. 'You look inordinately cheerful and so bloody *young!* You make me feel at least a hundred. What's it like outside? I told Arky not to open the curtains. My head's splitting from last night.' Last night, the Rowland-Graves had held a dinner party.

'It's nice outside, sunny and warm.'

Emily winced. 'I'd prefer it dull and cold.'

'I thought we could go shopping,' Ruby said hopefully as she sat on the edge of the bed.

'Sorry, dear. I'm going to a garden party this afternoon. I'm urgently in need of a rejuvenating bath and you know how long it takes me to get ready.'

It took hours of massaging the sagging skin, painting the ageing face, teasing the dyed hair into a satisfactory style, trying on at least a dozen outfits, deciding which shoes went best with the frock or costume that had been chosen, searching for appropriate jewellery, the most flattering hat.

'I need new shoes,' Ruby growled. 'All the ones I've got now are too small.'

'Oh, dear!' Emily bit her lip, feeling guilty that she was neglecting the girl. If Mim and Ronnie Rowland-Graves hadn't appeared on the scene, Emily would have leapt at the idea of shopping for shoes. But to her everlasting relief, Mim and Ronnie had. They'd led a fast, slightly *risqué* life in India and were set on doing the same in England. In their early fifties, their main aim in life was to have a good time. They paid no regard to the married status of their guests, nor their ages, as long as they shared their quest for excitement, which involved drinking too much, engaging in spicy conversation, and even spicier party games, all of which would have shocked Edwin to the bones were he still alive.

She stared at Ruby's thin face, no longer cheerful, still looking as if she hadn't eaten a decent meal in ages, and wondered if she was lonely by herself for so much of the time. Emily couldn't possibly have taken her to the Rowland-Graves's, which was no place for a young girl. She had an idea. 'If you like, later, I'll drop you off at Kirkby station and you can go to Liverpool and buy shoes yourself.'

Ruby couldn't have been more delighted had she been offered the Crown Jewels. She leapt off the bed and danced around the room. '*Can* I? Oh, *can* I? Oh, Emily, I'd *love* to. I've never been on a train. What time are you leaving? Shall I get changed?'

'But how will you get home from the station?' Emily was already wishing she hadn't been quite so hasty. Was she being irresponsible? No, she decided after a few seconds' thought. Had Ruby gone into service, she would have been given all sorts of onerous tasks to do, shopping among them. It would do the girl good to go out by herself.

'I'll walk home from the station. It's not far, only a few miles,' Ruby said fervently, her big, dark eyes suddenly anxious that the wonderful treat might be denied.

'Are you sure?'

'Absolutely certain.'

The big train came charging into Kirkby station like a monster, snorting clouds of dirty smoke. Ruby, in her best dress – white, patterned with rosebuds – climbed into a carriage, hugging herself with glee. She had two ten-shilling notes folded in her purse, as well as a further five shillings in coins for her fare and any other expenses that might occur.

All the way to Liverpool, much to the irritation of the only other passenger, a woman, she flew from one side of the carriage to the other to look at the view, at the way it changed from soft green fields to rows of cramped brick houses then to a forest of factories before drawing into Exchange station where she got off, marvelling at the vastness of the building and the steaming, panting trains.

Happiness bounced like a ball in Ruby's chest as she made her way through the crowded, vibrant city to Lewis's department store where, feeling terribly important, she bought a pair of Clarks' sandals for four and eleven, and black patent leather shoes with a strap and button for seven and six. It had been *almost* true to claim she'd grown out of the shoes she already had. She'd said it in an attempt to persuade Emily to take her shopping. And it had worked better than she'd hoped. It was nice being on her own, able to go where she pleased, not having to keep retreating to the Adelphi Hotel for coffee and a cigarette, as Emily felt the need to do.

Emerging from Lewis's, she stood on the busy pavement, buffeted by the crowds, breathing in the choking fumes and the various smells that she liked better than those of the country, wondering where to go next. Not back to Kirkby, it was too early.

She wandered along, starry-eyed, looking in shop windows – window-shopping Emily called it. Blacklers had a display of frocks and one in particular caught Ruby's eye: navy blue with bold red spots, it had a frilly neck with a red bow and flared sleeves like little skirts, and was only one and elevenpence, about a quarter of what Emily usually paid. It was a lady's frock, not a child's, but Ruby was tall enough to wear it. She went inside and tried it on, twirling around in front of the cubicle mirror.

'It looks the gear on you, luv,' the assistant said.

'I'll take it.' The frock was calf-length, whereas all her others came to just below the knees. She thought it made her look very adult. She handed the assistant half a crown which was sent whizzing high across the shop in a little tube attached to a wire towards a woman in a glass case who removed the tube and, a minute later, Ruby's change whizzed back with the bill. She never ceased to be facinated by this process.

Outside again, she decided to wear the frock on Saturday in case Jacob came. She crossed the road, dodging through the traffic, and just missed being mown down by a tramcar with Number 1 and its destination, Dingle, on the front.

'Dingle'. She said the word aloud. It sounded pretty, like something out of a fairy-tale. She noticed that the tram had stopped and people were getting on. It took barely a second for Ruby to decide to get on with them.

She'd always wanted to ride on a tram. She climbed to the top and sat on the hard front seat, which gave a perfect view.

The tram set off, clicking noisily along the lines, swerving round bends, breaking suddenly, when a queue appeared, waiting to board. Ruby clutched her parcels with one hand, and held on to the edge of her seat with the other, worried she might be thrown through the window as the tram rocked dangerously from side to side. They passed the soaring tower of the Protestant cathedral which had been started in the last century but still wasn't finished.

The conductor came. Ruby bought a penny ticket which would take her all the way to the Dingle. 'Will you tell me when we get there?' She'd heard him shouting the names of the stops.

'You'll know, luv. We don't go no further than the Dingle.'

The tram was rolling along a long, colourful and very busy road, full of traffic and lined with every conceivable sort of shop, interrupted frequently by little streets of terraced houses. Groups of men lounged outside the pubs that seemed to be on every corner, hands in pockets, idle. Women chatted eagerly over their bags of shopping, children hanging on to their skirts or chasing each other up and down the pavements, in and out of the shops.

Ruby's eyes were everywhere, taking it all in, the way the women were dressed, some almost as smart as Emily, some with shawls over their heads like poor Mrs Humble. There were men in suits and bowler hats, and jackletless men with braces showing, no collars to their shirts, tieless. She saw scrubbed, neatly dressed children, glowing with health, and felt a surge of pity when she saw the scabby-faced mites with bare, dirty feet who were much too thin.

It was like being at the very hub of the universe and Ruby, clutching the seat, knew with utter certainty that this was where she belonged: amid people, noise, and city smells. She felt at home in the clutter of the busy streets in a way she never would in Kirkby where there wasn't another house in sight.

'I'll come back,' she whispered to herself. 'I'll come back tomorrow or the next day, and one of these days, I'll come back for good.'

She got off at the tram sheds and walked up and down the tiny streets. Women sat contentedly on the whitened steps outside their neat houses, enjoying the brilliant sunshine. Children swung from the lamp-posts, played hopscotch on the pavement, whip and top, or two-balls against the walls.

Ruby sighed enviously and supposed she'd better be getting home.

On Saturday night, Emily went to the theatre wearing a new grey silk costume and a little matching hat with a veil, her fox fur laid casually around her shoulders despite the gloriously hot day.

'You'll be all right won't you, dear?' she said worriedly. 'You can read a book or listen to the wireless. I'll tell you what the play was about when I get home.'

'I'll be fine,' Ruby said stoutly.

As soon as Emily had gone, she went upstairs and changed into the spotted dress from Blacklers. It clung to her thin body and, she was pleased to note, emphasised her small breasts, making her look very grown-up, particularly when she piled her black hair on top of her head, securing it with a slide.

She went into Emily's room, searched through the jewellery box on the dressing table which had been left in a terrible mess, and helped herself to a pearl necklace and earrings – Emily had gone out wearing her 'good' pearls. She tried on a pair of red, high-heeled shoes. They were only a bit too big.

Downstairs, she switched on the wireless and was met by a thunderous blast of classical music which she turned off in disgust, deciding to play one of her favourite records instead: a selection of ballads sung by Rudy Vallee, and so hauntingly lovely, they made her go all funny inside.

Ruby began to sway as she watched the record spin around. 'Goodnight, Sweetheart' was one of her favourites. Unable to resist, she kicked off the shoes, flung her arms in the air, and danced around the room, very slowly, hugging herself. The music was causing a sweet, nagging ache in her tummy, it always did, making her want things she couldn't define. She closed her eyes and tried to imagine someone in the room with her, a man. They were dancing together. She was being kissed by invisible lips in a way she'd never seen people kiss before. Ruby had no idea where the thoughts came from. She must have been born with them.

Rudy Vallee began to sing 'Night and Day', and still Ruby danced, losing herself completely in the glorious, romantic music, unaware that she had an audience.

Outside the window, Jacob Veering, his face shiny after a thorough scrubbing, wearing his one and only suit, didn't think he had ever seen anything so beautiful as the strange young lady fluttering like a butterfly across the room. He had never known anyone like her. His tongue would form a lump in his throat whenever she spoke to him, and it was all he could do to answer.

Jacob already had a girlfriend, Audrey Wainwright, whose father owned a farm much bigger than Humble's. There was an unspoken agreement that they would marry one day and he would transfer his labour from Humble's farm to Wainwright's, where he would live and work for the rest of his life. He wasn't particularly looking forward to the future, but nor did he regard it with dread. As long as he could work on the land, have a place to live, enough to eat, and no one abused him, Jacob would be content, if not happy. Being a man he would need a wife and Audrey Wainwright would fill this role. He assumed she felt the same. The word 'love' had never been uttered during their relationship, but if either had noticed they didn't seem to mind.

But now, as he watched Ruby dance, sensations he'd never felt before were causing tremors in Jacob's normally stolid heart. It was pounding for one thing, so hard and so fast that he felt frightened. He had the urge to smash the window, climb inside, catch Ruby by her tiny waist and twirl her round and round till they both fell dizzily to the floor in each other's arms. Yet he knew he could never bring himself to touch her. She was out of bounds to someone like him. She was a creature from another world to which Jacob, the farmhand, didn't belong.

She looked so strong, and yet so frail, and there was an expression on her face that he envied, a dreamy, lost expression, as if she was somewhere else entirely than the room in which she danced. Jacob had never felt like that and he wondered what it was like. He also wondered if she remembered she had invited him to the house that night. Well, there was only one way of finding out. He knocked on the front door.

When she answered, Jacob gasped. Her eyes were starbright, her cheeks were flushed, and she bestowed upon him a warm look of welcome that caused his heart to pound even more.

'I didn't think you'd turn up!' She reached for his hand. 'Come and listen to the music. I've been dancing. Can you dance?'

'No,' Jacob said thickly. He allowed himself to be pulled inside and immediately felt ill at ease in the richly furnished house with carpets on the floor and ornaments and pictures all over the place. There were velvet chairs in the room into which she led him and the music was louder here. A man was singing about his heart standing still and Jacob wished his own heart would do the same. He couldn't take his eyes away from the little curls that clung damply to Ruby's slender neck and his hand was tingling from her touch.

She smiled at him. 'Would you like something to eat? There's a big apple pie for tomorrow, but Emily won't care if we eat it.'

'Wouldn't mind,' Jacob grunted, wishing he didn't sound so surly.

He was dragged into a big scullery where he gaped at the extraordinary cream stove, the shallow cream sink, the green painted cupboards, the black and white check-tiled floor. She took a golden-crusted pie out of the larder. 'Would you like tea or coffee?' She gestured to him to sit at the big table in the centre of the room.

'Tea.' He had never had coffee and had no idea what it was like. She made him feel very ignorant, a bit of an oaf, with her gramophone and coffee and a scullery the likes of which he'd never seen before – he had a feeling people like her called them 'kitchens'.

He watched as she poured water into what was definitely a kettle, but instead of putting it on the peculiar stove to boil, she attached it to the wall with a plug. Overcome with curiosity, he said, 'What's that?'

'It's an electric kettle. Haven't you seen electricity before?'

'They have it in the pub by the station, The Railway Arms.'

'I didn't even know electricity existed until I came to live with Emily. We had paraffin lamps in the convent and the food was cooked in an oven by the kitchen fire. It was called a range.'

'The convent?'

She put milk and sugar on the table and sat opposite him, folding her thin arms. 'The convent where I grew up.'

'But Mr Humble said you were Mrs Dangerfield's niece or something, a relative.'

'Oh, no.' She laughed and her wide mouth almost reached her ears. 'I'm an orphan. The convent was an orphanage, still is. Emily just wanted a friend and she picked me.' She preened herself.

'Don't you mind being an orphan?' Jacob missed not having a father, but at least could boast a mother, even if she hadn't been up to much.

Ruby shrugged carelessly. 'Seems a waste of time, minding. What help would it be?'

Jacob stared at her, blinking. The fact that she was an orphan, that she didn't truly belong in a grand house like this, had brought her, in a way, down to his level. At the same time, it only made her seem more remarkable and untouchable that she had so quickly made herself at home, fitting so easily into rich people's ways, though she didn't talk posh like Mrs Dangerfield.

The kettle boiled. She got up, switched it off, and made the tea. 'Do you take sugar?'

'Two spoons, ta. How did your mam and dad die?'

'I don't know if they're alive or dead. Sister Cecilia said I wasn't even a day old when I arrived at the convent. There was a note to say I was called Ruby O'Hagan, that's all.'

'O'Hagan sounds Irish. Ruby's nice.' Jacob blushed.

'So's Jacob. Would you like some pie?'

Jacob nodded. 'I'll have to be going soon. I'm meeting someone in the pub for a drink.' He didn't say it was his future father-in-law.

'Oh!' Ruby pouted. 'I thought you'd come for longer. You can come again next week. Come whenever you like, 'cept when Emily's here. You can tell if the car's in the drive.'

'OK, ta.'

The pie finished, Jacob left by the rear door. When he got to the front, he heard music. Looking back, he saw Ruby bending over the gramophone. Suddenly, she turned and began to dance. Jacob stood watching for ages and ages, and it was all he could do to tear himself away.

From that week on, life for Ruby was no longer dull. Two, three, sometimes four times a week, whenever Emily was out, she would catch the train to Exchange station and explore Liverpool – the centre of the city and its environs. She discovered the Pier Head where ferries sailed across the Mersey to Birkenhead, Seacombe, and best of all, New Brighton where, if she had enough money, she bought fish and chips, ice cream, and made herself pleasantly sick on the fairground.

'I hope you're not coming down with something,' Emily would say in a concerned voice when she couldn't eat her tea.

'I'll eat it later.' She usually did, better by then. Her appetite was voracious, though she never put on weight. Emily remarked she was growing taller.

She went by tram to every possible destination: Bootle, Walton Vale, Aigburth, Woolton, Penny Lane, getting off along the way, or at the terminus, where she roamed the streets, envious of the way people lived so closely together. A few times, she strolled along the Dock Road, possibly the busiest and most frenziedly noisy place of all, with its foreign smells, hooting, blaring traffic nose to tail, the funnels of enormous ships soaring over the dock walls. The pavements were packed with people jabbering away in languages that were rarely English. She had to push her way through, heart lifting at the exhilerating strangeness of every single thing.

The Dingle remained her favourite place, perhaps because she'd gone there first. A few of the tram conductors got to know her and greeted her as a friend.

The money for fares Ruby found in Emily's large collection of handbags where there were always a few coins that would never be missed. It wasn't stealing. She knew, if asked, Emily would give her money to buy sweets or comics or coloured pencils from the post office, but possibly not to travel the length and breadth of Liverpool by various means. It seemed less troublesome to help herself to money than tell a lie.

Sometimes Emily arrived home before her and when she got in Ruby would say she'd been for a walk.

'In the dark, dear!'

'It was light when I left. I didn't realise I'd walked so far.' Emily didn't notice she always made the same excuse.

Jacob usually turned up in the evenings when Emily was out. Since the night he had seen Ruby dance, Jacob had discovered that sitting in the Wainwrights', as he did most nights, with Audrey, her mam and dad, and two younger sisters, talking or playing cards, drinking tea and eating Mrs Wainwright's rather dry home-made scones, then retiring with Audrey to the stuffy parlour to exchange a few chaste kisses, had lost what little thrall it had. It had never held much, but seemed the thing to do when you were courting.

He still felt uncomfortable in Brambles with its satin cushions, pleated curtains, and electricity. He felt uncomfortable with Ruby who was teaching him to dance, had taught him to drink coffee, and told him things she'd heard on the wireless or read in Emily's newspaper, about people he didn't know who lived in countries he'd never heard of. He'd never opened a newspaper in his life and could read and write only a little.

She dazzled him. He was in awe of her, She knew everything. At night, he went to sleep with her graceful, twirling figure in front his eyes, hearing her voice. He forgot what Audrey looked like. He used some of the money he was saving for the wedding to buy a suit in Ormskirk market.

'We could have bought it in town on Saturday afternoon when you're off,' Ruby said when she admired the cheap suit which was navy blue with a lighter blue stripe. She squeaked with horror when Jacob said he had never been to Liverpool.

'Never *been*! Lord, Jacob, I've been dozens of times. *Dozens!*'

'I know.' Her frequent expeditions, by train, tram and ferry filled him with admiration. He hated leaving Kirkby. Even in Ormskirk, a small market town, he felt overwhelmed by so many people, panic-stricken in the narrow streets, his chest tight, wanting to run away to where there were open spaces and a clear, unrestricted sky, to where he could breathe. He only felt at home with the soil and the crops and the animals that he tended. There were times when he wished he'd never met Ruby, who'd caused such havoc in his heart that he no longer knew what he wanted.

Christmas was never-ending party time at the Rowland-Graves's. Emily ate Christmas dinner with Ruby – the food had mostly been prepared the day before by Mrs Arkwright – nursing the pleasant thought that later she would enjoy herself in a very different way.

She regarded herself as having been doubly blessed. She genuinely loved Ruby, who was a perfect companion; loyal, uncomplaining, intelligent, with a cheerful disposition. It was a pleasure to be met by her sunny, happy face whenever she entered the house. They'd been to Midnight Mass together and it was a delightful experience that she would have missed if the girl hadn't been there. At the same time, the Rowland-Graves were providing all the excitement and fun that Emily had always longed for. Life had never been so good or so fulfilling.

'Will you be all right on your own?' She asked the inevitable question while making preparations for the evening ahead.

Ruby was sitting on the bed, watching the painstaking proceedings. She gave the inevitable answer. 'I'll be fine.'

As soon as Emily had gone she put the light on in her bedroom without drawing the curtains, a signal to Jacob, watching across the fields, that it was safe to come.

Fifteen minutes later, Jacob came, drawn to the light like a moth to a flame.

Ruby had been at Brambles for two years and would shortly be sixteen. 'We should really have a party,' Emily said the week before. 'But you don't know anyone, do you?'

'Not a soul,' Ruby said innocently. Only Jacob, scores of bus conductors, a barrow lady called Maggie Mullen from whom she regularly purchased an apple, Mrs First, who had a sweetshop in the Dingle, a girl her own age,

Ginnie O'Dare, who worked by Exchange station and whom she often met on the train. There were loads more people she knew by sight. But none of these people could she ask to a party.

'We can't just let your birthday pass without doing something,' Emily said. If she took her out to tea, as she had done last year, it wouldn't interrupt her hectic social life. Perhaps it was guilt that made her decide to splash out on an expensive gold watch for a present.

'Can we go to the pictures?' Ginnie O'Dare was always on about the pictures and Ruby was curious as to what they were like.

'What a lovely idea! We'll go to a matinée. There's a Greta Garbo picture on in town, *Grand Hotel*. I'd love to see it.'

Unknown to Emily, Ruby went to see *Grand Hotel* another half a dozen times. She practised saying, 'I vant to be alone,' Greta Garbo style, in front of the mirror. She gave up tram rides for the cinema, sitting open-mouthed and totally absorbed in the cheapest seats during matinées in half-empty cinemas where she learnt more about human nature in the space of a few weeks than she'd done during her entire life. She discovered what treachery meant, jealousy and betrayal, and that she'd never realised people could so easily be provoked to murder. She learnt about love, how pure it could be, how good, yet sometimes very evil, driving people to do all sorts of terrible things in its name. Ruby knew the film stars were only acting out stories that had been written for them, yet they must be reflecting real life, the sort of life she hadn't known existed.

After a while, she felt as if Bette Davies, Joan Crawford, Claudette Colbert, were her friends. She fell in love with Van Heflin and would have liked Herbert Marshall for a dad.

It was about this time, a few months after Ruby's sixteenth birthday, that Emily Dangerfield fell in love herself.

Bill Pickering was forty-three, the first American she had ever met, which only added to his warm, relaxed charm. Tall, slender, deeply tanned, with luxuriant blond, wavy hair and a full moustache, he had lived the last ten years in Monte Carlo where he owned a chain of hotels. His clothes were well cut and expensive, extremely dashing, and he wore them with elegant grace. He had come to stay with his old friends, the Rowland-Graves, for the summer, feeling ever-so-slightly tired of Monte Carlo's ritzy glamour, leaving the hotels in the care of experienced staff.

Emily was thrilled when he began to flirt with her, flattered that a man sixteen years her junior should find her attractive. And she wasn't just imagining it. Mim Rowland-Graves had commented enviously that Bill was obviously smitten. Emily was already in love by the time he asked her out. 'I think it's time we got to know each other properly,' he said in his light transatlantic drawl.

She invited him to Brambles for drinks and to sample Mrs Arkwright's delicious miniature pork pies.

'I didn't know you had a daughter!' he exclaimed in surprise when introduced to Ruby.

'Ruby is my ward,' Emily explained, flattered again that he thought her young enough to have a sixteen-year-old child – mind you, she had vaguely admitted to being forty-nine.

'How do you do,' Ruby said nicely, liking Bill Pickering on the spot. He had a lovely smile that crinkled the skin around his light brown eyes.

'And how do *you* do. Ruby. Gee whizz, Em, this little lady will break a few hearts when she grows up,' he said, thus pleasing Ruby with the compliment and Emily with the diminutive 'Em', which made her feel as if they were more than just friends.

Emily showed him around the house, which he found very impressive. 'Great place, Em,' he enthused. 'Love the garden. Best house I've seen round these parts, in fact. Furnished with exquisite taste, as my old ma back in the States would say.'

'Thank you.' Emily blushed. 'I chose everything myself.'

From then on, Bill Pickering appeared frequently at Brambles. He played tennis with Ruby and sometimes let her win. Emily, watching wistfully from a deckchair, tried hard not to feel old.

'They're potty about each other,' Ruby told Jacob one night. 'They kiss all the time. Sometimes they go into Emily's bedroom and make the most peculiar noises.' She looked at him coyly. 'Have you ever wanted to kiss me?'

'Yes,' Jacob said daringly.

'Shall we try it? See what it's like?'

Before he could answer, she'd thrown herself on to his knee and pressed her mouth against his. For a few seconds he didn't respond, but the light pressure of her lips was creating turmoil in his stomach. He pulled her down so that they were squashed together in the velvet armchair and his arms were wrapped around her as tightly as a fist. Her ribs were like a little delicate ladder under his splayed hand, her shoulder blades as sharp as knives. He was kissing her fiercely now, rubbing his thumb against her soft breasts. And to his joy and astonishment she was responding, curling her arms around his neck, caressing the nape, touching his ears.

It went on and on the kiss, on and on, until it felt as if they'd been kissing for hours, until Jacob, unable to help himself, slid his hand under her skirt. Ruby groaned and opened her legs and he moved her gently to the floor and crouched on top of her. He looked into her eyes which were huge and black and slightly scared, framed like a picture with long, smoky lashes.

He wanted to ask if it was all right to do what he was about to do, but then she might say no, and he couldn't have borne it. Somewhere deep within the ferment in his brain he felt a tiny prick of conscience. He wondered how much she knew. What had she been told in the convent? Had Mrs Dangerfield informed her of the facts of life?

Then Ruby said, 'Don't stop,' and Jacob couldn't have stopped to save his life, though he retained enough sense to withdraw at the proper time. It wouldn't do for her to get pregnant.

Afterwards, she was unusually quiet and subdued. She looked puzzled, as if she wasn't quite sure what had happened. They went into the kitchen and it was Jacob who made the tea. Ruby sat in a chair, kicking her heels against it absently, like a child.

'Does this mean we'll get married?' she asked after a while.

Jacob's heart did a somersault. 'If you want,' he replied.

'I think I do. When?'

'When you're older,' he said gruffly.

'Where will we live?'

'I don't know.' Nor did he care. To be with Ruby, he'd live on one of them tramcars she was always on about. He'd go anywhere, do anything, if they could be together.

She was sipping the tea, watching him over the cup with her dazzling black eyes. 'Shall we go upstairs and do it again?' she whispered.

'I hope you're not coming down with something,' Emily said a few days later when it dawned on her that Ruby had been very quiet for several days.

'I feel all right, thank you.'

'Are you sure?' Even the reply wasn't quite like Ruby. Perhaps she was concerned what would happen to her when Emily and Bill got married – he had only hinted so far, but she was expecting a proposal any minute. 'I think the confirmed bachelor will shortly be confirmed no more,' Ronnie Rowland-Graves had said with a wink the other day. Ruby was smart and could no doubt sense the way the wind was blowing.

Bill was thinking of selling his hotels and living permanently in England. Emily was already making plans. They would live in Brambles at first, the house he so much admired, then look for a place in London. A flat in Mayfair or Belgravia would be ideal and perhaps a little hidey-hole in Paris, or even New York – they could travel to and fro on one of those great cruise liners which would be a holiday in itself. Whatever happened, once she became Mrs Pickering, there would be no more need for Ruby in her life.

Yet she couldn't just abandon the girl. She had been wondering if Adrian in Australia would be willing to take her until she was eighteen? Or perhaps the Rowland-Graves could be persuaded, though they wouldn't provide a particularly healthy atmosphere for someone so young.

She forgot about Ruby and concentrated on Bill, a less taxing way of occupying her mind. For the first time in her life she was properly in love. When she looked in the mirror she saw the lovely woman she'd once been. Her blissful happiness showed in her eyes and she could feel it in her heart. This coming weekend, Bill was taking her to the Lake District. She couldn't wait. She began to plan what to wear. It was when she was deciding which nightdress to take that she remembered Bill would see her first thing in the morning when she looked a miserable wreck. She prayed she'd wake early so there'd be time for the massive preparations required to make herself presentable for when Bill himself woke up.

It was fine when they left Kirkby after tea on Saturday, a clear August day, warm but not muggy. But they'd gone only twenty miles when the sky began to cloud over, getting ominously dark. Spots of rain splattered on to the windscreen and in the blinking of an eye became a deluge. They were in Emily's Jaguar as Bill couldn't drive. 'There just doesn't seem the need in Monte Carlo. I can easily walk to my hotels. Otherwise I use taxis.'

Emily hated driving in the rain. She reduced her speed and bent over the steering wheel clutching it tightly in both hands. A headache arrived as quickly as the rain and she could hardly see. The windscreen wipers didn't seem to be working properly and were making her dizzy. The headlights were useless, the beam absorbed by the pelting rain. Beside her, Bill made encouraging noises, but after a while, Emily drew into a lay-by and announced she couldn't go on. They'd travelled less than a quarter of the way, and at this rate they wouldn't get there till midnight.

'But, honey, the hotel's booked,' Bill cried.

'I'm sorry, but we'll just have to wait until the rain goes off. I'm no good at driving in this sort of weather.'

An hour later, the weather showed no sign of clearing.

'Where are we?' Bill asked.

'I've no idea. In the middle of nowhere, I suspect. I wonder, darling, would you mind very much if we went home? This is bound to have cleared up by morning and we can start off early. If we turn round at least I'll know where I'm going.'

'I don't mind a jot, hon.' He kissed her cheek. 'As long as I'm with you, that's all I care.'

The journey back was hazardous, but it wasn't long before she began to recognise the way and felt able to relax.

'Well,' Bill laughed when the Jaguar squelched to a halt outside Brambles. 'That was quite an adventure, unexpected though it was.'

'What time is it?'

'Not quite ten.'

'The house is in darkness. Ruby sometimes goes to bed early, but she always leaves a light on. I hope she's all right.'

'We'll soon see, hon.'

Ruby appeared on the landing in response to Emily's shout. She must have been about to get undressed as the buttons down the front of her frock were undone. There was something odd about her face. She looked uncomfortable. When she saw Bill, she drew the edges of her frock together – perhaps that was the reason.

'You didn't leave a light on, dear.'

'I wasn't expecting you back till Sunday.'

'You'd forgotten that, hadn't you, honey?'

Bill's intervention made Emily feel doddery and vague. To her surprise he went over to the foot of the stairs, looked up. 'Why don't you come down. Rube? Join me and Emily for a drink?'

'She's only sixteen,' Emily snapped. She had been thinking that now was a perfect time for him to propose, over drinks, rain lashing against the windows, lamps switched on instead of the central light, a romantic record on the gramophone ... She would have lit a fire had she known how.

'A little drop of sherry wouldn't hurt,' Bill smiled.

'I don't want any, thanks all the same,' said Ruby, tossing her head.

Bill continued to stand by the stairs. An irritated Emily followed his upward gaze – and caught her breath! Ruby had grown up without her noticing. There was something about her stance, feet slightly apart – bare feet – the way her hands clutched the frock so that the material was pulled taut over the breasts that seemed to have happened overnight. She looked like a woman, a woman very much aware of her sexuality as she stared haughtily back at a transfixed Bill.

Emily broke the spell. 'Would you like a bite to eat, darling?' Mrs Arkwright had roasted a large joint of beef that morning, enough for several days. She'd slice some on a plate with tomato, pickles, and bread and butter, open some wine.

'A bite to eat would be most welcome.' Bill jumped, as if he'd forgotten she was there.

'Would you mind putting on some music? I won't be long.'

Upstairs, a door slammed. Ruby had gone into her room. Emily's face was grim as she went into the kitchen. Pretty soon, Ruby would be gone for ever. No matter how much she loved the girl, there was no alternative. It was dangerous for her to stay.

She threw a lace cloth over a little occasional table and put it in front of the fireplace, lighting a candle for the centre. The dancing orange flame was reflected in the rose red wine so the bottle looked as if it was on fire. In the background, Paul Whiteman and his Orchestra were playing. 'Rhapsody in Blue'.

'This is very nice.' Bill seemed to have forgotten about Ruby and was eating the snack with boyish enjoyment. He winked. 'You'll make someone a wonderful wife one day, Emily.'

Emily fluttered her lashes. She had changed out of her tweed costume into a pair of Chinese silk lounging pyjamas in a stunning shade of yellow and felt rather daring. She was more than a little dismayed to hear him say 'someone'. There was only one person whose wife she wanted to be and she had thought he felt the same.

But apparently he did. He reached across and took her hand. 'And honey, I'd like that someone to be me.'

'Oh, darling!' She almost burst into tears, but remembered her mascara just in time. 'I'd like it too.'

He kissed her hand. 'Let's drink to us.' He picked up his glass.

'To us!' She had never been so deliriously happy.

'When I finish this delicious food, I'll kiss you like you've never been kissed before.'

Emily couldn't eat another thing. She lit a cigarette and poured the remainder of the wine. 'Shall I fetch another bottle?' There were still several cases left from Edwin's once considerable wine cellar.

'Why not!' He waved his fork. 'Let's celebrate. It's not every day a couple decide to get married.'

The second bottle quickly went and Emily felt quite gloriously tipsy. By now, they were sitting on the settee and Bill was kissing her thoroughly as he'd promised. Her heart thumped wildly in her chest as she responded with an almost fierce passion. She would never know another night like this.

Bill opened more wine and they began to discuss wedding arrangements. 'I think we should get hitched pretty soon, hon. We love each other, so what point is there in waiting?' His voice, like hers, had become slurred.

Emily couldn't have agreed more. 'I wouldn't want a grand affair. A register office would suit me.'

'Me, too.' he stroked her breast. Emily shivered with delight. 'And where shall we go for our honeymoon? How about Rome, my favourite city? I'll do this to you all day long.'

She sighed pleasurably. 'Rome's perfect. Where shall we live? Please say London. You know how much I love it. I've told you so many times.'

'Then London it shall be, my lovely Em.' He stretched his arms and glanced around the room. 'Though I love this house. It will be a shame to sell it, but if you're intent on London, we have no choice. I can't get rid of the hotels at the drop of a hat. It will take at least a year, possibly longer.'

Emily laughed. 'Then I'm afraid we're stuck in Brambles until then. I can't sell it. It isn't mine to sell.'

Bill reached for his glass, a strange expression on his face. Emily, trying to discern it, decided it was expression*less*, very still, telling nothing. 'I beg your pardon?' he said politely.

'Edwin left the property to the boys.' She wrinkled her nose. 'I can – we can – live here as long as we want, but I'm afraid that's all. If it hadn't been for Edwin's ridiculous will, I would have sold up the minute he died.'

'But I thought . . .' he paused. He was very pale.

'Thought what, darling?'

'Nothing. Will you excuse me for a moment?'

He walked unsteadily out of the room. She heard him trip on his way up to the bathroom which she badly needed herself after so much wine. She slipped off her shoes, lifted her feet on to the settee, and hugged her knees, a demure, girlish pose in which to welcome him back. Her mind felt blurred and, afterwards, Emily wondered how, while she was in such a blissfully confused state, the truth should arrive so clearly and so cruelly.

She was wondering idly why his face had changed so suddenly, then gone so pale. What was it he'd thought but wouldn't say?

The answer came unexpectedly, like a physical blow. *He'd assumed she owned Brambles.* It was the reason he'd wanted to marry her. He was after the money he'd thought she'd get from the sale of the house.

Edwin had been right about the will.

Bill was coming downstairs, entering the room. Their eyes met. Emily's were sick with horror. She felt as if her bones were corroding inside her body, that any minute she would collapse into a flabby, boneless lump of flesh. Everything he'd said had been a lie – and she'd fallen for it, she thought bitterly, silly old woman that she was.

'How many hotels do you have in Monte Carlo, Bill?'

He shrugged, her face, the tone of her voice, made it obvious she had guessed the truth. Her blood boiled when his handsome face twisted in a grin. 'None, though I've worked in quite a few.'

'What as, a waiter, or a kitchen hand, collecting the swill for the pigs? Or did you pimp for the rich guests, procure – I think that's the word – procure old tarts and young boys for a fat tip? That would be just up your street.'

He flushed an ugly red, every scrap of charm gone. He took a step towards her and she felt frightened for having spoken so venomously. But she was speaking from the heart which he had broken only a few minutes ago.

'The only old tart I know is you, Emily,' he sneered and she wondered how she could possibly have thought him likeable, let alone fallen in love. It was as if he'd shed an outer skin and revealed the real man underneath. 'You were very easy to seduce. And I'm not the only one who's a liar. Forty-nine! You're sixty if a day.'

'You bastard!' She picked up her glass and threw it at him. It merely glanced off his arm, but a few dregs of wine stained the sleeve of his grey tweed suit. It looked like blood.

'You're a bad loser, Emily.'

It dawned on her that he no longer spoke with an accent. Instead, he had a trace of Cockney whine. He wasn't even an American! She'd been set up!

All the love that had recently flowed so sweetly through her veins turned to acid. She launched herself at him, knocking over the little round table that still held the debris of their meal and catching Bill by surprise, so that he stumbled and almost fell. He blinked, raised his hand, and hit her hard across the face.

Emily screamed, just as Ruby rushed into the room wearing a dressing gown that was much too short.

'What do you think you're doing?' She leaped on Bill's back, wrapping her arms like a vice around his neck. Bill seized the arms, easily pulling them apart, and pinned the slight, valiantly struggling figure against the wall.

'You pig!' Ruby yelled, doing her best to bite his hands, kicking at him with her bare feet which only made Bill laugh.

He turned his laughing face to Emily. 'You know how I managed to kiss you without puking, Emily, dearest? I thought about Ruby. I pretended I was kissing her instead. Like this!' He bent his head and kissed the still wriggling Ruby full on the lips. Emily watched, horrified, as his hand reached for the belt of her dressing gown, undid it.

Suddenly, someone was pulling him away and Emily nearly fainted when she saw who it was – Jacob Veering! He was barefoot, like Ruby, naked to the waist, and the savagery of his anger was awesome. Emily was trying to digest the awful fact that the two young people must have been upstairs together, when Jacob pulled Bill round to face him as effortlessly as if he'd been a rag doll. He drew back his fist and aimed a blow that sent the man hurtling across the room, slamming him against the wall with a thud that shook the house. Bill's body bounced forward like a ball and he fell to the floor, where he lay face down, absolutely still.

Nobody spoke for several minutes. Then Emily said in a dull voice, 'You could have killed him!'

Ruby ran across the room, knelt beside the prone figure, and felt the limp wrists for a pulse, then turned the body over and laid her head against the chest. She straightened up, eyes huge and fearful, and shook her head.

'Oh, my God!' Emily screamed.

It was the girl, not the woman, who took charge of the situation. 'Jacob, you've got to get away,' Ruby said crisply, shaking the young man's arm. He looked at her dazedly, as if he was being shaken from a deep sleep. 'Jacob! Bill's dead. You've killed him.'

'He shouldn't have touched you.' Jacob's eyes blazed briefly, then his broad shoulders slumped, all anger gone.

'They'll hang you.' Ruby shook him again. 'You've got to get away.'

Jacob sighed. His arms hung hopelessly at his side. He looked lost. 'I don't know where to go, Ruby.'

Ruby flung her arms around his neck. 'I'll come with you. I know where we can go. But we must leave straight away. Emily will have to call the police soon. Come on, Jacob.' She dragged him towards the door. 'Let's get dressed.'

They left without a backward glance. Emily heard them go upstairs, heard their voices in the bedroom – Ruby's full of reckless urgency, Jacob's slow and muffled. They came down again. Ruby was wearing the ghastly spotted dress she'd bought in Blacklers, much too grown-up. It looked silly with her childish red shoes. There was a handbag and a white cardigan over her arm. She'd never seen Jacob in a suit before. It looked the cheapest you could buy. There was something terribly brave and vulnerable about the pair. They looked too young to be throwing themselves at the mercy of a capricious fate.

'You'll be all right, won't you, Emily?' Ruby said anxiously.

Emily nodded.

'You'll give us a chance to get away before you call the police?'

Emily nodded again. She would have spoken, offered money, suggested Ruby take a coat, asked if it was still raining, but her lips were too stiff to move.

'We're going now, Emily. Look after yourself.'

All Emily seemed able to do was nod.

'We might see each other again, you never know.'

Another nod.

Jacob grunted something. Shortly afterwards the front door opened and closed and a sense of emptiness descended over Brambles, along with an oppressive silence that was so palpable that Emily felt she could have reached out and touched it with her shaking hands. She hid her face in the velvet arm of the settee and wondered what would happen to her now. She was friendless. There was a feeling in her bones that the Rowland-Graves had been behind Bill's scheming. They had encouraged her pathetic belief he might be interested in a woman old enough to be his mother. She vowed never to see them again.

She thought of Ruby, making her way through the dark countryside with Jacob and wondered if the girl loved him as much as he obviously loved her. She was far too good for him in every way. Jacob might be physically strong, but Ruby would have to carry him through whatever life they might have together.

After a long while, Emily got wearily to her feet, averting her eyes from the body on the floor. It was time she got washed, made herself look respectable. She painted her old face, changed into a sensible frock, and wondered as she returned downstairs what to tell the police. What explanation could she give for her lover having been punched so hard by a local farmhand that it had killed him? Not the truth. It was too shameful and was bound to be pounced on by the press. She'd be a laughing stock.

Then Emily had an idea she desperately wished she'd had before. She gritted her teeth and dragged the still warm Bill by his heels to the bottom of the stairs. He'd been drinking, she'd say, and had fallen the whole way down. It would still cause a bit of a scandal, but would be more bearable than the truth. She put a cushion under his head so it would look as if she'd tried to care for him and checked there was no blood on the carpet where he'd lain. The carpet was clean. The injury that had killed him must have been internal.

She picked up the telephone, dialled the operator, asked for the police, and was waiting to be connected when she heard a noise, a groan, that sent shivers of ice down her spine. From the corner of her eye she saw a movement at the bottom of the stairs. Emily could scarcely bear to look, not sure if she could stand any more shocks that night. When she did, she saw Bill was trying to sit up, groaning, and holding the back of his head. He looked at her fearfully. 'Where's that bloody maniac who hit me?'

'Gone.' Emily replaced the receiver, weak with relief, and regretting she hadn't the sense to feel for a pulse herself. 'And I'd like you to be gone by the time I get back if you don't mind. If you're still here, I'll call the police and have you thrown out.'

He was struggling to his feet, holding on to the banisters. She felt no inclination to help. 'Where are you going?' he asked in an old man's voice.

'Never you mind.'

She was going to look for Ruby, fetch her back. There was no need, now, for her and Jacob to have gone. In the dark, lonely days that lay ahead she would need Ruby as she had never done before.

Outside, the rain had stopped. A brilliant moon, almost whole, shone out of a dense, black, cloudless sky, making long, glistening ribbons of the still wet roads. The tyres of the Jaguar sizzled in the wet as Emily drove for miles and miles in every direction, until she felt giddy, and realised she was passing places she'd already passed before.

Still Emily drove, hopeless now, looking for Ruby, until the moon disappeared and a glimmer of yellow light on the horizon signalled the night was over and a new day was about to dawn.

Jacob

4
1935–1938

She made an impressive sight, the pawnshop runner. Tall for a woman, taper thin, she proudly walked the streets of the Dingle in her polka-dot frock and shabby red shoes, her sleeping baby tucked in a black shawl. Her long hair was thick and wavy and as black as night and it billowed like a cloud behind her, reminding her many admirers of a ship in full sail. The baby was a girl and her name was Greta – no one was surprised that the remarkable pawnshop runner hadn't given her child a conventional name like Mary or Anne.

It was said she was only seventeen, though she looked older. Her long face with its sharp nose and wide mouth could appear pinched when she wasn't smiling, but as she seemed to be smiling all the time, not many people noticed, just as they didn't notice when her dark eyes grew sombre as they sometimes did when she looked at her child who wasn't thriving as well as she should. She lived in Foster Court, an appalling slum, where twenty or thirty people dwelt in a single house, whole families in just one room. And, yes, she had a husband – she wasn't *that* sort of girl. It was rumoured that he, the husband, drank his wages. The pawnshop runner supported him, just as she did her baby and herself.

Those who had spoken to her said she was clever. She used long words and knew all sorts of funny things, though she didn't talk posh. Her accent was more Irish than Scouse and she'd obviously fallen on hard times. Oh, and her name was Ruby – Ruby O'Hagan.

When Ruby and Jacob left Brambles, they'd headed straight for Kirkby station. 'It's too late for a train,' Ruby said, 'but we'll be safer inside the waiting room, out of sight.'

They walked quickly. The rain had stopped, the moon was out, though the midnight air was chilly. Ruby regretted not bringing a coat.

Jacob followed like an obedient animal. He hadn't said a word since they left the house. Ruby spoke to him gently. He'd killed Bill Pickering while protecting her. Who knows what Bill might have done if Jacob hadn't been there. She doubted if Emily had been in a fit state to help.

During the hours spent in the waiting room, she held his hand and murmured comforting words of support. 'We'll be all right,' she told him. 'We'll bury ourselves where no one knows us, the Dingle, I've been there loads of times. We'll find a nice place to live and get jobs. I've always wanted to work in a shop.' The more she thought about it, the more she tried to convince herself it was an adventure, the sort of thing they might have done, anyway, at some time in the future.

A train came puffing in just after six o'clock by which time a watery sun had risen in a pallid sky. Jacob had only seen trains in the distance and found the noise terrifying. He put his hands over his ears to shut it out, wishing he could shut out the world as easily.

When they reached Exchange station, Ruby remembered they hadn't bought tickets. She paid the fares at the barrier and looked worriedly in her purse. 'I've only got tenpence left. Have you got money, Jacob?'

He shook his head. He had more than five pounds saved, but it was in his loft on Humble's farm.

'We'd better walk to the Dingle,' Ruby was saying. 'We'll need to buy food later.'

For Jacob, the walk was a nightmare. So many tall buildings rearing skywards, threatening to collapse on top of him, tramcars almost as noisy as the trains, buses, cars, lorries, the occasional horse-drawn cart that made him think longingly of Waterloo, the horse that kept him company on the farm. Ruby said, 'It's only early, so it's not so busy as usual,' as if he'd like it better when it was, when he already hated it with all his heart.

It started to drizzle, and he felt as if they'd been walking for ever by the time they reached the Dingle, a rabbit warren of little streets. It was only then that Ruby paused, looking lost.

'How do we find somewhere to live?'

Jacob hoped she wasn't asking him because he had no idea. He had no idea about anything any more.

'I know, I'll ask in a shop,' she said cheerfully. She went into a sweet and tobacconists and emerged with a piece of paper clutched in her hand.

'There's a room to let in Dombey Street. The landlady's called Mrs Howlett. It's along this way, second on the right. I think we should take it, whatever it's like. If necessary, we can look around for somewhere better when we've got more time.'

He trudged behind her in a daze, wanting to die, yet knowing he would have followed her to the ends of the earth. She knocked on a house with steps up to the front door and it was opened by a nervous-looking girl of about eighteen.

'I've come about the room,' Ruby said importantly.

'Me mam's gone out a minute.' The girl had a nice, kind smile. 'Come and have a decko. She won't be long. It's upstairs at the back.'

The room was small and cramped and had too much dark furniture including a great double bed. Jacob felt his insides shrink. It was like being inside a coffin.

'It's nice,' Ruby said. She sat on the bed and bounced up and down a few times. 'We'll take it. How much is the rent?'

'Half a crown a week in advance, but you'll have to wait for me mam.'

'What does "in advance" mean?'

'It means me mam wants paying now. People have been known to do a moonlight flit and she ends up out of pocket.'

Ruby had never heard of a moonlight flit, but got the meaning. She didn't have half a crown, but she was wearing the gold watch Emily had bought for her birthday which had cost five guineas. She'd offer Mrs Howlett the watch as a deposit until she earned enough to pay the rent.

'I hope she lets you have it,' the girl said wistfully. 'It'd be nice to have young people for a change.'

The front door opened and a voice shouted, 'Dolly!'

'I'm upstairs, Mam,' the girl shouted back. 'There's people here about the room.'

'Coming.' Mrs Howlett puffed up the stairs like a train. She appeared in the doorway, a big, stout woman, red-faced from her exertions. Her small eyes took in the young couple, Ruby sitting on the bed, Jacob hunched and awkward, wishing he were anywhere else in the world.

'Where's your luggage?' she snapped.

'We haven't got—' Ruby began.

'And where's your wedding ring?'

'I haven't—'

Mrs Howlett gestured angrily towards the stairs. 'Get out me house immediately. I'm not having the likes of you under me roof.'

'But—'

'Out!' the landlady said imperiously.

It was the first time Jacob had ever seen Ruby stuck for words. She drew herself to her full height, tossed her head, and stalked downstairs. By the time she reached the bottom she must have recovered her composure, because she said in her loudest, most penetrating voice, 'Come on, Jacob. This place is a pigsty. I wouldn't live here if they paid me.'

They were outside, on the pavement, it was raining properly now, and Ruby was shaking, her face the colour of a ripe plum. Jacob longed to comfort her, as she had comforted him during the night, but nothing in his body seemed to be working, only his legs, which stumbled after Ruby wherever she chose to take him.

She took his hand. 'What shall we do now?' she whispered. It didn't feel like an adventure any more.

Jacob's head drooped. He didn't know.

The door of the house from which they'd just been evicted opened and Dolly crept stealthily out. 'Me mam's gone to the lavvy.' She touched Ruby's hand. 'I'm sorry, luv. I would have liked you to have the room, but mam's a stickler for convention.'

'She's got awful manners,' Ruby said spiritedly.

'I know.' Dolly sniffed. 'And I've got to live with 'em, an' all. Would you like a piece of advice, luv?' She ignored Jacob. Perhaps she thought him deaf and dumb as well as useless.

'What sort of advice?' Ruby enquired.

'If I were you, I'd buy meself a wedding ring from Woollies. They only cost a tanner.'

'I will, thanks. We only got married yesterday,' she lied shamelessly. 'It was very sudden and we couldn't afford to buy a proper ring. I didn't realise you could get them for sixpence.'

'Good luck – what's your name, luv?'

'Ruby.'

'Good luck, Ruby.'

Dolly smiled and was about to leave when Ruby said, 'Do you know if there's a room going anywhere else?'

'No, luv. There's bed and breakfast places around, though they might get a bit sniffy if you haven't got luggage and a ring. Anyroad, have you got the money?'

Ruby made a face. 'Only tenpence.'

'That's not nearly enough. Mind you, if you're stuck for cash, you could always pawn that lovely watch. In the meantime, you could try Charlie Murphy in Foster Court, number 2. He charges by the night, only thruppence, and he won't care if you're wearing a ring or not. But I warn you, it's a terrible fleapit. Scarcely fit for human beings to live in.'

'Your mam's just made me feel less than human, so that won't matter all that much.'

In all the times she had happily roamed the streets of the Dingle, Ruby had never come across anywhere like Foster Court. It was hidden, out of sight, between a billiard hall and a butcher's, a narrow alley, barely six feet wide, with a handful of four-storey dwellings on either side, the filthy bricks bitten and crumbling, as if they'd caught a repellent disease. Despite the rain, barefoot children were playing in the water that ran along the cracked flags separating the houses, paddling, splashing their hands. One little boy, wearing only ragged short trousers, was trying to sail a paper boat. There was a sickening lavatory smell and the place was very dark, buried within its own shadows, as if the sun, when it was out, had been forbidden to shine in the hideous man-made chasm that was Foster Court.

She was tempted to go no further, turn back, but it wouldn't hurt to know they had a place to sleep that night, even if it was horrible. It was only early. They could spend the rest of the day looking for work. If things went well, they might not have to come back. Mr Murphy could keep his threepence.

Ruby knocked on the unpainted door with the number 2 scratched on crudely with a knife. There was no letter box, as if letters were unknown in a place like this.

'Mr Murphy?' she said faintly when a ghostly figure appeared, an old man with a grey face and skin the texture of wet putty. His white hair was long and dirty, the ends the colour of tobacco, as if he was turning rusty with age.

'That's me, queen,' he said chirpily.

'I . . . we, we're looking for a room.'

'Are you now! Well, I've got a room. Second floor back, thruppence a night, payment up front.' He grinned, showing the occcasional yellow tooth. 'No parties, no drinking, no dancing.'

'We'd like to take it, please. Just for tonight.'

'Give us the ackers, queen, and it's yours. You can find your own way up. The lavvy's in the yard, the scullery's below stairs. I'll fetch you the keys.' He threw open the door, and Ruby winced when she saw the damp-stained walls, the uncarpeted stairs worn to a curve in the middle from the tread of a thousand feet. She wondered if the owners of the feet had felt as miserable as she did as she went up one flight of stairs, then another, Jacob behind, as he had been all day, not speaking, his face a mask of despair. The sound of a woman screaming came from one of the rooms, using language Ruby had never heard before. A baby wailed plaintively in another.

The first thing she noticed when she went in the room was the threadbare curtain on the window. One of the panes was missing and there was a piece of cardboard in its place.

'There's no bedding.' There was no sink either, no carpet or linoleum on the floor, no ornaments, hardly any furniture, no light, only a stub of metal tubing where a gas mantel should have been. The bed didn't have a headboard, the palliasse looked disgusting, and the bolster had turned an unhealthy shade of yellow. A small fireplace was heaped with ash. Ruby crept over to the window and saw a communal yard with just two lavatories for the use of the residents of all the properties on that side. Her heart sank and she turned away. Jacob was sitting on one of the wooden chairs beside a little square table with oilcloth nailed on top.

He spoke at last. 'Go home, Ruby,' he said in a voice as wretched as his face. 'Go back to Emily. I'll manage on me own.'

'Don't be daft!' Ruby said spiritedly. 'We're in this together.'

'I was thinking of turning meself in.'

'And letting them hang you!' she gasped.

'I didn't mean to kill him,' Jacob groaned.

'I know you didn't.' Ruby considered this fact. 'I suppose,' she said thoughtfully, 'you mightn't be tried for murder, but manslaughter instead. You'd be sent to prison for years.'

Jacob would rather hang than be shut for years in a cell with bars on the window, possibly never feel the sun again, smell the flowers, see the trees blossom in the spring and watch the leaves fall in autumn.

'Let's go and buy a cup of tea,' Ruby said encouragingly. 'Then look for a job.'

He shook his head and tucked his arms protectively across his chest. 'I'd sooner stay.' He needed to rest, come to terms with what he'd done, get used to the fact he was a murderer. The day had already been confused enough without having to look for work that he didn't want. He would never be happy working anywhere other than on the land. As far as today was concerned, he'd had enough. He'd look for a job tomorrow.

Ruby must have lost patience with him at last. She stamped her foot. 'If that's how you feel, Jacob Veering, I'll find a job on my own.'

Finding a job was just as difficult as finding a room when you didn't know where to look. Did you just walk into a shop and ask if there was a vacancy? Although not one to refrain from pushing herself forward, Ruby couldn't quite raise the nerve. And the shops she peered in appeared to be fully staffed. No one looked overworked. She passed a pub with a notice in the window, 'Cleaner Required', and sniffed in derision. She hated cleaning. She wanted to work in a shop. But how?

Some jobs were advertised in newspapers, but it meant writing a letter, waiting for a reply, going for interview with half a dozen other people, then waiting again for the interviewer to make up their mind – it had happened to Priscilla Lane in a picture she'd seen.

If only she'd brought a coat. Better still, her new mackintosh with check lining and a hood. Or an umbrella. It might be August, but it wasn't exactly warm, particularly if you were soaked to the skin. Her shoes had begun to squelch and the rain showed no sign of stopping. She thought balefully that it was the rain's fault she and Jacob were in such a mess. If it hadn't rained yesterday, Emily and Bill Pickering would be in the Lake District. For the first time, she wondered what had caused last night's fight? Alerted by the shouting, she'd arrived just in time to see Bill, whom she'd thought so nice, giving poor Emily a whack about the face. And now Bill was dead! Ruby tried not to think about it.

It was two o'clock by the time she came to Park Road, the route the tramcar took when it carried her to the Dingle. Briskly busy, lined with shops, there were even more people around on a Saturday afternoon. Ruby remembered it was where she'd decided, months ago, that this was the place she wanted to be, though she hadn't thought it would be under such horrible circumstances.

The first dress shop she came to, she plucked up courage and went in. A smart lady in black approached and wished her, 'Good afternoon, luv. What can I do for you? You look like a drowned rat, if you don't mind my saying.'

'Good afternoon,' Ruby gushed. 'I'm looking for a job – and I feel like a drowned rat at the moment.'

'Sorry, luv,' the woman said smilingly, 'but I only employ mature staff. I hope you have better luck somewhere else.'

Encouraged by the polite reception, Ruby made the same request several more times including a chemist and a haberdasher's when she ran out of dress shops. The chemist offered her a form to fill in and said she could bring it back any time, so obviously weren't anxious for another member of staff. 'We'll be taking an extra person on for Christmas,' the woman in the haberdasher's said helpfully. 'Try again in November.'

It was quarter past four, she was passing a cafe, and longed for a cup of tea – she'd had nothing to eat or drink since last night, though the thought of food made her nauseous. She went in, ordered a pot of tea for one, bringing the contents of her purse down to fourpence which was worrying. Tomorrow was Sunday and it would be a waste of time searching for work. If they had to stay in Foster Court a second night, it would cost another threepence and she'd be left with a penny. She'd intended buying Jacob something to eat and they'd need food tomorrow. She wished she hadn't bought the tea, though it was nice, sitting in the warmth, making the tea last out, giving her time to think, not that thinking had helped much so far.

Being short of money was a new experience. She recalled the abundant amount of coppers and silver that Emily left in her various bags that she'd helped herself to whenever she needed, for the pictures and her journeys around Liverpool.

It crossed her mind that the pennies she had left might be best spent calling Emily from a telephone box and asking for money – they could meet somewhere in town, because Ruby couldn't afford to go to Brambles. She gave the matter serious thought before deciding, reluctantly, that she couldn't rely on Emily not to tell the police. She might be followed when she returned to Foster Court and Jacob, who was wanted for murder.

A girl came to remove the tea things. 'Have you finished, luv? You look like a drowned rat.'

'Someone's already told me that. I'll be finished in a minute.' Ruby poured the last of the hot water into the pot and managed to squeeze out half a cup. 'By the way, I don't suppose you need any more staff?' It was worth a try.

'No. We're not much busy during the week. I only work Sat'days meself.'

'Thanks, anyway.'

Nothing had happened in Ruby's short life to make her feel as disheartened as she did now. She'd faced few problems – she couldn't remember what they were, but was sure she'd always come out on top. But now she felt beaten, not knowing which way to turn. If she kept on trying, she would get a job one day, next week perhaps, but she needed one *now*.

She looked at her watch. Five o'clock. Only a few people were left in the cafe and the sign on the door had been turned to Closed. She looked at her watch again. What was it Dolly Howlett had said? Something about pawning her lovely watch. Ruby had no idea what that meant.

The girl returned to clear the table. 'Excuse me,' Ruby said, 'but what does "pawn" mean?'

'Y'what?' The girl looked at her vacantly.

'Someone said today I could pawn my watch. I've never heard of it before.'

'Oh, *pawn*. It means taking it to a pawnshop and they'll lend money on it. You get a ticket in case you want to redeem your pledge, buy it back, as it were. Of course,' the girl smiled grimly. 'You have to pay more than they gave you. They're nothing but a racket, pawnshops. I'd steer clear of them if I were you.'

Ruby didn't have much choice. A ray of sunshine had appeared, making the immediate future look considerably brighter. 'Is there one near here, a pawnshop?'

'There's Overton's. Turn right outside the door and it's a few blocks away, on the corner. You'll know it by the three brass balls outside. You'd better hurry. They close at half five.'

'Thank you.

The window of Overton's was heavily barred and full of jewellery which an elderly man with rimless glasses and hardly any hair was in the process of removing. She opened the door and a bell jangled loudly. The man removed his head from the window.

'Yes?'

'I'd like to pawn—' Ruby began.

'Door's round the side,' the man snapped.

The side door was small and unobtrusive. Another bell rang when Ruby entered a small, dimly lit lobby, coming face to face with a metal grille over a wooden counter that was as curved in the middle as the stairs in Foster Court.

A man appeared, very like the one in the window, but younger and with slightly more hair that was combed over his bare scalp in an unsuccessful attempt to hide the fact he was bald. His eyes were the palest she had ever seen.

'We're closing in a minute,' he said abruptly. 'What do you want?'

'I want to pawn my watch, please.'

'Hand it over.'

There was a slit between the counter and the bottom of the grille. Ruby removed the watch which had an expanding strap and of which she was very fond and pushed it through. 'It cost five guineas,' she said. 'It's pure gold.'

'I can see that for meself, thanks.' He was examining the watch carefully, turning it over, running his fingers along the strap. He lifted his head and regarded her sharply with his pale eyes. 'Where did you get it?'

'It was a birthday present.'

'It ses on the back "Ruby O'Hagan".'

Emily had had the back engraved. 'I know, that's me.'

'Can you prove it?'

'How am I supposed to do that?' Ruby demanded sharply.

'Show me something with your name on; an official document of some sort – your birth certificate, or the receipt for the watch, a letter addressed to yourself would do.'

'I haven't got anything like that with me.' She didn't know if she'd ever had a birth certificate, Emily had the receipt for the watch, and no one had ever sent her a letter.

'Where do you live?'

Ruby paused, knowing instinctively not to say Foster Court where no one was likely to own a watch, let alone one worth five guineas. The man was watching her suspiciously and had noticed the pause. It dawned on her that she probably looked a sight, soaking wet, her hair plastered to her head, her cardigan all shrivelled. She should have tidied herself up before she came in. 'I live in Kirkby,' she replied.

'And you've come all this way to pawn a watch?' he said in mock disbelief.

'I'm staying in the Dingle for a few days with a friend.' Ruby was beginning to feel a touch desperate.

'What's the name of this friend?'

'Dolly Howlett. She lives in Dombey Street.' She rarely told lies because she was quite happy for people to know the truth, but today she seemed to be tying herself up in knots.

'I tell you what, bring Dolly Howlett along on Monday to vouch for you, and I'll let you have a guinea for your watch.'

'All right. Until then, I'd like it back if you don't mind.' She had no intention of entering a pawnshop again as long as she lived. The watch would have to be got rid of another way.

The man smiled, though it was more like a sneer. 'I don't think so. I'd like to check it against our list of stolen property. The police might be interested in this watch.'

Ruby lost her temper. 'Are you suggesting it's stolen?'

'Are you suggesting it's not?'

'Of course it's not. It's mine, I got it for my birthday.'

'Who off, the King?'

'No, off Emily. You can't just keep it. I need it.'

'If you need it, why are you trying to pawn it?'

'Because I want the money, stupid.'

The man scribbed something on a piece of paper and shoved it beneath the grille. 'Here's a receipt. You can have the money on Monday under the conditions already described. Now, if you don't mind, we're closed.' He pulled down a shutter behind the grille with a bang. An enraged Ruby hammered on the grille with her fist, to no avail. She marched round to the front, found the front door locked, and no sign of the other man inside. Despite more hammering, no one came.

It was the second time that day she'd been made to feel about two inches tall; first Mrs Howlett, now in a pawnshop. Angry tears stung Ruby's eyes mingling with the rain, still falling steadily. She couldn't go back for the watch even if she knew someone who could vouch for her. If the man contacted the police they might recognise the name on the back: Ruby O'Hagan, who'd left Brambles last night in the company of Jacob Veering. She'd lost her watch for ever.

What could she do now other than go back to Foster Court? At least she could get dry, have a rest. She thought about lying on the grubby palliasse, resting her head on the discoloured bolster, and her stomach turned. For the briefest of moments, she considered returning to Brambles, even if it meant walking there, spending the night to come and all the nights to follow, in her yellow and white bedroom wearing one of her pretty nighties – she remembered she hadn't brought a nightie with her. If asked, she would swear she had no idea where Jacob was. Emily would need her company after what had happened with Bill, with whom she'd seemed so much in love and he with her.

But she couldn't desert Jacob. She would never sleep easily that night, or any night, if she did. The memory of her treachery would haunt her the rest of her days. Jacob needed her far more than Emily ever would. What's more, he loved her and she loved him. She felt guilty for being so impatient when she'd left Foster Court and began to hurry. He was probably wondering why she'd been gone such a long time.

The shops were all closed now, hardly anyone was about. Trams rolled by, crowded, taking lucky people back to their homes or out for the night. Still smarting from the way she'd been treated in Overton's, Ruby eyed them enviously as she splashed through puddles, uncaring, her feet couldn't get more wet than they already were. She walked past the pub with the notice 'Cleaner Required' in the window, then stopped and retraced her steps. She'd been good at cleaning in the convent. She'd been good at everything. It was her attitude that was at fault according to the nuns. She made no secret of the fact she didn't like carrying out a single one of the tasks she was given to do and would like them even less if she was put into service and had to do them for a living.

'I wouldn't mind doing them for myself,' she would say with a superior expression on her face that drove the nuns wild, 'but not for anyone else.' She resented the notion she'd been put on earth solely to make other people's lives more comfortable.

But now Ruby was willing to throw her principles to the wind and apply for the job as cleaner in the Malt House as the pub was called according to the sign outside. The landlord's name was painted over the door: Frederick Ernest Quinlan.

She threw back her shoulders, confident again, and went through the swing doors into a large, brightly-lit room, with a polished floor and round, polished tables. The bar occupied most of one wall and was backed by a decorative mirror with a gold-painted border, reflecting the whole room. The mirror also reflected the back of the middle-aged barmaid, a tiny whisper of a woman, a whole head shorter than Ruby, wearing a mauve crocheted jumper and diamanté earrings, her hair as gold as the border on the mirror, except for the roots which were black. Expertly made-up, she looked worn out, despite the night having scarcely begun – there were only four customers present at such an early hour, all men.

'I'd like to see Mr Quinlan about the cleaning job,' Ruby said, coming straight to the point.

'Then you're out of luck,' the woman said tiredly. 'But I'm Mrs Quinlan and you can see me if you like. I need someone straight away.'

'I can start straight away, now if you want.'

A man entered and came over to the bar. 'A pint of best bitter, Martha, luv. Where's your Fred?'

Showing slightly more animation than before, the woman replied acidly, 'Where d'you think? In bed, bloody asleep.'

'So, Fred's in bed with a sore head,' the man chortled as he took the drink.

'Only a man would find it funny, the landlord drinking the profits and leaving his wife to tend the bar,' Mrs Quinlan remarked when the man went to take a seat.

'Is that what he does? That's disgraceful,' Ruby said sympathetically.

'Isn't it?' The sympathy was clearly appreciated. 'He manages to stagger down at midday, but by three o'clock, closing time, he's as drunk as a fiddle and ready for his bed. He might condescend to join us about nine in the evening to get tanked up again, which means he can't be raised next morning, leaving yours bloody truly to clear this place up. I'm working fourteen hours a bloody day, flat out, and I can't stand it any more. That's why I need a cleaner, mornings, eight till ten, half a crown a week. Fred thinks it an extravagence which is a bloody cheek when you consider the amount of ale he consumes a day.'

'It certainly is,' Ruby agreed. 'About the job . . .'

'Oh, yes.' Mrs Quinlan looked properly at Ruby for the first time, clearly liking what she saw, and no doubt influenced by the fact she was on her side against Fred. 'How old are you?'

'Sixteen.'

'I'll pretend I didn't hear that. Under eighteen, you're not allowed on licensed premises. You shouldn't be here, in fact.'

'In that case, I'm eighteen. My name's Ruby O'Hagan, by the way.'

'In that case, Ruby, you've got the job,' Mrs Quinlan said promptly, looking slightly happier than when Ruby had come in. 'I wouldn't expect you Sundays. I'll just have to clean the bloody place meself, but you can start Monday.'

'Make it three shillings a week and I'll work Sundays. And I'd appreciate being paid by the day, Mrs Quinlan, if you don't mind,' Ruby said daringly, having gauged Martha Quinlan was a good-natured person and open to such suggestions.

'I don't mind, luv. I don't mind so much, I'll pay you beforehand.' She opened the till. 'Here's a tanner for tomorrer. You've got an honest face. I trust you not to let me down. Oh, and call me Martha, everyone does.'

She'd done it! She'd got a job. Added to that the rain had stopped, she had tenpence in her purse again, and there was the most delicious smell that made her taste buds water.

A fish and chip shop! She was about to buy two-pennyworth of chips and take them back to Foster Court, but decided to fetch Jacob first. They could buy the chips together and go for a walk. It would do him good to get some fresh air.

But Jacob was fast asleep in their decrepit little room, fully dressed and snoring softly, his face buried in the yellow bolster, his nice new suit all creased as he lay, curled up like a baby, one arm shielding his face.

Ruby no longer felt hungry. She removed her damp cardigan, folded it into a pillow, and lay beside him, putting her arm around his waist. In no time at all, she was asleep herself.

Martha Quinlan was a hard taskmaster. Due to the fact she no longer had a watch to know the time, Ruby arrived more than half an hour early and got her out of bed. Without her make-up, in a shabby dressing gown, she looked wretchedly weary. It was midnight by the time she'd gone to bed, she complained. 'Fred came down and a couple of his cronies stayed long after closing time. I had to hang about and lock the bloody place up. I don't trust Fred to do it proper.'

The bar, so spruce and shining the night before, looked as if a hurricane had swept through it. The tables were laden with dirty glasses, empty cigarette packets, and overflowing ashtrays. There were more glasses on the floor, cigarette butts, spent matches, two dirty hankies, and a copy of yesterday's *Daily Herald*, which Ruby put aside to read later.

She set to, taking the glasses into the kitchen, emptying the ashtrays in a bucket, wiping the tables, sweeping the floor. She washed the glasses in hot, soapy water, dried them, and took them into the bar, hanging the tankards on the hooks provided, putting the others on a shelf underneath.

'I've finished,' she announced to Martha who was perched on a stool, smoking, and watching her with a hawk's eye.

'In a pig's ear, you've finished. Them tables need polishing and the glass marks removed, floor has to be buffed. You'll find everything you need in the kitchen. After that, I'd like the place dusted; window sills, doors, chairs, and them bottles behind could do with a wipe. Then you can take a look in the men's lavvies in the yard, mop 'em out. We only had a few women in last night and none of 'em used the lavvy, so the Ladies won't want touching.' She grinned. 'Oh, this is nice. I feel like a lady of leisure, I do. If you weren't here, I'd be doing all this meself. When you've finished, I'll make us a nice cup of tea and some toast.'

'How long have I been here?' Ruby felt as if she'd been slaving away for hours.

'Not long enough to earn even half the tanner you got last night,' Martha said with another grin. 'I suppose you think I'm finicky, Fred does, but I like to keep the place nice. There's some pubs just sprinkle a handful of sawdust on the floor each morning, but not me. Come on, luv,' she urged, 'get a move on. The sooner you finish, the sooner we can have that tea.'

'Do you want the bread cut thick or thin?' Martha asked an hour later, though to Ruby it felt more like ten. They were in the kitchen, the kettle was about to boil, and the grill was on waiting to toast the bread.

'Thick, please.'

'I'll put the jam on the table and you can help yourself. I suppose you're fair worn out.'

'Yes, but I'll get used to it,' Ruby said stoutly.

'I'm sure you will. You're a hard worker, I can tell. Thorough, like meself. We'll get along, you and me.' Martha turned the toast over. 'Do you live nearabouts?'

'Foster Court – but it's only temporary.'

Martha wrinkled her nose. 'By yourself?'

'No, with Jacob. He's my husband.'

'Jaysus, Mary and Joseph, girl,' Martha gasped. 'You're never married at your age!'

'We did it secretly, then we ran away from home. It only happened on Friday. I haven't even got a wedding ring yet.'

'Your poor mam and dad, I bet they're dead upset, wondering where you are.'

'I haven't got a mam and dad. I'm an orphan. Oh, look, the toast's burning.'

'She always burns the toast,' said a caustic voice and a woman came in, a much younger version of Martha. Her blonde hair was pinned in curls against her scalp and covered with a flesh pink net. She wore a flowered crêpe dressing gown and fluffy slippers. 'Is that piece mine, Mam?' she demanded.

'It's Ruby's. If you want toast, our Agnes, make your own.'

'I'm not Agnes, I'm Fay,' the young woman said crossly. 'I don't know how many times I've got to tell you.'

'As far as I'm concerned, miss, you were christened Agnes Quinlan, and Agnes Quinlan you'll stay. Fay!' Martha hooted. 'I've never heard such nonsense.'

The newcomer pouted. 'Agnes is a horrible name. What do you think, Ruby? Isn't Fay much nicer?'

'I like them both,' Ruby said tactfully, more interested in the toast.

'Just because she works in the Town Hall she wants her name changed,'

Martha sneered. 'Agnes isn't good enough for her any more. She's ashamed of living in a pub in the Dingle, an' all.'

'So would you be,' Agnes/Fay said hotly, if you worked with people from places like Aigburth or Woolton. Some even live in houses with names, not numbers.'

'Where you live's got a name, it's called the Malt House.'

'Oh, shurrup, Mam. I'm going back to bed. You can wake me up in time for midday Mass.'

'Ta, very much, *Agnes.*'

'She's me daughter,' Martha announced, as if Ruby hadn't already guessed, after Agnes/Fay had gone in a huff. 'She's too big for her boots these days. You'd think she was lady-in-waiting to the queen herself, not just a bloody receptionist in the Town Hall. Mind you,' her face grew fond, 'I'm proud of her. What mother wouldn't be? Though I'd appreciate some help with this place, but our Agnes wouldn't be seen dead behind the bar. As to cleaning, she wouldn't know where to start.' She sighed. 'Our Jim now, he's a different kettle of fish altogether. Always willing to lend a hand, but he's in the Merchant Navy and we only see him once in a blue moon. Would you like more toast, luv? That piece went quick. And, oh, I'll give you tomorrer's money now, if you like, seeing as how you're obviously short. It works out to fivepence a day.'

Jacob had been asleep when she left that morning. When she returned to Foster Court, having been to nine o'clock Mass in a church called St Finbar's on the way, he was still in bed, wide awake, staring glumly at the ceiling. His eyes flickered in her direction when she went in.

'I've got a job, cleaning,' she announced breezily, 'and I've got money, too. We can have fish and chips for our dinner. With your wages on top of mine, we can be out of here by the end of the week.'

He didn't answer, but rolled over, away from her, facing the wall.

'Your suit's in a terrible state,' Ruby continued in the same breezy voice. 'And my dress is even worse, it was damp when I lay down to sleep. We need an iron. We need all sorts of things: soap and towel, dishes, knives and forks. If we had a saucepan, I could make us something to eat in the kitchen downstairs. Perhaps tomorrow. Oh, and we definitely need bedding, except I'm not sure if we'll need our own once we're living somewhere else. Another thing, Jacob ... '

'I want to die, Ruby.'

'Jacob!' She leapt on to the bed and folded him in her arms. 'Don't talk like that. Everything's going to be all right, you'll see. We'll soon be out of here.'

'I don't want to be out of here,' he said despairingly. 'I don't want to be anywhere except back on the farm.'

'But that's not possible, Jacob. You can't go back to Humble's, not ever. But in a while, once we're on our feet, maybe we can move out to the countryside, find another farm.' She'd hate it, perhaps not as much as he hated the town, but she was hardier than him, she realised that now. She could stand up to things, make the best of them.

'I'm a murderer, Ruby.' He turned over and she shivered when she saw the dead empty eyes in a face that had lost all its colour, like the face of a corpse. 'I killed a man. I don't think I can live with it. That's why I want to die.'

'It was an accident, love. Oh, please don't be like this. I can't stand it.' She put her head on his chest and began to weep.

Jacob would have wept with her, but he was beyond tears, beyond everything, except sleeping and staring at the wall. And loving Ruby, yet wishing she would go away, back to Emily, leaving him to rot on the stinking bed. It made everything worse, seeing her so dishevelled when she'd always looked so smart, knowing the girl who could dance like a butterfly had got a job cleaning. It was enough that his old life was ruined. It wasn't possible to imagine feeling better, but he wouldn't feel so bad if Ruby hadn't been there, sharing the agony with him.

'Take your suit off, Jacob. It's getting ruined.' She began to help him off with his clothes, tugging at them.

Something stirred within him, a longing to forget, to lose himself within her. But even that didn't help. They made half-hearted love and the furore in Jacob's brain continued unabated and he forgot nothing.

Later, he couldn't bring himself to go with her to look for food although, despite everything, he was hungry. Ruby went alone, returning with a bottle of lemonade and two bars of chocolate – the fish and chip shop wasn't open on Sundays.

'We'll have something nice and tasty tomorrow,' she said comfortably, resting her hands on her rumbling stomach.

Next day, Jacob felt exactly the same, as if he was secured to the bed with invisible chains, capable only of using one of the unspeakable lavatories when it was dark and no one could see him.

'But we'll never get out of this place if you don't go to work!' Ruby cried. She had been to the Malt House and bought a comb, soap and towel on the way back. Her frock was off and she was in her silky petticoat, trying to remove the frock's creases with her hands, shaking it. Having fetched water from the kitchen in the lemonade bottle, she was pouring it into her hands, splashing it on her face and under her arms, drying herself with an energy that made Jacob wilt, knowing he couldn't match it to save his life. Then she combed her hair, tugging at the knots, looking almost her own self again, and suggested he went out and found a job.

'No,' said Jacob, wishing there were bedclothes he could hide under.

A few weeks later, there were. Ruby got them secondhand: thick, flanelette sheets, frayed at the hem, a bolster cover. There were other things: dishes, cutlery, a shaving brush and razor that Jacob hardly used, though Ruby had insisted he wear the moleskin pants and thick shirt she'd got for when he started work. It saved his suit, now hanging behind the door, waiting for when she could afford to have it dry-cleaned.

The saucepan she'd bought had disappeared off the kitchen stove, along with a quarter of a pound of stewing steak and potatoes for their tea, poor Ruby unaware she should have stayed and kept watch. Anyone could have taken it: the woman who lived on the first floor with her eleven children, the mad man in the basement who wore nothing but a dirty blanket and shouted obscenities at everyone, the two women on the ground floor who entertained a suspiciously large number of male visitors.

By this time, Ruby had another cleaning job because she wasn't earning enough at the Malt House. There were still things needed to make life bearable. She was desperate for an iron, a rope to hang the washing on, and doubted if there would ever be sixpence to spare for a wedding ring.

It was Agnes/Fay who got her the job in the Town Hall, evenings, six till eight, five days and half a crown a week, mopping floors, cleaning stairs, polishing the chairs and tables in the stately council chamber.

'Why do you do it?' Agnes/Fay, with whom she'd become quite friendly, wanted to know. 'You could get a proper job. You talk nice, you're presentable, at least you would be if you ever ironed your frock.'

'I'd sooner clean,' Ruby replied. She was so busy, she didn't have time to think about Jacob, mouldering away in Foster Court which she would do if she worked in a shop, as she would have preferred. Jacob was asleep when she left for the Malt House and ready for sleep again by the time she went to the Town Hall. It meant she could keep him company during the day. All he did was sleep, or lie on the bed staring at the ceiling while she talked to him, tried to cheer him up. He would leave the bed only to eat the food prepared in the cockroach-ridden kitchen, which Ruby did her best to use when it was empty of the sullen, angry women who lived elsewhere in the house.

Jacob had fallen apart. His hair was dirty, he smelt. His beard was a tangle of stiff, matted hairs. But it was Jacob's weakness that gave Ruby the strength to carry on. She told herself that one day he would get better, find a job, and they would live somewhere nice. Anywhere would be an improvement on Foster Court.

'Would you do us a favour, Ruby, luv?' Martha Quinlan said. 'I'm expecting a delivery from the brewery today, and I'm a bit short o'cash. Would you mind taking something to uncle's for me?'

'Uncle who?'

'Uncle no one, luv. I'll just have to pawn me engagement ring, not for the first time, I might add,' she said darkly.

'You want me to take your engagement ring to the pawnshop?'

'Otherwise known as uncle's, that's right, luv. I'll give you something, two and a half per cent's the going rate.'

'Two and a half per cent of what?' asked Ruby, mystified.

THE HOUSE BY PRINCES PARK

'Of whatever you get, girl. Are you thick or something this morning? Old Nellie, the pawnshop runner, popped her clogs last month. I've been stuck ever since.'

'Stuck for what?'

'Someone to take me valuables to the pawnshop, that's what,' Martha said impatiently. 'I've got me reputation to consider. I couldn't be seen going anywhere near the place meself.'

'All right.' Ruby forgot her vow never to enter a pawnshop again. 'Where shall I go?'

'Reilly's on Park Road pays the best rates. I'll give you a note. Mrs Reilly knows me by name, if not by sight.'

Mrs Reilly had a hard, businesslike manner, but was a great improvement on the man who'd stolen her watch. Like Overton's, the window at the front displayed jewellery and various items of silver. Ruby found an entrance round the back leading to a small room with the now familiar grille. She had to wait while a child, much to her amazement, pawned a man's suit.

'Have you taken over from Old Nelly?' the woman asked when Ruby eventually gave her the envelope containing Martha's ring and a note to say who it was from.

'No. I'm just doing a favour for Mrs Quinlan.'

'That's a pity. There's quite a few people who've missed Old Nelly since she passed on. Hang on a minute while I show me husband the ring.'

Ruby waited, the woman returned, 'Twenty-five shillings,' she said.

'What's two and a half per cent of that?' They hadn't taught percentages in the convent.

'Sevenpence a'penny.'

A few days later, Ruby was sent to redeem the ring with the promise of the same sum. It seemed an extraordinarily easy way of earning one and threepence.

'These people you mentioned,' she said to the woman behind the grille, 'What would I have to do?'

'Can you be trusted?'

'Mrs Quinlan trusted me with her ring.'

'So she did. This needs a bit of sorting. Come back tomorrow and I'll let you know.'

A few days later, Ruby crossed Dingle Lane into Aigburth Road, where the properties suddenly became larger, the streets wider. Brocade curtains hung in neat folds on the bay windows, every step had been ruthlessly scrubbed, door brasses glittered in the late October sunshine. She found the road she was looking for, went down the back entry, as she'd been instructed, and entered the house, number 14, through the yard where she was met by a dazzling display of net curtains. She knocked on the door and it was opened by an anxious woman of about forty who looked frantically around, as if expecting heads to appear over the adjacent walls to see who the visitor was.

Ruby was dragged inside a kitchen very like the one in Brambles, only smaller. The woman whispered hoarsely, 'Are you from Reilly's?'

'I am so,' Ruby announced grandly.

'I've got the stuff ready, some jewellery.' The woman's name was Mrs Somerfield. Her hands trembled as she reached inside a drawer and drew out a paper bag. 'How long will it take? I need the cash urgent like.'

'About an hour. I've someone else to see.'

Mrs Somerfield's eyes narrowed. 'Who?'

'That's confidential,' Ruby said officiously. 'You wouldn't want me telling the other person where I've been, would you?'

'God, no!'

'I'll be back as soon as I can.'

The next house was detached, backing on to Princes Park. It was a large, friendly, russet brick house, with an untidy tangle of roses around the door, and gardens front and back full of trees and overgrown shrubs. The bay windows were badly in need of a good clean and the grass urgently required mowing. Even so, it would be a perfect place to live, Ruby thought longingly, so close to the shops, yet affording a certain amount of privacy. She'd become quite keen on privacy after so long in Foster Court. A fluffy, striped kitten was sitting unhygienically on the table in the cosy, old-fashioned kitchen, giving itself a thorough wash.

Mrs Hart, the owner of this enviable house, was a friendly woman, tall and carelessly dressed, and remarkably open about her need for money. She gave Ruby a small parcel wrapped in tissue paper. 'It's Dresden, so be careful with it, won't you, dear. That son of mine will have me in the poorhouse before long. He's at university, living the life of Riley, and draining my pitiful finances – my husband only left me a small pension. I'm forever having moneylenders banging on the door or sending threatening letters. Would you like a cup of tea, dear? You look cold.'

'I'd love one, thanks.' Mrs Somerfield would just have to wait for the cash she urgently needed. Ruby sat down and stroked the kitten who obligingly washed her fingers.

'Have you taken over from Old Nelly?' asked Mrs Hart.

'I think I might have.'

5

By the time Christmas came, Ruby was earning almost as much from her role as a pawnshop runner as she did from cleaning. But she could never manage to get enough together to escape from Foster Court. Now that winter had descended, there was fuel to buy as well as food. She wore a shawl instead of a more expensive coat and could have done with a pair of stouter shoes.

Christmas was also the time when Ruby finally had to admit to herself the alarming fact that she was expecting a baby. She'd been deliberately ignoring the non-appearance of periods, the slight sickness in the mornings. She knew little about babies, but recognised the rudimentary signs. It must have happened the first Sunday in Foster Court when Jacob hadn't pulled out as he usually did. They hadn't made love since, which meant she was four months gone and the baby would arrive in May.

It was Martha Quinlan who pointed out what was becoming increasingly obvious. 'Are you in the club, luv?' she asked on Christmas Eve.

Ruby sat down with a thump on the chair she was polishing. 'Yes.' It was scary, saying the word, 'yes', agreeing that in five months' time she would have a baby and it was no use ignoring it any longer, hoping it would go away.

'Congratulations, luv. I expect you're dead pleased,' Martha said warmly. 'Though I can't say I'll be glad about losing you. I'll never get another cleaner as good.'

'Oh, I won't be leaving.' Ruby tried not to sound as worried as she felt. She couldn't afford to lose one of her jobs. 'I feel fine, and I can bring the baby with me once it's born. Can't I?'

Martha looked doubtful. 'I dunno, luv. We'll have to see.'

The news that he was about to become a father jolted Jacob out of his all-consuming lethargy. It was Christmas Day and Ruby, usually a source of never-ending chatter, was unnaturally quiet. Her peaked face bore a sober expression he'd never seen before and her dark eyes were inscrutable. She'd done her best to make the room look festive with a few pathetic strands of tinsel around the window and draped over the tiny fireplace, in which an equally pathetic fire smouldered, giving off more smoke than flames. There was a lamb chop for dinner followed by a piece of home-made cake, a present from the woman in the pub.

'What's wrong?' Jacob asked when they had finished eating, unable to stand the silence any longer. He had always found the chatter irritating, but found the silence worse.

'I'm having a baby,' she said matter-of-factly.

Jacob turned to look out of the window, at the brilliant afternoon sun sinking in the cloudless sky, at the ice-skimmed walls and roofs. There was a sprinkling of snow in the yard. The crazy man from downstairs was peeing against a lavatory wall, his feet bare, wearing only his blanket. Somewhere, a carol was being sung, 'Christmas is coming, the goose is getting fat . . .'

He sighed. 'I think you should go back to Emily.'

Ruby unexpectedly exploded, furiously waving her arms. 'I phoned Emily last night to wish her Merry Christmas, to see how she was, and she doesn't live in Brambles any more. She's gone abroad. So I can't go back even if I wanted.' She glared at him. 'Not that I do.'

Jacob wilted under the glare. 'What are we going to do, Ruby?' he asked in his hopeless, tired way.

She jumped up, stamped her foot, and began to pace up and down the room, her shoes clattering on the floorboards. 'We?' she screamed. 'What are *we* going to do? I know this much, Jacob Veering, *you're* not going to do anything other than lie rotting on the bed, never getting washed, so that you smell disgusting and look like a tramp. But I'll tell you this for nothing, it won't be on *this* bed, not any longer. You can rot somewhere else. I wish I'd never stuck by you. Better still, I wish we'd never met. I wish they'd hung you by the neck until you were dead.'

Jacob's shoulders hunched lower and lower under the onslaught. 'I wish I *were* dead, Ruby,' he whispered.

'In that case, why haven't you killed yourself? What's to stop you.' She flung her arm in the direction of the line slung across the room. 'There's a rope. I'm out long enough, working, so you've had plenty of opportunity.'

He felt a slight rumble of anger. 'That's a coward's way out.'

She laughed sarcastically. 'You're a coward already, letting yourself be kept by a woman.'

'Hold on a minute, Ruby—'

'I'll do no such thing. I'm not holding on another minute. You can get out, Jacob. I'll be better off without you. You're a dead weight. With you gone, there'll be more money for my baby.'

'But it's *our* baby,' he spluttered.

'No, Jacob.' She shook her head furiously. 'It's *mine*. If you're not willing to support it, you've no right to lay claim it's yours.' She threw her shawl around her. The fringed ends flicked against Jacob's cheek, stinging.

'Where are you going?'

'For a walk.'

'But it's Christmas Day!'

'I don't care if it's Judgement Day, I'm going for a walk.'

Ruby's anger was too hot to let her feel the cold as she walked swiftly along the empty streets of the Dingle. It was dusk now, and the lamplighter was doing his rounds

'Merry Christmas, miss,' he said as she walked through the pool of light that appeared like magic on the icy pavement.

'And the same to you.'

Curtains were being drawn against the dark and the coldness of the night, leaving only the occasional chink of light. Families had gathered together for the anniversary of the birth of Christ. For the first time in her life, Ruby felt very alone, but it didn't make her sad. Instead, she felt more angry with Jacob for letting her down, not pulling his weight. He'd become a burden she wasn't prepared to shoulder any more, not now that she was expecting a child. Resting her hands on her swelling stomach, she made a vow that her child would come first, always.

As she walked, Ruby wondered curiously if her mother was celebrating Christmas behind curtains somewhere in the land. In the past, occasionally, she'd thought about her mother, but never for long. What point was there? She could think about it till the cows came home, but it was a waste of time. Mrs, or Miss, O'Hagan might be dead. And if she was alive then she hadn't wanted her baby for some reason which, as far as Ruby was concerned, was more her mother's loss than hers. Until the last few months, she'd always been very happy, mother or no mother. Even now, most of the time, she wasn't *un*happy, not even about the baby once she'd got used to the idea. There were occasions, admittedly, when she had bouts of despair, but she managed to cope, somehow. If Jacob had done his share, she would have coped even better.

He'd better be gone when she got back, she thought grimly. If not, there'd be hell to pay.

When Ruby returned to Foster Court, Jacob had washed, shaved, combed his hair, put on his suit, and looked a new man. If it hadn't been for the hollow cheeks and flabby neck, he would have been the Jacob of old. He glanced at her shyly. 'I'll look for a job straight after Christmas, Ruby. I'm sorry about ...'

She didn't let him finish, but danced across the room and threw herself into his arms. 'Oh, Jacob, I love you. Everything's going to be perfect from now on.' She cupped his face in her hands. 'It is, isn't it, Jacob?'

'Yes, Ruby. I promise.'

Unemployment had been rising for years. When Jacob Veering set out in search of work, there were almost a million men in competition. Jacob, unskilled in everything except farm work, found there was a limit to the jobs he could do. The docks, the mainstay of male employment in the area, were out – even experienced dockers were being laid off. The wages he'd been hoping to earn, two pounds a week at least, possibly three, according to Ruby, seemed more like pie in the sky as he was turned down for job after job, each paying less than the one he'd last applied for and, despite the paltry wages, all with a dozen men after them who'd done the work before.

Jacob was almost tempted to take to his bed again, give up altogether, but Ruby was having their child, growing bigger and bigger, waiting for him, bright-eyed and expectant, when he returned to Foster Court after another dismal, unsuccessful day.

'Never mind. Your luck might change tomorrow,' she would say encouragingly when she saw his dejected face.

One night, she came home from the Town Hall in a rage. 'They're making me leave,' she said hotly. 'All because of the baby. I said I felt fine, but they wouldn't listen. They said I might fall and weren't prepared to answer for the consequences.' She grimaced. 'And Martha Quinlan keeps threatening to let me go. I make her feel uncomfortable, she says, working my legs off while all she has to do is watch. In fact, she's started giving me a hand. "It's not right," I keep telling her, "paying me to clean and doing it yourself." You'd think I was an invalid or something,' she finished indignantly.

He wondered if Ruby had been a weaker person, not so independent, he might have risen to the occasion months ago, not given in. But she sapped any confidence he might have had, made him feel less than a man. Nothing got her down. Her initiative knew no bounds. Undeterred by the loss of her job, next morning she neatly wrote out half a dozen postcards and took them to pawnbrokers in the vicinity:

RUBY O'HAGAN
PAWNSHOP RUNNER
Available to collect and redeem pledges
Far and wide

She was delighted with the response. Names and addresses were promptly supplied of people urgently in need of cash, but too ashamed to show their faces in the place where it could be had. From then on, she visited the shops every morning in case there'd been a telephone call or a note delivered when it was dark requesting the pawnshop runner to call.

Without exception, the customers were women, not solely from better-off places like Aigburth or Princes Park. There were poverty-stricken families in the Dingle, too proud to let their neighbours know they had to pawn the man's best suit on Monday to make ends meet, redeeming it for weekend use on Friday when the wages arrived. Ruby had to call at some ungodly hour, early morning or late at night, in case she was recognised, earning only a penny or twopence for her pains.

Not all the pathetic bundles of bedding, children's boots, canteens of cutlery, chiming clocks, or wedding rings, were redeemed. At the end of the week, Ruby might be told, 'Sorry, luv. I can't afford it. I'll get in touch once I've got the cash together.' Until then, beds would remain bare and childish feet unshod, or they might stay that way for ever.

Mrs Hart, the nicest of her customers, had so far never redeemed a pledge. Her big house was gradually being stripped of the pretty things that had been wedding presents or had belonged to her or her late husband's family since before she was born, to pay the ever-increasing debts of her son, the awful Max.

'I'd get much more for the damn things if I sold them,' she groaned, 'But I pawn them in the hope that one day I'll get them back, though where the money will come from, I've no idea.'

'They only keep them six months, then they're put up for sale,' Ruby said as she nursed the growing kitten, appropriately called Tiger.

At first she had been intrigued as to why so many apparently well-off women should so frequently require an urgent injection of cash. After a while she was able to tell the signs. There were women who drank, women who gambled, who overspent the housekeeping, who juggled a load of debts, borrowing from one source to pay off another. One sad lady she regularly called on was secretly supporting her dying father, unable to tell her husband because he wouldn't approve.

Some of the posh houses Ruby went in were anything but posh inside, with bare floors and mean furniture little better than Foster Court. The only decent things were the curtains on show to the outside world.

She was becoming a familiar figure on the streets of the Dingle. 'There's the pawnshop runner,' people would say as she walked by. 'Which tuppenny-a' penny toff are you off to see today, Ruby?' they would call, but Ruby would smile enigmatically and put her finger to her lips.

Martha Quinlan was no longer prepared to let an increasingly pregnant Ruby clean her bar and insisted she leave. 'You make me feel terrible, luv. But promise you'll still come for a cuppa regularly. I'll miss you something awful and so will our Agnes.'

'I'll miss you too.' Martha and Agnes/Fay had become her friends. She was sorry to lose her job, but was earning enough to manage without it, particularly now that Jacob was working, earning twenty-one and sixpence a week.

At long last, Jacob had found a job where his past experience was relevant – he knew about horses. For the past month he had driven a horse and cart around Edge Hill delivering coal. He hated it with all his heart. The black, pungent dust got up his nose and on his chest, making him cough and wheeze. At six o'clock, he came home covered in the stuff, his clothes stiff with it, his face and neck filthy. Ruby had to boil pans of water for him to wash in, though he never seemed able to get the dirt out of his hair. But she couldn't wash the clothes and the room stank of coal. Jacob could smell it even when he was asleep. One of the worst times of the day – and there were many – was getting out of bed and putting on the moleskin pants and the shirt that felt like a suit of armour they were so hard. And, finally, the leather waistcoat to protect his back and shoulders when he humped the heavy sacks down narrow entries into someone's back yard or emptied them down a manhole into the cellar.

Even the horse had no personality, not like Waterloo, the horse who'd been his companion on Humble's Farm. It was a dull, tired creature, as miserable as himself, showing no interest when he tried to talk to it.

Unlike Ruby, Jacob could see no end to this wretched existence. While she talked about leaving Foster Court and how their life would improve, he couldn't envisage a brighter future.

Winter was coming to an end, the nights were getting lighter, the days warmer. It was March and the baby was due in six weeks' time. A woman was coming to deliver it at Jacob's command, no matter what the hour. She charged ten shillings, but was very reliable and experienced.

Jacob came home one Friday, his spirits at their lowest. Charlie Murphy, their landlord, was sitting on the step, sunning himself in the evening sunshine. 'Nice day,' he remarked.

'Is it?' Jacob grunted. He hadn't noticed anything nice about it.

Charlie regarded him thoughtfully. 'Pay days are always a bit special, lad.'

'I suppose.' He always gave his entire wages to Ruby who handled the family's finances.

'While you're flush, d'you fancy putting a tanner on a horse running tomorrer? Twenty to one, a sure-fire winner.'

'How much would I get if it won?'

'It's bound to win, mate, and you'd get ten bob plus your place money which isn't a bad return in my book.'

'And if I put on a shilling I'd get twice as much?'

'You would so.' Charlie nodded emphatically.

'Then I'll risk a shilling,' Jacob said recklessly.

Ruby called him the biggest fool under the sun when he told her. He had to tell her because she counted the wages carefully, pointing out he was a shilling short. She still claimed he was a fool when the horse won and he gave her a pound, keeping the place money for himself. On Sunday night, he celebrated his win with a couple of pints of ale, the first he'd had since coming to Foster Court. In the pub he got chatting to a group of young men who called him 'Jake', and made him feel one of the crowd, a proper man, unlike at home where he felt worthless.

All the following week he felt better about himself. On Friday, Charlie Murphy was waiting on the step when he came home and Jacob put another shilling on a sure-fire winner running next day. The horse lost and Ruby flatly refused to give him a few coppers so he could drown his sorrows in drink.

'I still want things for the baby, a shawl, and where's the little mite to sleep I'd like to know?' she said crossly. 'We need a cot. You're being very irresponsible, Jacob.'

The next time he was paid, Jacob, feeling daring, deducted half a crown before giving Ruby his wages, a shilling for a bet, the rest for ale. He'd go to the pub, the Shaftesbury, tonight. She could rant and rave all she liked, but he'd put in a hard week's work and was entitled to a bit of relaxation over a pint. Other men did it. Why not him?

Ruby didn't rant and rave. 'I've worked hard, too, Jacob,' she said quietly. 'But if that's how you feel ...' She shrugged.

It *was* how he felt. In the pub he could forget about Foster Court, Ruby, and the coming baby. She made him boil his own water to wash in and silently perused the little notebook in which she kept a record of her pawnshop dealings while he changed into his newly cleaned suit. She didn't look up when he said 'Tara'.

In the Shaftesbury he was made welcome with shouts of, 'Hello, there, Jake, ould mate. We didn't think we'd be seeing you again. What are you drinking?'

There were eight of them altogether, including Jacob. He felt obliged to buy a round and by closing time he'd consumed eight pints of ale, more than he'd ever had before. He was pickled to the gills when he got home, to find Ruby sitting up in bed with a sleeping baby in her arms. A strange woman was folding blood-stained sheets. She looked at him with contempt.

'You've got a daughter, Mr O'Hagan,' she said in a voice full of loathing. 'Fortunately, your poor wife was fit enough to send one of the downstairs' kids to fetch me. Christ knows what she'd have done if I hadn't been here.'

'She'd have managed.' Sober, Jacob would have felt ashamed, but brimming with ale, he didn't care. Left alone, Ruby could have delivered the child on her own, cut the cord, done whatever else was necessary, saved herself ten bob. And he resented being called 'O'Hagan'. There was good reason for not admitting to Veering which would be on the police files, but having to use Ruby's name instead of his own only added to his feeling of inferiority.

'I'm off now, Mrs O'Hagan. Are you comfortable, luv?' Ruby nodded. She looked flushed and happy. 'I'll pop in tomorrow, see how you are like. You can pay me then.'

'Thank you.'

The woman left. Overcome with curiosity, Jacob swayed drunkenly towards the bed. 'It's a girl?'

'Yes, she's only little,' Ruby said distantly. 'Mrs Mickelwhite reckons about four pounds. It's because she came early. She wasn't due till next month. She needs fattening up.'

'What are you going to call her?' He took for granted he would have no say in the naming of his daughter and he was right.

'Greta, after Greta Garbo.'

He nodded, though he thought it a daft name. 'Look, Ruby, I'm sorry I wasn't around.' He felt it necessary to make amends. 'I wouldn't have dreamt of going out if I'd known the baby would come tonight.'

'It would have been nice if you'd been here to hold my hand,' she said reproachfully.

'Say if she had come when I was at work,' he reasoned.

'That's different. Work's necessary, not like ale.'

Jacob felt tempted to disagree, but held his tongue. 'Did it hurt bad, Ruby?' He suppressed a hiccup.

'No, it was very quick and hardly hurt at all. Mrs Mickelwhite said it was one of the easiest births she'd ever known. Would you like to hold her?' She must have decided to forgive him and carefully laid the tiny baby in his arms. It was muffled in clothes: a long, flannelette gown, knitted cardigan, bonnet, bootees, all well worn. Ruby had got them from a secondhand market stall. Only the shawl was new, a present from the woman in the Malt House.

The child felt as light as a feather in his arms, but to Jacob she weighed heavier than the sacks of coal he humped around Edge Hill. He stared at the perfect little face, the long lashes trembling on white, waxen cheeks, the prim, pale mouth, and wanted to run away and never come back. Some men might regard their first child as a blessing, but he saw it as a cross he would have to bear for the rest of his life. There would be no end to the years of dirty, back-breaking work, earning a measly few bob. He put his daughter back in Ruby's arms. 'She's lovely,' he said briefly.

'Isn't she?' She stared at the child adoringly. 'I love her more than life itself, Jacob.'

'Do you, now!' He felt jealous.

Within a week, Ruby had returned to work, the baby wrapped up warmly and tucked inside her shawl, acknowledging the congratulations from various passers-by with a queenly gesture of her hand, and moving the shawl a fraction to expose Greta's pretty, pale face to be admired.

Mrs Hart gave the baby a tiny silver bangle. 'My godmother bought that when I was born,' she said to Ruby. 'I'd like Greta to have it, otherwise it will end up in Reilly's along with everything else of value from this house.'

The christening took place the following Sunday, the day after Ruby's seventeenth birthday. It was a quiet affair: just Ruby, Jacob, and their daughter, who was turning out to be an ideal baby, sleeping all night, sucking contentedly at her mother's breast, burping on cue. Though she wasn't gaining weight, Ruby reckoned, balancing Greta in her arms. 'She's hardly any different from the day she was born,' she said worriedly.

'How can you tell?' Jacob wanted to know. He was fed up with Greta commanding her entire attention.

'I just can.'

The night of the christening he went to the pub, saying he wanted to wet the baby's head. The horse he'd backed the day before, which Ruby knew nothing about, had come in third and the odds had been good. He wasn't sure which was more important, the drink or the horses. It certainly wasn't Ruby, or their baby.

By the time Greta was three months old, Jacob was handing over barely half his pay. Every Friday he put a couple of bob on the horses. The occasional wins made his heart sing so sweetly they were worth the more frequent losses. The weeks passed more quickly, each day bringing Friday closer. There would be a feeling in his gut that this week he'd make a killing.

The hours flew by too, knowing the evening ahead would be spent in the Shaftesbury with his mates. Ruby could scowl all she liked; he was a man and he'd do as he pleased. The men in the pub boasted of how they gave their wives a clout if they stepped out of line. If Ruby didn't buck up her ideas, show him some respect, one of these days he'd box her bloody ears.

Charlie Murphy had been badgered into repairing the window in their room and Ruby had made curtains, bright red. There was a patchwork cover on the bed, a rag rug on the floor, and a lace cloth hid the scratches on the chest of drawers. Everywhere was spotless, the room a little, bright oasis in the otherwise cheerless house.

When Jacob came home one hot evening in August, covered with coal dust as usual, the evening sun was pouring through the open window giving the place an extra sparkle. Greta was lying on the bed wearing only a ragged nappy, cooing and lazily examining her toes. She wasn't an active child. She caught colds easily and was still underweight according to Ruby, who worried about her constantly.

The table was set. A large dish in the middle emitted a thin spiral of smoke through a hole in the lid indicating there was the inevitable stew for tea. Ruby acknowledged Jacob's presence with a brief nod. 'Tea's ready when you've had a wash.'

'Is there water boiled?'

'I'm not boiling water so you can get tarted up and go drinking in the pub. I've told you that before. You can boil your own water.' She sat down and opened a newspaper she must have found, an action that always particularly irked Jacob. He could hardly read and felt she was showing him up. 'I'll have a cup of tea while I wait,' she said.

'I'd sooner you boiled the water.' There was a threat in his voice and she looked at him in surprise.

'You'd sooner what?'

'I'd sooner you got off your backside and boiled some bloody water.' He took a step towards her.

Ruby laughed. 'This is the first time all day I've sat down and I've no intention of moving.'

It was the laugh that did it. He wanted her cowed. He was fed up with her being so superior, always on top, him in the wrong, making him feel like a naughty lad. Jacob raised his hand and slapped her across the face, hard enough to make her cry, beg his forgiveness.

Except it did no such thing. Ruby screamed, jumped to her feet, grabbed the saucepan that had held the stew, and swung it against his head. There was a cracking sound as metal hit bone and Jacob collapsed back on to the bed.

Ruby screamed again and grabbed Greta out of the way. She stood over him, saucepan in one hand and the baby in the other, her cheek as red as a flame. 'If you ever hit me again, Jacob Veering,' she said in a grating voice, 'So help me, I'll kill you stone dead.'

Jacob didn't doubt it.

'I tripped,' he explained later in the pub. 'Banged me head against the wall.'

'Sure it wasn't your missus that did it,' joked one of his mates. 'If so, I hope you gave her what for.'

'Me missus wouldn't dare!' He seethed all night at the unfairness of it all. The feeling grew the drunker he got. Other men got away with knocking their wives about, why not him? But then you couldn't compare Ruby with normal women. There was something unnatural about her. The harder things got, the greater she thrived, as if life was a battle she was determined to win. Something inside Jacob melted. This extraordinary woman belonged to *him*! A memory surfaced in his sozzled brain, of Ruby, the way she used to poke her head around the cowshed. 'Hello, Jacob,' she would say shyly.

She'd loved him then, but not now. He'd spoiled things. Jacob began to feel sorry for himself. As soon as he got home, he'd show Ruby how much he loved her, make everything better.

She was fast asleep, the window open, the curtains drifting to and fro in little puffy waves. His working clothes were hanging over the sill, though the room still smelled of coal dust. Greta was in her cot at the foot of the bed.

Jacob quickly undressed, trembling with desire not felt since he'd left Brambles. He wanted Ruby as he'd never wanted her before. She'd been little more than a child when they last made love, but now she was a woman, a desirable woman, famous throughout the neighbourhood.

He slid naked into bed, put his arm around her waist, and pulled her towards him.

She woke immediately. 'What are you doing?' she said warily, pushing him away.

'I love you, Ruby,' he whispered hoarsely. By now, there was a fire in his gut that had to be extinguished or he would go mad. The slippery, struggling, protesting body only added to his passion, egging him on, making the fire get hotter and hotter, until it was scarcely bearable.

'Jacob!' she spat. 'You're drunk, I can smell it. Let go of me. You'll wake Greta.'

He didn't care if he woke the world. The petticoat she slept in tore as he pulled it waist high, dragging her underneath him, positioning himself between the thin legs. He plunged inside her and shuddered with relief. She felt looser than he remembered, but then she'd had a baby since. It did nothing to dampen his enjoyment or inhibit his tumultuous, tumbling climax. He rolled off her, sated, satisfied, ready for sleep.

He never went to the Shaftesbury again, but to a pub where he was a stranger. He felt ashamed of what he'd done and all the things he hadn't done. They never spoke of the night when he'd taken Ruby against her will. Next morning, there were angry marks on her arms and a bruise on her face where he'd hit her earlier on.

By now, he needed the drink, not just to escape from the frigid atmosphere of Foster Court. In the pub he kept to himself, not wanting to make friends.

His shame increased when, a few months later, Ruby announced she was pregnant, her face accusing. It was his fault. Everything was his fault.

Their second daughter was born the following year, 1937, April again. Ruby called her Heather, after some actress, Heather Angel, who'd been in one of her favourite films of all time, *Berkeley Square*.

Unlike Greta, Heather was an active, boisterous baby, hardly sleeping, always crying, demanding her mother's breast, scarlet with incomprehensible anger. Ruby, the pawnshop runner, acquired a giant pram, pushing it along the streets of the Dingle, a baby at each end: quiet Greta, sitting up, and Heather, bawling her bad-tempered little head off.

The girl approached him first. Jacob wouldn't have dreamt of talking to a woman on his own initiative. It was Saturday night, the pub was crowded, a pianist was thumping out tunes he vaguely remembered from the time he'd spent in Brambles listening to the gramophone with Ruby.

'When they begin, the beguine,' the clientele roared lustily.

'You look lonely, luv,' the girl said, slipping on to the bench beside him. She was neither white nor black, but an attractive pale brown, with dark gingery hair a mass of curls and ringlets.

'I'm all right, thanks,' Jacob said stiffly, assuming she was on the game and looking for a customer. If so, she was out of luck. He had ninepence in his pocket, not enough to pay for the cheapest prostitute in all of Liverpool. Which was a shame, because she was very pretty. Her small, pointed breasts showed prominently through her red jumper, and she had smooth, satiny skin. He was a normal, virile man, with a normal man's desires – desires that went unfulfilled. He and Ruby slept in the same bed, but he was too scared to touch her.

'What's your name, luv?' the girl enquired.

'Jake Veering.'

'I'm Elizabeth Georgeson, but everyone calls me Beth. D'you come from round here?'

'No, Kirkby.'

'What are you doing in these parts, Jake?'

Jacob wasn't sure what he was doing there. Ruby had brought him and he'd meekly followed, but he couldn't tell the girl that.

'Lost me job,' he said, 'came looking for another.'

'Did you find one?'

'I'm a coalman, Edge Hill way.'

'Me Gran lives in Edge Hill,' she cried, smiling delightedly. 'I'll tell her to look out for you in future. I live in Toxteth meself.' She worked on the tool counter in Woollies in Lord Street. 'But I'm hoping to be transferred to cosmetics any minute.' Her brown, velvety eyes glowed. 'I can't wait.'

Her father was Jamaican, her mother Irish, and she had two brothers and three sisters, all living at home. She was eighteen, the same age as Ruby, which Jacob found incredible. Ruby seemed more like twenty-five, thirty, compared to this pretty, carefree girl, whose main ambition in life was to sell lipsticks and scent.

'You didn't mind me talking to you, did you, Jake?' she said later. 'You *did* look lonely, and I thought it was a shame, someone as nice as you sitting on their own.' She looked at him shyly. 'Have you got a girlfriend?'

Jacob swallowed. 'No,' he said boldly. He didn't want to drive her away. It made a change to be flattered. She wasn't on the game, but in the pub only because it was someone's birthday from work. She made him feel big, whereas Ruby made him feel small. She was soft, Ruby was hard. When closing time came, he daringly suggested they meet again next Saturday in the same pub.

She looked disappointed. 'But that's a whole week away! Couldn't we see each other sooner?'

'I'd like to but . . .' Jacob paused, but having told one lie, it was easy to tell another, '. . . I'm a bit short of cash. I send money to me mam in Kirkby every week, see. She's a widder and I've got three brothers, all younger than me. She has a job making ends meet since I left home.'

Beth looked at him emotionally. 'You're even nicer than I first thought. Tell you what, we'll go to the pictures Wednesday, it'll be my treat.'

From then on, they saw each other twice a week, which quickly became three. His wages rose by one and six a week and he didn't tell Ruby, but kept the money for himself. When Beth introduced him to her big, strapping father and red-haired mother, they regarded him with a critical eye and apparently liked what they saw. He said he was a Catholic and was welcomed with open arms into their home, regarded as Beth's suitor, just as he had been Audrey's what seemed like a million years ago. It was a position that Jacob liked, uncomplicated, with few demands, apart from the necessity to have a good time. He rather enjoyed his double life, though knew it couldn't last. One of these days Ruby would find out about Beth, or Beth about Ruby.

The double life came to an end in an unexpected way.

It was New Year's Eve, snowing, the grey sky was heavy with sludgy black clouds. In the coalyard, a mountain of glossy coal had been turned into a thing of beauty by a spangle of snowflakes. Jacob wore gloves as he threw the bulging sacks on to the cart, whistling cheerfully as he worked. His employer, Arthur Cummings, too old and frail to carry on the business by himself, was rubbing his gnarled hands in the doorway of the small house overlooking the yard where he lived alone. His wife had died two years before, they'd had no children.

'Watch'a doing tonight, lad?' he enquired.

He knew about Ruby and the girls. Christmas had proved complicated with two women having demands on his time. Beth had been told he was spending the holiday in Kirkby. He was seeing her tomorrow. 'Just staying in,' Jacob replied, 'having a drink with the wife.'

'Good lad,' Arthur said approvingly. 'You're welcome to share a bottle of Guinness with us when you're finished here. We can toast the New Year a bit early, like.'

Jacob nodded, though he'd no intention of accepting. Arthur was a nice man, obviously lonely, always offering cups of tea and trying to engage him in conversation. But Jacob couldn't be bothered. He finished loading the cart, patted the unresponsive horse whose name was Clifford, between the ears, and was about to leap on board, when Beth walked through the wooden gates, startling Clifford, who tossed his head and gave a nervous snort.

'What are you doing here?' he demanded a trifle shortly. The yard was neutral territory. Ruby had never thought to come near.

'I've got something to tell you, Jake.' She looked very pale and her eyes were swollen. 'I'm in the club.'

'In the what?'

'The club, Jake. I'm expecting a baby. I haven't told me mam and dad, but we'll have to get wed straight away. They'll guess, eventually, but it won't matter once we're married. We'll go to St Vincent de Paul's tonight and see Father O'Leary, arrange to have the banns called.'

Jacob froze with shock. 'I can't, tonight,' he stuttered. 'It's New Year's Eve. I promised to spend it with me mam.'

Beth looked disappointed. 'The next night, then.'

That night and the next, to Ruby's surprise, Jacob stayed in, terrified out of his wits. It occurred to him he wasn't married to Ruby and was therefore free to marry Beth. But he didn't want a wife, particularly not one who was pregnant. It would be a case of exchanging one miserable life for another, possibly worse. At least Ruby earned a goodly sum and had worked right through both pregnancies. Beth might want to leave Woollies and the responsibility for supporting her and the child would rest entirely on him. He began to see all sorts of qualities in Ruby that he hadn't appreciated before.

Beth knew he lived in Foster Court, but not the number. 'It's a hovel,' he told her. 'Only temporary. I'd sooner you didn't come.' Any minute she'd come looking for him or she'd turn up again at the coal yard. Even worse, she might send her father. Jacob didn't know which way to turn.

Another day passed. He told Arthur Cummings he needed a day off. 'I've a bit of business to see to. I'll work all day Sat'day instead.' He'd been a good worker and had never taken time off before. Arthur willingly agreed.

Next morning, he put on in his working clothes and hid in a doorway at the end of the court until he saw Ruby leave with the children in the pram, then went back and changed into his suit.

He had no idea how to escape the tangle his life had become, other than to run away, get a job on a farm, never look at a woman again for as long as he lived. There were railway stations in town where he could catch a train as far away from Liverpool as he could afford.

The city throbbed with the noise of traffic, he was jostled on the pavements, his head began to ache as he made his muddled way towards Lime Street station. He paused, trying to get his bearings. He was outside a shop that wasn't really a shop. 'Army Recruiting Office' said the sign over the window. It took him ages to work it out.

He hadn't expected to return to Foster Court, but he did. It would take at least two weeks for his application to join the Army to be processed. He'd given the address of the coal yard, Mr Cummings wouldn't mind, and he'd think of a reason for the different surname, Veering, if it was noticed. His first posting would be with the Army Educational Corps to have his reading and writing skills brought up to standard. Accommodation would be provided, food, his pay would be his own. Most importantly of all, he would be taken care of. From now on, his only obligation would be to King and country.

Tonight he'd go round Beth's before she sought him out, arrange to have the banns called, pick a date for the wedding. By the time it arrived, he would be gone.

Ruby didn't worry when Jacob didn't come home for his tea. She'd got used to the way he seemed to lead his own life these days. Sometimes, she wondered if she still loved him, or if she never had, that it had just been a childish crush. He was the first young man she'd ever met, undoubtedly handsome, but under different circumstances, she doubted if she would have given him a second glance. Without the incident with Bill Pickering, their romance would probably have petered out years ago.

But then she wouldn't have had her girls. They were on the bed, both asleep. She went over and touched Greta's white cheek. 'What would I have done without you?' she whispered. The pale lips were curved in a wistful smile and she was clutching the rag doll she had christened 'Babs'. She resembled her father, with the same butter-coloured hair, the same blue eyes and long, fair lashes. She had Jacob's placid temperament.

Poor Jacob! Ruby sighed. He was a nice man who'd been expected to act in a way that was quite beyond him. Jacob needed peace, quiet, to be left alone. Jacob, the farmhand, would have worked as hard as any man, harder than some.

Ruby made no attempt to touch her other daughter for fear of waking her. At nine months, Heather was a minx, crawling now, into everything. Twice she'd burnt her hand on the iron that had been hidden under the bed to cool. Mother and daughter were very alike. Heather had black hair and almost black eyes. Thin and wiry, very strong, she was almost as tall as Greta who was a year older, often sickly, and still underweight.

She supposed she may as well eat the stew going cold on the table. Stew was easiest to make on the gas ring in the kitchen – she wouldn't have dreamt of putting anything in the filthy oven. Cooking was difficult since Heather had started crawling. She didn't know whether to leave the child in the room with everything dangerous out the way, or take her downstairs where there were different hazards, including cockroaches which Heather couldn't be trusted not to catch and eat.

When, oh, when, would they get away from Foster Court!

It was only in the dead of night that the house was still and silence descended. For this reason, Ruby never minded the occasional times when she woke, able for once to hear the girls' gentle breathing and Jacob's soft snores. No babies were crying, no women screaming, doors slamming. No one was fighting. Sometimes, she would lie, quite content, until the wheels of the milk cart rattled along the main road, followed by the clink of bottles. As if this was a signal for the area to come to life, doors would open, voices could be heard, whistling, and the steady beat of booted feet as men marched towards the docks to start their day's work. At this point, Ruby would wake Jacob and get up herself and hope to reach the kitchen before anyone else to boil water for tea.

When she woke up that night, she realised something was wrong, something was missing. She remembered Jacob wasn't home by the time she'd gone to bed. And he still wasn't there.

She had no idea what time it was. Apart from the children's breath, the world was soundless. She sat up and lit the candle and for the first time noticed Jacob's suit wasn't behind the door on its cardboard hanger. She stayed sitting up, sick with worry and freezing cold, until the milk cart arrived, the dockers had gone to work, when she got dressed, fed the girls, put them in the pram, and pushed it round to the coal yard.

The sky was leaden and the January morning bitterly cold. When she arrived at the yard, a strange young man was loading the cart with sacks. A grey horse, already harnessed, stared moodily at the ground, tossing its head fearfully when it saw her.

'Where's Jacob?' Ruby demanded loudly. Had he lost his job and was too scared to tell her?

'You'd better give Arthur Cummings a knock. He'll tell you.' The young man grinned and nodded towards the small house standing on its own in the corner of the yard. 'Sounds as if he was a bit of a lad, our Jacob.'

'How would you know?' Ruby snapped.

An old man, very bent, with rheumy eyes, answered the door. For some reason, he looked extremely moidered. Ruby didn't waste time with polite niceties. 'Where's Jacob?'

'Who are you?'

'His wife.'

'But I thought . . .' He pulled at his snow-white hair and looked even more moidered.

'Thought what?'

'Well, his wife's already here.'

'I never said I was his wife. I'm his fiancée.' A girl had come into the hall from the back of the house. She wore a brown fitted coat and a Fair Isle tam-o'-shanter with matching mittens, and would have been exceptionally pretty had her eyes not been so red with weeping. 'Jake hasn't got a wife.'

'Oh, yes he has,' Ruby said fiercely. 'Me!' She pointed to the pram. 'And these are his children. But where the hell's their father, that's what I'd like to know. His name's Jacob, by the way, and you can't possibly be his fiancée.'

The girl screamed and burst into tears. 'Jaysus! It's even worse than I thought. He's double-crossed me on top of everything else.'

'Yes, but where is he?' Ruby insisted.

'He's joined the Army, girl,' Arthur Cummings said nervously. 'The Royal Tank Regiment. He said his wife knew.'

Arthur was a gentle old man, genuinely upset by his ex-employee's disgraceful behaviour as if, somehow, it reflected on him. He made a pot of tea, which, he said, he was as much in need of as his visitors. The pram was parked in the hall and the two women sat at a chenille-covered table in a comfortable back room which looked as if nothing had changed since the last century. A cheerful fire spat and crackled in the black grate.

There seemed little point in blaming each other. Jacob had duped them both. Perhaps it was perverse, but Ruby couldn't help liking the girl who was clearly heartbroken. She loved him, she sobbed, they were getting married next month. Last night they'd arranged to go window-shopping to look at wedding rings and intended to buy one on Saturday. When he didn't turn up, she'd been worried.

Ruby glanced at the sixpenny brass ring she'd bought from Woolworth's. She'd paid for it herself and her finger turned green if she didn't take it off when she went to bed. She wasn't sure how she felt other than totally betrayed. Jacob! Having an affair! She hadn't thought he had it in him. But adversity had never sat well on Jacob's shoulders and at that moment her own shoulders felt a fraction lighter, knowing that he had gone out of her life. She might cry, tonight and the next night and a few nights to come, if only because the thing that had started so sweetly had ended on such a sour note. But then it had turned sour a long while ago.

By now, Beth was weeping inconsolably. Ruby reached over and touched her arm. 'You'll have to try and forget him,' she said in the tone of a mother addressing a child. 'You're only young. You'll find someone else.'

'I'll never forget him and I don't want anyone else,' the girl wept. 'Me life's ruined. I can't go back to work. I've told everyone I'm getting married. Some of 'em have already got me a present. They were coming to St Vincent de Paul's to watch.'

'Tell them you've called it off,' Arthur suggested. He was sitting between them like a referee, having taken their predicament to his heart.

'That's a good idea,' Ruby said encouragingly. 'Say you've changed your mind.'

Beth looked at them, her face tragic. 'I would, I could, except . . . except, I'm having Jake's baby. When me dad finds out, he'll kill me.'

There was a knock on the door. 'Not another young lady looking for Jacob, I hope,' Arthur said plaintively when he went to answer it, but it was only his new employee announcing he was on his way.

The knock must have reminded Heather she was being neglected and she set up a plaintive wail.

'I'll have to be going,' Ruby announced. 'I've got things to do, important things, people to see.'

'But what about me?' Beth cried.

Ruby frowned. 'What about you?'

'You've got to help me.'

'No, I haven't. I've been left in a bigger pickle than you. I've got two children to support, rent to pay, a job to do.'

'But you haven't got a broken heart, not like me,' Beth said passionately. 'You're not the least upset, I can tell. No wonder he turned to me. You must have been neglecting him something awful. It's your fault he went away. You drove him to it.'

'Hold on a minute, girl,' Mr Cummings interjected. 'I don't think you're being entirely fair.'

'Nothing *is* fair.'

'Jacob only left home after he met you,' Ruby pointed out. 'It was probably learning about the baby that did it. He wasn't capable of supporting one family, let alone two.'

'He supported his mam and little brothers, didn't he?'

'Did he thump! He hasn't seen his mam in years and he was an only child. He could hardly bring himself to support his children. It was the bookie and the beer that took most of Jacob's money.'

'Oh!' Beth started to cry again.

Perhaps that last remark had been unnecessarily brutal. Ruby felt sorry for the girl. She looked too soft-hearted by a mile and was right to claim Jacob had been neglected, but it was his own fault. He'd been treated with the utmost sympathy when they'd first arrived at Foster Court. Another woman wouldn't have let him lie on that damned bed for more than a couple of days, let alone six months, supporting him, fussing over him. He'd probably still be there, she thought darkly, if Greta hadn't arrived. He'd treated his daughters with indifference, as if they were nothing to do with him, that somehow Ruby had managed to conceive them on her own.

'You're better off without him,' she said abruptly.

'How can you possibly say that!' the girl cried.

'She's been married to him for two years,' Mr Cummings put in. 'She should know. Meself, I considered him a nice lad, but he's gone down in me estimation as from this morning.'

Beth shivered. 'I'm nearly three months gone. I'll have to leave home before I start to show. I'd prefer to go sooner rather than later, under me own steam, as it were, because I'll be chucked out, anyroad, once me dad finds out. At least I'd avoid a good hiding.'

'That makes sense to me,' the old man opined, nodding his white head.

'Yes, but where would I go?' She spread her hands and shrugged helplessly. 'Could I stay with you?' She looked hopefully at Ruby. 'I'm sorry about what I said before. I didn't mean it.'

Ruby snorted. 'Believe me, you wouldn't want to stay with me. No one in their right mind would want to live in Foster Court. The room was cramped enough with Jacob and he was out most of the time. You and me'd be falling over each other and there isn't the space for another baby. And what happens when you stop work? Am I supposed to keep you?'

'I don't care how squashed it is. I tell you what,' Beth said eagerly, 'I'll do the cleaning in return for me keep. You won't have to lift a finger.'

'I can't exactly afford a housekeeper,' Ruby said tartly.

'You can pretend I'm the wife and you're the husband. I'll look after the children and make the meals while you go out to work. What sort of work d'you do?'

'She's the pawnshop runner,' Arthur said proudly.

'I don't want to be anyone's husband, thanks all the same,' Ruby snapped. 'Not only that, my main aim in life is to get out of Foster Court, not take in a lodger.' She folded her arms, a sign her mind was made up. In the hall, her younger daughter was screaming the fact she had completely lost patience with being ignored. 'I'll have to go before Heather takes the roof off.'

'I know what you can do,' Arthur said. 'Both of you. You can move in with me. There's two rooms empty upstairs and a parlour that's never used. I wouldn't want paying, like, just the cleaning and cooking done in return.' He sniffed pathetically. 'I haven't had a decent meal since me ould missus passed on. It'd be nice to have company for a change.' He looked from one to the other with his rheumy eyes. 'Oh, and I like kiddies,' he added as if another inducement was needed before they would agree. 'What do you say?'

'Yes!' Beth cried without hesitation.

Ruby contemplated the idea for several seconds. She liked Beth. They had something in common, both having been betrayed by the same man. And she liked Arthur and his comfortable little house. 'All right,' she said after a while, 'Beth can do the cleaning and cooking and look after the children. I'll pay for the food. It wouldn't be fair otherwise. But I am *not*,' she said warningly, 'under any circumstances, to be regarded as a husband.'

Arthur sighed happily. 'Then it's agreed?'

'Agreed,' the two women said together, and Ruby thought that Jacob would probably die of shock if he could have seen the way they smiled at each other and shook hands.

Beth

6
1938–1945

Beth's little boy fought his way into the world six months later on a sultry August night, causing his mother considerable agony and a certain amount of agitation to Arthur Cummings who paced the living room like an expectant father. 'Is she going to die?' he asked in a trembling voice when a scream more piercing than the others rent the air.

'Of course not,' Ruby snapped. Her own children having arrived without inconveniencing a soul, apart from herself, she had little patience with Beth's hysterical carryings-on. Mrs Mickelwhite, who'd delivered Greta and Heather, was in the bedroom with her now. Ruby ran upstairs to make sure the latest exhibition hadn't woken the girls, but they were fast asleep, one at each end of a single bed. She sat there while the screams in the next room rose to a crescendo, then suddenly stopped. A baby yelled lustily. Ruby waited until the gory bits were over and went into the bedroom, where Mrs Mickelwhite was putting a vast, chubby baby in Beth's arms. The new mother looked exhausted. Bathed in sweat, her gingery hair stood on end.

'He's at least ten pounds,' the midwife said with a satisfied cluck. 'His poor mother went through hell. What are you going to call him, luv?'

'Jake.' Beth stuck out her tongue at Ruby.

'Bitch!' Ruby said amiably. The two girls shared a love–hate relationship. Ruby accused Beth of being indolent and too extravagant, though secretly conceded these trifling faults were more than made up for by her sweet nature and kind heart. In turn, Beth told Ruby she was bossy and mean enough to skin a flint, though was forced to admit she was an incredibly hard worker and extremely caring. They'd argued over calling the baby Jake if it were a boy. Ruby didn't want to be reminded of Jacob, particularly in human form. Beth wanted reminding all the time. She called herself Beth Veering and had kept his shaving brush – Ruby had been about to throw it out – and it stood, like an ornament, on the dressing table in her room.

'Isn't he handsome?' Beth smiled proudly at her new son who was wide awake and waving his chubby fists like a boxer. A fluff of light brown hair covered his scalp and his skin was lighter than Beth's, a pale tan shade.

'He's beautiful,' Ruby said truthfully. She kissed Beth and shook hands with Jake.

'Where's his father?' Mrs Mickelwhite enquired.

'In the Army.'

'And where's your fella nowadays, Mrs O'Hagan? I met him a few times if you recall.'

'He's in the Army too.'

'They joined together.' Beth grinned.

'They're best friends.' Ruby grinned back.

'That's nice,' Mrs Mickelwhite remarked.

It was pleasant living with Arthur Cummings. The house was cosy, though very small. Beth complained it was cramped but, after Foster Court, Ruby appreciated not eating and sleeping in the same room and having a proper kitchen for their sole use. The washing got covered in coal dust and the lavatory was at the bottom of the yard, but at least it wasn't used by all and sundry and Beth managed to keep it more or less clean if she was nagged hard enough.

There was no need nowadays to take the girls as she sped to and fro between her customers and the various pawnshops. They were happy to be left with Beth and Arthur giving Ruby the opportunity to drop in on Martha Quinlan for a cup of tea and a chat, feeling quite the lady of leisure. Mrs Hart had also become a good friend and Ruby often called to see her and Tiger, even if nothing had to be pawned that day to pay off her incorrigible son's debts.

On Sundays, Beth's day off, Ruby reluctantly took over the cooking. Saturday, the old man babysat while the two women went to the pictures: the Dingle Picturedrome or the Beresford. At first, there'd been terrible arguments over what to see until they decided to take turns in choosing. Ruby preferred romances, Beth liked comedy best and anything starring Franchot Tone.

Everyone was happy with the arrangement. Arthur paid the bills and was provided with company in his old age, Beth had a roof over her own and her baby's head in return for doing the housework, although not very well, according to Ruby who bought the food. The money left over she shared with Beth, leaving enough to buy things she'd never been able to afford since leaving Brambles.

Even Jacob's replacement, the young man whose name was Herbie, proved his usefulness by seeing to Clifford the horse every night after they'd finished their day's work.

Arthur was the only one concerned about the war clouds that were gathering on the horizon. He read the *Daily Herald* every day and had his ear glued to the wireless. 'That Hitler chap's throwing his weight about far too much for my liking,' he said frequently. 'I've lived through enough wars in my lifetime. It's not meself I'm concerned about, I've had a good innings. It's you young 'uns.'

'There's nothing to worry about.' Ruby flatly refused to believe anyone, including Adolf Hitler, would be so stupid as to start the war some columnists claimed was imminent. She ignored the ominous signs: the booklet called, 'The Protection of Your Home Against Air Raids,' which had been delivered to every household in the land, followed by others describing how to mask the windows with tape to prevent them from shattering, or explaining what a gas mask was. Martha Quinlan had joined the Women's Voluntary Service, the WVS, and was learning first aid and hoping Fred would feel patriotic enough to run the Malt House in her absence.

Germany annexed Austria, threatened Czechoslovakia, mobilised its armed forces. Benito Mussolini installed a Fascist government in Italy. Still Ruby felt convinced that war would somehow be avoided.

In September, the British Prime Minister, Neville Chamberlain, met with Adolf Hitler in Munich, returning home waving a piece of paper guaranteeing, 'Peace in our Time'.

'See, I told you there wouldn't be a war,' Ruby crowed when she heard it on the wireless.

But the paper proved worthless and Germany blithely continued with its objective of conquering the entire continent of Europe.

Christmas, which they'd been so much looking forward to, was thoroughly spoiled by the arrival a few days beforehand of three adult-size gas masks – junior ones would be issued at a later date and there would be a special one for Jake, now five months old. Arthur was the most badly affected and seemed to sink into a depression from that day on from which he never recovered. The 1914–18 conflict had been termed 'the war to end all wars', yet now there was about to be another. He had lost faith in humanity, he moaned, there was no goodness left in the world, otherwise how could a man like Adolf Hitler prosper? 'Look what he's doing to the Jews!' He stopped going to Mass because he no longer believed in God and made a desperate fuss of the three small children he had so kindly taken into his home. 'What's going to happen to the poor little mites?' he would say despairingly.

They wondered what the New Year, 1939, would bring, and as the weeks and months passed, it seemed that war was becoming more and more inevitable. The signs were everywhere. Brick shelters were built on the corners of the streets, walls of sandbags appeared outside important buildings. First Aid Centres were established. Agnes/Fay Quinlan reported the staff had practised evacuating the Town Hall in case of an air raid. Martha said that when the war started, the children of Liverpool would be evacuated to places like Southport or Wales.

'Over my dead body,' Ruby swore. 'There's no one going to separate me from my kids.'

'It's not compulsory,' Martha assured her. 'Anyroad, mothers can go with their children if they want.'

'I wish they were grown-up like yours,' Ruby said with a heartfelt sigh. 'They wouldn't be such a worry.'

Martha gave her arm a little shake. 'Don't you believe it, luv. Kids are always a worry, no matter what their age. Our Jim's in the Merchant Navy. The seas will be the most dangerous place of all. By the way, he's home this weekend, the first time in months. We're having a bit of a do on Sat'day. You're welcome to come. I've never asked before because you couldn't get away due to the kids.'

'Can I bring Beth?' They could wear the new frocks they'd got for Christmas from C & A.

'Bring whoever you like, luv. How's your Jacob? Have you heard from him lately?'

'Not for a while.'

'Is he still in Aldershot?'

'As far as I know. That's where I last wrote to him, but he still hasn't answered. He was never much good at writing.' She'd heard that the Royal Tank Regiment was based in Aldershot. It wasn't a lie that Jacob had joined up. She just hadn't mentioned that it was his way of leaving his family for good.

'I bet his heart's in his mouth, wondering where he'll be posted when the fighting begins.'

'I bet it is.' She wondered if Jacob would be braver in the Army than he'd been in civilian life.

Ruby had never met Jim Quinlan before. He was, she supposed, unremarkable, though at times there was something almost beautiful about his still, tranquil face. She loved the way he always managed to give everyone his undivided attention, making them feel special, no matter how unimportant other people might think they were.

The Merchant Navy was his life. He'd signed on as a cadet with the Elder Dempster line sixteen years ago. Recently, he'd passed his First Master's Certificate and was now a First Officer, the equivalent of a captain, though so far he'd never had a ship of his own. There was scarcely a country on earth he hadn't visited on the ships, big and small, that carried goods and sometimes passengers, across the oceans of the world.

'So, this is the famous pawnshop runner,' he said when Martha introduced them in the Malt House on Saturday night. 'Mam often mentions you in her letters. It's nice to meet you in the flesh at last. You're every bit as pretty as she said.'

'Am I?' Ruby stammered, strangely tongue-tied, glad she was wearing her new emerald green frock. Emily would have approved of the plain style, but not the colour.

'You've got a husband in the Army, so I understand. And two children as well. How old are they?'

'Greta's three, Heather's two. Their birthdays were last month.'

'You don't look much more than a child yourself.' He smiled into her eyes.

'I had my birthday last month too. I'm twenty.'

'Twenty! You make me feel very old. I'm thirty-one.'

'That's not old,' she protested.

'Old enough to put pretty girls like you out of my reach – married ones in particular.'

Jacob would have to be killed as soon as the fighting started, Ruby decided. She would become a widow and put herself within the reach of Jim Quinlan.

Beth, sitting on her other side, joined in the conversation. 'I suppose you've got a girl in every port,' she said, fluttering her lashes and glancing at him coyly. She looked very pretty tonight in pale blue.

'Only every other port. Will you excuse me? Me mam wants me a minute.' Martha was beckoning to him from behind the bar.

'Is that how you caught Jacob?' Ruby said furiously when Jim had gone. 'Looking at him like a dying cow?'

'He'd be well used to cows, Jacob, after being married to you for so long.'

'Women who flirt make me sick.'

'You're only saying that because you can't flirt yourself.'

'I wouldn't want to. It's degrading. Men either take me for what I am, or they don't take me at all.'

'They don't take you at all as far as I can see. There's only been Jacob and he did a runner.'

'That was your fault, not mine.' Ruby put an end to the argument by going to the Ladies. When she came out, she leant against the wall and watched Jim Quinlan who was sitting with an elderly couple, nodding now and then, oblivious to the noise in the crowded bar. His face was brown from the sun, the skin smooth, not weatherbeaten as she would have expected from someone who spent so much time in the open air. Tiny lines were etched around his hazel eyes and the lashes were short and stubby, very thick. She imagined him standing on deck, shielding his eyes against the sun with a hand that was surprisingly long and slender and also very brown.

Ruby shivered, imagining going to bed with Jim Quinlan, waking up in his arms. The delicious thought was interrupted by Martha shoving a plate of sausage rolls in her ribs.

'Do us a favour, girl. Take these around. I'm up to me eyeballs behind the bar.'

'OK.' It would give her another chance to talk to Jim.

In June, Mrs Hart decided to leave the country for America. 'I've a sister there, Nora. She lives in Colorado, I think I told you before. Once this damn war starts, it won't be safe to cross the Atlantic.'

Ruby thought about Jim Quinlan who would have no choice but to cross the Atlantic no matter how unsafe. 'What about Max?' she asked.

'He's already been called up. He's joined the Royal Air Force – he learnt to fly at university.' She smiled. 'I'm pleased to say he appears to have turned over a new leaf.'

'Are you taking Tiger?' Tiger had grown to an enormous size, though still considered himself a kitten. She scratched his chin and he purred appreciatively.

'Unfortunately, I can't. Nora already has two cats, both female. Tiger would be in his element, but I doubt if the resultant kittens would be welcome. No, he's going to my friend in Childwall. I'm sure he'll be happy there, won't you, Tiger?' The cat didn't look particularly pleased about this arrangement and stared impassively at his owner. 'I wonder, Ruby, dear,' Mrs Hart went on, 'if you'd do me a big favour?' She took a small, brown envelope from out of the dresser drawer.

'You know I will,' Ruby assured her. Mrs Hart had become a dear friend and she was sorry she was leaving.

'If I give you the keys, will you keep an eye on the house for me? It seems silly to sell it. They say the war will only last a couple of months and I'll be back. Just look in every few weeks and make sure everything's all right. I'm having the mains cut off, so there shouldn't be any floods or gas leaks, but I've put Nora's address in there, so you can write and let me know if there's a problem. And help yourself to anything from the garden, dear. You've had apples off the tree, so you know how lovely and crisp they are, and there's rhubarb too. It tastes like wine.'

'I'll miss you,' Ruby said, taking the envelope.

'And I'll miss you, Ruby dear, and your two lovely little girls.' Mrs Hart looked close to tears. 'But it won't be for long, will it? In no time at all, I'll be back and we'll have tea together again; just you, me, and Tiger.'

It was a wonderful day, not hot, but comfortably warm, the golden sun dazzling in the cloudless blue sky, entirely appropriate for a *Sun*day. It was the sort of day that, under different circumstances, would have been regarded as a blessing from God, an example of how perfect the world could be when He felt in the mood.

In reality, the day was anything but perfect.

Ruby and Beth strolled through Princes Park. Jake was fast asleep in the pram that had once held Greta and Heather. The girls were scampering over the thick, dry grass, running in and out of the trees, calling to each other, their childish voices echoing sharply in the late afternoon air.

The faces of the young women were sombre. At eleven o'clock that morning, Great Britain had declared war on Germany after Hitler had invaded Poland, a country they had been bound by treaty to protect.

'What are we going to do, about being evacuated, that is?' Beth spoke in a low voice, as if half to herself.

'I think we should go, though I don't like leaving Arthur.'

'Me neither. But I suppose the children should come first.'

'Arthur would be the first to agree. He'd hate it if he thought we were staying in Liverpool because of him.' Ruby watched Heather pull her older, more fragile sister, up a slight incline. Heather watched over Greta like a mother hen with a chick. Tears sprang to her eyes at the thought of either of her daughters being harmed. Or Beth and Jake, come to that. She loved Beth like a sister and Jake as a son.

Arthur had made a fuss when they said they were going for a walk. He was expecting an air raid any minute. 'Don't go far,' he'd warned. So they hadn't.

Ruby looked anxiously at the sky, half expecting to see an enemy plane loaded with deadly bombs, but the blue sky was clear from horizon to horizon except for the brilliant sun. 'Martha Quinlan's helping to organise the evacuation. Shall we call in the Malt House on the way home and arrange to go tomorrow?' she said. 'They're running special coaches and trains for evacuees.'

Beth sighed. 'OK, but let's go on a train no matter where it takes us. It'll be murder stuck on a coach with the children.'

'A train it is.'

Coaches went to Wales, trains to Southport, Martha told them. They should turn up at Exchange station at ten o'clock next morning.

'Who will we stay with?' enquired Beth.

'No one knows, luv. I understand it's a bit like a meat market at the other end. You just have to stand around until you're picked.'

As they walked back, Beth said wistfully, 'I'd love to go and see my brothers. Ronnie's eighteen and Dick's twenty-one. They're bound to have been called up.'

'I'll come with you,' Ruby offered.

'No, ta, Rube. Thanks all the same, but me dad won't consider it too late to give me a walloping. I don't want to arrive in Southport with me arm in a sling.'

'I'll stay and keep the home fires burning,' Arthur promised manfully when they left next morning with Jake in his pushchair, a few hastily packed carrier bags, and gas masks slung over their shoulders. The old man was obviously on the verge of tears. His hands were visibly shaking and he looked particularly frail today. 'Never forget this is your home,' he said emotionally. 'You're free to come and go whenever you please.'

'Thanks, Arthur,' Ruby said, flinging her arms around his neck. 'It's the first *proper* home I've ever had.'

The train was packed with excited children, weeping children, and some pale with fear. A few mothers accompanied the smaller ones. A uniformed WVS lady distributed sandwiches en route and tied name labels around wrists. Ruby pinned her label to the collar of her green frock.

In Southport, they were herded into an open space beside the station where several cars were parked. The occupants immediately got out and began to walk among the new arrivals, assessing them openly. The nicely dressed children were pounced upon and quickly whisked away.

'Martha was right,' Ruby said hotly. 'I feel like a piece of meat. Any minute now someone's going to ask how much I cost a pound.' Nevertheless, she was glad they were all wearing their best clothes. The girls looked like the royal princesses in their frilly cotton frocks, and Jake was adorable in a blue and white sailor suit, a present from Arthur for his first birthday.

'Would you like to come with me, dear?' A tall, grey-haired woman with a mild good-natured face put her hand on Ruby's arm. She wore an expensive navy-blue serge coat and matching hat.

'Come on, Beth!' Ruby called. 'Greta, love, hold Heather's hand. I've got these bags to carry.'

The woman shook her head. 'I'm sorry, dear. I meant you and your little girls. I haven't room for any more.'

'In that case, I'll wait for someone who has,' Ruby said.

A WVS lady bustled up. 'Then you'll wait for ever, Mrs . . .' she peered at the label on Ruby's frock, '. . . O'Hagan. I doubt if anyone can accommodate two adults and three children.'

'You go, Ruby.' Beth gave her a little push. 'I'll meet you here, by the station, tomorrow. About two o'clock.'

'But I wanted us to be together!'

'That's out of the question, Mrs O'Hagan. Miss Scanlon has kindly offered to take you. I'd appreciate it if you left immediately. You're holding up the proceedings.'

Miss Scanlon led them towards a small Morris saloon. She chatted amiably throughout the journey. Ruby sat in the back, hardly answering, hugging the silent children and blinking back the tears. It was bad enough leaving Arthur; she hadn't expected to be parted from Beth as well.

'Here we are!' They stopped outside a smart semi-detached house on the outskirts of the town. 'I'll take the bags, you look after your little girls,' Miss Scanlon said helpfully. 'You must all feel very strange.'

The house was pleasant inside. The furniture was light oak. Patterned rugs were scattered over the polished floors and there were numerous bowls of roses: red roses, yellow, and a lovely peachy colour. Their heady perfume filled the house. Yet Ruby experienced the same sinking sensation she'd had on first entering Foster Court, when she went into the place where they were now to live.

Greta started to cry.

'Don't like here, Mammy,' Heather whispered.

'Shush, both of you.'

They were shown upstairs. 'I decided to let the evacuees have the big room, it accommodates more beds. I've moved into the back.' Miss Scanlon waved her arm at the double bed with its flowered eiderdown. Two campbeds were made up with blankets.

'It's kind of you to put us up,' Ruby muttered.

'I'm only too pleased to do my bit, Mrs O'Hagan.'

The bed was comfortable, they all slept well on their first night, the food was well cooked and plentiful. Miss Scanlon was doing her best to be friendly and make them feel at home.

But it *wasn't* home. Greta and Heather didn't know where to play and Ruby didn't know where to put herself. The parlour seemed out of bounds, the living room had Miss Scanlon in it most of the time and they felt in the way. The garden contained only rose bushes and a vegetable patch. It was impossible to run around – Heather tried and badly scratched her arm. The bedroom was the only place where they could be alone, yet it felt rude to shut themselves away for long periods.

It was a relief, after dinner, to catch a bus to the town centre to meet Beth.

The bus dropped them off in Lord Street, a lovely wide boulevard with trees down the centre, where Ruby used to go shopping with Emily. The weather was as lovely as the day before. 'We'll go to the sands later,' Ruby promised. 'After we've met Beth and Jake and had a cup of tea.'

'When we see Arfur?' Greta asked in a quivery voice.

'I'm not sure, love, soon.'

The small face crumpled. 'Wanna go home to Arfur.'

'We will, eventually.'

Beth was late. Ruby's nerves were already on edge, Greta made no secret of how miserable she felt, and Heather quickly got bored while they sat on a bench outside the station, complaining about her scratched arm.

Two hours later, when Beth and Jake still hadn't arrived Ruby, deeply concerned, gave up. By now, Greta was sobbing helplessly, demanding they go home to Arthur, and Heather was in a filthy temper. She took them for the promised cup of tea and a brief play on the sands, then caught the bus back to Miss Scanlon's.

'Have you got the telephone number of anyone in the WVS?' she asked the woman anxiously.

'I'm afraid not, dear. Is something wrong?'

'I've lost my friend. She didn't turn up and I've no idea where she is.'

'She can't have gone far, Mrs O'Hagan. I shouldn't let it worry you.'

It worried Ruby all night long. When Beth didn't turn up at the station the following day, it worried her even more. She called the Malt House from a telephone box and asked Martha Quinlan if she knew where Beth and Jake might be. Martha had no idea, but promised to try and find out.

'If you speak to her, tell her I'll be at the station at two o'clock every day until she comes.'

Two more days were to pass before a perspiring Beth bearing a carrier bag and a grizzling Jake turned up at Southport station. 'I think he's cutting a tooth.' Beth's pretty face collapsed and she burst into tears. 'Oh, Rube! We're living in this horrible place, miles from anywhere. This woman, Mrs Dobbs, she's got five children, and considers me a maid-of-all-work. I couldn't get away, there's no buses, and one of the kids broke the pushchair. I share a campbed with Jake and we've hardly slept at all.'

'Sit down, love,' Ruby said angrily. 'Here, give me Jake.'

'I'm not going back, Rube,' Beth sobbed. 'I've brought our things. I don't care about the pushchair. I walked for ages until I came to a bus stop. I've never prayed so much that you'd be here.'

'Of course you're not going back. Somehow or other, we'll find a WVS woman and she can get you somewhere else to stay.'

'No, she won't, Ruby. The other night, the day we came, we waited till it was dark, but no one wanted Jake and me. There was just us left and the woman in charge had to take us back to her house. Next day, she drove us into the depths of the countryside and dumped us on Mrs Dobbs.'

'But you and Jake looked dead respectable compared to most of the others. I thought you'd be taken straight after us.'

'You don't understand, do you, Ruby?' Beth stopped crying and managed to smile ruefully at her friend.

'What's there to understand?'

'We're coloured, me and Jake,' she said in a matter-of fact voice.

'I know you're coloured,' Ruby said impatiently, 'a very nice colour as it happens. What's wrong with that?'

'Not everyone's as tolerant as you. It's all right round Toxteth and Dingle where there's lots of black people, but there's parts of Liverpool where we wouldn't exactly be welcome.'

Ruby wiped Jake's tearful face with her hanky. He was a lovely baby with a lovely nature. It was beyond her comprehension how anyone could be prejudiced towards an innocent one-year-old child because he wasn't white. 'What's going to happen now?' she asked Beth.

'I'm going home, that's what, back to Arthur.'

'Come back with us,' Ruby said tersely. 'Miss Scanlon won't mind if I explain what's happened. There's plenty of room. I can sleep in the big bed with the girls and you and Jake can have a camp bed each.'

Miss Scanlon listened, her mild face expressionless, while Ruby explained the reason for Beth and Jake's presence, finishing with, 'You don't mind if they stay, do you?'

'Show your friend where's she's to sleep, then I'd like a word with you in private, Mrs O'Hagan.' Her voice was as expressionless as her face.

Ruby returned downstairs alone when the sleeping arrangements had been sorted out. She found Miss Scanlon in the kitchen. 'You wanted to speak to me?' she said with a smile, grateful that the woman had been so willing to help.

Miss Scanlon turned and Ruby felt her blood turn to ice when she saw the look of hatred in her eyes, her ugly twisted lips. 'I don't appreciate having niggers brought into my home,' she spat. 'I'd have turned her and her nigger baby out on the spot if it hadn't been for the fact I've got a weak heart and I couldn't have stood a scene. But I want them out tomorrow, first thing. After they've gone, *you* can wash the things they've used; the dishes, the cutlery, the bedding. I'm not touching them.'

It took several seconds for the odious words to sink in, and when they did Ruby could hardly speak for the ball of anger in her throat. 'Don't worry,' she said in a voice she hardly recognised as her own, 'they won't use any of your precious things, because they're going home, Beth and Jake. And me and my children are going with them.'

The woman must have realised she had gone too far. She immediately changed her tune. 'But there's no need for you to go, Mrs O'Hagan,' she cried. 'You and me, we'll get along fine. You talk nice, your children have lovely manners. Lord knows who I'll get landed with if you leave.'

'*You* don't talk nice, Miss Scanlon. Oh, your accent's posh enough, but what you say is filthy. I don't want someone like you anywhere near my girls. You're worse than Hitler with your views. Oh, and I hope tomorrow you get landed with a family of gorillas. At least they'll have better manners than you.'

'I don't know why we had to up and leave so suddenly,' Beth said on the train back to Liverpool. 'That woman seemed OK to me. I was looking forward to a nice long kip.'

'Has there been the faintest sign of an air raid since we left?'

'No, but . . .'

'Well, that's why we went away in the first place, isn't it?' Ruby raised her eyebrows, daring Beth to argue. 'To escape the raids. It seemed daft to stay. None of us were happy there. Were we, girls?' Greta and Heather emphatically shook their heads. 'Even Jake has bucked up since we got on the train.' Jake was gurgling happily at everyone. Ruby sighed blissfully. 'Another few stops and we'll be home.'

To their surprise, when the small company entered the coal yard, the door to Arthur's house was open and there was a strange young man standing in the hall.

'Who are you?' Ruby demanded.

'I'm Doctor Brooker,' the man said crisply. 'Who are you?'

'Ruby O'Hagan and I live here. All of us do.'

'You're acquainted with Mr Arthur Cummings?'

'I must be, mustn't I, if I live here? What does Arthur want with a doctor?'

'Would you mind coming inside, please?'

'Where's Arthur?'

'I'll tell you inside.'

'What's the matter, Rube?' Beth asked shakily.

'I don't know. Let's go in and find out.'

'I'm afraid there's bad news,' Dr Brooker said gravely when the women were seated. By now they had realised that must be the case, but weren't prepared for how bad the news actually was. 'I'm sorry to say that last night Arthur Cummings died peacefully in his sleep. He suffered no pain. Indeed, there was a smile on his face when he passed away. He was eighty-one years old. I pray I live so long myself and die so happily.' He spoke gently. 'Are you relatives?'

'No, friends,' Ruby whispered. Beth began to cry. The little girls caught her mood and cried with her, little hacking sobs, as it dawned on them that their dear Arthur was dead.

'I'm so sorry,' Dr Brooker murmured.

'Is he still here? I'd like to say goodbye – we all would.'

'He was taken to the morgue only minutes before you arrived. It's not long since his body was found. The young man, Herbie, was worried there was no sign of life when he returned this evening with the cart. Apparently, Mr Cummings always came out to greet him.'

'He'd still be alive if we hadn't gone away,' Ruby said, her voice suddenly harsh. 'It was us going that finished him off. Five days, the war only started five days ago, and already we've lost someone we love.'

It was the saddest night they'd ever known. The children were worn out and went to bed willingly. Greta and Heather were upset about Arthur, but not old enough to mourn. Ruby and Beth stayed up until the early hours, talking about their old friend, reminiscing, crying sporadically, taking turns to comfort each other. They blamed themselves for deserting him.

When Beth began to fall asleep in front of her eyes, Ruby made her go upstairs, then stayed in the chair, staring at the empty fireplace, while other thoughts flitted in and out of her mind. The scene with Miss Scanlon had brought home to her an aspect of life she hadn't known existed; colour prejudice. She would never repeat to Beth the terrible things that Miss Scanlon had said, but the words would forever stay seared on her soul.

Her thoughts turned to Jim Quinlan, as they often did when she was alone. They'd only met a few times since the party in the Malt House. Looking into his warm eyes, she'd hoped to see something more than the friendly interest he took in everybody's affairs, but had looked in vain. Ruby sighed. Even if he considered her the most desirable woman in the world, she couldn't imagine Jim Quinlan allowing himself to show a scrap of interest when he thought she was married.

Next morning, there were practical issues to consider. Would the landlord let them have the house? Beth wondered aloud.

'Not unless we take over the yard as well. They both go together. I don't know about you, but I don't fancy running a coal business.'

'I didn't think of that. Which reminds me, I'll just have a word with Clifford. Just because he's a horse, it doesn't mean he won't be as upset as anyone that Arthur's gone.'

Herbie arrived soon afterwards, wanting to know if he should deliver the coal as usual and who would pay him if he did. 'And there's more needs ordering. We're running low.'

'I think you should nip round the landlord's first, tell him about Arthur,' Ruby advised. 'Things need sorting out.'

'Would he let our dad take over the place, d'you think?' Herbie asked, his young face bright with hope. 'He lost his leg on the docks a few years back, our dad, then our mam did a bunk and we lost the house an' all. Me and him and our Mary have been living in rooms ever since. We could run the place together. Mary could do the paperwork, she's good at sums. We talked about it last night.'

'All you can do is ask, Herbie. If you move in, I won't have to worry about Clifford being looked after.'

Beth came up and overheard the last remark. 'No, but you can start worrying about something else, Ruby – where are *we* going to live?'

'I know exactly where we're going to live,' Ruby sang. 'In a nice, detached, five-bedroomed house overlooking Princes Park.'

'What if she comes back, this Mrs Hart?' Beth asked next day as they toured the house, upstairs and down. The girls ran ahead, gleefully exploring, Arthur forgotten. Jake tottered along on his chubby legs, clutching his mother's hand.

'She went to America to escape the war. She's not likely to come back now it's started, is she?'

'I'll be worried all the same.'

'So will I, a bit, but I'd sooner be worried than live somewhere like Foster Court. I'd write and ask Mrs Hart if it'd be all right if we stayed, but her sister's address turned out to be a laundry list when I opened the envelope with the keys. She was always a bit of a scatterbrain. Isn't everywhere lovely and big!'

The hall and the landing were enormous and four of the spacious bedrooms had bay windows with padded seats – one was still full of Max Hart's childish toys. The furniture was old and shabby and the carpets as faded as the curtains and the upholstered suites in the two big reception rooms at the front. Here and there, a young Max had scribbled with a crayon on the pale, knobbly wallpaper, though was unlikely to have been chastised by his indulgent mother. Mrs Hart hadn't thought to cover the furniture or put things away before she set sail for America. The beds hadn't been made, there was half-finished knitting in the kitchen where dishes had been left to drain. Ruby hadn't felt inclined to tidy up the times she'd come to make sure everything was all right.

'It looks as if she's just popped out to do a bit of shopping,' Beth remarked. 'It's creepy. She's even left a record on the gramophone with the lid up. It's full of dust.'

Ruby thought the place had a run-down, appealing charm that hadn't been evident in the more sumptuously furnished Brambles. 'Stop moaning and count your blessings,' she said sternly.

'Oh, I'm counting them, don't worry.' Beth smiled. 'I never dreamt I'd ever live in a house like this. Bagsy me a bedroom overlooking the park.'

'Bagsy me the other. Anyway,' Ruby frowned and looked thoughtful, 'I think it best if we kept to the back, downstairs too, we'll use the living room next to the kitchen, so as few people will notice us as possible, but we'll have to think of a story for the neighbours to explain why we're here – say we're housesitting, for instance, that we've got permission to stay. We'll have to get some blackout curtains. It's lucky Mrs Hart put sticky tape on the windows before she went away.'

'There's a sewing machine in the little bedroom, a treadle. Me mam had one the same at home. It'll do to sew the blackout curtains – and I can make us some clothes.'

They returned downstairs, leaving Greta and Heather trying out the inside lavatory. 'I'll arrange to have the mains turned on,' Ruby said, thinking aloud. 'I'll say I'm Mrs Hart's daughter if anyone asks. It means we'll have bills to pay, electricity, gas. Tomorrow, I'll start work again. Probably no one's noticed I've been gone – there wasn't time to tell them.'

'Oh, this is the gear!' Beth picked Jake up and gave him a little excited twirl. 'You're a miracle worker, Ruby O'Hagan, you really are. I'm ever so glad I met you.'

'You can thank Jake's dad for that. Don't forget, it was him you met first.'

7

It wasn't long, a matter of weeks, before Ruby was forced to declare the pawnshop runner another casualty of war. Most of her former customers no longer needed to pawn their valuables. Unemployment had vanished at a stroke and wages had risen. Women were taking over men's jobs, earning fabulous amounts in factories. They delivered post, read meters, joined the Forces, became tram and bus conductors, did all sorts of jobs that had once been the preserve of males.

The world had changed. There was a different spirit in the air. Germany had laid down a challenge and the British people had taken it up with enthusiasm. The pawnshop runner was out of date. She belonged to a world that no longer existed. Ruby would have to find another, quite different job.

Ironically, the new poor were women with families whose husbands had been called up. They were allowed a pitiful sum to make up for the breadwinner being away risking his life for his country.

'Why aren't you getting an allowance?' Beth enquired when Ruby, rather foolishly, conveyed this piece of information and expressed her disgust. 'You've got a husband in the Army.'

'I told you, it's pitiful.'

'How much is pitiful?'

'About twenty-five shillings,' Ruby replied, uncomfortably aware the conversation had taken a dangerous turn.

'Twenty-five bob!' Beth gaped. 'Don't be daft, we could do a lot with that.'

Ruby yawned. 'I can't be bothered applying.'

'I'm surprised you didn't get it automatically as soon as Jake joined up.'

'Are you?' She couldn't think of anything else to say.

Beth went into the kitchen and Ruby to the garden to watch the children play. She gave a sigh of relief, thinking the subject of allowances had been dropped, but her interrogator appeared a few minutes later.

'Why are you known as Ruby O'Hagan, not Veering?'

'Why not?' Ruby countered weakly.

'Because it's what happens when people get married, soft girl. The woman takes the man's name. Me, I was looking forward to becoming Mrs Veering.' Her eyes narrowed. 'You and Jake weren't married, were you? Don't argue,' she snapped, when Ruby opened her mouth to insist they were. 'I know for sure because there's no way in the world you'd turn down twenty-five bob without good reason.'

'Oh, all right, we weren't.' Ruby shrugged.

Beth went pale. 'So, he *could* have married me.' She burst into tears. 'I've always told meself he went away with a broken heart because we couldn't get wed.'

'Well you were wrong.' Ruby was inclined to give the occasional emotional outbursts concerning Jacob short shrift. 'I bet he went away happier than he'd been in a long time. He was escaping from us both, not to mention his children – including Jake.'

'You're as hard as nails, Ruby O'Hagan.'

'No, I'm not. I'm a realist. I've never seen the point of crying over spilt milk. We've got more important things than Jacob to think about at the moment – ourselves. I'm not making enough for us to live on. I need to find another job. Just try thinking about that!'

'I've already thought about it.' Beth sniffed and wiped her eyes with her sleeve. 'Why don't *I* get a job instead of you?'

Ruby stifled a laugh. Beth was upset enough, it wouldn't do to upset her further, but what on earth could she *do*? She thought the world of her, but to put it bluntly, Beth was useless. She wasn't very strong nor particularly clever. She glided dreamily through life and nothing could hurry her. Looking after children, doing housework, was the most she could be trusted with. 'What sort of job?' Ruby asked, feigning interest.

'In one of them munition factories. You said yourself the wages were good. I can be the husband for a change. You can stay at home and be the wife.'

'You think you can manage that, do you?'

'Well, I can try.'

'All right then, try.' Ruby hid a smile, knowing it would all end in the inevitable tears and she'd be looking for a job herself in a few weeks' time. She could take over Beth's! 'Let's see how you get on.'

Ten days later, Beth started work as a fly presser at A. E. Wadsworth Engineering, a small factory on the Dock Road that had recently converted to war work.

'I'm going to stamp out parts for aeroplanes,' she said importantly when she returned from the interview. 'The wages are three pounds, five and six a week. I get a five bob rise after six months. It's ever such hard work.' She grimaced. 'You should see the size of the press I have to operate. It's *huge*.'

The first day she came home, her hands wouldn't stop shaking and she went to bed straight away. During the night, Ruby heard her sobbing quietly, but decided to leave her to it, doubting that she'd last the week.

On the second day, her right arm was paralysed from using the heavy machine and she could hardly walk from the tram stop on her swollen feet. She refused anything to eat and cried again in bed.

Wednesday, she cried before she went to bed. The women she worked with were horrible and the men made fun of her. 'One of 'em said I had the strength of a gnat.'

'Cheek!' Ruby expostulated.

Thursday, she arrived with a bandage on her thumb. 'I caught it in the machine.'

'Is it still all there?'

'The machine or me thumb?'

'I don't care about the machine. What about your thumb?'

'It's just bruised, Rube. Don't worry.'

Ruby worried again on Friday when there was no sign of Beth by half-past five. She arrived two hours later, slightly unsteady on her feet, and looking twenty years older than at the beginning of the week. 'I went for a drink with me mates,' she announced. 'I'm a little bit tiddly.'

'Mates!' Ruby shrilled. 'What mates? I thought everyone was horrible or made fun. You've got a cheek! I took ages making your tea and now it's ruined. I'm not making another.'

'S'all right, Rube. I'm not hungry.' Minutes later, she was fast asleep in the chair.

Ruby wouldn't have felt quite as irritated at the way things had turned out if she hadn't found it so hard to look after three small children as well as clean a very large house and keep the garden tidy. Now that Jake was walking, he couldn't be let out of sight.

'We need a playpen,' she informed his mother.

'I'll buy one as soon as I can afford it,' Beth promised in the same airy tone Ruby used to adopt in Arthur's house when told something was urgently required.

Greta and Heather demanded constant attention. 'How am I supposed to play with you, keep an eye on Jake, clean this place, and prepare the food?' Ruby shrieked.

'Beth didn't shout at us,' growled Heather.

Six months later, in March, Beth got the promised five-shilling raise. She loved her job and claimed it made her feel very much part of the war effort.

Ruby sulked. She didn't feel she was contributing anything towards the war. By now, a playpen had been acquired, the girls were encouraged to help with the housework, and a rota had been drawn up so only a certain number of tasks were carried out each day. There was time for a walk to the shops each morning, a visit to the park in the afternoon, an occasional ride into town on the tram. She responded to the call to 'Dig for Victory', and planted vegetables in the garden.

But it wasn't enough. She was bored out of her skull. Martha Quinlan suggested she join the WVS and Ruby said she'd love to, 'But what would I do with the children?'

'We can have meetings in your nice big house,' Martha said. 'You don't have to be an active member like me. We meet regularly to roll bandages, knit blankets, make toys, do all sorts of useful things. Before Christmas, we made gift parcels for the troops. Last week, we stuffed mattresses for evacuees – some of the poor little mites still wet their beds.'

Ruby agreed. It was better than nothing.

There was a meeting the following week. The children were lectured beforehand on the necessity of behaving themselves, and about a dozen women of various ages turned up armed with refreshments and a pile of old sheets to be turned. This involved tearing the sheets in two, cutting away the frayed centre, and sewing the good ends together to make another, almost new. The women were delighted to discover the sewing machine and took turns using it, apart from Ruby who wanted nothing to do with the damn thing.

It turned out to be an unexpectedly enjoyable afternoon. They told jokes, some quite near the knuckle, gossiped, and sorted out the war between them. When they were leaving, one of the younger women approached Ruby. 'Would you mind if I brought my kids next week? I have to leave them with me mam and she moans like hell. They could play in the garden. One of us could be designated to look after them.'

'I'll do it,' Ruby offered, groaning inwardly. She didn't like children much apart from her own and Jake, but she disliked sewing even more. Still, she wanted to do something towards the war effort and it didn't mean she had to like it.

'I'll tell Freda. She can bring her kids too.'

'If you're looking after eight children, two more wouldn't make much difference, would it, Rube?' Beth remarked a few weeks later.

'What do you mean?' Ruby asked suspiciously.

'It's just that Olive Deacon, one of the women in the factory, is having to leave because her mam's gone in hospital and there's no one who'll have her two little boys. They're lovely, Rube, honest. Olive showed us their photey once.'

'Most kids look nice in photographs. And I'd be having them every day, not once a week like now.'

'Ah, come on, Rube,' Beth said in her most cajoling voice. 'If Olive leaves, they'll get someone else who won't be nearly as good. She's one of our best workers. In a way, it's your patriotic duty to look after her kids. She'll pay, naturally.'

'You bitch!' Ruby hissed. 'OK, I'll have them.'

Roy and Reggie Deacon were little horrors. They told lies, fought with the girls, and taught Jake to wee against the trees. One day, when Ruby thought they were innocently occupied upstairs, she discovered them playing with Max Hart's well-preserved toys and they had beheaded several wooden soldiers and unstuffed a bear. She comforted herself with the thought that Roy was starting school in September and without him Reggie might behave when he was outnumbered two to one by the girls.

But when September came, Roy's place was taken by a girl called Mollie whose mother also worked with Beth. Mollie was more badly behaved than Roy and Reggie put together and broke a pretty vase on her first day, one of the few valuable objects in the house that hadn't been pawned. Ruby gritted her teeth and told herself she was doing her patriotic duty though wasn't sure if she believed it. Nevertheless, she threw herself wholeheartedly into the task of looking after the children, just as she had done with the cleaning jobs which she'd loathed almost as much.

For almost a year, the bulk of the population had remained unaffected by the war. France had fallen, thousands of French and British troops had been rescued in the great evacuation of Dunkirk, the slaughter on the seas at the hands of German U-boats was horrific. Martha Quinlan was in a constant state of fear for Jim – so was Ruby, though she told no one. These events occurred outside the lives of ordinary people. Although food rationing was in place, the main inconvenience was the tiny amount of tea allowed. But when, in June, 1940, the air-raid siren sounded for the first time, the fact of war became a brutal reality.

Ruby had prepared a shelter in the vast cellar which was as big as the ground floor area of the house and separated into four sections by thick, brick walls. It was full of mysterious lengths of timber, boxes of books and old clothes, furniture even older than that upstairs, rolls of tattered linoleum and carpet. She cleaned one of the sections, laid a carpet, and furnished it with two discarded easychairs, a sofa with a curled end which she covered with a blanket to hide the holes, and a folding bed. Jake's cot, which he didn't use any more but could still squeeze into, was brought down. She fixed a splint on a table which had a broken leg, and filled a box with matches, candles, an assortment of books and board games, and a pack of cards. Then she prayed the shelter would never be used. But her prayers were in vain.

Beth was a light sleeper and heard the siren first. She woke Ruby and they ushered the children into the cellar. Jake stayed asleep and the others played snap and drank lemonade, while gunfire rumbled in the distance. After about an hour, the all clear sounded and they returned upstairs.

'Well, that wasn't so bad, was it?' Ruby commented.

'It was scarcely worth breaking our sleep for,' grumbled Beth.

The next time the siren went, the gunfire sounded closer and they thought they could hear a plane and hoped it wasn't German. The following day, they heard that six bombs had landed harmlessly in a field.

The siren continued to sound throughout July and bombs continued to drop on fields on the outskirts of the city. Ruby and Beth decided these incidents weren't worth getting out of bed for, but two weeks later, in August, four people were killed and several injured when a stick of bombs fell on Wallasey.

'Jaysus!' Beth gasped when she heard. '*Killed!*' They looked at each other with scared eyes.

Ruby nodded bleakly. 'It's the cellar from now on. No more staying in bed when the siren goes.'

It seemed to happen all of a sudden, as if the Luftwaffe had been playing with them and had now decided that it was no longer a game. The raids continued, getting heavier, lasting longer, until one night saw three separate raids on Liverpool causing serious damage throughout the city and killing more people.

The unthinkable had finally happened. In the cellar, Ruby and Beth listened to the planes droning overhead, the bombs screaming to earth, the inevitable explosions, and wondered how such madness could have been allowed to happen. Their worst nightmare had become a reality.

'I'm almost glad Arthur died when he did,' Ruby said softly. 'At least he missed all this.'

There was one good thing to be thankful for; Greta and Heather regarded the raids as a great adventure. They enjoyed playing games and being read to in the middle of the night and Jake usually slept through everything.

No matter how little sleep she'd had, Beth always left promptly for work. One morning, after Beth had gone and Mollie and Roy Deacon had arrived and the five children were in the living room with drawing pads, crayons, and Max Hart's wooden blocks, Ruby went into the kitchen and was washing the dishes when she heard scratching on the back door. She opened it to find a skeletal cat outside. It miaowed weakly when it saw her, walked shakily inside, then flopped in a heap of scraggy, tortoiseshell fur on to the floor.

'Tiger!' Ruby fell to her knees and stroked the strangely thin, furry body. 'Oh, Tiger, what's happened to you? You're no more than skin and bone.' Tiger regarded her pathetically with his amber eyes. 'Let's get you some milk.'

She poured milk into a saucer and the cat managed to raise his head and lap most of it up. He ate half a slice of bread and Marmite, then Ruby wrapped him in a piece of old blanket and cuddled him, sniffing tearfully, the dishes forgotten. Greta came in and was instructed to look under the stairs for his basket.

'I can remember seeing it there,' said her mother.

Tiger was put in front of the fire with stern instructions he wasn't to be touched. 'He's not well,' Ruby said. 'I'm nursing him better.'

'I can't stand cats,' Beth said when she came home and was informed of Tiger's presence.

'You'd better learn to stand this one because he's staying.'

'What if the woman he was left with comes looking for him?'

'It's taken weeks, possibly months, for him to get in such a state. If anyone was going to look for him, they'd have done it long before.'

'Ruby?' Martha Quinlan said in the tone of voice of someone about to ask a favour.

'Yes, Martha?' Ruby rolled her eyes and wondered what the favour was.

'You know Mrs Wallace who has a wart on her nose and who sometimes comes to meetings? Well, her granddaughter, Connie, lives in Essex, but she's coming to work in Rootes' Securities in Speke and needs somewhere to live. Her gran can't take her, the poor dear only lives in lodgings.'

'What d'you want me to do, build her a house?'

Martha grinned. 'No, luv, put her up. You've plenty of room. The extra few bob a week will come in handy, won't it? Connie's giving up a wonderful job in order to serve her country. She's a beautician in a posh London hotel, the Ritz, or something. She wanted to join the forces but they wouldn't take her because her sight's not too good, so she decided on munitions instead.'

'Don't they have munition factories down south?'

'Of course, luv, but her mam's dead, her dad's been transferred to Scotland for some reason, and her brother's in the Army. She thought it would be nice to be near her gran.'

'OK,' Ruby said with a sigh. It was a waste of time trying to refuse. Her patriotic duty would be called into question and she'd be made to feel guilty. 'Will she expect to be fed?'

'Only breakfast and an evening meal, luv.'

'Is that all?'

Mrs Hart's linen cupboard was raided and a bed prepared for Connie Wallace whose bespectacled, perfectly made-up face had to be seen to be believed. She was a plain woman made striking by the skilful use of cosmetics. Her eye shadow was two different shades of blue and the lashes were so long that Ruby and Beth were green with envy until told that they were false. Rouge was applied with a brush and lipstick with a pencil. 'They're from America,' she said. There was a beauty spot on her chin when she remembered.

Her spectacles were shaped like bird's wings, the frames black flecked with gold, also from America. 'I'm terrified of breaking them, because they can't be replaced till this ruddy war's over.'

In the cellar during the raids, she taught Ruby and Beth how to apply make-up so it showed off their best features, though the exercise usually ended in shrieks of laughter.

By now, the evidence of the damage caused by the raids was all around them. Houses had been replaced by mounds of rubble or just the roofless skeleton left, like a grotesque statue, the sky visible though the gaps that had once been windows. Churches had been damaged, hospitals, schools, cinemas, numerous factories. Hundreds of people had been killed and hundreds more injured.

Ruby wondered how she, how everyone, managed to carry on. Yet somehow they did, and mainly, they managed to do it with a smile and a cheerfulness that was catching, including Ruby herself. She had no choice. It was either that or be miserable and admit defeat, and there was no way Ruby O'Hagan would do either.

In November, two things happened, both totally unexpected.

Beth always arrived home with the *Liverpool Echo*, which Ruby would read if she had time. The paper wasn't only concerned with war news. Other things, mundane in comparison, were happening on the domestic front. People were getting married for one, and having their wedding photographs published. Ruby never read the weddings page, but one night a man's vaguely familiar face caught her eye as she was about to turn over. Interested, she scanned the text beneath.

'The marriage took place last Saturday at the Holy Name church, Fazakerley, between Mr William Simon Pickering and Miss Rosemary Louise McNamara . . .'

Her insides did a somersault and she read no more.

Bill Pickering! He wasn't dead. Jacob hadn't killed him after all. He'd been alive all this time.

'What's the matter, Rube?' Beth asked in a concerned voice. 'You've gone as white as a sheet.'

'Nothing.' It had all been in vain – the running away, the years spent in Foster Court. She could have stayed in Brambles and Jacob could have continued to work on the farm. By now, she would have long grown out of him, she felt sure of that. She bunched the paper in a ball and threw it across the room.

'I thought we were supposed to save waste paper?' said Beth.

'We are.' The gesture had got rid of some of her anger. Things that had happened couldn't be undone. Anyway, had things gone differently, she wouldn't have had her girls.

It was Beth who discovered Jacob Veering was dead. A woman at work had shown her a photograph of her brother who was in the Royal Tank Regiment and shortly due home on leave. 'He was with this other chap in the photey. They had their arms around each other. I couldn't believe me eyes when I saw the other chap was Jake. "Who's that?" I asked, pointing to him. Me heart was in me mouth. I wasn't sure what I wanted her to say, perhaps that Jake might be coming home with her brother. Instead, she said, "Oh, that's Jacob, one of Albie's friends. Poor chap got killed at Dunkirk." "Are you sure?" I asked. "Sure I'm sure," she said. "They were sitting next to each other waiting for a boat to fetch them home when the Jerries strafed the beach. Jacob was hit in the head. He died in Albie's arms. Albie was dead upset."

There was silence for a while, then Ruby sighed. 'Well, I'm glad he died in someone's arms.'

'Is that all you've got to say?'

'What d'you expect me to say, Beth?'

Beth was stronger now. She didn't cry. 'Oh, I dunno. I don't know what to say meself. I'm surprised I'm not more upset.'

'It means we're both widows, in a way. We're only twenty-two, we can have new relationships.' She thought of Jim Quinlan.

'I don't want a new relationship,' Beth said flatly. 'One was enough.'

Ruby wondered how she would tell people that the man who was supposed to be her husband was dead. She wasn't prepared to cry and mope around, pretend to be sad. Though, thinking about it, she *was* sad. Jacob was the father of her children, the first man she had ever loved. She hadn't even a photograph to show the girls when they grew up. 'This woman at work,' she said, 'would she loan you the photo to have a copy made?'

'What excuse would I give?'

'Use your imagination for a change and think of one.' Ruby went upstairs for a little cry.

By Christmas, they had another lodger, a fussy, mild-mannered young man called Charles Winner from Dunstable who took very seriously his position as the only man in the household. As an engineering draughtsman, he was in a reserved occupation and wouldn't be called up. He had moved to Liverpool to be near his girlfriend, Wendy, who was a WREN and had been posted to the Admiralty Operations Room in Water Street. Sometimes, Wendy slept overnight in the small bedroom, the only one now empty – at least Ruby presumed she slept in the small bedroom, but felt in no position to lay down the law if she didn't.

It seemed to have got around that Mrs Hart's house was somewhere people could stay if they were in Liverpool overnight, a few days, a week – Ruby suspected it was all Martha Quinlan's doing. If Wendy wasn't occupying the spare room, then more often than not someone else was: a serviceman on leave who couldn't stay with his family because they'd lost their house in a raid, or whose girlfriend lived in a place where men weren't allowed. Wives came to see their sailor husbands when their ships docked briefly in Liverpool. When all the bedrooms were in use, people kipped down on a settee in one of the living rooms. They brought their ration books so the coupons could be used to buy the extra food.

Ruby was up at six every morning preparing half a dozen breakfasts. The children ate at a later sitting. She was never sure how many people would turn up for tea. During the day she looked after hordes of children, somehow managed to shop, and washed endless sheets and pillowcases so that the rack in the kitchen was always full of washing that took ages to dry and there was never time to iron – by now, Mrs Hart's linen cupboard had been stripped bare.

'You'd never guess, Tiger,' Ruby commented more than once, 'but I swore I'd never enter domestic service.'

Tiger was his old self again, possibly bigger than before. He was a very understanding cat and purred sympathetically whenever she complained.

'Another thing, I wanted to keep our presence in the house as unobtrusive as possible, but people come and go by the minute and the noise is horrendous. The neighbours must wonder if it's been turned into a hotel or a school.'

'Don't worry about it,' Tiger purred.

Christmas was less than a week away. A box of decorations had been discovered in the cellar, a paper tree. The living room at the back, supposedly private, but which everyone considered they were at liberty to use whenever they pleased, was festooned with chains, the tree decorated with gold and silver stars. Ruby made a Christmas cake that contained no eggs, very little fruit, and had only a thin suggestion of icing. Beth won a pudding in a raffle at work, and Connie had come by a turkey by mysterious means she wasn't prepared to divulge. Charles Winner was staying in Liverpool because Wendy hadn't been allowed leave. 'But she's coming to dinner on Christmas Day,' he told Ruby when he presented her with two bottles of sherry.

'That's nice of her!' Ruby remarked, seeing herself stuck in the kitchen just like any other day.

But Beth and Connie, who'd made herself very much at home, offered to do the cooking on the day. 'You won't have to lift a finger, Rube,' Beth promised.

Ruby began to look forward to the festivities. Suddenly, she didn't mind the house being full. For the first time, there was money to buy presents for the children, though finding them in the shops wasn't easy. She'd managed to get Greta and Heather a doll each, little shopping baskets, hairslides. There was a wheelbarrow for Jake, a toy bus, and a lovely enamelled compact for his mother. She rubbed her hands together excitedly. This year, Christmas was going to be the gear.

Apart from a few light raids that had caused little damage, December had been remarkably free from the attentions of the Luftwaffe. Liverpool breathed a sigh of relief and everyone anticipated a peaceful holiday.

But they were wrong.

Five days before Christmas, the siren went at half-past six. Tiger, terrified, immediately made for the cellar. The children had eaten, but Ruby, Beth and Connie were in the middle of a meal. Charles wasn't yet home. They followed the big cat down the narrow wooden stairs with their food. When Ruby finished, she went back for the tea she wasn't prepared to waste, raid or no raid. She was about to return, when the front door opened and Charles came in accompanied by Wendy and another WREN, a pretty blonde. 'This is Rhona. She's on her way to see a friend, but I thought she could shelter with us until the raid's over. It's probably just a light one, but it's not worth taking the risk.'

'I hope you don't mind,' Rhona said.

'Of course, I don't mind.' Ruby gave her a warm, welcoming smile. 'You'd best get down the cellar quick. Take the pot and I'll fetch more cups.'

There'd never been a raid like it before. The world became one large, never-ending explosion. The house shook, dust drifted from the ceiling. Shut away as they were in the bowels of the earth, the sound of breaking glass could still be heard, the urgent clamour of fire engines, the occasional scream.

Even the children were frightened, not interested in games or stories tonight. The grown-ups hardly spoke, but looked at each other, biting their lips, when a bomb shrieked to earth, wondering if they were to be its target.

During a lull, Ruby went upstairs to make more tea, not caring if she used the entire week's ration. She drew back the curtains and looked at the crimson sky shot with streaks of black smoke. A fire crackled nearby. It was like a scene from hell.

'It looks as if it's been soaked with blood, the sky,' said a voice. It was Charles. 'I've come for the sherry,' he explained. 'I thought it might cheer us up a little. I know where I can get more tomorrow.'

'If there is a tomorrow.'

'Tomorrow always comes, Ruby.'

'It might not come for us,' Ruby said harshly. 'It's no good pretending everything's going to be all right, being positive, because we've lost control of our lives. In the past, no matter how bad things got, I'd grit me teeth and make them better. But now I can't. No one can.'

'In that case, you've just got to grit your teeth and hope for the best. Forget about the tea for now, let's have sherry instead. And I got you a box of chocolates for Christmas. I'll fetch them too.'

It cheered her that he'd thought to buy her a present. She'd got nothing for him or Wendy. She'd buy something – tomorrow!

Charles said, 'I don't know if it's just my imagination, but I can hear singing.'

'I'll just get some glasses.' Mrs Hart had some in her china cabinet. The children could have lemonade.

They returned to the cellar, where Rhona had removed her tunic, loosened her tie, and was leading a sing-song in a fine soprano voice. 'Good King Wenceslas looked down, on the feast of Stephen ...'

Greta and Heather had livened up miraculously. They were singing along, bright-eyed and full of smiles. Jake didn't know the words, but stared intently at Rhona's pretty face and tried to mouth them. Beth glanced at Ruby and winked. 'Isn't this the gear!' she whispered. 'I can't hear the bombs any more.'

The sherry and lemonade were poured, the chocolates opened, spirits were lifted. Connie and Wendy danced an Irish jig and Ruby sang, 'Yours till the stars lose their glory', astonished to find she knew all the words. Greta and Heather recited a poem they'd learnt from Roy Deacon, unaware it was full of innuendo and double entendres. The audience laughed until their sides ached and drank more sherry.

'Do your impersonation of Paul Robeson,' Wendy urged Charles, so he sang 'Old Man River' in a deep, mournful voice that made them want to cry. Rhona cheered them up again with a chorus of carols.

Outside, bombs fell, the earth was being shaken to pieces, but they didn't hear, or pretended not to hear. They were too loud, too boisterous, needing to shut out reality in favour of make-believe.

It meant they didn't notice the candle flicker when the cellar door opened, or see the young man wearing an air force blue greatcoat limp down the stairs. 'Evening folks,' the young man said, bringing the entertainment to an abrupt halt. 'Hope I'm not interrupting, but do you mind if I join in?'

'Who are you?' demanded Ruby, but she knew before the words were out of her mouth. She hadn't met him before, but a photograph of the curly-haired young man with the same mischievous, smiling features was on the sideboard upstairs.

It was Max Hart.

'This is Max,' she said quickly to the assembled company, praying he wouldn't demand to know what they were doing in his mother's house. But he didn't look as if he was about to make a scene. Instead, despite his smile, he appeared bone weary, his young face creased with exhaustion. 'Max, meet Beth, Connie, Charles ...' She reeled off the introductions.

'Take your coat off, luv, and sit down,' said Connie.

Removing the coat was easier said than done. Max could hardly raise his arms. Charles sprang forward to help.

'My God!' Charles gasped when the coat was off, revealing the blue-grey uniform underneath. 'You're a Flight Lieutenant and you've got the Distinguished Flying Cross.' He shook Max's hand vigorously, close to tears. 'This country owes everything to young men like you. You're the bravest of the brave. What was it Churchill said about the battle in the skies? "Never have so many owed so much to so few."'

Max Hart blushed uncomfortably. 'Would you mind if I had a drink?'

'It's only sherry,' said Ruby.

He managed a tired grin. 'That'll do fine.' He went on to explain it had taken two days to get from his base in Kent using public transport or hitching lifts. 'An ambulance at one point. In Bedford, a chap lent me his bike to get as far as Northampton where I left it with his cousin. The cousin used his entire petrol ration to take me to Birmingham.' He'd slept on a train and had arrived in Liverpool only an hour ago and, ignoring the danger, began to walk. 'Then this Civil Defence chap stopped and gave me a lecture and a lift. I've got ten days' leave on account of the fact I sprained my damn ankle. I was determined to spend Christmas in my own home, don't ask why.' He grinned again. 'I think I wanted to be assured there were a few remnants of normality left in the world, but instead I found Liverpool being blown to pieces and the house apparently haunted. It gave me a shock, I can tell you, when I heard singing from the cellar.'

'Didn't your mum tell you she said Ruby could have the house while she went to America?' Connie enquired.

'It must have slipped her mind,' Max replied with a straight face. 'Look, you were having a good time before I showed up. Please go on. It sounded fun, better any day than listening to the noise outside.' The bombardment was continuing unabated.

Rhona said, 'This is especially for you,' and began to sing, 'There's a boy coming home on leave . . .'

By midnight, they had begun to wilt, having run out of songs and energy, though the Luftwaffe showed no sign of wilting and the bombs continued to rain down. Thankfully, the children had gone to sleep. They talked instead.

'I know who you are,' Max said quietly to Ruby. 'The pawnshop runner. Mum said you were like an exotic stick insect.'

'I don't know if that's a compliment or not!'

'I'd take it as a compliment if I were you.' He winked. 'Out of interest, what are you doing here?'

She'd known this was coming. 'Your mam asked if I'd keep an eye on the house,' she explained, 'but when me and Beth were desperate for somewhere to live, I thought it wouldn't hurt to move in, just us two and the children. But I kept being told it was my patriotic duty to take in more people or look after other women's children. I suppose,' she added ruefully, 'it's all got out of hand. Lord knows what your mam'll say when she finds out.'

'Well, she won't find out from me. You're doing a great job while mum is having a grand time in the States according to her letters. Let's regard it as *her* contribution towards the war.'

'You're being very kind and understanding.'

'Don't mention it,' he said dismissively. 'I was halfway to Liverpool when I began to wonder if I was mad, wanting to spend Christmas alone in a cold house where there wouldn't be any food. I've rarely been so pleased about anything as finding you here. Bloody hell, Tiger!' he exclaimed when the big cat appeared and launched itself on to his knee. 'I didn't know you were still around.'

'There's an old wardrobe he regards as his own special shelter.'

'Me and Tiger used to be best friends when I was home from university.'
Tiger purred ecstatically as he feverishly licked the familiar face.

'It looks as if you still are.'

It was almost four when the all clear sounded. They looked at each other
thankfully, knowing they'd shared an experience they would never forget.
Charles insisted Max use his bedroom. 'I'll just get some clothes first . . .'

Ruby was the first to emerge from the cellar, half expecting the house to
have blown **away** and be met by open air. But Mrs Hart's house had
survived. A strange, sour smell turned out to be soot which had fallen down
all the chimneys. They went straight to bed. Heather shared Wendy's room
and Charles slept on a settee.

Four hours later, everyone had gone to work as usual. Ruby peeped in to
look at Max; he was dead to the world. Roy Deacon was delivered by his
mother, but there was no sign of Mollie. The family had been sheltering in
the understairs cupboard, Ruby learnt later, and the house had received a
direct hit. Mollie, four years old, was dead.

The heavy raids continued in the run-up to Christmas. Ruby wondered if
Hitler's aim was to wipe Liverpool and its people off the face of the earth as
the terror continued, night after night. Max Hart didn't leave the house and
spent much of his time in bed. He was having a lovely rest, he said, enjoying
being made a desperate fuss of. People kept bringing him little treats; cream
cakes, chocolate, a quarter bottle of whisky. The children had spent hours
making a Christmas card especially for him – he had vowed to keep it for
ever. The creases in his face had smoothed away, he looked more relaxed.

On Christmas Eve, Beth finished work at midday and announced she was
taking Greta and Heather out to buy their mam a present.

'They haven't got any money,' said Ruby.

'I'll soon remedy that. I'll take Jake an' all, let him get some fresh air.'

It was the first time Ruby could recall being in the house alone since
they'd moved in – she didn't count Max who was asleep upstairs. She
sprawled in an armchair, luxuriating in the unaccustomed silence. When
Beth returned, she might go out herself and buy a few last-minute presents.
Although it was distressing to witness the devastation caused by the last
day's raids, there was also the feeling of being lucky to be alive. So many
people had died: people who had worked with Beth or Connie, or she knew
slightly, such as Charlie Murphy who'd been their landlord in Foster Court.
Arthur's little house in the coal yard had been damaged, though the
occupants, Herbie and his family, were thankfully unhurt.

Ruby sighed and supposed she'd better get on with some work. She was
heaving herself reluctantly out of the chair when she heard a shout, quickly
followed by another and knew it could only be Max.

She raced upstairs and found him thrashing wildly about in the bed, covered in perspiration.

'Max!' She shook him. 'Max! Calm down. Everything's all right. You're quite safe.'

He opened his eyes and looked at her fearfully, like a small boy. 'I'm sorry. I was having this ghastly dream.'

'The dream's over now, love. You're safely at home with us.'

'God!' He shoved himself to a sitting position. 'It seemed so real.'

'What was it about?'

'I can only remember bits. I was in my plane, over Germany, and I'd lost my way. I didn't know how to get home. The world was drowned in blackness, not a light anywhere. I was worried for my crew, that I was letting them down. I began to panic ...'

Ruby stroked his brow. 'It was only a dream. Here, have a drop of your whisky. It'll calm you down.'

'You're very kind,' he said when she put the glass in his hand.

'Why shouldn't I be?' she asked, surprised.

'You can't have a very high opinion of me. I presume you know why Mum had to pawn so many of her things?'

'To settle your debts at university. Yes, but it doesn't alter what you are now: a pilot in the Royal Air Force who won a medal for bravery.'

'I got in with this crowd of chaps who had money to burn,' he said ruefully. 'I wanted the things they had; clothes, a car. I spent a fortune on booze. We played cards, the minimum stake was a quid.'

'That's all in the past,' Ruby soothed.

'As for my medal, I don't deserve it. I'd only been in the air a matter of seconds when I came face to face with a bloody Heinkel. I knew my plane had been hit, but just carried on with what I was there for, to bring down every Jerry plane in sight. I got the Heinkel and half a dozen others. When I got back to base, there was a bullet in my shoulder.' He gave an ironic shrug. 'I hadn't felt a thing, but they gave me a medal all the same. The thing is,' he went on, suddenly angry, 'every man in every damn aircrew deserves a medal for bravery.' He frowned irritably. 'Why is this house so damn quiet? It feels eerie. And where's that bloody cat?'

'Everyone's out except you and me. Tiger was up a tree when I last saw him.'

His face crumpled. 'I was as mad as hell when Mum said in a letter that she'd given him away.'

'He'll be here when you come back,' Ruby said consolingly.

'Will you be? Here when I come back, that is?'

'Only if you come back soon. As soon as the war ends, your mother will come home and we'll have to find somewhere else to live. Could I have your mother's address before you leave?'

'It's in my locker at the base. I'll have to send it to you.' He gave a satisfied sigh. 'It's nice, knowing you're here, keeping the place warm.'

He looked so young and vulnerable, had suffered so much, that Ruby felt an impulse to plant an affectionate, sisterly kiss on his cheek, though was unprepared for his response. Max immediately grabbed her and kissed her back in a way that was anything but brotherly.

'Max!' She was about to push him away, but hesitated. For months, he'd been risking his life for people like her. He could have died a hundred times. It wasn't much to ask, she thought impulsively, to give herself in return for the sacrifices he had made. She slid her arms around his neck.

'You're so lovely,' he was saying gruffly. 'I've been wanting to do this ever since we met.' There was desperation in the way his lean hands caressed her, as if he was trying to shed the nightmare that was now his life and lose himself in the curves and secrets of a woman's body. She wondered if any female body would have done as she let him remove her clothes, at the same time she felt concerned that Beth might come home.

Max said no more, just gave a rapturous groan when he plunged inside her.

Ruby tenderly stroked his face, pretending to respond, appear as passionate as he was, listening with one ear for Beth and the children. All that mattered was that Max momentarily forgot the violent times in which they lived.

'That was wonderful,' he whispered when it was over and she lay in his arms. 'I'll come back for you one day.' His face was soft with emotion and he was about to kiss her again when a shout from down below made them both jump.

'I'd better go.' Ruby struggled into her clothes. At the door, she paused. 'It was wonderful for me too, Max.'

The siren went that night at seven and the onslaught didn't stop until the early hours of Christmas morning.

Dinner would have been a sober affair if they hadn't done their best to appear in good spirits for the sake of the children who had never received so many presents. Their happiness was infectious and by the end of the meal the good spirits were quite genuine.

'After all,' Charles pointed out, 'if the good Lord has seen fit to spare us, we should celebrate that fact, not mope.'

Max Hart left on Boxing Day. It could take days to return to the base in Kent. A friend of Charles had offered to take the young airman as far as Manchester from where he might catch a train – or he might not. Nothing was certain any more.

The car arrived at eight o'clock that morning. Everyone gathered outside the door to say goodbye. Max hugged the children, kissed the women, shook hands with Charles. 'It's been the best Christmas of my life,' he told them with a happy sigh.

'See you next Christmas, if not before,' Connie called as he backed towards the gate, waving all the time.

'Try and make it before,' shouted Beth.

Ruby held her hands to her face, not knowing what to say. Max was about to get in the car when she ran down the path.

'Take care Max,' she cried. 'I'll never forget you.'

She watched the car, waving frantically, until it turned a corner and Max was gone.

She never saw him again and he never sent his mother's address.

8

In April, Greta started school. 'Why can't *I* go too?' demanded an outraged Heather.

'Because you're not old enough. You'll have to wait until next year.' Ruby badly missed her eldest daughter, though not Roy Deacon who'd started at the same time. It hurt, handing over the care of her precious child to strangers. Would they understand her nervous little ways, her shyness? Would she be bullied? If so, Ruby would descend upon the school and raise Cain. Heather sulked and worried Greta wouldn't cope without her.

Beth was informed that Ruby had exhausted her patriotic duty when it came to looking after other women's kids and not to bring any more home.

'Anything you say, Rube,' Beth replied easily. 'By the way, what's wrong with Charles?'

'I've no idea. I'll ask him.'

Charles was moping around like a sick puppy. Wendy had met someone else, he confessed when Ruby questioned the reason for his miserable face. The someone else was a sub-lieutenant in the Navy. 'It's the uniform,' he said gloomily. 'Men in civvies are at a distinct disadvantage these days.'

'I'll take him out of himself,' Connie Wallace vowed. 'I've always liked Charles and I don't give a damn about uniforms. After all, you can't wear 'em for the rest of your life. They've got to come off sometime, even if it's only for bed.'

Charles was taken out of himself so thoroughly that three months later the couple announced they were getting married.

'Straight away,' Connie said with a grin. 'Charles thinks it's silly to hang around while there's a war on, one of us could get killed any day,' which Ruby thought a touch morbid. She was pleased they wanted to continue living upstairs, sleeping in Connie's room which had a double bed and, if Ruby didn't mind, using the small bedroom for storage.

The wedding would take place two weeks on Saturday. Clothes rationing had just been introduced and Connie was given the choice of using all her precious coupons on a bridal gown or getting married in ordinary clothes.

'I always wanted a white wedding,' she said wistfully. 'But never mind, eh!'

But Beth had other ideas. She enjoyed showing off her skill on the sewing machine. A pair of Mrs Hart's lace curtains would make a fine wedding gown, she claimed. 'And there's enough for a veil, though you can't have it over your face, it's too thick.'

Roses from the garden would do for a bouquet and Martha Quinlan offered a supply of beer as her and Fred's present. The church wasn't far away so everyone could walk. The reception would be held in the house. There were some very old records under the gramophone for those who wanted to dance. Thirty guests had been invited.

'What am I supposed to give them to eat?' Ruby wanted to know. 'It takes me all my time to feed you lot.'

'Spam?' suggested Charles.

'Spam with what?'

'Just sliced on a plate with bread and pickles.'

'And when did you last see pickles in the shops?' Ruby replied tartly. 'I can't remember what a pickle looks like.'

'I'll show you what a pickle looks like.' Charles disappeared, returning minutes later with three large dust-covered jars which he put on the table with a thump. 'Pickled onions, pickled cabbage, pickled plums,' he announced, clearly enjoying the look of astonishment on Ruby's face.

'You don't pickle plums, you preserve them. Where did these come from?'

'The cellar. Max's mother must have done them.'

'Good gracious me! I never noticed before. Will they be all right after all this time? I don't want to spoil the wedding by poisoning the guests.'

'We'll try them out beforehand.'

'*You* can try them out beforehand, Charles. If you don't die, I'll serve them to your guests. It's a pity the apples aren't ripe yet, else I could have done something with them. And that rhubarb would make lovely wine, but one of the things they never taught us at the convent was how to make wine.'

Fortunately, the guests saw fit to contribute items of food towards the wedding do. The bridal pair began to bring home tins of Spam, fruit cocktail, peaches and cream that they'd been given. Charles's mother was fetching a cake from Dunstable, though as she said in her letter, it would be sadly lacking most of the essential ingredients.

Connie arrived one night with a basket containing a live rabbit. 'I got it off this chap at work. He can't feed it any more. Apparently, rabbit tastes just like chicken.'

Ruby screamed. 'Only when it's dead, and there's no way I'm going to kill the poor thing. It's beautiful.' The rabbit was sleekly black with two white paws. It was nibbling a piece of carrot, innocently unaware what fate might have in store.

'Chicken would be a real treat compared with Spam. Maybe Charles is willing to kill it,' Connie said thoughtfully.

'He can bone it and cook it too. I'd feel as if I was cooking Tiger.'

By the time Charles arrived, the children were playing with the rabbit and it had a name – Floppy. Tiger regarded it warily, unsure whether it was friend or foe.

Charles professed his unwillingness to lay a hand on the creature and Beth burst into tears at the very idea. 'I couldn't possibly eat it,' she cried. 'Anyroad, you can't take it off the children now. They love it.'

'You're nothing but a shower of yellow-bellies,' Connie said scathingly.

'Why don't *you* kill it?' demanded Charles.

His bride-to-be shuddered delicately. 'Oh, I couldn't. It's much too cuddly.'

Mrs Hart had several glorious hats stored in boxes in her wardrobe. Ruby borrowed a navy-blue straw boater that went perfectly with her new blue and white flowered frock which had puffed sleeves and a sweetheart neck.

'You'll not come across a frock like this again until this ruddy war's over,' the shop assistant said sadly. 'From now on, they'll be made from the minimum amount of material. Puffed sleeves are definitely out.'

Beth's suit was strawberry red moygashel with a pleated skirt – pleats were something else that would take a long time to come back. With it, she wore Mrs Hart's cream organdie picture hat trimmed with silky cabbage roses.

'Don't we look wonderful!' Ruby sang on the morning of the wedding when they were dressed in their finery. 'I feel very elegant in this hat and you look like a Southern belle in yours – Vivien Leigh had better look out.' She turned to the bride. 'But neither of us can hold a candle to you, Connie. You're a sight for sore eyes. Mrs Hart would be thrilled to bits if she could see you in her curtains.'

Connie's perfectly painted face, surrounded by a frill of lace, glowed with happiness, and her eyes behind her smart glasses were misty with love for Charles, whose wife she would shortly become. She looked at herself in the full-length mirror. The dress had a high neck, long, tight sleeves and a gathered skirt with the curtains' original scalloped hem. 'This is the loveliest wedding dress in the world,' she said huskily. 'I couldn't have got anything half as nice from the poshest shop in London.' She flung her arms around Beth. 'Thank you! You've made my wedding day extra-special. I'll be grateful for this as long as I live. And thank you, Ruby. You've worked wonders with the food. I bet Queen Elizabeth herself didn't sit down to such a grand do when she married the King.'

Ruby rescued her hat which had fallen off during Connie's emotional embrace. 'I bet she didn't sit down to rabbit either. I'm glad we didn't kill Floppy. It would have ruined the day – and such a glorious day too. The sun's hot enough to crack the flags and there's not a cloud in sight.'

Greta and Heather were bridesmaids, their frocks peach-coloured slipper satin made from the skirt of a genuine bridesmaid frock that had belonged to Agnes/Fay Quinlan. Jake was adorable in a borrowed page boy suit of blue velvet, only a mite too big.

People came to their doors on that lovely July day, to watch and wave, to clap and smile, to shout their good wishes, as the wedding procession made its way on foot to the church. Hearts were warmed and tears were shed as the bright little pageant passed, reminding them that great joy and happiness was still possible even if their country was embroiled in a vicious war.

They arrived at a scene of devastation, where two houses had recently stood. Connie removed a rose from her bouquet and threw it on to the tumble of bricks. She gave another rose to a very old woman who was smiling through her tears as they approached.

'God bless you, luv,' the woman gasped.

A third rose went to a young soldier, a fourth to a woman with two babies in a pram. By the time they reached the church, Connie had only one rose left. But it was enough.

Ruby doubted if Mrs Hart's house had ever rung to so much laughter. People laughed at the slightest thing or sometimes at nothing at all. It was as if on this one, special day, they had forgotten their troubles and were determined to enjoy themselves to the full. They danced and laughed, laughed and sang, and split their sides when the best man, a friend of Charles's, made a speech that wasn't remotely funny. 'Ladies and Gentlemen,' he began, and everyone collapsed into giggles.

The children couldn't contain their excitement. Their shrill, urgent cries could be heard above the music, their abundant energy evident by the way they flashed, like lightning, from room to room, where they were petted and made a desperate fuss of, to such an extent, Ruby began to doubt if she'd ever be able to control them again.

The Spam, bread and pickles rapidly disappeared, and the dry-as-dust cake went down a treat, much to the relief of Charles's grey-haired mother, elegantly clad in peacock blue brocade, who'd been worried it would be spat out in disgust.

'These plums are delicious,' she said to Ruby. 'Did you bottle them yourself?'

'No. They were a sort of gift, like most of the food.'

'You've done my son proud, Mrs O'Hagan. I only wish his brother and sister could be here, but Graham is in Egypt and Susie expecting a baby any minute. This is quite the nicest wedding I've ever been to. I can't wait to tell everyone what a wonderful send-off Charles had. I'm very grateful, and not just for the wedding. Charles tells me the household buzzes around you, that you're always here, always cheerful, keeping everyone going and looking after them so well.' She gave Ruby's shoulder an affectionate squeeze. 'That's quite an achievement for someone so young.'

'Why thank you.' Ruby had never looked at it that way before. It came as a pleasant surprise to know she was so highly appreciated.

'I suppose your husband's in the forces?'

'He was. He was killed in the evacuation of Dunkirk.'

Mrs Winner's face went pale with shock. 'Oh, my dear girl! I'm so terribly sorry. Charles never mentioned that.'

The strangest thing happened – it had happened before when she'd told people – Ruby felt her eyes fill with tears. 'I'm getting over it,' she said gruffly.

Later, when someone put an old Rudy Vallee record on the gramophone and he began to sing 'Night and Day', she thought of Jacob again, remembering the first night he'd come to Brambles and she'd danced for him. *That* Jacob had been so sweetly innocent, so very nice. The same Jacob had punched Bill Pickering across the room in order to defend her, because he loved her so much. In her eyes, it was *that* Jacob who'd died on the sands of Dunkirk, not the scared, pathetic man she'd lived with for two years. Ruby mourned the real Jacob, before he'd become twisted with fear, forced to live in a world he found totally alien.

At six o'clock, the newly married couple left for their two day honeymoon in New Brighton, a mere ferry ride across the Mersey, but a place easy to get to, and just as easy to get back from, better than going further afield and spending their precious time waiting on stations for trains that might never come.

The mood became quieter. The air was already cooler and they lounged in the garden, watching the shadows creep across the untidy grass with its clusters of tiny daisies and brilliant yellow dandelions, praying the siren wouldn't go to signal a raid. But since May, after an horrific week, when every night the city had been subjected to a relentless barrage of bombs and mines, when it seemed that Liverpool would completely disappear off the face of the earth, when thousands of people had been killed or injured, Hitler seemed to have given up. There'd been few raids since.

Ruby was sitting on the back step with Martha Quinlan, when suddenly the woman leapt to her feet. 'Jim! It's our Jim!' she cried.

'Hello, Mam. Dad said you were here.'

His voice was unusually dull, as were his eyes. He had lost his suntan and looked thin. Martha began to pat him all over, as if to make sure he was real, exclaiming in distress at his thinness.

'I wasn't expecting you, son. Oh, but I'm so pleased to see you I could cry.'

Jim raised a wry smile. 'That's a bit of a contradiction, Mam. I'm changing ships, that's why I'm here. I'm off again on Monday. I just thought I'd come and sample what ordinary life feels like for a change. It's easy to forget on a ship. Hello, Ruby. You look very smart.'

'How are you, Jim?' She felt concern that he looked so low. At the same time, her heart was racing. It was months since she'd seen him, almost a year, though he was rarely far from her mind. Did he think of her as often as she did him? she wondered. Did he think of her *ever*?

'I'm OK,' Jim shrugged. 'I was sorry to hear about your husband.'

Martha broke in before Ruby could reply. 'She's bearing up remarkably well, son. Beth too. Oh, so many widows,' she cried, 'so many fatherless children. What has the world come to!'

Mrs Wallace, Connie's gran, the only one of her relatives who could be there, came to announce she was going and to thank Ruby for the lovely day, followed shortly afterwards by several of Charles's friends. After seeing them out, she returned to the garden where Jim Quinlan was deep in conversation with Beth. She was about to join them, but there was something about the way their heads were bent together, an air of intimacy, that stopped her in her tracks. She felt a flush of jealousy. What were they talking about? Did they have to be so close?

Until then, she hadn't wanted the day to end. Now she wanted it to be over, for everyone to go. She had difficulty keeping her temper with the girls. The excitement had made them silly. They were showing off, rolling over on the grass in their bridesmaid's frocks. Tiger was discovered on the draining board licking a tin of conny-onny that had been almost full. The best man was drunk, having had far more than his fair share of the beer. Ruby resisted the urge to point this out.

And still Beth and Jim talked. It wasn't fair, Ruby raged inwardly. Beth was leaving everything to her. She was beginning to feel like the mother of the bride as the guests began to depart in greater numbers, shaking *her* hand, thanking *her* for the wonderful time they'd had.

'You put so much effort into everything.'

'Thank you so much. It's been a marvellous day.'

At last, there were only three people left: Mrs Winner, Martha, and Jim, all inside listening to the wireless. Beth had taken Ruby's not very subtle hint and was putting the children to bed, no easy task if the shrieks and yells coming from upstairs were anything to go by. Mrs Winner was sleeping in Charles's room and returning to Dunstable next day. She was dead on her feet, she said contentedly, but insisted on washing the dishes before retiring. 'I'll help tidy up in the morning.'

Martha yawned. 'We'd best get going, son. I've got to be up at the crack of dawn to clean that bloody pub. Thanks, Ruby. You did a cracking job today. I really enjoyed meself.'

Jim nodded briefly. 'Me too, for the short time I was here.'

'Come again tomorrow,' Ruby said eagerly. 'Sample a bit more ordinary life. Come to tea! There's some tinned fruit left.'

'Thanks all the same, but I've made arrangements for tomorrow.'

'Then I'll see you next time you're home.' How many months would pass before that happened? And then they might exchange no more than a few words, like today. For some reason she wanted to cry and was horribly pleased when mother and son left and Jim made no attempt to shout goodbye to Beth upstairs.

Beth came down not long after the front door closed. 'What's up with you?' she demanded. 'You've got a cob on, I can tell. I can't think why. I thought today was the gear.'

'I'm tired, that's all,' Ruby answered shortly.

'You don't usually have a face on when you're tired.'

'Well, I have this time. I'm going to bed. The house is in a state and there'll be loads to do tomorrow.'

She was halfway up the stairs, when Beth said. 'I hope you don't mind, but I'm going out tomorrow.'

'Going out!' An awful suspicion entered her mind. 'Where to?'

'To a matinée at the pictures with Jim Quinlan, then for a meal afterwards.'

'That's not fair!' Ruby said furiously, knowing she was being unreasonable. It was the first time Beth had done such a thing, but she wouldn't have cared had it been with someone else. 'Connie was your friend as well as mine. I organised the wedding. At least you could help with clearing up.'

Beth looked so penitent that Ruby felt ashamed. Had the positions been reversed, she would have told Beth where to go. 'I'm sorry, Rube. But I couldn't possibly have turned him down.'

'Why not?'

'He's in a bit of a state – well, more than a bit.' Her eyes filled with tears. 'He's expecting to die any minute.'

At midday on Sunday, after an emotional goodbye and a fervently expressed hope they would meet again, Mrs Winner left for Dunstable. Beth accompanied her on the tram and would take her to the station before meeting Jim Quinlan.

Ruby was glad he wasn't calling for her. She couldn't have stood watching them go off together. What was it about Beth that had made him confide in her? Had he thought she, Ruby, would laugh, make fun, dismiss his fears? Though it wasn't fear, according to Beth, more the total conviction he was going to die. 'And it's not the dying itself he's worried about, but the way it might happen. He doesn't mind if it's quick, but he has nightmares about freezing to death in the seas around Russia, or dying in a fire.'

'Why on earth should he think like that?' asked Ruby.

'When he left school, ten lads from his class joined the Merchant Navy. Now they're all dead except Jim. He doesn't see why God should spare him and not his mates. He said it doesn't seem right.' Beth shivered. 'Oh, Ruby! It's only natural he'd feel like that. There's death everywhere. I feel a bit the same when we're sheltering in the cellar, like we could die any minute. Why should we be allowed to live, when there's people dying all around us? At least raids stop eventually, but the danger never stops for the men at sea.'

When the two women had gone, Ruby walked through the empty house to where the children were playing in a desultory fashion in the garden, having expended a week's energy at the wedding the day before. It seemed strange, not having to think about preparing a meal for tonight. Charles and Connie were away, Beth was eating out. She'd just make something light for her own and the children's tea – beans on toast. It was Jake's favourite. There was plenty of tinned fruit for afters.

She paused in the kitchen to make a cup of Camp coffee – a bottle of the disgusting stuff had been provided for the wedding. She drank it on the back step, grimacing with each sip.

The children were playing school, Heather the teacher, Greta and Jake the class. Tiger and Floppy lay on the grass pretending to be interested observers. A lump came to her throat at this picture of sweet, childish innocence, and she thanked God that Mrs Hart had gone to America, leaving her house for them to commandeer.

But what would they do when the war was over? Where would they live then? She and Beth couldn't stay together for always. Ruby would have to get a job, which she didn't mind a bit. But what sort of job? She didn't think there would ever again be a need for the pawnshop runner. Anyway, she'd moved on from that. As for cleaning, she'd no intention ever again of wielding a duster or mopping a floor on behalf of anyone except herself. Her thoughts went back to the convent when the height of her ambition had been to work in a shop or a restaurant. She hadn't realised then that women could become teachers, doctors, actresses, that women went to university, flew planes, discovered radium like Marie Curie, had all sorts of fascinating jobs.

Much as Ruby wanted to, she couldn't imagine doing any of these things, not because she considered herself incapable – she would have had a shot at any one of them – but circumstances in the shape of two young children were against her.

Of course, the future could lead in a different direction. She might get married . . .

A scream jolted her out of her musings. The picture of sweet, childish innocence had been spoilt by a classroom revolt. Three-year-old Jake had got tired of being taught how to spell, particularly by such a hard taskmaster, and was making for the swing – a piece of rope suspended from a tree. Heather was trying to drag him back. 'It isn't playtime yet,' she yelled.

Ruby clapped her hands and the children froze. Heather glared at the little boy who had a mutinous look on his handsome face.

'Let him go, Heather,' Ruby ordered.

'He's being naughty, Mam.'

'No, he isn't. He wants to play on the swing, that's all. Let him go.'

Heather reluctantly released a joyous Jake. He seized the rope and began to swing with the liberated air of a child who'd spent the day in a real school.

It was a good job Beth wasn't there. She got annoyed when Heather bossed her son around.

'I'll have to put a stop to it,' Ruby thought. 'Not just with Jake, but with Greta too.' It had seemed touching once, the concern Heather felt for her sister, but since Greta started school, it was as if the younger girl resented the older being out of her control, dominating her totally when she was home. Ruby wasn't sure if it was fortunate or *un*fortunate that Greta didn't seem to mind, allowing herself to be ordered about without a murmur of complaint. She seemed content never to make a decision for herself, to play what Heather wanted, go where Heather went, unlike Jake, who preferred to run his young life on his own with only occasional interference from a grown-up. He was a lovely child with a lovely nature. Ruby felt sure he would become a fine young man, whereas Heather, she thought wryly, seemed destined to grow up a shrew and Greta a doormat.

She looked at her daughters. Greta was sitting patiently on the grass. Her tiny heart-shaped face, framed by a mop of babyish blonde hair, was fixed on that of her sister, waiting for her to return to her role as teacher. She was still small for her age, as if her body had never recovered from those first lean years in Foster Court when she always seemed to have a cold and there wasn't enough to eat – yesterday, quite a few people had assumed she was the four-year-old and Heather, an inch taller, was five.

Looking at Heather was like looking at herself: the same strong features, dark eyes, bony frame. 'But was I ever quite so sour?' Ruby wondered. The nuns had said she was wilful, always wanting her own way, but she hadn't stamped her feet in rage if she didn't get it, which Heather was apt to do.

'She'll grow out of it,' Ruby consoled herself. 'Or at least, I hope so.'

Not long after the wedding, a downstairs room became a bedroom for Marie Ferguson, a gruff, good-natured widow in her fifties who worked as a cook in Sefton hospital. She found it easier to live close by, rather than travel daily to her house in a small village near Wigan.

Marie quickly became a member of what was, by now, almost a family. Weekends, she was happy to babysit while Ruby and Beth went to the pictures or, occasionally, a dance.

Beth loved dancing, but Ruby was no good at small talk. She got bored when asked the same questions over and over again. 'What's your name? What do you do? Where do you live? Can I take you home?', the last being met with a firm '*No!*'

'They all seem so *young*,' she grumbled.

'You're not exactly old,' argued Beth.

'I *feel* old compared to them.'

'Anyroad, they're not all young. There's plenty in their thirties, even older. What's wrong with them?'

'They're married, that's what. Their poor wives would have a fit if they saw them dancing with other women, taking them home, where they'd get up to even worse mischief if they were allowed.'

Ruby had the feeling that she'd gone from young to old in the space of the few days it had taken to leave Kirkby with Jacob and move into Foster Court. Once, she'd loved to dance, but the urge had gone and dancing now seemed a frivolous way of occupying her time. She had lost her sense of fun, she realised sadly. She had grown up too quickly, become an adult too soon, a rather serious, very sober adult.

The following Easter, Heather started school. Ruby didn't like to admit, not even to herself, that she was relieved to see the back of her troublesome daughter. Jake was happy on his own, and equally happy to start school himself a year later, giving Ruby the long-cherished opportunity to do her bit, even if only part-time.

Martha Quinlan, always an opportunist on behalf of the WVS, immediately found her something to do. Liverpool Corporation were gradually repairing the thousands of houses damaged in the blitz, but this didn't include decorating the insides; the walls and ceilings stained when water tanks had broken, discoloured when a chimney-full of soot had fallen, or scorched by fire.

'It's the elderly that need help,' Martha explained. 'Young 'uns can distemper the walls in a jiffy. The old people get distressed when their homes look a mess, and painters and decorators are as hard to find as ciggies, not that they could afford 'em if they weren't.'

So Ruby spent four hours every morning painting houses. She learnt how to plaster holes and mix cement, arriving home stinking of turpentine, her black hair streaked with paint.

It was 1943 and the war showed no sign of ending, though the people were continually promised victory was 'just around the corner'. The invasion of France was expected any day, but in the meantime, another invasion had taken place, much to the delight of young women throughout Britain – and the dismay of the men.

The Yanks had arrived. Hordes of cheerful, outgoing, engaging young men in well-fitting uniforms, generous to a fault, had taken over the country. They were everywhere, pockets stuffed with chewing gum and cash, convinced that every British woman, young or old, could be had in exchange for a pair of nylons.

Nowadays, Ruby looked forward to the weekend dances. It was like entering a fresh, new world, talking to young men from places like Texas or California who had done things she'd only seen in films; worked on ranches, driven Cadillacs, played baseball, been to Radio City, Hollywood, Fifth Avenue, Niagara Falls ...

Or so they said. She only believed half she was told, but the Americans' good-natured high spirits came as a relief after the horror of the air raids and the continuing shortage of virtually every single thing that made life bearable, particularly food.

She went out with quite a few, never more than twice, otherwise she would have found herself engaged, a crafty way the Yanks had of getting women into bed who couldn't be got there by easier means. There was a measure of cynicism in Ruby's fraternisation with the 'enemy', as Charles called them, and she often returned home laden with oranges, candy, tins of ham, and other delicacies rarely seen in war-torn Britain and which Charles happily consumed, despite their dubious source.

Ruby had known Beth was in love before Beth knew herself. They were at a dance at the Locarno, a foxtrot had just ended, and Ruby returned to their spot under the balcony. Beth was already there, holding hands with a tall, black American sergeant.

'Rube, this is Daniel,' Beth said shyly, and there was a look on her face, and on Daniel's, that said everything.

It came as no surprise when they got married six months later in the same church where Connie had married Charles, though it was a very different sort of wedding. Beth wore a simple white frock she'd made herself and there were no bridesmaids. The only guests were Beth's immediate friends whom she now regarded as her family. There was hardly time for a sandwich and a glass of wine before Daniel and the best man had to return to the base in Burtonwood, where he would continue to live, while Beth and Jake remained in Mrs Hart's house.

Daniel Lefarge was a lawyer. Back in Little Rock, Arkansas, he fought for equal rights for Negroes. He was one of the few educated black men in the state.

'It's terrible there,' a wide-eyed Beth said to Ruby on the night of her wedding. Everyone else had gone to bed and they were finishing off the last of the wine. 'We're not allowed in restaurants or bars. We can't sit by whites on the buses. We have to use separate lavatories.'

Ruby raised her eyebrows. 'We?'

'Black people,' Beth said firmly. 'I'm black, like Daniel.'

'I always thought of us, of you and me, as the same.'

'If I was the same as you,' Beth explained, 'Daniel would have been refused permission to get married. Black servicemen aren't allowed to marry British girls if they're white. It was decided in the Senate because it would cause trouble when they returned home with a white bride.'

'That's daft!' Ruby expostulated.

'It may seem daft to you, but not to Americans, particularly in the South where Daniel comes from. White people there consider negroes less than human.'

'Will you be happy in that sort of atmosphere?' Ruby felt fearful for her gentle, sensitive friend, who didn't seem to realise the awfulness of what she was saying. 'Remember the time when we were evacuated to Southport? You were terribly upset.'

'I'd be happy anywhere with Daniel.' Beth's face shone. 'And so will Jake. They adore each other.'

In June, 1944, on D-Day, Daniel Lefarge was among the first American troops to storm the French beaches. From that day on, Beth lived in a state of terror. Daniel's letters were few and usually arrived weeks late. Beth rarely ate breakfast, but lingered behind the front door with a cup of tea, praying that the postwoman would come. If she did, and there was nothing from Daniel, her disappointment was evident in her tragic face. On more than one occasion, Ruby travelled all the way to A. E. Wadsworth Engineering to deliver a letter with a French postmark that had arrived after her friend had gone to work.

Another Christmas, the sixth of the war, and hopefully the last. Allied troops were slowly advancing across Europe and, at last, victory was in sight.

In the New Year, Charles and Connie found a place of their own, a little cottage in Kirkby, not far from Brambles where Ruby used to live. Beth was advised that shortly she would no longer have a job. Marie Ferguson was making plans to go home.

As soon as the conflict was over, Beth and Jake were going to live in America with Daniel's mother – he would join them as soon as he was demobbed. There would only be Ruby and her girls left in the house, to which its owner could return any day.

She took down the blackout curtains and began to put the house, as far as she could, back to its original order. There were marks, scars, wear and tear, things broken, missing, changed, that couldn't be hidden. Mrs Hart was unlikely to think Ruby, who'd only been asked to keep an eye on the place, had tamed the wild garden out of the kindness of her heart – even established a vegetable patch – or varnished the front door when the original varnish had worn away altogether and she'd felt ashamed of the bleached, bare wood.

She had every intention of facing Mrs Hart, confessing what she'd done, but preferred not to be living on the premises when the woman walked through her newly varnished door. But finding somewhere to live was proving difficult, if not impossible. She roamed the streets, anxiously perused the cards in newsagents' windows, scoured the *Echo*, but nearly half the properties in Liverpool had been destroyed or damaged. It wasn't just Ruby desperate for somewhere to live.

The months passed. February gave way to March, March was suddenly April, the Allies were approaching Berlin and victory was imminent, but still Ruby hadn't found a job or somewhere to live. She and Beth had built a little nest egg between them, but her half would quickly disappear if there wasn't a wage coming in. She had nightmares about returning to somewhere like Foster Court, and the bad dreams occurred almost nightly as time went by and still nothing had turned up.

At the beginning of May, it was reported that Hitler had killed himself. The following day, Berlin fell. A victory announcement was expected by the hour. Ruby, working in the home of Mrs Effie Gittings, was listening to the wireless in the next room while she distempered the parlour walls an insipid pale blue, the only colour available apart from white. Mrs Gittings kept abandoning the wireless to discuss the latest news and fetch cups of tea as insipid as the distemper.

'You work ever so neat,' the old lady said admiringly. 'It's nice having a woman do the decorating. Men make splashes on the furniture and look daggers if you dare complain. At least one good thing's come out of this terrible war; women have shown they can work as good as men in most jobs.'

Later, as Ruby trudged home, she had an idea that made her want to dance along the pavement. *She would become a painter and decorator!* She liked the idea of being her own boss, working her own hours, being home when the children finished school. As soon as she was settled elsewhere, she'd have leaflets printed and deliver one to every house in the Dingle. She would become well-known again, like the pawnshop runner, not that fame was her objective, but making a living was. The future suddenly looked challenging and exciting, full of hope, and by the time she reached the house, her decorating company had expanded to the extent it had a staff of ten, all women. She would think of a clever name to call herself, something catchy.

At the gate, she paused. The 'settled elsewhere' bit had still to be resolved. Some of her excitement faded. Before she could lift a paintbrush, she had to find a place to live.

Sighing, she opened the front door, ready to make for the wireless in case there'd been any news, but froze when she heard footsteps upstairs, heavy, male footsteps.

'Who's there?' she called shakily. For a brief second she wondered if it might be Max Hart.

A young man appeared at the top of the stairs, nothing like Max. 'Who the hell are you?' he demanded angrily. 'There's people living here, but there bloody well shouldn't be. This house is supposed to be empty.'

It had always been Ruby's belief, ever since she was a little girl and couldn't have put it into words, that the best form of defence was attack. Besides which, she disliked the young man on sight. He looked about twenty-one, five years younger than herself, was very tall, very thin, with brilliantined black hair and a pencil moustache. The trousers of his cheap, chalk-striped suit were several inches too short, exposing shabby brown boots. Not that she presented a pretty picture herself in her paint-stained slacks and jumper.

'Who the hell are *you*?' she replied spiritedly. 'How dare you break into my house!'

'Break in!' The man clumped downstairs brandishing a key. '*Your* house!' he snorted. 'This house belongs to Mrs Beatrice Hart, but not for long, 'cause I'm going to buy it.'

Ruby tossed her head haughtily and hoped she didn't look as shaken as she felt. 'She hadn't told us it was to be sold.'

The visitor frowned. 'Why should she?'

'Because she writes to me from Colorado,' Ruby lied. 'She's been living with her sister. Mind you, I haven't heard from her in a while. She said we could live here for the duration. Her son, Max, stayed with us for a time. Do you know where Max is?'

'Never heard of him.' The man's frown faded, though he still looked suspicious. 'Why didn't she say the house was occupied when she wrote and told the estate agent to sell?'

'I've known her for years, she was always very forgetful. Did you say she was *selling* the house?'

'Yes. She's got married again and she's staying in America. 'I'm surprised she didn't write and tell you *that*!'

'I expect she will.' They glared at each other. His eyes were brown, his cheeks hollow, lips thin and stern. There was something hungry about him, and she suspected he'd been raised in poverty worse than she'd ever known. To her horror, a little excited shiver coursed down her spine, shocking her to the core, because he wasn't a bit attractive.

'Anyroad,' he said bluntly, 'as soon as the final contracts are exchanged, you can scram sharpish. How many live here?'

'Me and my two children. There's also my friend and her little boy, but they'll be leaving soon. How long will it be before the contracts are exchanged?'

'A few weeks.'

Ruby nodded. Suddenly, the idea of leaving the house in which everyone had been so happy, despite the war, made her feel inordinately sad. She touched the wooden banister and sighed. 'It's a lovely house,' she murmured. 'You'll like living in it.'

'I'm not going to live in it. I've already got a house. I'm a property developer. Here's my card.'

His name was Matthew Doyle according to the badly handwritten card. 'You've spelt property wrong,' Ruby pointed out. 'It only has one "p" in the middle.'

'Thanks for telling me,' he sneered, but looked embarrassed.

'I hope you're not going to pull the place down.' She sighed again. 'It would be such a shame.'

'I will, one day, when the time is ripe. Until then, it'll be rented out.'

'What's happening to everything in it?'

'You mean the furniture and fittings?' He made an attempt to look knowledgable and superior. 'It's being sold as it is. I'll keep some stuff and sell the rest.'

'I see.' She wondered where he'd got the money from to buy the house. And why wasn't he in the Forces like most men of his age? There was something despicable about speculating, buying up property, while there was a war on and other men were risking their lives. Her lips curled in disgust.

'Why are you covered all over in paint?' Matthew Doyle enquired.

'I've been decorating an old lady's house.'

He chuckled. 'I've just bought a whole row of bomb-damaged houses. When they need painting, I'll get in touch.'

Ruby looked at him directly, hating him. 'Don't bother. I do it for nothing, something I doubt you'd understand.'

He flushed angrily. 'You know nothing about me.'

'I know enough. How much rent will you want for the house?'

'More than you can afford,' he replied, blinking at the sudden change of tack, 'seeing as you work for nothing, like. Unless you've got a husband who can pay what it's worth.'

'My husband died at Dunkirk. I'm a widow.' She knew he would never let her have the house which she couldn't possibly afford, but was hoping to get under his skin, make him ashamed, though doubted if he was capable of shame.

To her surprise, he didn't answer straight away, but seemed lost in thought. She watched him, hands stuffed in the pockets of his ill-fitting suit. There was something almost pathetic about such a badly dressed individual who couldn't spell passing himself off as a property developer. She'd like to bet the estate agents he dealt with laughed like drains behind his back, yet he could probably buy and sell the lot of them. She neither respected nor admired him, but there was something to be said – she couldn't think what it was just now – for someone who'd so clearly pulled himself up by his bootstraps to get on.

'You could turn it into a boarding house,' he said.

Ruby's jaw dropped. 'I beg your pardon!'

'Live downstairs and let the upstairs rooms. Take lodgers. Make their meals, do their washing, and they'll pay more.' He smiled sarcastically. 'Or is being a landlady too good for you?'

'Oh, Rube! That's wonderful news,' Beth cried when she came home.

'Is it?' Ruby loathed every aspect of housework and regarded with horror the idea of looking after a houseful of lodgers. But it seemed she had no choice. Matthew Doyle wanted eight pounds a week rent. If she let the upstairs rooms for four pounds each, she'd be left with eight pounds for herself. It sounded a lot, but there'd be mountains of food to buy and tons of washing powder. It seemed she was destined to wallow in domesticity for the rest of her life.

No! No, she wouldn't. Ruby tightened her fists and gritted her teeth. She'd hang on to her little nest egg, add to it week by week, *buy* a house if she couldn't find one to rent. Somehow, in some way, she'd *do* something with her life, no matter how long it took.

At twenty to eight that night, it was announced on the BBC that the following day was to be a national holiday.

The war in Europe was over.

They took the excited children to a street party by the Malt House, where bunting was strung from the upstairs windows, where the tables were laden with a feast that made young eyes glisten and mouths water. Ruby had been saving food for this momentous day and arrived with two dozen home-made fairy cakes, a jelly sprinkled with hundreds and thousands, a tin of cream, two bottles of ginger beer, and mounds of sandwiches filled with cress she'd grown herself.

It was a mad day, crazy. Total strangers flung their arms around each other and hugged and kissed as if they were the greatest friends. When the children finished eating, the grown-ups sat down to what was left over, by which time half the men were as drunk as lords. They sat on the pavement outside the pub, hugging their ale, reliving the war, fighting the battles all over again, savouring the victory, which they claimed they'd expected all along, having forgotten the dark times when everything seemed to be lost and Hitler was winning.

After tea, they danced; the hokey-cokey, knees up Mother Brown, the conga. Ruby and Beth waltzed together, and Beth said longingly, 'Don't be hurt, Rube, but I don't half wish I was dancing with Daniel. There'll never be another day like today. It would have been nice to have spent it together.'

Ruby felt a little knot of envy. What would it be like to fall in love, she wondered? *Properly* in love, not the childish love she'd felt for Jacob, or the hopeless way she loved Jim Quinlan. Would she ever know what real love was?

Jim was around somewhere. He looked withdrawn, a bit lost, not joyful that everything was over but he *was* still alive. Perhaps he felt that death had cheated him, that he had no right to be there, celebrating, when his friends were dead. Ruby had already decided to give up on Jim Quinlan, though he would always retain a special place in her heart.

Still, she had her girls. She looked up to see where they were. They were whizzing round in a circle with Jake, laughing helplessly, as if they, too, were drunk. The girls would miss Jake. He was their brother, although neither she nor Beth had ever felt able to tell them. It was hard to imagine the future without Beth. They'd lived through the war together, shared every single thing. Even Jacob, she thought with a smile.

Connie and Charles arrived. 'We decided you were the only people in the world we wanted to spend tonight with,' Connie cried. 'We've been to the house and guessed you might be here.' She embraced Ruby affectionately, then Beth.

Charles kissed them both. 'You'll always be part of our memories,' he said huskily. 'You took strangers into your house and made them feel at home. I'll always be grateful.'

He took them into the packed Malt House for a drink, where Martha was working frantically behind the bar. Above the din, Ruby managed to convey the news that she'd found somewhere to live. 'In other words, I'm staying put. Some chap's buying the house, a Matthew Doyle.'

'Matt Doyle!' Martha screeched. 'You'll have to be careful there, Ruby. He's nothing but a dirty, rotten spiv. He could get you anything on the black market – at a price.'

Dusk was falling when they went outside. The exhausted crowd started to sing, sitting on their doorsteps, lounging against the walls, happier than most had ever known. The moon came out, and then the stars. And still they sang, until a few began to drift away, and then more.

Ruby and Beth walked back through the lamp-lit streets, the weary children behind, dragging their feet. Mrs Hart's house came into view. Ruby had switched on the lights before they left, feeling extravagent and very daring. But it was worth it to see every window in every room brightly lit, welcoming them home, a sight never seen before in all the years they'd lived there.

Beth took Ruby's hand and squeezed it, as if in farewell. In another few weeks, she and Jake would be gone.

An era was over and a new one about to begin.

Ruby's girls

9
1957–1958

Heather O'Hagan sat on the bed and watched her sister in her frothy pink party dress get made up in front of the dressing table mirror. 'That lippy doesn't suit you,' she said critically. 'It's too dark.'

'D'you think so?' Greta put her head on one side and studied her reflection. 'I thought it made me look glamorous.'

'It makes you look like a tart. Fair-haired women should wear pale lippy.'

Greta pouted. 'You're always saying that, sis, but Marilyn Monroe doesn't, and *she* looks glamorous.'

'No, she doesn't. She looks like a tart.'

'Oh, all right.' Greta rubbed the offending lipstick off with her hankie and applied a lighter shade. 'What's that like?'

'Much better.' Heather smiled, having got her way. For as long as she could remember, she'd felt responsible for Greta, who could very easily make a complete mess of things without her help. She never seemed able to do things right. Say she'd worn that horrible maroon lippy at her party! It was all right Mam saying, 'People learn from their mistakes,' but they could learn better and less painfully with good advice.

Ruby opened the bedroom door. 'Greta, it's eight o'clock and your first guest has arrived.'

Greta quickly dabbed scent behind her ears, then tipped the bottle against a piece of cotton wool which she tucked inside her bra. She jumped to her feet. 'Who is it?'

'I don't know, love. It's a he, and he's very handsome. I told him to put some records on the gramophone.'

'It might be Peter King.' She rushed out of the room.

'Don't let him see you're interested,' Heather called.

'I think that's up to Greta, don't you?' Ruby said pointedly.

'But he's a drip, Mam. He's already got a girlfriend.'

'It can't be all that serious if he's come to Greta's party on his own.'

'I don't want her to get hurt, Mam.' She'd sooner be hurt herself, any day, than let Greta suffer a broken heart.

Ruby's face softened. 'I know. But you can't protect her for ever. Oh, there's the doorbell. Answer it, there's a love. I've sausage rolls in the oven that need seeing to and sandwiches still to make.'

'All right.' Heather stood and smoothed the hips of her plain black skirt, glancing briefly at her tall reflection in the mirror. With the skirt, she wore a white, tailored blouse, and her long, black hair was pinned back with a slide. The whole effect was deliberately severe because she didn't want to overshadow her sister on her twenty-first.

Frankie Laine was singing 'Jezebel' and everywhere smelled of a strange mixture of baking and scent – June, the girls' favourite. There was a lovely atmosphere, heady, excited, as if the walls of Mrs Hart's house knew there was going to be a party. Ruby still thought of it as Mrs Hart's house, even though it had belonged to Matthew Doyle for twelve years – twelve long, very tedious years, she thought, making a face as she took the sausage rolls out of the oven. The lodgers lived upstairs and the two downstairs reception rooms had been turned into bedrooms, one for Ruby, the other for the girls. The rather dark room at the back, where the party would be held, was their living room. Fortunately, the kitchen was big enough for the lodgers to eat in. *Un*fortunately, it meant she had to keep it scrupulously clean, or at least she tried.

Every time she thought she had enough saved for a deposit on a house of her own, houses had gone up another few hundred. It was like being in a race she stood no chance of winning. She'd probably end up the oldest landlady in the world.

The doorbell rang again. 'Will someone get that!' she yelled.

'I'll do it.' Mr Keppel appeared at the kitchen door. 'I'm just on my way out.'

'Thanks. Have a nice time.'

'It's the dress rehearsal tonight. I'm a bag of nerves.'

'I hope it goes well.' Mr Keppel had only been living upstairs a few months. He worked in a bank and his spare time was taken up with amateur dramatics. Ruby was going to the play's first night at the Crane Theatre on Monday. She was glad Mr Oliver and Mr Hamilton were away for the weekend, leaving only Mr Keppel, who was no trouble, and Mrs Mulligan, who was a pain.

A few seconds later, Martha Quinlan came into the kitchen, a shopping bag in each hand. 'This is the cake,' she puffed, putting one bag on the table. 'And the other's a couple of bottles of wine, for us, not the kids. D'you fancy a glass now?'

'I wouldn't say no. I'm a bit nervous, Martha. I've never thrown a party before.'

'It's not like you to be nervous. Remember that wedding during the war? I've never had such a nice time since.'

'That was different. People were more easily pleased. Let's see the cake.' Ruby had made the cake herself and Martha had iced it. 'Oh, it's lovely!' she exclaimed when the elaborate pink and white creation was removed from its tissue wrapping. 'Very artistic. Did you actually make the roses yourself?'

''Course, I did. That's what I went to night school for, cake decoration. I've got the candles separate.'

Martha was nearing seventy, grey-haired, slightly stooped, deeply wrinkled, but as hard-working as ever. It was almost a decade since Fred had retired as licensee of the Malt House, and the licence had passed to Jim and his wife, Barbara. The older couple still lived on the premises and Martha was often called upon to lend a hand behind the bar. According to her, Barbara was a lazy bitch. 'You'd never dream she'd been a nurse,' she frequently remarked. 'I used to think our Agnes was idle, but at least she bucked up her ideas when she got married and had kids. That Barbara won't have a baby, she's too scared.'

'Do you want white wine or red, luv?' she asked now.

'White, please.'

A bottle was expertly uncorked, the wine poured. Martha began to put twenty-one pink candles on the cake. 'How many's coming to the party?'

'Twenty, half girls, half boys – that sounds like more now,' she said when the doorbell rang. 'They're mostly Greta's friends from work, a few of Heather's. Charles and Connie might pop in later, but only if they can get a babysitter for the boys.'

'They can stay in the kitchen with us,' Martha said comfortably. 'We can have a nice natter. It will be quite like old times, except Beth won't be here.'

'She rang earlier to wish Greta a happy birthday.'

'How's she getting on?'

'Just fine,' Ruby lied, because Beth wouldn't have wanted Martha to know anything else. 'Jake's at university in Boston and her other three kids sound incredibly clever – much cleverer than mine. Daniel's got his own law firm and they've just bought a lovely new house. It's got central heating, a double garage, and its own swimming pool.'

Martha looked impressed. 'She certainly fell on her feet, didn't she, our Beth, when she married Daniel.'

Ruby gave a non-committal smile. Only she knew how unhappy Beth was. She recalled the very first letter she had written from Little Rock; how pretty the place was, how the sun always seemed to be shining, the clothes in the shops so smart, Daniel's brother, Nathan, was teaching Jake to play baseball. Everything sounded wonderful until Ruby reached the end and there was a PS which she could remember almost word for word.

'Oh, Rube,' Beth had written. 'I'm so miserable I could die. Daniel's mam doesn't like me, you'll never guess why; because I'm too pale.' The 'pale' was underlined. 'She says I'm "high yeller", whatever that is. And my poor Jake is almost white. We don't fit in anywhere, Jake and me. The whites hate us because we're black, and the blacks don't like us for not being black enough. Nathan's OK, but he's the only one. I can't wait for Daniel to be demobbed and come home.'

Daniel came home, but things only got a little better. With her husband deeply involved in his work, and his spare time taken up with advancing the cause of black people, Beth felt increasingly lonely and friendless. Everywhere was segregated; shops, restaurants, buses, even schools. She yearned to return to Liverpool. Yet she loved Daniel and couldn't bear to leave.

'Oh, listen!' Martha suddenly yelped. 'It's Bill Haley and the Comets singing "Rock around the Clock".'

'Someone must have bought Greta the record as a present.'

'Fred ses I'm turning childlike in me old age, but I love rock and roll.'

'I'm not averse to it myself. I wonder what time I should serve the food?'

'Nine-ish?' suggested Martha.

Ruby began to arrange the sausage rolls on a plate. 'I should have done this earlier, but I've been run off my feet all day. I hope fifty sarnies are enough; salmon paste and cheese – not together,' she added hastily. 'I made the little vol-au-vent things and the cheese straws last night.' She laughed. 'Lord! If the nuns could see me now, they'd be so proud. I used to hate cookery lessons – well, I hated everything they taught us, but some of it must have sunk in.'

At nine o'clock, she sailed into the noisy, crowded, smoke-filled living room with the refreshments and put them on the sideboard for the guests to help themselves. Most were dancing, a few attempting to talk above the din, and one couple were squashed in an armchair in a passionate embrace, though the young man quickly disengaged himself when he saw the food.

'I'll fetch the cake later,' she called, but no one heard.

Charles and Connie had arrived earlier, but could only stay a little while. They'd asked a neighbour to watch over their two little boys, but she wanted to be home for ten o'clock to see a play on television.

'I'd love a television,' Martha sighed. 'But our Fred claims they're nothing but a time waster. Mind you, he should know. If anyone knows how to waste time, it's bloody Fred.'

'A chap upstairs, Mr Hamilton, has one,' said Ruby. 'I switched it on once when I cleaned his room, but nothing happened. I was worried I'd broken it.'

It was Charles's opinion that televisions would never catch on. 'People are too intelligent to sit and watch a little screen all night long.'

Connie grinned. 'Then I must be very unintelligent, because I wouldn't mind having one a bit. I'd love to see *What's My Line,* and the lads would enjoy *Watch With Mother.*'

'I think this calls for an instant divorce,' Charles said sternly, grinning back.

They waited for Ruby to carry the cake with its twenty-one flickering candles into the other room, following behind with Martha, singing 'Happy Birthday to You . . .'

'You've done them kids dead proud, d'you know that, Ruby,' Martha said when Connie and Charles had gone and they were alone again in the kitchen.

'It's only a party, Martha.'

'I don't just mean the party, girl. I mean over their whole lives. And you've done it on your own, without a husband most of the time, and not a single relative around to give a hand. Yet they've turned out such lovely girls.' She gave Ruby a look of real affection. 'I'll not forget the day you came into the pub about the cleaning job. You looked as if you'd just got out the bath with your clothes on. Fred said I was a fool, advancing you sixpence. He didn't think I'd ever see you or the tanner again. But I knew I would.' She patted Ruby's hand. 'I wonder if your mam's around somewhere? If so, it's her that's the fool, giving up such a lovely daughter.'

'Oh, Martha, stop it.' Ruby blushed. 'You've had too much wine and it's made you maudlin. You'll be crying any minute.'

Martha seemed about to continue with her eulogy, but was interrupted by a knock on the kitchen door and Iris Mulligan came in, her stout, fiftyish body wrapped in a tweed dressing gown, a thick brown net covering her mousy hair, and her face greasy with Pond's cold cream. Mrs Mulligan had occupied a front upstairs room for nearly five years and was a champion complainer, almost certainly the reason she was there now.

'Is that noise going to go on for much longer, Mrs O'Hagan?' she whined. 'It's ten o'clock and some of us have to sleep.'

'I told you the other day we were having a party, Mrs Mulligan,' Ruby said plainly. 'I apologised in advance for the noise, remember? It's Friday, you don't have to work tomorrow. It's also my daughter's twenty-first. I'm afraid the noise will continue until midnight and then everyone will go home.'

'That seems most unreasonable, Mrs O'Hagan.'

'I'm afraid it can't be helped, Mrs Mulligan.'

'You'll just have to read a book,' Martha growled. 'Jaysus! How do you stand it?' she exlaimed when Iris Mulligan had departed in a huff.

Ruby shrugged. 'I've stopped taking any notice. She complains about every single thing. If it's not the noise, it's the food, or the other lodgers – Mr Oliver snores and Mr Hamilton has his television on too loud. At least she does her own washing and ironing, not like the men.'

'Fancy ending up at her age living in a room in someone's house! Has she got any kids?'

'No. Actually, Martha,' Ruby dropped her voice, concerned she might be overheard, 'someone told me her husband brought a woman home only half his age, and she was given the choice of putting up with it or getting out.'

'He couldn't do that!' Martha gasped.

'He did. She ended up with nowhere to live and without a stick of furniture. That's why she's here.'

'Bloody hell! My Fred doesn't seem so bad after that. No wonder the poor woman's miserable. I'd be the same if I was her.'

Next morning, the party was declared a great success. It had gone suspiciously quiet over the final half hour, but Ruby hadn't bothered to investigate. She could hardly complain if they were indulging in a bit of snogging when she'd got up to far worse with Jacob when she was only sixteen.

'Are you staying in town this afternoon?' she enquired over breakfast. The girls had appeared at half-past seven in their dressing gowns, as fresh as daisies, despite going to bed so late. Both worked in the city centre; Greta as a switchboard operator for a firm of accountants and Heather as filing clerk in the Royal Liver insurance company. Saturday, they finished at midday and usually spent the afternoon roaming the clothes departments of the big shops, always arriving home with something new. Ruby would have done the same at their age, but lack of money, followed by clothes rationing, had proved rather inhibiting.

'I might spend my birthday money on a new frock,' Greta announced, munching on a piece of toast.

'And I need new shoes.' Heather regarded her long, narrow feet. 'Wedge heels would be nice for a change.'

'I wouldn't mind new shoes myself.'

'You can have my red ones if you like, Mam. I don't like them anymore. The heels are too squat.'

'Squat!' Ruby hooted. She and Heather took the same size. 'I've heard of high heels and flat heels and Cuban heels, but never squat. I'll try them on later. It's come to something, a mother inheriting her daughter's cast-offs. You've got more money than sense, the pair of you.'

An hour later, she waved them off into the soft April sunshine, arms linked, heads bent towards each other, already deep in conversation. In her spindly-heeled sandals, Greta was almost as tall as her sister. She wore a stiff, taffeta petticoat under a flowered dirndl skirt, and her wide belt was pulled so tight it was a wonder she could breathe. On top, she wore a gathered peasant blouse with smocking on the yoke. Her hair was held back with wide pink ribbon. Ruby smiled. She would have looked perfect stuck on top of a Christmas tree.

Heather favoured a more tailored look. Her suit was classically styled grey flannel, worn with a white blouse, black shoes, and a black felt beret.

They made a striking pair; Greta small and pretty, a pale, natural blonde, Heather elegantly tall and very dark. Her sombre face could look quite beautiful when she smiled.

A van passed, and the driver had to brake sharply as he almost ran into a lamp-post, his attention distracted by the sight of Ruby's girls. He caught her eye, looked her up and down, and winked appreciatively. She would be thirty-eight in a few weeks' time, but could turn male heads as easily as her daughters.

Ruby closed the door and began to sort through the post which had just arrived. There were two belated birthday cards for Greta, letters for the lodgers, and an electricity bill for herself - she winced when she opened it and saw the amount. She left Greta's cards on the hall table and took the rest upstairs, shoving the letters under the appropriate doors.

Downstairs again, she met Tiger, ancient now, emerging from a marathon sleep in the cellar where he spent most of his time in his wardrobe. Floppy had disappeared years ago and hopefully hadn't ended his days as someone's dinner. She gave the big cat a cuddle and a saucer of milk, then went into the girls' room and tried on Heather's red shoes. The heels *were* a bit thick, but otherwise very smart. They fitted perfectly, but she had nothing to wear with them. She searched through Heather's clothes, found a nice navy-blue frock she hadn't seen her wear in ages, and wondered if she dropped a hint she'd be given the frock as well. It would have been nice to wander round the shops with the girls, buy herself new clothes, she thought ruefully, but every spare penny went in the bank towards a house.

In Owen Owen's, Greta was agonising over whether or not to buy a short-sleeved angora jumper. 'It's a lovely blue and ever so soft.' She rubbed the stuff between her fingers.

'It's daft buying a jumper in April,' Heather said. 'It'll itch like mad in the heat.'

'I could keep it till winter, sis.'

'But it's only got short sleeves!'

'Oh, all right.' Greta abandoned the jumper and made for a rack of blouses. 'These are pretty. Oh, see! They've got lace panels down the front. They'd go nice with your suit.'

'Mmm!' Heather frowned and began to pull out the various colours. Buying a blouse, buying clothes of any sort, was a serious matter, demanding total concentration. 'I wouldn't mind the black. I tell you what, let's keep these in mind and perhaps come back later. We haven't been to Lewis's yet, nor T. J. Hughes, and you still haven't seen a frock you like.'

'Shall we go for a coffee? We can think about the blouses and that white handbag I saw earlier.'

'That's a good idea! There's a new coffee bar at the top of Bold Street.'

On the way, they earnestly discussed the things they'd seen. If Greta bought the white bag, she would need white sandals to match. Heather wondered if diamanté earrings would be too dressy for work.

'You wear a diamanté brooch,' Greta pointed out.

'Yes, but earrings are different.'

They ordered coffees and took them to a table in the window, too embroiled in their own concerns to show interest in the people passing by. They'd led a cosseted, sheltered life, the O'Hagan girls. Foster Court had made no impression on their young minds. Their memories stretched back only as far as living cosily with Arthur in the coal yard. Lack of a father had never bothered them. A man had always been around; first Arthur, then Charles, then Mam's lodgers, to make a fuss of them. Other children, not just Jake, had been there to play with, in a house that was always full of people. They'd never felt lonely or unloved. So far, neither had been called upon to take a decision about anything remotely important apart from what clothes to buy or whether to go out with a particular young man.

Last night, Peter King had asked Greta for a date but, on Heather's advice, she had turned him down. Whenever possible, they went out in a foursome, because they enjoyed each other's company as much as they did that of the various young men. Greta, more so than Heather, knew that one day this would change, that a man would appear she would want to spend the rest of her life with to the exclusion of everyone else, including her sister. Heather couldn't imagine Greta coping with marriage, and certainly not motherhood, without her unwavering support. Sometimes, she wondered if she should remain unmarried, become a spinster, so that she would always be available for Greta.

'I think I'll buy something for Mam,' Greta said. 'A sort of "thank you" for the party.'

'I'll go halves,' offered Heather. 'What shall we get?'

'I was thinking about a scarf, a nice georgette one.'

'How about a scarf and a scarf ring?'

'Perfect.' They smiled at each other, imagining the way Mam's eyes would light up when she was given the presents. They loved Mam with all their hearts.

At first, neither saw the two young men outside the coffee bar window, waving their arms, pressing their faces against the glass, in an attempt to make themselves noticed. Greta gave a tiny scream when she became aware of a squashed nose and staring eyes only inches away. She burst out laughing, and the young man leapt back, did a thumbs up sign, said something to his equally contorted friend, and they made for the door.

'They're coming in!' Heather cried, aghast. 'Do you know them?'

'Not from Adam.'

'Then you shouldn't have laughed. 'Oh, look, they're coming to sit by us!'

The young men joined them at the table. 'Good afternoon, ladies,' said one. 'I'm Larry, and this is Rob. We've been looking everywhere for you two.'

Heather scowled. 'Don't talk soft.'

'It's true,' said Rob, looking hurt. 'I said to Larry earlier, "This avvy, we'll find the two best-looking girls in Liverpool and take them to the pics." We've been searching for ages and had almost given up when we saw you.'

'Gary Cooper and Grace Kelly are on at the Futurist in *High Noon.*' Larry sniffed pathetically. 'We couldn't possibly go on our own. We need someone to hold our hands.'

'I can't think why,' Heather snapped. 'Anyroad, we've already seen it and it's not the least bit frightening.'

'How about *Bride of the Gorilla*?' suggested Rob. 'It's on at the Scala. You can hide your head on me shoulder during the scary bits. I won't mind.'

'It sounds a load of rubbish.'

'Oh, Heather, it sounds fun.' To Heather's annoyance, Greta was smiling broadly at the intruders, whom she had to concede seemed quite harmless, even faintly funny, not to mention very good-looking. They were remarkably similar in appearance; fresh-faced, wholesome, well-built, almost six feet tall, with the same coloured hair, a sort of mid-brown, though Rob's was curly and Larry's straight. Both were nicely dressed in flannels, open-necked shirts, and tweed jackets.

'Are you brothers?' she enquired.

'Almost,' replied Rob. 'Our mams had us on the same night in the same hospital. They were in the next bed to each other. We've been best friends ever since and so have our mams.'

'Oh, that's nice, isn't it, sis?'

'I suppose so,' Heather grudgingly agreed.

'You're sisters!' Larry gaped. 'I'd never have guessed. You're not a bit like each other.'

'I take after me dad, and Heather's the image of our mam.'

'If that's Heather, who are you?'

'Greta.'

Larry inched his chair closer. 'Greta's always been me favourite name for a woman.'

'Liar!' Greta laughed.

'Me, I've always preferred Heather.' Rob grinned at Heather, and she could have kicked herself, because although she didn't mean to, she couldn't help but grin back.

'Now, about the pics ...' Larry began.

'We've got shopping to do first,' Greta said. 'And we'll have to ring Mam, tell her we'll be late.'

'We'll come shopping with you. Would you like another coffee before we go?'

'Yes, please,' the girls said together.

Ruby was sitting with her feet up, listening to the wireless, and wondering if she could afford a television, when her daughters turned up with two extremely pleasant, polite young men who looked like identical twins, yet weren't even related. One was called Larry Donovan, the other Rob White. They owned a car between them, a Volkswagen Beetle, and had given the girls a lift home. She understood they'd been to the pictures that afternoon to see *Bride of the Gorilla*, which had given them a good laugh.

Heather, usually so sober, had gone all girlish and coy, having paired off with an obviously smitten Rob. Greta and Larry couldn't take their starry eyes off each other.

After making something to eat, Ruby stayed in the kitchen, where she drank a glass of the wine left over from the night before and listened to the giggles and whisperings from the next room. It was one of the rare occasions she wished she had a husband so that when the time came he could sternly demand what Larry and Rob's intentions were towards his daughters. She had a feeling they were already serious. She'd noticed how Larry had managed to slip in the reassuring fact that they were Catholics.

Something miraculous had happened; two inseparable couples had met and fallen in love.

She felt herself go cold. She'd known it was inevitable that one day her girls would get married. Indeed, she had prayed they would settle down, have children, be happy. But now, when it seemed that this might happen, Ruby found it impossible to visualise life without them. She had fashioned her life around her daughters. They were always at the forefront of her mind whenever she made a decision, no matter how trivial. Virtually everything she had done had been done for her girls.

Imagine the house without music, without the wireless on too loud, no bright young voices, arguing, laughing, sometimes crying, shouting 'Tara, Mam,' or 'Mam, we're home'? There'd only be the lodgers who made hardly any noise at all except where Iris Mulligan was concerned.

Rubbish! Ruby drained the glass and returned it to the table with a thump. Without the girls, she could do all sorts of things. Give up being a landlady, for one. There would be no need for a house big enough for three, and she could afford to buy something smaller. Matthew Doyle could have his house back, though she'd be sad to leave. She'd get a job, doing something, she wasn't sure what, but she'd go to night school like Martha, learn a trade; book-keeping or typing. Or she could start her own business – she remembered she'd once thought of becoming a painter and decorator.

For the first time since she was a child she would have no ties. She could do anything she pleased.

Oh, but she would always miss her girls!

Sunday, the girls went to Southport for the day in Larry and Rob's car. They returned late, with the rest of the week already mapped out; Monday, the pictures to see *Carousel* with Gordon MacRae and Shirley Jones, Tuesday the Locarno, Wednesday a club called the Cavern that hadn't long opened and played New Orleans jazz, Thursday somewhere else . . .

Ruby lost track of the arrangements. The boys didn't seem short of money, both were toolmakers at the English Electric. When they'd gone, she wondered if she should offer some motherly advice, but couldn't think of any. 'Don't rush things,' perhaps, but doubted if the girls would take any notice – *she* wouldn't have. Years ago, she'd told them the facts of life and felt sure they were still virgins – at least they had been until that morning. It was best not to interfere. They'd go their own way whatever she said. Young people were very perverse and inclined to regard opposition as encouragement.

She got things off her chest in a letter to Beth. On re-reading it, she thought the weekend's developments sounded rather nice, a bit touching, and felt very pleased for her girls.

On Friday, just after she'd changed the beds upstairs and had four sets of sheets and pillowslips to wash, Matthew Doyle paid his monthly visit to collect the rent. It had crept up over the years to fifteen pounds a week. Ruby had raised her lodgers' terms accordingly.

He always breezed in, without an invitation, made himself at home in the kitchen and expected a cup of tea and a long chat as if, Ruby thought nastily, he found it necessary to emphasise the property was his. She found it incredible that a man in his position should still collect his own rents, and detested him as much now as when they'd first met. It riled her that she had to be nice to him, and she worried that one of these days he'd remember that the house had been bought as an investment with a view to having it knocked down and something else put in its place.

Nowadays, he was unrecognisable as the young man she'd met twelve years ago. Gone were the shabby clothes, the boots, the moustache. Today he wore a slick, grey suit over a sparkling white shirt, a silk tie. His expensive black shoes were highly polished and he carried a leather briefcase. It wasn't just his appearance that had changed, but his bearing – he exuded an airy, good-humoured confidence that she found highly irritating, and his accent had lost its rough edge.

Matthew Doyle had become a very rich man with a finger in all sorts of pies. It was Doyle Construction who were responsible for the block of flats being built in Crosby which had been the subject of much controversy – residents in the houses behind had thought they'd have a view of the River Mersey from their front windows for the rest of their lives. He had been elected to Liverpool City Council and his photo was frequently in the *Echo*, attending a charity function or a civic event with his pretty wife who was the daughter of another business tycoon. They lived in an old manor house in Aughton.

'I've brought Greta a present,' he announced, settling himself in the kitchen. He took a box out of the briefcase.

'What for?'

'Her birthday, of course. It's a bit late, but I'm afraid I couldn't get here before.'

'How did you know it was her birthday?'

'She told me last month.'

Greta actually *liked* him, as did Tiger, who had exerted himself sufficiently to rub against his legs. Matthew reached down and tickled his chin.

'Thanks for the present. I'm sure Greta will love whatever it is.'

'It's scent, good stuff. Made in France. Chanel something.' He was sprawled on a wooden chair, long legs stretched in front of him, very elegant.

Ruby turned away to put the kettle on when an excited little shiver made her spine tingle. It happened every time they met, as if her body wasn't listening to her brain. Damn the man!

'You don't think much of me, do you?' He was looking at her, laughter in his brown eyes, making fun of her. Lately, she could have sworn he'd started to flirt. Today she thought he seemed a bit edgy, unusual for him.

'You're all right,' she said grudgingly.

'You've never liked me from the moment we first met.'

'I wouldn't say that.'

'*I* would. You were thinking what a creep I was, making a few bob when most men of my age were in the Forces.'

'It happened to be true,' Ruby pointed out. 'And it wasn't exactly "a few bob", either.'

He nodded. 'You're right, 'cept when we met I was up to me ears in debt to the bank. I was desperate for ready cash. When I first looked over this place, I intended letting out the rooms meself, making a bomb.'

'Why didn't you?' She wondered where this was leading.

'You turned up, didn't you? Your need seemed greater than mine. I let you have the place for eight quid a week when I could have got twice as much.'

'I'm very grateful,' Ruby said stiffly. She hadn't asked for special treatment and wondered why he was telling her twelve years after the event.

He grinned. 'You might be grateful, but you still don't think much of me.'

Sometimes, she found it very difficult to be nice. She slammed a cup of tea in front of him. 'I think you're wonderful, will that do? Anyway, what's brought this on? Why is it suddenly so important that I like you after all this time?'

'Because *I* like *you*,' he said simply.

'And you've only just realised?'

'No, I've liked you since the day you walked through the front door covered in paint.' He shrugged. 'Being rich has its drawbacks.'

'I wouldn't know.' Now what was he on about?

'You lose contact with your roots,' he said forlornly. 'You never meet people who've been as poor as you were yourself. Everyone thinks you've always lived in a mansion and driven a Rolls-Royce.'

'Aah!' Ruby said with mock sympathy.

'It's got to me lately,' he went on, ignoring the interruption. 'I feel lonely, suffocated. I want to talk to someone from the same background as meself, remind meself of who I am, as it were.'

'There's plenty around.'

'Including you.'

'What makes you think we're from the same background?'

'We both lived in Foster Court.'

She gasped. 'I don't remember you.'

'I lived in number five with me gran.' He smiled, as if the memory wasn't totally unpleasant. 'I never went out, that's why you don't remember me. I used to sit in the window and watch the world go by. I'd see you every day, leaving number two in your shawl with your kids in a pram. Gran said you were the pawnshop runner.'

'Why didn't you go out?' She suspected he was like Jacob, set on avoiding a proper job of work.

'Because I had TB,' he said simply.

'Tuberculosis!' No wonder he hadn't joined the Forces. 'Are you better now?'

'Well, I'm not likely to cough up blood on your nice kitchen table, if that's what you're worried about.'

'I wasn't worried about any such thing,' Ruby said sharply.

'Sorry!' He raised his hands and backed away.

'Why are you telling me this?' she demanded irritably. 'You've never mentioned Foster Court before.'

'I'm playing on your sympathies,' he said with a grin. 'I told you, I need someone to talk to. Someone who won't slag off the working classes and argue over the quality of various wines. I'm sick of discussing contracts and arranging deals.'

Ruby folded her arms on the table. 'OK, so talk.'

'I'd prefer to do it over dinner,' he said slyly.

'You've got a cheek!' she cried indignantly. 'You've also got a wife.'

'Caroline's in the South of France, holidaying on daddy's yacht.'

'I don't care if she's holidaying on the moon. I'm not going out with a married man.'

'It would be entirely above-board. We'd sit in a restaurant with about fifty other people and talk, that's all.'

'No!' Ruby said flatly.

He got up and went over to the window. 'I'd forgotten how big this garden is. It must be at least a hundred and fifty feet deep and half as wide. I reckon I could get two pairs of semis on this plot, no problem.' He turned to face her. 'D'you know how much a semi goes for these days, Ruby?' He shook his head incredulously. 'Over two thousand quid.'

At this, Ruby felt so angry that she half expected a cloud of steam to emerge from her mouth. 'Are you trying to blackmail me?' she hissed.

'Yes.'

'Well, it hasn't worked. The answer's still "No".'

Ruby had been invited to tea to meet Larry and Rob's parents and sundry other relatives. She had her hair set and bought a new frock; red cotton to match Heather's cast-off shoes. It had a plain round neck, cap sleeves, and a swirling circular skirt. The boys took her in the car, squashed on the back seat between Greta and Heather, both reeking of Matthew Doyle's Chanel No 5.

She felt unusually nervous, expecting to feel out of things without a husband, a relative, even a friend to take with her in support, but found herself warmly welcomed into the bosoms of both families; the mams and dads, aunts and uncles, brothers and sisters, various grandparents, all crammed into the large Victorian terraced house in Orrell Park. Without exception, they made her feel very special, as if no one in the entire history of the world had given birth to two such outstandingly pretty daughters, such charming, old-fashioned girls, real bobby-dazzlers. Though it wasn't surprising, she was something of an eye-catcher herself, and could easily have been taken for their elder sister. What a pity their dad hadn't been around to see them grow up. He would have been dead proud. And what a struggle she must have had, bringing them up all on her own. Well, all they could say was, no one could possibly have done it better.

'Me and Moira often worried that one of the lads would meet a girl and leave the other bereft,' said Ellie, who was Rob's mother, or might have been Larry's – Ruby didn't think she would ever remember who was who. 'But, as it is, it's worked out perfectly, both falling in love at the same time. Mind you, they've always done things together.' Moira was Larry's mother, or possibly Rob's.

'I'm very pleased,' Ruby murmured.

'Of course, we wouldn't dream of letting you pay for the double wedding. That'd be too much to expect. Perhaps we could get together sometime and discuss the expense.'

'I didn't know they were planning on getting married,' Ruby said faintly, deeply hurt that no one had told her.

'Oh, they're having too good a time at the moment to make plans, but Moira and me assume it's on the cards. Don't you?'

Ruby smiled, relieved she hadn't been left out. 'I think I always have, right from the minute they first met.'

Ellie linked her arm. 'Come and have more sherry. You look as if you need it. I bet you feel shattered, meeting so many people in one go. I know I would. Oh, look, our Chris has arrived. I must introduce you to me disgraceful little brother.'

'What did he do that was so disgraceful?'

'He entered a seminary, became a priest, then gave it up. That was fourteen years ago, but our mam still hasn't got over the shock.'

She half expected an ex-priest to look romantic, slightly decadent, possibly debauched, but Ellie's brother, Chris Ryan, was none of these things. Instead, he was a distracted, untidy man about her own age, with a pleasant face and a lovely smile. She noticed he was wearing odd socks.

'Oh, look at your tie,' Ellie said fussily. 'Have you got it on upside down or something?'

'I don't seem able to get the knot right,' Chris said mildly, smiling at Ruby. 'So, you're shortly to become a member of our family, or I should say families. You must find it all very confusing. I'm never quite sure which of these people I'm related to, yet I've known at least half of them all my life.'

'Don't worry about it, luv.' Ellie patted his hand. 'If you need reminding, just ask me.' She winked at Ruby. 'Don't take any notice of him. He's putting it on. There's a brain as sharp as a razor in that ugly head. Excuse me a minute, while I fetch some sherry.'

'And a beer for me, please, sis.'

'Go on, ask,' said Chris when Ellie had gone.

'Ask what?'

'Ask why I stopped being a priest. I know Ellie will have told you. For some strange reason, she tells everyone. I think she revels a bit in having a disreputable brother.'

'I wanted to ask, but didn't like to,' Ruby confessed.

'That makes a change. Most people ask straight out.'

'OK, so why did you stop being a priest?'

'I'm afraid there was nothing scandalous about it. I didn't have an affair with a nun, as most people seem to think. I lost my faith, which coincided, quite fortunately, with the start of the war. It meant I had no crisis of conscience when I left and joined the Army.'

'Did you enjoy the Army?'

He made a rueful face. 'My only problem was, although I was anxious to fight for my country, I wasn't too keen on killing Germans. I was glad when it was all over and me and a German had never come face to face.' He took her elbow. 'I spy two empty seats. Let's sit down.'

'How do you use this razor-sharp brain of yours?' Ruby asked when they were seated.

He looked at her enigmatically. 'You'll never guess.'

'I'm not even going to try and guess what an ex-priest does.'

'I'm a policeman, a detective sergeant. Plain clothes, I'm pleased to say. I could never get used to wearing a helmet.'

Ruby shook her head. 'I can't see you in a policeman's uniform.'

'Thank the Lord you never will. I was hopeless on traffic duty. I used to bless everything and it went in the wrong direction.'

She laughed. 'Is that why you were promoted?'

'I suspect so. The powers-that-be probably wanted me out of harm's way.' He waved his hand dismissively. 'Enough about me, Ruby. Let's talk about *you*. What do you do?'

She told him she was a landlady and how it had come about, going back to the day she and Beth had returned from Southport and found Arthur

Cummings had died and they'd moved into Mrs Hart's house overlooking Princes Park. She told him a surprising amount, about Connie and Charles and all the other people who'd stayed, and how they'd sheltered in the cellar and enjoyed a sing-song during the raids, about Beth going to work, the children she'd looked after, Matthew Doyle, her lodgers, Greta's party the other week, how pleased she was the four young people had got together, that she liked Larry and Rob very much.

'Gosh! I've been talking for ages,' she said, flustered, when she'd finished. 'You're a very good listener. I'm surprised you didn't die of boredom.'

'I've been anything but bored.' He was watching her with a strange expression on his face, a face that seemed rather more than pleasant now that she looked at it properly. It was sensitive, intelligent, immensely attractive. Why hadn't she noticed before? His eyes were dark grey, his nose and mouth a bit too wide. All of a sudden, Ruby's heart began to beat excessively loud and painfully hard.

'Our Ellie never brought the sherry or the beer, did she?' Chris said lightly. 'Don't dare move from that chair while I fetch them.' He threw her a glance that sent her heart into overdrive. 'If I come back and find you gone, you'll become a wanted woman, and the entire constabulary of Liverpool will be dispatched to bring you in.'

10

The November sky was the colour of slate. It scowled through the windows of Mrs Hart's house where Ruby was in the kitchen making a list of O'Hagan guests for the forthcoming wedding. Beth was flying over from America, Martha and Fred Quinlan were coming, so were Connie and Charles. Greta and Heather had invited loads of friends from work, otherwise there'd only be six people on the brides' side of the church, including herself. Not that she cared. It wasn't her fault that she didn't have hordes of relatives.

The double wedding would take place on the Saturday before Christmas. Ruby was making a cake for Martha to ice. The Whites were paying for the flowers, the Donovans the cars, and the three families were sharing the cost of the reception. The wedding gowns were already in the hands of a dressmaker – Heather's regal white velvet, and Greta's determination to look like a fairy requiring dozens of yards of organdie and tulle.

Ruby was buying her own outfit, but couldn't decide on the colour. She changed her mind by the day. Pink was too light, brown too dark, red too bright, blue babyish, white or black out of the question. Purple had been her favourite for two whole days until Chris said it was the colour mourners wore to royal funerals.

'What about peach or apricot?' he suggested.

'Too fruity.'

'Green?'

'Unlucky.'

'There's no colours left. You've rejected the entire rainbow.'

'I'm considering burgundy or maroon.'

'Too miserable.'

'Grey?'

'Depressing.'

'You're a lot of help. I know, navy blue!'

'I'd feel as if I was with a woman copper.'

'I might not go,' Ruby said gloomily.

'That seems the only solution. I suggest that before our own wedding we join a nudist colony so we can get married with nothing on. All you'd have to worry about is the colour of your lipstick.'

Ruby stretched lazily and remembered she'd thrown a cushion at him. This last year, a kind fate had showered the O'Hagan women with the most generous of blessings, first the girls, then their mother.

She and Chris Ryan were in love. They had recognised this remarkable fact the first time they met. 'I love you,' Ruby whispered, as if he was in the room with her, able to hear, able to answer, say, 'I love you too.' Or maybe the precious message had carried across the miles and he *had* heard, sitting at his desk, or out on a case, or in that horrible bar where he went with his colleagues for a drink. She looked at her watch; almost noon. He could be anywhere.

The future stretched ahead, a glorious vision of endless days filled with happiness. As yet, they'd made no firm plans, apart from a wish to get married next summer. They hadn't decided where to buy a house, where to go on their honeymoon, should they have a big wedding or a small one?

'Small,' said Chris.

'Big,' said Ruby.

Once she was married and no longer a landlady, for the first time in her life she would be a lady of leisure, though knew she would quickly get bored. There'd be time to learn things, study, think about a career. Chris had suggested she become a teacher. One of his mates on the force had left and was now in a teachers' training college.

Ruby, who was inclined to think she could do anything on earth, thought it a marvellous idea, until she remembered aloud that she hadn't been very keen on looking after other people's children during the war.

'You'd be teaching them, not looking after them,' Chris pointed out. 'You might need qualifications before they'd let you in, but you can study for them at home.'

She promised to think about it. She also thought, though she didn't tell him, about the possibility of having more children of her own. For the umpteenth time she thought about it again, sitting at the kitchen table, making the guest list for her daughters' wedding. It would be different this time, having babies with a proper husband at her side, enough money to feed and clothe them, loads of Chris's relatives to provide support if she needed it. Ellie White and her family were delighted that Ruby and Chris were together.

The doorbell rang and the sound barely made an impression on Ruby's consciousness. She jumped when it rang again, and prayed it was Chris, who occasionally called if he was in the vicinity.

It wasn't Chris, but a strange woman in an expensive fur coat who was about to ring the bell again. 'I thought you weren't in,' she said in a quiet, cultured voice.

'Can I help you?' Ruby enquired. She looked too posh to be selling something.

'You're Ruby O'Hagan, aren't you? Oh, there's no need to ask, I recognised you months ago, the first time I saw you.'

Ruby searched her memory, but couldn't recall having seen the woman before and certainly not within the last few months. She looked in her sixties, with a small, tight, very ordinary face, greying hair. 'I'm sorry, have we met?'

'I suppose you could say we met briefly. My name's Olivia Appleby.' She swallowed nervously. 'I'm your mother.'

What did you say to a mother who'd dumped you in a convent when you were less than twenty-four hours old? Ruby had no idea. She showed Olivia Appleby into the living room, then went to make tea. In the kitchen, she tried to collect her thoughts, make sense of things while waiting for the kettle to boil. She took out the best china, set the tray with a lace cloth, put sugar in the little painted bowl and milk in the matching jug, polished the teaspoons on her skirt. When everything was ready, she took a deep breath, picked up the tray, and carried it into the next room.

'I suppose you don't know what to say,' remarked Olivia Appleby when she went in. She was sitting uncomfortably on the very edge of the settee, clutching her knees, as if she too found the situation difficult. The fur coat had been thrown on a chair and she wore a smart black suit underneath.

'How did you find me? How long have you known where I live?' Ruby asked. She was curiously empty inside, as if all emotion and feeling had drained from her body. She felt nothing for this well-spoken, well-dressed woman, neither love nor anger, but there was a vague sense of resentment that she'd turned up to disrupt her life after all this time.

'I've known about you for two months. Since then, I've been trying to pluck up the courage to come.' There was a slight tremor in her voice. 'I found you through, well it's a long story, but I'll tell you in as few words as possible.' She took a deep breath. 'When I was expecting you, I lived in Bristol with a woman called Madge Cookson. She was a midwife of sorts. You'd only been born a matter of hours when someone took you away.' A look of pain passed over her face. 'Madge swore she'd no idea where you'd gone.' She shrugged tiredly. 'We stayed in touch with the occasional letter, Christmas cards, that sort of thing. Earlier this year, in August, Madge died. When her son wrote to tell me, he enclosed a letter. On the envelope, Madge had written it was to be sent to me on her death. It said, the letter, that she'd promised never to tell where my baby had been taken, but didn't want to carry the secret to her grave and you'd gone to the Convent of the Sisters of the Sacred Cross in Abergele. She also said you'd kept your real name, Ruby O'Hagan.' She smiled wanly at Ruby. 'My first thought was truly horrible – I wished Madge hadn't lived until almost ninety, that she'd died years and years before, when you were still a child.'

'Who was the someone who took me away?'

'My father. He dragged you from my arms.' She cradled her arms and shivered violently. 'Do you mind if I smoke?'

'There's an ashtray around somewhere.' Ruby found one on the sideboard and put it beside the untouched tea. 'Have you been to the convent?'

'I went as soon as I read Madge's letter. It's no longer an orphanage, hasn't been for years.' She paused to light a cigarette, breathing in the smoke with an expression of relief, as if she'd been aching for a cigarette for ages. 'At first, I thought they'd refuse to give me the information I wanted, but the Mother Superior was young and very understanding. She couldn't see the harm after so many years. There was a mad search in the basement for files, and the long and short of it is I learnt you'd gone to live in Liverpool with an Emily Dangerfield.'

'Emily left, years ago.' Ruby felt as if she was listening to the story of some other child's life, not her own.

'I found that out straight away. I then resorted to the telephone directory, though I thought it unlikely you'd be in. You'd have married, I reasoned. But say you'd had a son? He'd be an O'Hagan. All I had to do was ask his mother's name. I found an R. O'Hagan at this address and drove here straight away, stopped the car outside.' She stubbed the cigarette out and immediately lit another. 'I saw you at an upstairs window. You're so like your father, I wanted to cry. I went away and cried somewhere else, then I drove home. That was September. Since then, I've been trying to pluck up the nerve to come back.'

Ruby knew there were dozens of questions she should ask, but couldn't think of a single one.

'I'm surprised you never married,' commented the woman who claimed to be her mother.

'I did. His name was Jacob and he was killed in the war. I kept my own name. It would take too long to explain why.' She didn't want to. All she wanted was for the woman to go away and never come back because it was disquieting to discover she had a mother when she'd managed quite well without one for thirty-eight years.

'I'm so sorry about your husband. Have you any children?'

'Two girls; Greta and Heather. They're getting married in December. It's a double wedding.'

'I suppose you're up to your eyes. I remember when my own daughter ...' She broke off, embarrassed. 'I meant, my *other* daughter. Oh!' she cried. 'I don't suppose there's any chance of us becoming friends? It's been too long.'

'I reckon so,' Ruby said slowly and felt ashamed when she saw the look of anguish on Olivia Appleby's pale, unhappy face.

'Perhaps I should go. I'm sure you're very busy and I'm probably holding you up.' She reached for her coat.

'Please, don't.' If she left, Ruby would kick herself later for not asking things she'd always been curious to know. It would also be very cruel. This woman had clearly grieved for her lost child far more than the child had grieved for its mother. She tried to imagine how she would have felt if one of her daughters had been torn from her arms when only a few hours old and she'd never seen her again, but it was impossible. 'Tell me about my father?' she said trying to make her voice sound warm and friendly.

The woman smiled properly for the first time, a sweet, almost childish smile. Her eyes lit up. 'His name was Thomas Gerald O'Hagan. We met in France towards the end of the First World War. I was a nurse, he was my patient.'

'Did he know about me?'

'No, he died before I knew I was pregnant. He was an American, born in Boston.'

'An American!'

'His father had a bookshop where Tom worked. We were going to get married after the war.' Her head drooped. 'He was my one and only love. I never fell in love again. I married Henry Appleby for companionship. He was a widower, much older than me. I never told him about you. I was only forty when he died.' She twisted the wedding ring on her finger. 'It was a good marriage. We were content with each other. We had three children – a daughter and two sons, all married now, leading their own lives, and providing me with grandchildren. I have eight,' she said with a touch of pride.

'Ten.'

She flushed. 'Ten, counting yours.' She leant forward and looked at Ruby anxiously. 'Tell me, have you been happy? I've thought of you constantly over the years; on your birthday, or whenever I saw a girl your age. Madge told me this would happen. I'd wonder what you were doing, where you were living, but most of all I longed to know if you were happy.'

'I've been happy most of the time.'

'I'm glad. Now, I really must be going. I've intruded long enough. All this must have come as a terrible shock.' She was putting on her coat, lighting another cigarette. 'You need time to think, get used to the idea of your mother appearing out of the blue. Perhaps we could meet again sometime. I'm sure we have loads of things to say to each other.'

'Perhaps we could,' Ruby said politely.

Olivia Appleby winced. 'I'll leave you my card. I'd love to have a photo of your daughters' wedding.' Her lips twisted wryly. 'My *grand*daughters' wedding. Oh, and I brought you something. I nearly forgot.' She fished in her bag and brought out a little velvet box. 'This is the ring that Tom, your father, gave me. It belonged to his "grandpop" – that's how he put it. It's engraved, "Ruby to Eamon, 1857". It's exactly one hundred years since Ruby and Eamon got married. Now you know where your name came from.'

'Thank you,' said Ruby.

They went towards the door, shook hands. Olivia Appleby was walking down the path towards a large, gleaming car Ruby hadn't noticed before. She opened the gate, turned and waved. There was something terribly sad about her bent shoulders, her wan face.

This woman was her *mother*! Yet she'd treated her like a stranger. She wouldn't have expected Ruby to fall into her arms, shower her with kisses, but she must have hoped for something more than the cold welcome she'd been given, some enthusiasm towards the idea of them meeting again.

She must be bitterly disappointed. How far did she have to drive, feeling as as she did? Ruby glanced at the card – Bath. She hadn't asked all sorts of things, important things, about her father, Olivia herself.

Ruby wanted to run down the path, persuade her mother to come back, ask the questions now. But she couldn't. There was still a feeling of faint resentment that she'd come at all.

Olivia had reached the car, opened the door, was about to get in.

'Just a minute,' Ruby shouted.

The wan face brightened hopefully. 'Yes, dear?'

'Why don't you come to the wedding? It's the third of December, a Saturday.'

'I'd love to.'

'I'll send an invitation to the address on the card.'

Her mother got in the car, smiling and nodding. 'Thank you very much.' She closed the door and drove away.

'You're very quiet,' Chris said that night. Larry and Rob had taken the girls out in the Volkswagen and they had the house to themselves, not counting the lodgers upstairs.

'I'm thinking.'

'Could you think aloud? It's more sociable.'

'Sorry.' She wrinkled her nose apologetically. For some reason, she couldn't bring herself to tell him about her mother's visit. Later, after he'd gone, she'd write to Beth, with whom she'd always shared the closest of her secrets.

'I hope you're not still cogitating on what colour frock to wear for the wedding?'

'No.' She laughed. 'I've decided I don't care. Any colour will do apart from khaki. Fuchsia would be nice.' She'd always been drawn to bright colours.

'You'd look lovely in khaki, but even lovelier in fuchsia.' They were on the settee in each other's arms. He traced the outline of her face with his finger. 'You've got a very determined chin.'

'You've got holy eyes. You'd have made a good priest. The women parishioners would have fallen madly in love with you.'

'I doubt if having holy eyes will advance my career in the police force,' he said drily.

'I've never got anywhere with my determined chin.'

He kissed her. 'There's plenty of time. Until then, could you point your chin in the direction of the bedroom and we can continue this conversation there? Better still, *dis*continue it and concentrate on other things.'

Two hours later, a blissfully exhausted Ruby and Chris were in the kitchen innocently drinking tea when the young people arrived home – it probably never crossed their minds they did anything else.

The day was bitterly cold. Tiny flakes of ice were being whipped to and fro in the bone-chilling wind, confetti for a winter wedding.

Heather's short veil was flung into a halo around her regal head, while Greta had to cling on to her longer one for fear she'd take off, be blown away, as it spread around her like two great, lacy wings.

There'd been a gasp from the watching crowd when Ruby's girls came out of the church. They had never looked so beautiful, and probably never would again, Ruby thought with tears in her eyes. Memories chased each other through her brain; Greta's first words, Heather's first determined, stumbling steps, playing with Jake in the garden of Mrs Hart's house, starting school.

But now her girls were married women. They belonged to someone else, two very nice young men whom Ruby felt convinced would make them happy. Their mother was no longer the most important person in their lives.

'Sad?' whispered Chris who was standing behind her while the photographer took pictures.

Ruby nodded and he slipped his arm around her waist and squeezed. 'It's only natural to feel sad, but I'll cheer you up tonight, I promise.'

'Not tonight. Beth's staying.'

'And you'd prefer me out the way!'

'If you don't mind. Only tonight. She's staying a week, but you can come tomorrow. Get to know her.'

'I mind so much, I'm busting a gut, but I'll just have to put up with it.' He grinned. He was the most understanding man she'd ever known and she was the luckiest woman in the world. There wasn't a single reason to be sad.

'Who's the lady in the mink?' Chris asked.

'Olivia Appleby, a friend from long ago.' She hadn't known the coat was mink until Martha Quinlan had remarked on the fact.

Her mother had asked for their relationship to be kept to themselves. 'I hope you don't mind,' she'd said over the phone, 'but I'm not up to the questions, the explanations, the accusing looks. Perhaps later . . .'

'I'll introduce you as Olivia Appleby and say you're a friend.' It was the way Ruby preferred. She wasn't up to facing people's reactions, either. Even the girls didn't know their grandmother was at the wedding. Only Beth knew the truth.

Beth! She looked across at her friend who was standing with Connie and Charles. She'd lost weight and her lovely hair had been brutally shorn to tight little curls close to her scalp, reminding Ruby of a convict. Above the exaggerated cheekbones in the once plump face, her eyes held an expression that a convict might; desperate, lonely. She was wearing a lovely mohair coat with fur trimming and suede boots. Beth clearly wasn't short of money, but she was short of other, more important things. It was obvious from her eyes.

The photographer had almost finished and some of the shivering guests had begun to pile into cars to drive to the hall where the reception was being held. Ruby and Chris were being taken in an official car. Charles had offered to take the Quinlans, her mother was bringing Beth.

Ruby made sure everyone was being looked after before getting in the car herself.

'Gee, Rube! I had a great time.' It was almost midnight when Beth threw herself into an armchair with an exhausted sigh. She already had a touch of an American accent.

Ruby collapsed wearily on to the settee. She'd danced herself silly and had kissed more people than she'd done in her entire life. It had been an enjoyable day, but highly emotional.

'I can't remember when I last enjoyed meself so much,' Beth said, 'though for all the expense, it wasn't as good as Connie and Charles's wedding all those years ago.'

'Martha said the same – and Connie and Charles.'

'That day will stand out in me mind for ever.' She looked curiously at her friend. 'I've often wondered why you got so ratty with me when it was over.'

Ruby made a face. 'Because Jim Quinlan asked you out.'

'You were keen on him?'

'Excessively keen. I can't think why. It was never reciprocated.'

'You've never mentioned that before.' Beth looked surprised. 'We usually told each other everything.' She unzipped her boots, threw them off, and tucked her legs beneath her. 'Have you got any wine? I feel pleasantly drunk and I don't want it to wear off.'

'I got some specially for my American guest. Red or white?'

'Either.'

When Ruby returned with the wine, she said, 'I didn't tell you about Jim because I was too embarrassed. I loved him, at least I had a crush on him, but he was only vaguely aware of my existence. Then he damn well went and asked you for a date. I was livid, I can tell you.'

'There's no need to tell me. I remember very well.'

'I'm sorry,' Ruby said penitently.

'How is Jim these days? I thought he might have come to the wedding.'

'He has the Malt House to look after, doesn't he? He's never been the same since the war. According to Martha, it knocked the stuffing out of him. His wife doesn't help. Martha claims she has affairs.'

'Poor Jim!' Beth sighed. 'Why is it some people lead incredibly happy lives and others are dead miserable?'

'If I knew that, Beth, I'd write a book about it and make a fortune. I suppose for most people it's a bit of both.'

Beth gave a short laugh. 'That more or less describes me, but leaning heavily towards the dead miserable.'

'Oh, Beth! What's wrong?' It didn't seem fair. Beth was so nice - and so was Jim. Yet she, Ruby, was deliriously happy and wasn't nice at all.

'Can I have more wine?'

'Help yourself – here, take the bottle. But promise not to get plastered.'

'I'm not making promises I might not keep.' She sighed again. 'It's Daniel, it's my kids, it's everything, Rube.'

'Is Jake all right?'

'Sort of. He's at university in New York, I think I told you. I insisted he went there. Daniel was annoyed, but black people can lead relatively normal lives in New York, not like in Little Rock. I shall try to persuade Jake to stay when he finishes the course, though I'll miss him dreadfully. He's the one person who keeps me sane.'

'I never think of Jake – or you – as black.'

'Well, we are,' Beth said flatly. 'Daniel and his friends fight against prejudice all the time. They sit in the white section of buses and wait to get thrown off or barge into hotels or restaurants, knowing they'll be chucked out, often brutally. No one cares that Daniel's a top-class lawyer, only that he's black. He's forever coming home with his head split open, covered in blood.'

'I suppose you could say that was admirable, Beth,' Ruby said cautiously. It was the sort of thing she hoped she would do herself.

'It is, it's just that he wants me to go with him, other women do. He considers I'm letting him down, which I suppose I am.' She looked appealingly at Ruby, her lovely velvet eyes moist. 'But I hate violence. I can't stand seeing the hate in people's eyes, their faces all contorted. I'd sooner hide in the house, send Rebecca – she's our housekeeper – to do the shopping. Daniel and his friends are contemptuous of me. They think I'm a coward – I freely admit that I am.'

'What about the other children?' She'd had two girls and another boy.

'I hardly feel they're mine.' Her voice was desolate. 'Daniel's mother sets them against me – she's never liked me much. I'm the wrong colour, the wrong wife for her son, the wrong mother for her grandchildren. She brought her children up to fight and she considers me weak and spineless. My way of dealing with prejudice would be to move to a place where people are more tolerant, where there's no need to fight. Poor Jake is thoroughly confused. He doesn't know whose side to be on.'

'I don't know what to say, Beth.' It was far worse than she'd thought.

'What *is* there to say, Rube?' She shrugged helplessly. 'Sometimes, I wish it was just me and Jake again.' She smiled. 'Except it never was just us, was it? It was you and your girls as well – and dear old Arthur for a while.'

Beth was sleeping in the girls' room. Next morning, just after nine, Ruby went in with two cups of tea. Beth was already awake. She sat up and stretched her arms.

'I slept like a log. This bed's lovely and soft.'

'That's Greta's. Heather prefers a hard mattress.'

'She would!' Beth laughed. 'What a little madam she was! Always bossing Jake around.'

'Not to mention Greta, but she's improved since she met Rob.'

'Good old Rob. Give us that tea, Rube. I'm desperate. Me mouth feels like a sewer.'

'You drank too much wine.' Ruby sat on the bed. 'Though you look better this morning.'

Beth rolled her eyes. 'Are you suggesting I looked awful yesterday?'

'No, but your face is less drawn. Actually, Beth,' Ruby said gratefully, 'I'm glad you're here. The house would have felt peculiar without the girls, knowing they'll never live here again.' There hadn't been time to tidy the room since her daughters had got ready for their wedding. Nighties had been flung over a chair, the dressing table was littered with make-up, face powder had been spilt, the top left off a bottle of June. Ruby put her tea on the floor and went to screw it back on. Heather must have been too excited to be her usual neat and tidy self.

'If I wasn't here, I'm sure you'd have had other company,' Beth glanced at her slyly. 'Chris Ryan, for instance.'

'He's never stayed the night.'

'I'm sure he'd jump at the chance if it was offered. Unless you're worried about your reputation?'

Ruby laughed. 'Since when have I cared about my reputation?'

'What if your lodgers found out and were so shocked they left?' It was a relief to see Beth's eyes dance.

'The men wouldn't. Mrs Mulligan might complain, but if she left I'd be glad to see the back of her. Mind you, she gave the girls a lovely tablecloth each for a wedding present, white damask.' She loathed white tablecloths herself, finding it impossible to get the stains out. Dark, check patterned cloths were best – the stains could hardly be seen.

'Where's Tiger? I haven't seen him since I came.'

'He spends most of his time in the cellar. Remember that wardrobe he hid in during the raids? He just comes up for food now and then, has a weary stroll around the garden, then it's back to the cellar.'

'I'll go down and say "hello" later. I've never liked cats, apart from Tiger. What are we going to do today?' she enquired.

'After Mass – do you still go to Mass?'

'Of course!'

'If we get well wrapped up, after Mass, we could go for a walk in the park, then come back for something to eat. I don't feed the lodgers on Sundays, it's my day off, so we'll have the place to ourselves. We're going to the Quinlans for tea, and tonight Chris is coming.'

'I'll feel like a gooseberry.'

'As long as you don't *look* like a gooseberry, it doesn't matter.'

The week flew by. They went to the pictures, to dinner, wandered around the shops that were decorated for Christmas. Beth bought presents to take back home. Sometimes Chris came with them, but Ruby didn't let on that it was better when he didn't. Beth looked upon the years they'd spent in the house by Princes Park as a golden time when everything was perfect. She talked about little else; 'Remember this, Rube. Remember that.' Ruby had never been inclined to look back, particularly not now that the future seemed so sweet, but she willingly indulged her friend, laughed with her, remembered this and that, held her hand when she cried. She felt more comfortable if Chris wasn't there during these nostalgic reminders of a period long before they'd met.

One afternoon, they walked to the house in Toxteth where Beth used to live. The woman who answered the door was young and had a baby in her arms. She had no idea who'd lived there before, and when Beth asked at the shop on the corner they knew nothing about a red-haired Irishwoman who'd been married to a tall man from Jamaica.

'Well, I suppose that's that,' Beth sighed. 'It would have been nice to see them. Now I'll never know where they are.'

On Friday, Beth's last night, Ruby fed her lodgers early, and Connie, Charles, and Martha Quinlan came to dinner. Chris was on duty, or so he claimed. Ruby wondered if he was just being tactful. He would say goodbye to Beth next morning at Lime Street station where she would catch the London train.

'It's a pity you've come all this way and can only stay a week,' Martha said to Beth. 'And the girls are coming home tomorrow. You've seen hardly anything of them.'

'I'd have preferred to stay longer, but it's Christmas soon and I've loads of things to do.' Beth looked wistful.

'Perhaps next time you could come and stay a whole month.'

'But don't leave it another twelve years until you do,' Connie put in.

'Hear, hear,' echoed Charles. 'And bring Jake with you. We'd love to see him.'

'He'd love to see you.' There were tears in Beth's eyes. She'd cried too much that week.

She cried again when everyone had gone, sobbed uncontrollably because she didn't want to go back to Little Rock. 'I'd forgotten what it was like to feel happy. I almost wish I hadn't come and been reminded.'

Next morning, she managed to remain dry-eyed when Ruby and Chris saw her on to the London train. She was flying home from Heathrow.

Ruby hugged her fiercely. 'Come to *our* wedding,' she urged. 'We haven't fixed a date yet, but it'll be some time next summer.'

'I'll try.'

The train chugged out of the station and they waved to each other until it turned a bend and Beth disappeared.

'I've had an idea where we should go for our honeymoon,' Chris said, putting his arm around a dejected Ruby's shoulders.

'Where?' she sniffed.

'If Beth doesn't come to us, then we could go to her. How about spending our honeymoon in the States, New York? We could fly down to Little Rock for the weekend.'

'Oh!' Ruby flung her arms around his neck. 'You are truly the most wonderful man in the world. Whatever did I do to deserve you?'

Everyone had been surprised when the two young couples had decided to honeymoon separately; Greta and Larry had gone to London, Heather and Rob to Devon. Though perhaps it wasn't all that surprising considering they intended to live together while they saved up a deposit for a house.

'One house or two?' Ruby had wanted to know.

'Don't be silly, mam,' Greta laughed. 'Two, of course.'

'Though we'll live close by so we can see each other every day and take our babies for walks,' Heather announced.

'Babies!' Ruby shrieked. 'Oh, my God! I might soon be a grandmother.'

To her chagrin, Greta had asked Matthew Doyle if he had a place to let. Ruby couldn't understand why he was always so obliging with her family – the girls had been given a beautiful dinner service each as a wedding present. He'd let them have a self-contained, furnished flat comprising the top half of a narrow, four-storied house in the Dingle not far from where Foster Court, now demolished, used to be.

Greta and Heather had had a wonderful time getting the flat ready to live in. They were like children with a doll's house. The rickety furniture was polished, the windows cleaned till they sparkled, pictures and new curtains put up. They would come home from work and excitedly show their mother the flowered teatowels they'd bought in their dinner hour, the various kitchen utensils. Even the purchase of half a dozen pink toilet rolls seemed to give them an inordinate amount of pleasure.

Now Beth had gone and Ruby's girls were expected home any minute to start their lives as married women.

Another era had ended. Another was about to begin.

11

Greta Donovan couldn't remember a time when she hadn't been happy, but she'd never thought it possible to be as happy as she was now. Life couldn't possibly be more perfect. Although Heather hadn't said anything, every now and then they would look at each other and smile, and Greta would just *know* she felt the same. There was something about Heather's face – and no doubt her own – a sort of glow, as if she was bubbling over inside, wanting to say things that couldn't be said because words hadn't been invented to describe how they felt.

Since she had become a married woman, Greta was convinced she'd grown taller, looked older, become a more responsible person. During the dinner break, she went with her sister to St John's Market and bought food for their tea. Back at work, she would earnestly discuss what they were having that night with the other married women, who would in turn tell her what they had planned. It was far more interesting than talking about clothes, not that she'd lost *all* interest in clothes.

Larry and Rob always went to a football match on Saturday. If it was an away game, they went in the Volkswagen or on the train if it was very far. The girls took the opportunity to clean the flat from top to bottom, polishing everywhere, changing the beds, and doing the washing. Mam said it was daft, they were doing work for work's sake, the bedding only needed to be changed every fortnight, and the furniture merely needed dusting, and then only if the dust could actually be seen. What Mam didn't realise, was her daughters *enjoyed* doing these things. Nowadays, Greta preferred the smell of polish to June.

What they liked most of all was cooking. There wasn't time to make anything lavish on weekdays, but the menu was varied so they didn't have the same meal twice in a week. Greta had discovered she was good at making omelettes which she usually served with sautéed potatoes and salad. Heather could make wonderful puddings, especially trifle, though they only had trifle on Sundays after an ambitious main course of something like Chicken Marengo or Pork and Apple Casserole from Mam's cookery book which she'd never used, preferring to stick to meals she'd learnt to make at the convent. The book had been given her by one of the lodgers, probably as a hint.

Often, Larry or Rob's parents would join them, or Mam and Chris. There wasn't room at the table for more then six people and even then it was a squeeze. Anyroad, they only had five chairs and a stool.

Sundays, Larry and Rob helped prepare the meal in the diminutive kitchen and washed up afterwards – they were the best husbands the world had ever known. Once a month, they all went out to dinner, but not anywhere expensive because they were saving up for a house.

With four wages coming in and such a tiny amount needed in rent – Matthew Doyle had let them have the flat surprisingly cheap – both couples had almost enough for deposits. The boys had already had money saved, not for any particular reason other than there didn't seem much to spend it on. The girls found this amazing, having saved nothing at all, and knowing they still wouldn't have saved a penny if their wages had been two or three times as much. There'd always seemed far too many essential things, like clothes, to spend money on.

Marriage, however, had brought them down to earth. Since the wedding, neither Greta nor Heather had bought a single item of clothing and hardly any make-up. They were very careful with the food, though Larry had asked with an amused grin if they really needed three different sorts of pepper.

Matthew Doyle had informed them when he came to collect the rent that there was a new estate of semi-detached houses planned in Childwall that would cost two thousand pounds which meant they'd only have to put down two hundred.

'What!' Mam had screamed when she was told.

'Two hundred pounds, Mam. That's all.'

'I'm not on about the deposit. Are you saying he collects *your* rent as well? What's the matter with the man? He's got hundreds of people working for him, yet he still goes round marking rent books.'

Matthew had arranged for them to be sent a brochure which showed a plan of the estate which was shaped like a letter U with a smaller U inside.

The following Sunday, after breakfast, they went in the car to look at the site, which was ideal; an old playing field, not far from a row of useful shops.

'Those houses would be best,' opined Mrs White, Rob's mother, when she and her husband came that afternoon. She pointed on the plan to the larger U. 'They're less overlooked, well away from the main road, and they've got bigger gardens. The ones on the curve have the biggest.'

'You and Larry can live on one curve, and me and Rob on the other,' Heather said excitedly. 'We can wave to each other in the morning and before we go to bed.'

'I suggest you put down a deposit immediately before they're snapped up,' Mr White put in. 'We'll let you have a loan if you haven't enough.'

Larry's mam and dad had also offered to lend them money and so had

Mam. People were being incredibly nice. Greta took the plans into work to show everybody and they were very nice as well. She was given the name of a good conveyancing solicitor and that of a man who fitted carpets on the cheap.

Greta lay in bed one Sunday morning studying the back of Larry's head. It was almost three months since they were married and Sunday was the best day of all. She felt even more exquisitely happy than usual. They would be in each other's company until it was time for Larry to leave for work tomorrow.

She always found the back of his head particularly endearing and longed to reach out and touch the short hairs on the nape of his boyish neck, kiss his right ear, the only one visible, which was a lovely, rosy pink. But the alarm clock showed only five past seven and she didn't want to wake him yet. He worked hard and needed his sleep. At eight o'clock, she'd sneak out and make a cup of tea. After they'd drunk it, they'd make love which was quite seriously the very, very best part of being married.

Until then, Greta was quite satisfied to lie in bed, look at Larry's head, think about the new house and what colours to choose for the walls and, most importantly of all, the tiny baby that was resting securely in her tummy. Only Larry knew about the baby – it felt awfully odd, almost daring, discussing your periods with a *man*. She was waiting to see the doctor until three had been missed which she would know by next Wednesday. It was just possible that their house might be finished before the baby arrived and things would work out ideally which, in Greta's short experience of life, things usually did.

Her thoughts were so enjoyable that by the time she looked at the clock again it was almost eight. She got up as quietly as she could and tiptoed downstairs to the kitchen. Heather was already there, about to put the kettle on. She looked flushed and starry-eyed and Greta suspected she and Rob had already made love, though didn't say anything. Sex with their husbands was the only subject the girls never discussed.

'Shall we go to ten o'clock Mass?' Heather enquired, a silly question in a way because they always did.

'I think so.' It would give all of them another hour and a half in bed. They didn't have breakfast until they came home from church, a *real* breakfast for a change; bacon, eggs, sausages and fried bread.

Heather said in a small voice, 'We haven't been to Holy Communion since we got married.'

'I know.' It was embarrassing to swallow the body of Christ after an hour or more of enthusiastic lovemaking. Perhaps Heather, like Greta, had a feeling God wouldn't have approved. 'Perhaps next week,' Greta said vaguely.

'Yes, perhaps,' Heather answered, just as vaguely.

It was Mam and Chris's turn to come to dinner; curried beef and rice followed by a meringue gâteau. Chris had brought a bottle of red wine. Greta was thrilled to bits that Mam had clicked with Rob's uncle and they would stay one big happy family.

The food went down extremely well, though Greta had a touch of indigestion afterwards which was probably due to the baby and she didn't mind a bit. The men, Chris included, went into the kitchen to wash up.

'I have a feeling,' Ruby said to Greta, almost slyly, 'that you've got news for us.'

'No, I haven't.' She'd noticed Mam had been staring at her intently throughout the meal.

'Are you sure?'

Greta felt her cheeks grow extremely hot and knew she was blushing. 'How did you guess?' she stammered.

'From your face, love. You look like the cat that ate the cream. Am I right?'

'I haven't the faintest idea what you're both talking about,' Heather complained.

'I'm expecting a baby,' Greta whispered.

'There! I knew it,' Ruby said triumphantly. 'When?'

'About the end of September, I reckon, but I haven't seen the doctor yet.'

'How long have you known?' her sister demanded angrily.

'Two months.'

'And you didn't tell me! Does Larry know?'

'Of course.'

'That's not fair!'

'Don't be silly, Heather.' Ruby looked annoyed. 'Larry's her husband.'

'*I'm* her sister. I wanted us to have our babies at the same time. Now I'm way behind.'

'It's not a race, luv. Oh!' Ruby groaned. 'I've got a horrible feeling I've put my foot in it.'

'It had sorted itself out by the time we left,' Ruby said in the car on the way home. 'Rob and Larry knew nothing about their little tiff. I think Heather regards them as a foursome, not two separate couples. She expects Greta to be as close to her as she is to Larry. Greta, strangely enough, has always been more independent. But me and my big mouth! I really set the cat amongst the pigeons.'

'I happen to love your big mouth,' Chris replied. 'Anyway, there'd have been an upset whenever Heather found out.'

'I suppose.' Ruby sighed. 'You know, I always feel uneasy when I've been to see them.'

Chris looked at her in surprise. 'Why? I've rarely known such a happy atmosphere. They obviously adore each other. It seems to me the two nicest young women in the world have found the two nicest young men. Honestly, darling, most parents worry if their children are miserable, not the other way round.'

'It's unreal,' Ruby said slowly. 'It's *too* happy, like a fairy-tale, or that film, *The Enchanted Cottage*. I keep feeling that somethings's going to spoil it, that it can't last.'

'Of course, it can't last. Eventually, they'll calm down, get used to being married, get on one another's nerves, lose their tempers, go running to their mam for a moan. But it doesn't mean they'll love each other any less.'

'You wouldn't think you were a bachelor. You sound as if you've had half a dozen wives. Does it mean we'll go like that?'

'No, not us.' He grinned. 'We'll prove the exception to the rule.'

It was April and about time she told Matthew Doyle and the lodgers that she would be abandoning the house by Princes Park at the end of July – she and Chris were getting married on 3 August, his fortieth birthday. 'I'll be getting the best present a man could ever have,' he said jubilantly. 'You!'

Ruby knew she was being unfair. The lodgers needed plenty of notice to find somewhere else to live and, for all his faults, Matthew Doyle had been a good landlord.

Yet she couldn't bring herself to say a word and was glad when Matthew broached the subject himself next time he came. He knew she was getting married, Greta had told him.

'Will your new husband mind sharing you with the lodgers?' he enquired. He was lounging in a kitchen chair, long legs stretched out, finishing in a pair of gleaming handmade shoes. As always, he wore an expensive suit, white shirt, silk tie.

'He won't be sharing me with anybody. We're buying a house.'

'Where?'

Ruby shrugged. 'I don't know yet. We've looked at a few places.'

'When did you intend telling me you were leaving?'

'I meant to,' she said uncomfortably, 'but kept putting it off.'

He looked at her sideways. 'Why?'

'I don't know.' She did, though. It was because she had the strangest feeling she was burning her bridges behind her, which she knew was ridiculous because nothing could possibly go wrong. 'I'm sorry,' she said. 'I'll be leaving at the end of July. I'll tell them upstairs tonight.'

'In that case, I'll apply for planning permission and have this place torn down.'

Everton were playing Arsenal in London. It was the last away match of the season. When Greta and Heather arrived home from work early on Saturday afternoon, the Volkswagen had gone from the place where it was usually parked outside the flat.

'I thought they were catching the train?' Heather remarked.

'They must have changed their minds, probably because the weather's cleared up.' It had poured with rain all night, but the sun had come out on their way to work. 'Shall we have a little snack before we start on the cleaning? Beans on toast, or something. I'm starving.'

'That's because you're eating for two,' Heather said stiffly. It was still a sore point that Greta hadn't confided in her the minute she'd found herself pregnant. It was for this reason, because she'd been so deeply hurt, that she hadn't told her sister she might possibly be pregnant too. She was only a week late, but was normally as regular as clockwork.

'I'll need maternity clothes soon.' Greta gave a little shudder of delight as they went upstairs. 'Shall we look for some next week in the dinner hour?'

'If you like.' Heather's voice was still stiff, but the idea of wandering around the maternity departments of the big shops was so appealing, that she added warmly, 'I'd *love* to!'

They smiled at each other.

As soon as they entered the flat, Heather put the kettle on and Greta switched on the wireless. She turned the knob, hoping to find something nice to listen to and stopped when she came to a woman singing, 'You'll Never Walk Alone', from *Carousel*, the best picture she'd ever seen.

'Listen!' she shouted.

'I can hear.' They sang along with the wireless while they prepared the beans on toast.

Ruby was humming along to the same music while she ironed the lodgers' sheets. She never ironed her own sheets and resented doing it for other people. But the beautiful words of the song were so uplifting, they made her feel quite cheerful. 'Only another couple of months,' she thought, 'and I'll never have to iron another sheet again.'

In a house in Orrell Park, Moira Donovan was searching through her friend's knitting patterns for a matinée jacket. The wireless was on in the background and the sun shone cheerily through the window.

'This looks nice,' she said, pulling a pattern out. 'I think I could manage that. It's a relatively simple stitch.'

'I'll do the lacy borders for you.' Ellie White offered. She was an expert knitter.

'Ta. I wonder if Greta will have a boy or a girl?' Moira mused.

'What does your Larry have to say?'

Moira laughed. 'Whatever Greta has will suit Larry. As long as it's healthy, he doesn't care, same as me.'

'I hope our Rob puts Heather in the club soon. We've always done things together. I'd like us to become grandmothers at the same time.'

'We're ever so lucky with our sons and their wives, Ellie,' Moira said soberly.

'I know. We're lucky all round. Oh, there's that song! What's the name of the picture it's from?'

'*Carousel.* The lads took the girls to see it not long after they met. Ever since, Larry's always sung it in the bath – if you could call it singing. It's more like a bellow.'

'You'll never walk alone,' Ellie began to sing.

Moira joined in.

The phone call came just after six o'clock. Ruby had several things on her mind. What to wear that night when she went out with Chris? Was she prepared to live in the north side of Liverpool when all she knew was the south? Had she made enough food for the evening meal now that Mr Oliver had turned up when he'd said he'd be away?

She went into the hall. The telephone was on a table with a wooden box beside it for anybody who wasn't an O'Hagan to put in the money if they made a call. They usually did. She picked up the receiver and briskly reeled off the number.

'Ruby. It's Albert White.' Albert was Rob's father.

'Oh, hello, Albert. How are you?'

'I've some terrible news, girl. Are you sitting down?'

There was nowhere to sit. A chair only encouraged longer calls. 'What's wrong, Albert?' Perhaps the house purchase had fallen through, which would be a shame. She hadn't the faintest intimation how earth-shattering the news would be.

'It's the lads, Ruby. I don't quite know how to say this, but there's been an accident . . .'

It had been raining in London by the time the match finished. The lads were on their way home when a lorry skidded on the wet surface and rammed straight into the Volkswagen. Larry and Rob had been killed instantly. The police had telephoned their colleagues in Liverpool who'd gone to tell the Whites because Rob, who'd been driving, still had his parents' address on his licence.

'Do my girls know?' Ruby screamed. There wasn't a phone in the flat.

'Not yet. Moira and Ellie have just set off in a taxi to tell them.' His gruff voice broke. 'Ruby, girl, I don't know how we're going to live with this.'

'I'm going to see my girls straight away.'

'Chris is on his way to collect you. Don't go by yourself, Ruby. Wait for Chris.'

She slammed down the phone. She had no intention of waiting for Chris or anyone. If she ran, she could be with her girls in ten minutes, maybe less.

'Mrs O'Hagan!' Iris Mulligan appeared on the stairs. 'Do you have to leave the kitchen door open when you've got the wireless on so loud? I was trying to take forty winks.'

'Oh, shut up,' Ruby said brutally.

'I beg your pardon?'

'Shut up your moaning.' She snatched a coat off the rail in the hall. It was an old one of Heather's, but she didn't notice.

'Is something wrong, Mrs O'Hagan?'

Ruby didn't answer. She opened the door and ran.

She actually lost her way in the streets that were as familiar to her as the back of her hand. By the time she reached the flat she had a stitch in her side and could hardly breathe. Moira Donovan and Ellie White were getting out of a taxi. Both were weeping and supported each other towards the door. They'd lost their sons and Rob had been an only child, but right then Ruby cared only for her girls.

The door was opened by Heather who was wiping her floury hands on a frilly apron. The sweet smell of baking wafted out.

'Hello!' She smiled, but the smile faded when she saw the expressions on the faces of the three women. 'What's wrong?'

'Oh, love!' Ruby fell upon her daughter, pressed her to her breast.

Greta appeared. 'What's the matter, Mam?'

'*Greta!* Come here.' Ruby reached with one arm for her other daughter and for the briefest of moments, they clung together until Greta broke away.

'Oh, Mam!' she wailed hysterically. 'It's Larry, isn't it? And Rob? They're not coming back. Oh, Mam!'

Her girls were beyond help. Nothing could console them. They cried in their mother's arms, in each other's. Rob and Larry's fathers arrived, but for the mother and her daughters, the other people in the room didn't exist.

Someone, a man, tried to embrace Ruby, comfort her, but she pushed him away.

Someone else made tea, sympathetic words were murmured, a doctor came and left sleeping tablets, it was the only thing he could do.

Then everybody went, leaving Ruby with her girls. There seemed no point in staying and they had their own grieving to do.

A week later, early one May morning, the two young men, the best of friends throughout their short lives, were buried together. It was the prettiest of days, sunny and warm. A slight, white mist drifted over the cemetery, but had cleared by the time the nightmare proceedings were over. Greta and Heather could hardly stand and there were no refreshments afterwards because it would only have prolonged the agony.

'Would you like me to come back with you?' Chris asked Ruby.

'No, thanks,' she answered politely. 'I'm not in the mood.'

He looked at her sadly. 'I see.'

Days passed, weeks, a month. Ruby stayed most of the time in the flat with the girls, tending to them, making sure they ate. Both were expectant mothers and needed their food. She had no idea what was happening with the lodgers and didn't care.

'You know what I'd like?' Heather said one day.

'What, love?'

'To go back and live in our old room.' Heather glanced around the dark, drab, little living room that had never seemed dark or drab before. 'I don't want to stay here anymore. Everything about it reminds me of Rob. It's not that I don't want to be reminded,' she went on, 'but this was our special place, where me and Rob belonged. It doesn't seem right to live here now that he's gone.'

'What about you, Greta?'

'I feel the same.'

'Then let's pack your things and go.'

Ruby felt in a muddle. In six weeks' time she was supposed to be marrying Chris. They'd intended buying a house. But she couldn't possibly leave her girls and this wasn't the time to be planning a wedding. Perhaps in the New Year, February or March, by which time the girls would have had their babies and everyone's grief mightn't feel so raw.

It was then she remembered Matthew Doyle had been informed she was leaving at the end of July and the lodgers told to find somewhere else.

The muddle needed to be sorted out. The first person to contact was Chris. Now she thought about it, she was surprised he hadn't been in touch before.

She rang the station and was told it was his day off, so called him at home. His voice was courteous, but lacked its usual warmth. She knew she'd been neglecting him, but surely he hadn't taken offence considering the tragic circumstances? They arranged for him to come and see her that night.

It was ages since she'd looked at herself in a mirror and when she did she was horrified. She'd aged. Her hair, usually so glossy, had become wire wool, her skin was pasty, her eyes were dead. It was important she make herself look presentable because there'd been something worrying about Chris's voice. She used conditioner when she washed her hair, splashed her face with cold water, put drops in her eyes, and decided to wear the red dress she'd had on when she and Chris had first met. Finally, she got made-up, taking particular care. Although she looked much better when she'd finished, she was still pale. She went into the girls' room and asked to borrow some rouge.

Greta and Heather were talking quietly, half lying, half sitting on their beds. The endless, wretched weeping had more or less stopped, but the life had gone out of them. They would never be the same again. Yet looking at them, in their old room, on their old beds, Ruby found it hard to believe that Larry and Rob hadn't been part of a dream, that they'd ever actually existed. Her girls were home and it was as if they'd never been away.

She flung her arms around Chris's neck and kissed him. She'd almost forgotten what he looked like. She smoothed his slightly tousled hair, straightened his tie. 'Oh, I've missed you,' she gasped.

'I don't think so, Ruby. I reckon you've only just remembered I exist.'

'Don't be silly.' She shook his arm. 'Come inside.'

They went into the living room where Chris sat in an armchair when she'd expected him to sit on the settee and take her in his arms.

'Would you like tea or coffee?' she asked, slightly scared. This wasn't a bit like him.

'No, thank you.'

'Chris, what's the matter?' She felt a curl of fear in her stomach. Something was terribly wrong.

'How are the girls?'

'Broken-hearted. I doubt if their hearts will ever mend.'

He nodded. 'They'll bear the scars for the rest of their days.'

'So will I,' Ruby said fervently.

'And so will an awful lot of other people.' He looked at her directly. 'You didn't think of that, did you? My sister lost her only child. She wanted to grieve with his wife, with Heather, so that they could comfort each other. It would have helped, yet Ellie was left to find out by accident that Heather is bearing the only grandchild she and Albert will ever have.'

'I don't know what you mean!' She felt genuinely puzzled.

'You shut everyone out, Ruby,' he said gently, kindly. 'It didn't enter your head that other people were suffering as much as the girls. You shut *me* out. I tried to offer comfort, but you didn't want it. You didn't want *me*. You pushed me away.'

'It wasn't deliberate,' she cried.

'I know, darling. I know you couldn't help it. But it wouldn't do, would it, to marry someone you can't turn to when something dreadful happens? I must mean very little to you.'

'You mean everything to me. *Everything*,' she added emphatically.

'It's felt more like nothing over the last few weeks,' he said ruefully. 'I doubt if it's possible to love a person too much, but you love your girls to the exclusion of everyone else. If we got married, I'd feel very much second best which, I'm afraid, just wouldn't do. I happen to feel that as your husband I should be the most important person in the world.'

'But you would be, you already are.' She wanted to run to him, throw herself on his knee, plead, but had the awful feeling that he would push her away, as he was claiming she'd pushed him.

'No, Ruby, I'm not. I only wish I were.'

'So, we're not getting married?' Her voice cracked.

'I don't think it's such a good idea.'

She got up, began to walk wildly to and fro across the room, then turned on him angrily. 'How can you do this to me, now, of all times?'

'Do you think I *want* to!' He beat the arm of the chair with his fist. It was the first angry gesture she'd ever known him make. 'It's the last thing I imagined doing. Oh, I don't expect our love for each other to be weighed on scales and your side must exactly match mine. But I need to feel *needed*, darling. The last weeks have shown how *unnecessary* I am to you.'

'Oh, Chris!' She began to cry and he took her in his arms.

'Don't, darling.' He was almost in tears himself. 'You'll get over me far quicker than I will you. I'll love you for as long as I live.'

'Is there no hope for us?' she sobbed.

'I'm sorry, Ruby.' He went over to the door. 'Can I see the girls before I go?'

'Of course.'

He kissed her forehead, released her, and left the room. She heard him knock on the bedroom door, and sat with her head in her hands remembering, too late, the times she'd turned him away, rebuffed him. Once, he'd come to the flat and she wouldn't let him in. She'd thought he'd understand, but would she have understood given the same circumstances? It was her own fault that she'd lost him.

She had no idea how long he stayed in the bedroom. When he came out he said, 'They seem slightly better than I expected. Perhaps young hearts are tougher than old. Do you mind if I make a suggestion?'

'Of course not.'

'Ring Ellie and Moira, invite everyone round. I hope this doesn't sound brutal, but you've hurt them badly. You moved the girls back here and didn't tell a soul, as if the Whites and the Donovans didn't exist. If you value their friendship I suggest you try to make things up before it's too late. Don't forget, Greta and Heather are now part of their families too.'

A month later, Greta was found to be expecting twins. 'Larry was a twin,' she said sadly when they got home from the clinic. 'But his brother died in Moira's womb.'

'I didn't know that!' Ruby exclaimed.

'Nor did I.' Heather scowled. 'Why didn't you tell us before?'

'Because Larry didn't want anyone to know, that's why. It was a secret between us two.' She sighed and patted her stomach. 'He would have been so pleased.'

The lodgers all wanted to stay – at least she must be doing something right, Ruby thought drily. Mr Hamilton and Mr Oliver hadn't got round to looking for somewhere else, Mr Keppel had found a place, but withdrew when he discovered he could probably stay put. Mrs Mulligan claimed she had tried, but had been unable to find anywhere remotely suitable.

There'd been a time, not long ago, when Ruby would have been glad to see the back of Iris Mulligan, but Iris had proved worth her weight in gold over the last few months. During the weeks when Ruby couldn't have cared less whether the lodgers ate again or if the clothes rotted on their beds, Iris had taken charge. She saw to the meals, did the washing, kept everywhere tidy, answered the phone, collected the rents, and arranged for the shopping to be done.

'I made sure the men did their share,' she told Ruby. 'Mr Oliver did the ironing, Mr Keppel peeled the spuds and set the table, and me and Derek,' she blushed ever so slightly, 'I mean, Mr Hamilton, did the shopping.'

Derek Hamilton, a crusty bachelor in his fifties, formerly her greatest enemy because his television was always on too loud, now appeared to be her greatest friend. The television was still too loud, but now it didn't matter because Iris was usually in Mr Hamilton's room watching with him, which meant one good thing had come out of the tragedy.

Ruby warned everyone not to feel too settled. She'd written to the landlord explaining the changed circumstances and was still waiting to hear back. Matthew Doyle might not be prepared to let her stay.

'I've already applied for outline planning permission,' Matthew Doyle announced when he eventually turned up. It was a sultry, hot July day, and he wore cotton slacks and an Aertex short-sleeved shirt with the top buttons undone exposing his scrawny neck. His thin arms were very brown. 'An architect is drawing up the plans.'

'What for?' Ruby enquired coldly.

'A block of four terraced properties with garages at the back. They'd go for eighteen hundred each in an area like this.'

Ruby bit her lip and supposed she'd better be nice to him, though it would be awfully hard. 'Couldn't you delay it for a few years?' she suggested sweetly, then spoilt it by adding, 'You must be made of money. Another few thousand wouldn't make much difference to your bank balance, would it?'

To her annoyance, he laughed out loud. 'Another person would have grovelled, but not you, Ruby. Even when you need a favour, you can't help being nasty.'

'I wasn't being nasty, just pointing out the obvious.'

He raised a sarcastic eyebrow. 'You think that's a tactful thing to do?'

'What do you want me to do?' she demanded. 'Get down on my knees and beg?'

'Some people might.'

'Well, I'm not some people, I'm me!' She swallowed. She was going about things the wrong way. 'I told you in my letter what had happened.'

'I already knew. I sent a wreath to the funeral. You didn't say anything about a wedding in the letter. I thought you were getting married in a few weeks?'

She hadn't mentioned it because it was none of his business. 'It's been postponed,' she said shortly.

'I understand.' He nodded, a gesture she found irritating because he couldn't possibly have understood. 'How are Greta and Heather? Can I see them?'

'They've gone out for a walk. Heather's bearing up, but Greta ...' she paused. 'Greta's still nowhere near her old self. She's expecting twins. She ...' She paused again.

'What?' Matthew prompted.

'She talks to Larry in her sleep, as if he was still alive, and keeps looking at her watch when it's time for him to come home. There's other things.' Like wanting to know where Larry's shirts were so she could iron them, making sandwiches for him to take to work.

'I refused to believe it when me gran died. I used to close me eyes and try to imagine she was there.' He smiled, his dark eyes soft with the memory. 'Sometimes, I actually managed it – and then we'd talk.'

For a minute, Ruby didn't know what to say. She couldn't imagine him having done anything that wasn't hard and calculating. 'How old were you then?'

'Thirteen. I was completely on me own. Me mam scarpered straight after I was born and dumped me on gran. I must have had a dad, but no one knew who he was.'

'How did you manage?' she asked, genuinely wanting to know.

He leant his sharp elbows on the table. 'The war started – you'd gone from Foster Court by then. I tried to get a job, but anybody would have been mad to take me on. I could hardly read and write except for the bit Gran taught me, and I was nothing but skin and bone. I looked like death warmed up – people still say the same about me now. Then Charlie Murphy took pity on me.'

'The landlord?'

'S'right. He was our landlord too. He could get things for people. At first it was just food; sugar, tea, fruit, all nicked from the docks. I'd deliver the stuff for him, collect the money, take orders. Charlie gave me a cut of the proceeds. It was a bit like being the pawnshop runner,' he said with a grin.

'That was perfectly honest and above board,' Ruby said hotly. 'What you did was criminal.'

'I knew that would rile you.' He actually had the nerve to reach across the table and pat her hand. As flesh touched flesh, Ruby had the same disturbing sensation in her stomach that he so frequently caused. She snatched her hand away.

'I thought Charlie was killed in the raids?' she said.

'He was. By then, I knew his contacts and took over the business, though everyone called it the black market. It was either that or starving to death.' He shrugged. 'I went from strength to strength, but I knew it would all stop when the war was over, so I started buying property. It wasn't long afterwards that I met you.'

'And you're still going from strength to strength?'

'I've just got back from Australia. I'm going into swimming pools. I only saw your letter yesterday.'

And he'd come straight away! Ruby was beginning to wonder if she'd misjudged him, when the front door opened and the girls came in. To her surprise, they both looked extraordinarily pleased to find him there, particularly Greta, who inexplicably burst into tears. 'Oh, it's lovely to see you,' she cried.

Matthew gave her a hug and a kiss. He wiped the tears away with an impeccably ironed white hankie. 'And it's lovely to see you, both of you.'

He left soon afterwards, without saying if she could stay in the house. Ruby was left to assume that she could.

'He's a strange man,' she mused aloud to the girls. 'Fancy someone in his position collecting rents.'

'I don't see anything strange about him,' Heather said defensively. 'And it's only *our* rents he collects, because he likes us and wants to be friends.'

Greta chimed in. 'I think he's smashing. Larry and Rob thought he was the gear. He used to get them tickets for . . . oh!' She clapped her hand to her mouth and ran from the room.

'For what?' asked a mystified Ruby.

'Football matches,' Heather said briefly. 'He used to get them tickets for football matches, the best seats. I'll go and see to her.'

That night, while the girls were in the lounge watching the newly acquired television, Ruby sat at the kitchen table and wrote a short letter to her mother, informing her of the recent tragedy and that she was no longer getting married. They hadn't seen each other since the girls' wedding. She finished with, 'I'll let you know when Greta's babies arrive in case you would like to come to the christening.'

She addressed the envelope, stamped it, and opened the writing pad again. Now Beth, whom she should have telephoned weeks ago, but it was easier to describe the events of that dreadful day on paper. The other way, she would have broken down, wept herself silly.

'Well, that's a load off my mind,' she sighed when Beth's much longer letter was finished and ready to post tomorrow.

Ruby cupped her chin in her hands and stared into space. It wasn't long since she'd sat in this very spot thinking everything was about to change. The girls had just got married, she was getting married herself.

But now it seemed she was destined to remain in Mrs Hart's house, and hardly anything had changed at all.

12
1963–1970

The woman was crying loudly outside the school gates, a small tubby woman of about thirty wearing blue and white striped cotton slacks and a bright red jumper. Her brown hair was cropped untidily short. Ruby stopped and enquired, 'Are you all right?'

'No, I'm not,' the woman sniffed and dabbed her eyes with a sodden handkerchief. 'I'm devastated if you must know. Me little boy's just started school and I don't know how I'm going to manage without him.'

'You will,' Ruby said with conviction.

'How would you know? Oh, of course. I just saw you taking three little girls into the classroom. They all seemed quite happy considering it's their first day. Which are yours? The twins or the red-haired one?'

'They're all mine in a way. I'm their gran.'

'Goodness me! You don't look nearly old enough to be a grandmother.'

Ruby was forty-four. She preened herself, being apt to take offence on the rare occasions she was assumed to be a grandparent. She and the woman began to walk together away from the school.

'Where are their mothers?' the woman enquired. 'That's if you don't mind me asking, like?'

'I don't mind at all. The twins' mother, Greta, hasn't been well for a while. She's at home. My other daughter, Heather, goes to work.' It had been necessary, not long after the babies were born, for the girls to have a room each to accommodate their offspring. Fortunately, Mr Oliver had announced he was leaving at about the same time, so Ruby had moved upstairs. It meant one less rent was coming in and although her daughters received an allowance from the state, it wasn't enough. Heather had returned to work and was now a clerk in a solicitor's office, leaving red-haired Daisy in Ruby's capable hands.

'I'm Pixie Shaw, by the way,' the woman said. She had stopped crying, though her eyes were still bloodshot. 'Me real name's Patricia, but me husband claims I look like a pixie, so that's where the name comes from.'

There was no way on earth that Ruby would have allowed anyone to call her Pixie. 'It's very nice,' she said unconvincingly. 'My name's Ruby O'Hagan.'

'I'd ask you back for a cup of tea, Ruby, 'cause I feel like talking to someone, but me house is a tip.'

Ruby took the blatant hint. 'You can come back to ours if you like.' Her own house was a tip, but she didn't care. Nor did she feel like talking to anyone, but felt even less like entering a house bereft of children where Greta would still be asleep. She'd get used to the silence eventually, enjoy it, but it would take a while. It didn't help that it was such a horrible morning, dark and forbidding, with black clouds bunched threateningly overhead.

'That'd be nice, ta. I didn't have time to tidy up before I left. Me and our poor Clint were bawling our heads off. Neither of us wanted him to go to school.'

'Clint!'

'He's called after Clint Eastwood from *Rawhide*. It was my favourite programme on the telly. Did you ever see it?'

'No, but my daughters did.' By the time Ruby collapsed in front of the television, it was usually time for the national anthem.

'It's finished now, but I miss it still. What are your granddaughters called?'

'Daisy's the red-haired one. She's four months younger than the others, but the headmistress thought it'd be best if she started at the same time rather than after Christmas. The twins are Moira and Ellie.' Naming the twins after their maternal grandmothers had finally healed the rift that Ruby's thoughtlessness had caused, though it could create confusion at family gatherings.

'Daisy's a pretty name,' Pixie remarked, leaving Ruby to assume that she didn't think much of Moira and Ellie. 'Ooh! Is this where you live?' she gasped when Ruby turned into the drive of the house. 'It's ever so big. What does your husband do?'

'He died in the war.'

'Oh, I'm sorry to hear that. How long have you lived here?'

'Twenty-four years.' Ruby sighed. She led the way around the back rather than go in the front which might disturb Greta.

'Have you never thought of having the kitchen modernised?' her new friend enquired, staring aghast at the wooden draining board piled high with dirty dishes, the ancient wooden dresser, the floor with its chipped black and white tiles.

'I like it as it is.' Ruby tossed her head. 'Anyway, it's not my house. It's only rented.' She was wondering if she'd made a mistake in inviting Pixie Shaw for a cup of tea. She wasn't sure if she liked the woman whose only resemblance to a pixie was that she was very small. Otherwise, she was most unattractive, with pale, watery grey eyes, a flat nose, and a little prim mouth.

'My husband completely gutted our kitchen. We've got lovely new units;

lime green laminated and an orange tiled floor. Mind you, we *own* the place, so it's worth our while to make improvements. Oh, you've got a cat? Or is it a dog?' She pointed to the earthenware bowl on the floor.

'It's a cat's bowl, but I'm afraid he's no longer with us. My daughter won't let me throw it away.' It had been a terrible year, 1958. So many deaths; Larry and Rob, then Martha Quinlan had died, shortly followed by Fred. One day, when Tiger didn't appear for his morning milk, she'd gone down into the cellar and found him curled in a ball in his wardrobe. His furry body was cold to the touch when she tried to wake him.

It had been Tiger's death that sent Greta completely over the edge. She'd wanted the twins to play with him, she sobbed.

'But, love, Tiger was already the oldest cat in the world.' Ruby had stroked her daughter's soft, fair hair. 'We were lucky to have had him for so long.'

'That only makes it worse. I'd known Tiger for nearly all me life, as well as Martha. Soon, everyone will die and I'll be the only one left.'

For a long while, she'd put milk out for Tiger every morning, called him in at night, looked for him in the wardrobe. Once, Ruby found her on the old settee they'd used during the raids. She was singing, 'We'll Meet Again', but stopped when her mother appeared. 'I just heard the siren go,' she said.

'She'll get over it,' the doctor said complacently. 'She's rather a fragile young woman who has had too much grief. Would you like her to go away for a while?'

'Where to?'

'A mental home, where she'll get treatment.'

'No, thanks. Tell me what sort of treatment and I'll give it to her here.'

'You must think of yourself, Mrs O'Hagan.' The doctor frowned. 'You're working yourself into the ground with three small children to look after, not to mention a sick daughter and the folks upstairs. You're not exactly young.'

'I'm not exactly old, either. I'll manage.'

Under no circumstances was Greta to be stressed. She took a tablet every morning to steady her nerves and another at night to make her sleep. The afternoons were her best time, when she usually played with the children. Ruby made sure she watched nothing on television that would upset her and limited her reading to women's magazines.

Greta, still in her dressing gown, came wandering into the kitchen while Ruby and Pixie were drinking the tea. She smiled dreamily at the stranger. 'Hello.'

'This is Pixie,' Ruby said. 'Pixie, this is my daughter, Greta.'

'Are you the one with the twins who's been ill?' Pixie enquired with a complete lack of tact.

Before Greta could answer, the telephone rang and Ruby went to answer it. It was Heather wanting to know if the children had settled in school and how was Greta? She rang every day to ask after her sister.

'The children seemed fine,' Ruby told her, 'And so does Greta as it happens. I brought some woman back and I can hear them in the kitchen chattering away like nobody's business.'

'What woman?'

'Her name's Pixie. She seems a bit silly to me, but Greta obviously likes her.'

'Make sure she doesn't upset her.'

'Of course, love.'

When Ruby returned to the kitchen, Pixie was saying, '*Three* widows, all living under the same roof! It sounds dead romantic, like a novel.'

Greta nodded. 'I suppose it does.'

Ruby regarded her daughter with shock and amazement. She couldn't recall the term 'widow' having been mentioned in the house before. Everyone was careful with their language when Greta was around.

'And your husband never got to see his kids!' Pixie gasped.

'No, nor did Heather's. She hadn't even told Rob she was pregnant with Daisy.'

'Oh! That's too sad for words. My husband, Brian, is thinking about buying a car but, meself, I've always considered them dangerous. He mightn't be so keen once I've told him about you and your sister.'

'Well,' Ruby said in a loud voice, 'It's about time I got on with some work.'

Pixie was better at dropping hints than taking them. Or perhaps the words hadn't registered. Greta picked up the cups which Ruby noticed had been refilled in her absence. 'Let's go in the other room. We can talk while Mam tidies up.'

'Have you got a picture of your wedding, Grete?'

'There's an album somewhere. Do you know where it is, Mam?'

'On the bottom shelf of the sideboard.' It hadn't been opened since the day Larry and Rob had died.

'Come on, Pix. I'll show you.'

Ruby sat down heavily when the pair disappeared into the lounge. For years, Greta had been treated with kid gloves, then along had come the tactless Pixie Shaw and her daughter had seemed more than willing to talk about Larry and the day that had forever changed all their lives. Perhaps Greta had been well for a long time, yet they'd all continued to walk on eggshells, treat her as an invalid. It had needed someone like the garrulous, nosy Pixie to show them she was better.

At midday, Pixie announced she had to leave to collect Clint from school. 'He wants to come home for his dinner.'

'Bring him round after school one day to play with the girls,' Greta suggested. 'Once he's made friends, he might stay for his dinner.'

'That's a good idea,' Pixie enthused. 'I fancied having him home for the company, but the morning's just whizzed by and I've hardly thought about

Clint at all. 'Fact, I'd have stayed longer if it weren't for him. 'Bye, Grete. See you tomorrow.'

Ruby closed the door on their guest. 'She's coming again?'

'You don't mind, do you, Mam? We're going to night school together. It starts next week. Pixie had already put her name down for leatherwork, but I thought I'd learn cake decorating, same as Martha. Pixie's decided to do it with me.'

'But Mam, that's not fair,' Heather complained that night after tea. She was drying the dishes while Ruby washed. Greta was watching television with the children who were tired after their first day at school. 'I've been asked loads of times at work to go to the pictures with the girls, but I always refuse because I'd sooner stay in with our Greta.'

'Surely you're glad she seems so much better?'

'Yes, but ...' Heather made a face. 'Perhaps I could go to night school with her and this stupid Pixie.'

'Don't be silly, love. You'd be bored out of your mind decorating cakes.' Ruby sighed as she put a casserole dish on the draining board. Her own mind was numb with the effort of feeding nine people and keeping everywhere clean. Mr Keppel had left to get married years ago, and Iris Mulligan and Mr Hamilton had found a house of their own where they'd gone to live in sin, Ruby supposed. Three students from Liverpool University, young men, now lived upstairs and seemed determined to eat her out of house and home. No matter how much food she made, every scrap had gone by the end of the meal.

Clint Shaw came to play on Saturday morning. The weather had bucked up; the sky was blue and the sun was shining. By the end of the week, Ruby had had enough of Pixie who'd been every day. She was relieved to find Clint a blond angel of a child, very sensitive, with none of his mother's brashness.

She watched through the window as the children played in the garden. It seemed only yesterday that she'd watched her daughters play with Jake on the same lawn under the same trees.

'How time flies,' she murmured.

Now it was Ellie who was the leader, the one who determined what games were to be played. She was the younger of the twins by an hour, yet the more forceful as well as the taller. But Moira wasn't prepared to be ordered about as Greta had been. There was rarely any argument; Moira just went her own sweet way no matter what Ellie said. They were obviously twins, alike in many ways, different in others. Apart from being fractionally smaller, Moira's rich brown hair was curly, her eyes a lovely light blue, her chin round, soft and dimpled. She was a self-contained little girl with a gentle, kindly smile, almost adult.

Ellie's hair was wavy and her expressive cobalt blue eyes were never still. She flashed like lightning around the garden, running the fastest, shouting the loudest, climbing the highest trees. Her pointed chin was always gritted, as if she had great problems to grapple with, and she suffered from a singular lack of patience, though having realised at a very early age it was a waste of time getting angry with her sister, she was inclined to turn on her cousin instead.

Daisy! Ruby's heart contracted when she looked at her third granddaughter, the solid, freckle-faced, red-haired Daisy, hanging timidly back from the others as usual. Such a pretty name for such a plain child – a woman had actually said that once in the clinic when Ruby had taken the girls for an injection.

No one knew where Daisy had got her looks from. The Whites had racked their brains, but neither could recall having had a relative with red hair, no matter how far back they went. Ruby had asked her mother, but Olivia couldn't help.

'There aren't any redheads in my family. As for your father, he had black hair, same as yours, but there could have been loads of ginger-haired O'Hagans in America. I wouldn't know.'

Ellie White, Rob's mother, probably didn't realise she made such an almighty fuss of her glowing, vivacious namesake, rather than her own son's child, the dull, slow-witted Daisy.

'How's Greta been today?' was the first thing Heather always asked when she came home from work, as if her sister was far more important than her daughter.

Ruby tried to make amends, make a fuss of the little girl who always seemed to be trying hard to look happy. But it was difficult. She didn't want it to appear too obvious to the twins – Moira wouldn't mind, she might even understand, but Ellie wouldn't be pleased if she thought her cousin was Ruby's favourite. Ellie could be spiteful at times.

Greta and Pixie came out of the lounge where they'd been talking animatedly. 'Is it all right if me and Pix go into town to do some shopping?' Greta asked.

'Me sister-in-law's getting married in November. I need an outfit for the wedding,' Pixie put in.

'We won't be long, Mam.'

'Why not ask Heather to come with you?' It was years since the girls had gone shopping together.

'She can shop in the lunch hour,' Greta said airily. 'Anyroad, she's in the bath.'

'All right, but don't you dare think about going out next Saturday. It's the twins' birthday party, there's twelve children coming, and I'll need all the help I can get.' She was already dreading it.

'Wouldn't dream of it, Mam.'

She must have been mad, inviting twelve strange children for four whole hours, when three hours would have done, or even two! The meal had been eaten in a flash and the kitchen floor was covered in jelly which the boys had flicked at the girls. There was also a scattering of crisps and crusts of bread. Two glasses had been broken and the tablecloth was soaked with ginger pop and lemonade.

Never again, Ruby vowed as she brushed the mess up, put the cloth in the laundry basket, and wiped the table, wincing at the screams coming from outside where the girls and Pixie were organising the games. Next party, she'd go out and leave them in complete charge.

For the next few hours, Ruby, never that keen on entertaining other people's children, cowered in the kitchen and listened to her garden being wrecked. Children came in frequently to demand a drink, something to eat, the lavatory, have a cut bathed, or to complain about something or other.

Pixie had brought a portable wireless which was being switched on and off. Ruby assumed they were playing musical chairs – without chairs – or statues or pass the parcel. She couldn't be bothered looking, just wanted everyone to go.

An unusually bright-eyed Daisy came running into the kitchen followed by Clint. 'Can I show him me colouring book, Gran?'

'Of course, love. Go in the bedroom, it's quieter there.'

She was pleased the two had paired off. Daisy needed a friend outside of the twins. When she looked in some time later, she and Clint were sprawled on the floor taking turns colouring in a picture.

Only another half an hour to go. Ruby sighed with relief as she filled a tray with glasses of lemonade and chocolate biscuits to take outside, where she was pleased to find a couple of mothers had arrived to collect their children – the sooner the better as far as she was concerned.

'I bet you've had a helluva day,' one of the women remarked. She looked about Ruby's age, very slim, with short brown curly hair and smiling eyes. 'I was dead relieved when my other kids grew out of birthday parties – I've a boy and girl in their twenties – but right out of the blue I had Will, and now I have to start all over again.' She groaned. 'He's five next week. The girls have been invited to his party.'

'Which is Will?'

'The blond one in the blue T-shirt. I won't ask if he's behaved himself, because I know for sure he won't have.' Ruby recognised the impish Will as the instigator of the jelly-flicking. 'He hasn't been so bad.'

'You're only being nice. You're Ruby, aren't you? I'm Brenda Wilding. Oh! And this is my husband, Tony. He's been parking the car.' A good-looking man with Will's blond hair joined them. 'Tony, this is Ruby.'

'Pleased to meet you, Ruby.'

'Excuse me! There's a child stuck up a tree. I'd better rescue him before his mother comes.'

'I'll do the rescuing,' Tony Wilding offered, 'If you fetch Will's coat we'll take him off your hands. We're in a bit of a rush, we're going to the theatre tonight.'

'He didn't have a coat, just a jumper,' Brenda laughed. 'It was cream when he put it on, but it'll be black by now.'

Ruby found the jumper, still recognisably cream, on the hall floor. When she took it into the garden, Brenda Wilding was leaning back against her husband who had slid his arms around her waist and was nuzzling her neck. Ruby stopped in her tracks and a feeling of pure envy swept over her. They must have been married for a quarter of a century, yet were still obviously in love.

More parents arrived and the garden thankfully emptied. Pixie noticed Clint was missing. 'And where's Daisy?' enquired Heather.

'They're in the bedroom,' Ruby said.

Ellie ran into the house. 'That's not fair,' she cried. 'He should be playing with *me*.'

Ruby couldn't see anything unfair about it, but said nothing. She'd had enough. 'I'm going to lie down for a while,' she announced. The students had gone hiking and weren't coming back for tea, but tomorrow there would be a grown-up party to which the Whites and the Donovans had been invited, which meant she had another hectic day ahead.

She threw herself face down on to the bed and punched the pillow. 'I'm fed up,' she informed it. 'Fed up to the bloody teeth. Why aren't *I* going to the theatre with a dishy husband?'

The pillow remained mute. 'Stupid thing!' Ruby gave it another punch, then buried her head in the feathery mound with a deep, heartfelt sigh. She hadn't been out with a man since Chris Ryan. Her entire life, from the age of seventeen, seemed to have been centred around children, first her own, and now her daughters'. And housework, endless housework. She was sick to death of cooking, washing, ironing, cleaning. She'd never been to the theatre, the last dance she'd gone to was during the war, and she couldn't remember when she'd last been to the pictures or out for a meal.

There was a knock on the door. She folded the pillow over her ears so she wouldn't hear if the person knocked again and gave a little shriek when she felt a hand on her back.

'Ruby,' said Matthew Doyle.

She sat up, outraged. 'This is a *bedroom*,' she gasped.

'I thought I could hear you crying.'

'I wasn't crying, but if I had been, I'd've thought it a reason to stay out, not come in.'

He had the cheek to sit on the edge of the bed. It irritated her that he seemed to regard himself as a member of the family, though that was Greta and Heather's fault. They encouraged him, asked him round, invited him for meals – he was coming to tomorrow's party. The little girls adored him and called him 'Uncle Matt'.

'I brought some presents for the twins. I got something for Daisy too, in case she felt left out. What's the matter, Rube?'

'Nothing.' She resented him calling her 'Rube'. And why couldn't he have brought the presents tomorrow?

'You look down in the dumps.'

There seemed little point in denying it. 'So what?' she said churlishly. It had been a tiring, unpleasant day, and seeing Brenda and Tony Wilding together had been the last straw, though she wasn't going to tell him *that*.

'You need cheering up.'

'Do I?' She did. She definitely did.

'Let's go out somewhere. I need cheering up too.'

'Why?'

'Caroline's divorcing me.'

Ruby wasn't surprised. He must spend more time with the O'Hagans than he did with his wife. 'What have you done?'

He shrugged. 'It's what I won't do that's the problem. She's fed up with Liverpool. Daddy's retired to the South of France, to Monaco, and she'd prefer to live there. I flatly refused and she ses I'm being awkward.'

'So, she's divorcing you for being awkward?'

'Seems like it.'

He'd never said anything horrible about Caroline, but he'd never said anything nice either. She sensed he wasn't particularly upset, but the end of a marriage, even if it hadn't been blindingly happy, was always sad.

'What about us going out?' he said encouragingly. 'Last time I asked – it must be five or six years ago – you turned me down because I was married. Now that hardly applies. I'll be a bachelor again in no time.'

'A divorcee,' she reminded him. 'You'll never be a bachelor again.'

'Don't nitpick. Let's have a night on the town.'

Normally, Ruby wouldn't have walked to the end of the road with Matthew Doyle, but tonight she felt tempted. She would never cease to dislike him, but he seemed to like *her*, and was easy to talk to. She would express astonishent when her daughters said they considered him good-looking. 'He's too gaunt and hungry-looking,' she would protest yet wonder why he so often caused a riot in her stomach. Always impeccably dressed, today he was wearing grey trousers with a knife-edge crease, a navy-blue blazer with brass buttons, and an open-necked shirt. He looked as if he was about to leap on to his yacht. She was surprised he wasn't wearing a white peaked cap.

If she stayed in, what did the evening ahead have to offer? Lord knows what time Pixie would leave. She was another who was coming to regard the house as a second home. If Pixie stayed, Heather would have a face on because she didn't like the way she monopolised Greta and the children wouldn't go to bed while Clint was still there.

She shuddered. A night out with almost anyone was preferable. 'OK,' she said. 'But I'll need a while to get ready.' She must look a wreck.

He jumped off the bed with alacrity. 'I'll wait downstairs.'

Ruby looked in the wardrobe for a dress fit for a night on the town but, as expected, could find nothing. Along with all the other things she hadn't done in years, she hadn't bought much in the way of clothes. The only thing faintly suitable was the fuchsia dress she'd bought for the girls' weddings which was badly creased. She took it downstairs to the kitchen, set up the ironing board, and was just finishing when Heather came in looking sulky.

'When's *she* going?' She nodded towards the lounge from which Pixie's shrill voice could be heard above the even shriller chatter of the children.

'I don't know, love. Soon, I expect. Clint's bound to be tired.'

Heather frowned. 'Why are you ironing your frock?'

'Matthew's taking me out,' Ruby said with a happy grin. She couldn't wait to get away. Tonight, her daughters' needs seemed second to her own.

'And you're leaving us by ourselves?'

Ruby put the iron down with a crash. 'For goodness' sake, Heather, you're twenty-six years old. Do you really expect your mother to stay in with you at your age? Greta's been so much better lately.'

'Oh, and I suppose that's all that matters!' Heather's sternly pretty face went red. 'Greta's better and there's no need to worry about me. Have you ever cared about how *I* feel? My husband died too, you know.' She burst into tears. 'The minute she's better, Greta doesn't want me any more.'

So *that's* what the tears were all about. Greta had been surprisingly thoughtless since Pixie had appeared on the scene. And it was an undoubted fact, Ruby thought guiltily, that no one had been overly concerned how Heather felt over the past five years. All their attention had been focused on Greta.

'I've always been sidelined,' Heather sobbed. 'Greta's everyone's pet.'

Ruby put her arms around her younger daughter. This was serious. Heather was a stalwart and hardly ever cried, not even when she was a child and had hurt herself. 'She wasn't Rob's, was she, love? Nor is she mine. It's just that she's always been so frail, she's needed more attention.'

'Just because I'm strong, it doesn't mean I don't want people to love me.'

Matthew appeared in the doorway. Ruby shook her head over her daughter's heaving shoulders and he gave a reluctant nod of understanding. The night on the town was off.

'There's something burning,' he remarked.

It was Ruby's frock, branded for ever with the shape of the iron and completely ruined.

A few weeks later, Heather asked her mother if she minded if she went abroad.

'Of course not, love,' Ruby said, pleased. 'A holiday would do you the world of good.'

'I didn't mean on holiday, Mam. I meant to work.'

Ruby didn't answer immediately. 'How long for?'

'I'm not sure. These two girls in the office are planning to hitch-hike around Europe getting jobs wherever they can. They might only be away weeks, but it could be months. They said I could go with them.'

'That sounds awfully dangerous, Heather.'

'It won't be, not with the three of us.'

'What about Daisy?' She already knew what the answer would be.

Heather squirmed uncomfortably. 'I can't take her, can I? Anyroad, she won't miss me. She's fonder of you than she is of me. Oh, Mam!' Her voice rose. 'The idea of getting away from everything seems like heaven. I can't stand it here any more. I had this stupid idea in me head that once Greta was herself again, it'd be like it was before, that we'd be best friends, go shopping together, to the pictures. But that's not going to happen, is it? Pixie's taken my place and things won't ever be the same again.'

Greta was entirely unrepentant when Ruby accused her of behaving disgracefully with her sister. 'You've driven her away from home. Heather's always thought the world of you, but all of a sudden you've dropped her like a hot brick.'

'Huh!' Greta snorted. 'Our Heather's always been far too possessive, so Pixie ses. She treats me like a child, not her older sister. In fact, *everyone* treats me like a child. No one seems to realise I'm a grown woman with two children.'

'You're not acting like a grown woman now. In fact, you never have.' It was the first time ever that Ruby had snapped at the daughter who'd always been such an agreeable little thing. 'I wouldn't expect the twins to come out with such a load of rubbish. What's got into you, Greta? You sound awfully hard.'

'I'm going to be hard from now on. Pixie ses being soft gets you nowhere.'

'Since when has Pixie been such a fount of wisdom. Oh!' Ruby got up and left the room. What a stupid thing to say. What was the matter with everyone? Were her daughters having teenage tantrums ten years too late? Maybe it was time she indulged in a few tantrums herself.

Pixie Shaw turned out to be a fickle friend. Six months later Greta was dropped for someone else as unceremoniously as she'd dropped her sister. Ruby found it hard to be sympathetic. She would never forget the way Greta had behaved, and if she'd done it once, she could do it again.

Clint continued to come and play after school. Ruby was glad. Although Daisy didn't appear to be missing her mummy, she clung to her gran as if worried she might also go away. Clint and Daisy got on well, though Ellie did her best to pry them apart.

'Oh, Mam, when's our Heather coming back?' now became Greta's constant cry.

'Who knows!' Postcards arrived regularly, there was the occasional letter. Heather was washing dishes in France, working as a chambermaid in an

Italian hotel, cleaning lavatories in Germany, harvesting fruit in Spain. Over Christmas, she worked in a restaurant in a ski resort in Austria. 'It doesn't matter that I only speak English because almost everyone else is foreign.' The card was posted in Innsbruck.

Ruby followed her progress in the atlas that had once been Max Hart's. His name was printed childishly in red crayon inside the tattered cover. She thought about him whenever she opened it and wondered what had happened to the brave, young airman who'd made love to her so desperately that first Christmas of the war.

She'd never imagined that all these years later she'd still be living in his mother's old house, doing the same things that she'd resented doing then. She'd had dreams, once, of doing other things, but every time there'd seemed a chance the dreams would come true, something happened to prevent it. Perhaps it would have helped if she'd known what the dreams were, but all she'd ever had was vague, airy-fairy ideas about studying something or other, starting her own business – the first woman-only decorating company, she remembered with a smile.

Heather came home the following summer. She'd been away nine months. When she reached Lime Street station, she telephoned to say she was about to catch the bus.

It was the most perfect of August days, brilliantly sunny, the air scented with flowers. The children were halfway through the summer holidays. Ruby left the front door open and every now and then someone would look to see if Heather was coming. It was her intention to let Daisy go first to welcome her mummy home.

'She's here,' Moira shouted, but Ruby had scarcely turned round to look for Daisy, before Greta was running down the path, flinging her arms around her sister, kissing her, crying, 'Oh, it's so good to have you back.'

'It's good to *be* back, sis,' replied a surprised and extremely delighted Heather.

A fortnight later, Greta started work as a receptionist with a firm of accountants in Victoria Street, not far from the solicitors where Heather had returned to work. They met each other at lunchtime, went shopping together on Saturday afternoons. They put their names down at night school for shorthand and typing so that one day they would get better-paid jobs.

Ruby wrote a long letter to Beth and told her of the events of the last few months. 'Greta is her old self again and she and Heather are back in each others' pockets, the best of friends. I'm not sure if that's good or bad. They're not likely to meet another Larry and Rob, which means they're stuck with each other, and I'm stuck in this bloody house. Sometimes, I feel like doing a Heather and disappearing for nine months, but fat chance! What would happen to poor little Daisy? I'm the only one who seems to notice she's alive. There's *always* a reason to stay. *Always*.'

She put down the pen, then took it up again and added another paragraph. 'I shouldn't complain. Despite everything, I'm happy. It's a lovely house to be stuck in and I laugh far more than I cry. My granddaughters are a joy, my girls seem content, we're not exactly poor. On the whole, life is good.'

Beth was also content at last. Things had marginally improved in Little Rock. She'd joined a black–white integration group, and had been appointed secretary, 'Only because no one else wanted to do it.' A year ago, she'd gone to Washington and had shaken hands with President Jack Kennedy only weeks before he was tragically killed and all America had gone into mourning. Daniel disapproved of her activities. 'He wants black supremacy, not equality.' They argued all the time. 'But he respects me at last. He's suddenly realised I've got a brain, and my awful mother-in-law has now decided she quite likes me, after all.'

Jake was married and Beth would shortly become a grandmother. Ruby shivered. The years were racing by with frightening speed.

Olivia Appleby came in September, late one Monday morning when the children were at school and the girls at work. Ruby only saw her mother four or five times a year and then it was for just a few hours. Her children, her *other* children, she would stress, would want to know where she was if she stayed overnight.

'They don't know about you or your father. It's a secret I've always kept close to my heart. I couldn't bear to talk about him to anyone else, only you.'

It seemed to Ruby that, as the years took her further and further away from Tom O'Hagan, the more clearly Olivia remembered him. His face she described in specific detail, and she could repeat the conversations they had word for word. She was only now recalling long forgotten things, such as railway lines glinting, 'like silver wire in the moonlight', the strange smell – 'it was just the other day I realised what it was, a mixture of night flowers and burnt flesh'.

When she came, Olivia asked if they could go into the garden. The day wasn't particularly warm, a weak sun appeared occasionally from behind pearly grey clouds. They sat in deck chairs under the trees that were just beginning to turn gold, Olivia a melancholy figure in her pale, linen suit and large framed hat, smoking the inevitable cigarette.

'I've brought you something,' she said in a whispery voice that Ruby could hardly hear. She seemed tired today, washed out. 'It's in my bag in the house.'

'Oh, what?' Ruby tried to sound enthusiastic. She was unable to describe exactly how she felt about her mother's visits; a mixture of resentment, embarrassment, and guilt – mostly guilt. She didn't doubt that Olivia would prefer to have found a far more loving daughter than herself.

'It's a matinée jacket, the only item of baby clothes I kept. I didn't even buy it, Madge did, but I thought you'd like to have it as a memento.'

'I'll treasure it for ever.'

The colourless lips twisted in a smile. 'My dear Ruby, you try so hard, but you're not a good enough actress to deceive. You find me a pain, don't you?'

'Of course not!' Ruby protested.

'Yes, you do, dear. Not that I blame you. It was selfish of me to come bursting into your life nearly forty years too late, but once I'd discovered where you lived, I *had* to get to know Tom's daughter.' She looked curiously at Ruby. 'Don't you ever wonder how your life would have gone if he hadn't been killed?'

Ruby shook her head. 'It seems a waste of time.'

'I've wasted an awful lot of time thinking about what might have been,' Olivia said with a sigh. 'I wish I were strong like you.'

'It's not a question of being strong.' The circumstances of her birth had been entirely beyond her control. It was pointless trying to imagine how it would be had things gone differently. 'It would have been nice, living in America, being part of a big family,' she said, hoping this would please Olivia.

'It would have been more than nice. It would have been perfect. I used to think of contacting Tom's family, even going to see them. She smiled thinly. 'I was too nervous, though. I would have felt like an intruder. Then I met my husband and by the time he died it was too late.'

'Would you like more tea?'

'I'd love some, dear.'

'I won't be a minute.'

'Do you think you'll ever get married again?' Olivia enquired when Ruby returned.

'I don't know. It's something else I don't think about. I've got my hands full as it is.'

'I'd like to see you settled before . . .' she broke off. 'It's a pity that Chris turned out to be such a fool.'

'A fool?' Chris Ryan had always seemed eminently sensible.

'Fancy giving you up for loving your girls too much! Did he expect to have taken their place in your heart?' She angrily flicked the ash off her cigarette. 'What conceit some men have. Have you heard from him since?'

'I've seen him lots of times – he's Ellie White's brother. We've talked a bit, but never about anything intimate. He's getting married soon, but I haven't met the woman.'

'What about that Matthew I seem to meet whenever I come to your house?'

Ruby laughed. 'Why are you so anxious to see me married?'

'I told you, I'd like to see you settled. Matthew seems very nice. He's also very rich, so I've been given to understand.'

'Until recently, he was also very married. Now he's divorced and he sometimes asks me out, but I always refuse.'

'Why?'

'Because I don't like him,' Ruby said simply. 'We shared some of our past and I'm the only one he can talk to about it. That's why he comes. Now he seems to regard us as his substitute family.'

'It's not always possible to escape the past,' Olivia murmured.

'Anyway, Matthew's got a girlfriend, so I'm afraid, Olivia, there's no sign of a husband on the horizon at the moment. I'm not exactly worried.'

Olivia looked pleased, she always did when Ruby used her name. She crushed a cigarette beneath her heel and lit another. 'Tell me about your husband. You hardly ever talk about him.'

'Jacob? There's nothing much to tell.' Ruby racked her brains for things to say about Jacob without revealing what a disaster it had been. She described meeting Jacob on Humble's Farm, invented their wedding, smartened up Foster Court so it sounded quite respectable, avoided her cleaning career – Olivia already knew she'd been the pawnshop runner. After she'd finished, Olivia asked about the convent, about Emily, then Beth.

'She seemed so nice, Beth. It's a pity she went away.'

'It certainly is.' Ruby's voice was hoarse with answering so many questions. She'd been talking for hours. They'd spoken about the same things, the same people, before, but today Olivia wanted to know every trivial little detail. 'I have to collect the children from school soon. Would you like to come with me?'

'No, thank you. I'll just sit here till you come back. I'm rather tired.' There were dark circles under her eyes and her cheeks were hollow. 'That's a pretty dress, dear. I meant to say before,' she commented when Ruby stood up.

'I bought it the day the twins had their sixth birthday party. I left the girls to get on with it and went shopping by myself. It was such a treat. I'd almost forgotten what town looked like.' For years, her life had been confined to a small patch of Liverpool; the park, the school, the shops in Ullet Road. 'I might do it more often.'

'It's about time you spread your wings a bit. You suit that colour.'

The dress was wine corduroy, very fine, with a cowl neck and short sleeves. 'Emily used to say I had terrible taste in clothes.'

'Emily didn't know what she was talking about.'

When Ruby returned from school with her granddaughters, three large, beautifully dressed dolls were perched on chairs around the kitchen table and Olivia was making a pot of tea.

'In order to avoid an argument, they're identical,' she said. 'Sorry I couldn't get them here in time for your birthday, girls. As you can see, I got one for Daisy too.'

The children fell upon the dolls with screams of delight. 'Why does Daisy get presents on our birthday, but we get none on hers?' Ellie wanted to know.

'So she won't feel left out,' said Ruby.

'What if me and Moira feel left out?'

'Do you?'

Ellie considered the question earnestly. 'No.'

'Well, there's your answer. Have you all thanked Olivia for the lovely present?'

'Thank you, Olivia,' they chorused. They hadn't seen enough of the woman who was their great-grandmother to grow fond of her, but were always pleased when she came, as were Greta and Heather who'd been told she was a 'friend from the past', someone Ruby had known when she'd lived in Brambles with Emily.

Olivia went with the children into the living room while Ruby made the tea and wondered why she hadn't gone by now – she rarely stayed more than a couple of hours. It was a long drive to Bath and she'd already said she was tired.

This was Ruby's busiest time. The children ate and returned to watch television and Olivia stayed in the kitchen and chain-smoked while her daughter prepared another meal.

'Are you sure you won't have anything?' Ruby asked.

'No, dear. I'm not at all hungry, though I wouldn't mind another cup of tea. I'll just wait and say hello to Greta and Heather, then I'll go.' She glanced at the heap of potatoes Ruby was peeling. 'What a brick you are, doing this every night of the week.'

'Except Sundays, when the students feed themselves and the girls do the cooking. During the war, I often made meals for a dozen people, sometimes more.'

'I helped the Red Cross in the last war, just dressing wounds, that sort of thing. Although I was qualified, I hadn't nursed for more than fifteen years.'

Ruby paused, a potato in one hand, the peeler in another. 'I'd be a hopeless nurse. I'd get impatient with people if they didn't get better.'

'You didn't get impatient with Greta when she was ill.'

'No, but she's family. I'm wonderful with family, horrible with everyone else.'

'Thank goodness I'm family,' Olivia gave one of her rare rusty laughs. 'Not that I think what you said is true. I'm sure you're not horrible to the students or the people you fed during the war.'

'Not openly, but I feel horrible inside.'

They smiled at each other, and Ruby thought it was rather nice to have her mother sitting companiably by the table while she worked. For the first time, she felt stirrings of what might turn into a relationship. 'You must come again soon,' she said.

Perhaps her mother sensed it too but, if so, why did she look so sad? 'I'll come as soon as I can,' Olivia said.

Beth rang on Christmas Day to say she'd become a grandmother and felt very odd.

'You'll soon get used to it,' Ruby assured her. 'What time is it there?'

'Eight o'clock. I'm not long up. It's a beautiful day.'

'We're just about to have our tea – the Donovans and the Whites are here. It's already pitch dark, freezing cold, and snowing.'

'It sounds mad, but I'd sooner be in Liverpool right now, particularly if it's snowing.'

'I'd sooner you were too, Beth.'

'Ah, well,' Beth sighed. 'Have you had a nice day so far?'

'Lovely. The children are over the moon with their presents.' Matthew had bought them a toy typewriter each and she'd felt obliged to invite him to dinner.

'We've come through, haven't we, Rube?'

'We have that, Beth. Merry Christmas.'

'And a Merry Christmas to you.'

It was four days after Christmas. Greta and Heather had returned to work and the children were playing snowballs in the garden. Ruby was making another batch of mince pies, everybody's favourite, when the telephone rang.

'Hello. Oh! Now there's pastry stuck to the damn thing.'

'I beg your pardon?' It was a woman at the other end, well-spoken, with a nothing sort of voice, expressionless.

'Sorry, it's just that I'm baking and I forgot to wipe my hands. Hello, again.'

'Is that Mrs O'Hagan?'

'Speaking.'

'We found a note on mother's pad to ring you if something happened. I'm sorry to say she died on Christmas morning.'

'Who is this? I'm afraid I don't understand.'

'I'm Irene Clark. My mother's Olivia Appleby. She's never mentioned you before. There was just this note on her pad . . .' The voice trailed away.

'Olivia's *dead*?' Ruby gasped incredulously.

'Were you a friend?'

'Yes.'

'Well, it can't have come as a surprise. She's known for months she was dying. All those cigarettes! Eighty a day for years. When did you last see her?'

'September.'

'Then you must have been one of her last visitors.'

'Actually, she came to see me.'

'How incredible. Where are you, by the way? Yours isn't a local number.'

'Liverpool.'

'Liverpool! Mother came all the way to Liverpool in September! Are you sure you're not confusing this year with last?'

'Perhaps I am,' Ruby couldn't be bothered arguing. She disliked the woman's dull, deadpan voice. She didn't sound the least upset that her mother had just died.

'Oh, well. I've let you know as she requested. The funeral's Monday if you want to come.'

'I'm afraid that won't be possible. I'm very sorry to hear about your mother. Thank you for ringing.' Ruby replaced the receiver and went back into the kitchen where she ferociously kneaded the pastry, then pounded it just as ferociously with the rolling pin. Too late – such thoughts always came too late – she realised she'd wasted the opportunity of getting to know her mother. Poor Olivia, with her sad, sweet smile, who'd lost her lover, then had her newborn baby snatched from her arms. Why wasn't I nicer, more friendly, more loving? Ruby asked herself in an agony of remorse, then chided herself for being a hypocrite. She'd had every opportunity of doing all those things, but she hadn't, and it was no use crying over spilt milk. Except she was. She wiped the tears away with the back of her floury hand and wondered if she should ring Olivia's house in case Irene Clark was there and apologise for being so unsympathetic. Fancy assuming the woman wasn't upset because she had a deadpan voice! Maybe her voice was like that *because* she was upset.

'Oh, what a horrible person I am!' Ruby wailed aloud. 'And I don't get better as I get older.'

The children came pouring in from the garden, mittens soaking wet, their noses cherry red, faces glowing with health. Daisy was sniffing audibly, close to reluctant tears, because Ellie had stuffed a snowball down her neck. For some reason, Ruby hugged the three of them extravagantly, even Ellie who'd been such an extremely naughty little girl.

By the end of the following year, Greta and Heather had become competent shorthand typists. Greta moved to a different firm, but Heather was promoted to secretary in the solicitors and began to study towards becoming a legal clerk.

In 1968, Beth's youngest child, Seymour, enrolled at Liverpool University and it seemed only natural for him to stay with the O'Hagans. He was eighteen, a stranger in a strange land, who'd abandoned his country to escape the draft. On the other side of the world a cruel and pitiless battle was being fought as America attempted to wrest North Vietnam from the control of the Communists. Daniel Lefarge wasn't prepared for his son to be sacrificed in what he considered was a white man's war. On this, he and Beth wholeheartedly agreed.

Seymour was a shy, withdrawn young man, not a bit like Jake, his half brother. He studied hard in his room upstairs, but always came down for the *Nine o'Clock News* on television, when he would watch, making no comment, when students in his home country were shown demonstrating against the war, or when scenes of the fighting appeared on the screen and the numbers of dead were announced.

After the long, hot summer break, Seymour didn't return to university for his second year. Ruby found his room empty of most of his things and a note on the bed:

'I don't like being a coward. By the time you read this, I will have given myself up to the American Embassy in London. Please remind Pop that all my life he taught me to fight and I can't just stop when it pleases him. I need to fight for my country, otherwise I won't be able to live with myself for the rest of my life. Tell Mom I love her.'

In the first month of the new decade, January 1970, Private Seymour Lefarge lost his young life in the jungles of North Vietnam. For a long time, Beth was inconsolable, but eventually the memory of her son was tucked away in a corner of her mind to be brought out and cherished during times when she was alone. Daniel, though, never recovered. From the moment he heard about Seymour's death, he was a changed man.

Ruby had only witnessed the sixties from afar. She was too old to have gone to the Cavern, an open-air pop concert, worn flowers in her hair, and sung songs extolling love and peace. Carnaby Street could have been on the moon for all the chance she'd had of seeing it and, although the Liverpool Sound had spread throughout the world, she'd only heard it on *Top of the Pops*.

Even so, she was aware that the sixties had mainly been a heady, idealistic decade when compared to the ugly violence of the seventies. In Vietnam, the conflict was escalating and, suddenly, there seemed to be wars all over the place. Politicians were kidnapped and murdered, planes hijacked. Even on mainland Britain, bombs were killing and maiming innocent people as a consequence of the troubles in Northern Ireland.

She remembered the day that war had been declared on Germany and she and Beth had taken the children to Princes Park. Jake was still in his pram. Then, she'd been terrified that her children would be hurt. More than thirty years later, Ruby wondered what sort of world awaited her granddaughters when they grew up.

Daisy and the twins

13
1975–1981

Clint's problem was he was far too polite, Daisy thought wretchedly. It wouldn't enter his head to tell Ellie he was in a hurry. If they didn't leave soon, they'd be late for the film and she'd been looking forward to seeing *Godfather II* for ages and didn't want to miss a single minute. It meant they'd have to go to a different film and she hadn't a clue what else was on.

Was she the only person in the world who saw through her cousin and realised what a horrid person she was? Didn't Auntie Greta, or Moira, or even Daisy's own mother, consider it unreasonable for Ellie to ask Clint in her sweet, helpless way – though the real Ellie wasn't even vaguely sweet or the least bit helpless – if he wouldn't mind fixing her portable radio just when he and Daisy were about to go out? Gran might have said something, but she was in the kitchen washing up. Daisy had rushed into the bedroom – no one had noticed – to sulk and seethe and feel wretched on her own.

Of course, she could have said something herself, but was worried she'd show herself in a bad light next to the sweet and helpless Ellie who was always as nice as pie when Clint was around. Daisy could hear her, giggling like a little girl, while he tried to fix her radio, which he knew as much about as Daisy did herself.

Gran stuck her head around the door. 'Haven't you gone yet, love? You're going to be late.'

'I'm waiting for Clint,' Daisy said in an agonised voice.

'I'll tell him to get a move on.'

Seconds later, Clint appeared, so heartbreakingly handsome that Daisy caught her breath. 'We'd better hurry,' he said, as if it had been *her* holding *him* up.

'It's too late to hurry,' she said mildly when she would have preferred to scream. 'We'll never get there in time. The film starts at quarter past seven.'

'That's the programme, Daise. We'll miss the trailers and the adverts, that's all. The picture's not till half past.'

They arrived just in time, but it seemed as if everyone else in Liverpool had wanted to see *Godfather II*, and the Odeon was almost full. They had to sit in separate seats and Daisy didn't enjoy it nearly as much as she'd expected.

When they came out, they went to McDonald's for a chocolate milk shake. Daisy felt much better. When she and Clint were alone together, they got on perfectly. She'd liked him since the day they'd started school, drawn towards the little boy who looked as shy and awkward as herself. She was thrilled when they'd become friends, though Ellie had always been a thorn in her side, wanting to monopolise him, take him away, determined never to leave them by themselves.

Clint preferred to do quiet things with Daisy; mainly draw and paint, but seemed unable to resist when Ellie dragged him off to play leapfrog or climb trees. Now they were all seventeen and Ellie found different reasons for prying them apart, like fixing her stupid radio, which Daisy suspected hadn't been broken in the first place.

At some time over the last twelve years, she had fallen in love with Clint Shaw, but had no idea how he felt about her. He *liked* her, that was obvious, otherwise she wouldn't have become his regular girlfriend, but whether he wanted to spend the rest of his life with her, Daisy didn't know. She was always on tenterhooks, praying every night that he would suggest they get married or at least engaged but, so far, the prayer hadn't been answered. It worried her that one of these days the penny would drop and Clint would realise how attractive he was and she'd be jilted for a girl equally attractive. Like Ellie.

They began to discuss the picture which Clint considered even better than *Godfather I*. Daisy pretended to have enjoyed it because it seemed sour to say how she really felt.

'I thought Robert De Niro was brilliant,' Clint enthused. He was a film buff and his ambition was to become a Hollywood director, though he never mentioned taking her with him.

'Me too, but I preferred the first film.'

'Why?' Clint wanted to know. He was always interested in her opinion.

'It was more suspenseful. I remember being on the edge of me seat the whole way through.'

'You might be right.' Clint nodded in agreement, but claimed he still thought the second *Godfather* superior to the first.

They had another milk shake, strawberry this time, then Clint took her home. At the gate, he kissed her chastely on the lips and squeezed her waist, which was the most he'd ever done, much to Daisy's disappointment. She sometimes had the horrible feeling in her agonised brain that he looked upon her as a sister and was never likely to do anything else.

Gran was the only one still up. She was on the settee watching an old film on the telly and patted the seat beside her.

'It's nearly finished,' she said. 'I saw this with Beth before the war.'

'What's it called?' Daisy asked so she could tell Clint.

'*Of Human Bondage*, with Bette Davis and Leslie Howard. Me and Beth cried our eyes out.'

There was a photo of Beth on the mantelpiece. She was in Washington holding a placard for the Third World Women's Alliance. Gran said she'd been such a meek and mild person and was amazed she'd become a political agitator, always on demonstrations and marches.

The picture finished, Gran sniffed a bit and turned the set off. 'Did you get to the Odeon on time?'

'Sort of. We had to sit in separate seats.'

'Oh, dear.' Gran squeezed her hand. 'Ellie doesn't mean anything, you know. She just likes to draw attention to herself, make her presence felt.'

'If *I* did that, no one would take any notice. Everyone notices Ellie.

'I don't think so. Clint is such a nice, obliging young man who hasn't learnt to say no. One of these days he'll get his priorities right, don't worry.' She yawned. 'I think I'll turn in. Would you like some cocoa?'

'I'll make it.' Gran worked herself to the bone every day looking after them and deserved being waited on when the opportunity arose.

To Daisy's surprise, Ellie was in the kitchen with one of the students, the Irish one called Liam. He'd probably been searching for something to eat. He was extremely good-looking and had red hair, sort of gold, much nicer than Daisy's carroty colour. Gran was threatening to take only women students next year in view of the amount of flirting that went on.

'They must think they've landed on a bed of roses, finding themselves in the same house as three pretty teenage girls.' Gran had said this in Daisy's presence and she was only being nice, because Daisy wasn't remotely pretty and as solid as a piece of rock. The students were forever asking Ellie and Moira to functions at the university; discos and concerts. Daisy wouldn't have gone, she had Clint, but it would be nice to be asked.

Liam smiled at her nicely when she went in. Ellie ignored her. While Daisy poured water in the kettle, Liam asked what A levels she was taking.

'None,' she replied. 'I go to work.'

'She had to leave school at sixteen because she didn't get a single O level,' Ellie informed him.

'I got one in Art,' Daisy argued, going red.

'Huh, *Art!*' Ellie said, as if Art was totally useless.

'Not everyone can be a genius,' Liam said reasonably.

Daisy's brain was in proportion to her looks, below average. She'd tried hard to study, but the words made no sense and danced all over the page. The headmistress had said it wasn't worth her while staying for A levels like the twins – it had once been suggested she go to a special school, but Gran had insisted she stay where she was. Uncle Matt had given her a job, but Daisy suspected he was only doing Gran a favour. She was as useless in an office as she'd been at school. Clint had also stayed to take three A levels and she felt very much out of things when everyone discussed the subjects they were taking. Clint and Ellie were in the same class for English.

Oh, God! Daisy clenched her teeth. Life was *torture!*

'Are you making cocoa?' Ellie enquired.

'Yes.'

'Make us a cup while you're at it. Would you like some, Liam?'

'I wouldn't say no.' He had a lovely, lilting Irish accent and at least had the grace to thank her when she sulkily shoved the mug in front of him. Ellie took hers without a word.

'Why were you so nasty with her?' Liam asked when Daisy had gone.

'Was I nasty?' Ellie looked at him in surprise. It was the way she'd always spoken to Daisy.

'You weren't exactly nice.'

'I suppose she gets on me nerves,' Ellie replied after a few moments' thought. 'I find her a drag, always have. She's so slow and witless. I think she must have sludge for brains.' She'd never understand in a million years what Clint Shaw saw in her.

'I wouldn't want to get on your wrong side.' He pretended to shudder.

'There's not much chance of that.' Ellie let her tongue roll provocatively over her pink lips. She allowed her knee to touch his under the table. The whole house would have been shocked to the core had they known she and Liam Conway made love regularly.

Another thing no one knew was that when Liam finished his degree in two months' time, Ellie was returning to Dublin with him. There was no suggestion of them getting married. Both agreed this was the last thing they wanted. Ellie intended to have all sorts of adventures and this was only the first. Liam didn't want to be hampered by a wife and family while he travelled around the world – he could speak French and Spanish fluently and had a smattering of German and Italian.

Liam wasn't the first man Ellie had slept with, though he was the oldest and the best-looking. There'd been two before, one a student, and the other a boy at school. She wasn't over keen on the sex part, though it was OK. What she enjoyed was the enormous feeling of excitement, knowing the risk she was taking, making love with a man when her grandmother was in the next room and the rest of the family were downstairs. There'd be hell to pay if she was discovered, but that made it even more daring.

Liam leant over the table and kissed her. 'Will I see you later?'

Ellie giggled. 'You might.' Or he might not. The longer she avoided it, the more he would want her when next she condescended to visit his room. *That* was exciting too.

'Is our Daisy coming down with something, Mam?' Heather enquired over breakfast next morning.

'You should know, love. She's your daughter,' Ruby replied as she made mounds of toast in preparation for the students.

'She seemed very quiet earlier.' Daisy was the first to leave in the mornings. Matthew Doyle's head office was in Crosby and she had to catch a bus and a train. 'Perhaps she doesn't like that job.'

'Why not ask her tonight?' It could be work that was getting Daisy down. On the other hand, it might be Ellie, or possibly Clint, or a combination of all three.

'I can't tonight. Greta and I are going to the Playhouse.'

'Can't you go to the Playhouse another night?'

'But we've already got the tickets,' Greta wailed.

'Perhaps you could have a word with her, Mam,' Heather suggested. 'Are you ready, sis?'

'I'll just get me coat.'

'Before you go, Greta, would you kindly remind the twins that it's time they were up?' Ruby said with heavy sarcasm that went completely unnoticed.

'All right, Mam,' Greta said with the air of someone who was doing her a favour.

Her daughters seemed to regard their children as entirely the responsibility of their mother. Ruby sometimes wondered if she'd given birth to twins and a red-haired child without having noticed.

She'd once written to Beth to ask her opinion as to why they should think like this, and Beth had replied that the death of the boys had knocked the girls' lives out of kilter. 'They returned to being daughters when they could no longer be wives,' she wrote. 'Having children of their own doesn't fit in with this role. *You're* the mother, so you should take care of their children, just as you took care of everything when they were little. Daisy and the twins are your concern, not theirs.'

At first, Ruby thought this a load of rubbish but after a while conceded it made, sort of, sense, and was preferable to thinking it was all her own fault for being too domineering in the past.

She waved the girls goodbye, as she did every morning. They linked arms as they walked down the path. From the back Greta, in her pink fluffy coat and high heels, looked more like a teenager than almost forty, and Heather was very much the career woman in a black suit, hair pulled severely back in a bun, giving the appropriate gravitas to someone who was now a legal clerk specialising in probate. Heather actually had her own secretary, something of which Ruby was immensely proud. Greta was still a shorthand typist and showed no wish to be anything else.

There was a noise, as if a herd of elephants were trampling down the stairs, and two of the students, Frank and Muff, arrived in search of breakfast. She wondered what their mothers would say if they could see them now; unshaven, hair uncombed, clothes filthy. It was her job to do their washing, but it hardly ever appeared and she had no intention of pressing them.

Once again, she wondered if she should ask for girls when the new term started in October. She preferred boys. They were no trouble, apart from consuming a horrendous amount of food. Lately though, she'd begun to feel uneasy.

The chief cause of her unease came into the kitchen and wished her a breezy, 'Good morning.'

Liam Conway, a brilliant language student, twenty-one, but with the confidence of a man twice his age, and the ability to charm the birds off the trees. She didn't like the way he looked at Ellie – or the way Ellie looked at him, come to that. Something was going on, Ruby felt convinced.

Perhaps it would be best in future if three virile young men and the same number of young women ceased to have temptation put in their way by being housed under the same roof.

'Hi, Gran.' Ellie parked herself at the table. Until Liam Conway had arrived, she'd always been late for breakfast. Nowadays, she was early. Ruby had felt obliged to lay down the law and insist she came fully dressed instead of in her dressing gown, putting the students off their food, though this morning Frank clearly found the white lace bra visible through her thin school blouse just as disconcerting, but Muff was too busy eating to look up.

Liam didn't even glance in her direction and Ruby sensed it was deliberate. Ellie made a great show of tossing her head and flashing her lovely blue eyes, accidentally on purpose reaching for the milk at the same time as he did so that their hands touched. Liam looked at her then and Ruby tried to fathom the expression on his face. His eyes had narrowed, he was looking at Ellie through lowered lids and biting his bottom lip.

Desire! He was looking at her seventeen-year-old granddaughter with desire!

A little voice in Ruby's head shouted, 'Help', and she decided that later she would write to Beth.

The three-storey office block in Crosby overlooked the River Mersey. Daisy sat at her desk, unable to take her eyes off the water that shimmered in the gentle April sunshine. The sky was powdery blue with clouds like scraps of lace floating across.

It would make a stunning painting; cerulean blue as a base for the sky, yellow ochre with white or chrome orange for the sand. The silvery water would present a challenge.

A few people were walking along the sands; a man with a dog, a woman pushing an empty pram, two small children running behind. The dog would run into the water, back to his owner, shake itself vigorously, then run off again. It was a collie and was obviously having a wonderful time, furiously waving its great flag of a tail.

The children kept stopping to pick up things from the sand which they would show to their mother, who put them in a shopping bag attached to the handle of the pram. Daisy imagined the bag being full of shells and stones and funny little scraps of seaweed which the children would play with when they got home.

She sighed enviously. She would give everything she owned – not that she owned much – to be one of the people on the sands, able to run into the water, collect shells.

It was hard to concentrate when paradise was only fifty or so yards away. And now a ship had appeared, a tanker. Daisy rested her head in her hands and wondered where it was going. Somewhere exotic, a foreign port, with foreign smells, where people wore strange clothes and rode on camels.

Daisy's longing to be anywhere else in the world rather than the place where she was now, was so strong, it felt like a sickly ball in her throat.

'Haven't you started on that filing yet?'

'I was just looking through it,' Daisy lied as she shuffled the pile of papers on her desk. She had been taken on to assist Uncle Matt's secretary whom he claimed was overworked. Theresa Frayn had treated her nicely at first, but had long ago become impatient with her slowness. She had never known anyone take so long to do filing or type a simple letter. If it hadn't been for Uncle Matt, Daisy suspected she'd have been shown the door months ago.

She began the painful task of sorting through the filing, putting the sheets in alphabetical order, conscious of Theresa glowering at her from across the room. The incoming letters weren't so bad. They had bold letterheads and were easy to understand, but the carbon copy replies were difficult. As she tried to make sense of the words, Daisy had a familiar feeling of disorientation, as if the world had turned upside down.

'Morning, girls.' Uncle Matt came into the office. He was wearing jeans and an anorak which meant he would be visiting a site during the day.

'Good morning, Matthew,' Theresa said girlishly, fluttering her lashes.

'Good morning, Mr Doyle.' Gran had stressed she mustn't call him 'Uncle Matt' in the office.

'Tea!' He pretended to gag. 'I desperately need a cuppa.'

Theresa got to her feet, anxious to please her handsome boss, but Uncle Matt said, 'Let Daisy do it.' He grinned. 'She makes a lovely cup of tea does our Daise.' It was one of the few things Daisy could do efficiently.

The day wore on. Uncle Matt went out, more people appeared on the sands, more ships glided across the glistening water, in and out of the port of Liverpool. Daisy copy-typed a specification and made such a hash of it that Theresa Frayn ripped it to pieces in front of her eyes. 'I'll do it again meself,' she snapped.

While Daisy was struggling with the typewriter, Ellie and Moira were walking home from school arm in arm, a boy on each side and two trailing behind. The Donovan twins were the prettiest girls in the sixth form and the fact they were so alike gave an added flavour to their already plentiful charms. They were usually accompanied by a court of admirers.

'What'cha doing tonight?'

'Fancy going to a disco?'

'How about the pics? I'll buy you some chocolates.'

The boys didn't mind which twin responded, each being as appealing as the other.

Ellie giggled and Moira stuck her nose in the air. She wouldn't be seen dead with a boy her own age, preferring older, more sophisticated men. Apart from Uncle Matt who was fifty-one and *too* old, she hadn't so far met one that she liked, but she would, one day. It didn't matter when, she wasn't in any hurry. It was Moira's intention to gain three top grade A levels, go to university, and become a teacher. Once this ambition had been realised and she had worked for a few years, she might think about getting married and starting a family.

'Come on, Ellie,' a boy called slyly, 'have a heart. John Perry said you're an easy lay.'

Moira glanced at Ellie. 'Aren't you offended?' she asked, but her sister just shrugged. If a boy had said that to her, she'd have slapped his face. They walked in silence for a while until Moira said, 'Unless it's true.'

Still Ellie didn't answer, but smiled instead, as if she wasn't a bit perturbed by the suggestion.

'I know some nights you go upstairs to Liam Conway's room.' Moira was an exceptionally light sleeper. Ellie or Daisy only had to turn over for her to wake up. It was months now since she'd first heard her sister creep upstairs. Shortly afterwards, the bed in Liam's room which was directly overhead would creak. About an hour later, Ellie would return. Moira hadn't said anything, being a firm believer in letting the world go by with the minimum of interference. People, her sister included, were masters of their own destiny, and if Ellie wanted to sleep with Liam Conway, then it was up to her. She was, however, a little disturbed at the idea that Ellie was sleeping around.

'Are you going to clat on me?' Ellie said casually.

'You know I won't.' Moira had never told tales in her life.

'Not that I care, like. I just wondered. Another thing, don't tell anyone this either, but when Liam goes back to Dublin in June, I'm going with him.'

'They mightn't let you.'

'They can't stop me. Anyroad, so as to avoid a fuss, I might just run away.'

'That would be very inconsiderate, Ellie.' Despite not wanting to interfere, Moira was extremely shocked. She also believed people should have standards. 'Mum would be terribly upset and it would break Gran's heart.'

Ellie looked momentarily abashed. 'Oh, I'll come back, don't worry,' she assured her sister. 'Dublin will just be the first of my adventures. I shall have loads more.'

'Aren't you worried you'll get pregnant?'

'I can't. I'm on the pill.'

Moira could never quite understand her twin. Sometimes, she wondered if Ellie's heart beat twice as fast as other people's, if her blood raced around her body when everyone else's merely flowed. She was never still, always agitated, impatient, wanting to do things first, be the centre of attention, be the loudest, the brightest, the most daring of all. Ellie had to have everything.

Yet she wasn't happy. Moira was the only person who recognised the turbulent nature of her sister hid a dissatisfaction that would never be soothed by normal means. Ellie craved excitement, it was the reason why, years ago, she'd stolen things from school. Fortunately, the culprit had never been discovered. It was why she'd started sleeping with men, why she wanted to run away.

'Did you do it with John Perry?' she asked.

'Yes.'

'Where?'

'Behind the gym, after school.'

'Say if you'd been seen! You'd have been made to leave and couldn't have done your A levels.'

'Who cares!' Ellie laughed. 'Anyroad, I wasn't seen, was I?'

Sometimes, Ellie would watch through the bedroom window when Clint brought Daisy home. All he did was kiss her, and then only the once. He didn't realise what he was missing. Half the girls in the sixth form were crazy about him and would have gone much further than just a kiss.

Yet Clint stuck to Daisy, despite Ellie having made it obvious that she fancied him. She'd like to bet he was a virgin, which was no wonder, having the ugly, clodhopping Daisy for a girlfriend.

Before she went to Dublin, Ellie resolved she'd do her utmost to seduce Clint Shaw, show him what it was like to be with a real woman! It would be a problem finding the opportunity, they were hardly ever alone together, but that only made the task more exciting.

Ellie rubbed her hands together. She could hardly wait!

Ruby regarded the painting with dismay. 'It's very nice, love,' she said, trying to put some enthusiasm into her voice.

'It's the view from the office window,' Daisy explained. 'I had to do it from memory.'

'You're lucky, having such a lovely view.'

'I suppose,' Daisy sighed. 'Though I find it very distracting.'

Daisy was very easily distracted when she had to work. It had been the same at school when she'd always been bottom of the class, except for Art, which was surprising considering the dreadful paintings she turned out. The latest was particularly crudely done, the paint laid on thickly like tar. Instead of being smooth, the sky was full of ridges and for some reason the river was white and grey lumps. There was a strange figure standing in the water which Ruby eventually recognised as a dog and the other, even stranger figure, on the sand – more lumps – was presumably its owner.

'What's this, love?' she asked, pointing to what looked like litter on the beach.

'Children. They're collecting shells and stuff. And that's their mother with a pram.'

'As I said, it's very nice.'

'Where shall I hang it? It still needs hooks and some string. Ellie doesn't like my paintings in our bedroom. She said they're ugly.'

'I'll put it in my room, shall I?' Most of Daisy's unframed work went in Ruby's room. Even Heather refused to hang her daughter's paintings in a place where they could be seen. Ruby had put some in the students' rooms and none had so far complained. 'Leave it where it is for now, love,' she said.

'OK, Gran,' Daisy said happily. 'I'll go and tidy the shed.' She painted in the garden shed where Mrs Hart's garden tools were still stored, including a roller that couldn't be budged.

Mrs Kilfoyle, who taught Art, had suggested Daisy go to college for the subject, but Heather had put her foot down and refused. 'I wouldn't take any notice of Mrs Kilfoyle. She's as daft as a brush. Our Daisy lazed her way through school. It's about time she buckled down to some proper work.'

Daisy had meekly agreed. 'Anyroad,' she confided to Ruby, 'I don't want to leave one school for another.' It was obvious she'd had enough. Not long afterwards, she arrived home laden with boxes of paint and squares of hardboard and set up work in the shed, where it was either freezing cold or like an oven depending on the weather. Even Heather felt guilty for not having provided the materials before.

'Oh, Mam! She mustn't have liked asking us to buy them. She waited till she was earning money of her own. I thought that O level was just a fluke.'

The paintings that emerged from the shed only confirmed that Heather had been right. The O level had indeed been a fluke.

Ruby's heart bled for her unhappy granddaughter. How would poor Daisy cope as she grew older? She fervently hoped she and Clint would get married. A genuinely nice boy, he was clearly fond of her – and she of him, though it would mean his mother, the loathsome Pixie, would become a member of the family.

Everyone had eaten, the dishes had been washed and dried, the kitchen looked unusually clean – a sight that Ruby always found slightly disturbing it was so unnatural. Daisy was out with Clint, and the twins were in the bedroom doing their homework. An evening in front of the television with Heather and Greta stretched ahead seductively.

Ruby was about to switch on *Coronation Street*, when Heather said, 'Mam, I thought I'd better tell you, me and Greta booked a holiday in Corfu today. We're going for a fortnight in July.'

'How kind of you – to tell me that is,' she said icily. 'Well, at least I'll know where you are when you disappear for two whole weeks.'

Heather looked taken aback. 'We didn't think you'd mind.'

'I'd like to have been consulted first. I assume you're not taking your children with you, that they're being left with me?'

'We couldn't afford for the five of us to go.'

'Oh, dear! But thank goodness you can afford to pay for two. I hope you both have a lovely time.'

'We'll cancel it if you like,' Greta offered, sensing her mother wasn't exactly pleased at the news.

'Though we'll lose the deposit,' Heather warned.

'I wouldn't dream of putting you to any inconvenience. Fortunately, your holiday doesn't clash with mine.' Ruby had never made up her mind so quickly about anything before.

'You're going away?' the girls gasped, more or less together.

'I'm going to stay with Beth in Washington for a week in June. It's International Women's Year and there's all sorts of things going on.'

'But how will we cope without you?' Greta wailed.

'Same way as I'll cope without you.'

'Have you booked the flight?' demanded Heather.

'No. I intended discussing it with you first,' Ruby lied shamelessly. She was fed up being taken for granted. 'All you have to do is get up early and make everyone's breakfast, then do the dinner when you come home. I'll change the beds before I go,' she said helpfully.

'Why couldn't you have gone later, like us, when the students will have gone?'

'You obviously haven't noticed, Heather, but we have foreign students in the summer. The upstairs rooms can't stay empty for three and a half months. We need the money.'

'Actually, Mam,' Greta grumbled, 'We could do with the whole house to ourselves. I wouldn't mind a room to meself, and neither would Heather, and the girls are too old for three to a room.'

'If you'd like to ask your boss for a two hundred per cent rise, then we can have the whole house to ourselves.'

'You're being dead sarcastic tonight, Mam. Why can't we get a cheaper house?'

Ruby guffawed. 'With a room each for the six of us! Which planet are you living on, Greta?'

'We could ask Uncle Matt to reduce the rent.'

'Don't you dare even *think* such a thing!' Ruby angrily thumped the arm of the settee and the girls jumped. 'We're fortunate to get it as cheap as we do. It's a lovely house and you're not exactly cramped sleeping two or three to a room. Nowadays, Matthew could sell this place for thousands and thousands of pounds. You should be thanking your lucky stars, not complaining. Now would someone mind switching on *Coronation Street*? I've already missed half.'

Ellie couldn't make head nor tail of Milton's *Paradise Lost*, which was part of the English A level. It was something to do with hell having been taken over by some guy called Beelzebub. When the class had finished, she asked Clint Shaw if he understood what it was about.

'Well, yes,' he stammered.

'Then help me with tonight's essay.' She fluttered her lashes and looked at him pleadingly. 'We could do it together.'

'I was going to do mine as soon as I got home. Me and Daisy are going out tonight.'

'Then I'll come with you,' Ellie said with alacrity. 'Your mum won't mind, will she?'

He didn't look terribly keen on the idea, but he'd never been able to refuse her anything. 'Mum won't be there. She goes to work.'

Ellie already knew that. Fate had provided the perfect opportunity to seduce Clint Shaw.

The Shaws lived in a street of substantial terraced houses off Wavertree Road, a street that Ruby had been very familiar with when she'd been the pawnshop runner, though the young people didn't know that. Ellie had been to the Shaws' house before. She thought it rather garish and over-furnished.

'I usually do me homework in the kitchen,' Clint mumbled.

'That's OK by me.'

They spread their books on the lime green table, sat on the lime green chairs, and he explained that *Paradise Lost* described the fall of man for having disobeyed God's laws. Satan was trying to exact revenge for being expelled from heaven.

'You make it sound so much clearer,' exclaimed Ellie, filling her eyes with admiration.

Clint blushed. Gosh, she marvelled as the blush spread over his smooth, fair skin, he was incredibly good-looking. How come he hadn't realised? Why didn't he play the field as boys did who were only half as attractive? His hair was thick and blond and almost straight apart from the ends which flicked up slightly, not quite reaching the collar of his school blazer, but not short enough to look old-fashioned. Everything about his face was perfect, from the fine eyebrows, grey eyes with lashes that most women would give their eye teeth for – not Ellie, who had equally long lashes of her own – straight nose, and slightly full mouth.

Gran used to wonder aloud where Clint had got his looks from. 'Not his mother, that's for sure.' She'd never liked Pixie. 'They must have come from his dad.' Brian Shaw had turned out to be a rougher, tougher version of his son.

'Can I have a glass of water?'

'I'll make tea if you like?'

'Oh, *please*.' She got to her feet when he did. 'I'll help, shall I?' By the sink, she brushed against him so that her breast touched his arm. Clint looked embarrassed and edged away. Ellie giggled, slid her hand inside his blazer, and tickled him. She lifted her head and bit his ear, then rubbed her lips against his cheek. 'You need a shave,' she whispered, before kissing him fully on the lips.

She would never forget his reaction. He shuddered violently, as if he'd just had an electric shock and pushed her away. '*Don't do that!*'

'Oh, come on, Clint. What harm would it do.' She approached him again and was about to put her arms around his neck, but he caught hold of her hands and held them tightly. 'That hurts,' she complained in a babyish voice.

'Leave me alone.' He flung her hands away, as if they were contaminated. There was a look on his face, as if he wanted to be sick.

'Why?' Ellie demanded.

'Because Daisy's me girlfriend. It wouldn't be fair on her.'

Neither spoke for quite some time, just stared at each other across the room. Then, with a shiver of comprehension, Ellie understood. She felt herself go very cold.

'No, that's not why,' she said slowly. 'It's nothing to do with Daisy. It's because you don't like women. You're a queer.'

'Just because I don't fancy you, it doesn't mean I'm a queer,' he blustered, looking even sicker.

'No, it doesn't,' Ellie conceded. 'But you'd have behaved the same with any woman. I just know.' She began to put the books back in her satchel.

Clint was trembling, leaning against the sink, supporting himself with his hands, as if his legs were about to give way. His face had lost all vestige of colour and his eyes were hot and feverish.

'Don't tell Daisy.' The hoarse voice was as agonised as his face. 'Don't tell anyone. *Please!*'

'Don't worry,' Ellie assured him. She felt scared and a little bit ashamed. 'I won't tell a soul.'

That night, Daisy came home early when everyone was still up. She burst into the living room, eyes shining. 'You'll never guess,' she cried.

'Guess what?' demanded a chorus of voices.

Ellie didn't speak. She sensed what her cousin was about to say.

'We didn't go to the pictures, but for a walk instead. Clint asked me to marry him. We're getting engaged. On Saturday, we're going to town to buy a ring. Only a cheap one,' she added quickly. 'He's only got a few pounds of pocket money saved.'

'Oh, that's wonderful, love.' Gran leapt to her feet and hugged Daisy warmly. 'What do you think, Heather?'

Heather frowned. 'You're awfully young, Daisy.'

'But Mum, we're not getting married for ages, not till Clint's at least twenty-one. We might go to live in London where it'll be easier for him to get the sort of job he wants, scriptwriting, or something.' She smiled blissfully.

'Congratulations, Daise!' Moira planted a kiss on Daisy's freckled cheek.

'I'll get the sherry and we'll drink a toast,' Gran cried. 'Someone fetch the glasses. What a pity Clint didn't come in so we could have congratulated him too.'

'You know Clint, he's terribly shy,' Daisy said with a proprietorial air. She examined the third finger of her left hand as if she could already see herself wearing the cheap ring.

'I hope you'll be very happy, Daisy.' Ellie gave her cousin a brief hug. She'd never had much time for Daisy, but she was family and meant more to her than Clint Shaw ever would. He saw nothing threatening about Daisy and was using her as a cover. Was she supposed to protect him at the expense of Daisy's happiness, let her go blithely ahead and *marry* the guy?

Yet she'd never seen Daisy as happy as she was now, as if a light had come on inside her. How could she spoil everything by telling the truth? Did Daisy know what a queer was? Would anyone, not just Daisy, believe her if she told them what she knew about Clint Shaw? Ellie doubted it.

14

She wanted to see the White House, Georgetown, the Lincoln Memorial, sail along the Potomac to Mount Vernon, visit museums and art galleries, which she wouldn't have dreamt of doing at home, but was the sort of thing people did on holiday. She bought a guidebook and made a list of sights to see.

Beth was delighted she was coming to Washington and had booked a room at her hotel. 'You'll love it, Rube. There'll be loads of exciting things to do, and you'll meet all my friends.'

As usual, Ruby's wardrobe was devoid of anything smart, but now she had a perfect excuse to renew it. Everyone in the house contributed in some way towards the holiday in Washington, even the students who clubbed together and bought a lovely black leather handbag to thank her for being such a great landlady. Before leaving, Ruby bade them a fond farewell. They would be gone by the time she came back.

Greta and Heather stayed in for three Saturdays in a row to see to things in the house, giving their mother time to roam the city shops and look for clothes. A delirious Ruby, drunk with excitement, purchased an elegant black linen suit, a blue frilly blouse and a plain white one to wear under it, two floaty, feminine Indian frocks in stunning jewel colours, a pair of daringly high-heeled shoes to go with the suit and gold sandals to go with the frocks.

Daisy bought her a pretty cotton nightdress – the ones she had were probably older than Daisy herself and only fit for ripping into dusters, and the twins took note of every single item in her filthy, ancient make-up bag. They replaced each thing with a new one; lipstick, powder, eye shadow, rouge. 'Cake mascara's dead old-fashioned, Gran,' Moira told her. 'Nowadays, it's in a wand. Oh, and we got you some kohl eyeliner.'

'I've never used eyeliner before, but I'll give it a go.' She'd try anything once.

'We bought a new make-up bag an' all and some perfume. It's only a little bottle,' said Ellie.

'I love *Je Reviens*. Oh! Aren't you lovely girls! I know I'll only be gone a week, but I'll miss everyone something rotten.'

'I'll miss *you*, Gran.' Ellie looked unusually tearful.

Now, here she was, on the plane, wearing the black suit, feeling like a member of the human race again.

The flight was enjoyable and she wasn't the least bit sick or frightened as Heather had warned she might be. She drank two gins and orange after the meal, then lost herself in a novel she'd been meaning to read for ages, feeling ever so slightly tipsy.

It was five o'clock on Saturday afternoon American time when Beth met her at Washington National airport. The occasional photos Beth had sent hadn't shown how much she'd changed. She wore no make-up and her skin had acquired the texture of old, polished wood. It was hard to believe she'd once been so soft and plump when now she looked the opposite, hardy and tough. Her eyes held a glint, rather than a sparkle, and she even moved differently, in short, hurried spurts when she'd used to glide, driving Ruby mad with her refusal to hurry. She wore jeans, a T-shirt, and shabby sports shoes. Her short, wiry hair was almost completely grey.

'You make me feel over-dressed,' Ruby cried after they'd hugged each other affectionately.

'You make me feel like an old bag lady,' Beth responded with a grin.

'What's that?'

'A woman tramp.'

'We've always been honest with each other, Beth. You do look a bit like a tramp.'

'I can't be bothered with doing meself up nowadays.'

'I spent ages doing myself up for you. I've just learnt to use eyeliner and I had my hair tinted. I've got a few grey ones.'

'I've got rather more than a few and they can stay grey for all I care. Come on, I've a cab outside.'

She linked Ruby's arm and began to lead her towards the exit. Ruby thought it a shame that the girl who, during the war, had melted the remains of half a dozen lipsticks in an unsuccessful attempt to make a whole one, no longer cared how she looked. She recalled the unctuous flattery they'd both heaped upon various American soldiers in the hope of acquiring nylons.

To her surprise, the cab driver turned out to be a woman.

'Ruby, this is Margot,' Beth said when they got in.

'Hi, Rube. Nice to meet 'cha.'

The three chatted amiably as the cab carried them through a warren of streets. Ruby's eyes were everywhere. It was hard to believe that she was in a foreign country. 'They're all straight,' she remarked.

'What was that, honey?' Margot asked.

'The streets, they're all straight. At home, they go all over the place.'

'We're more orderly this side of the Atlantic.'

'Where are we staying?' she asked Beth.

'Halfway between Old Downtown and the White House.'

'The White House is one of the first places I want to see.' If you went on a guided tour, it was possible to get a glimpse of President Ford going about his business.

'You'll see it tomorrow morning.'

'Goody!'

The hotel was clean and functional and seemed to be run and occupied entirely by women. Beth introduced Ruby to the desk clerk and virtually every other woman they met on the way up to the second floor.

'I always use this place when I stay in Washington,' she explained, opening the door on to a small, plain room, completely devoid of pictures or any sort of ornament. 'Would you like a rest?'

'No, thanks, though I wouldn't mind getting washed and changing into a frock.' The temperature felt at least ten degrees hotter than in England. 'Another thing, I'm starving.'

'We'll eat downstairs the minute you're ready.'

The restaurant was more like a school canteen, the tables big enough for eight. Ruby, freshly made-up and wearing a filmy green Indian frock and gold sandals, felt slightly overdressed when she went in with Beth who was still in her bag lady outfit. The food was plain and nourishing and reminded her of the convent. More women joined their table as the room quickly became crowded and a floundering Ruby was asked loads of questions about her home country to which she didn't know a single answer.

No, she hadn't a clue how many women were members of the British parliament, or how many were senior civil servants, leaders of unions, announcers on television, chief executives of this or managing directors of that.

'Margaret Thatcher was elected leader of the Conservative party earlier this year,' she told them in a lame attempt to show she wasn't completely ignorant, but they already knew.

No, she'd never been a member of a union, she confessed. 'I've never had a proper job, so there's never been the need.'

'Isn't there a housewives' union?' one of the women queried. 'I remember reading about it once.'

Ruby had no idea. Beth took pity on her and changed the subject. 'You'll never guess what she did before the war. Tell them about the pawnshop runner, Rube.'

The women listened, fascinated, while she described going to and from the various pawnshops with Greta in her arms, then both children in a pram. She got quite carried away – or perhaps she wanted to impress after the abysmal ignorance she'd just shown – so told them about Foster Court, the cleaning jobs, and Jacob's extended stay in bed.

'Gee, honey, you sure showed some enterprise.'

'I guess you've seen poverty most of us have never known.'

'I suppose I must have,' Ruby said modestly.

Everyone remained seated while the tables were cleared. 'What's happening now?' she asked.

'There's a meeting,' Beth replied.

'What's it about?'

'The glass ceiling.'

'Oh, right.' Ruby had never heard of the glass ceiling, but soon discovered it was what women encountered when they tried to climb the hierarchy of an organisation. It wasn't visible, but it was there. Women were promoted so far, but all sorts of sneaky, underhand things were done to prevent them rising further.

Ruby couldn't find much sympathy for the speaker, an aggressive, well-spoken journalist who claimed she'd been thwarted on numerous occasions when she'd applied for promotion. 'I wouldn't like to work for *her*,' she whispered. Beth just smiled.

When the meeting was over, an all-women rock group appeared to entertain them. By the time they'd finished, Ruby was ready for bed.

Next morning, she put on her other frock – turquoise with little gold beads around the neck – and applied her make-up with extra care for the visit to the White House, hoping her hand wouldn't shake as she drew a fine black line around each eye – Moira and Ellie claimed eyeliner made her look exotic and glamorous.

'I'm not too old for it at fifty-seven?' Ruby had asked them anxiously. 'I don't want to look like mutton dressed up as lamb.'

'You always look gorgeous, Gran. Everyone at school thinks you're our mother.'

Last night at the meeting there'd hardly been anyone wearing make-up, or frocks, come to that. They'd mostly been like Beth, in jeans and T-shirts.

'Will you be comfortable like that?' Beth enquired at breakfast.

'Why shouldn't I be?'

Beth shrugged. 'No reason. Let's not dawdle over coffee. People are already beginning to collect outside.'

'What for?'

'The march to the White House.'

An hour later, Ruby found herself in the blazing sunshine marching up and down Pennsylvania Avenue in front of an impressive white building holding a placard bearing the message, 'Equal Pay for Equal Work', a concept with which she fully agreed, but she'd been expecting something other than a march. Not only that, the gold sandals had started to pinch, her feet hurt, she was perspiring from every pore, and her throat was as dry as a bone. She was beginning to wonder if there'd ever be time to go sightseeing or whether the week ahead was to be a long series of demonstrations and marches.

'Have you come far?'

She turned to find a young woman beside her. 'England,' she replied in a cracked voice.

'We're from New Zealand. I'm with my mum. She's back there somewhere.' The girl gestured vaguely. 'They weren't doing much to celebrate International Women's Year at home and Mum was determined to experience at least a bit of it. It's wonderful, isn't it? The feeling of sisterhood, of women being in charge, able to do things that men have always insisted that they couldn't. I wonder if there'll ever be a woman President one day – of America, that is.'

'I don't see why not.'

'Well, there's not much sign of it yet,' the girl said, her face glowing with youthful indignation. 'Don't you feel as mad as hell when you see all the world leaders together on television and there's not a single woman amongst them?'

'I do. I feel outraged.'

'It's not fair, is it? Why should it only be men who have a say in how the world is run when more than half the population are women?'

'You're right. It's not a bit fair.'

'Oh, my mum's calling me. Well, it was nice talking to you. Perhaps we'll come across each other again some time.'

'I hope so.' Ruby smiled. For the first time, she was aware she was taking part in a great event. The women began to sing 'We Shall Overcome', and she joined in, moved and uplifted in a way she'd never felt before. Later, she'd buy jeans, a couple of T-shirts, and some comfortable shoes, and leave the pretty, entirely unsuitable frocks for when she got home. It seemed unlikely she'd sail along the Potomac, visit a single museum or gallery, and this was as near as she would get to the White House. Still, it was International Women's Year and she was determined to enjoy the experience to the full.

After a rally and numerous speeches, they returned to the hotel for dinner which was followed by a black factory worker describing how the female workforce had been sexually harrassed, then sacked when they'd demanded to be represented by a union. Three years later, after a vigorous campaign, they'd been reinstated and the union recognised. The entire room erupted in cheers when the woman finished.

Later, Ruby, Beth, and half a dozen other women went to a nearby basement club and drank too much wine. Ruby wondered aloud why every single person there was female. 'Are men banned?' she enquired.

'No, but they're not exactly welcome,' she was told.

'Why not?'

'It's a lesbian bar, honey.'

Had Beth become a lesbian? Ruby asked her when they got back to the hotel. They stopped in the foyer to buy coffee from the machine and went to sit in the lounge.

'Of course not, idiot.' Beth laughed. 'But we have to show solidarity with all our sisters, Rube, whatever their colour, race, or sexual disposition. Women should stick together.'

'That woman last night, the one on about the glass ceiling, she was pushy and aggressive and would make a terrible boss. I don't see why I should show solidarity with someone like her.'

'Why should only men be allowed to become terrible bosses?' Beth said reasonably. 'No one's saying all women are nice, but being nasty doesn't stop men from getting on.'

'Gosh, Beth, you've changed.' Ruby stared at her friend's gritty, determined face. 'There was a time when you never had a sensible idea in your head. Now you're full of them.'

'If my marriage had been different, I'd be at home baking cookies and keeping the house nice, bemoaning the fact that one of my kids was dead and the others were married. But I was forced to do something or go under. The more I did, the more I became involved and the more I changed. Things mattered that I'd never thought about before.'

Ruby nodded. 'And now it's Daniel stuck at home. Is he happy?'

'Not really. He can't stop mourning Seymour. I don't like leaving him, but he left me when *I* was unhappy. I suppose that sounds selfish, but I don't care.'

'You still loved Jacob, though he did much worse than that.'

'I still love Daniel. I'm just putting myself first.'

'I've never been able to do that,' Ruby said with a sigh. 'The girls have always come first with me, then *their* girls. They'd never manage without me.'

'Are you quite sure about that, Rube?' Beth's eyes narrowed. 'Are you honestly saying Greta and Heather wouldn't have somehow coped if you hadn't been around? People usually do. You know the old dictum, "No one's indispensable."'

'Are *you* saying I've wasted my life?' Ruby replied hotly.

'No, but you've done exactly what you wanted to do, Ruby. Don't get angry.' She put her hand on Ruby's arm. 'You'd make a lousy employee. If the boss looked at you sidewise, you'd bawl him out. You can't stand criticism. You need to be top dog, to be in charge. So, you created your own little world and crowned yourself its queen. Don't tell me you haven't been contented with your lot, for most of the time, that is.'

'I suppose I have, but what if Larry and Rob hadn't been killed and the girls hadn't come back home? What would I have done then?'

'Married Chris, trained for a career, ended up as someone important. You have to be *important*, Rube. Remember how much we all needed you during the war? You revelled in it.'

'Did I?'

'You certainly did.'

Ruby would have liked to continue the conversation, but more women came into the lounge and joined them, and a different conversation ensued well into the early hours.

The rest of the week flew by. By the time it ended, Ruby had learnt more about herself and the rest of the world than she had during her entire lifetime. In the past, she'd watched television or read the paper and complained loudly to whoever would listen about the injustices in the world, but apart from the years in Foster Court, she'd never had to struggle. She'd worked hard, but had never fought for anything in her life. Compared to many of the women she'd met that week, she'd had things easy. When she got home, she was determined do something, join something, read the books she'd bought from the numerous stalls and broaden her education. Most of her life had been spent in a rather comfortable rut – with the help of Matthew Doyle, she realised thirty years too late.

On her final afternoon, Beth took her on the metro to City Place, a bargain mall, where Ruby bought a long cream jacket to wear with the jeans she'd got earlier in the week – she'd travel home in the new outfit, give everyone a surprise. She chose little gifts, mainly ethnic jewellery, for the girls, and hesitated a while over a navy silk tie with a tiny embroidered White House on the front before deciding to buy it.

'Who's that for?' Beth asked.

'Matthew Doyle.' It wasn't much, but it was a gesture.

Ruby wasn't the only one leaving next morning. The night was spent wishing a tearful farewell to women with whom she'd become instant friends and was unlikely ever to see again. It finished with drinks and a singsong in the hotel where the warm, comradely atmosphere was thick with emotion and virtually the whole room was in tears.

Nothing would ever be the same again, Ruby thought dismally. Life would be unbearably dull back in Liverpool.

Saying goodbye to Beth next morning was the worst thing of all. They could hardly speak, just clung to each other at the airport until Beth pushed her away, saying gruffly, 'You'll miss the plane.'

'Bye, Beth.'

'Tara, Rube,' Beth said, lapsing into a Liverpool accent for the first time. Ruby burst into tears.

It had been an exhausting seven days. For most of the flight, she slept soundly, but woke up feeling not even faintly refreshed. Her legs could barely carry her when she walked down the steps and her feet touched the tarmac in Manchester airport.

She caught a taxi home; hang the expense. All she wanted was to see her family, give them their presents, then go to bed, where she would probably sleep for a week.

Mrs Hart's house looked smaller than she remembered and much shabbier. The front door opened when she was paying the taxi driver and

Greta came out. Ruby thought she'd come to help carry her bag as she didn't think she had the strength left to lift it.

Instead, Greta said in a tragic voice, 'Oh, Mam! Our Ellie's disappeared. According to Moira, she's run away to Dublin with that student, Liam Conway. Oh, Mam! What are we going to do?'

At that particular moment, Ruby had no idea.

It wasn't the only thing that had happened, just the worst. Three fifteen-year-old French students were arriving on Monday.

'Some woman rang to ask if it was all right,' Heather told her. 'I said it was.'

'But I wasn't expecting them until the week after!' Ruby cried. She'd like to bet no one had cleared up after Frank, Muff and Liam. From previous experience, the rooms were usually a tip, full of rubbish and unwanted belongings, when their occupants left for good.

Ellie wasn't the only one in disgrace. Daisy had given up her office job and was working as an usherette in the Forum.

'An usherette!' Ruby said faintly. 'Is that where she is now?'

'Yes.' Heather pursed her angry lips. 'She didn't discuss it with me first, just gave in her notice weeks ago and swore Matthew to secrecy. I'd have given him a piece of my mind, except he's already got troubles of his own.'

'What sort of troubles?' Had she really only been away a week? It felt more like a month, or six months.

The news about Matthew Doyle had been in the *Echo*. The dampcourses were faulty on an estate of 250 houses that his firm had built and the sub-contractors responsible had declared themselves bankrupt.

'Uncle Matt's got to put them right, but it's not covered by the insurance. It'll cost the earth,' Moira told her. Moira was also in disgrace, having known all along what her sister was planning to do, yet kept it to herself.

'Sly little monkey,' Greta snapped during the argument that followed.

'Not as sly as our Daisy,' Heather countered.

'I promised to keep it a secret,' Moira said, unperturbed. 'I wasn't prepared to break me promise. What do you think, Gran?'

'Don't ask me,' replied a distraught Ruby. 'I'm incapable of thought at the moment.'

'The holiday doesn't seem to have done you much good,' Greta said huffily.

'The holiday did me a world of good, but coming home's done me no good at all. I was only tired before. Now, I feel as if the world's collapsed around my ears.'

And no one had noticed she was wearing jeans.

Perhaps the events in Washington had made Ruby more tolerant. When she thought about it the next day, she couldn't see much harm in what her granddaughters had done. Ellie had acted very irresponsibly, but she would be eighteen in September, an adult. At the same age, Ruby had had two children and was living in Foster Court.

As for Moira, the girl had made a promise and felt morally obliged to keep it. Her loyalty was to her twin, not to her mother. And what would Greta have done if she'd been told of Ellie's plans – tied her headstrong daughter to the bed for the rest of her life?

Furthermore, it was entirely understandable that Daisy hasn't told anyone except Matthew she was leaving. Heather would have tried to stop her, yet the girl clearly wasn't cut out for office work. Ruby admired her enormously for having taken charge of her young life.

Daisy came with her to midday Mass. She loved her new job, she declared. 'All you have to do is show people to their seats, and you can tell by the colour of the tickets what section they should be in. Of course,' she went on importantly, 'you have to be careful not to shine the torch in anyone's eyes.'

'Doesn't it get a bit boring?' Ruby asked.

'Not really, Gran. I watched *The Sting* twice because Robert Redford's so gorgeous, but once the picture starts, you can stand outside the door and talk to the other usherettes. I don't feel even the littlest bit stupid and some of them are dead envious I'm engaged to Clint. He came one night to see *The Sting* – we let him in for nothing,' she added in a whisper, as if the manager of the Forum was within earshot.

'I'm glad you're happy, love. Did Matthew mind you going?'

'No. He wished me luck and said to take as long as I liked to find another job. Oh, Gran, I don't half feel sorry for him. He's in terrible trouble.'

'I know. I'll give him a ring when we get home.'

'All the houses are occupied and the downstairs rooms will have to be redecorated,' Matthew said despondently when Ruby phoned to ask exactly how much trouble he was in. 'Apart from putting right the dampcourse, floorboards have to be replaced, carpets have been ruined. It's going to cost millions to put right.'

'I'm so sorry, Matthew. Look, I was just about to start dinner. You're welcome to come if you want. I've brought you a little present back from Washington.'

'Have you?' He sounded pathetically pleased. 'I can't manage dinner. I'm due at the office any minute to go through figures with the accountants. The workforce have seen this as an ideal opportunity to demand a pay rise. I'll try and make it later.'

'I look forward to seeing you, Matt.'

He made a little harrumphing noise. 'I doubt that very much, Ruby. You're just being polite.'

Ruby replaced the receiver and went into the kitchen where she began to peel potatoes. Her thoughts went back to the day she'd first met the gangling, would-be property developer, with his misspelt visiting card and cheap suit. Over the years, she'd been horrible to him, ignoring his kindness, his wish to become friends, resenting the way he had attached himself to her family, bought the girls presents, invited himself around. But now she was deeply sorry he was in trouble and would do all she could to help.

Ruby had only been home a few days when she called the hotel in Washington for a moan. 'I almost wish,' she groaned, 'that I'd never gone away. If I'd stayed, nothing bad might have happened; Ellie would still be here, Daisy wouldn't have changed her job, Matthew's business would be all right.'

'I'd've thought you'd be pleased about Daisy?'

'I am.' Ruby sighed. 'But our Heather isn't.'

'You're nothing but a soft girl, Ruby O'Hagan,' Beth said scathingly. 'You're not *that* important. The entire household doesn't fall to pieces just because you're not there.'

'I know.' Ruby sighed again. 'One thing though, the French students wouldn't have come for another week. I could do without them at the moment. The boy's all right, Louis, except he expects me to teach him English. He follows me everywhere, making notes. One of the girls is terribly homesick, poor thing, and cries all the time. The other one keeps picking up boys and bringing them home. She'd have them in her room if I'd let her.'

'Never mind, Rube. It won't be for ever.'

Right then, Ruby found that difficult to believe. 'Another thing, Greta's driving us mad. She wants to go to Dublin to look for Ellie, but she's nervous about travelling on her own. Heather's too busy to go with her, Moira flatly refuses, and now she's badgering me.' There was a note of hysteria in her rising voice. 'As if I could possibly drop everything and go on what's bound to be a wild goose chase.'

'Calm down, Rube. Take a deep breath or something.'

'Whereabouts are you in the hotel?'

'In a booth in the foyer. The desk clerk said there was a call just as I was leaving. You only just caught me.'

'What are you doing this afternoon?'

'It's morning, actually. I'm going to an anti-apartheid rally in support of black families in South Africa.'

'I wish I were there,' Ruby said wistfully. 'I miss it something awful. That's really why I called, to hear what Washington sounds like, if only for a minute or two.'

'I'm leaving tomorrow, Saturday. Nearly everyone is. This time next week, we'll all be back in our dull little houses or tedious jobs, and we'll be feeling exactly the same as you, Rube.'

On top of everything else, Ruby was worried about Matthew Doyle. He looked ill, not a bit like his usual dashing, confident self. The owners of the affected houses had called a meeting and asked him to attend.

'I can't think why,' he said ruefully. 'They were so angry, they'd hardly let me speak. I was shouted down every time I opened me mouth. Everyone considers it *my* fault.'

'Write to them,' Ruby urged after a few moments' thought. 'Find out their names and send a letter to every single house. Explain what happened, that the sub-contractor responsible has made himself bankrupt and the onus of putting things right has fallen on you. Say you'll do it as quickly as possible, but ask for their patience. Appeal to their better natures.'

'I don't suppose it would do much harm,' he conceded. 'Mind you, that's not the only thing on me mind. I've got two big contracts that should have been started by now, but I can't spare the manpower. They've both got penalty clauses if they're not finished on time. At the rate things are going, they won't be finished at all. I need the entire workforce for that bloody estate.'

'Have you advertised for more tradesmen?'

'Yes, but the response was pretty poor. Word gets around. These days, Doyle Construction's considered a dodgy outfit to work for.'

'But that's not fair!' she gasped, outraged.

He suddenly grinned. 'I'm glad I've got you on my side. I should have taken you with me to the meeting. You'd have shouted the lot of them down.'

'I'd have tried,' Ruby said stoutly. 'What happened to the business in Australia, the swimming pools?'

'It went to Caroline when we got divorced.' He pretended to shudder. 'I'd sooner not think about Caroline. I've got enough on me plate. By the way, I meant to say before, you suit jeans.'

'Well, I'm glad someone's noticed.'

The French students left after a fornight and another three took their place, all girls, who couldn't stand English food. Ruby didn't care. She made salads and gave them an apple for afters. It was much easier.

She flatly refused to iron the frocks Greta and Heather were taking to Corfu the following week. 'You can iron them yourselves when you come home from work. All you do is watch television.'

'You've been dead funny since you got back from Washington, Mam,' Greta complained.

Ruby haughtily tossed her head. 'I'm making a statement.' She'd meant to do all sorts of things, but had been submerged by events. She hadn't touched any of the books she'd brought back – she didn't even know where they were.

'What's the statement about?'

'I'm not sure.' She was fed up being a maid-of-all-work. She wanted a life of her own, though what she intended doing with it, she had no idea. Something important.

Two weeks later, the girls returned from Corfu, both with an enviable tan. It quickly became obvious that they weren't speaking to each other.

It was about time the pair of them grew up, thought an impatient Ruby. 'What's wrong?' she enquired as soon as she got one of them on their own. It happened to be Heather.

'She only clicked with some chap, didn't she, our Greta?' Heather said indignantly. 'I was dropped like a hot brick. A few days later, I met this man – I didn't mean to, we just bumped into each other in a shop and started talking and he asked me for a drink. Then Greta's chap went home the first Saturday, and *I* was expected to drop mine, which I flatly refused to do. She had a lousy time the second week and seems to think it's all *my* fault.'

'Well, I hope you make things up pretty soon. I don't like an atmosphere in the house.' Ruby was surprised. It wasn't like Heather not to put Greta first. She thought her daughter looked rather sad. 'What was your chap like?' she asked.

'Actually, Mam, he was awfully nice. His name's Gerald Johnson. He lives in Northampton and works in a bank. He's got two kids and his wife was killed in a road accident, so straight away we had something in common. We got on ever so well, but neither of us felt the least bit romantic towards each other. I can't imagine getting involved with another man and Gerald feels the same about women.'

'Oh, well. I'm glad *you* had a nice time.'

Heather's stern face melted. 'Oh, I did, Mam! Gerald was lovely to talk to. We're going to write to each other. He might come and see us one weekend.'

'I thought neither of you wanted to get involved?'

'We don't, but it doesn't mean we can't be friends. Talking of friends, I'll go and have a word with our Greta. I don't like us not speaking. Mind you, it's entirely her own fault.'

'I love Dublin,' Ellie sang, flinging back the curtains of the tiny bedsit that had a distant view of the River Liffey. Fortunately, the room wasn't overlooked, so no curious observer could see she had nothing on.

'Jaysus! The sun's bright.' Liam pulled the bedclothes over his head. 'Why do I feel so hungover? Did I drink much last night?'

'Only gallons and gallons of Guinness.' Ellie, her eyes on the glittering river in the distance, began to sing raucously, 'Bridge Over Troubled Water'.

'Do you *have* to sound so happy? And so fucking loud?'

'Don't swear,' she said automatically.

'I'll swear as much as I fucking want.'

'I might leave you.'

'I don't care.'

Ellie ran across the room, threw herself on top of him, and yanked the sheet away. Liam shrieked. His eyes were full of sleep and he looked dreadful.

'Do you really mean that? About not caring if I left?' she demanded, tickling his chest.

'You know I don't.' He rolled over so that she was beneath him and pushed himself inside her. He was ready to make love at any time, whether it be morning, noon, night or day.

'That was nice,' he said, rolling off her.

'Only nice!' Ellie pouted.

'I've known it better.'

'With me or someone else?' she enquired, making a face.

'With you, of course, me darling girl.'

Ellie was about to wrap herself around him, but changed her mind when her nose came in contact with his smelly armpit. 'I'll have to get ready for work in a minute.'

'Me too.'

He worked in a supermarket stacking shelves and collecting trolleys. After a lifetime spent studying, he wanted a job that didn't tax his brain. It would only be for a few months. Once he got the result of his degree, he'd leave Dublin, go abroad. 'The world will be my oyster,' he boasted.

What would she do then? Ellie didn't know and didn't care. He was only the first of her adventures. She had a job in a restaurant which she quite enjoyed and Dublin was full of attractive men. Among Liam's many friends were students from Trinity College and he and Ellie were invited to parties almost every night. An American student, Dean, lived in the room above, and there were two girls on the floor below. If there wasn't a party, they'd all end up in someone's room and get drunk.

The university term had ended, but there were still loads of young men around that Liam had been to school or played rugby with, as well as girls he used to date. Whenever they went to a pub there was always a crowd Liam – and now Ellie – knew.

Sunday afternoons, they went for a drive in Liam's car, a yellow Hillman Imp, which he'd bought on his eighteenth birthday. It had been left with his brother, Felix, in the family home in Craigmoss, a village about ten miles from Dublin. When Liam's father died, his mother had gone to live with her sister in Limerick, and Liam's own sister, Monica, lived in London.

They'd caught the bus to Craigmoss to collect the car soon after they'd arrived in Ireland. 'Next Sunday, we'll go to Sandymount Strand – there's a beach,' Liam said as the bus lumbered through the pretty Irish countryside. 'James Joyce used to go for walks there.'

'Did he, now!' said Ellie, who'd never heard of James Joyce, despite having taken an A level in English.

The Conway house was depressing, both inside and out, she thought when they arrived. It was called Fern Hall and was very large, very tall, and situated on its own just outside the village, reminding her of the house in *Psycho*, a film she'd recently watched on television and hated – she'd had nightmares about it ever since.

Felix Conway lived alone in Fern Hall. He was five years older than Liam, a slighter, paler version of his handsome brother. His eyes were a lighter green, his receding hair not quite so red. He had a faint, whispery voice and wore round glasses with pearly white frames that Ellie thought made him look slightly sinister, like the house.

Even the meal was depressing, served in a miserable, musty-smelling dining room; cress sandwiches made from stale bread, digestive biscuits served in the packet, and weak tea.

Ellie didn't like the way Felix watched her from behind his round glasses, still and contemplative, as if he was trying to look into her soul. 'Why isn't he married?' she asked Liam on the way back to Dublin in the Hillman Imp.

'Don't ask me. He's been courting Neila Kenny ever since me horrible old daddy died. I don't know what they're waiting for. Their old age pensions perhaps.'

'Let's not go again, Liam. I didn't enjoy meself a bit.'

'You needn't go again, me darling Ellie, but I certainly shall. Felix is me brother and I quite like the guy.'

'Please yourself,' Ellie sniffed.

'I always do,' Liam replied with a smile she thought unnecessarily grim.

Since then, he'd only been to see Felix the once, on another Sunday afternoon, leaving Ellie on her own, but not for long. Dean was still upstairs, waiting for his family to arrive when they would go on a tour of Europe. He had come down to borrow something and was still there when Liam returned. 'I hope you two haven't been up to anything,' he said with a leery grin.

Ellie was a bit put out that it didn't seem to bother him if she and Dean had spent the time making mad, passionate love. But would she care if she found *him* with a girl under the same circumstances? She decided that she wouldn't. They were using each other, that's all. It made her feel sophisticated and very grown-up.

They had been in Dublin almost two months when Ellie discovered she had run out of contraceptive pills.

'Fuck!' Liam said when she told him in bed that night.

'There's no need to swear. I can easily get more. I'll look up a birth control clinic in the telephone directory tomorrow.'

'Are you mad or what?' He roared with laughter. 'This is Ireland, girl. It'd be easier finding a brothel than a clinic dishing out contraceptives.'

'Why's that?' enquired an astonished Ellie.

He laughed again. 'Some Catholic you are! Don't you know the Church is totally opposed to birth control? In Ireland, what the Church says goes.'

'That seems very unreasonable.'

'Unreasonable or not, that's the situation. Is there anyone in Liverpool who can send you more pills?'

'God, no!'

'I'll ask around at work. If necessary, we can drive across the border, get them there. Otherwise, I'll have to find meself another bed partner. The last thing I want to hear is the patter of little feet.'

Ellie hit him with a pillow. 'Neither do I. So remember, until I get more pills, you'd better be careful.'

Liam brought the pills home a few days later. They were in a little brown bottle.

'Are you sure they're the right ones?' There wasn't a name on the bottle when Ellie examined it.

'I should hope so. They cost five quid.'

'These are white, the others are blue.' She popped one in her mouth all the same.

'They're a different brand, that's all,' Liam said easily, more concerned with opening the letter with a Liverpool postmark that had arrived for him that morning, almost certainly the result of his degree. He gave a joyful shout. 'I got a First and was top of my year. I think this calls for a drink – champagne, the very best. Put your glad rags on, me darling girl. Tonight we're celebrating. Tomorrow, I'll buy the newspaper and start writing after jobs.'

As usual, there were plenty of people they knew in the pub. They got in with a crowd celebrating a wedding anniversary, and pretty soon they were all celebrating together.

Someone started to sing an Irish folk song accompanied by the plaintive strains of a fiddle. It was all terribly bohemian. Nothing like this ever happens in Liverpool, Ellie thought, entirely forgetting she'd never been inside a Liverpool pub, so wouldn't know.

15

Daisy shone the torch discreetly along the back row of the Forum. It was filled with couples snogging madly, not even faintly interested in what was happening on the screen, despite *The Conversation* with Gene Hackman being such an excellent film. Clint had already seen it three times for free. In his expert opinion, it was one of the best ever made.

Every seat was occupied. Daisy transferred the torch beam to the right aisle. 'There's two empty seats in the middle,' she said to the young couple who'd only just arrived and asked to be seated at the back. *The Conversation* had started fifteen minutes ago, but watching a film was clearly the last thing on their minds.

She switched the torch off and went outside where her fellow usherette, Paula, was having a smoke.

'That pair were probably the last,' Paula said. She was a lovely, cheerful woman, with dyed blonde hair and purple lips. 'I think I'll take the weight off me feet and sit down.'

Daisy sat on the padded seat beside her. 'They went in the back row. I don't understand why people come to the pictures just to neck. It's nothing but a waste of money.'

'Perhaps they've got nowhere else warm to go, luv. I don't think me and Chas saw a picture properly the whole two years we were courting.' She tittered. 'There was one on telly the other night, *My Sister Eileen* with Janet Leigh. I know me and Chas went to see it, but all we could remember was the name.' She gave Daisy a painful nudge with her elbow. 'Don't tell me you and your Clint always sit with your eyes glued to the screen when you're at the pics?'

'We do, actually,' Daisy said primly. 'He's a film fanatic. He watches every single minute, even if it's not very good.'

'Then you've obviously got somewhere else to neck.'

'Not really,' Daisy was about to say, but limited herself instead to a telling laugh. She and Clint had never necked or snogged or whatever you called it, but she wasn't prepared to reveal that to Paula.

'Anyroad, Daisy, luv,' Paula said, 'I've got something to tell you. That painting you gave me, I wasn't sure about it at first, but Chas, he really liked it. Anyroad, he hung it over the mantelpiece. "I never thought we'd ever have our own, original masterpiece," he said. Meself, I thought that was going a bit far.'

'You've told me all this before,' Daisy reminded her.

'I know, luv. I'm leading up to something else, aren't I? Our Brigid's boyfriend's sister goes to art college. Her name's Mary, and when she came the other night she was dead impressed with your picture. She wants to meet you, and I wondered, luv, would you like to come to tea on Sunday?'

'I'd love to. Can I bring Clint? We don't have much time together since I came to work here.'

'I took it for granted you'd bring him, Daise. What it must be like to be in love, eh?' She nudged Daisy again. 'Mind you, me and Chas still have our moments.'

As she journeyed home on the bus, Daisy thanked her lucky stars she'd exchanged her office job for that of an usherette. Not only could she do it as well as anyone else, but she'd made loads of friends. As far as work was concerned, nowadays she was dead happy.

She was happier at home too since Ellie had run off to Dublin with Liam Conway. It meant she had Clint all to herself. But life still wasn't perfect – would it ever be? Daisy wondered desperately, thinking about the conversation with Paula, the bit about the back row.

It was two months since she and Clint had got engaged and still all he did was kiss her by the gate. Lately, she'd starting kissing him back with all her might, pressing her lips against his as hard as she could, hoping he'd put his arms around her, groan a bit, the way the boys did in the back row when they started kissing the girls.

But the pressing had had no effect. She'd seen enough films to know that engaged couples did rather more than give each other a brief kiss whenever they had the opportunity, and it was usually the man who was keener than the woman. She'd like to bet that Ellie and Liam had *gone all the way*! Just the thought of it made Daisy go all funny. Perhaps *that* was why Clint had never properly kissed her. He was holding himself back, worried he'd lose control, and *they* would go all the way, which Daisy would have found quite scary, even though she loved him with all her heart and soul.

On reflection, it was probably best that things remain as they were. She'd stop kissing him back, just in case he lost control and it would all be highly embarrassing. There was probably a happy medium which she would have very much preferred, but it seemed that wasn't possible, men being what they were.

Ruby prepared the tiny fifth bedroom – it had hardly been used since the war – for when Gerald Johnson came to stay the weekend. It was only a month since he had met Heather in Corfu.

'I don't want anyone thinking it's serious,' Heather warned. 'We're friends, good friends, that's all.'

'Are you sure?' Greta asked suspiciously.

'Quite sure, sis.'

Gerald was an extremely pleasant young man. Lord, I'm growing old, Ruby thought with a groan. He's forty if he's a day, yet I look upon him as young.

He showed them photos of his children and his late wife and Heather showed him a photo of Rob.

As if to emphasise the relationship was purely platonic, they insisted on taking a petulant Greta with them to the pictures on Saturday night – they went to the Forum, where Daisy proudly showed them to their seats.

The A level results arrived and Moira was thrilled to find she'd got three Bs. She'd been provisionally accepted by two universities, one in Canterbury, the other in Norwich, depending on her grades. Now it was up to her to choose.

Greta was dismayed. 'You're not leaving home too!'

'You know I've always wanted to go to university, Mam,' Moira said with her usual calm reasonableness. 'I've discussed it with you loads of times.'

'Yes, but I never thought it'd *happen.*'

'I wish the twins had been thick, like Daisy,' Greta said tearfully to her mother. Ellie hadn't done all that badly considering her mind had been taken up with other things; two Cs and a D.

'Daisy's not thick.' Ruby sprang to the defence of her other granddaughter. 'She's just got an unusual mind.'

'Whatever! She's not thinking of leaving home, is she? Come October, I won't have any daughters left, not like our Heather. I might go to Dublin and fetch Ellie back, even if I do have to go on me own.'

Clint's results were the best in the school; three straight As. Daisy was terrified he'd also decide to go to university where he'd come into contact with girls as brilliant as himself and far better-looking than she was. She was pleased and flattered when he declared he couldn't bear to leave her.

'I think I'd go mad without you, Daise.'

Mad! It seemed an extreme word for someone only eighteen to use. He had a retiring disposition, not full of himself like most boys with only half his looks, but he'd always seemed entirely sane. He actually hugged her for quite a long time, and Daisy had the strangest thought, that he was scared to go to university. She tenderly stroked his cheek. 'Don't worry, Clint. I'll always be here for you.'

She rather hoped he'd tell her he loved her, or call her 'darling', both of which she longed for, but he just stiffened slightly and began to discuss the film they'd just seen.

Mam said she was daft. Didn't she realise Dublin was a huge place, a city?

Finding Ellie would be next to impossible. Where would she look? Who would she ask? Heather agreed it was a mad idea.

Greta sighed and gave up. No one seemed to realise how miserable she felt, losing both her daughters. For the first time in her life, she felt very alone and very small, merely the tiniest of specks in the vastness of the universe. Say if Ellie never came back! Moira would be gone and Heather could well marry that revolting Gerald Johnson. Greta couldn't stand him and didn't believe they were just friends. One of these days, Mam would die, then she'd have no one, not a soul in the world. She'd be truly alone, not just temporarily, like now.

'Oh, God!' It was a horrifying thought, unbearable. She'd sooner be dead.

She'd just have to get married again. But who to? Someone who'd look after her because, Greta thought fretfully, she wasn't able to manage by herself. She remembered there was a man who'd played a significant part in her life, who never forgot her birthday, bought presents at Christmas, made a fuss of her whenever he came to the house.

Matthew Doyle had always been a father figure in a way, yet he was only twelve years older than she was. She was as fond of him as he was of her. He was having financial problems at the moment, but she felt sure they would be overcome.

Greta decided Matthew would make a very satisfactory husband. Somehow, she'd have to put the idea in his head that she would make a satisfactory wife.

The wedding ring was the thinnest in the jeweller's shop and the cheapest. It was secondhand, almost certainly off the finger of a dead woman, and it fitted Ellie perfectly.

'Remember, Felix is the only person who knows we're not married,' Liam said on the way to Craigmoss in the Hillman Imp. It was a horrible day, quite different to the first time she'd gone, when the flowers had been out and the air smelt fresh. Today, the sky looked like grey soup, the trees were bare, everywhere felt damp. 'Everyone else thinks you're Mrs Liam Conway, I've got a job abroad, and you'll join me when you're ready. This being Ireland, an unmarried woman in the family way could have a pretty hard time. It's all right to have affairs, but it's not done to get pregnant.'

'If it wasn't for bloody Ireland, I wouldn't be pregnant,' Ellie reminded him in a hard voice. 'What were they, aspirin?'

'I wouldn't know.' Liam's voice was equally hard. 'I was told they were contraceptive pills. I paid a good price.'

'I'm paying an even higher price.'

'I'm sorry, Ellie, but I'm trying to do the right thing, aren't I?' he said reasonably, as if he thought she'd listen to reason when she felt completely at the end of her tether. 'If you'd gone back to England in the first place and got rid of the damn thing, there'd have been no need for these shenanigans.'

Ellie placed her hands over her swelling tummy. 'I couldn't have got rid of it,' she whispered. 'It would have been murder. He or she would have come back to haunt me.'

Liam laughed. 'You're a rum girl, Ellie; screwing like a rabbit one minute, back in the Dark Ages the next.'

He zoomed around a bend. They were getting nearer to Craigmoss, to Fern Hall, to Felix. Ellie shivered, remembering the way he'd looked at her with his pale green eyes. If only she hadn't been too scared to have an abortion, or felt too proud to go back to Liverpool. But she had planned to return when she'd had all sorts of adventures to boast about, not expecting an illegitimate baby.

'I'm surprised,' Liam said, 'That you didn't press me to marry you.'

'I'm not. It so happens I don't want to get married, and certainly not to you.'

'Oh, well.' He laughed. 'Then I won't propose.'

'Just in case you do, the answer's "No". One thing though, I think you might have stayed a bit longer, not landed me on Felix right before Christmas. It'll be dead horrible.' It was true he'd got a job abroad, as a translator with the United Nations in Geneva.

'They wanted me by mid-December, Ellie.'

She didn't believe him. He just wanted to get rid of her so he could have a good time, go to parties and stuff. The United Nations wouldn't need much in the way of translating done over the Christmas period.

The car turned into the drive of Fern Hall, stopped. Ellie got out. Liam fetched her suitcase from the boot. He'd given her the money to buy some pretty maternity frocks.

Felix came to the door, the pale ghost of his brother. He looked as damp as the weather. The outside walls of the house were wet, as if they were weeping, and she felt like weeping with them. She went inside and Felix prepared a meal; tinned soup with bread and margarine, and for afters, tinned fruit, followed by weak tea.

Then Liam said he had to be going, and she and Felix went with him to the door.

'I'll give you a ring over Christmas,' Liam promised.

Ellie didn't want him to stay – she'd gone off him completely – but even less did she want him to go. At least he had some life in him, unlike his brother. He pressed an envelope into her hand. 'That's my last week's wages, fifty quid. It should keep you going for a while. Look after yourself, Ellie. Don't forget, you're pregnant.'

As if she could!

Ellie's absence wasn't allowed to spoil the festive spirit in Mrs Hart's house. The living room was drenched with paper chains and tinsel and the tree was so big it would only fit in the hall. Heather spent an entire evening decorating it. Gerald Johnson was coming with his children – Lloren, ten, and Rufus, two years older – and she wanted it to look extra special. The students had gone home so accommodation wasn't a problem. Clint was invited to Christmas dinner along with his parents, the revolting Pixie Shaw and her husband, Brian.

'Flippin' hell, Ruby,' Pixie exclaimed when she came in, her eyes everywhere, 'This place hasn't changed a jot since I was last here. You've still got the same wallpaper and how you can stand working in that old-fashioned kitchen, I'll never know.'

'I like it,' Clint put in, unusually for him. 'It's got character.'

'So do I,' remarked Gerald. 'It's got charm as well.' He smiled at Heather, who blushed slightly and smiled back.

'*I* wouldn't want it any different.' Greta had never forgiven Pixie for severing their friendship many years before.

Even the normally unruffled Moira, home from university in Norwich, looked indignant. 'Me neither.'

'Oh, well, there's no accounting for taste,' said Pixie, entirely unabashed.

'The place *is* looking a bit shabby, Ruby.' Matthew glanced around the living room, as if he'd never looked it properly before.

'I sometimes touch the paintwork up or emulsion over the wallpaper.' Ruby didn't give a damn what anyone thought. Like her, the house was showing its age and could do with patching up a bit. 'Who'd like a drink before dinner?'

'I'd quite like a cocktail.'

'I'm afraid I haven't any cocktails, Pixie. There's red or white wine, sherry, or beer. Take your pick.'

'Oh, that's a shame. Brian bought us a cocktail shaker for Crimbo, didn't you, luv? If I'd known, I'd have brought it with me. I'll have a sherry. Sweet, if you've got it.'

'I've only got medium.'

'I'd love a beer,' said Brian.

Greta jumped to her feet. 'I'll get the drinks, Mam, while you get on with the dinner.'

'Would you like a hand, Ruby?'

'No thanks, Pixie. I can manage on my own.' Pixie was bound to notice she was still using the same saucepans and she might feel tempted to hit her with one.

Mid-afternoon, Pixie and Brian Shaw went home to their cocktail shaker. Not long afterwards the Whites and the Donovans arrived for tea. Ellie White tried not to look upset when she was introduced to Gerald Johnson and his children. Having lost her only son, perhaps she sensed she was about to lose his wife. Heather might claim she and Gerald were merely friends, but it was obvious to everyone else it was rather more than that.

'I suppose they'll move to Northampton when they get married,' she said privately to Ruby.

'There's been no mention of them getting married yet.'

'I wonder if Daisy will go with them? She's our Rob's daughter. Pretty soon, she'll be all I'll have left of him.'

'Daisy would never leave Clint. Did you know he's got a job with the Liverpool Playhouse? Only as a stagehand, helping to paint scenery, that sort of thing. He thinks it's all grist to the mill for when he goes to Hollywood to direct films – movies, he calls them.'

'Daisy told me.' Ellie smiled wanly. 'I wonder what Rob would have thought of Clint? It's hard to imagine him as a forty-year-old father making judgements on his little girl's boyfriend. In my mind, he's still only twenty-three.' She sighed, her eyes full of pain. 'Poor Rob, he never had the chance to grow old, did he? Nor Larry.'

Ruby was reminded of Ellie's words when they arrived at the Whites' house for tea the following day, minus Heather, who had gone with Gerald and the children to the pantomime at the Empire.

'I should have stopped her,' she thought uncomfortably. 'Not today, it was too late, the children were looking forward to it, but weeks ago, when she first came up with the idea of buying tickets. She should be here. Oh, Lord! I'm the most insensitive person who ever lived.'

Chris Ryan was there to remind her of her insensitivity to other people's feelings. He was with his wife who wasn't much older than Ruby's girls, and their son, a delicate little boy of ten who had severe asthma.

Before, at similar gatherings, Chris and Ruby had done no more than smile at each other, perhaps exchange a few polite words. Today, however, Chris followed her into the kitchen when she went for a glass of water after a hectic game of Charades.

'I was thinking about us the other week,' he said.

'Us!' Ruby replied, taken aback.

'You, me – us. Did you know we had a terrible scare with Timmy? It was about a month ago. We thought he was going to die.'

'Oh, Chris! I'm so sorry. I knew he had asthma, that's all.'

'He had a particularly bad attack. We didn't think he was going to make it.' His eyes clouded over. 'I can't think of a worse torture than watching the child you love suffer. You'd give everything you possessed if you could take the pain away, suffer it yourself. Nothing, no one else in the world matters. I guess that's how you felt about your girls when Rob and Larry died.'

'I guess it was,' Ruby said slowly.

Chris smiled drily. 'It's taken me all this time to understand. I was a bit of a prig, wasn't I?'

'I wouldn't say that.'

He leant against the wall, hands in pockets. When she'd been in love with him, Ruby had thought him very attractive with enormous charm. In her eyes, he probably wouldn't have changed had they stayed together. Now he was just an ageing man, almost sixty, with thinning hair. There was nothing exceptional about him.

'I wanted to see you for two reasons,' he said. 'One was to confess I'd been a prig, the other to say goodbye. The three of us are off to New Zealand in February. We might not see each other again. The Liverpool air's no good for Timmy, it's too damp, and I've been at a bit of a loose end since I stopped being a copper. I'm going to start my own security firm.'

'Good luck. I hope Timmy's health improves and you do well.' She held out her hand and Chris took it.

'I often think about the year we were engaged, how it would have been if we'd got married.' He held on to her hand and squeezed it. 'I wish I hadn't been such a fool, Ruby. I'll always regret it.'

Ruby pulled her hand away. 'Well, you shouldn't,' she said brusquely. 'It was over and done with a long time ago. You should look to the future, not the past. *I* always do.'

Not long after Christmas, Matthew Doyle put his big house in Aughton on the market – he urgently needed the cash – and came to stay with Ruby while he looked for somewhere cheaper.

'I thought you owned loads of houses and flats,' Ruby exclaimed when the idea was first muted.

'I got rid of them years ago. They were hardly worth the trouble,' he said.

'You didn't get rid of this one.'

'Because it's different, that's why. This is my second home, the place where, lately, I come and shelter when I'm in trouble.'

Ruby bit her lip. 'There's only the little bedroom where there's hardly room to swing a cat. The others have all got students.' It didn't seem right that the owner of the house should have the smallest room.

'The little bedroom will do me nicely, Rube. It shouldn't be for long.'

Ruby prepared the room for her temporary guest, painting the woodwork glossy white and the walls a pretty eggshell blue. She bought new bedding - brushed nylon that didn't need ironing - and a rug for beside the bed. She realised she was quite looking forward to having Matthew stay – if she hadn't been so horrible, they could have been friends years ago. There were times when she wondered if she was her own worst enemy.

'Very nice,' Matthew said approvingly the day he arrived, not long after breakfast when everyone had gone. It was the first of February, bitterly cold, despite the clear blue sky and the distant sun, not nearly strong enough to melt the layer of glittering ice that covered their part of the earth. The garden was a frosty wonderland and the bare trees looked eerily pretty in their cloak of white. It was a day Ruby would never forget and always regret, despite her frequently expressed belief that one should never look back and regret anything.

She took Matthew upstairs. 'I hope the bed's long enough.'

'Beds usually are.'

'Lately, you seem to be growing taller,' she remarked.

'I'm growing thinner, that's what. It's probably an optical illusion.'

'I'll feed you up. I hope you like plain cooking. I can't be bothered with anything fancy. I'll make us some tea.' She turned to leave, but he caught her arm.

'I appreciate this, Rube.'

'It's not much, considering all you've done for us.'

'Have you ever wondered why?'

'Sometimes.' Ruby shrugged carelessly. 'I assumed it was because I reminded you of Foster Court, of your gran. Me and the girls were your substitute family.'

'Is that really what you think?' He was frowning slightly and his eyes looked very dark. She could feel the tension in the long thin fingers on her arm.

'What else is there to think?'

'There could be another reason.' The fingers were trembling now.

'And what would that be?'

He released her arm and sat on the bed. 'I've always found it hard to talk to you. Because I wasn't short of a few bob, you thought I was being patronising. You like to be on equal terms with people or, better still, on top. Well, now it's different.' He looked at her directly and Ruby was reminded of the first time they'd met, when he'd been so unsure of himself. It was an expression she'd never seen since. 'By the end of the year, I'm likely to be skint, so now I can tell you how I feel – how I've felt, ever since you came through the door downstairs covered in paint. I . . .'

The phone rang. 'Just a minute,' Ruby said, and ran down to answer it.

It was Clint, wanting Daisy. 'She's at the dentist,' Ruby informed him. 'Didn't she tell you?'

'Oh, yes. I forgot.' He began a rambling explanation. They were meeting for lunch, but he'd be late. He'd see her in McDonald's instead of by the theatre. 'If I don't turn up at all, I'll drop in the Forum sometime this afternoon and say hello.'

There was a mirror by the telephone. Ruby stared at her reflection. She saw a woman who didn't look her fifty-seven years, a woman who nowadays would be described as handsome, as good-looking women were when they grew older. Her black hair was sprinkled with grey - the tint she'd had for Christmas had almost washed out. Her neck was lined, getting scraggy, she thought. Perhaps she'd better start wearing polo necks. After a while, as Clint's voice droned on about something or other, the reflection grew blurred, while at the same time the meaning of Matthew's words, of what he'd been about to say, became clear. He'd been about to tell her that he loved her! He'd almost got the words out, but she'd thought it more important to answer the phone.

There were footsteps on the stairs, brisk and fast. Matthew was coming down, his face stony. He was wearing a padded jacket, obviously on his way out.

'Clint,' she said hurriedly. 'I have to ring off.'

'Don't forget to tell Daisy.'

'No.' She slammed down the receiver just as Matthew opened the front door. 'What was it you wanted to tell me?' she called, surprised to find that she was trembling and her heart had leapt to her throat. It was vital that she hear the words he'd been about to say before she'd interrupted him so rudely.

'It doesn't matter now.' His voice was bitter. 'Anyroad, it was nothing important.'

The door slammed. Ruby groaned and sank on to the stairs, head in her hands. She'd made many mistakes in her life, but now she'd just made the biggest mistake of all.

Ellie hadn't thought it possible for Christmas to be so dead miserable. She'd gone with Felix to the little village church for Midnight Mass and woke up late next morning.

Christmas morning, she thought gloomily, and imagined waking up at home where there'd be loads of presents under the tree which would be opened after breakfast – Gran always made a lavish breakfast on such a special day and everyone would eat it together for a change. The telly would be on, even if no one was watching, and carols could be heard all over the house.

She supposed she'd better get up. Ellie put one foot on the floor, winced, and put it back under the covers. The linoleum was freezing and she didn't have any slippers. She managed to get dressed without getting off the bed. Her tummy was getting quite big, she noted, although the baby wasn't due till May, and she was already wearing maternity frocks. She threw back her shoulders, took a deep breath, and went downstairs.

'Good morning, Ellie.' Felix was in the parlour, a small, dark room at the back of the house, where a fire struggled to burn in the black grate and half a dozen Christmas cards stood on the mantelpiece. Liam hadn't sent one, nor had he, so far, made the promised telephone call. Ellie had no wish to speak to him if he did. 'Would you like some tea?' Felix enquired courteously.

'Please.' He treated her like an invalid, which she didn't mind, preferring to be waited on rather than the other way round.

He went to fetch the tea and Ellie sat in one of the old-fashioned armchairs and held out her hands to the fire. The armchair felt damp. Everything in the house felt damp; the walls, the floors, the furniture, her bed. It was no wonder Liam and his sister had left. Even their mother had gone the minute her husband died. He'd been a miser, according to Mrs McTaggart who came in three times a week to do the washing and clean. Eammon Conway had owned the village chemist which was a little gold mine, being the only one for miles, but had refused to spend a penny on his family or the house. Instead, the money had gone on the horses, so there was nothing for his wife and children when the fatal heart attack struck.

Now Felix ran the chemist's shop, but it was no longer a gold mine, Mrs McTaggart said sadly. A supermarket had since opened in the village, only small, but called a supermarket all the same. It sold aspirin and cough linctus, cold cures and corn plasters, all much cheaper than the chemist's, so people only called on Felix when they needed a prescription or had ailments that required medicine the supermarket didn't stock.

Felix brought her a cup of weak tea. 'What would you like for breakfast?' He stared at her intently from behind his pale-framed spectacles.

'Just some toast,' Ellie sighed. The look no longer bothered her. It was the way Felix looked at everyone, as if he was trying to see behind their eyes to some deep, inner part of them.

'We're having chicken for dinner,' he said proudly. 'Neila will be along in a minute to roast it.'

The chicken would be no bigger than a pigeon. Felix was finding it hard to survive on the profits from the chemist. There were times when Ellie felt quite sorry for him, which was odd, as she was inclined to regard inadequate people with contempt. But Felix never complained, never lost his temper, and had the patience of Job, as Gran would have said. She actually felt a sneaking liking for him. He wouldn't be nearly so hard up, she thought darkly, if he got rid of Neila Kenny, who'd been his father's assistant. Perhaps he didn't like to sack her because she was his girlfriend.

It was a strange relationship. She'd never seen them touch, let alone kiss. At first, she'd assumed they did those sort of things during the dinner hour when the chemist closed, but Mrs McTaggart said Neila went home for dinner and Felix treated himself to half a pint of Guinness in one of the local pubs.

Neila Kenny was older than Felix, a large, raw-boned woman of about thirty-five, with scrappy hair and a face that the most charitable person in the world would have to admit was ugly. The shabby, shapeless clothes she wore looked as if they'd come from a jumble sale. Her stony grey eyes regarded the newcomer with hostility and Ellie found her just a bit scary.

Her favourite person was Mrs McTaggart, who brought her home-made scones and girdle cakes, otherwise she would have starved – even the toast when Felix brought it would be horrid, either underdone or burnt. Craigmoss didn't have a gas supply and the ancient electric cooker was unpredictable.

There was no knowing whose fault it was – Neila's or the cooker's – that Christmas dinner turned out such a disaster; the chicken almost raw, the potatoes hard, the Brussels sprouts soggy.

Throughout the meal, Neila subjected her to the third degree, asking questions about Liam that she'd asked before, as if trying to catch her out in a lie. Where had they got married? she asked suspiciously. Was it a white wedding? Did they have a honeymoon? Why hadn't she gone with him to Geneva?

'I'm expecting a baby in case you haven't noticed,' Ellie replied in answer to the last.

'Your wedding ring's awfully thin. Is it secondhand?'

'Yes, it's all we could afford.'

Ellie stayed put while Neila cleared the table. From the lack of spoons, she assumed there wasn't to be a pudding and, so far, there'd been no sign of anything alcoholic to drink.

Neila retured with a tray containing three cups of tea and three mince pies. 'I hope these are all right. I got them from the supermarket. They've been warmed up a bit in the oven.'

Ellie burnt her tongue on the mincemeat filling. She yelped and left hurriedly to get a glass of water from the nineteenth-century kitchen which led to a miserable, barren garden. She stood by the sink, dangled her tongue in the icy water, and thought how stupid she must look, how dreadful everything was, and how incredibly unhappy she felt.

'Are you all right, Ellie?' Felix enquired from the door.

'Yes. Look, could we go to a pub for a drink? It'll be my treat.' She hadn't used any of the money Liam had given her and was desperate to get out of the house.

'The pubs are closed today. Anyway, the Craigmoss pubs don't welcome women, so you couldn't go if they were open.'

Time had never passed so slowly. There was nothing to do, nowhere to go except the village. After a couple of forays, Ellie decided never to go again. There was only a handful of shops; the supermarket which was pathetic, the chemist's, a tiny post office, a shop that sold wool, sewing things, baby clothes, and adult fashions she wouldn't have been seen dead in. People were quite friendly and stopped in the street to chat but, even so, Ellie had a feeling they didn't believe she'd married Liam and hoped to trip her up. What would they do if they discovered the truth, she wondered? Stone her to death, beat her with sticks and drive her from the village, ban her from Mass?

A library van visited Craigmoss once a week and Ellie spent most of the time with her head buried in a book. Felix insisted she visit the local doctor who examined her and advised she was putting on too much weight.

'You need more exercise,' Dr O'Hara said sternly. He made a note in his diary of when the baby was due – he would deliver it himself.

In order to keep sane, remind herself that a world existed outside the confines of Craigmoss, every few weeks Ellie caught the bus to Dublin, where she wandered round the shops, buying nothing, because it was important she keep Liam's money for when the baby arrived and she could leave Fern Hall. Her only extravagance was a cup of coffee. She would sit in the restaurant, savouring the rich aroma, and try to plan ahead, impossible in Fern Hall where her brain felt as damp as the house itself.

But even with a clear head, it was hard to imagine what she would do once she had a child. Best not to think about it, see how she felt when the time came. If it was well-behaved, she'd buy a sling and carry it on her back and it wouldn't stop her from having the adventures she had planned.

The weather improved and so did Ellie. The garden she'd thought barren suddenly sprang into life and the trees gradually became covered in pink and white blossom. She took a chair outside and read her book in the warm, spring sunshine. When Mrs McTaggart finished her work, they would have a cup of tea and a gossip.

Mrs McTaggart was a widow, comfortably plump, with red apple cheeks and three grown-up sons; two worked on farms nearby, and Brendan, the youngest, was in prison in Belfast.

'He's a terrorist,' his mother said proudly. 'He threw a bomb at someone. They still sent him to prison, even though it missed.'

'I like the name Brendan,' Ellie opined.

'You'd like Brendan himself. He's a lovely lad. He went to school with your Liam. They were a pair of imps, always in trouble.'

'What was Felix like when he was young?' She couldn't imagine Felix being young.

'Clever, far cleverer than Liam, if you don't mind me saying. It was always planned he'd go to university, but when the time came, he couldn't bring himself to leave, apart from which there wasn't the money. Liam was only thirteen, Monica a year older, and his poor mam was being driven silly by his philandering dad. So, Felix stayed. All them brains, but what does he do but get a job in the Rose as a barman.' Mrs McTaggart's normally cheery face was sober.

'That's a shame,' Ellie said encouragingly. It showed how bored she was that she found this stuff of interest.

'It is indeed! Maybe he'll get his reward in heaven, because he certainly hasn't had it on earth. Five years later, didn't his daddy go and die! By then, Monica had already left for London, Liam was ready for university himself, and Eammon Conway hadn't been in his grave for more than half an hour, before his wife ups and parks herself on her sister, leaving Felix with the chemist's and a house no one in the world would want to buy. Not to mention,' Mrs McTaggart added darkly, 'Neila Kenny.'

'What's Neila Kenny got to do with things?' demanded Ellie. 'And what did you mean by his philandering dad?'

'I shouldn't really tell you.'

'Oh, go on. I won't repeat it. I'll not be here much longer, will I? It doesn't matter what I know.'

'It's not that. It doesn't seem right to spread gossip.' She gave Ellie a reproachful look, as if spreading gossip was the last thing on earth she'd do. 'As to repeating it, I doubt if a soul in Craigmoss doesn't already know.'

'If everyone already knows, then it's not gossip.'

'Do you think not? Ah, well, I don't suppose it'd hurt.' She was obviously dying to spill the beans. 'The truth is,' her voice dropped to a whisper though the garden was empty except for themselves and a couple of birds, 'Neila Kenny was Eammon Conway's bit on the side for nigh on ten years.'

'Never!' Ellie was genuinely shocked. 'You mean they slept together?'

'I doubt if they slept much, but they definitely did the other,' the woman said smugly.

'For ten years! But this is Ireland! I thought you couldn't get contraceptives. How could they have made love for ten years without having babies all over the place?' Ellie was annoyed. She'd only made love for five minutes with the son of Eammon Conway before she was up the stick.

Mrs McTggart dropped her voice even lower. 'Neila's never had periods, so she can't have babies.'

'How the hell do you know *that*?'

'Everyone knows everything about everyone in Craigmoss,' said her informant, tight-lipped, as if she disapproved. 'But you see what's happened, Ellie? Felix has taken over his father's woman, just as he took over his shop and his house. Now he's stuck with her. One of these fine days they'll probably get married, or so everyone expects. There's some people, and Felix Conway is one, who are far too good for this world. That man's a saint.'

16

LOCAL BUILDING FIRM GETS MUCH NEEDED HELPING HAND, ran the headline in the *Echo*.

'Crisis-hit Doyle Construction has been taken over by Medallion, the company responsible for some of the most impressive buildings recently erected in London and other major British cities. A spokesman for Medallion said all outstanding contracts would be honoured and completed on time. Matthew Doyle, founder of Doyle Construction, is being retained as Managing Director of the Liverpool arm of this prestigious company, though he will not have a seat on the board . . .'

Ruby laid the paper down with a sigh. Matthew hadn't thought to tell her the good news himself – she assumed the news was good – he'd left her to find out for herself.

She sighed again because she knew this wasn't true. Matthew hadn't *wanted* to tell her himself. It wasn't thoughtlessness on his part. He hardly came to the house nowadays, and then only when he knew there'd be other people there, at evenings and weekends. He'd stayed upstairs only for a few weeks before purchasing a one-bedroom flat in a modern block in Gateacre. Greta had helped put up curtains.

How she must have hurt him! Ruby cringed. But then all she'd done was hurt him since they'd met. He must love her very much, she thought, to have put up with it, with her, for so long.

But did he still love her now, she wondered? Perhaps he'd given up. He'd been about to open his heart and in return had received the equivalent of a slap in the face. She wouldn't be surprised if he hated her.

Ever since, on the few times they'd met, she'd looked at him in a different light, not as a friend, not as the man she'd once found so very irritating, but as a lover. She realised she would quite like to go to bed with Matthew Doyle, lie in his arms, marry him if he asked. The excited thrill she'd had when they first met, which had never completely gone away, returned with a vengeance. The half-spoken acknowledgment of his feelings had unlocked the key to her own heart, sadly too late.

One of these days, Ruby vowed, she'd get Matthew by himself and *force* him to say the words he'd been about to say on that brilliant February morning. He may have given up on her, but she hadn't even started on him.

'Forty-one!' Greta grimaced at her reflection in the mirror. 'I don't *feel* forty-one. Do I look it?'

'No way, sis.' Heather was sitting on the bed, conscious that it was twenty years almost to the minute that she'd been in exactly the same position, doing the same thing, watching her sister get made-up on her birthday. Then, Greta had been twenty-one. 'Do I look forty?' she asked. It would be her own birthday in two weeks' time.

'Hardly thirty. Is this lippy all right?'

'It's a bit dark. You've got a thing about dark lippies. With your colouring, you need something lighter.'

'You always say that.'

'You shouldn't ask my opinion if you don't want it.'

Greta rubbed the lipstick off with a tissue and applied a paler one. 'Does that look OK?'

'Much better.'

'What shall I wear?' Greta got up and examined her half of the wardrobe.

Heather shrugged. 'Anything'll do. It's only the two of us going for a meal.'

'We should have had a party.'

'Who would we have invited?'

'Oh, I dunno. People from work?'

'They're all married,' Heather said. 'We'd have been the only single ones there.'

Greta took out a frilly chiffon frock and examined it critically. It would look good with her black velvet jacket. 'I'm surprised Gerald isn't coming for Easter,' she remarked. 'It's only next week. Moira will be home from Norwich, and there's Matthew, Daisy and Clint. We could have had a family party then. Mam would have been pleased.'

'I'm not seeing Gerald any more.'

'Why not?' Greta span round so fast she nearly fell over. She looked at her sister with amazement. 'I know you only started off as friends, but I thought it had got serious.'

'It had,' Heather said calmly. 'He asked me to marry him.'

'What did you say?'

'At first, I didn't know what to say. I thought about living in a strange town, leaving this house.' Heather glanced around the familiar room. 'I tried to imagine what it would be like, not seeing Mam every day, you, our Daisy. I wondered if Gerald's children would grow to love me, and would I ever love them?'

'And what did you decide?' Greta sat on her bed and the sisters looked at each other across the small space between, as they'd done thousands of times in the past.

'I decided I could do all those things.' She gave herself an approving nod. 'I said, "yes", to Gerald.'

'But I thought you weren't seeing him any more!'

'I'm not.' A wry smile drifted across Heather's stern features. 'I didn't tell anyone about getting married. I was waiting for the right opportunity, I suppose. One night, not long after he proposed, Gerald rang. We were discussing things, the future. He told me how much he earns in the bank. It was a lot less than I do, so I suggested it would be best if I got a job as a legal clerk in Northampton and he looked after the children.'

'What did he say?'

'He nearly hit the roof.' Her eyes rolled, as if she still felt shocked by the memory. 'He said it was the daftest idea he'd ever heard and he was surprised at me. Men went to work, women stayed at home and did the housework. Apparently, any other way and civilisation would crumble.'

'Cheek!' Greta gasped.

'Isn't it?' Heather said indignantly. 'I said it wouldn't hurt to discuss the matter and he lost his temper. That was how he felt and there was to be no discussion, so I told him I didn't want to marry a man whose mind was so made up he wouldn't talk about things. Then I put the phone down and we haven't spoken to each other since.'

'He's bound to call again, apologise.'

'Then he needn't bother. I've finished with him.'

'Oh, sis! And it happened just like that?'

'Just like that.' Heather snapped her fingers. 'One minute I loved him, next I never wanted to see him again for as long as I live.'

'That's amazing.'

'I know, and it's also a bit scary.' Heather's eyes grew round. 'Say I'd married him, and *then* discovered what he was like.' She jumped to her feet. 'C'mon, Grete, else it'll be too late to go out. I hope you're not intending to wear that frock, it's awfully thin, and it's cold outside.'

Greta couldn't be bothered arguing. She put the chiffon frock back in the wardrobe, and took out another, warmer one. 'I was rather hoping you'd get married,' she said.

'Why?'

'Then I wouldn't feel so bad if I got married meself.'

From past experience, Heather knew Greta would always do exactly as she wanted, including getting married. It had hurt, being used, then ditched when someone more appealing appeared on the scene like the time in Corfu, but it didn't stop her from loving her sister. The thought of life without Greta, living in this room on her own, was horrible, but it seemed Greta didn't feel the same.

'Have you got some chap up your sleeve?' she asked. Greta had gone out a few times recently and refused to say who with.

'Sort of.'

'What does that mean?'

Greta giggled. 'It means I've got some chap up me sleeve.'

Three months later, on a melting July day, Greta's missing daughter returned to the house by Princes Park with her beautiful two-month-old son whose name was Brendan.

'You're just in time for the wedding.' Moira had opened the door. She'd only been home from university a few days herself.

'Whose wedding?'

'Our Mum's. She's getting married to Matthew Doyle next Tuesday.'

The birth had been extraordinarily easy and quite painless. Ever since it had been imminent, Mrs McTaggart had been coming every morning, just in case, and Neila Kenny deserted the chemist's and came afternoons.

One morning, just after eleven, Ellie felt a twinge and phoned Dr O'Hara who came straight away. Two hours later she was the mother of a perfect baby boy. It was that easy.

'Why do some women make such a fuss?' she wanted to know when the doctor placed her newly-born son in her arms.

'Because some women have a much harder time than you. Ask Mrs McTaggart here what she went through. I was there.'

'Agony,' Mrs McTaggart said dramatically. 'Hours and hours of sheer agony, and each time was worse than the time before. What are you going to call him, Ellie?'

'Brendan,' Ellie said promptly.

The older woman went pink with delight. 'I hope he gives you as much pleasure as my Brendan gave me.'

Dr O'Hara raised his eyebrows. 'Does that include landing up in a Belfast jail?'

'It does indeed, Doctor. I'm proud of him, and so would his daddy be if he was alive.'

'I like the idea of having a son named after an Irish terrorist,' Ellie said with a gleeful smile. She looked down at the baby. He had a fluff of reddish hair, large blue eyes, a plump face and plump, pink hands. The blue eyes were fixed intently on her face. 'He's staring straight at me. He knows I'm his mother.'

The doctor gave Mrs McTaggart a knowing smile. 'Babies can't see properly for the first few weeks, Ellie.'

'I thought that was kittens.'

'It's babies too.'

The front door slammed, there were heavy footsteps on the stairs, and a red-faced, strangely bright-eyed Neila Kenny came rushing into the room. She looked just a little bit mad.

'I saw Doctor O'Hara's car outside. Oh, the baby's come! Is it a boy or a girl?'

'A boy,' Ellie said proudly. 'I'm calling him Brendan.'

'Let me look at him. Can I hold him? I wish he'd come this afternoon when I was here.'

'You can hold him some other time, Neila,' Dr O'Hara said. 'I'd like to see him at his mother's breast right now. She and Brendan need to get used to each other.'

Ellie felt a tiny bit embarrassed, undoing her nightie, and exposing her breasts in front of three people, one of whom she wholeheartedly detested. She wished Neila would go away, not stare at Brendan as if she'd like to eat him.

Her son attached himself to her left breast and began to suck loudly.

'Very good,' the doctor said approvingly.

'It hurts,' Ellie complained. 'Me breasts feel dead tender.'

'That's quite normal. Let him try the other breast once he's had his fill.'

'How will I know?'

'Brendan will let you know, don't worry.'

A few minutes later, Brendan set up an angry wail and was transferred to the right breast. To Ellie's intense irritation, Neila seemed to think it necessary to lend a hand. 'I can manage meself, thanks,' she snapped.

Mrs McTaggart offered to make a cup of tea, but the doctor refused and said he had to go. 'I'll come back tomorrow, make sure everything's all right, but don't hesitate to give me a call if there's a problem.'

'I'll be looking after her, Doctor,' said Neila, 'don't worry. I'll ring Felix in a minute, tell him to bring more nappies and one or two other things. He'll be thrilled to bits it's a boy.'

'You're all heart, Neila. Ellie's lucky to have you.'

Ellie didn't think so.

Before, time had crawled by. Now it flew. Brendan, already a big baby according to Dr O'Hara, seemed to grow bigger by the day, not surprising considering the amount of milk he consumed. Ellie's breasts were sore, and she had to grudgingly concede she couldn't have coped without Neila Kenny, who abandoned the chemist's altogether and came to Fern Hall every day. Ellie had assumed bathing a baby, changing nappies, were the sort of things that would come naturally to a mother, but they seemed to require a knack she didn't have. Brendan was terrifyingly slippery when he was wet, and it was impossible to hold a squirming baby with one hand and wash him with the other. Nappies got in a terrible tuck and came off faster than she put them on. Neila could do all these things with incredible efficiency having had five younger brothers and sisters to learn on.

Brendan was demanding, but a good baby, according to Mrs McTaggart, far better behaved than Brendan the First, who'd screamed his bad-tempered little head off for three whole months, so much so that Mr McTaggart, bless his heart, had threatened to throw his latest son out of the window.

The new Brendan slept in a cot beside Ellie's bed and required feeding twice, sometimes three times, a night, followed by the inevitable burping. Ellie would scarcely have closed her eyes, when she would be alerted by an urgent cry. '*I'm hungry again,*' Brendan would yell. Next morning, she would hand him over to an eager Neila before going back to bed for a few hours of much needed sleep.

The amount of washing was horrendous. So many baby clothes, bedclothes, dozens and dozens of nappies; dirty nappies, soaking nappies, nappies drying on the line, nappies dried and aired and ready for use. Mrs McTaggart helped when she could, but she had other tasks to do and only came three times a week.

Despite her utter weariness, there were some mornings Ellie went back to bed and couldn't sleep. Although she knew the cot was empty and Brendan was safely downstairs, her mind remained alert and expectant, as if any minute there would be a desperate appeal for food. After a few hours, she would give up trying to sleep and go downstairs where there was always work to do.

It was on such a morning, when Brendan was six weeks old, that Ellie came down, aching for a cup of tea, to find the front door open and Neila coming in with the baby in his carrycot on wheels.

'Have you been out for a walk?' she asked.

'I go most mornings, didn't you know?'

'You never said before. Did you go to the village?'

'We needed shopping done.' Neila removed a nylon shopping bag from the tray under the pram and stared at her aggressively. 'Do you mind?'

Ellie minded very much her baby being examined by the entire village and his likeness to Liam – very strong – commented on.

'Everyone's surprised,' Neila remarked, 'That you're not getting yourself ready to go to Geneva.'

'What's in Geneva?' Ellie nearly said, then remembered Liam was, and he was supposed to be her husband and she was supposed to be joining him when the baby was born. 'Do I look as if I'm ready to go Geneva?' she said irritably instead. The furthest she got was the garden. Her hair was lucky if it got combed once a week, she'd forgotten what make-up looked like, and was wearing a maternity frock because she'd put on so much weight none of her old clothes would fit.

'*I'm* surprised Liam hasn't rung, or you haven't rung him, or that you haven't written to him or he to you.' Neila lifted Brendan from the pram, put her large, red hand on his fluffy head and pressed it tenderly into the curve beneath her chin.

Ellie resented her baby being touched by the hateful Neila Kenny. 'You're surprised at an awful lot of things. If you must know, I've written to Liam twice since I had Brendan.'

'You didn't ask me or Felix to post the letter.'

'That's because I asked Mrs McTaggart.'

'Liam hasn't answered.'

'Do you examine the post?'

'I pick it up off the mat when I come in, don't I?'

'I wouldn't know. I'm not a spy like you.'

Neila's big hand spread over the baby's back, the other supported his bottom. She said angrily, 'I'm not a spy. I can't help but notice things, that's all.'

Unable to think of a reason why Liam hadn't replied to her imaginary letters, Ellie turned on her heel and went into the kitchen to put the kettle on. Neila followed, Brendan clinging to her the way a monkey clings to a tree, as if *she* were his mother.

'You never married him, did you, Ellie?' Neila spat from the kitchen door. 'He ran off and left you. He doesn't give a damn about you or Brendan.'

'Say that were true,' Ellie said tiredly, 'What business is it of yours?'

'I'm worried about Brendan, that's all.' The horrible woman kissed Brendan's rosy cheek. 'He needs his father.'

'*I* didn't have a father,' a seething Ellie pointed out. 'He died before me and me sister were born. Neither of us seem to have come to any harm.'

'Ah, but you had a proper home, a family. What sort of life will Brendan have with you on your own? No husband, no job, nowhere to live.'

Ellie realised with a shock that Neila was after her baby. She shivered. Although common sense told her the woman could do nothing harmful, she felt the need to get away from Fern Hall with all possible speed; tomorrow or the day after. The longer she stayed, the more possessive Neila would become. She held out her arms, forgetting the tea. 'He's due for a feed. I'll do it in the garden.'

It was June and the garden looked especially lovely. The crumbling walls were covered with trailing flowers, the trees with budding fruit. Ellie sat in a deckchair, opened her frock, and began to feed her always-hungry son. She wasn't sure if she loved Brendan, but he was *hers*, grown and nurtured in her womb. He was part of her, and she'd no more intention of letting him go than of getting rid of one of her limbs.

Next morning, Ellie was making her breakfast when Neila Kenny arrived, having washed her hair and made up her face for the first time in weeks. She'd also managed to struggle into a pair of jeans – all the hard work had made her lose some of the extra weight.

'You're up early,' Neila said, surprised, when they encountered each other in the kitchen. 'Where's Brendan?'

'Asleep in the garden. He only woke up once last night.' Perhaps he realised it was time he gave his mother a break. 'By the way, I'm going to Dublin tomorrow to see a friend, Amy. She lived in the same house as me and Liam.' She'd sooner not say she was leaving for ever and provoke a scene.

'And taking Brendan with you?'

'Naturally, Amy would love to see him.'

Neila frowned and looked as if she'd like to object. 'Will you be able to manage on your own? I'll come with you if you like. I wouldn't mind a stroll around the shops.'

'I wouldn't dream of it. You've already done enough. I'll always be very grateful to you and Felix,' Ellie said falsely. She would have to put the planned adventures on hold for a while. Neila was right about one thing. It would be impossible to get a job when she had a small baby and where would she live? Well, Ellie could think of one place where she would be welcomed with open arms – home. It was one thing crawling back after a few months with her pregnancy a badge of shame, but another altogether returning with her head held high, proudly, bearing the world's most beautiful baby, and pretending she'd had a super time over the last year. She would think of a reason for having left Liam so it didn't reflect badly on her – say he was dead, for example.

That night, after Neila had gone, she sat with Felix in the garden, nursing a sleepy Brendan in her arms. It was very peaceful, very still. The flowers shimmered in the golden light of the evening sun which was slowly setting into a mishmash of red, green and purple stripes, casting a dark, moving shadow across the grass, slowly stripping the blooms of their vivid colour. The air was heavily scented – Gran had flowers in the garden at home, Ellie remembered, that smelt wonderful at night. It was the first time in her life she had appreciated the beauty of nature and she thought it strange this should happen when she was on the point of leaving Fern Hall.

'You should get central heating,' she said.

'Eh!' Felix looked understandably taken aback by this strange remark.

'Central heating. It would make the house much warmer in the winter, get rid of the damp.' Now she thought about it, it was quite a pleasant house, gracious.

Felix's face softened into a gentle smile. 'I couldn't afford it, Ellie. It takes me all my time to pay the bills I have now.'

Ellie felt guilty, something else that was a first. He'd paid for Brendan's pram, his cot, mountains of baby clothes and nappies, and all the other things that were needed for a baby. It hadn't crossed her mind to say, 'thank you', yet it wasn't Felix's job to provide for his brother's child – a child he adored, always remarking how like Liam he was.

'Can't you turn the chemist's into something else?' she suggested. 'A tea room, for instance.' Lots of cars passed through Craigmoss on their way to and from Dublin or Dun Laoghaire, from where the ferry sailed to England – from where she and Brendan would sail tomorrow.

'People need a chemist for their prescriptions. It would be irresponsible to close it down.'

She wanted to shake some sense into him. It was time he put himself first, not conduct his life for the convenience of all and sundry. 'Fern Hall could provide bed and breakfasts,' she said. 'It's conveniently situated on the main road.'

'I'm not very good when it comes to business,' Felix said simply. 'It takes me all my time to run the chemist's.'

He needed a wife behind him, a pushy, determined wife, not the oaf-like Neila Kenny, who'd been his father's mistress and was someone else he felt responsible for. She was about to suggest other things he could sell from the chemist's, flowers for instance from the garden that could be put in buckets outside, but knew it was a waste of time. Life had beaten Felix and he'd lost the will to fight.

'I'll miss you and Brendan when the time comes for you to go,' he said in his husky whisper.

'I'll come and see you sometime.' Ellie genuinely meant it. 'At least, I'll try.'

'You'll always be welcome.'

It was a good job she didn't tell people at home that Liam was dead – she'd said they were 'incompatible' – because she'd only been in Liverpool two days when he rang to say Felix had tracked him down in Geneva, worried where Ellie was.

'He said you went to Dublin for the day and didn't come back,' Liam said accusingly. 'Did you *have* to walk out without a word? I told him it was just like you and I wasn't a bit surprised. He only wants to know if you're safe.'

'I'm quite safe, thanks, and I only left without saying anything because I was worried Neila Kenny would make a big fuss.'

'And why should Neila Kenny make any sort of fuss?'

'She was after Brendan, that's why, because she can't have children of her own. I think you should rescue your brother from Neila Kenny, Liam. Did you know she was your father's mistress for nearly ten years?'

'Y'what?' Liam gasped.

'You heard. He inherited her along with Fern Hall and the chemist's. Another thing, Felix bought all Brendan's stuff, so you owe him loads of money. *I* can't pay him back.'

There was silence for a moment while Liam digested these startling facts. 'What's he like, Brendan?' he eventually asked.

'Gorgeous. Everyone here loves him to death.'

'I might come and see him some time?'

'If you do, you're likely to get some dirty looks from me family.' Ellie gave the receiver a dirty look before slamming it down.

She couldn't have arrived home at a better time, amid preparations for her mother's wedding, with people too busy to question what she'd been up to, lecture her for turning up with Liam Conway's baby and brazenly announcing she wasn't married. Mum was pleased she'd got back in time to be a bridesmaid and was more concerned with getting her a frock the same as Moira and Daisy's than anything. And it was true what she'd said to

Liam; everyone loved Brendan to death, particularly Gran. An old cot had been unearthed from the cellar, a new mattress hurriedly bought, and mother and son were installed in an upstairs room, empty now that the students had gone for the summer. Unlike with Neila, Ellie didn't mind a bit when Gran took Brendan off her hands every morning, allowing her to have a long sleep in.

Ruby felt as if Brendan had been sent by heaven to take her mind off the fact that the man she loved was about to marry another woman. If the other woman hadn't been her daughter, she might have put up a fight, told him that she loved him, forced him to admit he loved her back, insisted he was making a mistake.

She had no idea what had prompted Matthew to ask Greta to be his wife, but he had, and there was no going back, mistake or no mistake. She'd made a mess of things with Jacob, then with Chris Ryan, and the worst mess of all with Matthew Doyle. 'You're a soft girl, Ruby O'Hagan,' Beth used to tell her, and Beth was right.

Greta and Matthew made a perfect couple. They had known each other for the best part of their lives. Greta had liked him from the start, in the days when Ruby had called him every name under the sun. Even Heather approved of the match, though Ruby knew it would break her heart to lose her sister now that the relationship with Gerald Johnson had fizzled out.

The sole topic of conversation became the wedding, which couldn't take place in church because Matthew was divorced. Greta didn't mind and although there was a time when Ruby would have minded very much, things had changed. Nowadays, all sorts of people got divorced and couldn't be expected to remain alone for the rest of their lives, particularly if they were the innocent party, like Matthew.

Now that he was on his feet again, Matthew was paying for everything. A hotel had been booked for the reception – a new one in Paradise Street, very expensive. The menu was discussed endlessly, how many guests should be invited. Flowers were ordered, cars booked. Daisy knew of a pop group if they wanted music. Heather was to be Matron of Honour, Daisy and Moira bridesmaids. Moira was ordered home from Norwich for the weekend so she could be bought a dress – pale blue voile with a pleated bodice and a gathered skirt. Appointments were made at the hairdresser's – there would be plenty of time for shampoos and sets because Greta wanted an afternoon wedding.

Ruby was dragged into town to help choose the bride's outfit. Greta still had a weakness for frills and flounces and ended up with a cream lace, knee-length frock that made her look like a Barbie doll, and a mixture of feathers and flowers pretending to be a hat. Ruby bought her own outfit at the same time; a simple mid-blue sheath with a short boxy jacket. Looking in the mirror, she thought Matthew was right to have chosen the daughter not the mother, because the mother looked a sight; old, grey, with drooping eyes and a neck like a piece of old rope. She threw back her shoulders. She was even getting a hump.

Matthew was buying a lovely house in Calderstones. The solicitors were doing their utmost to exchange final contracts before the newly wed couple returned from their honeymoon in the South of France. So far, everything was going smoothly, but for Ruby nothing was going smoothly at all.

Beth couldn't come to the wedding. 'I'm speaking at a conference,' she wrote. 'I'd feel awful, cancelling, though if it were *you* getting married, Rube, I'd be there if it meant snubbing President Carter himself.'

She hadn't seen Connie and Charles for ages and hoped an invitation to a wedding might tempt them back to Liverpool, if only for the day, but Connie rang to say Charles was too ill to travel. 'It's his heart, Ruby. He's not allowed to drive any more and he's not up to the train journey. Give Greta our love and tell her we're sending a present.'

If that wasn't bad enough, a few days later she saw in the *Echo* that Jim Quinlan had died. Over the years, she'd felt glad that he hadn't been attracted to her as she had been to him. There'd been a time when she would have married him like a shot – perhaps because he was so different to Jacob. Or maybe, without realising it, she'd just been casting round for someone to love and Jim had fitted the bill.

Why do people have to grow old, die? she wondered, and for the first time in her life, Ruby was overwhelmed by an all-consuming sadness, feeling as if her own life was hanging by a thread, and asking herself the inevitable question, 'What is it all for?'

Then Ellie returned from Dublin with Brendan, her first great-grandchild and, although Ruby never received an answer to her question, the sadness lifted, and she took the baby boy to her heart.

It was a daft idea, thought Heather, to have a Matron of Honour and three bridesmaids when you were only getting married in a registry office. For once, she'd kept her opinions to herself. After all, it was Greta's wedding, not hers. As for that dress, it was far too short, and you'd think Mam would have talked her into something at least ballerina length.

And there was something strange, not quite right, about being joined together in Holy Matrimony in an ordinary room by a man in a suit – there were actually women registrars, which would be even stranger.

'Do you take this woman . . . ?'

'Do you take this man . . . ?'

'I do,' Greta murmured in the girlish voice that had hardly changed since she was a child. Heather felt her eyes prickle with tears, not because she was losing her sister, but she knew that, unlike Greta, she would never say those words again. She couldn't have brought herself to say them to Gerald, nor to any other man on earth. She had said, 'I do' just once, to Rob, and she'd meant it for ever. Heather knew that she would remain Rob White's widow for the rest of her days.

There was a dreadful smell coming from Brendan. The little monkey had dirtied in his nappy, and in the middle of a wedding too. He was perched in the crook of Ruby's arm making cooing noises. She worried that she hadn't brought enough spare nappies, only three, and it would be hours before they could go home.

Considering it was a wedding, the atmosphere was rather flat. She missed the grandeur and dignity of a church, and wondered if second marriages always lacked the excitement of the first. The groom hadn't smiled once and Heather looked as if the world was about to end. At least Greta seemed pleased she was about to become Mrs Matthew Doyle.

Ruby glanced across at the Donovans and the Whites. Their faces were sober, no doubt remembering the day they'd attended a different wedding which they had thought would be a beginning, but had turned out to be the end.

Thank the Lord she'd come home when she did, Ellie thought as she danced with a dead gorgeous chap called Gary who was a sculptor, or something arty. She was having a great time. The reception had been a bit boring, especially the speeches, but Grannie and Grandad Donovan had been so pleased to see her and had made a desperate fuss of Brendan. Ellie had felt very proud, as if she'd performed a miracle.

'He's our Larry's *grandson*,' Grannie Donovan said tearfully. 'Is he like him or not?'

'The spitting image,' Grandad Donovan confirmed, making four different people Brendan had been declared the spitting image of that day.

At seven o'clock, the pop group arrived along with loads more people and the reception turned into a party. The Gigolos made up for in noise what they lacked in talent, but were easy to dance to – how come Daisy knew a pop group?

Not long afterwards, the bride and groom left for their honeymoon and the dancing stopped for the guests to cheer them on their way. Moira came over and whispered to her twin, 'I'll never get used to Mum being married. It seems really weird. Just look, Matthew's got his *arm* around her.'

'I suppose it is a bit weird,' Ellie agreed. She hadn't been home long enough to give the matter much thought, though the news had initially come as a shock. 'It means Matthew's our step-father.'

'Mum wants us to go and live with her in Calderstones. I don't know about you, but I said "no". I'd sooner stay in our old house with Gran. I think Mum's a bit annoyed.'

'She hasn't asked me yet, but I feel the same as you.' Ellie couldn't imagine her mother looking after Brendan while she had a long lie in, unlike Gran.

The music started again. Unable to resist, the twins grinned at each other and began to dance on the spot, twisting and turning in rhythm with the loud, throbbing beat. In no time, two young men appeared; Gary the sculptor, and a pony-tailed individual wearing shredded jeans who paired off with Moira.

Ellie prepared to dance the night away, entirely forgetting she was a mother with a hungry baby to feed. She was annoyed, even if it was hours later, when Gran tugged at her sleeve and announced Brendan was screaming fit to bust. 'Why can't he have a bottle?' she asked irritably.

'He's drunk both his bottles, love.'

'Does that mean I'll have to go *home*?' Ellie was outraged.

'I can't feed him, can I? Anyway, his nappy's soaking. That's the fifth today. I sent out for some of them disposable ones, but I don't like changing it again. The poor little chap needs a bath by now, else he'll get a rash. I'll ring for a taxi.'

'Where is Brendan?'

'With your other gran. He's wet her lovely new costume.' Ruby hurried away.

'Have you got a *baby*?' Gary looked at Ellie askance.

'Yes.'

'Oh! Excuse us a mo, there's a mate over there I want to talk to.'

Gary vanished into the crowd, without mentioning the party he'd invited her to on Saturday night, and Ellie knew it would always be like this. Her time was no longer her own now that she was responsible for another person's life. She couldn't go out whenever she felt like it, do whatever she pleased, and men would keep their distance if they knew about Brendan, worried they'd be landed with another man's child.

Ellie hardly spoke to her grandmother on the way home in the taxi, though it was hardly Gran's fault she'd had a baby. Mind you, Gran hardly spoke to *her*, which was odd because she was usually so cheerful. In fact, she'd seemed a bit down all day. Ellie didn't care, although she thought the world of her grandmother. She was too fed up to care about anything.

When Ellie woke, it was still dark and someone was sitting on the bed trying to shush a bawling Brendan. She sat up and switched on the bedside lamp. 'What time is it?'

'Three o'clock.' The someone was Daisy, still in her blue bridesmaid's frock. 'Me and Clint went back to Mary's house and I've only just got in. I heard Brendan cry and thought I might stop him before he woke you, but he must need feeding.'

'The bloody little sod always needs feeding.' Ellie opened her nightdress and Daisy put Brendan in her arms. 'I only fed him five hours ago.'

'You must be awfully tired not to have heard him.'

'I'm more than tired. I'm totally exhausted,' Ellie replied piteously.

'Why don't you put him on the bottle permanently and we can take turns looking after him during the night? I wouldn't mind, and nor would Gran. You can get tablets from the doctor to dry your milk up.'

'Can you?' It seemed a marvellous idea. Ellie decided to see the doctor first thing in the morning.

'Would you like us to make you some cocoa?'

'Please. Can I have a biscuit too? I'm starving.'

By the time her cousin came back, Brendan was halfway through his mother's second breast.

'What does it feel like?' Daisy asked.

'It either hurts or tickles, one or the other.'

'Me and Clint are going to have loads of children.'

'Are you now! Is that Clint's idea or yours?' Ellie suspected Clint was keeping well out of her way. They hadn't come face to face since she'd got back.

'Mine, I suppose. You know Clint, how shy he is. He doesn't like talking about certain things.'

Having babies being one of them, Ellie thought cynically. 'Are you two still getting married?'

'Yes, a year next January, 1979. You can be a bridesmaid with your Moira if you like,' Daisy offered generously.

'That'd be nice, ta.' Ellie looked at Daisy's innocent, wholesome face. She'd changed a lot in the last year, was far more confident, and had loads of friends, though was as dumpy and plain as she'd always been. The friends were artists, Moira said, and considered Daisy to be a fantastic painter. They'd held an exhibition and some of Daisy's paintings had actually been *sold*.

'You mean people gave money for them?' Ellie gasped.

'Yes, isn't it amazing?'

'Truly amazing.'

Brendan detached himself and smacked his lips with satisfaction. Ellie hoisted him on to her shoulder to bring up his wind.

'Shall I do that while you have your cocoa and biscuit?'

'Thanks, Daise.' Ellie gratefully handed her son across.

'I like the feel of him, the way he fits against me like the piece of a jigsaw puzzle.' She began gently to pat Brendan's back. 'He's a very masculine baby. He doesn't suit nightgowns. Do you mind if I buy him one of those all-in-one stretchy things?'

'I don't mind a bit.'

'I'll get one in Mothercare tomorrow.'

It was rather nice, leaning against the pillows, sipping the cocoa, and watching someone else burp her child.

'Were you pleased about your A levels?' Daisy asked.

'I did much better than expected.' Ellie had been astonished to find she'd done so well considering she hadn't revised a single subject.

'Are you going to look for a job?'

'I hadn't thought about it. What about Brendan?'

'Gran will look after him, won't she? She looked after us when your mum was ill and mine went to work.'

'I suppose she would,' Ellie said thoughtfully. After Daisy had gone and Brendan was back in his cot, snoring softly, Ellie snuggled under the clothes and considered what had just been said. She didn't want an ordinary job, like in an office or a bank, but fancied working in a night club or an advertising agency, becoming a model or an actress, travelling the world. She'd thought having Brendan had put a stop to these dreams, but if Gran was prepared to have Brendan while she went to work, she might be prepared to have him if she went away!

Only might! Ellie had a feeling that if she put this proposal to her grandmother, she would object. After all, looking after a baby for a few hours a day wasn't the same as looking after one the whole time. And Gran might insist Brendan needed his mother, even if it was only at night.

In that case, Ellie would just have to leave the way she'd left before, the way she'd left Felix and Fern Hall, without telling a soul, knowing her son was in safe hands. This time, she wouldn't even say anything to Moira who'd only disapprove.

And so it was that, two months later, in the middle of September, when Ruby crept into the room to collect Brendan and give him his bottle, Ellie's bed was empty. She wasn't in the bathroom, either, nor downstairs. A few hours later, when there was still no sign, Ruby came to the inevitable conclusion that, not for the first time, her granddaughter had run away.

17

So much money, enough to buy all the clothes she wanted, anything for the house, yet Greta felt bored. And it was such a beautiful house, mock Tudor, with five bedrooms, living, dining and breakfast rooms, and a kitchen with every conceivable modern device. The garden was a picture, neatly perfect, and a man came twice a week to weed and prune and cut the grass.

Matthew had had the place redecorated from top to bottom; new carpets everywhere. She had rarely enjoyed herself so much, choosing the colours, the curtains, wandering around the most expensive shops picking any item of furniture that took her fancy.

Now it was all done, the limewood wardrobe and the matching chests of drawers were full of new clothes, and suddenly there was nothing else to do. They had a cleaner as well as a gardener, and all Greta did was put the washing in the automatic machine, transfer it to the dryer, and make an evening meal for Matthew.

She wondered if she should have kept her job, but it hadn't seemed right, being married to a hugely successful businessman, living in such an impressive house, yet working as a shorthand-typist. If she'd had a profession, like Heather, it would have been different. Anyroad, she'd never liked work. Mam always said she was lazy, that she preferred her bed, which Greta had to concede was true.

It was upsetting that neither of her girls had wanted to live with her – four of the five bedrooms hadn't been used. It didn't matter that Moira was at university or Ellie had taken it into her head to run away again. At least she could have got their rooms ready for when they came back, furnished them in a way she knew they would have liked.

Matthew worked harder now that the company belonged to someone else. Some nights, it was ten o'clock by the time he got home and the meal was spoilt. Greta felt lonely on her own, which was ironic in a way, as she'd only married him so she *wouldn't* feel lonely. More and more, she found herself going round to see Mam. She hadn't realised when she'd lived there just how shabby and run down Mam's house was, and it made her more cross that the twins hadn't wanted to leave. It was Mam, not her, talking about Moira coming home from university for Christmas.

Now Heather was studying for a law degree through the Open University, getting up at unearthly hours of the morning to watch programmes on television. Evenings, when Greta went into her old room and sat on her old bed wanting to chat to her sister, Heather was usually studying or writing essays and made it obvious she didn't appreciate being interrupted.

During the day, Mam was usually busy with Brendan, nearly eight months old, a delightful baby, but a terrible handful. Poor Mam was up to her eyes with work, what with Brendan, three students, and Heather and Daisy to look after.

'Why don't I take Brendan off your hands?' Greta suggested one afternoon when Brendan was being given his tea and turning it into a game, holding the food in his mouth for ages, before slyly letting it dribble out so that Mam had to catch it with the spoon and put it back. His green eyes sparkled with mischief, and he kept slamming the tray on his high chair with his big hands and thumping it with his fat knees at the same time. He was a handsome child, perfectly built, with Liam Conway's eyes and hair a lovely golden red. Brendan would keep her busy during the day and she was sure Matthew would love a baby. They could get an au pair to look after him during the night and do things like change his nappies.

'I don't need him taking off my hands, love,' Ruby said mildly.

'But you've so much to do, Mam!'

'If you feel like helping, Greta, you can make the students' tea.'

Greta pouted. It wasn't the same. After all, Brendan was Ellie's son and Ellie was her daughter, which made her Brendan's Grandma. She had far more right to him than Mam. 'But that's not fair,' she said. 'We've got a much nicer house, a lovely garden. We could buy him far more things, toys and stuff, clothes.' Brendan's stretchy suit was so small, the feet had been cut off to accommodate his legs and he was wearing a pair of frilly girl's socks that she remembered had belonged to one of the twins.

'I'm sorry, love,' Ruby said, very slowly and deliberately, 'but when you said you'd take him off my hands, did you mean permanently?'

'Yes.'

'And why, all of a sudden, do you want a baby? Is it because you're bored all day in your much nicer house?'

'Yes, no. No, of course not,' Greta stammered, and all of a sudden she and Mam were having a terrible row, which they'd never done before. At least Greta was having a row, Mam didn't say much. She accused her mother of having stolen her children so that she'd hardly seen anything of them when they were little, and now she was stealing her grandson. She ended up storming out, screaming something about going to court, getting her grandson back, when she'd never had him in the first place.

When she got home, the house was in darkness and felt cold. She turned up the central heating, threw herself on to the bed, and burst into tears. Why wasn't she happy? She'd always been happy apart from the few years after Larry died, and she'd thought she'd be happier still in a smart house with pots of money. Although it hadn't been her intention to go one up on her sister, nevertheless she'd thought Heather would be envious of her new position in life, but nowadays Heather appeared serenely contented as she studied for her law degree.

Matthew didn't help much, though it wasn't deliberate. He was incredibly kind and thoughtful, took her out at weekends, was buying her a fur coat for Christmas, and complimented her on her cooking. Making love was oddly thrilling. Matthew had been part of her life for almost as long as she could remember and although she'd always considered him attractive, she'd never remotely thought of him as a lover. But now he was her husband, she went to bed with him every night, and felt instantly aroused by his touch, yet sensed that Matthew was only doing what was expected of him, that he was detached from the whole thing. Sometimes, even when he was being his kindest, she felt as if he was detached from the marriage itself.

Ruby was still shaking when her other daughter came home. She'd burnt the students' tea, but fortunately she'd taken boys again and they didn't seem to care what the food was like as long as it arrived in heaps – girls, she'd decided, were far too much trouble, always complaining about something or other.

'Where's Brendan?' Heather enquired.

'Asleep, for once. Look, love, d'you mind having an omelette? There's nothing else ready. I'm way behind today.'

'An omelette's fine. What's the matter, Mam?' Heather had noticed her mother's trembling hands.

Ruby sat down, close to tears. 'I had a terrible row with our Greta.' She explained what had happened. 'I don't know what's got into her. She's not been the same since she got married.'

Heather reached for her mother's hands. 'I'm sorry, Mam, but none of us really know what our Greta's like. Oh, she's as nice as pie while she's being spoilt and made a fuss of, loved by one and all, but she's got a selfish streak. She's always put herself first – it's what she was doing today, no matter how much it upset you. It's obvious she's not happy in that big house on her own and she sees Brendan as a way of filling the time, making her feel as if she's somebody again.'

'Oh, I don't hold with all this psychological claptrap, Heather. Beth's always coming out with stuff like that.'

'Can you think of another reason why Greta behaved the way she did?'

'No,' Ruby sighed after a few moments' pause.

'Ellie's the same,' Heather continued. 'She does her own thing and to hell with the consequences.'

'Your dad was a bit like that. He had no conscience. He'd sooner walk away than face up to things.' Ruby frowned. 'I hope Matthew's being all right with our Greta.'

'I'm sure Matthew's being fine, but he's not there all the time, is he? He's got other things to think of, and Greta's not the centre of the universe any more, like she was here – with you and me, at least.'

'Perhaps I should go and see her.'

'No,' Heather said in a hard voice. 'Let her stew in her own juice for a while, she'll soon be back. You see, Mam, Greta needs us far more than we need her.'

'That only seems more reason why I should go and see her.'

'She's forty-one, Mam. She's got to learn to stand on her own two feet. You've got enough to do with Brendan.'

A week later, Greta returned, by which time Moira was home and the Christmas decorations were up. She felt a twinge when she saw the worn paper chains, the balls and bells that opened and closed like concertinas, the elderly fairy on top of the tree, things she'd helped put up in the past, but this time it had been done without her.

Moira was lying on the living room floor playing with Brendan, teaching him how to put one block on top of another, but he clearly preferred flinging them as far as they'd go.

'Hi, Mum,' Moira sang, but didn't get up and kiss her.

Greta had come all set to apologise to her mother, but felt annoyed at the signs that life was continuing smoothly without her in the place she still regarded as home. She found Ruby in the kitchen emptying flour into a plastic bowl.

'Oh, hello, love.' She smiled, as if their last meeting had never happened. 'Does that look like a pound to you? I thought I'd make the mince pies early for a change, rather than in a rush on Christmas Eve.'

'I wouldn't know, Mam. I thought you were supposed to weigh it first.'

'I usually do, but Brendan's broken the scales.'

'Actually, Mam,' Greta said on an impulse. 'Me and Matthew thought you'd like to come to us for Christmas dinner. We've bought this huge turkey,' she lied, and imagined herself the star of the show, everyone saying what a wonderful job she'd done, admiring the house which they'd hardly seen.

'Greta, love, it's a bit late to ask now. I was expecting you and Matthew to come to us. Clint's coming, and I've already invited his mum and dad, and Jonathan will be here.'

'Who's Jonathan?'

'One of the students. He's from India, Karachi. It's too far for him to go home, so he's staying here.'

'Why is he called Jonathan if he's Indian?'

'Because he's a Christian. He'll be coming with us to Midnight Mass.'

'Matthew and I can't come to dinner on Christmas Day,' Greta said bluntly.

Her mother looked perplexed. 'But you just asked us!'

'If me family can't come, we'll go somewhere else. We've been asked to loads of places for dinner.' Greta knew she was cutting off her nose to spite her face, but felt deeply hurt that her invitation had been refused, unreasonable though it was at such a late date. She felt as if she didn't matter any more.

The dining room in the house in Calderstones had never been used since they moved in. She and Matthew usually ate in the little breakfast room which was much cosier. Perhaps it was a mistake to serve dinner on the vast table on Christmas Day, just the two of them, Matthew clearly puzzled that they hadn't been asked home.

They didn't say much during the meal. Afterwards, Greta cleared the table and watched the portable television in the kitchen, and Matthew watched the one in the lounge. It stayed that way until six o'clock, when it was time to get ready for the party in Southport being held by one of the executives from Medallion, the company who'd taken over Doyle Construction.

Greta put on a red crêpe frock with shoelace straps and a frilly hem, a bit like the sort Spanish dancers wore. Without Heather there to advise her, she painted her lips bright red to go with the frock and applied a little too much rouge and mascara. Matthew looked a bit surprised when she appeared, but didn't say anything, just helped her on with her new fur coat which was sealskin with a mink collar and cuffs, terribly glamorous.

At the party, quite a few men wanted to talk to her, tell her what a stunner she was, how much she suited red and, Greta, always used to being the centre of attention, felt like a star after all. She even gave one chap, an American whose name was Charlie Mayhew, her telephone number, and he promised to call and take her to lunch. She was sure Matthew wouldn't mind, but didn't tell him.

'She seemed such a sweet little thing,' Matthew muttered.

'Are you saying she isn't?' snapped Ruby.

'Not any more,' said Matthew.

It was two weeks after Christmas, and Matthew Doyle had appeared unexpectedly in the middle of the afternoon. Moira had gone for a walk with Brendan in his pram, and Ruby had taken the opportunity to wash the students' bedding. They were due back in a few days and she hadn't had the chance before.

'We've only been married six months and I've a horrible feeling it's already a failure,' Matthew said miserably.

'Why are you telling me this?' She wondered why she sounded so abrupt when she was so pleased to see him, even if the news he'd brought was distressing. Her heart had turned a somersault when she'd opened the door and found him outside.

'Because I've got to talk to someone and you're the only one I can.'

'Would you like a cup of tea?'

'I was hoping you'd ask.' He sat his long body on a kitchen chair, shoulders drooping.

Ruby ran water in the kettle and gave the washing machine a kick when it stopped. It was on its last legs and needed encouragement. 'What's wrong, Matthew?' she asked, kinder now.

'I dunno, Rube.' She felt warmed by the 'Rube'. It meant they were at least friends again. 'I don't know what I'm doing wrong. I don't know what's right any more. She's moody all the time, bad-tempered, bored. There was a time when I couldn't have visualised Greta being bad-tempered, but I've witnessed it quite a few times lately.'

'I've witnessed it myself. It shook me too.'

'Have you?' He didn't look surprised. 'She hasn't a good word to say for you or Heather, or Moira come to that. She seems to think you're all against her for some reason.'

'We're not.' Ruby said fervently. 'I'm worried sick about her. Heather seems to think she'll come round in her own time. I don't think Moira's noticed anything amiss.'

'She's got a thing about Brendan. She wants him.'

'Brendan's not a parcel to be handed round at whim. He's already had two different people looking after him.'

'That's what I more or less told her meself.'

'Are you sorry you asked her to marry you?'

'I didn't ask her, Rube. She asked me.'

'*What!*' Ruby was pouring boiling water into the teapot. It splashed on to her hand and she gave a little scream. 'Ouch!'

'Are you all right?' Matthew leapt to his feet, grabbed her hand, and put it under the cold tap. 'Does that feel better?'

'Much better, thanks. Why did you accept?' He was patting her hand gently with the teatowel. They were standing very close, touching. His breath was warm on her cheek.

'Because I'm a soft lad, because I was flattered, because I was feeling particularly low and vulnerable at the time.'

'Why were you feeling low and vulnerable?'

'You know the answer to that, Ruby.'

She turned away and faced the sink, unable to meet his eyes. 'I'm sorry, Matthew. I was stupid, rude. I was every horrible name you can think of. I've always been slow-witted. It didn't enter my head what you were trying to say until I was on the phone. I called you, but you didn't come back.'

'I was too bloody mad to come back.' There was a long pause during which both were very still. Then Matthew whispered softly, 'What would you have said if I had?'

'It's too late for that now, Matthew.' Ruby moved away. 'You can see that, can't you?'

He sighed. 'I'm not sure if I want to.'

'Then you must,' she said with a briskness she didn't feel. She would have preferred to weep, throw herself into his arms, make up for the hurt she'd caused him, but he was her daughter's husband, and it was much, much too late. Had he been married to anyone else, she would probably have felt pleased his marriage had failed. 'Oh, this damn washing machine!' It had stopped again. She gave it another kick. 'I'll never get this lot done in time.'

'For Christ's sake, Ruby, buy a new one.' Matthew was himself again. The conversation they'd just had might never have occurred. He returned to the table and she gave him a mug of tea.

Ruby laughed sardonically. 'What with?' Greta no longer contributed towards the household finances and Brendan was an extra expense, if a welcome one.

'I'll get you one for Christmas.'

'I couldn't possibly accept such an expensive present. Anyway, you already gave me some scent.'

'Climb down off your high horse, Rube. We're family now. You're my . . .' He paused.

'Mother-in-law?'

'My mother-in-law.' They grinned at each other and she was aware of an intimacy between them that had never been there before, though there was nothing sexual about it. 'As such,' Matthew went on, 'I'd prefer you forgot about the rent for this place from now on. I mean it, Ruby,' he said flatly when she opened her mouth to protest. 'If you send a cheque, I'll only tear it up.'

'If you insist,' Ruby said stiffly.

'I do. Oh, and don't thank me, Rube. I might have a heart attack.'

'All right, I won't.'

The following afternoon, Ruby left Brendan with an adoring Moira, and went to see her daughter, but found no one in. She telephoned that night and was pleased when Greta sounded quite her old self again.

'I was having lunch in town with a friend,' she said. 'Her name's Shirley and she lives next door. We're going again on Monday.'

'I'm pleased you've made a friend, love. When can we expect to see you again?'

'Oh, I dunno, Mam. Soon, I suppose.'

Charlie had taken her through the Mersey tunnel in his red sports car, then deep into the Cheshire countryside, to a little thatched pub where they'd had scampi and chips and two bottles of wine. Medallion were planning to set up business in the States, he told her. He had already spent six months with the head office in London, and was staying another six in Liverpool, the latest jewel in the Medallion crown, familiarising himself with the way things were run.

'And I'm sure you'll make my stay very pleasant,' he twinkled. He was very handsome, very charming, very sure of himself, with broad, athletic shoulders and an engaging smile.

Greta felt drunk and giggled a lot. She liked being the object of Charlie's undivided attention, which she never was with Matthew, whose mind always seemed to be elsewhere.

On Monday, they returned to the same pub, had a different meal accompanied by the same amount of wine. Charlie leant over and played with a lock of her fair hair.

'How about coming upstairs with me, gorgeous? All I have to do is book a room.'

She knew instinctively that he wouldn't ask her out again if she refused. It was what he'd been after all along. 'A roll in the hay,' Americans called it. Greta didn't answer straight away. It wasn't the sort of thing that she would have dreamt of doing once, but since she'd re-married, she no longer felt like her old self. Now she was bolder, more demanding, as if it had taken all this time to properly grow up. She enjoyed Charlie's company, the way he made her feel extra-special. What's more, she *wanted* them to make love as much as he did. Matthew would never know.

'Why not?' Greta giggled. And so Charlie booked a room and they went upstairs.

In June, Moira came home, having completed her second year at university and Brendan celebrated his first year on earth. Daisy swapped her day off with someone else so she could be there for his birthday tea and Heather came home early from work. Greta had been invited, but Ruby saw her daughter only rarely these days, and wasn't sure if she would come.

Brendan ruled the roost in the house, with every single person there attentive to his slightest whim. Moira often rang up from Norwich solely to ask how her nephew was, and Daisy and Heather were his slaves. Clint thought the world of him and Matthew considered the sun shone out of his little fat behind.

'He's being spoilt rotten,' Ruby would frequently cry, and although she loved him the most of all, she did her best to be firm with the little boy when he was naughty. But it was difficult – Brendan was even more adorable and funny and kissable when he was naughty than when he was good. Anyway, finding him on the floor with the shoe-cleaning box, having scrubbed himself all over with black polish, wasn't exactly *naughty*. It showed the child was clever and was trying to clean himself, even if the result was the reverse. When Brendan planted the clothes pegs around the edge of the lawn, it was because he'd thought they'd grow, and merely another sign of how brilliant he was. He could walk at ten months and had a vocabulary of half a dozen words, of which 'Bee', his name for Ruby, had been the first.

Ruby lived with the constant fear that he would be taken away. Greta's threats had frightened her, though there'd been no repeat since. Say if Ellie came home and, quite reasonably, wanted her son back? Ruby couldn't possibly refuse. She tried to prepare herself in advance for when this happened so it wouldn't come as a devastating shock. It was hard to imagine that each day spent with Brendan might be the last, but it was what Ruby did. It made the time they spent together very precious.

For his birthday, she had bought him denim overalls with red patches on the knees, a red T-shirt to go with the patches, and training shoes. Thus attired, Brendan presided over the table in his high chair, while the guests paid court and presented him with their gifts.

Halfway through the meal, Clint appeared, panting slightly, bearing a giant beach ball. 'I've got an hour off. I'll have to go back in a minute.' He beamed at the little boy. 'Happy birthday, Brendan.'

Brendan decided he preferred to play with the ball rather than finish his tea and the party transferred to the garden, where Daisy had to chase him with the birthday cake and implore him to blow out the single blue candle, which eventually went out of its own accord.

It was a fresh June day, slightly colder than it should have been, and the sun and the sky were exceptionally bright. The flowers in the garden were fully in bloom, the trees dressed with leaves of every possible shade of green.

Ruby sat on the grass and wondered how many children's parties there had been since she'd moved into the house. Then, Greta had only been three, Heather two, and Jake just a baby. She'd had birthday teas for the children she'd looked after during the war – Mollie, she remembered, had turned four only a few weeks before a bomb had demolished her house. The little girl had never had the chance to become five. The twins' parties had always been chaotic affairs with loads of friends invited. Daisy had preferred to have just her family present – and Clint, of course.

Clint was about to leave. He kissed Daisy chastely on the cheek. There wasn't much passion between them. Perhaps they knew each other too well, like brother and sister. Neither had had a relationship with another member of the opposite sex. Ruby wasn't sure if this was a good thing or a bad.

Just as Clint left, Matthew appeared carrying a tiny, three-wheeler bike. He waved to her, and Brendan immediately abandoned the ball and made for the bike. Matthew sat him on the seat and Moira and Daisy showed him how to turn the pedals with his feet. Heather shouted she was going to make some tea, and Matthew came and flopped down beside Ruby on the grass.

'I thought you were madly busy,' she said.

'I am. I pretended I was going somewhere vital and came here instead. It's too nice to be stuck in an office. These days, I spend too much time indoors. It goes with the job.' He removed his dark jacket and loosened his tie. His white shirt was beautifully ironed. At first, she'd been impressed, thinking it was Greta's work, but it turned out they went to the laundry. She asked if Greta was coming.

'She didn't mention it this morning, just that she was going to lunch with that friend of hers, Shirley.'

'What's she like, this Shirley?'

'Dunno, Rube.' He shrugged. 'I've never met her.'

'I thought she only lived next door?'

'No, Woolton somewhere. Greta met her in the hairdresser's.'

'But . . . oh, never mind. I must have got it wrong.' She hadn't though. Ruby distinctly remembered Greta saying that Shirley lived next door, but it wasn't worth an argument. It was a relief to know that Greta was all right again, had been so for months, though it would have been nice to see more of her.

'You look nice,' Matthew remarked. 'Is that a new frock?'

'No, I bought it for Washington. There's scarcely been an opportunity to wear it since.' It was the turquoise Indian cotton with beads around the neck.

He lay back on the grass and rested his head in his hands. 'Have the students gone?'

'The last one left at the weekend. It feels odd, knowing I won't be having more. Normally, I'd be expecting the foreign students to arrive any minute.' Months ago, they'd held a family conference and had decided the students could be dispensed with at the end of term now that the house was rent-free. On Monday, Moira was starting a summer job as a waitress so she could contribute towards her keep, and Daisy had reminded them she was getting married in less than a year and her contribution could only be relied on until Christmas – she and Clint were going to live in London, the only place for a person with a film career in mind.

Brendan had hurt his foot on the pedals of his bike. He gave a little whimper and trotted over to Ruby who rubbed it until it was better. 'Is that OK?'

'Yeth, Bee.' He returned to the bike, giving the ball a kick on the way as if to confirm the foot was in perfect condition.

Heather came out with a tray of tea and chocolate biscuits and handed them around.

'I wish you could do that to me, Rube,' Matthew said gloomily.

'Do what?'

'Make me better.'

She glanced at him sharply. 'Are you ill?'

'No, but I'm bloody fed up.'

'What with?' She hoped he wasn't going to say, 'Greta'.

'Me job. It's not my company any more. I'm just an employee like everyone else, responsible to those on high.'

'You should be thanking your lucky stars, not complaining. Sit up and drink your tea.'

He eased himself to a sitting position. 'Thanks for the sympathy. I knew you'd understand.'

'What is there to understand?' Ruby said cuttingly. 'Most people would give anything to be in your position.'

'Yes, but Rube, it's not *exciting* any more. I know exactly what I'll be doing from one day to the next.' He turned towards her, brown eyes wistful. 'You know what I'd like? To start again, by meself, like I did before, except this time I'd have more than a few bob in me pocket.'

'Why not do it, Matthew? There's nothing stopping you.'

'Isn't there?' His laugh came out like a bark. 'D'you think Greta would be pleased if the money suddenly dried up? Her favourite occupation is shopping. She's got enough clothes to sink a ship.'

'*I'd* help,' Ruby offered. 'I could type letters for you.'

'You can't type.'

'I can learn.'

'Oh, Rube, I don't half wish ...' He paused and said no more. Ruby didn't ask what the wish was because she already knew. She wished the same herself.

When Greta let herself in – she still had a key – the house appeared to be empty, but there were voices in the garden. Everyone had gone outside. Instead of joining them, she went into her old bedroom, sat on the bed, removed her sunglasses, and looked in the mirror at her red, swollen eyes. It was obvious she'd been crying and the tears had made little shiny rivulets on her powdered cheeks. Heather's compact was on the dressing table. Greta picked it up and the shiny marks were quickly obliterated, but there was nothing she could do about her eyes. She'd have to keep the sunglasses on.

An hour ago, she'd said goodbye to Charlie Mayhew for the last time. At that very moment, he was on his way to London. This time tomorrow he would be back in America. She would never see him again.

Charlie had been as upset as she was. They'd grown fond of each other over the last six months – well, more than fond. They were a little bit in love, but he had a wife and three young children and she had a husband and twin daughters but, Greta thought darkly, she may well have been childless for all she saw of them.

Making love for the final time had been bittersweet; both wonderful and terribly sad. She had sobbed in his arms that she didn't want him to go and he had cried a little too.

But he'd gone. He had to, and that Greta understood. It meant she had no choice but to return to her empty life. What was she to do with herself from now on? She lay on the bed, her head sinking into the soft pillow, and hoped someone would come in, ask what was the matter, make a fuss of her. She would say she didn't feel well to account for the red eyes.

No one came and there was laughter in the garden. She recognised Heather's low-pitched chuckle. She must have stayed off work for Brendan's party. Had Greta been living there, she would have stayed off too. They'd have had great fun getting everything ready. For the briefest of moments, Greta considered leaving Matthew and coming home. In no time at all, things would return to how they'd always been. The thought was tempting, except she'd have to go back to work and there'd only be the usual few pounds a week to spend. Greta felt torn between the idea of being a wealthy lady of leisure, albeit an unhappy one, and resuming her old, hard-up life, with Mam fighting a continual battle to make ends meet.

The lady of leisure easily won and Greta felt slightly better. She'd made a choice and it showed she had some control over her life. And it helped, knowing she could always come home if she felt *too* unhappy. Mam would welcome her with open arms.

Greta sat up and combed her hair. Her eyes already looked better. She went into the kitchen, where the door was wide open, and the first person she saw was Matthew, lying on the grass beside her mother. When had he ever come home during the day for *her*? Never! And there was something familiar about the way the pair were chatting so easily, as if Mam was his wife, not her.

As if that wasn't bad enough, Heather and Moira had their heads together, giggling helplessly over something. Her sister and her daughter, obviously the best of friends.

Brendan must have been given a bike for his birthday and Daisy was following him around, arms stretched protectively over his head in case he fell off.

Everyone was having a fine time without her, they probably hadn't noticed she wasn't there. She no longer meant anything to her family.

She turned on her heel and left. No one had seen her come, no one had seen her go. She wouldn't be missed.

18

At Daisy's request, it was the simplest of weddings. Her frock was cream jersey, calf length, without a single adornment, worn under a sky-blue velvet fitted jacket. For the first time, she wore lipstick, and carried a posy of white Christmas roses tied with blue ribbon. The only bridesmaid, Moira, carried a similar posy tied with pink to match her own plain frock. Clint had bought his first formal suit, dark grey, and throughout the ceremony, his handsome face was sombre.

Matthew, the sole male member of the O'Hagan clan – not counting Brendan – gave the bride away. There were only twenty guests, including the young couple's immediate families and a collection of friends.

The January day was icy cold. Heavy grey clouds lumbered slowly across the dull sky and several people remarked it looked as if it might snow. The guests were dressed appropriately for a winter wedding. Ruby had treated herself to a new coat, bright scarlet, and was relieved it wasn't the sort of wedding that required a hat, though neither Greta or the loathsome Pixie Shaw seemed to think so. Pixie's great fur contraption looked as if it was designed to be worn on the Russian Steppes, and Greta's face could hardly be seen behind a jungle of green feathers.

She found it all very moving. Daisy and Clint looked so unworldly. They didn't know much about anything and she wondered how they would cope in a big city on their own. One of their artist friends had arranged for them to live in a cheap bedsit in a place called Hackney. As a sort of honeymoon, they were spending their first two nights in a hotel by Piccadilly Circus.

Snow had started to fall by the time the short service was over, and everyone returned to the house for the buffet meal that Pixie had insisted on helping to prepare, giving her the opportunity to remark that everything reminded her of her grandma's house before the war.

The newly married couple only stayed a short while. After barely an hour, Daisy appeared in the living room, still in her wedding dress, with her best coat on top, and wearing a woolly hat and gloves to match. The lipstick had worn off and she hadn't bothered to renew it. Clint stood awkwardly behind with a suitcase.

'We're off now, Gran. The taxi's waiting.'

'Already, love?'

'The train takes four hours and we've got to find the hotel. The underground looks very complicated.'

'Have you said goodbye to your mother?'

'Yes, Gran. She's in the bedroom.'

'Have a lovely time now.' Her heart ached unbearably as she kissed them both. They were scarcely more than children. 'Don't forget, Matthew's arranged for all your things to be delivered on Monday. Make sure you're in or you won't have any bedding to sleep on.' The bedding, wedding presents, Daisy's painting gear, clothes, all the other things necessary for a place that contained nothing except furniture, had been packed in a crate to be collected early Monday morning by one of Medallion's lorries.

'Don't worry, Gran. We'll be there.'

''Bye, love. Bye, Clint. Look after her now.'

The guests crowded into the hall and watched the sturdy young woman and the slender young man go through the snow and climb into a taxi.

Ruby looked around for Heather, but she was nowhere to be seen. She found her in the bedroom, face down on the bed, sobbing her heart out. 'Oh, love!' She sat on the edge of the bed and laid her head against Heather's dark hair. 'I know how you feel. I feel the same myself.'

'She looked so *young*, Mam,' Heather wept. 'And she's not a bit hard, like some people. You can tell from her eyes. She's always been so good. Daisy's never given me a moment of trouble. Oh, I know she was useless at school, but at least she tried.'

'She'll be all right, love. She's probably tougher than we think.'

'You know, Mam, I could kill Ellie. She knew when the wedding would be. Daisy asked her to be bridesmaid and was dead upset when she didn't even send a card.'

'She didn't send a card for Christmas either.'

The door opened. 'So, this is where you are!' Greta cried. 'I thought you might have decided to go to London with Daisy.'

'Heather's a bit upset,' Ruby explained.

'I'm not surprised. I'll cry buckets when my two get married. Mind you, for all I know, Ellie's already married. She might even have another child.' Greta smiled. 'It doesn't upset me any more. I've too much to do. I'm going to Grenoble skiing next week with the girls.'

Not only had Greta learnt to ski, she'd learnt to drive and play bridge. The 'girls' were a group of fortyish women with nothing else to do with their time except play cards, attend coffee mornings, and hold dinner parties. Ruby considered them an idle, useless lot.

She'd changed a lot had Greta since she married Matthew, not just her personality, but also her looks. She was becoming prettier as she grew older. Gone were the childish, frilly clothes she'd always been so fond of. Now she wore chic, expensive outfits that clung to her shapely figure, and her hair was expertly cared for by one of the best hairdressers in Liverpool. Regular visits to a beauty parlour had taught her the most flattering way to apply make-up, so that she was always impeccably and beautifully turned out. Today, she wore an oatmeal tweed suit over a green silk blouse that matched the feathered hat she'd taken off when she got in.

'Would you like a nice, stiff whisky, Heather?' Greta asked.

'No, thanks.'

But Ruby insisted it would do her good. 'Fetch one for me while you're at it. Then I'd better see to the guests.'

Daisy and Clint sat opposite each other on the London train. Clint had found a newspaper and was doing the crossword.

'Two across, four letters, O.T. prophet.' He groaned. 'What does that mean?'

'Old Testament. Does Esau fit?'

'Isn't Esau a donkey?'

'No, that's Eeyore.' Daisy giggled.

'I'll leave it for now. Here's a ten-letter one, three down. Author of *The Forsyte Saga*.' He frowned. 'I should know that. I've got an A level in English.'

'Galsworthy,' Daisy said promptly.

He looked at her curiously. 'For someone who has such a hard job reading, you're pretty smart, Daise.'

Daisy went pink. 'It was on television. I remember things.' She could also remember the names of all the actors and the parts they'd played, as well as every detail of the plot.

'European capital, six letters, second letter's "i".'

'Vienna?'

'Eighteen down, a hermit.'

'Recluse?'

'Right. I'm impressed, Daise.'

'You've married a genius, Clint Shaw.'

'Seems like it.' His face closed up. He threw down the pen and turned to look out of the window. It was dark, and the snow was throwing itself against the glass. Lights could be seen twinkling in the towns and villages the train passed through on its way to London. The outlines of the buildings were blurred, merging into the black sky.

Today was a day she'd been looking forward to for most of her life, Daisy thought as she watched the lights flash by but, lately, it had become a day to dread. She felt confident she wasn't the only young woman in the world who'd been courting for five whole years yet was still a virgin. There must be others, even if they were rare. Even so, Daisy had a feeling there was something terribly wrong.

It would have been nice to discuss her worries with her mother or Gran but, not only would it have been embarrasing, she couldn't expect them to be shocked that she and Clint hadn't made love. They'd probably approve.

And if she'd expressed the fear that she wasn't even prepared to admit to herself, they would have tried to dissuade her from marrying him. They would never understand that she was prepared to take Clint for better or for worse because she loved him so completely.

She wasn't quite as innocent as people thought. It was three years since she'd gone to tea at Paula's and met Mary Casey, then at art school. Mary had been impressed with her painting and they'd become great friends. Through Mary, she'd got to know other young people who were artists of some kind and admired her work. Daisy and Clint quickly became one of the crowd. They went to parties where things went on and things were said that would have horrified her family, where joints were passed around – she'd taken a puff on more than one occasion, but it always made her sick. Daisy probably knew more about life than her mother and Gran put together.

Gran had booked the hotel by Piccadilly Circus. It was her wedding present. Naturally, she'd asked for a double bed.

The bed looked very large and a bit ominous – Daisy pretended to ignore it as she busily unpacked the clothes and put them away. 'Oh, look!' she cried. 'There's a kettle and tea things. Would you like a drink?'

'Yes, please.' Clint was in an armchair, watching her. She was surprised he hadn't switched the television on.

'Let's look for a restaurant when we've finished. I'm starving. It's only half-past eight. There might be one in Soho, it's no distance away.'

She was setting out the cups, pouring milk from the tiny containers, when Clint said, 'I need you, Daise. I can't tell you how much.' His eyes were very bright, as if he was about to cry.

'There's no need to tell me. I know.' She longed to take him in her arms, but the first move must come from him.

They held hands while they wandered around Soho, where every other building appeared to be a restaurant serving food from all over the world. They had spaghetti bolognaise and a glass of red wine in a trattoria and, after another wander around, returned to the hotel.

Daisy's trousseau consisted of a single nightie; white cotton with puffed sleeves and embroidery on the yoke. She took it into the bathroom, cleaned her teeth, washed her face, combed her hair, wishing it had a shape and wasn't just a halo of red fuzz. Then she put the nightie on.

The mirror revealed a most unglamorous bride, modestly attired, shapeless hair, face shining like a beacon and covered in freckles. Still, that was how she was.

Clint was sitting up in bed, clad in tartan pyjamas and watching television. Daisy's heart thumped madly as she lifted the covers and got in beside him. 'What's on?' she enquired.

'An old James Cagney movie, *Angels With Dirty Faces*.'

'I don't think I've seen it.'

'It's only just started.'

'Would you like some tea? Or there's coffee for a change.'

'Coffee would be fine.'

Had it not been their wedding night, Daisy would have quite enjoyed sitting companionably up in bed with Clint, drinking coffee and watching a film. As it was, she couldn't concentrate. What would happen when the film finished?

When 'The End' came on the screen, Clint got out of bed, switched the television off, got back in again, kissed her cheek, slid under the clothes, and said, 'Goodnight, Daise.'

'Goodnight.'

And that was that.

Daisy had done her best to make the room in Hackney look cosy, spreading their things around so it looked lived in. It was a vast, high-ceilinged room, and the dusty curtains on the tall windows had clearly been made for somewhere else as they were at least a foot too short. None of the ancient furniture matched and the top hinge was missing off one of the wardrobe doors so it had to be held when it was opened in case it fell off. A long time ago, the floor had been painted chocolate brown. Now most of the paint had worn away, and the minuscule rug may once have had a pattern, but if so it was no longer obvious.

She'd actually felt relieved to find there were twin beds. It was easier to sleep, not having Clint lying next to her, worrying what was wrong, *suspecting* what was wrong, but not being prepared to face it. The same thoughts haunted her all day long, but at least she could sleep.

Clint had an interview already arranged when they came to London and was now working for a company that made short promotional films. He wrote the scripts which boasted how successful a firm had been selling their goods abroad, describing how washing machines were put together, or how glass was blown. It was another step on the way towards him becoming a Hollywood director.

Daisy would have liked to be an usherette again, particularly in a West End cinema, but it would have meant they'd hardly see each other. She was a salesgirl in a little, exclusive shoe shop off Oxford Street.

'I really wanted someone a bit smarter,' the manageress said rudely at the interview, 'But I suppose you'll just have to do. The job's been vacant for ages. I just can't get anyone.'

It didn't seem possible for shoes to cost so much when there was so little of them. The heels were thin as cigarettes and the tops merely a few straps – Auntie Greta would love them. One day, when the manageress had gone to lunch, Daisy tried on a pair and immediately fell over.

She quite liked her job. At least she didn't have to read anything and although some of the women customers were ruder than the manageress, others were very nice. A few faces she recognised from television and it was lovely writing home to say she'd sold a pair of shoes to a well-known actress.

A couple of times a week, after they'd eaten, they went to the cinema. Clint enjoyed seeing films the minute they came out – it was usually weeks, sometimes months, before they were shown in Liverpool. Most nights they stayed in and watched television – Uncle Matt had given them a coloured portable for a wedding present – or Daisy painted at the easel she'd set up in front of the window, while Clint worked on his latest script. He had changed since coming to London, was more outgoing, obviously happier living there. Perhaps he was even happy being married.

One night when he came home, he told her he'd been asked out for a drink by one of the chaps from work. 'But I said, no, my wife was expecting me home.'

'I wouldn't have minded,' she exclaimed. 'You must go if you're asked again.'

His face fell. 'I thought you'd be worried if I was late.'

'You could have rung the phone downstairs in the hall. I can hear it from here.'

'Hmm.'

He seemed upset she didn't mind if he deserted her for a few hours, arrived home late. She realised he needed to be needed, to belong. He referred to her as 'my wife' whenever he had the opportunity; in shops, at the pictures, on the buses or the tube, as if he wanted to stress he was part of a couple.

The awkwardness of the first few nights was long over and they were the best and closest of friends – as they had always been, but now possibly closer. She loved him, he needed her. They shared the same opinions on most things, but enjoyed the arguments when they didn't.

Life would have been perfect, almost was, except for that one thing, which neither of them ever mentioned.

After two months in London, they went back to Liverpool for the weekend to find everything exactly the same as when they'd left.

But it will always be the same, Daisy thought. Nothing ever changes. People come and people go, but Gran will always be here, bossing everyone around, loving them. She had missed her gran more than anyone during the time in London.

On Sunday afternoon, they went to dinner with Clint's parents. During the meal, Pixie gave her a painful nudge. 'I thought you'd come because you had something nice to tell me!'

It took a few seconds for the penny to drop. Pixie had thought she might be pregnant. Daisy waited for Clint to supply an answer. When he didn't, she said seriously, 'We thought it was time we came to see everyone, that's all.'

They didn't stay long. They had a train to catch and the journey took longer on Sundays. Neither spoke on the way back to Gran's. Daisy was thinking about babies. She'd always wanted at least two. For the very first time, she felt angry with Clint, walking silently at her side. What was he thinking? Did he expect her to forget the idea of having babies? One of these days she'd have things out with him, but it was awfully difficult. She loved him so much and didn't want him to be hurt.

Moira had just sat the final paper for her English Literature degree. She put down her pen and, along with every other student in the room, uttered an audible sigh of relief. The invigilator began to collect the papers. She'd done well in all the exams, her thesis on Mary Shelley had been thoroughly researched, and she was confident she'd get a First. In October, she was starting a teacher training course. Once she'd qualified, she'd stay with Gran, teach in Liverpool for a year, then apply for a post further afield. It might be nice to work in London near Daisy, or go abroad. For Moira, the future stretched tidily ahead. She was looking forward to it.

As she shuffled out of the room, her thoughts turned to the summer ahead. She'd rest for a few days, then look for temporary work as a waitress during the holiday, as she'd done last year. The suitcase in her room was already packed. All she had to do was collect it and catch the train from Norwich to Liverpool. Her years at university were over and she couldn't wait to get away.

She turned a corner, lost in thought, and collided head on with a figure coming in the opposite direction. 'Look where you're going!' a male voice said indignantly. 'Now there's papers everywhere.'

'Sorry.' Moira returned from the future to the present. She knelt and began to gather up the scattered papers. 'This wouldn't have happened if you'd used a paper clip or kept them in a folder.'

'Perhaps I should be apologising to you,' the man growled as he knelt on the ground beside her.

'Don't be childish. I hope these pages are numbered or it'll take ages to sort them out.'

'I'll try not to think about you while I'm doing it.'

Moira got to her feet. 'Oh, pick them up yourself. You're very rude. I was only trying to help.'

The man stood at the same time and they glared at each other. Moira had had few boyfriends over the last three years – they would only have interfered with her studies – and this was the type she avoided like the plague. A few years older than herself, he had long, untidy hair, a Zapata moustache, and wore a flowered Indian shirt, cotton trousers, an earring, and plaited sandals on his otherwise bare – and dirty – feet. She'd never seen him before, which wasn't surprising, as the incomprehensible symbols and columns of figures on the fallen papers indicated he was a science student. Moira willingly conceded that she was useless at anything to do with science.

In view of his disgusting appearance, his earrings, and the fact he was clearly a bad-tempered individual, she wondered why their eyes held for such a very long time – it seemed like for ever – and why her heart was beating extremely fast and why her knees suddenly felt weak. It may have been because, despite everything, he was devastatingly attractive.

The man's eyes were glued on hers and he didn't seem to care that the remainder of his papers were being trampled on or blown to the wind. 'Sorry about before,' he said eventually in an odd, choked voice. 'I've just sat my final paper and I don't think I did all that well. We bumped into each other at the worst possible time.' He gulped. 'My name's Sam Quigley. Would you like a coffee?'

'I'm Moira Donovan, and I'd love a coffee.' Was it only minutes ago she couldn't wait to get away?

It was nice to have a wedding completely devoid of tension; the young couple so obviously mad about each other, money no object – Matthew Doyle, step-father of the bride, was paying for everything – and the groom with a First Class degree and a Master's degree in Applied Mathematics and already employed as a junior lecturer at Cambridge University.

Greta was upset that her daughter's own First Class degree had been a complete waste of time. Moira was engaged to be married when the result came through.

'Don't be daft, Mum,' Moira sang. 'I'm still going to be a teacher, aren't I?'

Ruby had worried that Sam, an otherwise commendable young man, might turn up for his wedding looking like an unwashed hippy, but as the weeks and months passed his appearance gradually improved. He discovered soap and water, socks, wore clean jeans, shaved off his moustache, had his hair trimmed to shoulder length, and remembered to comb it.

When Sam married Moira, flushed and beautiful in ivory lace, he looked a perfectly respectable member of society. Once again, Matthew was prevailed upon to give the bride away. 'Two granddaughters down, one to go,' Ruby murmured when the newly married pair came out of the church and posed for photographs. She wondered where Ellie was, what she was doing, why she didn't get in touch. She could at least write, let everyone know she was all right so they wouldn't worry.

Daisy certainly wasn't all right, though she was pretending to be, smiling stoically at everyone in sight. She'd lost weight and the creamy yellow bridesmaid's dress made her look pale. Like her mother, Daisy had always been a stoic, never showing her feelings when she was hurt. She was hurting now, Ruby could tell and wondered why. It might be because Clint hadn't come with her, he was too busy with his job, or it might be that was merely an excuse and it was for quite another reason that Clint hadn't come.

'Oh, you children are a worry,' she complained to Brendan who was doing his best to break free from her restraining hand and create havoc among the guests – Sam's widowed mother looked a nervous soul. 'In another twenty years, I could be standing here and it's *you* getting married. Mind you, by then I'll be going on for eighty and might not live that long.'

No one noticed Daisy creep out of the reception. She caught a bus to the house she still thought of as home and let herself in. It was the first time she'd been in the place alone and the familar objects looked different, almost threatening, without Gran or her mother there, or one of her cousins. It was hard to imagine a door wouldn't open any minute and someone would yell, 'Daisy!' or some other name. When she went to put the kettle on, the kitchen clock ticked more loudly than she remembered, and it was scary how the stairs creaked on her way upstairs to the lavatory.

Later, the tea made, Daisy sat in Gran's spot on the settee, switching the television on for company, but without the sound. Everyone seemed to have accepted her explanation for Clint's absence from the wedding. He was busy at work, she'd told them. He'd written to Moira to apologise for not coming. Daisy was supposed to be seeing his mum and dad tomorrow. She hated letting people down, but had no intention of going; she wasn't in the mood for Pixie Shaw and her probing questions.

It was exactly a week ago that Clint had gone to America. It was her decision, not his, that she didn't go with him. He'd written the script for a film promoting an electronics company that made those new-fangled video recorders. The film had been shown in California where the light, amusing tone of the narration had been much admired by a man called Theo Gregory who prepared videos for circulation. He'd managed to track Clint down. So far, they'd only spoken on the phone.

'Theo said my script wasn't pedantic and boring like these things usually are,' Clint told her excitedly. 'He wants me to write trailers. Just think, Daise, I'll have to watch the movies first! And Santa Barbara's not far from Los Angeles – *Hollywood*, Daisy.'

'That's wonderful, Clint.' At first, she was just as excited as he was. 'When will we go?'

'Soon. Don't tell anyone yet. I've got to sign a contract.' He looked sheepish. 'I've never signed a contract before. It's the sort of thing they do in America. The salary's amazing, about four times what I get now. You won't need to work, just paint.'

'It sounds marvellous!'

Two days later, Jason Wright, who lived downstairs, came to ask if he could borrow some milk. Jason was a sculptor who welded old bits of metal together with remarkable results. Daisy had seen his work as he was inclined to leave his door wide open when he was welding because of the dreadful smell.

'Just half a cup will do, Daisy,' he said at the door. 'I'm dying for some coffee and I can't stand it black. Oh, is that your painting? Do you mind if I have a look?'

'Come in.' She never felt shy or uncomfortable with fellow artists who were only interested in her work, not her appearance. 'Would you like some coffee now? You can have the milk as well. I'm just about to make a meal. My husband will be home in a minute.' Clint and Jason had never met.

'You're a mate, Daisy.' He came into the room and went over to the easel. He was a magnificently built young man, dark like a gypsy, with broad muscled arms and shoulders of which he was obviously proud as he always wore sleeveless T-shirts, even when it was cold. Today he was all in black, and his peeling leather trousers were tight on his bulging thighs. She admired the way the muscles rippled as he walked. One of these days, she might paint him.

'This looks interesting,' he said in front of the painting she'd only started a few days before. 'What's it going to be?'

'A womb,' she explained. 'My home, the house where I was brought up, was like a womb. I can't say I was all that happy there, but I felt dead safe, as if nothing could touch me. The outside world seemed very far away and it didn't affect us. Things that happened, the tragedies and the wars, could have been happening on a different planet. Our house was warm and comfortable, full of people. It was the best place on earth to come home to, the only place.' Somewhat inexplicably, Daisy felt close to tears.

'Wow!' Jason looked impressed. 'Did you go to art school?'

'No. I'm not being conceited or anything, but I paint for meself. It's the way I see things and I don't want to be taught any different.'

'What do you do with your paintings when they're finished?'

'They're over there.' She pointed to the stack of canvases on top of the wardrobe.

'Can I look at them too?'

'Of course.' Daisy went to get a chair.

'I'll get them down. Don't worry, I'll be careful.'

Jason was reaching up for the paintings when Clint came in. 'Oh, here's my husband. Clint, this is Jason from downstairs. He's a sculptor.'

'Hello,' Clint muttered.

The two young men stared at each other across the room. For several seconds, there was a surprising silence and Daisy was trying to think of something to say to break it, when she noticed Jason was looking at her husband with undisguised admiration in his dark eyes. Her gaze swiftly turned to Clint, and a feeling of horror swept over her when she realised that, caught unawares, he was returning the look.

The two young men were attracted to each other. Her worst suspicions had been confirmed.

Jason left without the milk he'd come for. That night, Daisy didn't talk about what had occurred. She didn't ask Clint why he was so edgy, just made the tea, watched the news on television, then got on with her painting.

When the contract from Theo Gregory arrived, Clint signed it immediately, put it in an envelope, and said he'd post it in the morning. 'If I'm to start work on the first of October, we need to see the landlord soon, give him a month's notice on this place.' He glanced around the tall, miserable room. 'I can't say I'll be sorry to see the back of it. It means we can't go to Moira's wedding. Do you mind?'

'There's no need to see the landlord,' Daisy said in a quiet voice. 'And I'll be going to Moira's wedding. I'm a bridesmaid and I can't let her down.' She paused. 'But I'm not going to America with you, Clint. I'm staying here.'

'*What?*' He looked at her in astonishment. 'What on earth do you mean, Daisy?'

'What I said, that I'm not coming with you.'

'But I *need* you, Daise,' he said frantically. His face had gone pale and he looked sick. 'I'll not go if you don't come. I'll tear the contract up.'

'Why do you need me? As a shield to hide behind, so people won't know the truth?' It struck her that he'd been extremely selfish. He'd taken advantage of her love, used it, expected her to live a life of lies, pretending a marriage that would never be real, where there would never be children.

'A shield?' By now, he was visibly shaking. 'I don't know what you're talking about, Daisy.'

'Yes, you do, Clint. Don't pretend you don't know what I'm trying to say. I think you should go to America, find yourself, admit what you are.'

He shrank into the chair, seemed to grow smaller in front of her eyes. 'What I am?'

'It's nothing to be ashamed of.' Daisy felt very wise and calm and sensible. 'I'll always be proud to call you my friend, but not my husband, Clint. It was wrong of you to marry me. Perhaps you thought I was so plain and unattractive that I'd never find a husband, that I'd be happy to make do with one who wouldn't want to sleep with me, kiss me properly, do all the things a proper husband does.'

'Oh, *God!*' He dropped his head into his hands and neither spoke for a long time. The only sound was the traffic outside which never stopped, not even at night. Then Clint pushed himself to his feet and came and knelt beside Daisy's chair, laid his head on her lap. 'Daisy, you're the loveliest girl I've ever known. I *wanted* to love you, I *do* love you.'

'But not in the right way, Clint. Oh!' She put her hand on his neck and stroked it. 'I wish you could, because I love you more than anyone on earth'. Even now, she felt tempted to stay with him, but he had to learn to stand on his own two feet. In the long run, they'd be better off without each other.

'I'm sorry, Daise.' His voice was muffled. She could feel his breath on her skirt. 'I've been terrified all me life that someone would find out. Someone did once,' he paused and made a face. 'They didn't tell anyone. But me dad would have killed me, and I daren't think what Mum would have said. It would have been torture at school. I tried not to admit it, even to meself. Even now I can't say the word that describes what I am.'

'There's no need to say it, we both know. From now on, you must be proud of what you are, not ashamed.' Daisy began to cry. 'Be happy in America, Clint. I'll be thinking of you all the time.'

Daisy cried again, sitting in Gran's place on the settee, watching people do meaningless things on television, not making a sound. At the wedding earlier, she'd felt envious of Moira, so clearly head over heels in love with Sam and he with her.

'Why don't you go back to your womb?' Clint had said, only days before he'd left. The painting had remained untouched since the night she'd forced him to admit the truth.

'Go home? Oh, no, I couldn't. I'd never be able to keep up the lies. Anyroad, it's going back and I'd sooner go forward.' Somehow. She'd asked him not tell anyone about America until Moira's wedding was over. There'd have been too many questions otherwise.

'You'll come and see me, won't you?' he said anxiously. 'Say at Christmas. The weather's fantastic in California.'

'I'll try.' Daisy knew she would probably never see him again.

'Don't forget, I'll send money. You can't afford to live in London on your own.'

'Thank you, Clint.'

'Oh, Daisy!' He cupped her face in his hands – he'd touched her more in the last few weeks than in all the years that had gone before. It was as if he could be himself at last. 'Don't thank me. You'd still be back in your womb if it weren't for me. I've messed up your life and I'm sorry.'

The key sounded in the door and Daisy went into the hall. Gran came in carrying a deceptively angelic Brendan who was fast asleep.

'He's out like a light,' she whispered. 'He must have run a hundred miles today. I don't know why it is kids have to go mad at weddings. I remember your mam and Greta going beserk at a wedding we had here during the war.'

'Here, let me take him.' Daisy held out her arms.

'Be careful, he weighs a ton.'

'Is his bed made?'

'I've no idea, but he's not likely to notice if it isn't. Just take his top clothes off. The little imp can sleep in his underwear.' Gran looked at her keenly. 'I didn't notice you leave the reception. Have you been crying, love?'

'There was just this sad film on the telly.' If only she could tell Gran everything! A trouble shared is a trouble halved, so people said. But Daisy had the feeling she would only cry again – and this time she would never stop.

When Daisy came home on Christmas Eve, she brought with her a large painting which she stood on the mantelpiece. 'This is for you. Gran.'

'Thank you, love.' Ruby was taken aback. 'What is it?' she asked politely. 'Home.'

'Home?' The painting consisted of a large circle – not a very good circle at that – filled with splodges. 'It's lovely, Daisy. Thank you very much. I don't suppose you'll be staying long, not with having to get back to work.'

'I've left the shop. Next week, I'm starting as an usherette in the Odeon in Leicester Square, so I've got seven whole days.' It meant the manageress of the shoe shop had been left in the lurch, what with the winter sales starting directly after Christmas, but the woman hadn't a polite bone in her body and didn't deserve any better.

'I'm surprised you didn't go to America for Christmas, stay with Clint.'

'Can't afford it, Gran. Anyroad, he shares a flat with a pile of other people. He couldn't have put me up.' The lies had already begun.

'That's a shame, love. You've hardly been married five minutes and already you're living apart.'

Daisy decided that after Christmas, as soon as the celebrations were over, she'd tell Gran and her mother the truth.

Matthew came later with presents for under the tree. Daisy had gone to bed. 'I can see what she's getting at,' he said when he saw the painting.

'Then explain it to me,' Ruby demanded. 'It makes no sense at all as far as I can see.'

He shook his head. 'One of these days the penny will drop and you'll understand.' He glanced from the painting to Ruby, then back again. 'You're very lucky, all of you. I wish I were in Daisy's painting, but there was never a chance of that and now it's too late.'

Ruby hadn't the faintest notion what he was talking about.

It was almost midnight when Moira and Sam arrived. Moira's career as a teacher hadn't got off the mark. She was three months pregnant and thrilled to bits. The baby was expected in June.

Nowadays, Pixie Shaw took it for granted she and her husband would be invited to Christmas dinner. Throughout the meal, Daisy was subjected to the third degree. 'Clint hardly tells us anything in his letters,' Pixie complained. She was annoyed Moira was having a baby and Daisy wasn't. 'And you got married so much earlier.'

'It's not a race, Pixie,' Ruby said tartly. 'Daisy and Clint will have children when it suits them, not you.'

'Hear, hear,' Heather echoed. There was no love lost between her and Pixie Shaw. 'I wouldn't dream of pressing Daisy to have a baby just so I can be a grandmother. It seems most unfair.'

For the first time ever, Ruby was glad when dinner was over. The meal had been full of tension. Next year, she'd tell Pixie they'd been invited out, though the strained mood hadn't only been Pixie's fault; Daisy was clearly upset, Greta was sulking about something, and Matthew hardly spoke. Even Brendan didn't help, he was aching to get back to his presents. She thanked the Lord that Moira and Sam were there, providing at least two happy faces.

Greta and Matthew must have had another row, which was all they seemed to do these days. Perhaps Greta had been spending too much money again. 'She'll have me bankrupt, so she will,' Matthew had groaned only a few weeks ago. 'She's only gone and bought a gazebo for the garden – in the middle of winter too!' Ruby had never dreamed her nice, agreeable daughter could be so thoughtlessly extravagant.

It was unreasonable to feel so cross when Moira and Sam decided to go for a walk, depriving the house of their cheerful company. She marched into the living room, determined to make everyone play a game and elicit a laugh or two, but Greta had already turned on the television and they sat like lumps for the rest of the afternoon watching *The Sound of Music*, a film Ruby had seen before and hadn't liked – and liked even less the second time around.

It was a lousy Christmas. Ruby was glad when it was over and things returned to normal. But not for long, because Daisy revealed the reason why Clint had gone to America on his own and completely spoilt New Year.

Matthew rang one afternoon in March when a brisk, urgent wind was playing havoc with the house, rattling the windows and whistling through the cracks around the doors.

'Ruby, something terrible's happened.' His voice shook.

'Oh, yes?' Ruby said coolly.

He mustn't have noticed her frosty tone. 'I got home from work early, about an hour ago. I was feeling dead rotten, I think I must be coming down with flu.'

'Dearie me.'

'I thought Greta was out – until I went upstairs and found me fucking wife in bed with another man. Oh, Rube!' he said hoarsely. 'I don't know what to do. I've got to talk to someone. Can I come round?'

'Not now, Matthew, Greta's here. My God!' Ruby gasped. 'I didn't realise . . . She's in a terrible state. She said you just turned on her for no reason at all.'

'And you believed her?' His bitter laugh tore at her heart. 'You mustn't have much of an opinion of me. No wonder that other fellow wouldn't marry you, Ruby. You put your family before every other bloody thing on earth, no matter what they do. Tell my wife to stay where she is. You're welcome to each other.'

'Matthew!' Ruby cried frantically. 'I'll come and see you straight away.' But she was talking to herself. Matthew had slammed down the receiver.

She went into the garden and screamed for Brendan. He was halfway up a tree he'd been forbidden to climb and made his way down, looking guilty, expecting to be told off. 'Come on,' Ruby said brusquely. 'We're going for a ride in a car.' She pulled him into the house, 'Get your coat,' she commanded.

'Yes, Bee.' Brendan said obediently. He was nearly four and aware something was wrong.

Ruby turned her attention to her daughter. Earlier, Greta had thrown herself on to the settee, sobbing her heart out. Matthew was an awful person, truly horrible. That afternoon, he'd flown into a rage, she'd no idea why.

'Greta,' Ruby said from the door. 'Get up immediately. I want you to take me to your house in the car.'

'What, Mam?' Greta raised her tear-streaked face, surprised.

'I said, drive me to your house. That was Matthew on the phone. You stupid girl, you've hurt him badly. You didn't tell me he'd found you in bed with another man. That's not the way you were brought up. Oh, I'm so ashamed!' Ruby stamped her foot in rage. She'd be sixty-two next month and it was about time she had a bit of peace. 'Who was he, the man?'

There was a pause.

'The husband of one of me friends.'

'Well, you won't be friends much longer once she finds out. If you don't get off that settee this very minute, I'll drag you outside. I'll have a go at driving the car myself if you won't do it.'

Greta got sullenly to her feet. 'I don't know why you're so concerned about Matthew.'

'Get a move on, girl,' Ruby snapped. 'I'm concerned about Matthew because he's been the best friend this family could have had. Are you coming or do I have to drive myself?'

No one spoke on the way to Calderstones, not even Brendan who was unusually subdued. When they reached the house, Ruby turned to her daughter. 'Give me the key.'

'I haven't got it. It's in me handbag at home.'

'*This* is your home,' Ruby said tartly. 'Or at least it was. I'll just have to knock and hope he answers.'

'He won't answer, 'cause he's not there. His car's gone.'

'Damn!' She'd let him down again.

Matthew still wasn't home by midnight. Next day, when Ruby rang Medallion and asked to speak to Mr Doyle, she was told he was on holiday.

'When will he be back?'

'He didn't say when he would return.'

'When he does, please tell him Mrs O'Hagan would like to speak to him urgently.'

'I'll relay that message to his secretary.'

The day after, Greta drove round to Calderstones to collect her things, after phoning first to make sure Matthew wasn't there. She returned, the car full of clothes, and tearfully reported that the house was up for sale.

'Oh, Mam, I've been such a fool,' she sobbed.

'You certainly have. Oh, come here, love.' Ruby held out her arms. It was impossible to stop loving someone because they'd been a fool – well, a bit more than a fool where Greta was concerned. But it would be a long time before she would forgive her for what she'd done.

Heather no longer wanted to share a room with her sister. She had bought a portable television so she could watch Open University programmes and study in bed. Greta would be in the way.

'Can I sleep with you, Mam?' Greta sniffed pathetically after a few nights on her own. 'I've never slept by meself before. It feels dead peculiar.'

'You certainly can't. I like my privacy too.'

'What about Brendan? Can I sleep with him?'

'Not when there's two empty bedrooms upstairs, no. By the way, have you done anything about getting a job?'

Greta sighed. 'Not yet.'

'Then I'd appreciate you doing it soon.'

'I'll look in the *Echo* tonight.'

'If nothing's there, try the Labour Exchange tomorrow.'

'All right, Mam,' Greta said with a martyred air, but Ruby was having none of it.

'It's entirely your own fault you're in this situation, so I want none of your pained looks. Heather's the only one in the house earning a wage. It's not up to her to keep you.'

A fortnight passed and Matthew still hadn't acknowledged her phone call. Ruby called Medallion again.

'Mr Doyle was made aware of your message,' she was told. 'He said to tell you he'll be in touch next time he's in Liverpool.'

'When will that be? Where is he now?'

'I'm afraid I've no idea when it will be, Mrs O'Hagan. Our firm has just been awarded a contract for three hospitals in Saudi Arabia. Mr Doyle will be overseeing the work.'

'Thank you.' Ruby rang off. Saudi Arabia! If Greta had been there just then, she would have strangled her.

Six months later, a letter from a solicitor dropped on the mat addressed to Mrs Greta Doyle. Matthew wanted a divorce on the grounds of adultery.

'He can't divorce me for adultery,' Greta pouted. 'He hasn't any proof. I'm going to write back and contest it.'

'He might try and get proof,' Ruby pointed out. 'He's sure to know the name of the chap he found you in bed with if he was a friend's husband and involve him, then the wife would be round here, making a scene. It'd be in the *Echo*, and your name would be mud. Not only that, the legal costs would be horrendous. You'd end up in debt for the rest of your life.' She had no idea what she was talking about. Every word she'd just said could be a lie. But Greta *had* committed adultery and no longer deserved to be married to Matthew.

'So what should I do?' Greta cried piteously.

'Just write to the solicitor and agree the divorce can go ahead as it stands.' There were times when honour demanded *not* putting your family first.

The following year, 1981, as soon as her divorce from Matthew was finalised, Greta got married for the third time. She was forty-five. Frank Fletcher was a sweet, if rather dull little man, a widower, with two grown-up sons, both married. He was a clerk in the shipping company where Greta worked, and owned a semi-detached house on the estate where she would have lived with Larry had life gone differently.

The wedding was held in a register office. There were just six guests; Ruby, Heather, and Frank's sons and their wives – none seemed too pleased that he was marrying again. Brendan had just started school and was otherwise occupied.

After the soulless ceremony, everyone went to Ruby's for something to eat. The Fletchers refused the wine and beer she'd bought, saying they preferred tea. After politely eating a few sandwiches, they went home, leaving only the enamoured Frank who could hardly believe his luck in landing such a pretty bride. The newly married couple left for their honeymoon in Scarborough in the afternoon.

Greta was still on honeymoon when Ruby tidied her room and was surprised to find the wardrobe full of her smart clothes. She mentioned the fact to Heather when she came home.

'She doesn't want them any more,' Heather told her. 'She said there'd be no need for stuff like that when she's married to Frank.'

'I wonder if any of them will fit us?'

When tea was over, they went upstairs to try on the clothes, accompanied by Brendan, who seized the hat Greta had worn to Daisy's wedding and put it on, grinning at them through the green feathers. The women went through the wardrobe and wished Greta was taller.

'I wonder if I could have a false hem put on this?' Ruby held up a blue crêpe frock.

'I could wear this jacket, but not the skirt. Look at this sweater! I bet it cost the earth. Oh, I can't do this!' Heather threw the sweater on to the floor and burst into tears.

'Neither can I.' Ruby dropped the blue frock as if it was too hot to touch. 'I feel like a grave robber.'

'I don't think she'll be happy married to Frank, Mam.'

'She might, love,' Ruby said sadly. 'You know, I should have been nicer to her when she came home, but I was so annoyed ...'

'Our Greta's never been any good on her own. I should have let her back in our room. We drove her away, Mam.'

'I wouldn't put it quite as strongly as that, love.' Ruby put her arm around her weeping daughter. 'She behaved disgracefully with Matthew. It would have been wrong to welcome her home and act as if nothing had happened.'

'It *wouldn't* have happened if Rob and Larry hadn't died.'

'That's something we'll never know, Heather. If it hadn't been Matthew, it might have been something else.' Ruby sighed. 'Brendan! Give us that hat before you wreck it. One of these days Greta might want to wear the damn thing.'

Brendan

19

1985

She was in a hotel room, an expensive hotel, not her own, and she was lying in a double bed, feeling like death. The other half of the bed had been occupied. She could see the indent of where a head had lain on the pillow and the bedclothes had been thrown back when the person had got out.

Who, Ellie wondered? Last night there'd been a party and she could recall getting plastered, but from then on her mind was a blank. She looked at her watch; half-past nine.

It wasn't the first time this had happened. Ellie worked for a London-based agency that provided pretty girls for all sorts of occasions; company dinners to which wives hadn't been invited, business exhibitions, sporting events. At the moment she was in Madrid with six other girls for a motor show – sports cars – and it was their job to drape themselves provocatively over the bonnets as an incentive to prospective purchasers to part with monumental amounts of cash. Last week it had been a computer exhibition in Sweden where they'd been expected to look charming and wise. Next month it was office equipment in Rome, though the work was mainly based in the British Isles.

The agency adopted a high moral tone. It had its reputation to consider and the girls were forbidden to have sexual relationships while employed on a job. Ellie only occasionally broke the rule, and always when she'd had too much to drink, like last night.

She sat up, clutched her reeling head, and noticed her clothes were on the floor beside the bed. The net curtains on the open window billowed outwards and she saw a stone balcony outside. The sun was shining brilliantly and it was already warm considering it was only May – she dreaded to think what Spain would be like in summer. People could be heard splashing about in a pool.

The room had two doors, one of which was ajar, revealing a bathroom. Ellie climbed out of bed and got washed, then put on the tight white skirt and red blouse, the uniform for the motor show. They were badly creased and there was a wine stain on the skirt. She'd prefer to be gone when the owner of the room came back. *If* he came back. There was no sign of anyone staying there; no suitcase, clothes, toilet gear. Maybe he'd already checked out.

When she opened her bag to get her make-up she found it stuffed with notes; Spanish pesetas. She had no idea what the exchange rate was, but there was plenty of them. The guy, whoever he was, must have thought she was on the game.

Ellie sat on the bed, feeling slightly ashamed. Still, she hadn't come to any harm. The cash was a plus and maybe the guy was just showing his appreciation. It was scary, though, to think she'd spent the night with a man she couldn't remember. He might have looked like King Kong for all she knew or he could have been a pervert.

There was a knock on the door and she stiffened. 'Who is it?' she called.

'It's Barry, darling.'

The girls jokingly referred to sixty-year old Barry as their chaperone. He booked hotels, made travel arrangements, saw that they were properly fed, and got to the various events on time. He was a little, roly-poly man, almost completely bald, with a warm smile that never reached his eyes. Ellie considered him two-faced, but so were most of the people she met these days – she probably was herself.

'How did you know where I was?' Ellie asked when she let him in.

'You and Bruno Pinelli seemed very much an item last night. This being his room, it seemed the first place to look. Bruno Pinelli,' he went on in response to Ellie's puzzled look, 'was at the show yesterday signing autographs. He's a racing driver, Italian, very good-looking. He invited a few of us back to the bar downstairs for a drink and it turned into quite a party. Then Bruno disappeared at exactly the same time as you did. It didn't take much in the way of brains to put two and two together.'

Ellie dredged up a vague memory of dark, flashing eyes and an exceptionally virile lover. 'I had a bit too much to drink,' she muttered.

'More than a bit, darling. You want to be careful. Next thing you know, you'll be an alcoholic.'

'Don't talk daft, Barry.' She laughed. 'I'm a social drinker. I never drink during the day.'

'Maybe not, but when you get near a bar, you can put a fish to shame. What's this?' He picked up the ashtray and frowned at the contents. 'Have you been smoking grass?'

Ellie couldn't remember. 'We must have done.'

'And you've left the evidence for anyone to find!' He looked grim when he took the ashtray into the bathroom. The lavatory flushed. He returned and said harshly, 'If humping guys and getting sloshed wasn't bad enough, now I find you've been smoking an illegal substance. If you don't pull your socks up, darling, I'll have to advise the agency to let you go.'

'That's decent of you – darling, ' she said icily.

'I don't have to give you a warning,' he replied, just as coldly. 'I could advise the agency today.'

'I've got the message, Barry.'

'Glad to hear it, Ellie.' He smiled, but his eyes didn't. 'You've got two hours before the show opens and you look like shit. I'll get room service to bring you something to eat and some black coffee. While you're waiting, put your war paint on, and I'll arrange to have a change of clothes brought over. Fact, I'll do both things right now.' He picked up the phone.

'What about this Bruno guy? Is he likely to come back?'

'No, he checked out early this morning.'

'Thanks, Barry – for everything.' She didn't like having to be grateful, but he could have her fired.

Not that it would matter all that much, Ellie thought when Barry had gone. It was a lousy job which had seemed exciting at first. Now she found it boring. Most jobs turned out boring in the end.

She sat in front of the dressing table and began to apply her make-up, difficult when her hands were shaking so badly. Barry was right, she looked like shit. Halfway through, a waiter arrived with the coffee and some rolls.

'You pay for this now, please,' the man said courteously handing her a bill. 'Señor Pinelli, he already settled his account.'

'How much is this in English money?'

'About ten pounds.'

Just for coffee and rolls! Ellie blanched. She didn't even want the rolls and dreaded to think what it would cost to stay in the place. The waiter appeared satisfied with two of the notes Bruno Pinelli had given her and left. Ellie finished her make-up, then sat at the small table in front of the window to drink the coffee. The room was on the first floor at the rear of the hotel. Outside, a shimmering blue pool looked a mile long and was set within an avenue of shady trees. A man was teaching a little boy to swim and, at the far end, a youth was poised on the edge of the diving board. He raised his arms, jumped, and soared downwards, hardly raising a splash, to the cheers of a group of watching teenagers and the few people so far occupying the loungers and umbrella-covered tables surrounding the majestic pool.

Ellie felt a pang of envy. These people didn't have to spend the rest of the day inside a stinking hot marquee, pretending to be nice to people, not caring whether they bought a car or not. Why hadn't she the money to stay at a place like this? What had gone wrong with her life?

She was twenty-six, getting on, getting nowhere. After she'd left home the second time, Ellie had hung around the pop scene for a while, hoping for a job in a promotional capacity, as an assistant of some sort, or in advertising. But nothing had happened. Nor had anything happened during the time spent working in the office of a fashion magazine. No one had suggested she become a model, though she was prettier than most of the successful ones. She'd remained unnoticed as a film extra and during the year with the television company where she'd never risen above making tea and doing the filing – an office girl. When she'd joined the agency two years ago, it had seemed a step up. At least she'd been taken on for her looks and her figure, her personality. But it was a dead end job without any chance of promotion.

Barry was wrong to say she'd become an alcoholic, though she wouldn't mind a good, stiff drink right now, help buck her up a bit. Trouble was, it didn't always work, and she'd have another stiff drink, then another, and end up drinking herself into oblivion.

There was another knock on the door. This time it was one of the girls, Trisha, with a fresh outfit.

'Barry sent this. Did you have a good time last night?' Trisha hadn't been to the party. She was eighteen, a lovely, fresh-faced girl who, right now, made Ellie feel old and rather grubby.

'Great.'

'Oh, well. I'll love you and leave you. See you later, Ellie.'

'See you.'

Ellie changed her clothes and brushed her hair. She was beginning to feel better and decided to eat one of the rolls, seeing as how it had cost an arm and a leg. She poured more coffee and took it on to the balcony. There were more people in the pool since she'd last looked and she regarded them jealously. A woman with ghastly red hair, a toad-like figure, and legs like duffle bags, was waddling her way towards a thickly cushioned chair under an umbrella. She wore a sack-like gingham frock and sat down with a thump that Ellie sensed rather than heard.

'I'd sooner be as poor as a church mouse than have a shape like that,' she said to herself.

The woman took a good look around before putting on a pair of large sunglasses and settling back against the cushions. There was something about the way she moved, the red of her hair, that was very familiar and a few seconds later an astonished Ellie realised it was her cousin, Daisy.

She crammed the remainder of the roll in her mouth and washed it down with coffee, then checked her reflection in the mirror. She looked svelte and smart, her long, brown hair gleamed, her make-up was perfect. Picking up her bag, she ran downstairs, found the way to the pool, and approached her cousin. Daisy had always made her aware of how lucky she really was.

'Hi, Daise!'

'Ellie!' Daisy gasped, removing the sunglasses. Her freckled face had gone fat and podgy and was covered in perspiration. 'What a lovely surprise. What on earth are you doing here?'

'I'm working in Madrid. I'm a model. I get sent all over Europe.'

'How wonderful!' Daisy looked incredibly impressed. 'Are you a fashion model? Have you come on a shoot or something?'

'Yes,' Ellie lied. 'How's things at home? It's ages since I wrote. I keep meaning to . . .' Her voice trailed away.

'All sorts of exciting things have happened since you left, Ellie.' Daisy wiped her face with a tissue – how awful to be so fat in hot weather. It was no wonder she was sheltering under the umbrella, she always turned as bright red as her hair in the sun. 'Your Moira's married for one. Sam, her husband, is terribly nice and terribly clever. He's a lecturer and they live in Cambridge and have two children, a girl and a boy.'

Ellie felt uneasily that Moira had got one up on her. Her twin had wanted to be a teacher, which she considered the dullest occupation in the world. But marrying a lecturer and living in Cambridge sounded the opposite of dull.

'Oh, and you've got a sister.'

'I know, you've just told me about her.' Had Daisy lost her mind as well as her figure? It hadn't been up to much in the first place.

'I mean, a *new* sister. I don't suppose you know, I mean, it's years since you were home, but Aunt Greta and Matthew Doyle got divorced and she married a chap called Frank Fletcher. To everyone's surprise – including your mum's – she had a baby at forty-six, a little girl called Saffron. She's three now. Isn't that a lovely name?'

'Lovely,' Ellie said faintly. 'How's Gran?'

'She's absolutely fine.' Daisy looked at her strangely. 'And so's Brendan. He'll be eight next month and he's the image of Liam Conway, ever so handsome.'

Ellie hadn't forgotten about her son. He just didn't seem all that important.

'Let's see, what else has happened?' Daisy put her finger to her podgy chin. 'My mum's now a qualified solicitor.'

'You don't say!' Ellie rolled her eyes impatiently.

'Matthew Doyle's been in Saudi Arabia for ages. I think I've covered the lot. What have you been doing with yourself all this time, Ellie?'

'All sorts of exciting things.' Ellie shrugged modestly. 'I was in the music industry for a while, then worked for a magazine and a television company. I made a few films – I only had little parts,' she said hastily, in case Daisy asked for details. 'Then I decided to become a model which is why I'm here. What about you, Daise? Did you marry Clint?' It was the question Ellie had been wanting to ask all along. She'd often wondered about Daisy and Clint.

'Yes.' Daisy smiled. 'But we got divorced a year afterwards. Clint is gay, Ellie, but he was too scared to admit it. Now he's come out, he's much happier. He's living in California, writing scripts – you know how he was about films – movies, he called them. His main ambition has always been to direct. There's plenty of time, he's still young. We write to each other regularly.'

Poor, pathetic Daisy had been left to come on holiday on her own! She'd never get another man looking as she did. Ellie felt sorry for her cousin and at the same time immensely superior. She resisted the temptation to say she already knew about Clint.

'I'm so sorry, Daise. Do you still paint?'

'No. I haven't painted in years. I only did it because I was unhappy.'

'And you're not unhappy now?' It was hard to keep the surprise out of her voice.

'Well, no.' Daisy laughed contentedly. 'I don't suppose I *look* happy in this state, but I'm perfectly happy inside. I'll be happier still when the baby's born.' She patted her swollen stomach. 'It's due in less than four weeks. I'm full of water. We thought we'd grab a quick break, else Lord knows when we'd get away.'

'We?' Ellie said faintly. Daisy was *pregnant*!

'Michael, Harry and me. That's them over there,' she pointed to the pool. 'Michael's teaching Harry to swim.'

Ellie's eyes swivelled towards the man she'd noticed earlier with the little boy. Daisy was married with a child and another on the way. Already hot, Ellie felt herself grow hotter. She wouldn't have cared what had happened to her sister and cousin if her own life had gone the way she'd planned. But it hadn't. Instead, the last eight years had been wasted in a vain search for excitement and adventure, while Moira and Daisy had been successfully getting on with their lives.

'Harry's three,' Daisy was saying, waving furiously in the direction of the pool. 'Here they are now.'

Daisy's husband had hoisted the little boy on to his shoulders and was wading towards them. He wasn't a handsome man, but had a pleasant, quirky face and a charismatic smile. Ellie thought him rather appealing.

'Sweetheart! I didn't notice you there. You should have stayed in bed and rested. Have you taken your water tablet?'

'We're on holiday, Michael. I can rest perfectly well in the fresh air, and yes, I've taken my water tablet. Michael, this is my cousin, Ellie. She's a model and in Madrid for a fashion shoot. Isn't it a coincidence that we met? It's ages since we've seen each other. Harry, this is Auntie Moira's twin sister, so she's another sort of aunt.'

Michael shook hands, apologising for it being wet. Harry merely glanced at Ellie, climbed out of the pool, and laid his head on his mother's stomach.

'Is it awake yet?'

Daisy and Michael exchanged complacent smiles and Ellie felt she could easily be sick at this vision of domestic bliss. She was about to jump to her feet, leave, when Michael said. 'He's been pleading for an ice cream. Would you like a cold drink, darling?'

'I'd love one. Something with lime in.'

'And how about you, Ellie?'

'No, thanks. I'll have to be going in a minute.'

'Come on, tough guy. Let's go find the ice cream man.' He ruffled Daisy's hair as he went past, and a feeling of raw jealousy swept like a pain through Ellie's body. She wanted to be loved like that, to have the same warm intimacy with a man that Daisy had with her husband, instead of feeling excluded, apart, alone.

'Where do you live, Daisy?' she asked, breaking the short silence that followed.

'London, a place called Crouch End. Michael's a doctor, he works terribly hard.'

How on earth had someone like Daisy managed to hook a doctor, such an attractive one at that. 'How did you two meet?'

Daisy wiped her red, melting face. 'We met at a clinic. Michael's dyslexic, same as me.'

'What?'

'Dyslexic. Remember I never learnt to read? Everyone thought I was daft.'

'No they didn't,' Ellie said falsely.

'Yes, they did, Ellie.' Daisy shook her head. 'I thought so meself. Anyroad, when me and Clint got married, we went to live in London, and I stayed after he'd gone to California. Oh, Ellie, I was dead miserable, working as an usherette, painting like a mad woman, hardly knowing a soul, and wondering what the hell I was doing with my life.' Despite the heat, Daisy shivered. 'Then Gran rang about this article she'd read on something called dyslexia. It explained why some perfectly intelligent people have trouble reading – they think in pictures, not words, though it's more complicated than that. The article gave the name of a clinic in London where you could go to be assessed. It turned out I was a perfect example of a dyslexic.'

'How come Michael managed to become a doctor if he couldn't read?'

Daisy laughed. 'He's got this dead pushy mother, Angela. She refused to accept he was as stupid as the teachers claimed. She coached him, taught him to read herself. It was Angela who wrote the article and started the clinic. The first time I went, Michael was there. You've no idea how wonderful it was knowing someone else had experienced the same problems as meself. Suddenly, everything fell into place and I didn't feel daft any more.' She sighed blissfully, remembering. 'Then Michael asked me out and things just went on from there. I never thought it was possible to be so happy. Oh!' she cried. 'Isn't it marvellous that the three of us have done so well; you, me, and your Moira!'

'Marvellous,' Ellie said thinly. 'Look, Michael's coming back. I'll just say goodbye, then I'll have to go.'

'It's been lovely meeting you, Ellie.' Daisy looked at her pleadingly. 'Write home soon, won't you? Your mum's always wondering where you are, Gran too. They worry themselves sick about you. Better still, when you're back in England, go and see them. They'd love to see you.'

Ellie dreamed that night about the house where she was born. It was Christmas, she was a little girl, and the walls inside had been painted silver. It was like a grotto and the tree was so big it filled the hall with its feathery branches. The girls' presents had been hidden all over the house. After breakfast there was a treasure hunt and they ran up and down the stairs, Ellie, her sister and her cousin, in and out of the rooms, screaming with joy when they found another mysteriously wrapped parcel. Ellie opened one and found the prettiest frock she had ever seen; pale blue silk with a lace collar, an old-fashioned, Victorian frock. She tried it on in front of the mirror in Gran's bedroom and sighed with pleasure; she was the most beautiful little girl in the world. When she grew up she would become something quite exceptional; a famous film star, an opera singer, a queen.

When Ellie woke, she found herself in the shabby hotel Barry had booked, with another long, hot day ahead in the marquee selling cars. She would have given anything for a drink to get her started.

Back in London in her tiny flat, Ellie looked through the red leather address book with a gold clasp that Daisy had given her as a birthday present when they were teenagers. It had seemed a stupid present at the time, but over the years it had gradually been filled. She opened the book at 'C', and his number was there, as she'd thought – Felix Conway.

She'd done a lot of thinking on the plane home from Spain. Her life was a mess, she was drinking too much, and it was important she do something about it. The time had come to settle down, in which case it was necessary to find a husband. She'd known many men over the years, but there'd only been one with whom she'd shared a sort of intimacy, not sexual, and not as close as that between Daisy and Michael, naturally, but she'd felt at ease with Felix Conway. She recalled the last night in the garden of Fern Hall when he'd evoked emotions she'd never had before or again. Felix, with his gentle voice and gentle smile, made her feel a nicer person, softer.

By now, he might have been long-married to Neila Kenny or some other woman, but a phone call wouldn't hurt. She couldn't imagine anything much having changed in Fern Hall and Felix would still be running the chemist's at a loss. What was needed was a guiding hand, someone who recognised the potential of the house and the shop. In other words, herself. It would be a challenge.

She collected together all her small change and took it downstairs to the communal phone, then dialled the number of the house in Craigmoss. Felix should be home by now. He answered almost immediately.

'Felix, it's Ellie. Do you remember me?'

'Of course.' His voice was faint, but he sounded pleased. 'I often think about you – and Brendan. He'll be eight soon. How are you both?'

'We're very well and Brendan's getting on famously at school. I wondered, Felix, if I could come and stay for a while? Would Neila mind?' she added cautiously.

'Neila? She left Craigmoss years ago. She's living somewhere in England with her brother.' He gave a whispery sigh. 'There's only me and I'd love to see you. When will you be coming?'

'In a couple of weeks or so.'

'Will you be bringing Brendan?'

'Yes,' said Ellie after a pause.

Brendan came home from school and threw his satchel on to the kitchen table. 'Where is she?'

'If you mean Ellie, love, she's gone to town to do some shopping.'

Ruby saw him visibly relax. She poured a glass of lemonade and he drank it thirstily. They'd both felt on edge since Ellie had arrived a week ago. The girl was completely devoid of tact, expecting her son to fall into her arms, treat her as a mother, when she was a total stranger as far as Brendan was concerned.

Over the years, Ruby had tried to talk to him about Ellie, show him her photograph, but Brendan wasn't interested. He was a well-adjusted, self-confident child, quite sure of his place in the world, and had never shown any sign of missing his parents. Old for his years, he made friends easily, and frequently brought home some of his mates from school, though not since Ellie had arrived. She made him embarrassed, tousling his hair, kissing him, buying him sweets he didn't like, calling him, 'kiddo', as if trying to make up for the fact that she was a mother who'd so far played no part in his young life.

It was rare Brendan looked miserable, but he did now, hunched at the table, nursing the empty glass. Ruby sat beside him. 'Would you like a scone?'

'With jam on?'

'Of course. We've got strawberry.'

'Then I'd like a scone, Bee.'

'I think I'll have one too, keep you company.' She did him two scones and one for herself. At the table again, they sat shoulder to shoulder, loving each other so much it hurt, and terrified that very soon they might be parted.

Ellie hadn't said anything, but Ruby could sense it in the air and could tell Brendan did too. They didn't discuss it, because putting their fear into words would only make it seem more real. Ellie hadn't given a reason for coming home, hadn't said if she was staying or going, and there was something about the calculating way she watched her son, asked repeated questions, as if trying to catch up on the time she'd lost, familiarise herself with his habits, his likes and dislikes, become his mother within a week.

In a little corner of her mind, Ruby had always feared something like this would happen. In a fatalistic sort of way, she had been prepared for it. But Brendan wasn't. It would be cruel beyond belief for Ellie, whom he didn't like, to suddenly remove him from the only home he'd ever known and the people who loved him.

Ruby knew she could point this out till the cows came home, but in the end she had no rights. Brendan belonged to Ellie. It was an irrefutable fact, and Ellie was selfish, she thought of no one but herself. If it suited her to reclaim her child, she would do it, regardless of the hurt it would cause. In her own way, Greta was the same. It seemed the worst of Jacob's genes, the ones that made a person selfish and uncaring, had been passed to his eldest daughter and then on to that daughter's child.

Ruby and Brendan were on the settee, watching *Blue Peter*, when Ellie and Heather came in together, having met on the bus on the way home. There was a stiffness between them. A grim-faced Heather went straight to her room. She'd always been dutiful and conscientious and disapproved of the way her niece behaved. In a few days' time, she was going to stay with her own daughter. Daisy's baby was expected soon and she was looking after Harry while his mother was in hospital. Everyone had got over the surprising revelation about Clint, apart from Pixie, and were thrilled that Daisy and Michael had found each other and were so obviously happy.

'See what I bought you, kiddo!' Ellie was laden with carrier bags. She opened one and produced a garish, flowered shirt.

Brendan blushed scarlet. 'I'm not wearing that!'

'Don't be rude, Brendan. It's lovely, very fashionable.'

'He prefers T-shirts, Ellie,' Ruby said mildly.

'Not for best, surely. Anyroad, he wears shirts for school.'

'Only reluctantly, and then they're grey.'

'I thought he could wear it when we go to Ireland.'

There was a long silence. Ellie pretended to sort through the shopping and didn't look at them.

'Ireland?' Ruby was aware her voice sounded querulous and old.

'Not far from Dublin, to be precise. I'm going to stay with a friend, Felix Conway, Liam's brother, and taking Brendan with me.'

'You can't just take him out of school!'

'I can do anything I like, Gran.' Ellie arrogantly tossed her long brown hair.

'How long will you be going to Dublin for?'

'I'm not sure, a while.'

'I don't want to go to Dublin,' Brendan said mutinously. He rarely cried, but his eyes were dangerously full of tears.

'It's only for a little holiday, kiddo.'

'You just said you weren't sure when you'd be back,' Ruby pointed out. 'I tell you what, let's talk about this some other time.' Tonight, for example, when Brendan was in bed and she could speak her mind. But Ellie wasn't willing to give an inch.

'No, Gran, let's talk about it now,' she said, her eyes steely hard. 'Brendan is my son and I want him. Oh, I know I've not been much of a mother, but I will be from now on. I'm taking him with me to Dublin and, if you want the truth, I might not come back. It's time I settled down and I quite fancy doing it in Craigmoss with Felix Conway.'

'And you don't give a damn what Brendan thinks, how he feels?'

'He's only eight. He'll soon get used to things.'

Brendan threw himself at the woman who claimed to be his mother and began to beat her with his fists. 'I'm *not* eight,' he screamed. 'I'm only seven.

You don't even know me *birthday*. I'm not going to Ireland with you.' He stamped his foot. 'I *won't*.'

Ruby lost her temper. 'Now see what you've done, you foolish girl. You must have been at the back of the queue, Ellie Donovan, when the Lord handed out good sense.' She pulled Brendan away, clasped the heaving figure in her arms, and could feel his heart beating madly against her own. It was a long time since she could remember being so angry, but if she let rip to her feelings, it would only distress Brendan more.

Ellie had the grace to look uncomfortable at the upset she had caused. She laid her hand on Ruby's arm. 'I'm sorry, Gran. I didn't want to hurt anyone, but he *is* mine. You must have realised this might happen one day. I've got plane tickets for tomorrow. I thought it best not to say anything before. He'll soon grow to love me, won't you, kiddo?' She ruffled Brendan's hair, but he tore himself away.

'I'll never love you,' he hissed. 'Never, never, never.'

The most mind-shattering things in life always happened suddenly, without warning. One minute everything was normal, next minute things had changed and would never be the same again. Jacob had deserted his family to join the Army, Arthur Cummings had died, the lads had been killed. Yet still life continued, sometimes better than before, sometimes worse.

During the sleepless night that followed, Ruby discovered she wasn't as hard as she used to be, not quite so confident. The thought of life without Brendan was scarcely bearable. Nothing and no one would ever take his place. Even so, had the circumstances been different, had she known he would be happy with his mother, she would have resigned herself to his going. But what made it even more unbearable, was knowing he would be desperately unhappy with Ellie. He would never grow to love her as she hoped.

Next morning, she went downstairs, her head thumping with tiredness. To her surprise, Heather was already up and looked at her with concern.

'I heard you tossing and turning all night, Mam. How do you feel?'

'How d'you think, love?'

'I wish there was something we could do to stop this.'

'There's nothing, Heather,' Ruby said wearily. 'You're a solicitor, you should know. Everything Ellie said was right.'

'Legally right, but morally wrong. Does our Greta know she's going?'

'Greta's coming later to say goodbye.'

When Brendan appeared, he was accompanied by Ellie and rather surprisingly wearing the new shirt. 'He put it on without a murmur,' Ellie said jubilantly.

'That's because he's a good boy.' Ruby held out her hand, praying she wouldn't cry. Brendan took it without a word.

Greta arrived alone. Saffron was at playgroup, she explained. Four generations of O'Hagans sat in the living room making stilted conversation, waiting for the taxi to take Ellie and her son to Lime Street station to catch the Manchester train, from where they would fly to Dublin. Brendan's clothes and toys had been packed the night before.

At exactly one minute past eleven, the taxi sounded its horn . . .

Brendan hardly spoke on the way to Manchester. His mother kept pointing things out through the window, as if she thought it was the sort of thing mothers were supposed to do. He acknowledged her comments with a brief nod of his head. She offered to buy him a can of drink when a trolley of food was pushed through the carriage, but he refused.

All Brendan could think of was Bee. Bee's face when he'd left her, Bee stroking his head when he felt sick, Bee singing him to sleep, reading to him, playing cards, watching football on the telly and screaming encouragement for the wrong side, then Bee's face when he'd left her yet again. Bee was his world. He didn't like his mother and never would.

The journey to Manchester didn't take long. They were catching a coach to the airport.

'I want to go to the lavvy,' he said when they went through the barrier.

'Say lavatory, kiddo. Or toilet's even better. You should have gone on the train.'

Brendan made a face behind his mother's back. 'I want to go to the toilet.'

'That's better. There's a Gents over there.'

'I'd like a drink now, please.'

'What sort?'

'Any sort.'

'They sell them in the newsagents. I'll meet you there. Don't get lost now.'

'No.' Brendan trotted into the Gents and re-emerged almost immediately. He saw his mother disappear into a shop and sped towards the platform where they'd just got off the train. A man in uniform caught his collar as he went through the barrier.

'And where d'you think you're off to, sonny?'

'I'm going to Liverpool with me mam,' Brendan explained nicely. 'I've lost her.'

'Well, you won't find her on this train. The next train to Liverpool's on platform 2. Where's your ticket?'

'Me mam's got it.'

'You'd better get a move on, or you'll lose her altogether. It's leaving in a minute.'

Brendan found platform 2 and ducked under the barrier when no one was looking. The train was only half full and he easily found a seat from where he could see the platform, ready to hide if his mother came looking for him.

It took twice as long to return to Liverpool as it had to go the other way, or so it seemed to Brendan, whose heart was in his mouth for the entire journey. He kept changing his seat, dodging into the lavatory whenever anyone in uniform appeared.

At last the train drew into Lime Street station where, to his utter astonishment, he found an anxious Bee waiting for him by the barrier. He'd thought he'd have to walk all the way home.

'Brendan!' She held out her arms. Her grey hair was waving all over her face and she had on the frayed jeans she wore to do the housework and a giant T-shirt that almost reached her knees, but in Brendan's eyes she had never looked so beautiful.

'Bee!' He flung himself at her. 'How did you know . . . ?' He couldn't find the words he wanted. How did she know to meet the train, that he'd be on it? But Bee knew what he meant.

'Your mother rang, love. She was terribly worried, but she guessed you were on your way home.'

Brendan's heart returned to his mouth. 'Is she coming after me?'

'No, love.' Bee took his hand. 'Seeing as we're in town, would you like to go to McDonald's for a hamburger? It's a lovely day.'

'No, ta, Bee. I'd sooner go home.' He didn't want to be seen for longer than necessary in the dead horrible shirt.

'So would I,' Bee said comfortably.

The phone call had come about an hour ago. Ellie had sounded frantic. 'Gran! Brendan's disappeared. He went to the Gents and was supposed to meet me in the newsagents, but he never came.'

'Did you send someone into the Gents to look for him?' Ruby said sharply.

'Yes, but he wasn't there. One of the ticket inspectors or something said a boy sounding like Brendan tried to get on the wrong train. He directed him towards the right one. He must be coming home.'

'What time does the train get in and I'll meet it?'

'Two thirty.'

'And what happens then, Ellie, when I've met the train?'

Ellie sighed. 'Nothing, I suppose. It doesn't seem such a good idea, taking Brendan to Dublin. I'll have his luggage sent back. Felix is going to be disappointed. He thought the world of him when he was a baby.'

'If it's your intention to make a life with Felix Conway, Ellie,' Ruby said gently, 'then it shouldn't matter whether you take Brendan with you or not.'

'Oh, Gran!' Ellie wailed. 'I desperately want to be happy.'

'Don't we all, love. Don't we all.'

Within a week, Brendan was his old self again, full of life, and inviting his mates home to play in the garden. Dublin and his mother had been forgotten.

But the incident had shaken Ruby. For some reason, she felt fearful, jumping at the least sound, always expecting something terrible to happen. She felt like a creature that had lost its outer shell and was now vulnerable to dangers never known before. Whenever the telephone rang, she'd get a sickly sensation in her stomach. It could only be bad news, though it never was.

Daisy had her baby, another boy. 'He's beautiful,' Heather reported from London. 'And she's going to call him Robert, after her father.'

Moira rang to say she and Sam were expecting another baby at Christmas. 'Me and Daisy are having a race, Gran. I've bet her I'll be the first to have five.'

Ruby was beginning to feel better, when something else happened, trivial when compared to losing Brendan but, for a while, she thought she was losing her mind.

It was August, sizzlingly hot, and she and Brendan had had a wonderful day in Southport, where they'd built castles in the sand, spent a fortune in the fairground, wandered along gracious Lord Street, and had tea in a glass-roofed arcade. While they ate, she told Brendan about Emily, who'd brought her to the very same place more than fifty years before. 'We could even have sat here, in this same spot.'

'And you were young, like me?' Brendan asked through a mouth full of cream cake, as if he couldn't conceive of such a thing.

'Older than you, fourteen.'

'What did you look like then?'

'Pretty. Everyone said I was pretty.'

'You're still pretty,' Brendan said loyally.

Ruby laughed. 'Thank you, love. During the war, me and Beth were evacuated to Southport, though we only stayed a few days. Your mam was three – I mean your gran.' The two small children she'd brought to Southport were now grandmothers! Despite all that had happened since, it seemed little more than yesterday that, on a similarly hot day, she'd waited by the station for Beth and Jake. She shrugged herself back to the present. 'I feel like buying things,' she said. 'A nice new summer frock for me. What do you fancy?'

'A goal,' Brendan said promptly.

'A goal?'

'You get them from Argos. A boy at school's got one. I went to his house once and it's the gear.'

'Will it be heavy to carry?' Ruby looked doubtful.

'I'll carry it, Gran. Don't worry,' Brendan said stoutly.

They returned happily to Liverpool; Brendan with his goal in a cardboard box and Ruby with a crushproof two-piece from Marks & Spencer that would never need ironing, to find the house had been burgled.

Not much had been taken; Heather's portable television, the Chopper bike Brendan had got for his birthday, Ruby's jewellery box which contained little of value, a few ornaments that had been gifts from people over the years. The burglar or burglars had left a mess behind – perhaps annoyed to have found so little of value in such a large house. The contents of drawers had been thrown on to the floors, dishes had been broken, a mirror smashed, chairs upturned, cupboards emptied.

The police were very sympathetic, but didn't hold out much hope of the goods being recovered. Ruby was advised to fit deadlocks on the doors and windows and have a burglar alarm installed.

'This place was a cinch to break into. Once they'd established no one was in, they merely kicked in the back door.'

For the first two days, Ruby was very calm. She concentrated on putting everything back where it belonged. The bike and the television were covered by insurance and would be replaced. Heather was arranging for the deadlocks and burglar alarm to be fitted.

It was when she began to list the contents of her jewellery box that something broke inside her. The police wanted details, 'In case an item's offered for sale. We provide jewellers with a list of stolen property.'

'But it was hardly worth anything,' Ruby cried. She'd never possessed a precious stone in her life.

'It could have been kids who burgled your home, Mrs O'Hagan, and they could still try and sell it. All we're asking for is a list. The stuff might even turn up at a car boot sale.'

Most of her jewellery had been presents from the girls; a tiny amethyst pendant on a silver chain with earrings to match were the first things that came to mind, bought when the girls had not long started work and couldn't have afforded more than a few pounds; gold stud earrings, very small; a silver cross and chain; a silver and amber bracelet brought back from Corfu. There was a brooch from Beth, a cheap thing that had gone dull with age.

As she wrote the things down, each brought back its own particular memory, when it had been given, why – a birthday, Christmas, or for no special reason at all. There was a scarf ring, she remembered, with a huge green stone which would have been worth thousands had it been real. Greta and Heather had bought it the day they'd met the lads. 'For being such a lovely mam,' Greta had said at the time.

Ruby felt as if the memories had been taken away and soiled. Her house had been soiled, her life had been invaded. A stranger or strangers had walked through the rooms touching her things, Heather's things, Brendan's.

Then she recalled the jewellery box had contained the ring Olivia had given her, the ring that had belonged to her father. 'It's my grandpop's wedding ring,' he'd said when he gave it to Olivia – she remembered the words exactly, she told Ruby. 'And the way he said it. I remember every single thing about that night.'

'Ruby to Eamon. 1857,' Ruby said aloud, and began to cry. She'd always meant to buy a gold chain and wear the ring around her neck, but had never got round to it. And now she didn't have the ring. It had been stolen.

She would never feel safe in the house again. What's more, she'd never be able to *leave* the house again. The thought of finding the rooms in turmoil a second time, their possessions strewn on the floor, made her feel physically sick. She was frightened to stay in, frightened to go out.

Ruby went into the kitchen and began to clean the room from top to bottom, wiping every surface, including the walls, so there would be no trace left of the intruders. Every single inch would have to be cleansed of their touch **and** the places where they'd breathed. There was a robotic urgency about **her** movements, and a slightly mad look in her eyes.

She worked herself to a standstill, but forced herself to start on the living room. As soon as she'd finished cleaning, she would wash everything; their clothes, the bedding, the curtains, all the things that had been contaminated by the thieves.

That night, she hardly slept, thinking of all the work that had to be done, listening to the creaks and groans of the old house, familiar noises that had once been comforting, but which she now found sinister. She got up twice to make sure Brendan was safely asleep in his bed and hadn't been murdered.

'Have you decided to spring clean in August, Mam?' Heather enquired a few days later when she came home from work and found Ruby up a ladder in her room cleaning the picture rail.

'I suddenly realised what a state the place was in. It needs a thorough going over.'

'It looks all right to me. Anyroad, since when have you cared what state the place was in? You look worn out. Would you like a cup of tea?'

'Please, love.' Heather didn't realise how hard she'd been working. Ruby hadn't told anyone how she felt. 'The meal's in the oven, it'll be ready soon. Brendan's round at a friend's house.'

Heather returned a few minutes later to report there was no tea. 'I'll just nip round to the shops and get some.'

'I could have sworn there was a packet in the cupboard,' Ruby said vaguely.

'Well, there isn't. I won't be long.'

'While you're there, will you get some sugar? We're nearly out of that too.' They were running out of all sorts of things. She usually bought the groceries on Thursdays, but was waiting until the weekend when Heather was home and the house wouldn't be left empty.

When she climbed down the ladder, her legs were shaking. She felt exhausted, yet there was so much to be done. Upstairs still hadn't been touched. She was working herself into the ground, hardly sleeping, all on account of a burglary in which not much had been taken. Far worse things happened to people on a daily basis – they'd happened to her – but she'd never felt like this before, completely gutted.

The phone went. It was Angela Burns, Daisy's mother-in-law, a pleasantly brisk woman with a finger in all sorts of pies. They'd met just once at the wedding. Angela wanted Heather. The two got on like a house on fire, although Angela was nearer Ruby's age. After a brief chat, she said she'd call back later when told Heather wasn't in.

Later, when Angela rang, Ruby shamelessly eavesdropped during the conversation with her daughter. It seemed Heather was being offered a job in London, a good one. She sounded excited, but then her voice dropped and Ruby had to strain to hear.

'I couldn't possibly leave just yet. I told you we'd had a burglary, didn't I? Well, it's badly affected my mother. She's in a bit of a state, though she pretends not to be, and I pretend not to notice. She hates to be thought weak.' There was a pause, then, 'Yes, yes. As soon as I can. I'm looking forward to it.'

When Heather returned, Ruby was innocently watching *Top of the Pops* with Brendan.

'Angela said Rob's thriving. You two must meet up again one day, Mam. You've never been to London, have you?'

'No, love.' And she never would. She couldn't possibly leave the house.

Later still, when Brendan and Heather were in bed, Ruby stayed up and watched an old film, knowing she'd never sleep. Would she ever sleep peacefully again? The film finished and for some reason, her eyes were drawn to Daisy's painting which still hung over the mantelpiece, though she'd been intending to move it for ages.

What did it mean? She'd often wondered. Perhaps that's why she kept it there, in the hope that one day she would understand. A wobbly circle with six splodgy figures inside, one much bigger than the others. If you stared hard enough, the figures seemed to move.

She went and made a cup of hot milk and returned to stare at the painting again. Six figures. Why six?

Matthew Doyle had understood. 'I can see what she's getting at,' he'd said. 'You're very lucky, all of you. I wish I were in Daisy's painting, but there was never a chance of that.'

Could the figures be herself, her daughters, and her granddaughters? Six people. Why were they lucky, these six people, sheltering with a circle, nothing touching them?

And *then* Ruby understood. This was Daisy's childhood world, the way she'd seen it before she married Clint and discovered how painful it could be. Greta, Ellie and Moira had also gone to experience the world outside for themselves. Soon Heather would also go and, of the six people, only Ruby would be left behind.

No wonder she'd been so upset by the burglary. It had shattered the circle. She was the large figure in the painting, cosseting and caring for her family, protecting them from harm. Perhaps it was a relic of Foster Court, the need to keep her children, and their children, safe.

'You created your own little world and crowned yourself its queen,' Beth told her that time in Washington.

But now Daisy's circle had been broken and couldn't be mended. Things would never be safe again. What's more, Ruby would just have to get used to it, not stay cowering in the house, scared out of her wits.

On impulse, she went into the hall and telephoned Beth. She spent most of her time in Washington these days, working for the Democratic Party. It was a long time since they'd spoken.

'Beth Lefarge's office,' said a male voice, only young.

'Is Beth there? It's Ruby O'Hagan speaking, her friend from Liverpool.'

'Hi, Ruby. Hold on, I'll see if she's free.'

Beth came on almost immediately. 'Ruby! It's ages since we spoke.'

'I was just thinking the same thing. Who's the young man? Or do you have a male secretary these days?'

'My secretary went home at five o'clock. Hank's my grandson. We were just wondering how to get more black voters involved in the next election. How's things, Rube?'

'Up and down. I was thinking about going to Dublin before the school holidays are over. Ellie lives there, Brendan's mother. It's about time they got to know each other properly. I'll see what Brendan has to say about it.' An astonished Ruby had been thinking no such thing. The words had just come out, perhaps because they were the right words. Brendan would be far better off with his mother than a woman of sixty-six. He had to learn to love Ellie before it was too late, as it had been too late with Ruby's own mother.

'And our Heather's got a job in London,' she went on. 'I'm not sure of the details, but she'll be leaving soon. She's been a good daughter, Heather, and I'm very pleased for her.' As it was, she was holding Heather back, when she should be offering encouragement.

'You'll be left in that big house all on your own,' Beth pointed out.

'It will be a while before Brendan will come to realise he'd be happier with Ellie. When he does – well, we'll just have to see.'

By then, it would be time to leave the house by Princes Park for ever.

The week in Dublin went unexpectedly well. Ellie was living in a pretty village, Craigmoss, several miles from the city. She already seemed less frenetic, more content, her turbulent brain at rest. Felix Conway was a lovely man, very kind, and a good influence on her wayward granddaughter. He brought out the best in her. Brendan had taken to him immediately and had seemed happy to stay with him and Ellie when Ruby had gone to Dublin for the day, a deliberate ploy on her part.

She had felt lonely, wandering around the strange city on her own, wondering what the future had in store. So many times in the past she had wanted to *do* something, though she'd never known what. Very shortly, for the first time in her life, she would be free to do anything she wanted and she still didn't know what.

Late September, and Ruby was in the garden, sitting in a deckchair under a tree, watching the occasional bronze leaf float to the ground.

'Catch a leaf and make a wish.' The girls had done it in the convent, but Ruby couldn't remember a single wish she'd made. What was she likely to have wished for in those days? Probably *not* to become a housemaid or a cook, in which case it hadn't come true. She'd been cooking and doing housework all her life.

A cloud drifted across the warm sun and she shivered. In a minute, she'd get on with her painting in case it rained. Daisy had left a load of hardboard pieces behind and some half-used tubes of paint and Ruby was painting a picture of the back of the house. It was a foolish idea that had come to her out of the blue. No one knew, not even Brendan who was at school. She was too embarrassed to let people know.

At first, she'd got more paint on her clothes than on the board, but now the painting was almost finished. But she'd been thinking that for weeks. Every time she thought the picture was complete, she'd feel impelled to include another tiny figure; a disjointed, unrecognisable figure, sitting, lying, or standing on the grass. A figure playing with a ball or a skipping rope, or sitting on the back step with a dab of white paint that was supposed to be a cup in what was supposed to be a hand. After a while, Ruby had realised she was painting the story of the early years in the house. The figures were her children, Beth and Jake, Connie and Charles, Martha Quinlan, Max Hart, the kids she'd looked after during the war, like little ghosts amidst the trees. The person on the step was herself.

There was one person missing from the painting and she wasn't sure where to fit him in; right in the middle where he truly belonged, or on the periphery where he'd always been.

She closed her eyes and saw the painting in her mind's eye. Right in the middle, she decided. She'd put him beside herself, outside the back door. Over the last tumultuous weeks, she'd wished he'd been around, if only as a friend, someone to talk to. She'd always been able to talk to Matthew Doyle.

When she opened her eyes, she became aware a man had come round the side of the house and was regarding her gravely. He was a striking man, very tall and very thin. His once black hair was almost completely grey and his face had been burnt deep golden brown by the sun. He was impeccably dressed, as always, in khaki cotton slacks and a green anorak.

For a moment, Ruby felt totally disorientated. Had her painting come to life, her wish come true?

'Matthew!' she mumbled. She tried to struggle to her feet, but gave up when it appeared she'd lost the use of her limbs.

He came towards her and sat on the grass, still grave. 'I understand you left a message at the office for me to call.'

'That was five years ago,' she gasped.

'Sorry about the delay, but I've been busy.'

She patted her hair and realised it hadn't been combed and she wasn't wearing a scrap of make up to disguise the multitude of wrinkles. She had on the old jeans she wore to paint in. 'Why didn't you let me know you were coming? I'd have got ready, properly dressed.'

He smiled at last and her heart turned over. 'The first time I saw you in this very house, you were covered in paint. It's how I always think of you.'

A little excited shiver ran down her spine, as it had done they day they'd met. 'You suit grey hair,' she said.

'I think that's the first compliment you've ever paid me.' He looked pleased. Close up, she saw he had enough wrinkles of his own around his brown eyes. His cheeks were gaunt and heavily lined. She thought he didn't look well.

'Are you home for good?' Ruby held her breath, waiting for the answer, and thinking what a silly way it was for an old woman to behave.

'I've retired, so yes, I'm home for good.'

'Where are you going to live?'

'That depends on you, Rube.' He looked at her directly, his expression serious, then turned to watch a leaf detach itself from a tree and land softly on the grass. 'Have you missed me?'

'Yes, Matthew, I've missed you. I've always hoped you'd come back.'

He nodded, satisfied. 'How's everyone?'

'Fine. Even Ellie seems to have settled down.' She told him about Greta's baby, all the other babies, Brendan coming back from Manchester alone on the train, the burglary. 'I thought I'd lost it for a while, but I managed to recover.'

'You're strong, that's why.'

Ruby shuddered. 'I didn't feel strong then. Would you like some tea, Matthew?'

'I was hoping you'd ask.'

She tried again to struggle out of the deckchair and he reached for her hand and pulled her to her feet.

They stayed holding hands as they strolled across the grass towards the house. It would be just like old times, him sprawled on a chair while she made the tea. Ruby felt a pang, thinking of what she'd missed because she'd ignored her true feelings.

But, she thought impatiently, she'd never believed in dwelling on the past. The present was more important. All of a sudden, she saw with vivid clarity what the future had in store, what she would *do*.

She would marry Matthew Doyle.

Matthew

Epilogue
Millennium Eve

They sat on a balcony overlooking the River Mersey, an elderly couple, warmly wrapped up against the cold. It had just gone half-past eleven. Only twenty-nine minutes remained of the twentieth century.

Daisy and Moira were having parties, but it was impossible to go to both. To avoid hurt feelings, they had decided to spend Millennium Eve at home, just the two of them, together.

'Are you warm enough, love?' Ruby said anxiously. Matthew was very frail these days. He hadn't known his lungs had been permanently damaged by the tuberculosis all those years ago until he found difficulty breathing.

'I'm fine, Rube.' His voice was slightly hoarse. 'I wouldn't miss this for anything.'

The river stretched in front of them, a black, satin ribbon, reflecting the bright lights of Wallasey and Birkenhead. The lights wobbled slightly in the gentle waves. It was a spectacular sight. Matthew loved it. In the summer, he would sit on the balcony of their riverside flat until long after it had gone dark.

The telephone rang for the umpteenth time – the sliding door had been left open so they could hear the phone and listen to the television. Ruby went to answer it. 'That was Beth,' she said when she came back. 'She's in Little Rock with the family. They're having a big do, but it's not midnight over there for hours yet. By the way, she's invited us to stay in Washington next summer.'

'I like Washington,' Matthew said. They'd been several times before. 'I'm already looking forward to it.'

Ruby prayed with all her heart he'd be fit enough to travel when the time came. She sat beside him on the wrought-iron bench, feeling fidgety. 'Would you like some tea?'

'For God's sake, Ruby,' he said irritably, 'can't you sit still a minute and look at the view?'

'Nothing's happening,' she complained.

'It will, soon, when the fireworks start.'

'I'll make myself a cup of tea in the meantime.' Ruby got to her feet and gave a little shriek when a pain shot through her leg.

'What's the matter?'

'It's my damn arthritis.' She was eighty-one and hated growing old – all the mysterious pains that appeared from nowhere, then disappeared as quickly as they'd come when she thought she was about to die.

She hobbled into the kitchen which couldn't have been more different than the one in the house by Princes Park; all stainless steel, efficient, functional, and easy to clean, which was the way kitchens ought to be. The contrast between the two rarely crossed her mind nowadays, though it had been a constant wonder when they'd first moved in. It was in 1988, when Brendan was eleven, that he'd gone to live in Dublin with Ellie and Felix, perhaps persuaded by the arrival of a baby sister and the need to belong to a proper family. Now he was managing the restaurant in Fern Hall that Ellie had started and which had proved such a great success. He had married an Irish girl, Katy, and would become a father very soon.

The house had been sold and Ruby had never gone back. She had no idea who lived there now. Leaving the place had hurt more than she'd ever imagined. The old walls held many memories, most of them good, and she preferred not to rake over them, though there were times when they unexpectedly returned, without warning, tugging at her heartstrings. Tonight, for instance, when Beth had rung, she'd put a face to the voice with its slight transatlantic twang, and found herself talking to the pretty, dewy-eyed girl she'd met in Arthur Cummings' house, not the gnarled old lady Beth was now.

The phone rang again. It was Robert, Daisy's son, on his mobile. 'We're on the Embankment, Bee.' Brendan's name for her had stuck with all the young people. 'The television camera's pointing straight at us. We're waving like mad, can you see us?'

'Just a minute, love. It's on the wrong channel. Yes, I can see you,' Ruby screamed, though without her glasses she could see only a crowd of blurred figures. 'Is Harry with you?'

'Yes, he's calling Mum on *his* mobile. We're going home as soon as the fireworks are over.'

'Have a nice time. Be careful now, and give Harry my love.'

'We'll ring again later, Bee.'

It would be nice, Ruby thought, when the camera moved to another location, to be on the banks of the Thames in the middle of all the excitement. Mind you, she could feel the excitement here. Buildings always seemed to know when something remarkable was about to happen. The air seemed to tingle.

'Who was that?' Matthew called.

'Robert. He's on the Embankment with Harry. I just saw them on television.'

'I wondered what the screaming was about. What are you doing in there? I'm feeling lonely.'

'Making myself a cup of tea, but I think I'll have something stronger, a Martini, to toast the New Year – the new century. Would you like some whisky?'

'Can't, Rube,' he answered gloomily. 'Not while I'm taking those tablets. You have one for me.'

'I'll fetch orange juice, you can make a toast with that.'

She'd hardly been on the balcony a minute, when the phone rang yet again. Matthew groaned. This time it was an ecstatic Ellie. 'Katy's just had the baby, Gran, by express delivery. It's a little girl. Brendan asked me to ring you first. They're going to call her Ruby.'

'Tell Brendan I'm very flattered.' Ruby sniffed. She quite fancied a little cry.

'Now I'm a grandmother!' Ellie sounded slightly shocked, as if she'd only just realised. 'It makes me feel dead ancient.'

'Wait till your grandchildren have grandchildren, Ellie. *Then* you'll feel ancient.'

'I'd better go now and give Mum a ring. She's at our Moira's. You'll come and stay soon, won't you, Gran, meet your namesake?'

'As soon as we can, love.' She was glad Greta was staying in Cambridge with Moira and Sam and their five children. New Year's Eve wasn't a good time for widows. Frank Fletcher had died five years ago and Saffron, their beloved little girl, now eighteen, had been in and out of a series of unstable relationships. She was at the moment living with a dodgy character who sold used cars – a distraught Greta suspected they were stolen.

Life was so unpredictable. Just as one daughter had lost a husband, the other had acquired one. Heather, at the age of fifty-six, had married a fellow solicitor, and was living close to Daisy in Crouch End. The sisters, once so close, hardly saw each other nowadays.

'Who was *that*?' Matthew sounded cross.

'Ellie. Katy's just had the baby, a little girl. They're going to call her Ruby.'

'Good. Are you coming out again?'

'In a minute.' Ruby was staring at Daisy's painting which hung over the mantelpiece. It went perfectly in the ultra-modern high-ceilinged room that had once been the top floor of a grain warehouse. She and Matthew were the only residents over fifty in the development – she liked living in a place designed for young people.

Visitors often admired Daisy's painting. Some asked what the artist was trying to convey, but Ruby never told them.

There were too many O'Hagans now to fit in the circle, too many for her to watch over, keep safe. She began to worry about Harry and Robert on the Embankment – things could get out of hand on a night like tonight.

'Am I going to see the New Millennium in on me own?' Matthew called plaintively.

'Coming.' She stepped out on to the balcony and closed the sliding door.

'We won't hear Big Ben.'

'It doesn't matter. It's getting cold inside with it open. We'll know when it's twelve o'clock, don't worry.' She leant her head on his shoulder and he immediately put his arm around her.

'I'm glad I'm with you,' he whispered.

'And I'm glad I'm with you.'

'Honest?'

Ruby sighed contentedly. 'Honest.'

They sat in silence for a while, the only sound the distant hum of the city, each preoccupied with their own thoughts. The past fifteen years with Matthew had been good years, almost perfect. They had travelled a lot, not only to Washington to see Beth, or to stay with relatives, but to places all over Europe. She had imagined this day, this very special New Year's Eve, many times in the past, wondering if she would still be alive to see it, where she would be, who with, and there wasn't a person in the world she'd sooner be with than Matthew. She said a prayer, thanking God for letting them both live long enough to welcome in the New Millennium, unlike the Donovans and the Whites, all dead now, along with Connie and Charles, and Daniel Lefarge, Beth's husband.

'It shouldn't be long now,' Matthew murmured.

As if on cue, the world suddenly erupted in a mighty cheer. In the distance, church bells chimed, a glorious sound, accompanied by the mournful wail of ships' hooters. Across the water, and on Kings Dock to their right, a thousand fireworks shot into the sky, exploding into a million stars. There were shouts and laughter from the balcony below. Somewhere close, a dog barked hysterically.

'Happy New Year, Matthew.'

'Happy New Century, Ruby.'

They kissed, a sweet, gentle kiss. There wasn't much passion left nowadays.

The noise went on, the fireworks, the cheering, the singing, as their small part of the world celebrated the advent of the twenty-first century.

After a while, Matthew began to shiver, so they went indoors and found the telephone ringing.

It was Greta. 'Happy New Year, Mam,' she sang.

'The same to you, love.' Ruby was glad she sounded happy. Moira came on, then Sam, followed, one by one, by the children, all five of them, anxious to wish Bee and Uncle Matt a Happy New Year.

Then Heather rang, Daisy and Michael, Brendan, the new father, as drunk as a lord. Harry called again from the Embankment. He and Robert were on their way home with a couple of girls they'd met. 'They're Swedish and drop dead gorgeous.'

Matthew had been watching television all this time. 'I think I'll tu.
he said when Ruby judged there were unlikely to be any more calls.

'Would you like some hot milk to take with you?'

'No, ta, Rube. I'm dead beat.'

But Ruby had never felt more wide awake. 'Goodnight, love. I'll join you
in a minute.' She kissed him, then watched him go, stooped and feeble, and
remembered the tall, dark young man in the cheap suit she'd met the day
the war ended. She sighed, went into the kitchen, but instead of milk,
poured another Martini, then put her coat back on and returned to the
balcony to watch the fireworks and listen to the bells and the sound of
people enjoying themselves. All of a sudden, she ached to be part of the
crowd, to dance and sing, celebrate this unique night. She was reluctant to
go to bed, curl up beside Matthew's warm body, while the rest of the world
was wide awake and having a wonderful time.

She went over to the bedroom door and listened. He was already asleep,
snoring softly. It wouldn't hurt to go out, just for half an hour, mingle with
the crowds, shake a few hands. She might well be a silver-haired old lady
with arthritis, but she still didn't want to miss anything.